D1014773

IRVING STONE

STONE

THREE COMPLETE NOVELS

IRVING STONE

THREE COMPLETE NOVELS

Lust for Life

The President's Lady

The Agony and the Ecstasy

AVENEL BOOKS · NEW YORK

This edition is published by Avenel Books,
distributed by Crown Publishers, Inc.
by arrangement with Doubleday & Company, Inc.
h g f e d c b a
1981 EDITION

Manufactured in the United States of America

CONTENTS

Lust for Life

PROLOGUE

LONDON

1

"Monsieur Van Gogh! It's time to wake up!"

Vincent had been waiting for Ursula's voice even while he slept.

"I was awake, Mademoiselle Ursula," he called back.

"No you weren't," the girl laughed, "but you are now." He heard her go down the stairs and into the kitchen.

Vincent put his hands under him, gave a shove, and sprang out of bed. His shoulders and chest were massive, his arms thick and powerful. He slipped into his clothes, poured some cold water out of the ewer, and stropped his razor.

Vincent enjoyed the daily ritual of the shave; down the broad cheek from the right sideburn to the corner of the voluptuous mouth; the right half of the upper lip from the nostril out, then the left half; then down the chin, a huge, rounded slab of warm granite.

He stuck his face into the wreath of Brabantine grass and oak leaves on the chiffonier. His brother Theo had gathered it from the heath near Zundert and sent it to London for him. The smell of Holland in his nose started the day off right.

"Monsieur Van Gogh," called Ursula, knocking on the door again, "the postman just left this letter for you."

He recognized his mother's handwriting as he tore open the envelope. "Dear Vincent," he read, "I am going to put a word to bed on paper for you."

His face felt cold and damp so he stuck the letter into his trouser pocket, intending to read it during one of his many leisure moments at Goupils. He combed back his long, thick, yellow-red hair, put on a stiff white shirt, low collar and a large knotted four-in-hand black tie and descended to breakfast and Ursula's smile.

Ursula Loyer and her mother, the widow of a Provençal curate, kept a kindergarten for boys in a little house in the back garden. Ursula was nineteen, a smiling, wide-eyed creature with a delicate, oval face, pastel colouring and a small, slender figure. Vincent loved to watch the sheen of laughter which, like the glow from a highly coloured parasol, was spread over her piquant face.

Ursula served with quick, dainty movements, chatting vivaciously while he ate. He was twenty-one and in love for the first time. Life opened out before him. He

3

thought he would be a fortunate man if he could eat breakfast opposite Ursula for the rest of his days.

Ursula brought in a rasher of bacon, an egg, and a cup of strong, black tea. She fluttered into a chair across the table from him, patted the brown curls at the back of her head, and smiled at him while she passed the salt, pepper, butter and toast in quick succession.

"Your mignonette is coming up a bit," she said, wetting her lips with her tongue. "Will you have a look at it before you go to the gallery?"

"Yes," he replied. "Will you, that is, would you . . . show me?"

"What a droll person he is! He plants the mignonette himself and then doesn't know where to find it." She had a habit of speaking about people as though they were not in the room.

Vincent gulped. His manner, like his body, was heavy and he did not seem able to find the right words for Ursula. They went into the yard. It was a cool April morning, but the apple trees had already blossomed. A little garden separated the Loyer house from the kindergarten. Just a few days before, Vincent had sown poppies and sweet peas. The mignonette was pushing through the earth. Vincent and Ursula squatted on either side of it, their heads almost touching. Ursula had a strong, natural perfume of the hair.

"Mademoiselle Ursula," he said.

"Yes?" She withdrew her head, but smiled at him questioningly.

"I . . . I . . . that is . . . "

"Dear me, what can you be stuttering about?" she asked, and jumped up. He followed her to the door of the kindergarten. "My *poupons* will be here soon," she said. "Won't you be late at the gallery?"

"I have time. I walk to the Strand in forty-five minutes."

She could think of nothing to say, so she reached behind her with both arms to catch up a tiny wisp of hair that was escaping. The curves of her body were surprisingly ample for so slender a figure.

"Whatever have you done with that Brabant picture you promised me for the kindergarten?" she asked.

"I sent a reproduction of one of Caesar de Cock's sketches to Paris. He is going to inscribe it for you."

"Oh, delightful!" She clapped her hands, swung a short way about on her hips, then turned back again. "Sometimes, Monsieur, just sometimes, you can be most charming."

She smiled at him with her eyes and mouth, and tried to go. He caught her by the arm. "I thought of a name for you after I went to bed," he said. "I called you *l'ange aux poupons.*"

Ursula threw back her head and laughed heartily. *"L'ange aux poupons!"* she cried. "I must go tell it to Mother!"

She broke loose from his grip, laughed at him over a raised shoulder, ran through the garden and into the house.

2

Vincent put on his top hat, took his gloves, and stepped out into the road of Clapham. The houses were scattered at this distance from the heart of London. In every garden the lilacs and hawthorn and laburnums were in bloom.

It was eight-fifteen; he did not have to be at Goupils until nine. He was a vigorous walker, and as the houses thickened he passed an increasing number of business men on their way to work. He felt extremely friendly to them all; they too knew what a splendid thing it was to be in love.

He walked along the Thames Embankment, crossed Westminster Bridge, passed by Westminster Abbey and the House of Parliament, and turned into number 17 Southampton, Strand, the London quarters of Goupil and Company, Art Dealers and Publishers of Engravings.

As he walked through the main salon, with its thick carpets and rich draperies, he saw a canvas representing a kind of fish or dragon six yards long, with a little man hovering over it. It was called *The Archangel Michael Killing Satan*.

"There is a package for you on the lithograph table," one of the clerks told him as he passed.

The second room of the shop, after one passed the picture salon in which were exhibited the paintings of Millais, Boughton, and Turner, was devoted to etchings and lithographs. It was in the third room, which looked more like a place of business than either of the others, that most of the sales were carried on. Vincent laughed as he thought of the woman who had made the last purchase the evening before.

"I can't fancy this picture, Harry, can you?" she asked her husband. "The dog looks a rare bit like the one that bit me in Brighton last summer."

"Look here, old fellow," said Harry, "must we have a dog? They mostly put the missus in a stew."

Vincent was conscious of the fact that he was selling very poor stuff indeed. Most of the people who came in knew absolutely nothing about what they were buying. They paid high prices for a cheap commodity, but what business was it of his? All he had to do was make the print room successful.

He opened the package from Goupils in Paris. It had been sent by Caesar de Cock and was inscribed, "To Vincent, and Ursula Loyer: *Les amis de mes amis sont mes amis.*"

"I'll ask Ursula tonight when I give her this," he murmured to himself. "I'll be twenty-two in a few days and I'm earning five pounds a month. No need to wait any longer."

The time in the quiet back room of Goupils passed very quickly. He sold on an average of fifty photographs a day for the Musée Goupil and Company, and although he would have preferred to deal in oil canvases and etchings, he was pleased to be taking in so much money for the house. He liked his fellow clerks and they liked him; they spent many pleasant hours together talking of things European.

As a young chap he had been slightly morose and had avoided companionship. People had thought him queer, a bit eccentric. But Ursula had changed his nature completely. She had made him want to be agreeable and popular; she had brought him out of himself and helped him to see the goodness in the ordinary pattern of daily life.

At six o'clock the store closed. Mr. Obach stopped Vincent on his way out. "I had a letter from your Uncle Vincent Van Gogh about you," he said. "He wanted to know how you were coming on. I was happy to tell him that you are one of the best clerks in the store."

"It was very good of you to say that, sir."

"Not at all. After your summer vacation I want you to leave the back room and come forward into the etchings and lithographs."

"That means a great deal to me at this moment, sir, because I . . . I'm going to be married!"

"Really? This is news. When is it to take place?"

"This summer, I suppose." He hadn't thought of the date before.

"Well my boy, that's splendid. You just had an increase the first of the year, but when you come back from your wedding trip I dare say we can manage another."

3

"I'll get the picture for you, Mademoiselle Ursula," said Vincent after dinner, pushing back his chair.

Ursula was wearing a modishly embroidered dress of verdigris faye. "Did the artist write something nice for me?" she asked.

"Yes. If you'll get a lamp I'll hang it in the kindergarten for you."

She pursed her lips to a highly kissable *moue* and looked at him sideways. "I must help Mother. Shall we make it in a half hour?"

Vincent rested his elbows on the chiffonier in his room and gazed into the mirror. He had rarely thought about his appearance; in Holland such things had not seemed important. He had noticed that in comparison to the English his face and head were ponderous. His eyes were buried in deep crevices of horizontal rock; his nose was high ridged, broad and straight as a shinbone; his dome-like forehead was as high as the distance from his thick eyebrows to the sensuous mouth; his jaws were wide and powerful, his neck a bit squat and thick, and his massive chin a living monument to Dutch character.

He turned away from the mirror and sat idly on the edge of the bed. He had been brought up in an austere home. He had never loved a girl before; he had never even looked at one or engaged in the casual banter between the sexes. In his love for Ursula there was nothing of passion or desire. He was young; he was an idealist; he was in love for the first time.

He glanced at his watch. Only five minutes had passed. The twenty-five minutes that stretched ahead seemed interminable. He drew a note from his brother Theo out of his mother's letter and reread it. Theo was four years younger than Vincent and was now taking Vincent's place in Goupils in The Hague. Theo and Vincent, like their father Theodorus and Uncle Vincent, had been favourite brothers all through their youth.

Vincent picked up a book, rested some paper on it, and wrote Theo a note. From the top drawer of the chiffonier he drew out a few rough sketches that he had made along the Thames Embankment and put them into an envelope for Theo along with a photograph of *Young Girl with a Sword,* by Jacquet.

"My word," he exclaimed aloud, "I've forgotten all about Ursula!"

He looked at his watch; he was already a quarter of an hour late. He snatched up a comb, tried to straighten out the tangle of wavy red hair, took Caesar de Cock's picture from the table, and flung open the door.

"I thought you had forgotten me," Ursula said as he came into the parlour. She was pasting together some paper toys for her *poupons*. "Did you bring my picture? May I see it?"

"I would like to put it up before you look. Did you fix a lamp?"

"Mother has it."

When he returned from the kitchen she gave him a scarf of blue marine to wrap about her shoulders. He thrilled to the silken touch of it. In the garden there was the smell of apple blossoms. The path was dark and Ursula put the ends of her fingers lightly on the sleeve of his rough, black coat. She stumbled once, gripped his arm more tightly and laughed in high glee at her own clumsiness. He did not understand why she thought it funny to trip, but he liked to watch her body carry the laughter down the dark path. He held open the door of the kindergarten for her and as she passed, her delicately moulded face almost brushing his, she looked deep into his eyes and seemed to answer his question before he asked it.

He set the lamp down on the table. "Where would you like me to hang the picture?" he asked.

"Over my desk, don't you think?"

There were perhaps fifteen low chairs and tables in the room of what had formerly been a summer house. At one end was a little platform supporting Ursula's desk.

He and Ursula stood side by side, groping for the right position for the picture.
Vincent was nervous; he dropped the pins as fast as he tried to stick them into the
wall. She laughed at him in a quiet, intimate tone.

"Here, clumsy, let me do it."

She lifted both arms above her head and worked with deft movements of every
muscle of her body. She was quick in her gestures, and graceful. Vincent wanted
to take her in his arms, there in the dim light of the lamp, and settle with one sure
embrace this whole tortuous business. But Ursula, though she touched him frequently
in the dark, never seemed to get into position for it. He held the lamp up high
while she read the inscription. She was pleased, clapped her hands, rocked back
on her heels. She moved so much he could never catch up with her.

"That makes him my friend too, doesn't it?" she asked. "I've always wanted
to know an artist."

Vincent tried to say something tender, something that would pave the way for
his declaration. Ursula turned her face to him in the half shadow. The gleam from
the lamp put tiny spots of light in her eyes. The oval of her face was framed in
the darkness and something he could not name moved within him when he saw her
red, moist lips stand out from the smooth paleness of her skin.

There was a meaningful pause. He could feel her reaching out to him, waiting
for him to utter the unnecessary words of love. He wetted his lips several times.
Ursula turned her head, looked into his eyes over a slightly raised shoulder, and
ran out the door.

Terror stricken that his opportunity would pass, he pursued her. She stopped for
a moment under the apple tree.

"Ursula, please."

She turned and looked at him, shivering a bit. There were cold stars out. The
night was black. He had left the lamp behind him. The only light came from the
dim glow of the kitchen window. The perfume of Ursula's hair was in his nostrils.
She pulled the silk scarf tightly about her shoulders and crossed her arms on her
chest.

"You're cold," he said.

"Yes. We had better go in."

"No! Please, I . . ." He planted himself in her path.

She lowered her chin into the warmth of the scarf and looked up at him with
wide, wondering eyes. "Why Monsieur Van Gogh. I'm afraid I don't understand."

"I only wanted to talk to you. You see . . . I . . . that is . . . "

"Please, not now. I'm shivering."

"I thought you should know. I was promoted today . . . I'm going forward into
the lithograph room . . . it will be my second increase in a year . . ."

Ursula stepped back, unwrapped the scarf, and stood resolutely in the night,
quite warm without any protection.

"Precisely what are you trying to tell me, Monsieur Van Gogh?"

He felt the coolness in her voice and cursed himself for being so awkward. The
emotion in him suddenly shut down; he felt calm and possessed. He tried a number
of voices in his mind and chose the one he liked best.

"I am trying to tell you, Ursula, something you know already. That I love you
with all my heart and can only be happy if you will be my wife."

He observed how startled she looked at his sudden command of himself. He
wondered if he ought to take her in his arms.

"Your wife!" Her voice rose a few tones. "Why Monsieur Van Gogh, that's
impossible!"

He looked at her from under mountain crags, and she saw his eyes clearly in the
darkness. "Now I'm afraid it's I who do not . . ."

"How extraordinary that you shouldn't know. I've been engaged for over a
year."

He did not know how long he stood there, or what he thought or felt. "Who is the man?" he asked dully.

"Oh, you've never met my fiancé? He had your room before you came. I thought you knew."

"How would I have?"

She stood on tiptoes and peered in the direction of the kitchen. "Well, I . . . I . . . thought someone might have told you."

"Why did you keep this from me all year, when you knew I was falling in love with you?" There was no hesitation or fumbling in his voice now.

"Was it my fault that you fell in love with me? I only wanted to be friends with you."

"Has he been to visit you since I've been in the house?"

"No. He's in Wales. He's coming to spend his summer holiday with me."

"You haven't seen him for over a year? Then you've forgotten him! I'm the one you love now!"

He threw sense and discretion to the winds, grabbed her to him and kissed her rudely on the unwilling mouth. He tasted the moistness of her lips, the sweetness of her mouth, the perfume of her hair; all the intensity of his love rose up within him.

"Ursula, you don't love him. I won't let you. You're going to be my wife. I couldn't bear to lose you. I'll never stop until you forget him and marry me!"

"Marry you!" she cried. "Do I have to marry every man that falls in love with me? Now let go of me, do you hear, or I shall call for help."

She wrenched herself free and ran breathlessly down the dark path. When she gained the steps she turned and spoke in a low carrying whisper that struck him like a shout.

"Red-headed fool!"

4

The next morning no one called him. He climbed lethargically out of bed. He shaved around his face in a circular swash, leaving several patches of beard. Ursula did not appear at breakfast. He walked downtown to Goupils. As he passed the same men that he had seen the morning before he noticed that they had altered. They looked like such lonely souls, hurrying away to their futile labours.

He did not see the laburnums in bloom nor the chestnut trees that lined the road. The sun was shining even more brightly than the morning before. He did not know it.

During the day he sold twenty *épreuves d'artiste* in colour of the *Venus Anadyomene* after Ingres. There was a big profit in these pictures for Goupils, but Vincent had lost his sense of delight in making money for the gallery. He had very little patience with the people who came in to buy. They not only could not tell the difference between good and bad art, but seemed to have a positive talent for choosing the artificial, the obvious, and the cheap.

His fellow clerks had never thought him a jolly chap, but he had done his best to make himself pleasant and agreeable. "What do you suppose is bothering the member of our illustrious Van Gogh family?" one of the clerks asked another.

"I dare say he got out of the wrong side of bed this morning."

"A jolly lot he has to worry about. His uncle, Vincent Van Gogh, is half owner of all the Goupil Galleries in Paris, Berlin, Brussels, The Hague, and Amsterdam. The old man is sick and has no children; everyone says he's leaving his half of the business to this chap."

"Some people have all the luck."

"That's only half the story. His uncle, Hendrik Van Gogh, owns big art shops in Brussels and Amsterdam, and still another uncle, Cornelius Van Gogh, is the head of the biggest firm in Holland. Why, the Van Goghs are the greatest family of picture dealers in Europe. One day our red-headed friend in the next room will practically control Continental art!''

When Vincent walked into the dining room of the Loyer's that night he found Ursula and her mother talking together in undertones. They stopped as soon as he came in, and left a sentence hanging in mid-air.

Ursula ran into the kitchen. "Good evening," said Madame Loyer with a curious glint in her eye.

Vincent ate his dinner alone at the large table. Ursula's blow had stunned but not defeated him. He simply was not going to take "no" for an answer. He would crowd the other man out of Ursula's mind.

It was almost a week before he could catch her standing still long enough to speak to her. He had eaten and slept very little during that week; his stolidity had given way to nervousness. His sales at the gallery had dropped off considerably. The greenness had gone from his eyes and left them a pain-shot blue. He had more difficulty than ever in finding words when he wanted to speak.

He followed her into the garden after the big Sunday dinner. "Mademoiselle Ursula," he said, "I'm sorry if I frightened you the other night."

She glanced up at him out of large, cool eyes, as though surprised that he should have followed her. "Oh, it doesn't matter. It was of no importance. Let's forget it, shall we?"

"I'd like very much to forget that I was rude to you. But the things I said were true."

He took a step toward her. She moved away.

"Why speak of it again?" Ursula asked. "The whole episode has quite gone out of my mind." She turned her back on him and walked down the path. He hurried after her.

"I must speak of it again. Ursula, you don't understand how much I love you! You don't know how unhappy I've been this past week. Why do you keep running away from me?"

"Shall we go in? I think Mother is expecting callers."

"It can't be true that you love this other man. I would have seen it in your eyes if you had."

"I'm afraid I've not got any more time to spare. When did you say you were going home for your holiday?"

He gulped. "In July."

"How fortunate. My fiancé is coming to spend his July holiday with me, and we'll need his old room."

"I'll never give you up to him, Ursula!"

"You'll simply have to stop this sort of thing. If you don't, Mother says you can find new lodgings."

He spent the next two months trying to dissuade her. All his early characteristics returned; if he could not be with Ursula he wanted to be by himself so that no one could interfere with his thinking about her. He was unfriendly to the people at the store. The world that had been awakened by Ursula's love went fast asleep again and he became the sombre, morose lad his parents had known in Zundert.

July came, and with it his holiday. He did not wish to leave London for two weeks. He had the feeling that Ursula could not love anyone else as long as he was in the house.

He went down into the parlour. Ursula and her mother were sitting there. They exchanged one of their significant looks.

"I'm taking only one grip with me, Madame Loyer," he said. "I shall leave everything in my room just as it is. Here is the money for the two weeks that I shall be away."

"I think you had better take all your things with you, Monsieur Van Gogh," said Madame.

"But why?"

"Your room is rented from Monday morning. We think it better if you live elsewhere."

"We?"

He turned and looked at Ursula from under the deep ridge of brow. That look made no statement. It only asked a question.

"Yes, we," replied her mother. "My daughter's fiancé has written that he wants you out of the house. I'm afraid, Monsieur Van Gogh, that it would have been better if you had never come here at all."

5

Theodorus Van Gogh met his son at the Breda station with a carriage. He had on his heavy, black ministerial coat, the wide lapelled vest, starched white shirt, and huge black bow tie covering all but a narrow strip of the high collar. With a quick glance Vincent took in his father's two facial characteristics: the right lid drooped down lower than the left, covering a considerable portion of the eye; the left side of his mouth was a thin, taut line, the right side full and sensuous. His eyes were passive; their expression simply said, "This is me."

The people of Zundert often remarked that the dominie Theodorus went about doing good with a high silk hat on.

He never understood to the day of his death why he was not more successful. He felt that he should have been called to an important pulpit in Amsterdam or The Hague years before. He was called the handsome dominie by his parishioners, was well educated, of a loving nature, had fine spiritual qualities, and was indefatigable in the service of God. Yet for twenty-five years he had been buried and forgotten in the little village of Zundert. He was the only one of the six Van Gogh brothers who had not achieved national importance.

The parsonage at Zundert, where Vincent had been born, was a wooden frame building across the road from the market place and *stadhuis*. There was a garden back of the kitchen with acacias and a number of little paths running through the carefully tended flowers. The church was a tiny wooden building hidden in the trees just behind the garden. There were two small Gothic windows of plain glass on either side, perhaps a dozen hard benches on the wooden floor, and a number of warming pans attached permanently to the planks. At the rear there was a stairway leading up to an old hand organ. It was a severe and simple place of worship, dominated by the spirit of Calvin and his reformation.

Vincent's mother, Anna Cornelia, was watching from the front window and had the door open before the carriage came to a full stop. Even while taking him with loving tenderness to her ample bosom, she perceived that something was wrong with her boy.

"Myn lieve zoon," she murmured. "My Vincent."

Her eyes, now blue, now green, were always wide open, gently inquiring, seeing through a person without judging too harshly. A faint line from the side of each nostril down to the corners of the mouth deepened with the passage of the years, and the deeper these lines became, the stronger impression they gave of a face slightly lifted in smile.

Anna Cornelia Carbentus was from The Hague, where her father carried the title of "Bookbinder to the King." William Carbentus's business flourished and when he was chosen to bind the first Constitution of Holland he became known throughout the country. His daughters, one of whom married Uncle Vincent Van Gogh, and a third the well known Reverend Stricker of Amsterdam, were *bien élevées*.

Anna Cornelia was a good woman. She saw no evil in the world and knew of none. She knew only of weakness, temptation, hardship, and pain. Theodorus Van Gogh was also a good man, but he understood evil very thoroughly and condemned every last vestige of it.

The dining room was the centre of the Van Gogh house, and the big table, after the supper dishes had been cleared off, the centre of family life. Here everyone gathered about the friendly oil lamp to pass the evening. Anna Cornelia was worried about Vincent; he was thin, and had become jumpy in his mannerisms.

"Is anything wrong, Vincent?" she asked after supper that night. "You don't look well to me."

Vincent glanced about the table where Anna, Elizabeth, and Willemien, three strange young girls who happened to be his sisters, were sitting.

"No," he said, "nothing is wrong."

"Do you find London agreeable?" asked Theodorus. "If you don't like it I'll speak to your Uncle Vincent. I think he would transfer you to one of the Paris shops."

Vincent became very agitated. "No, no, you mustn't do that!" he exclaimed. "I don't want to leave London, I . . ." He quieted himself. "When Uncle Vincent wants to transfer me, I'm sure he'll think of it for himself."

"Just as you wish," said Theodorus.

"It's that girl," said Anna Cornelia to herself. "Now I understand what was wrong with his letters."

There were pine woods and clumps of oaks on the heath near Zundert. Vincent spent his days walking alone in the fields, gazing down into the numerous ponds with which the heath was dotted. The only diversion he enjoyed was drawing; he made a number of sketches of the garden, the Saturday afternoon market seen from the window of the parsonage, the front door of the house. It kept his mind off Ursula for moments at a time.

Theodorus had always been disappointed that his oldest son had not chosen to follow in his footsteps. They went to visit a sick peasant and when they drove back that evening across the heath the two men got out of the carriage and walked awhile. The sun was setting red behind the pine trees, the evening sky was reflected in the pools, and the heath and yellow sand were full of harmony.

"My father was a parson, Vincent, and I had always hoped you would continue the line."

"What makes you think I want to change?"

"I was only saying, in case you wanted to . . . You could live with Uncle Jan in Amsterdam while you attend the University. And the Reverend Stricker has offered to direct your education."

"Are you advising me to leave Goupils?"

"Oh no, certainly not. But if you are unhappy there . . . sometimes people change . . ."

"I know. But I have no intention of leaving Goupils."

His mother and father drove him to Breda the day he was to leave for London. "Are we to write to the same address, Vincent?" Anna Cornelia asked.

"No. I'm moving."

"I'm glad you're leaving the Loyers," said his father. "I never liked that family. They had too many secrets."

Vincent stiffened. His mother laid a warm hand over his and said gently, so that Theodorus might not hear, "Don't be unhappy, my dear. You will be better off with a nice Dutch girl, later, later, when you are more established. She would not be good for you, that Ursula girl. She is not your kind.''

He wondered how his mother knew.

6

Back in London he took furnished rooms in Kensington New Road. His landlady was a little old woman who retired every evening at eight. There was never the faintest sound in the house. Each night he had a fierce battle on his hands; he yearned to run directly to the Loyers'. He would lock the door on himself and swear resolutely that he was going to sleep. In a quarter of an hour he would find himself mysteriously on the street, hurrying to Ursula's.

When he got within a block of her house he felt himself enter her aura. It was torture to have this feel of her and yet have her so inaccessible; it was a thousand times worse torture to stay in Ivy Cottage and not get within that penumbra of haunting personality.

Pain did curious things to him. It made him sensitive to the pain of others. It made him intolerant of everything that was cheap and blatantly successful in the world about him. He was no longer of any value at the gallery. When customers asked him what he thought about a particular print he told them in no uncertain terms how horrible it was, and they did not buy. The only pictures in which he could find reality and emotional depth were the ones in which the artists had expressed pain.

In October a stout matron with a high lace collar, a high bosom, a sable coat, and a round velvet hat with a blue plume, came in and asked to be shown some pictures for her new town house. She fell to Vincent.

"I want the very best things you have in stock," she said. "You needn't concern yourself over the expense. Here are the dimensions; in the drawing room there are two uninterrupted walls of fifty feet, one wall broken by two windows with a space between . . .''

He spent the better part of the afternoon trying to sell her some etchings after Rembrandt, an excellent reproduction of a Venetian water scene after Turner, some lithographs after Thys Maris, and museum photographs after Corot and Daubigny. The woman had a sure instinct for picking out the very worst expression of the painter's art to be found in any group that Vincent showed her. She had an equal talent for being able to reject at first sight, and quite peremptorily, everything he knew to be authentic. As the hours passed, the woman, with her pudgy features and condescending puerilities, became for him a perfect symbol of middle-class fatuity and the commercial life.

"There," she exclaimed with a self-satisfied air, "I think I've chosen rather well."

"If you had closed your eyes and picked," said Vincent, "you couldn't have done any worse."

The woman rose to her feet heavily and swept the wide velvet skirt to one side. Vincent could see the turgid flow of blood creep from her propped-up bosom to her neck under the lace collar.

"Why!" she exclaimed, "why, you're nothing but a . . . a . . . country boor!"

She stormed out, the tall feather in her velvet hat waving back and forth.

Mr. Obach was outraged. "My dear Vincent," he exclaimed, "whatever is the matter with you? You've muffed the biggest sale of the week, and insulted that woman!"

"Mr. Obach, would you answer me one question?"

"Well, what is it? I have a few questions to ask, myself."

Vincent shoved aside the woman's prints and put both hands on the edge of the table. "Then tell me how a man can justify himself for spending his one and only life selling very bad pictures to very stupid people?"

Obach made no attempt to answer. "If this sort of thing keeps up," he said, "I'll have to write to your uncle and have him transfer you to another branch. I can't have you ruining my business."

Vincent moved aside Obach's strong breath with a gesture of his hand. "How can we take such large profits for selling trash, Mr. Obach? And why is it that the only people who can afford to come in here are those who can't bear to look at anything authentic? Is it because their money has made them callous? And why is it that the poor people who can really appreciate good art haven't even a farthing to buy a print for their walls?"

Obach looked at him queerly. "What is this, socialism?"

When he reached home he picked up the volume of Renan lying on his table and turned to a page he had marked. "To act well in this world," he read, "one must die within oneself. Man is not on this earth only to be happy, he is not there to be simply honest, he is there to realize great things for humanity, to attain nobility and to surpass the vulgarity in which the existence of almost all individuals drags on."

About a week before Christmas the Loyers put up a dainty Christmas tree in their front window. Two nights later as he walked by he saw the house well lighted and neighbours going in the front door. He heard the sound of laughing voices inside. The Loyers were giving their Christmas party. Vincent ran home, shaved hurriedly, put on a fresh shirt and tie, and walked back as fast as he could to Clapham. He had to wait several minutes at the bottom of the stairs to catch his breath.

This was Christmas; the spirit of kindliness and forgiveness was in the air. He walked up the stairs. He pounded on the knocker. He heard a familiar footstep come through the hall, a familiar voice call back something to the people in the parlour. The door was opened. The light from the lamp fell on his face. He looked at Ursula. She was wearing a sleeveless green polonaise with large bows and lace cascades. He had never seen her so beautiful.

"Ursula," he said.

An expression passed over her face that repeated clearly all the things she had said to him in the garden. Looking at her, he remembered them.

"Go away," she said.

She slammed the door in his face.

The following morning he sailed for Holland.

Christmas was the busiest season for the Goupil Galleries. Mr. Obach wrote to Uncle Vincent, explaining that his nephew had taken a holiday without so much as a "with your leave." Uncle Vincent decided to put his nephew into the main gallery in Rue Chaptal in Paris.

Vincent calmly announced that he was through with the art business. Uncle Vincent was stunned and deeply hurt. He declared that in the future he would wash his hands of Vincent. After the holidays he stopped washing them long enough to secure his namesake a position as clerk in the bookshop of Blussé and Braam at Dordrecht. It was the very last thing the two Vincent Van Goghs ever had to do with each other.

He remained at Dordrecht almost four months. He was neither happy nor unhappy, successful nor unsuccessful. He simply was not there. One Saturday night he took the last train from Dordrecht to Oudenbosch and walked home to Zundert. It was beautiful on the heath with all the cool, pungent smells of night. Though it was dark he could distinguish the pine woods and moors extending far and wide. It reminded him of the print by Bodmer that hung in his father's study. The sky was overcast but the night stars were shining through the clouds. It was very early when he arrived at the churchyard at Zundert; in the distance he could hear the larks singing in the black fields of young corn.

His parents understood that he was going through a difficult time. Over the summer the family moved to Etten, a little market town just a few kilometres away, where Theodorus had been named dominie. Etten had a large, elm-lined public square and a steam train connecting it with the important city of Breda. For Theodorus it was a slight step up.

When early fall came it was necessary once again to make a decision. Ursula was not yet married.

"You are not fitted for all these shops, Vincent," said his father. "Your heart has been leading you straight to the service of God."

"I know, Father."

"Then why not go to Amsterdam and study?"

"I would like to, but . . ."

"There is still hesitation in your heart?"

"Yes. I can't explain now. Give me a little more time."

Uncle Jan passed through Etten. "There is a room waiting for you in my house in Amsterdam, Vincent," he said.

"The Reverend Stricker has written that he can secure you good tutors," added his mother.

When he received the gift of pain from Ursula he had inherited the disinherited of the earth. He knew that the best training he would get was at the University at Amsterdam. The Van Gogh and Stricker families would take him in, encourage him, help him with money, books, and sympathy. But he could not make the clean break. Ursula was still in England, unmarried. In Holland he had lost the touch of her. He sent for some English newspapers, answered a number of advertisements, and finally secured a position as teacher at Ramsgate, a seaport town four and a half hours by train from London.

7

Mr. Stokes's schoolhouse stood on a square in the middle of which was a large lawn shut off by iron railings. There were twenty-four boys from ten to fourteen years of age at the school. Vincent had to teach French, German, and Dutch, keep an eye on the boys after hours, and help them with their weekly ablutions on Saturday night. He was given his board and lodging, but no pay.

Ramsgate was a melancholy spot but it suited his mood. Unconsciously he had come to cherish his pain as a dear companion; through it he kept Ursula constantly by his side. If he could not be with the girl he loved, it did not matter where he was. All he asked was that no one come between him and the heavy satiety with which Ursula crammed his brain and body.

"Can't you pay me just a small sum, Mr. Stokes?" asked Vincent. "Enough to buy tobacco and clothes?"

"No, I will certainly not do that," replied Stokes. "I can get teachers enough for just board and lodging."

Early the first Saturday morning Vincent started from Ramsgate to London. It was a long walk, and the weather stayed hot until evening. Finally he reached Canterbury. He rested in the shade of the old trees surrounding the medieval cathedral. After a bit he walked still farther until he arrived at a few large beech and elm trees near a little pond. He slept there until four in the morning; the birds began to sing at dawn and awakened him. By afternoon he reached Chatham where he saw in the distance, between partly flooded low meadows, the Thames full of ships. Towards evening Vincent struck the familiar suburbs of London, and in spite of his fatigue, cut out briskly for the Loyers' house.

The thing for which he had come back to England, the contact with Ursula, reached out and gripped him the instant he came within sight of her home. In England she was still his because he could feel her.

He could not quiet the loud beating of his heart. He leaned against a tree, dully aching with an ache that existed outside the realm of words or articulate thought. At length the lamp in Ursula's parlour was extinguished, then the lamp in her bedroom. The house went dark. Vincent tore himself away and stumbled wearily down the road of Clapham. When he got out of sight of the house he knew that he had lost her again.

When he pictured his marriage to Ursula he no longer thought of her as the wife of a successful art dealer. He saw her as the faithful, uncomplaining wife of an evangelist, working by his side in the slums, to serve the poor.

Nearly every week-end he tried tramping to London, but he found it difficult to get back in time for the Monday morning classes. Sometimes he would walk all Friday and Saturday night just to see Ursula come out of her house on the way to church on Sunday morning. He had no money for food or lodgings, and as winter came on he suffered from the cold. When he got back to Ramsgate in the dawn of a Monday morning he would be shivering, exhausted and famished. It took him all week to recover.

After a few months he found a better position at Mr. Jones's Methodist school in Isleworth. Mr. Jones was a minister with a large parish. He employed Vincent as a teacher but soon turned him into a country curate.

Once again Vincent had to change all the pictures in his mind. Ursula was no longer to be the wife of an evangelist, working in the slums, but rather the wife of a country clergyman, helping her husband in the parish just as his mother helped his father. He saw Ursula looking on with approval, happy that he had left the narrow commercial life of Goupils and was now working for humanity.

He did not permit himself to realize that Ursula's wedding day was coming closer and closer. The other man had never existed as a reality in his mind. He always thought of Ursula's refusal as arising from some peculiar shortcoming on his part, a shortcoming which he must somehow remedy. What better way was there than serving God?

Mr. Jones's impoverished students came from London. The master gave Vincent the addresses of the parents and sent him there on foot to collect tuition. Vincent found them in the heart of Whitechapel. There were vile odours in the streets, large families herded into cold, barren rooms, hunger and illness staring out of every pair of eyes. A number of the fathers traded in diseased meat which the government prohibited from sale in the regular markets. Vincent came upon the families shivering in their rags and eating their supper of slops, dry crusts and putrid meat. He listened to their tales of destitution and misery until nightfall.

He had welcomed the trip to London because it would give him the chance to pass Ursula's house on the way home. The slums of Whitechapel drove her out of his mind and he forgot to take the road through Clapham. He returned to Isleworth without so much as a brass farthing for Mr. Jones.

One Thursday evening during the services the minister leaned over to his curate and feigned fatigue. "I'm feeling frightfully done in this evening, Vincent. You've been writing sermons straight along, haven't you? Then let's hear one of them. I want to see what kind of minister you're going to make."

Vincent mounted to the pulpit, trembling. His face went red and he did not know what to do with his hands. His voice was hoarse and halting. He had to stumble through his memory for the well-rounded phrases he had set down so neatly on paper. But he felt his spirit burst through the broken words and clumsy gestures.

"Nicely done, Vincent," said Mr. Jones. "I shall send you to Richmond next week."

It was a clear autumn day and a beautiful walk from Isleworth to Richmond along the Thames. The blue sky and great chestnut trees with their load of yellow leaves were mirrored in the water. The people of Richmond wrote Mr. Jones that they liked the young Dutch preacher, so the good man decided to give Vincent his chance. Mr. Jones's church at Turnham Green was an important one, the congregation large and critical. If Vincent could preach a good sermon there, he would be qualified to preach from any pulpit.

Vincent chose as his text, Psalms 119:19, "I am a stranger on the earth: hide not Thy commandments from me." He spoke with simple fervour. His youth, his fire, his heavy-handed power, his massive head, and penetrating eyes all had a tremendous effect on the congregation.

Many of them came up to thank him for his message. He shook their hands and smiled at them in a misty daze. As soon as everyone had gone, he slipped out the back door of the church and took the road to London.

A storm came up. He had forgotten his hat and overcoat. The Thames was yellowish, especially near the shore. At the horizon there was a dash of light, and above it immense grey clouds from which the rain poured down in slanting streaks. He was drenched to the skin, but he tramped on at an exhilarated speed.

At last he was successful! He had found himself. He had a triumph to lay at Ursula's feet, to share with her.

The rain pelted the dust on the little white path and swayed the hawthorn bushes. In the distance was a town that looked like a Durer engraving, a town with its turrets, mills, slate roofs and houses built in the Gothic style.

He battled his way into London, the water streaming down his face and sopping into his boots. It was late afternoon before he reached the Loyer house. A grey, murky dusk had fallen. From some distance he heard the sound of music, of violins, and wondered what was going on. Every room in the house had its lamp burning. A number of carriages stood out in the sheets of rain. Vincent saw people dancing in the parlour. An old cabby was sitting on his box under a huge umbrella, huddled away from the rain.

"What's going on here?" he asked.

"Weddin', I fancy."

Vincent leaned against the carriage, rivulets from his red hair streaming down his face. After a time the front door opened. Ursula and a tall, slim man were framed in the doorway. The crowd from the parlour surged out on the porch, laughing, shouting, throwing rice.

Vincent slunk around to the dark side of the carriage. Ursula and her husband got in. The cabby flicked his whip over the horses. They started slowly. Vincent took a few steps forward and pressed his face against the streaming window. Ursula was locked tight in the man's arms, her mouth full on his. The carriage drew away.

Something thin snapped within Vincent, snapped neat and clean. The spell was broken. He had not known it could be so easy.

He trudged back to Isleworth in the slashing rain, collected his belongings, and left England for ever.

BOOK ONE

THE BORINAGE

1

Vice-Admiral Johannes Van Gogh, highest ranking officer in the Dutch Navy, stood on the *stoep* of his roomy, rent-free residence at the rear of the Navy Yard. In honour of his nephew's coming he had donned his dress uniform; a gold epaulet perched on each shoulder. Above the ponderous Van Gogh chin jutted a strong, straight-ridged nose that met the convex cliff of the forehead.

"I'm glad to have you here, Vincent," he said. "The house is very quiet, now that my children have married out of it."

They mounted a flight of broad, angular stairs and Uncle Jan threw open a door. Vincent entered the room and set down his bag. A large window overlooked the Yard. Uncle Jan sat on the edge of the bed and tried to look as informal as his gold braid would permit.

"I was pleased to hear that you had decided to study for the ministry," he said. "One member of the Van Gogh family has always done God's work."

Vincent reached for his pipe and loaded the bowl carefully with tobacco; it was a gesture he often made when he needed an extra moment to think. "I wanted to be an evangelist, you know, and get right to work."

"You wouldn't want to be an evangelist, Vincent. They're uneducated people, and Lord knows what sort of garbled theology they preach. No, my boy, the Van Gogh dominies have always been University graduates. But no doubt you would like to unpack now. Dinner is at eight."

The broad back of the vice-admiral had no sooner gone out of the door than a gentle melancholy descended upon Vincent. He looked about him. The bed was wide and comfortable, the bureau spacious, the low, smooth study table inviting. But he felt ill at ease, as he did in the presence of strangers. He snatched up his cap and walked rapidly across the *Dam*. There he found a Jewish book-seller who offered beautiful prints in an open bin. After a good deal of searching, Vincent selected thirteen pieces, stuck them under his arm and walked home along the waterfront, breathing in the strong odour of tar.

As he was pinning up his prints lightly, so as not to injure the fabric of the walls, there was a knock on the door. The Reverend Stricker entered. Stricker was also

Vincent's uncle, but he was not a Van Gogh; his wife and Vincent's mother were sisters. He was a well-known clergyman in Amsterdam and by general admission a clever one. His black suit was of good material, smartly cut.

When the greetings were over the dominie said, "I have secured Mendes da Costa, one of our finest scholars of the classical languages, to tutor you in Latin and Greek. His home is in the Jewish quarter; you are to go there Monday afternoon at three for your first lesson. But what I came for was to ask your company at tomorrow's Sunday dinner. Your Aunt Wilhelmina and Cousin Kay are anxious to see you."

"I would like that very much. At what time shall I come?"

"We dine at noon, after my late morning service."

"Please present my compliments to your family," said Vincent, as the Reverend Stricker picked up his black hat and folio.

"Until tomorrow," said his uncle, and was gone.

2

The Keizersgracht, on which the Stricker family lived, was one of the most aristocratic streets in Amsterdam. It was the fourth horseshoe boulevard and canal which starts from the south side of the harbour, runs around the centrum and back to the harbour again on the north. It was clean and clear, far too important a canal to be covered with *kroos,* the mysterious green moss which for hundreds of years had laid a thick surface on the canals in the poorer districts.

The houses that line the street are pure Flemish; narrow, well built, tightly fitted together, a long line of prim Puritan soldiers standing at attention.

The following day, after listening to Uncle Stricker preach, Vincent set out for the dominie's house. A bright sun had waved away the ash-grey clouds that float eternally across the Dutch skies, and for a few moments the air was luminous. Vincent was early. He walked at a meditative gait and watched the canal boats being pushed upstream against the current.

They were largely sand boats, oblong except for the tapering ends; a water-worn black in colour, with great hollow spaces in the centre for the cargo. Long clothes-lines extended from prow to stern, on which hung the family wash. The father of the family thrust his pole into the mud, propped it against his shoulder, and struggled down the catwalk at twisted, tortuous angles while the boat slipped out from under him. The wife, a heavy, buxom, red-faced woman, sat immutably at the stern and worked the clumsy wooden tiller. The children played with the dog, and every few minutes ran down into the cabin hole that was their home.

The Reverend Stricker's home was of typical Flemish architecture; narrow, three-storied, with an oblong tower at the top containing the attic window, and decorated with flowing arabesques. A beam stuck out from the attic window with a long iron hook at the end of it.

Aunt Wilhelmina welcomed Vincent and led him into the dining room. A portrait of Calvin by Ary Scheffer hung on the wall, and a silver service gleamed on a sideboard. The walls were done in dark wood panelling.

Before Vincent could get used to the customary darkness of the room, a tall, lithe girl came out of the shadows and greeted him warmly.

"Of course you wouldn't know me," she said in a rich voice, "but I'm your cousin Kay."

Vincent took her outstretched hand and felt the soft, warm flesh of a young woman for the first time in many months.

"We've never met," the girl went on in that intimate tone, "and I think it rather curious, since I'm twenty-six, and you must be . . . ?"

Vincent gazed at her in silence. Several moments passed before he realized that an answer was necessary. In order to make up for his stupidity, he blurted out in a loud, harsh voice, "Twenty-four. Younger than you."

"Yes. Well, I suppose it's not so curious after all. You have never visited Amsterdam and I have never been in the Brabant. But I'm afraid I'm being a poor hostess. Won't you sit down?"

He sat on the edge of a stiff chair. With one of the swift, strange metamorphoses that changed him from an awkward, country boor to a polished gentleman, he said, "Mother often wished you would come to visit us. I think the Brabant would have pleased you. The country-side is very *sympatica.*"

"I know. Aunt Anna wrote and invited me several times. I must visit there very soon."

"Yes," replied Vincent, "you must."

It was only a remote portion of his mind that heard and answered the girl. The rest of him was soaking up her beauty with the passionate thirst of a man who has drunk too long at a celibate well. Kay had the hardy features of the Dutch women, but they had been filed down, chiselled away to delicate proportions. Her hair was neither the corn blond nor the raw red of her country-women, but a curious inter-mingling, in which the fire of one had caught up the light of the other in a glowing, subtle warmth. She had guarded her skin against the sun and wind; the whiteness of her chin crept into the flush of her cheek with all the artistry of a little Dutch master. Her eyes were a deep blue, dancing to the joy of life; her full-lipped mouth was slightly open, as though for its acceptance.

She noticed Vincent's silence and said, "What are you thinking about, Cousin? You seem preoccupied."

"I was thinking that Rembrandt would have liked to paint you."

Kay laughed low and with a ripe lusciousness in her throat. "Rembrandt only liked to paint ugly old women, didn't he?" she asked.

"No," replied Vincent. "He painted beautiful old women, women who were poor or in some way unhappy, but who through sorrow had gained a soul."

For the first time Kay really looked at Vincent. She had glanced at him only casually when he came in and noticed his mop of rust-red hair and rather heavy face. Now she saw the full mouth, the deep set, burning eyes, the high, symmetrical forehead of the Van Goghs, and the uncrushable chin, stuck slightly out toward her.

"Forgive me for being stupid," she murmured, almost in a whisper. "I understand what you mean about Rembrandt. He gets at the real essence of beauty, doesn't he, when he paints those gnarled old people who have suffering and defeat carved into their faces."

"What have you children been talking about so earnestly?" asked the Reverend Stricker from the doorway.

"We have been getting acquainted," Kay answered. "Why didn't you tell me I had such a nice cousin?"

Another man came into the room, a slender chap with an easy smile and charming manner. Kay rose and kissed him eagerly. "Cousin Vincent," she said, "this is my husband, Mijnheer Vos."

She returned in a few moments with a tow-headed boy of two, a vivacious child with a wistful face and the light blue eyes of his mother. Kay reached down and lifted the boy. Vos put his arms about the two of them.

"Will you sit on this side of the table with me, Vincent?" asked Aunt Wilhelmina.

Opposite Vincent, with Vos on one side and Jan propped up on the other, sat Kay. She had forgotten about Vincent now that her husband was home. The colour deepened in her cheek. Once, as her husband said something pointed in a low, guarded tone, she leaned over with a quick alertness and kissed him.

The vibrant waves of their love reached out and engulfed Vincent. For the first time since that fateful Sunday the old pain for Ursula arose from some mysterious source within him and flooded the outermost ramparts of his body and brain. The little family before him, with its clinging unity and joyous affection, brought him to a realization that he had been hungry, desperately hungry for love all these weary months, and that it was a hunger not easily destroyed.

3

Vincent arose just before sunrise each morning to read his Bible. When the sun came up about five o'clock he went to the window which overlooked the Navy Yard and watched the gangs of workmen come through the gate, a long uneven line of black figures. Little steamers sailed to and fro in the Zuider Zee and in the distance, near the village across the Y, he saw the swiftly moving, brown sails.

When the sun had fully risen and sponged the mist from the pile of lumber, Vincent turned from his window, breakfasted on a piece of dry bread and a glass of beer, and then sat down for a seven hour siege with his Latin and Greek.

After four or five hours of concentration his head became heavy; often it burned and his thoughts were confused. He did not see how he was going to persevere in simple, regular study after all those emotional years. He pounded rules into his head until the sun was already sliding down the other side of the heavens and it was time for him to go to Mendes da Costa for his lesson. On the way there he would walk along the Buitenkant, around the Oudezyds Chapel and the Old and South Church, through crooked streets with forges and coopers and lithograph shops.

Mendes reminded Vincent of the *Imitation of Jesus Christ* by Ruyperez; he was the classical type of Jew with profound, cavernous eyes, a thin, hollowed out, spiritual face, and the soft, pointed beard of the early rabbis. It was very close and sultry in mid-afternoon in the Jewish quarter; Vincent, gorged with seven hours of Greek and Latin, and more hours of Dutch History and Grammar, would talk to Mendes about lithographs. One day he brought his teacher the study of *A Baptism* by Maris.

Mendes held *A Baptism* in his bony, tapering fingers, letting the sharp stream of dusted sunlight from the high window fall upon it.

"It is good," he said in his throaty, Jewish voice. "It catches something of the spirit of universal religion."

Vincent's fatigue left him instantly. He launched into an enthusiastic description of Maris's art. Mendes shook his head imperceptibly. The Reverend Stricker was paying him a high price to instruct Vincent in Latin and Greek.

"Vincent," he said quietly, "Maris is very fine, but the time grows short and we had better get on with our studies, yes?"

Vincent understood. On the way home, after a two hour lesson, he would pause before the interiors of houses where the wood-choppers, carpenters, and ships' victualers were at work. The doors stood open before a big wine cellar, and men with lights were running to and fro in the dark vault.

Uncle Jan went to Helvoort for a week; knowing that he was alone in the big house behind the Navy Yard, Kay and Vos walked over late one afternoon to fetch Vincent for dinner.

"You must come to us every night until Uncle Jan gets back," Kay told him. "And Mother asks if you won't take Sunday dinner with us each week, after services?"

When dinner was over the family played cards, but since Vincent did not know how to play, he settled in a quiet corner and read August Gruson's "Histoire des

Croisades.'' From where he was sitting he could watch Kay and the changes of her quick, provocative smile. She left the table and came to his side.

''What are you reading, Cousin Vincent?'' she asked.

He told her and then said, ''It's a fine little book, I should almost say written with the sentiment of Thys Maris.''

Kay smiled. He was always making these funny literary allusions. ''Why Thys Maris?'' she demanded.

''Read this and see if it doesn't remind you of a Maris canvas, where the writer describes an old castle on a rock, with the autumn woods in twilight, and in the foreground the black fields, and a peasant who is ploughing with a white horse.''

While Kay was reading, Vincent drew up a chair for her. When she looked at him a thoughtful expression darkened her blue eyes.

''Yes,'' she said, ''it is just like a Maris. The writer and painter use their own medium to express the same thought.''

Vincent took the book and ran his finger across the page eagerly. ''This line might have been lifted straight from Michelet or Carlyle.''

''You know, Cousin Vincent, for a man who has spent so little time in classrooms, you are surprisingly well educated. Do you still read a good many books?''

''No, I should like to, but I may not. Though in fact I need not long for it so much, for all things are found in the word of Christ—more perfect and more beautiful than in any other book.''

''Oh, Vincent,'' exclaimed Kay, jumping to her feet, ''that was so unlike you!'' Vincent stared at her in amazement.

''I think you are ever so much nicer when you're seeing Thys Maris in the 'Histoire des Croisades'—though Father says you ought to concentrate and not think of such things—than when you talk like a stuffy, provincial clergyman.''

Vos strolled over and said, ''We've dealt you a hand, Kay.''

Kay looked for a moment into the live, burning coals under Vincent's overhanging brows, then took her husband's arm and joined the other card players.

4

Mendes da Costa knew that Vincent liked to talk to him about the more general things of life, so several times a week he invented excuses to accompany him back to town when their lesson was done.

One day he took Vincent through an interesting part of the city, the outskirts that extend from the Leidsche Poort, near the Vondel Park, to the Dutch railway station. It was full of sawmills, workmen's cottages with little gardens, and was very populous. The quarter was cut through with many small canals.

''It must be a splendid thing to be a clergyman in a quarter like this,'' said Vincent.

''Yes,'' replied Mendes, as he filled his pipe and passed the cone-shaped bag of tobacco to Vincent, ''these people need God and religion more than our friends uptown.''

They were crossing a tiny wooden bridge that might almost have been Japanese. Vincent stopped and said, ''What do you mean, Mijnheer?''

''These workers,'' said Mendes with a gentle sweep of his arm, ''have a hard life of it. When illness comes they have no money for a doctor. The food for tomorrow comes from today's labour, and hard labour it is, too. Their houses, as you see, are small and poor; they are never more than a stone's throw away from privation and want. They've made a bad bargain with life; they need the thought of God to comfort them.''

Vincent lighted his pipe and dropped the match into the little canal below him. "And the people uptown?" he asked.

"They have good clothes to wear, secure positions, money put away against adversity. When they think of God, He is a prosperous old gentleman, rather well pleased with himself for the lovely way things are going on earth."

"In short," said Vincent, "they're a little stuffy."

"Dear me!" exclaimed Mendes. "I never said that."

"No, I did."

That night he spread his Greek books out before him, and then stared at the opposite wall for a long time. He remembered the slums of London, the sordid poverty and suffering; he remembered his desire to become an evangelist and help those people. His mental image flashed to Uncle Stricker's church. The congregation was prosperous, well-educated, sensitive to and capable of acquiring the better things of life. Uncle Stricker's sermons were beautiful and comforting, but who in the congregation needed comfort?

Six months had passed since he first came to Amsterdam. He was at last beginning to understand that hard work is but a poor substitute for natural ability. He pushed aside his language books and opened his algebra. At midnight Uncle Jan came in.

"I saw the light under your door, Vincent," said the vice-admiral, "and the watchman told me he saw you walking in the Yard at four o'clock this morning. How many hours a day have you been working?"

"It varies. Between eighteen and twenty."

"Twenty!" Uncle Jan shook his head; the misgiving grew more perceptible on his face. It was difficult for the vice-admiral to adjust himself to the thought of failure in the Van Gogh family. "You should not need so many."

"I must get my work done, Uncle Jan."

Uncle Jan brought up his bushy eyebrows. "Be that as it may," he said, "I have promised your parents to take good care of you. So you will kindly get to bed, and in the future do not work so late."

Vincent pushed aside his exercises. He had no need for sleep; he had no need for love or sympathy or pleasure. He had need only to learn his Latin and Greek, his algebra and grammar, so that he might pass his examinations, enter the University, become a minister, and do God's practical work on earth.

5

By May, just a year after he came to Amsterdam, he began to realize that his unfitness for formal education would finally conquer him. This was not a statement of fact, but an admission of defeat, and every time one portion of his brain threw the realization before him, he whipped the rest of his mind to drown the admission in weary labour.

If it had been a simple question of the difficulty of the work, and his manifest unfitness for it, he would not have been disturbed. But the question that racked him night and day was, "Did he want to become a clever, gentleman clergyman like his Uncle Stricker?" What would happen to his ideal of personal service to the poor, the sick, the downtrodden, if he thought only of declensions and formulae for five more years?

One afternoon late in May, when he had finished his lesson with Mendes, Vincent said, "Mijnheer da Costa, could you find time to take a walk with me?"

Mendes had been sensitive to the growing struggle in Vincent; he divined that the younger man had reached a point where a decision was imminent.

"Yes, I had planned to go for a little stroll. The air is very clear after the rains. I should be glad to accompany you." He wrapped a wool scarf about his neck many times and put on a high collared, black coat. The two men went into the street, walked by the side of the same synagogue in which Baruch Spinoza had been excommunicated more than three centuries before, and after a few blocks passed Rembrandt's old home in the Zeestraat.

"He died in poverty and disgrace," said Mendes in an ordinary tone as they passed the old house.

Vincent looked up at him quickly. Mendes had a habit of piercing to the heart of a problem before one even mentioned it. There was a profound resilience about the man; things one said seemed to be plunged into fathomless depths for consideration. With Uncle Jan and Uncle Stricker, one's words hit a precise wall and bounced back fast to the tune of yes! or no! Mendes always bathed one's thought in the deep well of his mellow wisdom before he returned it.

"He didn't die unhappy, though," said Vincent.

"No," replied Mendes, "he had expressed himself fully and he knew the worth of what he had done. He was the only one in his time who did."

"Then did that make it all right with him, the fact that he knew? Suppose he had been wrong? What if the world had been right in neglecting him?"

"What the world thought made little difference. Rembrandt had to paint. Whether he painted well or badly didn't matter; painting was the stuff that held him together as a man. The chief value of art, Vincent, lies in the expression it gives to the artist. Rembrandt fulfilled what he knew to be his life purpose; that justified him. Even if his work had been worthless, he would have been a thousand times more successful than if he had put down his desire and become the richest merchant in Amsterdam."

"I see."

"The fact that Rembrandt's work brings joy to the whole world today," continued Mendes, as though following his own line of thought, "is entirely gratuitous. His life was complete and successful when he died, even though he was hounded into his grave. The book of his life closed then, and it was a beautifully wrought volume. The quality of his perseverance and loyalty to his idea is what was important, not the quality of his work."

They stopped to watch men working with sand carts near the Y, and then passed through many narrow streets with gardens full of ivy.

"But how is a young man to know he is choosing rightly, Mijnheer? Suppose he thinks there is something special he must do with his life, and afterwards he finds out he wasn't suited to that at all?"

Mendes drew his chin out of the collar of the coat, and his black eyes brightened. "Look, Vincent," he cried, "how the sunset is throwing a ruddy glow on those grey clouds."

They had reached the harbour. The masts of the ships and the row of old houses and trees on the waterfront were standing out against the colour and everything was reflected in the Zee. Mendes filled his pipe and passed the paper sack to Vincent.

"I am already smoking, Mijnheer," said Vincent.

"Oh yes, so you are. Shall we walk along the dyke to Zee burg? The Jewish churchyard is there and we can sit for a moment where my people are buried."

They walked along in friendly silence, the wind carrying the smoke over their shoulders. "You can never be sure about anything for all time, Vincent," said Mendes. "You can only have the courage and strength to do what you think is right. It may turn out to be wrong, but you will at least have done it, and that is the important thing. We must act according to the best dictates of our reason, and then leave God to judge of its ultimate value. If you are certain at this moment that you want to serve Our Maker in one way or another, then that faith is the only guide you have to the future. Don't be afraid to put your trust in it."

"Suppose I am not qualified?"

"To serve God?" Mendes looked at him with a shy smile.

"No, I mean qualified to become the sort of academic clergyman that the University turns out."

Mendes did not wish to say anything about Vincent's specific problem; he wanted only to discuss its more general phases and let the boy come to his own decision. By now they had reached the Jewish churchyard. It was very simple, full of old headstones with Hebrew inscriptions, and elderberry trees, and covered here and there with a high, dark grass. There was a stone bench near the plot reserved for the da Costa family, and here the two men sat down. Vincent put away his pipe. The churchyard was deserted at this hour of the evening; not a sound was to be heard.

"Every person has an integrity, a quality of character, Vincent," said Mendes, looking at the graves of his father and mother lying side by side, "and if he observes it, whatever he does will turn out well in the end. If you had remained an art dealer, the integrity that makes you the sort of man you are would have made you a good art dealer. The same applies to your teaching. Some day you will express yourself fully, no matter what medium you may choose."

"And if I do not remain in Amsterdam to become a professional minister?"

"It does not matter. You will return to London as an evangelist, or work in a shop, or become a peasant in the Brabant. Whatever you will do, you will do well. I have felt the quality of the stuff that goes to make you a man, and I know that it is good. Many times in your life you may think you are failing, but ultimately you will express yourself and that expression will justify your life."

"Thank you, Mijnheer da Costa. What you say helps me."

Mendes shivered a little. The stone bench under him was cold and the sun had gone down behind the sea. He rose. "Shall we go, Vincent?" he asked.

6

The following day, as twilight was falling, Vincent stood at the window overlooking the Yard. The little avenue of poplars with their slender forms and thin branches stood out delicately against the grey evening sky.

"Because I am no good at formal studying," said Vincent to himself, "does that mean I can't be of any use in the world? What, after all, have Latin and Greek to do with the love of our fellow men?"

Uncle Jan passed in the Yard below, making the rounds. In the distance Vincent could see the masts of the ships in the docks, in front the *Atjeh,* quite black, and the red and grey monitors surrounding it.

"The thing I wanted to do all along was God's practical work, not draw triangles and circles. I never wanted to have a big church and preach polished sermons. I belong with the humble and suffering *Now, Not Five Years From Now!"*

Just then the bell rang and the whole stream of workmen began pouring toward the gate. The lamplighter came to light the lantern in the Yard. Vincent turned away from the window.

He realized that his father and Uncle Jan and Uncle Stricker had spent a great deal of time and money on him in the past year. They would consider it entirely wasted if he gave up.

Well, he had tried honestly. He could not work more than twenty hours a day. He was obviously unfitted for the life of the study. He had begun too late. If he went out tomorrow as an evangelist, working for His people, would that be failure? If he cured the sick, comforted the weary, consoled the sinner, and converted the unbeliever, would that still be failure?

The family would say it was. They would say he could never succeed, that he was worthless and ungrateful, the black sheep of the Van Gogh family.

"Whatever you do," Mendes had said, "you will do well. Ultimately you will express yourself and that expression will justify your life."

Kay, who understood everything, had already surprised in him the seeds of a narrow minded clergyman. Yes, that was what he would become if he remained in Amsterdam where the true voice grew fainter and fainter every day. He knew where his place was in the world, and Mendes had given him the courage to go. His family would scorn him, but that no longer seemed to matter. His own position was little enough to give up for God.

He packed his bag quickly and walked out of the house without saying good-bye.

7

The Belgian Committee of Evangelization, composed of the Reverends van den Brink, de Jong and Pietersen, was opening a new school in Brussels, where instruction was to be free and the students had to pay only a small sum for their board and lodging. Vincent visited the Committee and was accepted as a pupil.

"At the end of three months," said the Reverend Pietersen, "we will give you an appointment somewhere in Belgium."

"Providing he qualifies," said the Reverend de Jong heavily, turning to Pietersen. De Jong had lost a thumb in mechanical labour while a young man, and that had turned him to theology.

"What is wanted in evangelical work, Monsieur Van Gogh," said the Reverend van den Brink, "is the talent to give popular and attractive lectures to the people."

The Reverend Pietersen accompanied him out of the church in which the meeting had been held, and took Vincent's arm as they stepped into the glaring Brussels sunshine. "I am glad to have you with us, my boy," he said. "There is a great deal of fine work to be done in Belgium, and from your enthusiasm I should say that you are highly qualified to carry it on."

Vincent did not know which warmed him more, the hot sun or the man's unexpected kindness. They walked down the street between precipices of six-story stone buildings, while Vincent struggled to find something to reply. The Reverend Pietersen stopped.

"This is where I turn off," he said. "Here, take my card, and when you have a spare evening, come to see me. I shall be happy to chat with you."

There were only three pupils including Vincent at the evangelical school. They were put in charge of Master Bokma, a small, wiry man with a concave face; a plumb line dropped from his brow to his chin would not have touched his nose or lips.

Vincent's two companions were country boys of nineteen. These two immediately became good friends, and to cement their friendship turned their ridicule on Vincent.

"My aim," he told one of them in an early, unguarded moment, "is to humble myself, *mourir à moi-même*." Whenever they found him struggling to memorize a lecture in French, or agonizing over some academic book, they would ask, "What are you doing, Van Gogh, dying within yourself?"

It was with Master Bokma that Vincent had his most difficult time. The master wished to teach them to be good speakers; each night at home they had to prepare a lecture to deliver the following day in class. The two boys concocted smooth, juvenile messages and recited them glibly. Vincent worked slowly over his sermons, pouring his whole heart into every line. He felt deeply what he had to say and when he rose in class the words would not come with any degree of ease.

"How can you hope to be an evangelist, Van Gogh," demanded Bokma, "when you cannot even speak? Who will listen to you?"

The climax of Bokma's wrath broke when Vincent flatly refused to deliver his lectures *extempore*. He laboured far into the night to make his compositions meaningful, writing out every word in painstaking, precise French. In class the following day the two boys spoke airily about Jesus Christ and salvation, glancing at their notes once or twice while Bokma nodded approval. Then it came Vincent's turn. He spread his lecture before him and began to read. Bokma would not even listen.

"Is that the way they teach you in Amsterdam? Van Gogh, no man has ever left my class who could not speak *extempore* at a moment's notice and move his audience!"

Vincent tried, but he could not remember in the proper sequence all the things he had written down the night before. His classmates laughed outright at his stumbling attempts and Bokma joined their merriment. Vincent's nerves were worn to a biting edge from the year in Amsterdam.

"Master Bokma," he declared, "I will deliver my sermons as I see fit. My work is good, and I refuse to submit to your insults!"

Bokma was outraged. "You will do as I tell you," he shouted, "or I will not allow you in my classroom!"

From then on it was open warfare between the two men. Vincent produced four times as many sermons as was demanded of him, for he could not sleep at nights and there was little use in his going to bed. His appetite left him and he became thin and jumpy.

In November he was summoned to the church to meet with the Committee and get his appointment. At last all the obstacles in his way had been removed and he felt a tired gratification. His two classmates were already there when he arrived. The Reverend Pietersen did not look at him when he came in, but Bokma did, and with a glint in his eye.

The Reverend de Jong congratulated the boys on their successful work and gave them appointments to Hoogstraeten and Etiehove. The classmates left the room arm in arm.

"Monsieur Van Gogh," said De Jong, "the Committee has not been able to persuade itself that you are ready to bring God's word to the people. I regret to say that we have no appointment for you."

After what seemed a long time Vincent asked, "What was wrong with my work?"

"You refused to submit to authority. The first rule of our Church is absolute obedience. Further, you did not succeed in learning how to speak *extempore*. Your master feels you are not qualified to preach."

Vincent looked at the Reverend Pietersen but his friend was staring out the window. "What am I to do?" he asked of no one in particular.

"You may return to the school for another six months if you wish," replied van den Brink. "Perhaps at the end of that time . . ."

Vincent stared down at his rough, square-toed boots and noticed that the leather was cracking. Then, because he could think of absolutely no word to say, he turned and walked out in silence.

He passed quickly through the city streets and found himself in Laeken. Without knowing why he was walking, he struck out along the towpath with its busily humming workshops. Soon he left the houses behind and came to an open field. An old white horse, lean, emaciated, and tired to death by a life of hard labour was standing there. The spot was lonely and desolate. On the ground lay a skull and at a distance in the background the bleached skeleton of a horse lying near the hut of a man who skinned horses.

Some little feeling returned to flood out the numbness, and Vincent reached forlornly for his pipe. He applied a match to the tobacco but it tasted strangely bitter. He sat down on a log in the field. The old white horse came over and rubbed his nose against Vincent's back. He turned and stroked the emaciated neck of the animal.

After a time there rose in his mind the thought of God, and he was comforted. "Jesus was calm in the storm," he said to himself. "I am not alone, for God has not forsaken me. Someday, somehow, I will find a way to serve Him."

When he returned to his room he found the Reverend Pietersen waiting for him. "I came to ask you to have dinner at my home, Vincent," he said.

They walked along streets thronged with working people on their way to the evening meal. Pietersen chatted of casual things as though nothing had happened. Vincent heard every word he said with a terrible clarity. Pietersen led him into the front room, which had been turned into a studio. There were a few water-colours on the walls and an easel in one corner.

"Oh," said Vincent, "you paint. I didn't know."

Pietersen was embarrassed. "I'm just an amateur," he replied. "I draw a bit in my spare time for relaxation. But I shouldn't mention it to my *confrères* if I were you."

They sat down to dinner. Pietersen had a daughter, a shy, reserved girl of fifteen who never once lifted her eyes from the plate. Pietersen went on speaking of inconsequential things while Vincent forced himself, for politeness' sake, to eat a little. Suddenly his mind became rivetted to what Pietersen was saying; he had no idea how the Reverend had worked into the subject.

"The Borinage," his host said, "is a coal mining region. Practically every man in the district goes down into the *charbonnages*. They work in the midst of thousands of ever-recurring dangers, and their wage is hardly enough to keep body and soul together. Their homes are tumbledown shacks where their wives and children spend most of the year shivering with cold, fever, and hunger."

Vincent wondered why he was being told all this. "Where is the Borinage?" he asked.

"In the south of Belgium, near Mons. I recently spent some time there, and Vincent, if ever a people needed a man to preach to them and comfort them, it's the Borains."

A gulp came into Vincent's throat, barring the passage of food. He laid down his fork. Why was Pietersen torturing him?

"Vincent," said the Reverend, "why don't you go to the Borinage? With your strength and enthusiasm you could do a great deal of fine work."

"But how can I? The Committee . . ."

"Yes, I know. I wrote to your father the other day explaining the situation. I had an answer from him this afternoon. He says he will support you in the Borinage until I can secure you a regular appointment."

Vincent jumped to his feet. "Then you will get me an appointment!"

"Yes, but you must give me a little time. When the Committee sees what splendid work you are doing it will surely relent. And even if it doesn't . . . de Jong and van den Brink will come to me for a favour one of these fine days, and in return for that favour . . . The poor people of this country need men like you, Vincent, and as God is my judge, any means is justified in getting you to them!"

8

As the train neared the South a group of mountains appeared on the horizon. Vincent gazed at them with pleasure and relief after the monotonous flat country of Flanders. He had been studying them only a few minutes when he discovered that they were curious mountains. Each one stood utterly by itself, rising out of the flat land with a precipitate abruptness.

"Black Egypt," he murmured to himself as he peered out of the window at the long line of fantastic pyramids. He turned to the man sitting next to him and asked, "Can you tell me how those mountains get there?"

"Yes," replied his neighbor, "they are composed of *terril*, the waste material that is brought up from the earth with the coal. Do you see that little car just about to reach the point of the hill? Watch it for a moment."

Just as he said this, the little car turned over on its side and sent a black cloud flying down the slope. "There," said the man, "that's how they grow. I've been watching them go up into the air a fraction of an inch every day for the past fifty years."

The train stopped at Wasmes and Vincent jumped off. The town was located in the hollow of a bleak valley; although an anaemic sun shone at an oblique angle, a substantial layer of coal smoke lay between Vincent and the heavens. Wasmes struggled up the side of the hill in two winding rows of dirty, red brick buildings, but before it reached the top, the bricks ran out and Petit Wasmes appeared.

As Vincent walked up the long hill he wondered why the village was so deserted. Not a man was to be seen anywhere; an occasional woman stood in a doorway with a dull and stolid expression on her face.

Petit Wasmes was the miners' village. It could boast of only one brick building, the home of Jean-Baptiste Denis, the baker, which sat right on the crest of the hill. It was to this house Vincent made his way, for Denis had written to the Reverend Pietersen, offering to board the next evangelist to be sent to their town.

Madame Denis welcomed Vincent heartily, led him through the warm kitchen-bakery with its smell of rising bread, and showed him his room, a small space under the eaves, with a window facing the rue Petit Wasmes, and rafters coming down at an abrupt angle at the rear. The place had been scrubbed by Madame Denis's thick, competent hands. Vincent liked it immediately. He was so excited he could not even unpack his things, but rushed down the few rough, wooden stairs which led into the kitchen to tell Madame Denis that he was going out.

"You won't forget to come back to supper?" she asked. "We eat at five."

Vincent liked Madame Denis. He felt in her the nature that understands things without going to all the trouble of thinking about them. "I'll be here, Madame," he said. "I just want to look about a bit."

"We have a friend coming tonight whom you should meet. He is a foreman at Marcasse and can tell you many things you will want to know for your work."

It had been snowing heavily. As Vincent walked down the road he observed the thorn hedges around the gardens and fields that had been turned black from the smoke of the mine chimneys. On the east side of the Denis house was a steep ravine in which were located most of the miners' huts; on the other side was a great open field with a black *terril* mountain and the chimneys of the Marcasse *charbonnage,* where most of the Petit Wasmes miners descended. Across the field there was a hollow road grown over with thorn bushes and torn up by the roots of gnarled trees.

Although Marcasse was only one of a string of seven mines owned by the Charbonnages Belgique, it was the oldest and most dangerous pit in the Borinage. It had a bad reputation because so many men had perished in it, either in descending or ascending, by poison gas, explosion, flooding water, or by the collapse of old tunnels. There were two squat, brick buildings above the ground, in which the machinery was operated for bringing up the coal and where the coal was graded and dumped into cars. The tall chimneys, which once had been of yellow brick, spread tangible, black smoke over the neighbourhood twenty-four hours a day. Around Marcasse were poor miners' huts with a few dead trees, black from the smoke, thorn hedges, dunghills, ash dumps, heaps of useless coal, and towering above it all, the black mountain. It was a gloomy spot; at first sight everything looked dreary and desolate to Vincent.

"No wonder they call it the black country," he murmured.

After he had been standing there for some time the miners began to pour out of the gate. They were dressed in coarse, tattered garments with leather hats on their heads; the women wore the same outfit as the men. All were completely black and looked like chimney sweeps, the whites of their eyes presenting a strange contrast to the coal-dust covered faces. It was not without reason that they were called *gueules noires*. The glare of the feeble afternoon sunlight hurt their eyes after they had laboured in the darkness of the earth since before dawn. They stumbled out of the gate, half blinded, speaking among themselves in a swift, unintelligible patois. They were small people with narrow, hunched-in shoulders and bony limbs.

Vincent understood now why the village had been deserted that afternoon; the real Petit Wasmes was not the small cluster of huts in the ravine, but the labyrinth city which existed underground at a depth of seven hundred metres, and in which almost the entire population spent the majority of its waking hours.

9

"Jacques Verney is a self-made man," Madame Denis told Vincent over the supper table, "but he has remained a friend to the miners."

"Don't all the men who get promoted stay friends with the workers?"

"No, Monsieur Vincent, it is not so. As soon as they move from Petit Wasmes to Wasmes they begin to look at things differently. For the sake of money they take the part of the owners and forget they once slaved in the mines. But Jacques is faithful and honest. When we have strikes he is the only one with any influence over the miners. They will listen to nobody's advice but his. But, poor man, he hasn't long to live."

"What's the matter with him?" asked Vincent.

"The usual thing—lung trouble. Every man who goes down gets it. He probably won't last the winter out."

Jacques Verney came in a little later. He was short and stoop shouldered, with the deep set, melancholy eyes of the Borain. Antennae of hair shot out from his nostrils, from the ends of his eyebrows and from the concha of his ears. His head was bald. When he heard that Vincent was an evangelist come to better the lot of the miners, he sighed deeply. "Ah, Monsieur," he said, "so many people have tried to help us. But life here goes on just as it always has."

"You think conditions bad in the Borinage?" asked Vincent.

Jacques was silent for a moment and then said, "For myself, no. My mother taught me to read a little, and through that I have become a foreman. I have a little brick house on the road leading down to Wasmes, and we are never in want of food. For myself I have nothing to complain . . ."

He was forced to interrupt himself for a violent fit of coughing; it seemed to Vincent that his flat chest would surely burst under the pressure. After walking to the front door and spitting into the road several times, Jacques again took his seat in the warm kitchen and gently pulled on the hairs of his ear, his nose, and his eyebrows.

"You see, Monsieur, I was already twenty-nine when I became a foreman. My lungs were gone by then. Nevertheless it has not been so bad for me these past few years. But the miners . . ." He glanced over at Madame Denis and asked, "What do you say? Shall I take him down to see Henri Decrucq?"

"Why not? It will do him no harm to hear the full truth."

Jacques Verney turned back to Vincent apologetically. "After all, Monsieur," he said, "I am a foreman and I owe some loyalty to 'them.' But Henri, he will show you!"

Vincent followed Jacques out into the cold night and plunged immediately into the miners' ravine. The miners' huts were simple wooden hovels of one room. They had not been put up with any plan, but ran down the side of the hill haphazardly at crazy angles, creating a labyrinth of dirt laden alleys, through which only the initiate could find their way. Vincent stumbled after Jacques, falling over rocks, logs, and heaps of refuse. About half-way down they came to Decrucq's shack. A light shone through the tiny window at the rear. Madame Decrucq answered the knock.

The Decrucq's cabin was exactly the same as all the others in the ravine. It had an earthen floor, moss covered roof, and strips of burlap stuck between the planks to keep the wind out. In each of the rear corners there was a bed, one of them already occupied by three sleeping children. The furnishings consisted of an oval stove, a wooden table with benches, one chair, and a box nailed to the wall, containing a few pots and dishes. The Decrucqs, like most Borains, kept a goat and some rabbits so that they might have meat occasionally. The goat slept under the children's bed; the rabbits had a bit of straw behind the stove.

Madame Decrucq swung open the upper half of the door to see who was there and then bade the two men enter. She had worked in the same *couches* with Decrucq for many years before their marriage, pushing the little cars of coal down the track to the tally board. Most of the juice was gone out of her. She was faded, worn and aged, and she had not yet celebrated her twenty-sixth birthday.

Decrucq, who had been leaning his chair against the cold part of the stove, sprang up at the sight of Jacques. "Well!" he exclaimed. "It is a long time since you have been in my house. We are glad to have you here. And I bid your friend welcome."

It was Decrucq's boast that he was the only man in the Borinage whom the mines could not kill. "I shall die in my bed of old age," he often said. "They can't kill me, for I won't let them!"

On the right side of his head a large square of red scalp-skin glowed like a window through the thatch of his hair. That was a memento of the day when the cage in which he was descending had plunged a hundred metres like a stone in a well and killed his twenty-nine companions. When he walked he dragged one leg after him; it had been broken in four places when the timbers in his cell collapsed and imprisoned him for five days. His coarse, black shirt bulged on the right side over the mound of three broken ribs that had never been set after an explosion of fire-damp had hurled him against a coal car. But he was a fighter, a game-cock of a man; nothing could put him down. Because he always talked so violently against the company, he was given the very worst *couches,* where it was hardest to get out the coal and where the working conditions were the most difficult. The more he took, the higher he flamed up against "them," the unknown and unseen but ever present enemy. A dimple, set just off centre in his stubby chin, made his short, compact face seem slightly askew.

"Monsieur Van Gogh," he said, "you have come to the right place. Here in the Borinage we are not even slaves, we are animals. We descend Marcasse at three in the morning; for fifteen minutes we can rest while we eat our dinner, and then we work on until four in the afternoon. It is black down there, Monsieur, and hot. So we must work naked, and the air is full of coal-dust and poison gas, and we cannot breathe! When we take the coal from the *couche,* there is no room to stand up; we must work on our knees and doubled in two. We begin to descend, boys and girls alike, when we are eight or nine. By twenty we have the fever and lung trouble. If we do not get killed by *grisou,* or in the cage (he tapped the red scalp-patch on his head), we may live until forty and then die of consumption! Do I tell lies, Verney?"

He spoke in such an excited patois that Vincent found difficulty in following him. The askew dimple gave his face an amused look, in spite of the fact that his eyes were black with anger.

"It is just so, Decrucq," said Jacques.

Madame Decrucq had gone to sit on her bed in the far corner. The faint glow of the kerosene lamp put her half in shadow. She listened to her husband while he spoke, even though she had heard the words a thousand times before. The years pushing coal cars, the birth of three children, and the succession of bitter winters in this burlap-stuffed hut had taken all the fight out of her. Decrucq dragged his bad leg from Jacques back to Vincent.

"And what do we get for all this, Monsieur? A one-room shack and just enough food to keep us swinging a pick. What do we eat? Bread, sour cheese, black coffee. Once or twice a year, perhaps, meat! If they cut off fifty centimes a day we would starve to death! We would not be able to bring up their *charbon;* that is the only reason they do not pay us less. We are on the margin of death, Monsieur, every day of our lives! If we get sick we are put out without a franc, and we die like dogs while our wives and children are fed by the neighbours. From eight to forty, Monsieur, thirty-two years in the black earth, and then a hole in that hill across the way so we can forget it all."

10

Vincent found that the miners were ignorant and untaught, most of them being unable to read, but at the same time they were intelligent and quick at their difficult work, were brave and frank and of a very sensitive temperament. They were thin and pale from fever, and looked tired and emaciated. Their skin was pasty and sallow (they saw the sun only on Sundays), marked with thousands of tiny black pores. They had the deep-set, melancholy eyes of the oppressed who cannot fight back.

Vincent found them attractive. They were simple and good natured like the Brabant people in Zundert and Etten. The desolate feeling of the landscape was gone too, for he perceived that the Borinage had character and that things spoke to him.

After Vincent had been there a few days he held his first religious meeting in a rough shed in back of the Denis bakery. He cleaned the place thoroughly and then carried in benches for the people. The miners came at five with their families, long scarfs wrapped about their necks and little caps on their heads to keep out the cold. The only light was from a kerosene lamp which Vincent borrowed. The miners sat in the dark on the rough benches, watched Vincent hovering over his Bible and listened attentively, holding their hands under their armpits to keep them warm.

Vincent searched very hard to find the most appropriate message for his opening sermon. He finally selected Acts 16:9, "A vision appeared to Paul in the night: there stood a man of Macedonia and begged him saying, 'Come over into Macedonia and help us.' "

"We must think of the Macedonian as a labourer, my friends," said Vincent, "a labourer with lines of sorrow and suffering and fatigue in his face. He is not without splendour or glamour, for he has an immortal soul, and he needs the food that does not perish, God's word. God wills that in imitation of Jesus Christ man should live humbly and go through life not reaching after lofty aims, but adapting himself to the lowly, learning from the gospel to be meek and simple of heart so that on the chosen day he may enter the Heavenly Kingdom and find peace."

There were many sick people in the village and each day he went the rounds like a doctor, bringing them whenever he could a bit of milk or bread, a warm pair of socks, or a cover to put over the bed. Typhoid and a malignant fever which the miners called *la sotte fièvre* descended upon the huts, giving the people bad dreams and making them delirious. The number of bedridden miners, emaciated, weak, and miserable, grew day by day.

The whole of Petit Wasmes called him Monsieur Vincent with affection, though still with a good bit of reserve. There was not a hut in the village to which he had not brought food and comfort, in which he had not nursed the sick and prayed with the miserable and brought God's light to the wretched. Several days before Christmas he found an abandoned stable near Marcasse, large enough to seat a hundred people. It was barren and cold and desolate, but the miners of Petit Wasmes filled it to the door. They listened to Vincent tell the story of Bethlehem and peace on earth. He had been in the Borinage only six weeks and had watched conditions grow more and more miserable with the passing of the days, but there, in an humble stable, lighted only by the smoky glow of a few small lamps, Vincent was able to bring Jesus Christ to the shivering blackjaws and warm their hearts with the promise of the Kingdom to Come.

There was only one flaw in his life, one factor to cause him any disturbance; his father was still supporting him. Each night he prayed for the time when he would be able to earn the few francs necessary for his humble needs.

The weather turned nasty. Black clouds overhung the whole region. Rain fell in torrents, making muddy creeks of the hollow roads and the earthen floors of the huts in the ravine. On New Year's day Jean-Baptiste walked down to Wasmes and returned with a letter for Vincent. The Reverend Pietersen's name was in the upper left-hand corner of the envelope. Vincent ran to his room under the eaves, trembling with excitement. The rain slashed away at the roof but he did not hear it. He tore open the envelope with clumsy fingers. The letter read:

Dear Vincent:

The Committee of Evangelization has heard about your splendid work and is therefore giving you a temporary nomination for six months, to begin the first of the year.

If at the end of June everything has gone well, your appointment will be made permanent. In the meanwhile your salary will be fifty francs a month.

Write to me often and keep looking upward.

Yours, fondly,
Pietersen.

He threw himself flat on the bed, letter clutched tight in his hand, exultant. At last he was successful! He had found his work in life! This was what he had wanted all the time, only he had not had the strength and courage to go straight to it! He was to receive fifty francs a month, more than enough to pay for his food and lodging and he would never have to be dependent upon anyone again.

He sat down at the table and wrote a tumultuous, triumphant letter to his father telling him that he no longer needed his help, and that he meant from that time on to be a source of credit and gratification to the family. When he finished writing it was already twilight; thunder and lightning were smashing over Marcasse. He ran down the stairs, through the kitchen, and flung himself joyously into the rain.

Madame Denis came after him. "Monsieur Vincent! Where are you going? You've forgotten your hat and coat!"

Vincent did not stop to answer. He ran to a mound nearby. He could see in the distance a great part of the Borinage, with the chimneys, the mounds of coal, the little miners' cottages, and the scurrying to and fro like ants in a nest of the black figures that were just coming out of the *houillères*. In the distance there was a dark pine wood with little white cottages silhouetted against it, a church spire a long way off and an old mill. A haze hung over the whole scene. There was a fantastic effect of light and dark formed by the shadows of the clouds. For the first time since he had been in the Borinage it all reminded him of the pictures of Michel and of Ruysdael.

11

Now that he was an authorized evangelist, Vincent needed a permanent place to hold his meetings. After a good deal of searching he found at the very bottom of the ravine, on a little road through the pine woods, a rather large house that was called Salon du Bébé, where the children of the community had once been taught to dance. After Vincent put up all his prints the house took on an attractive air. Here every afternoon he gathered the children between the ages of four and eight, taught them how to read, and told them the elementary stories of the Bible. It was the only instruction most of them received in their entire lives.

"How are we going to get coal to heat the room?" Vincent demanded of Jacques Verney, who had helped him secure the Salon. "The children have to be kept warm and the meetings at night can last longer if the stove is going."

Jacques thought a moment and then said, "Be here at noon tomorrow and I will show you how to get it."

When Vincent arrived at the Salon the next day he found a group of miners' wives and daughters awaiting him. They had on their black blouses, long black skirts and blue kerchiefs over their heads. All were carrying sacks.

"Monsieur Vincent, I have brought a sack for you," cried Verney's young daughter. "You must fill one, too."

They climbed through the maze of circuitous alleys formed by the miners' huts, passed the Denis bakery at the top of the hill, struck out across the field in the centre of which sat Marcasse, and skirted the walls of the buildings until they reached the black *terril* pyramid at the rear. Here they deployed, each one attacking the mountain from a different angle, climbing up its sides like tiny insects swarming over a dead log.

"You must go to the top before you will find any coal, Monsieur Vincent," said Mademoiselle Verney. "We have been picking the bottom of the heap clean for years. Come along, I'll show you which is the coal."

She scrambled up the black slope like a young goat, but Vincent had to go up most of the way on his hands and knees, for the stuff under his feet kept sliding away from him. Mademoiselle Verney scrambled on ahead, squatted on her haunches, and threw little pieces of caked mud at Vincent teasingly. She was a pretty girl with good colour in her cheeks and an alert, vivacious manner; Verney had been made a foreman when she was seven, and she had never seen the inside of a mine.

"Come along, Monsieur Vincent," she cried, "or you will be the last to get your sack filled!" This was an excursion for her; the company sold Verney fair coal at reduced rates.

They could not go altogether to the top for the little cars were dumping their loads of waste, first down one side, then down the other with mechanical regularity. It was no easy task to find coal on that pyramid. Mademoiselle Verney showed Vincent how to scoop up the *terril* in his hands and let the mud, rocks, clay and other foreign substances slip through his fingers. The amount of coal that escaped the company was negligible. The only thing the miners' wives ever found was a sort of shale composite which could not be sold in the commercial market. The *terril* was wet from the snow and rain, and soon Vincent's hands were scratched and cut, but he managed to get a quarter of a sackful of what he hoped was coal by the time the women had nearly filled theirs.

Each of the women left her sack at the Salon and rushed home to prepare the family supper, but not before promising to come to services that night and bring

her family. Mademoiselle Verney invited Vincent home to share their supper, and
he accepted with alacrity. The Verney house had two complete rooms; the stove,
cooking equipment, and tableware in one room, the family beds in the other. Despite
the fact that Jacques was fairly well off there was no soap in the house, for as
Vincent had learned, soap was an impossible luxury for the Borains. From the time
that the boy begins to descend the *charbonnage* and the girl begins to ascend the
terril until the day they die, the Borains never completely get the coal-dust off their
faces.

Mademoiselle Verney put a pan of cold water out in the street for Vincent. He
scrubbed up as best he could. He did not know how well he had succeeded, but
as he sat opposite the young girl and saw the black streaks from the coal-dust and
smoke still lining her face, he realized that he must look as she did. Mademoiselle
Verney chatted gaily all through the supper.

"You know, Monsieur Vincent," said Jacques, "you have been in Petit Wasmes
almost two months now, and yet you really don't know the Borinage."

"It is true, Monsieur Verney," replied Vincent in all humility, "but I think I
am slowly coming to understand the people."

"I don't mean that," said Jacques plucking a long antenna out of his nose and
looking at it with interest. "I mean you have only seen our life above ground. That
is not important. We merely sleep above ground. If you would understand what
our lives are like, you must descend one of the mines and see how we work from
three in the morning until four in the afternoon."

"I am very eager to go down," said Vincent, "but can I get permission from
the company?"

"I already have asked for you," replied Jacques, holding a cube of sugar in his
mouth and letting the tepid, inky, bitter coffee pour over it and down his throat.
"Tomorrow I descend Marcasse for safety inspection. Be in front of the Denis
house at a quarter before three in the morning and I will pick you up."

The entire family accompanied Vincent to the Salon, but on the way over,
Jacques, who had appeared so well and expansive in his warm house, shrivelled
up with a violent cough and had to go home again. When Vincent arrived at the
Salon he found Henri Decrucq already there, dragging his dead leg after him and
tinkering with the stove.

"Ah, good evening, Monsieur Vincent," he cried with a smile as broad as his
compact face would allow. "I am the only one in Petit Wasmes who can light this
stove. I know it from old, when we used to have parties here. It is *méchant,* but
I know all its tricks."

The content of the sacks was damp and only a small part of it was coal, but
Decrucq soon had the bulging, oval stove sending out good warmth. As he hobbled
about excitedly, the blood pounded to the bare spot on the scalp and turned the
corrugated skin a dirty beet-red.

Nearly every miner's family in Petit Wasmes came to the Salon that night to
hear Vincent preach the first sermon in his church. When the benches were filled,
the neighbouring families brought in their boxes and chairs. Over three hundred
souls crowded in. Vincent, his heart warmed by the kindness of the miners' wives
that afternoon, and the knowledge that he was at last speaking in his own temple,
preached a sermon so sincere and believing that the melancholy look on the Borains'
faces fell away.

"It is an old belief and a good one," said Vincent to his blackjaw congregation,
"that we are strangers on earth. Yet we are not alone, for our Father is with us.
We are pilgrims; our life is a long journey from earth to Heaven.

"Sorrow is better than joy—and even in mirth the heart is sad. It is better to go
to the house of mourning than to the house of feasts, for by sadness the countenance
of the heart is made better.

"For those who believe in Jesus Christ there is no sorrow that is not mixed with hope. There is only a constantly being born again, a constantly going from darkness to light.

"Father, we pray Thee to keep us from evil. Give us neither poverty nor riches, but feed us with bread appropriate to us.

"Amen."

Madame Decrucq was the first to reach his side. There was a mist before her eyes and a quiver at the corner of her mouth. "Monsieur Vincent," she said, "my life was so hard that I had lost God. But you have given Him back to me. And I thank you for that."

When they were all gone, Vincent locked the Salon and walked thoughtfully up the hill to the Denises'. He could tell from the reception he had received that night that the reserve was completely gone from the attitude of the Borains, and that they trusted him at last. He was now fully accepted by the blackjaws as a minister of God. What had caused the change? It could not have been because he had a new church; such things mattered not at all to the miners. They did not know about his evangelical appointment because he had not told them in the first place that he had no official position. And although he had preached a warm, beautiful sermon, he had delivered equally good ones in the wretched huts and in the abandoned stable.

The Denises had already gone to sleep in their little cubbyhole off the kitchen, but the bakery was still redolent of fresh, sweet bread. Vincent drew up some water from the deep well that had been enclosed in the kitchen, poured it out of the bucket into a bowl, and went upstairs to get his soap and mirror. He propped the mirror against the wall and looked at himself. Yes, his surmise had been correct; he had taken off only a small portion of the coal-dust at the Verneys'. His eyelids and jaws were still black. He smiled to himself as he thought of how he had consecrated the new temple with coal-dust all over his face, and how horrified his father and Uncle Stricker would have been if they could have seen him.

He dipped his hands into the cold water, worked up a lather from the soap he had brought with him from Brussels, and was just about to apply the suds vigorously to his face when something turned over in his mind. He poised his wet hands in mid-air. He looked into the mirror once again and saw the black coal-dust from the *terril* in the lines of his forehead, on the lids of his eyes, down the sides of his cheeks, and on the great ball of his chin.

"Of course!" he said aloud. "That's why they've accepted me. I've become one of them at last."

He rinsed his hands in the water and went to bed without touching his face. Every day that he remained in the Borinage he rubbed coal-dust on his face so that he would look like everyone else.

12

The following morning Vincent got up at two-thirty, ate a piece of dry bread in the Denis kitchen, and met Jacques in front of the door at a quarter to three. It had snowed heavily during the night. The road leading to Marcasse had been obliterated. As they struck out across the field toward the black chimneys and the *terril*, Vincent saw the miners scurrying over the snow from all directions, little black creatures hurrying home to their nest. It was bitterly cold; the workers had their thin black coats tucked up around their chins, their shoulders huddled inward for warmth.

Jacques first took him into a room where many kerosene lamps were hanging on racks, each under a specific number. "When we have an accident down below," said Jacques, "we can tell which men are caught by the lamps that are missing."

The miners were taking their lamps hastily and rushing across a snow-covered yard to a brick building where the hoist was located. Vincent and Jacques joined them. The descending cage had six compartments, one above the other, in each of which a coal truck could be brought to the surface. A compartment was just large enough for two men to squat comfortably on their haunches while going down; five miners were jammed into each of them, descending like a heap of coal.

Since Jacques was a foreman, only he and Vincent and one of his assistants crowded into the top compartment. They squatted low, their toes jammed up against the sides, their heads pushing against the wire top.

"Keep your hands straight in front of you, Monsieur Vincent," said Jacques. "If one of them touches the side wall, you will lose it."

A signal was given and the cage shot downward on its two steel tracks. The free way through which it descended in the rock was only a fraction of an inch larger than the cage. An involuntary shudder ran through Vincent when he realized that the blackness fell away for a half mile beneath him and that if anything went wrong he would be plunged to death. It was a sort of horror he had never known before, this rocketing down a black hole into the abysmal unknown. He realized that he had little to fear, for there had not been an accident with the hoist in over two months, but the shadowy, flickering light of the kerosene lamps was not conducive to reasoning.

He spoke of his instinctive trembling to Jacques, who smiled sympathetically. "Every miner feels that," he said.

"But surely they get used to going down?"

"No, never! An unconquerable feeling of horror and fear for this cage stays with them until their dying day."

"And you, Monsieur . . . ?"

"I was trembling inside of me, just as you were, and I have been descending for thirty-three years!"

At three hundred and fifty metres—half-way—the cage stopped for a moment, then hurtled downward again. Vincent saw streams of water oozing out of the side of the hole, and again he shuddered. Looking upward, he saw daylight about the size of a star in the sky. At six hundred and fifty metres they got out, but the miners continued on down. Vincent found himself in a broad tunnel with tracks cut through the rock and clay. He had expected to be plunged into an inferno of heat, but the passageway was fairly cool.

"This is not at all bad, Monsieur Verney!" he exclaimed.

"No, but there are no men working at this level. The *couches* were exhausted long ago. We get ventilation here from the top, but that does the miners down below no good."

They walked along the tunnel for perhaps a quarter of a mile, and then Jacques turned off. "Follow me, Monsieur Vincent," he said, *"mais doucement, doucement:* if you slip once, you will kill us."

He disappeared into the ground before Vincent's eyes. Vincent stumbled forward, found an opening in the earth, and groped for the ladder. The hole was just large enough to pass a thin man. The first five metres were not hard, but at the half-way point Vincent had to about-face in mid-air and descend in the opposite direction. Water began to ooze out of the rocks; mud slime covered the rungs of the ladder. Vincent could feel the water dripping over him.

At length they reached the bottom and crawled on their hands and knees through a long passage leading to *des caches* situated farthest from the exit. There was a long row of cells, like partitions in a vault, supported by rough timbers. In each cell a unit of five miners worked, two digging out the coal with their picks, a third dragging it away from their feet, a fourth loading it into small cars, and a fifth pushing the cars down a narrow track.

The pickers worked in coarse linen suits, filthy and black. The shoveller was usually a young boy, stark naked except for a burlap loin-cloth, his body a dull black, and the miner pushing the car through the three-foot passageway was always a girl, as black as the men, with a coarse dress covering the upper part of her body. Water was leaking through the roofs of the cells, forming a grotto of stalactites. The only light was from the small lamps whose wicks were turned down low to save fuel. There was no ventilation. The air was thick with coal-dust. The natural heat of the earth bathed the miners in rivulets of black perspiration. In the first cells Vincent saw that the men could work standing erect with their picks, but as he advanced down the passageway, the cells became smaller and smaller until the miners had to lie on the ground and swing their picks from the elbow. As the hours went on, the bodily heat of the miners raised the temperature of the cells, and the coal-dust thickened in the air until the men were gasping great mouthfuls of hot, black soot.

"These men earn two and a half francs a day," Jacques told Vincent, "providing the inspector at the checking post approves the quality of their coal. Five years ago they were earning three francs, but wages have been reduced every year since then."

Jacques inspected the timber proppings that stood between the miners and death. Then he turned to the pickers.

"Your propping is bad," he told them. "It is working loose and the first thing you know the roof will cave in."

One of the pickers, the leader of the gang, let forth a volley of abuse so fast that Vincent could catch only a few words.

"When they pay for propping," the man shouted, "we will prop! If we take the time off to prop, how will we get the coal out? We might as well die here under the rock as at home of starvation."

Beyond the last cell there was another hole in the ground. This time there was not even a ladder to descend. Logs had been shoved in at intervals to keep the dirt from pouring down and burying the miners below. Jacques took Vincent's lamp and hung it from his belt. "*Doucement,* Monsieur Vincent," he repeated. "Do not step on my head or you will send me crashing." They climbed down five metres more, foot following foot into the blackness, feeling for its timber to stand on while hands clutched the dirt in the sides, to keep from hurtling into oblivion.

At the next level there was another *couche,* but this time the miners did not even have cells to work in. The coal had to be picked out of a narrow angle in the wall. The men crouched on their knees, their backs pressed against the rock roof and threw their picks at the corner from which the coal was being taken. Vincent realized now that the cells above had been cool and comfortable; the heat at this lower level was like that of a blazing oven, thick enough to be cut with a blunt instrument. The men at work were panting like stricken animals, their tongues hanging out, thick and dry, and their naked bodies covered with a plaster of filth, grime and dust. Vincent, doing absolutely nothing, thought he could not bear the fierce heat and dust another minute. The miners were doing violent manual labour and their gorge was a thousand times higher than his, yet they could not stop to rest or cool off for a minute. If they did, they would not get out the requisite number of cars of coal and would not receive their fifty cents for the day's work.

Vincent and Jacques crawled on their hands and knees through the passageway connecting these beehive cells, flattening themselves against the wall every few seconds to let a car go by on the tiny tracks. This passage was smaller than the one above. The girls pushing the cars were younger, none of them over ten years of age. The coal cars were heavy and the girls had to fight and strain to get them along the tracks.

At the end of the passage there was a metal chute down which the cars were lowered on cables. "Come, Monsieur Vincent," said Jacques, "I will take you to the last level, seven hundred metres, and you will see something not to be found anywhere else in the world!''

They slid down the metal incline some thirty metres and Vincent found himself in a wide tunnel with two tracks. They walked for a half mile back in the tunnel; when it came to an end they pulled themselves up on a ledge, crawled through a *communiqué,* and lowered themselves on the other side into a freshly dug hole.

''This is a new *couche,''* said Jacques, ''the hardest place of any mine in the world to get the coal.''

Leading out of this excavation was a series of twelve minute black holes. Jacques shoved himself into one and shouted, ''Follow me.'' The opening was just large enough to pass Vincent's shoulders. He jammed his way into it and crawled on his stomach like a snake, digging his way along with his fingernails and toes. He could not see Jacques's boots, three inches ahead of him. The tunnel through the rock was only a foot and a half high and two and a half feet wide. The hole from which the passageway started had almost no fresh air, but it was cool compared to this stope.

At the end of the crawl Vincent came into a little dome-like hollow almost tall enough for a man to stand up. The place was pitch black and at first Vincent could see nothing; then he noticed four little blue glows along a wall. His body was wet with perspiration; the sweat from his brow brought the coal-dust down into his eyes, making them smart cruelly. He was panting for breath from the long crawl on his stomach and stood up with a feeling of relief to catch a little air. What he caught was fire, liquid fire that burned and choked him as it went down his lungs. This was the worst hole in all Marcasse, a torture chamber worthy of the Middle Ages.

''Tiens, tiens!'' cried a familiar voice, *''c'est Monsieur Vincent.* Have you come to see how we earn our fifty cents a day, Monsieur?''

Jacques went quickly to the lamps and inspected them. The arc of blue was eating up the light.

''He shouldn't come down here!'' Decrucq whispered in Vincent's ear, the whites of his eyes gleaming, ''he will have a hemorrhage in that tunnel and then we will have to haul him out with blocks and a pulley.''

''Decrucq,'' called Jacques, ''have these lamps been burning this way all morning?''

''Yes,'' replied Decrucq carelessly, ''the *grisou* is growing day by day. Once it will explode and then our troubles will be over.''

''These cells were pumped out last Sunday,'' said Jacques.

''But it comes back, it comes back,'' said Decrucq scratching the black scar in his scalp with pleasure.

''Then you must lay off one day this week and let us clean it out again.''

A storm of protest arose from the miners. ''We have not enough bread now for the children! It is impossible to live on the wages, let alone give up a full day! Let them clean it out when we are not in here; we must eat like all the others!''

''It's all right,'' laughed Decrucq, ''the mines can't kill me. They've tried it before. I shall die in my bed of old age. Speaking of food, what time is it, Verney?''

Jacques held his watch near the blue flame. ''Nine o'clock.''

''Good! We can eat our dinner.''

The black, sweating bodies with the white eyeballs ceased their labours, and squatting on their haunches against the wall, opened their kits. They could not crawl out into the slightly cooled hole to eat because they allowed themselves only fifteen minutes respite. The crawl going and coming would have taken almost that long. So they sat in the stagnant heat, took out two pieces of thick, coarse bread with sour cheese, and ate hungrily, the black soot from their hands coming off in great streaks on the white bread. Each man had a beer bottle of tepid coffee with which he washed down the bread. The coffee, the bread, and the sour cheese were the prize for which they worked thirteen hours a day.

Vincent had already been down six hours. He felt faint from lack of air and choking with the heat and dust. He did not think he could stand the torture very many more minutes. He was grateful when Jacques said they must go.

"Watch that *grisou,* Decrucq," said Jacques before he plunged into the hole. "If it gets bad, you'd better bring your gang out."

Decrucq laughed harshly. "And will they pay us our fifty cents for the day if we don't produce the coal?"

There was no answer to this question. Decrucq knew it as well as Jacques. The latter shrugged, and crawled on his stomach through the tunnel. Vincent followed him, completely blinded by the stinging, black sweat in his eyes.

After a half hour of walking they reached the *accrochage,* where the cage took the coal and men to the surface. Jacques went into a cave in the rock, where the horses were kept, and coughed up black phlegm.

In the cage, shooting upward like a bucket in a well, Vincent turned to his friend and said, "Monsieur, tell me. Why do you people continue to go down into the mines? Why don't you all go elsewhere, find other employment?"

"Ah, my dear Monsieur Vincent, there is no other employment. And we cannot go elsewhere because we do not have the money. There is not a miner's family in the whole Borinage that has ten francs put away. But even if we could go, Monsieur, we would not. The sailor knows that all sorts of dangers await him aboard his ship, yet, ashore, he is homesick for the sea. So it is with us, Monsieur, we love our mines; we would rather be underground than above it. All we ask is a living wage, fair working hours, and protection against danger."

The cage reached the top. Vincent crossed the snow-covered yard, dazed by the feeble sunlight. The mirror in the washroom showed him that his face was pitch black. He did not wait to wash. He plunged across the field, only half conscious, drinking in the fresh air and wondering if he had not suddenly caught the *sotte fièvre* and been suffering from nightmare. Surely God would not let His children work in such abominable slavery? Surely he must have dreamed all the things he had seen?

He passed the prosperous, comparatively well-to-do house of the Denis's and without thinking stumbled down the filthy labyrinth of alleys in the ravine to Decrucq's hut. At first no one answered his knock. After a bit the six year old boy came. He was pale and anaemic and undersized, but he had something of Decrucq's fighting courage about him. In two more years he would be descending Marcasse every morning at three, shoveling coal into cars.

"Mother went to the *terril,*" said the boy in a high, thin voice. "You must wait, Monsieur Vincent; I am taking care of the babies."

Playing on the floor with some sticks and a piece of string were Decrucq's two infants with nothing on but little shifts. They were blue with the cold. The oldest boy fed *terril* to the stove but it gave off very little heat. Vincent watched them and shivered. Then he put the babies to bed and covered them up to the neck. He did not know why he had come to this miserable shack. He felt that he must do something, say something to the Decrucqs, help them in some way. He must let them know that he at least realized the full extent of their misery.

Madame Decrucq came home, her hands and face black. At first she did not recognize Vincent through his filth. She ran to the little box that hid her provisions, and put some coffee on the stove. It was colder than tepid when she handed it to him, black, bitter and woody, but he drank it to please the good woman.

"The *terril* is bad these days, Monsieur Vincent," she complained. "The company lets nothing through, not even little grains. How am I to keep the babies warm? I have no clothes for them, only those little shirts and some sacking. The burlap gives them sores and rubs their skin off. If I keep them in bed all day, how will they grow?"

Vincent choked with unshed tears, but he could say nothing. He had never seen such abject personal misery. For the first time he wondered of what benefit prayers and the Gospel would be to this woman when her babies were freezing to death. Where was God in all this? He had a few francs in his pocket; he gave them to Madame Decrucq.

"Please buy woolen drawers for the children," he said.

It was a futile gesture, he knew; there were hundreds of other babies freezing in the Borinage. The Decrucq children would freeze again as soon as these drawers wore out.

He walked up the hill to the Denis's. The bakery kitchen was warm and cosy. Madame Denis heated him some water to wash in, and prepared him a nice lunch of the rabbit stew that had been left over from the night before. She saw that he was tired and overstrung from his experience so she put a trifle of butter out for his bread.

Vincent walked upstairs to his room. His stomach was warm and full. The bed was wide and comfortable; the sheets were clean, and on the pillow was a white pillow case. On the walls were prints by the great masters of the world. He opened his bureau and surveyed the rows of shirts, underclothes, socks, and vests. He went to the wardrobe and looked at his two extra pairs of shoes, his warm overcoat, and the suits of clothes hanging there. At last he realized that he was a liar and a coward. He preached the virtues of poverty to the miners but he himself lived in comfort and plenty. He was nothing more than a hypocritical slinger of words. His religion was an idle, useless thing. The miners ought to despise him and run him out of the Borinage. He pretended to share their lot, and here he had warm, beautiful clothes, a comfortable bed to sleep in, and more food in one meal than the miners had in a week. He did not even work for his ease and luxuries. He just went about telling glib lies and posing as a good man. The Borains ought not to believe a word he said; they ought not to come to his sermons or accept his leadership. His whole easy life gave the lie to his words. He had failed again, more miserably than ever before!

Well, he had only two choices; he could get out of the Borinage, run under the cover of night before they realized what a lying, weak-livered dog he was, or he could make use of the knowledge to which his eyes had been opened that day and really become a man of God.

He took all the clothes out of the bureau and packed them quickly into his bag. He also put in his suits, shoes, books, and prints, and closed the valise. He let it sit on the chair for the time being, and ran buoyantly out the front door.

At the bottom of the ravine there was a little creek. Just beyond that, the pine woods began the ascent of the other slope. In this woods there were scattered a few miners' cabins. After some inquiry, Vincent found one that was unoccupied. It was a board shanty without a window, built on a rather steep slope. The floor was the native earth trod down by long usage; the melting snow ran under the boards at the high end. Overhead there were rough beams holding the roof in place, and since the shack had not been used all winter, the knotholes and cracks between the boards let in icy blasts of air.

"Who owns this place?" Vincent demanded of the woman who had accompanied him.

"One of the business men in Wasmes."

"Do you know the rent?"

"Five francs a month."

"Very well, I'll take it."

"But Monsieur Vincent, you can't live here."

"Why not?"

"But . . . but . . . it is wretched. It is even worse than my place. It is the most wretched shack in Petit Wasmes!"

"That is exactly why I want it!"

He climbed up the hill again. A new feeling of peace had come into his heart. Madame Denis had gone to his room on some errand during his absence and had seen the packed valise.

"Monsieur Vincent," she cried when he came in, "what has gone wrong? Why are you going back to Holland so suddenly?"

"I am not going away, Madame Denis. I am staying in the Borinage."

"Then why . . . ?" A puzzled expression came over her face.

When Vincent explained, she said softly, "Believe me, Monsieur Vincent, you cannot live like that; you are not used to it. Times have changed since Jesus Christ; nowadays we must all live as best we can. The people know from your work that you are a good man."

Vincent was not to be dissuaded. He saw the merchant in Wasmes, rented the shack, and moved in. When his first salary check of fifty francs arrived a few days later, he bought himself a little wooden bed and a second-hand stove. After these expenditures he had just enough francs left to secure him bread, sour cheese, and coffee for the rest of the month. He piled dirt against the top wall of the cabin to keep the water out, stuffed the cracks and knotholes with sacking. He now lived in the same kind of house as the miners, ate the identical food, and slept in the identical bed. He was one of them. He had the right to bring them the Word of God.

13

The manager of the Charbonnages Belgique, which controlled the four mines in the vicinity of Wasmes, was not at all the sort of voracious animal that Vincent had been prepared to find. True, he was a bit stoutish, but he had kindly, sympathetic eyes and the manner of one who had done a little suffering on his own accord.

"I know, Monsieur Van Gogh," he said, after listening attentively while Vincent poured out the tale of woe of the miner. "It is an old story. The men think we are purposely starving them to death so that we can earn greater profits. But believe me, Monsieur, nothing could be farther from the truth. Here, let me show you some charts from the International Bureau of Mines in Paris."

He laid a large chart out on the table and indicated a blue line at the bottom with his finger.

"Look, Monsieur," he said, "the Belgian coal mines are the poorest in the world. The coal is so difficult for us to reach that it is almost impossible to sell it in the open market for a profit. Our operating expenses are the highest of any coal mine in Europe, and our profits are the lowest! For you see, we must sell our coal at the same price as the mines which produce at the lowest ton cost. We are on the margin of bankruptcy every day of our lives. Do you follow me?"

"I believe so."

"If we paid the miners one franc more a day our production costs would rise above the market price of coal. We would have to shut down altogether. And then they would really starve to death."

"Couldn't the owners take a little less profit? Then there would be more for the workers."

The manager shook his head sadly. "No, Monsieur, for do you know what coal mines run on? Capital. Like every other industry. And capital must receive its return or it will go elsewhere. The stocks of the Charbonnages Belgique pay only three percent dividends today. If they were reduced half of a percent the owners would withdraw their money. If they do that our mines will have to shut down, for we cannot operate without capital. And again the miners would starve. So you see, Monsieur, it is not the owners or managers who create this horrible condition in the Borinage. It is the unsatisfactory lay of the *couches*. And that condition, I suppose, we will have to blame on God!''

Vincent should have been shocked at this blasphemy. He was not. He was thinking of what the manager had told him.

''But at least you can do something about the working hours. Thirteen hours a day down there is killing off your whole village!''

''No, Monsieur, we cannot decrease the working hours because that would be equivalent to raising their wages. They would be turning out that much less coal for their fifty cents a day, and consequently our production cost per ton would be raised.''

''There is one thing that certainly can be improved.''

''You are going to speak of the dangerous working conditions?''

''Yes. At least you can decrease the number of accidents and deaths in the mines.''

The manager shook his head patiently. ''No, Monsieur, we cannot. We are unable to sell new stocks on the market because our dividends are too low. And we have absolutely no surplus of profit to invest in improvements.—Ah, Monsieur, it is a hopeless, vicious circle. I have gone around it many thousands of times. That is what has turned me from a firm, faithful Catholic to a bitter atheist. I cannot understand how a God in Heaven would purposely create such a condition and enslave a whole race of people in abject misery for century after century without one hour of providential mercy!''

Vincent could think of nothing to say. He walked home stunned.

14

The month of February was the most bitter one of the year. Naked winds swept through the valley and over the hilltop, making it almost impossible to walk through the streets. The miners' huts now needed the *terril* more than ever for warmth but the icy winds were so fierce that the women could not go out to the black mountain to search for it. They had nothing but their coarse skirts, blouses, cotton stockings, and kerchiefs to protect them against the biting winds.

The children had to stay in bed day after day to keep from freezing. Hot food was almost impossible to get because there was no coal for the stove. When the men came out of the blistering hot bowels of the earth they were plunged without a moment's preparation into the below zero weather, and had to struggle home across the snow-covered field in the cutting wind. Deaths from consumption and pneumonia occurred every day of the week. Vincent read a great many funeral services that month.

He had given up trying to teach the blue-faced children how to read, and was spending his days on the Marcasse mountain collecting what little coal he could, to be distributed among the huts where the misery was worst. He had no need to rub coal-dust on his face these days; he was never free from the mark of the miner. A stranger coming to Petit Wasmes would have called him, '' . . . Just another blackjaw.''

He had gathered almost half a sack of *terril* after many hours of work up and down the pyramid. The blue skin of his hands was torn by the ice-covered rock. At a little before four he decided to stop and take back what he had to the village so that at least a few wives might prepare hot coffee for their husbands. He reached the gate of Marcasse just as the miners began streaming out. Some of them recognized him and muttered a *bojou,* but the rest walked along with their hands in their pockets, shoulders caved inward, and eyes rivetted to the ground.

The last one out of the gate was a little old man whose cough racked his whole body so badly that he scarcely could walk. His knees trembled, and when the freezing wind from the snow-covered fields hit him, he staggered as though from a smashing blow. He nearly fell on his face in the ice. After a moment he gathered courage and began to cross the field slowly, presenting his side to the blast. He had a piece of burlap sack wrapped around his shoulders, a sack he had somehow secured from a store in Wasmes. Vincent saw that something was printed on it. He strained his eyes to make out what it said and deciphered the letters: FRAGILE.

After leaving his *terril* at the miners' huts, Vincent went to his own shack and laid all his clothes out on the bed. He had five shirts, three suits of underwear, four pairs of socks, two pairs of shoes, two suits of clothes and an extra soldier's coat. He left one shirt, one pair of socks and one suit of underwear on the bed. Everything else he stuffed into the valise.

The suit of clothes he left with the old man who had FRAGILE written across his back. The underwear and shirts he left for the children, to be cut up and made into little garments. The socks were distributed among the consumptives who had to descend Marcasse. The warm coat he gave to a pregnant woman whose husband had been killed a few days before by a cave in, and who had to take his place in the mine to support her two babies.

The Salon du Bébé was closed, as Vincent did not wish to take the *terril* away from the housewives. In addition, the families were afraid to tramp through the slush and get their feet wet. Vincent held little services at each hut as he made the rounds. As time went on, he found it necessary to devote himself to the practical duties of healing, washing, rubbing down, preparing hot drinks and medicines. At last he left his Bible at home because he never found time to open it. The Word of God had become a luxury that the miners could not afford.

The cold abated a little in March, but fever set in to take its place. Vincent spent forty francs of his February salary for food and medicine for the sick, leaving himself on starvation rations. He was growing thinner from lack of food; his nervous, jumpy mannerisms became more exaggerated. The cold sapped his vitality; he began to walk around with a fever. His eyes became two great fire holes in their sockets, and his massive, Van Gogh head seemed to shrink. Hollows appeared in his cheeks and under his eyes, but his chin stuck out as firmly as ever.

The oldest Decrucq child contracted typhoid; a difficult situation set in over the beds. There were only two of them in the house; the parents occupied one and the three children the other. If the two babies remained in the same bed with the boy, they might catch his disease. If they were put on the floor they would develop pneumonia. If the parents slept on the floor they would be unable to work the following day. Vincent realized immediately what must be done.

"Decrucq," he said when the miner came home from work, "will you help me a moment before you sit down to your supper?"

Decrucq was tired and ill from the pain in his scalp but he followed Vincent without question, dragging his dead leg after him. When they got to his hut Vincent threw one of the two blankets off the bed and said, "Take an end of this; we are going to move it up to your house for the boy."

Decrucq gritted his teeth. "We have three children," he said, "if God wills it so, we can lose one of them. But there is only one Monsieur Vincent to nurse the whole village, and I will not let him kill himself!"

He limped wearily out of the cabin. Vincent took the bed apart, loaded it on his shoulders, tramped to the Decrucq house and set it up. Decrucq and his wife looked at him over their supper of dry bread and coffee. Vincent transferred the child to his bed and nursed him.

Later that evening he went to the Denises' to ask if they had some straw he might take to his cabin to sleep on. Madame Denis was aghast when she heard what he had done.

"Monsieur Vincent," she exclaimed, "your old room is still unoccupied. You must come back here to live."

"You are very good, Madame Denis, but I cannot."

"I know, you are worrying about the money. But that does not matter. Jean-Baptiste and I make a good living. You can live here with us free, as a brother. Aren't you always telling us that all God's children are brothers?"

Vincent was cold, shivering cold. He was hungry. He was delirious with the fever he had been carrying about for weeks. He was weak from malnutrition, from lack of sleep. He was harrassed and nearly insane with the cumulative grief and suffering of the village. The bed upstairs was warm and soft and clean. Madame Denis would give him food to wipe out that gnawing at the pit of his stomach; she would nurse his fever and fill him with hot, powerful drinks until the cold was driven from the marrow of his bones. He shivered, weakened, almost collapsed on the red tile floor of the bakery. Just in time he caught himself.

This was God's ultimate test. If he failed now, all the work he had done before would have been futile. Now that the village was at its most horrible stage of suffering and deprivation, was he to backslide, be a weak, contemptible coward and grasp comfort and luxury the first moment it was thrust under his nose?

"God sees your goodness, Madame Denis," he said, "and He will reward you for it. But you must not tempt me from my path of duty. If you do not find me some straw, I'm afraid I'll have to sleep on the ground. But don't bring anything else, please, for I can't accept it."

He dumped the straw into one corner of his hut, over the damp ground, and covered himself with the thin blanket. He did not sleep all night; when morning came he had a cough, and his eyes seemed to have retreated even farther into his head. His fever had increased until he was only half conscious of his movements. There was no *terril* in the shack for the stove; he did not feel he could deprive the miners of even a handful of the stuff he collected from the black mountain. He managed to swallow a few mouthfuls of hard dry bread, and set out for his day's work.

15

March pushed its way wearily into April and conditions improved a bit. The winds disappeared, the slant of the sun became a little more direct, and at last the thaw came. With the melting of the snow the black fields became visible, the larks were heard, and in the woods the buds began to sprout on the elder trees. The fever died down and with the coming of warmer weather the women of the village were able to swarm over the Marcasse pyramid to get *terril*. Soon the cabins were blazing with cosy fires in their oval stoves; the children were able to stay out of bed during the day, and Vincent reopened the Salon. The entire village crowded in for the first sermon. A touch of a smile was coming back to the melancholy eyes of the miners; the people dared lift their heads just a little. Decrucq, who had appointed himself official fireman and janitor of the Salon, was cracking jokes over the stove and rubbing his scalp vigorously.

"Better times are coming," cried Vincent exultantly from his pulpit. "God has tried you and found you true. The worst of our suffering is over. The corn will ripen in the fields, and the sun will warm you as you sit before your homes after a good day's work. The children will run out to follow the lark and gather berries in the woods. Lift up your eyes to God, for the good things in life are in store for you. God is merciful. God is just. He will reward you for your faith and vigilance. Offer up thanks to Him, for better times are coming. Better times are coming."

The miners offered up fervent thanks. Cheerful voices filled the room and everyone kept saying to his neighbour, "Monsieur Vincent is right. Our suffering is over. The winter is gone. Better times are coming!"

A few days later, while Vincent and a group of the children were gathering *terril* behind Marcasse, they saw little black figures scurrying out of the building in which the hoist was located, and go running across the fields in all directions.

"What has happened?" exclaimed Vincent. "It can't be three o'clock yet. The sun isn't even in mid-heaven."

"There's been an accident!" shouted one of the older boys. "I've seen them run away like that before! Something's broken below!"

They scrambled down the black mountain as fast as they could, ripping their hands and clothes on the rocks. The field surrounding Marcasse was thick with black ants running to cover. By the time they all got down, the tide of movement had changed and the women and children were running across the field from the village, coming from every direction at a frightened speed, babies in their arms and infants tagging along behind.

When Vincent got to the gate he heard excited voices crying, *"Grisou! Grisou!* The new *couche!* They're caught! They're trapped in!"

Jacques Verney, who had been laid up in bed during the intense cold, came dashing across the field at top speed. He had grown thinner, his chest more cavernous. Vincent caught him as he went by and said, "What is it? Tell me!"

"Decrucq's *couche!* Remember the blue lamps? I knew it would get them!"

"How many? How many are there? Can't we get at them?"

"Twelve cells. You saw them. Five men to a cell."

"Can't we save them?"

"I don't know. I'm taking a volunteer crew down immediately."

"Let me come along. Let me help."

"No. I need experienced men." He ran through the yard to the hoist.

The little cart with the white horse drew up to the gate, the same cart that had carried so many dead and injured to the cabins on the hillside. The miners who had run across the fields began returning with their families. Some of the women cried hysterically, others stared ahead of them, wide eyed. The children whimpered and the foremen ran about, shouting at the tops of their voices, organizing rescue crews.

Suddenly the noise stopped. A little group came out of the hoist building and walked slowly down the stairs, carrying something wrapped in blankets. The hush was eloquent for a moment. Then everyone began shouting and crying at the same time.

"Who is it? Are they dead? Are they alive? For God's sake, tell us their names! Show them to us! My husband is down there! My children! Two of my babies are in that *couche!"*

The group stopped at the little cart with the white horse. One of the men spoke. "Three of the carriers who were dumping coal on the outside have been saved. But they are terribly burned."

"Who are they? For the love of Jesus tell us who they are! Show us! Show us! My baby is down there! My baby, my baby!"

The man lifted the blankets off the seared faces of two girls of about nine and a boy of ten. All three were unconscious. The families of the children fell upon them with mingled cries of lament and joy. The three blankets were laid in the cart with the white horse and driven across the hollow road of the field. Vincent and the families ran alongside like panting animals. From behind him Vincent heard the wail of fear and anguish mount ever higher and higher. He turned his head while he ran, and looked behind him, seeing the long line of *terril* mountains on the horizon.

"Black Egypt!" he cried aloud, giving vent to his pain. "Black Egypt, with the chosen people enslaved again! Oh, God, how could You? How could You?"

The children were burned almost to death. The skin and hair was seared off every part that had been exposed. Vincent went into the first cabin. The mother was wringing her hands in anguish. Vincent undressed the child and cried, "Oil, oil, quick!" The woman had a little oil in the house. Vincent applied it to the burns and then cried, "Now, bandage!"

The woman stood there staring at him, terror in her eyes. Vincent became angry and shouted, "Bandages! Do you want your child to die?"

"We have nothing," she blubbered. "There is not a piece of white cloth in the house. There has not been all winter!"

The child stirred and moaned. Vincent grabbed off his coat and shirt, and tore his undershirt from his body. He replaced his coat, ripped the other garments to strips, and bandaged the child from head to foot. He took the can of oil and ran to the second child. He bandaged her as he had the first. When he reached the third child the shirt and undershirt had been used up. The ten year old boy was dying. Vincent took off his trousers and woolen drawers, replaced the trousers and cut the drawers into bandages.

He pulled his coat tightly over his bare chest and ran across the field to Marcasse. From far off he could hear the lament, the unending cry of the wife and mother.

The miners were standing about the gate. Only one relief crew could work down below at a time. The approach to the ledge was narrow. The men were waiting their turn. Vincent spoke to one of the assistant foremen.

"What are the chances?"

"They're dead by now."

"Can't we get to them?"

"They're buried under rock."

"How long will it take?"

"Weeks. Maybe months."

"But why? But why?"

"That's how long it took before."

"Then they're lost!"

"Fifty-seven men and girls!"

"Every one of them gone!"

"You'll never see them again!"

Crews relieved each other for thirty-six hours. The women who had husbands and children below could not be driven away. The men above kept telling them rescue was sure. The women knew they were lying. The miners' wives who had lost no one brought hot coffee and bread across the field. The stricken women would touch nothing. In the middle of the night Jacques Verney was brought up in a blanket. He had had a hemorrhage. He died the following day.

After forty-eight hours Vincent persuaded Madame Decrucq to return home with the children. For twelve days volunteer rescue crews worked without stopping. No mining went on. Since no coal was brought up, no wages were paid. The few francs surplus in the village was soon gone. Madame Denis went on baking bread and distributing it on credit. She exhausted her capital and had to shut down. The company contributed nothing. At the end of the twelfth day they told the rescue crews to stop. The men were ordered back to work. Petit Wasmes had not one centime between it and starvation.

The miners struck.

Vincent's wages for April arrived. He went down to Wasmes and bought fifty francs' worth of food. He distributed it among the families. The village lived on it for six days. After that they went to the woods to collect berries, leaves, grass. The men went out of doors searching for things that lived; rats, gophers, snails, toads, lizards, cats, dogs. Anything that could be put into the stomach to stop the throbbing ache of hunger. At last there was nothing more to find. Vincent wrote to Brussels for help. No help came. The miners sat down to watch their wives and children starve under their eyes.

They asked Vincent to hold services for the fifty-seven lost souls in the mine, the ones who had gone before them. A hundred men, women, and children packed into Vincent's tiny hut. Vincent had had nothing but coffee for days. He had had almost no solid food since the accident. He was too weak to stand on his feet. The fever and despair had returned to his heart. His eyes were just two black pin pricks, his cheeks had been sucked in, the circular bones under his eyes protruded, a dirty, red beard matted his face. He had rough sacking wrapped around his body to take the place of underwear. Only one lantern illumined the shack. It hung from a broken rafter, giving but a flickering glow. Vincent lay on the straw in his corner, holding his head up on one elbow. The lantern flung fantastic, flickering shadows over the rough planks and the hundred mutely suffering souls.

He began speaking in a parched, feverish voice, every word filling the silence. The blackjaws, thin, emaciated, wracked by hunger and defeat, kept their eyes on him as they would on God. God was a long way off.

Strange, loud voices were heard outside the shack, lifted in indignation. The door was flung open and a child's voice cried, "Monsieur Vincent is in here, Messieurs."

Vincent stopped speaking. The hundred Borains turned their heads toward the door. Two well-dressed men stepped in. The oil lamp flared up for a brief moment. Vincent saw horror and fear written across the strange faces.

"You are welcome, Reverend de Jong and Reverend van den Brink," he said without rising. "We are holding funeral services for the fifty-seven miners who were buried alive in Marcasse. Perhaps you will say a word of comfort to the people?"

It took the Reverends a long time to find their tongues.

"Shocking! Simply shocking!" cried de Jong, giving his protuberant stomach a resounding smack.

"You would think you were in the jungles of Africa!" said Van den Brink.

"Heaven only knows how much harm he's done."

"It may take years to bring these people back to Christianity."

De Jong crossed his hands on his paunch and exclaimed, "I told you not to give him an appointment in the first place."

"I know . . . but Pietersen . . . who could ever have dreamed of this? This chap is absolutely mad!"

"I suspected he was insane all the time. I never did trust him."

The Reverends spoke in rapid, perfect French, not one word of which the Borains understood. Vincent was too weak and ill to realize the import of what they were saying.

De Jong stomached his way through the crowd and said to Vincent quietly but fiercely, "Send these filthy dogs home!"

"But the services! We haven't finished the . . . "

"Never mind the services. Send them away."

The miners filed out slowly, uncomprehending. The two Reverends faced Vincent. "What in the world have you done to yourself? What do you mean by holding services in a hole like this? What sort of a new barbarous cult have you started? Have you no sense of decency, of decorum? Is this conduct befitting a Christian minister? Are you utterly mad, that you behave like this? Do you wish to disgrace our Church?"

The Reverend de Jong paused for a moment, surveyed the mean, sordid shack, the bed of straw on which Vincent lay, the burlap wrapped around his body and his deep sunk, feverish eyes.

"It is a fortunate thing for the Church, Monsieur Van Gogh," he said, "that we have given you only a temporary appointment. You may now consider that appointment cancelled. You will never again be allowed to serve us. I find your conduct disgusting and disgraceful. Your salary is ended and a new man will be sent to take your place immediately. If I were not charitable enough to think you entirely mad, I would call you the worst enemy to Christianity that the Belgian Evangelical Church has ever had!"

There was a long silence. "Well, Monsieur Van Gogh, have you nothing to say in your own defense?"

Vincent remembered the day in Brussels when they had refused him an appointment. Now he could not even feel anything, let alone speak.

"We may as well go, Brother de Jong," said the Reverend van den Brink after a time. "There is nothing we can do here. His case is quite hopeless. If we can't find a good hotel in Wasmes, we'll have to ride back to Mons tonight."

16

The following morning a group of the older miners came to Vincent. "Monsieur," they said, "now that Jacques Verney is gone, you are the only man we can trust. You must tell us what to do. We do not wish to starve to death unless we have to. Perhaps you can get 'them' to grant our wishes. After you have seen them, if you tell us to go back to work, we will. And if you tell us to starve, we will do that, too. We will listen to you, Monsieur, and to no one else."

The offices of the Charbonnages Belgique had a funereal air. The manager was glad to see Vincent and listened to him in sympathy. "I know, Monsieur Van Gogh," he said, "that the miners are outraged because we did not bore through to the bodies. But what good would it have done? The company has decided not to reopen that *couche;* it doesn't pay for itself. We would have had to dig for perhaps a month, and what would have been the result? Simply to take the men from one grave and put them in another."

"Then what about the living? Can you do nothing to improve conditions down below? Must they work in the face of certain death every day of their lives?"

"*Oui,* Monsieur, they must. They must. The company has no funds to invest in safety devices. The miners are on the losing end of this quarrel; they cannot win because they have iron-clad economic laws against them. What is worse, if they don't return to work within another week, Marcasse will be shut down permanently. Then God knows what will happen to them."

Vincent walked up the long winding road to Petit Wasmes, defeated. "Perhaps God knows," he said to himself bitterly. "And then again, perhaps He doesn't."

It was clearly evident that he was of no more use to the miners. He had to tell them to go back to work for thirteen hours a day in the consumption pits, for starvation rations, with sudden death staring half of them in the face and a slow, coughing death all the others. He had failed to help them in any way. Not even God could help them. He had come to the Borinage to put the Word of God into their hearts, but what could he say further when faced by the fact that the eternal enemy of the miners was not the owners, but the Almighty Father Himself?

The moment he told the miners to go back to work, to take up their slavery again, he ceased to be of any value to them. He could never preach another sermon— even if the Committee would allow him—for of what good was the Gospel now? God had turned a stone deaf ear to the miners and Vincent had not been able to soften Him.

Then suddenly he realized something he had known for a long time. All this talk about God was childish evasion; desperate lies whispered by a frightened, lonely mortal to himself out in a cold, dark, eternal night. There was no God. Just as simply as that, there was no God. There was only chaos; miserable, suffering, cruel, torturous, blind, endless chaos.

17

The miners returned to work. Theodorus Van Gogh, who heard from the Committee of Evangelization, wrote, enclosing money and asked Vincent to return to Etten. Instead Vincent went back to the Denises'. He made a farewell trip to the Salon, took all the prints off the wall and put them up in his room under the eaves.

It was bankruptcy once again, and time to take stock. Only there was no stock. There was no job, no money, no health, no strength, no ideas, no enthusiasms, no desires, no ambitions, no ideals, and worst of all, no pivot upon which to hang his life. He was twenty-six, five times a failure, without the courage to begin anew.

He looked at himself in the mirror. His reddish beard covered his face in whorls. His hair was thinning out, his rich, ripe mouth had been squeezed down to a narrow line, and his eyes were lost somewhere in dark caverns. The whole personality that was Vincent Van Gogh seemed to have shrivelled, grown cold, almost died within itself.

He borrowed a little soap from Madame Denis and scrubbed himself from head to foot, standing up in a basin of water. He looked down at what had been a massive, powerful body and saw that it was thin and emaciated. He shaved carefully and neatly, wondering where all the strange bones in his face had come from so suddenly. He combed his hair in its old design for the first time in months. Madame Denis brought him up a shirt and suit of underwear belonging to her husband. He dressed and descended to the cheerful bakery kitchen. He sat down to dinner with the Denises; solid cooked food passed his lips for the first time since the catastrophe at the mine. It seemed curious to him that he should bother to eat at all. The food in his mouth tasted like warm wood pulp.

Although he had not told the miners that he had been forbidden to preach again, they did not ask him to, nor did they seem to care about sermons. Vincent rarely spoke to them any more. He rarely spoke to anyone. He exchanged only a *bonjour* in passing. He never entered their huts or engaged in their daily lives or thoughts. By some profound understanding and tacit agreement the miners refrained from discussing him. They adopted his attitude of formality but they never condemned the change. Mutely they understood. And life went on in the Borinage.

A note from home informed him that Kay Vos's husband had died suddenly. He was at too low an ebb of emotional exhaustion to do more than store the fact in some remote corner of his mind.

The weeks passed. Vincent did nothing but eat, sleep, and sit in a daze. The fever was slowly being driven out of his body. He was gaining strength and weight. But his eyes were two glass openings to a corpse-filled coffin. Summer came; the black fields and chimneys and *terrils* glistened in the sun. Vincent walked through the country-side. He did not walk for exercise or for pleasure. He never knew where he was going or what he passed along the way. He walked because he was tired of lying, sitting, standing. And when he got tired of walking, he sat or lay or stood.

Shortly after his money ran out he received a letter from his brother Theo in Paris, begging him not to idle away his time in the Borinage but to use the enclosed banknotes to take a decisive step and re-establish himself. Vincent turned the money over to Madame Denis. He did not remain in the Borinage because he liked it; he stayed because there was no place else to go, and it would take so much effort to get there.

He had lost God and he had lost himself. Now he lost the most important thing on earth, the one and only person who had always been instinctively sympathetic, and who understood him as he hoped to be understood. Theo abandoned his brother. All during the winter he had written once and twice a week, long, loving letters of cheer and interest. Now the letters stopped altogether. Theo, too, had lost faith; had given up hope. And so Vincent was alone, utterly alone, without even his Maker, a dead man walking in a deserted world and wondering why he was still there.

18

Summer thinned into fall. With the death of the meagre vegetation something came to life within Vincent. He could not yet face his own life, so he turned to the lives of others. He returned to his books. Reading had always been his finest and most constant pleasure, and now in the stories of other people's triumphs and failures, sufferings and joys, he found surcease from the ever haunting spectre of his own fiasco.

When the weather permitted he went out into the fields and read for the entire day; when it rained he either lay on his bed under the eaves or leaned a chair against a wall in the Denis kitchen, and sat there for hours, engrossed. With the passing of the weeks he absorbed the life stories of hundreds of ordinary people like himself, who strove, succeeded a little, and failed a great deal; and through them he slowly got a proper perspective on himself. The theme that ran through his brain: "I'm a failure. I'm a failure. I'm a failure," gave way to "What shall I try now? What am I best fitted for? Where is my proper place in the world?" In every book he read, he looked for that pursuit which might give his life direction again.

Letters from home described his existence as *choquant;* his father insisted that he was violating all decent social conventions by leading the life of an idler. When did he plan to get a job again, to support himself, to become a useful member of society and contribute his share to the world's work?

Vincent would have liked to know the answer to that himself.

At length he reached the saturation point in reading and could no longer pick up a book. During the weeks that followed his debacle, he had been too stunned and ill to feel anything emotionally. Later he had turned to literature to drown out his feelings, and had succeeded. Now he was almost completely well, and the flood of emotional suffering that had been stored up for months broke like a raging torrent and engulfed him in misery and despair. The mental perspective he had gained seemed to do him no good.

He had reached the low point in his life and he knew it.

He felt that there was some good in him, that he was not altogether a fool and a wastrel, and that there was a small contribution he could make to the world. But what was that contribution? He was not fitted for the routine of business and he had already tried everything else for which he might have had an aptitude. Was he always doomed to fail and suffer? Was life really over for him?

The questions asked themselves, but they brought no answers. And so he drifted with the days that slurred into winter. His father would become disgusted and stop sending money; he would have to give up eating at the Denis's and go on short rations. Then Theo would feel a little prick of conscience and send a few notes through Etten. By the time Theo lost patience, his father would once again feel his responsibility. Between them Vincent managed to eat about half the time.

One clear November day Vincent wandered over to Marcasse empty handed, empty minded, and sat on a rusty, iron wheel outside the wall. An old miner came through the gate, his black cap forward over his eyes, shoulders hunched over, hands in pockets, and knees jerking out bonily. Something about the man, he could not tell exactly what, attracted Vincent. Idly, without particular interest, he reached into his pocket, pulled out the stub of a pencil and a letter from home, and on the back of the envelope quickly sketched the little figure tramping across the black field.

Vincent opened his father's letter and saw that the writing covered only one side. After a few moments another miner came out of the gate, a young chap about seventeen. He stood taller, more erect, and there was a cheerful lift to the line of his shoulders as he struck out along the high stone wall of Marcasse toward the railroad tracks. Vincent had several full minutes to sketch him before he disappeared.

19

At the Denises', Vincent found several sheets of clean, white paper and a thick pencil. He put his two rough sketches on the desk and began copying them. His hand was clumsy and stiff; he could not get the line he had in mind on the paper. He used the eraser far more than the pencil, but kept plugging to reproduce his figures. He was so intent that he did not notice darkness creep across his room. He was startled when Madame Denis knocked on his door.

"Monsieur Vincent," she called, "supper is on the table."

"Supper!" exclaimed Vincent. "But it couldn't be that late already."

At the table he chatted animatedly with the Denises and there was a faint gleam in his eye. The Denises exchanged a significant look. After the light meal, Vincent excused himself and went immediately to his room. He lit the little lamp and pinned the two sketches on the wall, standing as far away from them as he could to get a perspective.

"They are bad," he said to himself with a curious grin, "very bad. But perhaps tomorrow I shall be able to do a little better."

He went to bed, placing the kerosene lamp on the floor beside him. He gazed at his two sketches without thinking about anything in particular; then his eyes saw the other prints he had on the wall. It was the first time he had actually seen them since that day, seven months ago, when he had taken them off the walls of the Salon. Suddenly he realized that he was homesick for the world of pictures. There once had been a time when he knew who Rembrandt was, who Millet, Jules Dupré, Delacroix and Maris were. He thought of all the lovely prints he had possessed at one time or another, the lithographs and etchings he had sent to Theo and his parents. He thought of all the beautiful canvases he had seen in the museums of London and Amsterdam, and in so thinking, he forgot to feel miserable, but fell into a deep, restful sleep. The kerosene lamp sputtered, burned bluely, and went out.

The following morning he awoke at two-thirty, thoroughly refreshed. He sprang lightly out of bed, dressed, took his big pencil and writing paper, found a piece of thin board in the bakery, and set out for Marcasse. He seated himself on the same rusty, iron wheel in the darkness and waited for the miners to begin coming in.

He sketched hastily and roughly, as he simply wanted to record his first impression of each personality. An hour later, when all the miners had gone down, he had five figures without faces. He walked briskly across the field, took a cup of coffee up to his room with him and when the light finally came, copied his sketches. He tried to put in all the strange little quirks of Borain appearance which his mind's eyes knew so well, but which he had not been able to catch in the dark, with his models walking out from under him.

His anatomy was all wrong, his proportions were grotesque, and his drawing was so outlandish as to be funny. And yet the figures came out as Borains and could have been mistaken for nothing else. Vincent, amused at his own clumsiness and *gaucherie,* tore up the sketches. Then he sat on the edge of the bed, opposite the Allebé of the little old woman carrying hot water and coals on a wintry street, and tried to copy it. He managed to suggest the woman, but he couldn't get her into relation with either the street or the houses in the background. He crumpled up the sheet, flung it into a corner and sat his chair before the Bosboom study of a lone tree against a cloudy sky. It all looked so simple; just a tree, a bit of loam, and clouds at the top. But Bosboom's values were precise and exquisite and Vincent learned that it is always the simplest piece of art which has practised the most rigid elimination and is therefore the most difficult to duplicate.

The morning passed outside the realm of time. When Vincent used up his last sheet of paper, he searched his belongings very thoroughly to see how much money he had. He found two francs, and believing he could get good paper and perhaps even a stick of charcoal in Mons, set out to walk the twelve kilometres. As he went down the long hill between Petit Wasmes and Wasmes he saw a few miners' wives standing before their doors. He added a cordial *comment ça va?* to his usual automatic *bonjour.* At Paturages, a little town half-way to Mons, he noticed a pretty girl behind a bakery window. He went in to buy a five centime bun, just to look at her.

The fields between Paturages and Cuesmes were a bright shade of green from the heavy rains. Vincent decided to come back and sketch them when he could afford a green crayon. In Mons he found a pad of smooth yellow paper, some charcoal, and a heavy lead pencil. There was a bin of old prints in front of the store. Vincent pored over them for hours although he knew he could buy nothing. The owner joined him, and they commented on one print after another just as though they were two friends going through a museum.

"I must apologize that I haven't any money to buy one of your pictures," said Vincent, after they had spent a long time looking at them.

The owner brought his hands and shoulders up in an eloquent Gallic gesture and said, "It doesn't matter, Monsieur! come again another time even though you have no money."

He walked the twelve kilometres home in a leisurely fashion. The sun was setting over the pyramid-dotted horizon and lit up the outer fringe of some floating clouds with a delicate shell pink. Vincent noticed how the little stone houses of Cuesmes fell into natural etching designs, and how peaceful the green valley lay below him when he gained the top of a hill. He felt happy, and wondered why.

The following day he went to the *terril* behind Marcasse and sketched the girls and women as they leaned over the slope, digging specks of black gold out of the mountainside. After dinner he said, "Please do not leave the table for a moment, Monsieur, Madame Denis. I wish to do something."

He ran to his room, brought back the drawing pad and charcoal, and quickly planted a likeness of his friends on the paper. Madame Denis came around to look over his shoulder and exclaimed, "But Monsieur Vincent, you are an artist!"

Vincent was embarrassed. "No," he said, "I am only amusing myself."

"But it is nice," said Madame Denis. "It almost looks like me."

"Almost," laughed Vincent, "but not quite."

He did not write home to tell them what he was doing because he knew they would say, and rightly, "Oh, Vincent is at one of his fads again. When will he settle down and do something useful?"

Besides, this new activity had a curious special quality; it was his and nobody else's. He could not bring himself to talk or write about his sketches. He felt a reticence about them that he had not felt for anything before, a disinclination to let strange eyes see his work. They were, in some crude and incomprehensible way, sacred, even though they might be wretchedly amateurish in every last detail.

Once more he entered the miners' huts, but this time he carried drawing paper and crayon instead of a Bible. The miners were not any the less glad to see him. He sketched the children playing on the floor, the wives bending over their oval stoves, the family at supper when the day's work was done. He sketched Marcasse with its tall chimneys, the black fields, the pine woods across the ravine, the peasants ploughing down around Paturages. If the weather was bad, he remained in his room, copying the prints on the walls and the rough drafts he had done the day before. When he went to bed at night, he felt that perhaps one or two of the things he had done that day were not so bad. He awakened the next morning to find he had slept off the intoxication of creative effort and that the drawings were wrong, all wrong. He threw them away without a qualm.

He had put down the beast of pain within him, and he was happy because he no longer thought of his unhappiness. He knew he ought to feel ashamed to keep on taking his father's and brother's money when he made no effort to support himself, but it did not seem to matter and he just went on sketching.

After a few weeks, when he had copied all the prints on the wall a great many times, he realized that if he was to make any progress he would have to have more to copy, and those of the masters. Despite the fact that Theo had not written to him for a year, he hid his pride under a pile of poor drawings and wrote to his brother.

Dear Theo:
    If I am not mistaken you must still have "Les Travaux des Champs" by Millet.
    Would you be so kind as to lend them to me for a short time and send them by mail?
    I must tell you that I am copying large drawings after Bosboom and Allebé. Well, perhaps if you saw them you would not be altogether dissatisfied.
    Send me what you can and do not fear for me. If I can only continue to work, that will somehow or other set me right again.
    I write to you while I am busy drawing and I am in a hurry to get back to it, so good night, and send me the prints as soon as possible.
                              With a hearty handshake in thought,
                                        Vincent.

Slowly a new hunger grew upon him, the desire to talk to some artist about his work, and find out just where he was going right and where he was going wrong. He knew that his drawings were bad, but he was too close to them to see exactly why. What he needed was the ruthless eye of a stranger who was not blinded by the creative pride of the parent.

To whom could he go? It was a hunger more cogent than any he suffered the winter before when he had lived for days on dry bread. He simply had to know and feel that there were other artists in the world, men of his own kind who were facing the same technical problems, thinking in the same terms; men who would justify his efforts by showing their own serious concern with the elements of the painter's craft. There were people in the world, he remembered, men like Maris and Mauve, who gave their whole lives to painting. That seemed almost unbelievable here in the Borinage.

One rainy afternoon, as he was copying in his room, there flashed before his mind the picture of the Reverend Pietersen standing in his studio in Brussels and saying, "But don't tell my *confrères* about it!" He knew that he had his man at last. He looked over the original sketches he had done, selected the figures of a miner, a wife bending over her oval stove, and an old woman gathering *terril*. He set out for Brussels.

He had only a little over three francs in his pocket, so he could not afford to take a train. The distance on foot was some eighty kilometres. Vincent walked that afternoon, all that night, and most of the following day, getting within thirty kilometres of Brussels. He would have gone straight on except that his thin shoes had worn through and he had pushed his toes through the top of one of them. The coat he had used all the previous year in Petit Wasmes was covered with a layer of dust, and since he had not taken even a comb or change of shirt with him, he could do little more than throw cold water over his face the next morning.

He put cardboard inside the soles of his shoes and started out very early. The leather began to cut him where his toes stuck through at the top; soon his foot was covered with blood. The cardboard wore out, water blisters took its place, changed to blood blisters, and then broke. He was hungry, he was thirsty, he was tired, but he was as happy as a man could be.

He was actually going to see and talk to another artist!

He reached the outskirts of Brussels that afternoon without a centime in his pockets. He remembered very distinctly where Pietersen lived and walked rapidly through the streets. People moved aside quickly as he passed, and then stared after him, shaking their heads. Vincent did not even notice them, but made his way along as fast as his crippled feet would permit him.

The Reverend's young daughter answered the bell. She took one horrified look at Vincent's dirty, sweat streaked face, his uncombed, matted hair, filthy coat, mud caked trousers and black, bloody feet, and ran screaming down the hall. The Reverend Pietersen came to the door, peered at Vincent for a moment without recognizing him, and then broke into a hearty smile of recognition.

"Well, Vincent my son," he exclaimed, "how good it is to see you again. Come right in, come right in."

He led Vincent into the study and drew up a comfortable chair for him. Now that he had made his objective, the cable of will broke within Vincent, and all at once he felt the eighty kilometres that he had tramped in the last two days on bread and a little cheese. The muscles of his back relaxed, his shoulders slumped, and he found it curiously difficult to breathe.

"A friend of mine nearby has a spare room, Vincent," said Pietersen. "Wouldn't you like to clean up and rest after your journey?"

"Yes. I hadn't known I was so tired."

The Reverend took his hat and walked down the street with Vincent, oblivious to the stares of his neighbours.

"You will probably want to sleep tonight," he said, "but surely you will come to dinner tomorrow at twelve? We will have a great deal to talk about."

Vincent scrubbed, standing up in an iron basin, and although it was only six o'clock, went to sleep holding his empty stomach. He did not open his eyes until ten the next morning and only then because hunger was pounding implacably on some anvil within him. The man from whom the Reverend Pietersen rented the room lent Vincent a razor, a comb, and a clothes brush; he did what he could to make himself look neat and found everything repairable except the shoes.

Vincent was ravenous for food, and while Pietersen chatted lightly about the recent events in Brussels, piled it in unashamedly. After dinner the two men went into the study.

"Oh," said Vincent, "you've been doing a lot of work, haven't you? These are all new sketches on the walls."

"Yes," replied Pietersen, "I'm beginning to find a great deal more pleasure in painting than in preaching."

Vincent said smilingly, "And does your conscience prick you occasionally for taking so much time off your real work?"

Pietersen laughed and said, "Do you know the anecdote about Rubens? He was serving Holland as Ambassador to Spain and used to spend the afternoons in the royal gardens before his easel. One day a jaunty member of the Spanish court passed and remarked, 'I see that the diplomat amuses himself sometimes with painting,' to which Rubens replied, 'No, the painter amuses himself sometimes with diplomacy!' ''

Pietersen and Vincent exchanged an understanding laugh. Vincent opened his packet. ''I have been doing a little sketching myself,'' he said, ''and I brought along three figures for you to see. Perhaps you won't mind telling me what you think of them?''

Pietersen winced, for he knew that criticizing a beginner's work was a thankless task. Nevertheless he placed the three studies on the easel and stood a long way off looking at them. Vincent suddenly saw his drawings through his friend's eyes; he realized how utterly amateurish they were.

''My first impression,'' said the Reverend, after some time, ''is that you must be working very close to your models. Are you?''

''Yes, I have to. Most of my work is done in the crowded miners' huts.''

''I see. That explains your lack of perspective. Couldn't you manage to find a place where you can stand off from your subjects? You'll see them much more clearly, I'm sure.''

''There are some fairly large miners' cabins. I could rent one for very little and fix it up as a studio.''

''An excellent idea.'' He was silent again and then said with effort, ''Have you ever studied drawing? Do you block the faces on squared off paper? Do you take measurements?''

Vincent blushed. ''I don't know how to do those things,'' he said. ''You see, I've never had a lesson. I thought you just went ahead and drew.''

''Ah, no,'' said Pietersen sadly. ''You must learn your elementary technique first and then your drawing will come slowly. Here, I'll show you what's wrong with this woman.''

He took a ruler, squared off the head and figure, showed Vincent how bad his proportions were, and then proceeded to reconstruct the head, explaining as he went along. After almost an hour of work he stepped back, surveyed the sketch, and said, ''There. Now I think we have that figure drawn correctly.''

Vincent joined him at the opposite end of the room and looked at the paper. There could be no doubt about it, the woman was now drawn in perfect proportion. But she was no longer a miner's wife, no longer a Borain picking up coal on the slope of her *terril*. She was just any perfectly drawn woman in the world, bending over. Without saying a word Vincent went to the easel, placed the figure of the woman bending over her oval stove beside the reconstructed drawing, and went back to join Pietersen.

''Hummmm,'' said the Reverend Pietersen. ''Yes, I see what you mean. I've given her proportion and taken away character.''

They stood there for a long time, looking at the easel. Pietersen said involuntarily, ''You know, Vincent, that woman standing over her stove isn't bad. She isn't at all bad. The drawing is terrible, your values are all wrong and her face is hopeless. In fact she hasn't any face at all. But that sketch has got something. You caught something that I can't quite lay my finger on. What is it, Vincent?''

''I'm sure I don't know. I just put her down as I saw her.''

This time it was Pietersen who walked quickly to the easel. He threw the sketch he had perfected into the wastebasket with a ''You don't mind, do you, I've ruined it anyway,'' and placed the second woman there all by herself. He rejoined Vincent and they sat down. The Reverend started to speak several times but the words did not quite form. At last he said, ''Vincent, I hate to admit it, but I really believe I almost like that woman. I thought she was horrible at first, but something about her grows on you.''

''Why do you hate to admit it?'' asked Vincent.

''Because I ought not to like it. The whole thing is wrong, dead wrong! Any elementary class in art school would make you tear it up and begin all over again.

And yet something about her reaches out at me. I could almost swear I have seen that woman somewhere before.''

"Perhaps you have seen her in the Borinage," said Vincent artlessly.

Pietersen looked at him quickly to see if he was being clever and then said, "I think you're right. She has no face and she isn't any one particular person. Somehow she's just all the miners' wives in the Borinage put together. That something you've caught is the spirit of the miner's wife, Vincent, and that's a thousand times more important than any correct drawing. Yes, I like your woman. She says something to me directly.''

Vincent trembled, but he was afraid to speak. Pietersen was an experienced artist, a professional; if he should ask for the drawing, really like it enough to . . .

"Could you spare her, Vincent? I would like very much to put her on my wall. I think she and I could become excellent friends.''

20

When Vincent decided he had better return to Petit Wasmes, the Reverend Pietersen gave him a pair of his old shoes to replace the broken ones, and railroad fare back to the Borinage. Vincent took them in the full spirit of friendship which knows that the difference between giving and taking is purely temporal.

On the train Vincent realized two important things; the Reverend Pietersen had not once referred to his failure as an evangelist, and he had accepted him on equal terms as a fellow artist. He had actually liked a sketch well enough to want it for his own; that was the crucial test.

"He has given me my start," said Vincent to himself. "If he liked my work, other people will, too.''

At the Denises' he found that "Les Travaux des Champs" had arrived from Theo, although no letter accompanied them. His contact with Pietersen had refreshed him, so he dug into Father Millet with gusto. Theo had enclosed some large sized sketch paper, and within a few days Vincent copied ten pages of "Les Travaux," finishing the first volume. Then, feeling that he needed work on the nude, and being quite certain he could never get anyone to pose for him that way in the Borinage, he wrote to his old friend Tersteeg, manager of the Goupil Galleries in The Hague, asking him if he would lend the "Exercises au Fusain" by Bargue.

In the meanwhile he remembered Pietersen's counsel and rented a miner's hut near the top of the rue Petit Wasmes for nine francs a month. This time the hut was the best he could find, not the worst. It had a rough plank floor, two large windows to let in light, a bed, table, chair, and stove. It was sufficiently large for Vincent to place his model at one end and get far enough away for complete perspective. There was not a miner's wife or child in Petit Wasmes who had not been helped in some way the winter before by Vincent, and no one ever turned down his request to come and pose. On Sundays the miners would throng to his cabin and let him make quick sketches of them. They thought it great fun. The place was always full of people looking over Vincent's shoulder with interest and amazement.

The "Exercises au Fusain" arrived from The Hague and Vincent spent the next two weeks copying the sixty studies, working from early morning to night. Tersteeg also sent the "Cours de Dessin" by Bargue; Vincent tackled this with tremendous vitality.

All five of the former failures were wiped completely from his mind. Not even serving God had brought such sheer ecstasy and constant, lasting satisfaction as creative art could give him. When for eleven days he had not one centime in his pocket and had to live off the few loaves he could borrow from Madame Denis, he did not once complain—even to himself—of his hunger. What did the hunger of his belly matter, when his spirit was being so well fed?

Every morning for a week he went to the gate of Marcasse at two-thirty and made a large drawing of the miners: men and women going to the shaft, through the snow by a path along a hedge of thorns; shadows that passed, dimly visible in the crepuscule. In the background he drew the large constructions of the mine, with the heaps of clinkers standing out vaguely against the sky. He made a copy of the sketch when it was finished and sent it in a letter to Theo.

Two full months passed this way, drawing from dawn to dark and then copying by the light of the lamp. Once again there came over him the desire to see and talk to another artist, to find out how he was getting on, for although he thought he had made some progress, achieved a little more plasticity of hand and judgment, he could not be sure. But this time he wanted a master, someone who would take him under his wing and teach him slowly and carefully the rudiments of the great craft. There was nothing he would not do in return for such instruction; he would black the man's boots and sweep the floor of his studio ten times a day.

Jules Breton, whose work he had admired since the early days, lived in Courrieres, a distance of a hundred and seventy kilometres. Vincent rode on the train until his money ran out, and then walked for five days, sleeping in hay ricks and begging his bread in exchange for a drawing or two. When he stood among the trees of Courrieres and saw that Breton had just built a fine new studio of red brick and generous proportion, his courage fled. He hung about the town for two days, but in the end, the chilly and inhospitable appearance of the studio defeated him. Then, weary, abysmally hungry, without a centime in his pocket, and the Reverend Pietersen's shoes wearing dangerously thin beneath him, he began the hundred and seventy kilometre walk back to the Borinage.

He arrived at the miner's cabin ill and despondent. There was no money or mail waiting for him. He went to bed. The miners' wives nursed him and gave him what tiny portions of food they could spare from the mouths of their husbands and children.

He had lost many pounds on the trip, the hollows were in his cheeks again, and fever ignited the bottomless pools of his green-black eyes. Sick as he was, his mind retained its clarity, and he knew that he had reached the point where a decision was imminent.

What was he to do with his life? Become a school teacher, book-seller, art dealer, mercantile clerk? Where was he to live? Etten, with his parents? Paris, with Theo? Amsterdam, with his uncles? Or just in the great void wherever chance might dump him down, working at whatever fortune dictated?

One day, when his strength had returned a little and he was sitting propped up in bed copying "Le Four dans les Landes" by Theodore Rousseau, and wondering how much longer he would have to indulge in this harmless little pastime of drawing, someone opened the door without knocking and walked in.

It was his brother Theo.

21

The passage of the years had improved Theo. Only twenty-three, he was already a successful art dealer in Paris, respected by his *confrères* and family. He knew and practised all the social amenities of dress, manners and conversation. He wore a good black coat, crossing high on his chest with satin piping on the broad lapels, a high stiff collar, and a white tie with a huge knot.

He had the tremendous Van Gogh forehead. His hair was dark brown, his features delicate, almost feminine. His eyes were soft and wistful and his face tapered in a beautiful oval.

Theo leaned against the door of the shack and gazed at Vincent in horror. He had just left Paris a few hours before. In his apartment there was lovely Louis Philippe furniture to sit upon, a wash bowl with towels and soap, curtains on the windows, rugs on the floor, a writing desk, bookcases, soft lamps and pleasant wallpaper. Vincent was lying on a dirty, bare mattress, covered by an old blanket. The walls and floor were of rough plank, the only furnishings a battered table and chair. He was unwashed and unkempt, his coarse, red beard splashed all over his face and neck.

"Well, Theo," said Vincent.

Theo crossed hastily and leaned over the bed. "Vincent, what in God's name is wrong? What have you done to yourself?"

"Nothing. I'm all right now. I was sick a while."

"But this . . . this . . . hole! Surely you don't live here . . . this isn't your home?"

"Yes. What's the matter with it? I've been using it for a studio."

"Oh, Vincent!" He ran his hand over his brother's hair; the lump in his throat prevented him from speaking.

"It's good to have you here, Theo."

"Vincent, please tell me what has been the matter with you. Why have you been sick? What was it?"

Vincent told him about Courrieres.

"You've exhausted yourself, that's what. Have you been eating properly since you're back? Have you been taking care of yourself?"

"The miners' wives have been nursing me."

"Yes, but what have you been eating?" Theo looked around him. "Where do you keep your stores? I don't see any."

"The women bring me in a little something every day. Whatever they can spare; bread, coffee, a little cheese, or rabbit."

"But, Vincent, surely you know you can't get your strength back on bread and coffee? Why don't you buy yourself some eggs and vegetables and meat?"

"Those things cost money here in the Borinage, the same as anywhere else."

Theo sat down on the bed.

"Vincent, for the love of God, forgive me! I didn't know. I didn't understand."

"That's all right, boy, you did all you could. I'm getting along fine. In a few days I'll be up and about again."

Theo ran his hand across his eyes as though to clear away some misty cobweb. "No. I didn't realize. I thought that you . . . I didn't understand, Vincent, I just didn't understand."

"Oh, come. It's all right. How are things in Paris? Where are you bound for? Have you been to Etten?"

Theo jumped up. "Are there stores in this forsaken town? Can I buy things here?"

"Yes, there are places down the hill in Wasmes. But draw up that chair. I want to talk to you. Lord, Theo, it's been almost two years!"

Theo ran his fingers lightly over his brother's face and said, "First of all I'm going to load you full of the best food I can find in Belgium. You've been starved, that's what's the matter with you. And then I'm going to give you a dose of something for that fever and put you to sleep on a soft pillow. It's a good thing I got here when I did. If I had only had the slightest idea . . . Don't move until I get back."

He ran out of the door. Vincent picked up his pencil, looked at "Le Four dans les Landes," and went on copying. In a half hour Theo was back, two small boys following him. He had two sheets, a pillow, bundles of pots and dishes and packages of food. He put Vincent between the cool, white sheets and made him lie down.

"Now how do you work this stove?" he asked, peeling off his beautiful coat and rolling up his sleeves.

"There's some paper and twigs. Light that first and then put in the coal."

Theo gazed at the *terril* and said, "Coal! Do you call this coal?"

"It's what we use. Here, let me show you how to work it."

He tried to get out of bed, but Theo was on him with a leap. "Lie down, you idiot!" he cried, "and don't move again or I shall be forced to thrash you."

Vincent grinned for the first time in months. The smile in his eyes almost put the fever to rout. Theo put two eggs in one of his new pots, and cut up some string beans in another. In a third he warmed some fresh milk, and held a flat toaster over the fire, with white bread on it. Vincent watched Theo hovering about the stove in his shirt-sleeves, and the sight of his brother close to him once again did him more good than any food.

At length the meal was ready. Theo drew up the table alongside the bed and spread a clean, white towel from his bag. He put a nice cut of butter into the beans, broke the two soft boiled eggs into a dish, and picked up a spoon.

"All right, boy," he said, "open your mouth. You're going to have a square meal for the first time in Heaven knows how long."

"Oh, come off, Theo," said Vincent, "I can feed myself."

Theo filled the spoon with egg and held it up for Vincent. "Open your mouth, young fellow," he said, "or I'll pour it in your eye."

When Vincent finished, he put his head back on the pillow with a deep sigh of contentment. "Food tastes good," he said. "I had forgotten."

"You're not going to forget again in a hurry."

"Now tell me, Theo, everything that's been happening. How are things at Goupils? I'm starved for news of the outside world."

"Then you'll have to stay starved for a little while longer. Here's something to put you to sleep. I want you to be quiet and give that food a chance to work."

"But, Theo, I don't want to sleep. I want to talk. I can sleep any time."

"Nobody asked you what you wanted. You're taking orders. Drink this down like a good fellow. And when you wake up, I have a nice steak and potatoes that will set you right on your feet."

Vincent slept until sundown, and awoke feeling greatly refreshed. Theo was sitting under one of the windows, looking at Vincent's drawings. Vincent watched him for a long time before he made a sound, a feeling of peace in his heart. When Theo saw that he was awake, he jumped up with a broad smile.

"Well! And how do you feel now? Better? You certainly were sleeping."

"What did you think of the sketches? Did you like any of them?"

"Wait until I put that steak on. I have the potatoes all peeled, ready to boil."

He attended to things at the stove and brought back a basin of warm water to the bedside. "Shall I use my razor, Vincent, or yours?"

"Can't I eat the steak without getting shaved?"

"No, sir. Nor without getting your neck and ears washed, and your hair neatly combed. Here, tuck this towel under your chin."

He gave Vincent a clean shave, washed him thoroughly, combed his hair, and put him into one of the new shirts he was carrying in his bag.

"There!" he exclaimed, backing away to survey the job he had done. "You look like a Van Gogh now."

"Theo, quick! The steak's burning!"

Theo set the table and put out the meal of boiled potatoes and butter, a thick, tender steak, and milk.

"My word, Theo, you don't expect me to eat that whole steak?"

"I certainly do not. Half of it belongs to me. Well, let's pitch in. All we would have to do would be to close our eyes, and we could imagine we were home at Etten."

After dinner Theo loaded Vincent's pipe with some tobacco from Paris. "Smoke up," he said. "I oughtn't to allow you to do this, but I guess real tobacco will do you more good than harm."

Vincent smoked in contentment, occasionally rubbing the warm, slightly moist stem of his pipe against his smooth cheek. Theo looked over the bowl of his pipe, through the rough boards, and all the way back to his childhood in the Brabant. Vincent had always been the most important person in the world to him, far more important than either his mother or father. Vincent had made his childhood sweet and good. He had forgotten that the last year in Paris; he ought never to forget it again. Life without Vincent was somehow incomplete for him. He felt that he was a part of Vincent, and that Vincent was a part of him. Together they had always understood the world; alone it somehow baffled him. Together they had found the meaning and purpose of life, and valued it; alone he often wondered why he was working and being successful. He had to have Vincent to make his life full. And Vincent needed him, for he was really only a child. He had to be taken out of this hole, put on his feet again. He had to be made to realize that he had been wasting himself, and be jerked into some rejuvenating action.

"Vincent," he said, "I'm going to give you a day or two to get your strength back, and then I'm taking you home to Etten."

Vincent puffed in silence for many minutes. He knew that this whole affair had to be thrashed out, and that unfortunately they had no medium but words. Well, he would have to make Theo understand. After that, everything would come all right.

"Theo, what would be the good of my going home? Involuntarily I have become in the family a kind of impossible and suspect person, at least somebody whom they do not trust. That's why I believe the most reasonable thing for me to do is to keep at a distance, so that I cease to exist for them.

"I am a man of passions, capable of doing foolish things. I speak and act too quickly when it would have been better to wait patiently. This being the case, must I consider myself a dangerous man, incapable of doing anything? I do not think so. But the question is to try to put these selfsame passions to a good use. For instance, I have an irresistible passion for pictures and books, and I want continually to instruct myself, just as I want to eat my bread. You certainly will understand that."

"I do understand, Vincent. But looking at pictures and reading books at your age is only a diversion. They have nothing to do with the main business of life. It is almost five years now that you have been without employment, wandering here and there. And during that time you have been going down hill, deteriorating."

Vincent poured some tobacco in his hand, rubbed it between his palms to make it moist, and stuffed it into his pipe. Then he forgot to light it.

"It is true," he said, "that now and then I have earned my crust of bread, now and then a friend has given it to me in charity. It is true that I have lost the confidence of many, that my financial affairs are in a sad state, and that my future is only too sombre. But is that necessarily deterioration? I must continue, Theo, on the path I have taken. If I don't study, if I don't go on seeking any longer, then I am lost."

"You're evidently trying to tell me something, old boy, but I'm blessed if I can gather what it is."

Vincent lit his pipe, sucking in the flame of the match. "I remember the time," he said, "when we walked together near the old mill at Ryswyk; then we agreed in many things."

"But, Vincent, you have changed so much."

"That is not quite true. My life was less difficult then; but as to my way of looking at things and thinking, that has not changed at all."

"For your sake I would like to believe that."

"Theo, you must not think that I disavow things. I am faithful in my unfaithfulness, and my only anxiety is, how can I be of use in the world? Cannot I serve some purpose and be of some good?"

Theo rose, struggled with the kerosene lamp, and finally lit it. He poured out a glass of milk. "Here, drink this. I don't want you to exhaust yourself."

Vincent drank it down too quickly, almost choking on its richness. Without even waiting to wipe the cream off his eager lips, he went on. "Our inward thoughts, do they ever show outwardly? There may be a great fire in our soul and no one comes to warm himself by it. The passers-by see only a bit of smoke coming through the chimney and continue on their way. Now look here, what must be done? Mustn't one tend that inward fire, have salt in oneself, wait patiently for the hour when somebody will come and sit near it?"

Theo got up and sat on the bed. "Do you know the picture that just flashed into my mind?" he asked.

"No."

"The old mill at Ryswyk."

"It was a nice old mill, wasn't it?"

"Yes."

"And our childhood was nice, too."

"You made my childhood pleasant, Vincent. My first memories are always of you."

There was a long silence.

"Vincent, I do hope you realize that the accusations I have made come from the family and not from me. They persuaded me to come here and see if I couldn't shame you into returning to Holland and a job."

"It's all right, Theo, the words they say are perfectly true. It's just that they don't understand my motives and don't see the present in relation to my whole life. But if I have come down in the world, you, on the contrary, have risen. If I have lost sympathies, you have gained them. That makes me very happy. I say it in all sincerity, and it will always be so. But I should be very glad if it were possible for you to see in me something else than an idle man of the worst type."

"Let's forget those words. If I have not written to you all year, it was through negligence, not disapproval. I've believed in you and had implicit faith in you since the earliest days when I used to take your hand through the high, grass fields at Zundert. And I haven't any less faith now. I need only to be near you to know that everything you do will eventually come right."

Vincent smiled, a broad, happy, Brabantine smile. "That was good of you, Theo."

Theo suddenly became the man of action.

"See here, Vincent, let's settle this thing right here and now. I have a suspicion that behind all these abstractions you've been dealing in, there is something you want to do, something that you feel is ultimately right for you and that will finally bring you to happiness and success. Well, old boy, just name it. Goupil and Company have raised my wages twice during the past year and a half, and I have more money than I know what to do with. Now if there is something you want to do, and you will need help right at first, simply tell me that you have at last found your real life work, and we'll form a partnership. You'll supply the work and I'll supply the funds. After we've put you on a paying basis, you can return the investment with dividends. Now confess, haven't you something in mind? Hadn't you decided long ago that there was something you wanted to do with the rest of your life?"

Vincent looked over at the pile of sketches Theo had been studying under the window. A grin of amazement, incredulity, and at last awareness spread across his face. His eyes opened wide, his mouth opened, his whole personality seemed to burst open like a *tournesol* in the sun.

"Well I'll be blessed!" he murmured. "That's what I've been trying to say all along, and I didn't know it."

Theo's eyes followed his to the sketches. "I thought so," he said.

Vincent was quivering with excitement and joy; he seemed to have suddenly awakened from some profound sleep.

"Theo, you knew it before I did! I wouldn't let myself think about it. I was afraid. Of course there's something I must do. It's the thing I've pointed towards all my life, and I never suspected it. I felt a tremendous urge to sketch, to put down what I saw on paper while I was studying in Amsterdam and Brussels. But I wouldn't allow myself to. I was afraid it would interfere with my real work. *My real work!* How blind I was. Something has been trying to push itself out of me all these years and I wouldn't let it. I beat it back. Here I am, twenty-seven, with nothing accomplished. What an idiot, an utterly blind and stupid idiot I've been."

"It doesn't matter, Vincent. With your strength and determination you'll be able to accomplish a thousand times as much as any other beginner. And you've got a long life ahead of you."

"I have ten years anyway. I'll be able to turn out some good work in that time."

"Of course you will! And you can live wherever you like; Paris, Brussels, Amsterdam, The Hague. Just take your choice and I'll send you money to live on each month. I don't care if it takes you years, Vincent, I'll never give up hope if you don't."

"Oh, Theo, all these bitter months I've been working toward something, trying to dig the real purpose and meaning out of my life, and I didn't know it! But now that I do know, I'll never be discouraged again. Theo, do you realize what it means? After all these wasted years I HAVE FOUND MYSELF AT LAST! I'm going to be an artist. Of course I'm going to be an artist. I've got to be. That's why I failed at all my other jobs, because I wasn't meant for them. But now I've got the one thing that can never fail. Oh, Theo, the prison is open at last, and you're the one who unbarred the gates!"

"Nothing can ever estrange us! We're together again, aren't we, Vincent?"

"Yes, Theo, for life."

"Now, just you rest and get well. In a few days, when you're better, I'll take you back to Holland, or Paris, or wherever you want to go."

Vincent sprang out of bed with a leap that carried him halfway across the cabin.

"In a few days, hell!" he cried. "We're going right now. There's a train for Brussels at nine o'clock."

He began pulling on his clothes with furious speed.

"But Vincent, you can't travel tonight. You're sick."

"Sick! That's ancient history. I never felt better in my life. Come on, Theo, boy, we've got about ten minutes to make that railway station. Throw those nice white sheets into your bag and let's be on our way!"

BOOK TWO

ETTEN

1

Theo and Vincent spent a day together in Brussels, and then Theo returned to Paris. Spring was coming, the Brabantine country-side called, and home seemed like a magic haven. Vincent bought himself a workman's suit of rough black velvet, of the material known as *veloutine,* some unbleached, muslin colored Ingres paper for sketching, and caught the next train home to Etten and the family parsonage.

Anna Cornelia disapproved of Vincent's life because she felt it brought him more pain than happiness. Theodorus disapproved on objective grounds; if Vincent had been someone else's son, he would have had nothing to do with him. He knew that God did not like Vincent's evil way of living, but he had a suspicion that He would like even less the casting off of a son by his father.

Vincent noticed that his father's hair had grown whiter and that the right lid drooped still lower over his eye. Age seemed to be shrinking his features; he grew no beard to make up for the loss, and the expression on his face had changed from "This is me," to "Is this me?"

In his mother Vincent found greater strength and attractiveness than before. Age built her up rather than tore her down. The smile engraved in curved lines between her nostrils and chin forgave one's errors before they were committed; the broadness and wideness and goodness of her face were an eternal "Yea" to the beauty of life.

For several days the family stuffed Vincent with revivifying food and affection, ignoring the fact that he had no fortune and no future. He walked on the heath among the cottages with the thatched roofs, watched the woodcutters who were busy on a piece of ground where a pine wood had been cut down, strolled leisurely on the road to Roozendaal, past the Protestant barn with the mill right opposite in the meadow and the elm trees in the churchyard. The Borinage receded, his health and strength came back with a rush, and within a short time he was eager to begin his work.

One rainy morning Anna Cornelia descended to the kitchen at an early hour to find the stove already glowing red, and Vincent sitting before it, his feet propped up on the grate, with a half finished copy after "Les Heures de la Journée" in his lap.

"Why son, good morning," she exclaimed.

"Good morning, Mother." He kissed her broad cheek fondly.

"What makes you get up so early, Vincent?"

"Well, Mother, I wanted to work."

"Work?"

Anna Cornelia looked at the sketch in his lap, then at the glowing stove. "Oh, you mean get the fire started. But you mustn't get up for that."

"No, I mean my drawing."

Once again Anna Cornelia glanced over her son's shoulder at the copy. It looked to her like a child's efforts to reproduce something from a magazine during a play hour.

"You are going to work at drawing things, Vincent?"

"Yes."

He explained his decision and Theo's efforts to help him. Contrary to his expectations, Anna Cornelia was pleased. She walked quickly into the living room and returned with a letter.

"Our cousin, Anton Mauve, is a painter," she said, "and he makes a great deal of money. I had this letter from my sister only the other day—Mauve married her daughter Jet, you know—and she writes that Mijnheer Tersteeg at Goupils sells everything Anton does for five and six hundred guilders."

"Yes, Mauve is becoming one of our important painters."

"How long does it take to make one of those pictures, Vincent?"

"That depends, Mother. Some canvases take a few days, some a few years."

"A few years! Oh, my!"

Anna Cornelia thought for a moment and then asked, "Can you draw people so that it looks like them?"

"Well, I don't know. I have some sketches upstairs. I'll show them to you."

When he returned, his mother had on her white kitchen cap and was placing kettles of water on the broad stove. The shining blue and white tiles of the wall gave the room a cheerful air.

"I'm fixing your favourite cheese bake, Vincent," said Anna Cornelia. "Do you remember?"

"Do I remember! Oh, Mother!"

He threw his arm about her shoulder roughly. She looked up at him with a wistful smile. Vincent was her eldest child and her favourite; his unhappiness was the only thing in life that grieved her.

"Is it good to be home with your mother?" she asked.

He pinched her fresh, wrinkled cheek playfully.

"Yes, sweetheart," he answered.

She took the sketches of the Borains and studied them carefully.

"But Vincent, what has happened to their faces?"

"Nothing. Why?"

"They haven't any."

"I know. I was only interested in the figure."

"But you can draw people's faces, can't you? I'm sure lots of women here in Etten would like to have their portraits painted. There's a living in that."

"Yes, I suppose so. But I'll have to wait until my drawing is right."

His mother was breaking eggs into a pan of sour cheese she had strained the day before. She paused with half the shell of an egg in each hand and turned from the stove.

"You mean you have to make your drawing right so the portraits will be good enough to sell?"

"No," replied Vincent, sketching rapidly with his pencil, "I have to make my drawing right so that my drawing will be right."

Anna Cornelia stirred the yolks into the white cheese thoughtfully and then said, "I'm afraid I don't understand that, son."

"Neither do I," said Vincent, "but anyway it's so."

Over the fluffy golden cheese bake at breakfast, Anna Cornelia broke the news to her husband. They had been doing a great deal of uneasy speculating about Vincent in private.

"Is there a future in that, Vincent?" asked his father. "Will you be able to support yourself?"

"Not just at first. Theo is going to help me until I get on my feet. After my drawing becomes accurate, I should be able to make money. Draftsmen in London and Paris earn from ten to fifteen francs a day, and the men who do illustrations for the magazines make good money."

Theodorus was relieved to find that Vincent had something—anything in mind, and was not going to drift idly as he had all these years.

"I hope, if you begin this work, Vincent, you will keep on with it. You'll never get anywhere changing from pillar to post."

"This is the end, Father. I'll not change again."

2

After a time the rain stopped and warm weather set in. Vincent took his drawing material and easel out of doors and began exploring the country. He liked best to work on the heath, near Seppe, though he often went to a big swamp in the Passievaart to draw the water lilies. Etten was a small, closely knit town and its people looked at him askance. The black velvet suit was the first of its kind to be seen in the village; never before had the natives known a full grown man to spend his days in the open fields with nothing but pencil and drawing paper. He was courteous to his father's parishioners in a rough, disinterested sort of way, but they wanted to have nothing to do with him. In this tiny, provincial settlement he was a freak, a sport; everything about him was bizarre; his clothes, his manner, his red beard, his history, the fact that he did not work, his incessant sitting in the fields and looking at things. They mistrusted and were afraid of him because he was different, even though he did them no harm and asked only to be let alone. Vincent had no idea the people did not like him.

He was doing a large study of the pine wood that was being cut down, concentrating on a lone tree at the border of a creek. One of the labourers who was clearing away would come and watch him draw, looking over his shoulder with a vacant grin, and occasionally breaking into a loud snigger. The sketch took Vincent some time. Each day the peasant's guffaws grew louder. Vincent decided to find out just what amused the man.

"You find it funny," he asked politely, "that I draw a tree?"

The man roared. "Yes, yes, it is so funny. You must be *fou!*"

Vincent deliberated for a moment and then asked, "Would I be *fou* if I planted a tree?"

The peasant sobered up instantly. "Oh, no, certainly not."

"Would I be *fou* if I tended the tree and took care of it?"

"No, of course not."

"Would I be *fou* if I picked the fruit off?"

"Vous vous moquez de moi!"

"Well then, would I be *fou* if I chopped the tree down, just as they have done here?"

"Oh, no, trees must be cut down."

"Then I can plant a tree, tend it, pick it, and cut it down, but if I draw one I am *fou*. Is that right?"

The peasant broke into his broad grin again. "Yes, you must be *fou* to sit there like that. All the village says so."

In the evenings he sat with the rest of the family in the living room. Around the immense wooden table the entire family gathered, sewing, reading, writing letters. His young brother Cor was a quiet child who rarely spoke. Of his sisters, Anna had married and moved away. Elizabeth disliked him so thoroughly that she did her best to pretend he had never come home. Willemien was sympathetic; she posed for Vincent whenever he asked her, and gave him an uncritical friendship. But their relationship was tied to earthly things.

Vincent worked at the table too, comfortable in the light of the huge yellow lamp which sat impartially in the centre. He copied his exercises or the sketches he had made in the fields that day. Theodorus watched him do one figure over a dozen times and always throw away the finished product with dissatisfaction; at last the dominie could contain himself no longer.

"Vincent," he said, leaning across the broad expanse of table, "don't you ever get them right?"

"No," replied Vincent.

"Then I wonder if you aren't making a mistake?"

"I'm making a great many, Father. Which one do you refer to?"

"It seems to me that if you had any talent, if you were really cut out to be an artist, those sketches would come right the first time."

Vincent glanced down at his study of a peasant kneeling before a bag in which he was putting potatoes. He could not seem to catch the line of the beggar's arm.

"Perhaps so, Father."

"What I mean is, you shouldn't have to draw those things a hundred times without ever getting them right. If you had any natural ability, they would come to you without all this trying."

"Nature always begins by resisting the artist, Father," he said, without putting down his pencil, "but if I really take my work seriously, I won't allow myself to be led astray by that resistance. On the contrary, it will be a stimulus the more to fight for victory."

"I don't see that," said Theodorus. "Good can never grow out of evil, nor can good work grow out of bad."

"Perhaps not in theology. But it can in art. In fact, it must."

"You're wrong, my boy. An artist's work is either good or bad. And if it's bad, he's no artist. He ought to have found that out for himself at the beginning and not have wasted all his time and effort."

"But what if he has a happy life turning out bad art? What then?"

Theodorus searched his theological training, but he could find no answer to this question.

"No," said Vincent, rubbing out the bag of potatoes and leaving the man's left arm suspended stiffly in mid-air. "At bottom, nature and a true artist agree. It may take years of struggling and wrestling before she becomes docile and yielding, but in the end, the bad, very bad work will turn into good work and justify itself."

"What if at the end the work remains poor? You've been drawing that fellow kneeling down for days and he's still wrong. Suppose you go on drawing him for years and years and he keeps on being wrong?"

Vincent shrugged. "The artist takes that gamble, Father."

"Are the rewards worth the gamble?"

"Rewards? What rewards?"

"The money one gets. And the position in society."

Vincent looked up from his paper for the first time and examined his father's face, feature by feature, as though he were looking at some strange being.

"I thought we were discussing good and bad art," he said.

3

He worked night and day at his craft. If he thought of the future at all, it was only to bring closer in fancy the time when he would no longer be a burden on Theo, and when the finished product of his work would approximate perfection. When he was too tired to sketch, he read. When he was too tired to do either, he went to sleep.

Theo sent Ingres paper, pictures from a veterinary school of the anatomy of a horse, a cow, and a sheep, some Holbeins in "The Models from the Artists," drawing pencils, quill pens, the reproduction of a human skeleton, sepia, as many francs as he could spare, and the admonition to work hard and not become a mediocre artist. To this advice Vincent replied, "I shall do what I can, but mediocre in its simple signification I do not despise at all. And one certainly does not rise above that mark by despising what is mediocre. But what you say about hard work is entirely right. 'Not a day without a line!' as Gavarni warns us."

More and more he had the feeling that the drawing of the figure was a good thing, and that indirectly it had a good influence on the drawing of landscape. If he drew a willow tree as if it were a living being—and it really was so after all—then the surroundings followed in due course, if only he concentrated all his attention on that same tree and did not give up until he had brought some life into it. He loved landscape very much, but ten times more he loved those studies from life, sometimes of startling realism, which had been drawn so well by Gavarni, Daumier, Doré, De Groux and Felicien Rops. By working on types of labourers, he hoped eventually to be able to do illustrations for the magazines and newspapers; he wanted to support himself completely during the long hard years in which he would perfect his technique and go on to higher forms of expression.

One time his father, who thought he read for entertainment, said, "Vincent, you are always talking about how hard you must work. Then why do you waste your time on all those silly French books?"

Vincent placed a marking finger in "Le Père Goriot" and looked up. He kept hoping that some day his father might understand him when he spoke of serious things.

"You see," he said slowly, "not only does the drawing of figures and scenes from life demand a knowledge of the handicraft of drawing, but it demands also profound studies of literature."

"I must say I don't gather that. If I want to preach a good sermon, I don't spend my time in the kitchen watching your mother pickle tongues."

"Speaking of tongues," said Anna Cornelia, "those fresh ones ought to be ready by tomorrow breakfast."

Vincent did not bother to upset the analogy.

"I can't draw a figure," he said, "without knowing all about the bones and muscles and tendons that are inside it. And I can't draw a head without knowing what goes on in that person's brain and soul. In order to paint life one must understand not only anatomy, but what people feel and think about the world they live in. The painter who knows his own craft and nothing else will turn out to be a very superficial artist."

"Ah, Vincent," said his father, sighing deeply, "I'm afraid you're going to develop into a theorist!"

Vincent returned to "Le Père Goriot."

Another time he became greatly excited at the arrival of some books by Cassagne which Theo sent to correct the trouble with his perspective. Vincent ran through them lovingly and showed them to Willemien.

"I know of no better remedy for my ailment," he said to her. "If I am cured of it, I shall have these books to thank."

Willemien smiled at him with her mother's clear eyes.

"Do you mean to tell me, Vincent," asked Theodorus, who was distrustful of everything that came from Paris, "that you can learn to draw correctly by reading ideas about art in books?"

"Yes."

"How very odd."

"That is to say, if I put into practice the theory they contain. However, practice is a thing one cannot buy at the same time with the books. If that were so there would be a larger sale of them."

The days passed busily and happily into summer, and now it was the heat that kept him off the heath, and not the rain. He sketched his sister Willemien in front of the sewing machine, copied for a third time the exercises after Bargue, drew five times over a man with a spade, *Un Bêcheur,* in different positions, twice a sower, twice a girl with a broom. Then a woman with a white cap who was peeling potatoes, a shepherd leaning on his staff, and finally an old, sick farmer sitting on a chair near the hearth, with his head in his hands and his elbows on his knees. Diggers, sowers, ploughers, male and female, that was what he felt he must draw continually; he must observe and put down everything that belonged to country life. He did not stand altogether helpless before nature any longer; that gave him an exultation unlike any he had ever known before.

The townspeople still thought him queer and kept him at arm's length. Although his mother and Willemien—and even his father in his own way—heaped kindness and affection upon him, in those innermost recesses to which no one in Etten or the parsonage could ever possibly penetrate, he was frightfully alone.

In time the peasants grew to like and trust him. He found in their simplicity something akin to the soil in which they were hoeing or digging. He tried to put that into his sketches. Often his family could not tell where the peasant ended and the earth began. Vincent did not know how his drawings came out that way but he felt they were right, just so.

"There should be no strict line between," he said to his mother who asked about this one evening. "They are really two kinds of earth, pouring into each other, belonging to each other; two forms of the same matter, indistinguishable in essence."

His mother decided that since he had no wife, she had better take him in hand and help him become successful.

"Vincent," she said one morning, "I want you to be back in the house by two o'clock. Will you do that for me?"

"Yes, Mother. What is it you wish?"

"I want you to come with me to a tea party."

Vincent was aghast. "But Mother, I can't be wasting my time that way!"

"Why will it be wasting your time, son?"

"Because there's nothing to paint at a tea party."

"That's just where you're wrong. All the important women of Etten will be there."

Vincent's eyes went to the kitchen door. He almost made a bolt for it. After an effort he controlled himself and tried to explain; the words came slowly and painfully.

"What I mean, Mother," he said, "is that the women at a tea party have no character."

"Nonsense! They all have splendid characters. Never a word has been breathed against one of them."

"No, dear," he said, "of course not. What I mean is, they all look alike. The pattern of their lives has fitted them to a specific mould."

"Well, I'm sure I can tell one from the other without any difficulty."

"Yes, sweetheart, but you see, they've all had such easy lives that they haven't anything interesting carved into their faces."

"I'm afraid I don't understand, son. You draw every labourer and peasant you see in the fields."

"Ah, yes."

"But what good will that ever do you? They're all poor, and they can't buy anything. The women of the town can pay to have their portaits painted."

Vincent put his arms about her and cupped her chin in his hand. The blue eyes were so clear, so deep, so kind and loving. Why did they not understand?

"Dear," he said quietly, "I beg you to have a little faith in me. I know how this job has to be done, and if you will only give me time I will succeed. If I keep working hard on the things that look useless to you now, eventually I will be able to sell my drawings and make a good living."

Anna Cornelia wanted to understand just as desperately as Vincent wished to be understood. She brushed her lips against her boy's rough, red beard and in her mind travelled back to that day of apprehension and fear when this strong, hard man body she held in her arms had been torn from her in the Zundert parsonage. Her first baby had been still-born, and when Vincent announced himself by yelling lustily and long, her thankfulness and joy knew no bounds. In her love for him there was always mingled a touch of sorrow for the first child that had never opened its eyes, and of gratitude for all the others that had followed.

"You're a good boy, Vincent," she said. "Go your own way. You know what is best. I only wanted to help you."

Instead of working in the fields that day, Vincent asked Piet Kaufman, the gardener, to pose for him. It took a little persuasion, but Piet finally consented.

"After dinner," he agreed. "In the garden."

When Vincent went out later he found Piet carefully dressed in his stiff Sunday suit, hands and face scrubbed. "One moment," he cried excitedly, "until I get a stool. Then I'll be ready."

He placed a little stool beneath him and sat down, rigid as a pole, all set to have his daguerreotype taken. Vincent had to laugh in spite of himself.

"But, Piet," he said, "I can't draw you in those clothes."

Piet looked down at his suit in astonishment. "What's the matter with them?" he demanded. "They're new. I only wore them a few Sunday mornings to meeting."

"I know," said Vincent. "That's why. I want to sketch you in your old working clothes, bending over a rake. That's the way your lines come through. I want to see your elbows and knees and omoplate. I can't see anything now except your suit."

It was the word omoplate that decided Piet.

"My old clothes are dirty and patched. If you want me to pose, you'll have to do me as I am."

And so Vincent went back to the fields and did the diggers bending over the soil. The summer passed and he realized that for the moment at least he had exhausted the possibilities of his own instruction. Once again he had the keen desire to enter into relation with some artist and continue his study in a good studio. He began to feel it absolutely necessary to have access to things well done, to see artists at work, for then he could tell what he lacked, and learn how to do better.

Theo wrote, inviting him to come to Paris, but Vincent understood that he was not yet ripe for that great venture. His work was still too raw, too clumsy, too amateurish. The Hague was only a few hours away, and there he could get help from his friend Mijnheer Tersteeg, manager of Goupil and Company, and from his cousin, Anton Mauve. Perhaps it would be better for him to settle in The Hague during the next stage of his slow apprenticeship. He wrote, asking Theo's advice, and his brother replied with the railroad fare.

Before moving permanently, Vincent wished to find out whether Tersteeg and Mauve would be friendly and help him; if not, he would have to go elsewhere. He carefully wrapped up all his sketches—with a change of linen this time—and set out for the capital of his country in the true tradition of all young provincial artists.

4

Mijnheer Herman Gijsbert Tersteeg was the founder of The Hague school of painting, and the most important art dealer in Holland. People from all over the country came to him for advice on what pictures they should buy; if Mijnheer Tersteeg said a canvas was good, his opinion was considered as definitive.

When Mijnheer Tersteeg succeeded Uncle Vincent Van Gogh as manager of Goupil and Company, the rising young Dutch artists were scattered all over the country. Anton Mauve and Josef lived in Amsterdam, Jacob and Willem Maris were in the provinces, and Josef Israels, Johannes Bosboom and Blommers were wandering about from town to town without any permanent headquarters. Tersteeg wrote to each one in turn and said,

"Why should we not all join forces here in The Hague and make it the capital of Dutch art? We can help each other, we can learn from each other, and by our concerted effort we can bring Dutch painting back to the world eminence it enjoyed in the age of Frans Hals and Rembrandt."

The response of the painters was slow, but in the course of the years every young artist whom Tersteeg picked out as having ability settled in The Hague. There was at this time absolutely no demand for their canvases. Tersteeg had chosen them, not because they were selling, but because he saw in their work the possibility of future greatness. He bought canvases from Israels, from Mauve, and Jacob Maris six years before he could persuade the public to see anything in them.

Year after year he went on buying patiently the work of Bosboom, Maris and Neuhuys, turning their canvases to the wall at the rear of his shop. He knew that these had to be supported while they struggled toward their maturity; if the Dutch public was too blind to recognize its own native genius, he, the critic and dealer, would see that these fine young men were not lost to the world forever through poverty, neglect, and discouragement. He bought their canvases, criticized their work, brought them into contact with their fellow painters, and encouraged them through the hard years. Day after day he fought to educate the Dutch public, to open its eyes to the beauty and expression of its own men.

By the time Vincent went to visit him at The Hague, he had succeeded. Mauve, Neuhuys, Israels, Jacob and Willem Maris, Bosboom, and Blommers not only had everything they painted sold at high prices by Goupil and Company, but they were in a fair way to becoming classics.

Mijnheer Tersteeg was a handsome man in the Dutch tradition; he had strong, prominent features, a high forehead, brown hair combed straight back, a flat, beautifully rounded, full-face beard, and eyes as pellucid as a Dutch lake sky. He wore a full black jacket in the Prince Albert manner, wide, striped trousers that fell over his shoes, a high, single collar and ready made, black, bow ties that his wife attached for him every morning.

Tersteeg had always liked Vincent, and when the latter was transferred to the London branch of Goupil and Company, he had penned a warm note of commendation about the boy to the English manager. He had sent Vincent the "Exercises au Fusain" to the Borinage and had included the "Cours de Dessin Bargue" because he knew it would be helpful. While it was true that Goupil and Company in The

Hague was owned by Uncle Vincent Van Gogh, Vincent had every reason to believe that Tersteeg was fond of him for his own sake. Tersteeg was not the man to cater.

Goupil and Company was located at number 20, Plaats, the most aristocratic and expensive square in all The Hague. Only a stone's throw away was the S'Graven Haghe castle which had been the beginning of the city, with its medieval courtyard, the moat that had been turned into a beautiful lake, and at the far end the Mauritshuis where hung Rubens, Hals, Rembrandt, and all the little Dutch masters.

Vincent walked from the station along the narrow, winding, busy Wagenstraat, cut through the Plein and Binnenhof of the castle, and found himself in the Plaats. It was eight years since he had last walked out of Goupils; the tide of suffering he had gone through in that short space of time welled over his body and mind, stunning him.

Eight years ago. Everybody had liked him and been proud of him. He had been his Uncle Vincent's favourite nephew. It was common knowledge that he would not only be his uncle's successor but his heir as well. He could have been a powerful and wealthy man by now, respected and admired by everyone he met. And in time he would have owned the most important string of art galleries in Europe.

What had happened to him?

He did not take the time to answer the question, but crossed the Plaats and entered Goupil and Company. The place was beautifully decorated; he had forgotten. He suddenly felt cheap and shoddy in his workingman's suit of rough black velvet. The street level of the gallery was a long salon hung in rich beige drapes; three steps above that was a smaller salon with a glass roof, and to the rear of that, a few steps higher still, a tiny, intimate exhibition room for the initiate. There was a broad staircase leading to the second floor where Tersteeg had his office and living quarters. The walls going up were pyramided with pictures.

The gallery smacked of great wealth and culture. The clerks were well groomed men with polished manners. The canvases on the walls were hung in expensive frames, set against costly hangings. Thick, soft rugs sank under Vincent's feet and the chairs, set so modestly in the corners, he remembered as priceless antiques. He thought of his drawings of the tattered miners coming out of the shaft, of their wives bent over the *terril,* of the diggers and sowers of the Brabant. He wondered if his simple drawings of poor, humble people would ever be sold in this great palace of art.

It did not seem very likely.

He stood gazing in awkward admiration at a sheep head by Mauve. The clerks who were chatting softly behind a table of etchings took one look at his clothes and posture and did not even bother to ask if there was something he wished. Tersteeg, who had been in the intimate gallery arranging an exhibition, came down the steps into the main salon. Vincent did not see him.

Tersteeg stopped at the bottom of the few steps and studied his former clerk. He took in the short cropped hair, the red stubble on his face, the peasant's boots, the workingman's coat buttoned up around his neck with no necktie concealed beneath it, the clumsy bundle he was carrying under his arm. There was something so altogether *gauche* about Vincent; it showed up cruelly, in high relief in this elegant gallery.

"Well, Vincent," said Tersteeg, walking noiselessly across the soft rug. "I see you are admiring our canvases."

Vincent turned. "Yes, they are fine, aren't they? How are you, Mijnheer Tersteeg? I bring you compliments from my mother and father."

The two men shook hands across the unbridgable chasm of eight years.

"You are looking very well, Mijnheer. Even better than when I last saw you."

"Ah, yes, living agrees with me, Vincent. It keeps me young. Won't you come up to my office?"

Vincent followed him up the broad staircase, stumbling all over himself because he could not tear his eyes from the paintings on the wall. It was the first time he had seen good work since that brief hour in Brussels with Theo. He was in a daze. Tersteeg opened the door of his office and bowed Vincent in.

"Will you sit down, Vincent?" he asked.

Vincent had been gawking at a canvas by Weissenbruch, whose work he had never seen before. He sat down, dropped his bundle, picked it up again, and then crossed to Tersteeg's highly polished desk.

"I've brought back the books you so kindly lent me, Mijnheer Tersteeg."

He unwrapped his bundle, pushed a shirt and pair of socks to one side, took out the series of "Exercises au Fusain," and laid them on the table.

"I worked on the drawings very hard, and you have done me a great service by lending them to me."

"Show me your copies," said Tersteeg, getting to the point.

Vincent shuffled about in the pile of papers and extricated the first series he had drawn in the Borinage. Tersteeg maintained a stony silence. Vincent then quickly showed the second copies he had made when he settled at Etten. This group elicited an occasional "Hummmm" but nothing more. Vincent then showed the third copies, the ones he had finished shortly before leaving. Tersteeg was interested.

"That's a good line," he said once. "I like the shading," he contributed another time. "You almost got that!"

"I felt it wasn't bad, myself," said Vincent.

He finished the pile and turned to Tersteeg for judgment.

"Yes, Vincent," said the older man, laying his long, thin hands out flat on the desk, with the fingers tapering upward, "you have made a little progress. Not much, but a little. I was afraid when I looked at your first copies . . . Your work shows at least that you have been struggling."

"Is that all? Just struggle? No ability?"

He knew he shouldn't have asked that question, but he could not keep it down.

"Isn't it too early for us to speak of that, Vincent?"

"Perhaps so. I've brought some of my original sketches along. Would you care to see them?"

"I should be delighted."

Vincent laid out some of his sketches of the miners and peasants. Immediately that awful silence fell, the silence famous all over Holland for having broken the indisputable news to hundreds of young artists that their work was bad. Tersteeg looked over the entire lot without even a "Hummmm" escaping his lips. Vincent felt sick. Tersteeg sat back, looked out the window and over the Plaats at the swans in the lake. Vincent knew from experience that if he did not speak first, the silence would go on forever.

"Don't you see any improvement at all, Mijnheer Tersteeg?" he asked. "Don't you think my Brabant sketches better than the ones from the Borinage?"

"Well," replied Tersteeg, turning back from the view, "they are better. But they are not good. There is something fundamentally wrong with them. Just what it is, I can't say offhand. I think you had better keep to your copying for a time. You're not ready to do original work yet. You must get a better grasp of elementals before you turn to life."

"I would like to come to The Hague to study. Do you think that a good idea, Mijnheer?"

Tersteeg did not wish to assume any obligations toward Vincent. The whole situation looked very peculiar to him.

"The Hague is a nice place," he said. "We have good galleries and a number of young painters. But whether it is any better than Antwerp, Paris, or Brussels, I'm sure I don't know."

Vincent left, not altogether discouraged. Tersteeg had seen some progress, and his was the most critical eye in all Holland. At least he was not standing still. He knew that his sketches from life were not all that they should have been, but he was confident that if he worked hard and long they would come right in the end.

5

The Hague is perhaps the cleanest and most well-bred city in all Europe. It is, in the true Holland manner, simple, austere and beautiful. The immaculate streets are lined with full-bosomed trees, the houses are of neat and fastidious brick, with tiny, lovingly kept gardens of roses and geraniums in front. There are no slums, poverty stricken districts, or careless eyesores; everything is kept up with that efficient asceticism of the Dutch.

Many years before, The Hague had adopted the stork as its official emblem. The population had grown by leaps and bounds ever since.

Vincent waited until the following day before calling on Mauve at his home Uileboomen 198. Mauve's mother-in-law was a Carbentus, a sister of Anna Cornelia, and since family ties were strong in those circles, he received Vincent warmly.

Mauve was a powerfully built man with sloping but tremendous shoulders and a large chest. His head, like that of Tersteeg and most of the Van Gogh family, was a more important factor in his appearance than the features of his face. He had luminous eyes, somewhat sentimental, a strong, straight bridged nose springing bonily from his brow without any declivity, a high, square forehead, flat ears, and salt-grey beard which concealed the perfect oval of his face. His hair was combed on the extreme right side, a great swash of it lying flat across the skull and parallel to his forehead.

Mauve was a man full of an energy which he did not dissipate. He painted, and when he got tired doing that he went on painting, and when that fatigued him he painted some more. By that time he would be refreshed and could go back to his painting again.

"Jet isn't home, Vincent," said Mauve. "Shall we go out to the atelier? I think we'll be more comfortable there."

"Yes, let's." He was eager to see the studio.

Mauve led him out to his large wooden atelier in the garden. The entrance was on the side near the house, but some little distance from it. The garden was walled in by hedges, giving Mauve complete isolation for his work.

A delicious smell of tobacco smoke, old pipes, and varnish greeted Vincent as he stepped in. The atelier was quite large, with pictures on easels standing about on a thick Deventer rug. The walls were warm with studies; in one corner was an antique table, and before it a small Persian rug. The north wall was half window. Books were scattered about, and on every available inch of flat space could be found the painter's tools. In spite of the life and fullness of the studio, Vincent could feel the definite orderliness that emanated from Mauve's character and dominated the place.

The formalities of family compliments engaged them only a few seconds; immediately they plunged into the only subject in the world that either of them cared a tinker's dam about. Mauve had been avoiding other painters assiduously for some time (he always maintained that a man could either paint or talk about painting, but he could not do both) and was full of his new project, a misty landscape in a minor key of twilight. He did not discuss it with Vincent, he simply poured it out to him.

Madame Mauve came home and insisted that Vincent remain for supper. He sat before the fireplace and chatted with the children after the pleasant meal, and thought of how fine it would be if he could only have a little home of his own, with a wife who loved him and believed in him, and children around to pronounce him Emperor and Lord by the simple title of father. Would that happy day never come for him?

It was not long before the two men were back in the studio again, pulling contentedly at their pipes. Vincent took out his copies. Mauve looked them over with the quick, discerning eye of the professional.

"They're not badly done," he said, "for exercises. But of what importance are they?"

"Importance? I don't . . . "

"You've only been copying, Vincent, like a schoolboy. The real creating had already been done by other men."

"I thought they might give me the feel of things."

"Nonsense. If you want to create, go to life. Don't imitate. Haven't you any sketches of your own?"

Vincent thought of what Tersteeg had said about his original studies. He debated whether or not to show them to Mauve. He had come to The Hague to ask Mauve to be his teacher. And if all he could show was inferior work . . .

"Yes," he replied, "I have been doing character studies right along."

"Good!"

"I have some sketches of the Borain miners and the peasants in the Brabant. They're not very well done, but . . . "

"Never mind all that," said Mauve. "Let me see them. You ought to have caught some real spirit there."

Vincent laid out his sketches to the accompaniment of a furious beating in his throat. Mauve sat down and ran his left hand along the great swash of hair, smoothing the grain of it on his head again and again. Soft chuckles escaped from behind his salt and pepper beard. Once he rammed his hand against the swash of hair, left it standing in a bush, and threw a quick look of disapproval at Vincent. A moment later he took the study of a labourer, rose and held it alongside of a rough draft figure on his new canvas.

"Now I see where I went wrong!" he exclaimed.

He picked up a drawing pencil, adjusted the light, and made a few rapid strokes, his eye on Vincent's sketch all the time.

"That's better," he said, stepping back. "Now the beggar looks as though he belongs on the land."

He walked to Vincent's side and put his hand on his cousin's shoulder.

"It's all right," he said. "You're on the road. Your sketches are clumsy, but they're authentic. They have a certain vitality and rhythm I haven't found very often. Throw away your copy books, Vincent; buy yourself a paint box. The sooner you begin working in colour, the better it will be for you. Your drawing is only half bad now, and you can keep improving it as you go along."

Vincent thought the moment auspicious.

"I am going to move to The Hague, Cousin Mauve," he said, "and continue my work. Would you be kind enough to help me sometimes? I need help from a man like you. Just little things, such as you showed me about your studies this afternoon. Every young artist needs a master, Cousin Mauve, and I will be grateful if you will let me work under you."

Mauve looked carefully at all the unfinished canvases in his studio. Whatever little time he took away from his work he liked to spend with the family. The warm aura of praise in which he had engulfed Vincent evaporated. In its place came withdrawal. Vincent, always highly sensitive to the changes in people's attitude, felt it instantly.

"I'm a busy man, Vincent," said Mauve, "and I have little opportunity to help others. An artist must be selfish; he must guard every second of his working time. I doubt if I could teach you much."

"I don't ask for a great deal," said Vincent. "Just let me work with you here sometimes and watch you build up a canvas. Talk to me about your work as you did this afternoon, so I'll see how a whole project is completed. And occasionally, when you are resting, you might look over my drawings and point out my mistakes. That's all I ask."

"You think you are asking only a little. But believe me, it is a serious matter, to take an apprentice."

"I wouldn't be a burden to you, I can promise that."

Mauve considered for a long time. He had never wanted an apprentice; he disliked having people about when he worked. He did not often feel communicative about his own creations, and he had never received anything but abuse for the advice he offered beginners. Still, Vincent was his cousin, Uncle Vincent Van Gogh and Goupils bought his canvases, and there was something about the crude, intense passion of the boy—the same crude, intense passion he had felt in the drawings—that appealed to him.

"Very well, Vincent," he said, "we'll have a try at it."

"Oh, Cousin Mauve!"

"I'm not promising anything, mind you. It may turn out very badly. But when you settle in The Hague, you come to the studio and we'll see if we can help each other. I am going to Drenthe for the fall; suppose you come at the beginning of winter."

"That is just when I wanted to come. I still need a few months more of work in the Brabant."

"Then it is settled."

A crooning voice sang inside of Vincent all the way home on the train. "I have a master. I have a master. In a few months I shall be studying with a great painter, and then I shall learn to paint, too. I will work, oh how I will work during the next few months, and then he shall see what progress I have made."

When he got home to Etten he found Kay Vos there.

6

Kay's great grief had spiritualized her. She had loved her husband devotedly and his death had killed something within her. The tremendous vitality of the woman, her high spirits, her enthusiasm and verve were completely gone. Even her warm, live hair seemed to have lost its sparkle. Her face had tapered down to an ascetic oval, her blue eyes had deep pools of brooding blackness in them, and the superb lustre of her skin had paled to a monotone. If she had less vitality than when Vincent knew her in Amsterdam, she now had in its place a more mellow beauty, a seasoned sadness which gave her depth and substance.

"It's nice to have you here at last, Kay," said Vincent.

"Thank you, Vincent."

It was the first time they had called each other by their Christian names without attaching the "Cousin." Neither knew quite how it had happened, nor for that matter did they even think about it.

"You've brought Jan with you, of course?"

"Yes, he's in the garden."

"It's the first time you've visited the Brabant. I'm glad I'm here to show it to you. We must take long walks over the heath."

"I would like that, Vincent."

She spoke kindly, but without enthusiasm. He noticed that her voice had deepened, become more vibrant. He remembered how sympathetic she had been to him in the house on the Keizersgracht. Should he speak to her about the death of her husband, offer his condolence? He knew that it was his duty to say something but he felt it would be more delicate not to throw her grief into her face again.

Kay appreciated his tact. Her husband was sacred to her and she could not discuss him with people. She, too, remembered those pleasant winter evenings on the Keizersgracht when she had played cards with Vos and her parents by the fire, while Vincent sat under a lamp in a far corner. Mute pain welled up within her and a mistiness covered her now black eyes. Vincent put his hand softly over hers and she looked up at him with a deeply pulsating gratitude. He saw how exquisite suffering had made her. Before, she had been only a happy girl; now she was a passionately suffering woman with all the richness that emotional misery can bring. Once again there flashed into his mind the old saying:

"From out of pain, beauty."

"You'll like it here, Kay," he said quietly. "I spend all day out in the fields sketching; you must come with me and bring Jan."

"I would only be in your way."

"Oh, no! I enjoy company. I can show you many interesting things as we walk."

"Then I'll be happy to come."

"It will be good for Jan. The air will make him sturdy."

She pressed his hand ever so slightly.

"And we'll be friends, won't we, Vincent?"

"Yes, Kay."

She released his hand and stared across the road at the Protestant Church, without seeing it.

Vincent went out into the garden, placed a bench nearby for Kay, and helped Jan make a little house of sand. He forgot for the moment the great news he had brought home from The Hague.

At dinner that night he told the family that Mauve had accepted him as a pupil. Ordinarily he would not have repeated any word of praise that either Tersteeg or Mauve might have given him, but the presence of Kay at the table made him want to appear in his best light. His mother was greatly pleased.

"You must do everything Cousin Mauve tells you," she said. "He is a successful man."

The following morning, Kay, Jan, and Vincent set out very early for the Liesbosch, where Vincent wanted to sketch. Although he never bothered to take anything with him to eat at midday, his mother packed a nice lunch for the three of them. She had an idea that it was some sort of picnic. On the way they passed a magpie's nest in the high acacia in the churchyard; Vincent promised to find an egg for the excited boy. They walked through the pine woods with its crunchy bed of needles, then across the yellow, white, and grey sand of the heath. At one spot Vincent saw an abandoned plough and wagon standing in the field. He set up his small easel, lifted Jan into the wagon, and made a quick sketch. Kay stood a little way off to one side, watching Jan romp. She was silent. Vincent did not wish to intrude upon her; he was glad enough just to have her company. He had never known it could be so pleasant to have a woman at his side while he worked.

They passed a number of cottages with thatched roofs, and then came to the road to Roozendaal. At length Kay spoke.

"You know, Vincent," she said, "seeing you before your easel reminded me of something I used to think about you in Amsterdam."

"What was that, Kay?"

"You're sure you won't be hurt?"

"Not at all."

"Then, to tell you the truth, I never did think you were cut out to be a clergyman. I knew you were wasting your time all along."

"Why didn't you tell me?"

"I didn't have the right to do that, Vincent."

She pushed several strands of red-gold hair under her black bonnet; a crooked furrow in the road threw her against Vincent's shoulder. He put his hand under her arm to help her regain her balance, and forgot to take it away.

"I knew you would have to work things out for yourself," she said. "No amount of telling would have done any good."

"Now I remember," said Vincent. "You warned me against becoming a narrow minded clergyman. That was a queer thing for a minister's daughter to say."

He smiled at her eagerly, but her eyes went sad.

"I know. But you see, Vos taught me a great many things I might not otherwise have understood."

Vincent dropped his hand to his side. The mention of Vos's name put a queer, intangible barrier between them.

After an hour's walk they reached the Liesbosch, and once again Vincent set up his easel. There was a bit of swamp he wanted to catch. Jan played in the sand and Kay sat behind him on a little stool he had brought along. She held a book in her hand but she did not read. Vincent sketched rapidly, with a certain *élan*. The study sprang up under his hand with more vigour than he had known before. He could not tell whether it was because of Mauve's compliments or Kay's presence, but his pencil had a surety of touch. He did several sketches in quick succession. He did not turn to look at Kay, nor did she speak to interrupt him, but her nearness gave him a glow of well-being. He wanted his work to be particularly good that day so Kay would admire it.

At lunch time they walked a short way to an oak grove. Kay spread the contents of the basket under a cool tree. The air was utterly still. The smell of the water lilies in the swamp mingled with the faint oak fragrance above them. Kay and Jan sat on one side of the basket, Vincent on the other. Kay served him. The picture of Mauve and his family, sitting about the homely supper table, came to his mind.

As he looked at Kay he thought he had never seen anyone so beautiful. The thick, yellow cheese was delicious and his mother's bread had its usual sweet tang, but he could not eat. A new and formidable hunger was awakening within him. He could not tear his gaze from Kay's delicate skin, the chiselled oval, the brooding, night-pool eyes, the full, sweet mouth that had been robbed momentarily of its ripeness, but which he knew would blossom again.

After lunch Jan went to sleep with his head pillowed in his mother's lap. Vincent watched her stroke the child's light hair, gazing down searchingly into the innocent face. He knew that she was seeing the face of her husband reflected in the child, that she was in their house on the Keizersgracht with the man she loved, and not on the Brabant heath with her Cousin Vincent.

He sketched all afternoon, part of the time with Jan on his lap. The boy had taken a liking to him. Vincent let him mark up several sheets of Ingres paper with black smudges. He laughed and shouted and ran about in the yellow sand, constantly returning to Vincent with questions, with things he had found, with demands that he be entertained. Vincent did not mind; it was good to have a warm, live little animal climbing over him affectionately.

Fall was coming on and the sun set very early. On the way home they stopped at the frequent pools to watch the sunset colourings settle on the water with butterfly wings, darken slowly, and disappear in the dusk. Vincent showed Kay his drawings. She saw them only slightly, and what she did see, she thought crude and clumsy. But Vincent had been good to Jan, and she knew only too well the nature of pain.

"I like them, Vincent," she said.

"Do you, Kay?"

Her praise released a locked flood-gate within him. She had been so sympathetic in Amsterdam; she would understand all the things he was trying to do. Somehow, she seemed the only one in the world who would. He could not talk to his family about his projects because they did not even know the vocabulary; with Mauve and Tersteeg he had to assume a beginner's humility which he did not always feel.

He poured out his heart in hurried, incoherent words. As his enthusiasm increased, he quickened his pace, and Kay had difficulty in keeping up with him. When he was feeling anything deeply, his poise fled and in its place came the old violent, jerky manner. Gone was the mannered gentleman of the afternoon; the provincial boor startled and frightened her. She felt his outburst to be so ill-bred, so immature. She did not know that he was paying her the rarest, the most valuable compliment that man can pay to woman.

He poured out to her all those feelings that had been bottled up within him since Theo had departed for Paris. He told her of his aims and ambitions, of the spirit with which he was trying to imbue his work. Kay wondered why he was getting so excited. She did not interrupt him, nor did she listen. She lived in the past, always in the past, and she found it slightly distasteful that anyone should live with so much joy and vigour in the future. Vincent was feeling his own effervescence too keenly to sense her withdrawal. He went on gesticulating until a name he spoke caught Kay's attention.

"Neuhuys? Do you mean the painter who lived in Amsterdam?"

"He used to. He's at The Hague now."

"Yes. Vos was his friend. He brought him home several times."

Vincent stopped short.

Vos! Always Vos! Why? He was dead. He had been dead over a year. It was time she forgot him. He belonged to the past, just as Ursula did. Why did she always have to bring the conversation back to Vos? Even in the Amsterdam days he had never liked Kay's husband.

Fall deepened. The carpet of pine needles in the woods turned to a crinkly rust-brown. Every day Kay and Jan accompanied Vincent into the fields while he worked. A touch of colour came into her cheeks from the long walks across the heath, and her step became more firm and confident. She took her sewing basket with her now and kept her fingers as busy as Vincent's. She began speaking more freely and liberally about her childhood, about the books she had read, and interesting people she had known in Amsterdam.

The family looked on with approval. Vincent's company was giving her an interest in life. Her presence in the house made Vincent far more amiable. Anna Cornelia and Theodorus thanked God for the opportune arrangement, and did everything they could to throw the two young people together.

Vincent loved everything about Kay; the slender, fragile figure encased so sternly in the long black dress; the perky, black bonnet she wore when she went into the fields; the natural perfume of her body in his nostrils when she bent in front of him; the way she puckered her mouth when she spoke rapidly; the probing glance of her deep blue eyes; the touch of her vibrant hand on his shoulder or arm when she took Jan from him; her throaty, enharmonic voice that shook him to the very depths of his nature, and which he heard singing in his head after he had gone to sleep; the live lustre of her skin, in which he burned to bury his famished lips.

He knew now that for many years he had been living only partially, that great funds of affection and tenderness in him had been dried up, the clear, cooling waters of love been refused to his parched palate. He was happy only when Kay was near him; her presence seemed to reach out and embrace him gently. When she went with him to the fields, he worked rapidly and with a flair; when she stayed at home, each line was drudgery. In the evenings he sat across the great wooden table from her in the sitting room, and although he copied his sketches, her delicate face was always between him and his paper. If occasionally he glanced up to see her sitting in the pale light of the huge yellow lamp and caught her eye, she would smile at him with a sweet passive melancholy. Often he felt he could not stay away from her for another moment, that he would have to spring up before the whole family and crush her to him fiercely, burying his hot, dry lips in the well of her cool mouth.

It was not only her beauty he loved, but her whole being and manner; her quiet walk, her perfect poise and bearing, the good breeding that she expressed with every slight gesture.

He had not even suspected how lonely he had been in the seven long years since he had lost Ursula. In all his life he had never heard a woman say one caressing word, look at him with the mist of tender affection in her eyes, run her fingers lightly over his face, and follow their trail with kisses.

No woman had ever loved him. That was not life, that was death. It had not been so bad when he had loved Ursula, for then—in his adolescence—he had only wanted to give, and it was the giving that had been refused. But now, in his mature love, he wanted to give and receive equally. He knew that life would be impossible unless his new hunger could be fed by Kay's warm response.

One night he was reading Michelet and he ran across the phrase, *"il faut qu'une femme souffle sur toi pour que tu sois homme."*

Michelet was always right. He had not been a man. Although he was twenty-eight, he was still unborn. The fragrance of Kay's beauty and love had been breathed upon him and he had become a man at last.

As a man, he wanted Kay. He wanted her desperately and passionately. He loved Jan, too, for the child was part of the woman he loved. But he hated Vos, hated him with all his strength, because nothing he could do seemed to drive the dead man from the foreground of Kay's mind. He did not regret her former love and marriage any more than he regretted the years of suffering that his love for Ursula had caused him. They both had been hammered on the forge of pain, and their love would be the purer for it.

He knew that he could make Kay forget this man who belonged to the past. He could make his love so burning in the present that the past would be wiped out. He was going to The Hague soon, to study under Mauve. He would take Kay with him, and they would set up a *ménage* like the one he had seen on the Uileboomen. He wanted Kay for his wife, to have her near him always. He wanted a home, and children who would bear the stamp of his features upon their faces. He was a man now, and it was time he stopped wandering. He needed love in his life; it would take the roughness out of his work, round off the crude edges, quicken it with the consciousness of reality that had been lacking. He had never known before how much of him had been dead without love; if he had known, he would have loved passionately the first woman he had come upon. Love was the salt of life; one needed it to bring out the flavour of the world.

He was glad now that Ursula had not loved him. How superficial his love had been then, how deep and rich it was now. If he had married Ursula he would never have known the meaning of true love. He would never have been able to love Kay! He realized for the first time that Ursula had been a shallow, empty headed child, with no fineness or quality. He had spent years of suffering over a *poupon!* One hour with Kay was worth a lifetime with Ursula. The road had been hard but it had led him to Kay, and that was its justification. Life would be good from now on; he would work, he would love, and he would sell his drawings. And they would be happy together. Every human life had its pattern that had to be worked out slowly to its ultimate conclusion.

In spite of his impulsive nature and impassioned state of mind, he managed to control himself. A thousand times, when he was alone with Kay in the fields and they were speaking of things that mattered not at all, he wanted to exclaim, "See here, let us drop all this pretense and casualness. I want to hold you in my arms, and kiss your lips over and over and over again! I want you to be my wife and stay with me forever! We belong to each other, and in our aloneness we need each other desperately!"

By some miracle he managed to restrain himself. He could not suddenly speak of love out of a clear sky; it would have been too crude. Kay never gave him the slightest opening. She always avoided the subjects of love and marriage. How and when was he to speak? He felt that he must soon, for winter was approaching and he had to go to The Hague.

At last he could bear it no longer; his will broke. They had taken the road toward Breda. Vincent had spent the morning sketching diggers at work. They ate their lunch by a little brook in the shadow of some elm trees. Jan was asleep on the grass. Kay was sitting beside the basket. Vincent knelt down to show her some drawings. While he spoke, rapidly, without knowing a word that he said, he could feel Kay's warm shoulder burning into his side; it was this contact that fired him beyond control. The sketches fell out of his hand, he caught Kay to him suddenly, fiercely, and a great wave of rough, passionate words broke from his lips.

"Kay, I can't bear not to tell you for another moment! You must know that I love you, Kay, better than I do myself! I've always loved you, from the first time I saw you in Amsterdam! I've got to have you near me always! Kay, tell me that you love me just a little. We'll go to The Hague to live, all by ourselves. We'll have our home, and we'll be happy. You love me, don't you Kay? Say you'll marry me, Kay dear."

Kay had made no effort to free herself. Horror and revulsion had sent her mouth all awry. She did not hear the words he said, but she caught their import, and a great terror arose within her. Her blue-black eyes stared at him cruelly and she raised a hand to mute the cry at her lips.

"No, never, never!" she breathed fiercely.

She wrenched herself free from his grasp, snatched up the sleeping child, and ran wildly across the field. Vincent pursued her. Terror lent speed to her legs. She fled before him. He could not understand what had happened.

"Kay! Kay!" he called out. "Don't run away."

The sound of his voice drove her on even faster. Vincent ran, waving his arms madly, his head bobbing about on his shoulders. Kay stumbled and fell in the soft furrow of the field. Jan whimpered. Vincent flung himself on his knees in the dirt before her and grasped her hand.

"Kay, why do you run away from me when I love you so? Can't you see, I've got to have you. You love me too, Kay. Don't be frightened, I'm only saying that I love you. We'll forget the past, Kay, and begin a new life."

The look of horror turned to hatred in Kay's eyes. She wrenched her hand away from him. Jan was now fully awake. The fierce, impassioned look on Vincent's face frightened the child, and the tumultuous words pouring from the strange man's lips put him into a terror. He flung his arms about his mother's neck and began to cry.

"Kay, dear, can't you say that you love me just a little bit?"

"No, never, never!"

Once again she ran across the field towards the road. Vincent sat there in the soft sand, stunned. Kay gained the road and disappeared. Vincent picked himself up and dashed after her, calling her name at the top of his voice. When he got to the road, he saw her a long way down, still running, the child clasped to her bosom. He stopped. He watched them vanish at a turning. He stood there quietly for a long time. Then he recrossed the field. He picked up his sketches from the ground. They were slightly dirty. He put the lunch things into the basket, strapped his easel to his back, and trudged wearily home.

The parsonage was thick with tension; Vincent felt it the moment he entered the door. Kay had locked herself in her room with Jan. His mother and father were alone in the sitting room. They had been talking, but stopped abruptly when he entered; he could feel half a sentence suspended in mid-air. He closed the door behind him. He saw that his father must be frightfully angry, for the lid of his right eye was almost closed.

"Vincent, how could you?" wailed his mother.

"How could I what?" He was not sure precisely what they were reproaching him for.

"Insult your cousin that way!"

Vincent could think of no answer to this. He unstrapped the easel from his back and placed it in a corner. His father was still too wrought up to speak.

"Did Kay tell you exactly what happened?" he asked.

His father loosened the high collar that was cutting into the red flesh of his neck. His right hand gripped the edge of the table.

"She told us that you threw your arms about her and raved like a madman."

"I told her I loved her," said Vincent quietly. "I don't quite see how that's an insult."

"Is that all you told her?" His father's tone was icy.

"No. I asked her to be my wife."

"Your wife!"

"Yes. What is so astonishing about that?"

"Oh, Vincent, Vincent," said his mother, "how could you even think of such a thing?"

"Surely you must have been thinking too . . . ."

"But how could I ever dream you would fall in love with her?"

"Vincent," said his father, "do you realize that Kay is your first cousin."

"Yes. What of it?"

"You can't marry your first cousin. That would be . . . that would be . . . "

The dominie couldn't even bring himself to pronounce the word. Vincent went to the window and stared out over the garden.

"What would it be?"

"Incest!"

Vincent controlled himself with an effort. How dare they muck over his love with second-hand words?

"That is sheer nonsense, Father, and completely unworthy of you."

"I tell you it would be incest!" shouted Theodorus. "I won't allow that sinful relation in the Van Gogh family."

"I hope you don't think you're quoting the Bible, Father? Cousins have always been allowed to marry."

"Oh, Vincent, my dear," said his mother, "if you did love her, why didn't you wait? Her husband is dead only a year. She still loves him devotedly. And you know you have no money to support a wife."

"I consider what you have done," said his father, "as distinctly premature and indelicate."

Vincent recoiled. He fumbled for his pipe, held it in his hand for a moment, and then put it back.

"Father, I must ask you firmly and decidedly not to use such expressions any more. My love for Kay is the finest thing that has ever happened to me. I won't have you calling it indelicate and premature."

He snatched up his easel and went to his room. He sat on the bed and asked himself, "What has happened? What have I done? I told Kay that I loved her and she ran away. Why? Doesn't she want me?"

"No, never, never!"

He spent the night tormenting himself by going over and over the scene. Always he ended at the same spot. That little sentence sounded in his ears like his death knell and his doom.

It was late the following morning before he could bring himself to go downstairs. The air of tension had been cleared away. His mother was in the kitchen. She kissed him when he came in, and patted his cheek sympathetically for a moment.

"Did you sleep, dear?" she asked.

"Where is Kay?"

"Father drove her to Breda."

"Why?"

"To catch a train. She's going home."

"To Amsterdam?"

"Yes."

"I see."

"She thought it would be better, Vincent."

"Did she leave a message for me?"

"No, dear. Won't you sit down to your breakfast?"

"No word at all? About yesterday? Was she angry with me?"

"No, she just thought she'd go home to her parents."

Anna Cornelia decided it would be better not to repeat the things Kay had said; instead she put an egg on the stove.

"What time does that train leave Breda?"

"At ten-twenty."

Vincent glanced at the blue kitchen clock.

"It's that time now," he said.

"Yes."

"Then there's nothing I can do about it."

"Come sit down here, dear. I have some nice fresh tongue this morning."

She cleared away a space at the kitchen table, laid a napkin and spread breakfast for him. She hovered over him, urging him to eat; she had the feeling that if only he would put enough into his stomach, everything would come all right.

Vincent saw it pleased her, so he swallowed everything she placed on the table. But the taste of "No, never, never" was in his mouth to make bitter every sweet bite he ate.

7

He knew that he loved his work far better than he did Kay. If he had been forced to choose between one and the other, there would have been not the slightest doubt in his mind. Yet his drawing suddenly went flat. He could no longer work with any interest. He looked over the sketches of the Brabant types on the wall and saw that he had made progress since his love for Kay had awakened. He knew that there was still something harsh and severe in his drawings, but he felt Kay's love could soften that. His love was serious and passionate enough not to be chilled by many "No, never, nevers;" he considered her refusal as a block of ice that he would press to his heart to thaw.

It was the little germ of doubt in his mind that prevented him from working. Suppose he could never change her decision? She seemed to have conscientious scruples even at the idea of a possible new love. He wanted to cure her of the fatal disease of burying herself too much in the past. He wanted to join his draftsman's fist with her lady's hand, and work for their daily bread and happiness.

He spent his time in his room, writing passionate, imploring messages to Kay. It was several weeks before he learned she did not even read them. He wrote almost daily letters to Theo, his confidant, strengthening himself against the doubt in his own heart and the concerted attacks of his parents and the Reverend Stricker. He suffered, suffered bitterly, and he was not always able to hide it. His mother came to him with a face full of pity and many comforting words.

"Vincent," she said, "you are only smashing your poor head against a stone dyke. Uncle Stricker says her 'No!' is quite decisive."

"I'll not take his word for anything."

"But she told him, dear."

"That she doesn't love me?

"Yes, and that she will never change her mind."

"We shall see about that."

"It's all so hopeless, Vincent. Uncle Stricker says that even if Kay loved you, he would not consent to the marriage unless you earned at least a thousand francs a year. And you know you are a long way from that."

"Well, Mother, he who loves lives, he who lives works, and he who works has bread."

"Very pretty, my dear, but Kay was brought up in luxury. She has always had nice things."

"Her nice things don't make her happy now."

"If you two were sentimental and married, great misery would come of it; poverty, hunger, cold, illness. For you know the family would not help with a single franc."

"I've been through all those things before, Mother, and they don't frighten me. It still would be better for us to be together than not to be together."

"But my child, *if Kay doesn't love you!*"

"If only I could go to Amsterdam, I tell you I could change that 'No!' to 'Yes!' "

He considered it one of the worst *petites misères de la vie humaine* that he could not go to see the woman he loved, that he could not earn a single franc to pay his railroad fare. His impotence put him in a rage. He was twenty-eight; for twelve years he had been working hard and denying himself everything but the bare necessities of life, yet in all the world, he had no way to command the pitifully small sum to buy a ticket to Amsterdam.

He considered walking the hundred kilometres, but he knew he would arrive dirty, hungry and worn. He did not mind the strain of it all, but if he should enter the Reverend Stricker's house as he entered the Reverend Pietersen's . . . ! After he had sent Theo a long letter in the morning, he sat down again in the evening and wrote another:

Dear Theo:
  I am in desperate need of money for the trip to Amsterdam. If I have just enough I go.
  I send along a few drawings; now tell me why they do not sell, and how I can make them salable. For I must earn some money for a railroad ticket to go and fathom that "No, never, never."

As the days went on he felt new, healthy energy arise. His love made him resolute. He had driven out the germ of doubt, and in his own mind he now knew that if he could only see Kay, help her to understand the sort of person he really was inside, he could change that "No, never, never" to "Yes! for ever, for ever!" He went back to his work with a new verve; although he knew that his draftsman's fist was still unwieldy, he felt a powerful confidence that time would wipe that out, just as it would Kay's refusal.

The following evening he sent a letter to the Reverend Stricker, stating his case clearly. He did not mince his words, and he grinned as he thought of the expletive that would be wrenched from his uncle's lips. His father had forbidden him to write the letter; a real battle was preparing in the parsonage. Theodorus saw life in terms of strict obedience and strict behaviour; he knew nothing of the vicissitudes of human temperament. If his son could not fit himself to the mould, then it was his son who was wrong, and not the mould.

"It's all the fault of those French books you read," said Theodorus across the evening table. "If you keep company with thieves and murderers, how can anyone expect you to behave like an obedient son and a gentleman?"

Vincent looked up from his Michelet in mild astonishment.

"Thieves and murderers? Do you call Victor Hugo and Michelet thieves?"

"No, but that's what they write about. Their books are full of evil."

"Nonsense, Father; Michelet is as pure as the Bible itself."

"I want none of your blaspheming here, young man!" shouted Theodorus in a righteous rage. "Those books are immoral. It's your French ideas that have ruined you."

Vincent rose, walked around the table, and placed "L'Amour et la Femme" before Theodorus.

"There is only one way for you to be convinced," he said. "Just read a few pages for yourself. You will be impressed. Michelet only wants to help us solve our problems and our little miseries."

Theodorus swept "L'Amour et la Femme" onto the floor with the gesture of a good man casting away sin.

"I don't need to read it!" he fumed. "We have a great-uncle in the Van Gogh family who was infected with French ideas and he took to drink!"

"*Mille pardons,* Father Michelet," murmured Vincent, picking up the book.

"And why Father Michelet, if I may ask?" said Theodorus icily. "Are you trying to insult me?"

"I hadn't thought of any such thing," said Vincent. "But I must tell you frankly that if I needed advice I would sooner go to Michelet than to you. It would be more likely to be in season."

"Oh, Vincent," implored his mother, "why must you say such things? Why must you break up family ties?"

"Yes, that's what you're doing," exclaimed Theodorus. "You're breaking up family ties. Your conduct is unpardonable. You had better leave this house and go elsewhere to live."

Vincent walked up to his studio room and sat down on the bed. He wondered idly why it was that whenever he received a tremendous blow he sat on the bed instead of a chair. He looked around the walls of his room at the diggers, the sowers, the labourers, the seamstress and the cleaning girl, the woodchoppers, and the drawings from Heike. Yes, he had made progress. He was going forward. But his work was not finished here yet. Mauve was in Drenthe and would not return for another month. He did not wish to leave Etten. He was comfortable; living elsewhere would be more expensive. He wanted time to crash through his clumsy expression and catch the true spirit of the Brabant types before he went away forever. His father had told him to leave the house, had actually cursed at him. But it had all been said in anger. If they really said, "Go!" and meant it . . . Was he really so bad that he had to be driven from his father's house?

The next morning he received two letters in the mail. The first was from the Reverend Stricker, an answer to his registered letter. There was also a note enclosed from the Reverend's wife. They summed up Vincent's career in no uncertain terms, told him that Kay loved someone else, that the other man was wealthy, that they wished his outlandish attacks upon their daughter to cease instantly.

"There are really no more unbelieving, hard hearted and worldly people alive than clergymen," observed Vincent to himself, crushing the Amsterdam letter in his hand with as much savage pleasure as though it had been the Reverend himself.

The second letter was from Theo.

"The drawings are well expressed. I will do my utmost to sell them. In the meanwhile I am enclosing twenty francs for that trip to Amsterdam. Good luck, old boy."

8

When Vincent left the Central railway station, night was beginning to close in. He walked rapidly up the Damrak to the Dam, past the King's Palace and the post office and cut across to the Keizersgracht. It was the hour when all the stores and offices were being emptied of their clerks and salesmen.

He crossed the Singel, and stopped for a moment on the bridge of the Heerengracht to watch the men of a flower barge eat their dinner of bread and herring at an open table. He turned left on the Keizersgracht, passed the long row of narrow Memish dwellings, and found himself in front of the short, stone steps and black railing of the Reverend Stricker's house. He remembered the first time he had stood there, at the beginning of his Amsterdam adventure, and he realized that there are some cities in which men are forever ill-fated.

He had rushed all the way up the Damrak and across the Centre at top speed; now that he arrived he felt a fear and hesitancy about entering. He looked upward and noticed the iron hook sticking out above the attic window. He thought what an excellent opportunity it afforded for a man to hang himself.

He traversed the wide, red brick pavement and stood on the curb, looking down into the canal. He knew that the next hour would determine the whole course of his external life. If he could only see Kay, talk to her, make her understand, everything would work out. But the father of a young girl possessed the key to the front door. Suppose the Reverend Stricker refused to admit him.

A sand barge came slowly upstream, being pushed to its nightly anchorage. There was a trail of moist yellow sand over the black side where the cargo had been shovelled out of the hollow. Vincent noticed that there was no wash strung from stern to prow, and idly wondered why. A thin, bony man stuck the side of his chest to the pole, and leaning against it heavily, pushed his way down the catwalk while the thick, clumsy boat slipped upstream from under him. A woman in a dirty apron sat at the stern, like a piece of water-carved stone, the hand behind her guiding the clumsy tiller. A little boy, a girl, and a filthy white dog stood on top of the cabin and gazed at the houses along the Keizersgracht wistfully.

Vincent mounted the five stone steps and rang the bell. After a moment the maid came. She peered at Vincent standing in the shadows, recognized him and thrust her adequate bulk into the doorway.

"Is the Reverend Stricker at home?" asked Vincent.

"No. He's out." She had received her orders.

Vincent heard voices inside. He pushed the woman aside brusquely.

"Get out of my way," he said.

The maid followed him and tried to bar his entrance.

"The family is at dinner," she protested. "You can't go in."

Vincent walked down the long hall and stepped into the dining room. As he did so he saw the very end of a familiar black dress disappear through the other door. The Reverend Stricker, his Aunt Wilhelmina, and the two younger children were at the table. Five places had been laid. At the place where the empty chair was pushed back at a crooked angle, there was a plate of broiled veal, whole potatoes, and string beans.

"I couldn't stop him, sir," said the maid. "He just pushed his way in."

There were two silver candlesticks on the table, with tall white candles giving off the only light. Calvin, hanging on the wall, looked eerie in the yellow glow.

The silver service from the carved sideboard gleamed in the darkness, and Vincent noticed the little high window under which he had first spoken to Kay.

"Well, Vincent," said his Uncle, "you seem to have less manners every day."

"I want to speak to Kay."

"She's not here. She's visiting with friends."

"She was sitting in this place when I rang the bell. She had begun her dinner." Stricker turned to his wife. "Take the children out of the room."

"Now, Vincent," he said, "you are causing a great deal of trouble. Not only I, but everyone else in the family has completely lost patience with you. You're a tramp, an idler, a boor, and as far as I can see, an ungrateful, vicious character. How dare you even presume to love my daughter? It is an insult to me."

"Let me see Kay, Uncle Stricker. I want to talk to her."

"She doesn't want to talk to you. She never wants to lay eyes on you again!"

"Kay said that?"

"Yes."

"I don't believe it."

Stricker was aghast. It was the first time he had been accused of lying since he had been ordained.

"How dare you say that I am not telling the truth!"

"I'll never believe that until I hear it from her own lips. And even then I won't."

"When I think of all the precious time and money I wasted on you here in Amsterdam."

Vincent sank wearily into the chair Kay had just vacated, and rested both his arms on the table.

"Uncle, listen to me a moment. Show me that even a clergyman can have a human heart under his triple steel armour. I love your daughter. I love her desperately. Every hour of the day and night I think of her and long for her. You work for God, then for God's sake show me a little mercy. Don't be so cruel to me. I know that I'm not successful yet, but if you'll give me a little time, I will be. Give me a chance to show her my love. Let me help her to understand why she must love me. Surely you must have been in love once, Uncle, and you know what agony a man can suffer. I've suffered enough; let me find a little happiness for once. Just give me a chance to win her love, that's all I ask. I can't bear this aloneness and misery another day!"

The Reverend Stricker looked down at him for a moment and then said, "Are you such a weakling and a coward that you can't stand a little pain? Must you be forever whimpering about it?"

Vincent sprang to his feet violently. All the softness was gone from him now. Only the fact that they were standing across the table from each other, separated by two tall candles in silver candlesticks kept the younger man from hitting the minister. A bruising silence hummed in the room while the two men stood staring at the sparkling points of light in each other's eyes.

Vincent did not know how much time passed. He raised his hand and placed it near the candle.

"Let me speak to her," he said, "for just as long as I can hold my hand in this flame."

He turned his hand over and placed the back of it in the flame. The light in the room dimmed. The carbon from the candle instantly made his flesh black. Within a few seconds it turned to a raw, burning red. Vincent did not flinch or take his eyes from his uncle. Five seconds passed. Ten. The skin on the back of his hand began to puff. The Reverend Stricker's eyes were wide with horror. He seemed paralysed. Several times he tried to speak, to move, but he could not. He was held in the grip of Vincent's cruel, probing eyes. Fifteen seconds passed. The puffed skin cracked open but the arm did not even tremble. The Reverend Stricker at last brought himself to consciousness with a violent jerk.

"You crazy man!" he shouted at the top of his voice. "You insane fool!"

He threw himself across the table, snatched the candle from under Vincent, and crushed the light with his fist. Then he leaned down to the candle nearest him and blew it out with a great puff.

The room was in utter darkness. The two men stood leaning on their palms, across the table from each other, peering into the darkness, unable to see, yet seeing each other only too clearly.

"You're mad!" cried the Reverend. "And Kay despises you with all her heart! Get out of this house and never dare to come back!"

Vincent picked his way slowly along the dark street and found himself somehow on the outskirts of the town. The familiar and pleasantly fetid odour of still water assailed his nostrils as he stood staring down into a brackish, dead canal. The gas lamp at the corner cast a light on his left hand—some deep instinct had kept his drawing hand at his side—and he saw that there was a black hole in the skin. He passed over a series of tiny waterways smelling faintly of a long forgotten sea. At last he found himself near the house of Mendes da Costa. He squatted down on the bank of a canal. He dropped a pebble on the heavy green blanket of *kroos*. It sank without even showing that there was water beneath.

Kay was gone from his life. The "No, never, never" had been wrung from the depths of her soul. Her cry had now become transposed, had become his property. It pounded through his head, repeating, "No, never, never shall you see her again. Never shall you hear the lilting croon of her voice, the smile in her deep blue eyes, the feel of her warm skin on your cheek. Never shall you know love, for it cannot live, no, not even for as long as you can hold your flesh in the burning crucible of pain!"

A great inarticulate surge of grief welled up in his throat. He raised his left hand to his mouth to stifle the cry, that Amsterdam and all the world might never know that he had been judged, and deemed unworthy. On his lips he tasted the bitter, bitter ash of unrequited desire.

BOOK THREE

THE HAGUE

1

Mauve was still in Drenthe. Vincent searched the neighbourhood of the Uileboomen, and found a little place behind the Ryn station for fourteen francs a month. The studio—it had been known as a room until Vincent took it—was fairly large, with an alcove for cooking and a large window facing the south. There was a stove squatting low in one corner with a long black pipe disappearing in the wall up by the ceiling. The wallpaper was a clean, neutral shade; out of the window Vincent could see the lumber yard belonging to the owner of the house, a green meadow, and then a vast stretch of dune. The house was located on the Schenkweg, the last street between The Hague and the meadows to the south-east. It was covered with black soot from the engines that banged in and out of the Ryn station.

Vincent bought a strong kitchen table, two kitchen chairs, and a blanket to throw over himself while he slept on the floor. These expenditures exhausted his small fund of money, but the first of the month was not far off and Theo would send the hundred francs that had been agreed upon as his monthly allowance. The cold January weather would not permit him to work out of doors; since he had no money to pay models he had to sit by and wait for Mauve to return.

Mauve came back to Uileboomen. Vincent went at once to his cousin's studio. Mauve was setting up a big canvas excitedly, the swash of hair across his forehead falling into his eyes. He was about to begin the big project of the year, a canvas for the Salon, and had chosen for his subject a fishing smack being drawn up on the beach at Scheveningen by horses. Mauve and his wife Jet had thought it extremely doubtful that Vincent would ever come to The Hague; they knew that nearly everyone has a vague prompting to become an artist at some time or other during his life.

"So you've come to The Hague after all. Very well, Vincent, we shall make a painter of you. Have you found a place to live?"

"Yes, I'm over at 138 Schenkweg, just behind the Ryn station."

"That's close by. How are you fixed for funds?"

"Well, I haven't the money to do a great deal. I bought a table and a couple of chairs."

"And a bed," said Jet.

"No, I've been sleeping on the floor."

Mauve said something in an undertone to Jet who went into the house and returned in a moment with a wallet. Mauve took out a hundred guilder note. "I want you to take this as a loan, Vincent," he said. "Buy yourself a bed; you must rest well at night. Is your rent paid?"

"Not yet."

"Then get it off your mind. How about the light?"

"There's plenty of it, but the only window has a southern exposure."

"That's bad; you had better get it fixed. The sun will change the light on your models every ten minutes. Buy yourself some drapes."

"I don't like to borrow money from you, Cousin Mauve. It's enough that you should be willing to teach me."

"Nonsense, Vincent; it happens once in every man's life that he has to set up housekeeping. In the long run it's cheaper to have things of your own."

"Yes, that's so. I hope to be able to sell a few drawings soon and then I'll pay you back."

"Tersteeg will help you. He bought my things when I was younger and just learning. But you must begin to work in water-colour and oil. There is no market for simple pencil sketches."

Mauve, in spite of his bulk, had a nervous manner of darting about at great speed. As soon as his eyes lighted on something he was looking for he thrust one shoulder out before him and flung himself in that direction.

"Here, Vincent," he said, "here's a painting box with some water-colours, brushes, palette, palette knife, oil, and turpentine. Let me show you how to hold that palette and stand before your easel."

He showed Vincent a few elements of technique. Vincent picked up the ideas very quickly.

"Good!" said Mauve. "I used to think you were a dullard, but I see it is not so. You may come here in the mornings and work on water-colours. I'll propose your name for a special membership of *Pulchri;* you can draw there several evenings a week from the model. Besides, it will give you some intercourse with painters. When you begin to sell you can take out a regular membership."

"Yes, I want to work from the model. I shall try to hire one to come in every day. Once I get the human figure, everything else will come of its own accord."

"That's so," agreed Mauve. "The figure is the hardest to get, but once you have it, trees and cows and sunsets are simple. Men who neglect the figure do so because they find it too hard."

Vincent bought a bed, drapes for the window, paid his rent, and tacked the Brabant sketches on the wall. He knew they were unsalable and he easily saw their defects, but there was something of nature in them; they had been made with a certain passion. He could not have pointed out just where the passion was, nor how it got there; he did not even realize its full value until he became friends with de Bock.

De Bock was a charming man. He was *bien élevé*, had pleasant manners and a permanent income. He had been educated in England. Vincent met him at Goupils. De Bock was the exact antithesis of Vincent in every way; he took life casually, nothing ruffled or excited him, and his entire make-up was delicate. His mouth was exactly as long as his nostrils were wide.

"Won't you come have a pot of tea with me?" he asked Vincent. "I'd like to show you some of my recent things. I think I have a new flair since Tersteeg has been selling me."

His studio was located in Willemspark, the aristocratic section of The Hague. He had his walls draped off in neutral velvets. Lounging divans with luxurious cushions filled every corner. There were smoking tables, amply filled bookcases, and oriental rugs. When Vincent thought of his own studio, he felt like an anchorite.

De Bock lit the gas under a Russian samovar and sent his housekeeper for some cakes. Then he took a canvas out from a closet and placed it on the easel.

"This is my latest," he said. "Will you have a cigar while you're looking? It may help the picture; you never can tell."

He spoke in a light, amused tone. Since Tersteeg had discovered him, his self-confidence had gone sky high. He knew Vincent would like the picture. He took out one of the long Russian cigarettes for which he was famous in The Hague, and studied Vincent's face for a passing judgment.

Vincent scrutinized the canvas through the blue smoke of De Bock's expensive cigar. He felt in De Bock's attitude that horrible moment of suspense when the artist shows one of his creations to strange eyes for the first time. What was he to say? The landscape was not bad, but neither was it good. It was too much like De Bock's character: casual. He remembered how furious and ill it made him when some young upstart dared condescend to his work. Although the picture was the sort that could be seen in its entirety with one glance, he continued to study it.

"You have a feeling for landscape, De Bock," he said. "And you certainly know how to put charm in it."

"Oh, thanks," said De Bock, pleased at what he thought was a compliment. "Won't you have a cup of tea?"

Vincent clutched the teacup with both hands, fearing that he might spill it on the rich rug. De Bock went to the samovar and drew himself a cup. Vincent wished desperately not to say anything against De Bock's work. He liked the man and wanted him for a friend. But the objective craftsman arose within him and he could not put down his criticism.

"There's only one thing I'm not sure I like about this canvas."

De Bock took the tray from his housekeeper and said, "Have a cake, old fellow."

Vincent refused because he did not see how he was going to eat a cake and hold a cup of tea on his lap at the same time.

"What was it you didn't care for?" asked De Bock lightly.

"Your figures. They don't seem authentic."

"You know," confided De Bock, stretching out leisurely on a comfortable divan, "I've often meant to plug away at the figure. But I never seem to get around to it. I take a model and work a few days, and then I suddenly become interested in some landscape or other. After all, landscape is very definitely my medium, so I needn't let the figure bother me much, need I?"

"Even when I do landscapes," said Vincent, "I hope to get something of the figure into them. Your work is years ahead of mine; besides, you're an accepted artist. But will you permit me to offer just one word of friendly criticism?"

"Love to have you."

"Well then, I should say your painting lacks passion."

"Passion?" inquired De Bock, cocking one eye at Vincent as he leaned over the samovar. "Which one of the numerous passions are you referring to?"

"It's rather hard to explain. But your sentiment seems a trifle vague. In my opinion it could stand a little more intensity."

"But see here, old chap," said De Bock, straightening up and regarding one of his canvases closely. "I can't spew emotion all over the canvas just because people tell me to, can I? I paint what I see and feel. If I don't feel any bloody passion, how am I to get it on my brush? One can't buy it at the greengrocer's by the pound, now can one?"

Vincent's studio looked almost mean and sordid after De Bock's, but he knew there were compensations for its austerity. He pushed the bed back into one corner and hid his cooking utensils; he wanted the place to be a painter's studio, not living quarters. Theo's money for the month had not yet arrived but he still had a few francs left from Mauve's loan. He used them to hire models. He had been in his studio only a short time when Mauve came to visit him.

"It took me only ten minutes to walk over," he said, looking about. "Yes, this will do. You should have north light, but this will do. It will make a favourable impression on those people who have suspected you of amateurism and idleness. I see you've been working from the model today?"

"Yes. Every day. But it's expensive."

And the cheapest way in the end. Are you short of funds, Vincent?"

"Thank you, Cousin Mauve. I can get along."

He did not think it wise to become a financial burden on Mauve. He had just a franc left in his pocket, enough to eat on for a day, but he wanted Mauve to give freely of his instruction; money was not really important.

Mauve spent an hour showing him how to daub in water-colours, and how to wash out again. Vincent made rather a mess of things.

"Don't let that disturb you," said Mauve cheerfully. "You will spoil at least ten drawings before you come to handle the brush well. Let me see some of your latest Brabant sketches."

Vincent brought them out. Mauve was such a master of technique that he could penetrate to the essential weakness of a piece of work in a very few words. He never said, "This is wrong," and then stopped. He always added, "Try it this way." Vincent listened closely, for he knew that Mauve spoke to him just as he would have spoken to himself if he had gone wrong in one of his own canvases.

"You can draw," said Mauve. "That year with your pencil will be of great value to you. I shouldn't be surprised to see Tersteeg buying your water-colours in a short time."

This magnificent consolation did Vincent little good two days later when he had not a centime in his pocket. It was already several days past the first of the month and the hundred francs had not yet arrived from Theo. What could be wrong? Was Theo angry with him? Could it be possible that Theo would go back on him now, at the very moment when he was on the threshold of a career? He found a stamp in his coat pocket; that enabled him to write to his brother and beg him to send on at least a part of the allowance so that he might eat and hire a model occasionally.

For three days he went without a bite of food, working at water-colour at Mauve's in the morning, sketching in the soup kitchens and third-class waiting rooms in the afternoons, and going either to *Pulchri* or Mauve's to work again at night. He was afraid that Mauve would discover his situation and become discouraged with him. Vincent realized that although Mauve had come to like him, his cousin would cast him aside without a second thought if his troubles began to have an effect upon Mauve's painting. When Jet invited him to dinner, he refused.

The low, dull ache at the pit of his stomach turned his mind back to the Borinage. Was he to be hungry all his life? Was there never to be a moment of comfort or peace for him anywhere?

The next day he swallowed his pride and went to see Tersteeg. Perhaps he could borrow ten francs from the man who supported half the painters of The Hague.

Tersteeg was in Paris on business.

Vincent developed a fever and could no longer hold the pencil. He went to bed. The following day he dragged himself back to the Plaats and found the dealer in. Tersteeg had promised Theo that he would look after Vincent. He lent him twenty-five francs.

"I have been meaning to look in at your studio for some time, Vincent," he said. "I shall drop around shortly."

It was all Vincent could do to answer politely. He wanted to get away and eat. He had thought on his way to Goupils, "If only I can get some money, I will be all right again." But now that he had the money he was more miserable than ever. He felt utterly and forlornly alone.

"Dinner will cure all that," he said to himself.

Food removed the pain in his stomach but not the pain of aloneness that lodged in some intangible spot within him. He bought some cheap tobacco, went home, stretched out on the bed and smoked his pipe. The hunger for Kay came back to him with terrific force. He felt so desperately miserable he could not breathe. He jumped up from the bed, opened the window and stuck his head out into the snow covered January night. He thought of the Reverend Stricker. A chill ran through him, as though he had been leaning too long against the cold stone wall of a church. He closed the window, snatched up his hat and coat, and ran out to a wine café that he had seen in front of the Ryn station.

2

The wine café had an oil lamp hanging at the entrance and another over the bar. The middle of the shop was in semidarkness. There were a few benches against the wall with mottled, stone topped tables before them. It was a workingman's shop with faded walls and a cement floor; a place of refuge rather than joy.

Vincent sat down at one of the tables. He leaned his back against the wall wearily. It was not so bad when he was working, when there was money for food and models. But to whom could he turn for simple companionship, for a casual and friendly word about the time of day? Mauve was his master, Tersteeg a busy and important dealer, De Bock a wealthy man of society. Perhaps a glass of wine would help him over the bad spot. Tomorrow he would be able to work, and things would look better.

He sipped the sour red wine slowly. There were few people in the shop. Opposite him sat a labourer of some sort. In the corner near the bar sat a couple, the woman in gaudy clothes. At the table next to him was a woman alone. He did not look at her.

The waiter came by and said to the woman roughly, "More wine?"

"Haven't a sou," she replied.

Vincent turned. "Won't you have a glass with me?" he asked.

The woman looked at him for an instant. "Sure."

The waiter brought the glass of wine, took the twenty centimes and went away. The tables were close together.

"Thanks," said the woman.

Vincent surveyed her closely. She was not young, not beautiful, slightly faded, one over whom life had passed. Her figure was slender but well formed. He noticed her hand as it clasped the glass of wine; it was not a lady's hand like Kay's, but the hand of one who worked much. She reminded him, in the half light, of some curious figure by Chardin or Jan Steen. She had a crooked nose that bulged in the middle, and a shadowy moustache on her upper lip. Her eyes were melancholy but there was, none the less, a touch of spirit in them.

"Not at all," he replied. "I'm grateful for your company."

"My name is Christine," she said. "What's yours?"

"Vincent."

"Do you work here at The Hague?"

"Yes."

"What do you do?"

"I'm a painter."

"Oh. That's a hell of a life too, aint it?"

"Sometimes."

"I'm a laundress. When I have strength enough to work. But that aint always."

"What do you do then?"

"I was on the streets for a long time. I go back to it when I'm too sick to work."

"Is it hard to be a laundress?"

"Yes. They work us twelve hours. And they don't pay nothing. Sometime, after I washed all day, I got to find a man to earn food for the kids."

"How many children have you, Christine?"

"Five. I'm carrying another one now."

"Your husband is dead?"

"I got them all from strangers."

"That made it difficult, didn't it?"

She shrugged. "Jesus Christ. A miner can't refuse to go down because he might get killed, can he?"

"No. Do you know who any of the fathers are?"

"Only the first son of a bitch. I never even knew their names."

"What about the one you're carrying now?"

"Well, I can't be sure. I was too sick to wash then, so I was on the streets a lot. But it don't matter."

"Will you have another glass of wine?"

"Make it gin and bitters." She reached into her purse, took out the butt of a rough, black cigar and lit it. "You don't look prosperous," she said. "Do you sell any paintings?"

"No, I'm just beginning."

"You look pretty old to be beginning."

"I'm thirty."

"You look forty. How do you live then?"

"My brother sends me a little money."

"Well it's no goddam worse than being a laundress."

"With whom do you stay, Christine?"

"We're all at my mother's."

"Does she know you go on the streets?"

The woman laughed uproariously but without mirth. "Christ yes! She sent me there. That's what she did all her life. It's how she got me and my brother."

"What does your brother do?"

"He's got a woman at the house. He pimps for her."

"That can't be very good for your five children."

"It don't matter. They'll all be doing the same some day."

"It's all a rum go, isn't it, Christine."

"Aint no good crying about it. Can I have another glass of gin and bitters? What did you do to your hand? You got a big black sore."

"I burned it."

"Oh, that must have hurt awful." She picked up his hand tenderly.

"No, Christine, it was all right. I wanted to."

She dropped his hand. "Why did you come in here all alone. Aint you got no friends?"

"No. My brother, but he's in Paris."

"Makes a guy feel lonesome, don't it?"

"Yes, Christine, horribly."

"I get like that, too. There's all the kids at home, and my mother and brother. And all the men I pick up. But you live alone anyhow, don't you? It aint people that count. It's having someone you really like."

"Hasn't there ever been anyone you cared for, Christine?"

"The first fellow. I was sixteen. He was rich. Couldn't marry me 'count of his family. But he paid for the baby. Then he died, and I was left without a centime."

"How old are you?"

"Thirty-two. Too old to have kids. The doctor at the free ward said this one will kill me."

"It won't if you have proper medical attention."

"Where in hell am I going to get it? I aint got nothing saved up. The doctors at the free ward don't care; they got too many sick women."

"Have you no way at all of getting a little money?"

"Sure. If I stay on the streets all night for a couple of months. But that'll kill me quicker than the kid."

They were silent for several moments. "Where are you going when you leave here, Christine?"

"I been at the tubs all day and I come in here to get a glass because I'm dead. They were supposed to pay me a franc and a half, but they put me off 'till Saturday. I got to get two francs for food. I thought I'd rest before I found a man."

"Will you let me come with you, Christine? I'm very much alone. I'd like to."

"Sure. Saves me the trouble. Besides, you're kind of nice."

"I like you too, Christine. When you picked up my burned hand . . . that was the first kind word a woman has said to me in I can't remember how long."

"That's funny. You aint bad to look at. You got a nice way."

"I'm just unlucky in love."

"Yes, that's how it is, aint it? Can I have another glass of gin and bitters?"

"Listen, you and I need not make ourselves drunk to feel something for each other. Just put in your pocket what I can spare. I'm sorry it isn't more."

"You look like you need it worse than me. You can come anyway. After you go, I'll find some other guy for the two francs."

"No. Take the money. I can spare it. I borrowed twenty-five francs from a friend."

"All right. Let's get out of here."

On their way home, threading their way through the dark streets, they chatted easily, like old friends. She told him of her life, without sympathy for herself, without complaint.

"Have you ever posed as a model?" Vincent asked her.

"When I was young."

"Then why not pose for me? I can't pay you much. Not even a franc a day. But after I begin selling, I'll pay you two francs. It will be better than washing clothes."

"Say, I'd like that. I'd bring my boy. You can paint him for nothing. When you get tired of me you can have my mother. She'd like to make an extra franc now and then. She's a charwoman."

At length they reached her house. It was a rough stone building of one floor and a court. "You don't got to see anyone," said Christine. "My room's in front."

It was a modest, simple little room in which she lived; the plain paper on the wall gave it a quiet, grey tone, like a picture by Chardin, thought Vincent. On the wooden floor there was a mat and a piece of old crimson carpet. An ordinary kitchen stove was in one corner, a chest of drawers in another, and in the centre a large bed. It was the interior of a real working woman's home.

When Vincent awoke in the morning and found himself not alone, but saw there in the twilight a fellow creature beside him, it made the world look so much more friendly. The pain and aloneness were gone from him and in their place had come a deep feeling of peace.

3

In the morning post he received a note from Theo with the hundred francs enclosed. Theo had been unable to send it until several days after the first. He rushed out, found a little old woman digging in her front garden nearby, and asked if she wouldn't come and pose for him for fifty centimes. The old woman assented gladly.

In the studio he placed the woman against a drowsy background, sitting next to the chimney and stove with a little teakettle off to one side. He was seeking tone; the old woman's head had a great deal of light and life in it. He made three fourths of the water-colour in a green soap style. The corner where the woman sat he treated tenderly, softly, and with sentiment. For some time his work had been hard, dry, brittle; now it flowed. He hammered his sketch on the paper and expressed his idea well. He was grateful to Christine for what she had done for him. Lack of love in his life could bring him infinite pain, but it could do him no harm; lack of sex could dry up the well springs of his art and kill him.

"Sex lubricates," he murmured to himself as he worked with fluidity and ease. "I wonder why Papa Michelet never mentioned that."

There was a knock on the door. Vincent admitted Mijnheer Tersteeg. His striped trousers were creased painstakingly. His round, brown shoes were as bright as a mirror. His beard was carefully barbered, his hair parted neatly on the side, and his collar was of impeccable whiteness.

Tersteeg was genuinely pleased to find that Vincent had a real studio and was hard at work. He liked to see young artists become successful; that was his hobby as well as his profession. Yet he wanted that success to be arrived at through systematic and preordained channels; he found it better for a man to work through the conventional means and fail, than break all the rules and succeed. For him the rules of the game were far more important than the victory. Tersteeg was a good and honourable man; he expected everyone else to be equally good and honourable. He admitted no circumstances which could change evil into good or sin into salvation. The painters who sold their canvases to Goupils knew that they had to toe the mark. If they violated the dictates of genteel behaviour, Tersteeg would refuse to handle their canvases even though they might be masterpieces.

"Well, Vincent," he said, "I am glad to surprise you at work. That is how I like to come in on my artists."

"It is good of you to come all this way to see me, Mijnheer Tersteeg."

"Not at all. I have been meaning to see your studio ever since you moved here." Vincent looked about at the bed, table, chairs, stove, and easel.

"It isn't much to look at."

"Never mind, pitch into your work and soon you'll be able to afford something better. Mauve tells me that you're beginning water-colours; there is a good market for those sketches. I should be able to sell some for you, and so should your brother."

"That's what I'm working toward, Mijnheer."

"You seem in rather better spirits than when I saw you yesterday."

"Yes, I was ill. But I recovered last night."

He thought of the wine, the gin and bitters, and Christine; he shivered at what Tersteeg would say if he knew about them. "Will you look at some of my sketches, Mijnheer? Your reaction would be valuable to me."

Tersteeg stood before the old woman in her white apron, standing out from the green soap background. His silence was not so eloquent as Vincent remembered it from the Plaats. He leaned on his walking stick for some moments, then hung it on his arm.

"Yes, yes," he said, "you're coming along. Mauve will make a water-colourist out of you, I can see that. It will take some time, but you will get there. You must hurry, Vincent, so that you can earn your own living. It is quite a strain on Theo to have to send you a hundred francs a month; I saw that when I was in Paris. You must support yourself as quickly as possible. I should be able to buy some of the small sketches very soon now."

"Thank you, Mijnheer. It is good of you to take an interest."

"I want to make you successful, Vincent. It means business for Goupils. As soon as I begin to sell your work, you will be able to take a better studio, buy some good clothes, and go out a bit into society. That is necessary if you want to sell your oils, later. Well, I must run on to Mauve's. I want to see that Scheveningen thing he is doing for the Salon."

"You'll look in again, Mijnheer?"

"Yes, of course. In a week or two. Mind you work hard and show me some improvement. You must make my visits pay, you know."

He shook hands and departed. Vincent pitched into his work once more. If only he could make a living, the very simplest living out of his work. He asked for nothing more. He could be independent. He would not have to be a burden on anyone. And best of all there would be no hurry; he could let himself feel his way slowly and surely toward maturity and the expression he was seeking.

In the afternoon mail there was a note from De Bock, on pink stationery.

Dear Van Gogh:
   I'm bringing Artz's model to your studio tomorrow morning so that we can sketch together.

                                                                    De B.

Artz's model proved to be a very beautiful young girl who charged one franc-fifty for posing. Vincent was delighted, as he would never have been able to hire her. There was a roaring fire in the little stove and the model undressed by it to keep warm. Only the professional models would pose naked in The Hague. This exasperated Vincent; the bodies he wanted to draw were those of old men and women, bodies that had tone and character.

"I've brought along my tobacco pouch," said De Bock, "and a little lunch that my housekeeper put up. I thought we might not want to disturb ourselves to go out."

"I'll try some of your tobacco. Mine is a trifle strong for the morning."

"I'm ready," said the model. "Will you pose me?"

"Sitting or standing, De Bock?"

"Let's try the standing first. I have some erect figures in my new landscape."

They sketched for about an hour and a half, and then the model tired.

"Let's do her sitting down," said Vincent. "The figure will be more relaxed."

They worked until noon, each bent over his own drawing board, exchanging only an occasional grunt about the light or tobacco. Then De Bock unpacked the lunch, and all three gathered about the stove to eat it. They munched the thin slices of bread, cold meats and cheese, and studied their morning's sketches.

"Queer, what an objective view you can get of your own work once you begin to eat," remarked De Bock.

"May I see what you've done?"

"With pleasure."

De Bock had put down a good likeness of the girl's face, but there was not even a faint suggestion of the individual nature of her body. It was just a perfect body.

"I say," exclaimed De Bock, looking at Vincent's sketch, "what's that thing you've got instead of her face? Is that what you mean by putting passion into it?"

"We weren't doing a portrait," replied Vincent. "We were doing a figure."

"That's the first time I ever heard a face doesn't belong on a figure."

"Take a look at your stomach," said Vincent.

"What's the matter with it?"

"It looks as though it were filled with hot air. I can't see an inch of bowels."

"Why should you? I didn't notice any of the poor girl's entrails hanging out."

The model went on eating without even a smile. She thought all artists were crazy, anyhow. Vincent placed his sketch alongside of De Bock's.

"If you will notice," he said, "my stomach is full of guts. You can tell just by looking at it that many a ton of food has wended its weary way through the labyrinth."

"What's that got to do with painting?" demanded De Bock. "We're not specialists in viscera, are we? When people look at my canvases, I want them to see the mist in the trees, and the sun setting red behind the clouds. I don't want them to see guts."

Every morning Vincent went out bright and early to find a model for the day. Once it was a blacksmith's boy, once an old woman from the insane asylum on the Geest, once a man from the peat market, and another time a grandmother and child from the Paddemoes, or Jewish quarter. Models cost him a great deal of money, money that he knew he ought to be saving for food for the end of the month. But of what good was it for him to be at The Hague, studying under Mauve, if he could not go full speed ahead? He would eat later, when he became established.

Mauve continued to instruct him patiently. Every evening Vincent went to the Uileboomen to work in the busy, warm studio. Sometimes he became discouraged because his water-colours were thick, muddy and dull. Mauve only laughed.

"Of course they're not right yet," he said. "If your work were transparent *now*, it would possess only a certain chic and would probably become heavy later on. Now you are pegging away at it and it becomes heavy, but afterwards it will go quickly and become light."

"That's true, Cousin Mauve, but if a man must earn money from his drawing, what is he to do?"

"Believe me, Vincent, if you try to arrive too soon, you will only kill yourself as an artist. The man of the day is usually the man of a day. In things of art the old saying is true, 'Honesty is the best policy!' It is better to take more trouble on a serious study than to develop a kind of chic that will flatter the public."

"I want to be true to myself, Cousin Mauve, and express severe, true things in a rough manner. But when there is the necessity of making one's living . . . I have done a few things I thought Tersteeg might . . . of course I realize . . ."

"Let me see them," said Mauve.

He glanced at the water-colours and tore them into a thousand pieces. "Stick to your roughness, Vincent," he said, "and don't run after the amateurs and dealers. Let those who like come to you. In due time you shall reap."

Vincent glanced down at the scraps of paper. "Thank you, Cousin Mauve," he said. "I needed that kick."

Mauve was having a little party that night, and a number of artists drifted in; Weissenbruch, known as the "merciless sword" for his fierce criticism of other men's work; Breitner, De Bock, Jules Bakhuyzen and Neuhuys, Vos's friend.

Weissenbruch was a little man with an enormous spirit. Nothing could ever conquer him. What he disliked—and that was nearly everything—he destroyed with a single lash of his tongue. He painted what he pleased and how he pleased, and made the public like it. Tersteeg had once objected to something in one of his canvases, so he refused to sell anything more through Goupil. Yet he sold everything he painted; nobody knew how or to whom. His face was as sharp as his tongue; his head, nose, and chin cutting. Everyone feared him and coveted his approbation. He had become a national character by the simple expedient of despising things. He got Vincent off into the corner by the fire, spat into the flames at frequent intervals to hear the pleasant sound of the hiss, and fondled a plaster foot.

"I hear you're a Van Gogh," he said. "Do you paint as successfully as your uncles sell pictures?"

"No. I don't do anything successfully."

"And a damn good thing for you. Every artist ought to starve until he's sixty. Then perhaps he would turn out a few good pieces of canvas."

"Tosh! You're not much over forty, and you're doing good work."

Weissenbruch liked that "Tosh!" It was the first time anyone had had the courage to say it to him for years. He showed his appreciation by lighting into Vincent.

"If you think my painting is any good, you better give up and become a *concierge*. Why do you think I sell it to the fool public? Because it's junk! If it was any good, I'd keep it for myself. No, my boy, I'm only practising now. When I'm sixty I shall really begin painting. Everything I do after that I shall keep by my side; when I die I'll have it buried with me. No artist ever lets go of anything he thinks is good, Van Gogh. He only sells his garbage to the public."

De Bock tipped Vincent a wink from the other side of the room, so Vincent said, "You've missed your profession, Weissenbruch; you ought to be an art critic."

Weissenbruch laughed and called out, "This cousin of yours isn't half as bad as he looks, Mauve. He's got a tongue in his head." He turned back to Vincent and said cruelly, "What in hell do you go around in those dirty rags for? Why don't you buy yourself some decent clothes?"

Vincent was wearing an old suit of Theo's that had been altered for him. The operation had not been successful, and in addition, Vincent had been wearing it over his water-colours every day.

"Your uncles have enough money to clothe the whole population of Holland. Don't they give you anything?"

"Why should they? They agree with you that artists should starve."

"If they don't believe in you they must be right. The Van Goghs are supposed to be able to smell a painter a hundred kilometres away. You're probably rotten."

"And you can go to hell!"

Vincent turned away angrily, but Weissenbruch caught him by the arm. He was smiling broadly.

"That's the spirit!" he cried. "I just wanted to see how much abuse you would take. Keep your courage up, my boy. You've got the stuff."

Mauve enjoyed doing imitations for his guests. He was the son of a clergyman, but there was room for only one religion in his life: painting. While Jet passed around tea and cookies and cheese balls, he preached the sermon about the fishing bark of Peter. Had Peter received or inherited that bark? Had he bought it on the installment plan? Had he, oh horrible thought, stolen it? The painters filled the room with their smoke and laughter, gulping down cheese balls and cups of tea with amazing rapidity.

"Mauve has changed," mused Vincent to himself.

He did not know that Mauve was undergoing the metamorphosis of the creative artist. He began a canvas lethargically, working almost without interest. Slowly his energy would pick up as ideas began to creep into his mind and become formulated. He would work a little longer, a little harder each day. As objects appeared clearly on the canvas, his demands upon himself became more exacting. His mind would flee from his family, from his friends and other interests. His appetite would desert him and he would lie awake nights thinking of things to be done. As his strength went down his excitement went up. Soon he would be living on nervous energy. His body would shrink on its ample frame and the sentimental eyes become lost in a hazy mist. The more he became fatigued, the more desperately he worked. The nervous passion which possessed him would rise higher and higher. In his mind he knew how long it would take him to finish; he set his will to last until that very day. He was like a man ridden by a thousand demons; he had years in which to complete the canvas, but something forced him to lacerate himself every hour of the twenty-four. In the end, he would be in such a towering passion and nervous excitement that a frightful scene ensued if anyone got in his way. He hurled himself at the canvas with every last ounce of his strength. No matter how long it took to finish, he always had will enough to the last drop of paint. Nothing could have killed him before he was completely through.

Once the canvas was delivered, he collapsed in a heap. He was weak, ill, delirious. It took Jet many days to nurse him back to health and sanity. His exhaustion was so complete that the very sight or smell of paint made him nauseated. Slowly, very slowly, his strength would return. In its wake would come his interest. He would begin to putter about the studio cleaning up things. He would walk in the fields, at first seeing nothing. In the end some scene would strike his eye. And so the cycle began all over again.

When Vincent had first come to The Hague, Mauve was just beginning the Scheveningen canvas. But now his pulse was rising day by day, and soon the mad, magnificent, most devastating of all deliriums would set in, that of artistic creation.

4

Christine knocked at Vincent's door a few nights later. She was dressed in a black petticoat and dark blue camisole, with a black cap over her hair. She had been standing at the washtub all day. Her mouth usually hung a little open when she was extremely fatigued; the pock-marks seemed to be wider and deeper than he had remembered them.

"Hello, Vincent," she said. "Thought I'd come see where you lived."

"You're the first woman to call on me, Christine. I bid you welcome. May I take your shawl?"

She sat down by the fire and warmed herself. After a moment she looked about the room.

"This aint bad," she said. "'Cept that it's empty."

"I know. I haven't any money for furniture."

"Well, I guess it's all you need."

"I was just going to fix supper, Christine. Will you join me?"

"Why don't you call me Sien? Everyone does."

"All right, Sien."

"What was you having for supper?"

"Potatoes and tea."

"I made two francs today. I'll go buy a little beef."

"Here, I have money. My brother sent me some. How much do you want?"

"I guess fifty centimes is all we can eat."

She returned in a few moments with a paper of meat. Vincent took it from her and attempted to prepare dinner.

"Here, you sit down. You don't know nothing about cooking. I'm a woman."

As she leaned over the stove, the heat sent a warm glow to her cheek. She looked rather pretty. It was so natural and homelike to see her cutting potatoes into a pot, putting the meat in with them to stew and simmer. Vincent leaned a chair against the wall and watched her, a feeling of warmth in his heart. It was his home, and here was a woman preparing dinner for him with loving hands. How often he had dreamed of this picture with Kay as his companion. Sien glanced about at him. She saw the chair leaning against the wall at a perilous angle.

"Here, you damn fool," she said, "you sit up straight. Was you wanting to break your neck?"

Vincent grinned. Every woman with whom he had ever lived in the same house— his mother, sisters, aunts and cousins—every last one of them had said, "Vincent, sit up straight on that chair. You'll break your neck."

"All right, Sien," he said, "I'll be good."

As soon as her back was turned, he leaned the chair against the wall again and smoked his pipe contentedly. Sien put the dinner on the table. She had bought two rolls while she was out; when they finished eating the beef and potatoes, they mopped up the gravy with their bread.

"There," said Sien, "I bet you can't cook like that."

"No, Sien, when I cook, I can't tell whether I'm eating fish, fowl, or the devil."

Over their tea Sien smoked one of her black cigars. They chatted animatedly. Vincent felt more at home with her than he did with Mauve or De Bock. There was a certain fraternity between them that he did not pretend to understand. They spoke of simple things, without pretense or competition. When Vincent spoke, she listened; she was not eager for him to get through so that she could talk about herself. She had no ego that she wished to assert. Neither of them wished to impress the other. When Sien spoke of her own life, its hardships and miseries, Vincent had only to substitute a few words to make her stories describe perfectly his own. There was no challenge in their words, no affectation in their silences. It was the meeting of two souls unmasked, stripped of all class barrier, artifice and distinction.

Vincent got up. "What are you going to do?" she asked.

"The dishes."

"Sit down. You don't know how to do dishes. I'm a woman."

He tipped his chair against the stove, filled his pipe, and puffed contentedly while she leaned over the basin. Her hands were good with the soap suds on them, the veins standing out, the intricate network of wrinkles speaking of the labour they had done. Vincent got pencil and paper and sketched them.

"It's nice here," she said when she finished the dishes. "If only we had some gin and bitters . . . "

They spent the evening sipping the bitters, while Vincent sketched Sien. She seemed content to rest quietly in a chair by the warm stove, hands in her lap. The glow of the heat and the pleasure of talking to someone who understood gave her vivacity and alertness.

"When do you finish with your washing?" he asked.

"Tomorrow. And a good thing. I couldn't stand much more."

"Have you been feeling badly?"

"No but it's coming, it's coming. The goddam kid wiggles in me now and again."

"Then you'll begin posing for me next week?"

"Is this all I got to do, just sit?"

"That's all. Sometimes you'll have to stand or pose naked."

"That aint so bad. You do all the work and I get paid."

She looked out the window. It was snowing.

"Wish I was home," she said. "It's cold and I aint got nothing but my shawl. It's a long walk."

"Do you have to come back to this neighbourhood again tomorrow morning?"

"Six o'clock. It's still dark then."

"You can stay here if you like, Sien. I'd be glad to have company."

"Won't I be in your way?"

"Not a bit. It's a wide bed."

"Can two sleep there?"

"Easily."

"Then I'll stay."

"Good."

"It's nice of you to ask me, Vincent."

"It's nice of you to stay."

In the morning she fixed him coffee, made the bed, and swept out the studio. Then she left him to go to her tubs. The place seemed suddenly empty when she was gone.

5

Tersteeg looked in again that afternoon. His eyes were bright and his cheeks red from the walk in the glowing cold.

"How does it go, Vincent?"

"Very well, Mijnheer Tersteeg. It is good of you to come again."

"Perhaps you have something interesting to show me? That is what I came for."

"Yes, I have some new things. Won't you sit down?"

Tersteeg looked at the chair, reached for his kerchief to dust it off, and then decided it might not be good manners. He sat down. Vincent brought him three or four small water-colours. Tersteeg glanced at them all hurriedly, as though he were skimming a long letter, then went back to the first and studied it.

"You're coming along," he said after a time. "These aren't right yet, they're a bit crude, but you show progress. You should have something for me to buy very soon, Vincent."

"Yes, Mijnheer."

"You must think about earning your living, my boy. It is not right to live on another man's money."

Vincent took the water-colours and looked at them. He supposed they were crude, but like every other artist, he was unable to see the imperfections in his own work.

"I would like nothing better than to support myself, Mijnheer."

"Then you must work harder. You must speed things up. I would like to have you do some things soon that I can buy."

"Yes, Mijnheer."

"At any event, I am glad to see you happy and at work. Theo has asked me to keep an eye on you. Do some good work, Vincent; I want to establish you in the Plaats."

"I try to make good things. But my hand doesn't always obey my will. However, Mauve complimented me on one of these."

"What did he say?"

"He said, 'It almost begins to look like a water-colour.'"

Tersteeg laughed, wrapped his wool scarf about his neck, said, "Plug on, Vincent, plug on; that is how great pictures are produced," and was gone.

Vincent had written to his Uncle Cor that he was established in The Hague, and had invited his uncle to visit him. Uncle Cor came often to The Hague to buy supplies and pictures for his art shop, which was the most important one in Amsterdam. One Sunday afternoon Vincent gave a party for some children with whom he had become acquainted. He had to keep them amused while he sketched, so he bought a bag of sweets and told them stories as he bent over his drawing board. When he heard a sharp knock on the door and a deep, booming voice, he knew that his uncle had arrived.

Cornelius Marinus Van Gogh was well known, successful and wealthy. For all that, there was a touch of melancholy about his wide, dark eyes. His mouth was a little less full than the other Van Gogh mouths. He had the family head; square across the wide, high brow, square across the strong jawbones, with a huge, rounded chin and a powerful nose.

Cornelius Marinus took in every last detail of the studio while giving the impression that he had not even glanced at it. He had probably seen the inside of more artists' studios than any man in Holland.

Vincent gave the children the rest of the sweets and sent them home. "Will you have a cup of tea with me, Uncle Cor? It must be very cold out."

"Thank you, Vincent."

Vincent served him and marvelled at how unconcernedly his uncle balanced the cup on his knee while chatting lightly about news of the day.

"So you are going to be an artist, Vincent," he said. "It's about time we had one in the Van Gogh family. Hein and Vincent and I have been buying canvases from strangers for the past thirty years. Now we'll be able to keep a little of the money in the family!"

Vincent smiled. "I have a running start," he said, "with three uncles and a brother in the picture selling business. Will you have a bit of cheese and bread, Uncle Cor? Perhaps you're hungry?"

C.M. knew that the easiest way to insult a poor artist was to refuse his food. "Yes, thank you," he said. "I had an early breakfast."

Vincent put several slices of thick, black bread on a chipped plate and then took out some coarse cheese from a paper. C.M. made an effort to eat a little.

"Tersteeg tells me that Theo is sending you a hundred francs a month?"

"Yes."

"Theo is young, and he should save his money. You ought to be earning your own bread."

Vincent's gorge was still high from what Tersteeg had said on the subject only the day before. He answered quickly, without thinking.

"Earn bread, Uncle Cor? How do you mean that? Earn bread . . . or deserve bread? Not to deserve one's bread, that is to say, to be unworthy of it, that certainly is a crime, for every honest man is worthy of his bread. But unluckily, not being able to earn it, though deserving it, that is a misfortune, and a great one."

He toyed with the black bread before him, rolling a piece of the inside into a round, hard pill.

"So if you say to me, Uncle Cor, 'You are unworthy of your bread,' you insult me. But if you make the rather just remark that I do not earn it always, that certainly is so. But what is the use in making the remark? It certainly does not get me any farther, if you say no more than that."

C.M. spoke no more about earning bread. They got along pleasantly enough until, quite by chance, Vincent mentioned the name of De Groux in speaking about expression.

"But don't you know, Vincent," said C.M., "that in private life De Groux has no good reputation?"

Vincent could not sit there and hear that said of the brave Father De Groux. He knew it would be far better to "Yes" his uncle, but he never seemed able to find a "Yes" when he was with the Van Goghs.

"It has always seemed to me, Uncle Cor, that when an artist shows his work to the public he has the right to keep to himself the inward struggle of his own private life, which is directly and fatally connected with the peculiar difficulties involved in producing a work of art."

"Just the same," said C.M., sipping the tea for which Vincent had offered him no sugar, "the mere fact that a man works with a paint brush, instead of a plough or a salesbook, does not give him the right to live licentiously. I don't think we ought to buy the pictures of artists who don't behave properly."

"I think it even more improper for a critic to dig up a man's private life, when his work is beyond reproach. The work of an artist and his private life are like a woman in childbirth and her baby. You may look at the child, but you may not lift her chemise to see if it is blood-stained. That would be very indelicate."

C.M. had just put a small bit of bread and cheese into his mouth. He spit it out hastily into the cup of his hand, rose, and flung it into the stove.

"Well, well," he commented. "Well well well well!"

Vincent was afraid that C.M. was going to be angry, but luckily things took a turn for the better. Vincent brought out his portfolio of smaller sketches and studies. He placed a chair by the light for his uncle. C.M. did not say anything at first, but when he came to a little drawing of the Paddemoes as seen from the peat market, that Vincent had sketched at twelve o'clock one night while strolling about with Breitner, he stopped.

"This is rather good," he remarked. "Could you make me more of these views of the city?"

"Yes, I make them for a change sometimes when I am tired of working from the model. I have some more. Would you care to see them?"

He leaned over his uncle's shoulder and searched through the uneven papers. "This is the Vleersteeg . . . this the Geest. This one is the fish market."

"Will you make twelve of them for me?"

"Yes, but this is business, so we must set a price."

"Very well, how much do you ask?"

"I have fixed the price for a small drawing of this size, either in pencil or pen, at two-francs-fifty. Do you think that unreasonable?"

C.M. had to smile to himself. It was such a humble sum.

"No, but if they turn out well, I will ask you to make twelve of Amsterdam. Then I shall fix the price myself so that you will get a little more for them."

"Uncle Cor, this is my first order! I can't tell you how happy it makes me!"

"We all want to help you, Vincent. Just bring your work up to standard, and between us we'll buy everything you make." He took up his hat and gloves. "Give my compliments to Theo when you write."

Intoxicated with his success, Vincent snatched up his new water-colour and ran all the way to the Uileboomen. Jet answered the door. She seemed rather worried.

"I wouldn't go into the studio if I were you, Vincent. Anton is in a state."

"What's the trouble? Is he ill?"

Jet sighed. "The usual thing."

"Then I don't suppose he'll want to see me."

"You'd better wait until another time, Vincent. I'll tell him you were here. When he calms down a bit he'll come round to see you."

"You won't forget to tell him?"

"I won't forget."

Vincent waited many days, but Mauve did not come. In his place came Tersteeg, not once but twice. Each time the report was the same.

"Yes, yes, you have made a little progress, perhaps. But they are not right yet. I still could not sell them in the Plaats. I'm afraid you don't work hard enough or fast enough, Vincent."

"My dear Mijnheer, I get up at five o'clock and work until eleven and twelve at night. The only time I stop is for a bite of food now and then."

Tersteeg shook his head uncomprehendingly. He looked at the water-colours again. "I don't understand it. The same element of roughness and crudeness that I saw the first time you came to the Plaats is still in your work. You ought to be getting over that by now. Hard work usually does it, if a man has any ability at all."

"Hard work!" said Vincent.

"Goodness knows I want to buy your things, Vincent. I want to see you begin earning your own living. I don't think it right that Theo should have to . . . But I can't buy until your work is right, now can I? You're not looking for charity."

"No."

"You must hurry, that's all, you must hurry. You must begin to sell and make your own living."

When Tersteeg repeated this formula for the fourth time Vincent wondered if the man were playing some game on him. "You must earn your own living . . . but I can't buy anything!" How in the devil was he going to earn his living if no one would buy?

He met Mauve on the street one day. Mauve was walking at a furious clip with his head down, going nowhere, shoving his right shoulder out in front of him as he walked. He almost seemed not to recognize Vincent.

"I have not seen you for a long time, Cousin Mauve."

"I've been busy." Mauve's voice was cool, indifferent.

"I know; the new canvas. How is it coming?"

"Oh . . ." He made a vague gesture.

"May I drop into your studio some time for a moment? I'm afraid I'm not making progress with my water-colours."

"Not now! I'm busy, I tell you. I can't be wasting my time."

"Won't you come in to see me some time when you're out for a walk? Just a few words from you would set me right."

"Perhaps, perhaps, but I'm busy now. I must be going!"

He darted forward, thrusting his body before him, nervously propelling himself down the street. Vincent stood staring after him.

What in the world had happened? Had he insulted his cousin? Had he in some way estranged him?

He was utterly amazed a few days later to have Weissenbruch walk into his studio. Weissenbruch never bothered with the younger painters, or for that matter the accepted ones, except to give their work a hearty damning now and then.

"Well, well," he said, looking about, "this certainly is a palace. You'll be doing portraits of the King and Queen here pretty soon."

"If you don't like it," growled Vincent, "you can get out."

"Why don't you give up painting, Van Gogh? It's a dog's life."

"You seem to thrive under it."

"Yes, but I'm successful. You'll never be."

"Perhaps not. But I'll paint far better pictures than you ever will."

Weissenbruch laughed. "You won't, but you'll probably come closer to it than anyone in The Hague. If your work is anything like your personality . . ."

"Why didn't you say so?" demanded Vincent, taking out his portfolio. "Want to sit down?"

"I can't see when I'm sitting."

He pushed the water-colours aside with a "This is not your medium; water-colours are too insipid for the things you've got to say," and concentrated on the pencil sketches of the Borains, the Brabantines, and the old people Vincent had drawn since coming to The Hague. He chuckled to himself gaily as he gazed at one figure after another. Vincent prepared for a stiff volley of abuse.

"You draw confoundedly well, Vincent," said Weissenbruch, his sharp eyes twinkling. "I could work from these drawings myself!"

Vincent had set himself to catch a heavy weight; Weissenbruch's words were so light they almost broke his back. He sat down abruptly.

"I thought you were called the 'merciless sword.' "

"So I am. If I saw no good in your studies, I would tell you so."

"Tersteeg has scolded me about them. He says they are too rough and crude."

"Nonsense! That's where their strength lies."

"I want to go on with those pen sketches, but Tersteeg says I must learn to see things as water-colours."

"So they can sell, eh? No, my boy, if you see things as pen drawings, you must put them down as pen drawings. And above all, never listen to anybody — not even me. Go your own way."

"It looks like I'll have to."

"When Mauve said you were a born painter, Tersteeg said no, and then Mauve took your part against him. I was there. If it happens again, I will take your part also, now that I have seen your work."

"Mauve said I was a born painter?"

"Don't let that turn your head. You'll be lucky if you die one."

"Then why has he been so cool to me?"

"He treats everyone the same, Vincent, when he's finishing a picture. Don't let it worry you; when the Scheveningen canvas is done he'll come round. In the meanwhile you may drop in at my studio if you want any help."

"May I ask you one question, Weissenbruch?"

"Yes."

"Did Mauve send you here?"

"Yes."

"Why did he do that?"

"He wanted to hear my opinion about your work."

"But why should he want that? If he thinks I'm a born . . . "

"I don't know. Perhaps Tersteeg put a doubt in his mind about you."

6

If Tersteeg was losing faith in him and Mauve was growing cooler every day, Christine was taking their place, and bringing into his life the simple companionship for which he longed. She came to the studio early every morning, and brought with her a sewing basket so that her hands might keep company with his. Her voice was rough and her choice of words unfortunate, but she spoke quietly, and Vincent found it easy not to hear her when he wanted to concentrate. For the most part, she was content to sit quietly by the stove, looking out the window or sewing little things for the new baby. She was a clumsy model and learned slowly, but she was eager to please. She soon fell into the habit of preparing his dinner before she went home.

"You mustn't bother about that, Sien," he told her.

"It aint no bother. I can do it better than you."

"Then of course you'll join me?"

"Sure. Mother's taking care of the kids. I like to stay here."

Vincent gave her a franc every day. He knew it was more than he could afford, but he liked her company; the thought that he was saving her from the tubs pleased him. Sometimes, if he had to go out during the afternoon, he would sketch her until late at night, and then she would not bother to go home at all. He enjoyed waking to the smell of fresh coffee and the sight of a friendly woman hovering over the stove. It was the first time he had ever had a *menage;* he found it very comfortable.

Sometimes Christine would stay over for no reason at all. "I think I'll sleep here tonight, Vincent," she would say. "Can I?"

"Of course, Sien. Stay as often as you like. You know I'm glad to have you."

Although he never asked her to do anything, she acquired the habit of washing his linen, mending his clothes, and doing his little marketing.

"You don't know how to take care of yourselves, you men," she said. "You need a woman around. And I'm sure they cheat you at the market."

She was by no means a good housekeeper; the many years of sloth in her mother's house had destroyed most of the will to cleanliness and order. She took care of things sporadically, in sudden bursts of energy and determination. It was the first time she was keeping house for anyone she liked, and she enjoyed doing things . . . when she remembered them. Vincent was dellghted to find that she wanted to do anything at all; he never even thought of reproving her. Now that she was no longer dead tired day and night, her voice lost some of its roughness: the vile words dropped out of her vocabulary one by one. She had learned to exercise very little control over her emotions, and when something displeased her, she would fly into a passionate rage, dropping back into her rough voice and using obscene words that Vincent had not heard since he was a young boy at school.

At such moments he saw Christine as a caricature of himself; he sat by quietly until the storm subsided. Christine was equally tolerant. When his drawing went all wrong, or she forgot everything he had taught her and posed awkwardly, he would burst into a fit of rage that fairly shook the walls. She let him speak his piece; in a very few moments calm was restored. Fortunately they never became angry at identical moments.

After he had sketched her often enough to become familiar with the lines of her body, he decided to do a real study. It was a sentence from Michelet that set him on the track: *Comment se fait-il qu'il ait sur la terre une femme seule désespérée?* He posed Christine naked on a low block of wood near the stove. He turned the block of wood into a tree stump, put in a little vegetation, and transposed the scene to the out-of-doors. Then he drew Christine, gnarled hands on her knees, the face buried in the scraggy arms, the thin hair covering the spine a short way down, the bulbous breasts drooping to meet the lean shanks, the flat feet insecurely on the ground. He called it *Sorrow*. It was the picture of a woman from whom had been squeezed all the juice of life. Under it he wrote the line from Michelet.

The study took a week and exhausted his supply of money; there were still ten days to go until the first of March. There was enough black bread in the house to last for two or three days. He would have to stop working from the model altogether and that would set him back some more.

"Sien," he said, "I'm afraid I can't have you any more until after the first of the month."

"What's the matter?"

"I have no more money."

"You mean for me?"

"Yes."

"I aint got nothing else to do. I'll come anyway."

"But you must have money, Sien."

"I can get some."

"You can't do any washing, if you're here all day."

" . . . well . . . don't worry . . . I'll get some."

He let her come for three more days, until his bread ran out. It was still a week to the first. He told Sien that he was going to Amsterdam to visit his uncle and that he would call at her house when he got back. He did some copying in his studio for three days on water without feeling much pain. On the third afternoon he went to De Bock's, hoping to be served tea and cake.

"Hello, old fellow," said De Bock, standing at his easel, "make yourself comfortable. I'm going to work straight through until my dinner engagement. There are some magazines over on the table. Just dig in."

But not a word about tea.

He knew Mauve would not see him, and he was ashamed to beg from Jet. He would rather have died of starvation than ask Tersteeg for anything after the latter had spoken against him to Mauve. No matter how desperate he became, it never occurred to him that he might earn a few francs at some craft other than his own. His old foe the fever came up, his knees developed rickets and he stayed in bed. Though he knew it was impossible, he kept hoping for the miracle that would send Theo's hundred francs a few days early. Theo did not get paid until the first.

Christine walked in the afternoon of the fifth day without knocking. Vincent was asleep. She stood over him, looking at the furrowed lines in his face, the paleness of the skin under his red beard, the parchment roughness of his lips. She placed a hand lightly on his forehead and felt the fever. She searched the shelf on which the supplies were usually kept. She saw that there was not a crumb of dry, black bread or a lone bean of coffee. She went out.

About an hour later Vincent began having dreams of his mother's kitchen in Etten and the beans she used to prepare for him. He awakened to find Christine mixing things in pots over the stove.

"Sien," he said.

She went over to the bed and put her cool hand on his cheek; the red beard was on fire. "Don't be proud no more," she said. "And don't tell no more lies. If we're poor, it aint our fault. We got to help each other. Didn't you help me the first night we met down the wine cellar?"

"Sien," he said.

"Now you lay there. I went home and got some potatoes and string beans. They're all ready."

She mashed the potatoes on the plate, put some green beans alongside, sat on his bed and fed him. "Why did you give me your money every day if you didn't have enough? It aint no good if you go hungry."

He could have stood the privation until Theo's money arrived, even if it had been weeks. It was always the unexpected piece of kindness that broke his back. He decided to see Tersteeg. Christine washed his shirt, but there was no iron to smooth it with. The next morning she gave him a little breakfast of bread and coffee. He set out to walk to the Plaats. One heel was off his muddy boots, his trousers were patched and dirty. Theo's coat was many sizes too small. He had an old necktie askew at the left side of his neck. On his head was one of the outlandish caps that he had a perfect genius for picking up, no one knew where.

He walked along the Ryn railroad tracks, skirted the edge of the woods and the station where the steam cars left for Scheveningen, and made for town. The feeble sun made him sensitive to his own anaemia. At the Plein he caught sight of himself in the window glass of a shop. In one of his rare moments of clarity he saw himself as the people of The Hague saw him: a dirty, unkempt tramp, belonging nowhere, wanted by no one, ill, weak, uncouth and *déclassé*.

The Plaats opened on a broad triangle to meet the Hof-vijvet alongside of the castle. Only the richest shops could afford to keep establishments there. Vincent was afraid to venture into the sacred triangle. He had never before realized how many millions of miles of caste he had put between himself and the Plaats.

The clerks in Goupils were dusting. They stared at him with unabashed curiosity. This man's family controlled the art world of Europe. Why did he go about so foully?

Tersteeg was at his desk in the upstairs office. He was opening mail with a jade handled paper knife. He noticed Vincent's small, circular ears that came below the line of his eyebrows, the oval of his face that tapered down through the jaws and then flattened out at the square chin, the head that was going smooth of hair above the left eye, the green-blue eyes that stared through him so probingly and yet without comment, the full, red mouth made redder by the beard and moustache in which it was set. He could never make up his mind whether he thought Vincent's face and head ugly or beautiful.

"You're the first customer in the shop this morning, Vincent," he said. "What can I do for you?"

Vincent explained his predicament.

"What have you done with your allowance?"

"I've spent it."

"If you have been improvident, you can't expect me to encourage you. There are thirty days to each month; you should not spend more than the proper share each day."

"I have not been improvident. Most of the money has gone for models."

"Then you should not hire them. You can work more cheaply by yourself."

"To work without models is the ruin of a painter of the figure."

"Don't paint figures. Do cows and sheep. You don't have to pay them."

"I can't draw cows and sheep, Mijnheer, if I don't feel cows and sheep."

"You ought not to be drawing people, anyway; you can't sell those sketches. You ought to be doing water-colours and nothing else."

"Water-colour is not my medium."

"I think your drawing is a kind of narcotic which you take in order not to feel the pain it costs you not to be able to make water-colours."

There was a silence. Vincent could think of no possible answer to this.

"De Bock doesn't use models, and he's wealthy. Yet I think you will agree with me that his canvases are splendid; the prices are going up steadily. I have been waiting for you to get some of his charm into your work. But somehow it doesn't come. I am really disappointed, Vincent; your work remains uncouth and amateurish. Of one thing I am sure, you are no artist."

Vincent's cutting hunger of the past five days suddenly severed the sinews in his knees. He sat down weakly on one of the hand carved Italian chairs. His voice was lost somewhere in his empty bowels, and he could not find it.

"Why do you say that to me, Mijnheer?" he asked, after a pause.

Tersteeg took out a spotless handkerchief, wiped his nose, the corners of his mouth, and his chin beard. "Because I owe it to both you and your family. You ought to know the truth. There is still time for you to save yourself, Vincent, if you act quickly. You are not cut out to be an artist; you ought to find your right niche in life. I never make a mistake about painters."

"I know," said Vincent.

"One great objection for me is that you started too late. If you had begun as a boy, you might have developed some quality in your work by now. But you are thirty, Vincent, and you ought to be successful. I was at your age. How can you ever hope to succeed if you have no talent? And worse yet, how can you justify yourself in taking charity from Theo?"

"Mauve once said to me, 'Vincent, when you draw you are a painter.' "

"Mauve is your cousin; he was being kind to you. I am your friend, and believe me, my kindness is of the better sort. Give it up before you find that your whole life has slipped out from under you. Some day, when you have found your real work and are successful, you will come back to thank me."

"Mijnheer Tersteeg, I have not had a centime in my pocket for a piece of bread in five days. But I would not ask you for money if it were only for myself. I have a model, a poor, sick woman. I have not been able to pay her the money I owe. She needs it. I beg you to lend me ten guilders until the money arrives from Theo. I will pay it back."

Tersteeg rose and stared out the window at the swans in the pond, all that was left of the original court water works. He wondered why Vincent had come to The Hague to settle, when his uncles owned art shops in Amsterdam, Rotterdam, Brussels, and Paris.

"You think it would be a favour if I lent you ten guilders," he said without turning about, his hands clasped behind his Prince Albert coat, "But I'm not sure that it wouldn't be a greater favour to refuse you."

Vincent knew how Sien had earned the money for those potatoes and string beans. He could not let her go on supporting him.

"Mijnheer Tersteeg, no doubt you are right. I am no artist and I have no ability. It would be very unwise for you to encourage me with money. I must begin earning my own living immediately and find my niche in life. But for the sake of our old friendship I ask you to lend me ten guilders."

Tersteeg took a wallet from the inside of his Prince Albert, searched for a ten guilder note, and handed it to Vincent without a word.

"Thank you," said Vincent. "You are very kind."

As he walked home along the well-kept streets with the neat little brick houses speaking to him eloquently of security, comfort, and peace, he murmured to himself,

"One cannot always be friends; one must quarrel sometimes. But for six months I will not go to see Tersteeg again, or speak to him, or show him my work."

He dropped in at De Bock's to find out just what this salable thing was, this charm that De Bock had, but he had not. De Bock was sitting with his feet up on a chair, reading an English novel.

"Hello," he said, "I'm in the doldrums. Can't draw a line. Pull up a chair and amuse me. Is it too early in the morning for a cigar? Have you heard any good stories lately?"

"Let me see some of your canvases again, will you, De Bock? I want to find out why your work sells and mine doesn't."

"Talent, old fellow, talent," said De Bock, getting up lazily. "It's a gift. Either you have it or you haven't. I couldn't tell you what it is myself, and I paint the blasted things."

He brought in half a dozen canvases still on their frames, and chatted lightly about them while Vincent sat there, poking holes through the thin paint and thin sentiment with burning eyes.

"Mine are better," he said to himself. "Mine are truer, deeper. I say more with a carpenter's pencil than he says with a whole paint box. What he expresses is obvious. When he gets all through he has said nothing. Why do they give him praise and money and refuse me the price of black bread and coffee?"

When he made his escape, Vincent murmured to himself, "There is a consumptive atmosphere in that house. There is something blasé and insincere about De Bock that oppresses me. Millet was right: *'J'aimerais mieux ne rien dire que de m'exprimer faiblement.'*

"De Bock can keep his charm and his money. I'll take my life of reality and hardship. That is not the road on which one perishes."

He found Christine mopping the wooden floor of the studio with a wet rag. Her hair was tied up in a black kerchief and a faint dew of perspiration glistened in the pock holes of her face.

"Did you get the money?" she asked, looking up from the floor.

"Yes. Ten francs."

"Aint it wonderful to have rich friends?"

"Yes. Here are the six francs I owe you."

Sien got up and wiped her face on the black apron.

"You can't give me nothing now," she said. "Not 'till your brother sends that money. Four francs won't help you much."

"I can get along, Sien. You need this money."

"So do you. Tell you what we'll do. I'll stay here 'till you get a letter from your brother. We'll eat out of the ten francs like it belonged to both of us. I can make it last longer than you."

"What about the posing? I won't be able to pay you anything for that."

"You'll give me my bed and board. Aint that enough? I'm glad enough to stay here where it's warm and I don't got to go to work and make myself sick."

Vincent took her in his arms and smoothed back the thin, coarse hair from her forehead.

"Sien, sometimes you almost perform a miracle. You almost make me believe there is a God!"

7

About a week later he went to call on Mauve. His cousin admitted him to the studio but threw a cloth over his Scheveningen canvas hastily before Vincent could see it.

"What is it you want?" he asked, as though he did not know.

"I've brought a few water-colours. I thought you might be able to spare a little time."

Mauve was cleaning a bunch of brushes with nervous, preoccupied movements. He had not been into his bedroom for three days. The broken snatches of sleep he had managed on the studio couch had not refreshed him.

"I'm not always in a mood to show you things, Vincent. Sometimes I am too tired and then you must for goodness sake await a better moment."

"I'm sorry, Cousin Mauve," said Vincent, going to the door. "I didn't mean to disturb you. Perhaps I may drop in tomorrow evening?"

Mauve had taken the cloth off his easel and did not even hear him.

When Vincent returned the following evening, he found Weissenbruch there. Mauve was verging on hysterical exhaustion. He seized upon Vincent's entrance to amuse himself and his friend.

"Weissenbruch," he cried, "this is how he looks."

He went off into one of his clever impersonations, screwing up his face in rough lines and sticking his chin forward eagerly to look like Vincent. It was a good caricature. He walked over to Weissenbruch, peered up at him through half shut eyes and said, "This is the way he speaks." He went off into a nervous sputtering of words in the rough voice that often came out of Vincent. Weissenbruch howled.

"Oh, perfect, perfect," he cried. "This is how others see you, Van Gogh. Did you know you were such a beautiful animal? Mauve, stick your chin out that way again and scratch your beard. It's really killing."

Vincent was stunned. He shrank into a corner. A voice came out of him that he did not recognize as his own. "If you had spent rainy nights on the streets of London, or cold nights in the open of the Borinage, hungry, homeless, feverish, you would also have ugly lines in your face, and a husky voice!"

After a few moments, Weissenbruch left. As soon as he was gone from the room, Mauve stumbled to a chair. The reaction from his little debauch made him quite weak. Vincent stood perfectly still in the corner; at last Mauve noticed him.

"Oh, are you still here?" he said.

"Cousin Mauve," said Vincent impetuously, screwing up his face in the manner that Mauve had just caricatured, "what has happened between us? Only tell me what I have done. Why do you treat me this way?"

Mauve got up wearily and pushed the swash of hair straight upward.

"I do not approve of you, Vincent. You ought to be earning your own living. And you ought not go about disgracing the Van Gogh name by begging money from everyone."

Vincent thought a moment and then said, "Has Tersteeg been to see you?"

"No."

"Then you don't care to teach me any more?"

"No."

"Very well, let us shake hands and not feel any bitterness or animosity toward each other. Nothing could ever alter my feeling of gratitude and obligation to you."

Mauve did not answer for a long time. Then he said, "Do not take it to heart, Vincent. I am tired and ill. I will help you all I can. Have you some sketches with you?"

"Yes. But this is hardly the time . . . "

"Show them to me."

He studied them with red eyes and remarked, "Your drawing is wrong. Dead wrong. I wonder that I never saw it before."

"You once told me that when I drew, I was a painter."

"I mistook crudity for strength. If you really want to learn, you will have to begin all over again at the beginning. There are some plaster casts over in the corner by the coal bin. You can work on them now if you like."

Vincent walked to the corner in a daze. He sat down before a white plaster foot. For a long time he was unable to think or move. He drew some sketching paper from his pocket. He could not draw a single line. He turned about and looked at Mauve standing before his easel.

"How is it coming, Cousin Mauve?"

Mauve flung himself on the little divan, his bloodshot eyes closing instantly. "Tersteeg said today that it's the best thing I've done."

After a few moments, Vincent remarked aloud, "Then it was Tersteeg!"

Mauve was snoring lightly and did not hear him.

After a time the pain numbed a little. He began sketching the plaster foot. When his cousin awoke a few hours later, Vincent had seven complete drawings. Mauve jumped up like a cat, just as though he had never been asleep, and darted to Vincent's side.

"Let me see," he said. "Let me see."

He looked at the seven sketches and kept repeating, "No! No! No!"

He tore them all up and flung the pieces on the floor. "The same crudity, the same amateurishness! Can't you draw that cast the way it looks? Are you unable to make a positive statement about a line? Can't you make an exact duplicate for once in your life?"

"You sound like a teacher at a drawing academy, Cousin Mauve."

"If you had gone to more academies, you might know how to draw by now. Do that foot over again. And see if you can make it a foot!"

He went through the garden into the kitchen to get something to eat, and returned to work on his canvas by lamplight. The hours of the night went by. Vincent drew foot after foot. The more he drew, the more he detested the poisonous piece of plaster sitting before him. When dawn sneaked gloomily in the north window, he had a great number of copies before him. He rose, cramped and sick at heart. Once again Mauve looked at his sketches and crumpled them in his hand.

"They're no good," he said, "no good at all. You violate every elemental rule of drawing. Here, go home and take this foot with you. Draw it over and over and over again. And don't come back until you get it right!"

"I'll be damned if I will!" shouted Vincent.

He flung the foot into the coal bin, shattering it to a thousand pieces. "Do not speak to me again about plaster, for I cannot stand it. I will draw from casts only when there are no more hands and feet of living people to draw from."

"If that's the way you feel about it," said Mauve icily.

"Cousin Mauve, I will not allow myself to be governed by a cold system, yours or anyone else's. I've got to express things according to my own temperament and character. I must draw things the way I see them, not the way you see them!"

"I care to have nothing more to do with you," said Mauve in the tone of a doctor speaking to a corpse.

When Vincent awoke at noon, he found Christine in the studio with her eldest son, Herman. He was a pale faced child of ten with fish-green, frightened eyes and a negligible chin. Christine had given him a piece of paper and pencil to keep him quiet. He had not been taught to read or write. He came to Vincent shyly, for he was wary of strangers. Vincent showed him how to hold the pencil and draw a cow. He was delighted and soon became friendly. Christine put out a little bread and cheese, and the three of them lunched at the table.

Vincent thought of Kay and beautiful little Jan. A lump arose in his throat.

"I aint feeling so good today, so you can draw Herman instead."

"What's the matter, Sien?"

"I dunno. My insides is all twisted."

"Have you felt like this with all the other children?"

"I been sick, but not like this. This is worse."

"You must see a doctor."

"It aint no use seeing the doctor at the free ward. He only gives me medicine. Medicine don't do no good."

"You ought to go to the state hospital at Leyden."

" . . . I guess I ought."

"It's only a short ride on the train. I'll take you there tomorrow morning. People go from all over Holland to that hospital."

"They say it's good."

Christine stayed in bed all day. Vincent sketched the boy. At dinner time he walked Herman home to Christine's mother and left him. Early in the morning they took the train to Leyden.

"Of course you've been feeling sick," said the doctor after he had examined Christine and asked her innumerable questions. "The child is not in position."

"Can anything be done, doctor?" asked Vincent.

"Oh, yes, we can operate."

"Would that be serious?"

"Not at this time. The child would simply have to be turned with the forceps. However, that takes a little money. Not for the operation, but for the hospital expenses." He turned to Christine. "Have you anything saved up?"

"Not a franc."

The doctor almost allowed himself a sigh. "That's usually the way," he said.

"How much would it cost, doctor?" asked Vincent.

"Not more than fifty francs."

"And if she doesn't have the operation?"

"There's not a chance in the world of her pulling through."

Vincent thought for a moment. The twelve water-colours for his Uncle Cor were almost done; that would be thirty francs. He would take the other twenty francs off Theo's April allowance.

"I'll take care of the money, doctor," he said.

"Good. Bring her back on Saturday morning, and I'll operate myself. Now just one thing more; I don't know what the relationship is between you two and I don't care to be told. That's not part of the doctor's business. But I think you ought to be informed that if this little lady ever goes back to walking the streets, she will be dead within six months."

"She'll never return to that life, doctor. I give you my word."

"Splendid. Then I'll see you on Saturday morning."

A few days later Tersteeg came in. "I see you are still at it," he said.

"Yes, I am at work."

"I received the ten francs you sent back in the mail. You might at least have come in to thank me for the loan personally."

"It was a long walk, Mijnheer, and the weather was bad."

"The walk was not too long when you wanted the money, eh?"

Vincent did not answer.

"It is just such lack of manners, Vincent, that turns me against you. It is why I have no faith in you and cannot buy your work."

Vincent sat himself on the edge of the table and prepared for another struggle. "I should think that your buying would be a thing quite apart from personal disputes and differences," he said. "I should think it would depend not on me but on my work. It is not exactly fair to let personal antipathy influence your judgment."

"Certainly not. If you could only make something salable, with some charm in it, I would be only too glad to sell it in the Plaats."

"Mijnheer Tersteeg, work on which one has plodded hard and into which one has put some character and sentiment, is neither unattractive nor unsalable. I think it is perhaps better for my work not to try to please everyone at first."

Tersteeg sat down without unbuttoning his topcoat or taking off his gloves. He sat with both hands resting on the knob of his cane.

"You know, Vincent, I sometimes suspect that you prefer not to sell; that you would much rather live off someone else."

"I would be very happy to sell a drawing, but I am happier still when a real artist like Weissenbruch says about a piece of work which you call unsalable, 'That is true to nature; I could work from that myself.' Although money is of great value to me, especially now, the principal thing is for me to make something serious."

"That might apply to a rich man like De Bock, but it certainly does not apply to you."

"The fundamentals of painting, my dear Mijnheer, have very little to do with a man's income."

Tersteeg put his stick across his knees and leaned back in his chair. "Your parents have written to me, Vincent, and asked me to do what I can to help you. Very well. If I cannot in full conscience buy your drawings I can at least give you a little practical advice. You are ruining yourself by going about in those unspeakable rags. You must buy yourself some new clothes and try to keep up appearances. You forget that you are a Van Gogh. Again, you should try to associate with the better people of The Hague, and not always go about with working people and the lower classes. You somehow have a penchant for the sordid and ugly; you have been seen in the most questionable of places and with the most questionable of companions. How can you ever hope to arrive at success if you behave that way?"

Vincent got off the corner of the table and stood over Tersteeg. If there was any chance to win back the man's friendship, this was the time and place. He searched about within himself to find a soft and sympathetic voice.

"Mijnheer, it is good of you to try to help me, and I will answer as sincerely and truthfully as I know how. How can I dress better when I have not a single franc to spare for clothes, and no way of earning one?

"To stroll on wharves, and in alleys and markets, in waiting rooms and even saloons, that is not a pleasant pastime, *except for an artist!* As such, one would rather be in the dirtiest place, where there is something to draw, than at a tea party with charming ladies. The searching for subjects, the living among working people, the drawing from nature on the very spot is a rough work, even a dirty work at times. The manners and dress of a salesman are not suitable for me, or for anyone else who does not have to talk with fine ladies and rich gentlemen to sell them expensive things and make money.

"My place is drawing diggers in a hole on the Geest, as I have been doing all day. There, my ugly face and shabby coat perfectly harmonize with the surroundings, and I am myself and work with pleasure. When I wear a fine coat, the working people I want to sketch are afraid of me and distrust me. The purpose of my drawing is to make people see things worth observing and which not everyone knows. If I sometimes have to sacrifice social manners to get my work done, am I not justified? Do I lower myself by living with the people I draw? Do I lower myself when I go into the houses of labourers and poor people, and when I receive them in my studio? I think my profession requires it. Is that what you call ruining myself?"

"You are very headstrong, Vincent, and will not listen to older men who can help you. You failed before, and you will fail again. It will be the same story all over."

"I have a draftsman's fist, Mijnheer Tersteeg, and I cannot stop drawing no matter how much you advise me! I ask you, since the day I began to draw, have I ever doubted or hesitated or wavered? I think you know quite well that I pushed onward, and that little by little I am growing stronger in the battle."

"Perhaps. But you are battling for a lost cause."

He rose, buttoned the glove on his wrist, and placed the high silk hat on his head. "Mauve and I will take care that you do not receive any more money from Theo. That is the only way to bring you around to your senses."

Vincent felt something crash in his breast. If they attacked him from the side of Theo, he was lost.

"My God!" he cried. "Why should you do this to me? What have I done to you that you should want to destroy me? Is it honest to kill a man just because he differs from your opinions? Can't you let me go my own way? I promise never to bother you again. My brother is the only soul I have left in the world. How can you take him from me?"

"It is for your own good, Vincent," said Tersteeg, and went out.

Vincent grabbed up his money purse and ran all the way downtown to buy a plaster foot. Jet answered the doorbell at the Uileboomen. She was surprised to see him.

"Anton isn't at home," she said. "He's frightfully angry at you. He said he doesn't ever want to see you again. Oh, Vincent I'm so unhappy that this has happened!"

Vincent put the plaster foot in her hand. "Please give this to Anton," he said, "and tell him that I am deeply sorry."

He turned away and was about to go down the steps when Jet put a sympathetic hand on his shoulder.

"The Scheveningen canvas is finished. Would you care to see it?"

He stood in silence before Mauve's painting, a large picture of a fishing smack being drawn up on the beach by horses. He knew that he was looking at a masterpiece. The horses were nags, poor, ill-treated old nags, black, white and brown; they were standing there, patient and submissive, willing, resigned and quiet. They still had to draw the heavy boat up the last bit of the way; the job was almost finished. They were panting, covered with sweat, but they did not complain. They had got over that long ago, years and years ago. They were resigned to live and work somewhat longer, but if tomorrow they had to go to the skinner, well, be it so, they were ready.

Vincent found a deep, practical philosophy in the picture. It said to him, *"Savoir souffrir sans se plaindre, ça c'est la seule chose pratique, c'est la grande science, la leçon à apprendre, la solution du problème de la vie."*

He walked away from the house, refreshed and ironically amused that the man who struck him the very worst of all blows should be the one to teach him how to bear it with resignation.

8

Christine's operation was successful, but it had to be paid for. Vincent sent off the twelve water-colours to his Uncle Cor and waited for the thirty francs payment. He waited many, many days; Uncle Cor sent the money at his leisure. Since the doctor at Leyden was the same one who was going to deliver Christine, they wished to keep in his good graces. Vincent sent off his last twenty francs many days before the first. The same old story began all over again. First coffee and black bread, then just black bread, then plain water, then fever, exhaustion, and delirium. Christine was eating at home, but there was nothing left over to bring to Vincent. When he reached the end of his rope, he crawled out of bed and floated somehow or other through a burning fog to Weissenbruch's studio.

Weissenbruch had plenty of money but he believed in living austerely. His atelier was four flights up, with a huge skylight on the north. There was nothing in the workshop to distract the man; no books, no magazines, no sofa or comfortable chair, no sketches on the walls, no window to look out of, nothing but the bare implements of his trade. There was not even an extra stool for a guest to sit down; that kept people away.

"Oh, it's you, is it?" he growled, without putting down his brush. He did not mind interrupting people in their own studios, but he was about as hospitable as a trapped lion when anyone bothered him.

Vincent explained what he had come for.

"Oh, no, my boy!" exclaimed Weissenbruch, "You've come to the wrong person, the very last man in the world. I wouldn't lend you a ten centime piece."

"Can't you spare the money?"

"Certainly I can spare it! Do you think I'm a goddam amateur like you and can't sell anything? I've got more money in the bank right now than I can spend in three lifetimes."

"Then why won't you lend me twenty-five francs? I'm desperate! I haven't even a crumb of stale bread in the house."

Weissenbruch rubbed his hands in glee. "Fine! Fine! That's exactly what you need! That's wonderful for you. You may be a painter yet."

Vincent leaned against the bare wall; he did not have the strength to stand up without support. "What is there so wonderful about going hungry?"

"It's the best thing in the world for you, Van Gogh. It will make you suffer."

"Why are you so interested in seeing me suffer?"

Weissenbruch sat on the lone stool, crossed his legs, and pointed a red-tipped brush at Vincent's jaw.

"Because it will make a real artist out of you. The more you suffer, the more grateful you ought to be. That's the stuff out of which first-rate painters are made. An empty stomach is better than a full one, Van Gogh, and a broken heart is better than happiness. Never forget that!"

"That's a lot of rot, Weissenbruch, and you know it."

Weissenbruch made little stabs in Vincent's direction with his brush. "The man who has never been miserable has nothing to paint about, Van Gogh. Happiness is bovine; it's only good for cows and tradesmen. Artists thrive on pain; if you're hungry, discouraged and wretched, be grateful! God is being good to you!"

"Poverty destroys."

"Yes, it destroys the weak. But not the strong! If poverty can destroy you, then you're a weakling and ought to go down."

"And you wouldn't raise a finger to help me?"

"Not even if I thought you the greatest painter of all time. If hunger and pain can kill a man, then he's not worth saving. The only artists who belong on this earth are the men whom neither God nor the devil can kill until they've said everything they want to say."

"But I've gone hungry for years, Weissenbruch. I've gone without a roof over my head, walking in the rain and snow with hardly anything on, ill and feverish and abandoned. I have nothing more to learn from that sort of thing."

"You haven't scratched the surface of suffering yet. You're just a beginner. I tell you, pain is the only infinite thing in this world. Now run on home and pick up your pencil. The hungrier and more miserable you get, the better you will work."

"And the quicker I'll have my drawings rejected."

Weissenbruch laughed heartily. "Of course they'll be rejected! They ought to be. That's good for you, too. It will make you even more miserable. Then your next canvas will be better than the one before. If you starve and suffer and have your work abused and neglected for a sufficient number of years, you may eventually—notice I say you may, not you will—you may eventually turn out one painting that will be fit to hang alongside of Jan Steen or . . . "

" . . . or Weissenbruch!"

"Just so. Or Weissenbruch. If I gave you any money now I would be robbing you of your chances for immortality."

"To hell with immortality! I want to draw here and now. And I can't do that on an empty stomach."

"Nonsense, my boy. Everything of value that has been painted has been done on an empty stomach. When your intestines are full, you create at the wrong end."

"It doesn't seem to me that I've heard about you suffering so much."

"I have creative imagination. I can understand pain without going through it."

"You old fraud!"

"Not at all. If I had seen that my work was insipid, like De Bock's, I would have thrown my money away and lived like a tramp. It just so happens that I can create the perfect illusion of pain without a perfect memory of it. That's why I'm a great artist."

"That's why you're a great humbug. Come along, Weissenbruch, be a good fellow and lend me twenty-five francs."

"Not even twenty-five centimes! I tell you, I'm sincere. I think too highly of you to weaken your fabric by lending you money. You will do brilliant work some day, Vincent, providing you carve out your own destiny; the plaster foot in Mauve's dustbin convinced me of that. Now run along, and stop at the soup kitchen for a bowl of free broth."

Vincent stared at Weissenbruch for a moment, turned and opened the door.

"Wait a minute!" cried Weissenbruch.

"You don't mean to tell me you're going to be a coward and weaken?" asked Vincent harshly.

"Look here, Van Gogh, I'm no miser; I'm acting on principle. If I thought you were a fool, I'd give you twenty-five francs to get rid of you. But I respect you as a fellow craftsman. I'm going to give you something you couldn't buy for all the money in the world. And there's not another man in The Hague, except Mauve, that I'd give it to. Come over here. Adjust that curtain on the skylight. That's better. Have a look at this study. Here's how I'm going to work out the design and apportion my material. For Christ's sake, how do you expect to see it if you stand in the light?"

An hour later Vincent left, exhilarated. He had learned more in that short time than he could have in a year at art school. He walked some distance before he remembered that he was hungry, feverish, and ill, and that he had not a centime in the world.

9

A few days later he encountered Mauve in the dunes. If he had any hopes of a reconciliation, he was disappointed.

"Cousin Mauve, I want to beg your pardon for what happened in your studio. It was stupid of me. Can't you see your way clear to forgive me? Won't you come and see my work some time and talk things over?"

Mauve refused point blank. "I will certainly not come to see you, that is all over."

"Have you lost faith in me so completely?"

"Yes. You have a vicious character."

"If you will tell me what I have done that is vicious, I will try to mend my ways."

"I am no longer interested in what you do."

"I have done nothing but eat and sleep and work as an artist. Is that vicious?"

"Do you call yourself an artist?"

"Yes."

"How absurd. You never sold a picture in your life."

"Is that what being an artist means—selling? I thought it meant one who was always seeking without absolutely finding. I thought it meant the contrary from 'I know it, I have found it.' When I say I am an artist, I only mean 'I am seeking, I am striving, I am in it with all my heart.' "

"Nevertheless, you have a vicious character."

"You suspect me of something—it is in the air—you think I am keeping something back. 'Vincent is hiding something that cannot stand the light!' What is it, Mauve? Speak to me frankly."

Mauve went back to his easel and began applying paint. Vincent turned away and walked slowly over the sand.

He was right. There *was* something in the air. The Hague had learned about his relation to Christine. De Bock was the one to break the news. He blew in with a naughty smile on his bud-like mouth. Christine was posing, so he spoke in English.

"Well, well, Van Gogh," he said, throwing off his heavy black overcoat and lighting a long cigarette. "It's all over town that you've taken a mistress. I heard it from Weissenbruch, Mauve and Tersteeg. The Hague is up in arms about it!"

"Oh," said Vincent, "so that's what it's all about."

"You should be more discreet, old fellow. Is she some model about town? I thought I knew all the available ones."

Vincent glanced over at Christine knitting by the fire. There was a homely sort of attractiveness about her as she sat there, sewing in her merino and apron, her eyes upon the little garment she was making. De Bock dropped his cigarette to the floor and jumped up.

"My God!" he exclaimed, "you don't mean to tell me *that's* your mistress?"

"I have no mistress, De Bock. But I presume that's the woman they're talking about."

De Bock wiped some imaginary perspiration from his forehead and looked Christine over carefully. "How the devil can you bring yourself to sleep with her?"

"Why do you ask that?"

"My dear old chap, she's a hag! The commonest sort of a hag! What can you be thinking about? No wonder Tersteeg was shocked. If you want a mistress, why don't you pick up one of the neat little models about town? There are plenty of them around."

"As I told you once before, De Bock, this woman is not my mistress."

"Then what . . .?"

"She's my wife!"

De Bock closed his tiny lips over his teeth with the gesture of a man tucking a buttonhole around a button.

"Your wife!"

"Yes. I intend to marry her."

"My God!"

De Bock threw one last look of horror and repulsion at Christine, and fled without even putting on his coat.

"What were you saying about me?" asked Christine.

Vincent crossed and looked down at her for a moment. "I told De Bock that you are going to be my wife."

Christine was silent for a long time, her hands working busily. Her mouth hung slightly open and her tongue would dart quickly, like the tongue of a snake, to moisten the rapidly drying lips.

"You would really marry me, Vincent? Why?"

"If I don't marry you, it would have been kinder of me to let you alone. I want to go through the joys and sorrows of domestic life in order to paint it from my own experience. I was in love with a woman once, Christine. When I went to her house, they told me I disgusted her. My love was true and honest and strong,

Christine, and when I came away I knew it had been killed. But after death there is a resurrection; you were that resurrection.''

"But you can't marry me! What about the children? And your brother may stop sending the money."

"I respect a woman who is a mother, Christine. We'll keep the new baby and Herman here with us, the others can stay with your mother. As for Theo . . . yes . . . he may cut off my head. But when I write him the full truth I do not think he will abandon me.''

He sat on the floor by her feet. She was looking so much better than when he had first met her. There was a little touch of happiness in her melancholy brown eyes. A new spirit of life had come to her whole personality. Posing had not been easy for her, but she had worked hard and patiently. When he first met her, she had been coarse and ill and miserable; now her whole manner was more quiet. She had found new health and life. As he sat there looking up into her crude, marked face into which a slight note of sweetness had come, he thought once again of the line from Michelet: ''*Comment se fait-il qu'il y ait sur la terre une femme seule désespérée?*''

"Sien, we'll skimp and be as saving as possible, won't we? I fear there will come a time when I shall be quite without means. I shall be able to help you until you go to Leyden, but when you come back I don't know how you will find me, with or without bread. What I have I will share with you and the child.''

Christine slipped off the chair, onto the floor beside him, put her arms about his neck and laid her head on his shoulder.

"Just let me stay with you, Vincent. I don't ask for much. If there's nothing but bread and coffee, I don't complain. I love you, Vincent. You're the first man's ever been good to me. You don't got to marry me if you don't want. I'll pose and work hard and do whatever you tell me. Only let me stay with you! It's the first time I ever been happy, Vincent. I don't want things. I'll just share what you have and be happy.''

He could feel the swelling child against him, warm and living. He ran his fingertips gently over her homely face, kissing the scars one by one. He let her hair fall down her back smoothing out the thin strands with tender strokes of his hand. She laid her flushed, happy cheek on his beard and rubbed softly against the grain.

"You do love me, Christine?''

"Yes, Vincent, I do.''

"It's good to be loved. The world may call it wrong if it likes.''

"To hell with the world,'' said Christine, simply.

"I will live as a labourer; that suits me. You and I understand each other and we do not need to mind what anybody says. We do not have to pretend to keep up a social standing. My own class cast me out long ago. I would rather have a crust of bread at my own hearth, however poor it may be, than live without marrying you.''

They sat on the floor, warmed by the red glow of the stove, entwined in each other's arms. It was the postman who broke the spell. He handed Vincent a letter from Amsterdam. It read:

Vincent:
   Have just heard of your disgraceful conduct. Kindly cancel my order for the six drawings. I will take no further interest in your work.

                                                                C. M. Van Gogh.

His whole fate now rested with Theo. Unless he could make Theo understand the full nature of his relationship with Christine, he too would be justified in cutting off the hundred francs a month. He could do without his master, Mauve; he could do without his dealer, Tersteeg; he could do without his family, friends, and *confrères* as long as he had his work and Christine. But he could not do without that hundred francs a month!

He wrote long, passionate letters to his brother, explaining everything, begging Theo to understand and not desert him. He lived from day to day with a dark fear of the worst. He did not dare to order more drawing material than he could pay for, or undertake any water-colours or push on.

Theo offered objections, many of them, but he did not condemn. He offered advice too, but not once did he infer that if his advice were not taken he would stop sending the money. And in the end, although he did not approve, he assured Vincent that his help would go on just as before.

It was now early May. The doctor at Leyden had told Christine she would be confined sometime in June. Vincent decided that it would be wiser if she did not move in with him until after the confinement, at which time he hoped to rent the vacant house next door on the Schenkweg. Christine spent most of her time at the studio, but her possessions still remained at her mother's. They were to be officially married after her recovery.

He went to Leyden for Christine's confinement. The child did not move from nine in the evening until half past one. It had to be taken with the forceps, but it was not injured at all. Christine suffered a great deal of pain, but she forgot it all when she saw Vincent.

"We will soon begin to draw again," she said.

Vincent stood looking down at her with tears in his eyes. It did not matter that the child belonged to another man. It was his wife and baby, and he was happy with a taut pain in his chest.

When he returned to the Schenkweg he found the landlord and owner of the lumber yard in front of the house.

"What about taking that other house, Mijnheer Van Gogh? It is only eight francs a week. I'll have it all painted and plastered for you. If you will pick out the kind of wallpaper you like, I will put it on for you."

"Not so fast," said Vincent. "I would like the new house for when my wife comes home, but I must write to my brother first."

"Well, I must put on some wallpaper, so pick the one you like best, and if you can't take the house, it won't matter."

Theo had been hearing about the house next door for several months. It was much larger, with a studio, living room, kitchen, alcove, and an attic bedroom. It was four francs a week more than the old place, but with Christine, Herman, and the baby all coming to the Schenkweg, they needed the new space. Theo replied that he had received another raise in salary and that Vincent could rely upon receiving a hundred and fifty francs a month for the present. Vincent rented the new house immediately. Christine was coming home in a week and he wanted her to find a warm nest upon her arrival. The owner lent him two men from the yard to carry his furniture next door to the new studio. Christine's mother came there to straighten things.

10

The new studio looked so real, with plain greyish-brown paper, scrubbed wooden floors, studies on the walls, an easel at each end, and a large, white, deal working table. Christine's mother put up white muslin curtains at the windows. Adjoining the studio was an alcove where Vincent kept all his drawing boards, portfolios and woodcuts; in a corner was a closet for his bottles, pots, and books. The living room had a table, a few kitchen chairs, an oil stove, and a large wicker chair for Christine near the window. Beside it he put a small iron crib with a green cover, and above it the etching by Rembrandt of the two women by the cradle, one of them reading from the Bible by the light of a candle.

He secured everything that was strictly necessary for the kitchen; when Christine came back she could prepare dinner in ten minutes. He bought an extra knife, fork, spoon, and plate against the day when Theo should come to visit them. Up in the attic he put a large bed for himself and his wife, and the old one with all the bedding in good order for Herman. He and Christine's mother got straw, seaweed, bedticking, and filled the mattresses themselves in the attic.

When Christine left the hospital, the doctor who treated her, the nurse of the ward, and the head nurse all came to say good-bye. Vincent realized more fully than before that she was a person for whom serious people might have sympathy and affection. "She has never seen what is good," he said to himself, "so how can she be good?"

Christine's mother and her boy Herman were at the Schenkweg to greet her. It was a delightful homecoming, for Vincent had told her nothing about the new nest. She ran about touching things; the cradle, the easy chair, the flower pot he had placed on the sill outside her window. She was in high spirits.

"The professor was awfully funny," she cried. "He said, 'I say, are you fond of gin and bitters? And can you smoke cigars?' 'Yes,' I answered. 'I only asked it,' he said, 'to tell you that you need not give it up. But you must not use vinegar, pepper, or mustard. And you should eat meat at least once a week.' "

Their bedroom looked a good deal like a hold of a ship, for it had been wainscotted. Vincent had to carry the iron cradle upstairs every night and down again to the living room in the morning. He had to do all the housework for which Christine was still too weak; making the beds, lighting the fire, lifting and carrying and cleaning. He felt as though he had been together with Christine and the children for a long time, and that he was in his element. Although she still suffered from the operation, there was a renewing and a reviving in her.

Vincent went back to work with a new peace in his heart. It was good to have a hearth of one's own, to feel the bustle and organization of a family about one. Living with Christine gave him courage and energy to go on with his work. If only Theo did not desert him he was certain that he could develop into a good painter.

In the Borinage he had slaved for God; here he had a new and more tangible kind of God, a religion that could be expressed in one sentence: that the figure of a labourer, some furrows in a ploughed field, a bit of sand, sea and sky were serious subjects, so difficult, but at the same time so beautiful, that it was indeed worth while to devote his life to the task of expressing the poetry hidden in them.

One afternoon, coming home from the dunes, he met Tersteeg in front of the Schenkweg house.

"I am glad to see you, Vincent," said Tersteeg. "I thought I would come and inquire how you are getting on."

Vincent dreaded the storm that he knew would break once Tersteeg got upstairs. He stood chatting with him a few moments on the street in order to gather strength. Tersteeg was friendly and pleasant. Vincent shivered.

When the two men entered, Christine was nursing the baby in her wicker chair. Herman was playing by the stove. Tersteeg gaped at them for a long, long time. When he spoke, it was in English.

"What is the meaning of that woman and child?"

"Christine is my wife. The child is ours."

"You have actually married her!"

"We haven't gone through the ceremony yet, if that's what you mean."

"How can you think of living with a woman . . . and children who . . . "

"Men usually marry, do they not?"

"But you have no money. You're being supported by your brother."

"Not at all. Theo pays me a salary. Everything I make belongs to him. He will get his money back some day."

"Have you gone mad, Vincent? This is certainly a thing that comes from an unsound mind and temperament."

"Human conduct, Mijnheer, is a great deal like drawing. The whole perspective changes with the shifted position of the eye, and depends not on the subject, but on the man who is looking."

"I shall write to your father, Vincent. I shall write and tell him of the whole affair."

"Don't you think it would be ridiculous if they received an indignant letter from you, and soon after, a request from me to come and visit here at my expense?"

"You intend to write, yourself!"

"Can you ask that? Of course I will. But you must admit that now is a very untimely moment. Father is being moved to the vicarage at Nuenen. My wife's condition is such that any anxiety or strain now would be murder."

"Then of course I shan't write. My boy, you're as foolish as the man who wants to drown himself. I only want to save you from it."

"I don't doubt your good intentions, Mijnheer Tersteeg, and that is why I try not to be angry at your words. But this conversation is very disagreeable to me."

Tersteeg went away, a baffled look on his face. It was Weissenbruch who delivered the first real blow for the outside world. He drifted in nonchalantly one afternoon to see if Vincent was still alive.

"Hello," he said. "I notice you managed to get along without that twenty-five francs."

"Yes."

"Now aren't you glad I didn't coddle you?"

"I believe about the first thing I said to you, that night at Mauve's, was 'Go to hell!' I repeat my invitation."

"If you keep this up, you'll become another Weissenbruch; you've got the making of a real man in you. Why don't you introduce me to your mistress. I've never had the honour."

"Bait me all you like, Weissenbruch, but leave her alone."

Christine was rocking the iron cradle with its green cover. She knew that she was being ridiculed, and looked up at Vincent with pain on her face. Vincent crossed to the mother and child and stood by their side, protectively. Weissenbruch glanced at the group, then at the Rembrandt over the cradle.

"I say," he exclaimed, "you make a corking motif. I'd like to do you. I'd call it *Holy Family!*"

Vincent sprang after Weissenbruch with an oath, but the latter got out the door safely. Vincent went back to his family. There was a bit of mirror hung on the wall beside the Rembrandt. Vincent glanced up, caught the reflection of the three of them and in one horrible, devastating instant of clarity saw through the eyes of Weissenbruch . . . the bastard, the whore, and the charity monger.

"What did he call us?" asked Christine.

"The Holy Family."

"What that?"

"A picture of Mary, Jesus, and Joseph."

Tears sprang to her eyes and she buried her head in the baby's clothes. Vincent went on his knees beside the iron cradle to comfort her. Dusk was creeping in the north window and threw a quiet shadow over the room. Once again Vincent was able to detach himself and see the three of them, just as though he were not a member of the group. This time he saw through the eyes of his own heart.

"Don't cry, Sien," he said. "Don't cry, darling. Lift up your head and dry your tears. *Weissenbruch was right!*"

11

Vincent discovered Scheveningen and oil painting at about the same time. Scheveningen was a little fishing village lying in a valley of two protective sand dunes on the North Sea. On the beach there were rows of square fishing barks with one mast and deep-coloured, weather beaten sails. They had rude, square rudders behind, fishing nets spread out ready for the sea, and a tiny rust-red or sea-blue triangular flag aloft. There were blue wagons on red wheels to carry the fish to the village; fisherwives in white oilskin caps fastened at the front by two round gold pins; family crowds at the tide's edge to welcome the barks; the Kurzaal flying its gay flags, a pleasure house for foreigners who liked the taste of salt on their lips, but not choked down their throats. The sea was grey with whitecaps at the shore and ever deepening hues of green fading into a dull blue; the sky was a cleaning grey with patterned clouds and an occasional design of blue to suggest to the fishermen that a sun still shines over Holland. Scheveningen was a place where men worked, and where the people were indigenous to the soil and the sea.

Vincent had been doing a good many street scenes in water-colour and he found that medium satisfactory for a quick impression. But water-colour did not have the depth, the thickness, the character to express the things he needed to say. He yearned for oil, but he was afraid to tackle it because he had heard of so many painters being ruined by going to oil before they learned to draw. Then Theo came to The Hague.

Theo was now twenty-six, and a competent art dealer. He travelled frequently for his house, and was everywhere known as one of the best young men in the business. Goupil and Company had sold out in Paris to Boussod, Valadon (known as *les Messieurs*) and although they had retained Theo in his former position, the art business was not what it had been under Goupil and Uncle Vincent. Pictures were now sold for the highest price obtainable—regardless of merit—and only the successful painters were patronized. Uncle Vincent, Tersteeg, and Goupil had considered it the very first duty of an art dealer to discover and encourage new and young artists; now only the old and recognized painters were solicited. The newcomers in the field, Manet, Monet, Pissarro, Sisley, Renoir, Berthe Morisot, Cezanne, Degas, Guillaumin, and the even younger men, Toulouse-Lautrec, Gauguin, Seurat and Signac, were trying to say something different from what Bouguereau and the academicians were repeating endlessly, but not one would listen to them. None of these revolutionists had ever had a canvas exhibited or offered up for sale under the roof of *les Messieurs*. Theo had developed a profound distaste for Bouguereau and the academicians; his sympathies were all with the young innovators. Every day he did what he could to persuade *les Messieurs* to exhibit the new paintings and educate the public to buy. *Les Messieurs* thought the innovators mad, childish, and completely without technique. Theo thought them the future masters.

Christine remained upstairs in the attic bedroom while the brothers met in the studio. When their first greetings were over, Theo said, "I had to come on business, too, but I must confess that my primary purpose in The Hague is to dissuade you from establishing any permanent relationship with this woman. First of all, what is she like?"

"Do you remember our old nurse at Zundert, Leen Verman?"

"Yes."

"Sien is that kind of person. She is just an ordinary woman of the people, yet for me she has something sublime. Whoever loves one ordinary, commonplace person, and is loved by her, is already happy, notwithstanding the dark side of life. It was the feeling of being of some use that brought me to myself again and made me revive. I did not seek for it, but it found me. Sien puts up with all the worries and troubles of a painter's life, and is so willing to pose that I think I shall become a better artist with her than if I had married Kay.''

Theo walked about the studio and finally spoke while staring intently at a water-colour. ''The only thing I can't understand is how you could fall in love with this woman while you were so desperately in love with Kay.''

''I didn't fall in love, Theo, not immediately. Because Kay turned me down, should all my human feelings be extinguished? When you come here you do not find me discouraged and melancholy, but you come into a new studio and a home in full swing; no mysterious studio, but one that is rooted in real life—a studio with a cradle and a baby's high chair—where there is no stagnation, but where everything pushes and urges and stirs to activity. To me it is as clear as day that one must feel what one draws, that one must live in the reality of family life if one wishes to express intimately that family life.''

''You know I never draw class distinctions, Vincent, but do you think it wise . . . ?''

''No, I don't think I've lowered or dishonoured myself,'' interrupted Vincent, ''because I feel my work lies in the heart of the people, that I must keep close to the ground, grasp life to the quick, and make progress through many cares and troubles.''

''I don't dispute all that.'' Theo crossed swiftly and stood looking down at his brother. ''But why does it necessitate a marriage?''

''Because there is a promise of marriage between her and me. I don't want you to consider her as a mistress, or as somebody with whom I am having a liaison without caring for the consequences. That promise of marriage is twofold; firstly a promise of civil marriage as soon as circumstances will permit, but secondly, it is a promise meanwhile to help each other, to cherish each other as if we were already married, to share everything together.''

''But surely you will wait a bit before you go into the civil marriage?''

''Yes, Theo, if you ask me. We will postpone it until I earn a hundred and fifty francs by selling my work, and your help will no longer be necessary. I promise you I shall not marry her until my drawing has progressed so far that I'm independent. By degrees, as I begin to earn, you can send me less each month, and at last I will not need your money any longer. Then we will talk about a civil marriage.''

''That sounds like the wisest thing to do.''

''Here she comes, Theo. For my sake, try to think of her only as a wife and mother! For that's what she really is.''

Christine came down the stairs at the rear of the studio. She had on a neat black dress, her hair was carefully combed back, and the touch of colour in her face almost obliterated the pock marks. She had become pretty in a homely sort of way. Vincent's love had surrounded her with an aura of confidence and well being. She shook hands with Theo quietly, asked if he wouldn't have a cup of tea, and insisted that he remain for supper. She sat in her easy chair by the window, sewing and rocking the cradle. Vincent ran excitedly back and forth across the studio, showing charcoal figures, street scenes in water-colour, group studies hammered on with a carpenter's pencil. He wanted Theo to see the progress of his work.

Theo had faith that some day Vincent would become a great painter, but he was never quite sure he liked the things Vincent had done . . . as yet. Theo was a discriminating amateur, carefully trained in the art of judging, but he never could make up his mind just what he thought of his brother's work. For him, Vincent was always in a state of becoming, never in the state of having arrived.

''If you begin to feel the need to work in oil,'' he said, after Vincent had shown him all his studies and spoken of his craving, ''why don't you begin? What are you waiting for?''

''For the assurance that my drawing is good enough. Mauve and Tersteeg say I don't know how . . . ''

" . . . and Weissenbruch says you do. You're the one who must be the final judge. If you feel that you've got to express yourself in deeper colour now, the time is ripe. Jump in!"

"But, Theo, the expense! Those confounded tubes cost their weight in gold."

"Meet me at my hotel tomorrow morning at ten. The sooner you begin sending me oil canvases, the quicker I'll get my money out of this investment."

During supper Theo and Christine chatted animatedly. When Theo left, he turned to Vincent on the stairs and said in French, "She's nice, really nice. I had no idea!"

They made a strange contrast, walking up the Wagenstraat the following morning; the younger brother carefully groomed, his boots polished, linen starched, suit pressed, necktie neatly in place, black bowler hat at a jaunty angle, soft brown beard carefully trimmed, walking along with a well poised, even pace; and the other, with worn out boots, patched trousers that did not match the tight coat, no necktie, an absurd peasant's cap stuck on the top of his head, beard scrambling out in furious red whorls, hitching along with jerky, uneven steps, waving his arms and making excited gestures as he talked.

They were not conscious of the picture they made.

Theo took Vincent to Goupils to buy the tubes of paint, brushes, and canvas. Tersteeg respected and admired Theo; he wanted to like and understand Vincent. When he heard what they had come for, he insisted upon finding all the material himself and advising Vincent on the merits of the various pigments.

Theo and Vincent tramped the six kilometres across the dunes to Scheveningen. A fishing smack was just coming in. Near the monument there was a little wooden shed in which a man sat on the lookout. As soon as the boat came in view the fellow appeared with a large flag. He was followed by a crowd of children. A few minutes after he had waved his flag, a man on an old horse arrived to go and fetch the anchor. The group was joined by a number of men and women who came pouring over the sand hill from the village to welcome the crew. When the boat was near enough, the man on horseback went into the water and returned with the anchor. Then the fishermen were brought ashore on the backs of fellows with high rubber boots, and with each arrival there was a great cheer of welcome. When they were all ashore and the horses had dragged the bark up on the beach, the whole troop marched home over the sand hill in caravan style, with the man on the horse towering over them like a tall spectre.

"This is the sort of thing I want to do with my paints," said Vincent.

"Let me have some canvases as soon as you become satisfied with your work. I might be able to find purchasers in Paris."

"Oh, Theo, you must! You must begin to sell me!"

12

When Theo left, Vincent began experimenting with his pigments. He did three oil studies; one a row of pollard willows behind the Geest bridge, another of a cinder path, and a third of the vegetable gardens of Meerdervoort where a man in a blue smock was picking up potatoes. The field was of white sand, partly dug up, still covered with rows of dried stalks with green weeds between. In the distance there were dark green trees and a few roofs. When he looked at his work in the studio, he was elated; he was certain that no one could possibly know they were his first efforts. The drawing, the backbone of painting and the skeleton that supported all the rest, was accurate and true to life. He was surprised a little because he had thought his first things would be failures.

He was busy painting a sloping ground in the woods, covered with moldered, dry beech leaves. The ground was light and dark reddish brown, made more so by the shadows of trees which threw streaks over it and sometimes half blotted it out. The question was to get the depth of colour, the enormous force and solidity of the ground. While painting, he perceived for the first time how much light there was still in that darkness. He had to keep that light, and keep at the same time the depth of rich colour.

The ground was a carpet of deep reddish brown in the glow of an autumn evening sun, tempered by the trees. Young birches sprang up, caught light on one side, and were sparkling green there, the shadowy sides of the stems were warm, deep black-green. Behind the saplings, behind the brownish red soil was a very delicate sky, bluish grey, warm, hardly blue, all aglow. Against it was a hazy border of green and a network of little stems and yellowish leaves. A few figures of wood gatherers were wandering around like dark masses of mysterious shadow. The white cap of a woman, who was bending to reach a dry branch, stood out brusquely against the deep red-brown of the ground. A dark silhouette of a man appeared above the underbrush; moulded against the sky, the figure was large and full of poetry.

While painting he said to himself, "I must not go away before there is something of an autumn evening feeling in it, something mysterious, something serious." But the light was fading. He had to work quickly. The figures he painted in at once by a few strong strokes with a resolute brush. It struck him how firmly the little tree stems were rooted in the ground. He tried to paint them in, but the ground was already so sticky that a brush stroke was lost in it. He tried again and again, desperately, for it was getting darker. At last he saw he was defeated; no brush could suggest anything in that rich loam-brown of the earth. With a blind intuition he flung the brush away, squeezed the roots and trunks on the canvas from the tubes of paint, picked up another brush, and modeled the thick, coloured oil with the handle.

"Yes," he exclaimed, as night finally claimed the woods, "now they stand there, rising from the ground, strongly rooted in it. I have said what I wanted to say!"

Weissenbruch looked in that evening. "Come along with me to *Pulchri*. We're having some tableaux and charades."

Vincent had not forgotten his last visit. "No, thanks, I don't care to leave my wife."

Weissenbruch walked over to Christine, kissed her hand, asked after her health, and played with the baby quite jovially. He evidently had no recollection of the last thing he had said to them.

"Let me see some of your new sketches, Vincent."

Vincent complied only too gladly. Weissenbruch picked out a study of Monday's market, where they were pulling down the stands; another of a line waiting in front of the soup kitchen; another of three old men at the insane asylum; another of a fishing smack at Scheveningen with the anchor raised, and a fifth that Vincent had made on his knees, in the mud of the dunes during a driving rain storm.

"Are these for sale? I'd like to buy them."

"Is this another of your poor jokes, Weissenbruch?"

"I never joke about painting. These studies are superb. How much do you want?"

Vincent said, "Name your own price," numbly, afraid that he was going to be ridiculed at any moment.

"Very well, how about five francs apiece? Twenty-five for the lot."

Vincent's eyes shot open. "That's too much! My Uncle Cor only paid me two and a half francs."

"He cheated you, my boy. All dealers cheat you. Some day they will sell for five thousand francs. What do you say, is it a deal?"

"Weissenbruch, sometimes you're an angel and sometimes you're a fiend!"

"That's for variety, so my friends won't get tired of me."

He took out a wallet and handed Vincent twenty-five francs. "Now come along with me to *Pulchri*. You need a little entertainment. We're having a farce by Tony Offermans. It will do you good to laugh."

So Vincent went along. The hall of the club was crowded with men all smoking cheap and strong tobacco. The first tableau was after an etching by Nicholas Maes, *The Stable at Bethlehem,* very good on tone and colour, but decidedly off in expression. The other was after Rembrandt's *Isaac Blessing Jacob,* with a splendid Rebecca looking on to see if her trick would succeed. The close air gave Vincent a headache. He left before the farce and went home, composing the sentences of a letter as he walked.

He told his father as much about the story of Christine as he thought expedient, enclosed Weissenbruch's twenty-five francs, and asked Theodorus to come to The Hague as his guest.

A week later his father arrived. His blue eyes were fading, his step becoming slower. The last time they had been together, Theodorus had ordered his oldest son from the house. In the interim they had exchanged friendly letters. Theodorus and Anna Cornelia had sent several bundles of underwear, outer clothing, cigars, homemade cake, and an occasional ten franc note. Vincent did not know how his father would take to Christine. Sometimes men were understanding and generous, sometimes they were blind and vicious.

He did not think his father could remain indifferent and raise objections—near a cradle. A cradle was not like anything else; there was no fooling with it. His father would have to forgive whatever there might have been in Christine's past.

Theodorus had a large bundle under his arm. Vincent opened it, drew out a warm coat for Christine, and knew that everything was all right. After she had gone upstairs to the attic bedroom, Theodorus and Vincent sat together in the studio.

"Vincent," said his father, "there was one thing you did not mention in your letter. Is the baby yours?"

"No. She was carrying it when I met her."

"Where is its father?"

"He deserted her." He did not think it necessary to explain the child's anonymity.

"But you will marry her, Vincent, won't you? It's not right to live this way."

"I agree. I want to go through the legal ceremony as soon as possible. But Theo and I decided that it would be better to wait until I am earning a hundred and fifty francs a month through my drawing."

Theodorus sighed. "Yes, perhaps that would be the best. Vincent, your mother would like you to come home for a visit sometime. And so should I. You will enjoy Nuenen, son; it is one of the most lovely villages in all the Brabant. The little church is so tiny, and looks like an Eskimo's igloo. It seats less than a hundred people, imagine! There are hawthorn hedges around the parsonage, Vincent, and behind the church is a flower filled yard with sand mounds and old wooden crosses."

"With wooden crosses!" said Vincent. "White ones?"

"Yes. The names are in black, but the rain is washing them away."

"Is there a nice tall steeple on the church, Father?"

"A delicate, fragile one, Vincent, but it goes way, way up into the sky. Sometimes I think it almost reaches God."

"Throwing a thin shadow over the graveyard," Vincent's eyes were sparkling. "I'd like to paint that."

"There's a stretch of heath and pine woods close by, and peasants digging in the fields. You must come home soon for a visit, son."

"Yes, I must see Nuenen. The little crosses, and the steeple and the diggers in the field. I guess there will always be something of the Brabant about me."

Theodorus returned home to assure his wife that things were not so bad with their boy as they had imagined. Vincent plunged into his work with an even greater zeal. More and more he found himself going back to Millet: *"L'art c'est un combat;*

dans l'art il faut y mettre sa peau.'' Theo believed in him, his mother and father did not disapprove of Christine, and no one in The Hague disturbed him any more. He was completely free to go ahead with his work.

The owner of the lumber yard sent him as models all the men who came for work and could not get it. As his pocketbook emptied, his portfolio filled. He drew the baby in the cradle by the stove many, many times. When the fall rains came he worked outdoors on oil torchon and captured the effects he wanted. He quickly learned that a colourist is one who, seeing a colour in nature, knows at once how to analyse it and say, "That grey-green is yellow with black, and hardly any blue."

Whether he was drawing the figure or landscape, he wished to express not sentimental melancholy but serious sorrow. He wanted to reach out so far that people would say of his work, "He feels deeply, he feels tenderly."

He knew that in the eyes of the world he was a good-for-nothing, an eccentric and disagreeable man, someone who had no position in life. He wanted to show in his work just what there was in the heart of such an eecentric man, of such a nobody. In the poorest huts, in the dirtiest corners, he saw drawings and pictures. The more he painted, the more other activities lost their interest. The more he got rid of them the quicker his eye grasped the picturesque qualities of life. Art demanded persistent work, work in spite of everything, and a continuous observation.

The only difficulty was that oil pigments were so frightfully expensive, and he laid his colour on so thick. When he squeezed it out of the tube onto the canvas in rich deep masses, it was like pouring francs into the Zuider Zee. He painted so fast that his canvas bill was enormous; he did at one sitting an oil that would have taken Mauve two months. Well, he could not paint thin, and he could not work slowly; his money evaporated and his studio became filled with pictures. As soon as his allowance arrived from Theo—who had arranged to send fifty francs on the first, tenth, and twentieth—he would rush down to the dealer and buy large tubes of ochre, cobalt, and Prussian blue, and smaller tubes of Naples yellow, *terra sienna,* ultramarine, and gamboge. Then he would work happily until the paints and the francs were exhausted, usually five or six days after the allowance arrived from Paris, and his troubles set in again.

He was amazed to find that so many things had to be bought for the baby; that Christine had to have constant medicines, new garments, special foods; that Herman had to buy books and supplies for the school he was sent to; and that the household was a bottomless pit into which he was forever pouring lamps, pots, blankets, coal and wood, curtains, rugs, candles, sheets, silverware, plates, furniture, and an endless stream of food. It was hard to know just how to apportion the fifty francs beween his painting and the three people who were dependent upon him.

"You look like a labourer rushing off to the wine shop the minute he gets paid," remarked Christine one time when Vincent snatched the fifty francs out of Theo's envelope and began gathering up empty tubes.

He built a new perspective instrument with two long legs that would stand up in the sand of the dunes, and had the blacksmith make iron corners for the frame. Scheveningen, with the sea, the sand dunes, the fisherfolk, the barks and horses and nets, lured him most. He trudged across the dunes every day, loaded down with his heavy easel and perspective instrument, to catch the changing nature of the sea and sky. As fall deepened and other artists began to hug their studio fires, he went out to paint in the wind, the rain, the mist and the storm. In the roughest of weather his wet paint often became covered with blowing sand and salt water. The rain drenched him, the mist and wind chilled him, the sand got into his eyes and nose . . . and he loved every last minute of it. Nothing but death could stop him now.

One night he showed Christine a new canvas. "But Vincent," she exclaimed, "how do you make it look so real?"

Vincent forgot he was speaking to an illiterate woman of the people. He might have been talking to Weissenbruch or Mauve.

"I don't know myself," he said. "I sit down with a white board before the spot that strikes me, and I say, 'That white board must become something!' I work for a long time, I come back home dissatisfied, I put it away in the closet. When I have rested a little I go to look at it with a kind of fear. I am still dissatisfied because I have too clearly in my mind the splendid original to be content with what I have made of it. But after all, I find in my work an echo of what struck me. I see that nature has told me something, has spoken to me, and that I have put it down in shorthand. In my shorthand there may be words that cannot be deciphered, there may be mistakes or gaps, but there is something in it of what the woods or beach or figure has told me. Do you understand?"

"No."

13

Christine understood very little of what he was doing. She thought his hunger to paint things a sort of costly obsession. She knew it was the rock upon which his life was built, however, and made no attempt to oppose him; the purpose, the slow progress and painful expression of his work were completely lost upon her. She was a good companion for ordinary domestic purposes, but only a very small part of Vincent's life was domestic. When he wished to express himself in words, he was forced to write to Theo; he poured out a long passionate letter almost every night, telling of all the things he had seen, painted, and thought during the day. When he wished to enjoy the expression of others, he turned to novels; French, English, German and Dutch. Christine shared only a fraction of his life. But he was satisfied; he did not regret his decision to take Christine to wife, nor did he attempt to force upon her the intellectual pursuits for which she was manifestly unqualified.

All this was very well during the long months of the summer, autumn, and fall, when he left the house as early as five and six in the morning, to be gone until the light of day failed completely and he had to trudge home across the dunes in the cool dusk. But when a terrific snow-storm served to celebrate the first anniversary of their meeting in the wine shop opposite the Ryn station, and Vincent had to work at home from morning until night, it became more difficult to maintain a satisfactory relationship .

He went back to drawing, and saved money on paints, but the models ate him out of house and home. People who would gladly work for next to nothing at the worst kind of menial labour would demand a large sum just to come and sit for him. He asked permission to sketch at the insane asylum, but the authorities declared they had no precedent for it, and besides they were laying new floors so he could not work there except on visiting days.

His only hope lay in Christine. As soon as she was well and strong he expected her to pose for him, work as hard as she had before the baby came. Christine had different ideas. At first she would say, "I'm not strong enough. Wait a bit. You aint in any hurry." When she was completely well again, she thought herself too busy.

"It's not the same now as it was, Vincent," she would say. "I got to nurse the baby. And I got to keep a whole house clean. There's four people to cook for."

Vincent arose at five in the morning to do the housework so that she would be free to pose during the day. "But I aint a model no more," she protested. "I'm your wife."

"Sien, you must pose for me! I can't afford to hire models every day. That's one of the reasons you're here."

Christine flared up into one of the unrestrained fits of temper that had been so common when she first met Vincent. "That's all you took me in for! So you could save money out of me! I'm just a goddam servant to you! If I don't pose you'll throw me out again!"

Vincent thought for a moment and then said, "You heard all those things at your mother's. You didn't think of them for yourself."

"Well, and what if I did? They're true, aint they?"

"Sien, you'll have to stop going there."

"Why? I guess I love my mother, don't I?"

"But they're ruining things between us. The first thing you know they'll have you back in their way of thinking. Then where will our marriage be?"

"Aint you the one tells me go there when there's no food in the house? Make some more money and I won't have to go back."

When he finally did get her to pose, she was useless. She committed all the errors he had worked so hard to eradicate the year before. Sometimes he suspected that she wiggled, made awkward gestures purposely so that he would become disgusted and not bother her to pose any more. In the end he had to give her up. His expense for outside models increased. Along with it, the number of days that they were without money for food also increased, and so did the amount of time that Christine was forced to spend at her mother's. Each time she came back from there he perceived a slight change in her bearing and attitude. He was caught in a vicious circle; if he used all his money for living, Christine would not go back to the influence of her mother; he could maintain their relationship on a wholesome plane. But if he did that, he would have to give up his work. Had he saved her life just to kill himself? If she did not go to her mother's several times a month, she and the children would starve; if she did go she would eventually destroy their home. What was he to do?

Christine ill and carrying a child, Christine in the hospital, Christine recovering from the confinement, was one sort of person; a woman abandoned, *désespérée*, on the verge of a miserable death, intensely grateful for a single kind word or helpful action; a woman who knew all the pain in the world and would do anything for a moment's surcease, who would make all sorts of fervent and heroic promises to herself and life. Christine well again, her body and face filled out with good food, medicine, and care, was another sort of woman. The memory of pain was receding, the resolution to be a good housewife and mother weakening; the thoughts and habits of her earlier life were coming back again slowly. She had lived loosely and on the streets, amid liquor, black cigars, vile language, and coarse men for fourteen years. With the strength of her body returning, the fourteen years of sloth overbalanced the one year of care and gentle love. An insidious change began to steal upon her. Vincent could not understand it at first; then slowly a consciousness of what was happening came over him.

It was just about this time, the beginning of the new year, that he received a curious letter from Theo. His brother had met on the streets of Paris a woman, alone, ill, despairing. She suffered from an ailment of the foot and could not work. She had been ready to kill herself. Vincent had taught Theo the way; he followed his master. He found a place for the woman in the home of some old friends. He secured a doctor and had examinations made. He paid for all the expenses of the woman's life. In his letters he called her his patient.

"Should I marry my patient, Vincent? Is that the best way for me to serve her? Should I go through the legal ceremony? She suffers much; she is unhappy; she was deserted by the only person she loved. What must I do to save her life?"

Vincent was deeply touched, and he wrote of his sympathy. But every day Christine was becoming more difficult. When there was only bread and coffee, she grumbled. She insisted that he leave off having models and use his money for the house. When she could not have a new dress, she neglected the old one and let it become covered with food and dirt. She stopped mending his clothes and linen. She fell once again under the influence of her mother, who persuaded her that Vincent would either run away or throw her out. Since a permanent relationship was impossible, what was the good of bothering about the temporary one?

Could he advise Theo to marry his patient? Was legal marriage the best way to save these women? Or was the most important thing a roof over their heads, good food to build their health, and kindness to bring them back to a love of life?

"Wait!" he cautioned his brother. "Do all you can for her; it is a noble cause. But the ceremony will help you not at all. If a love grows between you, then a marriage will grow, too. But see first if you can save her."

Theo was sending fifty francs three times a month. Now that Christine was growing careless in her housekeeping, the money did not last as long as it had before. Vincent was avaricious for models so that he could collect enough studies for some real canvases. He regretted every franc that had to be taken away from his drawing and sunk into the house. She begrudged every franc that had to be taken away from the house and sunk into the drawing. It was a struggle for their lives. The hundred and fifty francs a month could just have supplied him with food, shelter and materials; the attempt to make it provide for four people was heroic but impossible. He began owing money to the landlord, to the shoemaker, the grocer, the baker, and the colour dealer. To cap the climax, Theo went short on funds.

Vincent wrote imploring letters. "If you can please send the money just a little before the twentieth, at least not later. I have only two sheets of paper in the house and one last crumb of crayon. I have not a franc for models or food." Three times a month he wrote such letters; when the fifty francs arrived, he already owed it all to the tradesmen and had nothing to live on for the next ten days.

Theo's "patient" had to be operated on for tumor of the foot. Theo had her taken to a good hospital. At the same time he was sending money home to Nuenen, for the new congregation was small, and Theodorus's income was not always sufficient to meet the needs of the family. Theo was supporting himself and his patient, Vincent, Christine, Herman, Antoon, and the family at Nuenen. He was pushed to the last centime of his salary and could not send Vincent an extra franc.

At last it came about, in early March, that Vincent was left with one franc, a torn note that had already been refused by a tradesman. There was not a mouthful of food left in the house. The next money could not arrive from Theo for at least nine days. He was desperately afraid to put Christine into the hands of her mother for that length of time.

"Sien," he said, "we can't starve the children. You had better take them home to your mother's until Theo's letter arrives."

They looked at each other for a moment, thinking the same thoughts, but without the courage to utter them.

"Yes," she said, "I guess I got to."

The grocer gave him a loaf of black bread and some coffee for the torn bill. He brought models into the house and owed them their money. He became increasingly nervous. His work went hard and dry. He had been starving his body. The incessant financial worries were telling on him. He could not go on without working, yet every hour of work showed him that he was losing ground.

At the end of nine days, promptly on the thirtieth, the letter arrived from Theo with fifty francs. His "patient" had recovered from the operation and he had put her in a private home. The financial strain was telling on him, too, and he had grown despondent. He wrote, "I am afraid I cannot assure you of anything in the future."

That sentence almost drove Vincent out of his mind. Did Theo mean simply that he would not be able to send any more money? That in itself would not be so bad. But did it mean that from the almost daily sketches Vincent sent him to show the progress of his work, his brother had come to the conclusion that he was without talent and could hope for nothing in the future?

He lay awake at night worrying about it, wrote incessant letters to Theo begging for an explanation, and cast about desperately for some means of making his own livelihood. There were none.

14

When he went for Christine he found her in the company of her mother, brother, brother's mistress, and a strange man. She was smoking a black cigar and drinking gin. She did not seem at all pleased at the thought of going back to the Schenkweg.

The nine days at her mother's house had brought back the old habits, the destroying ways of life.

"I can smoke cigars if I want!" she cried. "You aint got no right to stop me if I get them myself. The doctor at the hospital said I could drink all the gin and bitters I wanted."

"Yes, as medicine . . . to improve your appetite."

She broke into a raucous laugh. "Medicine! What a ———— ————you are!" It was an expression she had not used since the very first days of their acquaintance.

Vincent was in a ragged state of sensitivity. He flew into uncontrollable rages. Christine followed his example. "You aint taking care of me no more!" she shouted. "You don't even give me something to eat. Why don't you make more money? What in hell kind of man are you, anyway?"

As the hard winter slipped into a grudging spring, Vincent's condition went from bad to worse. His debts increased. Because he could not give his stomach the right food, it went back on him. He could not swallow a bite. The ills of his stomach went to his teeth. He lay awake at night with the pain. The ache from his teeth went to his right ear, and all day it twitched jumpily.

Christine's mother began coming to the house, smoking and drinking with her daughter. She no longer thought Christine fortunate to be married. Once Vincent found her brother there, but he dodged out of the door as soon as Vincent entered.

"Why did he come here?" demanded Vincent. "What does he want of you?"

"They say you are going to throw me out."

"You know I'll never do that, Sien. Not as long as you want to stay."

"Mother wants me to leave. She says it aint good for me to stay here without something to eat."

"Where would you go?"

"Home, of course."

"And take the children into that house?"

"It's better than starving here. I can work and earn my own living."

"What would you work at?"

"Well . . . something."

"As a charwoman? At the tubs?"

". . . I guess."

He saw immediately that she was lying.

"So that's what they're trying to persuade you to do!"

"Well . . . it aint so bad . . . you make a living."

"Listen, Sien, if you go back to that house you're lost. You know your mother will send you on the streets again. Remember what the doctor at Leyden said. If you go back to that life, it will kill you!"

"It aint going to kill me. I feel all right now."

"You feel well because you have been living carefully! But if you go back . . . !"

"Jesus Christ, who's going back? Unless you send me."

He sat on the arm of her wicker chair and put his hand on her shoulder. Her hair was uncombed. "Then believe me, Sien, I will never abandon you. As long as you are willing to share what I have, I will keep you with me. But you must stay away from your mother and brother. They'll destroy you! Promise me, for your own sake, that you won't see them any more."

"I promise."

Two days later, when he came back from sketching at the alms house, the studio was empty. There was no sign of supper. He found Christine at her mother's, drinking.

"I told you I love my mother," she protested when they got home. "I guess I can see her all I want. You don't own me. I got a right to do as I please."

She fell into all the familiar, slovenly habits of her former life. When Vincent tried to correct them and explain that she was estranging herself from him, she would answer, "Yes, I know it quite well, you don't want me to stay with you." He showed her how dirty the house was, and how neglected. She answered, "Well, I am lazy and good-for-nothing; I always was that way and it can't be helped." If he tried to show her to what ultimate end her slothfulness was taking her she would reply, "I'm nothing but an outcast, that's true, and I'll end up by throwing myself in the river!"

The mother came to the studio nearly every day now, and took from Vincent the companionship he had so valued in Christine. The house fell into chaos. Meals became fitful. Herman was allowed to go around ragged and dirty, and stay away from school. The less Christine did, the more she smoked and drank her gin. She would not tell Vincent where she got the money for these things.

Summer came. Vincent went out of doors to paint again. This meant new outlays for paints, brushes, canvas, frames, bigger easels. Theo reported improved condition on his "patient," but serious problems in his relationship with her. What was he to do with the woman, now that she was better?

Vincent shut his eyes to everything in his personal life and continued to paint. He knew that his house was crashing about his ears, that he was being drawn into the abysmal sloth that had recaptured Christine. He tried to bury his despair in his work. Each morning when he set out on a new project, he hoped that this canvas would be so beautiful and perfect that it would sell immediately and establish him. Each night he returned home with the sad realization that he was still many years from the mastery he longed for.

His only relief was Antoon, the child. He was a miracle of vitality, and swallowed all kinds of eatables with much laughing and cooing. He often sat with Vincent in the studio, on the floor in a corner. He would crow at Vincent's drawings and then sit quietly looking at the sketches on the walls. He was growing up to be a pretty and vivacious child. The less attention Christine paid to the baby, the more Vincent loved him. In Antoon he saw the real purpose and reward for his actions of last winter.

Weissenbruch looked in only once. Vincent showed him some of the sketches of the year before. He had become frightfully dissatisfied with them.

"Don't feel that way," said Weissenbruch. "After a good many years you will look back on these early pieces of work and realize that they were sincere and penetrating. Just plug on, my boy, and don't let anything stop you."

What finally did stop him was a smash in the face. During the spring he had taken a lamp to the crockery man to have it repaired. The merchant had insisted that Vincent take some new dishes home with him.

"But I have no money to pay for them."

"It doesn't matter. There is no hurry. Take them and pay me when you get the money."

Two months later he banged on the door of the studio. He was a burly chap with a neck as thick as his head.

"What do you mean by lying to me?" he demanded. "What do you take my goods for and not pay me when you got money all the time?"

"At the moment I am absolutely flat. I will pay you as soon as I receive money."

"That's a lie! You just gave money to my neighbour, the shoemaker."

"I am at work," said Vincent, "and I don't care to be disturbed. I'll pay you when I get the money. Please get out."

"I'll get out when you give me that money, and not before!"

Vincent indiscreetly pushed the man toward the door. "Get out of my house," he commanded.

That was just what the tradesman was waiting for. As soon as he was touched, he smashed over his right fist into Vincent's face and sent him crashing into the wall. He struck Vincent again, knocked him to the floor, and walked out without another word.

Christine was at her mother's. Antoon crawled across the floor and patted Vincent's face, crying. After a few minutes Vincent came back to consciousness, dragged himself up the stairs to the attic and lay over the bed.

The blows had not hurt his face. He felt no pain. He had not injured himself when he had fallen heavily to the floor. But those two blows had broken something within him and defeated him. He knew it.

Christine came home. She went upstairs to the attic. There was neither money nor dinner in the house. She often wondered how Vincent managed to keep alive. She saw him lying across the bed, head and arms dangling over one side, feet over the other.

"What's the matter?" she asked.

After a long time he found the strength to twist about and put his head on the pillow. "Sien, I've got to leave The Hague."

". . . yes . . . I know."

"I must get away from here. Out to the country somewhere. To Drenthe, maybe. Where we can live cheaply."

"You want me to come with you? It's an awful hole, Drenthe. What will I do when you aint got no money and we don't eat?"

"I don't know, Sien. I guess you won't eat."

"Will you promise to use the hundred and fifty francs to live on? Not to spend it on models and paints?"

"I can't, Sien. Those things come first."

"Yes, to you!"

"But not to you. Why should they?"

"I got to live too, Vincent. I can't live without eating."

"And I can't live without painting."

"Well, it's your money . . . you come first . . . I understand. Have you a few centimes? Let's go over to the wine café across from the Ryn station."

The place smelled of sour wine. It was late afternoon, but the lamps had not yet been lit. The two tables where they had first sat near each other were empty. Christine led the way to them. They each ordered a glass of sour wine. Christine toyed with the stem of her glass. Vincent remembered how he had admired her worker's hands when she made that identical gesture at the table almost two years before.

"They told me you'd leave me," she said in a low voice. "I knew it, too."

"I don't want to desert you, Sien."

"It aint desertion, Vincent. You never done me nothing but good."

"If you are still willing to share my life, I'll take you to Drenthe."

She shook her head without emotion. "No, there aint enough for two of us."

"You understand, don't you, Sien? If I had more, I'd give you anything. But when I must choose between feeding you and feeding my work . . ."

She laid her hand over his; he could feel the rough parchment of her skin. "It's all right. You don't got to feel bad about it. You done all you could for me. I guess it's just time we was through . . . that's all."

"Do you want us to be, Sien? If it will make you happy, I'll marry you and take you with me."

"No. I belong with my mother. We all got to live our own lives. It'll be all right; my brother's going to take a new house for his girl and me."

Vincent drained his glass, tasting the bitter dregs at the bottom.

"Sien, I've tried to help you. I loved you and gave you all the kindness I had in me. In return I want you to do one thing for me, just one thing."

"What?" she asked dully.

"Don't go back on the streets again. It will kill you! For the sake of Antoon, don't go back to that life."

"Have we enough left for another glass of wine?"

"Yes."

She swallowed half the contents in a single gulp and then said "I only know that I can't earn enough, 'specially when I got to pay for all the children. So if I walk the street it will be because I must, not because I want to."

"If you get enough work you'll promise me, won't you, not to go back to that?"

"Sure, I promise."

"I'll send you money, Sien, every month. I'll always pay for the baby. I want you to give the little fellow a chance."

"He'll be all right . . . same as the rest."

Vincent wrote to Theo of his intention to go to the country and sever his connection with Christine. Theo answered by return mail with an extra hundred franc note to pay off his debts, and a strong word of approval. "My patient disappeared the other night," he wrote. "She's completely well now, but we couldn't seem to find any relationship to fit ourselves into. She took everything with her and left me no address. It's better that way. Now you and I are both unencumbered."

Vincent stored all the furniture in the attic. He wanted to come back to The Hague sometime. The day before he was to leave for Drenthe he received a letter and a package from Nuenen. In the package was some tobacco, and one of his mother's cheese bakes wrapped in oil paper.

"When are you coming home to paint those wooden crosses in the churchyard?" his father asked.

He knew at once that he wanted to go home. He was ill, starved, desperately nervous, fatigued and discouraged. He would go home to his mother for a few weeks and recover his health and spirits. A feeling of peace that he had not known for many months came over him when he thought of his Brabant country-side, the hedges and dunes and diggers in the field.

Christine and the two children accompanied him to the station. They all stood on the platform, unable to speak. The train came in and Vincent boarded it. Christine stood there with the baby at her breast, holding Herman by the hand. Vincent watched them until his train pulled out into the glaring sunlight, and the woman was lost forever in the grimy blackness of the station.

BOOK FOUR

NUENEN

1

The vicarage at Nuenen was a two-story, whitewashed, stone building with a tremendous garden in the back. There were elms, hedges, flower beds, a pond, and three pollard oaks. Although Nuenen had a population of twenty-six hundred, only one hundred of them were Protestant. Theodorus's church was tiny; Nuenen was a step down from the prosperous little market town of Etten.

Nuenen was in reality only a small cluster of houses that lined both sides of the road from Eindhoven, the metropolis of the district. Most of the people were weavers and peasants whose huts dotted the heath. They were God fearing, hard working people who lived according to the manners and customs of their ancestors.

On the front of the vicarage, over the door, were the black iron figures A° 1764. The entrance door led straight off the road and admitted to a wide hall which split the house in two. On the left-hand side, dividing the dining room and kitchen, was a rude stairway which led up to the bedrooms. Vincent shared the one over the living room with his brother Cor. When he awoke in the morning he could see the sun rise over the fragile tower of his father's church, and gently lay pastel shades on the pool. At sunset, when the tones were deeper than at dawn, he would sit in a chair by the window and watch the colour being thrown over the pool like a heavy blanket of oil, and then slowly dissolving into the dusk.

Vincent loved his parents; his parents loved him. All three made desperate resolves that the relationship was to be kept friendly and agreeable. Vincent ate a great deal, slept a great deal, walked sometimes on the heath. He talked, painted, and read not at all. Everyone in the house was elaborately courteous to him, as he was to them. It was a self-conscious relationship; before they spoke they had to say to themselves, "I must be careful! I don't want to disrupt the harmony!"

The harmony lasted as long as Vincent's illness. He could not be comfortable in the same room with people who did not think as he thought. When his father remarked, "I am going to read Goethe's 'Faust.' It has been translated by the Reverend Ten Kate, so it cannot be so very immoral," Vincent felt his gorge rise.

He had come home only for a two week vacation, but he loved the Brabant and wanted to stay on. He wished to paint simply and quietly from nature, trying to

135

say nothing but what he saw. He had no other desire than to live deep in the heart of the country, and paint rural life. Like good Father Millet, he wanted to live with, understand, and paint the peasants. He had the firm conviction that there were a few people who, having been drawn into the city and bound up there, yet retained unfading impressions of the country, and remained homesick all their lives for the fields and the peasants.

He had always known that he would come back to the Brabant some day and remain for ever. But he could not stay in Nuenen if his parents did not want him.

"A door must be either open or shut," he said to his father. "Let us try to come to an understanding."

"Yes, Vincent, I want that very much. I see that your painting is going to come to something after all, and I am pleased."

"Very well, tell me frankly whether you think we can all live here in peace. Do you want me to stay?"

"Yes."

"For how long?"

"As long as you wish. This is your home. Your place is with us."

"And if we disagree?"

"Then we must not get upset about it. We must try to live calmly and abide with each other."

"But what am I to do about a studio? You don't want me working in the house."

"I have been thinking about that. Why not take the wrangle room, out in the garden? You can have it all to yourself. No one need bother you."

The wrangle room was just off the kitchen, but there was no connecting door. It was a cubicle of a room, with one small window, high up, looking out onto the garden. The floor was of clay, always damp in winter.

"We'll light a big fire in here, Vincent, and dry the place out. Then we'll put down a plank floor so that you can be perfectly comfortable. What do you say?"

Vincent looked about. It was a humble room, very much like the peasants' huts on the heath. He could turn it into a real rural studio.

"If that window is too small," said Theodorus, "I have a little spare money now and we can make it larger."

"No, no, it's perfect just as it is. I'll get the same amount of light on the model that I would get if I were doing him in his own hut."

They brought in a perforated barrel and lit a big fire. When all the dampness had dried out of the walls and roof, and the clay floor was hard, they laid down the wooden planks. Vincent carried in his little bed, a table, a chair and his easels. He tacked up his sketches, brushed a rough GOGH into the whitewashed wall next to the kitchen, and settled down to become a Dutch Millet.

2

The most interesting people around Nuenen were the weavers. They dwelt in little thatched, clay and straw huts, generally of two rooms. In the one room, with a tiny patch of window letting in just a sliver of light, the family lived. There were square recesses in the walls, about three feet off the ground, for beds; a table, a few chairs, a peat stove, and a rough cabinet for the dishware and pots. The floor was of uneven clay, the walls of mud. In the adjoining room, about a third the size of the living room, and with half its height cut off by sloping eaves, was the loom.

A weaver who worked steadily could weave a piece of sixty yards in a week. While he weaved, a woman had to spool for him. On that piece of cloth the weaver made a net profit of four and a half francs a week. When he took it to the manufacturer, he often got the message that not before one or two weeks had passed could he take another piece home. Vincent found that they had a different spirit from the miners of the Borinage; they were quiet, and nowhere was there to be heard anything resembling rebellious speeches. But they looked as cheerful as cab horses, or the sheep transported by steamer to England.

Vincent quickly made friends with them. He found the weavers to be simple souls, asking only for enough work to earn the potatoes, coffee, and occasional strip of bacon on which they lived. They did not mind his painting while they worked; he never came without a bit of sweet for the child of the family, or a bag of tobacco for the old grandfather.

He found a loom of old, greenish-brown oak, in which the date 1730 was cut. Near the loom, before a little window which looked out on a green plot, stood a baby chair. The baby in it sat gazing for hours at the flying shuttle. It was a miserable little room with a clay floor, but in it Vincent found a certain peace and beauty which he tried to capture on his canvas.

He rose early in the morning and spent the entire day in the fields, or in the huts of the peasants and weavers. He felt at home with the people of the field and the loom. It had not been in vain that he had spent so many evenings with the miners, the peat diggers, and peasants, musing by the fire. By witnessing peasant life continually, at all hours of the day, he had become so absorbed in it that he hardly thought of anything else. He was searching for *ce qui ne passe pas dans ce qui passe*.

He went back to his love of drawing from the figure, but along with it he now had another love; colour. The half-ripe corn fields were of a dark golden tone, ruddy and gold bronze, raised to a maximum of effect by contrast to the broken cobalt tone of the sky. In the background were women's figures, very rough, very energetic, with sunbronzed faces and arms, with dusty, coarse, indigo clothes, and black bonnets in the form of berets on their short hair.

When he came swinging vigorously along the main road, easel strapped to his back, and wet canvas under his arm, the blinds of every house would open just a crack from the bottom, and he would run the gauntlet of curious and scandalized feminine eyes. At home he found that the old saying, "A door must either be open or shut," was not altogether true when applied to family relationships. The door of domestic felicity at the parsonage had a habit of remaining in some mysterious position that was very definitely neither open nor shut. His sister Elizabeth loathed him; she was afraid his eccentricities would ruin her marriage chances in Nuenen. Willemien liked him but thought him a bore. It was not until later that he became friends with his younger brother Cor.

Vincent ate his dinner, not at the family table, but in one corner, his plate on his lap, and the sketches of the day propped up on a chair before him, scrutinizing his work with piercing eyes, ripping it to pieces for imperfections and poor values. He never spoke to the family. They rarely addressed him. He ate his bread dry because he did not want to get in the habit of indulging himself. Occasionally, if the name of some writer whom he liked came up for discussion at the table, he would turn to them and speak for a moment. But on the whole he found that the less they had to say to each other, the better off they all were.

3

He had been painting in the fields for about a month when he began to have the very curious feeling that he was being watched. He knew that the people of Nuenen stared at him, that the peasants in the field used to rest on their hoes occasionally and gaze at him in wonder. But this was something different. He had a sense that he was not only being watched, but followed. For the first few days he tried to shake it off, impatiently, but he could not get rid of the sensation that a pair of eyes was staring holes through his back. Many times he searched the field about him with his glance, but he could see nothing. Once he thought he saw the white skirt of a woman disappear behind a tree when he turned suddenly. Another time, as he came out of a weaver's house, a figure scurried quickly down the road. Still a third time, when he was painting in the woods, he left his easel and walked to the pond for a drink. When he returned, he found fingerprints in the wet paint.

It took him almost two weeks to catch the woman. He was sketching diggers on the heath; there was an old abandoned wagon not far from him. The woman stood behind it while he worked. He picked up his canvas and easel suddenly, and pretended that he was making for home. The woman ran on ahead. He followed without arousing her suspicion, and saw her turn in at the house next to the parsonage.

"Who lives next door on the left, Mother?" he asked as they all sat down to dinner that night.

"The Begeman family."

"Who are they?"

"We don't know much about them. There are five daughters and a mother. The father evidently died some time ago."

"What are they like?"

"It's hard to tell; they're rather secretive."

"Are they Catholic?"

"No, Protestant. The father was a dominie."

"Are any of the girls unmarried?"

"Yes, all of them. Why do you ask?"

"I just wondered. Who supports the family?"

"No one. They seem to be wealthy."

"You don't know any of the girls' names, I suppose?"

His mother looked at him curiously. "No."

The following day he went back to the same spot in the fields. He wanted to catch the blue of the peasant figures in the ripe corn or against the withered leaves of a beech hedge. The people wore a coarse linen which they wove themselves, warp black, woof blue, the result of which was a black and blue, striped pattern. When this faded and became somewhat discoloured by wind and weather, it was an infinitely quiet, delicate tone which just brought out the flesh colours.

About the middle of the morning he felt the woman behind him again. Out of the corner of his eye he caught a sight of her dress in a copse behind the abandoned wagon.

"I'll catch her today," he murmured to himself, "even if I have to stop in the middle of this study."

He was getting more and more into the habit of *dashing a thing off*, getting down his impression of the scene before him in one great splurge of passionate energy. What had struck him most about the old Dutch pictures was that they had been painted quickly, that the great masters dashed off a thing from the first stroke and did not retouch it. They had painted in a grand rush to keep intact the purity of their first impression, of the mood in which the motif had been conceived.

He forgot about the woman, in the heart of his creative passion. When he happened to glance around an hour later, he noticed that she had left the woods and was now standing behind the wagon. He wanted to jump up and catch her, ask her why she had been following him all this time, but he could not tear away from his work. After a while he turned around again and noted to his surprise that she was standing in front of the wagon, gazing at him steadily. It was the first time she had come out into the open.

He went on working at a fever pitch. The harder he worked, the closer the woman seemed to come. The more passion he poured out on the canvas, the hotter the eyes became that were staring through his back. He turned his easel a fraction to get the light and saw that she was standing in the middle of the field, half-way between the wagon and himself. She looked like a woman mesmerized, walking in her sleep. Step by step she came closer and closer, pausing each time, trying to hold back, coming steadily forward, impelled toward him by some power beyond her control. He felt her at his back. He whirled about and gazed into her eyes. There was a frightened, feverish expression on her face; she seemed caught up in some baffling emotion which she could not master. She did not look at Vincent, but at his canvas. He waited for her to speak. She remained silent. He turned back to his work and in a final burst of energy, finished. The woman did not move. He could feel her dress touching his coat.

It was late afternoon. The woman had been standing in the field for many hours. Vincent was exhausted, his nerves worked up to a fine edge by the excitement of creation. He got up and turned to the woman.

Her mouth went dry. She moistened the upper lip with her tongue, then the lower lip with the upper one. The slight moisture vanished instantly and her lips became parched. She had a hand at her throat and seemed to have difficulty in breathing. She tried to speak, but could not.

"I am Vincent Van Gogh, your neighbour," he said. "But I suppose you know that."

"Yes." It was a whisper, so faint he could hardly hear it.

"Which one of the Begeman sisters are you?"

She swayed a little, caught him by the sleeve and steadied herself. Again she tried to moisten her lips with a dry tongue, and made several attempts to speak before she succeeded.

"Margot."

"And why have you been following me, Margot Begeman? I've known about it for several weeks."

A muted cry escaped her lips. She dug her nails into his arms to support herself, then fell to the ground in a faint.

Vincent went on his knees, put his arm under her head, and brushed the hair back from her brow. The sun was just setting red over the fields and the peasants were trudging their weary way home. Vincent and Margot were alone. He looked at her carefully. She was not beautiful. She must have been well on in her thirties. Her mouth stopped abruptly at the left corner, but on the right a thin line continued down almost to the jaw. There were circles of blue with little flesh freckles under the eyes. The skin seemed just on the point of going wrinkled.

Vincent had a little water with him in a canteen. He moistened Margot's face with one of the rags he used to wipe off paint. Her eyes shot open suddenly, and he saw that they were good eyes, a deep brown, tender, almost mystical. He took a little water on the end of his fingers and ran them over Margot's face. She shivered against his arm.

"Are you feeling better, Margot?" he asked.

She lay there for a brief instant, looking into his green-blue eyes, so sympathetic, so penetrating, so understanding. Then, with a wild sob that seemed wrenched from her inmost core, she flung her arms about his neck and buried her lips in his beard.

4

The following day they met at an appointed place some distance from the village. Margot had on a charming, high necked, white cambric dress and was carrying a summer hat in her hand. Although still nervous in his company, she seemed more self-possessed than she had been the day before. Vincent laid down his palette when she came. She had not even a fraction of Kay's delicate beauty, but compared to Christine, she was a very attractive woman.

He rose from his stool, not knowing what to do. Ordinarily he was prejudiced against women who wore dresses; his territory was more those who wore jackets and petticoats. The so-called respectable class of Dutch women was not particularly attractive to paint or look at. He preferred the ordinary servant girls; they were often very Chardin-like.

Margot leaned up and kissed him, simply, possessively, as though they had been sweethearts for a long time, then held herself to him, trembling for a moment. Vincent spread his coat on the ground for her. He sat on his stool; Margot leaned against his knee and looked up at him with an expression that he had never seen before in the eyes of a woman.

"Vincent," she said, just for the pure joy of uttering his name.

"Yes, Margot." He did not know what to do or say.

"Did you think bad things of me last night?"

"Bad things? No. Why should I have?"

"You may find it difficult to believe, but, Vincent, when I kissed you yesterday, it was the first time I had ever kissed a man."

"But why? Have you never been in love?"

"No."

"What a pity."

"Isn't it?" She was silent for a moment. "You have loved other women, haven't you."

"Yes."

"Many of them?"

"No. Just . . . three."

"And did they love you?"

"No, Margot, they didn't."

"But they must have."

"I've always been unfortunate in love."

Margot moved closer to him and rested her arm on his lap. She ran the fingers of her other hand over his face playfully, touching his high ridged, powerful nose, the full, open mouth, the hard, rounded chin. A curious shiver ran through her; she took her fingers away.

"How strong you are," she murmured. "Everything about you; your arms and chin and beard. I've never known a man like you before."

He cupped her face in his hands roughly. The love and excitement that throbbed there made it appealing.

"Do you like me a little?" she asked anxiously.

"Yes."

"And will you kiss me?"

He kissed her.

"Please don't think ill of me, Vincent. I couldn't help myself. You see, I fell in love . . . with you . . . and I couldn't keep away."

"You fell in love with me? You really fell in love with me? But why?"

She leaned up and kissed him on the corner of the mouth. "That's why," she said.

They sat quietly. A little way off was the Cimetière des Paysans. For ages the peasants had been laid to rest in the very fields which they dug up when alive. Vincent was trying to say on his canvas what a simple thing death was, just as simple as the falling of an autumn leaf, just a bit of earth dug up, a wooden cross. The fields around, where the grass of the churchyard ended beyond the little wall, made a last line against the sky, like the horizon of the sea.

"Do you know anything about me, Vincent?" she asked softly.

"Very little."

"Have they . . . has anyone told you . . . my age?"

"No."

"Well, I'm thirty-nine. In a very few months I shall be forty. For the last five years I have been telling myself that if I did not love someone before I left my thirties, I should kill myself."

"But it is easy to love, Margot."

"Ah, you think so?"

"Yes. It's only being loved in return that is difficult."

"No. In Nuenen it is very hard. For over twenty years I have wanted desperately to love someone. And I never have been able to."

"Never?"

She glanced away. "Once . . . when I was a girl . . . I liked a boy."

"Yes?"

"He was a Catholic. They drove him away."

"They?"

"My mother and sisters."

She rose to her knees in the deep loam of the field, soiling her pretty white dress. She placed both elbows on his thighs and rested her face in her hands. His knees touched her sides, gently.

"A woman's life is empty if she has no love to fill it, Vincent."

"I know."

"Every morning, when I awakened, I said to myself, 'Today, surely, I shall find someone to love! Other women do, so why shouldn't I?' Then night would come and I would be alone and miserable. An endless row of empty days, Vincent. I have nothing to do at home—we have servants—and every hour was filled up with longing for love. With each night I said to myself, 'You might just as well have been dead today, for all that you have lived.' I kept bolstering myself up with the thought that some day, somehow, a man must come along whom I could love. My birthdays passed, the thirty-seventh, and eighth, and ninth. I could not have faced forty without ever having loved. Then you came along, Vincent. *Now I too have loved at last!*"

It was a cry of triumph, as though she had gained a great victory. She leaned up, holding her mouth to be kissed. He stroked her soft hair back from her ears. She flung her arms about his neck and kissed him in a thousand wandering nibbles. Sitting there on his little painter's stool, his palette at his side, and the Cimetière des Paysans just in front, holding the kneeling woman close to him, and engulfed in the flow of her welled-up passion, Vincent felt for the first time in his life the luscious, healing balm of a woman's outpoured love. And he trembled, for he knew that he was on sacred ground.

Margot sat on the earth between his legs, her head back on his knee. There was colour in her cheeks and lustre in her eyes; she was breathing deeply and with effort. In the flush of her love she looked not more than thirty. Vincent, unable to feel anything at all, ran his fingers over the soft skin of her face until she clasped his hand, kissed it, and held the palm against her burning cheek. After a time she spoke.

"I know that you don't love me," she said quietly. "That would be asking too much. I only prayed to God to let me fall in love. I never even dreamed it would be possible for anyone to love me. It's loving that's important, isn't it, Vincent, not being loved."

Vincent thought of Ursula and Kay. "Yes," he replied.

She rubbed the back of her head against his knee, looking up at the blue sky. "And you'll let me come with you? If you don't want to talk, I'll just sit by quietly and never say a word. Only let me be near you; I promise not to disturb you or interfere with your work."

"Of course you can come. But tell me, Margot, if there were no men in Nuenen, why didn't you go away? At least for a visit? Didn't you have the money?"

"Oh, yes, I have plenty of money. My grandfather left me a good income."

"Then why didn't you go to Amsterdam or The Hague? You would have met some interesting men."

"They didn't want me to."

"None of your sisters are married, are they?"

"No, dear, all five of us are single."

A flash of pain went through him. It was the first time a woman had ever called him dear. He had known before how miserable it was to love and not be loved in return, but he had never suspected the utter sweetness of having a good woman love him with the whole of her being. He had looked upon Margot's love for him as a sort of curious accident to which he was no party. That one, simple word, spoken so quietly and fondly by Margot, changed his entire mental state. He gathered Margot to him and held her quivering body against his.

"Vincent, Vincent," she murmured, "I love you so."

"How queer that sounds, to hear you say you love me so."

"I don't mind now that I've had to go all these years without love. You were worth waiting for, my very own dear. In all my dreams of love I never imagined that I could feel about anyone the way I do about you."

"I love you too, Margot," he said.

She drew away from him slightly. "You don't have to say that, Vincent. Maybe after a while you will come to like me a little. But now all I ask is that you let me love you!"

She slipped out of his arms, put his coat off to one side, and sat down. "Go to work, dear," she said. "I must not get in your way. And I love to watch you paint."

5

Nearly every day Margot accompanied him when he went out to paint. Oftentimes he would walk ten kilometres to reach the exact spot on the heath that he wanted to work with, and they would both arrive tired and exhausted by the heat. But Margot never complained. The woman had undergone a startling metamorphosis. Her hair, which had been a mouse brown, took on a live blond tint. Her lips had been thin and parched; now her mouth went full and red. Her skin had been dry and almost wrinkled; now it was smooth and soft and warm. Her eyes seemed to grow larger, her breasts swelled out, her voice took on a new lilt, and her step became strong and vigorous. Love had opened some strange spring within her, and she was constantly being bathed in its elixir of love. She brought surprise lunches to please him, sent to Paris for some prints that he had mentioned with admiration, and never intruded on his work. When he painted, she sat perfectly still at his side, bathing in the same luxuriant passion that he flung at his canvases.

Margot knew nothing about painting, but she had a quick and sensitive intelligence, and a faculty for saying the right thing at the right moment. Vincent found that, without knowing, she understood. She gave him the impression of a Cremona violin that had been spoiled by bungling repairers.

"If I had only met her ten years ago!" he said to himself.

One day she asked him, as he was preparing to attack a new canvas, "How can you be sure that the spot you choose will come out right on the canvas?"

Vincent thought for a moment and then replied, "If I want to be active, I must not be afraid of failures. When I see a blank canvas staring at me with a certain imbecility, I just dash something down."

"You certainly do dash. I never saw anything grow as fast as your canvases."

"Well, I have to. I find paralysing the stare of a blank canvas which says to me, 'You don't know anything!' "

"You mean it's a sort of challenge?"

"Exactly. The blank canvas stares at me like an idiot, but I know that it is afraid of the passionate painter who dares, who once and for all has broken the spell of that 'you cannot.' Life itself turns towards a man an infinitely vacant, discouraging, hopelessly blank side on which nothing is written, Margot, no more than on this blank canvas."

"Yes, doesn't it."

"But the man of faith and energy is not frightened by that blankness; he steps in, he acts, he builds up, he creates, and in the end the canvas is no longer blank but covered with the rich pattern of life."

Vincent enjoyed having Margot in love with him. She never looked upon him with critical eyes. Everything he did she thought right. She did not tell him that his manners were crude, that his voice was rough, that there were harsh lines in his face. She never condemned him for not earning money, or suggested that he do anything but paint. Walking home through the quiet dusk, his arm about her waist, his voice soft from her sympathy, he told her of all the things he had done, of why he preferred painting the *rouwboerke* (peasant in mourning) to the Mayor, why he thought a peasant girl, in her dusty and patched blue petticoat and bodice, more beautiful than a lady. She questioned nothing and accepted everything. He was what he was, and she loved him completely.

Vincent was unable to get used to his new position. Every day he waited for the relationship to break, for Margot to become unkind and cruel, and confront him with his failures. Her love increased with the ripening of the summer; she gave him that fullness of sympathy and adoration which only a mature woman can bestow. Unsatisfied that she did not turn against him of her own accord, he tried to goad her into condemnation by painting his failures as black as he could. She saw them not as failures, but as simple accounts of why he did what he had to do.

He told her the story of his fiasco in Amsterdam and the Borinage. "Surely that was a failure," he said. "Everything I did there was wrong, now wasn't it?"

She smiled up at him indulgently. "The king can do no wrong."

He kissed her.

Another day she said to him, "My mother tells me you are a wicked man. She has heard that you lived with loose women in The Hague. I told them it was vicious scandal."

Vincent related the tale of Christine. Margot listened with some of the brooding melancholy in her eyes that had been there before love dissipated it.

"You know, Vincent, there's something Christ-like about you. I'm sure my father would have thought so, too."

"And that's all you can find to say to me when I tell you I lived for two years with a prostitute?"

"She wasn't a prostitute; she was your wife. Your failure to save her was not your fault, any more than was your failure to save the Borains. One man can do very little against a whole civilization."

"It's true, Christine was my wife. I told my brother Theo, when I was younger, 'If I cannot get a good wife, I shall take a bad one. Better a bad one than none at all.' "

There was a slightly strained silence; the subject of marriage had not come up between them. "There is only one thing I regret about the Christine affair," said Margot. "I wish I could have had those two years of your love for myself."

He gave up trying to break her love for him, and accepted it. "When I was younger, Margot," he said, "I thought that things depended on chance, on small accidents or misunderstandings that had no reason. But getting older, I begin to see deeper motives. It is the plight of most people that by a kind of fatality they have to seek a long time for light.''

"As I had to seek for you!"

They had reached the low door of a weaver's house. Vincent pressed her hand warmly. She gave him a smile of such sweet surrender that he wondered why fate had seen fit to keep love from him all these years. They entered the thatched hut. Summer had passed into fall and the days were growing dark. A suspension lamp hung over the loom. A piece of red cloth was being woven. The weaver and his wife were arranging the threads; dark, bent figures against the light, standing out against the colour of the cloth, casting big shadows on the laths and beams of the loom. Margot and Vincent exchanged an understanding smile; he had taught her to catch the underlying beauty in ugly places.

By November and the *chute des feuilles,* when all the leaves on the trees fell off in a few days, the whole of Nuenen was talking about Vincent and Margot. The village liked Margot; it distrusted and feared Vincent. Margot's mother and four sisters tried to break off the affair, but she insisted that it was only a friendship, and what harm could there be in walking in the fields together? The Begemans knew Vincent to be a drifter, and confidently expected him to leave any day. They were not greatly worried. The village was; it said over and over again that no good could come from that queer Van Gogh man, and that the Begeman family would regret it if they did not keep their daughter out of his hands.

Vincent could never understand why the people of the town disliked him so. He interfered with no one, injured no one. He did not realize what a strange picture he made in this quiet hamlet, where life had not changed in one word or custom for hundreds of years. It was not until he found that they thought him an idler that he gave up hope of making them like him. Dien van den Beek, a small shopkeeper, hailed him as he was passing one day, and threw down the gage for the village.

"Fall has come now and the nice weather is over, eh?" he asked.

"Yes."

"A man supposes you'll be going to work soon, eh?"

Vincent shifted the easel on his back to a more comfortable position. "Yes, I'm just on my way out to the heath."

"No, I mean work," said Dien. "Real work that you do all year."

"Painting is my work," said Vincent quietly.

"A man means work that you get paid for; a job."

"Going to the fields as you see me now is my job, Mijnheer van den Beek, just as selling goods is yours."

"Yes, but I sell goods! Do you sell what you make?"

Every soul to whom he had spoken in the village had asked that identical question. He was getting heartily sick of it.

"I sell sometimes. My brother is a dealer and he buys."

"You should go to work, Mijnheer. It is not good for you to idle this way. A man will grow old and he will have nothing."

"Idle! I work twice as long as you keep this store open."

"You call that work? Sitting and daubing? That's only play for children. Keep a store; plough in the fields; that's a real man's work. You're getting too old to be wasting your time."

Vincent knew that Dien van den Beek merely voiced the opinion of the village, and that to the provincial mind the words artist and worker were mutually exclusive. He gave up caring what the people thought, and ceased to see them when he passed them on the street. When their distrust of him had come to a positive climax, an accident happened that put him back in favour.

Anna Cornelia broke her leg on getting out of the train at Helmond. She was rushed home immediately. Although the doctor did not tell the family so, he feared for her life. Vincent threw aside his work without a second thought. His experience in the Borinage had made him an excellent nurse. The doctor watched him for a half hour and then said, "You are better than a woman; your mother will be in excellent hands."

The people of Nuenen, who could be as kind in times of a crisis as they could be cruel in times of boredom, came to the vicarage with dainties and books and comforting thoughts. They stared at Vincent in utter amazement; he changed the bed without moving his mother, bathed and fed her, took care of the cast on her leg. At the end of two weeks, the village had completely revised its opinion of him. He spoke to them in their own language when they came; they discussed how best to avoid bed sores, what foods a sick person should eat, how warm the room should be kept. Talking to him thus and understanding him, they decided that he was a human being after all. When his mother felt a little better and he could go out to paint for a short time each day, they addressed him with a smile, and by name. He no longer felt the blinds go up a tiny fraction from the bottom, one by one, as he walked through the town.

Margot was at his side at all times. She was the only one who was not amazed at his gentleness. They were speaking in whispers in the sick room one day, when Vincent happened to remark, "The key to many things is the thorough knowledge of the human body, but it decidedly costs money to learn it. There is a very beautiful book, 'Anatomy for Artists,' by John Marshall, but it is very expensive."

"Haven't you the money to spare?"

"No, and I shan't have until I sell something."

"Vincent, it would make me so happy if you would let me lend you some. You know I have a regular income, and I never manage to spend it."

"It's good of you, Margot, but I couldn't."

She did not press her point, but a couple of weeks later handed him a package from The Hague. "What is it?" he asked.

"Open it and see."

There was a little note tied on the cord. The package contained Marshall's book; the note read FOR THE HAPPIEST BIRTHDAY OF THEM ALL.

"But this isn't my birthday!" he exclaimed.

"No," laughed Margot, "its mine! My fortieth, Vincent. You gave me a present of my life. Do be good and take it, dear. I'm so happy today, and I want you to be, too."

They were in his studio in the garden. No one was about, only Willemien who was sitting with her mother in the house. It was late afternoon, and the falling sun pasted a slight patch of light on the whitewashed wall. Vincent fingered the book tenderly; it was the first time anyone but Theo had been so happy to help him. He threw the book on the bed and took Margot in his arms. Her eyes were slightly misty with the love of him. During the past few months they had done very little caressing in the fields; they were afraid of being seen. Margot always gave herself to his caresses so whole-heartedly, with such generous surrender. It was five months now since he had left Christine; he was a little nervous about trusting himself too far. He wanted to do nothing to injure Margot or her love for him.

He looked down into her kind brown eyes as he kissed her. She smiled at him, then closed her eyes and opened her lips slightly to receive his. They held each other tightly, their bodies fitting from mouth to toe. The bed was only a step away. Together, they sat down. In that locked embrace each forgot the loveless years that had made their lives so stark.

The sun sank and the square of light on the wall went out. The wrangle room was bathed in a mellow dusk. Margot ran her hand over Vincent's face, strange sounds coming from her throat in the language of love. Vincent felt himself sinking into the abyss from which there is only one precipitate return. He tore himself from Margot's arms and jumped up. He went to his easel and crumpled a piece of paper on which he had been working. There was no sound but the call of the magpie in the acacias and the tinkling bells of the cows coming home. After a moment Margot spoke, quietly and simply.

"You can if you want, dear," she said.

"Why?" he asked, without turning about.

"Because I love you."

"It wouldn't be right."

"I told you before, Vincent, the king can do no wrong!"

He dropped on one knee. Her head lay on the pillow. He noticed again the line on the right side of her mouth, that ran down to her jaw, and kissed it. He kissed the too narrow bridge of her nose, the too full nostrils, and ran his lips over the skin of her face that had gone ten years younger. In the dusk, lying receptively with her arms about his neck, she looked again the beautiful girl she must have been at twenty.

"I love you, too, Margot," he said. "I didn't know it before, but now I do."

"It's sweet of you to say that, dear." Her voice was gentle and dreamy. "I know you like me a little. And I love you with all my heart. That satisfies me."

He did not love her as he had loved Ursula and Kay. He did not even love her as he had loved Christine. But he felt something very tender for this woman lying so passively in his arms. He knew that love included nearly every human relationship. Something within him ached at the thought that he could feel so little for the only woman in the world who loved him unrestrainedly, and he remembered the agony he had undergone because Ursula and Kay had not returned his love. He respected Margot's overwhelming love for him, yet in some inexplicable way he found it a trifle distasteful. Kneeling on the plank floor of the dark wrangle room, with his arm under the head of the woman who loved him just as he had loved Ursula and Kay, he at last understood why the two women had fled from him.

"Margot," he said, "my life is a poor one, but I should be very happy if you would share it with me."

"I want to share it with you, dear."

"We could stay right here in Nuenen. Or would you rather go away after we're married?"

She rubbed her head against his arm, caressingly. "What is it that Ruth said? 'Whither thou goest, I will go.'"

6

They were in no way prepared for the storm that arose the next morning when they broke the news to their respective families. With the Van Goghs the problem was simply one of money. How could he take a wife when Theo was supporting him?

"First you must earn money and make your life straight; then you can marry," said his father.

"If I make my life straight by wrestling with the naked truth of my craft," replied Vincent, "the earning of money will come in due time."

"Then you must also marry in due time. But not now!"

The disturbance in the vicarage was only a little squall compared to what was going on next door in the house of women. With five sisters, all unmarried, the Begemans could face the world in a solid front. Margot's marriage would be a living proof to the village of the failure of the other girls. Madame Begeman thought it better that four of her daughters be kept from further unhappiness than that one of them be made happy.

Margot did not accompany him to the weavers that day. Late in the afternoon she came to the studio. Her eyes were puffy and swollen; she looked more her forty years than ever before. She held him close for a moment in a sort of desperate embrace.

"They've been abusing you frightfully all day," she said. "I never knew a man could be so many bad things and still live." ·

"You should have expected that."

"I did. But I had no idea they would attack you so viciously."

He put his arm about her gently and kissed her cheek. "Just leave them to me," he said. "I'll come in tonight after supper. Perhaps I can persuade them that I'm not such an awful person."

As soon as he set foot in the Begeman house he knew that he was in strange, alien territory. There was something sinister about the atmosphere created by six women, an atmosphere never broken by a masculine voice or footstep.

They led him into the parlour. It was cold and musty. There had not been people in it for months. Vincent knew the four sisters' names, but he had never taken the trouble to attach the names to the faces. They all seemed like caricatures of Margot. The eldest sister, who ran the household, took it upon herself to manage the inquisition.

"Margot tells us that you wish to marry her. May one presume to ask what has happened to your wife in The Hague?"

Vincent explained about Christine. The atmosphere of the parlour went several degrees colder.

"How old are you, Mijnheer Van Gogh?"

"Thirty-one."

"Has Margot told you that she is . . ."

"I know Margot's age."

"May one presume to ask how much money you earn?"

"I have a hundred and fifty francs a month."

"What is the source of that income?"

"My brother sends it to me."

"You mean your brother supports you?"

"No. He pays me a monthly salary. In return he gets everything I paint."

"How many of them does he sell?"

"I really couldn't say."

"Well, I can. Your father tells me he has never sold one of your pictures yet."

"He will sell them later. They will bring him in many times as much as they would now."

"That is problematical, to say the least. Suppose we discuss the facts."

Vincent studied the hard, unbeautiful face of the eldest sister. He could expect no sympathy from that quarter.

"If you don't earn anything," she continued, "may one be allowed to ask how you expect to support a wife?"

"My brother chooses to gamble a hundred and fifty francs a month on me; that's his affair, not yours. For me it remains a salary. I work very hard to earn it. Margot and I could live on that salary if we managed carefully."

"But we wouldn't have to!" cried Margot. "I have enough to take care of myself."

"Be quiet, Margot!" commanded her eldest sister.

"Remember, Margot," said her mother, "I have the power to stop that income if you ever do anything to disgrace the family name!"

Vincent smiled. "Would marrying me be a disgrace?" he asked.

"We know very little about you, Mijnheer Van Gogh, and that little is unfortunate. How long have you been a painter?"

"Three years."

"And you are not successful yet. How long will it take you to become successful?"

"I don't know."

"What were you before you took up painting?"

"An art dealer, teacher, book-seller, divinity student and evangelist."

"And you failed at all of them?"

"I gave them up."

"Why?"

"I was not suited to them."

"How long will it take you to give up painting?"

"He'll never do that!" exclaimed Margot.

"It seems to me, Mijnheer Van Gogh," said the old sister, "that you are presumptuous in wanting to marry Margot. You're hopelessly *déclassé*, you haven't a franc to your name, nor any way of earning one, you are unable to stick to any sort of job, and you drift about like an idler and a tramp. How could we dare to let our sister marry you?"

Vincent reached for his pipe, then put it back again. "Margot loves me and I love her. I can make her happy. We would live here for another year or so and then go abroad. She will never receive anything but kindness and love from me."

"You'll desert her!" cried one of the other sisters who had a shriller voice. "You'll get tired of her and desert her for some bad woman like the one in The Hague!"

"You just want to marry her for her money!" said another.

"But you won't get it," announced the third. "Mother will turn the allowance back into the estate."

Tears came to Margot's eyes. Vincent rose. He realized that there was no use wasting time on these viragoes. He would simply have to marry Margot in Eindhoven and leave for Paris immediately. He did not want to go away from the Brabant yet; his work was not finished there. But he shuddered when he thought of leaving Margot alone in that house of barren women.

Margot suffered in the days that followed. The first snow fell and Vincent was forced to work in his studio. The Begemans would not allow Margot to visit him. From the moment she got out of bed in the morning until she was permitted to feign sleep, she was forced to listen to tirades against Vincent. She had lived with her family for forty years; she had known Vincent only a few months. She hated her sisters, for she knew they had destroyed her life, but hatred is one of the more obscure forms of love and sometimes breeds a stronger sense of duty.

"I don't understand why you won't come away with me," Vincent told her, "or at least marry me here without their consent."

"They wouldn't let me."

"Your mother?"

"My sisters. Mother merely sits back and agrees."

"Does it matter what your sisters say?"

"Do you remember I told you that when I was young I almost fell in love with a boy?"

"Yes."

"They stopped that. My sisters. I don't know why. All my life they've stopped the things I wanted to do. When I decided to visit relatives in the city, they wouldn't let me go. When I wished to read, they wouldn't allow the better books in the house. Every time I invited a man to the house, they would rip him to pieces after he left so that I could never look at him again. I wanted to do something with my life; become a nurse, or study music. But no, I had to think the same things they thought, and live exactly as they lived."

"And now?"

"Now they won't let me marry you."

Much of the newly acquired life had gone out of her voice and carriage. Her lips were dry, and the tiny flesh freckles under her eyes stood out.

"Don't worry about them, Margot. We will marry and that will be the end of it. My brother has often suggested that I come to Paris. We could live there."

She did not answer. She sat on the edge of the bed and stared down at the floor planking. Her shoulders turned in a crescent. He sat beside her and took her hand.

"Are you afraid to marry me without their consent?"

"No." Her voice was without strength or conviction. "I'll kill myself, Vincent, if they take me away from you. I couldn't stand it. Not after having loved you. I'll kill myself, that's all."

"They wouldn't have to know. Do it first and tell them afterwards."

"I can't go against them. They're too many for me. I can't fight them all."

"Well, don't bother fighting them. Just marry me and that will be the end of it."

"It wouldn't be the end. It would be the beginning. You don't know my sisters."

"Nor do I want to! But I'll have another try at them tonight."

He knew it was futile, the moment he entered the parlour. He had forgotten the chilling air of the place.

"We've heard all that before, Mijnheer Van Gogh," said the sister, "and it neither convinces nor impresses us. We have made up our minds about this matter. We want to see Margot happy, but we don't want her to throw her life away. We have decided that if at the end of two years you still want to marry, we will withdraw our objections."

"Two years!" said Vincent.

"I won't be here in two years," said Margot quietly.

"Where will you be?"

"I'll be dead. I'll kill myself if you don't let me marry him."

During the flood of, "How dare you say such things!" and "You see the sort of influence he's had on her!" Vincent escaped. There was nothing more he could do.

The years of maladjustment had told on Margot. She was not nervously strong, nor was her health of the best. Under the frontal attack of the five determined women, her spirits sank lower and lower with each passing day. A girl of twenty might have fought her way out unscathed, but Margot had had all the resistance and will beaten out of her. The wrinkles showed on her face, the old melancholy returned to her eyes, her skin went sallow and rough. The line on the right side of her mouth deepened.

The affection Vincent had felt for Margot evaporated with her beauty. He had never really loved her or wanted to marry her; now he wanted to less than ever. He was ashamed of his callousness; that made him all the more ardent in his love making. He did not know whether she divined his true feelings.

"Do you love them more than you do me, Margot?" he asked one day when she managed to escape to his studio for a few minutes.

She shot him a look of surprise and reproach. "Oh, Vincent!"

"Then why are you willing to give me up?"

She cuddled into his arms like a tired child. Her voice was low and lost. "If I thought you loved me as I love you, I would go against the whole world. But it means so little to you . . . and so much to them . . ."

"Margot, you're mistaken, I love you . . ."

She laid her finger gently on his lips. "No, dear, you would like to . . . but you don't. You mustn't feel badly about it. I want to be the one who loves the most."

"Why don't you break away from them and be your own master?"

"It's easy for you to say that. You're strong; you can fight anyone. But I'm forty . . . I was born in Nuenen . . . I've never been farther away than Eindhoven. Don't you see, dear, I've never broken with anyone or anything in my life."

"Yes, I see."

"If it was something *you* wanted, Vincent, I would fight for you with all my strength. But it's only something I want. And after all, it comes so late . . . my life is gone by now . . ."

Her voice sank to a whisper. He raised her chin with his first finger and held it with his thumb. There were unshed tears in her eyes.

"My dear girl," he said. "My very dear Margot. We could live a whole life together. All you need to say is the word. Pack your clothes tonight while your family is asleep. You can hand them to me out the window. We'll walk to Eindhoven and catch the early morning train to Paris."

"It's no use, dear. I'm part of them and they're part of me. But in the end I'll have my way."

"Margot, I can't bear to see you unhappy this way."

She turned her face to him. The tears went away. She smiled. "No, Vincent, I'm happy. I got what I asked for. It's been wonderful loving you."

He kissed her, and on her lips he tasted the salt from the tears that had rolled down her cheek.

"It has stopped snowing," she said a little later. "Are you going to sketch in the fields tomorrow?"

"Yes, I think so."

"Where will you be? I'll come to you in the afternoon."

He worked late the next day, a fur cap on his head and the linen blouse drawn tightly around his neck. The evening sky was of lilac with gold, over dark silhouettes of the cottages, between the masses of ruddy-coloured brushwood. Above, the spare black poplars rose; the foreground was of a faded and bleached green, varied by strips of black earth and pale dry reeds along the ditch edges.

Margot came walking rapidly across the field. She was wearing the same white dress in which he had first met her, with a scarf thrown over her shoulders. He noticed a faint touch of colour in her cheeks. She looked like the woman who had bloomed so beautifully under love only a few weeks back. She was carrying a small work-basket in her hands.

She flung her arms about his neck. He could feel her heart beating wildly against him. He tipped her head back and looked into the brownness of her eyes. The melancholy was gone.

"What is it?" he asked. "Has something happened?"

"No, no," she cried, "it's . . . it's just that I'm happy . . . to be with you again. . . ."

"But why have you come out in this light dress?"

She was silent for a moment and then said, "Vincent, no matter how far away you go, I want you always to remember one thing about me."

"What, Margot?"

"That I loved you! Always remember that I loved you more than any other woman in your whole life."

"Why are you trembling so?"

"It's nothing. I was detained. That's why I was late. Are you nearly finished?"

"In a few moments."

"Then let me sit behind you while you work, just as I used to. You know, dear, I never wanted to be in your way, or hinder you. I only wanted you to let me love you."

"Yes, Margot." He could think of nothing else to say.

"Then go to work, my darling, and finish . . . so that we can go home together."

She shivered a little, drew the scarf about her, and said, "Before you begin, Vincent, kiss me just once more. The way you kissed me . . . that time . . . in your studio . . . when we were so happy in each other's arms."

He kissed her tenderly. She drew her dress about her and sat behind him. The sun disappeared and the short winter gloaming fell over the flat land. The quiet of the country evening engulfed them.

There was the clink of a bottle. Margot rose to her knees with a half stifled cry, then sank to the earth in a violent spasm. Vincent jumped up and flung himself before her. Her eyes were closed; across her face was spread a sardonic smile. She went through a series of quick convulsions; her body went rigid and arched backwards, with the arms flexed. Vincent bent over the bottle that was lying in the snow. A white, crystalline residue had been left just inside the mouth of the bottle. It was odourless.

He picked Margot up in his arms and ran madly across the fields. He was a kilometre away from Nuenen. He was afraid she would die before he could get her back to the village. It was just before the supper hour. People were sitting out in front of their doors. Vincent came in the far side of town and had to run through the full length of the village with Margot in his arms. He reached the Begeman house, kicked the door open with a smash of his boot, and laid Margot on the sofa in the parlour. The mother and sisters came running in.

"Margot took poison!" he cried. "I'll get the doctor!"

He ran for the village doctor and dragged him away from his supper table. "You are sure it was strychnine?" the medical man demanded.

"It looked that way."

"And she was still alive when you got her home?"

"Yes."

Margot was writhing on the divan when they got there. The doctor bent over her.

"It was strychnine, all right," he said, "but she took something along with it to kill the pain. Smells to me like laudanum. She didn't realize it would act as an antidote."

"Then she will live, doctor?" demanded the mother.

"She has a chance. We must get her to Utrecht immediately. She will have to be kept under close observation."

"Can you recommend a hospital in Utrecht?"

"I don't think a hospital advisable. We had better take her to a *maison de santé* for a time. I know a good one. Order your carriage. We must make that last train out of Eindhoven."

Vincent stood in a dark corner, silent. The carriage was brought around to the front of the house. The doctor wrapped Margot in a blanket and carried her out. Her mother and five sisters followed. Vincent brought up the rear. His family was standing next door, on the porch of the vicarage. The whole village had gathered before the Begeman house. A hard silence fell when the doctor came out with Margot in his arms. He lifted her into the carriage. The women got in. Vincent stood beside it. The doctor picked up the reins. Margot's mother turned, saw Vincent, and screamed,

"You did this! You killed my daughter!"

The crowd looked at Vincent. The doctor flicked the horses with the whip. The carriage disappeared down the road.

7

Before his mother had broken her leg, the villagers were unfriendly toward Vincent because they mistrusted him and could not understand his way of life. But they had never actively disliked him. Now they turned against him violently, and he could feel their hatred surrounding him on all sides. Backs were turned when he approached. No one spoke to him or saw him. He became a pariah.

He did not mind for his own sake—the weavers and peasants in their huts still accepted him as their friend—but when people stopped coming to the parsonage to see his parents, he realized that he would have to move.

Vincent knew that the best thing for him to do was to get out of the Brabant altogether and leave his parents in peace. But where was he to go? The Brabant was his home. He wanted to live there always. He wished to draw the peasants and weavers; in that he found the only justification for his work. He knew that it was a good thing in the winter to be deep in the snow, in the autumn deep in the yellow leaves, in the summer among the ripe corn, and in spring amid the grass; that it was a good thing to be always with the mowers and peasant girls, in summer with a big sky overhead, in winter by the fireside, and to feel that it always had been so and always would be.

For him Millet's *Angelus* was the closest man had ever come to creating anything divine. In the crudeness of peasant life he found the only true and lasting reality. He wanted to paint out of doors, on the spot itself. There he would have to wipe off hundreds of flies, battle the dust and sand, and get the canvases scratched as he carried them for hours across the heath and hedges. But when he returned he would know that he had been face to face with reality and had caught something of its elemental simplicity. If his peasant pictures smelled of bacon, smoke, and potato steam, that was not unhealthy. If a stable smelled of dung, that belonged to a stable. If the fields had an odour of ripe corn or of guano or manure, that too was healthy—especially for people from the city.

He solved his problem in a very simple manner. A short distance down the road was the Catholic church, and next to it the house of the caretaker. Johannus Schafrath was a tailor; he followed that trade when he was not taking care of the church. His wife Adriana was a good soul. She rented Vincent two rooms, with a sort of pleasure at being able to do something for the man against whom the whole village had turned.

The Schafrath house was divided in the middle by a large hallway; on the right, as one entered, were the quarters of the family. On the left was a large sitting room overlooking the road, and a smaller room behind it. The sitting room became Vincent's studio, the one behind it his storeroom. He slept upstairs in the beamed attic, one half of which was used for hanging out the Schafrath wash. In the other half was a high bed with a *veeren bed,* and a chair. When night came, Vincent would throw his clothes over the chair, jump into bed, smoke a bowl of tobacco, watch the glow fade into the darkness, and fall asleep.

In the studio he put up his drawings in water-colour and chalk; heads of men and women whose negro-like, turned up noses, projecting jawbones, and large ears were strongly accentuated. There were weavers and weavers' looms, women driving the shuttle, peasants planting potatoes. He made friends with his brother Cor; together they built a cupboard and collected at least thirty different birds' nests, all kinds of moss and plants from the heath, shuttles, spinning wheels, bed warmers, peasants' tools, old caps and hats, wooden shoes, dishes, and everything connected with country life. They even put a small tree in one of the rear corners.

He settled down to work. He found that bistre and bitumen, which most painters were abandoning, made his colouring ripe and mellow. He discovered that he had to put little yellow in a colour to make it seem very yellow, if he placed it next to a violet or lilac tone.

He also learned that isolation is a sort of prison.

In March his father, who had walked a great distance over the heath to visit a sick parishioner, fell in a heap on the back steps of the parsonage. When Anna Cornelia got to him he was already dead. They buried him in the garden near the old church. Theo came home for the funeral. That night they sat in Vincent's studio, talking first of family affairs, then of their work.

"I have been offered a thousand francs a month to leave Goupils and go with a new house," said Theo.

"Are you going to take it?"

"I think not. I have an idea their policy will be purely commercial."

"But you've been writing me that Goupils . . ."

"I know, *les Messieurs* are also after the big profits. Still, I have been with them for twelve years. Why should I change for a few more francs? Some day they may put me in charge of one of their branches. If they do, I shall begin selling the Impressionists."

"Impressionists? I think I've seen that name in print somewhere. Who are they?"

"Oh, just the younger painters around Paris; Edouard Manet, Degas, Renoir, Claude Monet, Sisley, Courbet, Lautrec, Gauguin, Cezanne, Seurat."

"Where did they get their name?"

"From the exhibition of 1874 at Nadar's. Claude Monet had a canvas there which he called *Impression: Soleil Levant*. A newspaper critic by the name of Louis Leroy called it an exhibition of *Impressionistes* and the name has stuck."

"Do they work in light or dark colours?"

"Oh, light! They despise dark colours."

"Then I don't think I could work with them. I intend to change my colouring, but I shall go darker instead of lighter."

"Perhaps you will think differently when you come to Paris."

"Perhaps so. Are any of them selling?"

"Durand-Ruel sells an occasional Manet. That's about all."

"Then how do they live?"

"Lord only knows. On their wits, mostly. Rousseau gives violin lessons to children; Gauguin borrows from his former stock exchange friends; Seurat is supported by his mother; Cezanne by his father. I can't imagine where the others get their money."

"Do you know them all, Theo?"

"Yes, I'm getting acquainted slowly. I've been persuading *les Messieurs* to give them a small corner for exhibition at Goupils, but they wouldn't touch an Impressionist canvas with a ten foot pole."

"Those fellows sound like the sort I ought to meet. See here, Theo, you do absolutely nothing to procure me some distraction by meeting other painters."

Theo went to the front window of the studio and stared out over the tiny grass plot that separated the caretaker's house from the road to Eindhoven.

"Then come to Paris and live with me," he said. "You're sure to end up there eventually."

"I'm not ready yet. I have some work to finish here, first."

"Well, if you remain in the provinces you can't hope to associate with your own kind."

"That may be true. But, Theo, there is one thing I cannot understand. You have never sold a single drawing or painting for me; in fact you have never even tried. Now have you?"

"No."

"Why not?"

"I've shown your work to the connoisseurs. They say . . ."

"Oh, the connoisseurs!" Vincent shrugged his shoulders. "I'm well acquainted with the banalities in which most connoisseurs indulge. Surely, Theo, you must know that their opinions have very little to do with the inherent quality of a piece of work."

"Well, I shouldn't say that. Your work is almost salable, but . . ."

"Theo, Theo, those are the identical words you wrote to me about my very first sketches from Etten."

"They are true, Vincent; you seem constantly on the verge of coming into a superb maturity. I pick up each new sketch eagerly, hoping that at last it has happened. But so far . . ."

"As for being salable or unsalable," interrupted Vincent, knocking out his pipe on the stove, "that is an old saw on which I do not intend to blunt my teeth."

"You say you have work here. Then pitch in and finish it. The sooner you get to Paris, the better it will be for you. But if you want me to sell in the meantime, send me pictures instead of studies. Nobody wants studies."

"Well, it's rather difficult to say just where a study leaves off and a picture begins. Let us paint as much as we can, Theo, and be ourselves with all our faults and qualities. I say 'us' because the money from you, which I know costs you trouble enough to procure for me, gives you the right to consider half of it your own creation."

"Oh, as for that . . ." Theo walked to the rear of the room and toyed with an old bonnet that hung on the tree.

8

Before his father's death Vincent had visited the parsonage only occasionally for supper or an hour of company. After the funeral his sister Elizabeth made it plain that he was entirely *persona non grata;* the family wished to keep up a certain position. His mother felt that he was responsible for his own life, and that it was her duty to stand by her daughters.

He was utterly alone in Nuenen now; in place of people, he put his study of nature. He began with a hopeless struggle to follow nature, and everything went wrong; he ended by calmly creating from his own palette and nature agreed with it and followed. When he was miserable in his aloneness, he thought of the scene in Weissenbruch's studio and the sharp-tongued painter's approval of pain. In his faithful Millet he found Weissenbruch's philosophy expressed more cogently: "I do not ever wish to suppress suffering, because often it is that which makes the artists express themselves most forcibly."

He became friends with a family of peasants by the name of De Groot. There were the mother, father, son, and two daughters, all of whom worked in the fields. The De Groots, like most of the peasants of the Brabant, had as much right to be called *gueules noires* as the miners of the Borinage. Their faces were negroid, with wide, dilated nostrils, humped noses, huge distended lips and long angular ears. The features thrust far forward from the forehead, the head was small and pointed. They lived in a hut of one room with holes in the walls for beds. There was a table in the centre of the room, two chairs, a number of boxes, and a suspension lamp that hung down from the rough, beamed ceiling.

The De Groots were potato eaters. With their supper they had a cup of black coffee and, perhaps once a week, a strip of bacon. They planted potatoes, dug up potatoes and ate potatoes; that was their life.

Stien de Groot was a sweet child of about seventeen. She wore a wide white bonnet to work, and a black jacket with a white collar. Vincent fell into the habit of going to visit them every evening. He and Stien laughed together a great deal.

"Look!" she would cry. "I'm a fine lady. I'm being drawed. Shall I put on my new bonnet for you, Mijnheer?"

"No, Stien, you're beautiful just as you are."

"Me, beautiful!"

She went off into gales of laughter. She had large cheerful eyes and a pretty expression. Her face was indigenous to the llfe. When she leaned over to dig potatoes in the field, he saw in the lines of her body a more authentic grace than even Kay had possessed. He had learned that the essential note in figure drawing was action, and that the great fault with the figures in the pictures of the old masters was that they did not work. He sketched the De Groots digging in the field, setting their table at home, eating steamed potatoes, and always Stien would peer over his shoulder and joke with him. Sometimes of a Sunday she would put on a clean bonnet and collar, and walk with him on the heath. It was the only amusement the peasants had.

"Did Margot Begeman like you?" she asked once.

"Yes."

"Then why did she try to kill herself?"

"Because her family wouldn't let her marry me."

"She was foolish. Do you know what I would have done instead of killing myself? I would have loved you!"

She laughed up into his face and ran to a clump of pine woods. All day long they laughed and played among the pines. Other strolling couples saw them. Stien had a natural gift for laughter; the smallest things Vincent said or did brought unrestrained shouts from her lips. She wrestled with him and tried to throw him on the ground. When she did not like the things he drew at her house, she would pour coffee over them or toss them into the fire. She came often to his studio to pose, and when she left, the place would be in chaos.

And so the summer and fall passed and winter came again. Vincent was forced by the snow to work in his studio all the time. The people of Nuenen did not like to pose and if it were not for the money, nobody would have come to him. In The Hague he had drawn almost ninety seamstresses in order to do a group picture of three. He wanted to paint the De Groot family at its supper of potatoes and coffee, but in order to get them right, he felt he first had to draw every peasant in the vicinity.

The Catholic priest had never favoured renting room in the caretaker's house to the man who was both heathen and artist, but since Vincent was quiet and courteous, he could find no reason to put him out. One day Adriana Schafrath came into the studio, all excited. "Father Pauwels wishes to see you immediately!"

Father Andreas Pauwels was a large man, red of face. He took a hurried look about the studio and decided he had never seen such mad confusion.

"What can I do for you, Father?" Vincent asked politely.

"You can't do anything for me! But I can do something for you! I shall see you through this affair, providing you do as you are told."

"What affair do you refer to, Father?"

"She is a Catholic and you are a Protestant, but I shall get a special dispensation from the Bishop. Be prepared to marry within a few days!"

Vincent came forward to look at Father Pauwels in the full light of the window. "I'm afraid I don't understand, Father," he said.

"Oh, yes you do. And all this pretense is of no use. Stien de Groot is with child! The honour of that family must be upheld."

"The devil she is!"

"You may well call on the devil. This is indeed the devil's work."

"Are you certain of this Father? You're not mistaken?"

"I don't go about accusing people until I have positive proof."

"And did Stien tell you . . . did she say . . . I was the man?"

"No. She refused to tell us his name."

"Then why do you confer this honour on me?"

"You've been seen together many times. Doesn't she come often to this studio?"

"Yes."

"Haven't you gone walking with her in the fields on Sunday?"

"Yes, I have."

"Well, what further proof do I need?"

Vincent was silent for a moment. Then he said quietly, "I'm sorry to hear about this, Father, particularly if it is going to mean trouble for my friend Stien. But I assure you that my relations with her have been above reproach."

"Do you expect me to believe that?"

"No," replied Vincent, "I don't."

That evening, when Stien returned from the fields, he was waiting for her on the step of their hut. The rest of the family went in to eat supper. Stien sank down beside him.

"I'll soon have somebody else for you to draw," she said.

"Then it's true, Stien?"

"Sure. Want to feel?"

She took his hand and put it on her abdomen. He was conscious of the growing protuberance.

"Father Pauwels just informed me that I was the father."

Stien laughed. "I wish it had been you. But you never wanted to, did you?"

He looked at the sweat of the fields caked in her dark skin, the heavy, crooked, coarse features, the thick nose and lips. She smiled at him.

"I wish it had been too, Stien."

"So Father Pauwels said it was you. That's funny."

"What's funny about it?"

"Will you keep my secret?"

"I promise."

"It was the *kerkmeester* of his church!"

Vincent whistled. "Does your family know?"

"Of course not. And I'll never tell them. But they know it wasn't you."

Vincent went inside the hut. There was no change in the atmosphere. The De Groots accepted Stien's pregnancy in the same spirit that they would have the cow's in the field. They treated him as they had before, and he knew they believed in his innocence.

Not so the village. Adriana Schafrath had been listening at the door. She quickly communicated the news to her neighbours. Within the hour, twenty-six hundred inhabitants of Nuenen knew that Stien De Groot was to be brought to bed with Vincent's child, and that Father Pauwels was going to force them to marry.

November and winter had come. It was time to be moving. There was no use in his remaining in Nuenen any longer. He had painted everything there was to paint, learned everything there was to learn about peasant life. He did not think he could go on living in the recrudescence of village hatred. Clearly the time had come for him to leave. But where was he to go?

"Mijnheer Van Gogh," said Adriana sadly, after knocking on the door, "Father Pauwels says you must leave this house at once and take lodgings elsewhere."

"Very well; as he wishes."

He walked about the studio, looking at his work. Two solid years of slaving. Hundreds of studies of weavers and their wives, of looms, and peasants in the field, of the pollards at the bottom of the vicarage garden, and the old church tower; the heath and hedges in the heat of the sun and the cool of a winter dusk.

A great heaviness fell upon him. His work was all so fragmentary. There were bits of every phase of peasant life in the Brabant, but no one piece of work that summed up the peasant, that caught the spirit of his hut and his steaming potatoes. Where was his *Angelus* of the Brabantine peasant? And how could he leave before he had painted it?

He glanced at the calendar. There were still twelve days until the first of the month. He called Adriana.

"Tell Father Pauwels that I have paid until the first and will not leave before then."

He gathered up his easel, paints, canvas, and brushes and trudged off to the De Groot hut. No one was at home. He set to work on a pencil sketch of the inside of the room. When the family returned from the fields, he tore up the paper. The De Groots sat down to their steamed potatoes, black coffee, and bacon. Vincent set up his canvas and plugged on until the family went to bed. All that night he worked on the picture in his studio. He slept during the day. When he awakened he burned his canvas with savage disgust and set out again for the De Groots'.

The old Dutch masters had taught him that drawing and colour were one. The De Groots sat down to the table in the same positions as they had all their lives. Vincent wanted to make it clear how these people, eating their potatoes under the lamplight, had dug the earth with those very hands they put in the dish; he wanted it to speak of *manual* labour, and how they had honestly earned their food.

His old habit of throwing himself violently at a canvas came in handy now; he worked with tremendous speed and vitality. He did not have to think about what he was doing; he had drawn hundreds of peasants, and huts, and families sitting before their steamed potatoes.

"Father Pauwels was here today," said the mother.

"What did he want?" asked Vincent.

"He offered us money if we would not pose for you."

"What did you tell him?"

"We said you were our friend."

"He has visited every house around here," put in Stien. "But they told him they would rather earn a sou posing for you than take his charity."

The following morning he destroyed his canvas again. A feeling, half of rage and half of impotence, seized him. He had only ten days left. He had to get out of Nuenen; it was becoming insufferable. But he could not leave until he had fulfilled his promise to Millet.

Every night he went back to the De Groots. He worked until they were too sleepy to sit up any longer. Each night he tried new combinations of colours, different values and proportions; and each day he saw that he had missed, that his work was incomplete.

The last day of the month came. Vincent had worked himself into a frenzy. He had gone without sleep and largely without food. He was living on nervous energy. The more he failed, the higher his excitement rose. He was waiting at the De Groots when they came in from the fields. His easel was set up, his pigments mixed, his canvas stretched on the frame. This was his very last chance. In the morning he was leaving the Brabant, forever.

He worked for hours. The De Groots understood. When they finished their supper, they remained at the table, talking softly in the patois of the fields. Vincent did not know what he was painting. He dashed off the thing without any thought or consciousness coming between his hand and the easel. By ten o'clock, the De Groots were falling asleep and Vincent was exhausted. He had done all he could with the canvas. He gathered his things, kissed Stien, and bade them all good-bye. He trudged home through the night, unaware that he was walking.

In the studio he set the canvas on a chair, lit his pipe, and stood regarding his work. The whole thing was wrong. It missed. The spirit wasn't there. He had failed again. His two years of labour in the Brabant had been wasted.

He smoked his pipe down to the hot dregs. He packed his bag. He gathered all his studies off the wall and from the bureau, and placed them in a large box. He threw himself on the divan.

He did not know how much time passed. He got up, ripped the canvas off the frame, threw it into a corner, and put on a new one. He mixed some paints, sat down, and began work.

*One starts with a hopeless struggle to follow nature, and everything goes wrong;
one ends by calmly creating from one's palette, and nature agrees with it and
follows.*

On croit que j'imagine—ce n'est pas vrai—je me souviens.

It was just as Pietersen had told him in Brussels; he had been too close to his
models. He had not been able to get a perspective. He had been pouring himself
into the mould of nature; now he poured nature into the mould of himself.

He painted the whole thing in the colour of a good, dusty, unpeeled potato. There
was the dirty, linen table cloth, the smoky wall, the lamp hanging down from the
rough rafters, Stien serving her father with steamed potatoes, the mother pouring
the black coffee, the brother lifting a cup to his lips, and on all their faces the
calm, patient acceptance of the eternal order of things.

The sun rose and a bit of light peered into the storeroom window. Vincent got
up from his stool. He felt perfectly calm and peaceful. The twelve days' excitement
was gone. He looked at his work. It reeked of bacon, smoke, and potato steam.
He smiled. He had painted his *Angelus*. He had captured that which does not pass
in that which passes. The Brabant peasant would never die.

He washed the picture with the white of an egg. He carried his box of drawings
and paintings to the vicarage, left them with his mother, and bade her good-bye.
He returned to his studio, wrote *The Potato Eaters* on his canvas, put a few of his
best studies with it, and set out for Paris.

BOOK FIVE

PARIS

1

"Then you didn't get my last letter?" asked Theo the next morning, as they sat over their rolls and coffee.

"I don't think so," replied Vincent. "What was in it?"

"The news of my promotion at Goupils."

"Why, Theo, and you didn't tell me a word about it yesterday!"

"You were too excited to listen. I have charge of the gallery on the Boulevard Montmartre."

"Theo, that's splendid! An art gallery of your own!"

"It really isn't my own, Vincent. I have to follow the Goupil policy pretty closely. But they let me hang the Impressionists on the *entresol,* so . . ."

"Who are you exhibiting?"

"Monet, Degas, Pissarro and Manet."

"Never heard of them."

"Then you'd better come along to the gallery and have a good, long look!"

"What does that sly grin on your face mean, Theo?"

"Oh, nothing. Will you have more coffee? We must go in a few minutes. I walk to the shop every morning."

"Thanks. No, no, only half a cup. Deuce take it, Theo, boy, but it's good to eat breakfast across the table from you once again!"

"I've been waiting for you to come to Paris for a long time. You had to come eventually, of course. But I do think it would have been better if you had waited until June, when I move to the Rue Lepic. We'll have three large rooms there. You can't do much work here, you see."

Vincent turned in his chair and glanced about him. Theo's apartment consisted of one room, a tiny kitchen, and a cabinet. The room was cheerfully furnished with authentic Louis Philippes, but there was hardly space enough to move around.

"If I set up an easel," said Vincent, "we'd have to move some of your lovely furniture out into the courtyard."

"I know the place is crowded, but I had a chance to pick these pieces up at a bargain and they're exactly what I want for the new apartment. Come along,

Vincent, I'll take you down the hill on my favourite walk to the Boulevard. You don't know Paris until you smell it in the early morning.''

Theo put on the heavy black coat that crossed up high under his immaculate, white bow tie, gave a final pat of the brush to the little curl that stood up on each side of the part in his hair, and then smoothed down his moustache and soft chin beard. He put on his black bowler hat, took his gloves and walking stick, and went to the front door.

"Well, Vincent, are you ready? Good Lord, but you are a sight! If you wore that outfit anywhere but in Paris, you'd be arrested!''

"What's the matter with it?'' Vincent looked down at himself. "I've been wearing it for almost two years and nobody's said anything.''

Theo laughed. "Never mind, Parisians are used to people like you. I'll get you some clothes tonight when the gallery closes.''

They walked down a flight of winding stairs, passed the *concierge's* apartment and stepped through the door to the Rue Laval. It was a fairly broad street, prosperous and respectable looking, with large stores selling drugs, picture frames and antiques.

"Notice the three beautiful ladies on the third floor of our building,'' said Theo.

Vincent looked up and saw three plaster of Paris heads and busts. Under the first was written, Sculpture, under the middle one, Architecture, and under the last, Painting.

"What makes them think Painting is such an ugly wench?''

"I don't know,'' replied Theo, "but anyway, you got into the right house.''

The two men passed Le Vieux Rouen, Antiquities, where Theo had bought his Louis Philippe furniture. In a moment they were in the Reu Montmartre, which wound gracefully up the hill to the Avenue Clichy and the Butte Montmartre, and down the hill to the heart of the city. The street was full of morning sunlight, of the smell of Paris arising, of people eating croissants and coffee in the cafés, of the vegetable, meat, and cheese shops opening to the day's trade.

It was a teeming bourgeois section, crowded with small stores. Workingmen walked out in the middle of the street. Housewives fingered the merchandise in the bins in front of the shops and bargained querulously with the merchants.

Vincent breathed deeply. "It's Paris,'' he said. "After all these years.''

"Yes, Paris. The capital of Europe. Particularly for an artist.''

Vincent drank in the busy flow of life winding up and down the hill; the *garçons* in alternately striped red and black jackets; the housewives carrying long loaves of unwrapped bread under their arms; the pushcarts at the curb; the *femmes de chambre* in soft slippers; the prosperous business men on their way to work. After passing innumerable *charcuteries, pâtisseries, boulangeries, blanchisseries* and small cafés, the Rue Montmartre curved to the bottom of the hill and swung into the Place Chateaudun, a rough circle formed by the meeting of six streets. They crossed the circle and passed Notre Dame de Lorette, a square, dirty, black stone church with three angels on the roof, floating off idyllically into the blue empyrean. Vincent looked closely at the writing over the door.

"Do they mean this *Liberté-Egalité-Fraternité* business, Theo?''

"I believe they do. The Third Republic will probably be permanent. The royalists are quite dead, and the socialists are coming into power. Emile Zola was telling me the other night that the next revolution will be against capitalism instead of royalty.''

"Zola! How nice for you to know him, Theo.''

"Paul Cezanne introduced me to him. We all meet once a week at the Café Batignolles. I'll take you there next time I go.''

After leaving the Place Chateaudun, the Rue Montmartre lost its bourgeois character and assumed a more stately air. The shops became larger, the cafés more imposing, the people better dressed, the buildings more prosperous looking. Music halls and restaurants lined the sidewalks, hotels made an appearance, and carriages took the place of trade wagons.

The brothers stepped along at a brisk pace. The cold sunlight was invigorating, the flavour of the air suggestive of the rich and complex life of the city.

"Since you can't work at home," said Theo, "I suggest you go to Corman's Studio."

"What's it like?"

"Well, Corman is just as academic as most masters, but if you don't want his criticism, he'll let you alone."

"Is it expensive?"

Theo tapped Vincent's thigh with his walking stick. "Didn't I tell you I was promoted? I'm getting to be one of those plutocrats that Zola is going to wipe out with his next revolution!"

At length the Rue Montmartre flowed into the wide, imposing Boulevard Montmartre, with its large department stores, arcades, and expensive shops. The Boulevard, which became the Boulevard des Italiens a few blocks farther on and led to the Place de l'Opéra, was the most important thoroughfare in the city. Although the street was empty at this hour of the morning, the clerks within the stores were preparing for a busy day.

Theo's branch of the Goupil Gallery was located at number 19, just one short block to the right of the Rue Montmartre. Vincent and Theo crossed the wide boulevard, stopped alongside of a gas lamp in the centre to let a carriage go by, and then continued on to the gallery.

The well groomed clerks bowed respectively as Theo walked through the salon of his gallery. Vincent remembered how he used to bow to Tersteeg and Obach when he was a clerk. In the air was the same aroma of culture and refinement, a smell he thought his nostrils had forgotten. On the walls of the salon were paintings by Bouguereau, Henner, and Delaroche. Above the main salon was a small balcony, with a flight of stairs at the rear leading to it.

"The pictures you'll want to see are up on the *entresol*," said Theo. "Come down when you're through and tell me what you think of them."

"Theo, what are you licking your chops about?"

Theo's grin became all the broader. *"A toute à l'heure,"* he said and disappeared into his office.

2

"Am I in a madhouse?"

Vincent stumbled blindly to the lone chair on the *entresol,* sat down and rubbed his eyes. From the age of twelve he had been used to seeing dark and sombre paintings; paintings in which the brushwork was invisible, every detail of the canvas correct and complete, and flat colours shaded slowly into each other.

The paintings that laughed at him merrily from the walls were like nothing he had ever seen or dreamed of. Gone were the flat, thin surfaces. Gone was the sentimental sobriety. Gone was the brown gravy in which Europe had been bathing its pictures for centuries. Here were pictures riotously mad with the sun. With light and air and throbbing vivacity. Paintings of ballet girls backstage, done in primitive reds, greens, and blues thrown next to each other irreverently. He looked at the signature. Degas.

There were a group of outdoor scenes along a river bank, caught with all the ripe, lush colour of midsummer and a hot overhead sun. The name was Monet. In all the hundreds of canvases that Vincent had seen, there was not as much luminosity, breath, and fragrance as in one of these glowing pictures. The darkest colour Monet used was a dozen times lighter than the lightest colour to be found in all the museums of Holland. The brushwork stood out, unashamed, every stroke apparent, every stroke entering into the rhythm of nature. The surface was thick, deep, palpitant with heavy globs of ripe, rich paint.

Vincent stood before a picture of a man in his woolen undershirt, holding the rudder of a little boat with the intense Gallic concentration characteristic of the Frenchman enjoying himself on a Sunday afternoon. The wife sat by, passively. Vincent looked for the name of the artist.

"Monet again?" he said aloud. "That's funny. There's not the slightest resemblance to his outdoor scene."

He looked again and saw that he was mistaken. The name was Manet, not Monet. Then he remembered the story of Manet's *Picnic on the Grass,* and *Olympia,* and how the police had had to rope off the pictures to keep them from being slashed by knives and spat upon.

He did not know why, but the Manet paintings reminded him of the books of Emile Zola. There seemed to be that same fierce quest after truth, the same unafraid penetration, the same feeling that character is beauty, no matter how sordid it may appear. He studied the technique closely, and saw that Manet put elemental colours next to each other without gradation, that many details were barely suggested, that colours, lines, lights and shades did not end with definite precision, but wavered into each other.

"Just as the eye sees them waver in nature," said Vincent.

He heard Mauve's voice in his ears. "Is it impossible for you to make a definite statement about a line, Vincent?"

He sat down again and let the pictures sink in. After a time he caught one of the simple expedients by which painting had been so completely revolutionized. These painters filled the air of their pictures solid! And that living, moving, replete air did something to the objects that were to be seen in them! Vincent knew that, for the academicians, air did not exist; it was just a blank space in which they placed rigid, set objects.

But these new men! They had discovered the air! They had discovered light and breath, atmosphere and sun; they saw things filtered through all the innumerable forces that live in that vibrant fluid. Vincent realized that painting could never be the same again. Photographic machines and academicians would make exact duplicates; painters would see everything filtered through their own natures and the sun-swept air in which they worked. It was almost as though these men had created a new art.

He stumbled down the stairs. Theo was in the main salon. He turned with a smile on his lips, searching his brother's face eagerly.

"Well, Vincent?" he said.

"Oh, Theo!" breathed Vincent.

He tried to speak, but could not. His eyes darted up to the *entresol.* He turned and ran out of the gallery.

He walked up the broad boulevard until he came to an octagonal building which he recognized as the Opera. Through the canyon of stone buildings he caught sight of a bridge, and made for the river. He slid down to the water's edge and dribbled his fingers in the Seine. He crossed the bridge without looking at the bronze horsemen, and made his way through the labyrinth of streets on the Left Bank. He climbed steadily upward. He passed a cemetery, turned to his right and came to a huge railway station. Forgetting that he had crossed the Seine, he asked a gendarme to direct him to the Rue Laval.

"The Rue Laval?" said the gendarme. "You are on the wrong side of the city, Monsieur. This is Montparnasse. You must go down the hill, cross the Seine, and go up again to Montmartre."

For many hours Vincent stumbled through Paris, not caring much where he went. There were broad, clean boulevards with imposing shops, then wretched, dirty alleys, then bourgeois streets with endless rows of wine shops. Once again he found himself on the crest of a hill on which there was a triumphal arch. To the east he looked down over a tree-lined boulevard enclosed on both sides by narrow strips of park, and ending in a large square with an Egyptian obelisk. To the west he overlooked an extensive wood.

It was late afternoon before he found the Rue Laval. The dull ache within him had been numbed by sheer fatigue. He went directly to where his pictures and studies were tied in bundles. He spread them all out on the floor.

He gazed at his canvases. God! but they were dark and dreary. God! but they were heavy, lifeless, dead. He had been painting in a long past century, and he had not known it.

Theo came home in the gloaming and found Vincent sitting dully on the floor. He knelt beside his brother. The last vestiges of daylight were blotted out of the room. Theo was silent for some time.

"Vincent," he said, "I know how you feel. Stunned. It's tremendous, isn't it? We're throwing overboard nearly everything that painting has held sacred."

Vincent's small, hurt eyes caught Theo's and held them.

"Theo, why didn't you tell me? Why didn't I know? Why didn't you bring me here sooner? You've let me waste six long years."

"Waste them? Nonsense. You've worked out your craft for yourself. You paint like Vincent Van Gogh, and nobody else in the world. If you had come here before you crystallized your own particular expression, Paris would have moulded you to suit itself."

"But what am I to do? Look at this junk!" He kicked his foot through a large, dark canvas. "It's all dead, Theo. And worthless."

"You ask me what you are to do? I'll tell you. You are to learn about light and colour from the Impressionists. That much you must borrow from them. But nothing more. You must not imitate. You must not get swamped. Don't let Paris submerge you."

"But, Theo, I must learn everything all over. Everything I do is wrong."

"Everything you do is right . . . except your light and colour. You were an Impressionist from the day you picked up a pencil in the Borinage. Look at your drawing! Look at your brushwork! No one ever painted like that before Manet. Look at your lines! You almost never make a definite statement. Look at your faces, your trees, your figures in the fields! They are your impressions. They are rough, imperfect, filtered through your own personality. That's what it means, to be an Impressionist; not to paint like everyone else, not to be a slave to rules and regulations. You belong to your age, Vincent, and you're an Impressionist whether you like it or not."

"Oh, Theo, do I like it!"

"Your work is known in Paris among the young painters who count. Oh, I don't mean those who sell, but those who are making the important experiments. They want to know you. You'll learn some marvellous things from them."

"They know my work? The young Impressionists know my work?"

Vincent got on his knees so that he could see Theo more clearly. Theo thought of the days in Zundert, when they used to play together on the floor of the nursery.

"Of course. What do you think I've been doing in Paris all these years? They think you have a penetrating eye and a draftsman's fist. Now all you need to do is lighten your palette and learn how to paint living, luminous air. Vincent, isn't it wonderful to be living in a time when such important things are happening?"

"Theo, you old devil, you grand old devil!"

"Come on, get off your knees. Make a light. Let's get all dressed up and go out for dinner. I'll take you to the Brasserie Universelle. They serve the most delicious

Chateaubriand in Paris. I'm going to treat you to a real banquet. With a bottle of champagne, old boy, to celebrate the great day when Paris and Vincent Van Gogh were joined together!''

3

The following morning Vincent took his drawing materials and went to Corman's. The studio was a large room on the third floor, with a strong north light coming in from the street. There was a nude male model posed at one end, facing the door. About thirty chairs and easels were scattered about for the students. Vincent registered with Corman and was assiged an easel.

After he had been sketching about an hour, the door to the hall opened and a woman stepped in. There was a bandage wrapped around her head and she was holding one hand to her jaw. She took one horrified look at the naked model, exclaimed *"Mon Dieu!"* and ran.

Vincent turned to the man sitting beside him.

"What do you suppose was the matter with her?"

"Oh, that happens every day. She was looking for the dentist next door. The shock of seeing a naked man usually cures their toothache. If the dentist doesn't move he'll probably go bankrupt. You're a newcomer, aren't you?"

"Yes. This is only my third day in Paris."

"What's your name?"

"Van Gogh. What's yours?"

"Henri Toulouse-Lautrec. Are you any relation to Theo Van Gogh?"

"He's my brother."

"Then you must be Vincent! Well, I'm glad to know you. Your brother is the best art dealer in Paris. He's the only one who will give the young men a chance. Not only that, he fights for us. If we are ever accepted by the Parisian public, it will be due to Theo Van Gogh. We all think he's mighty fine."

"So do I."

Vincent looked closely at the man. Lautrec had a squashed-down head; his features, the nose, lips, and chin, stuck far out from the flat head. He wore a full black beard, which grew outward from his chin instead of downward.

"What makes you come to a beastly place like Corman's?" asked Lautrec.

"I must have some place to sketch. What about you?"

"Damned if I know. I lived in a brothel all last month up in Montmartre. Did portraits of the girls. That was real work. Sketching in a studio is child's play."

"I'd like to see your studies of those women."

"Would you really?"

"Certainly. Why not?"

"Most people think I'm crazy because I paint dance hall girls and clowns and whores. But that's where you find real character."

"I know. I married one in The Hague."

"Bien!" This Van Gogh family is all right! Let me see the sketch you've done of the model, will you?"

"Take them all. I've done four."

Lautrec looked at the sketches for some moments and then said, "You and I will get along together, my friend. We think alike. Has Corman seen these yet?"

"No."

"When he does, you'll be through here. That is, as far as his criticism is concerned. He said to me the other day, 'Lautrec, you exaggerate, always you exaggerate. One line in each of your studies is caricature.' "

"And you replied, 'That, my dear Corman, is character, not caricature.' "

A curious light came into Lautrec's black, needle-point eyes. "Do you still want to see those portraits of my girls?"

"I certainly do."

"Then come along. This place is a morgue, anyway."

Lautrec had a thick, squat neck, and powerful shoulders and arms. When he rose to his feet, Vincent saw that his new friend was a cripple. Lautrec, on his feet, stood no higher than when he was seated. His thick torso came forward almost to the apex of a triangle at the waist, then fell in sharply to the tiny shrivelled legs.

They walked down the Boulevard Clichy, Lautrec leaning heavily on his stick. Every few moments he would stop to rest, pointing out some lovely line in the juxtaposition of two buildings. Just one block this side of the Moulin Rouge they turned up the hill toward the Butte Montmartre. Lautrec had to rest more frequently.

"You're probably wondering what's wrong with my legs, Van Gogh. Everyone does. Well, I'll tell you."

"Oh, please! You don't need to speak of it."

"You might as well know." He doubled over his stick, leaning on it with his shoulders. "I was born with brittle bones. When I was twelve, I slipped on a dance floor and broke my right thigh bone. The next year I fell into a ditch and broke the left one. My legs have never grown an inch since."

"Does it make you unhappy?"

"No. If I had been normal I should never have been a painter. My father is a count of Toulouse. I was next in line for the title. If I had wanted to, I could have had a marshal's baton and ridden alongside of the King of France. That is, providing there was a King of France . . . *Mais, sacrebleu,* why should anyone be a count when he can be a painter?"

"Yes, I'm afraid the days of the counts are over."

"Shall we go on? Degas's studio is just down this alley. They say I'm copying his work because he does ballet dancers and I do the girls from the Moulin-Rouge. Let them say what they like. This is my place, 19 *bis,* Rue Fontaine. I'm on the ground floor, as you might have guessed."

He threw open the door and bowed Vincent in.

"I live alone," he said. "Sit down, if you can find a place to sit."

Vincent looked about. In addition to the canvases, frames, easels, stools, steps, and rolls of drapery, two large tables encumbered the studio. One was laden with bottles of rare wines and decanters of multicoloured liqueurs. On the other were piled up dancers' slippers, periwigs, old books, women's dresses, gloves, stockings, vulgar photographs, and precious Japanese prints. There was just one little space among all this litter where Lautrec could sit and paint.

"What's the matter, Van Gogh?" he asked. "Can't you find a place to sit? Just shove that junk on the floor and bring the chair over to the window. There were twenty-seven girls in the house. I slept with every one of them. Don't you agree that it's necessary to sleep with a woman before you can fully understand her?"

"Yes."

"Here are the sketches. I took them down to a dealer on the Capucines. He said, 'Lautrec, why have you a fixation on ugliness? Why do you always paint the most sordid and immoral people you can find? These women are repulsive, utterly repulsive. They have debauch and sinister evil written all over their faces. Is that what modern art means, to create ugliness? Have you painters become so blind to beauty that you can paint only the scum of the earth?' I said, 'Pardon me, but I think I'm going to be sick, and I shouldn't like to do it all over your lovely carpet.' Is that light all right, Van Gogh? Will you have a drink? Speak up, what do you prefer? I have everything you could possibly want."

He hobbled about the chairs, tables, and rolls of drapery with agile movements, poured a drink and passed it to Vincent.

"Here's to ugliness, Van Gogh," he cried. "May it never infect the Academy!"

Vincent sipped his drink and studied Lautrec's twenty-seven sketches of the girls of a Montmartre sporting house. He realized that the artist had set them down as he saw them. They were objective portraits, without moral attitude or ethical comment. On the faces of the girls he had caught the misery and suffering, the callous carnality, the bestial debauch and spiritual aloofness.

"Do you like portraits of peasants, Lautrec?" he asked.

"Yes, if they're not sentimentalized."

"Well, I paint peasants. And it strikes me that these women are peasants too. Gardeners of the flesh, so to speak. Earth and flesh, they're just two different forms of the same matter, aren't they? And these women till the flesh, human flesh that must be tilled to make it produce life. This is good work, Lautrec; you've said something worth saying."

"And you don't think them ugly?"

"They are authentic and penetrating commentaries on life. That is the very highest kind of beauty, don't you think? If you had idealized or sentimentalized the women, you would have made them ugly because your portraits would have been cowardly and false. But you stated the full truth as you saw it, and that's what beauty means, isn't it?"

"Jesus Christ! Why aren't there more men in the world like you? Have another drink! And help yourself to those sketches! Take as many as you like!"

Vincent held a canvas up to the light, cast about in his mind for a moment, and then exclaimed, "Daumier! That's who it reminds me of."

Lautrec's face lit up.

"Yes, Daumier. The greatest of them all. And the only person I ever learned anything from. God! how magnificently that man could hate!"

"But why paint things if you hate them? I paint only things I love."

"All great art springs from hatred, Van Gogh. Oh, I see you're admiring my Gauguin."

"Whose painting did you say that was?"

"Paul Gauguin. Do you know him?"

"No."

"Then you should. That's a native Martinique woman. Gauguin was out there for awhile. He's completely *fou* on the subject of going primitive, but he's a superb painter. He had a wife, three children, and a position on the stock exchange that brought him thirty thousand francs a year. He bought fifteen thousand francs worth of paintings from Pissarro, Manet, and Sisley. He painted his wife's portrait on their wedding day. She thought it a delightful *beau geste*. Gauguin used to paint on Sundays; you know, the Stock Exchange Art Club? Once he showed a picture to Manet, who told him it was very good. 'Oh,' replied Gauguin, 'I am only an amateur!' 'Oh, no,' said Manet, 'there are no amateurs but those who make bad pictures.' That remark went to Gauguin's head like neat spirits and he's never drawn a sober breath since. Gave up his job on the Exchange, lived with his family in Rouen for a year on his savings, then sent his wife and children to her parents' home in Stockholm. He's been living off his wits ever since."

"He sounds interesting."

"Be careful when you meet him; he loves to torment his friends. Say, Van Gogh, what about letting me show you the Moulin Rouge and the Elysée-Montmartre? I know all the girls there. Do you like women, Van Gogh? I mean to sleep with? I love them. What do you say, shall we make a night of it sometime?"

"By all means."

"Splendid. I suppose we must go back to Corman's. Have another drink before you go? That's it. Now just one more and you'll empty the bottle. Look out, you'll knock that table over. Never mind, the charwoman will pick all that stuff up. Guess I'll have to move out of here pretty soon. I'm rich, Van Gogh. My father is afraid I'll curse him for bringing me into the world a cripple, so he gives me everything

I want. When I move out of a place I never take anything but my work. I rent an empty studio and buy things one by one. When I'm just about to be suffocated, I move again. By the way, what kind of women do you prefer? Blonds? Red heads?

"Don't bother to lock it. Notice the way the metal roofs flow down to the Boulevard Clichy in a sort of black ocean. Oh, hell! I don't have to pretend to you. I lean on this stick and point out beautiful scenes because I'm a God damned cripple and can't walk more than a few steps at a time! Well, we're all cripples in one way or another. Let's get along."

4

It looked so easy. All he had to do was throw away the old palette, buy some light pigments, and paint as an Impressionist. At the end of the first day's trial, Vincent was surprised and a bit nettled. At the end of the second day he was bewildered. Bewilderment was succeeded in turn by chagrin, anger, and fear. By the end of the week he was in a towering rage. After all his laborious months of experimentation with colour, he was still a novice. His canvases came out dark, dull, and sticky. Lautrec, sitting by Vincent's side at Corman's, watched the paint and curses fly, but refrained from offering any advice.

If it was a hard week for Vincent, it was a thousand times worse for Theo. Theo was a gentle soul, mild in his manners and delicate in his habits of life. He was an extremely fastidious person, in his dress, in his decorum, in his home and place of business. He had only a small fraction of Vincent's bruising vitality and power.

The little apartment on the Rue Laval was just large enough for Theo and his fragile Louis Philippes. By the end of the first week Vincent had turned the place into a junk shop. He paced up and down the living room, kicked furniture out of the way, threw canvases, brushes, and empty colour tubes all over the floor, adorned the divans and tables with his soiled clothing, broke dishes, splashed paint, and upset every last punctilious habit of Theo's life.

"Vincent, Vincent," cried Theo, "don't be such a Tartar!"

Vincent had been pacing about the tiny apartment, biting his knuckles and muttering to himself. He threw himself heavily into a fragile chair.

"It's no use," he groaned. "I began too late. I'm too old to change. God, Theo, I've tried! I've started twenty canvases this week. But I'm set in my technique, and I can't begin all over again. I tell you, I'm done for! I can't go back to Holland and paint sheep after what I've seen here. And I came too late to get in the main swing of my craft. God, what will I do?"

He jumped up, lurched to the door for some fresh air, slammed it shut, pried open a window, stared at the Restaurant Bataille for a moment, shut the window so hard he almost smashed the glass, strode to the kitchen for a drink, spilled half the water on the floor, and came back into the living room with a trickle of water running down each side of his chin.

"Well, what do you say, Theo? Must I give it up? Am I through? It looks that way, doesn't it?"

"Vincent, you're behaving like a child. Do quiet down for a moment and listen to me. No, no, don't pace the floor! I can't talk to you that way. And for goodness sake take off those heavy boots if you're going to kick that gilt chair every time you pass it!"

"But, Theo, I've let you support me for six long years. And what do you get out of it? A lot of brown-gravy pictures, and a hopeless failure on your hands."

"Listen, old boy, when you wanted to draw the peasants, did you catch the entire trick in a week? Or did it take you five years?"

"Yes, but I was just beginning then."

"You're just beginning with colour today! And it will probably take you another five years."

"Is there no end to this, Theo? Must I go to school all my life? I'm thirty-three; when in God's name do I reach maturity?"

"This is your last job, Vincent. I've seen everything that is being painted in Europe; the men on my *entresol* are the last word. Once you lighten your palette . . ."

"Oh, Theo, do you really think I can? You don't think I'm a failure?"

"I'm more inclined to think you're a jackass. The greatest revolution in the history of art, and you want to master it in a week! Let's go take a walk on the Butte and cool our heads. If I stay in this room with you another five minutes I shall probably explode."

The following afternoon Vincent sketched at Corman's until late, and then called for Theo at Goupils. An early April dusk had fallen, the long rows of six-story stone buildings were bathed in a coral-pink glow of dying colour. All of Paris was having its *apéritif*. The sidewall cafés on the Rue Montmartre were crowded with men chatting with their friends. From inside the cafés came the sound of soft music, playing to refresh the Parisians after their day of toil. The gas lamps were being lit, the *garçons* were laying table cloths in the restaurants, the clerks in the department stores were pulling down the corrugated iron shutters and emptying the sidewalk bins of merchandise.

Theo and Vincent strolled along leisurely. They crossed the Place Chateaudun, with its flurry of carriages from the six converging streets, passed Notre Dame de Lorette, and wound up the hill to the Rue Laval.

"Shall we have an *apéritif,* Vincent?"

"Yes. Let's sit where we can watch the crowd."

"We'll go up to Bataille's, on the Rue des Abbesses. Some of my friends will probably drop by."

The Restaurant Bataille was frequented largely by painters. There were only four or five tables out in front, but the two rooms inside were comfortably large. Madame Bataille always led the artists to one room and the bourgeois to the other; she could tell at first glance to which class a man belonged.

"*Garçon!*" called Theo. "Bring me a Kummel Eckau OO."

"What do you suggest for me, Theo?"

"Try a cointreau. You'll have to experiment for a while to find your permanent drink."

The waiter put their drinks before them on saucers with the price marked in black letters. Theo lit a cigar, Vincent his pipe. Laundry women in black aprons passed, baskets of ironed clothes under their arms; a labourer went by, dangling an unwrapped herring by the tail; there were painters in smocks, with wet canvases strapped to the easel; business men in black derbies and grey checked coats; housewives in cloth slippers, carrying a bottle of wine or a paper of meat; beautiful women with long, flowing skirts, narrow waists, and tiny plumed hats perched forward on their heads.

"It's a gorgeous parade, isn't it, Theo?"

"Yes. Paris doesn't really awaken until the *apéritif* hour."

"I've been trying to think . . . what is it that makes Paris so marvellous?"

"Frankly, I don't know. It's an eternal mystery. It has something to do with French character, I suppose. There's a pattern of freedom and tolerance here, an easy going acceptance of life that . . . Hello, here's a friend of mine I want you to meet. Good evening, Paul; how are you?"

"Very well, thanks, Theo."

"May I present my brother, Vincent Van Gogh? Vincent, this is Paul Gauguin. Sit down, Paul, and have one of your inevitable absinthes."

Gauguin raised his absinthe, touched the tip of his tongue to the liqueur and then coated the inside of his mouth with it. He turned to Vincent.

"How do you like Paris, Monsieur Van Gogh?"

"I like it very much."

"*Tiens! C'est curieux.* Still, some people do. As for myself, I find it one huge garbage can. With civilization as the garbage."

"I don't care much for this cointreau, Theo. Can you suggest something else?"

"Try an absinthe, Monsieur Van Gogh," put in Gauguin. "That is the only drink worthy of an artist."

"What do you say, Theo?"

"Why ask me? Suit yourself. *Garçon.* An absinthe for Monsieur. You seem rather pleased with yourself today, Paul. What's happened? Sell a canvas?"

"Nothing as sordid as all that, Theo. But I had a charming experience this morning."

Theo tipped Vincent a wink. "Tell us about it, Paul. *Garçon!* another absinthe for Monsieur Gauguin."

Gauguin touched the tip of his tongue to the new absinthe, wetted the inside of his mouth with it, and then began.

"Do you know that blind alley, the Impasse Frenier, which opens on the Rue des Forneaux? Well, five o'clock this morning I heard Mother Fourel, the carter's wife, scream, 'Help! My husband has hung himself!' I leaped out of bed, pulled on a pair of trousers (the proprieties)! grabbed a knife downstairs and cut the rope. The man was dead, but still warm, still burning. I wanted to carry him to his bed. 'Stop!' cried Mother Fourel, 'we must wait for the police!'

"On the other side my house overhangs fifteen yards of market gardener's bed. 'Have you a cantaloupe?' I called to the gardener. 'Certainly, Monsieur, a ripe one.' At breakfast I ate my melon without a thought of the man who had hung himself. There is good in life, as you see. Beside the poison there is the antidote. I was invited out to luncheon, so I put on my best shirt, expecting to thrill the company. I related the story. Smiling, quite unconcerned, they all asked me for a piece of the rope with which he had hung himself."

Vincent looked closely at Paul Gauguin. He had the great, black head of a barbarian, with a massive nose that shot down from the corner of his left eye to the right corner of his mouth. His eyes were huge, almond shaped, protruding, invested with a fierce melancholy. Ridges of bone bulged over the eyes, under the eyes, ran down the long cheeks and across the wide chin. He was a giant of a man, with overwhelming brutal vitality.

Theo smiled faintly.

"Paul, I'm afraid you enjoy your sadism a little too much for it to be entirely natural. I'll have to be going now; I have a dinner engagement. Vincent, will you join me?"

"Let him stay with me, Theo," said Gauguin. "I want to get acquainted with this brother of yours."

"Very well. But don't pour too many absinthes into him. He's not used to them. *Garçon. Combien?*"

"That brother of yours is all right, Vincent," said Gauguin. "He's still afraid to exhibit the younger men, but I suppose Valadon holds him down."

"He has Monet, Sisley, Pissarro, and Manet on the balcony."

"True, but where are the Seurats? And the Gauguins? And the Cezannes and Toulouse-Lautrecs? The other men are getting old now and their time is passing."

"Oh, then you know Toulouse-Lautrec?"

"Henri? Of course! Who doesn't know him? He's a damn fine painter, but he's crazy. He thinks that if he sleeps with five thousand women, he'll vindicate himself for not being a whole man. Every morning he wakes up with a gnawing inferiority because he has no legs; every night he drowns that inferiority in liquor and a woman's body. But it's back with him again the next morning. If he weren't crazy he'd be one of our best painters. Here's where we turn in. My studio is on the fourth floor. Look out for that step. The board is broken."

Gauguin went ahead and lighted a lamp. It was a shabby garret, with an easel, a brass bed, a table, and a chair. In an alcove near the door Vincent saw some crude and obscene photographs.

"From these pictures I would say you don't think very highly of love?"

"Where will you sit, on the bed or the chair? There's some tobacco for your pipe on the table. Well, I like women, providing they are fat and vicious. Their intelligence annoys me. I have always wanted a mistress who was fat and I have never found one. To make a fool of me, they are always pregnant. Did you read a short story published last month by a young chap by the name of Maupassant? He's Zola's protégé. A man who loves fat women has Christmas dinner served in his home for two and goes out to find company. He comes across a woman who suits him perfectly, but when they get to the roast, she is delivered of a bouncing baby boy!"

"But all this has very little to do with love, Gauguin."

Gauguin stretched out on the bed, put one muscular arm under his head and blew clouds of smoke at the unpainted rafters.

"I don't mean to say that I am not susceptible to beauty, Vincent, but simply that my senses wil have none of it. As you perceive, I do not know love. To say, 'I love you' would break all my teeth. But I have no complaints to make. Like Jesus I say, 'The flesh is the flesh and the spirit is the spirit.' Thanks to this, a small sum of money satisfies my flesh, and my spirit is left in peace."

"You certainly dismiss the matter very lightly!"

"No, whom one gets in bed with is no light matter. With a woman who feels pleasure, I feel twice as much pleasure. But I'd rather take the empty external gesture, and not get my emotions involved. I save them for my painting."

"I've been coming to that point of view myself of late. No, thanks, I don't think I could stand any more absinthe. Not at all, go right ahead. My brother Theo thinks highly of your work. May I see some of your studies?"

Gauguin jumped up.

"You may not. My studies are personal and private, like my letters. But I'll show you my paintings. You won't be able to see much in this light. Well, all right if you insist."

Gauguin went on his knees, pulled a stack of canvases from under the bed, and stood them one by one against the absinthe bottle on the table. Vincent had been prepared to see something unusual, but he could feel nothing but stunned amazement at Gauguin's work. He saw a confused mass of sundrenched pictures; trees such as no botanist could discover; animals the existence of which had never been suspected by Cuvier; men whom Gauguin alone could have created; a sea that might have flowed out of a volcano; a sky which no God could inhabit. There were awkward and angular natives, with the mystery of the infinite behind their naive, primitive eyes; dream canvases done in blazes of pink and violet and quivering red; sheer decorative scenes in which wild flora and fauna burst with the heat and light of the sun.

"You're like Lautrec," murmured Vincent. "You hate. You hate with all your might."

Gauguin laughed. "What do you think of my painting, Vincent?"

"Frankly, I don't know. Give me time to think about it. Let me come back and see your work again."

"Come as often as you like. There is only one young man in Paris today whose painting is as good as mine; Georges Seurat. He, too, is a primitive. All the rest of the fools around Paris are civilized."

"Georges Seurat?" asked Vincent. "I don't believe I've heard of him."

"No, you wouldn't have. There's not a dealer in town who will exhibit his canvases. And yet he's a great painter."

"I'd like to meet him, Gauguin."

"I'll take you up there later. What do you say we have dinner and go up to Bruant's? Have you any money? I've only about two francs. We'd better take this bottle with us. You go first. I'll hold the lamp until you're half way down, so you won't break your neck."

5

It was almost two in the morning before they got around to Seurat's house.

"Aren't you afraid we'll wake him up?" asked Vincent.

"Lord, no! He works all night. And most of the day. I don't think he ever sleeps. Here's the house. It belongs to Georges's mother. She once said to me, 'My boy, Georges, he wants to paint. Very well, then, let him paint. I have enough money for the two of us. Just so long as he is happy.' He's a model son to her. Doesn't drink, smoke, swear, go out nights, pursue the ladies, or spend money on anything but materials. He has only one vice; painting. I've heard he has a mistress and a son living close by, but he never mentions them."

"The house looks black," said Vincent. "How are we going to get in without waking the whole family?"

"Georges has the attic. We will probably see a light from the other side. We'll throw some gravel at his window. Here, you'd better let me. If you don't throw it just right it'll hit the third floor window and wake his mother."

Georges Seurat came down to open the door, put a finger to his lips, and led them up three flights of stairs. He closed the door of his attic behind him.

"Georges," said Gauguin, "I want you to meet Vincent Van Gogh, Theo's brother. He paints like a Dutchman, but aside from that he's a damn fine fellow."

Seurat's attic was of tremendous size, running almost the full length of the house. There were huge, unfinished canvases on the walls, with scaffolding before them. A high square table had been placed under the gas lamp; lying flat on this table was a wet canvas.

"I'm happy to know you, Monsieur Van Gogh. You'll pardon me for just a few moments, won't you? I have another little square of colour to fill in before my paint dries."

He climbed on top of a high stool and crouched over his canvas. The gas lamp burned with a steady, yellowish flare. About twenty tiny pots of colour formed a neat line across the table. Seurat touched the tip of the smallest painting brush Vincent had ever seen into one of the pots and began putting little points of colour on the canvas with mathematical precision. He worked quietly and without emotion. His manner was aloof and detached, like that of a mechanic. Dot dot dot dot. He held his brush straight up in his hand, barely touched it to the pot of paint, and then dot dot dot dot on the canvas, hundreds upon hundreds of minute dots.

Vincent watched him, agape. At length Seurat turned on his stool.

"There," he said, "I've got that space hollowed out."

"Would you mind showing it to Vincent, Georges?" asked Gauguin. "Where he comes from they paint cows and sheep. He didn't know there was a modern art until a week ago."

"If you'll sit on this stool, Monsieur Van Gogh."

Vincent climbed up on the stool and looked at the canvas spread out before him. It was like nothing he had ever seen before, either in art or life. The scene represented the Island of the Grande Jatte. Architectural human beings, made out of infinitely graduated points of colour, stood up like poles in a Gothic cathedral. The grass, the river, the boats, the trees, all were vague and abstract masses of dotted light. The canvas was done in all the brightest shades of the palette, lighter than those Manet or Degas or even Gauguin dared to use. The picture was a withdrawal into a region of almost abstract harmony. If it was alive, it was not with the life of nature. The air was filled with glittering luminosity, but there was not a breath to be found anywhere. It was a still life of vibrant life, from which movement had been forever banished.

Gauguin stood at Vincent's side and laughed at the expression on his face.

"It's all right, Vincent, Georges's canvases strike everyone that way the first time they look at them. Out with it! What do you think?"

Vincent turned apologetically to Seurat.

"You will forgive me, Monsieur, but so many strange things have happened to me in the last few days that I cannot find my balance. I trained myself in the Dutch tradition. I had no idea what the Impressionists stood for. And now I suddenly find everything I believed in, discarded."

"I understand," said Seurat quietly. "My method is revolutionizing the whole art of painting, so you could not be expected to take it all in with one glance. You see, Monsieur, up to the present, painting has been a matter of personal experience. It is my aim to make it an abstract science. We must learn to pigeonhole our sensations and arrive at a mathematical precision of mind. Every human sensation can be, and must be reduced to an abstract statement of colour, line, and tone. You see these little pots of colour on my table?"

"Yes, I've been noticing them."

"Each of those pots, Monsieur Van Gogh, contains a specific human emotion. With my formula they can be made in the factories and sold in the chemists' shops. No more haphazard mixing of colours on the palette; that method belongs to a past age. From now on the painter will go to the chemist's shop and simply pry the lids off his little pots of colour. This is an age of science, and I am going to make a science out of painting. Personality must disappear, and painting must become precise, like architecture. Do you follow me, Monsieur?"

"No," said Vincent, "I'm afraid I don't."

Gauguin nudged Vincent.

"See here, Georges, why do you insist upon calling this your method. Pissarro worked it out before you were born."

"It's a lie!"

A flush spread over Seurat's face. He sprang off his stool, walked quickly to the window, rapped on the sill with the ends of his fingers, then stormed back.

"Who said Pissarro worked it out before me? I tell you it's my method. I was the first to think of it. Pissarro learned his pointillism from me. I've been through the history of art since the Italian primitives, and I tell you, no one thought of it before me. How dare you . . .!"

He bit his lip savagely, walked to one of his scaffolds, and turned a hunched up back on Vincent and Gauguin.

Vincent was utterly amazed at the transition. The man leaning over his canvas on the table had had architectural features, perfect and cold. He had had dispassionate eyes, the impersonal manner of a scientist in a laboratory. His voice had been cool, almost pedagogic. The same veil of abstraction had been over his eyes that he threw over his paintings. But the man at the end of the attic was biting the thick, red under lip that stuck out from the full beard, and was angrily rumpling the mass of curly brown hair that had been so neat before.

"Oh, come, Georges," said Gauguin, winking at Vincent. "Everyone knows that it's your method. Without you there would have been no pointillism."

Mollified, Seurat came back to the table. The glow of anger died slowly out of his eyes.

"Monsieur Seurat," said Vincent, "how can we make painting an impersonal science when it is essentially the expression of the individual that counts?"

"Look! I will show you."

Seurat grabbed a box of crayons from the table and crouched down on the bare plank floor. The gaslight burned dimly above them. The night was completely still. Vincent knelt on one side of him, and Gauguin squatted on the other. Seurat was stil excited, and spoke with animation.

"In my opinion," he said, "all effects in painting can be reduced to formulae. Suppose I want to draw a circus scene. Here's a bareback rider, here the trainer, here the gallery and spectators. I want to suggest gaiety. What are the three elements of painting? Line, tone and colour. Very well, to suggest gaiety, I bring all my lines above the horizontal, so. I make my luminous colours dominant, so, and my warm tone dominant, so. There! Doesn't that suggest the abstraction of gaiety?"

"Well," replied Vincent, "it may suggest the abstraction of gaiety, but it doesn't catch gaiety itself."

Seurat looked up from his crouching position. His face was in the shadow. Vincent observed what a beautiful man he was.

"I'm not after gaiety itself. I'm after the essence of gaiety. Are you acquainted with Plato, my friend?"

"Yes."

"Very well, what painters must learn to portray is not a thing, but the essence of a thing. When the artist paints a horse, it should not be one particular horse that you can recognize in the street. The camera can take photographs; we must go beyond that. What we must capture when we paint a horse, Monsieur Van Gogh, is Plato's *horsiness*, the external spirit of a horse. And when we paint a man, it should not be the *concierge*, with a wart on the end of his nose, but manness, the spirit and essence of all men. Do you follow me, my friend?"

"I follow," said Vincent, "but I don't agree."

"We'll come to the agreement later."

Seurat got off his haunches, slipped out of his smock, and wiped the circus picture off the floor with it.

"Now we go on to calmness," he continued. "I am doing a scene on the Island of the Grande Jatte. I make all my lines horizontal, so. For tone I use perfect equality between warm and cold, so; for colour, equality between dark and light, so. Do you see it?"

"Go on Georges," said Gauguin, "and don't ask foolish questions."

"Now we come to sadness. We make all our lines run in a descending direction, like this. We make the cold tones dominant, so; and the dark colours dominant, so. There! The essence of sadness! A child could draw it. The mathematical formulae for apportioning space on a canvas will be set down in a little book. I have already worked them out. The painter need only read the book, go to the chemist's shop, buy the specified pots of colour, and obey the rules. He will be a scientific and perfect painter. He can work in sunlight or gaslight, be a monk or a libertine, seven years old or seventy, and all the paintings will achieve the same architectural, impersonal perfection."

Vincent blinked. Gauguin laughed.

"He thinks you're crazy, Georges."

Seurat mopped up the last drawing with his smock, then flung it into a dark corner.

"Do you, Monsieur Van Gogh?" he asked.

"No, no," protested Vincent, "I've been called crazy too many times myself to like the sound of the word. But I must admit this; your ideas are very queer!"

"He means yes, Georges," said Gauguin.

There was a sharp knock on the door.

"Mon Dieu!" groaned Gauguin, "we've awakened your mother again! She told me if I didn't stay away from here nights, she'd take the hairbrush to me!"

Seurat's mother came in. She had on a heavy robe and nightcap.

"Georges, you promised me you wouldn't work all night any more. Oh, it's you, is it, Paul? Why don't you pay your rent? Then you'd have a place to sleep at nights."

"If you'd only take me in here, Mother Seurat, I wouldn't have to pay any rent at all."

"No, thanks, one artist in the family is enough. Here, I've brought you coffee and brioches. If you must work, you have to eat. I suppose I'll have to go down and get your bottle of absinthe, Paul."

"You haven't drunk it all up, have you, Mother Seurat?"

"Paul, remember what I told you about the hairbrush."

Vincent came out of the shadows.

"Mother," said Seurat, "this is a new friend of mine, Vincent Van Gogh."

Mother Seurat took his hand.

"Any friend of my son's is welcome here, even if it is four in the morning. What will you have to drink, Monsieur?"

"If you don't mind, I'll have a glass of Gauguin's absinthe."

"You will not!" exclaimed Gauguin. "Mother Seurat keeps me on rations, Only one bottle a month. Take something else. Your heathen palate doesn't know the difference between absinthe and *chartreuse jaune.*"

The three men and Mother Seurat sat chatting over their coffee and brioches until the dawning sun struck a tiny triangle of yellow light on the north window.

"I may as well dress for the day," said Mother Seurat. "Come to dinner with Georges and me some evening, Monsieur Van Gogh. We shall be happy to have you."

At the front door Seurat said to Vincent, "I have explained my method rather crudely, I'm afraid. Come back often as you like, and we will work together. When you come to understand my method you will see that painting can never be the same again. Well, I must return to my canvas. I have another small space to hollow out before I go to sleep. Please present my compliments to your brother."

Vincent and Gauguin walked down the deserted stone canyons and climbed the hill to Montmartre. Paris had not yet awakened. The green shutters were closed tight, the blinds were drawn in the shops, and the little country carts were on their way home again after having dropped their vegetables, fruits, and flowers at the Halles.

"Let's go up to the top of the Butte and watch the sun awaken Paris," said Gauguin.

"I'd like that."

After gaining the Boulevard Clichy, they took the Rue Lepic which wound by the Moulin de la Galette and made its tortuous way up the Montmartre hill. The houses became fewer and fewer; open plains of flowers and trees appeared. The Rue Lepic stopped short. The two men took a winding path through the brush.

"Tell me frankly, Gauguin," said Vincent, "what do you think of Seurat?"

"Georges? I thought you'd ask that. He knows more about colour than any man since Delacroix. He has intellectual theories about art. That's wrong. Painters should not think about what they are doing. Leave the theories to the critics. Georges will make a definite contribution to colour, and his Gothic architecture will probably hasten the primitive reaction in art. But he's *fou,* completely *fou,* as you saw for yourself."

It was a stiff climb, but when they reached the summit, all of Paris spread out before them, the lake of black roofs and the frequent church spires emerging from the mist of night. The Seine cut the city in half like a winding stream of light. The houses flowed down the hill of Montmartre to the valley of the Seine, then struggled up again on Montparnasse. The sun broke clear and lit up the Bois de Vincennes beneath it. At the other end of the city the green verdure of the Bois de Boulogne was still dark and somnolent. The three landmarks of the city, the Opera in the centre, Notre Dame in the east and the Arc de Triomphe in the west, stood up in the air like mounds of variegated stone.

6

Peace descended upon the tiny apartment in the Rue Laval. Theo thanked his lucky stars for the moment of calm. But it did not last long. Instead of working his way slowly and minutely through his antiquated palette, Vincent began to imitate his friends. He forgot everything he had ever learned about painting in his wild desire to be an Impressionist. His canvases looked like atrocious copies of Seurats, Toulouse-Lautrecs, and Gauguins. He thought he was making splendid progress.

"Listen, old boy," said Theo one night, "what's your name?"

"Vincent Van Gogh."

"You're quite certain it's not Georges Seurat, or Paul Gauguin?"

"What the devil are you driving at, Theo?"

"Do you really think you can become a Georges Seurat? Don't you realize that there has only been one Lautrec since the beginning of time? And only one Gauguin . . . thank God! It's silly for you to try to imitate them."

"I'm not imitating them. I'm learning from them."

"You're imitating. Show me any one of your new canvases, and I'll tell you who you were with the night before."

"But I'm improving all the time, Theo. Look how much lighter these pictures are."

"You're going downhill every day. You paint less like Vincent Van Gogh with each picture. There's no royal road for you, old boy. It's going to take years of hard labour. Are you such a weakling that you have to imitate others? Can't you just assimilate what they have to offer?"

"Theo, I tell you these canvases are good!"

"And I tell you they're awful!"

The battle was on.

Each night that he came home from the gallery, exhausted and nervously on edge, Theo found Vincent waiting for him impatiently with a new canvas. He would leap savagely upon Theo before his brother had a chance to take off his hat and coat.

"There! Now tell me this one isn't good! Tell me that my palette isn't improving! Look at that sunlight effect! Look at this . . ."

Theo had to choose between telling a lie and spending a pleasant evening with an affable brother, or telling the truth and being pursued violently about the house until dawn. Theo was frightfully tired. He could not afford to tell the truth. But he did.

"When were you at Durand-Ruel's last?" he demanded, wearily.

"What does that matter?"

"Answer my question."

"Well," said Vincent sheepishly, "yesterday afternoon."

"Do you know, Vincent, there are almost five thousand painters in Paris trying to imitate Edouard Manet? And most of them do it better than you."

The battleground was too small for either of them to survive.

Vincent tried a new trick. He threw all the Impressionists into one lone canvas.

"Delightful," murmured Theo that night. "We'll name this one, *Recapitulation*. We'll label everything on the canvas. That tree is a genuine Gauguin. The girl in the corner is undoubtedly a Toulouse-Lautrec. I would say that your sunlight on the stream is Sisley, the colour, Monet, the leaves, Pissarro, the air, Seurat, and the central figure, Manet."

Vincent fought bitterly. He worked hard all day, and when Theo came home at night, he was chastised like a little child. Theo had to sleep in the living room, so Vincent could not paint there at night. His quarrels with Theo left him too excited and wrought up to sleep. He spent the long hours haranguing his brother. Theo battled with him until he fell asleep from sheer exhaustion, the light still burning, and Vincent gesticulating excitedly. The only thing that kept Theo going was the thought that soon they would be in the Rue Lepic, where he would have a bedroom to himself and a good strong lock on the door.

When Vincent tired of arguing about his own canvases, he filled Theo's nights with turbulent discussions of art, the art business, and the wretched business of being an artist.

"Theo, I can't understand it," he complained. "Here you are the manager of one of the most important art galleries in Paris, and you won't even exhibit one of your own brother's canvases."

"Valadon won't let me."

"Have you tried?"

"A thousand times."

"All right, we'll admit that my paintings are not good enough. But what about Seurat? And Gauguin? And Lautrec?"

"Every time they bring me new canvases, I beg Valadon to let me hang them on the *entresol*."

"Are you master in that gallery, or is someone else?"

"Alas, I only work there."

"Then you ought to get out. It's degrading, simply degrading. Theo, I wouldn't stand for it. I'd leave them."

"Let's talk it over at breakfast, Vincent. I've had a hard day and I want to go to sleep."

"I don't want to wait until breakfast. I want to talk about it right now. Theo, what good does it do to exhibit Manet and Degas? They're already being accepted. They're beginning to sell. It's the younger men you have to fight for now."

"Give me time! Perhaps in another three years . . ."

"No! We can't wait three years. We've got to have action now. Oh, Theo, why don't you throw up your job and open an art gallery of your own? Just think, no more Valadon, no more Bouguereau, no more Henner!"

"That would take money, Vincent. I haven't saved anything."

"We'd get the money somehow."

"The art business is slow to develop, you know."

"Let it be slow. We'll work night and day until we've established you."

"And what would we do in the meanwhile? We have to eat."

"Are you reproaching me for not earning my own living?"

"For goodness' sake, Vincent, go to bed. I'm exhausted."

"I won't go to bed. I want to know the truth. Is that the only reason you don't leave Goupils? Because you have to support me? Come on, tell the truth. I'm a millstone around your neck. I hold you down. I make you keep your job. If it wasn't for me, you'd be free."

"If only I were a little bit bigger, or a little bit stronger, I'd hand you a sound thrashing. As it is, I think I'll hire Gauguin to come in and do it. My job is with Goupils, Vincent, now and always. Your job is painting, now and always. Half of my work at Goupils belongs to you; half of your painting belongs to me. Now get off my bed and let me go to sleep, or I'll call a *gendarme!*"

The following evening Theo handed Vincent an envelope and said, "If you're not doing anything tonight, we might go to this party."

"Who's giving it?"

"Henri Rousseau. Take a look at the invitation."

There were two verses of a simple poem and some handpainted flowers on the card.

"Who is he?" asked Vincent.

"We call him *le Douanier*. He was a customs collector in the provinces until he was forty. Used to paint on Sundays, just as Gauguin did. He came to Paris a few years ago and settled in the labourers' section around the Bastille. He's never had a day of education or instruction in his life, yet he paints, writes poetry, composes music, gives lessons on the violin to the workers' children, plays on the piano, and teaches drawing to a couple of old men."

"What sort of thing does he paint?"

"Fantastic animals, largely, peering out of even more fantastic jungles. The closest he ever got to a jungle is the Jardin d'Acclimation in the Bois de Boulogne. He's a peasant and a natural primitive, even if Paul Gauguin does laugh at him."

"What do you think of his work, Theo?"

"Well, I don't know. Everyone calls him an imbecile and a madman."

"Is he?"

"He's something of a child, a primitive child. We'll go to the party tonight and you'll have a chance to judge for yourself. He has all his canvases up on the walls."

"He must have money if he can give parties."

"He's probably the poorest painter in Paris today. He even has to rent the violin he gives lessons on, because he can't afford to buy it. But he has a purpose in giving these parties. You'll discover it for yourself."

The house in which Rousseau lived was occupied by the families of manual labourers. Rousseau had a room on the fourth floor. The street was full of squalling children; the combined stench of cooking, washing, and latrines in the hallway was thick enough to strangle one.

Henri Rousseau answered Theo's knock. He was a short, thickset man, built a good deal on Vincent's lines. His fingers were short and stumpy, his head almost square. He had a stubby nose and chin, and wide, innocent eyes.

"You honour me by coming, Monsieur Van Gogh," he said in a soft, affable tone.

Theo introduced Vincent. Rousseau offered them chairs. The room was colourful, almost gay. Rousseau had put up his peasant curtains of red and white checked cloth at the windows. The walls were filled solid with pictures of wild animals and jungles and incredible landscapes.

Four young boys were standing by the battered old piano in the corner, holding violins in their hands nervously. On the mantel over the fireplace were the homely little cookies that Rousseau had baked and sprinkled with caraway seed. A number of benches and chairs were scattered about the room.

"You are the first to arrive, Monsieur Van Gogh," said Rousseau. "The critic, Guillaume Pille, is doing me the honour of bringing a party."

A noise came up from the street; the cries of children's voices and the rumble of carriage wheels over the cobblestones. Rousseau flung open his door. Pretty feminine voices floated up from the hall.

"Keep going. Keep going," boomed a voice. "One hand on the banister and the other on your nose!"

A shout of laughter followed this witticism. Rousseau, who had heard it clearly, turned to Vincent and smiled. Vincent thought he had never seen such clear, innocent eyes in a man, eyes so free from malice and resentment.

A party of some ten or twelve people burst into the room. The men were dressed in evening clothes, the women in sumptuous gowns, dainty slippers, and long white gloves. They brought into the room the fragrance of costly perfume, of delicate powders, of silk and old lace.

"Well, Henri," cried Guillaume Pille in his deep, pompous voice, "you see we have come. But we cannot stay long. We are going to a ball at the Princess de Broglie's. Meanwhile you must entertain my guests."

"Oh, I want to meet him," gushed a slim, auburn-haired girl in an Empire gown cut low across the breasts. "Just think, this is the great painter of whom all Paris is talking. Will you kiss my hand, Monsieur Rousseau?"

"Take care, Blanche," someone said. "You know . . . these artists . . ."

Rousseau smiled and kissed her hand. Vincent shrank into a corner. Pille and Theo chatted for a moment. The rest of the party walked about the room in pairs, commenting on the different canvases with gales of laughter, fingering Rousseau's curtains, his ornaments, ransacking every corner of the room for a new joke.

"If you will sit down, ladies and gentlemen," said Rousseau, "my orchestra will play one of my own compositions. I have dedicated it to Monsieur Pille. It is called *Chanson Raval.*"

"Come, come everybody!" shouted Pille. "Rousseau is going to entertain us. Jeanie! Blanche! Jacques! Come sit down. This will be precious."

The four trembling boys stood before a lone music rack and tuned their violins. Rousseau sat at his piano and closed his eyes. After a moment he said, "Ready," and began to play. The composition was a simple pastoral. Vincent tried to listen but the snickers of the crowd drowned out the music. At the end they all applauded vociferously. Blanche went to the piano, put her hands on Rousseau's shoulders and said, "That was beautiful, Monsieur, beautiful. I have never been so deeply stirred."

"You flatter me, Madame."

Blanche screamed with laughter.

"Guillaume, did you hear that? He thinks I'm flattering him!"

"I will play you another composition now," said Rousseau.

"Sing us one of your poems to it, Henri. You know you have so many poems."

Rousseau grinned childishly.

"Very well, Monsieur Pille, I will chant a poem to it, if you wish."

He went to a table, took out a sheaf of poems, thumbed through them and selected one. He sat down at the piano and began to play. Vincent thought the music good. The few lines he could catch of the poem he also thought charming. But the effect of the two together was quite ludicrous. The crowd howled. They slapped Pille on the back.

"Oh, Guillaume, you are a dog. What a sly one you are."

Finished with his music, Rousseau went out to the kitchen and returned with a number of thick, rough cups of coffee, which he passed about to the guests. They picked the caraway seeds off the cookies and threw them into each other's coffee. Vincent smoked his pipe in the corner.

"Come, Henri, show us your latest paintings. That is what we have come for. We must see them here, in your atelier, before they are bought for the Louvre."

"I have some lovely new ones," said Rousseau. "I will take them off the wall for you."

The crowd gathered about the table, trying to outdo each other in the extravagance of their compliments.

"This is divine, simply divine," breathed Blanche. "I must have it for my boudoir. I just can't live another day without it! *Cher Maître,* how much is this immortal masterpiece?"

"Twenty-five francs."

"Twenty-five francs! Only imagine, twenty-five francs for a great work of art! Will you dedicate it to me?"

"I will be honoured."

"I promised Françoise I would bring her one," said Pille. "Henri, this is for my fiancée. It must be the very finest thing you have ever done."

"I know just the one for you, Monsieur Pille."

He took down a painting of some sort of weird animal peering through a fairy tale jungle. Everyone howled at Pille.

"What is it?"

"It's a lion."

"It is not, it's a tiger."

"I tell you, it's my washerwoman; I recognize her."

"This one is a little larger, Monsieur," said Rousseau sweetly. "It will cost you thirty francs."

"It's worth it, Henri, it's worth it. Some day my grandchildren will sell this exquisite canvas for thirty thousand francs!"

"I want one. I want one," several of the others exclaimed. "I've got to take one to my friends. This is the best show of the season."

"Come along, everyone," shouted Pille. "We'll be late for the ball. And bring your paintings. We'll cause a riot at the Princess de Broglie's with these things. Au revoir, Henri. We had a perfectly marvelous time. Give another party soon."

"Good-bye, *cher Maître*," said Blanche, flicking her perfumed kerchief under his nose. "I will never forget you. You will live in my memory forever."

"Leave him alone, Blanche," cried one of the men. "The poor fellow won't be able to sleep all night."

They trouped down the stairs noisily, shouting their jokes at each other, leaving a cloud of expensive perfume behind them to mingle with the stench of the building.

Theo and Vincent walked to the door. Rousseau was standing at the table, looking down at the pile of coins.

"Do you mind going home alone, Theo?" Vincent asked quietly. "I want to stay and get acquainted."

Theo left. Rousseau did not notice Vincent close the door and then lean against it. He went on counting the money on the table.

"Eighty francs, ninety francs, one hundred, a hundred and five."

He looked up and saw Vincent watching him. The simple, childlike expression returned to his eyes. He pushed the money aside and stood there, grinning foolishly.

"Take off the mask, Rousseau," said Vincent. "I, too, am a peasant and a painter."

Rousseau left the table, crossed to Vincent and gripped his hand warmly.

"Your brother has shown me your pictures of the Dutch peasants. They are good. They are better than Millet's. I have looked at them many, many times. I admire you, Monsieur."

"And I have looked at your pictures, Rousseau, while those . . . were making fools of themselves. I admire you, too."

"Thank you. Will you sit down? Will you fill your pipe with my tobacco? It is a hundred and five francs, Monsieur. I will be able to buy tobacco, and food, and canvas to paint on."

They sat on opposite sides of the table and smoked in friendly, ruminative silence.

"I suppose you know they call you a crazy man, Rousseau?"

"Yes, I know. And I have heard that in The Hague they think you are crazy, too."

"Yes, that's so."

"Let them think what they like. Some day my paintings will hang in the Luxembourg."

"And mine," said Vincent, "will hang in the Louvre."

They read the thought in each other's eyes and broke into spontaneous, wholehearted laughter.

"They're right, Henri," said Vincent. "We are crazy!"

"Shall we go have a drink on it?" asked Rousseau.

7

Gauguin knocked on the door of the apartment the following Wednesday toward dinner time.

"Your brother asked me to take you over to the Café Batignolles this evening. He has to work late at the gallery. These are interesting canvases. May I look?"

"Of course. I did some of them in the Brabant, others in The Hague."

Gauguin gazed at the pictures for a long while. Several times he raised his hand, opened his mouth, and made as if to speak. He did not seem able to formulate his thoughts.

"Forgive me for asking, Vincent," he said, finally, "but are you by any chance an epileptic?"

Vincent was just slipping into a sheepskin coat which to Theo's dismay, he had found in a second-hand store and insisted upon wearing. He turned about and stared at Gauguin.

"Am I a what?" he demanded.

"An epileptic. One of those fellows who has nervous fits?"

"Not that I know of, Gauguin. Why do you ask?"

"Well . . . these pictures of yours . . . they look as though they were going to burst right out of the canvas. When I look at your work . . . and this isn't the first time it's happened to me . . . I begin feeling a nervous excitement that I can hardly contain. I feel that if the picture doesn't explode, I most certainly will! Do you know where your paintings affect me most?"

"No. Where?"

"In the bowels. My whole insides begin to tremble. I get feeling so excited and perturbed, I can hardly restrain myself."

"Perhaps I could sell them as laxatives. You know, hang one in the lavatory and look at it at a certain hour every day?"

"Seriously speaking, Vincent, I don't think I could live with your pictures. They'd drive me mad inside of a week."

"Shall we go?"

They walked up the Rue Montmartre to the Boulevard Clichy.

"Have you had dinner?" asked Gauguin.

"No. Have you?"

"No. Shall we go up to Bataille's?"

"Good idea. Got any money?"

"Not a centime. How about you?"

"I'm flat, as usual. I was waiting for Theo to take me out."

"Zut! I guess we don't eat."

"Let's go up and see what the *plat du jour* is, anyway."

They took the Rue Lepic up the hill, then turned right on the Rue des Abbesses. Madame Bataille had an ink-scrawled menu tacked to one of her imitation potted trees in front.

"Uummm," said Vincent, "*côté de veau petits pois*. My favourite dish."

"I hate veal," said Gauguin. "I'm glad we don't have to eat."

"*Quelle blague!*"

They wandered down the street and into the little triangular park at the foot of the Butte.

"Hello," said Gauguin, "there's Paul Cezanne, asleep on a bench. Why that idiot uses his shoes for a pillow is beyond me. Let's wake him up."

He pulled the belt out of his trousers, doubled it up, and gave the sleeping man a whack across the stockinged feet. Cezanne sprang off the bench with a yowl of pain.

"Gauguin, you infernal sadist! Is that your idea of a joke? I shall be forced to crack your skull one of these days."

"Serves you right for leaving your feet exposed. Why do you put those filthy Provence boots under your head? I should think they'd be worse than no pillow at all."

Cezanne rubbed the bottom of each foot in turn, then slipped on his boots, grumbling.

"I don't use them for a pillow. I put them under my head so no one will steal them while I'm asleep."

Gauguin turned to Vincent. "You'd think he was a starving artist the way he talks. His father owns a bank, and half of Aix-en-Provence. Paul, this is Vincent Van Gogh, Theo's brother."

Cezanne and Vincent shook hands.

"It's too bad we didn't find you a half hour ago, Cezanne," said Gauguin. "You could have joined us for dinner. Bataille has the best *côté de veau aux petits pois* I've ever tasted."

"It was really good, was it?" asked Cezanne.

"Good? It was delicious! Wasn't it, Vincent?"

"Certainly was."

"Then I think I'll go have some. Come and keep me company, will you?"

"I don't know whether I could eat another portion. Could you, Vincent?"

"I hardly think so. Still, if Monsieur Cezanne insists . . ."

"Be a good fellow, Gauguin. You know I hate to eat alone. Take something else if you've had enough veal."

"Well, just to oblige you. Come along, Vincent."

They went back up the Rue des Abbesses to Bataille's.

"Good evening, gentlemen," said the waiter. "Have you chosen?"

"Yes," replied Gauguin, "bring us three *plats du jour.*"

"*Bien*. And what wine?"

"You choose the wine, Cezanne. You know more about those things than I do."

"Let's see, there's Saint-Estephe, Bordeaux, Sauterne, Beaune . . ."

"Have you ever tried their Pommard?" interrupted Gauguin, guilelessly. "I often think it's the best wine they have."

"Bring us a bottle of Pommard," said Cezanne to the waiter.

Gauguin bolted his veal and green peas in no time, then turned to Cezanne while the latter was still in the middle of his dinner.

"By the way, Paul," he remarked, "I hear that Zola's 'L'Oeuvre' is selling by the thousands."

Cezanne shot him a black, bitter look, and shoved his dinner away with distaste. He turned to Vincent.

"Have you read that book, Monsieur?"

"Not yet. I just finished 'Germinal.' "

" 'L'Oeuvre' is a bad book," said Cezanne, "and a false one. Besides, it is the worst piece of treachery that has ever been committed in the name of friendship. The book is about a painter, Monsieur Van Gogh. About me! Emile Zola is my oldest friend. We were raised together in Aix. We went to school together. I came to Paris only because he was here. We were closer than brothers, Emile and I. All during our youth we planned how, side by side, we would become great artists. And now he does this to me."

"What has he done to you?" asked Vincent.

"Ridiculed me. Mocked me. Made me a laughing stock to all Paris. Day after day I told him about my theories of light, my theories of representing solids under surface appearances, my ideas of a revolutionary palette. He listened to me, he encouraged me, he drew me out. And all the time he was only gathering material for his book, to show what a fool I was."

He drained his wine glass, turned back to Vincent and continued, his small, sour eyes smouldering with passionate hatred.

"Zola has combined three of us in that book, Monsieur Van Gogh; myself, Bazille, and a poor, wretched lad who used to sweep out Manet's studio. The boy had artistic ambitions, but finally hanged himself in despair. Zola paints me as a visionary, another misguided wretch who thinks he is revolutionizing art, but who doesn't paint in the conventional manner simply because he hasn't enough talent to paint at all. He makes me hang myself from the scaffolding of my masterpiece, because in the end I realize that what I mistook for genius was only insane daubing. Up against me he puts another artist from Aix, a sentimental sculptor who turns out the most hackneyed, academic trash, and makes him a great artist."

"That's really amusing," said Gauguin, "when you remember that Zola was the first to champion Edouard Manet's revolution in painting. Emile has done more for Impressionist painting than any man alive."

"Yes, he worshipped Manet because Edouard overthrew the academicians. But when I try to go beyond the Impressionists, he calls me a fool and an idiot. As for Emile, he is a mediocre intelligence and a detestable friend. I had to stop going to his house long ago. He lives like a damned bourgeois. Rich rugs on the floor, vases on the mantelpiece, servants, a desk of carved and sculptured wood for him to write his masterpieces. Phew! He's more middle class than Manet ever dared to be. They were brother bourgeois under the skin, those two; that's why they got along so well together. Just because I come from the same town as Emile, and he knew me as a child, he thinks I can't possibly do any important work."

"I heard that he wrote a *brochure* for your pictures at the Salon des Refusées a few years back. What happened to it?"

"Emile tore it up, Gauguin, just before it was to have gone to the printers."

"But why?" asked Vincent.

"He was afraid the critics would think he was sponsoring me only because I was an old friend. If he had published that *brochure,* I would have been established. Instead he published 'L'Oeuvre.' So much for friendship. My pictures in the Salon des Refusées are laughed at by ninety-nine people out of a hundred. Durand-Ruel exhibits Degas, Monet, and my friend Guillaumin, but they refuse to give me two inches of space. Even your brother, Monsieur Van Gogh, is afraid to put me on his *entresol.* The only dealer in Paris who will put my pictures in his window is Père Tanguy, and he, poor soul, couldn't sell a crust of bread to a starving millionaire."

"Is there any Pommard left in that bottle, Cezanne?" asked Gauguin. "Thanks. What I have against Zola is that he makes his washerwomen talk like real washerwomen, and when he leaves them he forgets to change his style."

"Well, I've had enough of Paris. I'm going back to Aix and spend the rest of my life there. There's a hill rising up from the valley that overlooks the whole country-side. There's clear, bright sunlight in Provence, and colour. What colour! I know a plot of ground near the top of the hill that's for sale. It's covered with pine trees. I'll build a studio there, and plant an apple orchard. And I'll build a big stone wall around my ground. I'll mix broken bottles into the cement at the top of the wall, to keep the world out. And I'll never leave Provence again, never, never!"

"A hermit, eh?" murmured Gauguin into his glass of Pommard.

"Yes, a hermit."

"The hermit of Aix. What a charming title. We'd better be getting on to the Café Batignolles. Everyone will be there by now."

8

Nearly everyone was there. Lautrec had a pile of saucers in front of him high enough to rest his chin on. Georges Seurat was chatting quietly with Anquetin, a lean, lanky painter who was trying to combine the method of the Impressionists with that of the Japanese prints. Henri Rousseau was taking cookies out of his pocket and dipping them into a *café au lait,* while Theo carried on an animated discussion with two of the more modern Parisian critics.

Batignolles had formerly been a suburb at the entrance of the Boulevard Clichy, and it was here that Edouard Manet had gathered the kindred spirits of Paris about him. Before Manet's death, the École des Batignolles was in the habit of meeting twice a week at the café. Legros, Fantin-Latour, Courbet, Renoir, all had met there and worked out their theories of art, but now the École had been taken over by the younger men.

Cezanne saw Emile Zola. He walked to a far table, ordered a coffee, and sat aloof from the crowd. Gauguin introduced Vincent to Zola and then dropped into a chair alongside of Toulouse-Lautrec. Zola and Vincent were left alone at their table.

"I saw you come in with Paul Cezanne, Monsieur Van Gogh. No doubt he said something to you about me?"

"Yes."

"What was it?"

"I'm afraid your book has wounded him very deeply."

Zola sighed and pushed the table out from the leather cushioned bench to give his huge paunch more room.

"Have you ever heard of the Schweininger cure?" he asked. "They say if a man doesn't drink anything with his meals, he can lose thirty pounds in three months."

"I haven't heard of it."

"It hurt me very deeply to write that book about Paul Cezanne, but every word of it is true. You are a painter. Would you falsify a portrait of a friend simply because it made him unhappy? Of course you wouldn't. Paul is a splendid chap. For years he was my dearest friend. But his work is simply ludicrous. You know we are very tolerant at my house, Monsieur, but when my friends come, I must lock Paul's canvases in a cupboard so he will not be laughed at."

"But surely his work can't be as bad as all that."

"Worse, my dear Van Gogh, worse. You haven't seen any of it? That explains your incredulity. He draws like a child of five. I give you my word, I think he has gone completely crazy."

"Gauguin respects him."

"It breaks my heart," continued Zola, "to see Cezanne waste his life in this fantastic fashion. He should go back to Aix and take over his father's position in the bank. He could make something of his life that way. As things are now . . . some day he will hang himself . . . just as I predicted in 'L'Oeuvre.' Have you read that book, Monsieur?"

"Not yet. I just finished 'Germinal.' "

"So? And what do you think of it?"

"I think it the finest thing since Balzac."

"Yes, it is my masterpiece. It appeared *en feuilleton* in 'Gil Blas' last year. I got a good piece of money for that. And now the book has sold over sixty thousand copies. My income has never been as large as it is today. I'm going to add a new wing onto my house at Medan. The book has already caused four strikes and revolts in the mining regions of France. 'Germinal' will cause a gigantic revolution, and when it does, good-bye to capitalism! What sort of thing do you paint, Monsieur . . . What did Gauguin say your first name was?''

''Vincent. Vincent Van Gogh. Theo Van Gogh is my brother.''

Zola laid down the pencil with which he had been scribbling on the stone topped table, and stared at Vincent.

''That's curious,'' he said.

''What is?''

''Your name. I've heard it somewhere before.''

''Perhaps Theo mentioned it to you.''

''He did, but that wasn't it. Wait a minute! It was . . . it was . . . 'Germinal!' Have you ever been in the coal mining regions?''

''Yes. I lived in the Belgian Borinage for two years.''

''The Borinage! Petit Wasmes! Marcasse!''

Zola's large eyes almost popped out of his rotund, bearded face.

''So you're the second coming of Christ!''

Vincent flushed. ''What do you mean by that?''

''I spent five weeks in the Borinage, gathering material for 'Germinal.' The *gueules noires* speak of a Christ-man who worked among them as an evangelist.''

''Lower your voice, I beg you!''

Zola folded his hands over his fat paunch and pushed it inward.

''Don't be ashamed, Vincent,'' he said. ''What you tried to accomplish there was worth while. You simply chose the wrong medium. Religion will never get people anywhere. Only the base in spirit will accept misery in this world for the promise of bliss in the next.''

''I found that out too late.''

''You spent two years in the Borinage, Vincent. You gave away your food, your money, your clothes. You worked yourself to the point of death. And what did you get for it? Nothing. They called you a crazy man and expelled you from the Church. When you left, conditions were no better than when you came.''

''They were worse.''

''But my medium will do it. The written word will cause the revolution. Every literate miner in Belgium and France has read my book. There is not a café, not a miserable shack in the whole region, that hasn't a well-thumbed copy of 'Germinal.' Those who can't read, have it read to them over and over again. Four strikes already. And dozens more coming. The whole country is rising. 'Germinal' will create a new society, where your religion couldn't. And what do I get as my reward?''

''What?''

''Francs. Thousands upon thousands of them. Will you join me in a drink?''

The discussion around the Lautrec table became animated. Everyone turned his attention that way.

''How is *'ma methode,'* Seurat?'' asked Lautrec, cracking his knuckles one by one.

Seurat ignored the gibe. His exquisitely perfect features and calm, mask-like expression suggested, not the face of one man, but the essence of masculine beauty.

''There is a new book on colour refraction by an American, Ogden Rood. I think it an advance on Helmholtz and Chevral, though not quite so stimulating as de Superville's work. You could all read it with profit.''

''I don't read books about painting,'' said Lautrec. ''I leave that to the layman.''

Seurat unbuttoned the black and white checked coat and straightened out the large blue tie sprinkled with polka dots.

''You yourself are a layman,'' he said, ''so long as you guess at the colours you use.''

''I don't guess. I know by instinct.''

"Science is a method, Georges," put in Gauguin. "We have become scientific in our application of colour by years of hard work and experimentation."

"That's not enough, my friend. The trend of our age is toward objective production. The days of inspiration, of trial and error, are gone forever."

"I can't read those books," said Rousseau. "They give me a headache. Then I have to go paint all day to get rid of it."

Everyone laughed. Anquetin turned to Zola and said, "Did you see the attack on 'Germinal' in this evening's paper?"

"No. What did it say?"

"The critic called you the most immoral writer of the nineteenth century."

"Their old cry. Can't they find anything else to say against me?"

"They're right, Zola," said Lautrec. "I find your books carnal and obscene."

"You certainly ought to recognize obscenity when you see it!"

"Had you that time, Lautrec!"

"*Garçon*," called Zola. "A round of drinks."

"We're in for it now," murmured Cezanne to Anquetin. "When Emile buys the drinks, it means you have to listen to an hour's lecture."

The waiter served the drinks. The painters lit their pipes and gathered into a close, intimate circle. The gas lamps illuminated the room in spirals of light. The hum of conversation from the other tables was low and chordal.

"They call my books immoral," said Zola, "for the same reason that they attribute immorality to your paintings, Henri. The public cannot understand that there is no room for moral judgments in art. Art is amoral; so is life. For me there are no obscene pictures or books; there are only poorly conceived and poorly executed ones. A whore by Toulouse-Lautrec is moral because he brings out the beauty that lies beneath her external appearance; a pure country girl by Bouguereau is immoral because she is sentimentalized and so cloyingly sweet that just to look at her is enough to make you vomit!"

"Yes, that's so," nodded Theo.

Vincent saw that the painters respected Zola, not because he was successful—they despised the ordinary connotations of success—but because he worked in a medium which seemed mysterious and difficult to them. They listened closely to his words.

"The ordinary human brain thinks in terms of duality; light and shade, sweet and sour, good and evil. That duality does not exist in nature. There is neither good nor evil in the world, but only being and doing. When we describe an action, we describe life; when we call that action names—like depravity or obscenity—we go into the realm of subjective prejudice."

"But, Emile," said Theo. "What would the mass of people do without its standard of morality?"

"Morality is like religion," contributed Toulouse-Lautrec; "a soporific to close people's eyes to the tawdriness of their life."

"Your amorality is nothing but anarchism, Zola," said Seurat, "and nihilistic anarchism, at that. It's been tried before, and it doesn't work."

"Of course we have to have certain codes," agreed Zola. "The public weal demands sacrifices from the individual. I don't object to morality, but only to the pudency that spits upon *Olympia*, and wants Maupassant suppressed. I tell you, morality in France today is entirely confined to the erogenous zone. Let people sleep with whom they like; I know a higher morality than that."

"That reminds me of a dinner I gave a few years ago," said Gauguin. "One of the men I invited said, 'You understand, my friend, that I can't take my wife to these dinners of yours when your mistress is present.' 'Very well,' I replied, 'I'll send her out for the evening.' When the dinner was over and they all went home, our honest Madame, who had yawned the whole evening, stopped yawning and said to her husband, 'Let's have some nice piggy talk before we do it.' And her husband said, 'Let's not do anything but talk. I have eaten too much this evening.' "

"That tells the whole story!" shouted Zola, above the laughter.

"Put aside the ethics for a moment and get back to immorality in art," said Vincent. "No one ever calls my pictures obscene, but I am invariably accused of an even greater immorality, ugliness."

"You hit it that time, Vincent," said Toulouse-Lautrec.

"Yes, that's the essence of the new immorality for the public," agreed Gauguin. "Did you see what the *Mercure de France* called us this month? The cult of ugliness."

"The same criticism is levied against me," said Zola. "A countess said to me the other day, 'My dear Monsieur Zola, why does a man of your extraordinary talent go about turning up stones just to see what sort of filthy insects are crawling underneath them?' "

Lautrec took an old newspaper clipping out of his pocket.

"Listen to what the critic said about my canvases at the last Salon des Independents. 'Toulouse-Lautrec may be reproached for taking delight in representing trivial gaiety, coarse amusements and "low subjects." He appears to be insensible to beauty of feature, elegance of form and grace of movement. It is true that he paints with a loving brush beings ill-formed, stumpy and repulsive in their ugliness, but of what good is such perversion?' "

"Shades of Frans Hals," murmured Vincent.

"Well, he's right," said Seurat. "If you men are not perverted, you're at least misguided. Art has to do with abstract things, like colour, design, and tone. It should not be used to improve social conditions or search for ugliness. Painting should be like music, divorced from the everyday world."

"Victor Hugo died last year," said Zola, "and with him a whole civilization died. A civilization of pretty gestures, romance, artful lies and subtle evasions. My books stand for the new civilization; the unmoral civilization of the twentieth century. So do your paintings. Bouguereau is still dragging his carcass around Paris, but he took ill the day that Edouard Manet exhibited *Picnic on the Grass*, and he died the day Manet finished *Olympia*. Well, Manet is gone now, and so is Daumier, but we still have Degas, Lautrec and Gauguin to carry on their work."

"Put the name of Vincent Van Gogh on that list," said Toulouse-Lautrec.

"Put it at the head of the list," said Rousseau.

"Very well, Vincent," said Zola with a smile, "you have been nominated for the cult of ugliness. Do you accept the nomination?"

"Alas," said Vincent, "I'm afraid I was born into it."

"Let's formulate our manifesto, gentlemen," said Zola. "First, we think all truth beautiful, no matter how hideous its face may seem. We accept all of nature, without any repudiation. We believe there is more beauty in a harsh truth than in a pretty lie, more poetry in earthiness than in all the salons of Paris. We think pain good, because it is the most profound of all human feelings. We think sex beautiful, even when portrayed by a harlot and a pimp. We put character above ugliness, pain above prettiness, and hard, crude reality above all the wealth in France. We accept life in its entirety, without making moral judgments. We think the prostitute as good as the countess, the *concierge* as good as the general, the peasant as good as the cabinet minister, for they all fit into the pattern of nature, and are woven into the design of life!"

"Glasses up, gentlemen," cried Toulouse-Lautrec. "We drink to amorality and the cult of ugliness. May it beautify and re-create the world."

"Tosh!" said Cezanne.

"And 'Tosh!' again," said Georges Seurat.

9

At the beginning of June, Theo and Vincent moved to their new apartment at 54, Rue Lepic, Montmartre. The house was just a short way from the Rue Laval; they had only to go up the Rue Montmartre a few blocks to the Boulevard Clichy, and then take the winding Rue Lepic up past the Moulin de la Galette, almost into the countrified part of the Butte.

Their apartment was on the third floor. It had three rooms, a cabinet and a kitchen. The living room was comfortable with Theo's beautiful old cabinet, Louis Philippes, and a big stove to protect them against the Paris cold. Theo had a talent for home-making. He loved to have everything just right. His bedroom was next to the living room. Vincent slept in the cabinet, behind which was his studio, an ordinary sized room with one window.

"You won't have to work at Corman's any longer, Vincent," said Theo. They were arranging and rearranging the furniture in the living room.

"No, thank heavens. Still, I needed to do a few female nudes."

Theo placed the sofa across the room from the cabinet and surveyed the room critically. "You haven't done a complete canvas in colour for some time, have you?" he asked.

"No."

"Why not?"

"What would be the use? Until I can mix the right colours . . . where do you want this armchair, Theo? Under the lamp or next to the window? But now that I've got a studio of my own . . ."

The following morning Vincent got up with the sun, arranged the easel in his new studio, put a piece of canvas on a frame, laid out the shining new palette that Theo had bought him, and softened up his brushes. When it was time for Theo to rise, he put on the coffee and went down to the *pâtisserie* for crisp, fresh croissants.

Theo could feel Vincent's turbulent excitement across the breakfast table.

"Well, Vincent," he said, "you've been to school for three months. Oh, I don't mean Corman's, I mean the school of Paris! You've seen the most important painting that has been done in Europe in three hundred years. And now you're ready to . . ."

Vincent pushed aside his half-eaten breakfast and jumped to his feet. "I think I'll begin . . ."

"Sit down. Finish your breakfast. You have plenty of time. There's nothing for you to worry about. I'll buy your paints and canvas wholesale, so you'll always have plenty on hand. You'd better have your teeth operated on, too; I want to get you into perfect health. But for goodness sake, go about your work slowly and carefully!"

"Don't talk nonsense, Theo. Have I ever gone about anything slowly and carefully?"

When Theo came home that night he found that Vincent had lashed himself into a fury. He had been working progressively at his craft for six years under the most heartbreaking conditions; now that everything was made easy for him, he was faced with a humiliating impotence.

It was ten o'clock before Theo could get him quieted down. When they went out to dinner, some of Vincent's confidence had returned. Theo looked pale and worn.

The weeks that followed were torture for both of them. When Theo returned from the gallery he would find Vincent in any one of his hundred different kinds of tempests. The strong lock on his door did him absolutely no good. Vincent sat on his bed until the early hours of the morning, arguing with him. When Theo fell asleep, Vincent shook him by the shoulder and woke him up.

"Stop pacing the floor and sit still for a moment," begged Theo one night. "And stop drinking that damned absinthe. That's not how Gauguin developed his palette. Now listen to me, you infernal idiot, you must give yourself at least a year before you even begin to look at your work with a critical eye. What good is it going to do to make yourself sick? You're getting thin and nervous. You know you can't do your best work in that condition."

The hotness of a Parisian summer came on. The sun burned up the streets. Paris sat in front of its favourite café until one and two in the morning, sipping cold drinks. The flowers on the Butte Montmartre burst into a riot of colour. The Seine wound its glistening way through the city, through banks of trees and cool patches of green grass.

Every morning Vincent strapped his easel to his back and went looking for a picture. He had never known such hot, constant sun in Holland, nor had he ever seen such deep, elemental colour. Nearly every evening he returned from his painting in time to join the heated discussions on the *entresol* of Goupils.

One day Gauguin came in to help him mix some pigments.

"From whom do you buy these colours?" he asked.

"Theo gets them wholesale."

"You should patronize Père Tanguy. His prices are the lowest in Paris, and he trusts a man when he's broke."

"Who is this Père Tanguy? I've heard you mention him before."

"Haven't you met him yet? Good Lord, you mustn't hesitate another moment. You and Père are the only two men I've ever met whose communism really comes from the heart. Put on that beautiful rabbit-fur bonnet of yours. We're going down to the Rue Clauzel."

As they wound down the Rue Lepic, Gauguin told Père Tanguy's story. "He used to be a plasterer before he came to Paris. He worked as a colour-grinder in the house of Edouard, then took the job of *concierge* somewhere on the Butte. His wife looked after the house and Père began peddling colours through the quarter. He met Pissarro, Monet, and Cezanne, and since they liked him, we all started buying our colours from him. He joined the communists during the last uprising; one day while he was dreaming on sentry duty, a band from Versailles descended on his post. The poor fellow just couldn't fire on another human being. He threw away his musket. He was sentenced to serve two years in the galleys at Brest for this treachery, but we got him out.

"He saved a few francs and opened this little shop in the Rue Clauzel. Lautrec painted the front of it blue for him. He was the first man in Paris to exhibit a Cezanne canvas. Since then we've all had our stuff there. Not that he ever sells a canvas. Ah, no! You see, Père is a great lover of art, but since he is poor, he can't afford to buy pictures. So he exhibits them in his little shop, where he can live among them all day."

"You mean he wouldn't sell a painting even if he got a good offer?"

"Decidedly not. He takes only pictures that he loves, and once he gets attached to a canvas, you can't get it out of the shop. I was there one day when a well-dressed man came in, admired a Cezanne and asked how much it was. Any other dealer in Paris would have been delighted to sell it for sixty francs. Père Tanguy looked at the canvas for a long time and then said, 'Ah, yes, this one. It is a particularly good Cezanne. I cannot let it go under six hundred francs.' When the man ran out, Père took the painting off the wall and held it before him with tears in his eyes."

"Then what good does it do to have him exhibit your work?"

"Well, Père Tanguy is a strange fellow. All he knows about art is how to grind colours. And yet he has an infallible sense of the authentic. If he asks for one of your canvases, give it to him. It will be your formal initiation into Parisian art. Here's the Rue Clauzel; let's turn in."

The Rue Clauzel was a one block street connecting the Rue des Martyres and the Rue Henri Monnier. It was filled with small shops, on top of which were two and three stories of white-shuttered dwellings. Père Tanguy's shop was just across the street from an *école primaire de filles*.

Père Tanguy was looking over some Japanese prints that were just becoming fashionable in Paris.

"Père, I've brought a friend, Vincent Van Gogh. He's an ardent communist."

"I am happy to welcome you to my shop," said Père Tanguy in a soft, almost feminine voice.

Tanguy was a little man with a pudgy face and the wistful eyes of a friendly dog. He wore a wide brimmed straw hat which he pulled down to the level of his brows. He had short arms, stumpy hands, and a rough beard. His right eye opened half again as far as the left one.

"You are really a communist, Monsieur Van Gogh?" he asked shyly.

"I don't know what you mean by communism, Père Tanguy. I think everyone should work as much as he can, at the job he likes best, and in return get everything he needs."

"Just as simply as that," laughed Gauguin.

"Ah, Paul," said Père Tanguy, "you worked on the Stock Exchange. It is money that makes men animals, is it not?"

"Yes, that, and lack of money."

"No, never lack of money, only lack of food and the necessities of life."

"Quite so, Père Tanguy," said Vincent.

"Our friend, Paul," said Tanguy, "despises the men who make money, and he despises us because we can't make any. But I would rather belong to the latter class. Any man who lives on more than fifty centimes a day is a scoundrel."

"Then virtue," said Gauguin, "has descended upon me by force of necessity. Père Tanguy, will you trust me for a little more colour? I know I owe you a large bill, but I am unable to work unless . . ."

"Yes, Paul, I will give you credit. If I had a little less trust in people, and you had a little more, we would both be better off. Where is the new picture you promised me? Perhaps I can sell it and get back the money for my colours."

Gauguin winked at Vincent. "I'll bring you two of them, Père, to hang side by side. Now if you will let me have one tube of black, one of yellow . . ."

"Pay your bill and you'll get more colour!"

The three men turned simultaneously. Madame Tanguy slammed the door to their living quarters and stepped into the shop. She was a wiry little woman with a hard, thin face and bitter eyes. She stormed up to Gauguin.

"Do you think we are in business for charity? Do you think we can eat Tanguy's communism? Settle up that bill, you rascal, or I shall put the police on you!"

Gauguin smiled in his most winning manner, took Madame Tanguy's hand and kissed it gallantly.

"Ah, Xantippe, how charming you look this morning."

Madame Tanguy did not understand why this handsome brute was always calling her Xantippe, but she liked the sound of it and was flattered.

"Don't think you can get around me, you loafer. I slave my life away to grind those filthy colours, and then you come and steal them."

"My precious Xantippe, don't be so hard on me. You have the soul of an artist. I can see it spread all over your lovely face."

Madame Tanguy lifted her apron as though to wipe the soul of the artist off her face. "Phaw!" she cried. "One artist in the family is enough. I suppose he told you he wants to live on only fifty centimes a day. Where do you think he would get that fifty centimes if I didn't earn it for him?"

"All Paris speaks of your charm and ability, dear Madame."

He leaned over and once again brushed his lips across her gnarled hand. She softened.

"Well, you are a scoundrel and a flatterer, but you can have a little colour this time. Only see that you pay your bill."

"For this kindness, my lovely Xantippe, I shall paint your portrait. One day it will hang in the Louvre and immortalize us both."

The little bell on the front door jingled. A stranger walked in.

"That picture you have in the window," he said. "That still life. Who is it by?"

"Paul Cezanne."

"Cezanne? Never heard of him. Is it for sale?"

"Ah, no, alas, it is already . . ."

Madame Tanguy threw off her apron, pushed Tanguy out of the way, and ran up to the man eagerly.

"But of course it is for sale. It is a beautiful still life, is it not, Monsieur? Have you ever seen such apples before? We will sell it to you cheap, Monsieur, since you admire it."

"How much?"

"How much, Tanguy?" demanded Madame, with a threat in her voice.

Tanguy swallowed hard. "Three hun . . ."

"Tanguy!"

"Two hun . . ."

"TANGUY!"

"Well, one hundred francs."

"A hundred francs?" said the stranger. "For an unknown painter? I'm afraid that's too much. I was only prepared to spend about twenty-five."

Madame Tanguy took the canvas out of the window.

"See, Monsieur, it is a big picture. There are four apples. Four apples are a hundred francs. You only want to spend twenty-five. Then why not take one apple?"

The man studied the canvas for a moment and said, "Yes, I could do that. Just cut this apple the full length of the canvas and I'll take it."

Madame ran back to her apartment, got a pair of scissors, and cut off the end apple. She wrapped it in a piece of paper, handed it to the man, and took the twenty-five francs. He walked out with the bundle under his arm.

"My favorite Cezanne," moaned Tanguy. "I put it in the window so people could see it for a moment and go away happy."

Madame put the mutilated canvas on the counter.

"Next time someone wants a Cezanne, and hasn't much money, sell him an apple. Take anything you can get for it. They're worthless anyway, he paints so many of them. And you needn't laugh, Paul Gauguin, the same goes for you. I'm going to take those canvases of yours off the wall and sell every one of your naked heathen females for five francs apiece."

"My darling Xantippe," said Gauguin, "we met too late in life. If only you had been my partner on the Stock Exchange, we would have owned the Bank of France by now."

When Madame retired to her quarters at the rear, Père Tanguy said to Vincent, "You are a painter, Monsieur? I hope you will buy your colours here. And perhaps you will let me see some of your pictures?"

"I shall be happy to. These are lovely Japanese prints. Are they for sale?"

"Yes. They have become very fashionable in Paris since the Goncourt brothers have taken to collecting them. They are influencing our young painters a great deal."

"I like these two. I want to study them. How much are they?"

"Three francs apiece."

"I'll take them. Oh, Lord, I forgot. I spent my last franc this morning. Gauguin, have you six francs?"

"Don't be ridiculous."

Vincent laid the Japanese prints down on the counter with regret.

"I'm afraid I'll have to leave them, Père Tanguy."

Père pressed the prints into Vincent's hand and looked up at him with a shy, wistful smile on his homely face.

"You need this for your work. Please take them. You will pay me another time."

10

Theo decided to give a party for Vincent's friends. They made four dozen hard-boiled eggs, brought in a keg of beer, and filled innumerable trays with brioches and pastries. The tobacco smoke was so thick in the living room that when Gauguin moved his huge bulk from one end to the other, he looked like an ocean liner coming through the fog. Lautrec perched himself in one corner, cracked eggs on the arm of Theo's favourite armchair, and scattered the shells over the rug. Rousseau was all excited about a perfumed note he had received that day from a lady admirer who wanted to meet him. He told the story with wide eyed amazement over and over again. Seurat was working out a new theory, and had Cezanne pinned against the window, explaining to him. Vincent poured beer from the keg, laughed at Gauguin's obscene stories, wondered with Rousseau who his lady friend could be, argued with Lautrec whether lines or points of colour were most effective in capturing an impression, and finally rescued Cezanne from the clutches of Seurat.

The room fairly burst with excitement. The men in it were all powerful personalities, fierce egoists, and vibrant iconoclasts. Theo called them monomaniacs. They loved to argue, fight, curse, defend their own theories and damn everything else. Their voices were strong and rough; the number of things they loathed in the world was legion. A hall twenty times the size of Theo's sitting room would have been too small to contain the dynamic force of the fighting, strident painters.

The turbulence of the room, which fired Vincent to gesticulatory enthusiasm and eloquence, gave Theo a splitting headache. All this stridency was foreign to his nature. He was tremendously fond of the men in the room. Was it not for them he carried on his quiet, endless battle with Goupils? But he found the rough, uncouth clamour of their personalities alien to his nature. There was a good bit of the feminine in Theo. Toulouse-Lautrec, with his usual vitriolic humour, once remarked,

"Too bad Theo is Vincent's brother. He would have made him such a splendid wife."

Theo found it just as distasteful to sell Bouguereaus as it would have been for Vincent to paint them. And yet, if he sold Bouguereau, Valadon would let him exhibit Degas. One day he would persuade Valadon to let him hang a Cezanne, then a Gauguin or a Lautrec, and finally, some distant day, a Vincent Van Gogh.

He took one last look at the noisy, quarrelsome, smoke laden room, slipped out of the front door unnoticed, and walked up the Butte where, alone, he gazed at the lights of Paris spread out before him.

Gauguin was arguing with Cezanne. He waved a hard-boiled egg and a brioche in one hand, a glass of beer in the other. It was his boast that he was the only man in Paris who could drink beer with a pipe in his mouth.

"Your canvases are cold, Cezanne," he shouted. "Ice cold. It freezes me just to look at them. There's not an ounce of emotion in all the miles of canvas you've flung paint at."

"I don't try to paint emotion," retorted Cezanne. "I leave that to the novelists. I paint apples and landscapes."

"You don't paint emotion because you can't. You paint with your eyes, that's what you paint with."

"What does anyone else paint with?"

"With all sorts of things." Gauguin took a quick look about the room. "Lautrec, there, paints with his spleen. Vincent paints with his heart. Seurat paints with his mind, which is almost as bad as painting with your eyes. And Rousseau paints with his imagination."

"What do you paint with, Gauguin?"

"Who, me? I don't know. Never thought about it."

"I'll tell you," said Lautrec. "You paint with your genital!"

When the laugh on Gauguin died down, Seurat perched himself on the arm of a divan and cried, "You can sneer at a man painting with his mind, but it's just helped me discover how we can make our canvases doubly effective."

"Do I have to listen to that *blague* all over again?" moaned Cezanne.

"Shut up, Cezanne! Gauguin, sit down somewhere and don't clutter up the whole room. Rousseau, stop telling that infernal story about your admirer. Lautrec, throw me an egg. Vincent, can I have a brioche? Now listen, everybody!"

"What's up, Seurat? I haven't seen you so excited since that fellow spit on your canvas at the Salon des Refusées!"

"Listen! What is painting today? Light. What kind of light? Gradated light. Points of colour flowing into each other . . ."

"That's not painting, that's pointillism!"

"For God's sake, Georges, are you going intellectual on us again?"

"Shut up! We get through with a canvas. Then what do we do? We turn it over to some fool who puts it into a hideous gold frame and kills our every last effect. Now I propose that we should never let a picture out of our hands until we've put it into a frame and painted the frame so that it becomes an integral part of the picture."

"But, Seurat, you're stopping too soon. Every picture must be hung in a room. And if the room is the wrong colour, it will kill the picture and frame both."

"That's right, why not paint the room to match the frame?"

"A good idea," said Seurat.

"What about the house the room is in?"

"And the city that the house is in."

"Oh, Georges, Georges, you do get the damnedest ideas!"

"That's what comes from painting with your brain."

"The reason you imbeciles don't paint with your brains, is that you haven't any!"

"Look at Georges's face, everybody. Quick! We got the scientist riled up that time, all right."

"Why do you men always fight among yourselves?" demanded Vincent. "Why don't you try working together?"

"You're the communist of this group," said Gauguin. "Suppose you tell us what we'd get if we worked together?"

"Very well," said Vincent, shooting the hard, round yolk of an egg into his mouth, "I will tell you. I've been working out a plan. We're a lot of nobodies. Manet, Degas, Sisley, and Pissarro paved the way for us. They've been accepted and their work is exhibited in the big galleries. All right, they're the painters of the Grand Boulevard. But we have to go into the side streets. We're the painters of the Petit Boulevard. Why couldn't we exhibit our paintings in the little restaurants of the side streets, the workingman's restaurants? Each of us would contribute, say, five canvases. Every afternoon we would put them up in a new place. We'd sell the pictures for whatever the workers could afford. In addition to having our work constantly before the public, we would be making it possible for the poor people of Paris to see good art, and buy beautiful pictures for almost nothing."

"*Tiens,*" breathed Rousseau, his eyes wide with excitement, "that's wonderful."

"It takes me a year to finish a canvas," grumbled Seurat. "Do you think I'm going to sell it to some filthy carpenter for five sous?"

"You could contribute your little studies."

"Yes, but suppose the restaurants won't take our pictures?"

"Of course they will."

"Why not? It costs them nothing, and makes their places beautiful."

"How would we handle it? Who would find the restaurants?"

"I have that all figured out," cried Vincent. "We'll make Père Tanguy our manager. He'll find the restaurants, hang the pictures, and take in the money."

"Of course. He's just the man."

"Rousseau, be a good fellow and run down to Père Tanguy's. Tell him he's wanted on important business."

"You can count me out of this scheme," said Cezanne.

"What's the matter?" asked Gauguin. "Afraid your lovely pictures will be soiled by the eyes of workingmen?"

"It isn't that. I'm going back to Aix at the end of the month."

"Try it just once, Cezanne," urged Vincent. "If it doesn't work, you're nothing out."

"Oh, very well."

"When we get through with the restaurants," said Lautrec, "we might start on the bordellos. I know most of the Madames on Montmartre. They have a better clientele, and I think we could get higher prices."

Père Tanguy came running in, all excited. Rousseau had been able to give him only a garbled account of what was up. His round straw hat was sitting at an angle, and his pudgy little face was lit up with eager enthusiasm.

When he heard the plan he exclaimed, "Yes, yes, I know the very place. The Restaurant Norvins. The owner is a friend of mine. His walls are bare, and he'll be pleased. When we are through there, I know another one on the Rue Pierre. Oh, there are thousands of restaurants in Paris."

"When is the first exhibition of the club of the Petit Boulevard to take place?" asked Gauguin.

"Why put it off?" demanded Vincent. "Why not begin tomorrow?"

Tanguy hopped about on one foot, took off his hat, then crammed it on his head again.

"Yes, yes, tomorrow! Bring me your canvases in the morning. I will hang them in the Restaurant Norvins in the afternoon. And when the people come for their dinner, we will cause a sensation. We will sell the pictures like holy candles on Easter. What's this you're giving me? A glass of beer? Good! Gentlemen, we drink to the Communist Art Club of the Petit Boulevard. May its first exhibition be a success."

11

Père Tanguy knocked on the door of Vincent's apartment the following noon.

"I've been around to tell all the others," he said. "We can only exhibit at Norvins providing we eat our dinner there."

"That's all right."

"Good. The others have agreed. We can't hang the pictures until four-thirty. Can you be at my shop at four? We are all going over together."

"I'll be there."

When he reached the blue shop on the Rue Clauzel, Père Tanguy was already loading the canvases into a handcart. The others were inside, smoking and discussing Japanese prints.

"*Alors,*" cried Père, "we are ready."

"May I help you with the cart, Père?" asked Vincent.

"No, no, I am the manager."

He pushed the cart to the centre of the street and began the long climb upward. The painters walked behind, two by two. First came Gauguin and Lautrec; they loved to be together because of the ludicrous picture they made. Seurat was listening to Rousseau, who was all excited over a second perfumed letter he had received that afternoon. Vincent and Cezanne, who sulked and kept uttering words like dignity and decorum, brought up the rear.

"Here, Père Tanguy," said Gauguin, after they wound up the hill a way, "that cart is heavy, loaded down with immortal masterpieces. Let me push it for a while."

"No, no," cried Père, running ahead. "I am the colour bearer of this revolution. When the first shot is fired, I shall fall."

They made a droll picture, the ill-assorted, fantastically dressed men, walking in the middle of the street behind a common pushcart. They did not mind the stares of the amused passers-by. They laughed and talked in high spirits.

"Vincent," cried Rousseau, "have I told you about the letter I got this afternoon? Perfumed, too. From the same lady."

He ran along at Vincent's side, waving his arms, telling the whole interminable story over again. When he finally finished and dropped back with Seurat, Lautrec called Vincent.

"Do you know who Rousseau's lady is?" he asked.

"No. How should I?"

Lautrec snickered. "It's Gauguin. He's giving Rousseau a love affair. The poor fellow has never had a woman. Gauguin is going to feed him with perfumed letters for a couple of months and then make an assignation. He'll dress up in women's clothes and meet Rousseau in one of the Montmartre rooms with peepholes. We're all going to be at the holes watching Rousseau make love for the first time. It should be priceless."

"Gauguin, you're a fiend."

"Oh, come, Vincent," said Gauguin. "I think it's an excellent joke."

At length they arrived at the Restaurant Norvins. It was a modest place, tucked away between a wine shop and a supply store for horses. The outside was painted a varnish-yellow, the walls of the inside a light blue. There were perhaps twenty square tables with red and white checked tablecloths. At the back, near the kitchen door, was a high booth for the proprietor.

For a solid hour the painters quarreled about which pictures should be hung next to which. Père Tanguy was almost distraught. The proprietor was getting angry, for the dinner hour was near and the restaurant was in chaos. Seurat refused to let his pictures go up at all because the blue of the walls killed his skies. Cezanne would not allow his still lifes to hang next to Lautrec's "miserable posters," and Rousseau was offended because they wanted to stick his things on the back wall near the kitchen. Lautrec insisted that one of his large canvases be hung in the *lavabos*.

"That is the most contemplative moment in a man's day," he said.

Père Tanguy came to Vincent almost in despair. "Here," he said, "Take these two francs, add to it whatever you can, and hustle everyone across the street to a bar. If only I had fifteen minutes to myself, I could finish."

The ruse worked. When they all trooped back to the restaurant, the exhibition was in order. They stopped quarreling and sat down at a large table by the street door. Père Tanguy had put signs up all over the walls: THESE PAINTINGS FOR SALE, CHEAP. SEE THE PROPRIETOR.

It was five-thirty. Dinner was not served until six. The men fidgeted like schoolgirls. Every time the front door opened, all eyes turned to it hopefully. The customers of Norvins never came until the dot of six.

"Look at Vincent," whispered Gauguin to Seurat. "He's as nervous as a prima donna."

"Tell you what I'll do, Gauguin," said Lautrec, "I'll wager you the price of dinner that I sell a canvas before you do."

"You're on."

"Cezanne, I'll give you three to one odds." It was Lautrec.

Cezanne grew crimson at the insult, and everyone laughed at him.

"Remember," said Vincent, "Père Tanguy is to do all the selling. Don't anyone try to bargain with the buyers."

"Why don't they come?" asked Rousseau. "It's late."

As the clock on the wall drew nearer six, the group became more and more jumpy. At length all bantering stopped. The men did not move their eyes from the door. A feeling of tension settled over them.

"I didn't feel this way when I exhibited with the Independents, before all the critics of Paris," murmured Seurat.

"Look, look!" whispered Rousseau, "that man, crossing the street. He's coming this way. He's a customer."

The man walked past Norvins and disappeared. The clock on the wall chimed six times. On the last chime the door was opened and a labourer came in. He was shabbily dressed. Lines of fatigue were written inward and downward on his shoulders and back.

"Now," said Vincent, "we shall see."

The labourer slouched to a table at the other side of the room, threw his hat on a rack, and sat down. The six painters strained forward, watching him. The man scanned the menu, ordered a *plat du jour,* and within a moment was scooping up his soup with a large spoon. He did not raise his eyes from his plate.

"Tiens," said Vincent, *"c'est curieux."*

Two sheet-metal workers walked in. The proprietor bade them good evening. They grunted, dropped into the nearest chairs, and immediately plunged into a fierce quarrel about something that had happened during the day.

Slowly the restaurant filled. A few women came in with the men. It seemed as though everyone had his regular table. The first thing they looked at was the menu; when they were served, they were so intent upon their food that they never once glanced up. After dinner they lighted their pipes, chatted, unfolded their copies of the evening paper, and read.

"Would the gentlemen like to be served with their dinner now?" asked the waiter, about seven o'clock.

No one answered. The waiter walked away. A man and a woman entered.

As he was throwing his hat on the rack, the man noticed a Rousseau tiger peering through a jungle. He pointed it out to his comrade. Everyone at the painter's table stiffened. Rousseau half rose. The woman said something in a low tone and laughed. They sat down, and holding their heads close together, devoured the menu voraciously.

At a quarter to eight the waiter served the soup without asking. Nobody touched it. When it had grown cold, the waiter took it away. He brought the *plat du jour.* Lautrec drew pictures in the gravy with his fork. Only Rousseau could eat. Everyone, even Seurat, emptied his carafe of sour red wine. The restaurant was hot with the smell of food, with the odours of people who had laboured and perspired in the heat of the sun.

One by one the customers paid their checks, returned the cursory *bonsoir* of the proprietor and filed out.

"I'm sorry, gentlemen," said the waiter, "but it's eight-thirty, and we are closing."

Père Tanguy took the pictures off the walls and carried them out into the street. He pushed the cart home through the slowly falling dusk.

12

The spirit of old Goupil and Uncle Vincent Van Gogh had vanished forever from the galleries. In their place had come a policy of selling pictures as though they were any other commodity, such as shoes or herrings. Theo was constantly being harassed to make more money and sell poorer pictures.

"See here, Theo," said Vincent, "why don't you leave Goupils?"

"The other art dealers are just as bad," replied Theo wearily. "Besides, I've been with them so long. I'd better not change."

"You must change. I insist that you must. You're becoming unhappier every day down there. Let go of me! I can walk around if I like. Theo, you're the best known and best liked young art dealer in Paris. Why don't you open a shop for yourself?"

"Oh, Lord, do we have to go over all that again?"

"Look, Theo, I've got a marvelous idea. We'll open a communist art shop. We will all give you our canvases, and whatever money you take in, we'll live on equally. We can scrape together enough francs to open a little shop in Paris, and we'll take a house out in the country where we'll all live and work. Portier sold a Lautrec the other day, and Père Tanguy has sold several Cezannes. I'm sure we could attract the young art buyers of Paris. And we wouldn't need much money to run that house in the country. We'd live together simply, instead of keeping up a dozen establishments in Paris."

"Vincent, I have a frightful headache. Let me go to sleep now, will you?"

"No, you can sleep on Sunday. Listen, Theo . . . where are you going? All right, undress if you like, but I'm going to talk to you anyway. Here, I'll sit by the head of your bed. Now if you're unhappy at Goupils, and all the young painters of Paris are willing, and we can get a little money together . . ."

Père Tanguy and Lautrec came in with Vincent the following night. Theo had hoped Vincent would be out for the evening. Père Tanguy's little eyes were dancing with excitement.

"Monsieur Van Gogh, Monsieur Van Gogh, it is a wonderful idea. You must do it. I will give up my shop and move to the country with you. I will grind the colours, stretch the canvas, and build the frames. I ask only for my food and shelter."

Theo put down his book with a sigh.

"Where are we going to get the money to begin this enterprise? The money to open a shop, and rent a house, and feed the men?"

"Here, I brought it with me," cried Père Tanguy. "Two hundred and twenty francs. All I have saved up. Take it, Monsieur Van Gogh. It will help begin our colony."

"Lautrec, you're a sensible man. What do you say to all this nonsense?"

"I think it a damned good idea. As things go now, we are not only fighting all of Paris, but fighting among ourselves. If we could present a united front . . ."

"Very well, you are wealthy. Will you help us?"

"Ah, no. If it is to be a subsidized colony, it will lose its purpose. I will contribute two hundred and twenty francs, the same as Père Tanguy."

"It's such a crazy idea! If you men knew anything about the business world . . ."

Père Tanguy ran up to Theo and wrung his hand.

"My dear Monsieur Van Gogh, I beseech you, do not call it a crazy idea. It is a glorious idea. You must, you simply must . . ."

"There's no crawling out now, Theo," said Vincent. "We've got you! We're going to raise some money and make you our master. You've said good-bye to Goupils. You're through there. You're now manager of the Communist Art Colony."

Theo ran a hand over his eyes.

"I can just see myself managing you bunch of wild animals."

When Theo got home the next night he found his house crammed to the doors with excited painters. The air was blue with foul tobacco smoke, and churned by loud, turbulent voices. Vincent was seated on a fragile table in the middle of the living room, master of ceremonies.

"No, no," he cried, "there will be no pay. Absolutely no money. We will never see money from one year to the next. Theo will sell the pictures and we will receive our food, shelter, and materials."

"What about the men whose work never sells?" demanded Seurat. "How long are we going to support them?"

"As long as they want to stay with us and work."

"Wonderful," grunted Gauguin. "We'll have all the amateur painters in Europe on our doorstep."

"Here's Monsieur Van Gogh!" shouted Père Tanguy, catching a sight of Theo as he stood leaning against the door. "Three cheers for our manager."

"Hurrah for Theo! Hurrah for Theo! Hurrah for Theo!"

Everyone was enormously excited. Rousseau wanted to know if he could still give violin lessons at the colony. Anquetin said he owed three months rent, and that they'd better find the country house very soon. Cezanne insisted that a man be allowed to spend his own money, if he had any. Vincent cried, "No, that would kill our communism. We must all share and share alike." Lautrec wanted to know if they could have women at the house. Gauguin insisted that everyone be forced to contribute at least two canvases a month.

"Then I won't come in!" shouted Seurat. "I finish only one big canvas a year."

"What about materials?" demanded Père Tanguy. "Do I give everyone the same amount of colour and canvas each week?"

"No, no, of course not," cried Vincent. "We all get as much material as we need, no more and no less. Just like food."

"Yes, but what happens to the surplus money? After we begin selling our pictures? Who gets the profits?"

"Nobody gets the profits," said Vincent. "As soon as we have a little money over, we'll open a house in Brittany. Then we'll open another in Provence. Soon we'll have houses all over the country, and we'll be travelling from one place to another."

"What about the railroad fare? Do we get that out of the profits?"

"Yes, and how much can we travel? Who's to decide that?"

"Suppose there are too many painters for one house during the best season? Who gets left out in the cold, will you tell me?"

"Theo, Theo, you're the manager of this business. Tell us all about it. Can anyone join? Is there a limit to the membership? Will we have to paint according to any system? Will we have models out there at the house?"

At dawn the meeting broke up. The people downstairs had exhausted themselves rapping on the ceiling with broomsticks. Theo went to bed about four, but Vincent, Père Tanguy, and some of the more enthusiastic ones surrounded his bed and urged him to give Goupils notice on the first of the month.

The excitement grew in intensity with the passing of the weeks. The art world of Paris was divided into two camps. The established painters spoke of those crazy men, the Van Gogh brothers. All the others spoke endlessly about the new experiment.

Vincent talked and worked like mad all night and day. There were so many thousands of details to be settled; how they were to get the money, where the shop was to be located, how prices were to be charged, what men could belong, who would manage the house in the country and how. Theo, almost against his will, was drawn into the febrile excitement. The apartment on the Rue Lepic was crowded every night of the week. Newspaper men came to get stories. Art critics came to discuss the new movement. Painters from all over France returned to Paris to get into the organization.

If Theo was king, Vincent was the royal organizer. He drew up countless plans, constitutions, budgets, pleas for money, codes of rules and regulations, manifestos for the papers, pamphlets to acquaint Europe with the purpose of the Communist Art Colony.

He was so busy he forgot to paint.

Almost three thousand francs rolled into the coffers of the organization. The painters contributed every last franc they could spare. A street fair was held on the Boulevard Clichy, and each man hawked his own canvases. Letters came in from all over Europe, sometimes containing soiled and crumpled franc notes. Art loving Paris came to the apartment, caught the enthusiasm of the new movement, and threw a bill into the open box before they left. Vincent was secretary and treasurer.

Theo insisted that they must have five thousand francs before they could begin. He had located a shop on the Rue Tronchet which he thought well situated, and Vincent had discovered a superb old mansion in the forest of St. Germain-en-Laye that could be had for almost nothing. The canvases of the painters who wanted to join kept pouring into the Rue Lepic apartment, until there was no space left to move about. Hundreds and hundreds of people went in and out of the little apartment. They argued, fought, cursed, ate, drank, and gesticulated wildly. Theo was given notice to move.

At the end of a month the Louis Philippe furniture was in shreds.

Vincent had no time even to think about his palette now. There were letters to be written, people to be interviewed, houses to be looked at, enthusiasm to be kindled in every new painter and amateur he met. He talked until he went hoarse. A feverish energy came into his eyes. He took his food fitfully, and almost never found a chance to sleep. He was forever going, going, going.

By the beginning of spring, the five thousand francs were collected. Theo was giving notice to Goupils on the first of the month. He had decided to take the shop on the Rue Tronchet. Vincent put down a small deposit on the house in St. Germain. The list of members with which the colony would be opened was drawn up by Theo, Vincent, Père Tanguy, Gauguin and Lautrec. From the piles of canvases amassed at the apartment, Theo picked those he was going to show in his first exhibit. Rousseau and Anquetin had a bitter quarrel as to who was going to decorate the inside of the shop, and who the outside. Theo no longer minded being kept awake. He was now as enthusiastic as Vincent had been in the beginning. He worked feverishly to get everything organized so that the colony might open by summer. He debated endlessly with Vincent whether the second house should be located on the Atlantic or the Mediterranean.

One morning Vincent went to sleep about four o'clock, utterly exhausted. Theo did not awaken him. He slept until noon, and awoke refreshed. He wandered into his studio. The canvas on the easel was many weeks old. The paint on the palette was dry, cracked, and covered with dust. The tubes of pigment had been kicked into the corners. His brushes lay about, caked solid with old paint.

A voice within him asked, softly, "One moment, Vincent. Are you a painter? Or are you a communist organizer?"

He took the stacks of ill-assorted canvases into Theo's room and piled them on the bed. In the studio he left only his own pictures. He stood them on the easel, one by one, gnawing his hangnails as he gazed at them.

Yes, he had made progress. Slowly, slowly, his colour had lightened, struggled toward a crystal luminosity. No longer were they imitative. No longer could the traces of his friends be detected on the canvas. He realized for the first time that he had been developing a very individual sort of technique. It was like nothing else he had ever seen. He did not even know how it had got there.

He had strained Impressionism through his own nature, and had been on the verge of achieving a very curious means of expression. Then, suddenly, he had stopped.

He put his more recent canvases on the easel. Once he nearly cried out. He had almost, almost caught something! His pictures were beginning to show a definite method, a new attack with the weapons he had forged through the winter.

His many weeks of rest had given him a clear perspective on his work. He saw that he was developing an Impressionist technique all his own.

He took a careful look at himself in the mirror. His beard needed trimming, his hair needed cutting, his shirt was soiled, and his trousers hung like a limp rag. He pressed his suit with a hot iron, put on one of Theo's shirts, took a five franc note out of the treasury box, and went to the barber. When he was all cleaned up, he walked meditatively to Goupils on the Boulevard Montmartre.

"Theo," he said, "can you come out with me for a short time?"

"What's up?"

"Get your hat. Is there a café about where no one could possibly find us?"

Seated at the very rear of the café, in a secluded corner, Theo said, "You know, Vincent, this is the first time I've had a word alone with you for a month?"

"I know, Theo. I'm afraid I've been something of a fool."

"How so?"

"Theo, tell me frankly, am I a painter? Or am I a communist organizer?"

"What do you mean?"

"I've been so busy organizing this colony, I've had no time to paint. And once the house is started, I'll never catch a moment."

"I see."

"Theo, I want to paint. I haven't put in this seven years of labour just to be a house manager for other painters. I tell you, I'm hungry for my brushes, Theo, so hungry I could almost run away from Paris on the next train."

"But, Vincent, now, after all we've . . ."

"I told you I'd been a fool. Theo, can you stand to hear a confession?"

"Yes?"

"I'm heartily sick of the sight of other painters. I'm tired of their talk, of their theories, of their interminable quarrels. Oh, you needn't smile, I know I've done my share of the fighting. That's just the point. What was it Mauve used to say? 'A man can either paint, or talk about painting, but he can't do both at the same time.' Well, Theo, have you been supporting me for seven years just to hear me spout ideas?"

"You've done a lot of good work for the colony, Vincent."

"Yes, but now that we're ready to move out there, I realize that I don't want to go. I couldn't possibly live there and do any work. Theo, I wonder if I can make you understand . . . but of course I can. When I was alone in the Brabant and The Hague, I thought of myself as an important person. I was one lone man, battling the whole world. I was an artist, the only artist living. Everything I painted was valuable. I knew that I had great ability, and that eventually the world would say, 'He is a splendid painter.' "

"And now?"

"Alas, now I am just one of many. There are hundreds of painters all about me. I see myself caricatured on every side. Think of all the wretched canvases in our apartment, sent by painters who want to join the colony. They, too, think they are going to be great painters. Well, maybe I'm just like them. How do I know? What have I to bolster up my courage now? Before I came to Paris I didn't know there were hopeless fools who deluded themselves all their lives. Now I know. That hurts."

"It has nothing to do with you."

"Perhaps not. But I'll never be able to stamp out that little germ of doubt. When I am alone, in the country, I forget that there are thousands of canvases being painted every day. I imagine that mine is the only one, and that it is a beautiful gift to the world. I would still go on painting even if I knew my work to be atrocious, but this . . . this artist's illusion . . . helps. Do you understand?"

"Yes."

"Besides, I am not a city painter. I don't belong here. I am a peasant painter. I want to go back to my fields. I want to find a sun so hot that it will burn everything out of me but the desire to paint!"

"So . . . you want to . . . leave . . . Paris?"

" Yes. I must."

"And what about the colony?"

"I am going to withdraw. But you must carry on."

Theo shook his head. "No, not without you."

"Why not?"

"I don't know. I was only doing it for you . . . because you wanted it."

They were silent for some moments.

"You haven't given notice yet, Theo?"

"No. I was going to on the first."

"I suppose we can return the money to the people it belongs to?"

"Yes . . . When do you think you'll be going?"

"Not until my palette is clear."

"I see."

"Then I'll go away. To the South, probably. I don't know where. So that I can be alone. And paint and paint and paint. By myself."

He threw his arm about Theo's shoulder with rough affection.

"Theo, tell me you don't despise me. To throw everything up this way when I've put you through so much."

"Despise you?"

Theo smiled with infinite sadness. He reached up and patted the hand that lay on his shoulder.

" . . . No . . . no, of course not. I understand. I think you are right. Well . . . old boy . . . you'd better finish your drink. I must be getting back to Goupils."

13

Vincent laboured on for another month, but although his palette was now almost as clear and light as that of his friends, he could not seem to reach a form of expression that satisfied him. At first he thought it was the crudity of his drawing, so he tried working slowly, and in cold blood. The meticulous process of putting on the paint was torture to him, but looking at the canvas afterwards was even worse. He tried hiding his brush work in flat surfaces; he tried working with thin colour instead of rich spurts of pigment. Nothing seemed to help. Again and again he felt that he was fumbling toward a medium that would not only be unique, but which would enable him to say everything he wanted to say. And yet he could not quite grasp it.

"I almost got it that time," he murmured one evening in the apartment. "Almost, but not quite. If I could only find out what was standing in my way."

"I think I can tell you that," said Theo, taking the canvas from his brother.

"You can? What is it?"

"It's Paris."

"Paris?"

"Yes. Paris has been your training ground. As long as you remain here, you'll be nothing but a schoolboy. Remember our school in Holland, Vincent? We learned how other people did things, and how they should be done, but we never actually did anything for ourselves."

"You mean I don't find the subjects here sympathetic?"

"No, I mean that you're unable to make a clean break from your teachers. I'll be awfully lonely without you, Vincent, but I know that you have to go. Somewhere in this world there must be a spot that you can make all your own. I don't know where it is; it's up to you to find it. But you must cut away from your schoolhouse before you can reach maturity."

"Do you know, old boy, what country I've been thinking a lot about of late?"

"No."

"Africa."

"Africa! Not really?"

"Yes. I've been thinking of the blistering sun all during this damnably long and cold winter. That's where Delacroix found his colour, and maybe I could find myself there."

"Africa is a long ways off, Vincent," said Theo, meditatively.

"Theo, I want the sun. I want it in its most terrific heat and power. I've been feeling it pull me southward all winter, like a huge magnet. Until I left Holland I never knew there was such a thing as a sun. Now I know there's no such thing as painting without it. Perhaps that something I need to bring me to maturity is a hot sun. I'm chilled to the bone from the Parisian winter, Theo, and I think some of that cold has gotten into my palette and brushes. I never was one to go at a thing half-heartedly; once I could get the African sun to burn the cold out of me, and set my palette on fire . . ."

"Hummmm," said Theo, "we'll have to think that over. Maybe you're right."

Paul Cezanne gave a farewell party for all his friends. He had arranged through his father to buy the plot of land on the hill overlooking Aix, and he was returning home to build a studio.

"Get out of Paris, Vincent," he said, "and come down to Provence. Not to Aix, that's my territory, but to some place near by. The sun is hotter and purer there than anywhere else in the world. You'll find light and clean colour in Provence such as you've never seen before. I'm staying there for the rest of my life."

"I'll be the next one out of Paris," said Gauguin. "I'm going back to the tropics. If you think you have real sun in Provence, Cezanne, you ought to come to the Marquesas. There the sunlight and colour are just as primitive as the people."

"You men ought to join the sun worshippers," said Seurat.

"As for myself," announced Vincent, "I think I'm going to Africa."

"Well, well," murmured Lautrec, "we have another little Delacroix on our hands."

"Do you mean that, Vincent?" asked Gauguin.

"Yes. Oh, not right away, perhaps. I think I ought to stop off somewhere in Provence and get used to the sun."

"You can't stop at Marseilles," said Seurat. "That town belongs to Monticelli."

"I can't go to Aix," said Vincent, "because it belongs to Cezanne. Monet has already done Antibes, and I agree that Marseilles is sacred to 'Fada.' Has anyone a suggestion as to where I might go?"

"Wait!" exclaimed Lautrec, "I know the very place. Have you ever thought of Arles?"

"Arles? That's an old Roman settlement, isn't it?"

"Yes. It's on the Rhône, a couple of hours from Marseilles. I was there once. The colouring of the surrounding country makes Delacroix's African scenes look anaemic."

"You don't tell me? Is there good sun?"

"Sun? Enough to drive you crazy. And you should see the Arlesiennes; the most gorgeous women in the world. They still retain the pure, delicate features of their Greek ancestors, combined with the robust, sturdy stature of their Roman conquerors. Yet curiously enough, their aroma is distinctly Oriental; I suppose that's a result of the Saracen invasion back in the eighth century. It was at Arles that the true Venus was found, Vincent. The model was an Arlesienne!"

"They sound fascinating," said Vincent.

"They are. And just wait until you feel the mistral."

"What's the mistral?" asked Vincent.

"You'll find out when you get there," replied Lautrec with a twisted grin.

"How about the living? Is it cheap?"

"There's nothing to spend your money on, except food and shelter, and they don't cost much. If you're keen to get away from Paris, why don't you try it?"

"Arles," murmured Vincent to himself. "Arles and the Arlesiennes. I'd like to paint one of those women!"

Paris had excited Vincent. He had drunk too many absinthes, smoked too many pipefuls of tobacco, engaged too much in external activities. His gorge was high. He felt a tremendous urge to get away somewhere by himself where it would be quiet, and he could pour his surging, nervous energy into his craft. He needed only a hot sun to bring him to fruition. He had the feeling that the climax of his life, the full creative power toward which he had been struggling these eight long years, was not so very far off. He knew that nothing he had painted as yet was of any value; perhaps there was a short stretch just ahead in which he could create those few pictures which would justify his life.

What was it Monticelli had said? "We must put in ten years of hard labour, so that in the end we will be able to paint two or three authentic portraits."

In Paris he had security, friendship, and love. There was always a good home for him with Theo. His brother would never let him go hungry, would never make him ask twice for painting supplies, or deny him anything that was in his power to give, least of all full sympathy.

He knew that the moment he left Paris his troubles would begin. He could not manage his allowance away from Theo. Half the time he would be forced to go without food. He would have to live in wretched little cafés, lacerate himself because he could not buy pigments, find his words choking in his throat because there was no friendly soul with whom he could talk.

"You'll like Arles," said Toulouse-Lautrec the next day. "It's quiet, and no one will bother you. The heat is dry, the colour magnificent, and it is the only spot in Europe where you can find sheer Japanese clarity. It's a painter's paradise. If I weren't so attached to Paris, I'd go myself."

That evening Theo and Vincent went to a Wagnerian concert. They came home early and spent a quiet hour conjuring up memories of their childhood in Zundert. The next morning Vincent prepared the coffee for Theo, and when his brother had left for Goupils, gave the little apartment the most thorough cleaning it had had since they moved in. On the walls he put a painting of pink shrimps, a portrait of Père Tanguy in his round straw hat, the Moulin de la Galette, a female nude seen from the back, and a study of the Champs Elysées.

When Theo came home that evening he found a note on the living room table.

Dear Theo:

I have gone to Arles, and will write you as soon as I get there.

I have put some of my paintings on the wall so that you won't forget me.

With a handshake in thought,

Vincent

BOOK SIX

ARLES

1

The Arlesian sun smote Vincent between the eyes, and broke him wide open. It was a whorling, liquid ball of lemon-yellow fire, shooting across a hard blue sky and filling the air with blinding light. The terrific heat and intense clarity of the air created a new and unfamiliar world.

He dropped out of the third-class carriage early in the morning and walked down the winding road that led from the station to the Place Lamartine, a market square bounded on one side by the embankment of the Rhône, on the other by cafés and wretched hotels. Arles lay straight ahead, pasted against the side of a hill with a neat mason's trowel, drowsing in the hot, tropical sun.

When it came to looking for a place to live, Vincent was indifferent. He walked into the first hotel he passed in the Place, the Hotel de la Gare, and rented a ròom. It contained a blatant brass bed, a cracked pitcher in a washbowl, and an odd chair. The proprietor brought in an unpainted table. There was no room to set up an easel, but Vincent meant to paint out of doors all day.

He threw his valise on the bed and dashed out to see the town. There were two approaches to the heart of Arles from the Place Lamartine. The circular road on the left was for wagons; it skirted the edge of the town and wound slowly to the top of the hill, passing the old Roman forum and amphitheatre on the way. Vincent took the more direct approach, which led through a labyrinth of narrow cobblestone streets. After a long climb he reached the sun-scorched Place de la Mairie. On the way up he passed cold stone courts and quadrangles which looked as though they had come down untouched from the early Roman days. In order to keep out the maddening sun, the alleys had been made so narrow that Vincent could touch both rows of houses with outstretched fingertips. To avoid the torturing mistral, the streets wound about in a hopeless maze on the side of the hill, never going straight for more than ten yards. There was refuse in the streets, dirty children in the doorways, and over everything a sinister, hunted aspect.

Vincent left the Place de la Mairie, walked through a short alley to the main marketing road at the back of the town, strolled through the little park, and then stumbled down the hill to the Roman arena. He leaped from tier to tier like a goat, finally reaching the top. He sat on a block of stone, dangled his legs over a sheer drop of hundreds of feet, lit his pipe, and surveyed the domain of which he had appointed himself lord and master.

The town below him flowed down abruptly to the Rhône like a kaleidoscopic waterfall. The roofs of the houses were fitted into each other in an intricate design. They had all been tiled in what was originally red clay, but the burning, incessant sun had baked them to a maze of every colour, from the lightest lemon and delicate shell pink to a biting lavender and earthy loam-brown.

The wide, rapidly flowing Rhône made a sharp curve at the bottom of the hill on which Arles was plastered, and shot downward to the Mediterranean. There were stone embankments on either side of the river. Trinquetaille glistened like a painted city on the other bank. Behind Vincent were the mountains, huge ranges sticking upward into the clear white light. Spread out before him was a panorama of tilled fields, of orchards in blossom, the rising mound of Montmajour, fertile valleys ploughed into thousands of deep furrows, all converging at some distant point in infinity.

But it was the colour of the country-side that made him run a hand over his bewildered eyes. The sky was so intensely blue, such a hard, relentless, profound blue that it was not blue at all; it was utterly colourless. The green of the fields that stretched below him was the essence of the colour green, gone mad. The burning lemon-yellow of the sun, the blood-red of the soil, the crying whiteness of the lone cloud over Montmajour, the ever reborn rose of the orchards . . . such colourings were incredible. How could he paint them? How could he ever make anyone believe that they existed, even if he could transfer them to his palette? Lemon, blue, green, red, rose; nature run rampant in five torturing shades of expression.

Vincent took the wagon road to the Place Lamartine, grabbed up his easel, paints, and canvas and struck out along the Rhône. Almond trees were beginning to flower everywhere. The glistening white glare of the sun on the water sent stabs of pain into his eyes. He had left his hat in the hotel. The sun burned through the red of his hair, sucked out all the cold of Paris, all the fatigue, discouragement, and satiety with which city life had glutted his soul.

A kilometre down the river he found a drawbridge with a little cart going over it, outlined against a blue sky. The river was as blue as a well, the banks orange, coloured with green grass. A group of washerwomen in smocks and many-coloured caps were pounding dirty white clothes in the shade of a lone tree.

Vincent set up his easel, drew a long breath, and shut his eyes. No man could catch such colourings with his eyes open. There fell away from him Seurat's talk about scientific pointillism, Gauguin's harangues about primitive decorativeness, Cezanne's appearances beneath solid surfaces, Lautrec's lines of colour and lines of splenetic hatred.

There remained only Vincent.

He returned to his hotel about dinner time. He sat down at a little table in the bar and ordered an absinthe. He was too excited, too utterly replete to think of food. A man sitting at a nearby table observed the paint splashed all over Vincent's hands, face, and clothing, and fell into conversation with him.

"I'm a Parisian journalist," he said. "I've been down here for three months gathering material for a book on the Provençal language."

"I just arrived from Paris this morning," said Vincent.

"So I noticed. Intend to stay long?"

"Yes, I imagine so."

"Well, take my advice and don't. Arles is the most violently insane spot on the globe."

"What makes you think that?"

"I don't think it. I know it. I've been watching these people for three months, and I tell you, they're all cracked. Just look at them. Watch their eyes. There's not a normal, rational person in this whole Tarascon vicinity!"

"That's a curious thing to say," observed Vincent.

"Within a week you'll be agreeing with me. The country around Arles is the most torn, desperately lashed section in Provence. You've been out in that sun. Can't you imagine what it must do to these people who are subject to its blinding light day after day? I tell you, it burns the brains right out of their heads. And the mistral. You haven't felt the mistral yet? Oh, dear, wait until you do. It whips this town into a frenzy two hundred days out of every year. If you try to walk the streets, it smashes you against the buildings. If you are out in the fields, it knocks you down and grinds you into the dirt. It twists your insides until you think you can't bear it another minute. I've seen that infernal wind tear out windows, pull up trees, knock down fences, lash the men and animals in the fields until I thought they would surely fly in pieces. I've been here only three months, and I'm going a little *fou* myself. I'm getting out tomorrow morning!"

"Surely you must be exaggerating?" asked Vincent. "The Arlesians looked all right to me, what little I saw of them today."

"What little you saw of them is right. Wait until you get to know them. Listen, do you know what my private opinion is?"

"No, what? Will you join me in an absinthe?"

"Thanks. In my private opinion, Arles is epileptic. It whips itself up to such an intense pitch of nervous excitement that you are positive it will burst into a violent fit and foam at the mouth."

"And does it?"

"No. That's the curious part. This country is forever reaching a climax, and never having one. I've been waiting for three months to see a revolution, or a volcano erupt from the Place de la Mairie. A dozen times I thought the inhabitants would all suddenly go mad and cut each other's throats! But just when they get to a point where an explosion is imminent, the mistral dies down for a couple of days and the sun goes behind the clouds."

"Well," laughed Vincent, "if Arles never reached a climax, you can't very well call it epileptic, now can you?"

"No," replied the journalist, "but I can call it epileptoidal."

"What the devil is that?"

"I'm doing an article on the subject for my paper in Paris. It was this German article that gave me my idea."

He pulled a magazine out of his pocket and shoved it across the table to Vincent.

"These doctors have made a study of the cases of several hundred men who suffered from nervous maladies which looked like epilepsy, but which never resulted in fits. You'll see by these charts how they have mapped the rising curve of nervousness and excitement; what the doctors call volatile tension. Well, in every last one of these cases the subjects have gone along with increasing fever until they reached the age of thirty-five to thirty-eight. At the average age of thirty-six they burst into a violent epileptic fit. After that it's a case of a half dozen more spasms and, within a year or two, good-bye."

"That's much too young to die," said Vincent. "A man is only beginning to get command of himself by that time."

The journalist put the magazine back in his pocket.

"Are you going to stop at this hotel for some time?" he asked. "My article is almost finished; I'll mail you a copy as soon as it's published. My point is this: Arles is an epileptoidal city. Its pulse has been mounting for centuries. It's approaching its first crisis. It's bound to happen. And soon. When it does, we're going to witness a frightful catastrophe. Murder, arson, rape, wholesale destruction! This country can't go on forever in a whipped, tortured state. Something must and will happen.

I'm getting out before the people start foaming at the mouth! I advise you to come along!"

"Thanks," said Vincent, "I like it here. I think I'll turn in now. Will I see you in the morning? No? Then good luck to you. And don't forget to send me a copy of the article."

2

Every morning Vincent arose before dawn, dressed, and tramped several kilometres down the river or into the country to find a spot that stirred him. Every night he returned with a finished canvas, finished because there was nothing more he could do with it. Directly after supper he went to sleep.

He became a blind painting machine, dashing off one sizzling canvas after another without even knowing what he did. The orchards of the country were in bloom. He developed a wild passion to paint them all. He no longer thought about his painting. He just painted. All his eight years of intense labour were at last expressing themselves in a great burst of triumphal energy. Sometimes, when he began working at the first crack of dawn, the canvas would be completed by noon. He would tramp back to town, drink a cup of coffee and trudge out again in another direction with a new canvas.

He did not know whether his painting was good or bad. He did not care. He was drunk with colour.

No one spoke to him. He spoke to no one. What little strength he had left from his painting, he spent in fighting the mistral. Three days out of every week he had to fasten his easel to pegs driven into the ground. The easel waved back and forth in the wind like a sheet on a clothesline. By night he felt as buffeted and bruised as though he had been given a severe beating.

He never wore a hat. The fierce sun was slowly burning the hair off the top of his head. When he lay on his brass bed in the little hotel at night he felt as though his head were encased in a ball of fire. The sun struck him completely blind. He could not tell the green of the fields from the blue of the sky. But when he returned to his hotel he found that the canvas was somehow a growing, brilliant transcription of nature.

One day he worked in an orchard of lilac ploughland with a red fence and two rose-coloured peach trees against a sky of glorious blue and white.

"It is probably the best landscape I have ever done," he murmured to himself.

When he reached his hotel he found a letter telllng him that Anton Mauve had died in The Hague. Under his peach trees he wrote, "Souvenir de Mauve. Vincent and Theo," and sent it off immediately to the house on the Uileboomen.

The following morning he found an orchard of plum trees in blossom. While he was at work, a vicious wind sprang up, returning at intervals like waves of the sea. In between, the sun shone, and all the white flowers sparkled on the trees. At the risk every minute of seeing the whole show on the ground, Vincent went on painting. It reminded him of the Scheveningen days when he used to paint in the rain, in sandstorms, and with the storm-spray of the ocean dashing over him and his easel. His canvas had a white effect with a good deal of yellow in it, and blue and lilac. When he finished he saw something in his picture that he had not meant to put there, the mistral.

"People will think I was drunk when I painted this," he laughed to himself.

A line from Theo's letter of the day before came back to him. Mijnheer Tersteeg, on a visit to Paris, had stood before a Sisley and murmured to Theo, "I cannot help thinking that the artist who painted this was a bit tipsy."

"If Tersteeg could see my Arlesian pictures," thought Vincent, "he would say it was delirium tremens in full career."

The people of Arles gave Vincent a wide berth. They saw him dashing out of town before sunrise, heavy easel loaded on his back, hatless, his chin stuck forward eagerly, a feverish excitement in his eyes. They saw him return with two fire holes in his face, the top of his head as red as raw meat, a wet canvas under his arm, gesticulating to himself. The town had a name for him. Everyone called him by it.

"Fou-rou!"

"Perhaps I am a red-headed crazy man," he said to himself, "but what can I do?"

The owner of the hotel swindled Vincent out of every franc he could. Vincent could not get anything to eat, for nearly everyone in Arles ate at home. The restaurants were expensive. Vincent tried them all to find some strong soup, but there was none to be had.

"Is it hard to cook potatoes, Madame?" he asked in one place.

"Impossible, Monsieur."

"Then have you some rice?"

"That is tomorrow's dish."

"What about macaroni?"

"There was no room on the range for macaroni."

At length he had to give up all serious thoughts of food, and live on whatever came his way. The hot sun built up his vitality, even though his stomach was getting little attention. In place of sane food he put absinthe, tobacco, and Daudet's tales of Tartarin. His innumerable hours of concentration before the easel rubbed his nerves raw. He needed stimulants. The absinthe made him all the more excited for the following day, an excitement whipped by the mistral and baked into him by the sun.

As the summer advanced, everything became burnt up. He saw about him nothing but old gold, bronze and copper, covered by a greenish azure sky of blanched heat. There was sulphur yellow on everything the sunlight hit. His canvases were masses of bright burning yellow. He knew that yellow had not been used in European painting since the Renaissance, but that did not deter him. The yellow pigment oozed out of the tubes onto the canvas, and there it stayed. His pictures were sun steeped, sun burnt, tanned with the burning sun and swept with air.

He was convinced that it was no more easy to make a good picture than it was to find a diamond or a pearl. He was dissatisfied with himself and what he was doing, but he had just a glimmer of hope that it was going to be better in the end. Sometimes even that hope seemed a Fata Morgana. Yet the only time he felt alive was when he was slogging at his work. Of personal life, he had none. He was just a mechanism, a blind painting automaton that had food, liquid, and paint poured into it each morning, and by nightfall turned out a finished canvas.

And for what purpose? For sale? Certainly not! He knew that nobody wanted to buy his pictures. Then what was the hurry? Why did he drive and spur himself to paint dozens and dozens of canvases when the space under his miserable brass bed was already piled nearly solid with paintings?

The desire to succeed had left Vincent. He worked because he had to, because it kept him from suffering too much mentally, because it distracted his mind. He could do without a wife, a home, and children; he could do without love and friendship and health; he could do without security, comfort, and food; he could even do without God. But he could not do without something which was greater than himself, which was his life—the power and ability to create.

3

He tried to hire models, but the people of Arles would not sit for him. They thought they were being done badly. They were afraid their friends would laugh at the portraits. Vincent knew that if he painted prettily like Bouguereau, people would not be ashamed to let themselves be painted. He had to give up the idea of models, and work always on the soil.

As the summer ripened, a glorious strong heat came on and the wind died. The light in which he worked ranged from pale sulphur-yellow to pale golden yellow. He thought often of Renoir and that pure clear line of his. That was the way everything looked in the clear air of Provence, just as it looked in the Japanese prints.

Early one morning he saw a girl with a coffee-tinted skin, ash-blond hair, grey eyes, and a print bodice of pale rose under which he could see the breasts, shapely, firm and small. She was a woman as simple as the fields, every line of her virgin. Her mother was an amazing figure in dirty yellow and faded blue, thrown up in strong sunlight against a square of brilliant flowers, snow-white and lemon-yellow. They posed for him for several hours in return for a small sum.

When he returned to his hotel that evening, Vincent found himself thinking of the girl with the coffee-tinted skin. Sleep would not come. He knew that there were houses in Arles, but they were mostly five-franc places patronized by the Zouaves, negroes brought to Arles to be trained for the French army.

It was months since Vincent had spoken to a woman, except to ask for a cup of coffee or a bag of tobacco. He remembered Margot's loving words, the wandering fingers over his face that she followed with a trail of loving kisses.

He jumped up, hurried across the Place Lamartine and struck into the black maze of stone houses. After a few moments of climbing he heard a great hubbub ahead. He broke into a run and reached the front door of a brothel in the Rue des Ricolettes just as the gendarmes were carting away two Zouaves who had been killed by drunken Italians. The red fezzes of the soldiers were lying in pools of blood on the rough cobblestone street. A squad of gendarmes hustled the Italians to jail, while the infuriated mob stormed after them, shouting,

"Hang them! Hang them!"

Vincent took advantage of the excitement to slip into the Maison de Tolérance, Numero I, in the Rue des Ricolettes. Louis, the proprietor, welcomed him and led him into a little room on the left of the hall, where a few couples sat drinking.

"I have a young girl by the name of Rachel who is very nice," said Louis. "Would Monsieur care to try her? If you do not like the looks of her, you can choose from all the others."

"May I see her?"

Vincent sat down at a table and lit his pipe. There was laughter from the outside hall, and a girl danced in. She slid into the chair opposite Vincent and smiled at him.

"I'm Rachel," she said.

"Why," exclaimed Vincent, "you're nothing but a baby!"

"I'm sixteen," said Rachel proudly.

"How long have you been here?"

"At Louis's? A year."

"Let me look at you."

The yellow gas lamp was at her back; her face had been in the shadows. She put her head against the wall and tilted her chin up towards the light so that Vincent could see her.

He saw a round, plump face, wide, vacant blue eyes, a fleshy chin and neck. Her black hair was coiled on top of her head, giving the face an even more ball-like appearance. She had on only a light printed dress and a pair of sandals. The nipples of her round breasts pointed straight out at him like accusing fingers.

"You're pretty, Rachel," he said.

A bright, childlike smile came into her empty eyes. She whirled about and took his hand in hers.

"I'm glad you like me," she said. "I like the men to like me. That makes it nicer, don't you think?"

"Yes. Do you like me?"

"I think you're a funny man, *fou-rou.*"

"*Fou-rou!* Then you know me?"

"I've seen you in the Place Lamartine. Why are you always rushing places with that big bundle on your back? And why don't you wear a hat? Doesn't the sun burn you? Your eyes are all red. Don't they hurt?"

Vincent laughed at the naiveté of the child.

"You're very sweet, Rachel. Will you call me by my real name if I tell it to you?"

"What is it?"

"Vincent."

"No, I like *fou-rou* better. Do you mind if I call you *fou-rou?* And can I have something to drink? Old Louis is watching me from the hall."

She ran her fingers across her throat; Vincent watched them sink into the soft flesh. She smiled with her empty blue eyes, and he saw that she was smiling to be happy, so that he might be happy, too. Her teeth were regular but dark; her large underlip drooped down almost to meet the sharp horizontal crevice just above her thick chin.

"Order a bottle of wine," said Vincent, "but not an expensive one, for I haven't much money."

When the wine came, Rachel said, "Would you like to drink it in my room? It's more homey there."

"I would like that very much."

They walked up a flight of stone steps and entered Rachel's cell. There was a narrow cot, a bureau, a chair, and several coloured Julien medallions on the white walls. Two torn and battered dolls sat on top of the bureau.

"I brought these from home with me," she said. "Here, *fou-rou,* take them. This is Jacques and this is Catherine. I used to play house with them. Oh, *fou-rou,* don't you look droll!"

Vincent stood there grinning foolishly with a doll in each arm until Rachel finished laughing. She took Catherine and Jacques from him, tossed them on the bureau, kicked her sandals into a corner and slipped out of her dress.

"Sit down, *fou-rou,*" she said, "and we'll play house. You'll be papa and I'll be mama. Do you like to play house?"

She was a short, thickset girl with swelling, convex thighs, a deep declivity under the pointed breasts, and a plump, round belly which rolled down into the pelvic triangle.

"Rachel," said Vincent, "if you are going to call me *fou-rou,* I have a name for you, too."

Rachel clapped her hands and flung herself onto his lap.

"Oh, tell me, what is it? I like to be called new names!"

"I'm going to call you *Le Pigeon.*"

Rachel's blue eyes went hurt and perplexed.

"Why am I a pigeon, papa?"

Vincent ran his hand lightly over her rotund, cupid's belly.

"Because you look like a pigeon, with your gentle eyes and fat little tummy."

"Is it nice to be a pigeon?"

"Oh, yes. Pigeons are very pretty and lovable . . . and so are you."

Rachel leaned over, kissed him on the ear, sprang up from the cot and brought two water tumblers for their wine.

"What funny little ears you have, *fou-rou,*" she said, between sips of the red wine. She drank it as a baby drinks, with her nose in the glass.

"Do you like them?" asked Vincent.

"Yes. They're so soft and round, just like a puppy's."

"Then you can have them."

Rachel laughed loudly. She raised her glass to her lips. The joke struck her as funny again, and she giggled. A trickle of red wine spilled down her left breast, wound its way over the pigeon belly and disappeared in the black triangle.

"You're nice, *fou-rou,*" she said. "Everyone speaks as though you were crazy. But you're not, are you?"

Vincent grimaced.

"Only a little," he said.

"And will you be my sweetheart?" Rachel demanded. "I haven't had one for over a month. Will you come to see me every night?"

"I'm afraid I can't come every night, Pigeon."

Rachel pouted. "Why not?"

"Well, among other things, I haven't the money."

Rachel tweaked his right ear, playfully.

"If you haven't five francs, *fou-rou,* will you cut off your ear and give it to me? I'd like to have it. I'd put it on my bureau and play with it every night."

"Will you let me redeem it if I get the five francs later?"

"Oh, *fou-rou,* you're so funny and nice. I wish more of the men who came here were like you."

"Don't you enjoy it here?"

"Oh, yes, I have a very nice time, and I like it all . . . except the Zouaves, that is."

Rachel put down her wine glass and threw her arms prettily about Vincent's neck. He felt her soft paunch against his waistcoat, and the points of her bud-like breasts burning into him. She buried her mouth on his. He found himself kissing the soft, velvety inner lining of her lower lip.

"You will come back to see me again, *fou-rou?* You won't forget me and go to see some other girl?"

"I'll come back, Pigeon."

"And shall we do it now? Shall we play house?"

When he left the place a half hour later, he was consumed by a thirst which could be quenched only by innumerable glasses of clear, cold water.

4

Vincent came to the conclusion that the more finely a colour was pounded, the more it became saturated with oil. Oil was only the carrying medium for colour; he did not care much for it, particularly since he did not object to his canvases having a rough look. Instead of buying colour that had been pounded on the stone for God knows how many hours in Paris, he decided to become his own colour man. Theo asked Père Tanguy to send Vincent the three chromes, the malachite, the vermillion, the orange lead, the cobalt, and the ultramarine. Vincent crushed them in his little hotel room. After that his colours not only cost less, but they were fresher and more lasting.

He next became dissatisfied with the absorbent canvas on which he painted. The thin coat of plaster with which they were covered did not suck up his rich colours. Theo sent him rolls of unprepared canvas; at night he mixed the plaster in a little bowl and spread it over the canvas he planned to paint the following day.

Georges Seurat had made him sensitive to the sort of frame his work was to rest in. When he sent his first Arlesian canvases to Theo, he explained just what sort of wood had to be used, and what colour it had to be painted. But he could not be happy until he saw his paintings in frames that he made himself. He bought plain strips of wood from his grocer, cut them down to the size he wanted, and then painted them to match the composition of the picture.

He made his colours, built his stretchers, plastered his canvas, painted his pictures, carpentered his frames, and painted them.

"Too bad I can't buy my own pictures," he murmured aloud. "Then I'd be completely self-sufficient."

The mistral came up again. All nature seemed in a rage. The skies were cloudless. The brilliant sunshine was accompanied by intense dryness and piercing cold. Vincent did a still life in his room; a coffee pot in blue enamel, a cup of royal blue and gold, a milk jug in squares of pale blue and white, a jug in majolica, blue with a pattern in reds, greens and browns, and lastly, two oranges and three lemons.

When the wind died down he went out again and did a view on the Rhône, the iron bridge at Trinquetaille, in which the sky and river were the colour of absinthe, the quays a shade of lilac, the figures leaning on their elbows on the parapet blackish, the iron bridge an intense blue with a note of vivid orange in the black background and a touch of intense malachite green. He was trying to get at something utterly heartbroken and therefore utterly heartbreaking.

Instead of trying to reproduce exactly what he had before his eyes, he used colour arbitrarily to express himself with greater force. He realized that what Pissarro had told him in Paris was true. "You must boldly exaggerate the effects, either in harmony or discord, which colours produce." In Maupassant's preface to "Pierre et Jean" he found a similar sentiment. "The artist has the liberty to exaggerate, to create in his novel a world more beautiful, more simple, more consoling than ours."

He did a day's hard, close work among the cornfields in full sun. The result was a ploughed field, a big field with clods of violet earth, climbing toward the horizon; a sower in blue and white; on the horizon a field of short, ripe corn; over all a yellow sky with a yellow sun.

Vincent knew that the Parisian critics would think he worked too fast. He did not agree. Was it not emotion, the sincerity of his feeling for nature, that impelled him? And if the emotions were sometimes so strong that he worked without knowing he worked, if sometimes the strokes came with a sequence and coherence like words in a speech, then too the time would come when there would again be heavy days, empty of inspiration. He had to strike while the iron was hot, put the forged bars on one side.

He strapped his easel to his back and took the road home which led past Montmajour. He walked so rapidly that he soon overtook a man and a boy who were dallying ahead of him. He recognized the man as old Roulin, the Arlesian *facteur des postes*. He had often sat near Roulin in the café, and had wanted to speak to him, but the occasion had never arisen.

"Good day, Monsieur Roulin," he said.

"Ah, it is you, the painter," said Roulin. "Good day. I have been taking my boy for a Sunday afternoon stroll."

"It has been a glorious day, hasn't it?"

"Ah, yes, it is lovely when that devil mistral does not blow. You have painted a picture today, Monsieur?"

"Yes."

"I am an ignorant man, Monsieur, and know nothing about art. But I would be honoured if you would let me look."

"With pleasure."

The boy ran ahead, playing. Vincent and Roulin walked side by side. While Roulin looked at the canvas, Vincent studied him. Roulin was wearing his blue postman's cap. He had soft, inquiring eyes and a long, square, wavy beard which completely covered his neck and collar and came to rest on the dark blue postman's coat. Vincent felt the same soft, wistful quality about Roulin that had attracted him to Père Tanguy. He was homely in a pathetic sort of way, and his plain, peasant's face seemed out of place in the luxuriant Greek beard.

"I am an ignorant man, Monsieur," repeated Roulin, "and you will forgive me for speaking. But your cornfields are so very alive, as alive as the field we passed back there, for instance, where I saw you at work."

"Then you like it?"

"As for that, I cannot say. I only know that it makes me feel something, in here."

He ran his hand upward over his chest.

They paused for a moment at the base of Montmajour. The sun was setting red over the ancient abbey, its rays falling on the trunks and foliage of pines growing among a tumble of rocks, colouring the trunks and foliage with orange fire, while the other pines in the distance stood out in Prussian blue against a sky of tender, blue-green cerulean. The white sand and the layers of white rocks under the trees took on tints of blue.

"That is alive, too, is it not, Monsieur?" asked Roulin.

"It will still be alive when we are gone, Roulin."

They walked along, chatting in a quiet, friendly manner. There was nothing of the abrasive quality in Roulin's words. His mind was simple, his thoughts at once simple and profound. He supported himself, his wife, and four children on a hundred and thirty-five francs a month. He had been a postman twenty-five years without a promotion, and with only infinitesimal advances in salary.

"When I was young, Monsieur," he said, "I used to think a lot about God. But He seems to have grown thinner with the years. He is still in that cornfield you painted, and in the sunset by Montmajour, but when I think about men . . . and the world they have made . . ."

"I know, Roulin, but I feel more and more that we must not judge God by this world. It's just a study that didn't come off. What can you do in a study that has gone wrong, if you are fond of the artist? You do not find much to criticize; you hold your tongue. But you have a right to ask for something better."

"Yes, that's it," exclaimed Roulin, "something just a tiny bit better."

"We should have to see some other works by the same hand before we judge him. This world was evidently botched up in a hurry on one of his bad days, when the artist did not have his wits about him."

Dusk had fallen over the winding country road. The first chips of stars poked through the heavy cobalt blanket of night. Roulin's sweet innocent eyes searched Vincent's face.

"Then you think there are other worlds besides this, Monsieur?"

"I don't know, Roulin. I gave up thinking about that sort of thing when I became interested in my work. But this life seems so incomplete, doesn't it? Sometimes I think that just as trains and carriages are means of locomotion to get us from one place to another on this earth, so typhoid and consumption are means of locomotion to get us from one world to another."

"Ah, you think of things, you artists."

"Roulin, will you do me a favour? Let me paint your portrait. The people of Arles won't pose for me."

"I should be honoured, Monsieur. But why do you want to paint me? I am only an ugly man."

"If there were a God, Roulin, I think he would have a beard and eyes just like yours."

"You are making fun of me, Monsieur!"

"On the contrary, I am in earnest."

"Will you come and share supper with us tomorrow night? We have a very plain board, but we will be happy to have you."

Madame Roulin proved to be a peasant woman who reminded him a little of Madame Denis. There was a red and white checked cloth on the table, a little stew with potatoes, home-baked bread and a bottle of sour wine. After dinner Vincent sketched Madame Roulin, chatting with the postman as he worked.

"During the Revolution I was a republican," said Roulin, "but now I see that we have gained nothing. Whether our rulers be kings or ministers, we poor people have just as little as before. I thought when we were a republic everyone would share and share alike."

"Ah, no, Roulin."

"All my life I have tried to understand, Monsieur, why one man should have more than the next, why one man should work hard while his neighbour sits by in idleness. Perhaps I am too ignorant to understand. Do you think if I were educated, Monsieur, I would be able to understand that better?"

Vincent glanced up quickly to see if Roulin were being cynical. There was the same look of naive innocence on his face.

"Yes, my friend," he said, "most educated people seem to understand that state of affairs very well. But I am ignorant like you, and I shall never be able to understand or accept it."

5

He arose at four in the morning, walked three and four hours to reach the spot he wanted, and then painted until dark. It was not pleasant, this trudging ten or twelve kilometres home on a lonely road, but he liked the reassuring touch of the wet canvas under his arm.

He did seven large pictures in seven days. By the end of the week he was nearly dead with work. It had been a glorious summer, but now he was painted out. A violent mistral arose and raised clouds of dust which whitened the trees. Vincent was forced to remain quiet. He slept for sixteen hours at a stretch.

He had a very thin time of it, for his money ran out on Thursday, and Theo's letter with the fifty francs was not expected until Monday noon. It was not Theo's fault. He still sent fifty francs every ten days in addition to all the painting supplies. Vincent had been wild to see his new pictures in frames, and had ordered too many of them for his budget. During those four days he lived on twenty-three cups of coffee and a loaf of bread for which the baker trusted him.

An intense reaction set in against his work. He did not think his pictures worthy of the goodness he had had from Theo. He wanted to win back the money he had already spent in order to return it to his brother. He looked at his paintings one by one and reproached himself that they were not worth what they had cost. Even if a tolerable study did come out of it from time to time, he knew that it would have been cheaper to buy it from somebody else.

All during the summer ideas for his work had come to him in swarms. Although he had been solitary, he had not had time to think or feel. He had gone on like a steam-engine. But now his brain felt like stale porridge, and he did not even have

a franc to amuse himself by eating or going to visit Rachel. He decided that
everything he had painted that summer was very, very bad.

"Anyway," he said to himself, "a canvas that I have covered is worth more
than a blank canvas. My pretensions go no further; that is my right to paint, my
reason for painting."

He had the conviction that simply by staying in Arles he would set his individuality
free. Life was short. It went fast. Well, being a painter, he still had to paint.

"These painter's fingers of mine grow supple," he thought, "even though the
carcass is going to pieces."

He drew up a long list of colours to send to Theo. Suddenly he realized that not
one colour on his list would be found on the Dutch palette, in Mauve, Maris, or
Weissenbruch. Arles had made his break with the Dutch tradition complete.

When his money arrived on Monday, he found a place where he could get a
good meal for a franc. It was a queer restaurant, altogether grey; the floor was of
grey bitumen like a street pavement, there was grey paper on the walls, green blinds
always drawn, and a big green curtain over the door to keep the dust out. A very
narrow, very fierce ray of sunlight stabbed through a blind.

After he had been resting for over a week, he decided to do some night painting.
He did the grey restaurant while the patrons were at their meal and the waitresses
were scurrying back and forth. He painted the thick, warm cobalt sky of night,
studded with thousands of bright Provençal stars, as seen from the Place Lamartine.
He went out on the roads and did cypresses under the moonlight. He painted the
Café de Nuit, which remained open all night so that prowlers could take refuge
there when they had no money to pay for a lodging, or when they were too drunk
to be taken to one.

He did the exterior of the café one night, and the interior the next. He tried to
express the terrible passions of humanity by means of red and green. He did the
interior in blood red and dark yellow with a green billiard table in the middle. He
put in four lemon-yellow lamps with a glow of orange and green. Everywhere there
was the clash and contrast of the most alien reds and greens in the figures of little
sleeping hooligans. He was trying to express the idea that the café was a place
where one could ruin oneself, run mad, or commit a crime.

The people of Arles were amused to find their *fou-rou* painting in the streets all
night and sleeping in the daytime. Vincent's activities were always a treat for them.

When the first of the month came, the hotel owner not only raised the rent on
the room, but decided to charge Vincent a daily storage fee for the closet in which
he kept his canvases. Vincent loathed the hotel and was outraged by the voraciousness
of the owner. The grey restaurant in which he ate was satisfactory, but he had
sufficient money to eat there only two or three days out of every ten. Winter was
coming, he had no studio in which to work, the hotel room was depressing and
humiliating. The food he was forced to eat in the cheap restaurants was poisoning
his stomach again.

He had to find a permanent home and studio of his own.

One evening, as he was crossing the Place Lamartine with old Roulin, he noticed
a *For Rent* sign on a yellow house just a stone's throw from his hotel. The house
had two wings with a court in the centre. It faced the Place and the town on the
hill. Vincent stood looking at it wistfully.

"Too bad it's so large," he said to Roulin. "I'd like to have a house like that."

"It is not necessary to rent the whole house, Monsieur. You can rent just this
right wing, for example."

"Really! How many rooms do you think it has? Would it be expensive?"

"I should say it had about three or four rooms. It will cost you very little, not
half what the hotel costs. I will come and look at it with you tomorrow during my
dinner time, if you like. Perhaps I can help you get a good price."

The following morning Vincent was so excited he could do nothing but pace up and down the Place Lamartine and survey the yellow house from all sides. It was built sturdily and got all the sun. On closer inspection Vincent found that there were two separate entrances to the house, and that the left wing was already occupied.

Roulin joined him after the midday meal. They entered the right wing of the house together. There was a hallway inside which led to a large room, with a smaller room opening off it. The walls were whitewashed. The hall and stairway leading to the second floor were paved with clean red brick. Upstairs there was another large room with a cabinet. The floors were of scrubbed red tile, and the whitewashed walls caught the clean, bright sun.

Roulin had written a note to the landlord, who was waiting for them in the upstairs room. He and Roulin conversed for some moments in a fast Provençal of which Vincent could understand very little. The postman turned to Vincent.

"He insists upon knowing how long you will keep the place."

"Tell him indefinitely."

"Will you agree to take it for at least six months?"

"Oh, yes! Yes!"

"Then he says he will give it to you for fifteen francs a month."

Fifteen francs! For a whole house! Only a third of what he paid at the hotel. Even less than he had paid for his studio in The Hague. A permanent home for fifteen francs a month. He drew the money out of his pocket, hurriedly.

"Here! Quick! Give it to him. The house is rented."

"He wants to know when you are going to move in," said Roulin.

"Today. Right now."

"But, Monsieur, you have no furniture. How can you move in?"

"I will buy a mattress and a chair. Roulin, you don't know what it means to spend your life in miserable hotel rooms. I must have this place immediately!"

"Just as you wish, Monsieur."

The landlord left. Roulin went back to work. Vincent walked from one room to another, up and down the stairs again, surveying over and over every inch of his domain. Theo's fifty francs had arrived just the day before; he still had some thirty francs in his pocket. He rushed out, bought a cheap mattress and a chair and carried them back to the yellow house. He decided that the room on the ground floor would be his bedroom, the top room his studio. He threw the mattress on the red tile floor, carried the chair up to his studio, and went back to his hotel for the last time.

The proprietor added forty francs to Vincent's bill on some thin pretext. He refused to let Vincent have his canvases until the money was handed over. Vincent had to go to the police court to get his paintings back, and even then had to pay half the fictitious charge.

Late that afternoon he found a merchant who was willing to give him a small gas stove, two pots, and a kerosene lamp on credit. Vincent had three francs left. He bought coffee, bread, potatoes and a little meat for soup. He left himself without a centime. At home he set up a kitchen in the cabinet on the ground floor.

When night closed over the Place Lamartine and the yellow house, Vincent cooked his soup and coffee on the little stove. He had no table, so he spread a paper over the mattress, put out his supper, and ate it sitting cross-legged on the floor. He had forgotten to buy a knife and fork. He used the handle of his brush to pick the pieces of meat and potato out of the pot. They tasted slightly of paint.

When he finished eating, he took the kerosene lamp and mounted the red brick stairs to the second floor. The room was barren and lonely, with only the stark easel standing against the moonlit window. In the background was the dark garden of the Place Lamartine.

He went to sleep on the mattress. When he awakened in the morning he opened the windows and saw the green of the garden, the rising sun, and the road winding up into the town. He looked at the clean red bricks of the floor, the spotlessly whitewashed walls, the spaciousness of the rooms. He boiled himself a cup of coffee and walked about drinking from the pot, planning how he would furnish his house, what pictures he would hang on the walls, how he would pass the happy hours in a real home of his own.

The next day he received a letter from his friend Paul Gauguin, who was imprisoned, ill and poverty stricken, in a wretched café in Pont-Aven, in Brittany. "I can't get out of this hole," wrote Gauguin, "because I can't pay my bill, and the owner has all my canvases under lock and key. In all the variety of distresses that afflict humanity, nothing maddens me more than the lack of money. Yet I feel myself doomed to perpetual beggary."

Vincent thought of the painters of the earth, harassed, ill, destitute, shunned and mocked by their fellow men, starved and tortured to their dying day. Why? What was their crime? What was their great offense that made them outcasts and pariahs? How could such persecuted souls do good work? The painter of the future——ah, he would be such a colourist and a man as had never yet existed. He would not live in miserable cafés, and go to the Zouave brothels.

And poor Gauguin. Rotting away in some filthy hole in Brittany, too sick to work, without a friend to help him or a franc in his pocket for wholesome food and a doctor. Vincent thought him a great painter and a great man. If Gauguin should die. If Gauguin should have to give up his work. What a tragedy for the painting world.

Vincent slipped the letter into his pocket, left the yellow house, and walked along the embankment of the Rhône. A barge loaded with coal was moored to the quay. Seen from above, it was all shining and wet from a shower. The water was of yellowish white, and clouded pearl grey. The sky was lilac, barred with orange to the west, the town violet. On the boat some labourers in dirty blue and white came and went, carrying the cargo on shore.

It was pure Hokusai. It carried Vincent back to Paris, to the Japanese prints in Père Tanguy's shop . . . and to Paul Gauguin who, of all his friends, he loved the most dearly.

He knew at once what he had to do. The yellow house was large enough for two men. Each of them could have his own bedroom and studio. If they cooked their meals, ground their colours, and guarded their money, they could live on his hundred and fifty francs a month. The rent would be no more, the food very little. How marvellous it would be to have a friend again, a painter friend who talked one's language and understood one's craft. And what wonderful things Gauguin could teach him about painting.

He had not realized before how utterly lonely he had been. Even if they couldn't live on Vincent's hundred and fifty francs, perhaps Theo would send an extra fifty francs in return for a monthly canvas from Gauguin.

Yes! Yes! He must have Gauguin with him here in Arles. The hot Provence sun would burn all the illness out of him, just as it had out of Vincent. Soon they would have a working studio going full blaze. Theirs would be the very first studio in the South. They would carry on the tradition of Delacroix and Monticelli. They would drench painting in sunlight and colour, awaken the world to riotous nature.

Gauguin had to be saved!

Vincent turned, broke into a dog-trot and ran all the way back to the Place Lamartine. He let himself into the yellow house, dashed up the red brick stairs, and began excitedly planning the rooms.

"Paul and I will each have a bedroom up here. We'll use the rooms on the lower floor for studios. I'll buy beds and mattresses and bedclothes and chairs and tables, and we'll have a real home. I'll decorate the whole house with sunflowers and orchards in blossom."

"Oh, Paul, Paul, how good it will be to have you with me again!"

6

It was not so easy as he had expected. Theo was willing to add fifty francs a month to the allowance in return for a Gauguin canvas, but there was the matter of the railroad fare which neither Theo nor Gauguin could provide. Gauguin was too ill to move, too much in debt to get out of Pont-Aven, too sick at heart to enter into any schemes with enthusiasm. Letters flew thick and fast between Arles, Paris, and Pont-Aven.

Vincent was now desperately in love with his yellow house. He bought himself a table and a chest of drawers with Theo's allowance.

"At the end of a year," he wrote to Theo, "I shall be a different man. But don't think I'm going to leave here then. By no means. I'm going to spend the rest of my life in Arles. I'm going to become the painter of the South. And you must consider that you have a country house in Arles. I am keen to arrange it all so that you will come here always to spend your holidays."

He spent a minimum for the bare necessities of life, and sunk all the rest into the house. Each day he had to make a choice between himself and the yellow house. Should he have meat for dinner, or buy that majolica jug? Should he buy a new pair of shoes, or get that green quilt for Gauguin's bed? Should he order a pine frame for his new canvas, or buy those rush-bottom chairs?

Always the house came first.

The yellow house gave him a sense of tranquillity, because he was working to secure the future. He had drifted too much, knocked about without rhyme or reason. But now he was never going to move again. After he was gone, another painter would find a going concern. He was establishing a permanent studio which would be used by generation after generation of painters to interpret and portray the South. He became obsessed with the idea of painting such decorations for the house as would be worthy of the money spent on him during the years in which he had been unproductive.

He plunged into his work with renewed energy. He knew that looking at a thing a long time ripened him and gave him a deeper understanding. He went back fifty times to Montmajour to study the field at its base. The mistral made it hard for him to get his brush work connected and interwoven with feeling, with the easel waving violently before him in the wind. He worked from seven in the morning until six at night without stirring. A canvas a day!

"Tomorrow will be a scorcher," said Roulin one evening, very late in the fall. They were sitting over a bock in the Café Lamartine. "And after that, winter."

"What is winter like in Arles?" asked Vincent.

"It's mean. Lots of rain, a miserable wind, and a biting cold. But winter is very short here. Only a couple of months."

"So tomorrow will be our last nice day. Then I know the very spot I want to do. Imagine an autumn garden, Roulin, with two cypresses, bottle green, shaped like bottles, and three little chestnut trees with tobacco and orange coloured leaves. There is a little yew with pale lemon foliage and a violet trunk, and two little bushes, blood-red, and scarlet purple leaves. And some sand, some grass, and some blue sky."

"Ah, Monsieur, when you describe things, I see that all my life I have been blind."

The next morning Vincent arose with the sun. He was in high spirits. He trimmed his beard with a pair of scissors, combed down what little hair the Arlesian sun had not burned off his scalp, put on his only whole suit of clothes, and as a special fond gesture of farewell to the sun, wore his rabbit-fur bonnet from Paris.

Roulin's prediction had been right. The sun rose, a yellow ball of heat. The rabbit-fur bonnet had no peak, and the sun pried into his eyes. The autumn garden was a two hour walk from Arles, on the road to Tarascon. It nestled askew on the side of a hill. Vincent planted his easel in a furrowed cornfield, behind and to the side of the garden. He threw his bonnet to the ground, took off his good coat, and set the canvas to the easel. Although it was still early morning, the sun scorched the top of his head and threw before his eyes the veil of dancing fire to which he had become accustomed.

He studied the scene before him carefully, analysed the component colours, and etched the design on his mind. When he was confident that he understood the scene, he softened his brushes, took the caps off his tubes of pigments, and cleaned the knife with which he spread on his thick colour. He glanced once more at the garden, burnt the image on the blank canvas before him, mixed some colour on the palette, and raised his brush.

"Must you begin so soon, Vincent?" asked a voice behind him.

Vincent whirled about.

"It is early yet, my dear. And you have the whole long day to work."

Vincent gaped at the woman in utter bewilderment. She was young, but not a child. Her eyes were as blue as the cobalt sky of an Arlesian night, and her hair, which she wore in a great flowing mass down her back, was as lemon-yellow as the sun. Her features were even more delicate than those of Kay Vos, but they had about them the mellow maturity of the Southland. Her colouring was burnt gold, her teeth, between the smiling lips, as white as an oleander seen through a blood-red vine. She wore a long white gown which clung to the lines of her body and was fastened only by a square silver buckle at the side. She had a simple pair of sandals on her feet. Her figure was sturdy, robust, yet flowing downward with the eye in pure, voluptuous curves.

"I've stayed away so very long, Vincent," she said.

She placed herself between Vincent and the easel, leaning against the blank canvas and shutting out his view of the garden. The sun caught up the lemon-yellow hair and sent waves of flame down her back. She smiled at him so whole-heartedly, so fondly, that he ran a hand over his eyes to see if he had suddenly gone ill, or fallen asleep.

"You do not understand, my dear, dear boy," the woman said. "How could you, when I've stayed away so long?"

"Who are you?"

"I am your friend, Vincent. The best friend you have in the world."

"How do you know my name? I have never seen you before."

"Ah, no, but I have seen you, many, many times."

"What is your name?"

"Maya."

"Is that all? Just Maya?"

"For you, Vincent, that is all."

"Why have you followed me here to the fields?"

"For the same reason that I have followed you all over Europe . . . so that I might be near you."

"You mistake me for someone else. I can't possibly be the man you mean."

The woman put a cool white hand on the burnt red hair of his head and smoothed it back lightly. The coolness of her hand and the coolness of her soft, low voice was like the refreshing water from a deep green well.

"There is only one Vincent Van Gogh. I could never mistake him."

"How long do you think you have known me?"

"Eight years, Vincent."

"Why, eight years ago I was in . . ."

" . . . Yes, dear, in the Borinage."

"You knew me then?"

"I saw you for the first time one late fall afternoon, when you were sitting on a rusty iron wheel in front of Marcasse . . ."

". . . Watching the miners go home!"

"Yes. When I first looked at you, you were sitting there, idly. I was about to pass by. Then you took an old envelope and a pencil from your pocket and began sketching. I looked over your shoulder to see what you had done. And when I saw . . . I fell in love."

"You fell in love? You fell in love with me?"

"Yes, Vincent, my dear, good Vincent, in love with you."

"Perhaps I was not so bad to look at, then."

"Not half so good as you are to look at now."

"Your voice . . . Maya . . . it sounds so queer. Only once before has a woman spoken to me in that voice . . ."

". . . Margot's voice. She loved you, Vincent, as well as I do."

"You knew Margot?"

"I stayed in the Brabant for two years. I followed you to the fields each day. I watched you work in the wrangle room behind the kitchen. And I was happy because Margot loved you."

"Then you did not love me any more?"

She caressed his eyes with the cool tips of her fingers.

"Ah, yes, I loved you. I have never ceased to love you since that very first day."

"And you weren't jealous of Margot?"

The woman smiled. Across her face went a flash of infinite sadness and compassion. Vincent thought of Mendes da Costa.

"No, I was not jealous of Margot. Her love was good for you. But your love for Kay I did not like. It injured you."

"Did you know me when I was in love with Ursula?"

"That was before my time."

"You would not have liked me then."

"No."

"I was a fool."

"Sometimes one has to be a fool in the beginning, to become wise in the end."

"But if you loved me when we were in the Brabant, why didn't you come to me?"

"You were not ready for me, Vincent."

"And now . . . I am ready?"

"Yes."

"You still love me? Even now . . . today . . . this moment?"

"Now . . . today . . . this moment . . . and for eternity."

"How can you love me? Look, my gums are diseased. Every tooth in my mouth is false. All the hair has been burnt off my head. My eyes are as red as a syphilitic's. My face is nothing but jagged bone. I am ugly. The ugliest of men! My nerves are shattered, my body gone sterile, my insides poisoned from tip to toe. How can you love such a wreck of a man?"

"Will you sit down, Vincent?"

Vincent sat on his stool. The woman sank to her knees in the soft loam of the field.

"Don't," cried Vincent. "You'll get your white gown all dirty. Let me put my coat under you."

The woman restrained him with the faintest touch of her hand.

"Many times I have soiled my gown in following you, Vincent, but always it has come clean again."

She cupped his chin in the palm of her strong white hand, and with her fingertips smoothed back the few charred hairs behind his ear.

"You are not ugly, Vincent. You are beautiful. You have tormented and tortured this poor body in which your soul is wrapped, but you cannot injure your soul. It is that I love. And when you have destroyed yourself by your passionate labours, that soul will go on . . . endlessly. And with it, my love for you."

The sun had risen another hour in the sky. It beat down in fierce heat upon Vincent and the woman.

"Let me take you where it is cool," said Vincent. "There are some cypress trees just below on the road. You will be more comfortable in the shade."

"I am happy here with you. I do not mind the sun. I have grown used to it."

"You have been in Arles long?"

"I came with you from Paris."

Vincent jumped up in anger and kicked over his stool.

"You are a fraud! You've been sent here on purpose to ridicule me. Someone told you of my past, and is paying you to make a fool of me. Go away. I'll not talk to you any more!"

The woman held his anger with the smile of her eyes.

"I am no fraud, my dear. I am the most real thing in your life. You can never kill my love for you."

"That's a lie! You don't love me. You're mocking me. I'll show your game up."

He seized her roughly in his arms. She swayed inward to him.

"I'm going to hurt you if you don't go away and stop torturing me!"

"Hurt me, Vincent. You've hurt me before. It's part of love to be hurt."

"Very well then, take your medicine!"

He pressed her body to him. He brought his mouth down on hers, hurting her with his teeth, crushing his kiss upon her.

She opened soft, warm lips to him and let him drink deeply of the sweetness of her mouth. Her whole body yearned upward to him, muscle to muscle, bone to bone, flesh to flesh, in complete and final surrender.

Vincent thrust her away from him and stumbled to his stool. The woman sank down on the ground beside him, put one arm on his leg, and rested her head against it. He stroked the long, rich mass of lemon-yellow hair.

"Are you convinced now?" she asked.

After many moments Vincent said, "You have been in Arles since I came. Did you know about *Le Pigeon?*"

"Rachel is a sweet child."

"And you don't object?"

"You are a man, Vincent, and need women. Since it was not yet time to come to you and give myself, you had to go where you could. But now . . ."

"Now?"

"You need to no longer. Ever again."

"You mean that you . . .?"

"Of course, Vincent dear. I love you."

"Why should you love me? Women have always despised me."

"You were not meant for love. You had other work to do."

"Work? Bah! I've been a fool. Of what good are all these hundreds of paintings? Who wants to own them? Who will buy them? Who will give me one grudging word of praise, say that I have understood nature or portrayed its beauty?"

"The whole world will say it one day, Vincent."

"One day. What a dream. Like the dream of thinking that I will one day be a healthy man, with a home and a family and enough money from my painting to live on. I have been painting for eight long years. Not once in all that time has anyone wanted to buy a picture I've painted. I've been a fool."

"I know, but what a glorious fool. After you are gone, Vincent, the world will understand what you have tried to say. The canvases that today you cannot sell for a hundred francs will one day sell for a million. Ah, you smile, but I tell you it is true. Your pictures will hang in the museums of Amsterdam and The Hague, in Paris and Dresden, Munich and Berlin, Moscow and New York. Your pictures will be priceless, because there will be none for sale. Books will be written about your art, Vincent, novels and plays built around your life. Wherever two men come together who love painting, there the name of Vincent Van Gogh will be sacred.''

"If I could not still taste your mouth on mine, I would say I was dreaming or going mad.''

"Come sit beside me, Vincent. Put your hand in mine.''

The sun was directly overhead. The hillside and valley were bathed in a mist of sulphur-yellow. Vincent lay in the furrow of the field beside the woman. For six long months he had had no one to talk to but Rachel and Roulin. Within him there was a great flood of words. The woman looked deep into his eyes, and he began to speak. He told her of Ursula and the days when he had been a Goupil clerk. He told her of his struggles and disappointments, of his love for Kay, and the life he had tried to build with Christine. He told her of his hopes in painting, of the names he had been called, and the blows he had received, of why he wanted his drawing to be crude, his work unfinished, his colour explosive; of all the things he wanted to accomplish for painting and painters, and how his body was wracked with exhaustion and disease.

The longer he talked, the more excited he became. Words flew out of his mouth like pigments from his tubes. His whole body sprang into action. He talked with his hands, gesticulated with his arms and shoulders, walked up and down before her with violent body contortions. His pulse was rising, his blood was rising, the burning sun sent him into a passion of feverish energy.

The woman listened quietly, never missing a word. From her eyes, he knew she understood. She drank in all he had to say, and still was there, eager and ready to hear more, to understand him, to be the recipient of everything he had to give and could not contain within himself.

He stopped abruptly. He trembled all over with excitement. His eyes and face were red, his limbs quivering. The woman pulled him down beside her.

"Kiss me, Vincent," she said.

He kissed her on the mouth. Her lips were no longer cool. They lay side by side in the rich, crumbly loam. The woman kissed his eyes, his ears, the nostrils of his nose, the declivity of his upper lip, bathed the inside of his mouth with her sweet, soft tongue, ran her fingers down the beard of his neck, down his shoulders and along the sensitive nerve-ends of his arm pit.

Her kisses aroused in him the most excruciating passion he had ever known. Every inch of him ached with the dull ache of the flesh that cannot be satisfied by flesh alone. Never before had a woman given herself to him with the kiss of love. He strained her body to him, feeling, beneath the soft white gown, the heat of her life flow.

"Wait," she said.

She unbuckled the silver clasp at her side and tossed the white gown away from her. Her body was the same burnished gold as her face. It was virgin, every beating pulse of it virgin. He had not known that the body of a woman could be so exquisitely wrought. He had not known that passion could be so pure, so fine, so searing.

"You're trembling, dear," she said. "Hold me to you. Do not tremble, my dear; my sweet, sweet dear. Hold me as you want me."

The sun was slipping down the other side of the heavens. The earth was hot from the beating rays of the day. It smelled of things that had been planted, of things that had grown, been cut away and died again. It smelled of life, rich pungent smells of life ever being created and ever returning to the stuff of its creation.

Vincent's emotion rose higher and higher. Every fibre of him beat inward to some focal core of pain. The woman opened her arms to him, opened her warmth to him, took from him what was the man of him, took into herself all the volcanic turbulence, all the overwhelming passion that hour by hour wracked his nerves and burst his body, led him with gentle caressing undulations to the shattering, creative climax.

Exhausted, he fell asleep in her arms.

When he awoke, he was alone. The sun had gone down. There was a solid cake of mud on one cheek, where he had buried his perspiring face in the loam. The earth was coolish and smelled of buried, crawling things. He put on his coat and rabbit-fur bonnet, strapped the easel to his back, and took the canvas under his arm. He walked the dark road home.

When he reached the yellow house, he threw the easel and blank canvas on the mattress in his bedroom. He went out for a cup of coffee. He leaned his head in his hands on the cold stone-topped table and thought back over the day.

"Maya," he murmured to himself. "Maya. Haven't I heard that name somewhere before? It means . . . it means . . . I wonder what it means?"

He took a second cup of coffee. After an hour he crossed the Place Lamartine to the yellow house. A cold wind had come up. There was the smell of rain in the air.

He had not bothered to light the kerosene lamp when he had dropped his easel. Now he lit a match and set the lamp on the table. The yellow flare illumined the room. His eye was caught by a patch of colour on the mattress. Startled, he walked over and picked up the canvas that he had taken with him that morning.

There, in a magnificent blaze of light, he saw his autumn garden; the two bottle green, bottle shaped cypresses; the three little chestnut trees with tobacco and orange coloured leaves; the yew with pale lemon foliage and a violet trunk; the two blood-red bushes with scarlet purple leaves; in the foreground some sand and grass, and over all a blue, blue sky with a whorling ball of sulphur-lemon fire.

He stood gazing at the picture for several moments. He tacked it lightly on the wall. He went back to the mattress, sat on it cross-legged, looked at his painting and grinned.

"It is good," he said aloud. "It is well realized."

7

Winter came on. Vincent spent the days in his warm pleasant studio. Theo wrote that Gauguin, who had been in Paris for a day, was in vile frame of mind, and was resisting the Arlesian idea with all his strength. In Vincent's mind the yellow house was not to be simply a home for two men, but a permanent studio for all the artists of the South. He made elaborate plans for enlarging his quarters as soon as he and Gauguin put the place into working order. Any painter who wished to stay there would be welcome; in return for his hospitality he would be obliged to send Theo one canvas a month. As soon as Theo had enough Impressionist pictures on hand, he was to leave Goupils and open an Independent Gallery in Paris.

Vincent made it very clear in his letters that Gauguin was to be the director of the studio, master of all the painters who worked there. Vincent saved every franc he could in order to furnish his bedroom. He painted the walls a pale violet. The floor was of red tile. He bought very light, greenish lemon sheets and pillows, a scarlet covering, and painted the wooden bed and chairs the colour of fresh butter. The toilet table he painted orange, the basin blue, the door lilac. He hung a number of his pictures on the wall, threw away the window shutters, and then transferred the whole scene to canvas for Theo, so that his brother might see how restful his room was. He painted it in free flat washes, like the Japanese prints.

With Gauguin's room it was another matter. He was not willing to buy such cheap furniture for the master of the studio. Madame Roulin assured him that the walnut bed he wanted for Gauguin would come to three hundred and fifty francs, an impossible sum for him to muster. Nevertheless he began buying the smaller articles for the room, keeping himself in a constant state of financial exhaustion.

When he had no money for models, he stood before a mirror and did his own portrait over and over. Rachel came to pose for him; Madame Roulin came one afternoon a week and brought the children; Madame Ginoux, wife of the owner of the café where he took his drinks, sat for him in her Arlesienne costume. He slashed the figure onto the canvas in an hour. The background was pale lemon, the face grey, the clothes black, with raw Prussian blue. He posed her in a borrowed armchair of orange wood, her elbows leaning on a green table.

A Zouave lad with a small face, the neck of a bull, and the eye of a tiger agreed to sit for a small sum. Vincent did a half length of him in his blue uniform, the blue of enamelled saucepans, with braid of a faded reddish orange, and two pale lemon stars on his breast. There was a reddish cap on the bronzed, feline head, set against a green background. The result was a savage combination of incongruous tones, very harsh, common and even loud, but fitting the character of the subject.

He sat at his window for hours with pencil and drawing paper, trying to master the technique which would enable him with a few strokes to put down the figure of a man, a woman, a youngster, a horse, a dog, so that it would have a head, body, and legs all in keeping. He copied a good many of the paintings he had made that summer, for he thought that if he could turn out fifty studies at two hundred francs each within the year, he would not have been so very dishonest in having eaten and drunk as though he had a right to it.

He learned a good many things during the winter: that one must not do flesh in Prussian blue, for then it becomes as wood; that his colour was not as firm as it should have been; that the most important element in southland painting was the contrast of red and green, of orange and blue, of sulphur and lilac; that in a picture he wanted to say something comforting as music is comforting; that he wished to paint men and women with that something of the divine which the halo used to symbolize, and which he sought to give by the actual radiance and vibration of his colouring; and lastly, that for those who have a talent for poverty, poverty is eternal.

One of the Van Gogh uncles died and left Theo a small legacy. Since Vincent was so keen to have Gauguin with him, Theo decided to use half the money to furnish Gauguin's bedroom and send him to Arles. Vincent was delighted. He began planning the decorations for the yellow house. He wanted a dozen panels of glorious Arlesian sunflowers, a symphony of blue and yellow.

Even the news of the free railway fare did not seem to excite Gauguin. For some reason which remained obscure to Vincent, Gauguin preferred to dawdle in Pont-Aven. Vincent was eager to finish the decorations and have the studio ready when the master arrived.

Spring came. The row of oleander bushes in the back yard of the yellow house went raving mad, flowering so riotously that they might well have developed locomotor ataxia. They were loaded with fresh flowers, and heaps of faded flowers as well; their green was continually renewing itself in strong jets, apparently inexhaustible.

Vincent loaded the easel on his back once again and went into the country-side to find sunflowers for the twelve wall panels. The earth of the ploughed fields was as soft in colour as a pair of sabots, while the forget-me-not blue sky was flecked with white clouds. Some of the sunflowers he did on the stalk, at sunrise, and in a flash. Others he took home with him and painted in a green vase.

He gave the outside of his house a fresh coat of yellow, much to the amusement of the inhabitants of the Place Lamartine.

By the time he finished his work on the house, summer had come. With it came the broiling sun, the driving mistral, the growing excitement in the air, the tortured, tormented, driven aspect of the countryside and the stone city pasted against the hill.

And with it came Paul Gauguin.

He arrived in Arles before dawn and waited for the sun in a little all-night café. The proprietor looked at him and exclaimed, "You are the friend! I recognize you."

"What the devil are you talking about?"

"Monsieur Van Gogh showed me the portrait you sent him. It looks just like you, Monsieur."

Gauguin went to rouse Vincent. Their meeting was boisterous and hearty. Vincent showed Gauguin the house, helped him unpack his valise, demanded news of Paris. They talked animatedly for several hours.

"Are you planning to work today, Gauguin?"

"Do you think I am a Carolus-Duran, that I can get off the train, pick up my palette, and turn you off a sunlight effect at once?"

"I only asked."

"Then don't ask foolish questions."

"I'll take a holiday, too. Come along, I'll show you the town."

He led Gauguin up the hill, through the sun-baked Place de la Mairie, and along the market road at the back of the town. The Zouaves were drilling in the field just outside the barracks; their red fezzes burned in the sun. Vincent led the way through the little park in front of the Roman forum. The Arlesiennes were strolling for their morning air. Vincent had been raving to Gauguin about how beautiful they were.

"What do you think about the Arlesiennes, Gauguin?" he demanded.

"I can't get up a perspiration about them."

"Look at the tone of their flesh, man, not the shape. Look at what the sun has done to their colouring."

"How are the houses here, Vincent?"

"There's nothing but five franc places for the Zouaves."

They returned to the yellow house to work out some sort of living arrangements. They nailed a box to the wall in the kitchen and put half their money into it—so much for tobacco, so much for incidental expenses, including rent. On the top of the box they put a scrap of paper and a pencil with which to write down every franc they took. In another box they put the rest of their money, divided into four parts, to pay for the food each week.

"You're a good cook, aren't you, Gauguin?"

"Excellent. I used to be a sailor."

"Then in the future you shall cook. But tonight I am going to make the soup in your honour."

When he served the soup that night, Gauguin could not eat it.

"How you mixed this mess, Vincent, I can't imagine. As you mix the colours in your pictures, I dare say."

"What is the matter with the colours in my pictures?"

"My dear fellow, you're still floundering in neo-impressionism. You'd better give up your present method. It doesn't correspond to your nature."

Vincent pushed his bowl of soup aside.

"You can tell that at first glance, eh? You're quite a critic."

"Well, look for yourself. You're not blind, are you? Those violet yellows, for example; they're completely disordered."

Vincent glanced up at the sunflower panels on the wall.

"Is that all you find to say about my sunflowers?"

"No, my dear fellow, I can find a good many things to criticize."

"Among them?"

"Among them, your harmonies; they're monotonous and incomplete."

"That's a lie!"

"Oh, sit down, Vincent. Stop looking as though you wanted to murder me. I'm a good deal older than you, and more mature. You're still trying to find yourself. Just listen to me, and I'll give you some fruitful lessons."

"I'm sorry, Paul. I do want you to help me."

"Then the first thing you had better do is sweep all the garbage out of your mind. You've been raving all day about Meissonier and Monticelli. They're both worthless. As long as you admire that sort of painting, you'll never turn out a good canvas yourself."

"Monticelli was a great painter. He knew more about colour than any man of his time."

"He was a drunken idiot, that's what he was."

Vincent jumped to his feet and glared at Gauguin across the table. The bowl of soup fell to the red tile floor and smashed.

"Don't you call 'Fada' that! I love him almost as well as I do my own brother! All that talk about his being such a drinker, and off his head, is vicious gossip. No drunkard could have painted Monticelli's pictures. The mental labour of balancing the six essential colours, the sheer strain and calculation, with a hundred things to think of in a single half hour, demands a sane mind. And a sober one. When you repeat that gossip about 'Fada' you're being just as vicious as that beastly woman who started it."

"Turlututu, mon chapeau pointu!"

Vincent recoiled, as though a glass of cold water had been thrown in his face. His words and tense emotion strangled within him. He tried to put down his rage, but could not. He walked to his bedroom and slammed the door behind him.

8

The following morning the quarrel was forgotten. They had coffee together and then went their separate ways to find pictures. When Vincent returned that night, exhausted from what he had called the balancing of the six essential colours, he found Gauguin already preparing supper on the tiny gas stove. They talked quietly for a little while; then the conversation turned to painters and painting, the only subject in which they were passionately interested.

The battle was on.

The painters whom Gauguin admired, Vincent despised. Vincent's idols were anathema to Gauguin. They disagreed on every last approach to their craft. Any other subject they might have been able to discuss in a quiet and friendly manner, but painting was the meat and drink of life to them. They fought for their ideas to the last drop of nervous energy. Gauguin had twice Vincent's brute strength, but Vincent's lashing excitement left them evenly matched.

Even when they discussed things about which they agreed, their arguments were terribly electric. They came out of them with their heads as exhausted as a battery after it had been discharged.

"You'll never be an artist, Vincent," announced Gauguin, "until you can look at nature, come back to your studio and paint it in cold blood."

"I don't want to paint in cold blood, you idiot. I want to paint in hot blood! That's why I'm in Arles."

"All this work you've done is only slavish copying from nature. You must learn to work extempore."

"Extempore! Good God!"

"And another thing; you would have done well to listen to Seurat. Painting is abstract, my boy. It has no room for the stories you tell and the morals you point out."

"I point out morals? You're crazy."

"If you want to preach, Vincent, go back to the ministry. Painting is colour, line, and form; nothing more. The artist can reproduce the decorative in nature, but that's all."

"Decorative art," snorted Vincent. "If that's all you get out of nature, you ought to go back to the Stock Exchange."

"If I do, I'll come hear you preach on Sunday mornings. What do you get out of nature, Brigadier?"

"I get motion, Gauguin, and the rhythm of life."

"Well, we're off."

"When I paint a sun, I want to make people feel it revolving at a terrific rate of speed. Giving off light and heat waves of tremendous power. When I paint a cornfield I want people to feel the atoms within the corn pushing out to their final growth and bursting. When I paint an apple I want people to feel the juice of that apple pushing out against the skin, the seeds at the core striving outward to their own fruition!"

"Vincent, how many times have I told you that a painter must not have theories."

"Take this vineyard scene, Gauguin. Look out! Those grapes are going to burst and squirt right in your eye. Here, study this ravine. I want to make people feel all the millions of tons of water that have poured down its sides. When I paint the portrait of a man, I want them to feel the entire flow of that man's life, everything he has seen and done and suffered!"

"What the devil are you driving at?"

"At this, Gauguin. The fields that push up the corn, and the water that rushes down the ravine, the juice of the grape, and the life of a man as it flows past him, are all one and the same thing. The sole unity in life is the unity of rhythm. A rhythm to which we all dance; men, apples, ravines, ploughed fields, carts among the corn, houses, horses, and the sun. The stuff that is in you, Gauguin, will pound through a grape tomorrow, because you and a grape are one. When I paint a peasant labouring in the field, I want people to feel the peasant flowing down into the soil, just as the corn does, and the soil flowing up into the peasant. I want them to feel the sun pouring into the peasant, into the field, the corn, the plough, and the horses, just as they all pour back into the sun. When you begin to feel the universal rhythm in which everything on earth moves, you begin to understand life. That alone is God."

"*Brigadier,*" said Gauguin, "*vous avez raison!*"

Vincent was at the height of his emotion, quivering with febrile excitement. Gauguin's words struck him like a slap in the face. He stood there gaping foolishly, his mouth hanging open.

"Now what in the world does that mean, 'Brigadier, you are right'?"

"It means I think it about time we adjourned to the café for an absinthe."

At the end of the second week Gauguin said, "Let's try that house of yours tonight. Maybe I can find a nice fat girl."

"Keep away from Rachel. She belongs to me."

They walked up the labyrinth of stone alleys and entered the Maison de Tolérance. When Rachel heard Vincent's voice, she skipped down the hallway and threw herself into his arms. Vincent introduced Gauguin to Louis.

"Monsieur Gauguin," said Louis, "you are an artist. Perhaps you would give me your opinion of the two new paintings I bought in Paris last year."

"I'd be glad to. Where did you buy them?"

"At Goupils, in the Place de lÓpéra. They are in this front parlour. Will you step in, Monsieur?"

Rachel led Vincent to the room on the left, pushed him into a chair near one of the tables, and sat on his lap.

"I've been coming here for six months," grumbled Vincent, "and Louis never asked my opinion about his pictures."

"He doesn't think you are an artist, *fou-rou*."

"Maybe he's right."

"You don't love me any more," said Rachel, pouting.

"What makes you think that, Pigeon?"

"You haven't been to see me for weeks."

"That was because I was working hard to fix the house for my friend."

"Then you do love me, even if you stay away?"

"Even if I stay away."

She tweeked his small, circular ears, then kissed each of them in turn.

"Just to prove it, *fou-rou*, will you give me your funny little ears? You promised you would."

"If you can take them off, you can have them."

"Oh, *fou-rou*, as if they were sewed on, like my dolly's ears."

There was a shout from the room across the hall, and the noise of someone screaming, either in laughter or in pain. Vincent dumped Rachel off his lap, ran across the hall and into the parlour.

Gauguin was doubled up on the floor, convulsed, tears streaming down his face. Louis, lamp in hand, was gazing down at him, dumbfounded. Vincent crouched over Gauguin and shook him.

"Paul, Paul, what is it?"

Gauguin tried to speak, but could not. After a moment he gasped, "Vincent . . . at last . . . we're vindicated . . . look . . . look . . . up on the wall . . . the two pictures . . . that Louis bought from Goupils . . . for the parlour of his brothel. *They are both Bouguereaus!*"

He stumbled to his feet and made for the front door.

"Wait a minute," cried Vincent, running after him. "Where are you going?"

"To the telegraph office. I must wire this to the Club Batignolles at once."

Summer came on in all its terrific, glaring heat. The country-side burst into a riot of colour. The greens and blues and yellows and reds were so stark they were shocking to the eye. Whatever the sun touched, it burnt to the core. The valley of the Rhône vibrated with wave after wave of billowy heat. The sun battered the two painters, bruised them, beat them to a living pulp, sucked out all their resistance. The mistral came up and lashed their bodies, whipped their nerves, shook their heads on their necks until they thought they would burst or break off. Yet every morning they went out with the sun and laboured until the crying blue of night deepened the crying blue of day.

Between Vincent and Gauguin, the one a perfect volcano, the other boiling inwardly, a fierce struggle was preparing itself. At night, when they were too exhausted to sleep, too nervous to sit still, they spent all their energy on each other. Their money ran low. They had no way to amuse themselves. They found an outlet for their pent up passions in mutual exacerbation. Gauguin never tired of whipping Vincent into a rage and, when Vincent was at the height of his paroxysm, throwing into his face, *"Brigadier, vous avez raison!"*

"Vincent, no wonder you can't paint. Look at the disorder of this studio. Look at the mess in this colour box. My God, if your Dutch brain wasn't so fired with Daudet and Monticelli, maybe you could clean it out and get a little order into your life."

"That's nothing to you, Gauguin. This is my studio. You keep your studio any way you like."

"While we're on the subject, I may as well tell you that your mind is just as chaotic as your colour box. You admire every postage stamp painter in Europe, and yet you can't see that Degas . . ."

"Degas! What has he ever painted that can be held up alongside of a Millet?"

"Millet! That sentimentalist! That . . .!"

Vincent worked himself into a frenzy at this slur at Millet, whom he considered his master and spiritual father. He stormed after Gauguin from room to room. Gauguin fled. The house was small. Vincent shouted at him, harangued him, waved his fists in Gauguin's powerful face. Far into the tropical, oppressive night they kept up their bruising, battering conflict.

They both worked like fiends to catch themselves and nature at the point of fructification. Day after day they battled with their flaming palettes, night after night with each other's strident egos. When they were not quarreling viciously, their friendly arguments were so explosive that it was impossible to summon sleep. Money came from Theo. They spent it immediately for tobacco and absinthe. It was too hot to eat. They thought absinthe would quiet their nerves. It only excited them the more.

A nasty, lashing mistral came up. It confined the men to the house. Gauguin could not work. He spent his time scourging Vincent into a continuous ebullition. He had never seen anyone grow so violent over mere ideas.

Vincent was the only sport Gauguin had. He made the most of it.

"Better quiet down, Vincent," he said after the fifth day of the mistral. He had baited his friend until the storm within the yellow house had made the howling mistral seem like a mild and gentle breeze.

"What about yourself, Gauguin?"

"It so happens, Vincent, that several men who have been a good deal in my company, and in the habit of discussing things with me, have gone mad."

"Are you threatening me?"

"No, I'm warning you."

"Then keep your warnings to yourself."

"All right, but don't blame me if anything happens."

"Oh, Paul, Paul, let's stop this eternal quarreling. I know that you're a better painter than I am. I know that you can teach me a great deal. But I won't have you despising me, do you hear. I've slaved nine long years, and by Christ, I have something to say with this beastly paint! Now admit it, haven't I? Speak up, Gauguin."

"Brigadier, vous avez raison!"

The mistral died down. The Arlesians dared go out in the streets again. The blistering sun came back. An uncontainable fever settled over Arles. The police had to cope with crimes of violence. People walked about with a smouldering excitement in their eyes. No one ever laughed. No one talked. The stone roofs broiled under the sun. There were fights and knife flashes in the Place Lamartine. There was the smell of catastrophe in the air. Arles was too engorged to stand the strain any longer. The valley of the Rhône was about to burst into a million fragments.

Vincent thought of the Parisian journalist.

"Which will it be?" he asked himself. "An earthquake or a revolution."

In spite of it all, he still painted in the fields without a hat. He needed the white, blinding heat to make fluid within him the terrific passions he felt. His brain was a burning crucible, turning out red-hot canvas after canvas.

With each succeeding canvas he felt more keenly that all his nine years of labour were converging in these few surcharged weeks to make him, for one brief instant, the complete and perfect artist. He was by far surpassing his last summer's work. Never again would he produce paintings that so utterly expressed the essence of nature and the essence of himself.

He painted from four in the morning until night stole the scene from him. He created two, and sometimes even three complete pictures a day. He was spilling out a year of his life blood with every convulsive painting that he tore from his vitals. It was not the length of his stay on earth that mattered to him; it was what he did with the days of his life. For him time would have to be measured by the paintings he poured out, not by the fluttering leaves of a calendar.

He sensed that his art had reached a climax; that this was the high spot of his life, the moment toward which he had been striving all these years. He did not know how long it would last. He knew only that he had to paint pictures, and more pictures . . . and still more and more pictures. This climax of his life, this tiny point of infinity, had to be held, sustained, pushed out until he had created all those pictures that were gestating in his soul.

Painting all day, fighting all night, sleeping not at all, eating very little, glutting themselves with sun and colour, excitement, tobacco and absinthe, lacerated by the elements and their own drive of creation, lacerating each other with their rages and violence, their gorges mounted higher and higher.

The sun beat them. The mistral whipped them. The colour stabbed their eyes out. The absinthe swelled their empty bowels with turgescent fever. The yellow house rocked and throbbed with the tempest in the tropical, plethoric nights.

Gauguin did a portrait of Vincent while the latter was painting a still life of some ploughs. Vincent stared at the portrait. For the first time he understood clearly just what Gauguin thought of him.

"It is certainly I," he said. "But it is I gone mad!"

That evening they went to the café. Vincent ordered a light absinthe. Suddenly he flung the glass and the contents at Gauguin's head. Gauguin dodged. He picked Vincent up bodily in his arms. He carried him across the Place Lamartine. Vincent found himself in bed. He fell asleep instantly.

"My dear Gauguin," he said very calmly the next morning, "I have a vague memory that I offended you last evening."

"I forgive you gladly and with all my heart," said Gauguin, "but yesterday's scene might occur again. If I were struck I might lose control of myself and give you a choking. So permit me to write to your brother and tell him that I am coming back."

"No! No! Paul, you can't do that. Leave the yellow house? Everything in it I made for you."

During all the hours of the day the storm raged. Vincent fought desperately to keep Gauguin by his side. Gauguin resisted every plea. Vincent begged, cajoled, cursed, threatened, even wept. In this battle he proved to be the stronger. He felt that his whole life depended upon keeping his friend in the yellow house. By nightfall Gauguin was exhausted. He gave in just to get a little rest.

Every room in the yellow house was charged and vibrating with electrical tension. Gauguin could not sleep. Toward dawn he dozed off.

A queer sensation awakened him. He saw Vincent standing over his bed, glaring at him in the dark.

"What's the matter with you, Vincent?" he asked sternly.

Vincent walked out of the room, returned to his bed, and fell into a heavy sleep.

The following night Gauguin was jerked out of his sleep by the same strange sensation. Vincent was standing over his bed, staring at him in the dark.

"Vincent! Go to bed!"

Vincent turned away.

At supper the next day they fell into a fierce quarrel over the soup.

"You poured some paint into it, Vincent, while I wasn't looking!" shouted Gauguin.

Vincent laughed. He walked to the wall and wrote in chalk,

Je suis Saint Esprit
Je suis sain d'esprit

He was very quiet for several days. He looked moody and depressed. He hardly spoke a word to Gauguin. He did not even pick up a paint brush. He did not read. He sat in a chair and gazed ahead of him into space.

On the afternoon of the fourth day, when there was a vicious mistral, he asked Gauguin to take a walk with him.

"Let's go up to the park," he said. "I have something to tell you."

"Can't you tell me here, where we're comfortable?"

"No, I can't talk sitting down. I must walk."

"Very well, if you must."

They took the wagon road which wound up the left side of the town. To make progress they had to plunge through the mistral as though it were a thick, leathery substance. The cypresses in the park were being swayed almost to the ground.

"What is it you want to tell me?" demanded Gauguin.

He had to shout into Vincent's ear. The wind snatched away his words almost before Vincent could catch them.

"Paul, I've been thinking for the past few days. I've hit upon a wonderful idea."

"Forgive me if I'm a little leery of your wonderful ideas."

"We've all failed as painters. Do you know why?"

"What? I can't hear a word. Shout it in my ear."

"DO YOU KNOW WHY WE'VE ALL FAILED AS PAINTERS?"

"No. Why?"

"Because we paint alone!"

"What the devil?"

"Some things we paint well, some things we paint badly. We throw them all together in a single canvas."

"Brigadier, I'm hanging on your words."

"Do you remember the Both brothers? Dutch painters. One was good at landscape. The other was good at figures. They painted a picture together. One put in the landscape. The other put in the figures. They were successful."

"Well, to bring an interminable story to its obscure point?"

"What? I can't hear you. Come closer."

"I SAID, GO ON!"

"Paul. That's what we must do. You and I. Seurat. Cezanne. Lautrec. Rousseau. We must all work together on the same canvas. That would be a true painter's communism. We would each put in what we did best. Seurat the air. You the landscape. Cezanne the surfaces. Lautrec the figures. I the sun and moon and stars. Together we could be one great artist. What do you say?"

"Turlututu, mon chapeau pointu!"

He burst into raucous, savage laughter. The wind splashed his ridicule into Vincent's face like the spray of the sea.

"Brigadier," he cried, when he could catch his breath, "if that's not the world's greatest idea, I'll eat it. Pardon me while I howl."

He stumbled down the path, holding his stomach, doubled over with delight.

Vincent stood perfectly still.

A rush of blackbirds came out of the sky. Thousands of cawing, beating blackbirds. They swooped down on Vincent, struck him, engulfed him, flew through his hair, into his nose, into his mouth, into his ears, into his eyes, buried him in a thick, black, airless cloud of flapping wings.

Gauguin returned.

"Come on, Vincent, let's go down to Louis's. I feel the need of a celebration after that priceless idea of yours."

Vincent followed him to the Rue des Ricolettes in silence.

Gauguin went upstairs with one of the girls.

Rachel sat on Vincent's lap in the café room.

"Aren't you coming up with me, *fou-rou?*" she asked.

"No."

"Why not?"

"I haven't the five francs."

"Then will you give me your ear instead?"

"Yes."

After a very few moments, Gauguin returned. The two men walked down the hill to the yellow house. Gauguin bolted his supper. He walked out the front door without speaking. He had almost crossed the Place Lamartine when he heard behind him a well known step; short, quick, irregular.

He whirled about.

Vincent rushed upon him, an open razor in his hand.

Gauguin stood rigid and looked at Vincent.

Vincent stopped just two feet away. He glared at Gauguin in the dark. He lowered his head, turned, ran towards home.

Gauguin went to a hotel. He engaged a room, locked the door and went to bed.

Vincent entered the yellow house. He walked up the red brick stairs to his bedroom. He picked up the mirror in which he had painted his own portrait so many times. He set it on the toilet table against the wall.

He looked at his red-shot eyes in the mirror.

The end has come. His life was over. He read that in his face.

He had better make the clean break.

He lifted the razor. He felt the keen steel against the gooseflesh of his throat.

Voices were whispering strange tales to him.

The Arlesian sun threw a wall of blinding fire between his eyes and the glass.

He slashed off his right ear.

He left only a tiny portion of the lobe.

He dropped the razor. He bound his head in towels. The blood dripped onto the floor.

He picked up his ear from the basin. He washed it. He wrapped it in several pieces of drawing paper. He tied the bundle in newspaper.

He pulled a Basque beret down over the thick bandage. He walked down the stairs to the front door. He crossed the Place Lamartine, climbed the hill, rang the bell of the Maison de Tolérance, Numero I.

A maid answered the door.

"Send Rachel to me."

Rachel came in a moment.

"Oh, it's you, *fou-rou.* What do you want?"

"I have brought you something."

"For me? A present?"

"Yes."

"How nice you are, *fou-rou.*"

"Guard it carefully. It is a souvenir of me."

"What is it?"

"Open, and you will see."

Rachel unwrapped the papers. She stared in horror at the ear. She fell in a dead faint on the flagstones.

Vincent turned away. He walked down the hill. He crossed the Place Lamartine. He closed the door of the yellow house behind him and went to bed.

When Gauguin returned at seven-thirty the following morning, he found a crowd gathered in front. Roulin was wringing his hands in despair.

"What have you done to your comrade, Monsieur?" asked a man in a melon shaped hat. His tone was abrupt and severe.

"I don't know."

"Oh, yes . . . you know very well . . . he is dead."

It took Gauguin a long time to gather his wits together. The stares of the crowd seemed to tear his person to pieces, suffocating him.

"Let us go upstairs, Monsieur," he said stammeringly. "We can explain ourselves there."

Wet towels lay on the floor of the two lower rooms. The blood had stained the stairway that led up to Vincent's bedroom.

In the bed lay Vincent, rolled in the sheets, humped up like a guncock. He seemed lifeless. Gently, very gently, Gauguin touched the body. It was warm. For Gauguin, it seemed as if he had suddenly got back all his energy, all his spirit.

"Be kind enough, Monsieur," he said in a low voice to the police superintendent, "to awaken this man with great care. If he asks for me, tell him I have left for Paris. The sight of me might prove fatal to him."

The police superintendent sent for a doctor and a cab. They took Vincent to the hospital. Roulin ran alongside of the carriage, panting.

9

Doctor Felix Rey, young interne of the hospital of Arles, was a short, thickset man with an octagonal head and a weed of black hair shooting up from the top of the octagon. He treated Vincent's wound, then put him to bed in a cell-like room from which everything had been removed. He locked the door behind him when he went out.

At sundown, when he was taking his patient's pulse, Vincent awoke. He stared at the ceiling, then the whitewashed wall, then out of the window at the patch of darkening blue sky. His eyes wandered slowly to Doctor Rey's face.

"Hello," he said, softly.

"Hello," replied Doctor Rey.

"Where am I?"

"You're in the hospital of Arles."

"Oh."

A flash of pain went across his face. He lifted his hand to where his right ear had once been. Doctor Rey stopped him.

"You mustn't touch," he said.

" . . . Yes . . . I remember . . . now."

"It's a nice, clean wound, old fellow. I'll have you on your feet within a few days."

"Where is my friend?"

"He has returned to Paris."

" . . . I see . . . May I have my pipe?"

"Not just yet, old fellow."

Doctor Rey bathed and bandaged the wound.

"It's an accident of very little importance," he said. "After all, a man doesn't hear with those cabbages he has stuck on the outside of his head. You won't miss it."

"You are very kind, Doctor. Why is this room . . . so bare?"

"I had everything taken out to protect you."

"Against whom?"

"Against yourself."

" . . . Yes . . . I see . . ."

"Well, I must go now. I'll send the attendant in with your supper. Try to lie perfectly still. The loss of blood has made you weak."

When Vincent awoke in the morning, Theo was sitting by his bedside. Theo's face was pale and drawn, his eyes bloodshot.

"Theo," said Vincent.

Theo slipped off the chair, went on his knees beside the bed, and took Vincent's hand. He wept without shame or restraint.

"Theo . . . always . . . when I wake up . . . and need you . . . you're by my side."

Theo could not speak.

"It was cruel to make you come all the way down here. How did you know?"

"Gauguin telegraphed yesterday. I caught the night train."

"That was wrong of Gauguin to put you to all that expense. You sat up all night, Theo."

"Yes, Vincent."

They were silent for some time.

"I've spoken to Doctor Rey, Vincent. He says it was a sunstroke. You've been working in the sun without a hat, haven't you?"

"Yes."

"Well, you see, old boy, you mustn't. In the future you must wear your hat. Lots of people here in Arles get sunstroke."

Vincent squeezed his hand gently. Theo tried to swallow the lump in his throat.

"I have some news for you, Vincent, but I think it had better wait a few days."

"Is it nice news, Theo?"

"I think you'll like it."

Doctor Rey walked in.

"Well, how's the patient this morning?"

"Doctor, may my brother tell me some good news?"

"I should say so. Here, wait a minute. Let me look at this. Yes, that's fine, that's fine. It'll be healing fast, now."

When the Doctor left the room, Vincent begged for his news.

"Vincent," said Theo, "I've . . . well, I . . . I've met a girl."

"Why, Theo."

"Yes. She's a Dutch girl. Johanna Bunger. She's a lot like mother, I think."

"Do you love her, Theo?"

"Yes. I've been so desperately lonely without you in Paris, Vincent. It wasn't so bad before you came, but after we had lived together for a year . . ."

"I was hard to live with, Theo. I'm afraid I showed you a bad time."

"Oh, Vincent, if you only knew how many times I wished I could walk into the apartment on the Rue Lepic and find your shoes on the sideboard, and your wet canvases all over my bed. But we musn't talk any more. You must rest. We'll just stay here with each other."

Theo remained in Arles two days. He left only when Doctor Rey assured him that Vincent would make a rapid recovery, and that he would take care of his brother, not only as a patient but as a friend.

Roulin came every evening and brought flowers. During the nights Vincent suffered from hallucinations. Doctor Rey put camphor on Vincent's pillow and mattress to overcome his insomnia.

At the end of the fourth day, when the Doctor saw that Vincent was completely rational, he unlocked the door of the room and had the furniture put back.

"May I get up and dress, Doctor?" asked Vincent.

"If you feel strong enough. Come to my office after you have had a little air."

The hospital of Arles was of two stories, built in a quadrangle, with a patio in the centre, full of riotously coloured flowers, ferns, and gravel walks. Vincent strolled about slowly for a few minutes, then went to Doctor Rey's office on the ground floor.

"How does it feel to be on your feet?" asked the Doctor.

"Very good."

"Tell me, Vincent, why did you do it?"

Vincent was silent for a long time.

"I don't know," he said.

"What were you thinking of when you did it?"

" . . . I . . . wasn't . . . thinking, Doctor."

Vincent spent the next few days recovering his strength. One morning, while he was chatting with Doctor Rey in the latter's room, he picked up a razor off the washstand and opened it.

"You need a shave, Doctor Rey," he said. "Would you like me to give you one?"

Doctor Rey backed into a corner, the palm of his hand out before his face.

"No! No! Put that down!"

"But I'm really a good barber, Doctor. I could give you a nice shave."

"Vincent! Put that razor down!"

Vincent laughed, closed the razor, and put it back on the washstand.

"Don't be afraid, my friend. That's all over now."

At the end of the second week Doctor Rey gave Vincent permission to paint. An attendant was sent down to the yellow house to get the easel and canvas. Doctor Rey posed for Vincent just to humour him. Vincent worked slowly, a tiny bit each day. When the portrait was finished he presented it to the Doctor.

"I want you to keep this as a souvenir of me, Doctor. It is the only way I have of showing my gratitude for your kindness."

"That is very nice of you, Vincent. I am honoured."

The doctor took the portrait home and used it to cover a crack in the wall.

Vincent stayed at the hospital two weeks longer. He painted the patio, baking in the sun. He wore a wide straw hat while he worked. The flower garden took him the full two weeks to paint.

"You must drop in to see me every day," said Doctor Rey, shaking hands with Vincent at the front gate of the hospital. "And remember, no absinthe, no excitement, and no working in the sun without that hat."

"I promise, Doctor. And thank you for everything."

"I shall write your brother that you are now completely well."

Vincent found that the landlord had made a contract to turn him out and give the yellow house to a tobacconist. Vincent was deeply attached to the yellow house. It was his sole root in the soil of Provence. He had painted every inch of it, inside and out. He had made it habitable. In spite of the accident, he still considered it his permanent home, and he was determined to fight the landlord to the bitter end.

At first he was afraid to sleep alone in the house because of his insomnia, which not even the camphor could overcome. Doctor Rey had given him bromide of potassium to rout the unbearable hallucinations that had been frightening him. At length the voices that had been whispering queer tales in his ears went away, to come back only in nightmares.

He was still far too weak to go out and work. The serenity returned but slowly to his brain. His blood revived from day to day and his appetite increased. He had a gay dinner with Roulin at the restaurant, quite cheerful and with no dread of renewed suffering. He began working gingerly on a portrait of Roulin's wife, which had been unfinished at the time of the accident. He liked the way he had ranged the reds from rose to orange, rising through the yellows to lemon, with light and sombre greens.

His health and his work picked up slowly. He had known before that one could fracture one's legs and arms, and after that recover, but he was rather astonished that one could fracture the brain in one's head and recover after that, too.

One afternoon he went to ask after Rachel's health.

"Pigeon," he said, "I'm sorry for all the trouble I caused you."

"It's all right, *fou-rou*. You musn't worry about it. In this town things like that are not out of the way."

His friends came in and assured him that in Provence everyone suffered either from fever, hallucinations or madness.

"It's nothing unusual, Vincent," said Roulin. "Down here in Tartarin's country we are all a trifle cracked."

"Well, well," said Vincent, "we understand each other like members of the same family."

A few more weeks passed. Vincent was now able to work all day in the studio. Thoughts of madness and death left his mind. He began to feel almost normal.

Finally he ventured out of doors to paint. The sun was burning up the magnificent yellow of the cornfields. But Vincent could not capture it. He had been eating regularly, sleeping regularly, avoiding excitement and intense enthusiasm.

He was feeling so normal he could not paint.

"You are a *grand nerveux*, Vincent," Doctor Rey had told him. "You never have been normal. But then, no artist is normal; if he were, he wouldn't be an artist. Normal men don't create works of art. They eat, sleep, hold down routine jobs, and die. You are hypersensitive to life and nature; that's why you are able to interpret for the rest of us. But if you are not careful, that very hypersensitiveness will lead you to your destruction. The strain of it breaks every artist in time."

Vincent knew that to attain the high yellow note which dominated his Arlesian canvases he had to be on edge, strung up, throbbingly excited, passionately sensitive, his nerves rasped raw.

If he allowed himself to get into that state, he could paint again as brilliantly as he had before. But the road led to destruction.

"An artist is a man with his work to do," he murmured to himself. "How stupid for me to remain alive if I can't paint the way I want to paint."

He walked in the fields without his hat, absorbing the power of the sun. He drank in the mad colours of the sky, the yellow ball of fire, the green fields and bursting flowers. He let the mistral lash him, the thick night sky throttle him, the sunflowers whip his imagination to a bursting point. As his excitement rose, he lost his appetite for food. He began to live on coffee, absinthe, and tobacco. He lay awake nights with the deep colours of the country-side rushing past his bloodshot eyes. And at last he loaded his easel on his back and went into the fields.

His powers came back; his sense of the universal rhythm of nature, his ability to smash off a large canvas in a few hours and flood it with glaring, brilliant sunshine. Each day saw a new picture created; each day saw a rise in his emotional gauge. He painted thirty-seven canvases without a pause.

One morning he awoke feeling lethargic. He could not work. He sat on a chair. He stared at a wall. He hardly moved all through the day. The voices came back to his ears and told him queer, queer tales. When night fell he walked to the grey restaurant and sat down at a little table. He ordered soup. The waitress brought it to him. A voice rang sharply in his ear, warning him.

He swept the plate of soup to the floor. The dish smashed in fragments.

"You're trying to poison me!" he screamed. "You put poison in that soup!"

He jumped to his feet and kicked over the table. Some of the customers ran out the door. Others stared at him agape.

"You're all trying to poison me!" he shouted. "You want to murder me! I saw you put poison in that soup!"

Two gendarmes came in and carried him bodily up the hill to the hospital.

After twenty-four hours he became quite calm and discussed the affair with Doctor Rey. He worked a little each day, took walks in the country, returned to the hospital for his supper and sleep. Sometimes he had moods of indescribable mental anguish, sometimes moments when the veil of time and of inevitable circumstance seemed for the twinkling of an eye to be parted.

Doctor Rey allowed him to paint again. Vincent did an orchard of peach trees beside a road, with the Alps in the background; an olive grove with leaves of old silver, silver turning to green against the blue, and with orange-coloured ploughed earth.

After three weeks, Vincent returned to the yellow house. By now the town, and especially the Place Lamartine, was incensed against him. The severed ear and the poisoned soup were more than they could accept with equanimity. The Arlesians were firmly convinced that painting drove men mad. When Vincent passed they stared at him, made remarks out loud, sometimes even crossed the street so as to avoid passing him.

Not a restaurant in the city would allow him to enter the front door.

The children of Arles gathered before the yellow house and made up games to torment him.

"*Fou-rou! Fou-rou!*" they cried out. "Cut off your other ear."

Vincent locked his windows. The shouts and laughter of the children drifted through.

"*Fou-rou! Fou-rou!*"

"Crazy man! Crazy man!"

They made up a little song which they sang beneath his window.

> *Fou-rou* was a crazy man
> Who cut off his right ear.
> Now no matter how you shout,
> The crazy man can't hear.

Vincent tried going out to escape them. They followed him through the streets, into the fields, a jolly crowd of singing and laughing urchins.

Day after day their number increased as they gathered before the yellow house. Vincent stuffed his ears with cotton. He worked at his easel, making duplicates of his pictures. The words of the children came through the cracks and the walls. They seared into his brain.

The young boys became more bold. They clambered up the drain pipes like little monkeys, sat on the window sills, peered into the room and shouted at Vincent's back.

"*Fou-rou,* cut off your other ear. We want your other ear!"

The tumult in the Place Lamartine increased. The boys put up boarding on which they could climb to the second floor. They broke the windows, poked their heads in, threw things at Vincent. The crowd below encouraged them, echoed their songs and shouts.

"Get us the other ear. We want the other ear!"

"*Fou-rou!* Want some candy? Look out, it's poisoned!"

"*Fou-rou!* Want some soup? Look out, it's poisoned!"

> *Fou-rou* was a crazy man
> Who cut off his right ear.
> Now no matter how you shout,
> The crazy man can't hear.

The boys perched on the window sill led the crowd below in a chant. Together, they sang with an ever rising crescendo.

"*Fou-rou, fou-rou,* throw us your ear, throw us your ear!"

"FOU-ROU, FOU-ROU, THROW US YOUR EAR, THROW US YOUR EAR!"

Vincent lurched up from his easel. There were three urchins sitting on his window sill, chanting. He lashed out at them. They scampered down the boarding. The crowd below roared. Vincent stood at the window, looking down at them.

A rush of blackbirds came out of the sky, thousands of cawing, beating blackbirds. They darkened the Place Lamartine, swooped down on Vincent, struck him, filled the room, engulfed him, flew through his hair, into his nose and mouth and eyes, buried him in a thick, black, airless cloud of flapping wings.

Vincent jumped onto the window sill.

"Go away!" he screamed. "You fiends, go way! For God's sake, leave me in peace!"

"FOU-ROU, FOU-ROU, THROW US YOUR EAR, THROW US YOUR EAR!"

"Go away! Let me alone! Do you hear, let me alone!"

He picked up the wash basin from the table and flung it down at them. It smashed on the cobblestones below. He ran about in a rage picking up everything he could lay his hands on and flinging them down into the Place Lamartine to be hopelessly smashed. His chairs, his easel, his mirror, his table, his bedclothing, his sunflower canvases from the walls, all rained down on the urchins of Provence. And with each article there went a flashing panorama of his days in the yellow house, of the sacrifices he had made to buy, one by one, these simple articles with which he was to furnish the house of his life.

When he had laid the room bare, he stood by the window, every nerve quivering. He fell across the sill. His head hung down toward the cobblestone Place.

10

A petition was immediately circulated in the Place Lamartine. Ninety men and women signed it.

To Mayor Tardieu:

We, the undersigned citizens of Arles, are firmly convinced that Vincent Van Gogh, resident at Place Lamartine, 2, is a dangerous lunatic, not fit to be left at large.

We hereby call upon you as our Mayor to have this madman locked up.

It was very close to election time in Arles. Mayor Tardieu did not wish to displease so many voters. He ordered the superintendent of police to arrest Vincent.

The *gendarmes* found him lying on the floor below the window sill. They carried him off to jail. He was put in a cell, under lock and key. A keeper was stationed outside his door.

When Vincent returned to consciousness, he asked to see Doctor Rey. He was refused permission. He asked for pencil and paper to write Theo. It was refused.

At length Doctor Rey gained entrance to the jail.

"Try to restrain your indignation, Vincent," he said, "otherwise they will convict you of being a dangerous lunatic, and that will be the end of you. Besides, strong emotion can only aggravate your case. I will write to your brother, and between us we will get you out of here."

"I beg you, Doctor, don't let Theo come down here. He's just going to be married. It will spoil everything for him."

"I'll tell him not to come. I think I have a good plan for you."

Two days later Doctor Rey came back. The keeper was still stationed in front of the cell.

"Listen, Vincent," he said, "I just watched them move you out of your yellow house. The landlord stored your furniture in the basement of one of the cafés, and he has your paintings under lock and key. He says he won't give them up until you pay the back rent."

Vincent was silent.

"Since you can't go back there, I think you had better try to work out my plan. There is no telling how often these epileptic fits will come back on you. If you have peace and quiet and pleasant surroundings, and don't excite yourself, you may have seen the last of them. On the other hand, they may recur every month or two. So to protect yourself, and others about you . . . I think it would be advisable . . . to go into . . ."

". . . A *maison de santé*?"

"Yes."

"Then you think I am . . . ?"

"No, my dear Vincent, you are not. You can see for yourself that you are as sane as I. But these epileptic fits are like any other kind of fever. They make a man go out of his head. And when a nervous crisis comes on, you naturally do irrational things. That's why you ought to be in a hospital, where you can be looked after."

"I see."

"There is a good place in St. Remy, just twenty-five kilometres from here. It's called St. Paul de Mausole. They take first, second, and third-class patients. The third class is a hundred francs a month. You could manage that. The place was formerly a monastery, right up against the base of the hills. It is beautiful, Vincent, and quiet, oh, so quiet. You will have a doctor to advise you, and sisters to take care of you. The food will be plain and good. You will be able to recover your health."

"Would I be allowed to paint?"

"Why, of course, old fellow. You'll be allowed to do whatever you wish . . . providing it doesn't injure you. It will be just like being in a hospital with enormous grounds. If you live quietly that way for a year, you may be completely cured."

"But how will I get out of this hole?"

"I have spoken to the superintendent of police. He agrees to let you go to St. Paul de Mausole, providing I take you there."

"And you say it is really a nice place?"

"Oh, charming, Vincent. You'll find loads of things to paint."

"How nice. A hundred francs a month isn't so much. Perhaps that's just what I need for a year, to quiet me down."

"Of course it is. I have already written to your brother, telling him about it. I suggested that in your present state of health it would be inadvisable to move you very far; certainly not to Paris. I told him that in my opinion St. Paul would be the very best thing for you."

"Well, if Theo agrees . . . Anything, just so long as I don't cause him more trouble . . ."

"I expect an answer any hour. I'll come back when I get it."

Theo had no alternative. He acquiesced. He sent money to pay his brother's bills. Doctor Rey took Vincent in a carriage to the station where they boarded the train for Tarascon. At Tarascon they took a little branch line that wound up a green, fertile valley to St. Remy.

It was two kilometres up a steep hill, through the sleeping town, to St. Paul de Mausole. Vincent and Doctor Rey hired a carriage. The road led straight to a ridge of black, barren mountains. From a short way off Vincent saw, nestled at their base, the sod-brown walls of the monastery.

The carriage stopped. Vincent and Doctor Rey got out. On the right of the road there was a cleared, circular space with a Temple of Vesta and a Triumphal Arch.

"How in the world did these get here?" demanded Vincent.

"This used to be an important Roman settlement. The river, which you see down there, once filled this whole valley. It came right up to where you're standing. As the river receded, the town crawled lower and lower down the hill. Now nothing is left here except these dead monuments, and the monastery."

"Interesting."

"Come, Vincent, Doctor Peyron is expecting us."

They left the road and walked through a patch of pines to the gate of the monastery. Doctor Rey pulled an iron knob which sounded a loud bell. After a few moments the gate opened and Doctor Peyron appeared.

"How do you do, Doctor Peyron?" said Doctor Rey. "I have brought you my friend, Vincent Van Gogh, as we arranged by mail. I know that you will take good care of him."

"Yes, Doctor Rey, we will take care of him."

"You will forgive me if I run, Doctor? I just have time to catch that train back to Tarascon."

"Of course, Doctor Rey. I understand."

"Good-bye, Vincent," said Doctor Rey. "Be happy, and you will get well. I will come to see you as often as I can. By the end of a year I expect to find you a completely well man."

"Thank you, Doctor. You are very kind. Good-bye."

"Good-bye, Vincent."

He turned and walked away through the pines.

"Will you come in, Vincent?" asked Doctor Peyron, stepping aside.

Vincent walked past Doctor Peyron.

The gate of the insane asylum locked behind him.

BOOK SEVEN

ST. REMY

1

The ward in which the inmates slept was like a third-class waiting room in some dead-alive village. The lunatics always wore their hats, spectacles, canes, and travelling cloaks, just as though they were on the point of leaving for somewhere.

Sister Deschanel brought Vincent through the long corridor-like room and indicated an empty bed.

"You will sleep here, Monsieur," she said. "At night you will pull the curtains for privacy. Doctor Peyron wishes to see you in his office when you are settled."

The eleven men sitting about the unlit stove neither noticed nor commented upon Vincent's arrival. Sister Deschanel walked down the long narrow room, her starched white gown, black cape, and black veil standing out stiffly behind her.

Vincent dropped his valise and looked about. Both sides of the ward were lined with beds sloping downward at an angle of five degrees, each surrounded by a framework on which were hung dirty cream-coloured curtains. The roof was of rough beams, the walls were whitewashed, and in the centre was a stove with an angular pipe coming out of its left side. There was a lone lamp in the room, hung just above the stove.

Vincent wondered why the men were so quiet. They did not speak to each other. They did not read or play games. They leaned on their walking sticks and looked at the stove.

There was a box nailed to the wall by the head of his bed, but Vincent preferred to keep his belongings in his valise. He put his pipe, tobacco, and a book in the box, shoved the valise under the bed and walked out into the garden. On the way he passed a row of dark, dank looking rooms, locked tight and abandoned.

The patio cloister was utterly deserted. There were large pines beneath which grew tall and unkempt grass mixed with rampant weeds. The walls enclosed a square of stagnant sunlight. Vincent turned to his left and knocked on the door of the private house in which Doctor Peyron and his family lived.

Doctor Peyron had been a *médecin de marine* at Marseilles, after that an oculist. A severe case of gout had caused him to search for a *maison de santé* in the quiet of the country.

240

"You see, Vincent," said the Doctor, gripping a corner of the desk with each hand, "formerly I took care of the health of the body. At present I take care of the health of the soul. It is the same *métier*."

"You have had experience with nervous diseases, Doctor. Can you explain why I cut off my ear?"

"That is not at all unusual with epileptics, Vincent. I have had two similar cases. The auditory nerves become extremely sensitive, and the patient thinks he can stop the hallucinations by cutting off the auricle."

" . . . Oh . . . I see. And the treatments I am to have . . .?"

"Treatments? Well . . . ah . . . you must have at least two hot baths a week. I insist upon that. And you must stay in the baths for two hours. They will calm you."

"And what else am I to do, Doctor?"

"You are to remain perfectly quiet. You must not excite yourself. Do not work, do not read, do not argue or get upset."

"I know . . . I am too weak to work."

"If you do not wish to participate in the religious life of St. Paul, I will tell the sisters not to insist upon it. If there is anything you need, come to me."

"Thank you, Doctor."

"Supper is at five. You will hear the gong. Try to fit into the pattern of the hospital, Vincent, as quickly as you can. It will speed your recovery."

Vincent stumbled through the chaotic garden, passed the crumbling portico at the entrance to the third-class building, and walked by the row of dark, deserted cells. He sat on his bed in the ward. His companions were still sitting about the stove in silence. After a time he heard a noise from another room. The eleven men rose with an air of grim determination and stormed down the ward. Vincent followed them.

The room in which they ate had an earthen floor and no window. There was just one long, rough, wooden table with benches about it. The sisters served the food. It tasted mouldy, as in a shoddy boarding house. First there was soup and black bread; the cockroaches in the soup made Vincent homesick for the restaurants of Paris. Next he was served a dish of chick peas, beans, and lentils. His companions ate with all their might, brushing the crumbs of black bread from the table into their hands, and then licking them off with their tongues.

The meal finished, the men returned to the identical chairs about the stove and digested their food with intense concentration. When the supper had gone down, they rose one by one, undressed, pulled the curtains and went to sleep. Vincent had not as yet heard them utter a sound.

The sun was just setting. Vincent stood at the window and looked over the green valley. There was a superb sky of pale lemon, against which the mournful pines stood out in designs of exquisite black lace. The sight moved Vincent to nothing, not even the faint desire to paint it.

He stood at the window until the heavy Provençal dusk filtered through the lemon sky and absorbed the colour. No one came into the ward to light the lamp. There was nothing to do in the darkness but think of one's life.

Vincent undressed and went to bed. He lay there wide-eyed, staring at the rough beams of the ceiling. The angle of the bed pitched him downward toward the base. He had brought Delacroix's book with him. He fumbled in the box, found it and held the leather covering against his heart in the darkness. The feel of it reassured him. He did not belong with these lunatics who surrounded him, but with the great master whose words of wisdom and comfort flowed through the stiff binding and into his aching heart.

After a time he fell asleep. He was awakened by a low moaning in the bed next to his. The moans became louder and louder, until they broke into cries and a flood of vehement words.

"Go away! Stop following me! Why do you follow me? I didn't kill him! You can't fool me. I know who you are. You're the secret police! Well, search me if you like! I didn't steal that money! He murdered himself on Wednesday! Go way! For God's sake, leave me alone!"

Vincent jumped up and pushed aside the curtain. He saw a blond haired young boy of twenty-three, tearing at his nightgown with his teeth. When the boy saw Vincent, he sprang to his knees and clasped his hands fervently before him.

"Monsieur Mounet-Sully, don't take me away! I didn't do it, I tell you! I'm not a sodomist! I'm a lawyer! I'll handle all your cases, Monsieur Mounet-Sully, only don't arrest me! I couldn't have killed him last Wednesday! I haven't the money! Look! It isn't here!"

He tore the covers off him and began ripping up the bed in a paroxysm of maniacal frenzy, crying out all the while against the secret police and the false accusations against him. Vincent did not know what to do. All the other inmates seemed to be sleeping soundly.

Vincent ran to the next bed, slipped aside the curtain and shook the man in it. The fellow opened his eyes and stared at Vincent stupidly.

"Get up and help me quiet him," said Vincent. "I'm afraid he will do himself some harm."

The man in bed began to dribble at the right corner of his mouth. He let out a stream of blubbering, inarticulate sounds.

"Quick," cried Vincent. "It will take two of us to hold him down."

He felt a hand on his shoulder. He whirled about. One of the older men was standing behind him.

"No use bothering with this one," said the man. "He's an idiot. Hasn't uttered a word since he's been here. Come, we'll quiet the boy."

The young blond had dug a hole in the mattress with his fingernails and was crouched on his knees above it, pulling out the straw and stuffing. When he saw Vincent again, he began shouting legal quotations. He beat his hands against Vincent's chest.

"Yes, yes, I killed him! I killed him! But it wasn't for pederasty! I didn't do that, Monsieur Mounet-Sully. Not last Wednesday. It was for his money! Look! I have it! I hid the wallet in the mattress! I'll find it for you! Only make the secret police stop following me! I can go free, even if I did kill him! I'll cite you cases to prove . . . Here! I'll dig it out of the mattress!"

"Take his other arm," said the old man to Vincent.

They held the boy down on the bed, but his ravings rang out for over an hour. Finally, exhausted, his words sank to a jarred mumbling and he dropped off in a feverish sleep. The older man came around to Vincent's side.

"The boy was studying for the bar," he said. "He overworked his brain. These attacks come on about every ten days. He never hurts anyone. Good night to you, Monsieur."

The older man returned to his bed and promptly fell asleep. Vincent went once again to the window that overlooked the valley. It was still a long time before sunrise and nothing was visible but the morning star. He remembered the painting Daubigny had made of the morning star, expressing all the vast peace and majesty of the universe . . . and all the feeling of heartbreak for the puny individual who stood below, gazing at it.

2

The next morning after breakfast the men went out into the garden. Beyond the far wall could be seen the ridge of desolate, barren hills, dead since the Romans first crossed them. Vincent watched the inmates play lackadaisically at bowls. He sat on a stone bench and gazed at the thick trees covered with ivy, then at the ground dotted with periwinkle. The sisters, of the order of St. Joseph d'Aubenas, passed on their way to the old Roman chapel, mouse-like figures in black and white, their eyes drawn deep into their heads, fingering their beads and mumbling the morning prayers.

After an hour at mute bowls, the men returned to the cool of their ward. They sat about the unlit stove. Their utter idleness appalled Vincent. He could not understand why they did not even have an old newspaper to read.

When he could bear it no longer, he went again into the garden and walked about. Even the sun at St. Paul seemed to be moribund.

The buildings of the old monastery had been put up in the conventional quadrangle; on the north was the ward of the third-class patients; on the east Doctor Peyron's house, the chapel, and a tenth century cloister; on the south the buildings of the first and second-class inmates; and on the west, the courtyard of the dangerous lunatics, and a long, dead-clay wall. The locked and barred gate was the only exit. The walls were twelve feet high, smooth and unscalable.

Vincent returned to a stone bench near a wild rose bush and sat down. He tried to reason with himself and get a clear idea of why he had come to St. Paul. A terrible dismay and horror seized him and prevented him from thinking. In his head he could find neither hope nor desire.

He stumbled toward his quarters. The moment he entered the portico of the building he heard the queer howling of a dog. Before he reached the door of the ward, the noise had changed from the howl of a dog to the cry of a wolf.

Vincent walked down the length of the ward. In the far corner, his face to the wall, he saw the old man of the night before. The man's face was raised to the ceiling. He was howling with all the strength of his lungs, a bestial look on his face. The cry of the wolf gave way to some strange jungle call. The mournful sound of it flooded the room.

"What sort of a menagerie am I a prisoner in?" Vincent demanded of himself.

The men about the stove paid no attention. The wails of the animal in the corner rose to a pitch of despair.

"I must do something for him," said Vincent, aloud.

The blond boy stopped him.

"It is better to leave him alone," he said. "If you speak to him, he will fly into a rage. It will be over in a few hours."

The walls of the monastery were thick, but all through lunch Vincent could hear the changing cries of the afflicted one straining through the vast silence. He spent the afternoon in a far corner of the garden, trying to escape the frenetic wails.

That night at supper, a young man whose left side was paralyzed, grabbed up a knife, sprang to his feet, and held the knife over his heart with his right hand.

"The time has come!" he shouted. "I shall kill myself!"

The man on his right side rose wearily and gripped the paralytic's arm.

"Not today, Raymond," he said. "Today is Sunday."

"Yes, yes, today! I won't live! I refuse to live! Let go of my arm! I want to kill myself!"

"Tomorrow, Raymond, tomorrow. This isn't the right day."

"Let go of my arm! I shall plunge this knife into my heart! I tell you, I've got to kill myself!"

"I know, I know, but not now. Not now."

He took the knife from Raymond's hand and led him, weeping in a rage of impotence, back to the ward.

Vincent turned to the man next to him, whose red-rimmed eyes were watching his trembling fingers anxiously as he tried to carry the soup to his mouth.

"What is the matter with him?" he asked.

The syphilitic lowered his spoon and said, "Not a day has passed for a whole year that Raymond has not tried to commit suicide."

"Why does he try it here?" asked Vincent. "Why doesn't he steal the knife and kill himself when everyone has gone to sleep?"

"Perhaps he does not wish to die, Monsieur."

While Vincent was watching them play bowls the following morning, one of the men suddenly fell to the ground and went into a convulsive paroxysm.

"Quick. It's his epileptic fit," shouted someone.

"On his arms and legs."

It took four of them to hold his arms and legs. The writhing epileptic seemed to have the strength of a dozen men. The young blond reached into his pocket, pulled out a spoon, and thrust it between the prostrate man's teeth.

"Here, hold his head," he cried to Vincent.

The epileptic went through a rising and falling series of convulsions, their peaks mounting ever higher and higher. His eyes rolled in their sockets and the foam lathered from the corners of his mouth.

"Why do you hold that spoon in his mouth?" grunted Vincent.

"So he won't bite his tongue."

After a half hour the shuddering man sank into unconsciousness. Vincent and two of the others carried him to his bed. That was the end of the affair; no one mentioned it again.

By the end of a fortnight, Vincent had seen every one of his eleven companions go through his own particular form of insanity: the noisy maniac who tore his clothes off his body and smashed everything in sight; the man who howled like an animal; the two syphilitics; the suicide monomaniac; the paralytics who suffered from excess of fury and exaltation; the epileptic; the lymphomaniac with a persecution mania; the young blond who was being pursued by secret police.

Not a day went by without some one of them having a seizure; not a day passed but that Vincent was called to calm some momentary maniac. The third-class patients had to be each other's doctors and nurses. Peyron looked in but once a week, and the guardians bothered only with the first- and second-class residents. The men stayed close together, helped each other in the moments of affliction, and had endless patience; each of them knew that his turn was coming again, soon, and that he would need the help and forebearance of his neighbours.

It was a fraternity of *fous*.

Vincent was glad that he had come. By seeing the truth about the life of madmen he slowly lost the vague dread, the fear of insanity. Bit by bit he came to consider madness as a disease like any other. By the third week he found his comates no more frightening than if they had been stricken by consumption or cancer.

He often sat and chatted with the idiot. The idiot could only answer with incoherent sounds, but Vincent felt that the fellow understood him and was pleased to be talking. The sisters never spoke to the men unless it was imperative. Vincent's portion of rational intercourse each week consisted of his five minute conversation with Doctor Peyron.

"Tell me, Doctor," he said, "why do the men never talk to each other? Some of them seem intelligent enough, when they are well."

"They can't talk, Vincent, for the minute they begin to talk, they argue, get excited, and bring a seizure upon themselves. So they've learned that the only way they can live is by remaining utterly quiet."

"They might just as well be dead, mightn't they?"

Peyron shrugged. "That, my dear Vincent, is a matter of opinion."

"But why don't they at least read. I should think that books . . ."

"Reading starts their minds churning, Vincent, and the first thing we know, they have a violent attack. No, my friend, they must inhabit the closed world of their own. There is no need to feel sorry for them. Don't you remember what Dryden said? 'There is pleasure, sure, in being mad, which none but madmen know.' ''

A month passed. Not once did Vincent have the least desire to be elsewhere. Nor did he notice in any of the others a definite wish to get away. He knew this came from the feeling that they were all too thoroughly shattered for the life outside.

And over the ward hung the fetid odour of decaying men.

Vincent held the spirit of himself together rigidly, against that day when the desire and strength to paint should return to him. His fellow inmates vegetated in idleness, thinking only of their three meals a day. In order to discipline himself against this surrender, Vincent refused to eat any of the stale and slightly spoiled food. He swallowed only a little black bread and soup. Theo sent him a one-volume edition of Shakespeare; he read "Richard II," "Henry IV," and "Henry V," projecting his mind to other days and other places.

He fought valiantly to keep grief from gathering in his heart like water in a swamp.

Theo was now married. He and his wife Johanna wrote to Vincent often. Theo's health was poor. Vincent worried more about his brother than he did about himself. He begged Johanna to give Theo wholesome Dutch food once more, after ten years of restaurant fare.

Vincent knew that work distracted him infinitely better than anything else, and that if he could only throw himself into it with all his strength, it might possibly be the best remedy. The men in the ward had nothing to save them from a rotting death; he had his painting which would take him out of the asylum a well and happy man.

At the end of the sixth week, Doctor Peyron gave Vincent a little room for a studio. It was done in greenish-grey paper, and had two curtains of sea-green with a design of very pale roses. The curtains, and an old armchair covered with an upholstery splashed like a Monticelli, had been left behind by one of the wealthier inmates who had died. The room looked out on a slanting cornfield, and freedom. There were thick black bars across the window.

Vincent promptly painted the landscape that he saw from the window. In the foreground was a field of corn ruined and dashed to the ground after a storm. A boundary wall ran down a slope, and beyond the grey foliage of a few olive trees were some huts and hills. At the top of the canvas Vincent put a great grey and white cloud drowned in the azure.

He returned to the ward at supper time, exultant. His power had not left him. He had come face to face with nature again. The feeling for work had held him and forced him to create.

The insane asylum could not kill him now. He was on the road to recovery. In a few months he would be out. He would be free to return to Paris and his old friends. Life was beginning for him once more. He wrote Theo a long, tumultuous letter, with demands for pigments, canvas, brushes, and interesting books.

The next morning the sun came out, yellow and hot. The cicadas in the garden began to sing with a harsh cry, ten times stronger than that of the crickets. Vincent took his easel out and painted the pine trees, the bushes and the walks. His ward mates came to look over his shoulder, but remained perfectly silent and respectful.

"They have better manners than the good people of Arles," murmured Vincent to himself.

Late that afternoon he went to see Doctor Peyron. "I am feeling perfectly well, Doctor, and I should like your permission to go outside the grounds to paint."

"Yes, you are certainly looking better, Vincent. The baths and quiet have helped you. But don't you think it a bit dangerous to go out so soon?"

"Dangerous? Why, no. How?"

"Suppose you . . . had an attack . . . in the fields . . .?"

Vincent laughed. "No more attacks for me, Doctor. I'm through with them. I feel better than I did before they began."

"No, Vincent, I'm afraid . . ."

"Please, Doctor. If I can go wherever I wish, and paint the things I love, don't you see how much happier I will be?"

"Well, if work is what you need . . ."

And so the gate was unlocked for Vincent. He loaded his easel on his back and went in search of pictures. He spent whole days in the hills behind the asylum. The cypress trees about St. Remy began to occupy his thoughts. He wanted to make something of them, like his sunflower canvases. It astonished him that they had not yet been painted as he saw them. He found them as beautiful in line and proportion as an Egyptian obelisk; splashes of black in a sunny landscape.

The old habits of the Arlesian days returned. Each morning at sunrise he trudged out with a blank canvas; each sundown saw it transcribed from nature. If there was any lessening of his power and ability, he could not perceive it. Every day he felt stronger, more sensitive, surer of himself.

Now that he was again master of his own destiny, he no longer feared eating at the asylum board. He devoured his food avidly, even the cockroach soup. He needed food for his working strength. He had nothing to fear now. He was in complete control of himself.

When he had been in the asylum three months, he found a cypress motif that lifted him out of his troubles, beyond all the suffering he had endured. The trees were massive. The foreground was low with brambles and brushwood. Behind were some violet hills, a green and rose sky with a decrescent moon. He painted the clump of brambles in the foreground very thick, with touches of yellow, violet and green. When he looked at his canvas that night he knew that he had come up out of the pit and was standing once more on solid earth, his face to the sun.

In his overwhelming joy he saw himself once again a free man.

Theo sent some extra money, so Vincent secured permission to go to Arles and recover his pictures. The people in the Place Lamartine were courteous to him, but the sight of the yellow house made him very ill. He thought he was going to faint. Instead of visiting Roulin and Doctor Rey, as he had planned, he went in search of the landlord, who had his pictures.

Vincent did not return to the asylum that night as he had promised. The following day he was found between Tarascon and St. Remy, lying face downward in a ditch.

3

Fever clouded his mind for three weeks. The men in the ward, whom he had pitied because their attacks were recurrent, were very patient with him. When he recovered sufficiently to realize what had happened, he kept repeating to himself.

"It is abominable. It is abominable!"

Toward the end of the third week, when he was beginning to walk about the barren, corridor-like room for a little exercise, the sisters brought in a new patient. He allowed himself to be led to his bed very docilely, but once the sisters were gone, he broke into a violent rage. He ripped all the clothes off his body and tore them to shreds, shouting at the top of his voice all the time. He clawed his bed to pieces, smashed the box nailed to the wall, pulled down the curtains, broke the frame, and kicked his valise into a shapeless mass.

The inmates never touched a newcomer. At length two guardians came and hauled the maniac away. He was locked in a cell down the corridor. He howled like a savage beast for two weeks. Vincent heard him night and day. Then the cries ceased altogether. Vincent watched the guardians bury the man in the little cemetery behind the chapel.

A terrible fit of depression came over Vincent. The more his health returned to normal, the more his brain could reason in cold blood, the more foolish it seemed to him to go on painting when it cost so much and brought in nothing. And yet if he did not work, he could not live.

Doctor Peyron gave him some meat and wine from his own table, but refused to let him go near his studio. Vincent did not mind so long as he was convalescing, but when his strength returned and he found himself condemned to the intolerable idleness of his companions, he revolted.

"Doctor Peyron," he said, "my work is necessary for me to recover. If you make me sit about in idleness, like those madmen, I shall become one of them."

"I know, Vincent, but it was working so hard that brought on your attack. I must keep you from that excitement."

"No, Doctor, it wasn't work. It was going to Arles that did it. I no sooner saw the Place Lamartine and the yellow house, than I became ill. But if I never go back there again, I'll never have another attack. Please let me go to my studio."

"I am unwilling to take the responsibility in this matter. I shall write to your brother. If he gives his consent, then we'll let you work again."

ₜ The return letter from Theo, urging Doctor Peyron to allow Vincent to paint, brought a revivifying piece of news. Theo was to become a father. The news made Vincent feel as happy and strong as he had before the last attack. He sat down immediately and wrote Theo a glowing letter.

"Do you know what I hope, Theo? It is that a family will be for you what nature, the clods of earth, the grass, the yellow corn, and the peasants are for me. The baby that Johanna is designing for you will give you a grip on reality that is otherwise impossible in a large city. Now certainly you are yourself deep in nature, since you say that Johanna already feels her child quicken."

Once again he went to his studio and painted the scene from the barred window, the cornfield with a little reaper and a big sun. The canvas was all yellow except for the wall, which ran down the slope at a steep, sharp angle, and the background of violet-tinted hills.

Dr. Peyron acquiesced in Theo's wish, and allowed Vincent to go outside the grounds to work. He painted the cypresses which flowed up out of the ground and poured into the yellow roof of sun. He did a canvas of women gathering olives; the soil violet, and farther off yellow ochre; the trees with bronze trunks and green-grey foliage; the sky and the three figures of the women a deep rose.

On his way to work he would stop and talk to the men labouring in the fields. In his own mind he considered himself below these peasants.

"You see," he told one of them, "I plough on my canvases, just as you plough in your field."

The late Provençal autumn came to a focal point of beauty. The earth brought forth all its violets; the burnt-up grass flamed about the little rose flowers in the garden; the green skies contrasted with the varying shades of yellow foliage.

And with the late autumn came Vincent's full strength. He saw that his work was getting on. Good ideas began to spring anew in his mind; he was happy in letting them develop. Because of his long stay he began to feel the country keenly. It was very different in character from Arles. Most of the mistral was stopped by the hills which overlooked the valley. The sun was far less blinding. Now that he had come to understand the country about St. Remy, he did not want to leave the asylum. In the early months of his stay he had prayed that the year would pass without breaking his mind. Now that he was wrapped in his work, he did not know whether he was staying in a hospital or a hotel. Although he felt entirely well, he thought it foolish to move to some chance place and spend another six months getting acquainted with strange terrain.

Letters from Paris kept him in high spirits. Theo's wife was cooking at home for him, and his health was recovering rapidly. Johanna was carrying the baby without difficulty. And every week Theo sent tobacco, chocolate, paints, books, and a ten or twenty franc note.

The memory of his attack after the Arlesian trip vanished from Vincent's mind. Again and again he reassured himself that if he had never gone back to that cursed city, he would have had six months of normal health to his credit. When his studies of the cypresses and olive groves dried, he washed them with water and a little wine to take away the oil in the *pâte*, then sent them to Theo. He received Theo's announcement that he was exhibiting a number of his canvases at the Independents with disappointment, for he felt that he had not yet done his best work. He wanted to hold off until he had perfected his technique.

Letters from Theo assured him that his work was going ahead at a remarkable pace. He decided that when his year was up at the asylum, he would take a house in the village of St. Remy and continue his painting of the Southland. He felt once again the exultant joy that had been his in the Arlesian days before Gauguin arrived, when he was painting his sunflower panels.

One afternoon, when he was working calmly in the fields, his mind began to wander. Late that night the guardians of the asylum found him, several kilometres away from his easel. His body was wrapped about the trunk of a cypress.

4

By the end of the fifth day his senses returned to normal. What hurt him most deeply was the way his fellow inmates accepted the seizure as being inevitable.

Winter came on. Vincent could not find the will to get out of bed, The stove in the centre of the ward now glowed brightly. The men sat about it in frozen silence from morning until night. The windows of the ward were small and high, letting in very little light. The stove heated and spread the thick odour of decay. The sisters, withdrawn even farther into their black capes and hoods, went about mumbling prayers and fingering their crosses. The barren hills in the background stood out like death heads.

Vincent lay awake in his slanting bed. What was it that Scheveningen picture of Mauve's had taught him? *"Savoir souffrir sans se plaindre."* Learn to suffer without complaint, to look on pain without repugnance . . . yes, but in that he ran the risk of vertigo. If he gave in to that pain, that desolation, it would kill him. There came a time in every man's life when it was necessary to fling off suffering as though it were a filthy cloak.

Days passed, each exactly like the last. His mind was barren of ideas and hope. He heard the sisters discuss his work; they wondered if he painted because he was crazy, or if he was crazy because he painted.

The idiot sat by his bedside and blubbered to him for hours. Vincent felt a warmth in the man's friendliness and did not chase him away. Often he talked to the idiot, for there was no one else who would listen.

"They think my work has driven me crazy," he said to the man one day, as two of the sisters passed. "I know that at bottom it is fairly true that a painter is a man too much absorbed by what his eyes see, and is not sufficiently master of the rest of his life. But does that make him unfit to live in this world?"

The idiot only drooled.

It was a line from Delacroix's book that finally gave him the strength to get out of bed. "I discovered painting," said Delacroix, "when I no longer had teeth or breath."

For several weeks he did not even have the desire to go into the garden. He sat in the ward near the stove, reading the books that Theo sent from Paris. When one of his neighbours was taken with an attack, he did not look up or get out of his chair. Insanity had become sanity; the abnormal had become the normal. It was so long since he had lived with rational people that he no longer looked upon his fellow inmates as irrational.

"I'm sorry, Vincent," said Doctor Peyron, "but I cannot give you permission to leave the grounds again. In the future you must stay within the walls."

"You will permit me to work in my studio?"

"I advise you against it."

"Would you prefer me to commit suicide, Doctor?"

"Very well, work in your studio. But only for a few hours a day."

Even the sight of his easel and brushes could not destroy Vincent's lethargy. He sat in the Monticelli armchair and stared through the iron bars at the barren cornfield.

A few days later he was summoned to Doctor Peyron's office to sign for a registered letter. When he slit open the envelope, he found a check for four hundred francs made out in his name. It was the largest sum of money he had ever possessed at one time. He wondered what on earth Theo had sent it for.

My Dear Vincent:

At last! One of your canvases has been bought for four hundred francs! It was *Red Vineyard,* the one you painted at Arles last spring. It was bought by Anna Bock, sister of the Dutch painter.

Congratulations, old boy! Soon we'll be selling you all over Europe! Use this money to come back to Paris, if Doctor Peyron agrees.

I have recently met a delightful man, Doctor Gachet, who has a home in Auvers-sur-l'Oise, just an hour from Paris. Every important painter since Daubigny has worked in his home. He claims he understands your case thoroughly, and that any time you want to come to Auvers, he will take care of you.

I'll write again tomorrow.
Theo

Vincent showed Doctor Peyron and his wife the letter. Peyron read it thoughtfully, then fingered the check. He congratulated Vincent on his good fortune. Vincent walked down the path, the soft stuff of his brain springing to firm life again with feverish activity. Half-way across the garden he saw that he had taken the check with him but left Theo's letter in the Doctor's office. He turned and walked back quickly.

He was about to knock on the door when he heard his name mentioned inside. He hesitated for a moment, irresolute.

"Then why do you suppose he did it?" demanded Madame Peyron.

"Perhaps he thought it would be good for his brother."

"But if he can't afford the money . . .?"

"I suppose he thought it was worth it, to bring Vincent back to normal."

"Then you don't think there's any chance of it being the truth?"

"My dear Marie, how could there be? This woman is supposed to be the sister of an artist. How in the world could a person with any perception . . .?"

Vincent walked away.

At supper he received a wire from Theo.

NAMED THE BOY AFTER YOU   JOHANNA AND VINCENT FEELING FINE.

The sale of his picture, and the marvelous news from Theo made Vincent a well man over night. In the morning he went early to his studio, cleaned his brushes, sorted the canvases and studies that were leaning against the wall.

"If Delacroix can discover painting when he no longer has teeth or breath, I can discover it when I no longer have teeth or wits."

He threw himself into his work with a dumb fury. He copied *The Good Samaritan* after Delacroix, *The Sower* and *The Digger* after Millet. He was determined to take his recent misfortune with a sort of northern phlegm. The life of art was shattering; he had known that when he began. Then why should he take to complaining at this late date?

Exactly two weeks to the day after receiving the four hundred franc check, he found in the mail a copy of the January issue of the *Mercure de France*. He noticed that Theo had checked an article on the title page called "Les Isolées."

That which characterizes all the work of Vincent Van Gogh [he read] is the excess of force, and the violence in expression. In his categorical affirmative of the essential character of things, in his often rash simplification of form, in his insolent desire to look at the sun face to face, in the passion of his drawing and colour, there lies revealed a powerful one, a male, a darer who is sometimes brutal, sometimes ingenuously delicate.

Vincent Van Gogh is of the sublime line of Frans Hals. His realism goes beyond the truth of those great little burgers of Holland, so healthy in body, so well balanced in mind, who were his ancestors. What marks his canvases is his conscientious study of character, his continuous search for the quintessence of each object, his deep and almost childlike love of nature and truth.

This robust and true artist with an illumined soul, will he ever know the joys of being rehabilitated by the public? I do not think so. He is too simple, and at the same time too subtle, for our contemporary bourgeois spirit. He will never be altogether understood except by his brother artists.

G.-Albert Aurier.

Vincent did not show the article to Doctor Peyron.

All his strength and lust for life came back to him. He painted a picture of the ward in which he slept, painted the superintendent of the buildings, and then his wife, made more copies after Millet and Delacroix, filled his nights and days with tumultuous labour.

By going carefully over the history of his illness, he saw clearly that his seizures were cyclical in nature, coming every three months. Very well, if he knew when they were to come, he would be able to take care of himself. When his next attack was due, he would stop work, go to bed, and prepare himself for a brief indisposition. And after a few days he would be up again, just as though he had been suffering from nothing more than a slight cold.

The only thing that now disturbed him at the asylum was the intense religious nature of the place. It seemed to him that with the coming of the dark winter, the sisters had suffered a hysterical seizure. Sometimes, as he watched them mumble their prayers, kiss their crosses, finger their beads, walk with their eyes glued to their Bibles, tiptoe into the chapel for prayer and services five and six times a day, he had difficulty in determining who were the patients in this insane asylum, and who the attendants. Since his days in the Borinage he had had a horror of all religious exaggerations. At moments he found the sisters' aberrations preying upon his mind. He drove himself more passionately into his work, trying to wipe the image of the black-hooded, black-caped creatures from his mind.

He gave himself forty-eight hours leeway before the end of the third month, going to bed in perfect health and spirits. He pulled the curtains of the bed about him so that the sisters, shaken by their ever rising religious exaltation, could not destroy his peace of mind.

The day arrived when his seizure was due. Vincent awaited it eagerly, almost with affection. The hours dragged by. Nothing happened. He was surprised, then disappointed. The second day passed. He still felt completely normal. When the third day drew to an end without mishap, he had to laugh at himself.

"I've been a fool. I've seen the last of those attacks, after all. Doctor Peyron was wrong. From now on I don't have to be afraid. I've been wasting my time, lying in bed this way. Tomorrow morning I'm going to get up and work."

In the dead of the night, when everyone was asleep, he climbed quietly out of bed. He walked down the stone floored ward in his bare feet. He made his way in the dark to the cellar where the coal was stored. He fell to his knees, scooped up a handful of coal-dust, and smeared it over his face.

"You see, Madame Denis? They accept me now. They know I am one of them. They did not trust me before, but now I am a *gueule noire*. The miners will let me bring them the Word of God."

The guardians found him there shortly after dawn. He was whispering chaotic prayers, repeating broken bits of scripture, answering the voices which were pouring queer tales into his ear.

His religious hallucinations continued for several days. When he came back to his senses, he asked one of the sisters to send for Doctor Peyron.

"I think I would have avoided this attack, Doctor," he said, "if it had not been for all the religious hysteria I am exposed to."

Doctor Peyron shrugged, leaned against the bed, and pulled Vincent's curtains behind him.

"What can I do, Vincent? It is just so, every winter. I do not approve but neither can I interfere. The sisters do good work, in spite of all."

"Be that as it may," said Vincent, "it is hard enough to keep sane among all the madmen, without being exposed to religious insanity in the bargain. I had passed the time for my attack . . ."

"Vincent, do not delude yourself. That attack had to come. Your nervous system works itself up to a crisis every three months. If your hallucinations had not been religious, they would have been of some other nature."

"If I have another, Doctor, I shall ask my brother to take me away."

"As you say, Vincent."

He returned to work in his studio on the first real day of spring. He painted the scene out of his window again, a field of yellow stubble being ploughed. He contrasted the violet-tinted ploughed earth with the strips of yellow stubble against the background of hills. The almond trees began to blossom everywhere, and once again the sky became pale lemon at sunset.

The eternal re-creation of nature brought forth no new life in Vincent. For the first time since he had grown accustomed to his companions, their mad babblings and periodic seizures tore his nerves and ripped into his vitals. Nor was there any escape from the mouse-like, praying creatures in black and white. The very sight of them sent shivers of apprehension through Vincent.

"Theo," he wrote to his brother, "it would make me unhappy to leave St. Remy; there is much good work to be done here yet. But if I have another attack of a religious nature, it will be the fault of the asylum, and not my nerves. It will only take two or three more of them to kill me.

"Be prepared. If I have another religious seizure, I shall leave for Paris the instant I am able to get out of bed. Perhaps it would be best for me to come north again, where one can rely on a certain amount of sanity.

"What about this Doctor Gachet of yours? Will he take a personal interest in my case?"

Theo replied that he had spoken to Doctor Gachet again, and shown him some of Vincent's canvases. Doctor Gachet was eager to have Vincent come to Auvers and paint in his house.

"He is a specialist, Vincent, not only in nervous diseases, but in painters. I am convinced that you could not be in better hands. Any time you wish to come, just wire me and I will catch the first train for St. Remy."

The heat of early spring came on. The cicadas began to sing in the garden. Vincent painted the portico of the third-class ward, the walks and trees in the gardens, his own portrait in the mirror. He worked with one eye on his canvas and the other on the calendar.

His next seizure was due in May.

He heard voices shouting at him in the empty corridors. He answered them, and the echo of his own voice came back like the malignant call of fate. This time they found him in the chapel, unconscious. It was the middle of May before he recovered from the religious hallucinations that went twisting through his brain.

Theo insisted upon coming to St. Remy to get him. Vincent wanted to make the trip alone, with one of the guardians putting him on the train at Tarascon.

Dear Theo:

I am not an invalid, nor yet a dangerous beast. Let me prove to both you and myself that I am a normal being. If I can wrench myself away from this asylum with my own strength, and take up a new life in Auvers, perhaps I shall be able to conquer this malady of mine.

I give myself one more chance. Away from this *maison des fous*, I feel confident that I can become again a rational person. From what you write me, Auvers will be quiet and beautiful. If I live carefully, under the eyes of Doctor Gachet, I am convinced that I will conquer my disease.

I shall wire you when my train leaves Tarascon. Meet me at the Gare de Lyon. I want to leave here Saturday, so that I can spend Sunday at home with you and Johanna and the little one.

BOOK EIGHT

AUVERS

1

Theo could not sleep all that night for anxiety. He left for the Gare de Lyon two hours before Vincent's train could possibly arrive. Johanna had to stay home with the baby. She stood on the terrace of their fourth floor apartment on the Cité Pigalle and peered through the leaves of the great black tree that covered the front of the house. She eagerly watched the entrance of the Cité Pigalle for a carriage which would turn in from the Rue Pigalle.

It was a long distance from the Gare de Lyon to Theo's house. To Johanna it seemed an endless time of waiting. She began to fear that something had happened to Vincent on the train. But at length an open *fiacre* turned in from the Rue Pigalle, two merry faces nodded to her, and two hands waved. She strained to catch a glimpse of Vincent.

The Cité Pigalle was a *rue impasse*, blocked off at the end by a garden court and the jutting corner of a stone house. There were only two long buildings on either side of the prosperous and respectable looking street. Theo lived at number 8, the house nearest the impasse; it was set back from a little garden and had a private *trottoir* all its own. It took the *fiacre* but a few seconds to draw up before the big black tree and the entrance.

Vincent bounded up the stairs with Theo at his heels. Johanna had expected to see an invalid, but the man who flung his arms about her had healthy colour, a smile on his face, and an expression of great resoluteness.

"He seems perfectly well. He looks much stronger than Theo," was her first thought.

But she could not bring herself to look at his ear.

"Well, Theo," exclaimed Vincent, holding Johanna's hands and looking at her approvingly, "you certainly picked yourself a fine wife."

"Thanks, Vincent," laughed Theo.

Theo had chosen in the tradition of his mother. Johanna had the same soft brown eyes as Anna Cornelia, the same tender reaching out in full sympathy and compassion. Already, with her child but a few months old, there was the faint touch of the coming matriarch about her. She had plain, good features, an almost stolid oval

253

face, and a mass of light brown hair combed back simply from a high Dutch brow. Her love for Theo included Vincent.

Theo drew Vincent into the bedroom, where the baby was sleeping in his cradle. The two men looked at the child in silence, tears in their eyes. Johanna sensed that they would like to be alone for a moment; she tiptoed to the door. Just as she put her hand on the knob, Vincent turned smilingly to her and said, pointing to the crocheted cover over the cradle,

"Do not cover him too much with lace, little sister."

Johanna closed the door quietly behind her. Vincent, looking down at the child once more, felt the awful pang of barren men whose flesh leaves no flesh behind, whose death is death eternal.

Theo read his thoughts.

"There is still time for you, Vincent. Some day you will find a wife who will love you and share the hardships of your life."

"Ah, no, Theo, it's too late."

"I found a woman only the other day who would be perfect for you!"

"Not really! Who was she?"

"She was the girl in 'Terre Vierge,' by Turgenev. Remember her?"

"You mean the one who works with the nihilists, and brings the compromising papers across the frontier?"

"Yes. Your wife would have to be somebody like that, Vincent; somebody who had gone through life's misery to the very bottom . . ."

" . . . And what would she want with me? A one-eared man?"

Little Vincent awakened, looked up at them and smiled. Theo lifted the child out of the cradle and placed him in Vincent's arms.

"So soft and warm, like a little puppy," said Vincent, feeling the baby against his heart.

"Here, clumsy, you don't hold a baby like that."

"I'm afraid I'm more at home holding a paint brush."

Theo took the child and held him against his shoulder, his head touching the baby's brown curls. To Vincent they looked as though they had been carved out of the same stone.

"Well, Theo boy," he said resignedly, "each man to his own medium. You create in living flesh . . . and I'll create in paint."

"Just so, Vincent, just so."

A number of Vincent's friends came to Theo's that night to welcome him back. The first arrival was Aurier, a handsome young man with flowing locks and a beard which sprouted out of each side of his chin, but conjured up no hair in the middle. Vincent led him to the bedroom, where Theo had hung a Monticelli bouquet.

"You said in your article, Monsieur Aurier, that I was the sole painter to perceive the chromatism of things with a metallic, gem-like quality. Look at this Monticelli. 'Fada' achieved it years before I even came to Paris."

At the end of an hour Vincent gave up trying to persuade Aurier, and presented him instead with one of the St. Remy cypress canvases in appreciation for his article.

Toulouse-Lautrec blew in, winded from six flights of stairs, but still as hilarious and ribald as ever.

"Vincent," he exclaimed, while shaking hands, "I passed an undertaker on the stairs. Was he looking for you or me?"

"For you, Lautrec! He couldn't get any business out of me."

"I'll make you a little wager, Vincent. I'll bet your name comes ahead of mine in his little book."

"You're on. What's the stake?"

"Dinner at the Café Athens, and an evening at the Opéra."

"I wish you fellows would make your jokes a trifle less macabre," said Theo, smiling faintly.

A strange man entered the front door, looked at Lautrec, and sank into a chair in a far corner. Everyone waited for Lautrec to present him, but he just went on talking.

"Won't you introduce your friend?" asked Vincent.

"That's not my friend," laughed Lautrec. "That's my keeper!"

There was a moment of pained silence.

"Hadn't you heard, Vincent? I was *non compos mentis* for a couple of months. They said it was from too much liquor, so now I'm drinking milk. I'll send you an invitation to my next party. There's a picture on it of me milking a cow from the wrong end!"

Johanna passed about refreshments. Everyone talked at the same time and the air grew thick with tobacco smoke. It reminded Vincent of the old Paris days.

"How is Georges Seurat getting along?" Vincent asked Lautrec.

"Georges! Mean to tell me you don't know about him?"

"Theo didn't write me anything," said Vincent. "What is it?"

"Georges is dying of consumption. The doctor says he won't last beyond his thirty-first birthday."

"Consumption! Why, Georges was strong and healthy. How in the . . .?"

"Overwork, Vincent," said Theo. "It's been two years since you've seen him? Georges drove himself like a demon. Slept two and three hours a day, and worked himself furiously all the rest of the time. Even that good old mother of his couldn't save him."

"So Georges will be going soon," said Vincent, musingly.

Rousseau came in, carrying a bag of home-made cookies for Vincent. Père Tanguy, wearing the same round straw hat, presented Vincent with a Japanese print and a sweet speech about how glad they were to welcome him back to Paris.

At ten o'clock Vincent insisted upon going down and buying a litre of olives. He made everyone eat them, even Lautrec's guardian.

"If you could once see those silver-green olive groves in Provence," he exclaimed, "you would eat olives for the rest of your life."

"Speaking of olive groves, Vincent," said Lautrec, "how did you find the Arlesiennes?"

The following morning Vincent carried the perambulator down to the street for Johanna so that the baby might have his hour of sunshine on the private *trottoir*. Vincent then went back to the apartment and stood about in his shirt sleeves, looking at the walls. They were covered with his pictures. In the dining room over the mantelpiece was the *Potato Eaters,* in the living room the *Landscape From Arles,* and *Night View on the Rhône,* in the bedroom, *Blooming Orchards.* To the despair of Johanna's *femme de ménage,* there were huge piles of unframed canvases under the beds, under the sofa, under the cupboard, and stacked solid in the spare room.

While rummaging for something in Theo's desk, Vincent came across large packages of letters tied with heavy cord. He was amazed to find that they were his own letters. Theo had carefully guarded every line his brother had written to him since that day, twenty years before, when Vincent had left Zundert for Goupils in The Hague. All in all, there were seven hundred letters. Vincent wondered why in the world Theo had saved them.

In another part of the desk he found the drawings that he had been sending to Theo for the past ten years, all ranged neatly in periods; here were the miners and their wives from the Borinage period, leaning over their *terril;* here the diggers and sowers in the fields near Etten; here the old men and women from The Hague, the diggers in the Geest, and the fishermen of Scheveningen; here the potato eaters and weavers of Nuenen; here the restaurants and street scenes of Paris; here the early sunflower and orchard sketches from Arles; and here the garden of the asylum at St. Remy.

"I'm going to have an exhibition all my own!" he exclaimed.

He took all the pictures off the walls, threw down the packages of sketches, and pulled piles of unframed canvases from under every piece of furniture. He sorted them out very carefully into periods. Then he selected the sketches and oils which best caught the spirit of the place in which he had been working.

In the foyer, where one entered from the hallway of the house, he pinned up about thirty of his first studies, the Borains coming out of the mines, leaning over their oval stoves, eating supper in their little shacks.

"This is the charcoal room," he announced to himself.

He looked about the rest of the house and decided that the bathroom was the next least important space. He stood on a chair and tacked a row of Etten studies about the four walls in a straight line, studies of the Brabant peasants.

"And this, of course, is the carpenter's pencil room."

His next selection was the kitchen. Here he put up his Hague and Scheveningen sketches, the view from his window over the lumber yard, the sand dunes, the fishing smacks being drawn up on the beach.

"Chamber three," he said; "water-colour room."

In the little spare room he put up his canvas of his friends the De Groots, the *Potato Eaters*; it was the first oil in which he had expressed himself fully. All about it he pinned dozens of studies of the weavers of Nuenen, the peasants in mourning, the graveyard behind his father's church, the slim, tapering steeple.

In his own bedroom he hung the oil paintings from the Paris period, the ones he had put on Theo's walls in the Rue Lepic the night he left for Arles. In the living room he crowded every last blazing Arlesian canvas he could fit on the walls. In Theo's bedroom he put up the pictures he had created while in the asylum at St. Remy.

His job finished, he cleared the floor, put on his hat and coat, walked down the four flights of stairs, and wheeled his namesake in the sunshine of the Cité Pigalle, while Johanna held his arm and chatted with him in Dutch.

Theo swung in from the Rue Pigalle at a little after twelve, waved to them happily, broke into a run, and scooped the baby out of the perambulator with a loving gesture. They left the carriage with the *concierge* and walked up the stairs, chatting animatedly. When they came to the front door, Vincent stopped them.

"I'm going to take you to a Van Gogh exhibition, Theo and Jo," he said. "So steel yourself for the ordeal."

"An exhibit, Vincent?" asked Theo. "Where?"

"Just shut your eyes," said Vincent.

He threw the door open and the three Van Goghs stepped into the foyer. Theo and Johanna gazed about, stunned.

"When I was living in Etten," said Vincent, "father once remarked that good could never grow out of bad. I replied that not only it could, but that in art it must. If you will follow me, my dear brother and sister, I will show you the story of a man who began crudely, like an awkward child, and after ten years of constant labour, arrived at . . . but you shall decide that for yourselves."

He led them, in the proper chronological sequence, from room to room. They stood like three visitors in an art gallery, looking at this work which was a man's life. They felt the slow, painful growth of the artist, the fumbling toward maturity of expression, the upheaval that had taken place in Paris, the passionate outburst of his powerful voice in Arles, which caught up all the strands of his years of labour . . . and then . . . the smash . . . the St. Remy canvases . . . the crucial striving to keep up to the blaze of creation, and the falling slowly away . . . falling . . . falling . . . falling . . .

They looked at the exhibit through the eyes of casual strangers. Before them they saw, in a brief half hour, the recapitulation of one man's stay on earth.

Johanna served a typical Brabant lunch. Vincent was happy just to taste Dutch food once again. After she had cleared away, the two men lit their pipes and chatted.

"You must be very careful to do everything Doctor Gachet tells you, Vincent."

"Yes, Theo, I will."

"Because, you see, he's a specialist in nervous diseases. If you carry out his instructions, you are sure to recover."

"I promise."

"Gachet paints, too. He exhibits each year with the Independents under the name of P. Van Ryssel."

"Is his work good, Theo?"

"No, I shouldn't say so. But he's one of those men who have a genius for recognizing genius. He came to Paris at the age of twenty to study medicine, and became friends with Courbet, Murger, Champfleury, and Proudhon. He used to frequent the café La Nouvelle Athens, and soon was intimate with Manet, Renoir, Degas, Durante, and Claude Monet. Daubigny and Daumier painted in his house years before there even was such a thing as Impressionism."

"You don't say!"

"Nearly everything he has was painted either in his garden or his living room. Pissarro, Guillaumin, Sisley, Delacroix, they've all gone out to work with Gachet in Auvers. You'll find canvases of Cezanne, Lautrec and Seurat on the walls, too. I tell you, Vincent, there hasn't been an important painter since the middle of the century who wasn't Doctor Gachet's friend."

"Whoa! Wait a minute, Theo, you're frightening me. I don't belong in such illustrious company. Has he seen any of my work yet?"

"You idiot, why do you suppose he's so eager to have you come to Auvers?"

"Blessed if I know."

"He thought your Arlesian night scenes in the last Independents the best canvases in the whole show. I swear to you, when I showed him the sunflower panels you painted for Gauguin and the yellow house, the tears came to his eyes. He turned to me and said, 'Monsieur Van Gogh, your brother is a great artist. There has never been anything like the yellow of these sunflowers before in the history of art. These canvases alone, Monsieur, will make your brother immortal.' "

Vincent scratched his head and grinned.

"Well," he said, "if Doctor Gachet feels that way about my sunflowers, he and I shall get along together."

2

Doctor Gachet was down at the station to meet Theo and Vincent. He was a nervous, excited, jumpy little man with an eager melancholy in his eyes. He wrung Vincent's hand warmly.

"Yes, yes, you will find this a real painter's village. You will like it here. I see you have brought your easel. Have you enough paints? You must begin work immediately. You will have dinner with me at my house this afternoon, yes? Have you brought some of your new canvases? You won't find that Arlesian yellow here, I'm afraid, but there are other things, yes, yes, you will find other things. You must come to my house to paint. I will give you vases and tables that have been painted by everyone from Daubigny to Lautrec. How do you feel? You look well. Do you think you will like it here? Yes, yes, we will take care of you. We'll make a healthy man out of you!"

From the station platform Vincent looked over a patch of trees to where the green Oise wound through the fertile valley. He ran a little bit to one side to get a full view. Theo spoke in a low tone to Doctor Gachet.

"I beg of you, watch my brother carefully," he said. "If you see any symptoms of his trouble coming, telegraph to me at once. I must be with him when he . . . he must not be allowed to . . . there are people who say that . . ."

"Tut! Tut!" interrupted Doctor Gachet, dancing from one foot to the other and rubbing his little goatee vigorously with his index finger. "Of course he's crazy. But what would you? All artists are crazy. That's the best thing about them. I love them that way. I sometimes wish I could be crazy myself! 'No excellent soul is exempt from a mixture of madness!' Do you know who said that? Aristotle, that's who."

"I know, Doctor," said Theo, "but he is a young man, only thirty-seven. The best part of his life is still before him."

Doctor Gachet snatched off his funny white cap and ran his hand through his hair many times, with no apparent purpose.

"Leave him to me. I know how to handle painters. I will make a well man of him in a month. I'll set him to work. That will cure him. I'll make him paint my portrait. Right away. This afternoon. I'll get his mind off his illness, all right."

Vincent came back, drawing big breaths of pure country air.

"You ought to bring Jo and the little one out here, Theo. It's a crime to raise children in the city."

"Yes, yes, you must come on a Sunday and spend the whole day with us," cried Gachet.

"Thank you. I would like that very much. Here comes my train. Good-bye, Doctor Gachet; thank you for taking care of my brother. Vincent, write to me every day."

Doctor Gachet had a habit of holding people at the elbow and propelling them forward in the direction he wished to go. He pushed Vincent ahead of him, kept up a nervous flow of talk in a high voice, scrambled up his conversation, answered his own questions, and deluged Vincent in a sputtering monologue.

"That's the road to the village," he said, "that long one, straight ahead. But come, I'll take you up this hill and give you a real view. You don't mind walking with the easel on your back? That's the Catholic church on the left. Have you noticed that the Catholics always build their churches on a hill, so that people will look up to them? Dear, dear, I must be getting old; this grade seems steeper every year. Those are lovely cornfields, aren't they? Auvers is surrounded by them. You must come and paint this field some time. Of course it's not as yellow as the Provençal . . . yes, that's the cemetery on the right . . . we put it up here on the crest of the hill, overlooking the river and the valley . . . do you think it makes much difference to dead people where they lie? . . . we gave them the loveliest spot in the whole Oise valley . . . shall we go in? . . . you get the clearest view of the river from inside . . . we'll be able to see almost to Pointoise . . . yes, the gate is open, just push it . . . that's right . . . now isn't this pleasant? . . . we built the walls high to keep the wind out . . . we bury Catholics and Protestants alike here . . ."

Vincent slipped the easel off his back and walked a little ahead of Doctor Gachet to escape the flow of words. The cemetery, which had been laid at the very crest of the hill, was a neat square in shape. Part of it ran downward on the slope. Vincent went to the back wall, from where he could see the whole Oise valley flowing beneath him. The cool green river wound its way gracefully between banks of brilliant verdure. To his right he saw the thatched roofs of the village, and just a short distance beyond, another slope on the top of which was a chateau. The cemetery was full of clean May sunshine and early spring flowers. It was roofed by a delicate blue sky. The complete and beautiful quiet was almost the quiet from beyond the grave.

"You know, Doctor Gachet," said Vincent, "it did me good to go south. Now I see the North better. Look how much violet there is on the far river bank, where the sun hasn't struck the green yet."

"Yes, yes, violet, violet, that's just what it is, vio . . ."

"And how sane," murmured Vincent. "How calm and restful."

They wound down the hill again, past the cornfields and the church, and took the straight road on the right to the heart of the village.

"I regret I cannot keep you at my house," said Doctor Gachet, "but alas! we have no room. I will take you to a good inn, and every day you will come to my house to paint, and make yourself at home."

The doctor took Vincent by the elbow and propelled him beyond the Mairie, down almost to the river bank, where there was a summer inn. Gachet spoke to the proprietor, who agreed to give Vincent room and board for six francs a day.

"I will give you a chance to get settled now," cried Gachet. "But mind you come to dinner at one o'clock. And bring your easel. You must do my portrait. And let me see some of your new canvases. We will have a grand chat, yes?"

As soon as the doctor was out of sight, Vincent picked up his belongings and stalked out the front door.

"Wait a moment," said the proprietor. "Where are you going?"

"I am a labourer," replied Vincent, "not a capitalist. I cannot pay your six francs a day."

He walked back to the Place and found a little café exactly opposite the Mairie, called Ravoux's, where he could get room and board for three francs fifty a day.

Ravoux's café was the meeting place of the peasants and labourers who worked around Auvers. Vincent found a little bar on the right as he walked in, and all the way down the side of the dark, dispirited room, rough wooden tables and benches. At the rear of the café, behind the bar, was a billiard table with a soiled and torn green covering. It was the pride and joy of Ravoux's. A door at the rear led to the back kitchen; just outside this door was a flight of stairs winding up to three bedrooms. From his window Vincent could see the steeple of the Catholic church, and a small patch of the cemetery wall, a clean, crisp brown in the mild Auvers sunlight.

He took his easel, paints and brushes, a portrait of the Arlesienne, and set out to find Gachet's. The same road which came down from the station, and led past Ravoux's, sneaked out of the Place again on the west and climbed another grade. After a short walk, Vincent came to a spot where three roads forked. He saw that the one on his right led up the hill past the chateau, and the one on his left wandered down through fields of peas to the river bank. Gachet had told him to take the centre road, which continued along the contour of the hill. Vincent walked slowly, thinking of the doctor to whose care he had been committed. He noticed how the old thatched houses were being replaced by prosperous villas, and the whole nature of the country-side was changing.

Vincent pulled a brass knob stuck in a high stone wall. Gachet came running to the tinkle of the bell. He led Vincent up three flights of steep stone steps to a terraced flower garden. The house was of three stories, solid and well built. The doctor flexed Vincent's arm, seized the joint of the elbow and pushed him around to the back yard, where he kept ducks, hens, turkeys, peacocks, and a retinue of ill-assorted cats.

"Come into the living room, Vincent," said Gachet, after giving a complete life history of each of the fowls in the yard.

The living room at the front of the house was large and had a high ceiling, but there were only two small windows looking out on the garden. In spite of the size of the room it was so crammed full of furniture, antiques, and bric-a-brac that there was hardly enough space for the two men to move about the table in the centre. The room was dark from lack of window space, and Vincent noticed that every last piece in it was black.

Gachet ran about picking up things, thrusting them into Vincent's hands, taking them away again before Vincent had a chance to look at them.

"See. See that bouquet on the wall? Delacroix used this vase to hold the flowers. Feel it. Doesn't it feel like the one he painted? See that chair? Courbet sat in it by the window when he painted the garden. Aren't these exquisite dishes? Desmoulins brought them back from Japan for me. Claude Monet put this one into a still life. It's upstairs. Come with me. I'll show it to you."

At the dinner table Vincent met Gachet's son, Paul, a vivacious and handsome young lad of fifteen. Gachet, who was a sick man with a poor digestion, served a five course dinner. Vincent was accustomed to the lentils and black bread of St. Remy; he became distressed after the third course and could go no further.

"And now we must go to work," cried the doctor. "You will paint my portrait, Vincent; I will sit for you just as I am, yes?"

"I'm afraid I must come to know you better, Doctor, or it won't be an understanding portrait."

"Perhaps you are right, perhaps you are right. But surely you will paint something? You will let me see how you work? I am eager to watch you."

"I saw a scene in the garden I would like to do."

"Good! Good! I will set up your easel. Paul, carry Monsieur Vincent's easel into the garden. You will show us where you want it, and I will tell you if any other painter has done that exact spot."

While Vincent worked, the doctor ran about him in little circles, gesticulating with rapture, consternation and amazement. He poured a constant stream of advice over Vincent's shoulder, interspersed with hundreds of sharp exclamations.

"Yes, yes, you caught it that time. It's crimson lake. Look out. You'll spoil that tree. Ah, yes, yes, now you've caught it. No. No. No more cobalt. This isn't Provence. Now I see. Yes, yes, it's *épatant*. Careful. Careful. Vincent, put a little spot of yellow in that flower. Yes, yes, just so. How you make things live. There's not a still life in your brush. No. No. I beg of you. Be careful. Not too much. Ah, yes, yes, now I catch it. *Merveilleux!*"

Vincent stood the doctor's contortions and monologue as long as he could. Then he turned to the dancing Gachet and said, "My dear friend, don't you think it bad for your health to get yourself so excited and wrought up? As a medical man, you should know how important it is to keep calm."

But Gachet could not be calm when anyone was painting.

When he finished his sketch, Vincent went inside the house with Gachet, and showed him the portrait of the Arlesienne he had brought. The doctor cocked one eye and looked at it quizzically. After a long and voluble discussion with himself as to its merits and faults, he announced,

"No, I cannot accept it. I cannot fully accept it. I do not see what you have tried to say."

"I haven't tried to say anything," replied Vincent. "She is the synthesis of the Arlesiennes, if you like. I simply tried to interpret her character in terms of colours."

"Alas," said the doctor mournfully, "I cannot fully accept it."

"Do you mind if I look about the house at your collection?"

"But of course, of course, go look your fill. I will stay here with this lady and see if I cannot come to accept her."

Vincent browsed through the house for an hour, led from room to room by the obliging Paul. Thrown carelessly in one corner he found a Guillaumin, a nude woman lying on a bed. The canvas had obviously been neglected, and was cracking. While Vincent was examining it, Doctor Gachet came running up excitedly and poured out a string of questions about the Arlesienne.

"Do you mean to tell me you have been looking at her all this time?" demanded Vincent.

"Yes, yes, it is coming, it is coming, I am beginning to feel her."

"Forgive my presumption, Doctor Gachet, but this is a magnificent Guillaumin. If you don't have it framed soon, it will be ruined."

Gachet did not even hear him.

"You say you followed Gauguin in the drawing . . . I do not agree . . . that clash of colours . . . it kills her femininity . . . no, not kills, but . . . well, well, I will go look again . . . she is coming to me . . . slowly . . . slowly . . . she is jumping out of the canvas to me."

Gachet spent the rest of the long afternoon running about the Arlesienne, pointing at her, waving his arms, talking to himself, asking and answering innumerable questions, falling into a thousand poses. By the time night fell, the woman had completely captured his heart. An exulted quiescence fell upon him.

"How difficult it is to be simple," he remarked, standing in peaceful exhaustion before the portrait.

"Yes."

"She is beautiful, beautiful. I have never felt such depth of character before."

"If you like her, Doctor," said Vincent, "she is yours. And so is the scene I did in the garden this afternoon."

"But why should you give me these pictures, Vincent? They are valuable."

"In the near future you may have to take care of me. I will have no money to pay you. So I pay you in canvases instead."

"But I would not be taking care of you for money, Vincent. I would be doing it for friendship."

"*Soit!* I give you these pictures for friendship."

3

Vincent settled down once again to be a painter. He went to sleep at nine, after watching the labourers play billiards under a dull lamp in Ravoux's café. He arose at five. The weather was beautiful, with gentle sunshine and the fresh verdancy of the valley. His periods of illness and enforced idleness in St. Paul had taken their toll; the paint brush slipped in his hand.

He asked Theo to send him Bargue's sixty charcoal studies to copy, for he was afraid that if he did not study proportion and the nude again, he would be badly caught out. He looked about Auvers to see if he could find a little house in which he might settle permanently. He wondered if Theo had been right in thinking that, somewhere in the world, there was a woman who would share his life. He laid out a number of his St. Remy canvases, anxious to retouch and perfect them.

But his sudden activity was only a momentary gesture, the reflex of an organism that was yet too powerful to be destroyed.

After his long seclusion in the asylum the days seemed to him like weeks. He was at a loss to know how to fill them, for he did not have the strength to paint all the time. Nor did he have the desire. Before his accident in Arles no day had been long enough to get his work done; now they seemed interminable.

Fewer scenes in nature tempted him, and when he did begin work he felt strangely calm, almost indifferent. The feverish passion to paint in hot blood every minute of the day had left him. He now sketched in what was for him a leisurely fashion. And if he did not finish a canvas by nightfall . . . it no longer seemed to matter.

Doctor Gachet remained his only friend in Auvers. Gachet, who spent most of his days at his consulting office in Paris, often came to the Café Ravoux at night to look at pictures. Vincent had often wondered at the look of utter heartbreak in the doctor's eyes.

"Why are you unhappy, Doctor Gachet?" he asked.

"Ah, Vincent, I have laboured so many years . . . and I have done so little good. The doctor sees nothing but pain, pain, pain."

"I would gladly exchange my calling for yours," said Vincent.

A rapt eagerness lighted up the melancholy in Gachet's eyes.

"Ah, no, Vincent, it is the most beautiful thing in the world, to be a painter. All my life I wanted to be an artist . . . but I could spare only an hour here and there . . . there are so many sick people who need me."

Doctor Gachet went on his knees and pulled a pile of canvases from under Vincent's bed. He held a glowing yellow sunflower before him.

"If I had painted just one canvas like this, Vincent, I would consider my life justified. I spent the years curing people's pain . . . but they died in the end, anyway . . . so what did it matter? These sunflowers of yours . . . they will cure the pain in people's hearts . . . they will bring people joy . . . for centuries and centuries . . . that is why your life is successful . . . that is why you should be a happy man."

A few days later Vincent painted a portrait of the doctor in his white cap and blue frock coat, against a cobalt blue background. He did the head in a very fair, very light tone, the hands also in a light flesh tint. He posed Gachet leaning on a red table on which were a yellow book and a foxglove plant with purple flowers. He was amused to find, when he finished, that the portrait resembled the one he had done of himself in Arles, before Gauguin arrived.

The doctor went absolutely fanatical about the portrait. Vincent had never heard such a torrent of praise and acclaim. Gachet insisted that Vincent make a copy for him. When Vincent agreed, the doctor's joy knew no bounds.

"You must use my printing machine in the attic, Vincent," he cried. "We'll go to Paris, get all your canvases, and make lithographs of them. It won't cost you a centime, not a centime. Come, I will show you my workshop."

They had to climb a ladder and push open a trap door to get into the attic. Gachet's studio was piled so high with weird and fantastic implements that Vincent thought he had been plunged into an alchemist's workshop of the Middle Ages.

On the way downstairs, Vincent noticed that the Guillaumin nude was still lying about, neglected.

"Doctor Gachet," he said, "I simply must insist that you have this framed. You are ruining a masterpiece."

"Yes, yes, I mean to have it framed. When can we go to Paris and get your paintings? You will print as many lithographs as you like. I will supply the materials."

May slipped quietly into June. Vincent painted the Catholic church on the hill. He wearied in the middle of the afternoon and did not even bother to finish it. By dint of great perseverence he managed to paint a cornfield while lying flat on the ground, his head almost in the corn; he did a large canvas of Madame Daubigny's house; another of a white house in the trees, with a night sky, an orange light in the windows, dark greenery and a note of sombre rose colour; and lastly, an evening effect, two pear trees quite black against a yellowing sky.

But the juice had gone out of painting. He worked from habit, because there was nothing else to do. The terrific momentum of his ten years of colossal labour carried him still a little farther. Where scenes from nature had thrilled and excited him before, they now left him indifferent.

"I've painted that so many times," he would murmur to himself as he walked along the roads, easel on his back, looking for a motif. "I have nothing new to say about it. Why should I repeat myself? Father Millet was right. *'J'aimerais mieux ne rien dire que de m'exprimer faiblement.'* "

His love for nature had not died; it was simply that he no longer felt the desperate need to fling himself at a scene and recreate it. He was burned out. During the whole month of June he painted only five canvases. He was weary, unspeakably weary. He felt empty, drained, washed out, as though the hundreds upon hundreds of drawings and paintings that had flowed out of him in the past ten years had each taken a tiny spark of his life.

At last he went on working only because he felt he owed it to Theo to capitalize on the years of investment. And yet, when he realized, in the very middle of a painting, that Theo's house was already jammed with more canvases than could be sold in ten lifetimes, a gentle nausea would arise within him, and he would push away his easel with distaste.

He knew that another seizure was due in July, at the end of the three month period. He worried for fear he would do something irrational while the attack was upon him, and ostracize himself in the village. He had not made any definite financial arrangements with Theo when he left Paris, and he worried about how much money he was going to receive. The alternating heartbreak and rapture in Gachet's eyes was driving Vincent's gorge up, day by day.

And to cap the climax, Theo's child became ill.

The anxiety over his namesake almost drove Vincent frantic. He stood it as long as he could, then took a train to Paris. His sudden arrival in the Cité Pigalle heightened the confusion. Theo was looking pale and ill. Vincent did his best to comfort him.

"It isn't only the little one I'm worrying about, Vincent," he admitted at last.

"What then, Theo?"

"It's Valadon. He has threatened to ask for my resignation."

"Why, Theo, he couldn't! You've been with Goupils for sixteen years!"

"I know. But he says I've been neglecting the regular trade for the Impressionists. I don't sell very many of them, and when I do, the prices are low. Valadon claims my shop has been losing money for the past year."

"But could he really put you out?"

"Why not? The Van Gogh interest has been completely sold."

"What would you do, Theo? Open a shop of your own?"

"How could I? I had a little money saved, but I spent it on my wedding, and the baby."

"If only you hadn't thrown away those thousands of francs on me . . ."

"Now, Vincent, please. That had nothing to do with it. You know I . . ."

"But what will you do, Theo? There's Jo and the little one."

"Yes. Well . . . I don't know . . . I'm only worrying about the baby now."

Vincent stayed around Paris a number of days. He kept out of the apartment as much as possible, so as not to disturb the child. Paris and his old friends excited him. He felt a slow, gripping fever arise within him. When little Vincent recovered somewhat, he took the train back to the quiet of Auvers.

But the quiet did him no good. He was tormented by his worries. What would happen to him if Theo lost his job? Would he be thrown out into the streets like some vile beggar? And for that matter, what would happen to Jo and the baby? What if the baby died? He knew that Theo's frail health could never stand the blow. Who was going to support them all while Theo searched for a new job? And where was Theo going to find strength for the search?

He sat for hours in the dark café of Ravoux's. It reminded him of the Café Lamartine, with its odours of stale beer and acrid tobacco smoke. He jabbed around aimlessly with the billiard cue, trying to hit the discoloured balls. He had no money to buy liquor. He had no money to buy paints and canvases. He could not ask Theo for anything at such a crucial moment. And he was deathly afraid that when he had his seizure in July, he would do something insane, something to cause poor Theo even more worry and expense.

He tried working, but it was no good. He had painted everything he wanted to paint. He had said everything he wanted to say. Nature no longer stirred him to a creative passion, and he knew that the best part of him was already dead.

The days passed. The middle of July came, and with it the hot weather. Theo, his head just about to be chopped off by Valadon, frantic with worry over his baby and the doctor bills, managed to squeeze out fifty francs to send to his brother. Vincent turned them over to Ravoux. That would keep him until almost the end of July. And after that . . . what? He could not expect any more money from Theo.

He lay on his back under the hot sun in the cornfields by the little cemetery. He walked along the banks of the Oise, smelling the cool water and the foliage that lined its banks. He went to Gachet's for dinner and stuffed himself with food that he could neither taste nor digest. While the doctor raved on excitedly about Vincent's paintings, Vincent said to himself,

"That's not me he's talking about. Those can't be my pictures. I never painted anything. I don't even recognize my own signature on the canvas. I can't remember putting one single brush stroke on any of them. They must have been done by some other man!"

Lying in the darkness of his room he said to himself, "Suppose Theo doesn't lose his job. Suppose he is still able to send me a hundred and fifty francs a month. What am I going to do with my life? I've kept alive these last miserable years because I had to paint, because I had to say the things that were burning inside of me. But there's nothing burning inside me now. I'm just a shell. Should I go on vegetating like those poor souls at St. Paul, waiting for some accident to wipe me off the earth?"

At other times he worried about Theo, Johanna, and the baby.

"Suppose my strength and spirits return, and I want to paint again. How can I still take money from Theo when he needs it for Jo and the little one? He ought not spend that money on me. He ought to use it to send his family to the country, where they can grow healthy and strong. He's borne me on his back for ten long years. Isn't that enough? Shouldn't I get out and give little Vincent a chance? I've had my say; now the little one ought to have his."

But at the base of everything lay the overwhelming fear of what epilepsy would eventually do to him. Now he was sane and rational; he could do with his life what he wished. But suppose his next attack should convert him into a raving maniac. Suppose his brain should crack under the strain of the seizure. Suppose he became a hopeless, drivelling idiot. What would poor Theo do then? Lock him in an asylum for the lost ones?

He presented Doctor Gachet with two more of his canvases and wormed the truth out of him.

"No, Vincent," said the doctor, "you are all through with your attacks. You'll find yourself in perfect health from now on. But not all epileptics are that fortunate."

"What eventually happens to them, Doctor?"

"Sometimes, when they have had a number of crises, they go out of their minds completely."

"And is there no possible recovery for them?"

"No. They're finished. Oh, they may linger on for some years in an asylum, but they never come back to their right minds."

"How can they tell, Doctor, whether they will recover from the next attack, or whether it will crack their brains?"

"There is no way of telling, Vincent. But come, why should we discuss such morbid questions? Let's go up to the workshop and make some etchings."

Vincent did not leave his room at Ravoux's for the next four days. Madame Ravoux brought him his supper every evening.

"I'm well now, and sane," he kept repeating to himself. "I am master of my own destiny. But when the next seizure catches me . . . if it cracks my skull . . .

I won't know enough to kill myself . . . and I'll be lost. Oh, Theo, Theo, what should I do?''

On the afternoon of the fourth day he went to Gachet's. The doctor was in the living room. Vincent walked to the cabinet where he had put the unframed Guillaumin nude some time before. He picked up the canvas.

"I told you to have this framed," he said.

Doctor Gachet looked at him in surprise.

"I know, Vincent. I'll order a stick frame from the joiner in Auvers next week."

"It must be framed now! Today! This minute!"

"Why, Vincent, you're talking nonsense!"

Vincent glared at the doctor for a moment, took a menacing step toward him, then put his hand in his coat pocket. Doctor Gachet thought he saw Vincent grip a revolver and point it at him through the coat.

"Vincent!" he exclaimed.

Vincent trembled. He lowered his eyes, pulled his hand from his pocket, and ran out of the house.

The next day he took his easel and canvas, walked down the long road to the station, climbed the hill past the Catholic church, and sat down in the yellow cornfield, opposite the cemetery.

About noon, when the fiery sun was beating down upon his head, a rush of blackbirds suddenly came out of the sky. They filled the air, darkened the sun, covered Vincent in a thick blanket of night, flew into his hair, his eyes, his nose, his mouth, buried him in a black cloud of tight, airless, flapping wings.

Vincent went on working. He painted the birds above the yellow field of corn. He did not know how long he wielded his brush, but when he saw that he had finished, he wrote *Crows Above a Cornfield* in one corner, carried his easel and canvas back to Ravoux's, threw himself across the bed and went to sleep.

The following afternoon he went out again, but left the Place de la Mairie from the other side. He climbed the hill past the chateau. A peasant saw him sitting in a tree.

"It is impossible!" he heard Vincent say. "It is impossible!"

After a time he climbed down from the tree and walked in the ploughed field behind the chateau. This time it was the end. He had known that in Arles, the very first time, but he had been unable to make the clean break.

He wanted to say good-bye. In spite of all, it had been a good world that he had lived in. As Gauguin said, ''Besides the poison, there is the antidote.'' And now, leaving the world, he wanted to say good-bye to it, say good-bye to all those friends who had helped mould his life; to Ursula, whose contempt had wrenched him out of a conventional life and made him an outcast; to Mendes da Costa, who had made him believe that ultimately he would express himself, and that expression would justify his life; to Kay Vos, whose ''No, never! never!'' had been written in acid on his soul; to Madame Denis, Jacques Verney and Henri Decrucq, who had helped him love the despised ones of the earth; to the Reverend Pietersen, whose kindness had transcended Vincent's ugly clothes and boorish manners; to his mother and father, who had loved him as best they could; to Christine, the only wife with which fate had seen fit to bless him; to Mauve, who had been his master for a few sweet weeks; to Weissenbruch and De Bock, his first painter friends; to his Uncles Vincent, Jan, Cornelius Marinus, and Stricker, who had labeled him the black sheep of the Van Gogh family; to Margot, the only woman who had ever loved him, and who had tried to kill herself for that love; to all his painter friends in Paris; Lautrec, who had been shut up in an asylum again, to die; Georges Seurat, dead at thirty-one from overwork; Paul Gauguin, a mendicant in Brittany; Rousseau, rotting in his hole near the Bastille; Cezanne, a bitter recluse on a hilltop in Aix; to Père Tanguy and Roulin, who had shown him the salt in the simple souls of the earth; to Rachel and Doctor Rey, who had been kind to him with the kindness he needed;

to Aurier and Doctor Gachet, the only two men in the world who had thought him a great painter; and last of all, to his good brother Theo, long suffering, long loving, best and dearest of all possible brothers.

But words had never been his medium. He would have to paint good-bye.

One cannot paint good-bye.

He turned his face upward to the sun. He pressed the revolver into his side. He pulled the trigger. He sank down, burying his face in the rich, pungent loam of the field, a more resilient earth returning to the womb of its mother.

4

Four hours later he staggered through the gloom of the café. Madame Ravoux followed him to his room and saw blood on his clothes. She ran at once for Doctor Gachet.

"Oh. Vincent, Vincent, what have you done!" groaned Gachet, when he entered the room.

"I think I have bungled it; what do you say?"

Gachet examined the wound.

"Oh, Vincent, my poor old friend, how unhappy you must have been to do this! Why didn't I know? Why should you want to leave us when we all love you so? Think of the beautiful pictures you have still to paint for the world."

"Will you be so kind as to give me my pipe from my waistcoat pocket?"

"But certainly, my friend."

He loaded the pipe with tobacco, then placed it between Vincent's teeth.

"A light, if you please," said Vincent.

"But certainly, my friend."

Vincent puffed quietly at his pipe.

"Vincent, it is Sunday and your brother is not at the shop. What is his home address?"

"That I will not give you."

"But, Vincent, you must! It is urgent that we reach him!"

"Theo's Sunday must not be disturbed. He is tired and worried. He needs the rest."

No amount of persuasion could get the Cité Pigalle address out of Vincent. Doctor Gachet stayed with him until late that night, tending the wound. Then he went home for a little rest, leaving his son to care for Vincent.

Vincent lay there wide-eyed all night, never uttering a word to Paul. He kept filling his pipe and smoking it constantly.

When Theo arrived at Goupils the following morning, he found Gachet's telegram awaiting him. He caught the first train for Pontoise, then dashed in a carriage to Auvers.

"Well, Theo," said Vincent.

Theo dropped on his knees by the side of the bed and took Vincent in his arms like a little child. He could not speak.

When the doctor arrived, Theo led him outside to the corridor. Gachet shook his head sadly.

"There is no hope, my friend. I cannot operate to remove the bullet, for he is too weak. If he were not made of iron he would have died in the fields."

All through the long day Theo sat by his bed, holding Vincent's hand. When nightfall came, and they were left alone in the room, they began to speak quietly of their childhood in the Brabant.

"Do you remember the mill at Ryswyk, Vincent?"

"It was a nice old mill, wasn't it, Theo?"

"We used to walk by the path along the stream, and plan our lives."

"And when we played in the high corn, in midsummer, you used to hold my hand, just as you're doing now. Remember, Theo?"

"Yes, Vincent."

"When I was in the hospital at Arles, I used to think often about Zundert. We had a nice childhood, Theo, you and I. We used to play in the garden behind the kitchen, in the shade of the acacias, and Mother would make us cheese bakes for lunch."

"That seems so long ago, Vincent."

" . . . Yes . . . well . . . life is long. Theo, for my sake, take care of yourself. Guard your health. You must think of Jo and the little one. Take them into the country somewhere so they can grow strong and healthy. And don't stay with Goupils, Theo. They have taken the whole of your life . . . and given you nothing in return."

"I'm going to open a tiny gallery of my own, Vincent. And my first exhibition will be a one-man show. The complete works of Vincent Van Gogh . . . just as you laid it out in the apartment . . . with your own hands."

"Ah, well, my work . . . I risked my life for it . . . and my reason has almost foundered."

The deep quiet of the Auvers night fell upon the room.

At a little after one in the morning, Vincent turned his head slightly and whispered, "I wish I could die now, Theo."

In a few minutes he closed his eyes.

Theo felt his brother leave him, forever.

5

Rousseau, Père Tanguy, Aurier and Émile Bernard came out from Paris for the funeral.

The doors of the Café Ravoux were locked and the blinds pulled down. The little black hearse with the black horses waited out in front.

They laid Vincent's coffin on the billiard table.

Theo, Doctor Gachet, Rousseau, Père Tanguy, Aurier, Bernard, and Ravoux gathered about, speechless. They could not look at each other.

No one thought of calling in a minister.

The driver of the hearse knocked at the front door.

"It is time, gentlemen," he said.

"For God's sake, we can't let him go like this!" cried Gachet.

He brought all the paintings down from Vincent's room, then sent his son Paul running home to get the rest of his canvases.

Six of the men worked putting up the paintings on the walls.

Theo stood alone by the coffin.

Vincent's sunlight canvases transformed the drab, gloomy café into a brilliant cathedral.

Once again the men gathered about the billiard table. Gachet alone could speak.

"Let us not despair, we who are Vincent's friends. Vincent is not dead. He will never die. His love, his genius, the great beauty he has created will go on forever, enriching the world. Not an hour passes but that I look at his paintings and find there a new faith, a new meaning of life. He was a colossus . . . a great painter . . . a great philosopher. He fell a martyr to his love of art."

Theo tried to thank him.

". . . I . . . I . . ."

The tears choked him. He could not go on.

The cover was placed on Vincent's coffin.

His six friends lifted it from the billiard table. They carried it out of the little café. They placed it gently in the hearse.

They walked behind the black carriage, down the sunlit road. They passed the thatched cottages and the little country villas.

At the station the hearse turned to the left and began the slow climb up the hill. They passed the Catholic church, then wound through the yellow cornfield.

The black carriage stopped at the gate of the cemetery.

Theo walked behind the coffin while the six men carried it to the grave.

Doctor Gachet had chosen as Vincent's last resting place the spot on which they had stood that very first day, overlooking the lovely verdant valley of the Oise.

Once again Theo tried to speak. He could not.

The attendants lowered the coffin into the ground. Then they shovelled in dirt and stamped it down.

The seven men turned, left the cemetery, and walked down the hill.

Doctor Gachet returned a few days later to plant sunflowers all about the grave.

Theo went home to the Cité Pigalle. His loss pushed out every aching second of the night and day with unassuagable grief.

His mind broke under the strain.

Johanna took him to the *maison de santé* in Utrecht, where Margot had gone before him.

At the end of six months, almost to the day of Vincent's death, Theo passed away. He was buried at Utrecht.

Some time later, when Johanna was reading her Bible for comfort, she came across the line in Samuel:

And in their death they were not divided.

She took Theo's body to Auvers, and had it placed by the side of his brother.

When the hot Auvers sun beats down upon the little cemetery in the cornfields, Theo rests comfortably in the luxuriant umbrage of Vincent's sunflowers.

The President's Lady

BOOK ONE

1

They emerged from the dark woods and were suddenly in the hot September sunshine. At the bottom of the hill their horses stopped to drink from the shallow stream.

"Would you like to rest for a spell, Rachel, and freshen? We'll be home by sundown."

"I'd rather push on, Samuel, if it's the same to you."

He seemed relieved. Why was her own brother so constrained with her? No matter how serious the charges, she had expected support from her family.

They crossed the bottom lands and made their way up the trail to a timbered knob. She paused for a moment to let the cool wind of the uplands blow through her abundant black hair, refreshing her. For the first time in the four days since they had left Harrodsburg she began to feel clearheaded.

It's strange, she thought, during the long week that it took for my husband's message to reach the Cumberland and for my brother to come for me, I was too wretched to worry about anybody but myself. Yet the moment we were on the trail for home I began to think about Samuel and how hard he has taken my misfortune. If I greet my mother and brothers and sisters with the same stricken face I showed to Samuel, I'll make them all as wretched as I was.

I must think this thing through, come to some sort of understanding with myself before we reach home. Was I really guilty of misconduct? If so, how? If I wasn't guilty, then why has this happened to me? I've got to dig down to the root, no matter how bitter it may be to chew on.

She looked across at her brother, the change in her mood communicating itself to him. She had a mirror in her saddlebag, but she had no need for one at this moment: she and Samuel, who was a year younger, were alike as twins. She saw his warm brown eyes, so quick to pain and hurt, proffering her a tiny tentative smile; the thin, curved black eyebrows; the small but immaculate white teeth, showing between the expressive lips; the thick black hair, worn over the ears, pulled back tight and tied low on the neck with a thong; his contour, inclined to exposed roundness, unprotected against the world. He had not been judging her; his confused and troubled expression had been but a true reflection of her own.

Though she had not seen her family for three years there had never been any question in her mind as to which one of her seven brothers would make the dangerous trip to fetch her. They were the youngest and gayest of the Donelson family; when her father was home he had taught her to read and write, but when he was away on surveying trips or treaty-making with the Indians, she and Samuel had studied together from the leather-bound handwritten arithmetic book in which they learned about division of decimals and the double rule of three. Samuel had been clever with books, and their father, who was an intensely religious man, had imagined that at long last he had a son who would follow in the footsteps of his great-grandfather, the clergyman who had helped to found the first Presbyterian church in America.

"Why has he done this to you, Rachel?" Samuel cried out, released at last to discuss their difficulty. "What was his provocation?"

"Provocation? Well, a letter. Sent from Virginia to Crab Orchard, to be delivered to me secretly. Lewis intercepted it."

"But what could be in such a letter?"

"I never saw it. According to Lewis, a proposal that I elope with Peyton Short to Spanish Territory. Also a credit for me to buy anything I might need for a trip down to New Orleans."

Samuel gazed at her in bewilderment.

"When did all this nonsense start?"

Tears came into her eyes. She said to herself, Samuel is right; perhaps if I could find my way back to the beginning of our troubles . . . When did they start?

Probably at the house-raising bee to which Lewis had taken her at Bardstown, when he had suddenly become enraged because she was laughing heartily at a story told by one of his friends, an amusing fellow who insisted upon keeping his lips close to his listener's ear. Lewis had come to her side, yanked her unceremoniously by the arm and taken her away from the party.

Before their marriage her husband had told her that he loved her for her bubbling good spirits, for the way she came into a room filled with people who were feeling dull or unhappy and by her very warmth and genuine liking for folks somehow made them come alive. Then why had he turned against her?

She shook her head angrily, provoked with herself for being unable to reach disciplined conclusions. But when in her twenty-one years had she needed to be logical and disciplined in her thinking?

It had not been very long after the abrupt withdrawal from the party at Bardstown that Lewis Robards began accusing her of being too friendly with the young men of the neighborhood and with those who frequented the Robards home. Had she smiled too warmly at greeting this one? Her husband had said so in unmistakable terms later that night. Had she danced with too much vivacity at her first anniversary party? Lewis's face had gone purple with rage when he locked the door of their bedroom and turned to accuse her. Had she listened too sympathetically to a newcomer's account of his difficulties in adjusting himself to the rude frontier life in Kentucky? But she had been interested in the young chap and the recounting of his hardships, for he had come from within a few miles of the old Donelson home in Virginia.

After each quarrel she had lain awake saying to herself, if Lewis no longer likes me to be friendly, then I must be more reserved. If he doesn't want me to dance or sing, I will be quiet.

She would mind her resolution for a number of days, then forget herself and be gay with old friends, tell stories and let her laughter ring out . . . and Lewis would join in the funmaking, his arm fondly about her; until a day or a week later, when he would again seize upon some harmless incident to stage a humiliating scene in public.

But her real difficulties had not begun, she remembered, until there were a series of Indian attacks around Harrodsburg, with a half dozen killings. Lewis's mother, who had managed the plantation since her husband's death, decided they had better take in a few young men who were experienced in the ways of defending a stockade.

The first boarder was a plump, florid-faced lawyer from Virginia, impetuous, and with a rather loud voice. Peyton Short was a man who liked to talk, it didn't matter what the subject, and he had chosen Rachel as the object of his monologues. She had not thought him clever, but she understood that talking, even at random, eased his loneliness. On warm summer evenings the Robards family, which now included Lewis's brother George and his wife, sat out on the front porch; Peyton Short usually managed to pull his chair up close to Rachel's to tell of the day's doings. Lewis became uneasy.

"Rachel, couldn't you avoid him? He's so confoundedly . . . present."

"Yes, I'll try."

But she found that Mr. Short was not the kind of man one could easily avoid. One evening Lewis came back from the slave quarters to find them alone on the dark porch; her mother-in-law had just gone inside, and Rachel was looking for an opening in the encircling ring of words. Accusing her of having a tête-à-tête, Lewis went straightway to his mother and demanded that Peyton Short be put out of the house. Mrs. Robards refused to listen to what she called his "patent foolishness." Nor did Lewis feel any need to keep his private affairs to himself; everyone in the neighborhood knew that he was jealous of Peyton Short.

They had little peace until John Overton came to live with them. He was a distant cousin of the Robards, homely in a winsome fashion, a little fellow with straw-colored hair and a pale skin, possessor of a dry sense of humor which for a fair time served as an anodyne to the distressed household.

Then, for Rachel, a new element entered into Lewis's jealousy: now his outbursts seemed to bear no relationship to the immediate goings-on: his most violent attacks came when she had not exchanged ten words with Peyton Short in as many days. Once Short stopped her, when her eyes were red, and said:

"You'll never find happiness with a man like Lewis Robards. He has neither the sense to love you nor the pride to protect you. But not all men are such fools, Mrs. Robards."

She had not understood his words; in truth she had not listened. But a few weeks later, after Peyton Short had gone home to Virginia, Lewis had burst in upon her, thrusting the crumpled Peyton Short letter into her face.

She reined in her horse, feeling ill, as though she were back in her room at the Robards house at the beginning of those days of waiting, waiting for any one of the paralyzing eventualities: news from Virginia that her husband had been killed in the duel to which he had challenged Short; word that her family had received her husband's letter requesting that someone be sent to fetch her, but had decided not to interfere; that she would have to remain unwanted in a house where her husband had renounced her; or that one of her brothers would arrive and take her away, to . . . what?

2

Samuel helped her off the horse. She sat down at the base of a big tree, leaning her head against it. Her brother kneeled in front of her, wiping the perspiration from her brow with his unbleached cotton handkerchief.

"Are you taken bad, Rachel?"

"Just give me a few moments to rest, Samuel."

"Is there something I can do for you? A drink of water, maybe?"

"I'll be all right."

They were now only a few miles from the Donelson stockade. She understood why Samuel had been unable to ask questions or offer sympathy: separation of husband and wife had never happened in their part of the country. On a frontier where all relationships were based on confidence, where men were of necessity away for months at a time and the hospitality of their homes often meant survival to settlers moving westward on the trails, she had been judged unworthy of this basic trust.

Everyone on the Cumberland would know that she had been repudiated. How badly had she injured her family? What would be her position among her friends and neighbors? Would she be an outcast?

She could see these uncertainties reflected in Samuel's eyes as he leaned over and smoothed her hair back from her forehead. She simply could not reach home in this state; yet there were just a few more miles before they started climbing down the rim into the Cumberland basin.

Often in the past four days she had imagined that she was thinking her way through to the core of the problem, but it always eluded her. No matter how severe she might be in her self-judgment, blaming herself for each of Peyton Short's poor jokes at which she had laughed, she still could find nothing in her attitude that logically should have led to her present predicament. It almost seemed as though this was something that had happened to her from the outside, and to which she was not a party.

Very well then, if the original cause did not lie in herself, where did it lie? In Peyton Short, surely, for having written such a foolish letter; but hadn't there been two years of intermittent quarrels before Short arrived at the Robards house?

Forcing her mind backward torturously, she compelled herself to remember the times her husband's jealous outbreaks had come when the family had seen no outsiders; how at such times Lewis had simply refetched old accusations. She had wondered why he had brought up these largely forgotten matters; once she had asked him this question specifically. He had not answered.

Now fragments began to fit together, broken bits of action and explanation, basic uneasinesses. One of her husband's characteristics was to go away for a night, giving an offhand reason or excuse. But all along she had had an inkling of the handsome young mulatto who had been a house servant during the years before their marriage; at intervals she had surprised a fleeting smile on the girl's face, had caught something intangible between them as Lewis issued an order and the girl silently accepted it. She realized now she had sensed the bitter truth . . . even though she had rejected the evidence. By the same token, couldn't that be the reason for Lewis's conduct? She relived the scene in her upstairs bedroom, with Lewis shouting, "I've written your mother to send someone to get you out of my house. And I'm leaving tonight for Virginia to kill Peyton Short!"

Mrs. Robards had taken Rachel in her arms and turned to her son with blazing eyes to tell him that he had gone stark mad. Lewis's older sister insisted that Rachel had never given Peyton Short anything but hospitable courtesy. Jack Jouitt, her husband, had tried to calm Lewis by telling him that he was the only one in all Kentucky ludicrous enough to believe that Rachel Donelson Robards could be guilty of any part of this clandestine affair. John Overton had said in his shy manner: "Lewis, I could write you a letter tonight inviting you to join me in horse stealing and murder, but that would hardly make you a horse thief or a murderer." But it was Mrs. George Robards who had said coldly to Lewis, "All this arises from your own improper conduct."

Rachel rose, walked unevenly to where the horses were drinking, and stood with one hand grasping her saddle, the other clenched tight as there rushed into her mind the formerly unrelated evidence: her husband had left her side, sometimes even their bed, to go out to the slave quarters; inevitably when he had returned he had accused her of a crime against their love and marriage . . . transferring to his wife his own capacity for betrayal.

Her hand fell from the saddle and she stood with her head lowered. After a time a feeling of relief came over her: if she could not live with her husband, she could at least live with herself; she could face her family and her neighbors and friends.

Her husband had hurt her, hurt her severely, but she had not hurt herself, she had not injured her own dignity or self-respect.

She loosened a strap on the saddlebag, took out her traveling kit and emptied its contents onto the grass: an oblong mirror, a silver-backed comb and brush, a piece of scented soap from Richmond, a clean rough-fibered towel. Glancing down at her brown linsey-woolsey dress she saw that it was soiled from travel. From the saddlebag she took a fresh blue linen dress, then slipped out of the rumpled one, kneeling at the side of the creek in her white petticoat. She was small-boned, barely five feet two in height, with rounded shoulders and firm pear-shaped breasts; her hips were delicately modeled and her waist both slender and short, allowing for unusually fine long legs.

She scrubbed her face, neck and arms, splashing a good deal of the cool water over her bare shoulders, then removed the small combs that held her long black tresses in place, and brushed the cool water through her hair. She gathered the bulk of it low on her neck, tied it with a white ribbon and sat on the bank in the warm afternoon sunshine, gazing into the mirror. Her enormous brown eyes, set wide apart and framed by thin curved black brows, had recovered from their days of weeping and confusion: they were soft and clear. After having been set grimly in a thin line, her mouth was once again full and red-lipped. There was a spot of color high on her ivory-tinted cheeks. Her face, usually a little on the round side, was now slender-cheeked.

It becomes me, she thought. I'm only twenty-one. Surely life can't be over for me?

She put on the dark blue linen dress with the flaring skirt and white collar, wide and V-necked, looking like a bright shawl. Then she called out to her brother, who had borrowed her soap and was washing his hands and face in the creek.

"We can go now, Samuel. I'm feeling much better. I'm really anxious to see Mother and the family again. You haven't told me much about French Lick. Are there a lot of new settlers?"

He helped her into the saddle, mounted his horse and they went swiftly down the trail, the horses sensing their changed spirit and the eagerness to reach home. She turned to look at her brother and saw that he was smiling at her.

"You'll never recognize the old place, Rachel. They've even changed the name to Nashville. There must be about forty new cabins there, with two taverns, a store and a courthouse. It's really quite a big town you're coming home to."

3

Rachel was shocked to learn that her mother was already known throughout the Cumberland as the Widow Donelson. Their joy in this reunion was restrained, for Colonel Donelson had been killed on the trail since they last met; and now the Widow Donelson's youngest daughter and namesake was in trouble. Rachel could perceive little change in her mother in the three years since she had last seen her: about five feet two, a touch on the plump side, her hair a deep brown, her skin, except for the intricate network of lines radiating from the large brown eyes, still as soft in texture as Rachel had remembered it from her childhood. Only the warm bright light that had shown behind her mother's eyes was gone.

Rachel Stockly's family had settled in Virginia sometime before 1609 as original members of the Virginia Company; they had been large land and slave owners, and when seventeen-year-old Rachel Stockly married nineteen-year-old John Donelson and went with him to the western frontier of Virginia she took with her a substantial dowry, education and family tradition. They had come in handy, all three, in clearing the wilderness, raising eleven children, building a prosperous plantation and managing it while her husband served in three terms of the Virginia House of Burgesses.

"Rachel, perhaps you don't want to talk about it yet?"

They were sitting in the big room beneath the oblong porthole windows, sunlight flooding over their faces, so amazingly alike in coloring and bone structure, and in the quality of their unhappiness. Across the room the tall wooden cogwheeled clock sounded the buzzing whir of inside works before clanging out its metallic strokes.

"It seems so strange to me. I remember Lewis as a gay and carefree young man."

"Yes, we all thought so." Rachel's voice was soft and unhurried, with considerable body, as though coming from deep within her; both she and her mother had carried over the musical intonations of Virginia.

A familiar step sounded outside the room. Rachel had always been told that she was the prettiest of the Donelson girls, but looking up quickly she realized all over again that her sister Jane was the truly beautiful one of the family: a willowy figure, five feet six in height, halfway between the extremes of tall lean Catherine and short pudgy Mary; with fluffy blond hair that filled a dark room as radiantly as the September sunshine, light green eyes, cool and appraising, a sharp frosty tongue, realistic but not malicious. Jane had waited until she was twenty-six before marrying, an age called middle-yeared on the frontier, insisting that she must have a great man . . . or none at all; and had relentlessly passed by her young admirers, waiting until she found Colonel Robert Hays in Nashville, then knowing instantly that this was her man and this was her love.

Mrs. Donelson watched Rachel and Jane greet each other warmly, for these two younger of her four daughters had grown up as close friends. Rachel had known that Jane would come to her immediately. When their mother was called from the room, Jane asked:

"Rachel, what is wrong?"

Rachel hesitated for a moment; her pride made it difficult for her to speak even though she and Jane had always been confidantes. Then, forthrightly, she told Jane about the quarrels Lewis had precipitated because of his jealousy, of her own bewilderment and unhappiness over them; she described the humiliating scenes Lewis had created at parties and dances; and finally repeated Lewis's denunciation of her in their bedroom the last time she had seen him.

Jane listened attentively, her eyes never leaving her sister's face.

"His mother said he had gone stark mad, his sister and her husband, Jack Jouitt, believe that I have done no wrong, they told him so, but his ears were shut to them. His sister-in-law even accused him . . . Oh, Jane, there's a slave girl . . ."

Her calm left her and she sought refuge in Jane's arms, holding her face against her sister's long graceful neck. Jane stroked her hair.

"Samuel tells me that William is against me?"

"Oh yes, William the Cautious is thoroughly outraged and was dead-set against Samuel going for you." Jane's tone was icily refreshing, her voice a full octave higher than her sister's. "He has told people in the neighborhood that you've just come home for a visit and that you'll be returning to Harrodsburg next month. Johnny is also up in arms about what he calls the insult to our family name."

"It isn't only the humiliation, Jane, or even what William would call the disgrace of being put out of my husband's home; that's bad enough when you consider it has never happened to anyone we ever knew. But what am I to think about the future? Even a widow is better off; at least her position is clear. Do I remain Mrs. Lewis Robards all my life, and yet never lay eyes on my husband again? Jane, I mean to be strong . . . but my husband doesn't want me in his home, my brother doesn't want me here . . ."

"Rachel, why did you ever marry Lewis?"

She pulled away from Jane's embrace, her gentle brown eyes meeting her sister's cool dispassionate green eyes head-on.

"Then you never . . . liked him?"

"Oh, Captain Robards was the best-looking of the young men who took you to parties and dances; he dressed better than anyone else around and seemed to be more exuberant. The men he commanded during the war certainly idolized him . . ."

". . . but none of these things impressed you?"

"No, because I always felt that, inside himself, he was . . . uneasy. He took me to a few parties, you remember, while you were growing up. If he had a unified character, I couldn't find it; I never learned what he really wanted or believed."

"It's still . . . difficult," Rachel admitted slowly.

"Lewis is weak," pronounced Jane, "and you are strong because you're sure inside yourself. You're bright, and Lewis's mind is less active. In short, Rachel, I think you could have married considerable more man."

"I loved him, Jane."

Jane chose her words carefully as she asked the all-important question.

"And what about now, Rachel? Do you still love Lewis? Or perhaps you would rather answer that to yourself?"

Did she still love Lewis? She had suffered at his hands, had lost a great many of her romantic illusions. Now, after three years, she understood her husband in the sense that Jane had understood him from the beginning. This unfocused quality, his unwillingness to relieve his mother as manager of the prosperous Robards plantation, or to involve himself for long in any task; his inability to have confidence in himself . . . or her.

"If only we had children . . ." she replied resolutely. "Perhaps children are what he needs to settle him down, to give him a sense of permanence."

The Widow Donelson's station was some ten miles north of Nashville, just beyond where the Kentucky Road joined the Cumberland Road. The following morning, thinking to divert her, Samuel suggested that they ride into the town of Nashville; there had been only one stockade on the bluff overlooking the river when the Donelsons had abandoned the Cumberland after the disastrous summer of 1780.

Their first stop was Lardner Clark's store, a double-sized log cabin, mud-chinked, the only light coming from the open front door and from the grease lamps hung on the back wall. There were long roughhewn counters on either side; on the left, little piles of clothing and household goods: pans, dishware, candles; on the opposite side, sugar, salt, spices, whisky, smoked meats; and at the back the shelves containing axes, cow bells, a few farming implements, rifles, powder and shot,

There were three families in the store when Rachel and Samuel entered. The first to see them were the John Rainses, who had come to the Cumberland with the Donelsons. They greeted Rachel warmly, expressed their delight at seeing her again and wished her a happy visit with her family. The second group were new acquaintances of Samuel's; when he introduced his sister, the young wife of the couple said:

"You'll come visit us soon as you settle? Sam, you be sure to bring her now, there's so few young people in the station where we live,"

Rachel squeezed the young woman's hand. Then she felt a pair of eyes staring at her from the back of the store.

"Why, it's Martha Dinsmore, from Harrodsburg."

She started toward Mrs. Dinsmore, but even in the semi-darkness she saw that the woman's expression was forbidding. Rachel stopped short. Mrs. Dinsmore turned away with no sign of recognition, pushing her wide skirts forward and around her, as though to keep them clear of sin.

The blood rushed to Rachel's head. She thought she heard Mrs. Dinsmore say:

"Where there's smoke there's bound to be fire."

Did I really hear those words, she asked herself, or is it just my imagination? How could the news have come down the trail so quickly? Her father used to say: "Bad news travels fast because it has so many helping hands." If Martha Dinsmore knew and could feel this way, there would be others.

She felt Samuel gripping her arm.

"Rachel, you've turned a sour-apple green. You mustn't pay attention to people like that. There are always a few who get pleasure from believing the worst."

"I'll never expose myself again. I'm going to stay home until it's all over . . . till it's all over . . ."

4

She stepped out onto the hard-bitten earth of the yard, which was enclosed by a high stockade fence sheltering the spacious two-story main house, a large barn and six smaller cabins used for the kitchen, dairy, storehouse, smokehouse, guest cabin, forge and leather shed. It was the first of March, five months since she had come back to the Donelsons'. The sky was a brittle blue, the sun bright but the air cool. She walked to the kitchen to inspect the sides of venison, bear and buffalo that were broiling on their spits, the wild turkeys and geese roasting on their suspended hempen cords, the pigeon pies baking in deep coal beds along with dozens of hoecakes and johnnycakes. It was a double birthday, for her oldest brother Alexander, who was forty, and her youngest, Samuel, exactly half that age. This had always been the gayest day in the Donelsons' year; back in Virginia the entire countryside had been invited in for the feast.

Rachel was the only one of the four daughters now living at home; the Widow Donelson had turned over the household management to her, pretending to want a winter of rest. Rachel had been thankful for the busiest months of her life, supervising the making of the soap and candles, carding and spinning of the wool into yarn, stuffing the new pillows and mattresses.

She stood in the open door of the cabin watching Moll, the deep-bosomed, gray-haired Negress in a dress of drab hunter's cloth who had helped to raise her and had been bequeathed to her in her father's will, along with Moll's husband, George. Inside she saw her brother William, who managed the plantation, drinking a hot toddy with the Reverend Craighead, who had had Christmas dinner at the Donelsons' and routed his circuit riding so that the first of March would see him back in Nashville. William was a heavy-boned slow-moving man; he had never become reconciled to her living away from her husband. In the opposite corner, tightening catgut, sat James Gamble, who traveled from station to station, Bledsoe's to Eaton's to Freeland's to the Donelsons', carrying his fiddle fondly in a sack of soft doeskin, and telling everyone, "I love her, but I never squeeze her so as to break down the bridge or put her out of tune." He took no pay for his fiddling; he and his wife, as he called the violin, entertained at weddings, christenings, holidays, birthdays, logrollings, house-raisings, and were even called in to soothe the pains of the sick and wounded.

She stepped into the kitchen where Moll was spooning the juices out of the low-lying pan and basting the turkeys with them.

"Have we plenty of meat roasting, Moll? It's beginning to look as though I asked the whole Cumberland Valley."

"And about time, Miz Rachel." She spoke quietly so William and the Reverend Craighead would not hear. "I don't take to you lockin' yourself up the whole winter like you done . . . not even one dance or quiltin' bee or house-raisin'."

Rachel let her gaze wander about the kitchen, which had been equipped to cook for a hundred. Almost the entire east wall was a huge stone fireplace; across the top of the room were long poles of dried apples, peppers and pumpkin rings. Strung on the lug pole were her mother's favorite iron pot, weighing some forty pounds, the rotating clock jack for roasting meats, the smaller brassware pots and highly polished copper kettles. On the hearth stood the potato boiler, the dye tub and Dutch oven.

"I haven't been lonely," she murmured, "with ten brothers and sisters. And I really haven't wanted to see . . . outsiders."

Moll carefully measured out the precious coffee for the pot of water hanging on the crane over the fire, then turned for a penetrating look at Rachel. They were friends and trusted each other.

"You ha'n't done nothin', Miz Rachel. If you're not married no more, then I seen lots of fine young men come here for militia meetin's and taxes payin', and they's plenty you could have for husband. How long you think you goin' hide that pretty young face of yourn inside the house, even refusin' to go to suppers to Miz Jane's? How long you gonna be like a prisoner?"

Rachel went to the open doorway of the kitchen and stood gazing at the big and prosperous Donelson stockade, at the young apple and peach orchards which her seven brothers had planted, at the plowed fields which the boys would seed with corn, cotton, wheat, indigo and tobacco, Beyond was the pasture with a herd of thirty milk cows and the family's twenty-odd horses. Except for the high pointed palings which surrounded the station, their new home was coming to look more and more like the Virginia plantation they had been obliged to sell back in 1779, when she was twelve years old and her father had suffered reverses through the failure of his infant ironworks, the first to be established in that part of the country. That was when the entire family had set forth on the flatboat *Adventure* for the voyage down the Holston and Tennessee, then up the Ohio and Cumberland rivers, a two-thousand-mile journey through wild country and uncharted waters.

Images floated through her mind of how they had lived in tents on the south side of the Stone River while they felled the trees, broke the fields to the plow, planted cotton, surveyed a six-forty for each of the boys, and combined with their few neighbors to stave off the Indian attacks. She remembered how heartbroken her father had been when their crops had been flooded out and they were forced to take refuge at Mansker's station, spending more of their hours repulsing Indian attacks than working their fields. In the fall, when John Donelson realized he could not establish the legality of their land titles, they had chosen to retreat over the Kentucky Road to Harrodsburg where the family had settled for five years, until shortly after her marriage to Lewis Robards, and had then returned en masse to French Lick, determined that this time they would not be driven out,

And now, after only three years, they had built the most prosperous plantation in the Cumberland Valley. What a pity her father could not have lived to see this; for the settling of the Cumberland had been the last great dream of his life. People had said that the failure of the ironworks had been only an excuse for old Colonel Donelson, that he had the wilderness fever. The colonel had been killed on the Kentucky Road just a few days after he had visited Rachel in Harrodsburg, while returning from a business trip to Virginia. He had always said, "There isn't an Indian alive who can kill me," and for more than forty years had proven his contention by traversing the wilderness, surveying and treaty-making with the Indians for the Virginia government. He had been shot to death not far from Nashville and his brief case rifled; the Donelsons believed that his two companions on the trail, strangers to the frontier, had murdered their father.

She shook her head with a quick dispelling movement as though to unloose these pictures, then started back toward the main house. Suddenly she stopped, seeing a figure framed in the open doorway of the guest cabin. The man had his back to her; he turned and she exclaimed in astonishment:

"Why, it's John Overton!"

Through her mind flashed the thought, He comes from the Robards'. He will have news for me . . . perhaps a letter . . .

Eagerly, she crossed the yard to greet him.

John Overton was a small man, all clashing angles and nervous movements, and though he was only twenty-three years old his almost colorless straw hair barely covered his scalp. His chin was bony and turned up, his nose was bony and turned down, and between them his bloodless lips seemed to be not only overwhelmed but lost; his eyes were such a light vapor gray that half the time they seemed not to be there at all, and you imagined yourself to be looking out the back of his head. Yet after five minutes of talking with him Rachel always forgot that he was ugly, at the end of ten minutes she no longer imagined him to be plain, and at the end of an hour she believed him to be a beautiful human being. Behind Overton's seemingly transparent eyes there was at work a first-rate brain: fast, rangy, disciplined, logical, humorous, yet with the flinty incorruptibility of his Scottish ancestors. Inside himself, where he lived and breathed and fought, he was a big man; only newcomers were deceived by his unlikely shell.

"How good it is to see you again, Rachel. And how well you're looking."

"And you too, John." She hesitated a moment. "Are you passing through our country on business?"

"No, I've decided to settle in Nashville and open my law office here. So of course I came straight to the Donelsons' and asked your mother if she would take me in."

A slow flush crept up Rachel's cheeks: Overton's coming directly to the Donelsons' was an act of faith on his part; he had been a witness to the Peyton Short episode, had even risked Lewis's anger by refuting him. A man of John Overton's rigorously ethical nature would never have come here if he had considered his relative injured; he would have had as little as possible to do with the Donelson clan. And certainly if he had at any time suspected Rachel of wrongdoing he would not have been so indiscreet as to expose her to further gossip. She felt deeply grateful to him.

"I'm happy you are going to be part of our family, John. And I know you're going to be a fine lawyer. You have the talent and temperament for it."

His lips pursed while he judiciously weighed in his own mind the possibilities of his becoming a good lawyer. He was a bookish man; the passion in his life was the law, its nature, philosophy, logic and structure.

"All I know, Rachel, is that I have a great love for the law, and if love be sufficient . . ."

"Love is sufficient for nearly everything, John . . ."

She broke off. They stood facing each other in silence, both thinking of Lewis Robards. She had had no word from her husband in the five months since she had returned to Nashville, nor had there been any report on the outcome of his duel with Peyton Short. From the timbre of the silence she knew she had been right in assuming that Overton brought news from Harrodsburg, yet she sensed that he would never so much as mention Lewis Robards until she gave him permission to do so.

She gazed at him for a moment longer in silence. Was his news good or bad? And for that matter, how would she differentiate between the two when she herself hardly knew what she wanted from the future? John Overton's reticent expression confided little. And she knew that she did not want to, could not, in fact, hear his news now. Perhaps when the party was over.

"I must finish my tour of inspection," she said abruptly. "Once again, John, the heartiest of welcomes."

5

It was night, the children had been awakened from sleep and bundled up, the guests had departed. Her family had retired, exhausted from the day-long festivities. She could still hear the happy sound of the hundred or more voices, the singing, the heart-warming laughter and gaiety.

But now everything was quiet in the big room, the last of the candles extinguished, the lamps snuffed, the fire banked and cooling; behind her the tall clock made its buzzing whir, then clanged out twelve strokes.

She stood at the porthole, slipped a wooden bolt and opened the heavy wooden shutter, gazing up at the lone star in the March night. She tried to warm herself by pulling more compactly into the yellow wool dress, crossing her arms on her chest and holding the long sleeves tightly, pressing so hard against the bleached bone buttons that she felt them dig into her flesh. Her heart felt as cold in her bosom as the star up in the chill sky. She felt lonely and sad; the Donelsons had done everything they could to make her feel welcome, yet as she stood trembling at the window she felt not only unwanted but rejected. During these months she had recoiled emotionally from all serious thinking about her husband, but with John Overton at hand she must try to determine her feelings about Lewis. Then, when she heard Overton's news, she would be prepared, she would know how to deal with it.

She had loved Lewis Robards; he had seemed to her the handsomest, most romantic figure she had met, one of the most admired of the war heroes in Kentucky. He had wooed her with ardor and impetuousness. She had loved him during the first peaceful year of their marriage.

And now? Did she love him still? Did she think of him harshly? Or did she pity him, think of him as ill? That had been the way his mother had explained his rages. Mrs. Robards had said:

"It's something the war did to Lewis. He was so happy during the years we were fighting: life was a great adventure for him then. He liked the hardships, the dangers, the command of his men, the forced marches and swift attacks. He was living hard and bright and true, every minute of it. But when the war ended . . . when he came home to . . . inaction . . . overseeing the spring planting . . . he felt as though the best part of his life had already been lived. He became bored, morose, irritable. That was why I thanked God for you, Rachel; I was sure that with you he would find a new life and new happiness."

Yes, she felt sorry for Lewis, in the way she would for a child who was forever stumbling in the dark and hurting himself. Had he been in the room now she would have cradled his head on her breast and wept for him, for his twisted unhappy life.

She murmured half aloud to the dark room and to the lone light in the sky, All my dreams and plans and hopes are tied up in my marriage. Without it I am nothing, I have no place, no hearth, no future. I am a woman dispossessed. I want my husband back and a home of my own . . .

She watched the sun rise. When it was well above the horizon and she heard the first stirrings throughout the house, she walked across the yard to speak to John Overton. Spring had broken early that year: the jonquils were banked thick as butter on the slopes leading down to the river, running clear again after its cargo of mud; the cardinals, silent all winter, were singing in the tall yellow poplars. While she tried to slow down the beating of her heart she counted the sparrows, chickadees and woodpeckers exchanging perches on the highest limbs of oaks, beeches and sycamores. In a corner of a freshly furrowed field she heard an old cock quail calling bobwhite. The earliest violets were showing through the fresh vernal grass and across the river a young peach orchard had begun to show its pink blossoms. She felt quieter now.

"John, I feel that Lewis has asked you to bring a message to me. I appreciate your not saying anything until I was ready . . ."

Overton bowed slightly, took his silver-rimmed spectacles from an inside coat pocket and slipped them on. For a moment Rachel thought he was going to read her a paper of some sort, then she remembered that John used his glasses not to see more clearly the print in front of his eyes, but rather the thoughts behind them.

"Rachel, Lewis has cleared you completely. I've heard him tell his friends in Harrodsburg that he has been the blindest fool."

A long soughing breath escaped from her, one that seemed to have been held in pent-up suspense since the day her husband had written to the Donelsons to come and take their daughter away.

"Your husband assured me of how much he regretted your separation; he told me that he was convinced his suspicions were unfounded, that he loves you and wishes to live with you again. He requested that I use my exertions to restore harmony,'"

"You can imagine how happy I am to hear this, John. And the duel with Peyton Short? Neither of them was hurt?"

The flow of communication was suddenly shut off. She saw John's jaw set a little, as though he had locked his back teeth.

"There were no serious results."

The silence fell again. Rachel perceived that she would have to make the next move; there was something unpleasant here, something in which Overton had been offended.

"Please go on, John," she said softly.

"I told Lewis that I would undertake to restore harmony, providing he would put down his jealousy and treat you kindly as other men treat their wives. For I would not like this to happen to you again, Rachel."

His sympathy broke through the structure of her constraint.

"Oh, John, I felt so . . . degraded,"

"Lewis says that if you will come back to him he will never again cause you unhappiness."

She tried to separate her tumultuous feelings, not the least of which was the fact that she would be vindicated in the eyes of the world. Now that her husband had declared his confidence in her, she would go back to him, of course; for when had she ever wanted to be apart? But could she feel secure in Harrodsburg where Lewis had humiliated her so often and so abjectly by his torrential scenes? Could she return to the Robards home where that young girl would be in daily evidence? Above all, how could that same unfocused life for the two of them, with Lewis unwilling or unable to take the responsibility of running the plantation, passing his days in hunting and long stretches of idleness, ever breed anything but the same unhappiness she had already known?

Her face was averted while she was thinking; John Overton left her in peace, disturbing her neither with words spoken nor with words thought. Now she turned back to him. She had a forthright manner, with little that was complex or devious in her nature; her gaze was direct, she looked people straight in the eye the instant they met and continued to hold this personal contact as long as they spoke together: she was entirely willing that others should know what she was thinking, since there was rarely anything harsh, hidden or condemnatory in her thoughts. Nor did she have any inner protective veil with which to shield her eyes and their mirrorings.

"John, there is nothing I want more than to be with my husband again. I'm convinced that our problems at the Robards home make it impossible for us to live there happily. My father registered a fine piece of land for us just a few miles from this station, a square-mile preemption that can be turned into a good plantation. Would you be so kind as to write to Lewis and tell him that I reciprocate his feelings, but that I feel we have a far greater chance of success if he will come here to Nashville where we can build a house on our land and start an entirely new life for ourselves?''

6

She heard a hammering on the iron front-door knocker, gentle at first, then insistent. When no one answered, she left her bedroom on the second floor and came down the rough plank stairs. She opened the door and saw a tall young man with a thick mop of sandy-red hair. Apparently he had grown a little discouraged, for he was half turned, looking toward the heavy log gate which had been barred behind him. She was glad he had turned away momentarily, for it gave her a chance to study this odd-looking creature in the ill-fitting black homespun suit. He seemed the tallest man she had ever laid eyes on, surely some six and a half feet, she thought; and with a thinness to match his height.

The back of his head seemed disproportionately massive to the slender features which she could see in profile, with the high forehead and flat-ridged nose; but then everything about him seemed a little disproportionate: the incredibly long face, the long thin neck which appeared too delicate to support such a heavy head; the oblong torso and the gangling arms and legs. He looked like a youth whose figure had stretched to its outermost limits and would now require a full decade to fill out; yet in spite of this sense of physical immaturity he held himself rigidly erect, and there was a suggestion of power, as though this scraggly body were having difficulty containing its own force.

The man felt her presence; he wheeled sharply. She found herself gazing up into the largest and most brilliant pair of blue eyes she had ever encountered, vibrant and piercing in their quality. He seemed to be towering at least three heads above her, yet there was nothing formidable about him; rather she felt a warm glow and discovered to her astonishment that both she and the young stranger were smiling at each other amusedly.

''Please forgive my intrusion, ma'am, but I am Andrew Jackson of Nashville, a friend of John Overton's.''

''But of course, Mr. Jackson. We've been hearing tales of your exploits ever since you came here. I am Mrs. Lewis Robards.''

He bowed slowly from the waist, acknowledging the introduction; and everything about him, not only his courtly gesture, but the angular tilt of his big head, the opening of his sensitive, slightly moist lips, the smile in his brilliant blue eyes, all of these bespoke a deep, ingrained courtesy. She noted a scar on the left side of his forehead, saber-thin, arcing from his hairline down to the thick undisciplined eyebrow.

''Then you'd be Widow Donelson's daughter from Kentucky?''

Rachel felt the color rise to her cheeks. Had he heard of her difficulties?

''I've come to ask a favor, Mrs. Robards. Since I reached Nashville, beginning of last November, I've been living at the inns. John Overton tells me there's room in the cabin he's occupying. Do you think your mother would take me in? I am a crack shot with a rifle and have had considerable experience in fighting the Indians.''

He blushes like a schoolboy, she thought. But then he is a boy. Surely he can't be over twenty?

"I would consider it a great honor to be able to join this family," she heard him saying. "Oh, Mrs. Robards, if you could know how tired I am of the brawling and drinking and the greasy eatables at the Red Heifer!"

"Well, Mr. Jackson, we certainly are glad to have all the protection we can get. Our neighbor Captain Hunter was killed last week by some Creeks and when our men pursued them, they killed Major Kirkpatrick." She hesitated for a moment. "But I am not the mistress of this station. My mother and my brother William are in Nashville for the day."

She saw him turn and gaze wistfully at the full saddlebags on his horse; he had brought all his possessions with him. He was a bold man, sure enough, with a lean scrawny sense of independence, but she also felt that he was a little lonely.

"You said that John Overton is willing to share his cabin with you?"

"Oh yes, we have just formed a partnership, the long of the law I guess you'd call it: I'm long on height and he's long on the law. He said we could hold our office right here."

"But aren't you attached to the court? An officer . . . ?"

"Indeed I am, ma'am; Judge McNairy and I brought that court with us from North Carolina. I carry the hifalutin title of attorney general; that only means I proscute criminals where and as I find them. Rest of the time I'm just like all other lawyers, looking mighty hard for cases."

Again that queer combination of strength: the lawbreaker would be caught and prosecuted, his voice left no doubt about that: and humility, the young lawyer hopefully awaiting clients.

Rachel felt certain that her mother and William would welcome this young man, in fact they had spoken several times of bringing someone in to share the cabin with Overton; yet she had no authority to give him assent. Neither could she turn him away.

"In any event, you must stay to supper with us, Mr. Jackson. The family will want to meet you."

"Thank you, Mrs. Robards, I was frankly hoping you would invite me."

"Why not take your things out of the saddlebags and bring them over to the cabin in the meanwhile? Then you can turn your horse out in the canebrake."

He did as he had been bidden. Rachel walked across the yard with him while he supported the bulging bags on his bony shoulders, a rifle nursed under each arm. She pushed open the door to the cabin. The log house was fourteen by twenty-two feet inside, with a small sleeping room at the back containing a big double bed, a stand, a pitcher and a bowl of water. The front room was about fourteen by twelve with two good-sized porthole windows and a fireplace with a shelf above it on which John Overton kept the volumes of his law library. There was a heavy walnut table, two chairs made of hickory, a rude cupboard in which Overton's extra suit and shirts were stored, deerhorn racks on which were hung one rifle, two pistols and several buckhorns for powder, and an iron grease lamp suspended from the wall.

Andrew Jackson stood in the middle of the room, the top of his massive red hair barely an inch beneath the crossbeams which held up the roof, gazing at the fieldstone fireplace, then at Overton's books, at the pistols and powder horns and colorful striped cotton curtains at the windows.

"This is about the prettiest cabin I've been in," he said softly. "Are you superstitious, Mrs Robards? I am. For instance, I like to start new ventures on a Tuesday, like today, but I'll never begin anything on a Friday."

"That wouldn't be the Irish in you, by chance?"

He grinned, rubbing the freckles that ran like a speckled band straight across his nose and high cheekbones. There was an openness, a guilelessness about his smile that was like her own: suggesting to her a man who had little to conceal, and even less temperament with which to conceal it. His mouth was large, the teeth strong, compact.

"My mother always said I carried two things that gave away Carrickfergus on me: my face and my temper."

He went down on his haunches beside his bags, took out a half dozen books including Matthew Bacon's *Abridgement of the Law*, packets of ammunition, tea, tobacco and salt, two blankets and some spare clothing, which he hung in the cupboard.

"I'll just unpack a few little possessions and put them away. Then if your mother or your brother should say no, I'll come over quietly, get my things and slip them into my saddlebags."

Rachel watched his quick, awkward movements which somehow had considerable grace in them; and she was aware of a tiny smile, not on her lips, but somewhere inside her head.

At that instant the young man turned, rose, stood towering above her. They gazed at each other in silence, even as they had in that first surprised moment at the front door of the Donelson home.

7

She had refused all invitations to parties in the neighborhood, even when they were held in the homes of old friends, fearful lest people misunderstand if they found her dancing and enjoying herself. She had not wanted anyone to think that she was flouting her husband, or that she did not grasp the true implication of her situation. But John's good news spread over the Cumberland Valley, abetted, she knew, by her brothers who had informed the countryside of Lewis Robards' impending arrival and of his public acknowledgment that he had been wrong.

Now she felt free again and happy.

Sunday was gathering day for the Donelson clan. At the head of the polished split-log table sat Mrs. Donelson, and at the foot Rachel's oldest sister Mary, the plump pigeon of the family, fat-cheeked, cheerful, homey, a magnificent cook, whose twelve children went up in regular steps like rungs of the ladder to a hayloft, and whose oldest child was almost Rachel's age. Next to Mary sat her husband, John Caffrey, who had wanted to add on rooms or build new cabins as his progeny increased year by year; but Mary had refused, insisting that she wanted her children under her feet. Across from John Caffrey sat the next sister, Catherine, tall, stringy, gray, unrelentingly vocal at home with her nine children, but always silent at these family reunions. With her was her husband, Thomas Hutchings, a quiet but sympathetic man.

In the first seat on the right sat John, Jr., not because he was the oldest; Alexander, the first-born and perennial bachelor of the sharp yellow teeth and migratory feet, had gladly given up this place of ascendancy to Johnny who, because he bore his father's name, had become the titular head of the family. Opposite Johnny sat Alexander, next to him, William the Cautious, and then Samuel. Rachel's regular seat was next to Samuel's. Across from her were Robert and Jane Hays, and immediately next to Jane was Stockly, the sometime lawyer and politician of the family. John Overton sat next to Rachel with Andrew Jackson across from him, next to Stockly. The two last seats at the bottom of the board were occupied by Leven, who was two years older than Rachel but still an immature boy, and Severn, who was the ill member of the family, hollow-cheeked and with a severe cough.

Rachel noticed Jane watching Andrew Jackson intently, for the spring term of the Davidson County court was to open the following morning, and Samuel, who was fascinated by the two young boarders, was asking endless questions about the law. Andrew Jackson had been circuit riding up in Sumner County just before joining the Donelsons, and he had amusing tales to tell about Joshua Baldwin, who had been indicted by the Grand Jury for altering his name to Joshua Campbell; of William Pillows, who had been convicted of biting off the upper end of Abram Denton's ear; and of John Irwin, who had been sentenced to declare publicly that the "rascally and scandalous report I have raised and reported concerned Miss Polly McFadin is false and groundless, and I had no right, reason or cause to believe the same."

Samuel had been drifting aimlessly during the months since Rachel had been at home, not knowing whether he wanted to be a teacher or preacher or perhaps surveyor; he had taken on a new vitality since the lawyers had entered the family circle. Further to stimulate his interest, Rachel too began asking questions about court procedure. John Overton said:

"Samuel, I heard your mother say that you were riding up to Nashville in the morning to do some shopping at Lardner Clark's. Mr. Jackson and I have a number of interesting cases to try, so why don't you bring your mother and sister to court?"

"Won't Judge McNairy be upset at having lady visitors?" asked Rachel.

"Surprised, perhaps," replied Overton, "but on the pleasurable side. Besides, my partner is an officer of the court and I'm sure he'd be glad to intercede for you."

The next morning Rachel and her mother donned their severe black wool riding dresses which best resisted the dust of the ten-mile ride into town. In Mr. Clark's general store they bought a loaf of sugar, some whole spices to be ground at home and a bolt of unbleached muslin. Several of the women greeted Rachel, hugging her and saying how well she was looking. Then they walked up the rutted street to where a large number of horses were hitched to the stocks and whipping posts in front of the courthouse, which was built of hewn logs, chinked with a dried mortar-like mud. On the south side was a twelve-foot porch crowded with men who had ridden many miles to watch the day's litigation. They were dressed in buckskin trousers, leather leggings, buffalo-hide moccasins and the long deerskin hunting shirt with the uneven knife-cut fringes over the shoulders. Rachel saw a number of friends among them, bowed and exchanged greetings.

Samuel took each of the women by an arm. As they went toward the open door Rachel drew back with an instinctive shudder of distaste: for the interior was filthy, with mud, dirt and dust over everything, tobacco spittle in the corners, the two doors askew, the window shutters sagging, the entire place reeking of neglect. At the end of the small room was a long table behind which sat a young man of twenty-six, John McNairy, the first judge to have been appointed by the legislature of North Carolina for this Western District. There were also a number of split-log benches for the spectators and litigants, who now turned to gape at the two ladies standing in the doorway.

"I think we had better go," said Rachel, feeling self-conscious.

At that moment Jackson and Overton came from the end of the courtroom where they had been discussing the calendar with Judge McNairy, the only three men in the courtroom dressed in store suits and white shirts.

"Here, let me make you comfortable," said Jackson.

He pulled a bench into line, wiping it vigorously with an enormous colored handkerchief. Samuel sat down, his eyes bright and his hands clasped tightly in his lap. Neither Rachel nor her mother moved. Rachel's eyes continued to study the courthouse. Finally she turned to the two men and said:

"Yesterday when you were discussing the law I commented to myself on what a great respect both of you have for your profession. Then I come into this . . . forgive me . . . pigsty. How can you work here? How can you establish any dignity?

How can anyone respect the law, or lawyers, or any decision that the judge might make?''

The men looked at each other for a moment in blank silence.

"Mrs. Robards is completely right," said Jackson, as though seeing the interior for the first time. "Why didn't we think of it for ourselves?"

"I am just a fresh-baked lawyer, Rachel," Overton said, "but our friend Mr. Jackson here is the attorney general. Anything he says the court will have to take under advisement."

Rachel turned to Jackson expectantly, but he ducked one shoulder, grinning.

"Mr. Overton," he said, "I hereby appoint you special counsel for the city of Nashville to plead the case of this neglected courthouse."

John's silver spectacles moved up and down on his nose as his decision fluctuated. After a moment he walked ceremoniously up the crooked center aisle.

"Your Honor, it is a rule of equity," he said in his slow, meticulous voice, "that every suitor shall come into court with a clean shirttail. Without unnecessary offense to the majesty of the law, the ermine of judges or the purity of anybody, I defy suitor or advocate, much more this honorable court, to maintain pure thoughts and white linen in such a pigsty."

Rachel shrank; she had used the descriptive term for private rather than public consumption. Judge McNairy's eyes circled the courtroom slowly from left to right, then he too said in a slow drawl:

"Counselor is right. Is David Hay in court? Mr. Hay, I herewith order you to repair the courthouse by making two doors well fixed and hung, with three window shutters well hung, and the benches repaired. Each day that the court meets you shall see that it is swept, washed and cleansed, compensation to be arranged when this court adjourns."

She saw Jackson and John exchange an exaggerated wink. She and her mother sat down beside Samuel, who was chuckling. At that moment Hugh McGary burst into the courtroom, his face hard-set with anger.

"Andrew, I'm not going to need you for that case against Casper Mansker. I'm going to kill him right here in the courthouse and take possession of that slave. We had a written agreement, then he goes and loses the bill of sale on purpose."

Jackson rose, put a long-fingered hand on McGary's shoulder and said in a placating voice:

"Now, Hugh, I think this can be settled peaceably. Casper Mansker is one of the oldest settlers around here and everybody says his word is better than a bushel of salt."

A voice behind Rachel called, "Did I hear someone ask for me?"

"Yes, Hugh McGary and I were looking for you, Mr. Mansker," Jackson replied quickly. "My client and I have just been thinking we ought to find a friendly compromise. Let's go sun ourselves on the south porch, gentlemen, then we'll really be settling this matter out of court."

Rachel saw Jackson link his arms through old Mr. Mansker's and McGary's, and take them not so much by physical force as by force of will out of the court's jurisdiction.

"He isn't at all like the stories they tell about him," commented Mrs. Donelson. "He's really quite gentle."

"What kind of stories have you been hearing, Mother?" asked Rachel.

"Well, there's the story of that bully in Sumner County who purposely stepped on his foot in the public square, and then came back to step on it a second time just to make sure Mr. Jackson knew it was on purpose."

"And what did our peaceable Mr. Jackson do?"

"Why, he picked up a rail from the top of a fence and knocked the man down."

They heard a tremendous clatter of hoofs and the noise of a shouting band. By turning her head Rachel could see a group of men in filthy buckskin shirts carrying rifles, their faces grimy, hair uncombed. She watched while they sprang off their horses, several of them picking quarrels with men standing on the porch.

Samuel asked if something couldn't be done. She had not noticed that Andrew Jackson had returned to the courtroom.

"If I was an officer of the court a few minutes ago," he replied slowly, "making jokes about appointing John as special counsel to get the place cleaned up, then I guess I am still the attorney general when Spill Cimberlin heaves into sight."

He extracted a court citation from a sheaf of papers he was holding in his left hand, walked to the door and cried in a strong voice:

"First case on the docket is the State versus Spill Cimberlin, charged with theft, disturbing the peace, assault and contempt of the court."

Rachel rose so that she could see through the doorway to the crowd beyond. Spill Cimberlin shifted his rifle to a more comfortable position under his arm, came within a few inches of Jackson and stuck his face forward so that his nose was almost touching the younger man's.

"There ain't no damned court on this whole frontier that's man enough to try me."

"That's no way to speak about your own courts, Spill," replied Jackson. "The law is here to protect you as well as to punish you. If you've done wrong, then by gumshun you're going to be punished."

"And who's going to punish me, a skinny green saplin' like you?"

There was a silence during which Rachel watched the muscles in Jackson's jaw work up and down. He turned, went a short distance to his saddlebags, pulled out his own two pistols and cocked them as he whirled about. He walked straight at Spill Cimberlin, the guns aimed at the man's head. Rachel went cold; Cimberlin's rifle needed only the slightest bit of raising. When Andrew got within three feet of Cimberlin he said in a voice that carried the length of the main street of Nashville:

"Step up to the bar of justice and be tried by His Honor, or I'll blow your meager brains out."

There was an insucking hush. If Cimberlin was going to do anything, this was the second when he must fire. But the man slowly sagged at the shoulders. Excited talk broke out; Rachel turned to her mother,

"Would Mr. Jackson really have shot him?"

"Mr. Cimberlin seemed to think so," replied Mrs. Donelson with a smile.

Judge McNairy banged his gavel.

"By the way, Mother," Rachel asked, "what has happened to your picture of our new boarder as a peaceful man?"

As they were leaving court after adjournment, Jackson fell in step beside Rachel.

"Weren't you frightened?" she queried. "Mr, Cimberlin could have killed you awful dead."

"Oh, I was just showing off," he replied, pleased with himself. "Besides, I like to graze danger."

8

That evening at supper, while thundershowers pounded down intermittently on the roof, they lingered at the table with the light of the pine knots and logs on their faces. Mrs. Donelson asked:

"Don't you have any family of your own here in the West, Mr. Jackson?"

"No, Mrs. Donelson, I'm an orphan. Have been since I was fourteen. My father died a few days before I was born, hurt himself trying to lift a whole tree log up at our place in the Waxhaws. I had two brothers; Hugh, the oldest, he died after the battle at Stono Ferry. My mother rescued my younger brother Robert and me from the British military prison at Camden, but Robert died two days after we got home, of infected wounds and smallpox.''

He stopped abruptly; his long expressive face lost its pallor and became suddenly very red while the livid scar on his forehead stood out like a silver scimitar.

"When I pulled through the smallpox, my mother heard that my cousins, Joseph and William Crawford, had been taken by the British and were lying sick in a prison ship off Charleston, so she gathered up all the medicine she could find and made the journey with two other women. I don't know how many days she spent in that prisonhold trying to cure the boys, but she contracted ship's fever too and didn't get very far on the way home, just a couple of miles out of Charleston. I don't even know where she is buried. It's an unmarked grave in an open plain. I've searched several times, but nobody seems to know.''

His voice trailed off, the enormous head was lowered, the heavy lids closed. Rachel had never heard him speak this way before; for the first time she sensed the tenderness in the man and his overpowering need for love. When he looked up again there were tears in his eyes.

"That's why, Mrs. Donelson, I think the greatest thing in the world any man can have is a family, the bigger the better.''

"I wish I had another daughter for you.''

"Seeing as how there are no more Donelson girls,'' said Rachel, "as soon as my husband and I are settled in our new house we'll scour the countryside and give a lot of wonderful parties. Unless there is some girl waiting for you back in Jonesboro or Salisbury?''

He gazed at her for a moment from across the hearth, then answered in a bantering tone:

"Oh, sure, ma'am, dozens of them, whole jury panels full.''

"What are their names?''

"Names? Oh yes.'' He ran his thin tapering fingers through the mass of red hair, pulling some of it down over his forehead. "Let's see, there was . . . why, of course, Susan Smart, in the Waxhaws, used to tell me I had agreeable eyes and that I was a leaning-forward fellow. Then there was Nancy Jarret in Salisbury. Pretty girl, Nancy. Could ride a horse as fast as a March wind. But her mother didn't approve of me, said I drank and gambled too much.''

"And did you?''

"Oh, I suppose so. I was a wild lad as a student. But there wasn't much else to do when taverns were the only place a man could find to live. When I was sixteen and my grandfather left me a legacy of three hundred pounds, I went to Charleston and lost that money on the racing ponies so fast my head is still spinning. But since joining the Donelson family I've become a sober, responsible citizen. Don't even gamble any more, and won't . . . until I can build me the finest stable of racing horses on the frontier.''

But it was from John Overton that the Donelson family got its real grasp of Andrew Jackson's character. John commented quietly:

"He towers over all other men I've ever known. You've noticed that scar on his forehead, of course.''

There was a general nodding of heads.

"Back in 1781, it was, Andrew and his two brothers were fighting under their uncle, Major Crawford, against the British Dragoons who had invaded the Waxhaws. The Dragoons attacked our men in the local church, setting it on fire. Andrew and his young cousin Thomas Crawford managed to escape but they were overtaken and Crawford was made a prisoner. The next morning when Andrew made his way back to the Crawford home to tell them what had happened to their son, a company of Dragoons surprised the family. The British officer commanded Andrew to clean his high jack boots, which were splashed and crusted with mud. Andrew was only fourteen and just about came up to the middle button of the officer's red coat, but he cried out: 'Sir, I am a prisoner of war and claim to be treated as such!'"

"I can just hear the tone of voice in which he said it," commented Samuel.

"The commanding officer lifted his sword and swung it down on Andrew's head. Andrew threw up his arm, which was gashed to the bone; that's how he saved his life, but the tip of the sword cut his forehead."

There was silence while the seven brothers went back into their memories; they had all fought in the War for Independence.

"What did Mr. Jackson do about that?" Rachel asked, which brought a quick laugh, for her tone suggested that Andrew Jackson would somehow take command of the situation and avenge himself.

"Just what you would expect: the British officer ordered him to lead them to the home of a Waxhaw fighter, a man by the name of Thompson. Andrew avoided the regular road and led the British through a winding path and across an open field; Thompson could see them from half a mile away and escaped. Somehow the English officer didn't like that any better than he liked Andrew's refusal to polish his boots. He made Andrew march forty miles to the British military prison at Camden without allowing him even a drink of water."

Rachel gazed into the fire, observing to herself that she too would have need of such stamina.

9

It was a magnificent May afternoon with the red haw and forsythia in bloom, the late-arriving purple martins and the wrens chattering in the trees, the air filled with the fragrance of honeysuckle, when Rachel saw a party of traders come down the trail with Lewis Robards leading three heavily laden pack horses. She watched him from the porthole of the big room, sitting his horse with easy, almost arrogant grace. He appeared heavier, and from the lines in his face rather older than the passage of months should have indicated.

In the weeks since she had received the letter from her husband telling her that he would be happy to wind up his affairs in Harrodsburg and come to the Cumberland to live, she had looked forward to this moment when he would reach the station. She ran quickly to the door to welcome him.

The bulging panniers on either side of Lewis's pack horses had been filled not with his personal possessions, but with expensive and carefully selected gifts for each member of the family: a sapphire ring for herself, a French dressing mirror for her mother, a boxed compass for Alexander, a set of tools for William, one of the new Youmans rifles for John, Jr., the complete works of Shakespeare for Samuel, a wallet for Stockly, the money-maker of the clan, a hunting knife for Leven, an illuminated Bible for Severn, and for John Overton, out of gratitude for this reconciliation, a leather-bound set of lawbooks with his name tooled on the backstrap.

Lewis was greeted warmly by everyone except Samuel, who could not wipe from his mind the picture of his sister's tear-streaked face when he had taken her out of the Robards home eight months before. But as the day progressed Rachel saw with a kind of gnawing anxiety that her husband was very uncertain of himself. After supper the men fell to talking about land values, the difficulties of clearing titles farther out in the wilderness.

"Speaking of titles," said Overton, "I've checked that six-forty of yours, Lewis, in Clover Bottom. Rachel asked me to make sure the records were clean and legal. They are."

"Thank you, John, but I wasn't as much concerned over the title to the land as I am the amount of Indian raids. It's still pretty wild country, isn't it?"

William replied gravely, "Yes, there have been several attacks out that way in the past month. Mrs. Hargart and her two children were killed."

"Then it would hardly be safe to expose Rachel to such danger, would it?"

There was an uncomfortable silence. Rachel trembled as she felt old misgivings sweep over her. Yet she knew that none of her brothers considered Lewis a coward. The silence came because no man could tell any other how deep he should go into Indian country, or what attitude he should take toward the omnipresent threat of attack; yet all of them had lived on the frontier, all of them had been attacked and had fought the Indians. She knew what her brothers would be thinking: if nobody pushed out the frontier, risking Indian attacks, then this land would always be sparsely settled and unsafe.

"If you will permit me an opinion, Captain Robards," she heard Andrew Jackson say, "I've always felt that the Indians never attack where they know a man is fast with his rifle. Your presence would be all the protection Mrs. Robards would need."

Lewis flushed with pleasure at the compliment. Rachel felt her own atnxiety ease. Now she sat back quietly as Lewis told the first news of George Washington's inauguration as President a couple of weeks before on April 30, 1789, in New York; this brought double pleasure to the Donelsons because Washington had been their friend in Virginia.

"After Mr. Washington took the oath, the chancellor of New York cried, 'Long live George Washington, President of the United States,'" and the crowd thundered back, 'Long live George Washington, President of the United States.'"

"Sounds too much like 'Long live the King' to me," growled Jackson. "We're a new country and a new government, with a new kind of elected executive. Why don't we make up our own saying?"

No one took his grumbling seriously. Instead they asked each other whether the establishment of the new government might at last bring them some paid militia and some permanent protection against the Indians, a job which their mother state, North Carolina, had been unwilling to continue since it was obvious that these Cumberland people would soon be forming a state of their own. They spoke of agitating to have North Carolina cede this territory to the Federal government so they could be set up as a territory, for they were in desperate need of roads, a mail service and trading routes for merchandise from the East.

There was also the difficulty of knowing what kind of money was going to be legal tender. English sterling was still acceptable but it had almost disappeared from circulation; the Spanish gold florins which had found their way up the Natchez Trace from New Orleans were considered reliable, but the immediate need was for a standard form of money so that men could be paid for their services in hard cash instead of goods.

"I've been practicing law here in Nashville for half a year," said Jackson, "and if all the square miles I've received as fees could be strung together there'd be enough to make a whole county. If I don't get paid in land they give me mink skins, linsey, rye whisky, tallow, beeswax, cured bacon, peach brandy, beaver, otter, raccoon and fox furs. I ought to open a trading post."

Rachel was surprised to find what a wonderful background for thinking could be provided by men discussing with all seriousness the trying problems of the day; how strange it was that she could hear them clearly, take in and understand what they were saying, yet at the same time push her own thoughts forward step by step.

Her husband was attached to John Overton; they had remained friends at the Robards home even after Overton had defended her. Andrew Jackson and her husband had gotten off to an excellent start, for Mr. Jackson's compliment was something that Lewis would cherish for a considerable time. However, they were all going to live together here in fairly close quarters, until the new Robards home and plantation had been begun. She resolved to give up the robust relationship she had enjoyed with the young lawyers during the past months. Every life had to be lived inside its own boundaries; and if her husband's nature formed the palings which closed them in, then she would try to live happily and securely inside that fence.

10

During the next weeks Rachel and Lewis rode out to their land, studying it with a view to clearing, planting, putting in orchards and choosing a site for their cabin. They saw the family only at dinner. She greeted John Overton and Andrew Jackson formally when they met, then moved on to whatever chore she was doing.

Late one afternoon she was crossing the yard from the dairy cabin where she had been preparing buttermilk for bleaching linen thread, when Andrew Jackson rode in. She didn't know how he accomplished it so quickly but before she had gone three steps he stood directly in her path, his long thin shoulders hunched over toward her, his eyes searching hers.

"Mrs. Robards, have I said or done something to offend you? If so, I assure you I never meant it. You know that I have only the deepest . . ."

She hastened to reassure him.

"No, no, it's nothing you've done, Mr. Jackson. It's just . . . that since my husband's return I've been so busy . . ."

As she raised her head she saw in his eyes an expression that was rather like Moll's the day she had told Rachel she was living like a prisoner. Jackson quickly veiled his feelings, said, "Please forgive me for embarrassing you, Mrs. Robards," and was gone.

At dinner she no longer listened with interest to the legal discussions, even though the law firm of Overton and Jackson had converted the Donelson cabin into the most active law office west of the Blue Ridge. Samuel's problems had been solved: he was now reading law in the guest cabin, where he had moved everything but his bed. When it came time for Colonel Donelson's will to be probated it seemed only natural that John Overton should handle it. When Stockly needed money for a new business venture and mentioned this at the dinner table, it seemed only friendly for Andrew Jackson to volunteer the loan; when Overton and Jackson rode circuit and were paid in barter for their services, paid such things as woolen cloth, good flax linen, country-made sugar or tobacco, they brought the stuff home to the Donelsons to be thrown into the family larder.

With seven brothers, each engaging in a dozen different activities, there were bound to be unending discussions, councilings and group enterprises participated in by the Donelsons and their two paying guests. Only Lewis refrained. He was as clever and as educated as the rest, but he had no interest in the growth of Nashville or the hundred ways in which the Donelson clan was planning and working to establish the frontier and to make money.

It was two months after his coming to the Donelsons' that he told Rachel he had decided against developing the land at Clover Bottom.

"But Lewis, you promised in your letter . . ."

"What do I need another plantation for?" he demanded. "I've already got one back in Harrodsburg."

"Don't you really want to start the way everyone else does, and build your own life?"

"I would if I had to, but I can't see much sense in going through all that work when I already have what it would take us ten years to build here."

"Then what do you want to do?"

"Why must I do something? You like this house, don't you? You're comfortable. And I've been hunting; I've also made a few profitable land swaps in Nashville. Would you think it more important if I went around blabbering like those two walking lawbooks you're so attached to?"

Rachel pulled back.

"I'm sorry, Lewis, I didn't mean to hurt your feelings."

"Why don't they move into Nashville and build themselves an office there? It surely can't be convenient for them to ride ten miles into town and back every day."

"But they're both alone, Lewis, and they're happy here with us."

His skin grew dark; for a moment it seemed as though he would hold back, but the temptation was too strong.

"And you're happy with them."

Rachel took a deep breath. It was so painfully familiar.

"Oh, Lewis, let's start the cabin at Clover Bottom."

"So now you want to run away? His voice had grown louder with every passing sentence. "Well, I'm not going to let Andrew Jackson drive me out of here."

Rachel was shocked. There was a knock at the door. It was Mrs. Donelson.

"Lewis, for shame!" she exclaimed as she entered the room. "You've been shouting so loud that everybody downstairs has heard you."

Lewis stormed out of the house, jumped on one of his horses and rode off at a killing pace. A few hours later he was back, contrite. He asked, "Am I forgiven?" and Rachel replied, "Yes, of course." To avoid further trouble she stopped eating in the dining room with the rest of the family.

The peace lasted for two, almost three weeks. Then one noon, when she was in the kitchen with her mother and Moll, making a meat and vegetable hotchpot, Lewis burst in, shouting:

"I won't stand him around here any more. You get that fellow off this place or I'll run him off myself!"

Rachel could only stammer: ". . . what man . . . are you talking about?"

He waited until Moll had left, her step unhurried, reluctant.

"You know perfectly well who I mean. Andrew Jackson. He insulted me. If it had been my home I would have shot him dead!"

"Mr. Jackson? But how? Mr. Jackson admires you, he wouldn't insult . . ."

"He admires my wife, not me. He's trying to make me look ridiculous so he can get you away from me."

She sank onto the log bench alongside of Moll's sand-scrubbed workboard, saddened. She caught only fragments of her mother's questions and of Lewis's loud replies. Apparently Andrew had made a generalization about some absentee land cases and Lewis had taken the remark personally. She did not know when Lewis left but when she turned around from the fireplace she saw John Overton standing in the doorway; it was a warm summer day and he was in his shirt sleeves, the cuffs turned back, his writing fingers stained with ink. She felt exposed; she had no way of concealing her emotions except to go into a room and close the door behind her. So many people were able to mask their feelings; if only she could!

"Forgive me for intruding, but I heard the . . . the commotion. Is Lewis at it again?"

Mrs. Donelson nodded with grim hopelessness, then left the kitchen.

Rachel spoke. "John, I must ask you to do something dreadful."

"You want us to go?"

"No . . . not you . . . just Mr. Jackson."

"We'll both go, Rachel." He put his hand out and covered hers where it lay clasped on the table, her thumb clenched under her fingers. "But I am reluctant to do this: Lewis Robards is probably the only man on the frontier who doesn't understand the implications of insulting Andrew Jackson, of accusing him unjustly."

He began pacing up and down the kitchen. Rachel had never seen him thoroughly angry before; his eyes had the solidity of gray marble.

"In another month Andrew and I start on circuit. No one in Nashville will think it strange if we don't come back to the Donelsons'. But if we are obliged suddenly to move out people are bound to ask 'Why?' I shall ask Lewis to let things go along until we leave for the next court session at Jonesboro."

It took only a few moments for them to reach the Robards' bedroom.

"John, I've always trusted you," cried Lewis, "and now you are turning against me."

"As your cousin," interrupted Overton, "I feel it my duty to hit you over the head with a tree trunk. But as your attorney I'm going to give you some advice."

"I don't want your advice," snapped Robards.

"Lewis, when I left your home to come to Nashville I agreed to serve as your emissary because I thought you had learned your lesson. And now you are behaving in the same unmanly fashion. When you have quieted down you will realize that there has not been an untoward word or gesture between your wife and Andrew Jackson. I eat and sleep and work and travel and spend every moment of my life with that man; I know his character. If you drive him out of here you will have to go around again as you did at Harrodsburg, apologizing and explaining that it was nothing more than your feverish imagination."

"You may interpret it that way," replied Lewis, his voice dry and harsh. "I'm beginning to think that maybe I was right about Peyton Short, after all."

Rachel sat stunned and sickened.

"I beg your forgiveness, Rachel," said John, "for everything that has happened. I influenced you to let your husband come back; I sent Andrew Jackson here. My intervention today has caused Lewis to reopen old wounds and insult you again. I will tell Andrew tonight and we will be gone in the morning."

She slept fitfully. When she awakened the sun was already bright. She drew the curtains and saw John Overton standing between his horse and Jackson's, both laden with heavy saddlebags. Her eyes traveled to the fence by the orchard and there they found her husband and Andrew Jackson. Lewis had his fist raised as though to strike Jackson; Jackson drew back several steps. Her husband lowered his arm. Andrew Jackson turned and walked to the horses. He and John mounted and disappeared out the gate.

She dressed hurriedly, scooped cold water onto her face from the bowl and ran quickly into the yard.

"Your chivalrous Mr. Jackson!" snorted Lewis. "He said he apologized if he had done anything to offend me, but that he couldn't leave without first telling me that you had done nothing to warrant my anger. The man is a coward, Rachel; I offered to thrash him and he refused to fight."

Rachel turned toward the house. Andrew Jackson knew that if he and Lewis Robards rolled on the ground like a couple of drunken brawlers the whole of Nashville would hear about it by nightfall. Mr. Jackson had afforded her a protection her husband had not cared to provide.

Quiet descended on the Donelson station, but it was the wrong kind of quiet. By a tacit agreement the outlying Donelsons, Jane and Robert Hays, Catherine and Thomas Hutchings, Mary and John Caffrey, Johnny and his wife Mary, were remaining away from the parental stockade. Alexander and Leven and Stockly, even William, were avoiding Lewis; Samuel was seething with resentment.

"How could you put John and Andrew out of our home?" he demanded of his mother. "If Father were alive he never would have allowed this."

Mother and son turned to look at Rachel. Samuel fumbled with an apology.

"I'm sorry, Rachel. I didn't mean to make you any further unhappiness."

She knew what she would have to do.

"You happen to be right, Samuel. Lewis and I have spoiled everything here. I can't have the family staying away from the house. We'll start building our cabin at Clover Bottom."

After several days of argument with Lewis, Rachel was forced to say firmly:

"Lewis, I cannot feel comfortable here any longer. I am a married woman and am entitled to live under my own roof. Everybody will help us make a clearing and erect our cabin."

"I don't need their charity," he replied; "I've got the means to build a home. I'll hire my own workmen. I'll pay for what I get and be beholden to no one."

He bought two husky Negroes in Nashville and hired the town's carpenter to see that the cabin was built to Rachel's specifications. Once they were installed he set the slaves to cutting down trees in a wide circle about the cabin for protection against the Indians, then plotted the fields and slopes to determine which sections of the land could best be used for crops. While Rachel was busy furnishing her first home, Lewis hunted, molded bullets, cleared the thickets. When winter came on and darkness fell early he spent the long afternoons sitting by the fire, staring at the flames.

Finally they were shot at. Lewis stacked large piles of bullets beneath each porthole, stayed awake nights with his guns loaded and cocked, grew thin and jumpy. During the first heavy snowstorm he caught cold and came down with fever. Rachel sent for Samuel, who rode out to the clearing, wrapped Lewis in bearskins and carried him to the Donelsons'.

New Year's Day of 1790 dawned clear and bright. The family gathered for a dinner of roast wild turkey and suckling pig. Lewis had made a good recovery, but remained in bed. Rachel sensed that the day he was completely well would be a difficult one for them both. At first she had imagined that his lethargy was part of his convalescence; now she began to perceive that the spirit had gone out of the man.

In early April he informed her that he had to go back to Harrodsburg. She was puzzled both by the offhand way in which he spoke and by his choice of words.

"You *have to*, Lewis? Is something wrong?"

". . . well, Mother hasn't been feeling well . . . and there are a number of business matters that have to be settled: some slaves to be sold, there have been good offers for our outlying land that we never put under cultivation . . ."

The family took Lewis's announcement calmly. Moll laundered his linen, packing it neatly in one of the saddlebags; George groomed his horses and repaired their hoofs; Rachel supervised the preparation of enough food to carry him comfortably.

On the morning of his departure Rachel and Mrs. Donelson had breakfast with him and then walked him down to the front gate where Thomas Crutcher, an old friend, was waiting to start out with him for Harrodsburg. Lewis kissed them both on the cheek, thanked them for their hospitality and rode off.

Rachel leaned heavily against the log gate. While this was infinitely less unpleasant than being put out of her husband's home, Lewis's smile and farewell embrace could not conceal from her the fact that she once again was caught in the halfway point between being married and unmarried. In Harrodsburg she had been convinced by her husband's attitude that their marriage was over; difficult as it had been to face that hard fact, it was something definite that one could grasp and somehow grapple with. How did she endure this new kind of void, with no part of the future that she could either predict or control?

11

Two weeks had passed when John Overton came to call. The two lawyers were again holding forth in the April session of the court in Nashville, and were promptly invited for Sunday dinner. John managed to get a few minutes alone with Rachel.

"Rachel, do you know what Lewis's plans are?"

"No."

"Then I'd better tell you what I heard. On their second night out Lewis and Crutcher camped on the Barrens, and Lewis's saddle horse strayed off. The next day he was depressed about the loss. Crutcher tried to cheer him by saying that some hunter would find the horse and take him back to Nashville where Lewis could claim him. Lewis said he'd be damned if he'd be seen in the Cumberland again, that he hated the valley, the people and the life there. Crutcher is convinced he never intends coming back to Nashville."

She thanked him and slipped away to her bedroom. There was no shock to her in the story Overton had brought, only the confirmation of what she had suspected. There was a knock on the door. It was Moll to tell her that dinner was ready. She bathed her eyes in cold water, put on a too bright smile and went down to the dining room.

There were half a dozen excited conversations going on simultaneously around the table, for the Cumberland had at last secured its freedom from North Carolina and become a territory of the Federal government. Rachel seated herself between Samuel and Alexander, noting idly that her mother had ordered their finest linen board cover and napkins for the occasion. For the moment the pewter plates stood empty; Rachel looked down the long table at the chattering guests; only Andrew Jackson seemed constrained, silent. Then her brother John said grace and George and Benjamin, the best of the serving men, came from the kitchen with huge chargers of roasted meats and fresh vegetables in heaping basins. She asked Samuel to pour her some milk from the great jug of heavy leather sitting in the center of the board. Its coolness steadied her nerves. She heard her mother ask from her position at the head of the table:

"John, how are you and Mr. Jackson getting along over at Casper Mansker's?"

"Well, the Manskers are giving us every courtesy but we have no room for our office, we are practicing law across the bedcover."

"I don't mind that so much," said Jackson, "I can practice law in a hayloft. But the cooking is bad. John and I lay awake nights thinking of Sunday dinners like this."

"We haven't had any tenants in your cabin since you left," said William blandly. "Wouldn't you like to move back into your old office?"

"I think it's a wonderful idea," said Stockly. "I still owe Andrew some money and I think he ought to be around to protect his investment."

"And I could continue my studies," cried Samuel.

"There's nothing Andrew or I would like better," said Overton. "But is it . . . wise?"

"For my part," replied Mrs. Donelson quietly, "I can tell you that I was heartily against your moving out in the first place. However the question of what is wise or unwise in this particular case must rest with Rachel."

All eyes turned on her. She thought with an inner grimace that during the past year she had had to grow used to doing her thinking in public. But there was no fumbling or hesitation in her mind. Was there any reason why some twenty Donelsons should be controlled by one absent and hostile Robards? She turned to the two lawyers who were sitting up-table from her.

"I know of no reason why you shouldn't come back. Move into your cabin again, gentlemen. We enjoy having you here."

After dinner a number of them walked into the orchard to see the first blossoms on the peach trees. They had gone only a few steps beyond the fence when Andrew Jackson fell into step beside her.

"I want to thank you for your kind invitation, Mrs. Robards, but I just can't move back here. There's never been any young woman whose friendship has meant so much to me. That's why I was so distressed at causing you trouble."

"You didn't cause the trouble, Mr. Jackson. You just got caught in it, same as I did."

"Do you know what I am denying myself?" he cried out. Then, lowering his voice, he continued more calmly, "I will keep office in the cabin with John; but for the time being I think I had better continue living at Mansker's. I feel that I must do this to protect you, Mrs. Robards."

Rachel turned an unsmiling face up to him. "I don't think you need concern yourself about Lewis Robards."

He studied her, perplexed, his lips a little parted. She thought how peculiar it was that one could look at a man's face every day for two months as she had the year before and not really know its detail until a moment of crisis when one's vision was sharpened by the tautness of emotion. It was not a symmetrical structure: the high arched forehead was too narrow, his right eye was larger and somewhat more deeply recessed than the left, the left side of his lips seemed slightly fuller than the right, and his long jutting nose slashed across from the right eye to the left corner of his mouth. All these things she saw vividly, certain that they were not the ingredients of handsomeness; then why did it seem to her the most attractive face she had ever known? Her questioning was cut short as he managed to speak.

"I don't understand."

"I don't believe he's ever coming back to Nashville . . . ."

It was the most beautiful spring anyone could remember in the ten years of the Cumberland settlement. The magnolia tulips were in bloom and the early scent of lilac was already in the air. The small flowering redbud and dogwood trees showed pink and white among the ferns on the green hillsides; throughout the woods the wild grapevines were climbing among the tree trunks, the grass was already high and pastel green, and the yellow jasmine was rich with summerlike fragrance.

Rachel found her naturally buoyant spirits coming back in full force, and a tremendous need to be gay, to sing and make jokes, to be happy over the simple fact that she was twenty-two and alive in a beautiful springtime. She went to the neighborhood dances; on Sundays the Donelsons and their friends packed picnic lunches and rode along the river, finding quiet shallows where the water was caught in a winding bend, and where they could wade in the coolness. Once she joined John and Andrew Jackson and the pretty daughter of a settler who had just arrived in Nashville, walking along the river road with the warm sun streaming onto their faces. She liked to walk; her gait was easy and unhurried as she moved through space with her own compact graceful rhythm; her head was set a little too low on her shoulders for complete effortlessness, but her long slim legs kept pace with Andrew's tempered stride.

John and the pretty blond girl were up ahead. Rachel and Andrew Jackson talked about what they wanted out of life. For Rachel this was not difficult to tell, though it had been so difficult to achieve: a husband with whom she could live in love and peace; children; a home up here on the bluff overlooking the lazy green Cumberland.

It seemed that Mr. Jackson had no desire to become a great lawyer.

"I haven't the talent for the law that John has," he said. "Oh, I do well enough, but the law isn't something I've wanted all of my life, it was just the field that happened to be open to young fellows with spirit. What I really want to be is a planter. That was what my father wanted back in the Waxhaws. I'd like to put hundreds of acres under cultivation, see the crops grow clean and strong in the sun. And I'd like to raise blooded horses."

"But the law is an open door to politics," protested Rachel. "Stockly says we're going to become a state within a few years. Would you like to be a congressman, or a governor, perhaps?"

"No," he said quickly. "I have no political ambitions. I even surveyed a beautiful site down near Natchez in the Spanish territory when I was there on business last year." He turned to gaze headlong at her. "But now I just want to live here in the Cumberland."

A party of traders came in from Harrodsburg; they carried a packet of letters for Mrs. Lewis Robards. Rachel sat in the big chair beneath her window and arranged them chronologically by glancing at the opening lines in each letter, then read them through swiftly, almost without thinking or feeling, before going back to let each sentence carry its own weight.

First, Lewis assured her that being home again had brought a complete return of his energies; that his mother's illness had left her feeble and he had taken over the management of the plantation; that he was now employing two soldiers who had fought with him in the war to help him work the plantation and defend it; and that he had sold a number of slaves, male and female. He apologized for having caused her anxiety, assured her that he loved her, and wouldn't she come to Harrodsburg as quickly as possible?

She sank deep into reverie; how cleverly the letters had been put together, how carefully they had been designed to dispel her fears. The subject of the young slave had never been discussed between them, yet apparently he had sensed her knowledge of the relationship and was assuring her that the girl had been sold; he was assuring her too that since his new employees were trained fighters there would be no more boarders over whom he could become jealous. Lastly, he was making it clear that he had assumed the management of the plantation and would now be responsible and occupied.

In all of her days of determination not to return to Harrodsburg she had never once imagined that her husband would use this approach. She was glad that Lewis still loved her; she was grateful to him for being willing to reconstruct his life so that they might have a chance to live well together. Just how great that chance was she did not know. She was no longer eighteen years old, no longer able to give herself over to daydreams. She had been happy during this past month, yet what would happen to her over the months and years of being a woman without a defined status or position? Where was her chance for a home of her own, for children?

She must try again.

12

She packed her belongings and waited for news of a trading party that would be going down the Kentucky trail to Harrodsburg. The Donelson clan gathered to see her off, but was reluctant to have her leave.

She reached the Robards home late in the afternoon with the bright June sun lighting up the rambling stone house. She had anticipated being met by Lewis at Crow's station where she branched off the Kentucky Road, but no one had been there to greet her. The leader of the trading party insisted upon escorting her directly to the Harrodsburg house, but there was no sign of welcome here, either. She tied her horse to the hitching post, walked up the four broad log steps and knocked on the iron knocker.

She was escorted to the library, the door closed behind her. There sat Lewis, sprawled across a chair in a perspiration-soaked linen shirt and wrinkled woolen trousers, his booted legs stretched straight in front of him, crushing the striped nankeen coat which lay beneath them. His eyes were bleary and his face red from drinking. She stood with her back squared against the door, gazing at her husband in bewilderment. He made no effort to rise.

"It didn't take you very long, did it?"

"Take me . . . long? Five days, instead of four; there was a sick woman traveling with the party."

"I was no sooner out of sight than you invited him back to the blockhouse."

All of her expectancy had crashed at the first sight of her husband's unfocused eyes. Now her hope went along with it.

"Lewis, what are you saying?"

"Don't play the innocent with me."

"Do you mind if I sit down?"

"Friend of mine came in from Nashville, told me that Andrew Jackson was living at your house again."

"Mr. Jackson is not living at our station, Lewis. We invited him to return but he refused."

"Refused? When he's there every day?"

"John is living with us again, but Mr. Jackson comes only on his free days. He said he thought it would be better if he did not live there since you had once demanded that he leave."

Lewis pulled himself heavily out of the chair and stood with his face close to hers. "Then you admit that you invited him back?"

"It's not a matter of admitting, Lewis. Mother wanted him and so did the boys. After all, it is their house; he is like a member of our family."

"Yes," replied Lewis with an insinuative leer, "an intimate member."

She was too sick at heart to search deeply the implications of what her husband had said, but she sensed that for the first time he was accusing her directly of infidelity. She hung her head in shame: shame for herself and shame for Lewis. Then she turned, went out into the hall and up the stairs to her mother-in-law's bedroom.

She needed only one look at the thin face framed in the nightcap on the pillow to know that Mrs. Robards was seriously ill. She went to her side and kissed her. Mrs. Robards cupped Rachel's face in her hands. The long-sleeved gown with the ribbons tied at the wrist concealed her thinness, but her voice was strong.

"Rachel, my dear, there's nothing in the world I've wanted more than to have you become mistress of this house."

"Yes, darling, I know that."

"Lewis was a good boy, we loved him devotedly, my husband and I . . . but there can be no life for you . . ."

"You mustn't exhaust yourself. I'm going to stay here and help nurse you . . ."

"No, Rachel," the older woman interrupted. "We must get you back home . . . at once." She closed her eyes for a moment, then whispered,

"He promised me he would sell the girl, but he brought her back yesterday. He has been doing nothing but drinking and shouting. I'm frightened for him. You must write to your family at once. I will see that the message goes to Nashville with the first party to leave. You can stay in that little room yonder."

During the long warm days Rachel nursed Mrs. Robards, feeding her, at the doctor's orders, chicken broth and a medicinal tea brewed from bloodroot and wild ginger. She saw nothing of Lewis except at a distance, when she sat in her little room at the square window with wooden inside shutters and watched him riding to Harrodsburg or returning late at night slumped in his saddle. Her hope for her marriage was gone.

She slept little, only for an hour or two at a time; in the middle of the night she would rise, open the shutter and gaze out into the phosphorescent full-moon night. There was time and stillness in which to think back over her life. In a sense she would be free, free from pain, from humiliation, from falsely raised hopes. The years stretched ahead; but she had neither the will nor the clarity to face them. She would live one day at a time, find a moment or a task or a sight in each to warm her and bring her a reason for living.

Suddenly she blinked her eyes hard for she saw a figure on horseback come up the road, riding fast, and sitting his horse with ungainly ease . . . looking for all the world like Andrew Jackson! She leaned out the window, studying the figure that was coming toward her. Her letter to her family saying that she was leaving Lewis forever had gone from Harrodsburg ten days ago; she had expected that someone would arrive for her; but surely it would have been Alexander or Samuel or Stockly? Surely they would not have sent Andrew Jackson? Lewis would take this for a personal affront, an insult deliberately administered by the Donelson family. How could they have done this, she asked herself over and over again, when I have so many brothers?

But it was Andrew, there could no longer be any doubt about that, dressed in tight-fitting buckskin trousers and a leather hunting jacket. He dismounted with a quick sliding motion that enabled him to reach the ground at the same instant that the horse drew up before the porch. He pounded on the door with his fists, and it was as though that pounding were coming from her heart.

Except for necessities, her possessions had never been unpacked. She went quickly into her mother-in-law's room to bid her farewell, telling her that it was Mr. Jackson who had come for her, and that she wanted to get away before Lewis could return, that she dreaded the thought of a public quarrel and, still worse, of another duel.

"You need have no fear of that, my dear," replied the old woman; there was a quality in her voice that not only brought Rachel up short but put an end to her nervousness. The tone, rather than the words, brought back to her the scene with John Overton when she had asked him about Lewis's duel with Peyton Short, and he had evaded a direct answer. Gropingly she said:

"But Lewis fought a duel with Peyton Short."

Mrs. Robards turned her head slightly on the pillow. She had been a proud woman and a high-spirited one all her life. She could look neither at Rachel nor herself in this painful moment.

"This is a sad thing for a mother to have to reveal about her son. But you are entitled to know." She turned her head on the pillow; her eyes met Rachel's. "When Lewis found Peyton Short in Richmond, Mr. Short asked Lewis if he insisted on fighting a duel or if he would accept a money settlement."

"A money set . . . But for what?"

"For damages done to Lewis's feelings because of that letter. Lewis said he would consider a settlement. Mr. Short paid him a thousand dollars in sterling at Gault's Tavern."

Rachel felt her face flame. How could a man so insanely jealous that he would banish his wife accept money from the other man?

Tears welled in Mrs. Robards' eyes. Rachel kissed her mother-in-law's cheek, hard, and fled from the room.

This then was what had offended John, and what he had kept from her. This was why even William the Cautious had withdrawn his opposition to her remaining at the Donelsons'. Her whole family must have known, and thought to spare her further humiliation. But what difference could it have made if she had known? Where was there a pattern for separation or divorce that she could take refuge in? What else could she have done but send for her husband?

Alongside this news all concern about Andrew Jackson's having come for her was forgotten. By the time she reached the front door her chestnut mare had been saddled and brought up from the stable to the front of the blockhouse. She and Jackson exchanged a quick glance of greeting; it was not until they were several miles on their way to the Kentucky Road that he first addressed her.

"Shall we light straight out for Nashville or wait for the next party? There has been some Indian activity along the road during the past few weeks."

"How did you come?"

"Alone."

"Then that's the way we'll go back."

It appeared to be the answer he had expected; he made no comment.

"Besides, I'd like to get distance between us and Harrodsburg as quickly as we can. Lewis will return soon, and I'm sure he will follow us."

"Follow?" He wheeled his horse sharply so that he was facing her. "For what purpose? We understood from your letter . . ."

"He won't be coming in pursuit of me, he'll be coming after you. That was why I had to write home . . ."

It was a little before sundown when they reached the Boar's Head where they were provided with an excellent supper of fresh baked bread and butter, chicken fricassee, apple dumplings and coffee. Rachel had a room to herself, with a candle on the night stand, clean muslin sheets, a huge feather mattress and a goose-down patchwork quilt. Andrew had to share the last available bed with two other men. She was sure she would not so much as close her eyes because of all that had happened to her that day, but she had no more than put her head on the soft feather pillow than she heard Mr. Jackson's voice calling to her that the sun would be up soon and to dress quickly.

She put on the light blue calico summer gown which had only a moderate amount of material in the skirt to make it comfortable for side-saddle riding, and with the sleeves cut just below the elbows for coolness. It was the most austere dress she had ever sewn, with a high neckline but no collar. She slipped into moccasins, a short doeskin cloak, and left her room in the first ash-gray light of dawn. A hot breakfast was waiting on the downstairs board.

They were on the road again by the time the top curve of the sun pushed itself over the horizon. Their horses too were rested and they made good time as they streaked across the open meadows with the mist drying on the grasses. They stopped when the sun was perpendicular and hot, washed themselves in a cool stream, gave the horses a drink and had some of the bread and cheese from their saddlebags. In the afternoon the horses tired, and for the first time she realized how seriously Jackson was on guard, his whole being cocked at every tree and bush as they went through a copse of cedars. Suddenly he pulled in his horse.

"Can you shoot straight?"

"Sometimes."

"Then take this pistol. A group of Indians, I can't tell how many, perhaps only three or four, have been paralleling our course through the woods. They've just pulled out ahead of us to get to that spot up above. Do you see that fallen tree about twenty yards this side of the open space?"

"Yes."

"I'm going to pull off the road just beyond that log."

He started his horse at a medium pace. She followed behind him. When he passed the big cedar log he gave his horse the spur and dashed into the woods. She came behind him as quickly as she could. He fired his rifle, then called to her, "Use your spur!" and in an instant they were out of the clearing and back onto the trail.

"I missed," he said, "but it served the same purpose. They'll leave us alone from now on." He turned to her. "Were you scared?"

"No, I didn't see anything. Besides, I was too interested in watching you. If I'd been an Indian I'd have been sure there was a whole militia regiment behind you."

"That's the best tactic," he replied, pleased. "It will bring you out unscathed nearly every time."

She joined his laughter at the use of the word "nearly"; and the laughter dissipated the tension between them.

13

That night they stayed at the cabin of a family which had come over the Wilderness Trail with Daniel Boone in 1776. It was a one-room log cabin with a divided loft for sleeping rooms, chickens and dogs in the hard-packed-earth yard, hogs around the corncribs and children running in and out of the open door. There was cold broiled ham, milk and hoecake for supper served on a tree stump in the yard. Rachel shared a bed with several daughters of the family on the ground floor while Andrew climbed up the roughhewn ladder to the loft, where he wrapped himself in a blanket and slept with his head on a pillow of straw. In the middle of the night Rachel was awakened by the tossing of the children. She got her huge bearskin, spread it on the floor as a mattress and slept soundly the rest of the night.

On the third day the Indian danger was past and so was the threat of Lewis Robards catching up with them. They let the horses set their own pace, riding side by side. The day was soft and warm; they listened to the sounds of the wild life about them, feeling a sense of peacefulness and of companionship.

"You aren't frightened by the wilderness, are you?" he asked.

"I was brought up with it. All of us Donelsons were. We made that trip with Father on the *Adventure,* you know."

"I had forgotten. You couldn't have been very old?"

"Just twelve. But there were many children younger than me. In fact, one of them was born on the trip."

"That *Adventure* voyage was the most amazing ever made on the western frontier."

"Father and the boys built the *Adventure* on the Holston River, up near Fort Patrick Henry. It had a hull of squared logs and sides well bulwarked against gunfire, with a roof over a considerable part of the hull, bunks for sleeping and a stone hearth for cooking. We launched it the first of November 1779. There were thirty boats altogether, most of them flatboats, with a few pirogues. I guess about two hundred folks started the journey; there must have been more than fifty of us on our boat."

Colonel James Robertson, Donelson's partner in the venture, had left earlier in the fall with the best Indian fighters, heads of the families and considerable livestock to take an unexplored overland route through the Cumberland Gap and the Kentucky Trace. Colonel Donelson was to bring the women and children, and about thirty able-bodied men to handle and defend the boats on the longer but comparatively safer river journey, using the big flatboats to transport household goods, supplies, farm implements, sacks of seed, tools, slaves and building material.

"Father and Colonel Robertson were going to found a whole new community, maybe a whole new state . . . like Virginia. But the truth is Father had a bad case of 'wilderness fever.' I can still remember the excitement in his voice when he described rolling green valleys and broad rivers flowing through them which no white man had ever seen, let alone settled."

They left Fort Patrick Henry three days before Christmas, but could go only three miles the first day to the mouth of Reedy Creek because there was already ice on the water.

"For two months we had to live on our boats, and in tents in the snow. At the end of February we started again, but within a matter of hours the *Adventure* got stuck on Poor Valley Shoals. So did two of the other boats. We finally had to jump into the icy water holding sacks of food and tools in our arms to lighten the boats. Mother entrusted me with the monogrammed family silver, our most valuable possession."

As she talked the sun lighted her eyes with specks of hazel; there was a smile of nostalgia on her lips. Jackson watched her as her hands played with the reins, and admired the easy poise with which she sat her horse.

It had been rainy and blustery all through the early days of March as the *Adventure* floated down the great valley of the Tennessee. Gray sedge grass sprinkled with young trees and growths of brier and bramble covered the open savannas near the river; back of it all they could see through the streamers of rain clouds the great mountain ranges they were leaving behind them.

"Hardly an hour passed without some kind of accident somewhere along the line. Mr. Henry's boat was capsized by the force of the current. We all had to stop to rescue the little children and snatch floating articles as they went by."

By the time they had passed the mouth of the Clinch they were in hostile Indian country. The cold was still great. Colonel Donelson put into the mouth of South Chickamauga Creek where one of the Dragging Canoe's towns had stood, and here Mrs. Ephraim Peyton gave birth to a child. The next day the flotilla ran the gantlet of the Chickamauga towns. The boats were fired on, and Mr. Payne was killed from ambush on Moccasin Bend.

"Most of the upsets and hardships had been fun for us kids. Then we had a real tragedy: when Thomas Stuart's flatboat broke out with smallpox Father ordered the boat to keep at a distance. The Indians captured it and killed the whole party, twenty-eight people. We could hear their cries, but there was nothing we could do to help them."

When the *Adventure* flotilla approached the entrance to the Suck they could see bands of warriors along the rocky paths parallel with the river. The boys stood with their rifles trained on the shore while the older men guided the boats through the whirlpools and crosscurrents of the narrow gorge. Rachel had fired as many shots as any of the younger boys, but she wasn't sure she had ever hit anything.

"Some of the men in Abel Gower's boat were wounded. Young Nancy Gower, she was my age, seized the rudder and steered until the men reorganized. When the flotilla got under way again Mrs. Gower saw that Nancy's skirt was stained with blood. She had been shot through the thigh but she didn't tell anybody about it. Now there's a girl I've always admired."

Jackson smiled gently in the darkness. They rode in silence for a few minutes, the trees and the dusk closing them in like walls of a room.

The Indians continued to harass the *Adventure* until it emerged from the narrows and entered the Great Bend of the Tennessee. They thought they had lost Jonathan Jennings and his boat, but it had been grounded on a reef and had been submitted to a galling fire by the Indians.

"Worst of all, Mrs. Peyton, who had had to help unload the boat and pull it off the reef, lost her newborn baby in the confusion. Mother practically carried Mrs. Peyton in her arms for the rest of the trip."

At last spring broke through. In a week they floated two hundred and fifty miles to the junction of the Tennessee and Ohio rivers; the weather turned fair and the young green began showing in sheltered places beyond the cane thickets and gaunt white sycamores that fringed the banks. They poled the boats up the uncharted Ohio River against high and rapid currents. Their provisions were exhausted, most of the men were wounded or ill and the families discouraged because they did not know how many miles were still left to the journey.

"My father held most of the flotilla together through sheer will power, hoisting sails when there was wind, shooting buffalo and wild swan to live on. At the end of April, when we reached French Lick and the blockhouses that Colonel Robertson had built, we had lost thirty-three people. Father wanted to be out by himself. He moved us eight miles farther up on the Cumberland and another couple of miles up Stone River to Clover Bottom. I should have thought Mother would have had enough of the wilderness, but she made no objection whatever, saying that the land was richer on Stone River.

"Our first station consisted of tents; we put in cotton and corn, but just about everything went wrong: the river overflowed and drowned our crops, the Indians scarcely let a day go by without attacking; another Indian treaty would have to be made before we could perfect our land title. Father had to move us over this very road to Harrodsburg. It took him four years to get back to French Lick . . . it has taken me just as long . . ."

She stopped abruptly. Jackson was silent; he spurred his horse, stepping out along the path in front of her.

She thought, We Donelsons have had difficulties before, plenty of them, and we've always managed to survive. Father used to say, "If you can't solve a problem you just have to outlive it." But those other hardships, when she was young, they had been easy to bear because they were all in it together. This new trouble had happened to her apart. Perhaps that's what growing up meant: your troubles were yours alone and you had to overcome them by yourself.

She was glad she had told the story of the *Adventure;* thinking about the past had heartened her for the present.

14

Jackson had brought her an invitation to stay at the blockhouse of her sister Jane and Colonel Robert Hays in Haysboro, the community of stations that had been founded by Robert, his parents and his brothers. Their plantation was in rather wilder country than her mother's house; there were grapes, cherries and ripe blackberries in the forest to be picked. Rachel was glad to be returning here instead of to the Donelsons'. Jane's offhand manner would have a remedial effect upon her. Mr. Jackson turned her over to Jane, waved aside their efforts to thank him and rode off for Nashville.

Rachel's sanctuary lasted two days, long enough for Lewis Robards to reach the Hays plantation. He came along the dogtrot, chatting in an amiable voice with Jane.

"You have company, Rachel," called Jane, as though an acquaintance had just ridden out from Nashville. Her lids were raised the tiniest fraction over her Cumberland-green eyes, a signal for, I'll be close by. She's looking unusually lovely, Rachel thought; if only I could have her coolness and detachment.

"Aren't you going to welcome your husband after he's ridden more than two hundred miles to see you?"

Lewis's voice was low, charming. He had stopped somewhere for a bath and a shave and had changed into a smartly fashioned corduroy suit, a bit on the warm side for the first of July, she mused idly, with a spotless white silk shirt and polished black boots.

"The kind of welcome I had expected when I reached Harrodsburg?"

"I behaved badly, Rachel. I had been inflamed by the stories I'd heard."

"What kind of man believes every chance story that gossips may care to repeat about his wife?"

"My kind of man, I guess: a little stupid, a little hysterical."

"And you don't take it amiss that it was Andrew Jackson who brought me here?" asked Rachel bluntly.

"Certainly not," he replied. "If it was more convenient for your mother to send Jackson, then there is no reason why he shouldn't have come." He went to her impulsively, with one of his tenderest smiles. "I trust you, I love you, and I want you to come back with me. We'll leave for home in the morning."

"No, Lewis."

"No? But there are no more doubts in my mind. It won't ever happen again, my dear. I give you my word of honor."

"You've broken your word many times before."

"But there must be some way I can convince you . . ."

"It would do no good."

He peered at her intently, as though there were some explanation that might not be contained in her words.

"No good?"

"I no longer love you."

"That's a lie!"

"I bear you no ill will, Lewis, but I have no affection left for you, none at all. Under these conditions I could never live with you again."

The placating manner vanished.

"I don't believe you! Besides, it has no importance. You are my wife and you must do as I say. We will return to Harrodsburg in the morning."

His voice had risen. She replied with a firmness he had never before heard.

"Lewis, I never intend to see you again."

There could be no mistaking the finality in her voice. He stood close to her, his fist clenched in front of her face.

"Then it was true."

"What was true, Lewis?"

"My suspicions of you and Andrew Jackson! The fact that he came to Harrodsburg for you clinches the case!"

"But it's only a few moments since you told me that there was nothing wrong in Mr. Jackson's coming for me."

"That was before I knew."

"Knew what?"

"That you were in love with Andrew Jackson."

She had never realized that a few spoken words could have the solid substance of a physical object: that they could be a splinter under your fingernail, a fence rail that hit you over the head . . . or a sharp knife that penetrated deep into your bosom.

Did she love Andrew Jackson?

A hundred images of him revolved quickly on the screen behind her eyes: Andrew standing at the front door on the first day of his arrival, tall and skinny as a split log, looking lonely and forlorn, as though he had no homeplace; Andrew in the courtroom facing the bully and his guns, with "Shoot!" in his eyes; Andrew dancing at a party, indefatigable as a windmill, and similar in style. Andrew refusing to polish the British officer's boots. Andrew riding on the trail down from Harrodsburg, his whole being glued to both sides of the road. He was a man among men, she knew that, a fearless one and a leader like her father; strong, reliable, teeming with energy and ambition, and at the same time gentle and sympathetic. But as for love . . . How could she love anyone when she had been so badly hurt by love?

She turned her back on Robards.

"Please go now, Lewis."

"You are my wife and I'm going to stay right here until you are ready to return to Harrodsburg. Colonel Hays would never put me out."

To that extent Lewis was right: Colonel Hays refused her entreaties to ask Lewis to leave.

"I can't do that, my dear. He is still a member of our family, and I can't have it said that I refused hospitality."

She saw that she was embarrassing her brother-in-law.

"Forgive me, Robert, you are right. Would you be so kind as to ride me over to Mother's house?"

"No, Rachel, I think that's just as wrong as putting Lewis out. If your mind is fully made up, then in a few days Lewis will become discouraged and leave of his own accord. In the meantime you are perfectly safe here with us."

She spent the next days in the house with Jane, spinning and embroidering, going out in the evening for a breath of cool air under the thick-leafed oak trees.

"I'm uneasy about your berrypicking party tomorrow," she told her sister as they sat before Jane's large dressing table brushing their hair before retiring. Jane had loaned her a muslin nightdress and a bottle-green twill robe. "You and Robert invited Mr. Jackson, remember?"

"I'm sure we can rely on Mr. Jackson," said Jane soothingly, braiding her hair into two thick blond plaits. "And you'll come too," she added doggedly. "You always loved to eat the berries right off the bush, with the hot sun on them."

But in the morning their mother arrived, upright, corseted, in a light yellow cotton dress and ruffled white linen cap. Leven had brought her from church. Rachel remained in the cool log house to tell her what had happened at Harrodsburg.

"It's really the end, then," said Mrs. Donelson with a sigh of finality. "But how are you going to get free of Lewis?"

"I am free of him. In my mind, I mean, and that's the most important place. He can never hurt me again."

"Yes, my dear, but life consists of something more than not being hurt."

They heard a clatter of hoofs. Rachel went to the window, pushed aside the printed India chintz curtains which concealed the omnipresent board coverings and saw Robert Hays jump off his horse with unaccustomed haste, toss the reins to a yard boy and storm into the house. Samuel, who had ridden in with him, remained in the yard, mopping his forehead with a big muslin handkerchief.

Colonel Hays was white-faced. "Your way would have been the lesser of two evils, Rachel."

"Then it was Lewis. What has he done?"

"Made some nasty remarks about you . . . and Andrew Jackson, loud enough for the whole party to hear. I've come to the end of my patience. He'll have to be gone from here before dark."

Mrs. Donelson had moved past her daughter and son-in-law, and was gazing out the front door of the house.

"If they don't bury him in the blackberry patch," she interjected with a grim smile. "There goes Andrew to find him; he's just been talking to Samuel."

By nightfall Lewis was gone, leaving the countryside in an uproar. Rachel put the story together from garbled and conflicting reports: a young girl who had been berrypicking related that Andrew Jackson had said to Lewis, "If you ever connect my name with Mrs. Robards in that way again, I will cut the ears out of your head, and I am tempted to do it anyhow!" One of the more excitable boys said that Lewis had ridden to the nearest magistrate, secured a peace warrant against Andrew and had it served by two deputies. Still another version was that Lewis had run into the cane, with Jackson in pursuit.

She did not see Andrew Jackson after the quarrel, but she knew that in any event he would have refused to discuss the matter with her. By now she realized that the whole affair had degenerated into a distasteful farce. But it was blunt, untactful Leven who really upset her. He caught her alone in the yard under the oak tree.

"I have a word for you from your husband. He said, 'You can tell Rachel for me that I shall haunt her.' Can you imagine a man being willing to die just for the pleasure of keeping his wife unhappy?"

That's not what he meant, Rachel said to herself. He meant that I'll never see the end of all this trouble.

15

She lived like a bird on the wing that sharp blustery fall, with no permanent place of abode, visiting back and forth among her sisters and brothers to be with their children, particularly the newborn whom she helped usher into the world and took care of until their mothers came back to full strength. The youngsters awaited her visits eagerly and talked about Aunt Rachel so much that her family took to calling her, as though it had settled her peculiar status: Aunt Rachel. When the children were ill she nursed them, sitting by their bed during the day and night; if they got into trouble or needed a confidante, she performed that service too. If the man of the family had to go away she moved in with sister or sister-in-law to keep her company and offer added protection.

"You're a circuit rider now," teased John Overton one raw mid-November day when he and Jackson had picked her up at her brother John's and were taking her to her mother's, "the same as Andrew and I."

"A circuit-riding aunt," she said with a laugh. Her cheeks were a bright red from the cold, though she was snugly warm in the fur-trimmed bonnet and boots, and the heavy wool dress fastened securely under her chin.

Overton was amused, but Jackson was not.

"I'm sorry, but I don't happen to like that Aunt Rachel title. It has the implication of a middle-aged lady."

They arrived at Mrs. Donelson's stockade at sundown. Jackson was still living at Mansker's, but was invited to stay for supper. They went into the main house, removing their heavy coats, wool caps and mufflers.

"I think it's nonsense that you don't move back here altogether, Mr. Jackson," said Rachel as they stood in front of the fire, rubbing their hands before the flames. "I am not here more than one day a week, if that's what is keeping you out."

"I'm not going to give anybody a chance to do any more talking." His voice was determined.

"We are all still living our lives under the dark shadow of Lewis Robards," she replied a little sadly.

There had been no direct word from Lewis during the fall months, only news that came indirectly as a result of unguarded conversations around Harrodsburg. At first the threats did not disturb her: the talk about his legal rights, that he would come to Nashville and claim her. One day she found Overton alone in his office.

"I know he can't do that, John," she said, "but I'd feel so much better if I were completely free. Isn't there any possibility of a court action or a divorce?"

Overton, who was writing a brief from voluminous notes, moved his papers and iron inkpot to another corner of the desk, began taking down thick volumes and running through the passages he had annotated in anticipation of this inevitable question.

"Practically none, Rachel. Our law here derives from the English law, and even in London a man has to get an act through Parliament before he can have what's known as a legal separation. Each state makes its own laws about divorce; if you and Lewis had been married in Pennsylvania, he might conceivably have secured a divorce. New York does not allow court action for a divorce, and in Virginia the legislature has to grant each divorce separately. To the best of my knowledge it is impossible for a woman to secure a divorce in this country. In fact, it's almost impossible for her to get into a law court at all, except as a spectator.''

''Then there's nowhere I can go, nothing I can do, to make sure Lewis will have no right to disturb me again?''

Overton rose, put a chopped log into the small fireplace and watched the flames catch the peeling bark.

''Well, there is one possible way: you might be able to secure a separation down in the Spanish territory, say at New Orleans or Natchez. But that would never be considered legal up here; if you should ever marry again you would be considered guilty of bigamy. And if you had children . . .''

The hope drained out of her face. ''I see.''

''However, if you were to remain in the Spanish territory, and remarried down there, any second marriage might be considered legal.''

Shortly before Thanksgiving a letter reached Rachel informing her that Lewis had apparently convinced a segment of the Harrodsburg folk that the Donelsons were keeping his wife away from him against her will, and that he was organizing a band of his cronies to swoop down on the Cumberland and take her back with him by force.

The news was brought to Rachel on a blustery autumn morning when she was at home with her mother making pies and candies for Thanksgiving. Samuel went over to the guest cottage to summon John and Andrew. Each of the three men read the letter in turn.

''Can he really do this?'' she asked of no one in particular.

''He can try.''

''What do you mean by that, Mr. Jackson?''

''He can ride in with some armed men and start shooting; unless they took you by surprise and unprotected, they couldn't capture you . . .''

''But there is always the chance?''

''There is always the chance.''

''The men around Nashville can shoot just as fast as the ones from Harrodsburg,'' said Samuel bitterly.

Tears came into her eyes. ''I must go away, far away.''

''But where would you go, Rachel?'' her mother asked.

''It doesn't matter, Mother, just so long as there are thousands of miles between Lewis Robards and me.''

''Colonel Stark is leaving for Natchez soon,'' said Alexander as he entered the room. ''I've seen him outfitting his boat. Perhaps he would take Rachel along. She could stay there with Tom or Abner Green's family.''

''Yes, you would be welcome there,'' said Mrs. Donelson with excited relief. ''The Green boys have been asking us to come down and see the beautiful estates they've built.''

''That's a mighty dangerous voyage,'' commented Jackson; ''almost two thousand miles down the Cumberland, the Ohio and the Mississippi rivers, much of it inhabited by hostile Indians.''

''It won't be any worse than our trip on the *Adventure,*'' said Rachel.

''You had ample protection then; your father was a great expedition leader. Colonel Stark is an elderly man. Unless there are experienced Indian fighters along . . .''

She stood with her feet planted firmly, digging her toes into her thinsoled shoes and the floor beneath them, arching upward from her slender hips, her shoulders thrown back, every line of her face and figure stoutly determined.

''I'm going!''

She and Samuel found Colonel Stark at the landing, smoking a smelly ancient pipe, coonskin cap covering his cold ears, supervising the loading of barrels of salt, bales of cotton and hogsheads of whisky onto the boat. It was a twenty-foot-wide, one-hundred-foot-long, broad-bottomed structure, some two thirds of which was covered by a round roof, with carefully carpentered side walls containing cutouts for windows. He stopped in the midst of his labors and knocked the ashes from his pipe. The river was muddy, but a sharp current kept it covered with whitecaps. Two other flatboats were also loading, as part of the flotilla.

"Now, Miss Rachel, you know I'd do anything for you I could. But I simply can't shoulder the responsibility."

"Why not, Colonel Stark? You're taking your wife."

"We have risked our lives before, moving on to new country. But if anything happened to you . . ."

"Colonel, we'll take full responsibility," said Samuel. "Rachel's simply got to get away."

"Tell you what I'll do, Miss Rachel: there's a young fellow in this town who's a real Indian fighter. I was with him when we lifted the siege last year on Robertson's station. He can smell an Indian a hundred miles away with the wind blowing in the wrong direction. I'm referring to Andy Jackson, of course."

There was nothing in the old colonel's voice except admiration for young Jackson.

"But Colonel, that's simply out of the question! I can't ask Mr. Jackson to make this trip."

"Why not?"

"Well, a hundred reasons: he has his law practice, he's an officer of the court. John Overton says that Mr. Jackson is going to appear in fifty cases that are coming up for trial here in Nashville in the next few months."

"He's young, he'll have thousands of law cases."

"No, Colonel, I simply could not ask him. However, I will sell my possessions and hire a couple of good militiamen to come along."

"Better ask Andy Jackson, Miss Rachel; he might be awful hurt if you don't give him first chance."

Two days later, having made inquiries about engaging the riflemen to make the trip under Colonel Stark's command, Rachel went back to the dock. She was surprised to have the colonel greet her with a broad smile.

"It's all arranged, Miss Rachel, you can come along, and my wife will be mighty proud to have you."

"Then you've changed your mind . . . ?"

"Gettin' too old to change my mind, Miss Rachel. When you left here I simply went down to the courthouse and put the proposition up to Andy Jackson."

"You didn't!"

"Certainly did. Told him I wouldn't take you unless he came along. He seemed mighty upset. Said he'd need a couple days to mull it over. Wasn't more than an hour ago that he told me he'd come along, and when did we leave?"

She wondered whether there would ever come a time when she would again feel some single and unified emotion over what was happening to her. She was glad that Andrew Jackson was coming along, she was touched by this tribute to their friendship; but what obligations to each other were they undertaking by this move? And what would Nashville say?

Arriving home late in the afternoon, she made straight for the law cabin. John Overton was alone, immersed in a batch of documents. It was a dark, gloomy, dirty-gray day, and he had lighted not only the candles on his desk but the grease lamps on the walls as well.

"John, do you know what Andrew Jackson has done?"

"Yes, he's turned all his cases over to me and he's going down to Natchez with Colonel Stark."

"I came to tell him I couldn't allow it; but from your tone of voice, it would seem that you approve."

"Yes, I must say I do. Andrew paced this cabin for two days and nights with that long chin of his on that bony bosom. I finally asked, 'What the devil is eating you?' He told me that he was the unhappiest of men, that he believed you to be the finest woman he had ever known, and that he had unintentionally been the cause of your troubles for the past two years. He feels that he must get you safely out of Nashville and installed with your friends in Natchez, and then he will have done everything he could and should."

She cried in a hurt tone, "Kindly tell your law partner that he has no further obligation to me! I'm hiring a couple of militiamen. Besides, the family would never approve of his going."

"I think they will."

"What makes you so sure, John?"

"Because I think your mother, and Samuel and Jane at least, are now convinced that you and Andrew Jackson belong together."

She dropped onto the log bench reserved for clients and thought back to the time five months before when Lewis Robards had accused her of being in love with Andrew Jackson. It had been untrue then. But now, since she had terminated her relationship with Lewis . . . yes, now it was true. She loved Andrew Jackson. She had known for some time, but the occasion had never arisen for her to face the fact. Did he love her? They had never discussed love or their own personal relationship; her strange position had made this a subject which they both wanted to avoid. But now at least there was no need to conceal it from herself: she loved Andrew Jackson with all her heart.

She looked up at John, wondering how much she could tell him. If Andrew did not share her love, then she must never embarrass him by an expression of it. John's back was to her, as though he wished to afford her the opportunity of thinking in private. Now he turned, sensing that she was ready to continue.

"Have no fears, my dear Rachel," he said softly, "nor any misgivings. Andrew loves you too. He has told me so."

There was a long but gentle silence between them, so unlike the hostile and violent silences she had come to know these past years. She felt hollow and weak at what had been revealed. Unconsciously she pushed back her long black cloak that was trailing the floor, and ran her fingers through the ridges of her dark red corduroy skirt. Her hair suddenly felt too tight on her head, as though imprisoning her thoughts. She untied the dark red ribbon that held the heavy black tresses in place. Instantly she felt released, able to speak.

"Then don't you see, John, that's all the more reason why he must not go along on this trip."

"I would say all the more reason for him to accompany you. Every man has the right to protect the woman he loves."

"You won't tell him of anything that's been said here?"

"No, Rachel, nor would I have told you of his feelings if I had not considered it necessary to your future well-being. This is a secret I think you are going to have to keep from each other for a considerable time. That will make it possible for you to travel on this long journey together as friends, friends who would do nothing to compromise each other's good name or position. It is not in the character of either of you to make Lewis Robards look as though he had been right in his accusations!"

16

The morning of January 20, 1791, was cold and leaden-skied. Samuel took her to the landing with her two heavy portmanteaus strapped on a pack horse, one containing woolen clothes for the journey down-river, the other her light summer linens and lawn dresses. She picked up her skirts as she walked along the muddy bank, then across a plank and onto the boxlike boat which had been built of green timber sawed from the forests immediately behind the river and put together with wooden pins. She stood irresolutely for a moment until Andrew, stooping low, came through the door of the cabin. It was the first time she had seen him in the heavy buckskin shirt and breeches since their trip home from Harrodsburg the summer before. He greeted her with a pleasant but casual smile, assured Samuel that he would watch over her and then, when she kissed her brother good-by, picked up her two cases and led her toward the prow.

She stepped over the sill and found herself in the front portion of the cabin where Mrs. Stark, in a huge leather apron over her cotton dress, was directing her serving couple in the preparation of the noonday dinner. She turned toward Rachel with an open-armed gesture; she was a big shapeless bustling woman who moved about with astonishing speed in a pair of floppy buffalo moccasins; her greatest need, as Rachel was to learn over the ensuing weeks, was for talk.

"Well, now, welcome, Rachel. The colonel has dragged me up and down rivers and trails so much of our lives that whenever I land anyplace, even a flatboat, I hang up my pots and curtains and make believe it's a permanent home."

She took Rachel by the arm, leading her through the middle compartment of the flatboat in which were stored the bales of cotton, barrels of salt and smoked venison, buffalo and pork, which had to be protected from the weather, into the rear third of the cabin, which constituted the sleeping quarters. There were two bunks fastened to the log wall with leather hinges. A thick curtain of buffalo hide was pegged to the rafters; it fell heavily over the doorway.

"You and I will live here, child; it will give us good privacy."

It was still early in the morning when they shoved off the Nashville landing into fog and heavy rain, the two other flatboats following. Rachel remained in her little compartment; out the square hull window she could see that a group had assembled to say good-by to the Starks. She had made no attempt to conceal her own departure for Natchez; that would have been just as impossible as it would have been to conceal the reason for her flight.

The rain and cold continued for a full week. Rachel rarely left her quarters, reading, sewing, helping Mrs. Stark make a pair of intricate bedcovers. In addition to the Starks and Andrew there were five traders on board, spelling each other at the sweeps which kept the boat away from the banks and from collision with boulders. Colonel Stark did most of the steering himself, clinging hour after hour to a board fastened to a long pole.

The meals were simple, roast saddle of venison or buffalo, corn bread, stews and preserved dried fruits, strong draughts of whisky for the men when they came in after the long hours in the cold. They ate in two shifts, Rachel sitting with Mrs. Stark, the colonel and one or two of the traders, Andrew relieving Colonel Stark at the steering rudder. There wasn't much talk; the dark skies and penetrating cold dissipated any will toward conviviality.

During the first week they tied up at various settlements and at Fort Massac, bringing the settlers much-needed salt, coffee and sugar from Pittsburgh, taking in exchange packets of furs which would be sold down-river. The Starks and the traders from the three boats went ashore to deliver letters and exchange news with the people in the forts. Rachel and Andrew sat at the scrubbed plank table in front of the blazing log fire, his red hair plastered down from the many hours under a heavy wool cap. He spent his leisure studying his briefs and the lawbooks which John Overton had loaned him. The Andrew Jackson she had known, the man with the teeming energy and radiating inner force, the sparkling eyes and the deeply emotional nature, had remained in Nashville; the uncommunicative young man sitting opposite her needed but a pair of silver-rimmed spectacles to be John Overton. These periods of quiet, almost of solitude, were their only moments alone together.

It took them ten days to navigate the Cumberland and Ohio rivers. On the eleventh morning she awakened to find that their tiny flotilla was already several miles along the Mississippi, with the sun shining brightly overhead. As the days passed and they drifted swiftly down the swollen river the weather grew warmer and once again, just as she had from the decks of the *Adventure,* she saw spring grass and flowering shrubs on the banks to tell them that they were moving southward into a radiant spring. The next day at noon, when Colonel Stark came in for his dinner, Rachel went out to the stern of the boat and stood beside Andrew. He had donned a clean doeskin shirt which was open at the throat, letting the sun beat on his lean face and neck. She had packed her heavy winter woolens and was wearing a yellow linen dress, light enough for the warm days ahead, yet sturdy and suitable for life aboard the flatboat. The wind blew her hair and rippled through the open-work collar.

"I feel as though I'd been dead," she murmured, "and have suddenly been reborn."

His fingers gripped the steering pole as he moved the craft to avoid a floating log. She watched the muscles in his arms and shoulders work smoothly under the soft shirt: he was not a powerfully built man, not even a strong man, for there was little flesh on his frame.

"Not dead," he answered. "Just dormant, like those sycamores that have been standing bare and now are beginning to leaf."

Straight ahead it seemed as though the river were coming to an abrupt end, but it was only making a sharp turn. After a moment he spoke to her again.

"I think you'll like the South, Rachel; the air is warm and fragrant, the land is fertile, the whole countryside seems friendly and soft. Natchez isn't very big yet, only about twenty or thirty houses, but quite a few Americans have built plantations up and down the river. The forests are tremendously deep: cottonwood, willow, giant oaks. The sky over the river at sunset is crimson, or indigo; there are herons and pelicans and forests full of deer."

They had been attacked twice by Indians, once from a high bluff when they had steered too close to the bank and another time from an island thicket which had looked innocent enough as they approached. There were a number of bullet holes in the superstructure, but only one man had been injured, slightly, by an already spent bullet.

Then late one February afternoon they became separated from the other two boats and were obliged to tie up to an abandoned landing at the foot of a dense forest. Andrew pointed out to Colonel Stark how close the cypress trees came down to the shore, how the bank made a lagoon so that the Indians could surround them on three sides and subject them to a murderous crossfire. However, the colonel was unwilling to risk the river currents in the impenetrable darkness. Andrew took the youngest of the traders onshore with him. Colonel Stark tried to dissuade them from going.

"I want every man to remain on board so we have our fullest fighting strength."

"You've got to have advance warning, Colonel, and the only way you can get it is for us to go ashore."

He cleaned his rifle, filled his shot pouch, picked a flint, summoned his companion, who had been molding bullets, and the two men slipped noiselessly onto the old timbers of the landing, leaving orders for one of the traders to remain awake with an ax in hand, ready to cut the tie rope at the first sound of a shot. Rachel followed him to the edge of the railing.

"But how will you get back on board if we cut this rope?" she asked. "The current will sweep us out into the river."

"Don't worry about us," he murmured. "Just stay under cover."

She watched him until he had disappeared into the darkness, then went to her cabin, pulled the bunk from the wall and lay down fully clothed. After a time Mrs. Stark came in, undressed, pushed her own bunk down on its supporting legs, methodically folding the bedspread. She then got under the covers and began to talk, quietly and pleasantly, of other trips, other alarms. Rachel listened with only one ear, for the other was listening for sounds on the outside; even so she could hear everything Mrs. Stark said, could even answer, and tell stories of her own. An alligator lying along the bank was putting up a tremendous howling and bellowing.

Suddenly in the middle of one of her own sentences Mrs. Stark fell fast asleep. Rachel rose quietly and went out on deck to find the sky black, with no vestige of a moon. The guard was asleep. She stood peering into the darkness. The night was now still except for the call of some swamp birds. Then she saw the flash of a gun on the beach, followed by a burst of fire. The sleeping traders on the deck were awake at once. The guard grabbed the ax, but Rachel was waiting and seized his arm.

"Don't touch that rope."

"But Jackson gave orders . . ."

"I don't care what orders he gave. Here, give me that ax. I'll cut this rope the instant those two men are on board, and not before."

He stared at her, hearing the ring in her voice, shrugged, handed her the ax and picked up his rifle. Two more shots were fired, then she saw Andrew and his companion move swiftly up the plank and drop onto the deck. She brought the ax down sharply. The flatboat edged out into the river.

She and Andrew stood at the prow watching the currents, with Colonel Stark steering as best he could. She heard Andrew chuckling to himself.

"Tell me the joke," she said, "I should like to laugh."

Without turning his head, he replied, "So you refused to let them cut that tie line, eh? Don't you know you could have been massacred?"

"I like to graze danger," she said, mimicking his tone. "I might ask the same question of you."

"Fighting Indians is a bigger part of the circuit rider's job than trying law cases."

"Even so, how could we have left you on the beach and pulled away to safety?"

"From the evidence before this court, I would say you couldn't."

He put his arm about her in a slow encircling movement, holding her with his long sinewy fingers, crushing her shoulder against his in a momentary grip of avowal. Then, almost before she knew it had happened, he moved away.

17

Thomas Marston Green's home, Springfield, was the most luxurious Rachel had ever seen, bringing to mind the stories her father had told her about George Washington's Mount Vernon. It was a sturdy structure of red brick with six majestic pillars across the front, each standing on a solid rectangular base, deep shade galleries hung with vines to ensure coolness, a lacelike wooden balustrade protecting the second-floor porch; long narrow windows and tall green shutters, everything else painted a soft white. The social rooms were high-ceilinged, with carved cornices, hand-trimmed mantels, glistening crystal chandeliers, a side-lighted central doorway and an elegant foyer paneled in wood. The house had been built high above the murky swamps, was wind-swept, and stood framed at the end of a row of magnificent oaks.

The Greens quickly assembled all the Americans in the neighborhood for a welcoming dinner party. When Rachel saw the turquoise gown and the satin slippers which young Tom Green's wife was planning to wear, she knew there was nothing in her portmanteau that would stand comparison. Mrs. Green loaned her a lace-trimmed pale blue satin with a delicate lace cap; it required only a moderate amount of alteration to make it fit quite well. When she walked into the dining room on old Colonel Thomas Green's arm she found a hundred candles in the chandelier throwing a glow of light on the silver, crystal goblets and polished wood.

"You've transplanted the very best of Virginia down here in the South," she exclaimed breathlessly.

The old colonel was pleased; he turned to Andrew, who was just behind them, his black Nashville suit set off by a fine linen shirt with a lace jabot and lace cuffs which made him feel almost as elegant as the handsomely attired men about him.

"Every man carries his home with him no matter how far he travels. Isn't that true, Jackson? Of course we have a few things extra down here: mosquitoes, alligators, swamps, heat, but we take the bad with the good."

Colonel Thomas Green had been a friend of her father's in Virginia. He was a heavy-set man of about seventy with a magnificent splurge of white hair topping a leathery tan face. The unquestioned leader of the American colony in Louisiana, he had suffered greatly in his efforts to split off this region from Spanish ownership, set up a new county called Bourbon and attach it to the state of Georgia. The Georgia legislature had authorized Green's acts, but the coup had failed and Thomas Green had been thrown into prison in New Orleans. His wife had died of shock and grief. The Spaniards had pardoned him after this tragedy but he had been obliged to transfer all of his property to his young sons, not only this plantation at Springfield but also the Villa Gayoso, some eight miles south on Cole's Creek which he had previously bought from the Spanish governor of Natchez and where Abner, the second of his two sons, now lived.

"Too bad your father didn't live to see Springfield, Rachel," said the old colonel, "he would have moved down here and built a house just like it."

Rachel knew that her father had loved the Cumberland deeply, and that nothing could have persuaded him to move again; but she did not think it necessary to tell Colonel Green this. His son Tom at the head of the long mahogany table said:

"Since we can't have Colonel Donelson, perhaps we can have his daughter. How about it, Rachel?"

Tom Green's young wife nodded her agreement. "We feel as though we have scored a victory every time another American family joins us."

The elder Green lifted a goblet of Spanish madeira as he turned to Andrew, who had been handling a number of involved cases in Nashville for all three members of the Green family. The servants were bringing in bottles of light wine from the cool cellar and silver bowls of oranges, bananas, melons and grapes.

"You're staying this time, aren't you, Jackson? That's a fine piece of land you have over at Bayou Pierre, and you can have just as much more of it as you are willing to pay the survey costs on. We'd like to have you with us when we start our next revolt against the Spaniards."

The men plunged into a discussion of the comparative onerousness of being ruled by the Spanish or English. The Greens hated the Spanish as much as Andrew did the English, and so the race ended in a dead heat: how many years was it going to take to persuade the government at Philadelphia that Louisiana was a natural and contiguous part of the mainland? that the United States would have to acquire it in order to assure free navigation on the Mississippi, and to keep open the now-Spanish ports of Natchez and New Orleans? that it wouldn't require more than a few hundred men with rifles to chase the Spanish out forever? Surely Spain was farther away than England, and had even less business here on this American continent?

Rachel was disturbed by the suggestion of the Greens that she and Andrew remain in Natchez and establish another American family. Just how much were they assuming? They had asked no questions, in fact had treated them as guests who had arrived simultaneously but from opposite directions. Yet love was difficult to conceal; put a man and a woman who loved each other into even as spacious a room as this, and as large an assemblage; place them at opposite ends of the table, and still everyone would be sure to know.

She saw little of Andrew, for he spent a number of days in Natchez, some thirty miles down-river from Springfield, where he was discussing the settlement of cases with the clients he had acquired a year and a half before, and taking on new claims for men who had left land or other business assets behind them when they had come down the Mississippi. After that one fleeting moment at the prow of the boat in the seclusion of the dark Mississippi night there had been no intimate word or gesture between them.

Then early on a bright, fragrant Sunday morning they rode the two miles to Bayou Pierre to see Andrew's tract of land on the bluff overlooking the river. Rachel dressed in sheer pink lawn over her several billowing pink petticoats, with a wide velvet ribbon at the waist and a matching ribbon on her wide-brimmed bonnet. Looking into the mirror of her dressing table, she decided that she was beginning to look well again. Poor Andrew, he would have to carry all his life that scar on his forehead from the officer's saber; how fortunate that one's inner scars could not be seen every time one looked into a mirror; for, not being seen, they could be forgotten, and perhaps vanish completely.

They made their way to the small log cabin that Andrew had built and saw the outlines of the racecourse he had staked out. They stood before the door of the little house looking over the wide, slow-moving waters and the vast forest of cypress and oaks rolling horizonward to merge with the pastel sky. It was a beautiful spot, almost too beautiful; it gave her a poignant feeling of nostalgia.

"You will have to be going back soon, won't you, Andrew?"

"Yes. The spring court in Nashville opens on April twelfth."

"How long will it take you to go up the Chickasaw Trace?"

"A year and a half ago, about twenty days. There's a group of boatmen starting back at midweek. I'll travel with them. I'll carry a supply of imported silks and satins, some spices and Spanish segars."

His voice fell off; he stood gazing over the river for a moment. There was no breeze and the sun glared hotly on the water; in the distance wild birds were calling. When he turned his eyes were unguarded and full of his love for her. He untied the strings of her bonnet, took it off her head and ran his fingers through her hair.

"Rachel, I don't have to go back at all. We can stay right here together, the two of us."

"But how, Andrew?"

"I've been asking in Natchez: you could get an annulment there from the Spanish authorities. It would be legal."

"Not really legal, just a way around the law is what John called it. You took your oath to the United States government when they installed you as attorney general of the territory; I can't let you go back on your word. And you have the biggest law practice there, even John says so."

"I couldn't be a lawyer, perhaps. I couldn't hold public office, and I'd have to become a Spanish subject, but I can do just as well down here." There was a tiny edge to his voice. "Look about you. Isn't it proof I had this whole Bayou Pierre plantation staked out?" He rushed on, not wanting to give her a chance to answer. "The main house was to be over on the edge of the bluff; straight across I was going to build stables. The land is good for cotton, tobacco, indigo. There's money to be made, tremendous sums of money. One day we'd have a plantation as lovely as Springfield.''

She slipped into his embrace, held herself against him.

"Yes, you can do all that. You can do it anywhere, Nashville, Natchez, or the moon; but my dear, how could you ever be happy as a subject of Spain? You'd have no voice here, and no vote. You're an independent man . . .''

"It wouldn't be for long; this country will be American. I wouldn't mind helping the Greens bring it into the Union. I could go back to Nashville, take care of my cases, sell my lands and load everything movable on a flatboat.''

"No, Andrew, I can't take the responsibility. If you ever became unhappy down here, or if somehow we failed . . . one morning you might wake up to find you had wasted your life in Louisiana. Oh, you'd never reproach me, you'd do your best to keep your feelings hidden even from yourself; but I can't put this burden on our marriage. Our love is right and good; our marriage must be right and good too, from the first instant.''

His eyes, ordinarily so clear and penetrating, were confused and hurt. She drew back.

"But what are we going to do?'' he cried, as though the volume of his voice could knock down the walls which enclosed them. "We are caught. We are helpless. Robards holds all the weapons.''

"No, Andrew, that isn't true. He stands empty-handed. We have the only weapon that counts: love.''

"Rachel dear, I am not a fickle man, I have never loved before, and I'll not love again. Only you. Always you.''

"Thank you, my darling.''

He put his arms about her and kissed her full on the mouth.

"We would have to believe in miracles,'' he murmured.

She cupped his face in her hands, kissing him on one cheek and then the other.

"I do believe in miracles, Andrew. The fact that we have found each other, that we are standing here together, that you have your arms about me, that I can kiss you, so, all this is proof that miracles can happen.''

18

After six weeks with the colonel and the Tom Greens she was invited to visit down-river at Villa Gayoso, surrounded by huge oaks which dripped gray moss. Mrs. Abner Green was a woman of thirty, soft-spoken, but an exacting mistress of her household; it was the better part of her kindness which soon made Rachel see that she was not to live here as a guest, but rather as a part of the family, with her own daily chores, participating in the spinning and weaving, training the servants in the making of colored candles and scented soap for which her mother had given her a recipe.

There was no word from Andrew, nor from any of the Donelsons; southward movement over the Natchez Trace was practically unknown, and with the coming of summer the boat traffic on the Mississippi ceased. The weeks passed and she felt her strength and sense of well-being, of joy in life, return in full measure. The tinkling of the fountain, the enclosed patio so deeply shaded by vines of wild grapes, the twittering of small birds, the heavy scent of the magnolias, the deep colorings of the surrounding country, these were the only pleasures she needed. And as the slow, lazy, hot days of summer drifted by her eyes became bright and luminous, her step became buoyant.

"My dear, you are lovely," commented Mrs. Green as they sat on the broad gallery beneath deep roofs where Rachel sang softly and played the harpsichord.

Whatever she had suffered from Lewis Robards and her disillusionment, from the harassment of the past years, had been expunged by these months of tranquil living, a tranquillity which took so strong a hold that she felt she could wait out the rest of her life here.

Two months later she was sitting at the window of her bedroom having a tumbler of milk from the springs in which the dairy products were kept cool all summer, and watching a rust-colored sunset. She heard hoofbeats coming up the main road. Horsemen came and went all day, and she'd heard perhaps half a dozen in the past hour, but there was only one horseman who rode like this, who changed the rhythm of the horse to fit his own, so that no matter what its peculiar gait or tempo it must move precisely as Andrew Jackson moved through space: headlong, almost cyclonic, and always knowing its destination.

She picked up the skirts of her crisp white cotton dress and ran down the winding staircase. There stood Andrew in the doorway, hot, disheveled, in wrinkled buckskins, his boots white with dust, and wearing a three weeks' beard. As she went forward to greet him she saw that something crucial had happened, something that would change their lives. She led him toward the dark oak-paneled library, with its tall narrow windows open to the pungent fragrance of the tropical garden, resolved not to think or feel or even to fear until he had told her the purpose of his visit. He closed the door securely behind him.

They met in the center of the room. She felt his lips, dry and cracked from the long days on the trail, bruising her own. He held her securely for several moments, then blurted out:

'There's news . . . ''

"About . . . Lewis."

"Yes. He has divorced you."

She gasped, felt a sharp pain in her chest.

"Divorced me? But how?"

"The Virginia legislature. He persuaded his brother-in-law, Jack Jouitt, to introduce a bill. The legislature passed it."

Her eyes widened, and a question began to formulate itself on her lips. He spoke quickly.

"You're free now, my dear. We can be married as soon as you are ready."

She had not been diverted.

"The Virginia legislature gave him a divorce? But on what grounds?"

". . . well . . . desertion."

She gazed at him, unable to get breath into her lungs.

"And what else, Andrew? The Virginia laws don't allow divorce merely for desertion."

"That's what the bill says."

How badly he lies, she thought. Aloud, she said, "Tell me the rest. I must know."

". . . *adultery*."

She felt as though she had been struck across the face. She tasted blood on her lips, not knowing she had bitten through the skin. The only voice she could muster was so faint that she imagined she was saving the words inside her own head.

"Adultery! But . . . with whom . . . ?"

He enveloped her in his long arms and held her rigidly as though fearing she might fall.

"With me."

". . . you . . . but when . . . ?"

"When we . . . 'eloped' . . . the bill calls it. From the Robards' home."

"Eloped? But the family sent you. Lewis knows that. When he came to my sister Jane's and tried to persuade me to go back home with him, he said there had been nothing wrong in your coming for me. He never would have come for me if he had believed for a single instant . . ."

She burst into tears, hot scalding tears, while he stroked her hair and kissed her temples and spoke soft words to comfort her. After a time she looked up, her eyes wet, the tears still on her cheeks.

"I had expected he would try to kill me. This is worse."

"Only in the sense that still another injustice has been done. But let's look at it from our point of view: he could have kept us from each other for years; we might never have been able to marry or to have each other's love. Don't you see, dearest, this is the end of our troubles. A bitter end, I grant you that, but it means that we can have our life together. We can have a home and children and never be separated again."

There was a constriction about her heart which she thought must burst it.

"How could Jack Jouitt do a thing like that to me? He was my friend. He fought for me when Lewis was making trouble over Peyton Short. He believed in me during all those early years, had faith in me, but if now he is convinced . . ."

"I don't believe Jack has lost any faith in you. Perhaps he introduced the bill because he knows this is the only way you can ever get your freedom. It could have been an act of kindness . . ."

"To label me an adulteress!"

He dropped his eyes, unable to face her blazing indignation.

"Do they know what they have convicted me of? Does the charge of adultery mean the same to a man as it does to a woman? It can't, or they wouldn't have sat so calmly in their seats and voted . . . without even giving me a chance to appear and defend myself, voted me guilty of the vulgarest of all sins! By what majority did they decide that I am a liar, a cheat, a fraud . . . ?"

He put his hand lightly over her lips.

"What they have accused you of, they have accused me of. We are together in this . . . as we will always be in everything that happens to us."

Her anger was spent now; she sat limply on a chair, her head lowered, unable to face him, seeing only the waxed and polished stone floor. After a moment she whispered:

"Half of those men have known me since I was a child. Father sat with them in the House of Burgesses; they've been guests in our home, watched me grow up. They know that the Donelsons have never been . . . low . . . And John Overton, what does he think of this?"

"When I first heard that the legislature had granted Robards that divorce I wanted to go out and shoot him. I would have too, except that John stopped me. He said, 'Let's look at these facts calmly, as lawyers should. The divorce on these terms is Robards' final act of indignity. Nevertheless it opens the heavily barred door to your future. Now you and Rachel can be married. We would all wish it to be under different circumstances; but these are the circumstances Providence has seen fit to impose. Forget the bad part of it and think only that you and Rachel can begin your lives together.'"

She sighed deeply. "John is right; he's always right." She hesitated for a moment. "How did you learn all this?"

"Your family heard about it first. Probably half a dozen men brought in word from Richmond."

"Was it published in a paper?"

"No, I think not. It reached the Cumberland the way most news does, by word of mouth."

"Then everybody . . . knows . . . in Nashville . . . ?"

It was his turn to be angry now; the harshness in his voice brought her head up abruptly.

"Everyone knows that Robards has secured his divorce. But there's not a soul in the Cumberland Valley who could believe you guilty of anything more than having married an insanely jealous man. Everyone also knows that I came down here for our wedding. We are going to have a fine home and a fine life together, Rachel, and that will be the last we will ever hear of this wretched affair. None of our friends or neighbors can believe us guilty of duplicity. And if any enemy should ever raise his voice to accuse us, or to injure your name, I shall know how to deal with him."

She rose and walked to the window. She stared out into the darkness of the garden, hearing the water of the fountain and the croaking of frogs in the still evening air. Andrew walked to the candelabrum above the fireplace and lighted a single candle.

"Our marriage will give them more food for talk," murmured Rachel. "It will look as though Lewis was right after all, and that the Virginia legislature was justified in giving him his divorce."

She leaned her hot cheek against the dark oak panel of the window frame. She did not hear him come near, but suddenly she was whirled about and shaken rudely by the shoulders.

"All this has nothing to do with us! We can't let that kind of thinking keep us from our love." He released his grip on her shoulders and stood quietly, his face pale. "You do love me?"

She saw now that he was suffering as greatly as she. In her compassion she lifted her face to his, kissed him.

"Yes, Andrew. I will always love you."

"Then that is all we need. We can live at peace with ourselves. Our love will be a fortress that no amount of hostility or cruelty from the outside can ever penetrate."

"Yes, my darling, you are right."

"We will honeymoon here in my cabin at Bayou Pierre. It is so beautiful, overlooking the river. Tom Green will provide anything we need, and we can be utterly alone, perhaps more alone than we will ever be again in our lives."

"Give me a few days. I want to have a wedding gown made, so that you will be proud of me, and think me beautiful."

They stood together, silent in the dark room, holding tightly to each other.

This we will always have, she thought: our love. It will brighten our lives and sustain us through hardships. But Andrew, my dearest, you are wrong when you say this is the end of our troubles.

BOOK TWO

1

They spent a languorous two months in the stillness of Bayou Pierre, where the gray moss dripped from the huge live oaks and the air was heavily perfumed. Then they set out on the thousand-mile trip up the dangerous Natchez Trace, reaching Nashville on the first of October.

On the morning after their arrival at the Donelsons' Andrew rode into town with John Overton to rent for their law office a newly erected cabin immediately across from the courthouse. Andrew kissed her goodby with special tenderness.

"This will be the first time we've been separated in three months." He turned to Overton, who was waiting for him, grinning impishly. "John, we're looking for a homesite. Got a likely piece you'd care to sell us?"

"You can have any parcel I own as a wedding present, but those six-forties of ours are out in the wilderness with tepees sitting all over them."

By midmorning the five Donelson women had foregathered in the big room around cups of coffee.

"Thank goodness the last of my daughters is securely married," commented Mrs. Donelson with so much relief in her voice that her daughters laughed.

"There are times when I think it was you who arranged for Mr. Jackson to rescue me from Harrodsburg," replied Rachel, blushing. "And I wouldn't be at all surprised if it was you who first gave Colonel Stark the idea of insisting that Mr. Jackson make the trip to Natchez."

"I'm neither admitting nor denying," replied her mother; "I say all's well that ends well."

Mary, the plump, romantic sister, said, "Tell us about the wedding and your honeymoon, Rachel. Is it beautiful down there in Louisiana?"

Rachel sat quietly for a moment, her hands clasped in the lap of the deep blue Spanish silk robe which Andrew had bought her in Natchez. Her eyes were glowing.

"The ceremony was held in Tom Green's drawing room under a heavy cut-glass chandelier, with a hundred lighted candles. I can remember looking up several times and praying, 'Dear God, don't let that chandelier fall, I'm just about to begin to be happy.'"

"There was nothing to worry about," commented Jane matter-of-factly; "Andrew would have caught it before it hit you."

Rachel nodded her head.

"You're right, Jane, I should have waited all these years for Andrew Jackson, just as you did for Robert Hays."

"That's foolish backwards talk," observed Mrs. Donelson tartly. "You should thank Almighty God, instead of indulging in regrets."

"Now you three stop arguing," cried Mary, "I want to know about the wedding party, and what Bayou Pierre is like."

"Like heaven; the air is so soft you feel you can reach out and take a handful, as though it were silk, and sew yourself a gown. We danced cotillions for hours, then Andrew and I slipped away and rode over to Bayou Pierre. There was a full moon, and the Mississippi was so light you could see every drop of water separately. The nights are just as soft and warm as the day . . ."

"It must be a wonderful place to be in love," interrupted Mary dreamily.

"Any place is a good place to be in love," snapped Catherine; she had spent thirty years being embarrassed by her older sister's unabashed romanticism.

"You're right, Cathy, love is a place," replied Rachel. "It has its own foliage and trails and houses, even its own sun and moon and stars. Nashville looked just as beautiful to me yesterday as Natchez did; the air was as fragrant and the sun as warm."

"I hear you had some trouble coming up the Trace," said Jane, whose station in Haysboro was a clearinghouse for frontier news. "Indians, or those bands of no-good whites?"

"Neither, really. Andrew has a trouble-repellent manner: he peers so hard at the woods and the trail that he sends out a signal which says, 'Better keep away, we're prepared for you.' The only quarrel was with Hugh McGary."

"I'm sorry to hear that," said Mrs. Donelson. "Remember that first day we saw Andrew in court, Rachel; he persuaded Hugh to settle peaceably with Casper Mansker."

"Andrew says that Hugh has never forgiven him for that; it's the only time he's ever recommended compromise rather than fight, and look what it got him."

"Stop going down side paths," chided Jane, "and tell us precisely what did happen."

"Well, when we were about to cross the Tennessee River, Andrew and Hugh decided the Indians were going to attack that night. Hugh picked a camp spot, reasoning it would be better to entrench ourselves and greet the first Indian shots with a good round volley. Andrew said he wasn't going to get shot at like a sitting goose; he wanted to push ahead in the dark. Hugh claimed that only made us better targets; Andrew insisted the Indians never attacked a party going at top speed. The men voted to move out under cover of dark and leave the fires burning behind them as a decoy. We traveled all night and there was no attack. That proved Andrew right, but of course Hugh might have been able to beat them off with one volley . . . or they might never have attacked at all. Anyway, from that moment on the men looked to Andrew for their orders. Hugh resented it. He didn't exchange a single word with either of us for the last two weeks of the trip; when we parted in Nashville he walked away without saying good-by."

"Andrew knew the McGarys back in the Waxhaws, didn't he?" asked Mrs. Donelson.

"Yes, they are related: Hugh's brother Martin married Andrew's cousin. I did what I could to prevent the quarrel, even suggested that possibly Hugh was right. Andrew said, 'Possibly he is, but I'm not taking the one chance in a thousand that a British bullet in one of those guns should hit you.' "

"The McGarys are an unforgiving lot," said Mrs. Donelson.

"My husband can take care of himself," replied Rachel. It was the first time she had said *my husband* of Andrew Jackson. And here in the Donelson big room with her sisters around her, the words sounded good.

They had been back in Nashville only a few days when Andrew greeted her in a fever of excitement.

"Rachel, what do you suppose has happened?"

"You've been appointed governor of the territory!"

"Even better. I've been elected a trustee of Davidson Academy."

She kissed him soundly.

"Congratulations, my darling." And even while she held her lips to his, a number of tensions suddenly relaxed. She had not known that she was worrying about the kind of reception their marriage would receive in Nashville; for hers had been the first divorce in the Cumberland Valley. She had been accused before the Virginia legislature of eloping with Andrew Jackson. All Nashville knew this. By their marriage they had apparently proven the action of the legislature to have been right. She would not have been surprised if some of the families had resented this. Several nights on the Natchez Trace she had lain awake wondering whether Andrew's swift flight to Natchez and their immediate marriage might not be held against them.

Now they had no sooner returned than General James Robertson, her father's partner in the founding of Nashville, the Reverend Thomas B. Craighead, head of the Davidson Academy and the only clergyman in the community, Lardner Clark, who owned the supply store, General Daniel Smith, Revolutionary War hero and second-in-command under Governor Blount of the territory, Anthony Bledsoe, brother of Isaac Bledsoe, who with Casper Mansker had first explored the Cumberland Valley in 1771 . . . these most important men in the territory had by their gesture pushed aside potential criticism, and made it known that Andrew was one of theirs.

She had imagined that her husband's pleasure derived from the same source as her own. To her astonishment his exultation was on an entirely different level.

"Forgive me if I gloat, my dear, but that's just the last position I would have imagined I would ever be elected to. One of the heads of the academy! Do you know how much formal schooling I've had? A month or two at Queen's Museum at Charlotte. Oh, I went for a few years to an old-field school in the Waxhaws, it was just a one-room place, built among the stumps of a field that had been worked over and abandoned. Even taught readin' and writin' in one of them for a short spell when I was sixteen. All I've learned I've had to hew out of the few books I stumbled across. But that Davidson Academy, I'm going to pitch in and help make it one of the best schools this side of the Blue Ridge Mountains. Then our youngsters will be able to get themselves a real education."

"Amen," said Rachel under her breath.

The following Sunday they visited her brother Johnny to see the new daughter, and Rachel's namesake, who had been born while Rachel was in Natchez. Johnny was thirty-six, with Jane's green eyes, fluffy blond hair and slender face. He had married Mary Purnell when she was sixteen years old, taking her on the *Adventure* trip as a honeymoon. Their first child had been born in the open camp of Clover Bottom in 1780, but had not survived the difficulties of that first rude settlement. Little Rachel, now four months old, had three brothers and a sister, all healthy and vigorous.

Johnny owned some three hundred and thirty acres of Jones Bend, a snug and fertile peninsula bounded on three sides by the slow-moving green Cumberland and across the river from the Widow Donelson's station. The constant danger and death of the *Adventure* trip had had opposite effects on Johnny and Mary: of Johnny it had made a wanderer, a man who enjoyed staking out a new claim, clearing it, building a home, birthing a child and then moving on to the next six-forty. Mary detested not only change but movement itself. On the death of her first-born she had promised God that if He would give her children who would stay alive she would never cease thanking Him. Over the household hung a fervent religious spirit, for whenever Mary could spare a few minutes from her family duties she went into the lean-to sanctuary Johnny had built for her, fell on her knees and fulfilled her promise to God.

Dinner was ample, both with victuals and noise, for the four older children were propped up at the puncheon table. Johnny caught a quizzical expression on Andrew's face.

"They're forever talking and scratching and bawling, Andrew, but wait till you have five of your own, it'll sound like a heavenly chorus."

"I'll take twice as many as your five," replied Andrew, "and a hundred times the bawling."

After dinner Rachel, Andrew and Johnny walked down to the river. The woods were a blaze of glorious October colors: reds, russets and purples, light greens fading into dark greens. As they walked over the fields they tried to count the different kinds of trees and shrubs: beech, maple, hickory, ash, hackberry, mulberry, walnut, sweet gum, haw, poplar, redbud, dogwood, sycamore.

"You're going to have a fine plantation here in a couple of years, Johnny."

"No, I'm not, Andrew."

Rachel stopped in her tracks, holding back on her brother's arm.

"Johnny, surely you're not going to . . ."

"Yes, I am. I'm posting notice that it's for sale."

"Isn't the soil good?" asked Andrew.

"Nothing wrong with the place; it's me. I want to move on. I know a place about three miles from here, bigger. It can be more prosperous. No reason why a man shouldn't rise in the world."

"Now, Johnny, don't try to pull the woolsey over my eyes," said Rachel. "You don't care at all about moving upward, you just want to move sideways."

Johnny grinned. They walked in silence until they came to the river, then half slid down the trail. The river was not wide here, in the horseshoe bend, but it was deep, of a superb jade green. Andrew was the first to speak.

"How much are you asking for the place?"

"One hundred pounds. Know somebody who might be interested?"

"Might. However, I'm not helping put Mary on the move. The minute you get an offer, let me know about it. I'll see if my client won't better the price."

"You know what I like about this place, Andrew?" murmured Rachel as they walked across the path to their horses.

"What?"

"It's almost an island, surrounded on three sides by the river. If someone wanted to build a good stout fence across the back . . ."

She saw by his expression that he knew what she meant. He reached out encircling arms.

"It could be our first home," he said softly. His eyes roamed the acreage. "You don't think it's too isolated, Rachel? I have to be away so much, circuit riding to Jonesboro and Sumner County. The Creeks are still harassing these isolated spots."

"Surely you wouldn't counsel Andrew Jackson's wife to run away from a few Indians?"

2

Love was not only a place, but a time. She had no need for the kind of calendar that Andrew kept in his office in Nashville. Every waking moment was intensified, every look, every thought, every feeling was stamped sharply upon her mind; and yet filled as the days were, they sped by so fast that it was impossible to retain them.

Yes, and love was a climate too. It was deep into winter now, there was snow on the ground, the trees were bare, the overcast skies the color of the copper pots that the new smithy was fashioning at the end of the public square. Yet in her happiness she did not know that it was winter: the snow was warm, the heavy skies were brilliant, the raw wind was gentle and invigorating. True, there was a tornado, but that tornado was her husband. They were not to take over Johnny's place until spring, but already Andrew was building a barn for the livestock, adding a small kitchen to the main room so that Moll could spend part of the day with her, throwing up cabins for the Negroes, erecting stout fences across the back of the property, burning off the cane and undergrowth, grubbing the small trees, belting the larger ones to make way for productive fields; and at the same time riding circuit, hundreds of miles over wilderness trails to serve in Jonesboro, Gallatin and Clarksville as prosecuting attorney for the territory, and then as civil attorney for the hundreds of clients throughout the district who wanted him to speak the legal language for them in the courts.

The affection of the Donelson family for Andrew served as a cohesive which brought the eleven brothers and sisters together at every possible opportunity. Robert Hays formed a partnership with him on a land deal; Samuel read law with him and had been promised a partnership; Stockly was selling much of the goods which Andrew received in lieu of cash for his services; they had fun together on the snowy winter afternoons and evenings, convoking mock court around the blazing fire with Rachel, Johnny, William, Severn and Mrs. Donelson as audience, while Judges Jackson and Hays appointed neophyte Samuel as Lord Chief Joker and General Humbugger of North America.

She had once heard the adage that "the proper study of mankind is man." Then wasn't it doubly true that the proper study for a wife was her husband? There were men in Nashville who said that Andrew Jackson was quarrelsome, that he had an uncontrollable temper. Yet how could this be when he was so gentle with her? Sometimes he would come home angry or disgruntled, he would tell her of what some scalawag had done, his voice would rise, the blood pound into the pale scar on his forehead, and soon he would be pacing up and down the room as though it were a court of law, trying the offender before her. Yet she had only to speak a few quiet words, put a finger on his sleeve placatingly, and he would stop short, shake his head, say:

"I'll meet thousands just like him in my lifetime. How foolish of me to take him seriously. But thanks for letting me unbosom myself."

She had perceived that her husband suffered from a raw sensitivity. Slowly she learned the reasons why: he had grown so fast that he could not always control his gangling frame, and the other children had called him awkward. As an outsized boy of ten he had tried to run with the fifteen- and sixteen-year-olds, but he had not had the physical stamina to stand up with them. His mouth had been too large for his face, his desire to express himself greater than his ability to control the moisture that gathered in either corner of his lips; but if any of his friends laughed at him or so much as mentioned the word "slobbering" in his presence, he found himself involved in a fight. One of the young men who had grown up with him in the Waxhaws told her:

"I could throw Andrew three times out of four, but he would never stay throwed!"

Once his playmates had secretly loaded a gun to the muzzle and given it to him to fire so that they could watch it kick him over. The recoil had knocked young Andrew several feet through the air; but their pleasure had been short-lived for he had sprung up from the ground and cried:

"By God, if one of you laughs, I'll kill him."

Nobody had doubted it.

Andrew's mother had wanted him to become a preacher because he had been the bookish one of her three sons, having taught himself to read and write at the age of five; and also because Dr. Richardson of the Waxhaw Church had been able to acquire a prosperous plantation, a two-story manse and the finest library on the frontier. Andrew had taken his turn as the public reader in the Waxhaws, where a large proportion of the men and women could neither read nor write. When the weekly folio arrived from Charleston, or the Philadelphia newspapers came in once a month, the community would gather at the house of his uncle, Squire Robert Crawford, to hear the news. Andrew read regularly to some forty assembled people in a shrill and penetrating voice, never growing hoarse, going straight through his assigned articles without stopping to spell out the words.

Yes, it was fascinating to learn, slowly, all there was to know about a man; and to possess that knowledge in the warm, bright light of love. Yet when she thought of his sensitive, tempestuous nature, and of their troubled past, she trembled for him . . . and for herself.

On the first of May they moved into Poplar Grove. Their nine Negroes were established in well-chinked cabins, the stock had a stout barn and the fields had been planted with tobacco and corn. Rachel took from home the walnut secretary her father had willed her; her mother gave her a liberal share of the Donelson silverware which had come on the *Adventure,* and promised her the big clock. Her sisters and sisters-in-law had been weaving and spinning a good part of the winter and now presented her with quilts stuffed with soft down, pillows and mattresses; rugs, fine linen board covers and napkins; bedcovers; yards of cotton, striped and plain; ticking; dressed doeskins, soft and pliable, and lengths of bleached and unbleached muslin. Andrew had Lardner Clark send to Philadelphia for the largest canopied bed he could find; it completely filled Mary Donelson's former prayer room. They stood in the center of the cabin, which Moll and George had scrubbed with lye, holding hands.

"It's our first home, and I love it," said Rachel emphatically.

"Part of the chinking has come loose," replied Andrew. "I'll start redoing it in the morning. And it's much too dark; Mary must have made John cut those portholes that small."

They went out into the fields and walked the boundaries of their land, ". . . beginning at sugar tree, red oak and elm on the bank of the river, the lower end of the tract running thence north sixty degrees . . ."; they listened to the cardinals, starlings, coveys of sparrows, redheaded woodpeckers, quail. On the bluff overlooking the river they enumerated the flowers and plants that had burst into bloom: jonquils, red haw as golden as the forsythia was yellow, the magnolia tulips, lilacs, green willows, privet, violets. Andrew sketched for her the disposition of their acreage: these fields would be for cotton, these for corn, these for tobacco, these for indigo, these for orchards, here the canebrake would be left for the cattle to graze in, and here they would have a corral for their horses and colts.

"We will put the place on a paying basis just as soon as possible," he said. "Then when we are ready we will be able to sell it for a good price."

"Oh, darling, please don't move us out so soon. We haven't even spent our first night here."

"But this is not our final home, Rachel," he protested. "It's just one step on the way up."

"Where is up from being happy?" she asked. "So long as we love each other, it won't matter where we are."

He kissed her anxious mouth.

"You are a sentimentalist, and I love you for it, but there's no reason why we can't love each other just as much in a big house and on a large plantation as we can here in Johnny's rather crudely built cabin. Because you see, my dear, I am ambitious for us: I want to accumulate land: miles and miles of land, great herds of cattle and horses, and raise fine crops for market. I want us to be secure."

"All I want is to be secure in our love."

Had she spoken too softly? Hadn't he heard? Probably not, for his eyes were glazed and his mouth set.

"I want us to be rich, very rich. The one thing I never want to see is the ugly face of poverty."

She slipped her hand softly into his, thinking, I was wrong to imagine that unseen scars vanish; sometimes they stay with us all our lives.

"We are never going to be poor, darling," she said reassuringly. "How could we be with your energies and talents? But I could sleep on a straw pallet in front of the fire and eat our meat off the stick it'd been broiled on, and it wouldn't frighten me. I have no faith in *things:* they come and go so fast."

"That's true," he said a little impatiently, "but I promise that you will have the best of everything . . . whatever else may happen to you because you married hotheaded Andrew Jackson."

3

She remarked the arrival of new seasons not so much by the changing weather or foliage as by the fact that during January, April, July and October Andrew attended court sessions in Nashville. While he was riding to the quarter sessions at Jonesboro, Gallatin and Clarksville one of her bachelor brothers came to stay. Her sisters visited frequently with their children. Jane, whose station at Haysboro almost adjoined Poplar Grove, spent one full day a week. As Jane watched her younger sister go about the endless tasks of a self-sustaining plantation, she commented:

"You're happy now, Rachel, aren't you?"

"Yes, completely . . . or I will be, when I have children."

"No hope yet?"

". . . none. Is there a special prayer?"

"Not that I know of. For some women they come a little too fast, and for others a little too slow, but we Donelsons all seem to get our share."

"I keep remembering that."

Time went quickly; she and Andrew had been married a full year. They were sitting on the front porch watching the moon arch upward across the stars. Andrew had taken to smoking a pipe since they had moved to Poplar Grove; he slowly consumed one bowl of tobacco, knocked out the powder-gray ash against his boot heel and turned to her with a touch of amusement in his eyes.

"Well, my dear, I've brought you home a first-anniversary present. You are now married to a judge advocate."

"You mean like Judge McNairy?"

"No, not a judge at all, really. It's just that I am now the lawyer for our county militia. Last year I sent a plan to Governor Blount for the organization of our militia system; he liked it so well he forwarded it to the Secretary of War. I guess that's why they gave me the appointment. Anyway, I am now a captain."

"May I kiss you, Captain Jackson?"

"I'll take that kiss, thank you, ma'am, but you can leave off the title. Nobody is going to call me captain just because I straighten out a few warrants or contracts. I'll use the title of captain when I've earned it, fighting the Indians and the British."

With Andrew away almost half the time the responsibility of running the plantation was hers: in June there was the corn to be cultivated, the flax to be pulled, tied in stacks and arranged for drying; the hemp sowed; in July the wheat and timothy hay had to be harvested, the turnips planted; August was the best month to preserve the fruits and vegetables and also to clear new lands. In the early fall all buildings had to be repaired and chinked against the oncoming winter, meat had to be butchered and stored; there was the winter supply of candles to be made from the fats that had accumulated over the summer.

Her mother had been an expert in this difficult task and had trained each of her four daughters diligently. Before dawn the coals in the kitchen fireplace were stirred and a good fire started under the two huge iron kettles which hung on the lug pole; the melted tallow was given two scaldings and skimmings and put into the half-filled pots of boiling water. Two long poles were laid from chair to chair and across these were placed, like the rungs of a ladder, eighteen-inch candle rods which had been used in the Donelson family since Rachel was a child. Each rod had eight straight candlewicks with double-twisted wicking. The rods were dipped into the hot tallow in the pot at regular intervals and given sufficient time to cool and harden between dips so that they could grow steadily. For Rachel this had always been the most exciting operation of the year: she used everyone at the station to keep the fires high, the tallow pots constantly replenished, large sections of bark underneath the rods to protect the scoured floors from the drippings. At the end of the process the candles were packed into compartments of candle boxes, covered over carefully and stored where they would neither melt nor discolor.

The presence of Moll was a comfort to her. No one knew how old Moll was, least of all Moll herself. Her fine black skin was smooth in texture and a colorful contrast against the soft white of her hair; she went about her duties tirelessly, humming spirituals under her breath, knowing the tunes to dozens of these hymns but not one complete line from any of them. She was an inexhaustible mine of information, for as well as Rachel had been trained by her mother, this was the first actual opportunity she had had to function as a plantation wife. So many of the tiny details had escaped her: the recipe for making red dye out of logwood; the exact moment when the lye was strong enough for making soap; the right combination of woods and the degree of warmth for the smokehouse; how to make bayberry-bush candles which burned more slowly and gave off a pleasant scent.

Each day she loved Andrew so deeply that she knew there could be no going beyond it either in the depth of her emotion or the joy of loving completely, and being loved. Yet always the next day was infinitely sweeter, their love heightened and more complete: for did not each new morning promise still another day of wonderful memories to feed and grow upon?

It was a late December afternoon with the snow up to the doorsill when Andrew and John Overton returned from their fall circuit. They had a hilarious time unloading the bags on the saddle horses.

"I am going to have to open a general store," said Andrew. "Look what we've got here: bags of salt, cow bells, axes, loaves of sugar, bridles, a saddle, sacks of corn meal, bear and beaver hides, beeswax, smoked hams and venison, two rifles with horns full of powder, lead for bullets, and a bolt of bright calico for Moll. I was also paid with one cow, two horses, five pigs and eight sheep; I kept the horses and swapped the cow and sheep for land warrants."

But most important there was a pearl brooch for her, as a coming-home gift. She dressed for supper that night, brushing her hair until it gleamed in the candlelight, then piling it high on her head. She put on her long-sleeved red wool dress, its collar framing her tanned throat, the low neckline of the bodice a perfect setting for the new brooch on its silver chain. Her husband told her that she was beautiful. At dinner they held hands under the table.

"When I see you two together," said John, "I feel a little sorry about being a bachelor."

"But John, why should you stay a bachelor? There are a lot of nice young girls in the Cumberland looking for husbands."

John raised his hand before his face as though in self-defense. After a moment he said without emotion, as though it were a question of law:

"What woman could love me, Rachel, when I'm so homely?"

She rose and put her arm about his shoulders.

"John Overton, how can you be so kind to everyone else and so cruel to yourself? One day a woman is going to look at your gentle, sympathetic eyes and she will think you beautiful . . ."

John and Andrew gazed at each other in astonishment, then burst into hearty laughter.

"Now, Rachel, even my mother didn't think I was beautiful."

"Well, I'm not beautiful either," said Andrew, still laughing. "My face is as long as a pony's . . ."

"Oh, Andrew, stop; our faces are as God made them. A woman doesn't love a man because of the amount of hair on his head or the shape of his nose; she loves him because of some inner quality: strength, perhaps . . . or integrity."

The law practice of Andrew Jackson and John Overton was growing so fast that for the term of April 1793, in which there were a hundred and fifty-five cases docketed in Nashville, Andrew had been retained as counsel on seventy-two of them, while John had a considerable portion of the remainder.

"Rachel, why don't we build a guest cabin for John? We could set it up as an alternate office with a supply of lawbooks, and then I'd be home more."

"Good. I'll build it in the spring, while you're away."

Rachel and the Donelsons set to work at once to make the necessary bedframe, desk and chairs. As her own contribution Rachel loomed a bed coverlet of indigo-dyed hard-twisted wool in the intricate design known as Bachelor's Fancy. She asked her brother Samuel if he would stay with her for the two months that the men would be away. Samuel accepted at once.

"It's a wonderful opportunity for me. I'll have those lawbooks all to myself."

Andrew had been gone only a week when there began a series of Indian attacks the like of which Rachel could not remember. The son of Colonel Bledsoe and his friend were killed opposite Nashville, and on February 17 another son of Bledsoe was fired on and pursued by Indians to within fifty yards of his stockade. Five days later two sons of Colonel Saunders were scalped; a couple of days after, Captain Samuel Hays, brother of Robert, was killed near the front door of John Donelson's new house. General Robertson issued orders that every home, stockade and group of men working in a clearing were to keep night and day guard.

Rachel was caught in a dilemma: she could not go to her mother's and leave her hands at the mercy of the Indians, but if she took their Negroes with her the Indians would burn the station to the ground.

"I'm not letting my husband come home to a mess of charred embers," she declared.

"No," said Samuel, "but you can't let him come home to a scalped wife, either. Maybe Mother can spare us Alexander or Leven for the night watch."

Andrew and John returned home on April 9, the day Colonel Isaac Bledsoe was killed while working in the fields. Andrew's relief at seeing Rachel safe found its outlet in a torrential denunciation of all Indians. When he finally exhausted himself, John said in his driest legal tone:

"Surely you will admit that the Indians have a case too?"

"Sure, a case of whisky from the British and a case of rifles from the Spanish."

John said, "Pun me no puns," then added, "Bad as the Creeks and Cherokees have behaved, they can't hold a candle to us. The history of this country can be told in terms of the white man moving onto the Indian's lands, killing off his game, cutting down his forests and tilling his fields. We have bribed them, corrupted them and broken practically every treaty."

Rachel felt Andrew's gorge rise. He jumped up from his chair, shouting:

"By God, John, I'll not have you taking the side of the Indians against me in my own house! Furthermore, I just heard that the Federal government wants everybody to celebrate the Fourth of July this year. What are we supposed to bottom our celebration on?"

"On our independence," replied John. "The thing you got that scar for, remember?"

"What independence?" cried Andrew belligerently. "Do we have a vote? Do we have representation in Congress? Does the government build us roads or deliver our mail or provide us with troops to police the frontier?"

This was the Jackson temper she had heard about. She went to Andrew, put her finger on his arm. He gazed at her hand for a moment and dropped heavily into his chair, rubbing the back of his hand over his eyes.

"I think it's a wonderful idea," she said. "We could have a big party here; I've never given a party all by myself. Besides, it's most time for our second anniversary. We could plan an outdoor dinner for the Fourth of July, then anyone who doesn't want to celebrate the day politically can celebrate our anniversary."

More than a hundred adults and uncountable swarms of children came to their Fourth of July party. In the cool of the morning they went berrypicking in the woods and when the sun got hot the youngsters splashed in the river. On a smooth piece of ground under a shade oak some of the men were gambling over rattle and snap, with jugs of cool spring water to mix with their whisky; another group of men were down at the corral racing their horses for good-sized wagers. On the north side of the house, where the grass was the coolest, three fiddlers led by James Gamble provided untiring music for the contradance and the jig.

She made her way from group to group to be sure that everyone had all he wanted of food and drink and company and fun. Every once in a while she would go looking for Andrew just to exchange the bright pleased smile of hosts who know that their guests are enjoying themselves. John Rains sat in the shade of the doorstep and gathered listeners. The year before he had raised a bumper crop of tobacco, built a flatboat and carried his cargo down to New Orleans where tobacco prices were high, but the Spaniards had confiscated not only his crop but the logs out of which he had built his boat; and he had had to walk all the way up the Natchez Trace, empty-handed.

"Sometimes it beats me why we bother to stay here at all, friends. Certainly those white-wigged New Englanders don't want us to be part of the United States. It was our own government gave the Spanish control of that Mississippi."

Looking about her, Rachel saw that every one of these men had fought against the British. Andrew spoke for them when he said:

"Our Congress said we're too young and too weak to quarrel with the Spaniards, and the mouth of the Mississippi wasn't important anyway, so they give Spain control over the navigation on the Mississippi for twenty years. The English are still occupying forts in the Northwest, Detroit and Maumee, that they agreed to get out of ten years ago. But does our government force them out? No, we are too young and too weak. We watch them incite the Indians against the settlers and send them on the warpath against us. We're going to have to fight that war for independence all over again; but next time, by God, we'll make it stick."

John Overton sighed, then said, "Now, Andrew, a baby has to crawl before it can walk. If Spain had begun a war with us over the Louisianas our government might have collapsed. It's going to take years for us to grow strong enough to put the British out of those northern forts. We can't risk brawling with every nation that wants to quarrel with us."

"No wonder everybody despises us," growled Andrew.

When the blazing hot July sun finally settled itself onto the western horizon the guests started home.

"Was my party a success?" asked Rachel when they were alone. "People become so angry when they get involved in politics."

Andrew was astonished. "Why darling, everyone had a wonderful time! Political arguments are one of the treats."

Rachel glanced at her husband quizzically. Maybe so, but for herself she liked the way people had called her Mrs. Jackson, ma'am; she liked the feel of the name, it had a solidity for her, and so did the attitude of the guests that this Jackson marriage and this Jackson love and this Jackson home were permanent.

4

It was a melancholy gray-black day, with the fall sky as heavy as the timbered roof over her head when she heard him coming heavily homeward. Was it possible that she could know from the gait of the horse that something was wrong with the rider? Alarm fragments flashed through her mind: he was ill, he had been wounded, something had gone wrong in court. . . . These past two months since he had gone away had been difficult ones: Catherine's nine children had been desperately ill from eating spoiled meat, and Rachel had spent two weeks getting them back on their feet; her sister Mary had gone down with neuralgia, Rachel taking over the management of her brood of twelve; only two days before Jane's station had been attacked by Indians and two of the men defenders killed. And now Andrew . . .

She was slow in getting out of her chair, in opening the door and moving into the yard. One piercing look at her husband's expression and she was almost felled by the instinctive blow that whatever was wrong concerned them: Rachel and Andrew Jackson. He slid off his horse, unsmiling, did not speak or kiss her, but held his cheek against hers so that she could not see his eyes. She bruised her skin on the rough stubble of his cheek in bringing her mouth round to his, felt his reluctant lips hard.

They made their way into the house. The big room was cheerful, logs crackling in the fire, the wall lamps lighted against his return. He slumped into his chair by the fire while she went past the wide stone chimney into the small kitchen, returning in a few moments with hot coffee. When he had gulped down most of it, and spots of color had risen on his cheeks, she sat herself at his feet.

"What has gone wrong, my dear?"

He stared at her almost blankly for a moment, as though the thing that had happened was a nightmare of the road, having no possible reality here in their home with the fire crackling and the lamps spreading a bright glow. He tried several times to form words and get breath behind them before he finally garnered the strength.

". . . it's . . . what you might expect. Robards."

"Lewis? But how?"

"He's . . . done something."

"But what could he do? We're safe, we're married . . ."

She stopped short, her body frozen. Could it be possible . . . had Andrew shaken his head? Or had it been the way he had blinked his eyes and swallowed?

"Andrew, what are you trying to say, that we're not . . . ?"

"No, no!"

He pulled himself out of the chair and sank to his knees in front of her, his long arms clasped passionately about her as she sat immobile on the hard hooked rug.

"We're married. We always have been. We always will be."

In a hoarse voice she said, "Lewis is trying to make trouble. He's challenged our marriage in Natchez . . ."

"No."

". . . everyone said it was legal, the only way we could be married down there."

"It's not that. I only wish it was." He picked himself up, walked blindly about the room for a moment, then returned to her. The words came out in a rush. "He is only now starting suit for a divorce! The report that he got a divorce from the Virginia legislature was not true. They refused his petition. When I rode down the Trace to bring you the news, in July of '91, and we were married . . ."

She pulled back, gazing at him with terror-stricken eyes.

"I was still married to Lewis Robards!"

Her head began to spin. Andrew caught her, his fingers digging into her shoulders.

"I'll kill any man who even dares question . . ."

She did not hear his words, only his tone. She thought, At last Lewis Robards has had his way. He has made me an adulteress.

As she walked into the Donelson dining room and found the family assembled in their ritualistic places around the long table, she saw with stark clarity the character expression on each face; it was like a recapitulation of all the crises in the Donelson family.

At the head of the table sat her mother, with an expression which said, I'm hurt by this, but I still think that no price is too high to have paid for Andrew Jackson. In her father's place at the head of the table sat Johnny, whose expression intimated that at the moment he was more concerned about what was happening to the Donelson name than he was about what had happened to the Jackson marriage. Opposite him sat Alexander, who had no interest in women, love or marriage, and whose expression said, What can you expect if you are foolish enough to marry? At the second seat on the left she saw William the Cautious, sorry that his sister was in trouble, but remembering that he had told her to stay with Lewis Robards. Next to William sat Samuel, his usually creamy skin now mottled with anger, his soft brown eyes deeply hurt: a complete and authentic replica of herself, had she looked in a mirror.

Her regular seat was next to Samuel's. She dropped into it. Andrew sat beside her. She glanced across the table and saw Jane seated next to Alexander, Jane, who was recalling even now, with a gesture of distaste, the scene caused by Lewis at the Hays home. Next to Jane was Stockly, the former lawyer, too busy trying to figure out the legal complexities of this affair to be concerned over his sister's suffering. Coming back to her own side of the table, she saw Colonel Robert Hays reaching a hand in front of Andrew to clasp hers reassuringly. He was the most dazed one at this table, for he was a genuinely good and tender man, a fighter, second-in-command of the militia under General Robertson, yet a person of such utter decency that he could not conceive of any other human being behaving this way. Next to Robert Hays sat her brother Severn, hollow-cheeked, who rarely gathered at the family conferences any more; and across from him was Leven, without experience or responsibility, whose puzzled look inquired, What are you all so upset about? At the end seats on their side of the table were her two brothers-in-law, John Caffery and Thomas Hutchings, married to Mary and Catherine. They nodded to her sympathetically, but their expressions said, This is a Donelson affair; we'd be glad to do anything we could to help, but for the time being we'll remain silent. At the end of the table, facing their mother and Johnny, were her two sisters, Mary and Catherine, Mary who had grown plumper and jollier with the arrival of each of her dozen children, and Catherine, who had grown more wiry, and who still sat through these Donelson conclaves in silence.

She felt there was someone missing, yet all of her ten brothers and sisters were here, as well as her four in-laws. Then the door opened and John Overton came in, the water running from his broad-brimmed hat. He took off his sodden boots, slipping into his accustomed place alongside of Leven. Now her family was complete. The council of war could begin.

Stockly was the first one in voice.

"For heaven's sake, Andrew, what has happened? We can't make it out."

Andrew nodded his head down-table to John Overton.

"I guess we'd better let John start. He's the one found out about it."

All eyes traveled down the long table to Overton. When he spoke it was as though he were placing the words one by one in a bowl in the center of the table, for people to help themselves.

"When Andrew and I started for Jonesboro, I learned that the divorce was scheduled to be heard at the Court of Quarter Sessions at Harrodsburg."

Everyone sat waiting quietly. Then Stockly asked:

"What was the matter with the divorce granted by the Virginia legislature?"

John Overton looked steadfastly across at Andrew. He nodded to John to continue.

"We were misinformed. The legislature refused Robards' petition for a divorce. What they actually passed was what we call an enabling act, which merely gave Robards the right to plead his case before a judge and jury."

"But he didn't do it at that time?" inquired Mrs. Donelson sternly.

"No, he waited until April of this year. The court wouldn't hear his case then, and it was put over until this September."

Robert Hays leaned forward across the table, his hands clasped before him. His disciplined mind insisted upon getting at the core of matters.

"How could we have believed there was a divorce in the spring of 1791? Who was responsible for spreading that report?"

"I heard it myself from three or four different sources," said Johnny, "men who came from Harrodsburg and Richmond."

"We accepted rumor as truth," replied Andrew bitterly.

"There was more substance than word-of-mouth, Andrew," said Overton. "While you were in Natchez I stopped with the Robards family for several days. It was the assumption of everyone in that family that Lewis and Rachel were divorced. Mrs. Robards told me she was happy that Rachel was free."

These were the first words Rachel had really heard. She looked across at John, blinking her eyes at him as though this might bring further understanding.

"Mrs. Robards said that we were divorced?"

"Yes, and so did her daughter, Jack Jouitt's wife."

"They wouldn't . . . misrepresent," said Rachel tonelessly. "They have always liked me."

"Robards deceived them too," cried Samuel.

"Now, Sam, that may be a little harsh," said Robert Hays. He reached into his coat, took out a letter and unfolded it on the table. "It was only a month or two after the so-called divorce that I got this letter from Robards asking me to sell his land and send him his half of Rachel's inheritance from her father." He placed the letter in the center of the board and pointed out the sentences:

> I shall depend on you and Mr. Overton that there is no advantage taken of me in my absence. You will please to write by the first Opportunity if the Estate is divided as I may get my Right. If there is any Opportunity offered of selling my land you will please to let Me know.

Her mind shut out the voices that beat like the rain against the shutters. She lived again through her wedding under the exquisite chandelier at Springfield, through the happy weeks of honeymooning at Bayou Pierre. Should they have stayed in the Spanish territory after all, where this kind of trouble could never have reached them? But that was being disloyal to the happiness she and Andrew had had these past two years. Inside her head an agonized voice was crying: Why? Why has this happened to me? What sins have I committed that this brand should be burned forever into my living flesh? I was only a girl when I met Lewis Robards. I never knowingly hurt him. I tried to be a good wife. If I had done something wrong, then I could understand that I should suffer, and do penance. But of what, Almighty God, am I guilty? For what am I being punished?

She heard John Overton speaking quietly, heard each tiny sound in the room, the very breathing and murmuring of the seventeen people around the table, with a terrifying distinctness.

"Robert is right about the letter," commented Overton; "since Lewis asks for his division of the land he owned here and his half of Rachel's legacy from her father, that can only indicate that he believed he was already divorced."

"But how can all this be?"

Rachel had not been watching the table and did not know who had cried out in such naked pain. Suddenly, from the fact that everyone had turned and was looking at her with pity in their eyes, she realized that it had been her own voice and her own pain. She felt Andrew's hand reach over to take hers. Everyone waited for him to speak, but he could not. John Overton assumed the burden.

"Perhaps it's because the whole subject of . . . divorce . . . is so new. Lewis's petition for a divorce was only the second that had come before the Virginia legislature. When the legislature passed the Enabling Act, I think nobody except a few lawyers knew what it really meant; everyone else appears to have assumed that the bill actually granted the divorce, instead of merely the right to go into court to prove the charges."

"And now the case is to be tried. In Harrodsburg!" cried Rachel in anguish.

There was a silence which Andrew broke into, his voice hoarse with self-reproach. ". . . the fault is mine. No one else's. I'm a lawyer. Or supposed to be a lawyer. What right had I to accept the report of the divorce, regardless of how many people repeated it? My first duty to Rachel, to all of you, was to get a copy of the Virginia bill. I should never have gone to Natchez without it."

"Now, Andrew, there's no call for you to castigate yourself," said Stockly. "I used to be a lawyer too, and it never occurred to me that there could be anything wrong. That trip to Richmond would have taken you months . . ."

". . . and we were the first to tell you that the divorce had been granted," broke in Mrs. Donelson; "we had heard it while you were on your way up the Trace after taking Rachel down to Natchez with Colonel Stark."

"Wait a bit," said Alexander in his lazy, loose-jointed way, "I'm just remembering. That spring of '91 I was staying in General Smith's house for a spell; one day he pointed to a Richmond paper and told me he read a notice of the Robards divorce."

But Rachel saw from the way Andrew had his jaw set that no one would ever acquit him to himself.

"I got back here in April and didn't leave until the latter part of July. I could have sent a messenger to Richmond to bring back a copy; I could have gone myself between court sessions if I had taken enough horses and ridden hard . . . I was guilty of the worst kind of stupidity and carelessness. If I served my clients as badly as I served my wife, they would never let me practice law."

Jane Hays had been listening carefully.

"I don't think these post-mortems and soul-searchings are going to help us a bit." Her voice had an astringency which dried up their emotion. "You said, John, that Robards asked for a divorce trial in April of this year. How does it happen that none of us heard about it when there is so much travel back and forth between here and Harrodsburg? And why is Robards trying again now?"

Overton replied, "Early this year Lewis Robards met a woman by the name of Hannah Winn. When he decided he wanted to marry her, he went into court to get a divorce."

"Then he knew all along he was not divorced!" This was Samuel's explosion again. "For two years he let Rachel live . . . implicating herself . . ."

"I don't know about that, Sam. Let's give Robards the benefit of the doubt. Let's assume that when he went for a marriage license he found he couldn't get one . . . because he was not divorced. Or let's assume that his intended father-in-law insisted upon a thorough search of the records. Under the provisions of the Enabling Act, Robards was obliged to advertise eight weeks consecutively in a Kentucky newspaper so that the defendant, in this case Rachel, could learn about the impending suit and enter her defense.''

"We get all the papers from Kentucky,'' said William. "We never saw any such notice. Nobody in the Cumberland ever told us about having seen it.''

"No,'' agreed Overton. "The notice was never published in the papers. I checked on that in Harrodsburg.''

"On what grounds will he seek his divorce?'' persisted Jane.

"Through fraud!'' It was Andrew who had answered tangentially, his face blazing. "His petition to the legislature charged that Rachel had eloped with me from his home in July of 1790, and that we had lived together thereafter. He lied, and he knew he lied, because he followed us to your home and begged Rachel to come back with him.''

"That was my fault,'' cried Samuel. "I had gone for Rachel once, I could have gone a second time.''

"Yes,'' agreed Severn grimly; "there are a lot of us who should have gone. But there seemed such good reasons at the time to stay home.''

"If there is any blame to be taken here, I will take it,'' announced Mrs. Donelson. "Andrew was like one of my sons. We didn't know that Lewis was quarreling over him again. There was no conceivable reason why he shouldn't have gone.''

"We can defend . . .'' shouted Stockly, but John waved his hand quietly to interrupt.

"There is no need. Robards is no longer bringing that Harrodsburg trip into the case. The divorce papers state that Robards will introduce evidence that Rachel and Andrew lived as a married couple a year later, on the way up the Natchez Trace in September of 1791.''

"But that was after we were married!'' Rachel was aghast.

"He can't do that!'' cried Stockly.

"You are right, Stockly; his original petition to the Virginia legislature charged that Rachel had eloped with Andrew from his home in July of 1790, and it is on that basis that the legislature gave him permission to sue for a divorce. It is that charge he must prove. He has also failed to provide the necessary eight-day notice to the defendant. We can go into that court in Harrodsburg and demonstrate that the divorce will be fraudulently secured; but the more effectively we defend ourselves in Harrodsburg . . . the more surely we throw out Rachel's marriage to Andrew.''

There were commingled gasps around the table.

"We've got to stay out of the case,'' snapped Jane.

Rachel buried her head in her arms, her body shaking convulsively; for how could one do anything but weep when one was trapped as she was trapped? If she did not defend herself in Harrodsburg, if she did not take this opportunity to go into court and establish her innocence, was that not proof, eternal and indisputable, that she admitted her guilt?

"Do you know who will testify against Rachel at the trial?'' It was Johnny, wanting to identify the enemies of the Donelson family. "I think we ought to know.''

"Hugh McGary. He testified that he had observed Rachel Robards and Andrew Jackson sleeping under the same blanket on the journey north. The jury will accept that as proof of the charges. It is our misfortune that . . . adultery . . . is the sole grounds on which a divorce can be granted.''

Andrew jumped up from the bench and strode out the door into the rain. Rachel raised her head, stared after him, saying, "There is no marriage. It was never legal. It is not legal now; it won't be legal even after Lewis's divorce . . .''

Johnny asked Overton, "Are those records in Harrodsburg permanent?''

"Permanent?"

"Do they stay there forever, or are they thrown out at the end of, say, a court year?"

"Records are never thrown out."

"We could always burn down the courthouse," observed Alexander dryly.

"But it's totally unfair," cried Samuel. He turned to his sister, his eyes blazing. "Rachel, we've got to go into court and defend you. We can prove fraud against Robards, and falsehood as well. The jury will acquit you of the charges. You will be vindicated."

There was a heavy silence, a silence filled with frustration. Mary came in from the kitchen with pots of coffee and milk, followed by two servants with chargers of food. She would take no part in this discussion, but she would keep a supply of food coming in, maintaining, "Even the worst looks better when you have something hot in your stomach."

Mrs. Donelson handed Rachel a cup of coffee. Rachel drank slowly, the hot fluid scorching her throat. John Overton turned to her, his eyes deeply sympathetic.

"We must not defend you against those charges in the Harrodsburg court, Rachel. If Lewis can't get a divorce to marry his Miss Winn . . . neither will you be able to marry Andrew!"

5

It was pitch-black and raining harder than ever when they started for home. Moll, waiting in the little kitchen, gave them hot toddies against the chill, then retired to her own cabin. Overton bade them good night, went to the door, then hesitated.

"Perhaps we ought to look on the more constructive side of this tangle," he suggested blandly. "Suppose Lewis Robards had not wanted to marry Hannah Winn. It might then have been five or ten years before you found out that there never had been an actual divorce. That might really have had serious implications."

"You mean . . . if he should have gone seeking a divorce . . . after children had been born?"

"Yes, Rachel."

He turned his head slightly so that he was focusing on Andrew. "I think Lewis means to keep this trial as quiet as possible. Uncontested, the divorce will be over in a few hours. Robert Hays and I will sign your marriage bond for a new ceremony. That ceremony can also be short and quiet."

"As something we are ashamed of, eh?" Andrew broke in.

"John's trying to help us."

"We're married." Andrew's jaw was set. "We've been married since August 1791."

"Neither of you has ever told me the details of your marriage at Natchez," said Overton a little sternly. "If the Virginia legislature had granted the divorce in 1791 there may never have been any reason to question that Spanish territory ceremony. But now that we're in the middle of a hotchpot . . ."

Rachel stared at him dully. She saw Andrew clenching and unclenching his fists in black anger. He was a fighter: to strike out when he believed himself right was as natural as breathing; but how could he expose her to the battle? No matter how quiet the trial might be, the whole countryside would be twattling again, reviewing her story, embellishing it with these newest, delectable morsels.

Overton put a hand on Andrew's shoulder.

"Andrew, you have no choice; you must get a Nashville license and be married according to the American law."

Rachel stood before him supplicatingly.

"John is right. We must be married again."

Andrew walked away from her, went to the hearth and stood staring wildly into the fire, his hands clasped behind him, pushing roughly against the small of his back, talking into the flames:

"You are wrong, both of you. Terribly wrong. Don't you see what this means . . . we publicly admit that we have not been married these past two years. We plead guilty to the charges thrown against us in that Harrodsburg court, forever exposed to any enemy or scoundrel who wants to plague us with the record." He walked to the door. "Good night, John."

When John was gone he gazed for a moment into the dark night, then turned to Rachel. The anger had drained from his face; in its place came hurt pride.

"In our own eyes we are married, and so are we in the eyes of our family and friends. No one else matters. We've got to stand firm on this one base: that no purpose is served by going through a second ceremony when the first one was legal and adequate."

And now his expression told her why he was so adamant: he was taking upon himself all the blame for allowing her name to be thrown into a public courtroom in Harrodsburg, where her former friends and relatives could hear her character maligned; for everything she was suffering now and everything she would suffer in the future because, together, they had been convicted of adultery. And because she understood this, she knew how to quiet her husband and gain his consent.

She stood with her back to the fire, letting the heat burn in warmth and renewed strength. Andrew remained at the door, avoiding her eyes, sunk deep in his own injured feelings and even deeper in his remorse. She waited patiently until at last he came to her, took her in his arms and now, just as he had tasted the salt of her tears on his lips earlier that day, she felt his tears damp on her cheek. In the whole defeated cast of his body she saw his horror of this trial, the frustration of not being able to contest it, the terrible things they would be forced to admit thereby, and yet the total lack of any other course.

"There's so little we'd need do to stop Robards. Courts don't like to give divorces; the slightest intimation from us of irregularity and it would be all over. . . . We have every right and every weapon to defend ourselves; and yet we have to let him appear as the injured party, to paint us black as he pleases; there is not one word we can utter in our own defense. Do you know how hard it is for me to take that?"

"Yes, my dear, as hard as it was for me to take the news you brought to the Villa Gayoso. You quieted me then, and comforted me with your love, by showing me that at last we were free: free to love and free to marry. It was a bitter price to pay for that freedom, Andrew, but you were right. No price is too great if we can spend our lives together. So now it is I who must tell you not to weep, not to storm, and not to defend us. We must not dwell on the injustice, but think only of our two years of wonderful happiness, and all the years of happiness that are to come."

She put her index finger lightly across his lips as he opened them to protest, then took it away and kissed him.

"Do it for me, my darling. Even though you may be right, and I may be wrong, even though you don't want to, and it galls you, do it for my sake, because I want it, because it will help me. Do it because you love me and because . . . when our children come . . . there must be no question, no man must ever be able to hurt them because of something we refused to do before they were born,"

"Yes, Rachel, I'll do it for you. I'll do anything you want . . . always."

BOOK THREE

1

The bleating had turned from the plaintive to the urgent; they quickened their steps, leaning forward against the lateral wind which swept the big flakes downward.

"How did it get out of the barn?" She turned her face full to Andrew in order that the wind would not carry away the words.

"I don't know; George and I locked everything secure last night when this snow began."

A leafless poplar loomed up ahead. At the base in trampled snow they found one of their ewes, licking the moisture off a newly born lamb. Even as Rachel and Andrew reached her side the ewe weakened, began to stiffen in the snow. Andrew went to his knees to examine the animals.

"Is the little one still alive?" She dropped to the ground beside him, pushing the wool hood back off her head so she could see better.

"Just barely."

"Then let's get it up to the house quickly."

Andrew stripped off the long leather coat which he wore over a buckskin shirt and spread it on the snow, lifting the lamb onto its thick warmth. He looked over at the sheep.

"I'm sorry to lose her; she was a stouthearted renegade: broke out of the pasture to mate, and then out of the barn to lamb."

"Isn't that the fate of all renegades?"

Andrew rose with the lamb in his arms. "Only those who don't plan their uprisings for the proper season."

She ran ahead, her black leather boots making holes in the snow, cried out to Moll to bring in warm milk, and spread a plaid wool blanket before the blazing log fire. Moll came quickly with a tumbler of milk.

"Should we put in a drop of whisky?" asked Andrew. He was brushing snow off his hunting shirt, making damp spots on the floor.

"Yes, in you. Moll, please get Mr. Jackson a hot toddy."

They sat in silence, Andrew in his big chair, the soles of his boots exposed to the fire, sipping his drink. She was on the edge of the hearth, her cape tossed aside and her full wool skirt crushed under her as she concentrated on getting the warm milk between the lamb's lips. She caught a curious expression in Andrew's eyes, and said softly, "How precious all life is, even that of a stray lamb we didn't know existed a few moments ago."

Andrew lit his pipe while Rachel stroked the lamb's curly white wool. When his pipe was half ash, he said quietly:

"Rachel, I'm thinking of opening a store."

She looked up at him in astonishment.

"A store? You mean like Lardner Clark's . . . ?"

"Yes, but out here in the country. Even in the raw weather of these past weeks there must have been a full hundred families come over the Cumberland Gap in their Conestoga wagons, and a lot of them are settling out this way. There's a desperate need for goods."

She made no attempt to hide her amazement.

"But Andrew, why? You are attorney general for the territory, the most popular young lawyer . . ."

"Because I want cash money!" His voice sounded doubly loud because he rarely interrupted. "As a lawyer I'm still getting paid in land and livestock, but people will pay cash for what they buy in a store, three times what I can buy the merchandise for in Philadelphia."

The lamb stirred; she moved it gently so that she could nestle its head between her breasts.

"Andrew, how long before we'll know whether it will live?"

"If it's on its feet by nightfall. Now what I'd like to do is gather up all our lands, John will throw in with me, go to Philadelphia, sell them for cash and use that cash to buy stock for the store. Then, when we take our cash profits from the store, we can buy even bigger tracts of land . . ."

". . . to sell in Philadelphia?"

"Yes. The land companies will buy up everything you've got."

"But isn't that going around in a circle?"

"So does the sun. Look at your brother Stockly: he's accumulated hundreds of thousands of acres. Rachel, this is going to become the greatest trading center of the West, the meeting place for goods coming down from Philadelphia and up the Mississippi from New Orleans. The man who opens a trading post here will become the richest man on the frontier."

"It's hard for me to think of you as a shopkeeper, Andrew. Do you have the special kind of shrewdness that has made Lardner Clark so successful?" She noted that the lamb had only its lower teeth at birth, and that its eyes were a light blue behind the nearly shut lids. "Sooner or later you will make just as much money out of your law."

He moved in his chair with a restless gesture, crossing one booted foot over the other.

"It's not that I'm getting tired of the law, but the cases are so alike: conflicting land claims, disputes over the sale of goods, who started a quarrel and who finished it. I've never concealed from you the fact that with me the law is only a means . . ."

Moll bustled in from the kitchen in her gray cotton dress and black apron to see how the lamb was faring. Andrew walked to the window to stare out into the snow. His red hair shone in the brilliant firelight. Though it was not yet four in the afternoon, darkness had fallen.

"I've got it all figured out: together John and I own about fifty thousand acres, and I have thirty thousand in my own name. They've cost us about ten cents an acre; I can get a dollar in Philadelphia. The round trip will take me about two months. There's a cabin on the main road I can buy cheap. Two or three trips to Philadelphia, then we'll be able to open stores up and down the Cumberland Valley, with trading posts in Natchez and New Orleans."

He was pacing the main room of the cabin now, showering off enough sparks to shock the lamb into life.

"But what about your cases, and your attorney general work?"

"John will handle the cases on circuit, Sam can do the paper work in the office. As far as the attorney generalship is concerned, you know the court is delinquent in its pay to me, five years delinquent, ever since we became a territory. So I guess I can be delinquent for one quarter session . . ."

Strange man, she thought: he has this tremendous hunger to accumulate wealth, and yet he can work for five long years without receiving a cent of pay, and never let it be known.

"It'll only be a matter of a few years, Rachel, and then we can have the great plantation I've always dreamed of. I want the finest in the Cumberland for you . . . the finest in all the world. Then we'll be at the top. No one will ever be able to climb up high enough to attack us."

She lowered her head until her chin nestled on the softness of the lamb's head. For a full year now, since they had been remarried, she had known that he was determined to have . . . wealth, power. The higher he rises in the world, she thought, the more untouchable he thinks we will be. For herself, the need for seclusion, for the ability to live her days without being the focus of strange eyes and strange ears and, even worse, strange tongues, now seemed uppermost. It was not that she wanted to shut herself up, but only to live behind an impenetrable privacy. It was a hunger greater than she had ever known for food or drink or sleep, or even laughter.

They had been happy at Poplar Grove until . . . that news from Harrodsburg. During those first two years Andrew had been content: the land was good, they could live comfortably off its yield, it was in no way different or better than twenty others in the neighborhood. Folks still referred to it as the John Donelson station, which meant added anonymity . . . until people had forgotten, until she and Andrew had established themselves. Yet these things which brought her comfort and protection had become increasingly galling and unacceptable to Andrew. It is odd, she thought, that the need for that second ceremony has influenced no one but Andrew and myself. It's going to drive him on relentlessly. If I try to keep him as small and inconspicuous as I want to be, it would kill him.

She raised her head. Her voice was clear.

"I'm sure the store will be a success, Andrew. I'll help all I can."

She felt a slow movement against her bosom. It was the lamb raising its head, the slim legs twitching.

"Look, darling, his eyes are open."

The animal gave a little bleat or two and shook itself.

"You can set him on his own feet now, my dear," said Andrew. "He wants to walk."

She put the lamb down gingerly, holding him just beyond her skirts. He stood there for a moment weakly, looked about the room, backed away in fright from the fire, then suddenly ran straight-legged down to the other end of the cabin and back to Rachel.

2

She rarely left Poplar Grove, even for a brief trip into Nashville. She had developed a sixth sense about people and could tell at the first piercing glance whether her story was so close to the top of their minds that its edges spilled over into their eyes. She feared the probing glances, the guarded talk, the repetitions of the tale: all invasions of her intimate life. She flinched from meeting strangers, even when she encountered them in the homes of her sisters and knew them to be friends of the family. She was no longer always able to keep her gaze steadfast; at the subtlest intimation of prying, querying, her eyes fled in confusion and pain. In her own home, on her own grounds, she had a lulling sense of security. She was happy to have people come to her, for anyone who took the trouble to make the long ride must be a friend, uncritical and accepting; surely only well-wishers broke bread at your board?

She had need of her calm, for the messages from Andrew were disturbing. Owing to a depression that had settled over the East the arrangements he had made by correspondence for the sale of his lands had fallen through by the time he reached Philadelphia. The land he had planned to sell at one dollar an acre he had brought down by slow degrees to twenty cents, and still no takers. At the end of three weeks of vexation he wrote:

> Through difficulties such as I have never experienced before, they put me in the Dam'st situation ever man was placed in. I would not undertake the same business again for all the lands . . .

Samuel and John Overton frequently came to Poplar Grove to have supper with her; John had recently moved to his own cabin, which he had named Travellers Rest, about five miles south of Nashville. He read the message without his glasses, then put on his specs to see more clearly what he was thinking.

"I told him we ought to keep our land and sell it parcel by parcel to settlers as they came through," said John. "But he was so anxious to go to Philadelphia . . .''

With her husband away she lived in a suspended world in which she filled every hour with endless tasks, making infant gowns for the new baby expected by Johnny and Mary, knitting coarse oversocks for the winter and white hosiery with clocking, sewing a broadcloth riding habit for herself and a fine linen shirt with a double pleated frill of woven linen cambric for Andrew . . . all of her feelings stored against the hour of his return. The Nickajack Expedition of the militia had driven away the hostile Indians and for the first time since coming to the Cumberland she could walk her fields without fear of attack, could plant a rose garden and vegetable patch behind the house. She kept the lamb by her side as a pet. In the first bright April sunshine she directed the field hands in the plowing and planting of the crops, striding across the furrows in her high boots and long skirt of heavy cotton twill, a large straw hat shading her face. By mid-May the rows were showing fresh green lines, and the ewes and cows and horses began dropping their young. There were going to be good crops to harvest, plenty of livestock for food, tallow, wool and leather. She too felt young and vital and fecund; at night her loins ached for her husband, and the child she might carry.

She was prepared to find Andrew disgruntled and upset, but there had been no way to prepare herself for the sight she encountered when she came up from the barn in the heat of a scorching June day to find him sitting slumped in the saddle in front of their cabin. This was hardly the same person who had started out so hopefully three and a half months before; his eyes were sunk in their sockets, his cheeks gray and hollow; the wrinkled brown clothes hung on his body as though he were made of cross-sticks.

She led him into the house, saw to it that he had a bath with plenty of hot water and soap, then got him into a clean white linen sleeping gown and tucked him into bed. He ate lightly, squeezed her hand and fell into a sleep of exhaustion. She let the dark bear-skin blind fall over the window to shut out the sunlight, then gently closed behind her the door of Mary Donelson's former prayer room.

When he awakened he wanted to get up at once.

"Right now I'm stronger than you are," she replied resolutely. She stood with her hands on her hips, her apron berry-stained from making preserves, her brown eyes reflecting her happiness at having him home. "You are going to stay in bed for several days."

When they took their first walk across the fields to the river he was delighted with everything he saw.

"You're a wonderful manager, darling, you do a better job than I do."

They slid down the bank to the water's edge. Rachel took off her moccasins and waded at the edge of the shore, her skirts held above her knees. Andrew caught catfish and told her what had happened in Philadelphia. He had been on the verge of leaving the city without a sale of any of the land, and consequently without any merchandise for the store he wanted to open, but rather than admit defeat had sold their holdings to David Allison, a former Nashville lawyer who had gone east and become wealthy buying and selling western lands.

"Only trouble was I had to take Allison's personal notes. We went to Meeker and Cochran where I bought forty-eight hundred dollars' worth of goods, then Allison took me to Evans and Company where they sold me another sixteen hundred dollars' worth on his paper."

His greatest excitement seemed to center about the packet of books he had toted all the way from Philadelphia: Comte Maurice de Saxe's *Memories on the Art of War,* Frederick William von Steuben's *Regulations for the Order and Discipline of the Troops of the United States,* and Vegetius's *De Re Militari,* known as the military bible.

"By the way, my love, I don't think I've ever told you," he said *sotto voce,* "I intend to become major general of our militia."

She threw back her head, laughed heartily, shook loose the long black hair that had been held up by only one small comb. She put her arms about his neck and made him pull her up until their lips were on a level.

"Do I detect a note of disbelief in that laughter?"

"No, General Jackson; it was pure joy. Now I know you are well again."

3

On the Fourth of July, before the heat rose, they walked their horses to the old log cabin Andrew had purchased as his store. The interior was black, with tiny portholes and smoked walls, everything saturated with dust, cobwebs, ashes and the grease that had run down from the wall lamps.

Rachel grimaced. "I'll bring George over this afternoon with a bucket of lye water, also a saw to cut some window holes. By the way, who's going to sell your goods? Surely you're not planning to stand behind the counter?"

"I wouldn't mind. I like the feel of goods and money changing hands. But I've got to ride the circuit again in September, and if Governor Blount's count of our population goes over sixty thousand we'll have a constitutional convention and form ourselves into a state."

She caught the eagerness in his voice. "Apparently you think we are going to have sixty thousand people? And even more apparently, you intend to go to the convention. I thought you weren't interested in politics?"

"Answering your questions, madam, in the backwards order of their presentation: making an independent state of this territory is not politics: we've got to become a state in order to have representatives in Congress. If you saw some of those nabobs in Philadelphia, with their green silk breeches and powdered hair . . . it's hard for me to understand why those aristocrats ever broke away from England when they spend their whole lives aping everything British."

"Now, Andrew . . ."

He smiled. "All right, I won't fight them today. Answering your other question, I certainly do hope to be elected to that convention. Governor Blount told me in Knoxville that he's going to put my name in nomination. I've got a lot of ideas about how this new state should be set up. As far as population is concerned . . ."

he chuckled, "there's not a citizen of this territory so mean-spirited that he wouldn't step up and be counted at least three times."

On August 1, Samuel, who had brought Andrew's merchandise by flatboat from Limestone, Kentucky, arrived in Nashville. It took several days to move the goods onto the shelves: nails, axes, cooking utensils, nankeens, striped calicoes, a few bolts of satins and laces, shoes, hats, stationery, pepper, tobacco. Three weeks later they were paying their first visit to John Overton's Travellers Rest, and inspecting the young apple and peach orchard he had just set out, when Samuel arrived with a letter for Andrew which a trader had brought in from Philadelphia. It was marked *Important*.

It was a short message, but from the way the blood drained out of Andrew's face Rachel could see that it was too long at any length.

He looked up, his eyes dazed, his mouth for the moment wide and uncontrolled.

"It's from Meeker and Cochran in Philadelphia. David Allison is in trouble. His notes

". . . now falling due are not generally or regularly paid. We take this early opportunity to make known to you that we have little or no expectation of getting paid from him, and that we shall have to get our money from you, which we shall expect at maturity."

She stood on the garden path listening half to the low hum of conversation among the three men and half to her own insistent voice. Andrew owed Meeker and Cochran forty-eight hundred dollars, half of which he would have to pay on December 1. How were they going to sell enough of the stock to get the cash?

"I'll find a market somewhere," announced Andrew grimly.

"You can't, there isn't that much 'ready' in the entire Cumberland Valley," said John.

"The whole fault is mine, John: I promise you won't lose on it."

Rachel watched John Overton weigh this promise carefully.

"Whatever we manage to collect from Allison we'll divide half and half. Money can squeeze the life out of a friendship quicker than a grizzly bear."

She was saddened not by the loss of the money, which could be earned again, but by Andrew's suffering. It would be a blow to his pride: the fact that he had been defrauded, his judgment proven unsound, his working capital wiped out. He was not the kind of man to indulge in regrets, but to what new ends would he drive himself to reach that state of affluence which appeared to be his primary need?

They rode up the winding path that led to the top of Hunter's Hill, the highest eminence in the countryside, overlooking the Cumberland and Stone rivers. They reached the crest at about noon. Andrew spread a blanket on the lee side of the hill; they could hear the wind above them blowing away the few remaining autumnal leaves.

"We should have brought Lamb with us," said Rachel. "He would have liked to gambol up here."

"You are taking a gambol every time you let him out of the house. You seem to forget that the lamb is now a sheep. One day he'll be jumping the fence to join his kind."

"You could have made a double pun by spelling that last word with an *e* instead of a *d*, and it wouldn't have been any worse than the first one."

After lunch they stretched out side by side in the center of the blanket, her head nestled comfortably on his shoulder. He wrapped the rest of the blanket around them, then began speaking in a light, jocular tone.

"I brought you up here under false pretenses. I really wasn't so anxious for the picnic I dunned you into."

"Oh?"

"It's just that I have a story to tell you and I thought you would like to be sitting on top of the world when you heard it."

"Wherever you are is the top of the world."

"Thank you." He paused. "I've sold the store."

"For enough to meet the Meeker and Cochran note?"

"No, there's no one with cash who'll buy; Elijah Robertson's paying me with thirty-three thousand acres of good land worth a quarter an acre. The Philadelphia people will give me time to sell. We won't come out too badly once I've sold the land. I don't like failure, no man does. But I've learned a lot; I'll not make those mistakes next time . . ."

He lay quietly, looking down at her and stroking the hair back from her forehead, tracing the high arch of her brows with his fingers. Then he said, "Governor Blount sent me word yesterday that the population count is finished. He wants me to help write the new constitution."

She thought, This is what he really came up here to tell me.

"Good. You'll be helping to set up the state that Father dreamed about when he brought us all to the Cumberland. I'd like to see you at the convention speaking to all those men."

"Then it's done! You'll come with me."

She rose from the blanket, walked a little distance and gazed below her at the smoke rising from piles of burning underbrush, at the fences and groves of trees and the creeks and branches shining in the sun.

"Oh, I didn't really mean watch you in the flesh; I meant that I'll read the accounts in the *Intelligencer* and picture you standing there."

She did not hear him come up behind her.

"It's a magnificent view, isn't it?" he asked.

"The finest I've ever seen."

"Could you be happy here?"

"One would live above so much of the . . . struggle . . . that goes on below."

"I'm mighty relieved to hear you say that."

She turned about swiftly.

"Andrew, what do you mean?"

"My dear, you've been picnicking on your own land. I bought Hunter's Hill."

"But how could you? We've been so strapped . . ."

"I'm going to build you the finest home in the whole new state, Rachel. It's going to be the first house of cut lumber in the Cumberland Valley. I brought nails and glass back from Philadelphia and have kept them hidden away. And wait until you see the furniture: beautiful brocade settees, walnut tables, French wallpapers . . ."

"With what, darling? We've just failed in our first business venture. You say the new land is worth twenty-five cents an acre, but you may only get ten cents, or five."

In his excitement he was towering over her like a slender cypress trunk.

"Ah, my dear, that's the time you must dare to pull yourself up to the heights, when you have failed and everyone thinks you are on the road down. Then you yourself, and only yourself, can reverse that trend! You must search out the highest peak in the landscape, climb it and claim it as your own. Then when people see you, as they'll see us at the top of Hunter's Hill in a magnificent home, they'll look up to us. Rachel, the whole world will come to your door . . ."

She slipped her hand into his. "Whatever you want, Andrew, I know you can do."

4

The day before he was to leave for the Constitutional Convention in Knoxville Andrew announced he was posting notice that Poplar Grove was for sale.

"Oh, Andrew, must we sell?"

The words had escaped her. They had lived nearly four years at Poplar Grove: a woman didn't trade a home and happy memories quite as easily as a man did. She added quietly, "Couldn't we just rent, to Samuel, for instance? He's going to propose to Polly Smith any day now."

"We need cash money for the cut lumber from the mill. That's for labor, and they won't take personal notes."

He had instructed her to show the place. The first family or two of prospective buyers were not difficult for her, they were brought by friends and she could pretend it was a social visit. But by the middle of January when complete strangers began drawing up before her door in their wagons, with big-eyed children peering out from under the canvas and the fathers saying from a hunched-over position on the hard wagon seat, "You Miz Jackson, ma'am? We hear tell this place is for sale. We're looking for a likely place, now," she packed her portmanteau and fled across the river to her mother's house.

"You want we should make it look bad, Miz Rachel?" Moll asked. "George and me, we can heap the furniture like a shambles . . ."

"But how we gonna make that sweet earth and the fat animals look bad?" demanded George tartly.

Rachel found herself laughing for the first time in days.

Once she reached the Donelson station she felt brighter, for there was always activity and people here: slow-moving, slow-speaking William the Cautious had fallen in love with young Charity Dickinson and was courting her with all the fast-moving, fast-talking ardor of a seventeen-year-old. There was no regular mail service from Knoxville but the steady flow of travelers brought news each day. Andrew and Judge McNairy had been selected as the two local delegates to help design the government, and Andrew was working fourteen hours a day to create what he called a Jeffersonian constitution: two legislative houses instead of one; the right of all men to vote after six months' residence; only a two-hundred-acre ownership necessary for election to the legislature. Rachel read the newspaper report of Andrew's speech when proposals had been offered to name the new state after George Washington or Benjamin Franklin:

> Georgia was named after a King, the Carolinas, Virginia and Maryland after Queens, Pennsylvania after a colonial proprietor, Delaware after a Lord; and New York after a Royal Duke. Since Independence there is no reason for copying anything from England in our new geography. We should adopt for our new state the Indian name of The Great Crooked River, Tennessee, a word that has as sweet a flavor on the tongue as hot corncakes and honey.

She returned to Poplar Grove the day before Andrew was due.

"I see you practically worked yourself to the bone trying to sell Poplar Grove before I got back," he commented.

"I hope everybody hates it."

"Vain hope. I've got a buyer, your brother Alexander. Met up with him in Knoxville. He's paying five hundred thirty pounds . . . in cash, enough for me to order my cut lumber and other coin-on-the-barrelhead items to start building Hunter's Hill."

John Overton came to spend the evening. "Do I start calling you congressman now?" he asked Andrew.

"Congressman! I'm not interested in politics."

"Then you can put those military books away, General, because you're evidently not interested in the militia, either. That army is going to evaporate unless Congress repays the thousands of dollars spent for the Nickajack Expedition."

Andrew shook his head in despair.

"Now there's a choice assignment! The War Department forbade us to go out on that expedition against the Indians. General Robertson has had to resign because of his row with Secretary of War Pickering over the battles we fought. The Federal government has declared the whole expedition illegal, null, void . . . and now all you want me to do is to get the Congress to pay for it!"

Rachel found that Andrew's prophecy about Hunter's Hill proved sound: he no sooner started construction of the house, which attracted visitors from all over the Cumberland, than people began to speak of his tremendous success. He acknowledged their accolade by starting on a land-buying spree that surpassed anything he had ever done before: each day he brought home new titles: on March 11, a thousand outlying acres for two hundred and fifty dollars; on April 18, another five thousand acres for four hundred dollars; on April 19, a six-forty for twenty cents an acre; on May 9, three separate purchases: twenty-five hundred acres for two thousand dollars, three thousand acres for three thousand dollars, one thousand acres for one thousand dollars; on May 14, five thousand acres . . .

When she added up the books she found that he had bought some twenty-six thousand acres and spent more than sixteen thousand dollars . . . all on his personal notes. He sometimes sold land too; in her strong-box Rachel held signed papers from at least a dozen men in the Cumberland. Each man's credit was as good as his reputation; but let any one fail, man or reputation, and the whole structure would collapse. Rachel was convinced that this was a pure gambling game, like rattle and snap, played more for excitement and fun than for profit.

Both the excitement and the fun drained out when she learned that Andrew was contemplating buying the six-forty on which she had lived with Lewis Robards. This land, which was part of Clover Bottom, had been sold by Lewis to a Mr. Shannon who was now offering it to Andrew. She was amazed at the ardency with which she did not want to own that land again.

"The fields are innocent . . . and fertile," said John Overton; for at the last moment Andrew, unable to bring Robards' name past his teeth, had asked John to discuss the purchase with Rachel. "It adjoins Hunter's Hill. That particular piece will be indistinguishable from all the rest."

"Then you think I ought to approve?" she asked, swallowing so hard that her audible gulp filled the momentary silence.

"No . . . But is it worth making an issue of?"

"I see." She blinked several times, as though clearing cobwebs from her mind. "Well, I'll get over this feeling. We'll run the furrow straight down from Hunter's Hill to the river."

As soon as word got around that the Jacksons had bought the former Robards six-forty to add to their holdings, a wave of argument swept the valley. It had not occurred to Rachel that it would cause a controversy, with everyone taking sides and resurrecting the Robards-Jackson affair for the many newcomers of the region. She had imagined her reluctance to be something private and personal, and now here she was the center of discussion again, her past revealed and distorted. As far as she could gather, half of the people condemned them for bad judgment: this land could bring nothing but ill luck; the other half accused them of bad taste in wanting to show the world that they had been victorious over Lewis Robards and had thus symbolically absorbed him.

But she did not sense the extent of the argument until she learned that John Overton, who abhorred all forms of physical violence, had actually been involved in a fight in Nashville, and had had his eye blacked for his trouble. When he reached the Jacksons' at Rachel's urgent request, the lid over his right eye was still highly discolored, the bridge of his nose too tender to support his spectacles.

"That's the first time in my life I ever tried to knock a man down," he admitted sheepishly. "Of course I missed by a country mile."

"I don't know whether to be ashamed of you or proud." Then, no longer able to sustain her effort at humor, she cried, "Oh, John, how long will this go on? It's been five years since Andrew and I were first married, and three since that . . . divorce."

"I don't know," he replied grimly; "I thought so much time had elapsed and Andrew had become so important in the state that the whole affair would be forgotten."

"But it's never going to be, is it?"

They moved into Hunter's Hill on a Tuesday toward the end of May; it was the day of the week on which Andrew liked to begin new ventures. The house seemed enormous to Rachel, with its parlor and dining room on either side of the entrance hall, and Moll's kitchen to the left beyond a porte-cochere. The furniture Andrew had selected in Philadelphia was installed in the parlor: a settee and upholstered chairs covered in double damask with flowered figures standing out from the satin background, and on the floor a sixteenth-century Tabriz animal carpet he had purchased at an estate auction.

Behind the two front rooms was a music room, completely empty, and Andrew's study in which he reverently placed her father's wide walnut desk, then lined the fireplace wall with bookshelves. He took the four big outside drawers of the desk for his papers, and gave Rachel the eight smaller enclosed drawers with the brass knobs, for her household bills and account books. Upstairs there were four bedrooms fitted precisely over the four downstairs rooms, but only their own bedroom had furniture in it, the four-poster which they brought from Poplar Grove. The half-empty rooms doubled her sense of hollowness. Even as the small cabin at Poplar Grove had seemed to hold her close, to protect her, so the vast areas of Hunter's Hill seemed to expose her on all sides. Her husband might find the eminence of Hunter's Hill dominating and powerful; she felt it only made them the more vulnerable.

That summer Andrew worked in the fields to raise the small crop that had been planted in the spring. On July 30 the Tennessee legislature voted him his five years' back pay as attorney general. He used the money to build a road up the hill to the front door, while Rachel supervised the erection of a dairy, smokehouse, storehouse, stable and log cabins for the Negro families.

"We've come to the end of our troubles," he declared with satisfaction. "If I could get back to Philadelphia . . ."

She hated the thought of another separation, but kept all emotion out of her voice.

"You'd really like to be our first congressman, wouldn't you?"

"There's so much I could do," he shot back. "John was right about the money for the Nickajack Expedition. If I could get Congress to appropriate that fund . . . and could collect some of my own money from Allison, enough to buy merchandise for another store . . ."

She gazed at him in awe.

"Andrew, you're going to be the busiest representative in all of Philadelphia!"

5

With what did a childless woman fill the rooms of this big house? she asked herself. It was the first year since their marriage that she and Andrew had been separated at Christmas, for he had been elected to Congress, and left for Philadelphia in November. In an effort to cheer the house with voices and laughter and good memories she planned a Christmas Eve dinner for the family: Mary and John Caffrey and their twelve children, Catherine and Thomas Hutchings and their nine, Jane and Robert Hays and their four, John and Mary and their eight, the latest of which was only a month old; Stockly, Leven, Alexander and Severn, still bachelors; William and Charity, newly married, as were Samuel and Polly Smith; John Overton and her mother.

Because it was really a children's party, Rachel used rock candy for the sauces; two enormous boards were covered with candied and spiced fruits, pickled walnuts, marmalades, honey and jellies, apple-mose and half a dozen different kinds of pie, along with pear and quince tarts. There was a gift for each of her nieces and nephews: ribbons, bonbons, gloves, rag dolls, embroidery equipment; for the boys: knives, shot pouches, moccasins, hunting shirts. Each child ran to Aunt Rachel to embrace her; the sight of the young ones, the children she so ardently wanted to bring into the world, made her cry out in hunger. When the families had bundled up their youngsters and piled them into the carriages and onto saddles, sometimes as many as four hanging on behind their father, she was alone again.

She lay awake in the high four-poster, the curtains pulled on all sides to afford her an island of warmth and security. But the weather had been raw and the wind had a penetrating quality which invaded the house, the shut door of her bedroom, even the closed-in darkness of the bed. Exhausted and let-down after the big party, she listened to the creaking noises of a new house solidifying itself against winter's attacks, wondering how she would endure the months that lay ahead. All the dictates of logic and expediency had made her agree that Andrew should go east to the Congress; but in the stark shivering clarity of the lonely night she knew that the more past business he settled the freer he would be to set up future business. All of his savings for eight years had been wiped out when David Allison's paper had gone bad; all of his work as well as profit from his store had been nullified when he had been obliged to sell hurriedly; and only that afternoon she had learned that the Blount paper for which he had traded his thirty-three thousand acres had become practically worthless because the Bank of England had suspended its specie payments and thrown the East into a panic. From his letter she could not tell whether Andrew was maddest at having lost his money or at learning that America was still controlled by the Bank of England. She thought of him on this Christmas Eve in some strange inn or boardinghouse, separated from her by a thousand miles and weeks of hard travel . . . for what purpose?

There was no dawn, just an ash-gray light filtering through the windows. She got out of bed, went to the wardrobe and took out the blue silk robe Andrew had bought her in Natchez. The silk was ice to her touch. She went through the center hallway and out the side door, then stood very still: for the light had come up in the east now, and below her the river was frozen solid, the first time it had frozen over since the Donelsons had come west on the *Adventure*. She went into the kitchen building where George had left the fire banked, boiled some water in a pan for coffee, and drank the fluid as hot as she could. Its heat relaxed her; she went back to bed and fell asleep.

She was awakened by a considerable hubbub outside the house, and through the window saw the entire population of Hunter's Hill gathered about a highly polished black carriage with red wheels and a pair of matched iron-gray horses.

She dressed as quickly as she could and descended to the front porch. As she walked toward the carriage she saw that it was empty, then in an unbelieving flash a brilliant red monogram on the door: *R.J.* George opened the door with a flourish and bowed Rachel in. She put her foot on the little iron pedestal. George closed the door behind her. Only then did she realize that Andrew had ordered this carriage for her and had given instructions that it be delivered on Christmas Day. She remembered how hard pressed he had been for cash before leaving for Philadelphia, how he had manipulated and exchanged lands and paper; yet he had thought of her alone on Christmas morning.

Tears sprang to her eyes. She sat as warm and secure as though he were beside her, his arm gripped tightly about her shoulder. How weak she had been: as long as she loved her husband and he loved her they would not be separated. Love was a mighty bridge which crossed frozen rivers and frozen hours: it enabled a man and a woman to walk hand in hand across a sunlit field even when a thousand miles separated them and the field was snow-covered under a leaden sky.

In his next letter Andrew told how the moment he had reached Philadelphia he had ordered a black coat and breeches to be made by a tailor.

> They fit me quite well, and I thought I presented a handsome figure. But when I got to the Congress to be sworn in, I found myself the only one with a queue down my back tied with an eelskin. From the expressions of the more elegant nabobs about me, I could see that they thought me an uncouth looking personage with the manners of a rough backwoodsman.

She sensed how this must have galled him, for his manners were courtly; recalling her father's friends from the Virginia House of Burgesses, she knew that Andrew's manners were as gentlemanly as theirs.

In addition his very first act in Congress had antagonized not only a considerable portion of the legislators, but Tennessee as well. This news she learned when she went on a Sunday to her mother's home for dinner; as she came into the big room she perceived several sentences dangling in mid-air like the wool threads of an unfinished coverlet. She said in an impersonal voice:

"Very well, my husband has done something you don't like. Let's get it over with and not spoil Mother's Sunday dinner."

"Let's don't," replied Jane. "You're not responsible for your husband's political ideas."

"My dear Jane, the newspapers will reach me tomorrow."

Samuel lifted his head.

"You remember President Washington's farewell speech to the Congress? The House drew up an elaborate eulogy to make in return. Andrew voted against giving it, said it was a blanket approval and that some of Mr. Washington's acts sorely needed criticizing . . ."

Her eyes swept the room in a quick ring. "Has someone had a letter?"

Robert Hays pulled a paper out of his pocket, then read:

> ". . . Every day's paper proves the fact that the British are daily Capturing our vessels, impressing our seamen and Treating them with the utmost severity and brutality, but from the president's speech it would seem that the British were doing us no injury."

"I suppose it's all right for him to hate England so intensely while he's here at home," commented William, "but he has no right to make it appear that that's the way everybody in Tennessee feels. If he's not careful he'll get us into a war with the British."

Jane took the letter from her husband's hand and gave it to Rachel, murmuring, "The last paragraph is for you."

Rachel's eyes went quickly to the bottom of the page:

I make one request that you attend to my Dear Little Rachel and soothe her in my absence. If she should want anything get it for her if you can and you shall be amply rewarded.

She returned the paper, a smile on her lips.

During the latter weeks of January the cold intensified until one morning she found ice on the ground and her plants and young shade trees frozen. Moll was missing at breakfast. Rachel knew that she must be very sick indeed if she remained in her cabin. George too was ill. Rachel put her hand to Moll's forehead.

"You've got fever."

Moll leaned up in bed, her teeth chattering. "Sampson and Silvey is bedded too, and Winnie and James and their Orange. Must be the fluenzy."

She made a quick tour of the cabins: the grippe was of epidemic proportions. Among the older folks only one family had escaped, and Moll's niece Mitty. She sent them to bring blankets from the big house and to stack up the logs beside the fireplaces, then dispatched one of the younger boys to Nashville for the doctor. She herself went into the kitchen to brew the bitter tea of herbs and marshmallow root which her own mother used to fight the grippe. She and Mitty carried the steaming pot from cabin to cabin, plying the sick ones with the liquid.

For the next week she nursed her people night and day. She had always respected Andrew for his attitude toward their "black family." She had never seen him deny one of them a pass to visit friends, he never rationed their food or fuel, he refused to separate members of a family, gave them individual kitchens.

"I can't be as easygoing as you are, Andrew," she had once told her husband. "You're not responsible to anyone but yourself, but when you go away and set me tasks to do, I'm responsible to you."

"I think they understand that," Andrew answered; "in any event they accomplish more for you than they do for me."

No sooner had she been able to leave off making night rounds among her sick than she was awakened one midnight by the sound of a horse coming heavily up the road, and by someone pounding on the front door. She opened the window and called:

"Who's there?"

"Mrs. Jackson, ma'am, beggin' ya pardon for wakin' ya this hour at night, it's Tim Bentley, ya neighbor over beyond Willow Spring."

"What can I do for you, Mr. Bentley? What's wrong?"

The man shouted up at the window, the words coming in a frenzied jumble.

"It's the wife, Sarah, and the baby . . . I mean it should be the baby but it just won't get itself borned. I think Sarah's going to die, ma'am, the baby and she both . . ."

"Go around the side to the kitchen house and wake George; tell him to saddle me a horse."

In a matter of minutes she was racing downstairs. In the yellow glow of the porch lamp she saw the face of Tim Bentley. He could not have been more than twenty, but his skin was sallow, he had weak eyes and a chin that vanished at a precipitate angle under his lower lip. She told George to saddle another horse and bring along soap, blankets, sheets, towels, candles and food.

It required little light to indicate the ramshackle nature of the Bentley cabin: the notching was of such an uneven character that one end of the roof had begun to sag; inside, the logs that made up the floor showed gaps of cold damp earth beneath, while the one window had been pasted over with successive layers of brown paper drenched in bear's oil. There were two pots hanging over the fire, a small table stood near the hearth . . . and in the corner a wooden bed with a young girl lying in it, covered by a ragged blanket. The only preparation for the expected baby

appeared to be a crude cradle on which rested a linen christening gown they had
apparently brought from the East.

Rachel said, "Hello, Mrs. Bentley, I'm your neighbor, Mrs. Jackson, from up
on the hill. I'm going to stay right here with you until your baby is born. Why
didn't you call someone before?"

"We was hopin' to see it through by ourselves. But it's lasted so long . . . the
pains was so hard. . . . The minute I heard your horses I felt better." She hesitated.
"Are you *the* Mrs. Jackson, ma'am?"

"Who is *the* Mrs. Jackson?"

"The one they talk about so much? But you don't look at all like that kind. That
Mrs. Jackson wouldn't come help me."

Rachel stroked the girl's hair soothingly.

"I want very much to help you. I've never had the good fortune to have a baby
myself, but my sisters have, dozens of them, and I've helped them. So you see,
everything is going to be all right . . ."

While speaking, she had slowly lifted the blanket. Now she glanced down and
saw one of the baby's feet protruding. She recognized it as a breech birth; the baby
had failed to turn to the proper position so that the head could emerge first. Her
sister Mary's first child had been a breech birth; Mary had had the services of the
competent French *sage femme* who delivered the youngsters in their county, since
women were never attended by male doctors. Rachel remembered the birth vividly,
for the midwife had commented that these cases were rare, and that many of the
breech babies died in delivery. She spoke to the girl with considerably more calmness
than she was feeling herself.

"Your baby is beginning to show itself, Sarah. Before another hour you will be
holding it in your arms."

She wiped the girl's face with a cold cloth; every few moments she raised the
blanket, watching the baby's second foot emerge, a little later the buttocks, then
the two shanks. She recalled the midwife saying that it was best not to try to help
the baby at this point. Between times she had the father build up the spindly fire
until there was a good blaze. When George arrived with the supplies she washed
her hands with hot water and soap, then fixed a basin of water for use at the bedside.
She removed the old blanket under Mrs. Bentley and replaced it with a clean sheet;
she lined the crib with the quilt George had brought. When she lifted the cover
again the baby's hips had fought their way out.

"You're doing fine."

After she was able to take a deep breath, Mrs. Bentley replied, "I can tell I am."

With the next pain the baby's navel appeared. Rachel grew tense. Mrs. Bentley
grabbed the sides of the bed, making a strong effort, and with that the baby emerged
to the shoulders. Remembering how the midwife had done it, Rachel released the
arms and hands, picked up the two feet and held them so that the trunk was
perpendicular to the bed and at right angles to the mother; then with her free hand
she applied pressure to the lower part of the mother's abdomen.

A minute passed, then two. Nothing was happening. Soon the pressure on the
cord would stop the flow of blood to the infant. Rachel doubled her hand into a
fist and threw her whole weight on Mrs. Bentley's abdomen. At that instant the
mother let out a scream . . . and the baby was born. It was a girl.

Rachel tied the umbilical cord in two places with string, then cut between. Next
she spanked its buttocks, hard; and it cried. She sponged the infant, wrapped on a
tight bellyband to protect the navel, dressed her in the christening gown and lay
her in the cradle before the fire. About twenty minutes had elapsed. She washed
Mrs. Bentley with warm water, put her in one of her own white gowns, covered
her with the blankets from Hunter's Hill, gave her a cup of coffee and some of
Moll's apple cake.

It was some forty hours later before she finally reached home, having installed Mitty in the Bentley cabin. She went into the parlor, sank into a chair in front of the cold hearth. She knew that she should be cold and numb and exhausted; but she wasn't feeling cold at all. Or tired. Or alone. She had not been able to bear a child of her own, but that baby, it would have been dead without her help. This too was a way of creating life. She could feel the infant in her arms, its blood racing against her blood, warming it, warming away the dull ache that had settled in her when she had heard, "Are you *the* Mrs. Jackson?"

6

As long and severe as the winter had been, just so quickly was it gone, with the sun bright overhead and the grass growing green on the hillside. The hickories began to show their fine leaves, the buds opened on the honeysuckle and dogwood; the pelicans came flying in long trains, lighting on the surface of the river below. Andrew had said, "My ambition is to become a gentleman planter." Hunter's Hill had the makings of a rich plantation, the land a fine black mold lying on a bed of limestone; if they farmed it diligently it would not be long before he could build his racecourse and train thoroughbreds. Then he wouldn't have to ride fifty miles, or a hundred, every time he heard there were going to be blooded horses raced somewhere in this county or the next.

At that moment her first real interest in Hunter's Hill was born. The hands worked hard to clear new fields, and their crop this year would be a big one. Even her fear of the former Robards land vanished; it was good earth that could help them create a great plantation here, perhaps the biggest and best in the Cumberland. If that was what was needed to keep Andrew happily at home, then she must go about her plowing and planting with ardor.

She was out in the fields in a short-sleeved cotton dress with a wide skirt, her hair piled in a knot under the wide-brimmed straw hat, when John Overton brought her the news that Andrew had persuaded the Congress to reverse the War Department, legitimatize the Nickajack Expedition and pay back every dollar that Sevier and the rest of the militiamen had invested out of their own pockets.

"At last," she exclaimed, rooting her feet deep into the earth, as though she were a tree that grew there, "something good has happened in Philadelphia!"

On one of her visits to the Bentley cabin, carrying hyson tea, sugar and ginger for Sarah and lightweight cloth for the baby's gowns, she learned that Sarah had served a three-year apprenticeship as a seamstress in Baltimore. Since it was apparent that Tim would have trouble providing for his family, Sarah came to Hunter's Hill one day a week, bringing the baby with her, and sewed draperies of the loose-woven material Rachel had loomed for her spare bedrooms. Rachel passed Sarah along to Jane, who gave her an occasional day's sewing, and also introduced her to a friend in Nashville who was delighted with the way Sarah could fit the fashionable new styles.

Hunter's Hill was fully planted by the time Andrew reached home on April 1. He had not enjoyed his session in the Congress, but as far as Rachel could make out his feeling was more of bafflement than disappointment.

"I just don't feel comfortable in Philadelphia, Rachel. Those Federalist nabobs, I think they've never stopped regretting they admitted us as a state. The House is so crowded, and there were so many spouters. It's for men of a certain temperament, men who like to work with large groups, with plenty of persuasion and debate and compromise. I'm not good at that kind of thing. I like to work alone. Just between you and me and the front hitching post, I'd still like to master one field . . ."

"Say, the state militia?"

He grinned, "Yes, the militia. I assembled a library of military books in Philadelphia. I'll take this plantation off your hands now, darling. From the look of it we're going to be rich come next November."

"Well, not rich," she said smilingly, "but I do think we'll eat good."

He put his arms about her waist, which was as slim as when he had met her, and held her lightly, studying her face. Despite the wide brim of the straw hat she wore in the fields her skin was tanned almost as deep as the brown of her eyes.

"I like you when you make jokes," he said. "And you're going to have your husband home for good. I'm free of all involvements. No more politics, no more circuit riding, no more stores, no more debts. From now on I'm going to be a domesticated animal."

The house that had been so empty these many months was now crowded with visitors from all over the state; not only the foot soldiers who had received their long-due pay, but also the young officers who had been compensated for the money they had laid out for ammunition and supplies came to express their thanks, and remained for serious discussions of what was needed to revitalize the state troops. Rachel had never traveled circuit with Andrew and had not known the relationship between these men and her husband; now she saw that they looked to him for leadership. Many of them brought their wives. They came as friends, enthusiasts, admirers, their loyalty discernible in every word and gesture. She welcomed them all: there was food and drink and entertainment; when the bedrooms were filled in the main house there was always a guest cabin that could be requisitioned, and for the single men an emergency cot in Andrew's study. Strangers who came for an hour, diffidently, knew by the heartiness of their reception that they could stay as long as they liked. What they did not know was that a considerable part of her emotion was gratitude: for here at last was a circle she need not question or doubt, friends who would be her stanch defenders. To them she was Mrs. Jackson, ma'am, and not *the* Mrs. Jackson.

Andrew had carried home Caesar's *Commentaries* in his saddlebag, reading at night before snuffing the candle. Now his boxes of books arrived: military engineering, books on military discipline, on fortifications. But the studies he seemed to take the greatest pleasure in were the ones on the Revolutionary War: David Ramsay's *The History of the American Revolution,* Joseph Galloway's *A Short History of the War in America*. When she saw him reading in these volumes with such intentness and relish, she found herself perplexed. Basically her husband was a gentle soul. How then could he become so intrigued with the art of organized destruction? War meant people killing each other; she hated every aspect of it. Stumblingly, she tried to tell him of her feelings.

"But my dear, you know I'm not bellicose by nature." There was an injured note in his voice. "I wouldn't take a first step to encourage war with England or Spain. But if you could be in the Congress for a little while and see how close we actually are . . . ."

He paced the floor and made a wide gesture with his arm to include every new military volume in the room.

"The good general does not lose men in war; his campaigns are so well planned and provisioned that he crushes the opposing army with a few swift blows. But if the commanding officer is untrained, stupid, commits his men needlessly, they butcher not only their own troops but those of the enemy. Only the strong, the equipped, the prepared can keep out of war or, if dragged in, end it quickly and without great loss. The weak are set upon and attacked by every passing bully."

"You make it sound very logical and humane. But do you mind if I just pray for peace . . . among my other prayers . . . ?" She burst into tears. "Oh, husband, how I wish we had a child!"

He took her in his arms.

"Darling, God knows what to give, what to withhold."

"Somewhere in the back of my mind I had given myself until my thirtieth birthday . . ."

". . . and that's tomorrow, June thirtieth!" He released her, strode to the door and began bellowing for George. "You wait here, and don't go out no matter what commotion you hear in the hall."

She sat in Andrew's work chair, her hands folded in her lap, hearing his muffled orders, the movement of feet. After a considerable amount of hammering he came back to the room, his coat off, a smudge across his forehead and his shirt ripped just inside the elbow.

"Andrew, what in heaven's name have you been doing to yourself?"

"Come along, but close your eyes." He led her through the hall, then released her hand. "All right, you can open them now."

In the center of the formerly empty music room was a shiny black pianoforte, smaller and squarer than any she had seen before, standing on four delicately carved legs in front and two at the rear. She went to it, breathlessly ran her fingers over the keys.

"Oh, Andrew, it's beautiful. We couldn't bring ours from Virginia, it would have filled the entire cabin of the *Adventure*."

She played a few chords. From behind her she heard strange sounds. She whirled about in astonishment.

"Why, it's a flute! You never told me you could play a flute."

He lowered his arms, gazing raptly at the ebony instrument.

"I couldn't. There was a man living at Mrs. Hardy's boardinghouse who used to practice in the parlor every night. He offered to teach me, I thought how pleasant it would be if we could play duets."

She jumped off the little bench and flung her arms impetuously about his neck.

"Andrew Jackson, you are the strangest and most improbable creature God ever created! And I am the luckiest of wives."

She had never seen his joy at being home or working in his own fields so great; nor had she ever seen him more effective. Watching him run the big plantation, she decided all over again that he was really a first-rate farmer: she was a conservative farmer, unwilling to try anything new; but time and again she was amazed to find how free and open Andrew's mind was: if he read of a new tool or an improved seed, he would send away for it; if he learned of a breeder who was raising a higher-quality stock, he would experiment in the hope of improving his own breed. He said that most men farmed by intuition, and that that was good if their intuition was good, but farming could become a science if a man would take the trouble to make himself expert at it.

In the early evenings after supper Rachel ran slow scales for him while he practiced the ascending notes on his flute, then they would try the songs they had learned together, *Within a Mile,* and *As Dawn in the Sunless Retreats*. Afterward they would go into his office where he worked on one of his military books, drawing up his own battle maps as he read *The Art of War* by Chevalier de la Valiere. She sat quietly by, reading in the New Testament or one of the volumes of Virgil which Samuel had given her for her last birthday. They retired late, yet frequently when she was awakened by the first rays of the sun she would find Andrew long since risen and reading by candlelight at the little mosaic table under the window.

"Andrew, you shouldn't get up in the middle of the night. You should sleep until dawn."

"Sleep? It's a pure waste, when you're as happy as I am, and interested in as many things." He paced between the window and the bed. "The trouble with that first store was that it was too small to maintain itself; it couldn't have amounted to much even if the Allison paper hadn't gone bad."

His voice became excited as he stood looking down at her.

". . . what I'd really like to do this fall is set up a trading center on the Stone River. I'd build a landing so the boats could bring us everything we wanted; we could run our own ferry. We wouldn't sell just to single customers, we'd make it a real trading center, the biggest between Philadelphia and New Orleans; we'd ship our crops to the highest bidder, North or South, and in return we'd take from them whatever was needed here in the Cumberland. We'd build our own whisky still and lumber mill . . ."

She did not answer. The more he built the busier he would be . . . and the surer to stay home.

7

Out of her bedroom window she saw coming up the road a carriage with two women in it. When they alighted at the front door she recognized them as Mrs. Somerset Phariss, president of the newly formed Nashville Culture Club, and Miss Daisy Deson, secretary of the club. The group was composed solely of Nashville ladies; she had heard about the organization from Jane, who had commented:

"They blackballed Hilda Hinston because she's not from one of the *old* families. Why do they have to start by being snobbish? Why can't they just grow into it gracefully over the years?"

She took a quick look in her dressing mirror, combed into place the loose ends of her hair, straightened the collar of her dress and went down the stairs.

Mrs. Phariss was the cultural leader of Nashville. Married to the wealthy third son of an English peer, and herself a graduate of one of the best girls' academies in Boston, she was still using her impeccably preserved New England accent to express her opinion of everything she found uncouth or provincial on the frontier. She was a big woman, with an enormous bosom, yet modishly dressed. Her companion, Daisy Deson, was a slim attractive young woman of thirty-five who came from one of the best-liked families in the Cumberland. She had charm and talent, but in the midst of being sweet and delightful could suddenly lash out with a single sentence of such penetrating cruelty that everyone in the room would wither under the blow. She had been losing prospective husbands by this method for a full twenty years.

The two women accepted Rachel's offer of a cold drink with hearty thanks. Mrs. Phariss then went about inspecting the house,

"What an interesting pianoforte. It's one of the new Zumpe's isn't it, made in London? This is a double Belfast damask, you can tell by the precise way the flower figures stand out. But perhaps you wondered why we drove out?"

"I think it was most friendly of you." Rachel's voice said only words. Precisely what did these ladies want of her?

"Mrs. Jackson," said Mrs. Phariss, "it's my feeling that town society should join forces with the country society. By working together we can throw off the primitive aspect of our backwoods life, and have our community's social and cultural affairs resemble the finest of the eastern cities. We would like you to join our Culture Club, and attend our meetings every Tuesday. Each week there will be a different attraction: a literary reading, a musicale, an inspirational talk . . . In our membership, which already totals thirty, we have only the *crème de la crème,* I assure you."

Rachel blanched at the thought of walking into a room filled with thirty strange women.

"But I never go out . . . I'm not at all social."

"Come now, Mrs. Jackson, you're being too modest," said Miss Deson, glancing about the large, elaborately furnished parlor. "We've heard about the dinner parties you've given here at Hunter's Hill for the young militia officers, and Mr. Jackson's political friends from Philadelphia . . ."

"No, no," Rachel interrupted; "people just drop in, that's all. And everybody who comes is welcome."

"Well, I know you will want to join the Culture Club," said Mrs. Phariss firmly as she rose from the settee. "The wife of our congressman has a public obligation."

After the women had bid her adieu, telling her they expected her for tea at Mrs. Peter Huygen's house the following Tuesday, Rachel wandered down the hall and into the study. Sitting at the walnut desk covered with Andrew's books and papers, she could see her father sitting before this same desk in the Virginia home, writing letters, drawing his survey maps. She felt the reassuring presence of both men, and a warm glow crept over her. It was kind of Mrs. Phariss and Miss Deson to invite her to join the Culture Club, even though the invitation had sounded more like an order; it was an act of espousal.

Tuesday morning she rose early and set out the new costume she had prepared to wear to the meeting, her town outfit she had called it the evening before when she had modeled the soft brown twill skirt and pelisse for Andrew. The color suited her eyes and sunburned complexion, and the styling gave her added height. The skirt needed a bit of rehemming, but Sarah would do that when she came by. Rachel wondered if all women were as exacting as she, when dressing for a group of other women; she couldn't remember ever having been so finicky.

Sarah arrived while Rachel was at breakfast and went quickly to the sewing room. When Rachel joined her she saw that the girl's eyes were red, the lids damp and swollen. The new skirt lay across her lap but she had given up all pretense of sewing. Rachel stared for an instant, then put a hand on Sarah's shoulder.

"What's wrong, Sarah? Are you ill?"

"No, I'm not sick, Mrs. Jackson, ma'am, unless it's my heart is sick. I can't sew on your skirt for the tea party today, because I can't let you go to that meetin'. They don't want you, really. All day yesterday I sewed at Mrs. Phariss's house; about ten of the ladies was there, and they was fighting over you something awful."

Rachel took the skirt from Sarah and handed the girl her own linen handkerchief.

"Oh, Mrs. Jackson, you're so good, you came to help me when you didn't even know me, and you saved my baby, and found me work. You take care of Mrs. Krudner and her young ones when they be sick, and she's just a poor widow woman. We love you here in the country, you don't belong with them . . . city folk. They say you are a bad woman."

The blood drained from Rachel's face; her fingertips felt like ice.

"Go on, Sarah."

"That Martha Dinsmore, she said she knew you when your husband sent you home to your mother from Kentucky for misbehavin'; Mrs. Quincy said she heard all about you in Harrodsburg, and the trial where they accused you of wrongdoin' . . . and your divorce . . . and she wouldn't belong to any club that let you be a member."

Rachel was too stiff to sink into the chair beside her, much as she ached to relieve the weight on her legs. For a moment Sarah's voice faded out; then she was listening again, intently to every word.

"A couple of ladies said if that was the case they didn't want to associate with you, and that no divorced lady could be considered respectable, and they was surprised at Mrs. Phariss to suggest you come in. Mrs. Phariss said her husband thinks Mr. Jackson is going to be a very important man in Tennessee, maybe even governor someday, and that in the East where she comes from it's considered important for a club to have the wives of men in politics, and that all your furniture come from Philadelphia, and your house would be elegant for big balls. . . . When

I left Mrs. Phariss's at four o'clock they was still arguin' and fightin' . . . Oh, Mrs. Jackson, ma'am, you can't go to that meetin' with those ladies who think you're sinful.''

She looked up at Rachel pleadingly. Rachel would have liked to comfort her; but what good to explain to this child that she was already married to Mr. Jackson when they came up the Natchez Trace with Hugh McGary? What good to explain that she and Mr. Jackson had been married for two full years before they learned that Lewis Robards had never actually divorced her; and that she couldn't go into the Harrodsburg court to defend herself?

Out of the bedroom window she saw George bringing her carriage up the drive. He had spent hours shining and polishing it. She lifted Sarah from the chair.

''You go ahead home, Sarah; we won't do any sewing today. And when you get downstairs, tell George I shan't be needing the carriage.''

She took the unfinished skirt, folded it and set it in her big cedar chest. Then she went into her own bedroom and pulled the cord to summon Moll. Perhaps some hot coffee would warm her, dissipate the chill.

8

There had always been the chance that when the moment came Andrew might change his mind and decide to go back to Congress; yet the only politics that interested him during the summer were the troubles of his friend and sponsor, Senator Blount, who had been expelled from the Senate for conspiring with the English to drive the Spaniards out of Louisiana and Florida. He had even rejected the overtures of Blount's friends and political backers who had arrived from Knoxville to inform him that he was the unanimous choice to finish out the unexpired senatorial term.

But most of the crops had been brought in; his yield of seventy-six bushels of corn to the acre was the top figure in the valley; the market was good and the crops sold for high prices. Andrew became restless. She recognized the symptoms. There was a time to cultivate one's fields and raise the crops and harvest them, and this was the time for home and hearth; but there was also a time to be out in a man's world, fighting for the things one believed in. All this was in his character, and had been from the beginning. When the Blount delegation urged him to reconsider the senatorial job, she saw that he was carrying their offer around in his pocket, taking it out every few moments to gaze anew at its contour and complexion.

''Actually it's not so bad an idea as it seemed at first,'' he offered tentatively. ''I think I might like the Senate better than I did the House. I might be able to arrange a new Indian conference, and get back the land we lost under the Holston Treaty. Besides, if we went up to Philadelphia for the Senate, we could buy the merchandise for our new store . . .''

The fear that she would have to remain alone at Hunter's Hill for another long period turned into near-panic as she thought of facing Philadelphia society.

''. . . no, I couldn't . . . I have to stay here to manage . . .''

''We can afford an overseer now that we've had such a good season, Rachel. Why shouldn't you want to go out and see the world?'' There was a tinge of impatience in his voice. ''You're happy when the world comes to you.''

Silently she cried, All who seek us here are on our side, they have committed themselves, they believe in me. But when I must go out to meet strangers I become frightened, I withdraw. No, Andrew, I can't go with you.

*   *   *

He left for the Senate on a Friday, in the midst of a torrential downpour, complaining that it was the wrong day to start a journey; but since he was due in Philadelphia on November 13, he could wait no longer.

The rain continued for several more days; even when it ceased the skies remained leaden and the prospect dismal. She thought what bad luck it was always to be left at the most disagreeable time of the year. Or was it simply the most disagreeable because she was alone? Surely she would not have given up the magnificent spring and summer days with Andrew when they rode over the fields in the bright sunshine, or sat out on the porch during the warm evenings watching the countryside bathed in the light of the full moon.

No, she would not change that; but the Senate term probably would extend into the beginning of next summer; that could be seven or eight months without Andrew. She wished she could somehow fall asleep and not wake up until the following spring, the way grizzly bears did. Then she remembered that her father would disapprove of this thinking: for Colonel Donelson had believed it a sin to wish away the days of the short life God had granted one.

A few days later Jane came to visit and to read Rachel a portion of Andrew's letter to Robert Hays:

"I beg of you to try to amuse Mrs. Jackson and prevent her from fretting. The situation in which I left her—(Bathed in Tears) fills me with woe. Indeed, it has given me more pain than any event in my life, but I trust She will not remain long in her dolefull mood, but will again be cheerfull. Could I learn that was the case I could be satisfied."

"I'm not doleful," protested Rachel. "I'm just plain miserable."

She went to bed as soon as Jane left, slept long and deeply. When she awoke her mouth and lips were dry, and the heat she felt could not be the warmth of the room on this raw autumn day.

"You all right, Miz Rachel?" asked Moll with a troubled face. "I'll bring some coffee."

As always when she was alone, her despair at remaining childless returned to grip her. Women had children after they were thirty, but these were generally added to a long line. Her line seemed to have ended before it began. Why? Her sisters all had children; her brothers' wives all had children. Even Lewis Robards and his wife Hannah now had a son. She alone had never borne a child, to know its love and companionship.

She closed the curtains around her bed. Her mind went back to the first days Andrew had lived in the Donelson stockade. He had said, "I think the greatest thing a man can have is a family." Of how much was she depriving her husband by remaining childless? Last summer he had told her, "Darling, God knows what to give and what to withhold," but she knew that he was not a religious man, resigned to the dictates of God's will. He had said those words to comfort her. The stores he opened, the politics in which he professed not to be interested, the numerous business affairs in Philadelphia, could these be justifications rather than real desires? If there were half a dozen youngsters at Hunter's Hill could he have torn himself away? This was her failure, that she could not perpetuate his name.

Was there another, more serious failure? Was she a different woman from the one with whom Andrew had fallen in love? From that instant she had heard the news of Lewis Robards' Harrodsburg divorce, and learned that she was hopelessly trapped, her gay, warm, demonstrative nature had undergone a change, been replaced by the figure of the woman on horseback, riding across the fields alone at night to visit a cabin where someone was sick. The inescapable engulfment had turned her inward, banked the fires of her open, cheerful spontaneity, and in her self-consciousness made her search people's eyes to see if they thought her innocent or guilty. Would Andrew have loved her if she had been like this when he had first met her?

She grew thin and pale and, after a time, unwilling to distinguish between the gray darkness of night and the gray darkness of day. Only Jane knew that she was ill, and helped her, giving the Donelsons highly plausible reasons why Rachel was not coming to the Sunday dinners. She did not keep track of how long she lay abed torturing herself with self-reproaches, the victim of twisted and poisoned images, but at length the cycle wore itself out. She awakened one morning to find a warm November sun flooding into her bedroom. She groped at the head of the bed for the bellpull, shocked at the white boniness of her hands. When Moll came running she managed a little smile; Moll stopped short in her tracks, clasped her hands between her deep breasts and exclaimed:

"The Lawd be praised, Miz Rachel's come home again!"

"Moll, I'm actually hungry . . . for the first time since I learned that Mr. Jackson was going to the Senate."

Jane came in while she was sitting in her big iron bathing tub, splashing herself with warm water.

"As Moll says, 'The Lawd be praised.' For a while there I thought you had renounced all the pleasures of the flesh."

Rachel gazed down at herself, shaking her head despairingly.

"Doesn't look as though I have much flesh left."

"Moll will put the weight back on your bones; my only worry was that your spirit was getting a little thin."

"Almost to the point of vanishing, my dear. But I think I'm all right now: a great discovery has just come to me."

"Good, I'll leave you alone with it. Get some sunshine on that peaked little face of yours."

"Oh, Jane, I haven't become ugly?"

"No, darling, you could never be ugly; you have a light inside you that shines out warm and bright, and that light will keep you beautiful all your life."

Moll helped her to dress, selecting a warm woolen cape and a bright red knitted coverlet, and Rachel sat on the front porch with her face in the sun, thinking that she had not been joking with Jane when she had told her sister that she had made a discovery. She had thought that her love for Andrew was as great and full as it was possible for a woman to know. Now she realized that she had been cheating him, hoarding, holding back the love and devotion she was reserving for children.

It would be different now. There were no reservations in her mind, no more locked compartments. How much greater her love would be. Nor could she ever be really lonely or unhappy again; the important thing was to know the full extent of one's love and to give oneself to it. She would be able to face the calendars, accept her responsibility and do her work. She would not only survive, but be happy in that survival. Her father had been right: the days vouchsafed to one were so precious and so few.

She had not thought very much about her looks since they had come to Hunter's Hill; she had had to be out in the fields in the strong wind, in the rain, in the hot biting sun. Nights she had been routed from her sleep by neighbors, had gone out in the snow and slush, sat up until dawn in cramped cabins, returning home in time to see the sun rise and to begin the day's work. Andrew had told her she was beautiful, spoke of the velvet quality of her eyes, the softness of her skin, the richness of her long dark hair, the gracefulness of her figure. Had she become an old woman at thirty? Had she thrown away whatever attractiveness she may have possessed?

That afternoon she dressed in her prettiest winter costume over which she wore a heavily lined capote, and had George drive her into Nashville. A good many houses had been erected, both on the main street and along the river, some of them of brick. In the public square she found the Methodist church, the first real church Nashville had known. From the outside the courthouse looked exactly the same as it had when she and her mother and Samuel had gone in to watch Andrew and John try their cases.

She headed directly for Lardner Clark's store and bought some new hairbrushes, a skin cream, some French cologne and a soft scented face powder. Then, a little guiltily, she picked up a small pot of rouge, wondering if she would ever have the daring to use it. She remembered Andrew telling her of the law that had been passed in Pennsylvania decreeing that a marriage might be annulled if it could be proved that during the courtship the wife had "deceived and misled" her prospective husband by the use of cosmetics. But there was nothing in the law that made it illegal for a married woman to hold her husband through a tiny touch of artifice!

She had George carry her purchases out to the carriage, then drove back to Hunter's Hill as fast as she could get there. She sat down before her dressing mirror, and her face shone back at her from the mirror. My hair will need considerable brushing night and morning, she thought, and some of that liquid soap Jane uses. Next she looked for the beginnings of crow's-feet about her eyes. But her skin was firm. Her mouth was full and red-lipped. Her face was thinner, the cheekbones showed slightly, the plumpness was gone from under her chin.

She felt young again, almost like a young girl waiting for her lover to return.

9

Few visitors came to Hunter's Hill that winter of 1797 while Andrew was away. To the people of the neighborhood who had learned that she was available no matter what the nature of the illness or adversity, she became Aunt Jackson. They borrowed a plow horse, an ax, seed for planting, meat and meal. There was not a cabin for miles around where she had not tended the sick, comforted the afflicted, helped bury the dead. She became a familiar sight riding alone through the fields and woods, bringing medications and a rapidly growing knowledge of the illnesses of the Cumberland. She went where she was called, not asking who it was or what the trouble, passing no judgment and wanting no return.

From Andrew's letters, the senators were doing little but sitting in their big red chairs with their binoculars trained on the war between England and France. He had ordered a handsome brown outfit with a velvet collar and vest, and had had his hair cut short. He was staying in a comfortable hostelry where he had attended a dinner party given by former Senator Aaron Burr. Apart from trying to get a raise for John Overton, who had been appointed inspector of revenue, and a job as marshal for Robert Hays, his only important effort was convincing the Senate that an Indian treaty conference should be held in Tennessee.

By the end of January, when both Houses and President Adams had consented to the treaty, the signs of his restlessness began to multiply: he sent home specifications for the store he wanted her to build, and bought six thousand dollars' worth of stock for their new trading center. She was to inquire among her young nephews to see if there was one who would like to come into business with them. Her sister Catherine's boy, John Hutchings, a mild-mannered lad of twenty-two, was delighted at the prospect.

She was sleeping soundly one soft spring night when she awakened to find Andrew standing above her. He had left Philadelphia on April 12 and accompanied his stock of goods to the Ohio Falls, riding the last hundred and eighty miles in three days and nights. He was completely done in.

"I've been drenched by sleet and rain every day for a week; my first horse went lame, the second took sick and died. Some of the cabins I stopped at were the poorest I've ever seen; once the spaces were so wide between the floor logs that I woke up to find a snake in my bed."

"Serves you right. Stay home with your wife."

She was rewarded with a smile, his first. She put on a robe and went to her dressing mirror to comb her hair. After a moment she raised her eyes higher on the mirror and saw Andrew kneeling behind her, gazing at his own countenance.

"You send me away looking clean and fat and sleek and see how I come back to you: I look twice my thirty years. I could hang my rifle on either cheekbone, my eyes are sunk so deep they're coming out the other end. Good thing you didn't marry me for my beauty."

She turned, cupped his rough bearded face in her hands and replied in a gentle voice, "Oh, but I did. And you never looked better to me than you do this very instant."

He put his arms about her and kissed her on the lips.

"Oh, Andrew," she whispered, holding her cheek against his, "to maintain one's love amongst the difficulties of living . . ."

". . . is like maintaining one's life in the midst of a war."

She had been under the impression that Andrew had quit Philadelphia because the Senate had adjourned; a few days later she learned that the Senate was still very much in session. She came upon him in his study, writing his resignation to Governor Sevier.

"I simply had to get out. When our people see the results of the Indian Conference, and all the lands that will be restored to Tennessee, they won't be angry at my resignation. That's what I went up there for, and I came home when my job was done."

He became a whirlwind of activity: the new store proved successful; with the first cash that came in he built a landing and flatboat to serve as a ferry; he worked with the overseer in the fields from dawn until noon, bought a cotton gin he had seen in Philadelphia, and rode over the countryside explaining to the planters how fast the gin worked, offering to process their cotton on a percentage basis. He hadn't bought his first thoroughbred yet, but every time he crossed into Sumner County he managed to find his way to the Hartsville Course for the races. While in Philadelphia he had bought an extensive law library, and was again riding into Nashville to handle a few of the matters that old clients were urging him to take.

"I'm very glad to see you interested in the law again, Andrew," she commented. "I never could understand why you should want to be through with it,"

"A lawyer can never be through with the law."

Her hours with him were sweeter than they had ever been: this was what she had; this was what she would always have. Sometimes, watching him carry on the tasks of half a dozen men, she realized that he was not only her child but a whole brood of children; and that to keep him happy and working would require all of her strength and devotion.

One evening late in the fall John Overton rode out from their Nashville office with Andrew. Both men were deep in talk as they entered the house.

"What is it, Andrew?"

"Well, there's a vacancy coming up for the state Superior Court. The legislature has to elect a new man in December. Mr. Blount, General Robertson, Governor Sevier too, they think my name should be put up,"

"I agree with them," she exclaimed heartily. "Tell me more about it."

"The appointment is for six years, pays six hundred a year . . . in cash. It's an independent office, outside of political factions and quarrels. I'd have to ride circuit, same as I did when I was attorney general, but I'd still be able to run the plantation and the store . . ."

Rachel pushed back the hair from her brow, and smiled broadly. This is good, she thought. This is secure. Judges are above . . . gossip; no one would ever dare talk against a judge . . . or his wife . . .

10

She did not wait for the legislature to elect Andrew, but spun, dyed and wove some linen cloth. The prospect of six years without change, and a steady routine, kept her making lighthearted jokes as she draped the black material over Andrew's shoulders.

"Judging by the amount of material it takes to cover you," she teased, "you are going to be a very big judge. Pun me no puns."

"But can we afford all this drapery?" he asked as she swathed the material around him, "on a mere six hundred dollars a year?"

"Do you know what I like best about this job? That I will know what to expect tomorrow. Does that seem monotonous to you?"

"I'll draw you a chart for every day in the year. Undrape me now, lady, I've a heap of things to do."

He always had a heap of things to do; he could not abide inactivity: he had built a distillery; he had bought property at Gallatin and Lebanon and was erecting cabins to serve as branch stores. The cotton gin had arrived from Philadelphia and cotton was coming up the river to their landing on flatboats and over the dirt roads in oblong wagons. After the planters had delivered their cotton and bought their supplies Andrew invited them to Hunter's Hill for a visit, a drink and a meal. She found that if she set the noonday table for twenty, the same number her parents had always set for, she would not miss by more than a couple, one way or the other. These men liked Andrew and had confidence in him; in the same sense that his success in the Congress for the Nickajack Expedition had made him the leader of the young militiamen, so his bringing in of the first cotton gin and his successful marketing of the cotton had made him their business leader.

He was formally elected to the Supreme Court on December 20, 1798. John Overton came frequently to discuss the impending cases and to theorize about the law.

"Now John, you know I have no gift for abstract thought. Give me a set of facts between two contestants and I'll reach a fair decision."

"But that decision has got to emerge from a universal principle of law."

"And so it will, John, when you are sitting on the Bench; for my own part I'm still going to try to do what is right between two parties. That's what the law means to me."

John paced the study, idly inspecting a group of books stacked on a side table. "What are these military tomes open for?" he asked. "I thought you were reading Blackstone?"

Rachel too had noticed that Andrew was again studying military science. He had a deep-rooted respect for the law and for the position of a judge, but when she saw him consuming the military books with his eyes sparkling, his body poised tensely over the desk, every particle of him vibrantly alive and excited, she could not help but perceive that this was the field in which he had the greatest hunger.

"Andrew, I do believe you would like to become a professional soldier. I mean, a permanent officer of the Federal Army."

"What army?" he snorted. "We have none! Congress, the President, yes, the voters too, they're all deathly scared of a standing army . . . because the armies in Europe were always used against the people."

"That *is* something to be frightened about, Andrew. Even Mr. Jefferson is against . . ."

"Yes, where governments are ruled by monarchs. We could use our army to protect ourselves. England has never really given us up. She'll be back with her troops one day . . . just as sure as you and I are sitting at this desk together."

Looking down at his maps on which he had drawn troops and cannon and horses, it seemed like a game he was playing; yet the ringing conviction in every taut line of his figure portrayed a passion so strong that it at last convinced her too.

Dr. Henning sent a message that her mother had come down with pneumonia. Rachel went immediately to nurse her, and as soon as she was able to travel Andrew brought her to Hunter's Hill. Rachel thought her mother at seventy-six still beautiful; the lines had deepened about her eyes but there was no trace of white in her hair. Andrew fussed about her, saying, "You're going to stay with us permanently now."

"You're very kind, Andrew. But Colonel Donelson and I built our station together, and when it comes time for me to die I want to die at home and be buried there."

Mrs. Donelson watched her daughter's routine with approval,

"You remind me of myself, Rachel . . ."

". . . and Andrew reminds you of Father?"

"Yes. His activities here can no more keep him content than our plantation in Virginia was ever big enough to hold your father. But it was that same will to do things that made me fall in love with him in the first place . . . and kept me in love with him always."

Rachel leaned forward, her elbows on her knees and her face cupped in her hands.

"I used to pray, 'Dear God, make my husband happy here, so that he will want to stay home with me.' "

"And now?"

"Now I pray, 'Dear God, let him find a task and a mission that will be big enough to justify his talents and his energy.' "

Contrary to her expectation that Andrew s elevation to the Bench would put their private lives beyond petty gossip, she found that his becoming a judge had caused the disparagement to be directed against him as well. For the next ten years they would live their lives in the poisoned atmosphere of rumor: every acrion, every thought would be colored and influenced by it. How easily it spread, how quickly it was absorbed into the blood stream and became a near-truth! Even the brief happy days of respite, when they were free of attack, proved to be in themselves periods for the storing up and creating of material for the next siege. How unerringly rumor fastened onto the vulnerable facts, and sucked its sustenance from them, twisting and perverting until the character lay dead. Despite the fact that Andrew won praise throughout the state for getting rid of weak and crooked sheriffs, for buttressing the authority of the local officers of the court and instilling a rigid respect for the Bench wherever he sat, there were those in Nashville, many of the women of the Culture Club, who set out to prove that Mrs. Jackson was a backwoodswoman who was at home only among the poor and ignorant newcomers to the area, and that Mr. Jackson did not have the dignity or decorum required of a judge. They kept alive his criticism of George Washington, and in particular used him as a whipping boy in the encomiums when Washington died. They accused him of having represented the militia in the House rather than the whole state of Tennessee; and of having left his work unfinished when he walked out on his job as senator. They resurrected stories of his quarrels, one with Judge McNairy, caused by McNairy's brother carrying unfounded tales, which Andrew and his old friend had patched up; another with Senator Cocke, who claimed Andrew had been illegally appointed by Governor Sevier to replace him in the Senate, and which had almost ended in a duel; a third with Governor Sevier three years before, when the first major general of the Tennessee militia was to be elected, and Andrew had defeated the governor's maneuver to delegate the power of military appointments to men of his own choosing. The two men had called each other some unsavory names but in the end had apologized and resumed their friendship.

Rachel thought that John Overton and Samuel looked at her rather strangely when she urged them not to discuss these tales with Andrew; weeks later she learned that her husband was working equally to suppress the whispering campaign against her. Picking up the first of the talk outside his store one day, he had sent a friend to try to locate the source, and to see if the center of the activity was not in the kitchen of Betsey Harbin. The friend had been obliged to write back:

> I can't learn that Betsey has said anything injurious of Mrs. Jackson.

Andrew had then inquired if a certain Mrs. Ball was the talebearer. The investigator had replied:

> I pledge you that Mrs. Ball did not either directly or indirectly say anything intending to injure the reputation of Mrs. Jackson.

Rachel was shattered at the thought of Andrew devoting his time and energy to combating kitchen gossip. This matter of the unceasing talk about their past had never been discussed by either of them; it was too painful. Each had borne his own burden and pretended he knew nothing of what was going on. Now she sought her husband in his study.

"Andrew, I just can't let you waste your time and energy trying to fight gossip; it's a Hydra-headed monster. Not all the combined armies in the world can stop women from talking."

"But why should they want to hurt us?"

"The fault has been mine. I did not obey Mrs. Phariss's demand that I join her group. I'm going to become a member of the Culture Club, go to their meetings and give parties for them here . . ."

The declaration took all her strength. She sought shelter in his arms. He sat on a corner of his desk and held her close.

"Rachel, make no mistake about it, if they can conquer you with these methods you will not only be their slave but you will be at the mercy of every last person who stoops to slander to gain his ends. We've committed no crime, we've broken none of the commandments, we've hurt no man or woman, and we've helped a good many. We've got to be strong inside ourselves."

She was startled at the grim tone of his voice.

"All I want, Andrew, is for people to stop talking about us."

"We have stanch and loving friends all over Tennessee. In Knoxville and Jonesboro I have been asked again and again, 'Won't you bring Mrs. Jackson with you the next time you come?' By the Eternal, Rachel, you are going with me!"

It was her first trip with Andrew since they had come up the Natchez Trace. For this journey into society she would need traveling dresses, gowns for tea with the ladies of Knoxville and for visits to the courts, cloaks and shawls, slippers and gloves, hats and extra ivory combs. She would make the clothing, the accessories would be bought at Tatum's or Clark's in Nashville. She took inventory of the bolts of cottons and heavier linens stacked on the sewing-room shelves, then estimated how much lace, velvet and sheer linen batiste she would need for the three-month circuit. Sarah Bentley came every morning to sew. Rachel peered over her shoulder at the measurements; no question about it, striding the furrows of newly planted fields had added two inches to her hips!

She filled her hatboxes and Andrew's two aged trunks, then sent to Jane's for another. Her scented handkerchief was clutched into a tiny ball by the time she and Andrew drove down Hunter's Hill in their carriage.

In Knoxville Governor Sevier gave them an official banquet to which everyone in the government was invited. The Blount family held a magnificent ball; William Blount, the former senator, had died a few months before, but Willie, his half brother, was equally devoted to Andrew. At Hartsville they were the guests of honor for the opening of the racing season. She had not realized how many families she had entertained at Hunter's Hill, but every stop on the circuit was the occasion for a gala party. Her trepidation lessened, her natural buoyancy and gaiety rose as she found herself surrounded by old friends from early morning until she and Andrew could escape to their bed late at night. Lying by her husband's side she would close her eyes and think of the most gratifying picture she would take back to Hunter's Hill: Andrew presiding over the Knoxville court, handsome in his black gown, his tall lean figure towering over the courtroom, his face serious, his eyes somber, treated with vast respect by officers, lawyers and clients alike. She knew that he always had his brace of pistols resting on a little table out of sight but within immediate reach, for there was considerable brawling and turmoil in the courts, particularly in those closest to the newly established Indian frontier.

She was constantly amazed at the growth of Tennessee. When Colonel Donelson had ended his *Adventure* journey and the family had put up their tents on Clover Bottom, his group combined with Colonel Robertson's had made up about two hundred people. Now there were more than a hundred thousand people living in the state, with immigrant families pouring in so fast that in some places on the main road their carriages could not move because of the solid stream of wagons coming west. The wilderness through which she and Andrew had made their way on the last leg of the journey up the Natchez Trace was dotted with thriving settlements, the Trace was a tol'able road and on every side she saw cabins, barns, cultivated fields of corn, cotton and tobacco. Where she and Andrew had slept on the ground, cooking their supper over an open fire, there were now comfortable inns, county seats, courthouses, churches.

There was also a mail service to carry news home to her mother and Jane. From Jane she learned that the reports of the many banquets and balls with which she was being honored had had the effect of silencing her detractors.

11

Hunter's Hill and the stores were running at a profit for the time being.

"It's a good thing," groused Andrew. "I've been working for the county, the territory, the state and the nation for some twelve years now and I've yet to make my first dollar over expenses. You sure can't get rich working for the government."

"You're not supposed to, Andrew. Generals don't get rich, either. But they did name that new district Jackson County, after you."

Their serenity was frequently interrupted by outside events: John Overton lost the girl he was courting to a rival; Stockly, who had cleared some two hundred thousand dollars on gigantic speculations, was indicted along with his father-in-law by North Carolina for land fraud, though Governor Sevier refused to honor the request for extradition; in June their stillhouse burned down, consuming upward of three hundred gallons of whisky and rendering the still useless by melting down the caps and worms. At the end of the summer Mrs. Donelson died and was buried on her own plantation as she had requested. Severn, the sickly member of the family, promptly married Elizabeth Rucker, nineteen years younger than himself.

At the turn of the century practically every one in Tennessee voted the Republican ticket for the election of Thomas Jefferson and Aaron Burr, both of whom were sympathetic to the western states. When by a technicality Burr received the same number of electoral votes as Jefferson, the election was thrown into the House, where the defeated and disgruntled Federalists, who hated Jefferson as a revolutionist, did everything in their power to subvert the election and put Burr into the presidency. Aaron Burr was loved in Tennessee because he had been one of the leaders in the fight to have the state admitted to the Union, but even the Tennesseans wondered why he did not step up to the dais of the House and make the simple declaration that he had run for the vice-presidency, an act of forthright honesty that would have put an immediate end to the paralyzing controversy.

They made a new friend, John Coffee, a captain in the militia and the only man who, in Rachel's estimation, dwarfed her husband physically. Andrew had the determined strength of the man of will and grit, but Coffee wore his easily; powerfully built, he was gentle as the lamb she had raised at Poplar Grove, and so enormous he filled any room he entered. Andrew asked:

"Jax, I try to tell the truth most of the time but it seems to me that I frequently miss by a fraction. How do you manage to drive the center every shot?"

Coffee's face was round and full; his skin sunburned from his outdoor life as a surveyor and from running his own flatboat containing casks of salt to outlying river settlements.

"I'm not clever enough to distinguish between the various kinds of truth," he replied. "They all look alike to me."

Andrew was again plunged into state politics. Governor John Sevier, having served three consecutive terms, was obliged by the constitution to step aside for one session. Up to this time Tennessee politics had been controlled by the Blounts and Sevier on a friendly basis; now the Blount faction, to which Andrew belonged, decided to form its own party and elect its own governor. At a caucus in Blount's home early in the year they selected Andrew's friend and colleague, Judge Archibald Roane. Andrew resisted the considerable pressure put on him to stand for the Congress again.

"I don't want to leave the state," he confided to Rachel. "Major General Conway is ill; within a year I think our militia is going to need a new commanding officer . . ."

Major General Conway died. The election was posted for a new commanding officer. John Sevier immediately announced his candidacy; just as promptly Andrew was nominated by a group of militiamen. Knowing how passionately he wanted this post, Rachel imagined he would resign from the Bench to fling himself into the campaign. Instead he told her:

"I've always believed that the office should seek the man and not the man the office. I'm not saying a chap hasn't the right to be ambitious for a job, to study and prepare himself for it, yes, and even to let people know that he has mastered the field . . ."

"Then you really believe you have a chance?"

"Yes, a good one."

Among the officers of the militia seventeen cast their votes for Sevier, seventeen cast their votes for Andrew Jackson. According to the state constitution the deciding vote had then to be cast by the newly elected Governor Roane. Former Governor Sevier, chagrined at the tie, sent a message to Andrew requesting that he withdraw. Andrew replied that he would not walk out on the men who had supported him, and that he thought the properly constituted authority should make the decision. Bitterly angry, Sevier announced:

"What has this redheaded upstart ever done that entitles him to be military commander in chief of Tennessee? His whole warlike experience and service may be summed up in leading fifteen or twenty men on the trail of about a dozen Indians. He has the reputation of a fighting man, his friends say. Fighting whom?"

Governor Roane cast the deciding vote for Andrew. He was jubilant. Rachel said:

"I thought you were a small boy chasing rainbows."

Andrew laughed. "I'll not let anybody call me general until I win some battles. Nevertheless, the whole discipline of the militia has deteriorated during Conway's illness, and my first task is to rebuild the fighting spirit. The state of Tennessee is going to know they've got a new commanding officer. I'll never rest until it is a first-class fighting force."

She felt his eagerness to begin; yet how could it be possible for a man to sit in the Supreme Court and at the same time be a major general of the militia?

For his first general muster in Nashville in May, Andrew had a uniform made, the first he had ever owned. The collar was high, coming up just under his ears, with a long double-breasted coat, a row of buttons down either side, gold-braid epaulets and a broad brightly colored sash.

He tried to persuade Rachel to come with him to the muster, which was the grand event of the year for Nashville. All officers were dressed in their gayest trappings, the soldiers in fringed hunting shirts; the best marksmen in the state would be present for the shooting match. In many aspects the muster was actually a county fair, ringed by peddlers, farmers with horses, cows and pigs to trade, housewives selling their prize preserved fruits, cake men selling ginger cakes, the potters and ironmongers displaying their finest handiwork. It was Andrew's duty to supervise the inspection of the foot soldiers, making sure every commissioned officer had side arms, that every private was provided with either a musket, a cartouche box with nine charges of powder and ball, or a rifle, powder horn, shot pouch, spare flint, one picker and worm. With the horse troop he had to ascertain that every soldier had a good mount at least fourteen hands high, with a serviceable saddle, bridle, pistol, sword and cap, shoe boots, spurs, cartouche box and cartridges. The men received no pay and provided their own horses, uniforms, guns and ammunition, a situation which Andrew was determined to remedy as soon as he could wangle funds out of the state legislature.

He had ridden his fastest horse to the muster, but the bad news reached Hunter's Hill ahead of the returning general. Captain John Coffee brought it, his usually amiable face set in grim lines as he explained:

"The reason I'm here is I'm afraid Mr. Jackson will do something rash. You must calm him. It seems there was a young fellow at the muster, Charles Dickinson, a friend of Sevier's. They say he's the most brilliant young lawyer in Nashville. Trained by John Marshall. Dickinson was standing with a group of friends when the general rode onto the parade ground. Someone asked:

" 'What great military exploit has Mr. Jackson performed that entitles him to such exalted rank and gorgeous trappings?'

"Dickinson had been drinking; he replied in a voice loud enough for everyone to hear:

"Why, gentlemen, he has done a most daring exploit. He has captured another man's wife!"

Rachel placed her weight against the mantel, trembling.

"Dickinson has a reputation as the best shot in the Cumberland Valley, ma'am," continued Coffee. "Andrew's a great commanding officer, but I can outshoot him ten to one. Don't let him challenge Dickinson to a duel; if there's going to be shooting, I want to be at the other end."

She thanked Jax for his offer to fight in her behalf, then ran up to her room and threw herself face down across the bed. She wanted sufficient time to quiet her pounding heart before she had to cope with her husband.

It was unbelievable to her that a gentleman could make such a coarse joke because Andrew had defeated his friend in an election. He had been drinking, Coffee said, and that was some mitigation; but how close to the top of his mind their story must have been if it could spring to his lips so spontaneously.

She thought, Andrew and I have been married a full ten years now. Would they never forget? Charles Dickinson's remark would be repeated all over Tennessee, in every home and shop and tavern . . . her name the loose thread in the idle talk.

Suddenly she sat upright in the center of the bed, for Andrew was winding his way up Hunter's Hill. Her head cleared: bad as Dickinson's remark had been, it had merely intimated that Andrew had won her away from her husband. She would have to make Andrew accept this and allow the affair to pass over. Not that he would forget; but he must not provide the community with further fuel to keep alive their bright fires of scandal.

Reluctantly, Andrew agreed.

12

She sat at the walnut desk with her ledger spread out before her. Andrew came quietly behind her, leaned over and kissed the top of her head.

"A lucky thing your father taught you to figure in that arithmetic book: Hunter's Hill is now supporting all our other activities."

She turned about at the seriousness in his voice, ill concealed under the banter.

"I'm having problems at the store," he confided. "John Hutchings is fine as a clerk, but I've been involved in so many things that the management has fallen on his shoulders . . . and he's just too green."

He also was having considerable trouble with Thomas Watson, whom he had taken in to handle his huge cotton operation, and from whom he had been unable to get any accounting.

The unfortunate incident at the master muster proved to be the start of a series of disturbances. What had appeared to be a friendly break with former Governor Sevier now began to look like a political fight to the finish. After several years in which Andrew's opinions as a judge had been accepted with confidence, two new decisions brought condemnation upon his head. The first was one in which he was sitting with the two other judges of the circuit as a court of appeal involving a case which he himself had tried under Judge McNairy while he was attorney general. Now, as an appeal judge, he reversed himself; and was charged with being inconsistent, changeable, unreliable.

"I can't see that I had much choice," he expostulated to Rachel as they sat over their supper table scanning the criticism in the Knoxville newspapers. "I could have agreed with my reasoning of ten years ago and be called consistent, or decided according to what I thought was legal and proper for today."

The second outburst followed shortly after. Finding that a petitioner was one with whom he had been on unfriendly terms, Andrew summoned the petitioner's lawyer and urged him to ask for a postponement so that the case could be brought before another judge. He was immediately accused of being unable to decide a case on its legal merits. The probability that these attacks were politically inspired was of little comfort to her.

John Sevier, now qualified to run again for the governorship, announced his candidacy. Governor Roane announced his candidacy also. Sevier and his political followers let loose a thunderous blast, accusing Roane, Jackson and their supporters of double-dealing. Andrew maintained that Sevier was no longer fit to be governor.

"I can prove that he was deeply involved in that Glasgow land-fraud case. I'm going to expose him by showing how they changed the sale price on the warrants and falsified the dates. Why, they've stolen almost a sixth of the state of Tennessee."

Rachel was shocked: wasn't this the same affair in which Stockly had been involved several years before?

"Andrew, won't people accuse you of doing it for political purposes, to defeat Sevier in the election? Can't Governor Roane be re-elected without this exposure?"

"No. Sevier is too good an actor. He'll stump the state with that saber rattling at his side and relive the thirty battles he won during the War for Independence."

And he'll win, Rachel thought. His group will come into power again, and Andrew's group will go out. If he wants to stay on the Bench, they'll defeat him.

But she found herself unprepared for the clamor caused by Andrew's accusing letter in the Tennessee *Gazette* of July 27, 1803. Everyone in the state read it or had it read to him; and they discussed with equal avidity Sevier's defense in the *Gazette* of August 8. Andrew left Hunter's Hill to hold court in Jonesboro, took ill on the way and was so racked by diarrhea he was hardly able to remain on his horse. He had no sooner reached the inn than a mob of Sevierites threatened to tar and feather him. Andrew stood with both pistols cocked. The crowd saw "Shoot!" in his eyes; it melted away.

The contest was no longer between two governors; people now asked, "Who are you siding with, Sevier or Jackson?" A few weeks later they elected Sevier by a full one-third majority.

"Who do you suppose had the worst time," Rachel asked Jane, "the Christians who were in the Coliseum being devoured by lions, or their sympathizers in the stands, watching them be devoured?"

"The sympathizers," replied Jane; "they had to wake up the next morning and remember what they had seen the day before."

I'm in an even worse position, thought Rachel; I feel as if I were in the catacombs . . . waiting my turn . . .

On Saturday, October 1, 1803, after the adjournment of his court, Andrew made his way toward the front door of the Knoxville courthouse. In the sunshine he saw John Sevier standing on the top step with a crowd below him. Before he could turn away he heard Sevier say:

"Judge Jackson is an abandoned rascal, a man whom the people have made a judge and thereby promoted to the unmerited status of a gentleman." He shook his cavalry saber in its scabbard, then continued, "I won independence for this state, I drove out the Indians, I formed your first government . . ."

Andrew strode to the top of the steps; he stood face to face with the fifty-eight-year-old Sevier.

"I do not contest your past services to the state of Tennessee, Governor. But by the same token I believe that I have performed public services too, and most of them have met with the approval of my fellow citizens."

"Services?" cried Sevier in a thunderous voice which carried to the other end of the public square. "I know of no great service you have rendered to the country except taking a trip to Natchez with another man's wife!"

Murder sprang into Andrew's eyes.

"Great God! Do you mention *her* sacred name?"

Sevier drew his sword. Andrew swung his heavy walking stick. Shots were fired in the crowd. A bystander was hurt. Friends intervened, carrying Andrew off in one direction and Sevier in another.

Andrew instantly challenged Sevier to a duel.

The remark made by Charles Dickinson had been uttered by an irresponsible young man who had been drinking and who later had denied having made it. But this charge by Governor Sevier in a public square could never be denied or retracted. The passage of the years would not matter now; the length or extent of Andrew's service, or her own years of hard work, simple living, of neighborly kindliness would never wash away the sin of having lived a troubled youth.

For Governor Sevier had accused them before the world of wanton, deliberate adultery . . . John Sevier was the best-known and most influential man in Tennessee; as governor of the state he was its first citizen. If it were acceptable for him to heap calumny upon her character, what reason would there be for anyone, ever, to keep silent on the subject of Rachel and Andrew Jackson? Her personal life had become a political weapon.

When the ache had passed into a pulsating numbness her thoughts returned to Knoxville and to Andrew. The illegality of dueling in Tennessee would not stop him; the two men would meet across the border of the Indian country. The governor of the state, and a member of the Supreme Court, dueling on the frontier; what further scandal this would create!

Travelers and friends came in from Knoxville bringing news. Sevier had ignored Andrew's first challenges, confiding to his friend that his advanced years and large family should make it unnecessary for him to satisfy Jackson's demand. When Andrew's friends urged him to drop the challenge out of respect for his judicial robes he offered to resign immediately. When Sevier failed to answer his challenge, he placed an advertisement in the *Gazette*.

To all who shall see these presents Greeting. Know ye that I Andrew Jackson, do pronounce, publish, and declare to the world, that his excellency John Sevier, Captain General, and commander in chief of the land and naval forces of the state of Tennessee, is a base coward and poltroon. He will basely insult but has not courage to repair.

ANDREW JACKSON

Andrew left with his seconds for Southwest Point on the Cherokee boundary. For five days he awaited Sevier's arrival . . . and for five days Rachel plodded through her tasks, dreading the news, yet unable to believe that the two men would seriously injure each other. Surely they had been friends too long to fire for a kill? Many duels were fought but few had serious consequences, at worst a leg wound; adversaries frequently fired into the air, their pent-up anger spent with the bullet,

At last word came: just as Andrew was leaving Southwest Point, Sevier rode up with his party. In the melee Andrew drew his pistols and so did Sevier, advancing on each other with epithets. Members of both parties made overtures, the principles damned each other still once again, but put up their arms.

It was the end of the duel. But not of the strife.

On November 5, Governor Sevier pushed two bills through the legislature, the first of which split the Tennessee militia into two districts; the other provided for a second major general, to have equal status with General Jackson. The next morning Governor Sevier appointed former Senator William Cocke head of the eastern division of the militia, and dispatched him to Natchez with five hundred militiamen to make sure that Spain did not interfere with the transfer of the Louisiana Purchase to the United States. After rigorously training his troops and bringing them to peak form, Major General Jackson had been left twiddling his thumbs at home, his men of the western division deprived of the mission for which they had prepared.

When Rachel walked into his study she found Andrew slumped in his chair, his arms dangling lifelessly to the floor, his face ashen and his usually clear, determined eyes lost in some obscure mist. She had seen him through all manner of complication, adversity and despair, but she had never seen him so completely beaten. What disturbed her most was not that there were no words on his lips, but actually that there were no words being formulated anywhere in his brain. The final victory had been Sevier's; the ultimate defeat Andrew's . . . and hers.

13

On New Year's Day of 1804 they sat alone in their big room before a banked fire. It took no complicated profit-and-loss system or surrounding pile of ledgers for them to know where they stood after their years at Hunter's Hill. They had extended considerable credit at their stores, but a drive to collect the money owed them had been fruitless. The furs and pelts, salt, wheat, tobacco and other merchandise he took in exchange in the stores had been shipped out blind, for he could no longer get prices quoted in advance, and when the merchandise reached the port of New Orleans, or Philadelphia, it was sold for whatever it could bring. Most of the cotton crop in the Cumberland Valley had failed; there were now twenty cotton gins operating in the countryside, and Andrew was getting little outside cotton for processing or sale. In addition he had been obliged to bring suit against his former partner, Thomas Watson. His personal notes were piling up in New Orleans and Philadelphia, with the interest charges mounting; and he had the immediate obligation of paying back one thousand dollars in cash which had been loaned to him in Pittsburgh.

"There's no help for it, Rachel, I simply must resign the judgeship and devote my full time to getting us straightened out financially. Money, money, money! The deeper we get into business, the larger our stocks and transactions and sales, the worse off we become."

"Ah, the agonies of getting rich," she replied in a light tone; but he was not to be diverted.

Though he still held the title of major general, his command had virtually disappeared. Many of the officers were blaming him for being robbed of their expedition. It also was apparent that he had lost considerable prestige as the result of the personal feuds. The fact that he had quarreled only after his wife had been publicly slandered was lost in the ensuing embroilment.

Because of the investigation his charges against Sevier had started, the title to a considerable portion of their own lands, particularly those in the Indian country, had fallen under a shadow. All of their lands around Nashville were worth more than when he had bought them, and he should have been able to take a sufficient profit to quiet his most demanding creditors; but no one had any cash with which to buy and all he could get were other people's personal notes.

"It looks almost hopeless," he confessed in complete dejection. "We've got to get a fresh start."

She was shocked to learn a few weeks later that his "fresh start" might include shaking the dust of Tennessee from his boots.

"I think we've had enough of the Cumberland Valley, Rachel."

"But where would we go?"

"Now that Louisiana has been turned over to us, President Jefferson has to appoint a governor. Our congressmen in Washington are on my side; they think I have the proper qualifications: the legal training to help write and enforce the laws, the military experience to set up a militia. It's a great opportunity. Spain is angry at the transfer and she'll fight if she can. England is still searching our ships and impressing seamen; if war comes she will bring her troops in through Louisiana just as sure as she will go through the northern lakes . . ."

What an odd solution to our problems, she thought; Thomas Green urged us to stay right there in Natchez in the first place. How much turbulence might have been avoided; how pleasant life might have been.

". . . as governor, everything would be provided: a home, servants, carriages, military staff, and the salary would be clear cash." He came to her and took her in his arms; his voice was low and caressing. " . . . I remember how much you loved those beautiful homes in Natchez. We'd meet new people, make new friends. There'll be plenty of opportunity for a military man down there; we'll make Sevier eat his words about us."

It was not until this moment that she saw clearly why he wanted to go: to leave behind them the incessant talk, the insults to their love and marriage. It was not that he felt defeated, nor that he lacked the stamina to fight back; he had all these requisites and more. He was simply removing his wife from the battlefield.

She took his head between her hands and pressed her lips to his; she felt the tense bony strength of him.

"You'll be the First Lady of the territory," he murmured, "Remember what I told you at Poplar Grove? We've got to get to the top, then no one will be able to climb up high enough to attack us."

There was no word from Washington about the appointment during February. A load of iron which he had ordered from Pittsburgh and which was supposed to constitute half a cargo was sent on alone; when it arrived in Nashville the boatman demanded three hundred and seventy-five dollars for freightage in cash. Andrew tried for days to collect enough to release the cargo, but could not gather anything beyond the little pile of English, Spanish and American coins which John Coffee dumped onto their dining board, obviously his lifetime savings, and the few dollars that John Overton found himself able to contribute.

"Think of it, Rachel: we own a plantation worth ten thousand dollars. We have thousands of dollars' worth of merchandise in the stores, and other thousands already shipped north and south. The total value of all the lands in our name must be a hundred thousand dollars . . . yet after trying desperately for a full week to find three hundred and seventy-five dollars in cash, I cannot raise that insignificant sum."

"Can't you make a quick sale of the iron and use part of the payment for the freight?"

"I've already tried. The only 'ready' available is the two hundred dollars due me in judge's salary."

Toward the end of February, in an effort to recoup their losses by one bold stroke he instructed John Coffee to make the trip north to the Illinois where a fabulous salt lick had been discovered, and to offer fifteen thousand dollars, if necessary as high as thirty thousand, for it . . . in their personal notes.

Rachel was staggered by the move, even though Jax accepted the instructions without question; how could Andrew be planning to spend another fifteen to thirty thousand dollars when he couldn't raise three hundred and seventy-five dollars to cover a freight charge?

During the next weeks her amazement grew. By that time Andrew had gone to Washington City en route to Philadelphia. The Secretary of War received him in a friendly spirit, confiding to him that the War Department would need two boats built within the next six weeks, to be used in the transportation of troops down the Mississippi. The Secretary also wanted chains for the ferryboats across the Tennessee River; could Andrew provide them?

John Coffee brought Andrew's letter up to Hunter's Hill where Rachel read it a dozen times, shaking her head in disbelief.

"A fabulous man, my husband. The War Department wants boats? He'll build them. They want chains? He'll make them. I'm sure he hasn't ten dollars in his pocket, nor are there more than ten dollars in our strong-box. That's either magnificent folly or magnificent wisdom. Which do you think Jax?"

"Must be wisdom, Mrs. Jackson," Coffee replied with a slow smile, "because when Mr. Jackson orders me to repair the boat that was damaged at the mouth of the Spring Branch, and have a second one ready in six weeks, he knows I'm going to have them ready. When things got to be done, money's no help, it only gets in your way."

"Surely if Andrew provides these boats, the Secretary of War will let him fill them with his own troops and command the expedition?"

"Couldn't say, Mrs. Jackson; it seems likely."

She did not know when Andrew received the news, but one of the Philadelphia papers brought her the account of President Jefferson's appointment of William C. C. Claiborne as governor of Louisiana. Andrew's scheme of flight, of creating a new life for them, the rebuilding of his pride and prestige, had gone the way of most political appointments. They would have to stay home now and cope with their difficulties as best they could.

14

Andrew reached Hunter's Hill on June 19. They both knew that they would have to sell everything they owned for whatever price they could get. Andrew gazed lovingly at the pianoforte and the walnut desk.

"We'll keep those for our new home," she said.

"What new home?"

"Wherever we are going. Where are we going?"

"I don't know. There are one or two tracts we might save, that Hermitage land, for instance, across the river."

"What's it like?"

"Well, it's a fine piece of land, gently rolling, with abundant springs. There are beautiful trees, one cleared field. I bought it from Robert Hays's brother. The deed hasn't even been recorded yet."

"And a house? Is there a house on it, Andrew?"

"No, just an old blockhouse that was turned into a trading post. Hasn't been used for years. And a couple of smaller cabins close by."

"Could we go see it?"

He ran his hand through his hair, traced the boniness of his face and laid his palms across his troubled eyes.

"I can't move you there. It hurts . . . my pride. A crude, half-decayed cabin on a wild piece of land, just as though we were . . . poor settlers. How low I've brought you."

She stood before him, her feet anchored firmly, determination in her soft brown eyes and in her low musical voice as she said:

"Andrew, ask George to saddle our horses."

After crossing the Stone River they rode for two miles, then took a trail that curved around a burnt summer meadow. Andrew told her she was now on the Hermitage land. They walked their horses through a cool stand of hickory, soon coming upon a bubbling spring and a branch which ran into the adjoining woods. Close by were a group of four log cabins, shaded by catalpa trees. They dismounted.

She stood for a moment before the former trading post. It was already a number of years old but the men who had constructed it had done an expert job: the logs were well matched, the notches evenly cut. There was a look of sturdiness about the two-storied, almost square building, an appearance of pride and independence.

"Could we go in, darling?"

He lifted the heavy leather latch and stood aside for her to enter. She walked in, the sun streaming over her shoulder. It was a single room, twenty-four feet wide and twenty-six feet long; the puncheon floor was as clean as though someone had broomed it the night before. The logs had been fitted with a master mechanic's skill, and the passage of the years had polished them to a high sheen, a luminous silver-gray which threw light upward, illuminating the massive beams. The mortar between the logs had mellowed to the same shade of warm silver. She walked to the fieldstone fireplace which could consume a cord of wood on a cold day; the stones had been selected with care and shared in the silver-gray luminosity of the rest of the room. She stood before the fireplace, deeply moved.

"Andrew, it's beautiful."

"It's just a log cabin, like all the others . . ."

"Oh no, my dear, it's not like any of the others. That name, Hermitage, doesn't it mean . . . a place of refuge?"

BOOK FOUR

1

At the end of August 1804 they wound their way down the hill, Andrew in the lead wagon, Rachel in the carriage transporting their personal possessions, silver, clothing, linens; with Moll, George and the Negro families they had retained following with the dishes, cooking utensils, farm equipment and stores; the livestock was shepherded at the rear. Hunter's Hill had been sold with all its furnishings except the big four-poster in which they had slept since returning from their honeymoon at Bayou Pierre, the pianoforte Andrew had brought her from Philadelphia, the clock and desk inherited from her parents, the bookcases and books from Andrew's study.

That afternoon Rachel stood in the center of her big room, amidst the blanket-wrapped furniture, surveying her domain. At hand were Andrew, Samuel, John Overton and John Coffee ready to set things where she directed. After sending the heavy bed upstairs, she had the men place against the right wall the brocade satin settee which had arrived direct from Philadelphia, and facing it three mahogany chairs. This would be the sitting room. Along the back wall of the big room she placed her pianoforte, Andrew's music rack and flute; this would be the music room; and farther down the same wall Andrew's desk, and behind it the bookshelves for his books. In the corner by the settee she stood the big clock from the Donelson dining room; before the fireplace she left room for the dining-room table and chairs which they did not yet have. She had not curtained the windows because Andrew had promised to triple their size. Moll and George had set the gleaming copper and iron pots on the hooks by the fireplace and were cooking the first dinner at the Hermitage.

"What's the date today?" asked Rachel. "I want to note it down in my calendar. August twenty-fifth? Why Samuel, it's your little Andy's fourth birthday. You ride right over home now, get Polly and the three youngsters, and we'll celebrate our move-in supper and Andy's birthday at the same time."

Samuel was pleased; he went off at once for his family, returning before dark. It was eight years since their marriage, but golden-haired Polly of the symmetrical figure, laughing blue eyes and vivacious spirit was prettier and merrier than ever,

Rachel propped Andy high up on pillows at the end of the long boards which they had set up for a table. The boy was such a close reproduction of Samuel, and hence of herself, as to be almost a caricature: smooth olive skin and round face, with its slightly plump chin, warm, sensitive brown eyes and thick head of black hair, worn low on his neck. Rachel managed to rustle up a few presents, Andrew opened a bottle of his best French wine and everybody drank to long life and good fortune for the youngster and the new home.

374

The effect of the retrogression in the Jackson fortunes, of Andrew's resigning his judgeship and taking himself out of politics, was immediate: friends were sorry they had met with reverses, enemies were glad they had got their comeuppance. After everyone had said, "You know that the Jacksons had to sell Hunter's Hill and move into an abandoned store over on the Hermitage?" all interest vanished. To Rachel this was God's most beneficent gift; she had an instinct for measuring how much talk was going on about them. From the moment she moved into the Hermitage she found the air sweet and good.

Their expenses and responsibilities at the Hermitage were cut to a negligible fraction; although Hunter's Hill had been difficult to sell because of the omnipresent lack of cash, an old acquaintance by the name of Colonel Ward had advanced five thousand dollars in Virginia currency which had enabled Andrew to meet his most pressing debts. He became easygoing, full of laughter and good will, and had an inner quietude. He avoided the more rabid Sevier clique in Nashville, in particular young Charles Dickinson, but recaptured many of the friends he had alienated during the late quarrels. His chief pleasure was fixing up the Hermitage as Rachel wanted it, putting in big window lights in the main house and guest cabins, building a springhouse and buttery. Late each afternoon when his work was finished in the fields, or in the newly planted peach and apple orchards, or at the office-cabin he had built for himself just below the house, he would come to the door and call for her and they would walk hand in hand across their gently rolling land, stopping to inspect the trees and meadows and to follow the brook which flowed from their copious spring.

Occasionally on a warm morning during the colorful fall and the unusually mild winter they rode their horses into Nashville. In the evenings they sat before the fire, reading, had dinner with John Overton at Travellers Rest, or entertained themselves by playing duets. To Rachel it seemed as though ten heavy years had fallen off Andrew's shoulders; and when he had the opportunity to buy a race horse he had long admired, Indian Queen, and won his first race with her for a hundred-dollar side bet, he looked once again like the twenty-two-year-old boy she remembered standing at the front door of the Donelsons', asking if he might be taken in.

"I'm going to build a stable around Indian Queen," he told her.

"Of wood, or of race horses?"

"Both. I've already picked a site where they will have good grazing and plenty of water. By the way, I hear that the Anderson brothers don't have enough money to finish their racecourse in Clover Bottom."

They were standing on a knoll of the Hermitage lands which commanded a view of their little group of cabins. She caught the note of excitement in his voice.

"And we do!"

"Are you encouraging me to buy? You're supposed to be the conservative member of our family."

"I'm only conservative when it comes to making money. When it comes to making fun I'm as radical as any man who signed the Declaration. One of the first things you ever told me you wanted was blooded horses and a racecourse of your own; I think we ought to try to get the things we want originally, instead of all the ones that crop up along the road that we have no real use or desire for."

He gathered her up and kissed her quickly, delighted with her approval.

With the privacy in their lives and the constant companionship, their love flowered fresh and vital; she felt almost as though they were just married and had moved into their first home here on the Hermitage. She found herself adding a bow to the neckline of her dress, an ornament in her hair, an extra row of eyelet-hole embroidery to her nightcap. When Andrew walked to the wall which separated their bedroom from the small room beyond and, rapping on it with his knuckles, said, "I could take this wall down if you like, and give us a really large bedroom," she became suddenly aware that she had been guarding this little room next to her own. She

was in robust health, just thirty-seven, and only the other day she had heard of
Thomas Hutchings' cousin who had borne her first baby at thirty-nine. The hope
she had imagined to be extinguished would never die.

"Could we leave it . . . for a while, anyway?"

"Oh sure, it was just for your pleasure."

At the beginning of March, while she was working in front of the house preparing
the garden she had planned all winter, she saw a rough emigrant wagon coming
down the trail, escorted by a procession of silent horsemen. At the rear she recognized
John Coffee, slouched over in the saddle, his head down. He spurred his horse,
dismounted and asked quickly:

"Where is Mr. Jackson?"

"In his office. What has happened, Jax?"

"Please let me get Mr. Jackson."

His long strides ate up the twenty feet separating the house from Andrew's cabin.
None of the riders dismounted, or met Rachel's eyes. Andrew came running, took
her by the arm and led her into the house.

"Darling, it's . . . Samuel."

She could only stammer, "Sam . . . Samuel . . . but what . . . ?"

Andrew looked at Coffee supplicatingly. The big fellow said as gently as he
could, "A surveyor friend of mine . . . found him . . . quite a few miles out on
the trail. We don't know how long he had been there . . . or what happened."

"But he isn't . . . Jax, Samuel's not dead!"

"I'm afraid he is. Shot. We don't know how, or why. He's been dead for at
least twenty-four hours."

Andrew lifted her, in a state of shock, onto the settee, and covered her with a
warm quilt. Samuel, her closest and dearest brother. She had known it would be
Samuel of all her seven brothers who would make the long trip to Harrodsburg for
her. She saw before her now the pained concern in his warm brown eyes as he
brought her down the Kentucky Road toward home. He had been so happy with
the law, and his Polly and their three beautiful boys.

Samuel was buried the following day, next to his mother. They never learned
who had shot him, nor even what he was doing out on that remote trail. His death
was like their father's. Polly returned to her parents' home, but asked Rachel if
she would like to take Andy to the Hermitage. The little room beside their bedroom
was quickly furnished for him. He was a frolicsome boy, quick to laughter as well
as tears, with a winning smile and a bright mind. His arrival filled the Jackson
home with movement and play; and filled Rachel's heart with the kind of love for
which she had yearned.

She and Andrew would take Andy upstairs to bed, kiss him good night and watch
him fall asleep with the suddenness of a rock dropped into a pond.

"The room is filled," she said softly, "and with a child. But hardly in the way
I wanted or anticipated." After a pause she asked, "Andrew, do you think we
could keep Andy . . . raise him as our own son?"

Andrew put his arm around her shoulders.

"I'd be most willing. We'll speak to Polly."

2

Andrew officially purchased a two-third interest in the Anderson racecourse; John
Coffee, who had become a partner in the Jackson, Hutchings store at Clover Bottom,
put up his personal notes for the other third. Andrew was wild with joy.

"We'll build a tavern and stalls for farmers and merchants who come on racing days. And when we learn how to train the fastest horses, there's money to be made on the betting."

Work was resumed at once on the beautiful meadow with the rising hill on which a large crowd could stand and watch the races. Early each morning, after Rachel and Andy had breakfasted together, they walked to the corral to see Andrew train Indian Queen. In the afternoons they rode over to Clover Bottom, the boy on a white pony, where Andrew was dividing his time between the building of the tavern and timing the young jockey, Billey Phillips, for he had already added a number of quarter horses and fast mares to their stable.

The spring races had already been scheduled for Hartsville, but by fall they were to inaugurate the Clover Bottom course. At the end of April Indian Queen was to run against Greyhound, Lazarus Cotton's champion gelding. Andrew bet a thousand dollars in notes on Indian Queen to win. They set out for Hartsville the day before, since the thirty miles by carriage would take eight or nine hours, even though they crossed the river at Hendersonville on Hubbard Saunders' ferry. The road led through level valleys of pasture, grainfields and young orchards, crossed shallow creeks whose clear water flowed over pebbly beds, and then climbed the grass-covered uplands.

There was a large crowd gathered by the time the Jackson carriage reached the course. Rachel bet everything she had on Indian Queen, then wagered her pair of gloves against the walking stick of Lazarus Cotton, owner of Greyhound. Theirs was not the important race of the day; the big one came later when Greyhound was to race against Truxton, one of the most famous horses out of Virginia; nevertheless, interest was high in the Jackson entry. Suddenly, seeing their rather small mare against the famous Greyhound, Rachel had her first doubts.

"Are you sure Indian Queen can win?"

"Now, don't worry," said Andrew. "All Greyhound is going to see of that Queen is the dust coming up from her hind hoofs."

But it was Indian Queen who ate dust the first time around the track; and if the second time around she ate no dust, it was because it had already settled.

"Think of the fun we've had training her," Rachel said consolingly as she saw Andrew's disappointment. "It was worth every cent we lost."

It was Greyhound's day; the big gelding went on to beat Truxton as handily as he had Indian Queen. In the din she heard Andrew saying against her ear:

"Let's go round to the stables."

Truxton was an enormous bay stallion with white feet. Andrew put his arms up slowly, bringing the horse's head down onto his shoulder.

"This is the greatest horse I've ever seen on a racecourse. He should have beaten Greyhound."

"Why didn't he?"

"Because he was poorly trained. If I could take him home to the Hermitage with us for one month, he would beat Greyhound by ten lengths."

"But Andrew, he's not our horse . . ."

"You wouldn't like to place a small bet on that, would you, Mrs. Jackson? There's his owner coming toward us now; have you ever seen an unhappier man?"

Mr. Verell approached his horse with reluctance. "I had everything I owned on him, and quite a lot of money I didn't have. They'll be seizing Truxton for debt, twelve hundred dollars' worth."

"I'll make you a fair offer, Mr. Verell: I'll assume that debt and pay you three geldings in addition, worth over three hundred dollars. If Truxton wins an important race for me this year, I'll pay you two geldings as a bonus."

"That is indeed a fair offer, Mr. Jackson. I'll take it."

Andrew's eyes sparkled with excitement. Rachel saw him snap his head as he made a fast decision. He turned to the crowd clustered in front of Greyhound's stall.

"Mr. Cotton, I've just bought Truxton. I have five thousand dollars' side money says he can beat your Greyhound one month from today on this same course."

Rachel gasped; five thousand dollars! In paper, of course, like the land sales; but even so it was a lot of money. She heard Mr. Cotton say:

"Done! June twelfth, right here. Five thousand, side bet!"

The month that intervened was the most hectic they had ever known. There was considerable plowing and seeding to be done at the Hermitage, but the better part of their time was spent at Clover Bottom working with Truxton. The horse had power and speed; the one thing he lacked was stamina.

"That's because they treated him too delicately," Andrew explained, "They were afraid to work him hard for fear of exhausting him. We'll get him trimmed down until there's nothing left but pure fighting horse."

Rachel turned to Andy who was standing beside her.

"Truxton doesn't know it yet," she said, "but your Uncle Andrew has just inducted him into the militia."

Toward the end of May Andrew rode into Nashville to preside over a dinner being given for Aaron Burr, whose term as vice-president of the United States had recently been concluded, and to bring him back to the Hermitage. He rode his finest horse into town, taking along a milk-white mare for Colonel Burr. Rachel went about preparing the largest of her three guest cabins. As she worked with young Mitty, replenishing the candles and soap and putting a number of the latest journals on the table, she knew that Colonel Burr would be considered the most important visitor, socially, to have come to Nashville. She had an uneasy feeling that if Colonel Burr rode to the isolation of the Hermitage straight from the Nashville dinner, their newly acquired peace might be strained.

Returning to the main cabin she stood looking at the long, highly polished dining-room table of cherry wood and the dozen curved-back chairs that had arrived only a few days before. What if she were to give a dinner party for Colonel Burr the following Sunday, inviting a number of Andrew's friends and a few of the less rabid Sevierites? It might be a good idea to include as well Mr. and Mrs. Somerset Phariss, and Miss Daisy Deson.

In the midafternoon she and Andy went out to gather dogwood, forsythia and violets for the cabin; as they walked among the blossoms she thought of the strange career of the man who would shortly be her guest. Colonel Burr had been a resourceful commanding officer in the Revolutionary War; Andrew was not disturbed by the fact that he had been sent down from General Washington's staff and was frequently in conflict with his superior officers. He had been a brilliant and prosperous lawyer in New York, then United States senator during the time Andrew had been in the House, when the two men had first become acquainted. Rising from comparative obscurity to become Thomas Jefferson's running mate in the 1800 election, he had half destroyed his political career by allowing the House to wrangle and vote for days as to who should be president. The previous July he had shot and killed Alexander Hamilton, first Secretary of the Treasury, in a duel in Weehawken, been indicted by the state of New Jersey for murder, and obliged to flee south. However he had returned to Washington at the beginning of the year to finish out his term as presiding officer of the Senate. The chief topic of conversation in the days preceding his arrival had been:

"What is Aaron Burr doing in Nashville?"

Andrew and the colonel reached home at dusk. Rachel was surprised to find Burr a small man, slight of form; yet he was a striking figure, holding himself with military erectness and superb poise. She thought him handsome, with dramatically curved eyebrows, all-consuming jet-black eyes, a sensuous mouth and slender oval face that looked as though it had been carved out of pale ivory. His full sideburns had a fringe of pure white, making him seem older than his forty-nine years. Though she was captivated immediately by the warmth and enveloping quality of his voice, she thought she detected, in the first moment of their meeting, a touch of bitterness.

Sunday dawned clear and warm. By one o'clock when the first guests began arriving, a refreshing breeze was stirring the branches of the catalpa trees. The servants, dressed in immaculate white, circulated with trays of sherry for the ladies; the men gathered about Andrew's liquor chest, plunging at once into a discussion of politics. Rachel wore a filmy pale pink batiste, and her eyes glowed with excitement; both Mrs. Phariss and Daisy Deson had considered her invitation an important one: they were richly gowned in silk and lace, with brilliant fans and very large hats.

Rachel had spent a number of uneasy hours on her menu, then realized that she was being foolish: she would offer the same simple and abundant hospitality that she had begun in Poplar Grove and which actually had changed little in character whether dispensed in a one-room log cabin or a large and beautiful mansion. The guests had barely finished their appetizer when she knew that this was going to be the most successful dinner party she would ever give. She watched Colonel Burr with the gratitude of a hostess who senses that her guest of honor has the entire table entranced, for Aaron Burr's magnetism leaped out to capture everyone. John Overton turned to her and said softly:

"The colonel has the most agile mind I've ever encountered."

Colonel Burr in turn complimented Judge Overton on the recording of his decisions, telling him this would be the beginning of codified law in Tennessee. Colonel Burr expressed himself with utter clarity on any subject, his voice captivated everyone who came within its aura as a beautiful woman does with a subtle perfume. Jane Hays tipped Rachel the tiniest wink from the end of the table, while Robert Hays accepted eagerly when Colonel Burr offered to take their seventeen-year-old son Stockly to New Orleans and train him for the law. The color stood high on Daisy Deson's cheeks.

Yet underneath Aaron Burr's charm and brilliance she thought she perceived . . . could it be? . . . death? But surely this was only because the blood of Alexander Hamilton was still so fresh on his hands? Old General Robertson, who had accepted her invitation reluctantly, said as much.

The most important part of Colonel Burr's talks with Andrew had concerned the Spanish in Florida and Texas: Andrew and his guest agreed that they must be ejected. Rachel had assumed that this was the answer to Colonel Burr's future: he was heading south to investigate the situation in Florida and prepare the way for American occupation. However, as he now talked to the various people around the dinner table she became a bit confused: to Mr. Phariss, who was interested in new settlements in the South, he intimated that the purpose of his present trip was to recruit settlers for a colony on the Ouachita River in Louisiana; to John Overton's brother Thomas, who had only recently settled in the Cumberland, he dropped a hint that one of the purposes of his trip was to prepare for the invasion of Texas; to Thomas Eastin, editor of the Nashville *Impartial Review*, he intimated that he was on unofficial business for the United States government, preparatory to taking over the governorship of Louisiana.

Andrew enjoyed himself thoroughly, and was particularly pleased when Colonel Burr assured him his wines were as fine as any he himself had served. For Rachel the day was successful because the Culture Club ladies had been enchanted with the colonel.

It's so easy this way, she thought. Why didn't I do it before?

3

It was hot the mid-June morning the Jackson caravan started for the Hartsville course. Rachel took her beautiful thirteen-year-old niece Rachel Hays with her and her nephew Sandy Donelson. Andy sat on John Coffee's lap; in a dozen other carriages were their friends from the neighborhood who had wagered everything on Truxton that could conceivably serve as a medium of exchange.

But when they reached the racecourse, jammed with a thousand spectators, she found that only their particular group had any faith in Truxton. Andrew plunged deeper and deeper; he bet the equivalent of fifteen hundred dollars in wearing apparel, and a number of his best six-forties. When the wife of one of the Greyhound backers said to Rachel:

"I understand Mr. Jackson has Truxton so exhausted the poor horse may not be able to run the whole course," Rachel caught the fever and replied:

"I'll wager my carriage and matched horses against yours, Mrs. Sitgreaves, that you've been listening to the wrong judges of horseflesh."

At last Truxton and Greyhound were led to the starting line. Andrew's face was pale under the bushy red-orange hair, his eyes the deepest blue she had ever remembered them.

"I just had a brief talk with Truxton."

"And what is the latest word from the horse's mouth?"

"He says not to worry about his being overtrained."

"I think it's us who are overtrained: if we lose we are going to have to walk home."

"In our long underwear," he agreed. "But if we win, I'll get back all of my grandfather's legacy that I lost in Charleston."

"Andrew, I'm happy." She folded her hands in her lap and looked up at him serenely from under the beribboned bonnet that cast a warm light on her olive skin. "I like to win because it's more fun that way, but if we lose we don't lose anything important."

The crowd suddenly went still, then the starter gave the signal. Greyhound took an immediate lead, setting a killing pace, though it was not too much of a margin as they came down the stretch after the first time around the course. Rachel turned to Andrew questioningly. Andrew, who was sitting tense but quiet, said:

"We're letting Greyhound set the pace. Wait till they round the curve."

The horses began the long straightaway opposite the spectators. Truxton seemed literally to shoot through the air, his flying hoofs making a continuous white blur against the landscape. He finished a full twenty lengths ahead of a thoroughly tired Greyhound.

"Too bad the race wasn't three times around the track," gloated Andrew, "that poor overtrained turf nag of ours would have passed Greyhound a second time."

She said impulsively, "Now Andrew, be charitable in your victory."

"Oh, I'll be charitable," he cried; "in fact I'm even going to give Lazarus Cotton a chance to recoup his losses by selling me Greyhound. Let's go back to the stables. He can be had mighty cheap right now."

Greyhound was bought for only a portion of their day's winnings. Rachel sold back to Mrs. Sitgreaves her carriage and horses at a modest figure so there would be no hard feelings. When they added their winnings the sum was sufficient to pay off the remainder of their indebtedness in Philadelphia. Rachel considered it ironic that after having worked very hard for so many years and rarely been out from under a burden of debt, their retirement had made them prosperous. Andrew set out to travel the state looking for a dozen more horses to add to his stable.

Captain Joseph Erwin, who owned two of the fastest racers in the West, Tanner and Ploughboy, posted notice that he would run Tanner against any horse in the world at the opening meet at Clover Bottom for a five-thousand-dollar side bet. Andrew accepted the challenge for Greyhound. Rachel heard about it with regret, for Captain Erwin was Charles Dickinson's father-in-law, and Mr. Dickinson had half his father-in-law's bet.

After a summer of training, Greyhound beat Tanner in three straight one-mile heats. It was a gala day for the Jacksons, who now owned not only the finest string of race horses in Tennessee but also its finest course. To Rachel's intense relief Captain Erwin took his defeat gracefully, paying the five-thousand-dollar bet, while Andrew's tavern, crowded for several days before the big race, dispensed free cider and ginger cakes.

Captain Erwin made only one request, that Andrew give him a return match at the end of November, this time with Ploughboy. The side bet was to be two thousand dollars, and eight hundred dollars in forfeit money to be paid if either withdrew from the race. Andrew accepted the match for Truxton. Charles Dickinson again had half his father-in-law's bet, and also was half owner of Ploughboy.

When the hour arrived for Truxton and Ploughboy to go to the post, Captain Erwin announced that Ploughboy had gone lame and that he would pay the eight hundred dollars. Rachel waited in her carriage while Andrew went back to the stables to collect the forfeit. Considerable time elapsed before he returned, his face the color of the red earth around Nashville.

"Why, Andrew, what's happened?"

"Something strange; the captain is too honorable to have done it intentionally . . ."

"Done what?"

"Well, you know we agreed on a list of notes to be used for payment, all notes due and payable on demand. However Captain Erwin offered me paper that's not due until next January. I told him I had to have half the forfeiture in due notes, as I had agreed to give that much to the trainer, who is leaving Nashville . . ."

"But you settled everything amiably?" Her voice was anxious. "You and Captain Erwin have known each other for a good many years."

Andrew hesitated for a moment, then spoke to the driver. They started on the way home.

"Charles Dickinson stepped in and offered his own due notes for four hundred dollars."

Two days after the forfeit, Thomas Overton rode out to the Hermitage. They heard him come riding up with the breakneck speed of a courier from Washington City, and went to the door of the springhouse where they were turning their cloth-wrapped cheeses.

"Why is he always in such a desperate hurry?" Rachel asked.

"It's his way of creating excitement."

Thomas was the exact opposite of John, his younger brother: redfaced, heavy-built, a hairy man with bristling rust-colored eyebrows, a beard which began just under the circle of his eyes, and an enormously thick head of rust-brown hair. He had been a valuable officer in the Revolution, and a general in the North Carolina militia: a fierce fighting man who became restive and unhappy when there was nothing to fight about. The Jacksons were hard pressed to understand how he could be John's blood brother.

"That has always puzzled Thomas too," John once told them wistfully; "but the answer is really a simple one: growing up in his shadow I developed an organic dislike of loud voices and bellicose arguments."

Thomas flung himself out of the saddle to the ground.

"What's the hurry?" asked Andrew with a laugh.

"Hurry! I'm already two days late. John gave me this message to deliver to you at the racecourse two days ago; then the race wasn't run, and I hung around the tavern . . . Guess Dickinson did too. He's a loose talker when he's imbibed too much . . .''

Rachel sat down on the edge of the cheese press, thinking, It's going to start all over again. That first time he attacked us it was because we won the militia election; now it's because we won a horse race.

"Was it something about the forfeit notes?" asked Andrew.

"No, it was something Mrs. Jackson said at the races."

Rachel jumped up.

"Something I said? But I never laid eyes on Mr. Dickinson . . .''

"It was when Captain Erwin announced Ploughboy couldn't run. Seems like you turned to your nephew Sandy Donelson and said, 'It's just as well, for Truxton would have left Ploughboy out of sight.'''

Rachel stared at Thomas in dread. He continued:

"One of Mr. Dickinson's friends heard what you said and repeated it to him. Dickinson shouted, 'Yes, about as far out of sight as Mrs. Jackson left her first husband when she ran away with the general.' Begging your pardon, Mrs. Jackson, ma'am . . .''

Rachel was shocked at how surely she had known what was coming. She flashed Andrew a look of despair.

"Oh, Andrew, this time the fault is mine. Why did I have to make such a prideful boast? It wasn't good manners on my part. I struck at Mr. Dickinson with my bragging words; and now he's struck back at me."

"Struck back is right: with a sharp-edged sword, a weapon of war."

"Apparently Mr. Dickinson is at war with us," she said helplessly. "But Andrew, I can't understand: what injury have we ever done him? Why does he hate us so?"

"It has nothing to do with you. It has only to do with his ambitions: he wants to become the political leader of Nashville, and he thinks I stand in his way."

"But you're no longer in politics, Andrew."

He made a ducking, deprecatory gesture of a shoulder.

"True. But I still have friends . . . and influence. Dickinson thinks I'm bad for Tennessee: that I'm a crude, ignorant backwoodsman who might have been all right in the days of the Indian raids, when the Cumberland Valley was still a wilderness, but that the state has now outgrown me and my kind; and we have to be put out of the way in order for Tennessee to become respected in Washington."

"He has actually said these things about you?" she asked, incredulous.

"Yes."

"And you have never confronted him with them?"

"No. He has a right to attack me politically."

She linked her arm through his.

"I'm proud of you, Andrew."

"Well, I'm not so proud of myself. I've kept the peace, but the only result seems to be that Mr. Dickinson is beginning to think me a coward. If I had stopped his talk earlier he would never have dared to bring up our marriage again. I wonder how many lives he thinks he has?"

The whole timbre of his voice had changed. She searched his face and saw that it was dark, his lips set firmly over the clenched teeth.

"Andrew, you won't fight him?"

He smoothed the worried lines in her forehead.

"No. I'm going to Captain Erwin's tonight and ask him to use his influence over his son-in-law. I'll tell the captain that I want no quarrel with Dickinson, and that he must stop trying to pick a quarrel with me."

She took his hand and held it against her cheek.

They rose early and prepared to receive company: Captain Erwin had promised he would bring his son-in-law out to the Hermitage that morning. Rachel thought how strange it was that she would now meet Charles Dickinson for the first time; how could it be that a man would set himself up as her mortal enemy without ever having laid eyes on her?

"I have great hopes for this meeting," she confided to Andrew; "I always think it difficult for people to hate each other once they have met and shaken hands."

She had been given many descriptions of Charles Dickinson by her friends and family: Dickinson was one of the best-looking men in the Cumberland Valley, with finely molded features and enormous eyes set wide apart; he was young, only twenty-seven, carried himself with a flashing poise, and even at this hour of the morning was immaculately garbed in royal-blue nankeens, an Irish-linen shirt and a handsome broad-brimmed hat. There had been stories of his excessive drinking, yet none of it showed on his smooth light skin.

It was apparent to Rachel that Mr. Dickinson had hated every foot of this journey out to the Hermitage, but it was also apparent that he would obey his father-in-law, a man half his size and twice his age, with a small mop of white hair standing straight up almost in the middle of his head, and twinkling eyes set deep under bony brows. Captain Erwin shook hands with Rachel, then turned to his son-in-law and said:

"May I present Mr. Charles Dickinson?"

Mr. Dickinson bowed low without looking at her. She had wanted to welcome him warmly, but the very remoteness of his bow made it impossible.

"Won't you sit down, gentlemen?" she asked. "You'll have a stirrup cup after your ride?"

Dickinson sat rigidly at the end of the settee, took the cup from Moll, touched it to his lips without drinking, then set it on the table beside him.

"Mr. and Mrs. Jackson, I have been accused of making a personal remark about you. I do not believe I passed that remark, for I have no memory of it. However, I had been drinking . . . Captain Erwin insists that I owe you an apology even if I can't remember having given offense. I herewith offer that apology."

How clear he had made it that he was offering this apology to satisfy his father-in-law. Andrew stood, legs apart, in front of the fireplace, his piercing blue eyes devouring every movement in the room. She waited for him to say something, but apparently he did not feel anything was expected of him. To fill the painful silence she said:

"Thank you, Mr. Dickinson; Mr. Jackson and I genuinely hope that we can be friends."

Mr. Dickinson rose. He advanced a few steps toward Andrew, then said in a cold voice:

"Mr. Jackson, I wish further to state that if I did make any derogatory remark, I was amply provoked."

"In what way, sir?"

"I have been informed that you accused Captain Erwin and myself of deliberate trickery over those forfeit notes."

"That is not true, Mr. Dickinson. I have known Captain Erwin for many years and consider him one of the most honest of men. I think the misunderstanding arose when Captain Erwin thought he had the right to pay the forfeit out of any notes of the stake, while as the winner I believed I had the right to choose the due notes. As for yourself, you did pay me in due notes."

Rachel felt chilled, as though the temperature had fallen twenty degrees. It was clear that Mr. Dickinson was not the slightest bit mollified by Andrew's explanation.

"I have it on excellent authority that you did make these statements."

"Then, sir, your informant told a damned lie. Who is he?"

"Thomas Swann, a friend of mine and a lawyer in Nashville."

"Very well, let us summon him."

"That I cannot do; it might lead Mr. Swann to think I want to throw the burden off my shoulders onto his."

Captain Erwin came to his son-in-law's side.

"Mr. and Mrs. Jackson accepted your apology even though you prefaced it by saying you did not believe you made the remark. Mr. Jackson now tells us that he merely said a different list of notes was offered by me, though not by you, and that he has never thought the difference in my list was premeditated. I think this amounts to the same kind of apology you proffered the Jacksons, and I for one am going to accept theirs. It behooves you to do the same."

He turned to Rachel, took her hand and smiled in the most friendly fashion.

"My wife and daughter are expecting us home."

When they left Rachel asked, "Who is this Thomas Swann?"

"One of Dickinson's toadies. He thinks that if he caters to the Dickinson crowd he can get some of their law work, maybe even a political office."

"Well, I'm glad it is settled."

4

She had underestimated the piercing power of trouble. Two days later Andrew received a letter from Thomas Swann telling him that Mr. Dickinson had informed him that Mr. Jackson had called him, Mr. Swann, a damned liar. Rachel read aloud:

"The harshness of this expression has deeply wounded my feelings; it is language to which I am a stranger, which no man acquainted with my character would venture to apply to me, and which I shall be under the necessity of taking proper notice of.

"I am, sir, Your obt. servt.,
"THOS. SWANN"

"Mr. Dickinson should not have gone to Thomas Swann with this," she said gently.

Andrew was angry, but this time stone-cold angry.

"I've suspected for a long time he does not want this quarrel ended, he wants it to continue and to grow. I shall answer Mr. Swann in a day or two."

She did not see the letter that Andrew sent to Thomas Swann but she knew it was aimed at Dickinson. When she heard that Charles Dickinson had departed on a flatboat voyage to Natchez she was relieved; but the next day a letter reached them which he evidently had written just before leaving. The last of it cut across her eyes with the sharpness of a sword's tip.

As to the word coward, I think it is as applicable to yourself as any one I know, and I shall be very glad when an opportunity serves to know in what manner you give your anodynes, and hope you will take in payment, one of my most moderate Cathartick.

Yours at Command,
CHARLES DICKINSON

She studied the words *anodyne* and *Cathartick*; all she could figure was that both words were being used as synonyms for ammunition. She hoped that Mr. Dickinson would have a long and pleasurable stay in Natchez, long enough to let this hopelessly tangled hullabaloo die down.

Rather, it grew apace. Andrew would no longer tell her the details, and she assembled the facts through her usual fragmentary sources. With Charles Dickinson gone, Thomas Swann was keeping the fire burning. He "demanded the satisfaction which as a gentleman he was entitled to receive." Andrew replied that if Swann challenged him he would be obliged to cane him. The next day Swann challenged; whereupon Andrew returned to Winn's Tavern and hit Swann over the shoulder with his cane.

Her consolation during these cold months was little Andy, who was now almost six. The weather was too raw to take him to school in town each day, so she undertook the teaching herself, training him from the same family arithmetic ledger and books from which she and Samuel had been instructed by their father. They walked a little each day, but the trees were bare and the earth heavy with rain. Everything was lying fallow. It was her frank opinion that the whole Swann dispute was due to the fact that they were in the deep of winter, with too little work that needed doing. She prayed for spring to come early, for the sun to get warm and the land to dry so that the men could throw their energies once again into their many tasks.

At this point General James Robertson, founder of the first settlement in the Cumberland, intervened. He was a solidly built man who stood with his head inclined a little forward, his white hair brushed down as a bang and cut square across his forehead. He was quiet, thoughtful, with forthright eyes, his once-fair skin darkened and reddened by exposure. He had been like a father to Andrew, backing him in the militia and helping Blount to push him along politically.

"Andrew, I've been watchin' you squabble with that young Tom Swann. I rode out here to beg you: don't fight."

"Swann's doing most of the fighting, General."

"Son, your courage and reputation don't require you to duel. If you lose your family suffers; if you win it will be a pyrrhic victory. Duelin's got to go, Andrew, it's nothing better than murder."

"There are times when dueling is justified."

"No, my boy." The general's hands were trembling a little, so he spread them out flat on the table before him to keep them still. "You can't take the life of a fellow mortal. If you kill young Swann, you might be miserable as long as you live . . . just like Aaron Burr. You know he was indicted for murder?"

"He will never be tried; but anyway I give you my word: under no circumstances will I duel with that puppy, Thomas Swann."

Rachel had remained silent during this exchange, deeply grateful to the older man for making this long trip to protect her; for she knew that he was thinking of more than Andrew's physical well-being.

With the beginning of February the dispute left the realm of semi-private, oral argumentation and broke into public print. Thomas Swann published a long and detailed attack on Andrew in the Nashville *Impartial Review*. Andrew published an even longer defense, documented with affidavits by friends who had overheard any part of the discussions. John Erwin, a relative of Mrs. Dickinson, inserted a third statement in the paper, urging people to reserve their judgment until Mr. Dickinson returned and could present his case. The only one who appeared to be enjoying the row was Thomas Eastin, owner of the *Impartial Review:* he charged for all of these articles at regular commercial rates.

Spring came at last. The sun dried the ground, the plows turned over the earth, the men went to work . . . Andrew returned to Clover Bottom to train Truxton for the big race against Ploughboy. And as Rachel had suspected, everybody dropped the discussion of the forfeit-note quarrel, transferring their excitement to the April contest. The betting was extraordinarily heavy.

It was overcast the morning of the Truxton-Ploughboy race, but the somber grays of the outdoors could not match Andrew's gloom; two days earlier Truxton had injured his thigh, and the swelling would not yield to massage or liniment. They left for Clover Bottom early. The crowd of spectators was already tremendous.

"This is the largest number of people I ever saw assembled," commented Andrew. "I would sure hate to disappoint them by calling off the race."

"But Andrew, if Truxton has a swollen thigh . . . ?"

His long bony chin set stubbornly.

"I'm just not convinced that a swollen thigh would keep Truxton from winning."

The men who had helped to train the horse, and had large sums of money bet on him, John Coffee, John Verell, Sam Pryor, all began speaking at once: Truxton would have to exert himself to the utmost to beat Ploughboy, even when in perfect condition.

"I never saw a horse more eager to win," said Andrew. "Gentlemen, I will gladly assume any part or all of your bets."

The two horses were led to the starting line. The word was given, and they shot forward. Truxton took a slight lead. The spectators were still, watching the two great animals circle the meadowland. Now as they came into the stretch, Truxton forged steadily ahead.

Their big stallion won the first heat easily; but he was limping badly. One of his front legs also had gone lame, the shoe having sprung. Captain Erwin's supporters were shouting that the race was over.

"It's too late to forfeit now, isn't it, Andrew?" Rachel asked.

"Yes. We either have to run the second heat or withdraw and pay the full amount of our wager."

To herself she thought, We may lose our money, but it's just as well: Truxton's opening win will satisfy Andrew, while Captain Erwin and Charles Dickinson will get their money back and also have the right to claim a victory.

But she had bargained without her husband.

"Truxton's going to run," he announced. "If he can beat Ploughboy with one bad leg . . . he can do it with two."

And Truxton did, by a full sixty yards, in a sudden heavy rain, running the two miles in one second short of four minutes. Andrew and his friends had won ten thousand dollars; Captain Erwin and his supporters were utterly crushed. It was the most humiliating defeat in the history of western racing. Rachel's heart pounded as she left the course.

5

If Andrew had experienced any despair over the reversal in his fortunes or the need to sell Hunter's Hill, his regrets now disappeared completely as his victories with his race horses established him as the top turfman of Tennessee. Captain Erwin paid his debt, congratulating Andrew on having infused a great fighting spirit into his horse. Swann's diatribes had been silenced by the state authorities in Knoxville, who apparently had threatened to suspend his attorney's license, in which act Rachel was certain she saw General Robertson's influence. Reports filtered back to them that Charles Dickinson had engaged in considerable pistol practice on his way down the Mississippi, but Rachel dismissed this as gossip.

One night toward the end of May, Andrew came home from the store upset. Shortly after sundown Thomas Overton reached the Hermitage. Rachel, working on the small loom in her bedroom, heard the men's voices downstairs, Overton's high, almost querulous, Andrew's low and vibrant. He came upstairs after about

twenty minutes, told her he had to go into town on urgent business, and that he
would not be back until the following evening. She searched his face for some clue
to the matter, but he kissed her, completely preoccupied, and left the room.

The next day passed quickly, for she had a number of chores: preserving fruits
for candied desserts and appetizers, cleaning the heavy winter bedclothes before
putting them away, sewing a light-weight suit for Andy. A neighbor returning from
Nashville brought the message that Andrew would not be back that night. The
following noon George brought her a copy of the *Impartial Review*. In it was an
article by Charles Dickinson; she had not even known that he had returned to
Nashville. She scanned the first part, finding it to be a long review of the quarrel
over the forfeit notes. Then she read:

> General Jackson states that Mr. Swann has acted the puppet and lying valit, for a
> worthless, drunken, blackguard, scoundrel, etc. etc. Should Andrew Jackson have
> intended these epithets for me, I declare him (notwithstanding he is a major general
> of the militia) to be a worthless scoundrel, a poltroon and a coward. A man who, by
> frivolous and evasive pretexts, avoided giving the satisfaction, which was his due to
> a gentleman whom he had injured. This had prevented me from calling on him in the
> manner I should otherwise have done; for I am well convinced, that he is too great
> a coward to administer any of those anodynes he promised me in his letter to Mr.
> Swann.

She sat on a hard dining chair, unable to move or even think until she heard
Andrew's horse coming across the field. She ran to the open door, shading her
eyes from the midday sun. He alighted in the yard, gathered her in his arms for a
moment and, glancing at the newspaper she still held, murmured:

"Bad news travels fast because it has so many helping hands."

He led her into the house. Moll was cooking supper. She took a quick look at
Rachel's face, then left, soundlessly.

"That's why you went into Nashville Thursday night: you had heard that Charles
Dickinson was back."

"I went to see this article before Eastin set it up in type. Well . . . I saw it."

"Andrew, you didn't challenge!"

He took her hand in his.

"I had to. I wanted the whole thing settled this morning . . . before you could
learn about it . . . but Dickinson's seconds had a lot of excuses."

"You are going to duel with him," she said numbly. "When . . . and where?"

"A week from today, at Harrison's Mill, Kentucky."

The air in the room became still. She felt something on her cheek, reached up
and found tears: he would be traveling the Kentucky Road, the one on which he
had brought her home from the Robards' fifteen years before, when her old life
had ended . . . and her new life begun. How closely these two journeys were
bound; and how inescapable was the past!

"Darling, you're not going to let this hotheaded boy shatter our lives?"

He walked away from her.

"I have no choice."

"This is not going to be like other duels, is it? You are both going to shoot
to . . ."

"Yes."

She felt faint. Andrew brought her a mug of cool water. She took a sip, then
looked up at him and cried, "For the dear God's sake, why must you do this? Do
you no longer love me or care what happens that you can risk your life without
reason or purpose?"

He took the water from her, dipped his fingers into it and ran them over her
forehead.

"I do love you, my darling. I'll love you until my dying day."

"If he kills you, Andrew! There will be nothing left for me of love . . . or life."

He walked to the sideboard, cut a piece of loaf sugar and ground it in some whisky, downing the mixture in a swift draught. When he turned back to her his face was pale.

"If I ignore these insults men will spit on me when I walk down Market Street. My name will become a laughingstock. I will be the butt of derision throughout all Tennessee."

"Dueling is savage. Everyone who respects the law would respect you for declining to fight. General Robertson told you in this very room that your courage and reputation did not require this kind of vindication. He said that if you lose your family would suffer, and if you win it would be a pyrrhic victory . . ."

She watched him make his way almost blindly to a big chair and slump into it, holding his face in his hands.

"Oh, Rachel, I've tried so many things, and I've failed at so many. The one thing that has sustained me has been my sense of honor. This is what I live by. Take that away and it would be like severing a tent pole with an ax. I've never run away from anything or failed to fulfill my obligations. Make me do so just one time and you have destroyed me. What would you have left? I would no longer be a man."

"It would take far more courage to ignore this braggadocio letter and face the men on Market Street than it would to stand at Harrison's Mill with an almost complete stranger, both of you determined to kill each other."

"Perhaps so; but it's a kind of courage I don't possess. If Dickinson had sent this letter to me privately, then perhaps I might have found some way to answer him privately. But there won't be a man, woman or child who won't have read this article. I'm still a major general of the militia, and there are hundreds of militiamen who will read it and know instantly that I must fight Dickinson. If I fail I'm not the only one who stands in disgrace: the whole militia does, for if their leader is a coward, so are they. I fight, or I resign. I fight, or I stop racing our horses. I fight, or I sell our store and tavern, yes, and our home too. I fight, or I lose everything."

She waited for a moment, then asked quietly:

"Andrew, are you dueling with Charles Dickinson over the disputed forfeit notes . . . or the ugly things he has said about us and our marriage?"

"How can I say? If Charles Dickinson did not hate me so terribly he would never have made those attacks on you. By the same token, if I did not hate him so much for his slanders, this quarrel over the forfeit notes might not have gone so far."

"But if you know this, others will know it too. They will say the duel was fought over me."

"There is no way to stop the loose talk so long as we leave that man free to blacken us. I must close his mouth once and for all."

"It will be the end for both of us . . . and what a dreadful end to our love, and our hopes for each other."

"No, it will be a good end: we will have fought for our love. But if we let this go by we will die every hour and every day of our lives: die from bullets of gossip and vile charges." He paced the full length of the room. "Dickinson wants to be the great man of Tennessee. Everywhere he turns it seems I somehow thwart him." He could not restrain a wry grin. "Even his great Ploughboy is humiliated and disgraced by our Truxton."

She went to him, took his hands in hers.

"He's the best shot in this part of the country. He can hit a coin three times in the air before it falls, sever a string at twenty yards."

"He's gone to great pains to have these stories circulated."

"Then . . . he can . . . miss you?"

"Not totally. But I give you my promise I'll not miss him either."

"Oh, Andrew, I don't want you to be guilty of killing another man. Think of his wife . . . and their baby son."

He stood staring at her for a moment, then turned away, went to the door and called out:

"Moll, would you be so good as to serve dinner now? And ask George to bring up a bottle of wine from the springhouse."

She had expected to find some change in his routine in the days that preceded his departure for Harrison's Mill, some final preparations he would make or instructions he would leave, papers he might straighten out, accounts balanced. But he did none of these things. He went about his day's work in the fields, spending the early mornings at the stables on Clover Bottom exercising the horses; in the evenings they sat before the fire, reading or talking with friends who had come in for supper. He never again alluded to the oncoming duel.

He was to leave Thursday morning at five. They went to bed early the night before. Andrew fell into a sound sleep. Rachel did not close her eyes. Through her mind went all the happiness they had known, the successes and failures; and how wonderful Andrew had been: his soft, gentle love at Bayou Pierre, and at Poplar Grove; the big house he had built on Hunter's Hill to make her the great lady of Tennessee; the carriage he had had delivered to her on Christmas Day when they were so hard pressed for funds, the gifts he had brought back from Philadelphia when he had been deep in trouble and anxiety.

He awoke at four. They breakfasted together. There was so much she wanted to tell him: how much she loved him, how fine their years together had been, and how dear their love; yet she realized she could not utter one word, that she must not indicate by a single gesture that she feared she might never see him again. Instead, when it was time to go and they had clasped each other fervently, she said:

"Don't ride too hard; get some rest after lunch; and be careful . . . "

He smiled wistfully at her, said, "I'll be careful."

"Come home as quickly as you can. I'll be waiting for you. I'll have a whisky ready, and a hot supper on the fire."

There was gray light in the east by now. She stood at the doorway waving as he went across the fields. Then she turned back into the house. It was dark and still.

6

She went about her chores for the day, feeling strangely suspended in both time and space, as though she were standing above the world and watching a woman by the name of Rachel Jackson desperately trying to fill redundant moments and hours with unthinking physical activity.

Jane arrived at midday with a small portmanteau. She said nothing about the duel or Andrew's absence: she was simply there as she always had been when Rachel was in trouble. The Hayses were in trouble too, Rachel knew; some of Robert's investments had gone bad and he had had to sacrifice most of his holdings. There was even some talk of their losing their plantation.

Jane slept with her that night. Several times Rachel fell into a nightmare, racked by throttled screams. She felt Jane's arm about her, comforting her. At the first sign of the sun Rachel looked over at her sister, saw that she was sleeping, got out of bed quietly, dressed and left the house. It was already warm but after she passed the springhouse and went into the woods she found the air closed in and cool.

She walked a very long time, having no way of telling when it was precisely seven o'clock and the shots would be fired, but feeling in her heart that if anything serious were to happen to Andrew she would sense it. The woods were like a series of walls within walls, through which no human eye or voice could penetrate, giving her privacy and seclusion. It was dark, yet the trees were friendly, as though they knew she needed protection against a cruel and chaotic world. She moved over the soft moss-covered earth as effortlessly as though she were floating in still warm waters in some nascent period before it had been necessary for her to think or struggle.

The sun had risen fairly high and was beginning to clear the treetops. She took her bearings and after a time found the trail that led her home. It was ten o'clock when she reached her cabin. Jane was sitting out in front knitting, with Andy playing at her feet. She looked up, made a swift appraisal of Rachel's face, then said:

"For a time there I thought you'd gone to Harrison's Mill to fight the duel for him."

"There's been no news, Jane?"

"No. How could there be? It's still a number of hours before Andrew could reach home, no matter how fast he rode." Jane rose, linked her arm through her sister's. "You need rest. It must be several nights since you really closed your eyes."

"I believe I *could* sleep . . . for an hour or two."

She put her head on the pillow, remembered Andrew's boyhood chum telling her, "I could throw Andrew three times out of four, but he would never stay throwed," and fell into a bottomless slumber. It was late afternoon by the time she awoke. Downstairs she could hear Moll humming and Jane's voice as she read to Andy. She poured some cold water into the bowl on the dresser, washed quickly, combed her hair and slipped on a white linen dress, wearing her pearl brooch, the first gift of jewelry Andrew had given her. Even as she descended the stairs she heard the noise of fast-moving horses, and by the time she reached the door she saw Andrew coming down the trail flanked on either side by Thomas Overton and Dr. May, whom she recognized as a Nashville surgeon. She was at his side as he lifted himself gingerly off his horse.

"Thank God, darling! Are you all right?"

"Oh, he pinked me."

"And Mr. Dickinson? How is he?"

"Well, I don't know precisely. He was hit. I sent Dr. May over to offer his assistance, but it was declined."

The men followed Rachel into the house and to the bedroom upstairs where they helped Andrew off with his coat and shirt. His chest was bandaged, but the blood had soaked through.

"I tried to get Mr. Jackson to stay at David Miller's tavern on the Red River for a couple of days until this wound healed," Dr. May said, "but he insisted he had to get home to prove to you that he was alive."

"How bad is it?"

"Painful, but not dangerous: the ball broke a rib or two and raked his breastbone."

She sat beside him, holding his hand while the surgeon cleansed the wound and redressed it. Andrew gritted his teeth, saying to her between gasps:

"Mr. Dickinson had not been bragging. His aim was perfect. He shot for exactly where he supposed my heart was beating. But you know how loosely that blue frock coat fits me? Standing sideways, as we did, it billowed out in front of me. I never thought it would do me any good in this world to be skinny, but it sure enough saved my life . . . by a half inch."

Dr. May took a handkerchief out of his pocket and wiped the perspiration from his face. "Right now I think we all could do with a good strong whisky. Mr. Jackson will have his in bed."

"Just one word to you, gentlemen, before you leave," said Andrew, leaning up on one elbow. "When you report this wound in Nashville, please be so kind as to use my words: 'Mr. Jackson was pinked, nothing more.' "

The men agreed, then accompanied Rachel downstairs. Thomas Overton had two fast drinks, then plunged into a recital of the duel.

"On our ride out to Red River the general and I discussed how the duel should be fought. As you know, the pistols were to be held downward until the word was given, then each man was to fire as soon as he pleased. It was scarcely possible that both pistols could be discharged at the same instant, therefore the one who was the quickest might end the duel with one shot. Should we try to get the first shot, or should we permit Dickinson to have it? We agreed that Dickinson would be sure to get the first fire . . ."

". . . please, Mr. Overton . . ."

"I'm telling it fast as I can, Mrs. Jackson. Well, when I gave the word 'Fire!' Dickinson raised his pistol like lightning and fired. I saw a puff of dust fly from the breast of the general's coat, watched him raise his left arm and place it tightly across his breast. Dickinson fell back a pace or two, saying in a faltering tone, 'Great God, have I missed him!' 'Back to the mark, sir,' I cried . . . "

"Mr. Overton, do you mind . . . ?"

"The general took aim at Mr. Dickinson and pulled the trigger. The gun neither snapped nor went off, it stopped at half cock. The general drew the trigger back, took second aim and fired. He did not miss, I assure you. That will be an end to Mr. Dickinson's challenging men he is positive he can kill at twenty-four paces."

Rachel took a supper tray upstairs to Andrew, propped him against soft pillows and, when his arm hurt, fed him.

Before long he fell into a quiet sleep. When Robert Hays came for Jane, Overton and Dr. May left with them. Rachel undressed and climbed into bed gently, not wanting to wake Andrew. She slept only intermittently, knowing she could not rest until she had had reassuring news about Charles Dickinson. She had never hated him, she had only considered him ungallant in attacking a defenseless woman. If Mr. Dickinson were fatally wounded, the responsibility would be as much hers as it was Andrew's; she did not want any man to be killed because of her.

The news came soon enough, out from Nashville.

The following morning before Andrew was awake, Moll summoned her quietly from the bottom of the stairs. Rachel put on her dressing gown and slippers and descended to find a militiaman waiting. He asked to see General Jackson. When she insisted that Andrew could not be awakened, the officer said:

"I have been sent to tell the general that Charles Dickinson died last night at nine o'clock.

She reached for a chair to steady herself. When the man left she fell to her knees on the floor.

"Oh, God, have pity on the poor wife; pity the babe in her arms." Then, from deep in the recesses of her mind, there came the whispered words, "And have pity on us too."

BOOK FIVE

1

Rachel brooded over the death of Charles Dickinson. She watched with anxiety as the Cumberland Valley people reversed the roles of the duelists: somehow in their grief Andrew Jackson had become the invincible marksman who had mercilessly killed a younger and less experienced opponent. Captain Erwin's letter in the *Impartial Review*, stating that although Andrew technically had been within his rights in pressing the trigger a second time he had actually violated the unwritten code of dueling, found credence in Nashville; and the honor for which he had risked his life was being seriously tarnished. Among the women, Mrs. Somerset Phariss, who was a cousin of Charles Dickinson, now charged Rachel with having egged on Mr. Jackson because of Mr. Dickinson's two attacks on her, insinuating that Charles Dickinson's blood was on Rachel Jackson's hands. When Nashville turned out for Dickinson's funeral the sentiment ran so strong that a mass protest meeting was called.

It was no longer necessary for her to set her table for twenty; they ate alone. Even those friends who had believed the duel inevitable had been distressed by young Dickinson's death; their remaining away from the Hermitage was a confession of repugnance. Rachel understood this, for had not she too been repulsed by the all-too-fresh blood on Aaron Burr's hands? Her understanding lengthened her despair as Andrew's clients, his associates, his cronies from Nashville, the throng of admirers from the racecourse and the men who had come from all over the state to counsel, make land deals or swap horses vanished like morning frost. His friends who controlled Tennessee politics also dropped him, no longer seeking his advice or patronage. By dying, Charles Dickinson had obliterated Andrew's political position and influence far more effectively than he could have by staying alive. Only his young aides in the militia of West Tennessee remained loyal, riding out to the Hermitage for a handclasp and a drink, outlining campaigns by means of which they could drive the Spanish from Florida. To them the duel had been an affair of honor, necessarily fought and resolved.

Andrew was allowed to leave his bed after noonday dinner, but he had to spend the afternoon reclining on the red settee, waiting for his broken ribs to mend. Rachel dressed the wound carefully, but it did not heal as the surgeon had predicted. Thomas Overton and Dr. May kept their word, telling no one that the Dickinson bullet had missed Andrew's heart by less than an inch.

Rachel pleaded, "Andrew, you've got to let Dr. May give an accurate report of your wound. A lot of the people who are angry with you because they think you are unscathed would feel differently if they knew how close Dickinson came to killing you."

"Where or how badly Dickinson hit me is my private affair," he answered abruptly; "there's no need for me to share that knowledge with those short-memoried folks who have turned against me."

"Be generous, Andrew, let them salvage their pride. Perhaps it would make Mr. Dickinson's family feel a little better."

Pain twisted Andrew's mouth as he sat up.

"He had no generosity for you; he struck at you in public. He had no generosity for me; he went to that dueling ground absolutely certain that I had no chance of emerging alive. He laid bets in Nashville that he would kill me at the first fire."

"Yes, Andrew, I know. But the air around us is black with hate, and with talk . . . the old talk . . . of Lewis, and our first two years together, and how I did not defend myself in Harrodsburg, and the jury's verdict against us . . ."

She felt Andrew's hand in hers; his face was pale, gaunt.

"Darling, you must trust me. I did what I had to do; I could no longer have lived with you or asked you to love me if I had let Charles Dickinson continue to humiliate us. We'll be vindicated."

She took his face in her hands and kissed his bloodless lips.

"All right, Andrew. Whatever you did, we did together; and whatever you must suffer we will suffer together." She hesitated for a moment, then added quickly, "That mass meeting got up a petition to have Editor Eastin put the next issue of the *Impartial Review* in mourning 'As a tribute of respect for the memory, and regret for the untimely death of Mr. Charles Dickinson . . .' "

"The paper in mourning, eh," he interrupted harshly, "with a nice official black band. By what right? If only I could ride into town . . ."

She rose from his side and went to the window, where she stood with her back to him, ostensibly straightening the curtain.

"Why not write a letter of protest? Eastin will be going to press tomorrow. I will take it in."

The next morning she waited in the outer office of the newspaper until the sandy-complexioned young man came forward from the composing room, a black apron covering his trousers, his hands smeared from the type he had been setting. She handed him Andrew's letter. He read it, leaning on his elbows behind the counter, his head bobbing.

"Now, Mrs. Jackson, you know we don't take sides on our paper. We make every effort to live up to our name, *Impartial Review*."

Rachel's eyes flashed fire.

"Your *Review* would have been a lot more *Impartial* if you had never run any of those letters by Thomas Swann, the Erwins, Mr. Dickinson, Mr. McNairy or General Jackson."

The editor's ink-smudged mouth dropped open with shock.

"But Mrs. Jackson, when a gentleman hands us a statement and pays the prevailing rates, we've no basis for refusing him. Any more than we can refuse seventy-three of our leading citizens the right to buy a black band around one issue of the paper."

She had no liking for the subtle or devious; this young newspaper owner was being clever with her.

"I assume you will list the names of all seventy-three of the men who are paying for the border?"

". . . well . . . no, there had been no mention of that."

"Then put on your coat, go out to your seventy-three purchasers and tell them that General Jackson insists you publish their names. We cannot have it look as though the *Impartial Review* were taking this stand editorially, can we?"

Eastin flushed.

"It's not common practice, ma'am, but I'll do what you say. We strive to please everybody."

Twenty-six of the mourners withdrew their names; the rest stood firm. To stress his impartiality, Eastin ran Andrew's letter without charge. The black border caused the controversy to heighten in intensity, while her own trip into town provided further ammunition for those who were charging her with complicity.

It was the hottest summer she could remember; the cattle lay panting under the trees, the hogs stood waist-deep in the pond and the dry clay earth became gray dust on the roads. Dr. May forbade Andrew to train his horses for the fall races. He promptly withdrew his entries.

It was a gratuitous withdrawal, for the Nashville Jockey Club claimed that people would no longer go to a track owned by Andrew Jackson. All races were to be transferred to Hartsville.

Despite her unceasing efforts to bring him back to health he remained thin to the point of emaciation. In the fall she went into the fields to supervise the bringing in of the crops; the earth was a caldron and the dust choked her. When she came in from work she went directly to the springhouse where Moll set out tubs of the cool water. Discarding her dust-caked bonnet and dress, she bathed and washed her hair, and piled it high on her head with the gold combs Andrew had given her. Then she donned a white or pale yellow cotton dress, low-necked and short-sleeved, and went to the main house to drink a glass of cool wine with Andrew before their dinner. In the evening they sat under catalpa trees, using their fans to keep off the dry-weather flies.

Judge Overton visited as frequently as his arduous duties permitted, John Coffee came to spend the week ends. Of the Donelson family they saw Jane, who rode over in the afternoons, bringing her young daughter Rachel, while Mary and Catherine usually drove out on Saturday with a carriage full of grandchildren. William disapproved the duel; Johnny was silently protesting the further trouble Andrew had caused the clan; Alexander and Leven were too indifferent or too lazy to come or to send a sympathetic word. Only Severn, with whom neither she nor Andrew had been on intimate terms, sensed what they were suffering in their isolation. He bought the piece of land immediately adjoining the Hermitage and insisted that the Jacksons visit him frequently.

As soon as the doctor said Andrew could ride in the carriage he went over to Clover Bottom to his store. After three trips he stopped going and Rachel did not need to ask why: she had known that the store stood empty. She had also managed to conceal from her husband that Colonel Ward had defaulted on his second-half payment for Hunter's Hill. To add to their problems their last flotilla of seven boats of produce for New Orleans had been hit by a storm, three had been totally lost, and because of damage to the others they had arrived at the market too late to earn back their cost.

Rachel accepted these financial upsets philosophically, convinced that they were an inescapable part of their life pattern. But in the dark sleeplessness of the nights she murmured over and over, Oh, Andrew, if only you had raised your pistol high into the air that second time and fired at the sky, how great a man you would have been! You would have emerged as the merciful victor who had been too big to extract your pound of flesh! Yet in the few seconds that had passed between the click of Andrew's trigger and the recocking for a second shot, he had known he was seriously hit. Could a man wounded, perhaps dying, take pity on an opponent whose one grim determination had been to destroy him? And who was she to pass judgment? She who had reached out for love, gone quickly into a second marriage, knowing it was an unheard-of thing she was doing, that divorce was unknown in Tennessee and the frontier, that Lewis Robards would never allow her to become totally free . . . that the stigma would make her forever the source of contention and strife.

2

One night toward the end of September they heard a rider come up the trail. Andrew got out of bed, went to the big window which stood open and exclaimed:

"Why, it's Colonel Burr."

He put on his dressing gown and slippers. Rachel sat up in bed.

"Andrew, can I go down with you?" she asked.

He glanced at her, her braids wound tightly about her head, her eyes excited by this unexpected visit.

"Come ahead," he said with a grin; "if the colonel feels so friendly as to break in upon us late at night, that means we can be *en famille*."

Colonel Burr's face lit up with an affectionate smile when they opened the door to him.

"How wonderful to see you and the general again, Mrs. Jackson. I've been looking forward to it for days. That is the only excuse I can offer for my bad manners in intruding upon you at this late hour."

"Indeed, Colonel, I would have been deeply hurt if you had not," boomed Andrew.

Rachel gathered about her the folds of her voluminous flannel robe and made her way to the springhouse where she secured a cold fried chicken, a loaf of Moll's bread, some chilled butter and a bottle of white wine. She found her husband and the colonel deep in a discussion of the hostilities with Spain; Andrew was never more intensely alive. Only now did she realize how dormant he had lain all summer, how terribly he missed being at the center of the happenings in Tennessee. As she spread a cloth over the table and set out the dishes and glasses she listened to Colonel Burr report that Spain's armed forces, operating inside American territory, had imprisoned five United States citizens and had cut down an American flag flying over a friendly Indian nation.

"By the Eternal," Andrew exclaimed, "it looks as though our moment has come!"

"I have purchased a tract of two hundred thousand acres on the Washita," continued Burr, "and several hundred young fighting men have already signed to settle there with me. When the war breaks with Spain we'll be a self-constituted army, ready to move on Texas and Mexico."

"All of Nashville will be glad to hear your news, Colonel," said Andrew eagerly. He turned to Rachel. "My dear, I want you to invite to dinner all the people who were at our first dinner for Colonel Burr."

Rachel shrank as the two men looked toward her. Would anyone come? Did she dare to ask the Pharisses, Daisy Deson and her father, the others who had helped to pay for the black border? Should she risk their rejection for this chance to bridge the gap of coolness and hostility that had sprung up since the duel? John Overton could help her; he was in close contact with Nashville. She would have to speak to him first.

John was one of the managers of the Nashville Dancing Assembly, whose first ball was to be held that Saturday night at the new Talbot Hotel. Rachel asked if the Dancing Assembly would like to invite Colonel Burr as its guest of honor. John considered the proposal, decided it would lend social importance to the occasion, and sent announcements to all subscribers of the Assembly.

The next afternoon he returned her visit.

"Seems as though I acted without my usual judicial calm in inviting Colonel Burr for Saturday night."

"Has there been objection?"

"Yes. Several men have come to my office to say they did not think we should honor Colonel Burr. It seems the colonel is charged with engaging in a number of questionable activities."

"Such as?" she asked uneasily.

"Such as: Mr. Daviess, attorney for the United States at Frankfort, is arraigning the colonel in Federal Court on charges of planning to injure a power with which the United States is at peace."

"Oh, you mean his preparations for a war against the Spanish. Andrew approves . . ."

"Such as: at Cannonsburg, Ohio, he told Colonel Morgan that the Union would not last, that the fumbling and imbecility of the Federal government was so great that a separation of the states could not be more than four or five years off; and that with two hundred men he could drive Congress, with the President at its head, into the Potomac."

"But that's treason!" She was dumfounded. "Do they have proof of these charges?"

"No proof. All bottomed on rumor . . . In any event we've reached a working compromise: Colonel Burr will be ticketed but he's not to be our guest of honor . . . And of course you and Andrew will attend the ball."

Colonel Burr went to Nashville on Friday to stay at the Talbot Hotel. Andrew donned his uniform as general of the militia, but Rachel was more timid. She thought it the better part of discretion to wear her simple black gown.

John greeted them, turned to Rachel with a wistful smile and said, "As manager of the ball, madam, may I have the great honor of taking you in?"

She flushed with pleasure; this was John's way of showing the hostile world precisely where he stood. Almost a decade and a half before he had demonstrated his belief in her innocence by coming to the Donelson stockade from Harrodsburg and asking to be taken in as a boarder. How many times in the intervening years had he had to renew that show of faith?

She had a single moment of uneasiness when Andrew entered the ballroom with the colonel on his arm and began presenting him to the members of the Assembly. To her relief they were received cordially; for the most part, Burr's efforts to instigate a war against Spain were looked upon with favor in Nashville. The colonel had a firm handclasp and a brilliant smile for everyone. Rachel followed Andrew with her eyes; how wonderful to see him talking and laughing with friends whom he had not seen since the duel. She observed that Captain Erwin and his family, as well as a nucleus of Charles Dickinson's friends and relatives, had not attended.

At the beginning of November Andrew received from Burr a packet of three thousand dollars in Kentucky bank notes, with an order to build five flatboats and to outfit them. By the same messenger he asked Andrew for a list of men whom he could recommend to the War Department for commissions. Andrew turned the money over to Jax with instructions to start building the boats, then joined General Robertson in drawing up a list of able soldiers.

A few days later a handsome young man knocked at the door, took off his military cap to show a head of tight blond curls, introduced himself as Captain Fort, a friend of Colonel Burr. He was invited to stay the night. After dinner while the two men were smoking their pipes in front of the fire and Rachel was sitting behind them on the settee knitting a cap for Andy, the conversation took a strange turn. Though Andrew had not moved, she had seen his back stiffen and felt his intense concentration upon the glowing bowl of tobacco.

"This separatist movement is the best thing that could have happened," Captain Fort was saying smoothly. "It will give the western states a focus and a capital, and people to run the new nation."

Rachel recognized the deep calm which characterized Andrew's conversation in moments of crisis.

"And where is this new capital to be?"

"New Orleans. We will seize the port, then move on to conquer Mexico. This done, we'll unite the western part of the Union to the conquered country."

"And how is this to be effected?" Andrew's tone had risen slightly in warmth, but the captain was too absorbed to notice it.

"By the aid of Federal troops, with General Wilkinson at their head."

Andrew knocked out the gray ash on the hearth, straightened up and looked fiercely at Fort.

"Is Colonel Burr in on this scheme?"

"My information comes from a high officer who is well acquainted with Colonel Burr. General Wilkinson is one of our leaders."

All doubt had fled from their minds at the identical instant. There was a betrayed look on Andrew's face. He controlled himself with a determined effort, dismissing Captain Fort curtly. When he was gone, Andrew closed the door and bolted it. He was trembling.

"My God, is Burr really a traitor?"

"Sit down, my dear, before you fall into the fire. Now, tell me: is such a scheme to separate the West from the East really treason, or is it the foolishness of an overwrought mind?"

"I gave him military lists! Jax is building boats for him, and buying provisions!"

He turned and, with his eyebrows raised high, said, "Do you know what can happen if these charges are true?"

"Not . . . altogether."

"Aaron Burr has put me in a position where I too can be charged with treason!"

The news came by courier from Frankfort that Aaron Burr had been arraigned in Federal Court. That same morning they received a letter from Burr. Andrew read it aloud:

"MY DEAR GENERAL,

"I give you my most sacred pledges that I have never held any views inimical or hostile to the United States and if anyone should charge me with the intention of separating the Union they must charge me with insanity at the very same instant.

"And so I do," declared Andrew emphatically. "If he shows up at the Hermitage again, he'll be turned away."

Immediately after Burr's release from the Frankfort court because of lack of witnesses to testify against him, he arrived at the Hermitage, his smile warm and charming. Rachel planted herself squarely on the threshold.

"I'm sorry, Colonel Burr, but General Jackson is not at home."

"I'm indeed sorry to have missed him. Would you permit me to wait for his return?"

"The general has gone to Sumner County."

"Then could you perhaps give me some information about the five boats I ordered, and the provisions that were to have been laid in?"

"I can give you no information."

She saw Burr flinch, and felt her own distress: it was the first time she had ever denied anyone hospitality.

"If you are concerned about those absurd charges, Mrs. Jackson, I think I should tell you that I was completely exonerated in the Kentucky court."

"Colonel Burr, there is nothing I can do. Might I suggest the tavern at Clover Bottom? I am sure they can make you comfortable."

Burr pulled himself up to his full five feet four, bowed in imperious fashion, turned, mounted his horse and disappeared across the fields. Rachel watched him until he was out of sight.

When Andrew returned he rounded up John Coffee and Thomas Overton and rode over to the Clover Bottom Tavern for a final accounting, taking along some two thousand dollars, the balance of the Kentucky bank notes not expended. He returned several hours later, dropped into a chair and threw a batch of papers onto the table. His eyes were of many opinions. Rachel asked:

"What happened, Andrew?"

He ran his hand through the papers, said with a smile that had as much awe as bewilderment in it:

"Frankly, I don't know. He very nearly convinced me that those charges were pure nonsense. Do you know what he has in his possession? A blank commission, signed by President Jefferson." He looked down between his widespread knees, studying the carpet pattern. "If Governor Sevier gave me such a blank commission for my militia I could name any officer to any rank. But what does a blank commission from President Jefferson mean? That Burr can write himself in as a general?"

"Did you see the President's signature?"

"Only a quick look. . . . Anyway we gave him back his money and told him he could take delivery of the two boats we finished. I don't know how far he can get in them, without provisions. I wouldn't be surprised if Stockly Hays came walking home within a week."

"Surely Jane and Robert are not going to let Stockly go with him after all that's happened!"

"Robert says it's a matter of honor; he gave his word to Burr that Stockly would go along. If he were my boy, I'd keep him here. But I think there's no danger on the voyage down the Mississippi. I've told Stockly to leave the flotilla at the first sign of anything suspicious."

Burr departed with his two boats at dawn on December 22. Five days later the explosion came in the form of a proclamation from President Jefferson which had been more than a month in transit. The people were warned that an illegal conspiracy against Spain had been set in motion; all military and civil officials were ordered to seize the conspirators. Everyone around Nashville read the separatist movement between the lines.

Rumors flew into the Hermitage faster than feathers in a high wind: Burr's army of invasion was assembling where the Cumberland River met the Ohio; he had a hundred boats and a thousand men under arms with vast stores of guns and ammunition stashed on Blennerhassett Island. Rachel worried about Stockly Hays; Andrew worried about the treachery of General Wilkinson in New Orleans; and Nashville worried about Andrew Jackson.

General Robertson came out to the Hermitage to report that the Dickinson clique had written to Governor Sevier demanding Andrew's removal as a general of the militia: in times of crisis any officer involved in an insurrection could be court-martialed. When Aaron Burr was burned in effigy in the public square, the figure looked more like gangling Andrew Jackson than it did the short-statured Burr. Rachel asked herself why it was that some men and women were storm centers all their lives, while others lived out their years in comparative quiet.

Then the insurrection collapsed: General Winchester informed General Jackson that when Burr left the mouth of the Cumberland he had only eleven boats and one hundred and ten men; Captain Bissell reported from Fort Massac that Colonel Burr had nothing on board his boats that a man could not be taking to market; Andrew's scout sent back word that Burr had no arms. Burr surrendered to the authorities just above Natchez and was returned north as a prisoner.

3

They were returning from a day of early spring hunting, with Andy riding his Indian Princess between their two horses and trying to contaln his pride over the deer slung across his saddle, when Rachel saw Polly waiting for them under the trees. As she drew close it was evident from Polly's expression that her sister-in-law had reached a moment of decision and wasn't liking it too well. Had she come to take Andy away? But what reason could there be? The boy had flourished, learning to ride and shoot; according to the young tutor they had hired for him, he was making progress in the books.

The reason was quickly forthcoming.

"Rachel, I'm going to marry Colonel Saunders," declared Polly. "Pappy advised it, he thinks it's best for me and the boys."

Rachel stood with her head lowered. How lonely the house would seem without Andy. Despite their preoccupation since the duel, she had moved about her work or gone to bed at night always conscious of the boy in the next room. So many times he had pulled them out of a momentary despair with some foolish antic or pressing need. She had already been dreading the fact that he must go off to the academy next autumn, and she would be deprived of his companionship during the week. She looked at Andy, wondering how he would adjust himself to the middle-aged Colonel Saunders, a prosperous but dour man whose nickname was Johnny Dry.

Her question got itself answered two days before the wedding: along the trail came Polly and Andy. The boy slid off Indian Princess and ran to Rachel. Polly dismounted wearily.

"It just won't work . . . because neither of them want it to work. Andy has been misbehaving frightfully. He organized all sorts of annoyances, like cutting the stirrups off the colonel's saddle. The colonel whupped him; it's more than the poor man can endure."

She glanced toward her son, who had his arms wrapped tightly about Rachel's neck while she ran her fingers through his hair. Polly smiled, and her eyes were resigned. "I know he was only trying to get back here. He loves you both."

"We love him too."

"Yes, you do; and that's why I guess this is the best arrangement for everybody. I want Andy to be happy; but I also want the colonel to be happy. So he's yours . . . to raise . . . . and keep, as long as you want him." The color drained from Polly's cheeks; she was still, very still.

Rachel went to the younger girl, put her arms around her. Polly began to sob.

"If the time ever comes . . . if I should need him . . . want him . . . ."

Rachel answered quickly. "He'll always be your son, Polly. We won't ask to adopt him; he'll be our nephew. We'll just raise him, and teach him, and love him . . . as Samuel's boy."

At the beginning of May when they were in the midst of plantlng Indian corn in a newly cleared field a subpoena arrived from the Federal court in Richmond, summoning Andrew Jackson to appear and testify in the trial of the United States versus Aaron Burr. Andrew sent immediately for John Overton; he was considerably upset.

"I'm being called a traitor; that's the dirtiest word in our language!"

Rachel picked up the subpoena. She shook her head vigorously as if to say, Shame on you!

"Andrew, they're only asking you to come to Richmond to help carry on the trial and convict Aaron Burr . . . if he is guilty."

John arrived in response to their summons. Andrew turned two dining chairs to face the hearth. Both men stretched their legs toward the banked ashes.

"I know this is a bad season for you to leave," started John; "I'm also afraid that the trial may drag on considerably. You are not legally obliged to go to Richmond. But in all good conscience, is there any way for you to ignore this subpoena? After all, you've been a judge, and you must assist the Federal court in Richmond to function."

"If war with Spain had started," countered Andrew, "Colonel Burr would have been a hero instead of a villain."

"Ifs don't count," replied John tartly. "There'll be no hysteria in Chief Justice John Marshall's court. When you get on that stand, you stick to the facts: precisely what Burr said or wrote to you, what he ordered, paid for. Leave your opinions home with Rachel, who will take tender care of them in your absence."

There was no mistaking the stern warning in John's voice; Rachel saw Andrew's face go red as he bolted up from his chair and stood glaring down at John.

"Since you sent for me," said John coolly, "I assumed that you wanted my advice; and having ridden eight miles in very much of a hurry, you are going to get it whether you like its flavor or not."

"Oh, I always intended to go," growled Andrew, deflated.

The two men burst into laughter. Rachel sat quietly listening to their discussion of the impending trial, and what they knew about similar trials for treason; whether or not Aaron Burr's copious but ambiguous talk would be sufficient to get him convicted.

"Andrew, John, do you think it's at all possible . . . that you two could go into the law together again someday? It isn't too late, is it?"

"I'd be willing," said Overton, his eyes bulking up like warm gray granite. "How about you, Andrew?"

"Frankly, I don't know. I must have forgotten most of my law by now."

'But you haven't forgotten how to shoot."

A silence fell. At the sound of the word "shoot" all three of their minds went back, not to the rough-and-tumble days when Andrew had had to carry his guns to enfore respect for the law and the courts, as John had intended, but to the Dickinson duel. Rachel felt hollow at the bottom of her stomach: the unfortunate little joke had answered her question better than an hour-long discussion: it was too late.

Andrew left for Richmond in the middle of June. Standing in the cornfield talking with Andy, she thought how more than half the time she was left to manage the plantation alone. Andrew had the energy to manage a dozen farms as big as the Hermitage, while the need to pace the work in the fields left her exhausted; but somehow there was always something to keep him from it. The penetrating sun was burning her face as deeply red as John Coffee's, the skin on her hands was becoming parched, a furrow deepened between her brows, pale, crinkling lines appeared about her eyes where she squinted to gaze over the expanse of work still to be done, or to the horizon to judge the next day's weather. Despite the sunbonnet she draped about her head like the other laborers in her fields, her hair was baked dry by the omnipresent heat. She was obliged to wear big boots while striding the rows; to her consternation she found that her shoes were almost impossible to get on.

She thought of the time at Hunter's Hill when she had become ill because of Andrew's absences, and had feared that she had lost so much of her attractiveness that her husband might no longer love her. Now she was forty; her figure was beginning to thicken at the waist. She sent in to Tatum's for the new French creams, rubbed oil through her hair in the mornings when she found it dry and brittle, ordered field gloves in which to work.

And, as ever, their separation served no purpose. During the solid month that Andrew spent in Richmond the case had not come to trial. He returned disgruntled.

"The first twenty days we sat there doing nothing because General Wilkinson refused to obey his summons. Then Chief Justice Marshall tried to get President Jefferson to testify, and Mr. Jefferson refused to come. There we sat, trying to convict one man of treason because he put together a few flatboats, while the English warship *Leopard* raked our ship the *Chesapeake,* killing and wounding twenty-one of our seamen on the flimsy pretext that we had a couple of English seamen aboard. That broadside was fired so close to the capital it must have rattled the dishes right off Mr. Jefferson's dinner table. But does he get mad? Does he protest to the British? Does he promise to blow their ships out of the water if they don't stop waging war on us? Hardly! He turns to polite diplomacy . . . which the British love. I made an hour's speech on the courthouse steps, best darn speech I ever made in my whole life. 'Mr. Jefferson has plenty of courage to seize peaceable Americans and persecute them for political purposes,' says I, 'but he is too cowardly to resent foreign outrage on the Republic. Millions to persecute an American,' I told that crowd, 'but not a cent to resist England.' ''

Rachel shook her head at him in amused despair.

"My, my, that's going to make you popular with the Administration.''

An article in the *Impartial Review* informed her that Mr. Andrew Jackson had been indicted for trespass, assault and battery against Mr. Samuel Jackson, no relation, charged with having attacked Samuel Jackson with a sword cane, on the premises where he had a shop and living quarters. The trial was to take place in four weeks.

This was the first time her information service had failed her. It was strange, for the brawl had taken place right out on Market Street with rocks being thrown, the two men fighting with their fists and then being separated by spectators.

Acting on an impulse she went back to Moll's and George's cabin.

"George, did you know that Mr. Jackson had a fight in Nashville with Samuel Jackson ?''

"Yes, Miz Rachel, we all knowed it. Miz Jane says be sure not to mention it.''

The now elderly couple dropped their eyes. Rachel walked back to the house, her feet dragging. This quarrel which had been so studiously kept from her could only mean a new outburst of gossip. Who was this Samuel Jackson, a newcomer to Nashville? Was there perhaps a Mrs. Jackson, a new member of the Culture Club, who had come in from Kentucky with a fresh re-reading of the record that Rachel Robards had been declared by a jury, "Guilty as charged"? How virulent this new outburst must be if Andrew had again taken to violence to combat it: Andrew, who had cried at the time that the record would live to plague them.

Gazing moodily out a side window she recognized the coal-black mare that Robert Hays had given his daughter several years before. Eighteen-year-old Rachel came into the house, draping her capote over a chair in front of the fireplace. The ride had brought high color to her cheeks, but her green eyes, so like her mother's, were red-rimmed, Rachel poured some milk into a copper boiling pan from the large leather jack, then stirred in a little chocolate and maple syrup. The girl turned the mug of hot chocolate in her hands, staring into the flames and stalking the right moment to begin. Rachel sat across the dining table, watching the light of the fire through the youngster's soft blond hair, thinking how much she would have liked to have a daughter.

Suddenly her niece burst into tears, folding her arms over her face as a child might. Rachel went quickly around the table and stood before her.

"What is it, Rachel?'' she asked softly.

"George Blakemore and those ruffians he goes about with: Shadrach Nye, Benjamin Rawlings . . . they're saying the most dreadful things." The girl raised her head; her eyes were thoroughly frightened. "I know you will help me, and Uncle Andrew will make them stop . . ."

"There's nothing we'd rather do than help you, darling."

"That George Blakemore, at the tavern last night, he told a lot of men, 'Like aunt, like niece.' "

Rachel quivered.

"Oh, Aunt Rachel, they've said so many ugly things about you. And now they're saying them about me. I know I like pretty clothes, and spend too much of Papa's money . . ."

"That's purely a family matter, my dear, and of no interest to an outsider." She tilted the girl's head upward until their eyes were on a level, then said firmly, "Now you must tell me what they are accusing you of."

"Of having a baby!"

The words had shot out. She averted her head and began weeping again.

"Of having a . . . ?" For a moment Rachel was too stunned to grasp the implication of what had been said. Then she murmured, "Oh, my dear," and took the girl in her arms, feeling as utterly sick as she had that day so long ago when Andrew had brought home the news that they had not been legally married.

"Who could start such a malignant rumor?"

"I don't know. A wagoner who was hauling Joel Childrips' property over to Forks Camp saw the Hudson boy and told him he'd heard Rachel Hays had a fine son. George Blakemore told Boyd, 'Have you heard the news? Miss Rachel Hays had a child; Davis told me he saw her with the child in her arms, about to suckle it.' "

"Oh, Rachel, there's been some dreadful mistake. Go on home, dear. Your uncle and I will handle it."

Andrew had already heard the rumor.

"Andrew, who could possibly start a story like that? Do you know?"

"Yes, I traced it down. Samuel Jackson's wife."

"Samuel Jackson! The one you . . . fought with?"

"Yes."

"And that was the reason for your quarrel?"

"Yes. I wrote him a note telling him to silence his wife or I would hold him responsible. He refused."

"Oh, darling, I thought it was about us. Jane thought so too. She tried to protect me."

"I'll go into Nashville first thing in the morning, and make every last one of those men sign an affidavit that they are liars. Where are my pistols?"

And so he did, bringing six signed statements home to Rachel to put in her strongbox. The talk dried up instantly, no one wanting to share Charles Dickinson's fate. What Andrew had never been able to do for them, he had swiftly accomplished for young Rachel Hays.

4

She had never seen him so irascible or depressed. He had troubles enough, she knew, for most of them were too close at hand and too familiar to be concealed; he had to sell his racecourse at a loss; he and Jax closed their store, and not even their desperate dunning succeeded in raising any appreciable part of the twenty thousand dollars owed them by customers. No purchaser could be found for the store, the tavern or the boatyard. Jax gave Andrew his personal notes for half the debt, then went back to surveying for a living. Her own account books showed that there was no use farming the Hermitage except for their own food: the merchants were taking all the profit, leaving them no return for their year of hard labor except swollen feet, a sore back and the glory of having raised a crop.

Though Aaron Burr had been acquitted in the Richmond court, most of the Cumberland Valley felt he had committed no treason only because his conspiracy had been discovered in time. Andrew incurred additional disfavor by defending Burr and damning his accusers. Enlistments in his militia ceased altogether; interest in the musters fell to such a low point that not enough soldiers assembled on drill days to warrant a review. When the presidential election rolled around Andrew canvassed the countryside for James Monroe in an effort to defeat Secretary of State Madison, whom Jefferson wanted as his successor. If his effort earned no votes for Mr. Monroe, it earned for himself a renewed vote of hostility from the government in Washington City.

And now, after seventeen years of marriage, a strangeness fell between them; Andrew went about his chores silently, glumly; even little Andy's company could not raise him out of the doldrums. He glowered when she made little jokes, and when she once timidly suggested that they try a few of their duets he put her off with a curt wave of the hand. He rarely talked to her: she moved quietly through the hours, saying little, waiting for the opportunity to bring their common problems into the open. It was a considerable time before she grasped that the basis of his melancholy was that nothing interested him any more, and consequently he had nothing to do. When in desperation she persuaded him to race one of their two-year-olds he heard a last-minute rumor in the stables, dashed out to the starting line and held up the race at the point of his pistols. He began going into town to spend his afternoons at the Nashville Inn, word seeping back to the Hermitage that he was drinking too much, pounding his fists on the table and getting red of face.

She had always imagined that her most unhappy periods were those of Andrew's long absences; but this was worse. No matter what she might have suffered in terms of personal loneliness she had had the reassurance that he was doing an important job, that they were building for the future, and that her husband loved her. But where was the mighty soaring bridge which enabled them to meet and clasp hands when they were together in the same house yet separated by a chasm of despair? How could it be that a man who had done the work of a dozen men, with energies enough on the side to be a student of all that went on, how could that same man only a month or a year later have insufficient energy or interest to take care of his simplest duties? Every day was Friday now; lucky Tuesday had disappeared from the week. In their early days he had said that their love was a fortress, impregnable from without. Had it decayed from within?

She knew intuitively that talk with an unhappy man was dangerous: it could flare into argument or angry retort, words which would be difficult to forget. Yet surely there was something even more dangerous than the possibility of provoking Andrew: the possibility of his doing himself irremedial damage. She did not believe him to be quarrelsome by nature; he liked people, was loyal to his friends, wanted to be loved. But circumstances seemed to combine in an infinite variety to rob him of his tranquillity, to violate his innate sense of justice. Was this too part of their life pattern? Must it always be so? Or did men go through cycles in their lives, just as the earth did? Now he was lying hard and barren beneath a winter snow; but surely if the soil was good, and the proper season came, it would yield?

In her need she found company and friendship with her brother Severn. His cabin, just beyond the Hermitage spring, reminded her of Poplar Grove. It was small but cozy, with an adjoining lean-to similar to the one Johnny's Mary had used for her prayers, big enough to hold the large bed in which the four older children slept. The baby's trundle was kept in the main room.

It was strange about Severn: Rachel had never been close to him, his illness had made him shy and he had kept himself apart from the family. He looked like no one Rachel had ever seen, bearing not the slightest resemblance to his parents or to any of his brothers or sisters. Now that they had won each other's confidence she learned that Severn read in the Bible for an hour upon awakening and also before going to sleep at night. Perhaps that is the source of his tranquillity, she thought; anyone who grows up hand in hand with death must have a feeling of intimacy with God. When she listened to Severn speak with reverence of God's will she knew that of the eleven Donelson children, he alone had inherited his father's religious nature; and that seemed doubly wondrous to her; for Severn not to have inherited his father's eyes or chin or voice or wilderness fever but precisely the one thing he needed to sustain him: devoutness. In her confused and frightened frame of mind, when Jane's cool asepticism would have been unacceptable, she had found a brother whose very nature fitted her need.

In return she was able to help Severn, whose wife Elizabeth was growing increasingly unable to cope with her brood; she had borne five children in the eight years of their marriage, not a staggering amount by Donelson standards: Johnny's wife Mary was about to have her thirteenth, Mary Caffrey had twelve: but Elizabeth had had a bad period after the birth of each child. During Andrew's frequent absences, that now began to extend from the day in town to several days on the road, Rachel and little Andy walked over to Severn's bringing a lunch basket and sweets; sometimes she took the four older youngsters back home with her. When Elizabeth was with child again she cried to Rachel:

"It isn't that I don't love them, but I just don't have the strength to bear them and nurse them and keep them out from under my feet."

Rachel thought, Oh, Liz, if you could know how terribly I have wished that God would bless me with just one. She recalled Jane's saying shortly after she had moved into Poplar Grove, "For some women they come a little too fast, for others a little too slow, but we Donelsons all seem to get our share." Jane, how wrong you were!

Andrew had been away for a week when she received word that he was on his way home after working with a group of Sumner County folks who were planning to move down to the new Mississippi Territory. She heated a tub of water, dressed in a soft brown muslin with the full skirt which she preferred to the newly fashionable narrow ones, and hung her pearl brooch on the end of her silver chain. She had Mitty polish the large candelabrum and put it in the center of the white huckaback-linen board cover, set the dining-room table festively, placing a vase of riotously colored autumn leaves at one end. The papaws were ripening, and she piled some in a pewter bowl on the sideboard next to Andrew's decanters. When he arrived home shortly before dark and saw the special preparations, he asked:

"Party?"

"For two."

"I see." Then with a wry smile, "Welcoming home the prodigal son?"

"The prodigal husband."

'I guess you could call me that; and it would be the kindest thing that has been said of me in quite a while."

"You should stay home more often and listen to your wife. I can think of all sorts of nice things I would like to say if I thought you were interested."

"I'm always interested in anything you have to say, Mrs. Jackson."

"Not for the past few months you haven't been, Mr. Jackson."

He walked over to the table and selected a pickled walnut from a pewter porringer. Then, slowly, almost apologetically, he moved toward where she was standing, took her in his arms and kissed her.

"Darling, you haven't kissed me for so very long, or taken me in your arms."

"I know, I've been too unhappy; when you hate yourself and the whole world around you . . ."

"But Andrew, you've always been so strong, so sure of yourself."

"I don't know. Everything just seems to have . . ."

"Could one of the reasons be that you are quarreling so constantly with Mr. Jefferson and President Madison? What would you do if you were in their shoes? Each section of the country has its special problems, and its separate demands. With the war still going on in Europe each foreign country has its demands too."

"I'll admit poor Mr. Madison is beset by everyone . . . including me." He grinned, the first sign that the good soil of Andrew Jackson was sprouting life again. "God help anyone who has to be president!" Then he waved his arms high above his head and brought his fists plunging through the air. "But by the Eternal, I'd be tougher with the British; I'd kick them out of those forts in the North . . ."

He picked up one of his clay pipes, filled it with tobacco, then crouched on the hearth, lighting it with a small live coal. "Those families over in Sumner County have reports that the land is fertile in the Mississippi Territory, and that a man can own as much of it as he can survey. There's a Federal judgeship open down there; if it paid only a thousand dollars a year, I'd take it."

He looked up into her face. "I think we can get the appointment this time; it's not a big enough job for Mr. Madison to bother about. Well, my dear, what do you think?"

What could she think? The last time he had wanted "to shake the dust of the Cumberland Valley from my boots," he had thought to go in splendor as governor of the new and vast Louisiana Territory, with a governor's mansion, and high social standing. Now, only five years later, he was content to plunge into the wilderness, swing an ax to level the fields and build himself another log cabin . . . if only he could get a thousand-dollar-a-year judgeship!

Two events, one political and one personal, brought them great pleasure: the election of their old friend Willie Blount as governor; and the marriage of John Coffee to Johnny's daughter Mary. The wedding party at the Mansion was the happiest reunion the Donelson family had known in a long time. Rachel and Andrew were pleased to have their good friend Jax a member of the family; by way of a wedding present they took from their strongbox Jax's notes for his portion of the store debts and tore them up.

When Severn's Elizabeth was ready to be delivered, Rachel hired the best midwife in the neighborhood and went herself to assist in the nursing. The child got itself born without difficulty, but there was a complication which the midwife did not explain. A half hour later it resolved itself in the form of a second child, a twin boy. Elizabeth burst into tears.

"Why does it have to be two when I have barely the strength to nurse one?"

One of the twins began to cry. Rachel took the baby, wrapped him in a soft blanket and put him on her shoulder with his head nestled against her neck. She was standing this way when Severn and Andrew came into the room. Andrew stood above her, gazing down at the infant in her arms, sensing how her heart ached with the need to keep this newborn babe right where he was. Then, suddenly, Elizabeth called from the bed:

"Keep that boy. We only expected one. We wouldn't be losing anything."

Rachel turned her head slowly.

"Yes, Rachel, keep that boy you have in your arms," said Severn softly, "we know how you've longed for a child, and he'll be well off."

Rachel looked about her, managing to bring Andrew's face into focus. His eyes were bright. Weak with expectancy, she sank into a chair, still holding the child.

"You can't be serious, Liz. This is your child. You just bore him. Wait until you recover your strength before you make such an important decision."

"If we could bring some happiness to you, Rachel and Andrew," said Severn, "and at the same time help Liz and the boy . . ."

Andrew's expression left little doubt about how he felt.

Elizabeth asked: "Do you have a woman at home who can wet-nurse him?"

"Yes. Orange has a little one."

"Then take him right this instant. Andrew, you go into Nashville tomorrow and file adoption papers."

When they reached the Hermitage, Andrew drew a chair up to the fire for her. She sat holding the baby in her arms and looking down into its face. Andrew watched her silently. Her eyes were fathomless, all the mystery and magic of life reflected in them. The years had fallen away.

They named him Andrew Jackson, Jr. Andrew brought her the adoption papers, signed and approved by the court, to put into her strongbox. Jane brought her the Hays trundle, which Rachel placed beside her bed. She had trouble falling asleep at night because she was listening so intently to the child's breathing; if a twig fell on the roof she was out of bed and leaning over the crib before she was awake. He was a long lean baby, with a thatch of black hair and pastel blue eyes; he cried little, except in the early morning when he was hungry. Rachel kept the fire roaring in the cabin to make sure he did not catch cold; Andrew could hardly breathe for the heat.

One day George reported that Mr. Jackson would not be home to dinner. When Andrew reached the Hermitage later that evening he was excitedly leading a new filly across the yard. Rachel ran up to him and examined the little roan race horse. Her eyes sought Andrew's, a small smile playing about her lips: could it be her husband's nose had been put out of joint?

The filly was so small and light in weight that it hardly seemed she could last out a long race.

"That's why I got her cheap," said Andrew gleefully as he came in from the yard where he had been training her. "I've entered her in the big race on Saturday with a thousand-dollar side bet against the course champion."

To everyone's astonishment except Andrew's, the little roan won handily, streaking around the course so fast her hoofs hardly seemed to touch the turf. Rachel could not tell from Andrew's chuckles whether his pleasure came from this renewed proof of his sense of horseflesh, or the fact that he had won what would have been a year's salary from the Mississippi judgeship . . . which had just been given to someone else.

"You know what I'm going to do with this thousand dollars?" he asked.

"No, what?"

"I heard of a stand of arms for sale in Hiwassie, and I'm going to use this money to buy them. I'm starting out tomorrow to see and talk to every militiaman who's ever served under me; if I can't persuade them back into the ranks, or convince them that we'll be training for an actual war, then I'll simply have to bribe them with whatever it is they need: a horse, or a sword, or a gun. I've got to build that militia from inside myself; there is no other place it can come from."

He was gone all day now, touring the countryside. Rachel would watch him leave the Hermitage a little after dawn, when she rose to tend the baby. It's so important that he be happy, she repeated to herself, for when he is unhappy he tears himself apart, and then the seamside of his fabric shows through.

For herself the baby had an annealing effect; a buoyancy permeated her outlook and her actions. She felt light on her feet, running the hundreds of errands needed for the child, and light of heart as she played the pianoforte after dinner. She was happy and grateful; she no longer turned inward, wondering what people knew or thought about her. She met strangers as easily as she did friends. Her sanguinity coincided with Andrew's renewed faith in himself, his own return to patience and lightness of touch. She realized that therein lay the curse and the genius of a good marriage: that what happened to one member happened equally to both.

She was the only one who knew that Andrew was spending his own money on the militia. He told her, "We should never count pennies on this subject," yet she was amused to see that he brought home the record of every dollar spent, asking her to post it in his militia account book.

"So you really think we'll be paid back, Andrew?"

"If war comes, every dollar will be returned; if not, it'll be like coming in second in a horse race."

As a result of his new fighting spirit, and Governor Blount's espousal, Sunday was once again open house at the Hermitage. A group of bright young aides-de-camp came for the afternoon and supper: Thomas Hart Benton, a law student, Robert Butler, recently married to Rachel Hays, John Reid, a bank clerk, William Carroll, who owned a successful hardware store in Nashville, and William B. Lewis, a neighbor. Eight years had passed since Andrew had taken command, so that he was able to draw a whole new generation of subalterns from among Rachel's nephews. When the weather was warm she spread long tables under the catalpa trees; when it turned cool she served inside, using her cherry-wood dining table as a buffet, with some thirty men standing in groups eating and discussing military problems. Andrew, Jr., learning to walk, made the adventuresome journey from one military leg to another as though he were wandering through a forest of young trees.

For the first master muster the following spring Rachel rode in her carriage to the drill grounds. There formerly had been some two thousand members of the militia, but surely, she told herself, there could not be more than two hundred assembled here? Few of the townspeople had bothered to come, the wrestling matches had disappeared, there were only a few old women selling ginger cakes. Yet even to her inexperienced eye it was clear that there were many new guns in evidence, as well as fine horses and considerable of what Andrew called *acouterments*. Andrew was pleased.

"Wait till word gets around about the new spirit and the new muskets," he told her; "the volunteers will start drifting back of their own accord."

It seemed only a few months before a visiting officer declared General Jackson's militia the most perfect of its kind in the country. Rachel found herself thinking, If war must come, let it come now so that Andrew can prove he has been right.

5

And so he was. On June 21, 1812, Billey Phillips, their former jockey and now a presidential courier, brought the news from Washington to Nashville: the United States had declared war on Great Britain!

Rachel was swept by a hundred inner gales. War, then, as Andrew had predicted that first night at supper at the Donelson stockade, more than twenty years before. She thought of the line he was so fond of quoting: someone had spoken to Benjamin Franklin of the Revolution as the War for Independence, and Mr. Franklin had replied, "Sir, the war for independence is yet to come!" Well, it was here now, and she knew that whatever might happen to the country, the government or the army it was a war that Andrew Jackson would never abandon until it had been won.

The weeks of July 1812 passed in a fever. Andrew rose at dawn and tried to supervise the farming of the Hermitage, but he was so preoccupied with military affairs that the effort was galling to him. Once again she made her way into the fields, releasing him for the thousand tasks involved in getting his troops armed and trained: for there was no help forthcoming from either the state or the Federal government, and he had to send out his own purchasing agents to places like Newport in Kentucky to bring back the necessary muskets and ammunition. To Rachel, who had watched him drawing up his maps, he explained:

"If President Madison approves, I can move my militia to Canada within ninety days and take Quebec. The British forces there are still feeble. We could sweep straight through Canada before they'd have a chance to reinforce their garrisons."

Since the Creeks, now heavily armed and incited by British agents, had already begun their war at the Tennessee border, Andrew stood poised with his men, ready to move in either direction upon receipt of an order. Then, late in July, the message arrived. Andrew was away, so Rachel tore open the sealed envelope. She read:

> The tender of Service by Genl. Jackson and the volunteers under his command is Received by the President with peculiar satisfaction and in accepting their services, he cannot withhold an expression of his admiration of the zeal and ardour by which they are animated.
>
> WILLIAM EUSTIS
> Secretary of War

The news of Secretary of War Eustis's note had been released by Governor Blount, and with it the announcement that a general of the United States Army was to be appointed from the West and dispatched at once to Canada. When Andrew reached home he barely glanced at the note which she stood waving at him as he came across the yard to the house.

The War Department has accepted my plan for a march on Quebec!" he exclaimed. "Rachel, remember at Hunter's Hill, when you said to me, 'Why Andrew, I do believe you would like to be a regular officer in the United States Army'? Well, my dear, it has come to pass."

"You've received the appointment?"

"It should be here on the next dispatch. I've alerted the militia. We'll be ready to move within a few hours."

The appointment came through the very next day, but it was for James Winchester, Andrew's second-in-command, who was made a brigadier general in the regular army and ordered to leave at once with Kentucky troops to join General William H. Harrison in Canada. Andrew sat on a bench outside their cabin, his face an earth-red in color, a dazed expression in his eyes, looking straight through Rachel.

"Perhaps it's because General Winchester had such a fine record in the Revolution?" she offered. When he did not answer, she continued, "Or it may be that they want you for the southern campaign? You've been telling the War Department for years that when the British struck they'd come in through Louisiana."

This helped a little; he gulped a few times and moved his head as though searching for the early August stars through the trees.

The first news of the war in the North was catastrophic: General Hull, who commanded the largest part of the American troops in Canada, had surrendered Detroit and his entire army. For days Andrew wandered about the Hermitage, unable to eat or sleep or discuss anything else. This time she did not try to bring him out of his gloom: it was too deep to be dissipated by any comforting word.

He did not find release from his lethargy for almost a full week, and then only because he learned that four hundred first-class rifles, of a better caliber than anything his militia had ever owned, were available on the Indian frontier. He secured twenty-eight hundred dollars from Governor Blount, signed his own personal paper for another thirty-two hundred dollars and sent the swiftest scouts in Tennessee to buy the rifles before anyone else could stumble across them.

At long last, in October, Governor Blount received seventy blank commissions from the War Department. Andrew assured Rachel that this was the authorization for which they had been waiting: if they could not push the British out of Canada, at least they would now be able to reach Louisiana before the British fleet could transport its victorious northern troops to New Orleans. She and Andrew were having a late supper after having taken Andy back to the Cumberland Academy, which had formerly been the Davidson Academy, when General Robertson came in from Knoxville. They could tell he was angry by the way he kept pushing back his bang of pure-white hair.

"I got bad news for you, son: the President and Secretary of War are ignorin' your militia. Governor Blount has been ordered to call out and equip fifteen hundred new volunteers."

Andrew sat stunned, his extraordinarily large mouth open and out of control, foam working in one corner. Rachel asked:

"But how can that be? They know that Andrew has twenty-seven hundred men trained and ready. They already accepted . . ."

General Robertson answered softly, as one does in the presence of a stricken man.

"Governor Blount is convinced that the President and the War Department don't want Andrew in their army."

"No," Andrew shot back, finding speech at last, "they want General Hull, who surrenders without a shot. I might fight, and embarrass them."

"Confidentially, son, the governor is afraid you won't take a subordinate position under General Wilkinson. But maybe I can find some way . . ."

"All I ask is a chance to fight; but to have to sneak into the war through the back door . . ."

Rachel sat quietly, her hands folded in her lap, half listening to the discussion, half hearing her own inner voices. The War Department had made it mercilessly clear that they were afraid of Andrew and mistrusted him. Why? Because of the Burr affair? Because of his early political quarrels with Sevier and Jefferson? Because he had had no real war experience? She would not let herself think what would happen to her husband if he were denied the right to participate in this war of which he had kept Tennessee aware these many years.

"Once you're inside the house, Andrew," she proffered, "the interior looks the same regardless of whether you came in the front door or the back."

He smiled at her wanly, said, "Agreed!" then turned to Robertson. "Just get me into the war, by fair means or foul, and nobody will ever get me out."

Her family reported that their every enemy in the state was working to convince Governor Blount that since the War Department had rejected Mr. Jackson, he must do likewise. Rachel watched Andrew grow thinner and jumpier with the passing of the days, but she knew that Willie Blount must be suffering equally: for he had now signed sixty-nine of the commissions, and had only one left. Would he abandon his old friend and commander of his western division? It seemed to Rachel that Andrew had not uttered ten words since the blank commissions had reached Tennessee.

On November 1, the governor's respect for Andrew conquered his fear of the War Department: Andrew was commissioned a major general of the volunteers, ordered to call a rendezvous of his troops and to move as quickly as possible to New Orleans to reinforce General Wilkinson.

Andrew brought home an overseer, an elderly man by the name of Dinwiddie, who did not look to Rachel as though he would be of much help. During the next ten days she showed Mr. Dinwiddie over the Hermitage and laid out her plan of work. She saw almost nothing of Andrew, who was trying to assemble a thousand horses for Colonel John Coffee's cavalry, a flotilla of flatboats to transport his militia down the Mississippi, muskets, powder and shot, medical supplies, blankets, tents and uniforms, of which there were almost none available except what the volunteers offered themselves. When he issued his order for the rendezvous in Nashville, Rachel asked:

"Darling, can you give me any idea of how long you may be gone?"

"No, my dear, only the British know the answer to that. They are in complete control in the North, raiding and burning all through New England, with no one to stop them. Their ships can move thousands of men southward to invade through the Floridas and Louisiana."

"Then let me come into Nashville and stay for the last days of your encampment? There's room for us at Tabitha's."

Tabitha was Johnny's daughter who had married Polly's brother, George Smith. She awoke on the morning of the rendezvous to the most penetrating cold she had experienced in the Cumberland. She waited until the fire was crackling in the downstairs hearth before venturing to dress her son. Her sled had been brought out; she and the boy huddled beneath a big bear robe, while Andrew rode alongside on his black charger, man and horse sending up streamers of frosty breath. The Cumberland River had frozen during the night, a sight she had not seen since the unhappy dawn at Hunter's Hill when she had despaired of her husband's long absences. Andrew leaned over to tell her what bad luck it was to have this terrible cold on the day the troops were to rendezvous, and how glad he was that the quartermaster, Major William B. Lewis, had assembled a thousand cords of wood at the cantonment.

When they reached Nashville Rachel went directly to Tabitha's house. At four o'clock she put on a heavily lined capuchin, mittens and boots, and waited for young Thomas Hart Benton to take her to the cantonment. The ground was snow-covered, but the camp itself, where more than two thousand men stood stomping about the fires, had been turned into a slough of mud. Benton led her to Andrew's tent; he was writing orders on a crudely contrived table.

"Andrew, they're saying in town that it's going to be the coldest night in the history of Tennessee. Couldn't you billet the men in the homes and stores and taverns?"

"I have no authority to do that," he said. "Besides, if we can't survive one night of cold how are we going to stay alive through a whole war?"

It was pitch-black by the time she reached her niece's house. Little Andrew was asleep. Rachel sat before the fire reading in Psalms 91:5:

Thou shalt not be afraid for the terror by night; nor for the arrow that flieth by day.

The cold so permeated the very stones of the hearth that by seven o'clock she began heating the sheets of her bed with the copper warming pan filled with hot coals. She slept intermittently, worried about Andrew and the men who had insuffcient blankets to lie in the snow.

The next morning Andrew sent her a message that his troops had weathered their first bout with adversity. At the breakfast table she asked her redheaded niece:

"Tabitha, is that artist, Josh Clenning, still painting vases and fans? Do you think he can catch a likeness on ivory?"

"I think so, Aunt Rachel. Why don't we go ask him?"

During the following weeks Andrew managed occasionally to come into Tabitha's for a cup of coffee late at night. He strode up and down the front room in his dark blue uniform, boots and sword, his red hair now graying at the temples, a cyclone of activity, telling Rachel of his problems. The two months' advance pay which the soldiers wanted to leave behind with their families had not arrived from Washington City. He was attempting to assemble provisions and boats on his own credit, and had used his own personal note for sixteen hundred dollars on urgent supplies; would she be sure to meet it when it came due in ninety days? He did not tell her with what.

Rachel went each morning for a sitting at Josh Clenning's, but apparently the artist did not think the general and his troops were going to leave Nashville; he only shrugged when Rachel tried to hasten his work.

Finally, in the first week of January, Colonel John Coffee rode off with his six hundred and seventy cavalrymen, heading down the Natchez Trace. Three days later she stood on the bank of the river, Andrew, Jr., in her arms, while she and the entire population of Nashville waved and cried their farewells to General Jackson and his fourteen hundred infantrymen. Andrew had said to her that morning as he kissed her goodby:

"Be of good heart, my dear, I can take care of myself. You know I'll be doing the one job I've wanted most in life to do."

Yes, she knew this; and she was resigned. She said, "Darling, he promised me he would have it ready. I wanted you to have it as my farewell gift."

"Oh, a surprise?"

"A painting of me, on ivory. I wanted you to carry it in your pocket."

"Not a chance. It'll go around my neck on a chain, and I'll never take it off, night or day. If it's finished within the next ten days send it by Dinwiddie to the juncture of the Cumberland and Ohio. It will be my good-luck piece."

She stood on the bank, watching the last of the boats shove off from the shore in the cold gray January light, with Andrew's lead boat slowly pulling out of sight.

6

It was not until she had entered the front door and Moll had taken her cape that she perceived the change that had come over her home in the short time since she had left it; for this would be Andrew's first long absence from the Hermitage. When he had been away for a week or a month she had felt his presence within the rooms, heard his voice, seen his lanky figure moving about with that awkward grace of extraordinarily tall men. Now he was gone: his voice, his figure, his presence; and the room had become not only enormous but empty.

She sat on the edge of one of her parlor chairs while Moll took the boy upstairs, not tired physically yet pervaded by a sense of letdown. Did soldiers' wives gear themselves to be brave and cheerful, and never let their husbands see any of the trembling or fear? And when the men had gone, when they returned to the silence of their homes, having used up the grit meant to last a year or perhaps a lifetime, did they all suffer alike? Did they feel weak and hollow, not knowing how long it might take before they could stand on their feet again? And why was it that not even the presence of a beloved son could make up for the absence of a beloved husband?

Moll and the boy came downstairs; he was in his night clothes and ready for supper. Rachel read to him for a little while, then put him to sleep early, in her own bed, for he had been up since dawn. Moll was sitting in a little rocker by the fire when she returned to the big room. Her hair had turned white and her face had thinned considerably with the years, but otherwise she gave no sign that she had passed her seventieth birthday.

"You didn't have to wait for me, Moll; I'm not planning to eat anything."

"I know *you* ain't, Miz Rachel, but *I'm* plannin'. General Jackson, he tell me before he leave, I'm to take care of you. Remember up on the Hill how skinny you got 'cause you wouldn't eat? Now you come over to the table and have some of this here pot pie."

She ate a little of the veal to satisfy Moll, then felt better and warmer. She went upstairs, undressed quickly, put on a long flannel nightgown, not bothering to braid her hair or put on a nightcap. She moved the boy onto his pillow, tucked the blankets around his shoulders, then slipped into her old and badly worn blue silk Spanish robe. She was weary from the long trip, from the days of waiting and the constant anxiety that at any moment Andrew might be relieved of his command; but she knew she could not sleep, for her loneliness was wide awake within her.

Downstairs, she put fresh logs on the fire and sat very close to its heat, her elbows planted firmly on her knees, her palms extended toward the flames. The nights would be the worst; during the day she could placate time with her chores, she would have the company of her son, she would invite over several of Severn's children; yet the greatest burden a woman had to bear was to be left behind with so little to do beyond the repetitious and, when alone, meaningless chores of housekeeping. It was the fate of women, she reflected, never to be the doers in the sense that men were, but always to serve as passive instruments to whom things happened.

She rose and moved about the room, touching old and familiar objects: her mother's gridiron hanging by the side of the fireplace, the big wooden clock, her pianoforte and Andrew's flute lying in its case, her father's walnut desk. She opened it, saw one of Andrew's clay pipes lying there and beside it a wooden bowl of tobacco. Unthinking, she picked up the pipe, stuffed it with tobacco, then went to the fireplace, took the pipe tongs and lifted a small coal from the fireplace, holding it to the bowl as Andrew did. The smoke tasted acrid in her mouth; it had an almost insupportably heavy body. She spat it out quickly. After a few moments she puffed in the smoke again; the sensation was not so unpleasant this time. She sank onto her chair, drawing little bits of smoke and then blowing them toward the crackling logs. She felt closer to Andrew. The pain eased a little.

She fell into a reverie, her mind returning to her early years on the Virginia plantation, and to her father, who had begun each day of his life with prayer. One of the first things he had tried to teach her was that God was not an idea or a remote presence, but actually part of herself. She could hear his voice saying to her, "We are all integral parts of God." To her father, she knew, God had been very close. When she had come upon him praying silently and asked if he wasn't afraid God might not be able to hear him, John Donelson had smiled indulgently as he replied, "No, my dear, God hears what we think even clearer than what we say."

She had never fully accepted or even understood her father's concept of the Deity. To her, God had been the all-powerful ruler of the universe, the distant and frequently terrifying force which controlled her and everybody else, whether they liked it or not. She had never been able to achieve any sense of intimacy in her prayers, for He had seemed to her to live too far away, up beyond the heavens, to be able to see or even care about one solitary soul. She knew other people besides her father who walked with their hand in God's; her brother Severn was one of these. She had prayed when Andrew had been away, but it had always been with more fear than love, and to some remote omniscience in whom she had neither abiding faith nor genuine hope.

Now she found herself on her knees by the hearth, praying for her husband with more devoutness and humility than she had ever known. Her sense of the remoteness and untouchability of God fell away; she felt His presence not merely in her house, the simple log cabin on the Hermitage, but in her being, hearing her silent prayer:

Please, let my husband find his fulfillment . . . and keep him safe.

A few days later Josh Clenning sent her picture out to the Hermitage. She took the ivory from the cotton in which Mr. Clenning had wrapped it, then stood by the window with the sun beating down on her likeness. Her heart dropped when she realized that this was by no means the picture of a young or beautiful girl. Why hadn't she had a picture painted when she had first met Andrew, when her skin had been flawlessly smooth? Then she would not have had to send her husband this picture of a forty-five-year-old woman, slightly plump under the chin.

But that was foolishness; Andrew was no longer young either: the embattlements had put rings under his eyes, wrinkles at their corners, and deep lines starting on either cheek above his nostrils and curving their way down to the corners of his uneven mouth. Thanks to the heritage from her mother, her hair was still richly black, her skin kept its slightly pink glow, the brown of her eyes was as dark and vibrant as when she had been twenty-one. There was strain there, suffering and uncertainty; these qualities hovered about her mouth too. But there was nothing frightening about losing one's youth so long as one's love struck ever deeper with the passage of the years.

She turned away from the window, wrapped the miniature securely in a box, then wrote Andrew a letter. When she had finished she summoned Mr. Dinwiddie. He returned a few days later with a reply from Andrew. She mounted the stairs, curled up on the bed and took out the sheet of paper that was covered with his cramped but clear writing.

MY LOVE:

I have this evening received your affectionate letter by Dinwiddie. He has carefully handed me your miniature. I shall wear it near my bosom; but this was useless for without your miniature my recollection never fails me of your likeness.

I thank you for your prayers. I thank you for your determined resolution to bear our separation with fortitude. I shall write to you often. If I can get the arms on board tomorrow I shall sail early on Monday morning.

It is now 1 o'clock in the morning—the candle nearly out. May the angelic hosts that reward and protect virtue be with you until I return, is the sincere supplication of your affectionate husband.

She lay quietly for a considerable time, the letter held firmly at her bosom, thinking nothing, feeling all. Then she rose, went down to the walnut desk, took paper and pen and began to write.

MY DEAR HUSBAND:

Your letter of the 18th of January from the mouth of the Cumberland river came safe to hand. It was everything to me. I rejoiced.

Do not, my beloved husband, let the love of country, fame and honor, make you forget. Without you, I would think them all empty shadows. You will say this is not the language of a patriot, but it is the language of a faithful wife.

Our little Andrew is well. Pray, my dear, write me often. It's a cordial—it's a balm to my mind in my lonesome hours. I treasure them up as a miser his gold.

Think of me your dearest friend on earth.

The reports that filtered back to her were good; John Coffee's cavalry and Andrew's flotilla were making excellent progress toward New Orleans. It was the news from the North that was disastrous: Brigadier General Winchester, having been captured by the British in Canada and assured that if he would counsel his troops to surrender they would be well treated, had given up his two regiments. Most of the Kentuckians had then been massacred by northern Indians who had been fighting alongside the British. Old General Robertson, so calm and philosophical by nature, was in an absolute rage as he paced the floor of the Hermitage.

"What has happened to the American army?" he demanded. "First Hull surrenders, not only himself, but Detroit. Now Winchester surrenders, and his two regiments with him, and we lose all those fine boys. If we'd fought that way in the Revolution we would still be British subjects. By the Eternal, Rachel, if they'll only give Andrew Jackson a chance to fight . . ."

He broke off abruptly. She caught the innuendo in his "If they'll only . . ."
She went to the old man's side, linking her arm through his.

"What has happened to upset you about Andrew?"

". . . well . . . He's being accused of having stated that the same county could
not contain himself and General Wilkinson, that he has his dueling pistols with
him."

She brushed aside the reference to dueling pistols. "When Andrew took his
commission he knew he would have to serve under General Wilkinson. He said it
was a bitter pill, but that he will obey like any other good officer."

Robertson ran his hand through his thinning white hair, sending it forward over
his brow until it came on an even line with his eyebrows.

"We know that, my dear friend, but does the War Department?"

She told herself that it was futile to worry about what such stories might do to
injure Andrew. Surely the Secretary of War was not going to dismiss an able general
on the basis of sheer rumor, not after the other generals had been so sorely defeated
and there were so few left to stand up against the British arms?

The first letter Andrew wrote her from Natchez told her that General Wilkinson
had ordered him to remain there and not to go down the river to New Orleans. He
had obeyed, pitching his tents four miles from the town in a handsome plain with
wood and water convenient. He had also written to Governor Blount and to the
War Department saying that he had followed Wilkinson's orders. His letter reassured
her.

Then, less than a month after Andrew had left with his troops, a new Secretary
of War took office in Washington City, Mr. John Armstrong. Almost instantly
upon sitting down to his desk he wrote a dispatch to Major General Jackson, a
copy of which found its way to the Hermitage:

War Department
February 5, 1813

Sir,

The causes for embodying and marching to New Orleans the Corps under your
command having ceased to exist, you will on receipt of this letter, consider it as
dismissed from public service and take measures to have delivered over to Major
General Wilkinson all articles of public property which may have been put into its
possession. You will accept for yourself and the Corps the thanks of the President of
the United States. I have the honor to be Sir, With great respect,

Your Most Obedient Servant,

She was staggered by this development. Dear God, would it never cease? She
studied the text a hundred times in an effort to make some sense out of it. *"The
causes for embodying and marching to New Orleans the Corps under your command
having ceased to exist. . . ."* What could the new Secretary of War mean? The
cause for Andrew's moving his troops to New Orleans could only cease to exist
when the war was over!

Of all the things that might have happened to Andrew, she decided, this was
the worst possible blow: after having taken two thousand men a thousand miles in
the dead of winter, having almost bankrupted himself by paying out his own money
to get whatever equipment and supplies were needed, he was now curtly dismissed!
The War Department had not wanted General Jackson in the army in the first place,
and now they had succeeded in booting him out.

7

Two weeks later Major William B. Lewis, Andrew's supply officer in Nashville,
came to her with a letter he had received from Andrew in which he asked that

transportation be sent down to the Tennessee River to afford passage for his officers and men, particularly for the sick.

"I can't send him even a single horse through army channels," Major Lewis told her. "So I've started taking up private subscriptions. I have about six hundred dollars, but Captain Erwin stopped me from collecting in Nashville on the grounds that I was aiding and abetting a mutiny."

"A mutiny!" She was thunderstruck. "On what grounds?"

"On the grounds that General Jackson was ordered to dismiss the corps under his command, but refused to do so, insisting upon marching them back to their homes."

She planted her feet firmly on the braided rag rug, stood with her legs apart as she did in the fields, and held her head high in the air.

"Well, good for General Jackson! What an idea of the War Department, to discharge all those soldiers so far from home, with no way and no supplies to get back."

Six weeks later, summoned by a courier, she rode her fastest horse into town to find the troops drawn up in the square. The men were gaunt and threadbare after their month trip up the Trace. Remembering the crowds that had turned out to bid them farewell three months before, how cannon had been fired, flags waved and speeches made, she now looked about the square to see that there was only a handful of onlookers.

As she walked toward where Andrew stood shaking the hands of his officers, she realized that she had not seen him so fleshless since his first return from Philadelphia, that hot June day in 1795 when she had come up from the barn to find him sagging on his horse in front of their cabin at Poplar Grove. But there was nothing thin about his spirit; he kissed her on the mouth, hard, the sharp bones of his body hurting her wherever they touched. As he stood there, his arm fiercely about her, watching his men leave through the many exits of the square, his emotion was not one of hurt pride, or even anger, but sheer grim determination that the War Department must not be so willfully stupid as to dismiss their fighting troops. As they rode home, their horses close together, he related how General Wilkinson had provided him with twenty days' rations, nothing more.

"I had to hire wagons and wagoners, and buy up whatever medicines I could find out of my own funds; when the food ran out or we needed additional horses I bought those too."

She looked at him quizzically.

"You bought, my dear? With what?"

"My personal notes. Drawn on Wilkinson's quartermaster."

A few days later they made a trip into town, Andrew to buy a dragon plow and a two-inch auger, Rachel to present her compliments to Sarah Bentley, who was opening a little shop to make gowns and dresses for the women of Nashville. Their carriage had no sooner entered Market Street than several people on the streets cried out, "There's General Jackson!" When Andrew had tied the horses in front of the Nashville Inn they were quickly surrounded by a group of young men. Someone called:

"Three cheers for Old Hickory!"

"Would this Old Hickory be you?" Rachel demanded, seeing him flush.

"Might. Let's go inside and find out why I've changed from a useless character to a hero overnight."

In the lobby of the inn she heard half a dozen stories at once: of how Andrew had walked all the way home, his mounts being used to carry the sick; of how he had turned over his share of the food to those who were weakened by the tropical fevers; of how he had nursed the boys and walked alongside the wagons, sometimes holding their hands, and bringing every last one home alive. Sandy Donelson said:

"Uncle ate less than anybody, walked farther, worked harder and slept the least; that's why we said he was tough."

"Sure," one of the soldiers added, "tough as hickory. We called him hickory for a considerable spell up the Trace, hating him for getting us into the mess. Then, when we saw he was going to bring us all in, we started calling him Old Hickory. We was proud to be serving under him."

John Overton pushed through the crowd, linked one arm through Rachel's and the other through Andrew's, escorting them to his office. He lifted a pile of law books and briefs from a chair, dusted it with his handkerchief. Then he turned to Andrew.

"That damned Wilkinson! He has refused to honor your notes. They've all been sent here to Nashville for collection."

Andrew's jaw locked. She watched him gulp.

"I guaranteed everyone from whom I took food, wagons, horses, medicines, that the United States Army would pay on demand, and that if they wouldn't, I would."

"How much does your paper amount to?"

"I don't know. Thousands of dollars."

"Thousands?" exclaimed Rachel. "Oh, darling, I had to sell a big part of last year's crop and much of our livestock to meet that sixteen-hundred-dollar note you left behind."

John said quietly, "I have some money put aside, it's yours for the using."

Andrew shook his head.

"How much easier it would have been for me to have dismissed my men at Natchez! I had money in my pocket, three good horses to carry me home. But could I be an obedient soldier? No! I gave Jax half my cash because his cavalry was starving, and then had to bring every last one of my men back here."

Rachel rose and stood beside him.

"And if the War Department refuses to honor the notes?"

He took her hand in his.

"Then we'll have to sell the Hermitage."

That night she heard the bleating of a young lamb. She went to the door and saw a little white animal, a few days old, which had strayed out of the barn. She picked it up and took it to Andrew, who was smoking before the fire.

"Remember that lamb we saved at Poplar Grove?" she asked. "This one looks enough like him to be his brother."

"His great-grandchild." He stroked the soft curly white wool. Rachel went to the desk, took one of his pipes and filled it with tobacco.

"I started smoking while you were away," she said. "When I was lonely I found it consoling."

He beckoned for her to come and sit by him. He put one arm about her shoulders and brought her head and cheek close to his.

"I leave you alone a terrible lot, don't I?"

She rubbed her cheek against his; he was unshaven and she found it pleasurable to feel her soft skin on the rough stubble of his beard.

"If I wanted to unboosom myself, I could tell you just how much."

He picked up a live coal in the tongs and held it in the bowl of her pipe. She sat looking into the glow of the ash, wondering where their next hearth would be. There was a brusque knock at the door. Andrew called, "Enter." Thomas Hart Benton came into the room, closed the door behind him and covered the space to the hearth all in one movement. He was thirty-one, a man of unceasing energies and ambition, handsome in a hacked-out fashion, with a powerfully made head, a great shock of hair, a huge jutting and crooked nose, devouring eyes, an orator's mouth, a massive chin. Benton said:

"General, I've come to say good-by, and to ask if you'll give me a letter of recommendation to the War Department. I'm going to apply for a position in the regular army."

"The regular army, eh? I don't think my recommendation will carry much weight right now, but I'll write them a letter telling them I think you were one of the finest officers in the corps."

"While you are writing that letter, why not restate the case of your promissory notes?" asked Rachel. "Colonel Benton can tell them the story."

The next day Andy came home, the spring term being over, and her family of four was together again. She let the two big Andrews teach little Andrew how to ride his pony and pretty soon her three men were riding across the fields, making for the river for a swim and a mess of catfish. She knew that there was a fire eating at her husband's vitals: for here he sat in enforced idleness while the war went from bad to worse, the American officers constantly being outmaneuvered and crushed by the more experienced English commanders, and no one in Washington willing to summon him or so much as let him fire a gun: yet he concealed all this from his son and nephew, giving them the companionship they so sorely missed during his absence and biding his time with more patience and fortitude than she had ever seen in him.

She returned from Severn's to find Andrew closeted with his brigade inspector, Major William Carroll, who had just been challenged by another of Andrew's officers, Littleton Johnston. From what she could gather, Carroll had refused to fight Johnston on the ground that the latter was not a gentleman, whereupon Jesse Benton, Colonel Thomas Hart Benton's younger brother and a friend of Johnston, had brought a second challenge; Carroll, assuming that Jesse Benton was willing to become a principal in the duel, had come out to the Hermitage to ask the general to deliver the challenge to Benton.

Rachel exclaimed: "Andrew, surely you are not going to let those two young men fight? Only we know how terrible . . . ."

She broke off. Andrew replied quietly:

"I'll do everything in my power to stop them."

But when he returned home the next day she learned that in spite of his efforts he had been ineffective. Jesse Benton had decided that he must fight if he were to continue to live in Tennessee; while Carroll, instead of being dissuaded by Andrew's arguments, asked that the duel be fought at ten paces instead of the usual thirty. Carroll also insisted that his commanding officer serve as his second.

"I just couldn't find any way of saying no to him, Rachel. He's such a poor shot with a pistol, and Jesse Benton is a good one."

"But if you're on the dueling ground," she protested, "it will look as though you are condoning the affair!"

Monday morning, when Andrew came home from the duel, he was wearing a broad smile.

"Young Benton wheeled so fast he couldn't aim, and only hit Carroll in the thumb. Then he suddenly doubled up at the waist and exposed the broadest part of his anatomy to Carroll. And that's precisely where he got shot. He'll have to eat his meals standing up for a week or two."

On the Fourth of July they received a letter from Thomas Benton from Washington City informing them that the War Department had ordered General Wilkinson to pay General Jackson's notes in full. Rachel felt as though a hundred-pound sack of meal had been unlashed from her back. They were deeply grateful to Benton for his assistance; Andrew wrote thanking him. However, others in Nashville were reaching Benton with a series of inflammatory letters about the duel, charging Andrew Jackson with having been the instigator. Andrew explained the circumstances;

Benton replied that Andrew had conducted the duel in a "savage, unequal, unfair and base manner." Friends brought word to the Hermitage that Colonel Benton was about to challenge General Jackson; Andrew became so incensed that he promised to horsewhip his aide on sight.

She was operating the churn in the shade of the catalpas, with both boys helping her, when Robert Hays appeared in view, his horse breathing hard.

"There's been a ruckus in town, Rachel; Andrew's got himself a little hurt. I think you best come in with me."

As they drove off, Robert linked his arm through hers, telling her as simply as he could what had happened: Tom and Jesse Benton had come from their home in Franklin the night before and put up at the City Hotel. Andrew and John Coffee had tied their horses at the Nashville Inn, then cut across the square to the post office. On the way back they had passed the City Hotel, and there in the doorway had stood Tom Benton, glowering at them. Andrew had raised his riding whip; Benton went into his breast pocket for his pistol; Andrew snatched his pistol out of his back pocket, pressing it against Tom Benton's chest and backing him down a long hall. Jesse Benton suddenly appeared behind them and fired, hitting Andrew in the shoulder.

Robert Hays led her quickly through the lobby of the Nashville Inn and up the stairs to Andrew's room. There were several men clustered about his bed.

"Please, ask them to leave," she said, feeling faint.

Only dimly did she hear Hays reply, "They're all doctors."

She went to the head of the bed. Andrew's face was lifeless, his lids closed tight over his eyes; he hardly seemed to be breathing. His left shoulder was heavily bandaged but soaked through with blood. She put her fingers lightly on his brow. His lids shot open.

"There's only one touch like that . . ."

Dr. May came to her side.

"I'm sorry, Mrs. Jackson, but the general is badly wounded: one bullet broke a bone in his shoulder, the second is lodged against his armbone. We've agreed, these other doctors and I, that the arm cannot be saved; if we do not amputate, gangrene . . ."

The room went black; the voices of the men became like sharp-beaked birds flying inside her skull. Then she heard Andrew say hoarsely:

"Thank you, gentlemen, but I'll keep my arm!"

The youngest of the doctors present, Felix Robertson, son of General Robertson, said:

"With all due apologies to my fellows in medicine, Mrs. Jackson, I don't think the arm needs to be amputated. I've applied strong pressure to stop the bleeding, and put poultices of slippery elm on the wounds."

By now she had regained control of herself. She thanked the doctors, dismissed them all except young Robertson, and sent Stockly Hays out to the Hermitage for sheets and food. With Andrew's great loss of blood had come a strong thirst; every few minutes throughout the night and following day she fed him sips of milk or tea. Though he was in bad pain he did not complain. Dr. Robertson bent the elbow and fixed his forearm to his chest with bandages. By the end of the second day he was able to take small quantities of solid food. Robert Hays came to report that Nashville was in an uproar, that the Bentons nearly had been murdered by some of Andrew's former soldiers, and had left town hastily, promising never to return. Sentiment also had turned strongly against Captain Erwin and his group for inciting the quarrel.

"On the strength of that good news," said Andrew, "I think I'll go home."

She prevailed upon him to remain in the room for another two days, until Dr. Robertson had changed the poultice and assured them that the danger of infection was past. Then they returned to the Hermitage. Two of their field hands carried him into the house and up the stairs, his arm still tightly bound, his smashed shoulder useless. Dr. Robertson informed her that there would be a long siege, probably months before he could be up and around, or have the use of his left side.

She was able to keep him quietly in bed for precisely twenty-four hours: for the very next day news reached Nashville that the Creeks had attacked Fort Mims, on the southern border of Mississippi Territory, massacring four hundred men, women and children. A delegation including Governor Blount and John Coffee arrived at the Hermitage to inform General Jackson that the state militia was disconsolate because he could not take command. Rachel waylaid them downstairs.

"Governor Blount, you know the general is ill. He hasn't the strength to stand on his feet, let alone ride a horse for hundreds of miles, and fight a war."

No one answered her, for all eyes had turned toward the stairs. There, coming down slowly, his good right arm holding his shattered left one, was Andrew, his face long and bony, his lips set, his eyes bright as hot coals. When he reached the bottom of the stairs he walked across the room, put his arm about Rachel's waist.

"Gentlemen, it is no time for a patriot to be sick when his country needs his services. We'll be ready to march in a few days. I shall command in person."

She helped him into his uniform, made a sturdy sling for his arm. She took his hand, holding it against her cheek for a moment. How could he fight a war when he had to be helped into his saddle?

8

By vigorous training at Fayetteville Andrew again whipped two thousand recruits into a cohesive force. Hardly a day passed but that she had a visit from a friend or relative who had been sent up the long trail from his headquarters seeking beef and flour for the troops, for the provisions on which the army was to march never reached Fort Deposit. Despite this, an early dispatch carried the news that he had forded the Coosa River and the following dawn took the Creeks by surprise. Three hundred of the Indians were killed.

The victory-starved nation, defeated and humiliated so often in the past year and a half, was singing General Jackson's praises. After eleven years of fanatical preparation, this was his first actual battle; and he had emerged triumphant.

In spite of the exultation of the press, the flatboats on which his provisions from East Tennessee had been loaded were still stuck there, the river being too low for the boats to navigate; the officers and soldiers of the militia, who had been existing on squirrels and then acorns, decided there was no use starving to death; large segments of the troops threatened to leave. General Jackson lined the road with loyal men, promising to fire on all deserters, and actually had to execute one young mutineer. When General Cocke arrived with fifteen hundred troops, Andrew dismissed the mutinous regiment, only to learn that the new arrivals had but ten days further to serve. His command was reduced to a hundred and thirty cold, starved and ragged men.

All work on the Hermitage came to a standstill; Fields, the new overseer, was drinking and quarreling with the hands; the acreage that Andrew had asked to be cleared was still untouched. And for the first time in her many years as a farmer, Rachel did not care. All of her energy and her desire was concentrated on this war with Britain, for Andrew had written that the Creeks were armed with new British rifles, and that the British agents had made extravagant promises to the Indians if they would continue to harass the United States troops until British soldiers could arrive to defeat the Americans. Young Andrew was a solace to her in her anxiety, for he liked to talk about Papa, and she was humbly grateful to anyone who would let her talk about her husband . . . even her son!

Andrew made no effort to conceal his illness from her: the wounds inflicted by Jesse Benton's bullets had not healed; in the cold the pain was so excruciating that he could sleep for only a few moments at a time. He was stricken with diarrhea because he had no food beyond what he could grub from the fields by way of acorns and nuts. Sometimes for hours on end he could retain consciousness only by remaining on his feet, his arms dangling over a tree limb to hold him up. On certain aggravated days he lay prostrate in his tent, unable to twitch a hand or foot, and when it was necessary to march, moved along on sheer will power.

When Governor Blount ordered him to bring his troops home he replied, "What, retrograde under these circumstances? I will perish first!"

His plight was so admittedly desperate that she found herself unable to eat or sleep. The snow broke large limbs off the trees. After helping to control an epidemic of the grippe which swept the Hermitage, including little Andrew, she herself collapsed, running such a high fever that Dr. May decided to bleed her. He also gave her frequent doses of calomel. When she wrote to Andrew her hands shook as though she had palsy.

It was not the bleeding or calomel that put an end to her anxieties: it was Andrew's victory at Emuckfau. Reinforced by eight hundred recruits delivered to him in person by Colonel Robert Hays, he led his scant and greatly outnumbered reserves into action, charging the Creeks before they had a chance to charge him. Colonel John Coffee was seriously wounded, Sandy Donelson, Johnny's boy, was among those killed.

Once again a beaten Administration and a starved press hailed the victory, calling it the greatest ever enjoyed against the Indians. Andrew Jackson became the most exalted commander in the field. Five thousand volunteers poured into the Indian country to report to General Jackson.

Buoyed by the presence of a company of United States regulars, Andrew attacked the Creek bastion at Horseshoe Bend and fought the Creeks across their own exposed plain. In a ferocious hand-to-hand encounter he had lost forty-nine men, but by the end of the day only a handful of the Creeks survived, their leader had surrendered, all British guns were captured, the Creek war ended. The British would have to find themselves new allies in the South.

Early in May, some five weeks later, with the sun warm overhead and the peach trees a mass of delicate blooms, a courier brought a note from Andrew asking her to meet him the following noon, five miles out on the road to Nashville. She knew she wouldn't sleep, so she spent the early hours of the evening washing her hair, bathing, shaping her nails and selecting the costume she would wear. Since their troubles over the Dickinson duel she had done little sewing. She had always loved pretty clothes, but the enforced isolation, and Andrew's apparent disregard of what she was wearing, had discouraged her. Now she found her wardrobe dull, and she searched her memory for some clue to which gown he would find the most attractive. She finally selected a brown cambric with rows of trimming around the neck and hem because it seemed the gayest, and because they had had a happy time together when she had worn it last, at Jane's twenty-fifth anniversary.

It was ten o'clock when her carriage reached the designated spot on the route, having passed hundreds of Cumberland Valley folk who were lining the road waiting for a sight of General Jackson. There were two hours to wait, but as she sat quietly against the cushions of the carriage, her hands folded in her lap, and thought back to the illnesses, to the actual physical terrors of the past seven months, she felt as though she might like to sit for a very long time in this suspended state, recouping her strength and composure.

Then she heard a rushing clatter and her carriage was surrounded by a dozen mounted men. Before she could distinguish their faces her carriage door was flung open and Andrew was by her side, crushing her to him. She had time for only one swift look at his face, but even in that fleeting instant she saw that his eyes were more truly alive and fulfilled than she had ever seen them before.

9

In the hail of Indian bullets that had fallen, not one piece of lead had touched him. A week at the Hermitage, with food and warmth, saw the grayness disappear from his face. There were many guests during the day; the dining table was crowded with friends and admirers; in the warm June evenings they sat quietly under the trees, watching the moon pull up into the heavens on the first half of its journey. Their time together was doubly sweet because they knew it would be short; the battles against the Creeks had been but the barest prologue to what would happen when the British terminated their long war in Europe and were free to pour the might of their Empire against Louisiana.

John Overton came back from the court at Knoxville bringing word of what people were saying in East Tennessee and Kentucky. There were already those who were inclined to boom him for governor. Even Sevier's followers were speaking of him in terms of respect. What ill feeling there was, was confined to militiamen and volunteers who had abandoned him before the big victories, and who now maintained that they had only wanted to return for food and winter clothing, but that General Jackson's arbitrary conduct had prevented them from so doing. The family of John Woods, whom Andrew had had executed for desertion, was claiming that this was an illegal act; and General Cocke, whom Andrew had had court-martialed for failure to report with his troops, had supporters who were charging that Andrew Jackson's purpose in this trial was to hog all the credit for himself.

"But these whiners are few in number," John concluded. "I only tell you about them because I know they are going to try to irritate you and involve you in bickering, their aim being to lessen your fame. If you will pardon these hints, I beg you not to notice them but just to let them write or speak as they wish. And don't thank me to keep out of your private affairs!"

"I won't, Counselor," Andrew replied. "There'll be no more of those Benton shootings or Samuel Jackson fights. I'm not the same man who got into those controversies; I've got a real antagonist now, and I'm saving my ammunition for the British."

She and Andrew had a month's honeymoon. They were never apart, riding for the day into the cooler hill country, picnicking on cold chicken and buttermilk, gazing down on the river valley and the flatlands while they talked helter-skelter of the hundreds of things they had perforce stored up for just such moments of leisure and intimacy. In the evenings she read Cowper's poems to him, or Virgil, while he sat smoking his pipe; or she triumphantly took him to dinner at Jane's or Johnny's or William's. The already neglected Hermitage was further neglected.

Then one morning a courier arrived from the War Department with two sealed dispatches. The first ordered him to "proceed without delay to Fort Jackson and consummate a treaty with the Creeks."

"That's fine," he cried, "but hear this next bit for idiocy." He began pacing, his long legs eating up the modest distance from wall to wall.

If the hostile part of the Creeks is really broken down, if they are prostrate before us, and even begging from us the means of subsistence, why retain in service any portion of the militia?

JOHN ARMSTRONG

He tossed the letter into the air, as he did all communications that irritated him.

"Now you know why we've lost every land battle since this war began, why they captured Detroit without a shot, annihilated Winchester's troops at Frenchtown, defeated Van Rensselaer at Queenstown, chewed up Dearborn's detachments and made such a fool out of Wilkinson in Canada that he had to be retired."

"Maybe the other letter is better?"

He returned to the table, picked up the second envelope and broke the seal. This time he stood awkwardly, embarrassed and apologetic.

"I take back everything I said about the Secretary of War. He is a man of infinite wisdom and discernment. Listen to this:

"War Department, May 28, 1814.

"SIR,

"Since the date of my letter of the twenty-fourth, Major General Harrison has resigned his commission in the army, and thus is created a vacancy in that grade, which I hasten to fill with your name."

They both held their breath for an instant, then Andrew, his whole body surging with excitement, exploded:

"By the Eternal! After all these years, they've finally taken me into their regular army. You see, miracles are not impossible . . ."

She reached her arms up about his neck, and he lifted her until their lips were on a level.

"May I be the first to congratulate you, Regular Army General Jackson? And don't tell me I can't call you general until you've won some battles. Tell me just what the appointment means."

In the surge of his joy he kissed her harder than she had been kissed in years. Then he set her down and stood with his head cocked to one side, his smile composited of gratification, determination . . . and happiness for the both of them.

"I will have command of the Seventh Military District, which includes Tennessee, the territory of Mississippi and Louisiana. It will also mean that you are not going to be left behind any more. As soon as I set up headquarters I'll send for you. Wherever I go from now on you will go with me."

"Please God! But what about the Hermitage?"

"It will go up for sale: lock and stock. My salary and allowance as a general will come to almost six thousand dollars a year."

They embraced again. This time they were joined by little Andrew, who had come into the room and tugged at his father's shirt, enviously. They picked him up and held him between them, kissing him and each other, all three laughing and crying in turn.

Toward the end of June news reached the Hermitage that the British were in Paris, and that Napoleon had fallen. The long war in Europe was over. Andrew was crushed by the defeat of his hero, but to Rachel he spoke only of the gigantic British fleet of a thousand vessels and the brilliant commanding officers and trained troops who would now be free to descend upon the United States in their full might.

She bade him good-by as he left for Fort Jackson. He had promised to send for her in a very few weeks.

"Darling, you told me I was to get a new carriage for my journey south, and travel in the style becoming to the wife of a major general of the United States Army. How about you stopping off at Murfreesboro and getting yourself a new uniform? Surely your shoulder will hold up an epaulet of the *regular* army?"

The little joke eased the moment of separation.

That very day she had the trunks and portmanteau aired in the July sun and brought up to her bedroom. If their permanent headquarters was to be in Mobile she might not need much in the way of stylish clothing, but if they were to settle in New Orleans, then her wardrobe would be inadequate. She decided to have Sarah Bentley sew her some new dresses.

Jane helped pick out the silks and satins, the hats and muffs and thin-soled slippers at the Nashville stores, spending many hours with her at Sarah Bentley's establishment while they pored over the color illustrations published in London, and discussed the latest fashion edicts.

"But Jane," protested Rachel, "you don't want me to arrive in New Orleans with these half-naked gowns. In the first place Andrew wouldn't recognize me, in the second he wouldn't approve, and in the third place, my dear sister, I'm a frontierswoman, slightly weather-beaten . . . ."

"You're going into the most elegant city in America," said Jane. "Those French-women get their gowns direct from Paris, or at least their styles come from there. I'd like to see you give them a run for their money."

Time went quickly for her. She completed her packing and made her final arrangements. A courier arrived with a letter from Andrew:

> Fortune that fickle dame, mars all my wishes—I have this moment received an express from Alabama Heights that will compel me to Mobile with all the regular Troops here. If I can spare Col Butler I shall send him to bring you down the river to me, at Natchez or New Orleans.

She re-read the line, *"Fortune that fickle dame, mars all my wishes,"* and smiled to herself as she heard Andrew's voice saying, "Pun me no puns." The Creek treaty must have been concluded to his entire satisfaction if he was in the mood to joke.

There was nothing amusing in the next intelligence: the British ships *Hermes, Carron* and *Sophia* had arrived at the Spanish town of Pensacola with land forces and large supplies of arms and ordnances; the *Orpheus* was also expected in a few days, with fourteen warships and transports carrying ten thousand troops. Fourteen more warships and transports had already arrived at Bermuda with Lord Wellington's army.

General John Coffee, and Rachel Hays's husband, Colonel Robert Butler, came to the Hermitage to say farewell. They had orders from General Jackson to leave Nashville as quickly as possible with one thousand cavalrymen. Andrew confided to her in a short note, brought to the Hermitage by an officer whom he had sent back to raise a battalion of artillery:

> Before one month the British and Spanish expect to be in possession of Mobile and all surrounding country. There will be bloody noses before this happens.

The army that had smashed Napoleon was advancing rapidly on the shores of America, and Andrew Jackson was promising to bloody their noses! When she thought of the mass mutinies of the year before, of his abandonment in the wilderness fort with a hundred officers and men, and no supplies, she was staggered by his inner strength. At the same time she was admittedly frightened. It would be Andrew's will to win pitted against the might of the British army that had just captured Washington City, burned the Capitol, shelled Baltimore, plundered Alexandria, occupied the state of Maine, burned the eastern seaboard, captured Nantucket and all of Cape Cod. New England was so deathly sick of the war that a convention had been held in Hartford at which secession sentiments bulked large, and delegates were appointed to go to Washington City and insist on peace at any price. Between the seasoned British army and the surrender of the American government stood . . . her husband!

She learned from dispatches in the Nashville papers that Andrew, believing the British would first have to capture Fort Bowyer, guardian of Mobile Bay, in order to take Mobile, had sped there with a hundred and sixty men and spent twelve days in repair work, setting up his cannon just as the British fleet attacked. One British ship was destroyed, another blown out of the water . . . after which the rest of the fleet fled to sea. It was his first victory against the British. What the newspapers did not tell her and she had to learn from her husband was that when he next decided to move his three thousand troops on Pensacola and needed rations for eight days, he once again had been obliged to buy the supplies with his own money.

The Hermitage lands had found a buyer in Philadelphia for twenty dollars an acre. Rachel knew that Andrew would use every dollar of the sale to provision his men. She wished there were some way the War Department could be induced to supply its troops. It really wasn't Andrew's private war, though he would probably say it was. And if it was his private war, it was hers too.

In the meanwhile her trunks remained in her bedroom. "With a war on my hands," wrote Andrew, "would you mind waiting just another few weeks?" It was now three full months since he had left, after his promise that they would never be separated again; but how could she put the burden of her safety, and her son's, upon him, when he had drawn his troops up before Pensacola, and the Spanish governor was refusing to put the English out of Fort Barrancas or surrender the arms and ammunition within the town? The next word she received was that he had stormed the Pensacola fortifications in the face of heavy guns and British warships, capturing the city and forcing the British to blow up Fort Barrancas and once again put to sea. He had then moved into New Orleans.

She went to Nashville to buy a sturdy carriage and a pair of strong horses. Then suddenly the letters stopped.

The heavy rains started early in December; it would be impossible to use her carriage and team of horses. The rivers were rising rapidly and were already navigable; now she would have to go by river. Robert Hays engaged a boat for her and she stood like a fledgling on a limb, poised for flight. At last young Stockly brought her marching orders: he had been instructed to bring Aunt Rachel and Cousin Andrew down the Mississippi to New Orleans and General Jackson.

She paid four hundred and twenty dollars in cash for the journey, but not wanting the money to be wasted, she began loading the boat with their bacon, beef, oats and corn, all of which should bring a profit in New Orleans. Robert Hays set her departure for December 28. At the family Christmas dinner at Haysboro Jane took her aside and said:

"Sister, Colonel Anderson is leaving for New Orleans with several other officers on January tenth; Robert feels you should have that extra military protection. We simply can't risk having you captured by the British."

"Oh, Jane," she wailed, "I know you're right, but it's six months since I've seen my husband. In the past year Andrew's been with me only four weeks!"

That there was a gigantic struggle pending near New Orleans she could not doubt; nor did she any longer care. Her patience was utterly exhausted. She remembered Andrew asking her, when they had come down the Kentucky Road for the first time, "Can you shoot?" She was so determined to join him that she would have been willing to shoot her way down the entire Mississippi. The Philadelphia purchase of the Hermitage had come to the signing point; Jane was keeping Moll, George, Mitty and Hannah until the Jacksons could find out where they were settling permanently. Everything else on the Hermitage was to be sold at the best price Robert Hays could get.

She was packing the last of her personal possessions in the big room downstairs when the door was opened and Jane with Robert and their daughter Rachel entered.

She had been so preoccupied she had not even heard them ride up; now as she raised her head she saw that they were big-eyed. They sat down just as Severn and Elizabeth entered. She heard more horses coming down the trail, and still more. From the excited expressions, from the spontaneous cries of "It has happened, the great battle of New Orleans!" and Thomas Overton's "Only General Jackson would have had the unmitigated gall to surprise the British"; from the glowing look of Johnny Donelson, who arrived with his wife and daughter, Mary Coffee, and boasted, "If he had sat in New Orleans with his few troops, the British could have attacked from a dozen sides!" she realized that this was not a planned gathering. The next to arrive were Sarah and Tim Bentley, then her bachelor brothers Alexander and Leven, whom she saw only at weddings and funerals, followed shortly by William and Charity, who had apparently picked up Catherine and John Hutchings on the way. The last to arrive was John Overton, who had ridden over from Travellers Rest in his gardening clothes, needing a shave. Looking around the room, with every one of the seats filled, she saw that once again the Donelson family and its intimates had assembled in a council of war.

She stood in the middle of the floor, waiting, while a dozen excited discussions were crisscrossing the oblong room. She moved her hearing among them, trying to separate collisions and sort out phrases; but the din was tremendous:

". . . Kentucky militia arrived exhausted and without guns" . . . "captured his few little gunboats on Lake Borgne" . . . "shipment of rifles from the War Department that stupid contractor sent by slow freight to save money". . . "British undiscovered only eight miles from New Orleans" . . . "good thing he broke into those warehouses . . . warm clothing" . . . "hadn't heard from Washington for sixty days . . ."

"Stop! Please, everybody! Be quiet!" She walked to the fireplace. "I understand there has been a major battle? Robert, won't you please tell me what happened?"

Colonel Robert Hays stood beside her, his massive shoulders squared back. She remembered that it had been loyal, loving Robert who almost singlehanded had assembled and delivered the troops with which Andrew had defeated the Creeks. He was the handsomest man anywhere in the Donelson family, and now his fine features were alight with pride as he fitted together for her the pieces of the story that had reached them an hour before:

The British, with a force of nine to ten thousand men, had landed at Lake Borgne, pushed through five miles of impassable swamp, then seized the Villere plantation, eight miles from New Orleans. Major Villere was captured, but escaped and reported the news to General Jackson. Though he had only one thousand regulars, and two thousand militia, Andrew summoned his aides, brought his fist down on the table with such force that it nearly smashed under the impact, and cried:

"By the Eternal, they shall not sleep on our soil! We must fight them tonight."

Within two hours he was leading his troops out of the city. At seven that night he surprised the British in their camp, gathered around their fires. It was hand-to-hand fighting, with Generals Coffee and Carroll leading the assault. The British were disorganized and hurt, but best of all, the British major who had burned the Capitol at Washington City had been captured. In the morning Andrew pulled his troops back of Rodriguez Canal, then built his defenses with every shovel, musket and able-bodied man from New Orleans pressed into service: for the British before him were constantly being reinforced. He fortified everything from the river to the swamp and woods, entrenched his few cannon, erected walls of baled cotton.

Two limited attacks were launched against him on December 28 and January 1. Then on the morning of January 8, the famous British General Pakenham fired a silver-blue rocket announcing the great attack. General Jackson was ready with his troops, deployed in a deep-dug defense arc. At seven in the morning the fog broke. Andrew, standing on his parapet above Rodriguez Canal, saw a field of stubble cane before him, frosted silver and, a little more than six hundred yards away, British soldiers by the thousands, white belts across red tunics, muskets at the ready.

They charged. Andrew gave his order: the twelve-pounders went off; then the first rank of men fired, stooped to unload, the second rank fired, then the third. They were all woodsmen, dead shots; the close-packed British lines fell. Others came on; Andrew's men and cannon, protected by their defenses, poured in more fire. The Highlanders attacked, but the Americans reloaded so fast the Scots went down without even shooting their guns. The British commanding officers were being eliminated one after the other: Generals Pakenham and Gibbs dead, Colonel Dale dead, General Keane injured. Fewer than a hundred English soldiers ever reached Rodriguez Canal, a few lived to scale the embankment . . . and died. After only an hour and a half of fighting the British withdrew, their morale shattered, their fighting force spent. Seven hundred British soldiers lay dead on the field before Andrew as he again mounted the parapet to survey the result of the battle. Fourteen hundred more were wounded, disabled and dying. When he saw some five hundred Britons rising from the heaps of their dead comrades and coming forward to surrender, he said:

"I never had such a grand or awful idea of the resurrection."

Moments later he learned that he had lost but seven men, and that, incredible as it seemed, the British army had inflicted wounds on only six others. The Donelson family had particular reason to rejoice: their husbands, sons and nephews had fought doggedly and well, and not one had been hurt. Rachel's memory reached back to the library at Hunter's Hill where Andrew had sat poring over his military books, where he had proclaimed, "The good general does not lose men in war; his campaigns are so well planned he crushes the opposing army with a few swift blows."

The British, beaten and broken, made their way back to their ships. Andrew chose not to pursue them. He received a note from the British commanding officer, General Keane, on board his ship, offering remuneration for his beloved battle sword, lost on the plain before Rodriguez Canal.

"Did Andrew have the sword?" asked Rachel excitedly. "I hope he returned it? It could be a symbol for that other sword that cut his head so cruelly when he was a boy."

"Oh yes, he returned it," said Robert Hays. "And sent with it a letter expressing his feeling for the misfortunes of all the brave English soldiers who had fallen in battle."

"Now his victory is complete," she murmured to herself, an ache of joy in her heart, "over the British . . . and over himself."

After a pause, Johnny said, "Perhaps Andrew will be home soon? Maybe you don't have to leave for New Orleans in the morning."

"I'm going!" she announced with a finality that silenced all further discussion. She turned to her brother-in-law. "But this does change one thing. If the war is really finished, Andrew will want a home to come back to. Don't sign those Hermitage papers when they come through from Philadelphia."

They ate and drank and told family anecdotes until the winter sun moved reluctantly over the horizon. Then they rode into Nashville and to the river landing. An icy wind whipped up whitecaps on the river. As Rachel took little Andrew firmly by the hand and walked across the loading plank she suddenly stopped in the midst of her passage and stood with her head bent, time and the years dissolving; she was a young girl again, only twenty-three, her brother Samuel had brought her to this very same landing to put her on board Colonel Stark's flatboat bound for Natchez. Unmoving, not hearing the cries of farewell from her family, she saw with memory's eye the tall, redheaded, twenty-three-year-old Andrew Jackson emerge from the Starks' boat to take her portmanteau and welcome her on board. What an arduous, troubled voyage it had been; but Andrew had said, in Tom Green's home, when he had brought her the report of her divorce and the news that they could be married:

"Our love shall be a fortress."

She turned to wave her last smiling farewells to her family on the riverbank, then continued up the gangplank onto the boat.

And so it had been.

BOOK SIX

1

She sat out in the blue flagstone courtyard, the morning air filled with the scent of cape jasmine and crepe myrtle. The breakfast table was placed next to colorful flower beds and a trickling fountain. As she looked up she saw the graceful curving stairs which rose from the courtyard to the roof, and the wrought-iron balconies of the second and third floor. Two *gardiennes* came out in calico gowns with gay madras handkerchiefs tied about their heads and held up by high combs. They carried freshly baked croissants and coffee. From outside the spiked iron fence she heard the vendors in the streets crying out their wares:

"*Belles des figues! Bons petits calas! Tout chauds!*"

It was her first big city and practically a foreign one; Philadelphia or New York, she thought, would have seemed less strange. The entire culture, from the small cakes at eleven o'clock coffee down through the performance at the Théâtre d'Orléans, was French. It was not only the exotic feel of New Orleans which fascinated her, it was the lush, tropical aspect, so diametrically opposed to the lean sinewy countryside of the Cumberland.

Dr. Kerr was Andrew's military surgeon; he had graciously turned over his home and staff to the Jacksons. Opposite her at breakfast sat thirty-year-old Major John Reid, who had been Andrew's secretary since the beginning of the Creek wars. Reid was a handsome chap with a mass of jet black curls falling over his forehead, heavy black sideburns and black eyebrows, one of which shot upward like an exclamation point. He seemed considerably thinner than when Rachel had last seen him at the Hermitage.

"Small wonder," he replied in a thin voice. "The general has me up all night and every night writing hundreds of dispatches."

Andrew came quickly down the outside stairway.

"Good morning, my dear," he said as he stood with an arm about her shoulder. "This is the first time I've slept past five o'clock since I left home."

"You should have had me with you this whole time," she replied with a smile, feeling warm and happy inside herself. "Then Major Reid would have gotten some sleep too, instead of your keeping him up all night writing letters."

Andrew laughed. He dropped into a chair beside her as Major Reid excused himself. She poured him a cup of coffee. They sat with the sun on their faces, holding hands under the table. Rachel murmured, "New Orleans may be a bad place to wage a war, but it's certainly a wonderful place for love."

"I remember your saying that any place is a good place for love."

"This country takes me back to our honeymoon at Bayou Pierre. Remember Tom Green telling us we ought to stay?"

He leaned across the table, pressed his cheek to hers.

"Would you like to live down here? Andrew is wild about the place; he spent all day yesterday on the levee watching the ships. I could have permanent headquarters in New Orleans, we could buy a beautiful house like this one out of the Hermitage sale."

"There wasn't any sale."

"Oh?"

"I stopped it when the news reached me. I thought that your victory would make everything right again. Those crowds lining the streets of New Orleans yesterday shouting your name as we went by in the carriage. . ."

"That was yesterday," he interrupted grimly; "a temporary truce declared in honor of your arrival. Right now I have two wars on my hands, one with the British and the other with the merchants and legislators of New Orleans who want to get back to business as usual. Governor Claiborne is due at my headquarters right now."

"Isn't he the one who got the job as governor of the Louisiana Territory that you wanted so badly back at Hunter's Hill? Now you're his commanding officer."

"Governor Claiborne doesn't think so; the purpose of his visit this morning is to force me to lift martial law and let the ships sail out of the harbor with the cotton and tobacco that's been in the warehouses for two years. He's also going to order me to dismiss all the Louisiana militia and volunteers, and take myself and my own troops out of his jurisdiction. According to Claiborne, the war is over."

"Well, isn't it?" she asked anxiously. "Your friend Edward Livingston came back from the British flagship yesterday with news that a treaty peace with England had been signed at Ghent."

"He also brought news that the British had captured Fort Bowyer!" He snapped this out at her almost angrily, then apologized with a self-deprecatory smile. "Forgive me, but we are still in danger here and so few seem to understand it. The British are maintaining a complete spy system; they know how many troops we have, where they are stationed, where our big guns are located and the morale of our men. They may strike again at any hour."

"But why would they want to, my dear, if they know the peace treaty has been signed? What could they hope to gain?"

"They have never acknowledged Napoleon's right to sell us Louisiana; if they can drive me and my men out of here they will claim this country as their own in spite of any peace treaty with the rest of the United States."

He jumped up, having eaten nothing. She held herself against him.

"It wasn't a very long truce, was it, dear? Only one day and one night. But I'm so terribly grateful even for that." A melodious clock inside the house chimed eight times. "Would you drop me at Madam Livingston's on your way to headquarters? Sister Jane was right, I have no proper clothes for these elegant Frenchwomen. Mrs. Livingston is having the finest seamstress in New Orleans at her home this morning to make me a gown for the George Washington Ball on Wednesday."

Two days later Andrew handed her into their carriage. It had rained the night before and the streets were filled with puddles of mud. Andrew carried her dainty ballroom slippers, while she held the bouffant velvet skirt up out of the mud. Mrs. Edward Livingston, who was the social leader of both the French and American colonies of New Orleans, had turned her second-floor salon into a fitting room; for the better part of two days Rachel had stood on a raised platform in the middle of the floor while the best of the French couturières draped yards of material about her and a swarm of voluble French needlewomen fitted and sewed, then cut and resewed until the gown was precisely what Madam Livingston wanted.

"It must be the most exquisite gown at the Exchange Ball," she had demanded of her couturière. "General Jackson and his lady are our guests of honor; no one may outshine them."

And so it had been: for Louise Livingston had driven her sewing staff relentlessly and between them they had designed this luxurious deep violet gown of the softest velvet with its short-sleeved bodice of sheer lace. Draped over her dark hair she wore a mantilla of the same lace, while her evening bag was of the same shade of deep violet as the wide velvet skirt. There was a strand of matched pearls at her throat, with small opals around the clasp of her bag.

She did not know how Louise Livingston would look in her gown, in fact how any of the hundreds of gorgeous Creole women would look; but when she saw the delight in Andrew's face as his eyes devoured her, she knew that, for her own purposes at least, Mrs. Livingston had succeeded. What a joy it had been to gaze at herself in a full-length mirror, and to see herself so elegantly gowned. She actually looked ten years younger, and twenty pounds lighter. How Jane's eyes would have flashed with pride could she have seen her. She was doubly pleased with herself for she had sold her bacon, beef, oats and corn for a sufficient profit to pay for the new costume.

As the carriage bumped slowly along the muddy streets Rachel thought of the woman who had given up her own role as queen of this ball so that she might be the center of attention. Louise Livingston was only thirty years old, yet she occupied the position in New Orleans society to which Mrs. Phariss aspired in Nashville; but Mrs. Phariss lacked the native charm, breadth of character and the innate love of people which Louise Livingston possessed so naturally. She had married at the age of thirteen in Santo Domingo, lost three infant children before being widowed at sixteen, and had then seen her father and two brothers killed in the uprising from which she, her mother, grandmother and infant sister and brother had escaped to Louisiana. The most beautiful of the New Orleans matrons, she was also a woman of the highest intelligence, giving Edward Livingston important help in the writing of his legal briefs. Rachel thought how companionable it must be to collaborate with one's husband in this capacity; she found herself wishing she had been born smarter so that she could have been of greater assistance to Andrew.

The members of the French Exchange had worked hard to transform their building into a glittering replica of a Parisian ballroom. The ground floor, on which the long dinner tables had been set up, was magnificently decorated with flowers, colored lamps, transparencies and the most brilliant crystal chandeliers she had seen since Tom Green's Springfield. She was escorted to her seat by Edward Livingston, a tall, slender, stoop-shouldered man with a genial disposition and an all-pervading sense of human dignity.

She found herself placed opposite the motto, *Jackson and Victory Are One*. There were gold hams on the table, and jeweled ornaments. In the center was a pyramid on the top of which was written *Vive Jackson* in large letters. So many toasts were drunk to Andrew as the "Hero of our country" and "Savior of New Orleans," that by the time they went upstairs to the second-floor ballroom for the dancing she felt a little dizzy. Everyone was very friendly. She found herself talking animatedly with handsome, impeccably garbed men and soignée women. She danced minuets and waltzes for hours. At the end of one dance Andrew linked his arm through hers and, smiling down from his tremendous height, said:

"You're beautiful, my darling."

"It's this velvet gown you're looking at; it does wonderful things for my eyes."

"No, it's you, your face, you are glowing with happiness. You're the loveliest lady here."

"Tell me, *General Jackson and Victory Are One*," she teased, "now that you've whupped the British, do you think you might be able to stay home for a while?"

"Forever."

"Can we go there soon?"

"How soon?"

"Tomorrow?"

"You sound just like the Louisiana militiamen. Wouldn't you like a few years of this kind of life, Rachel? Dinners and receptions and balls and new gowns and dances and laughter and music? Because you can have it now, if you wish."

"I've seen more already than in my whole life past. And I will cherish the memory of this night as long as I live. But now that I've had it, I'm content. I'm ready to go back to the Hermitage. That's what you want too, isn't it?"

He did not answer.

The weeks that followed were a phantasmagoria of band concerts, plays in the Théâtre d'Orléans, ballets and pantomimes in the Théâtre St. Philippe, dinner parties in the sumptuous homes of the first Creole families, trips to the battlefield with young Reid and Jax to show her where every company was placed, and how they had fought. She walked along the broad tree-shaded levee, inspected old Spanish forts, journeyed through the lakes and bayous, finding Italian-styled villas surrounded by gardens and magnificent wild-orange groves.

Her son Andrew spent all day at headquarters with his father, where he had become the pet of the staff. Headquarters was the elegant Daniel Clark residence at 106 Royal Street, one of the few brick buildings in New Orleans.

"I'm going to have to spend my time at headquarters too," Rachel chided her husband as she stood in the big front room which he used as his office. "My dear, do you know that every day for the past week you have worked from eight in the morning until eleven at night? Your face is so pale and thin."

"If only I could get word from Washington City that the war is really over. . . . This whole city is about to rise up in mutiny: today there is a long article in the Courrière telling me to get out of New Orleans and let the Louisiana soldiers return to the farms for their planting. I've clapped the author of that article in jail as an agent provocateur. And if Federal Judge Dominick A. Hall insists on releasing him, I'll lock Hall up too. I'll lock up the whole confounded town rather than let this army disintegrate before official word of the peace reaches me."

"As a beginning, let's go home and lock ourselves up and forget about your troubles until morning."

They were awakened early by the noise of a crowd coming down the street shouting, "La paix! La paix!" Andrew sprang out of bed, donned a robe and went downstairs. From behind the batten blinds she watched him take a dispatch from a travel-stained courier, then heard the groan of disappointment that went up from the crowd. Andrew returned to her, flinging the dispatch onto the table top. She waited for him to explain.

"It's absolutely unbelievable. This packet contains nothing more than authorization by Secretary Monroe for me to raise the state troops that have been fighting with me for months."

The rains fell heavily, converting the city and the outlying country into a quagmire; provisions were difficult to get from the New Orleans merchants, and hundreds of soldiers came down with influenza, fever and dysentery. Andrew's portrait in the Exchange Coffee House was destroyed by an angry mob. Rachel learned from her nephews that the Hero of New Orleans had become the Villain of New Orleans, a dictator who was holding his military control over the city for his own gratification. Andrew had a birthday coming, on March 15, his forty-eighth; Rachel wanted to give him a party, but there was so much hostility and sickness that she hardly knew whether a celebration would be appropriate.

Then on March 13, 1815, official news of the ratification of the peace treaty at long last reached New Orleans. The British fleet departed for home. Andrew lifted martial law, dismissed the Louisiana troops and sent the Tennessee, Mississippi and Kentucky troops home. The sun came out, the throngs were in the street again shouting, "Jackson and Peace," and Rachel sent invitations all over the city, to relatives and aides and to the French people who had been kind to her, inviting them to a birthday party for the general.

After dinner when her guests were assembled in the second-floor drawing room with coffee and liqueurs, Andrew sat in a comfortable chair, his legs stretched out in front of him, surrounded by his officers and nephews, by John Coffee, Edward Livingston and Dr. Kerr. Rachel listened from across the room while he talked of his mother, telling how she had rescued him and his brother from the British prison at Camden thirty-four years before. Seeing that everyone was well fortified, she slipped out to her bedroom to adjust the combs in her hair. As she stood before the mirror which hung above the handsome Louis XIV chest her eyes came down to a letter on top of the chest where Andrew had put it. She recognized the signature of a cousin on her mother's side, John Stokely, who held an important government position in Washington City. Suddenly, as though the lines had been raised by use of forceps, the words stood out:

> We are entitled to a President from the West, your activity and uniform success has rendered you very popular amongst the American people and I do conceive that you ought to fill the chair of the Chief Magistrate of this Union.

She stood leaning against the chest, one hand clutched at her breast, too stunned to think articulately. After a time her mind returned to the Hermitage, with John Overton standing before her, his silver specs lying over the hump of his nose, saying, "He might just as well go right to the top, where he belongs. There is only one real and indisputable top in this country, my dear Rachel, and when a man rises that high he is freed from all petty bickerings, jealousies and quarrels."

She sat down on the edge of the gilt-backed French chair, her heart pounding high in her throat. If they had been plunged into a caldron of heated emotions and animosity when Andrew ran for comparatively modest offices, if they found themselves and their love and marriage embroiled in scandal, accusations, bitternesses, feuds, duels and killings, what in the dear God's name would happen to them if he should ever get involved in a campaign for the presidency of the United States? And what had been said at that family council of war in her mother's home when they first learned of Lewis Robards' impending Harrodsburg divorce? "Those records will be there forever, for anyone to use for his own purposes."

If Andrew ran for the presidency would not his enemies and opponents dig up those records and use them in an effort to defeat him? Politics was a lethal business. Whatever she had suffered by way of malicious gossip, invasion of privacy and willful traduction, at least it had been confined to the Tennessee country. Wouldn't the difficulties of her first marriage to Lewis Robards and the illegality of her Natchez marriage to Andrew Jackson now be spread over the entire nation, made a matter of public domain?

Her terror passed. In its place came a clarity amounting almost to prescience: the storms, the scandals, the accusations and denials, the revelation of her most intimate life, all of these things which had seemed so violent and omnipresent would be but passing winds compared to what she would undergo in the future. And yet, if it all were to come to pass, would she make any effort to stop it? What a glorious fulfillment for Andrew Jackson, the penniless orphan who had pulled himself up the perpendicular mountainside by his bootstraps, sitting in the Chief Executive's chair which had been occupied by such fine and highborn gentlemen as George Washington, John Adams and James Madison.

2

New Orleans showered gifts upon the Jacksons, the magnificent furnishings from their bedroom in the Kerr home, a set of topaz jewelry for Rachel, a diamond pin for Andrew. They had once again completed the cycle: hero into villain and back again to hero.

Only Federal Judge Dominick Hall did not join in the adoration; instead he issued an order for Andrew's arrest on a charge of contempt of court.

"Andrew, you don't have to obey that summons, do you?"

"Why, Mrs. Jackson, that's no way for the wife of a former judge to speak. I threw Hall into jail to protect our military position; he has a right to try to throw me into jail to protect the position of the courts."

She rode to court with Andrew and Edward Livingston. The room was so crowded that attendants had to clear a lane for them down to the defense table. Judge Hall refused to hear the Livingston defense, fining Andrew a thousand dollars for contempt. For the briefest moment she feared that Andrew might rise in anger against the fine, but instead he accepted it graciously; when finally they made their way through the cheering throngs and into their carriage the people of New Orleans unhitched the horses and pulled them through the streets to the square before the Exchange. As she listened to Andrew say his farewells to the thousand admirers jammed into the square, she thought:

My brother Severn was right: the identical qualities which led to his failures have also brought about his success.

They left New Orleans at the end of the first week in April 1815. The streets and country roads were lined for miles by every class of Louisiana society crying out their gratitude and benedictions. They went by water to Natchez, but from there on they had to travel by horseback and carriage up the Trace, following the route they had taken home from their honeymoon at Bayou Pierre, that fateful journey on which Andrew had quarreled with Hugh McGary over an imminent Indian attack, so embittering McGary that two years later he had been willing to go before a Harrodsburg jury and testify that he had seen Rachel Robards and Andrew Jackson sleeping under the same blanket.

The Natchez Trace was still deeply rutted; sometimes she felt as though her spine would be jarred through the top of her head; when she could stand the jouncing no longer she joined her husband and son on horseback. This trip took them several weeks longer than the earlier one, for every hamlet along the way had its population in the street for a tumultuous reception. For Rachel the best of all the parties was the one given them by the now greatly expanded Green family, in the room with the exquisite glass chandeliers under which she and Andrew had been married.

She had difficulty in understanding the almost frenzied crowds that took over their party at the Tennessee border: the families that had ridden in from every direction to shout their names; the enormous throngs that led them into Nashville as though they were a triumphal procession; or the assemblage in the courthouse square, so tremendous that it seemed as if every last soul in Tennessee had come to pay homage. It was not until they had ridden out to the Hermitage, to be welcomed at the gates by their neighbors, and she had had the chance to read the first eastern newspapers she had seen since her departure from New Orleans and to study the details of the Treaty of Ghent, that she began to grasp what her husband had come to mean to the people of the country. Even to her untrained mind it was apparent that this peace treaty was a humiliating document, signed by the American negotiators after three years of continuous defeats. The British had not even agreed to end their seizure of American vessels or the impressment of American seamen! Andrew's triumph at New Orleans had actually come after the signing of the peace terms at Ghent and thus legally had accomplished nothing, yet it had accomplished everything, turning three years of defeat into victory, restoring the self-confidence of the American people and, as the eastern editors added, teaching the British a lesson they would never forget.

Sitting up in bed, propped comfortably with pillows and enjoying the tray Mitty had brought up to her, she pushed the journals aside and stared sightlessly out the big window overlooking the Hermitage fields. If what these editors said was true, would not the pressure on Andrew to run for the presidency next year be almost inescapable? She recalled how just a few hours before their departure their friend Edward Livingston had said:

"You know, General, the road north from New Orleans could lead directly to Washington City."

She had remained silent and, she hoped, expressionless; Andrew had laughed good-naturedly, thanked Livingston for the compliment, then said in terms of finality that the idea was absurd.

But was it? Nobody who came out to the Hermitage seemed to think so. The air was filled with presidential talk: the Federalist party, which had backed the Hartford Convention and declared for surrender in the war, was now passing from existence. Whoever the Republicans nominated was certain to be elected. James Monroe was the favorite, yet there were many who felt that the Virginia dynasty of twenty-four years, starting with George Washington, coming through Thomas Jefferson and James Madison, had reached its proper and logical conclusion. Another man was wanted, an outsider with a fresh face and a strong will and new ideas; who better fitted these qualifications, people were asking, than the Hero of New Orleans?

But if Andrew knew all this talk was going on he gave no sign of it; only once did he speak to her about the campaign which had already begun for his nomination:

"Don't worry, my darling, it would take a writ of habeas corpus to get me back into politics."

Twenty-four hours before she was to leave the Hermitage to meet her husband in New Orleans the Hermitage had been for sale. Now the Hermitage lands which had been so badly neglected the year before were teeming with activity, the forest cleared and planted in cotton by the new overseer hired by Robert Hays. As far as her eyes could see there were rows upon rows of young cotton plants showing healthy and green in the warm May air: for in the months following Andrew's victory at New Orleans his neighbors had come to the Hermitage wanting to do something for the general by way of showing their appreciation, and indefatigable Robert Hays had taken such good advantage of their offers that the barns had been repaired, the cabins chinked, the apple and peach trees pruned, new orchards set out from John Overton's stock of young trees. Pretty Jane Caffrey, one of Mary's daughters, had moved into the Hermitage to take care of the house. She had everything shined and gleaming for their return.

Rachel felt a little ashamed, as she wandered the fields, visited with the hands and neighbors, drank in the particular beauty of the Cumberland Valley, that she could ever have been willing to abandon this home. By what strange twists of fate were people's lives destroyed or saved by a mere matter of hours? After the Charles Dickinson duel Andrew had lost nearly every friend in the Cumberland; he had become despondent, quarrelsome, had drunk too much and made scenes in public. He had lost his joy in this fine plantation and even in his blooded horses, and she had wondered if life were over for them, if it were to continue to be a mud-rutted downhill road to some obscure end. And she, seeing him restless, frustrated, unable to find his place in the world, had been equally willing to leave the Hermitage, to go seeking a more fertile land in which Andrew might prosper.

How wrong that would have been for Andrew, who this very moment was attending a dinner being given to him at the Bell Tavern in Nashville, at which the most important men in the state had gathered to present him with a ceremonial sword sent as a gift from Mississippi; and where even Mr. Phariss and Mr. Deson would go out of their way to shake his hand. How wrong it would have been for her, who had never wanted to be anything but First Lady in her husband's affection and to live peacefully and happily on her plantation, surrounded by friends, relatives and neighbors as she was doing today.

The Hermitage once again seemed to be the crossroads of the West, literally hundreds of people pouring in: not only their countless relatives and the folk of the Cumberland Valley who wanted to thank the general personally, but all the political figures from the East who had business anywhere within several days' ride, and all of the army officers and officials and businessmen of the South making their way up the Trace toward the capital or New York. No one came empty-handed: each day saw dozens of gifts brought or delivered: for Rachel, a sewing box inlaid with mother-of-pearl, Chinese mandarin scent bottles, a beaded purse, rare laces, a guitar, a shell jewel case, initialed bedspreads, leather-bound Bibles, beautiful English bone china and glassware; and for Andrew, canes and swords and books, rare wines and fruits.

For herself Rachel maintained the pattern she had set at Hunter's Hill: all who sought her out were welcome, all who came were her friends. She received them graciously, gave freely of herself. But she rarely left the Hermitage grounds. She went into Nashville only when it was necessary, con enting herself with visits to the numerous Donelsons and their offspring, and to he long-time neighbors.

Moll and George had grown too old to handle the volume of work, so big Hannah took over the cooking, assisted by Mitty and Orange. Young Jane proved to be such a capable housekeeper and was so fascinated by the flow of celebrities to the Hermitage that she asked:

"Aunt Rachel, couldn't I just stay here with you permanently? I could take all the work off your hands and you could give your full attention to Uncle Andrew."

Andrew's health was by no means good. He had suffered six months of the almost universal military dysentery, and for weeks on end had gone with no more nourishment than the rice he could hold on his stomach. They had both assumed that all he needed was a regular routine and a lot of good solid food, but now, safely ensconced at home, he grew more rather than less ill. Even the special foods that Moll insisted she alone could prepare for him he was unable to retain. He had been holding himself together these many months by will power and now that there was no need to remain upright he suddenly collapsed and had to go to bed altogether. The flow of visitors was cut off. She sat by his bedside feeding him chicken broth, accompanying each spoonful with a prayer that he would be able to keep it down.

"You have simply used up the energies of six years in the past six months, Andrew. You need a great deal of rest. We are going to start from the beginning and raise you as though you were an infant."

"Sounds pleasant," he said faintly from his pillow.

"We have absolutely nothing to worry about," she reassured him. "Cotton prices are soaring and we are going to have a bumper crop."

"I wanted to go to Washington to make my reports. . . explain the Judge Hall affair, participate in the reorganization of the army . . . but it can wait."

"Of course it can. When the warm weather comes you must take your son fishing. And Andy feels badly that I insisted he remain in school instead of going to New Orleans with me, so you are going to have to spend time with him, riding and hunting. Major Reid will be here to begin his book about the history of your wars. And I must get you strong and handsome again because you have to have a painting made to send to Congress for that medal they are awarding you."

He lifted the ivory miniature of her which still hung on its silver chain about his neck.

"Perhaps I'll send them this instead."

3

By October, after a lazy summer, he became restless. He decided he must go to Washington City: to designate the military posts that were needed in the wilderness; to explain why the Creek opposition to the land treaty should be disregarded; to secure permission to move all Indian tribes west of the Mississippi so that they could not again be armed and used by a hostile European nation; and to drive out the Spanish, who still held Florida, and were thus in a position to allow enemy troops to invade the United States.

She knew that the little group of would-be president-makers, John Overton, John Reid, John Eaton, a wealthy lawyer and planter of Franklin, William Lewis and William Carroll were anxious that Andrew expose himself on all sides, thus increasing his chances for the nomination. She asked herself, Does he want the presidency? Is that why he is making this trip? Was he giving in to the urge that in the early years had led him to become a congressman and a senator?

And if Andrew asked her to accompany him, would she go? The reasons for which she had formerly refused to travel, the fear of meeting strangers, of being looked down at as *the* Mrs. Jackson, had been pushed deep into the background with Andrew's success and her own wonderful stay in New Orleans. Her problem was no longer whether she was willing to make the journey to Washington City, with its attendant dinners, balls and receptions, but whether she would not, by accompanying him, give evidence that she favored his drive for the presidency and was attempting to help her husband win both the nomination and the office of Chief Executive. In her heart she knew the answer: she did not wish to aid Andrew in this ambition. Yet if her husband invited her to accompany him, she would go; she had had enough of separations . . .

The inns at which they stayed each night were comfortable, but she was glad when they neared Lynchburg and the home of Major Reid's parents, where they were to rest for a few days. The elder Reids, genteel folk, were overjoyed at receiving the Jacksons. As Rachel and Andrew were about to descend for supper young Reid came running up the stairs.

"General, there's a delegation downstairs from Lynchburg; the town is tending you a formal banquet tomorrow. Thomas Jefferson is riding in from Monticello to preside!"

Rachel saw the flash of joy cross Andrew's face. She reached out a hand to him. He squeezed it hard. With his eyes brilliant he murmured:

"Mr. Jefferson would have reason to hate me, I've been a wasp stinging at him all these years; and yet he's so fine a gentleman as to ride almost a hundred miles to be at a dinner for me."

Yes, thought Rachel, you can forgive each other now that the war with Britain has been fought and won.

The tableau that presented itself to her eyes as she entered the ballroom of the hotel the following afternoon at three o'clock, her hand lightly on Mr. Jefferson's arm, was even more impressive to her than the Exchange Ball in New Orleans: their three hundred hosts stood at attention while she and Andrew walked slowly down the center aisle of the ballroom on either side of Mr. Jefferson. She had only a fleeting impression through dinner of the succeeding courses as they were placed before her and taken away, for underneath the quiet talk she felt a submerged tension, as though everyone were expecting something of critical importance and no one was quite sure what it would be. At last, when the tables had been cleared, the chairman rose, gestured for silence and turned to Thomas Jefferson. Mr. Jefferson got up slowly from his chair, stood with a wine goblet raised, the white hair falling thickly over his ears, his eyes luminous and infinitely wise, his face at seventy-two still patrician and beautiful. He extended his glass toward Andrew and in a low, carrying voice said:

"Honor and gratitude to those who have filled the measure of their country's honor."

The three hundred men rose in their chairs, extended their glasses toward Andrew and drank to him. Rachel's head began to spin: she knew quite well the importance of Mr. Jefferson's gesture; within a few days it would be in every newspaper in America and would be the chief topic of conversation in Washington City.

What did it all mean: merely that Mr. Jefferson was putting into words the thanks of the nation for Andrew's indestructible will to victory? Or was it, as indicated in the expressions of many standing above her, something of far greater significance: that Thomas Jefferson was putting his public seal of approval on Andrew Jackson as the next president of the United States?

But how could that be? James Monroe was one of Mr. Jefferson's oldest and dearest friends and had served Mr. Jefferson and Mr. Madison these last sixteen years in the most important governmental posts. It was inconceivable that Mr. Jefferson would jettison his old comrade whom he had trained for the presidency in favor of a man who had long been his adversary.

Her thoughts took but a few swift seconds. Silence filled the room, silence fraught with the deepest of drama. Everyone's eyes were fixed on Andrew: how would he respond to this toast? Would he use this banquet room as a political stump, making known his willingness to contest the presidency? Or would he let the moment pass, respond with routine courtesy, indicating nothing of what he felt or wanted?

Andrew rose on the other side of Mr. Jefferson. His eyes were masked. After what seemed to her an intolerable time, during which she could hear the silence adumbrating about the banquet hall, he raised his glass, smiled down at Mr. Jefferson and said:

"James Monroe, late Secretary of War."

The great hall broke into bedlam, with men waving their arms and cheering and crying out to each other across the length of the room: for in these six short words Andrew Jackson had bowed himself out of the presidential race of 1816, officially nominating James Monroe of Virginia. Everything that would happen between now and the election would be an anticlimax because there would be no one in all America to rise up and contest Mr. Monroe.

The picture of that moment was stamped forever on Rachel's mind: Andrew standing above the noise and the multitude, a half-wistful smile raising the left corner of his mouth, happy that he had at last committed himself and that the questioning and suspense were over; yet at the same time the tiniest touch sad that he had voluntarily given up this chance of becoming the first man of his country. And on Mr. Jefferson's face too she caught a strange expression: was it, she asked herself, one of not too completely disguised relief? Had Mr. Jefferson taken a long gamble? Had he, knowing his man, made the *beau geste* of riding the hundred miles, officiating at this banquet and paying the greatest honor to General Jackson, believing that in turn Mr. Jackson would make the *beau geste* of acclaiming James Monroe? But whatever had been Mr. Jefferson's thinking, there could be no doubt in her mind of his enormous pleasure: he had not wanted Mr. Jackson to be president, he had passionately wanted his friend, neighbor and protégé in that office.

Washington City had been the source of so much of Andrew's aggravation that in her mind it had become a place of evil. She therefore approached the city with considerable trepidation. The town itself was a frightful disappointment to her, with its deeply rutted, muddy streets and ugly brick houses standing unshaded and solitary amidst the fields and swamps. This impression of rawness, almost of desolation, was heightened by the damage that had been caused by the British burning of the Capitol, the President's House, the Treasury and Departments of State and War, only part of which had been repaired.

On their first morning in Washington City Andrew awakened at dawn; she found him pacing the hotel room looking nervous and constrained. She sat bolt upright in bed.

"Andrew, what's wrong?"

"It's just that I'm scheduled for a joust with the War Department today. They, and the President too, have been receiving letters from New Orleans protesting my arrest of Judge Hall and Louallier, who wrote that inflammatory letter in the *Cour-rière*."

"But they know you were fighting a war!"

"It's always the people who never get near a battlefield who want you to fight according to gentlemen's rules."

That morning Major Reid took her and little Andrew for a tour of the city, but she insisted on being back early, before Andrew could return from the War Department. He came in in high spirits, exclaiming, "I did all that worrying for nothing! I had no sooner started to justify my use of martial law to Secretary Dallas than he said that explanations were not in order, that everything I did in New Orleans was quite all right, and the President as well as the heads of departments were happy and satisfied. I tried to get him to approve a fifteen-thousand-man standing army, but the best I could do was ten thousand."

Relieved, she said, "I'm glad you've come back in such good spirits because we are due at the Monroes' for dinner at three, and frankly I'm a bit nervous."

"Of the Monroes? Why? He is one of the most loyal and friendly men I've ever known."

"Oh, it's not Mr. Monroe I'm worried about, it's his wife. I've heard her called an aristocratic woman; they say she comes from the highest New York society and is very regal in her manner."

"You are going to be received as no woman has ever been received by any other woman."

"Why?"

"Because we are helping her to achieve her life ambition to become First Lady."

For Rachel the ugliness of the city was more than made up for by the tremendous cordiality of its citizens; it seemed that every last family wanted to entertain for them: there was a brilliant ball at McKeowin's Hotel, attended by every important personage in the government; President Madison entertained formally for them at the Octagon House, a sumptuous dinner to which had been invited the entire diplomatic corps, including members of the British Embassy. To Rachel's infinite amusement Andrew and the British Ambassador had a long and cordial conversation.

The following morning a well-known Washington artist, Anna Peale, asked Rachel to sit for her portrait. Andrew was flattered by the idea, and insisted that she do so. Rachel posed in a dark blue velvet gown, with a soft lace collar and matching lace cap.

That Saturday evening as they were retiring Andrew said, "I've planned a trip out to Mount Vernon for tomorrow. I've never been there and I thought it would make a nice day in the country for us." When she raised her eyebrows he rushed ahead with, "You're remembering how I refused to vote for the encomium after Mr. Washington's farewell address. Even great presidents need criticism."

She looked up at him out of laughing eyes.

"A principle to which you have made a considerable contribution."

"Yes," he said sheepishly. "I have made life unpleasant for a few of them, haven't I?"

The day was warm for mid-December; their visit to Washington City had been eminently successful; they felt lighthearted and young as they left their carriage at the foot of the hill and by gentle ascent reached the summit which overlooked the Potomac River on one side, and on the other a superb panorama of the Virginia countryside. The Custis family received them with the utmost hospitality, showing them through the simple but beautiful home. They wandered through the flower garden laid out and trimmed with exactness, then walked down the hill on the far side of the house to the small vault, overgrown with cedar, where President Washington had been buried.

Later, after being served refreshments by the family of Washington's adopted son, Andrew and Rachel sat on the front porch overlooking the beautiful Potomac and the many craft plowing gently along its surface.

"Next to Bayou Pierre," Andrew murmured, "this must surely be the most beautiful prospect in the world."

"Yes, along with the view of our own countryside, from that knoll on the Hermitage."

He turned his face full to her, studying her meaning for a moment.

"My dear, we could build the equivalent of Mount Vernon in Tennessee: a lovely house and garden like this, overlooking the fields and forest, with the Cumberland and Stone rivers in the distance."

"Andrew, I had no such thought and you know it! I am completely happy in our cabin. I don't ever want to move."

"You won't be so happy when we get back in January and you feel that north wind come through the logs."

"I've survived that north wind for eleven years now; besides, I heard you ask Robert Butler to rechink the entire cabin."

He did not reply. She saw by his sense of inner excitement that he had not been dissuaded.

4

They sold their cotton crop for the highest price they had ever received, thirty-eight cents a pound; for the first time in years they were out of debt, with more than twenty-two thousand dollars to their account in the Nashville bank. The death of young Reid, whom they had left only two weeks before, was a severe blow. Andrew turned over the materials for the biography to John Eaton, with the proviso that all of the proceeds from the book were to go to Reid's widow and children.

They had been home less than three weeks when Andrew announced that he had to make a tour of the Indian country: the Creeks were complaining about the harshness of the treaty he had given them, and were not only refusing to move off certain lands they had ceded to the United States but were rousing their neighbors, the Cherokees and Chickasaws, and threatening to resume fighting. Rachel felt there was no immediacy to the problem.

"I suppose it sounds wifely of me," she insisted, "but do you really have to go? Jax is surveying down there and surely he would let you know if trouble were brewing."

"As long as I am on salary," he replied stubbornly, "I'm going to continue doing the best job I know how. I can't bear to report unfit for duty while eating the public bread."

No sooner had he ridden down the trail to the Tennessee border than a virulent epidemic which the doctors called "cold plague" broke out, felling whole families. Once again Rachel became a familiar figure in the countryside, riding across the fields at night wrapped in a dark cape and hood, carrying provisions and medication and warm friendliness. Day after day she closed the eyes of friends and neighbors who died while she sat by their bedside, ignoring the doctor's warning that since six and seven members of a family were dying within hours of each other the disease was highly contagious.

By the time spring came, and an end to the plague, almost a third of the population of the Cumberland had been wiped out. Rachel took to her bed, her own strength gone. Desperately as she missed Andrew, she was glad that she would have a few weeks in which to recuperate.

He was gone five months in all, returning in time for their nephew Andy's graduation from Cumberland Academy. During the exercises the headmaster told the parents how badly the school needed a new dormitory. Rachel plucked at Andrew's sleeve.

"Remember back at Poplar Grove when you were elected to the board of trustees, you said you were going to help make it a great school. Did you ever do much for them?"

"A little free legal advice here and there."

"Then don't you think this would be a good time to fulfill your promise?"

"You mean . . . the whole building?"

"The headmaster said it would only cost a thousand dollars. Our Andrew is going to be entered in the fall . . ."

He stood up and, when recognized, said, "Mr. Headmaster, I'd like to announce that you now have your new dormitory."

The next day, during a party for Andy's classmates, an itinerant portrait painter appeared on the scene, a most personable young man with a sweet smile and a lovable manner. He introduced himself as Ralph Earl, son of a Connecticut painter, and asked if he might have the pleasure of painting General Jackson's portrait. Rachel saw that her niece Jane was smitten at first sight; and since Andrew also liked the chap's air of inner quietude and confidence, she assigned him a guest cottage. He went to work at once, painting Andrew in his full-dress uniform.

The Earl sittings were soon interrupted however, for General Jackson received a formal notification from the new Secretary of War, William Crawford, that his treaty with the Creeks had been set aside, and that vast tracts of land had been returned to the Cherokees. Andrew was wild with anger, insisting that the news was the worst since the burning of Washington City; it put him flat on his back with an attack of diarrhea. When he was able to sit up and Rachel brought him his writing materials, he wrote Secretary Crawford a blistering letter. She feared that the strenuous effort and anger might bring on another attack, but instead it had a healing effect and by the next morning he was on his feet again, gaunt and concave of stomach, but ready to head the mass meetings of indignation that were being called throughout Tennessee.

President Madison named him as commissioner, with instructions to return to the Indian country and buy from the Cherokees the lands which he had taken from them and that Secretary Crawford had given back.

Once again they were separated. Once again she was alone. But the feeling of being only half alive when her husband was away was replaced by a feeling of complete bafflement when he returned to the Hermitage after several months and fell into a series of quarrels, disputes and conflicts that kept them in an uproar. She made no attempt to keep the details of the interlocking feuds straight in her mind; letters and episodes tumbled over each other in such fast sequence that it would have been impossible in any event.

He was still quarreling violently with Secretary of War Crawford, who was refusing to put the newly purchased Cherokee land on the market so that it could be bought by American settlers; with the Kentucky newspapers who were defending the Kentucky troops who had given way under British fire at New Orleans, and whom he had excoriated in his report to the War Department; and finally with the War Department itself, which had taken one of Andrew's officers off a topographical assignment and summoned him to New York without informing General Jackson of the transfer. Outraged, Andrew issued an order to his entire division instructing them to disregard all orders from the War Department unless they came through him.

In the midst of the cyclone, John Overton brought her the news that under the newly elected President Monroe, William Crawford was to become Secretary of the Treasury, and that the position of Secretary of War was now available to Andrew. It would mean leaving the Hermitage and settling in Washington City, probably for several years; and as a Cabinet member, a return to national politics. But then didn't all of Andrew's activities, including the winning of wars, end in political embroilments? Since he was always going to be involved, might it not be advisable to be at the center of the conflict? As Secretary of War he could issue the orders which would fulfill his life ambition: the solid settling of all lands between Tennessee and the Gulf of Mexico with American families. Tentatively, as they sat before the fire after dinner smoking their pipes, she suggested this line of reasoning to him.

He looked up at her in astonishment.

"You must be terribly upset by my difficulties, my dear, if you can make such a recommendation. I don't want to sit behind a desk; I want to march back south and send the Dons home from Florida."

And that was precisely what he did, leaving her for a fourth long journey within the period of two years.

The Hermitage was in the hands of a capable overseer; she no longer had to go into the fields, to be exposed to the hard labor, to the drying heat of the sun. Yet it seemed that each day brought its own misfortune: Severn took to bed with a hacking cough and died from it. John Overton became so ill he had to resign his judgeship and retire to Travellers Rest. Her nephew, John Hutchings, who had been Andrew's business partner for so many years, died at his home in Huntsville. Rachel brought his four-year-old son, Andrew Jackson Hutchings, now an orphan, back home with her. Only two pleasant things happened: her niece Jane and the portraitist, Ralph Earl, fell in love and asked her permission to be married. Rachel gave them a big wedding party at the Hermitage, and they moved into what had gradually become Earl's studio. Also that spring, 1817, the biography of Andrew was published, and enthusiastically received.

Andrew returned from the Seminole-Florida war after a half year's absence, though Rachel could not have said just how long it was; with her release from farming she had given up all calendars. His hands were shaking as though he had palsy and he had a cough as bad as the one that had killed Severn. He had a mysterious pain in his side which kept him from sleeping, and his left shoulder, broken by the Benton bullet five years before, had stiffened so severely that he had no use of the arm. She summoned Dr. Bronaugh from Nashville; John Overton rose from his sickbed to spend an hour locked in the upper bedroom with Andrew. He came downstairs shaking his head in mystification.

"That's quite a man you married yourself to: he doesn't think he can survive this illness but he's writing President Monroe that it's urgent for us to take St. Augustine and Cuba at once; and that all he needs is the President's order to lead an expedition southward."

"But surely no one would give him such an order!"

John studied her face for a moment, the silver specs down over the hump of his nose and his eyes frankly puzzled.

"Then you don't know what's happening?" he asked blandly.

Before a week was out she learned that her husband's seizure of Florida had caused an international scandal: Spain was demanding an immediate return of Pensacola, with indemnities and severe punishment of General Jackson. England was threatening war over his court-martial and execution of Lieutenant Ambrister of the Royal Colonial Marines, who had led the Indians in their fight during the Seminole war, and Alexander Arbuthnot, a Scotsman, also charged with spying and helping the enemy. Negotiations for the purchase of Florida, which had been progressing slowly, now collapsed. The press of America as well as of England

and Europe cried out for General Jackson's scalp. It wasn't possible for her to keep the newspapers out of the Hermitage, nor to bar her gates to the loyal officers who were organizing to fight the movement in Congress which would impeach Andrew and relieve him of his command. Apparently the only two men in the country who were defending her husband's course were John Quincy Adams, Secretary of State, and someone using the pseudonym of Aristedes, who was publishing a brilliant series of pro-Jackson articles in the Tennessee papers. Only by accident did she learn that Aristedes was their own John Overton.

She had had Andrew sitting up in a chair for a few hours each day, but this fresh crisis put him back in bed again. There he remained for two solid months, neither his temper nor his health helped any by President Monroe's apologetic return of Pensacola and St. Marks to Spain, thus nullifying Andrew's second conquest of Florida.

Yet this was the very moment that he told her he was ready to begin building the fine house he had promised her at Mount Vernon; apparently he had been planning its details during the six months he had been away. They went across the fields one hot August day, Andrew walking with slow and faltering steps, leaning heavily on his cane; at the top of a slight rise overlooking their cabins, the spring and the deep woods beyond, he stopped.

"This has always been your favorite spot." Raising his stick and pointing with it, he said, "There's a better elevation over there, you'll get a wider view. Wouldn't you prefer to build on that highest level?"

She smiled to herself, realizing that by his oblique question he had taken the subject of the new house out of the realm of disputation. The humble Hermitage cabin, which satisfied her completely, was no longer adequate to his *amour-propre*. She had no logic on her side, only sentiment: they had plenty of money in the bank, and their little cabin was really inadequate for the amount of entertaining they were obliged to do. Since Andrew wanted the big home, she might just as well enter into the plan with enthusiasm. But she would hold out for the lower knoll.

"We have so many pleasant memories of this spot," she pleaded. "That other hill has a little too much . . . eminence . . . for me. You know . . . I get vertigo."

He chuckled softly, then with his stick began outlining the house he had in mind: it was to be a two-story brick building with a big hall downstairs, two good-sized rooms on either side, and four rooms upstairs directly over the four below. He had been his own architect; he would be his own builder.

The harvest season brought them another excellent crop, but when they found a limestone quarry on their own land she agreed that they should take several of their more skilled hands out of the fields to start the foundation work. They spent days together wandering over their acreage until they located a good bed of clay; when the topsoil had been removed and lime sprinkled over the deposit, they let their son ride the mule who was treading the lime into the clay to give it the proper hardness. They built their own kiln, experimenting with the fires in an effort to get the kind of brick they wanted, and rode through the forest, marking the best poplar trees for timbers and structural lumber. Then he received an order from Washington City to go back into the Indian country and arrange a treaty with the Chickasaws.

She was left with the actual building of the house. Because the responsibility was now hers, and she had to make decisions about the fireplace and the wine cellar, she found that she was building into her new home an ever-growing interest and emotion. It wasn't going to be too grand a place after all: just a square brick building with a little picket fence around it. There would still be plenty of seclusion, for the house stood a hundred yards back from the road, completely screened by tall trees.

When Andrew returned in mid-November, having been delayed by an excursion into Alabama where he had bought a large cotton plantation next to the one on which John Coffee now lived, he approved the way the building had taken shape.

Six weeks later he started out for Washington City to be on hand when his enemies in the Congress started impeachment proceedings against him. He left on horseback in the midst of torrential rains, rejecting her suggestion that he take their carriage. Within a week she had a letter from Knoxville, telling her that she had been right after all; he had been unable to stay on his horse and had had to borrow a carriage for the journey.

She filled her days with the completing of the big house, building a separate kitchen just across the porch from the dining room and sinking a deep well which brought up cool water by windlass and bucket, staking out her first garden inside the low white picket fence. And as always when Andrew was away, the deepest tragedies struck: young Jane Earl died in childbed, just ten months after her wedding, and was buried in the family plot next to Mrs. Donelson, Samuel, Stockly and Severn. Within a few days Robert Hays was stricken and died, and Rachel lost her dearest and most loyal friend.

Jane went to live with one of her sons in West Tennessee, Andy was at West Point, young Andrew was in school in Nashville, and Earl wandered off, heartbroken at the loss of his wife. Yet Rachel could hardly say she was alone, for the air crackled with news about Andrew: the Committee on Military Affairs attacked him for the executions of Ambrister and Arbuthnot; Speaker of the House Henry Clay of Kentucky stepped down from the dais to attack the Creek Treaty and the conquest of Pensacola, charging Andrew Jackson with being a military chieftain who would one day destroy the liberties of the American people.

Rachel mounted Duke, Andrew's favorite horse, the superb stallion who had carried his master through the Battle of New Orleans and the Florida wars, now getting old but still beloved of the family. She rode over to Travellers Rest, where she found Overton puttering in a greenhouse amidst his young trees.

"I simply can't understand the ferocity of these attacks, John."

"Mr. Clay wants to be our next president," replied John. "He'd kill his own grandmother if he thought she stood in his way. The same applies to Mr. Crawford. Each gentleman thinks Andrew Jackson is standing in his way."

"But Andrew has said he doesn't want the presidency."

Overton buttoned up his collar against the cool of the greenhouse.

"Messrs. Clay and Crawford remain unconvinced: neither one will have a peaceful night's sleep until Andrew is relieved of his commission and punished for taking Florida. But our side will have its turn. Let me give you some of these purple flags to take home; they'll grow wonderfully in your new garden."

For the next two weeks the Nashville papers were filled with the fiery defense set up by their friends, who described Andrew's every action as part of an over-all military strategy designed to safeguard the American people. When the final vote was taken Andrew was vindicated. Philadelphia gave him a four-day celebration, New York a five-day reception while he was on his way to visit Andy at West Point. In his letters Andrew assured her that during even the most tumultuous hours of the debate he had remained quietly in his hotel room and had not entered personally into the controversy; was it not natural then for a man who had just triumphed over his bitterest adversaries to glory a little in public acclaim? She was convinced that if Andrew's military career had not been attacked he would have remained a general and a gentleman planter; but would he be content to remain so now with the ovations of Philadelphia and New York fresh in his ears?

5

She had the house completed, with carpets in the bedrooms, draperies at the windows and her cherry-wood table installed in the dining room by the time Andrew returned from Washington in mid-April. Her settee and the chairs were on the worn side, the pianoforte needed a resurfacing, but she enjoyed the sense of continuity that the old pieces brought to a house still smelling slightly of paint. Despite the fact that she now had eight rooms instead of the three in which they had lived for fifteen years at the cabin, it nonetheless had for her a feeling of compactness; Andrew had designed it on a somewhat smaller scale than Hunter's Hill. The entrance hall and stairs were of dark polished wood; to the left as one entered was the front parlor and dining room, with a nice view of the hill which rolled gently down to the old Hermitage buildings. The rooms were almost square, about twenty by twenty. Across the hall to the right was Andrew's office into which she moved her father's walnut desk and two walls of bookshelves. Behind Andrew's room was a passage with a side door leading out, and just beyond that a bedroom for young Andrew, who could get up as early as he liked and slip out of doors without disturbing the rest of the family.

Andrew walked about for an entire day determining where they would put up the fine wallpapers he had brought back from the East and what furniture was needed to complete the rooms. They had their first supper that night under the many candles of the crystal chandelier; Hannah had done the cooking, but Moll and George insisted upon serving the food. After dinner they walked outside to look at the house against the night sky; it had a simple grace and dignity that made them proud. Andrew brought forth a box from his waistcoat pocket, then leaned over to kiss her.

"It seems I'm forever leaving you home to finish something I started."

Rachel opened the box to find a set of beautiful mosaic jewelry, a necklace, earrings and belt clasp. She took the necklace from the case and held it draped over her palm. Andrew stood behind her to fasten the catch, then kept his arms about her. He went away so often, and stayed away so long, yet he always returned to her completely, bringing his full self, his full spirit, his full love and desire. She turned in his arms, found herself clasped against him. He couldn't help what he did; he was driven. He had great spirit, vision, courage, leadership; half the time she knew him to be physically more dead than alive; but the fire never went out, the fire which fed on itself, creating its own fuel even while consuming it.

At the beginning of June they received a note from President Monroe, who was touring Georgia, accepting Andrew's invitation to visit at the Hermitage for a few days. Rachel took the news in stride. It did not seem to her extraordinary that she should be offering hospitality to the President of the United States; her father before her had entertained George Washington, Patrick Henry and the other leaders of the House of Burgesses; the Donelson stockade had been the stopping-off station for all important visitors from the East, and now it seemed only natural to her that Mr. Monroe should come to the Hermitage.

She decided that he must have the big front bedroom over the parlor, and went that day into Nashville to buy a sturdy mahogany bed with a canopy, a marble-topped table with a comfortable chair for the center of the room and a mahogany dresser that fitted nicely into the corner beyond the fireplace. The last of the white curtains and damask draperies were hung the evening before his arrival.

"We finished this house just in time," said Andrew, watching her preparations with approval. "It's more fitting to entertain the President here."

"Oh, I think I could have made Mr. Monroe as comfortable in the cabin."

James Monroe proved to be the most undemanding of guests. A deep and abiding affection between the President and Andrew was apparent in their every word to each other as they lingered over a late supper, the three of them in the cozy intimacy of the dining room. Mr. Monroe was to have only two or three free days before going into Nashville for entertainment by the Female Academy, and a grand ball; Rachel saw to it that he had complete relaxation.

But after Andrew had left to make part of the return journey with the President she found that apparently the only center of quiet during his stay had been inside the red brick walls of the Hermitage; the newspaper editors and politicos all over the country were asking just what were the implications of President Monroe's visit to the Jacksons? In one Washington City newspaper Rachel read that this visit was planned by the President to give official approval to all of General Jackson's acts, starting with the Creek treaties and going straight through the capture of Florida; from a second group she learned that the visit had to do with internal politics: Mr. Monroe had reasoned that if the Jacksons received him in their home as a guest they would not shortly thereafter attempt to wrest the presidency from him; that in fact General Jackson, in affording hospitality to Mr. Monroe, had taken this means of announcing to the country that he was supporting Mr. Monroe for re-election in 1820. Their own friends in Tennessee maintained that by going directly to the Hermitage before he visited Nashville, Mr. Monroe was announcing publicly that he favored the succession of General and Mrs. Andrew Jackson to the President's House in Washington City in 1824.

This was indeed news to Mrs. Jackson.

Andrew had been gone only a few days when a panic descended upon the West with terrifying force; it was not merely that there would be no market for their cotton or for anything else they might raise on the Hermitage, but that the three years of prosperity following the Battle of New Orleans, during which countless new factories had been opened and vast quantities of outlying lands put under cultivation, were now ended with the suddenness of a cannon shot. Local banks which had sprung up by the dozens, issuing credit on unbroken lands and unplanted crops, had their voluminous paper money called in by the Bank of the United States in Philadelphia. Fortunately for her, Andrew had done no borrowing and had been far too busy to buy or start planting new farms; in fact he had opposed the new paper-money banks as being financially unsound; but most of their friends and neighbors had borrowed heavily for their speculations.

From her bedroom she now saw them ride wearily up the road and turn into the Hermitage. Could Mrs. Jackson lend them five hundred dollars . . . a thousand? If they had that much cash they could hold off the banks. . . . She had gone through several of these crises before, and was pretty well convinced that it would be throwing good money after bad; but she had lived with Andrew long enough to know that he too would want to help as much as he could.

She made substantial loans to twenty families; in a few cases the money saved their homes. But by the time she had loaned out half of her available cash she had also come to a realization that they themselves would be deeply involved in the depression. She stopped the lending until Andrew returned. He approved of what she had done, then continued to parcel out their money until he had not a dollar of cash left. After they had processed their cotton, and sold it at a pitiful price, he told Rachel:

"We now have cash loans out to a hundred and twenty-nine men; and are down to rock bottom. It's the fault of the Biddle crowd in Philadelphia that owns the Bank of the United States: if they hadn't forced the local banks to redeem their paper in specie, we might have worked out of this crisis. I really ought to get back to Washington City: Clay and Crawford are doing everything they can to scuttle our treaty with Spain for the purchase of Florida. But I need several hundred dollars for travel expenses . . ."

"I was never so happy to be without a sou," she said with a laugh. "And this is one time you can't borrow from John Overton: I think he's about to propose to Dr. May's widow. If she accepts he's going to have to build an extra wing for her five children. We're all hoping she will accept; after all, John is fifty-four now, and he's lived alone too long.''

The Widow May did accept; almost the whole Cumberland Valley attended the wedding at Travellers Rest.

Spain finally signed the treaty. Rachel was happy because Andrew would not be going off to war again. Instead there came a letter from President Monroe offering him the governorship of Florida.

"Doesn't this governorship come a good many years too late?'' she asked.

"Admittedly the appointment is anticlimactic. However, President Monroe seems to think I'm the logical person to organize an American government down there, since I know the most about it.''

"You could also be the illogical person: the Spanish governors hate you, and not without reason.''

He chewed on this for a number of moments, then sighed deeply.

"You're perfectly right. I have neither the strength nor the appetite for the task. I'll sit down right now and write to President Monroe, refusing the office.''

"You partially want that appointment, don't you?''

"That's my curse: I partially want everything. Wasn't it your father who used to say, 'Every man is his own jailer, and every man his own prison'?''

They slept late and were in the midst of a leisurely breakfast when a group of riders came up the road from Nashville. John Overton, Dr. Bronaugh and Felix Grundy were ushered in.

"We came to congratulate you on being the first American governor of Florida.''

"Then you can take your glasses off, John, because you are not going to get a clear view of the governor through them; I sent a letter last night, declining the position.''

"You didn't!'' It was Dr. Bronaugh, Andrew's military surgeon.

"We think you should hold a few such posts in the government, preparatory to the presidency.''

"And we're convinced that's why President Monroe made the appointment,'' added Felix Grundy.

She watched the dull brick color mount in Andrew's cheeks.

"Do you think I'm such a damned fool as to think myself fit for president of the United States? No sir; I know what I am fit for. I can command a body of men in a rough way; but I am not fit to be president.''

They were silent for a moment, then John said quietly, "This is only further proof of your good sense, Andrew. Couldn't we go into the library?''

She went up to her bedroom and resumed work on the bedspread she was making for a guest room. It was noon before the meeting in the library broke up. One of the men went out the front door and rode rapidly away in the direction of town. Andrew came up the stairs.

"I told them that if my letter of refusal had not yet left the post office I would withdraw it and send an acceptance letter in its place.'' He grimaced. "But you know the mail leaves the Nashville post office at noon, and it's past that now. We are perfectly safe.''

She wanted to exclaim, Andrew, it isn't like you to let a major decision hinge upon whether a messenger can reach the Nashville post office before the mails leave! It must be that he really wants to go, she thought, and with his own eyes and his own hands effectuate the transfer of Florida.

She was no whit surprised when the messenger returned, triumphantly bearing the letter. She sat quietly while he wrote an acceptance.

They descended the Mississippi to New Orleans by steamboat in eight days, their freshly painted carriage trimmed with morocco skins securely lashed in the hold. They brought with them their son, also Lieutenant Andy, just out of West Point, and as special company for Rachel, Narcissa Hays, Jane's twenty-year-old daughter. There were two hundred passengers on board where only fifty could be cared for comfortably.

"I guess I'm old-fashioned," she told Andrew one midnight as they stood at the prow, wrapped in greatcoats. "I prefer Colonel Stark's flatboat." She turned to put her arm through his. ". . . particularly when you were steering it."

It seemed to her as though all of New Orleans had assembled at the pier to welcome them, with a full band of martial music. That night they were conducted to the Grand Theatre by a guard of honor, and when they entered their box the audience rose to its feet, shouting: *"Viva Jackson! Long live the Jacksons!"* Later a delegation came into the box to place a crown of laurel on Andrew's head. Rachel shrank from the gesture of worship and sat staring at the shiny green leaves uneasily: by some optical illusion the laurel had turned to thorns. When the lights were extinguished and the curtain went up she found herself unable to follow the play.

The next morning she rose early and went on a buying spree to accumulate the new bedsteads, sideboard and dining table needed to complete the Hermitage. Louise Livingston knew the finest shops, making sure that she purchased only the best materials. Andrew's salary as governor was five thousand dollars, and Rachel reasoned it was wise to put some of the money into furnishings which they would enjoy for the rest of their lives, including the wonderful new French mattresses. By the end of their week's stay in New Orleans she had bought seven packing cases of furniture, which Edward Livingston arranged to send north.

They took a boat on Lake Pontchartrain, crossed the Gulf and landed at Mobile Bay. When they were within fifteen miles of Pensacola, where Andrew was to set up headquarters and take over the government, he decided he would go no further, but remain at the home of a friendly Spaniard, Señor Manuel, to which he had been invited.

"You and the children take the carriage into Pensacola," he explained to Rachel. "There's a comfortable house waiting for us on Main Street. It wouldn't be proper for me to go into the town until Governor Callava is ready to deliver the province to me officially."

Assured that it would be only a matter of a day or two, Rachel gathered up her son, her niece and her nephew and they rode the fifteen miles into Pensacola. The town lay on the bay, and from her balcony she had a fine view over the water, with a sea breeze from ten o'clock in the morning until ten at night.

Before the sun became too warm she went for a walk about the town, flanked by Narcissa and her two Andrews. Pensacola lay in a perfect plain, the land nearly as white as flour, yet productive of fine peach trees, oranges in abundance, grapes, figs and pomegranates. The Spanish residents, expecting a change of government, had neglected their gardens, flowers were growing wild, and the many public squares were overgrown with thick shrubs, weeping willows and pride of China. The streets were crowded with the most amazing polyglot she had ever seen: Spanish, French, Negroes from the islands, Indians in native costume; there were so few Americans that she heard only an occasional word of English in the streets.

There were daily notes from Andrew telling her of the hundred difficulties in his way: he did not believe it proper to call on Governor Callava before the governor called on him; the ships bearing American troops were missing; the Spanish governor was insisting on taking the guns in the fortifications. He would join her in a few days.

Dawn in Pensacola was the loveliest time; she arose while it was still dark, had a cup of coffee, then sat out on the balcony watching the ships coming into the harbor, most of them now loaded with Americans seeking political appointments or business opportunities. It was only two weeks since her arrival, yet the town had become so jammed that it was no longer possible for her to take her daily promenade down Main Street or through the square. On Sunday morning she decided to hold services for her family in her own living room. The town was still in an uproar from its Saturday-night brawl. Instead of holding the services she sat down at her desk and wrote letters to friends in Tennessee asking if they might know of a clergyman who would be attracted to this heathen land.

It took another two weeks of exasperating negotiations before Andrew was able to make his entry into Pensacola, arriving in time for a six o'clock breakfast, to which Governor Callava had been invited, but which he had declined. At ten o'clock Rachel stood on her balcony watching the Spanish troops drawn up in the square, their flag still flying, and the Americans marching down the street to take a position opposite them. The Spanish flag was lowered halfway, then she saw Andrew give a command and the American flag rose in its place. At long last Andrew Jackson had made a bloodless and permanent conquest of Florida! The Spanish people below her burst into tears and walked disconsolately out of the square; her own exultation faded in the face of her sympathy for them.

Within a very few days her sympathy veered to her husband. While the Spanish residents were prospering under the influx of Americans, Andrew was encountering little but obstruction and aggravation: the men he had invited down from Nashville to take part in the government were stranded because President Monroe had sent his own administrative staff into Florida. Aside from such minor tasks as cleaning the drunks off the streets on Sunday mornings, he had little to do. The rains began to fall as though the heavens had burst; her son came down with a fever, so Rachel sent the boy home with Colonel Butler. Because he was idle and frustrated, Andrew got into a row over the archives with ex-Governor Callava: Andrew insisted that the records be handed to the new American government, Callava refused, Andrew had him arrested and seized the records in Callava's house. That night, closeted in their bedroom, he confessed:

"You were right, I should never have come. The whole thing's been a wild-goose chase."

"Not entirely," she replied consolingly. "If you hadn't come you might always have had an unfinished feeling in your mind about Florida. But if your job is done now, why don't we just pack our trunks and go home?"

6

They returned to the Hermitage during the first week of November, after having been gone eight months. They found that a large portion of their crop had been destroyed by freshets, hailstorms and a deluge of rain. The *National Intelligencer* carried further deluge; they read of the demand being made for a congressional investigation of Governor Jackson's official behavior in Florida, in particular his jailing of the former Spanish Governor Callava, and his seizing of the Spanish archives.

"It's Crawford and Clay again," declared Andrew. "They are still trying to eliminate me from presidential consideration. I'm going to write a letter saying that I admire the talents of Secretary of State John Quincy Adams, and that I shall support him for the presidency when Mr. Monroe retires. That will put an end to their hellish machinations. Can you understand that?"

"Yes, I can understand it. But can you write the letter?"

"Just find a comfortable position anywhere behind my shoulder."

He was right; the congressional investigation was dropped.

At the beginning of February 1822, Andy came home for a conference with his aunt and uncle; he was bored with army life and attracted to the law. Since his uncle was now convinced that the United States was safe from invasion, he consented to Andy's resigning from the army and entering Transylvania Law College in Kentucky. At the same time Ralph Earl returned; he had been wandering for several years, unable to reconcile himself to the loss of his wife. He asked if he might stay at the Hermitage, since it was the only home he knew and he no longer could flee from his memories. Could he do a portrait of Mrs. Jackson, and several of Mr. Jackson? Rachel and Andrew assured him he could remain as part of the family for the rest of his days if he so desired.

With the coming of spring Andrew got out on the farm to supervise the planting. Rachel saw that he was in better health and in better spirits than at any time during the past ten years. With the passing months letters arrived from many states telling them how popular he was with the voters; there was an unending number of newspaper articles wondering when the wily Mr. Jackson was finally going to show his hand. He answered none of the letters which asked him to make political comments or commitments; the newspaper articles amused him. Each week saw a group of excited friends at the Hermitage estimating the popularity of various candidates, showing letters from their friends indicating that Pennsylvania would go for Jackson, or New York would, or he need only appear in Boston to assure himself of Massachusetts. If these presidential handicappers made any impression on Andrew, she could find no evidence of it. To Johnny's daughter Mary, who had married Jax and was living in Alabama, Rachel wrote:

> I do hope they will leave Mr. Jackson alone. He is not a well man and never will be unless they allow him a rest. He has done his share for the country. He has not spent one-fourth of his days under his own roof. Now I hope it is at an end. They talk of his being President. Major Eaton, General Carroll, Mr. Campbell, Doctor Bronough and even the Parson and I can't tell how many others—all of his friends who come here—talk everlastingly about his being President. In this as in all else, I can only say, the Lord's will be done. But I hope he may not be called again to the strife and empty honors of public place.

However, it was a letter from her sister Jane that really upset her:

> You will miss your fine farm and comfortable house for the city of Washington, when the General is elected President.

If sensible, hardheaded Jane had been convinced that Andrew would be the next president, then whom in all God's world could they ever persuade that they intended to remain by their hearth for the rest of their lives?

It would have been difficult for her to tell the exact moment at which Andrew began to grow restless. The action of the Tennessee legislature in officially nominating their favorite son for the presidency in July of 1822 could surely excite any man who was genuinely interested in the office. However, Andrew did not take the move seriously; he merely commented to her that the usual method of nominating presidents, that of a caucus of congressmen who dictated the party's choice, was now obsolete. Yet no matter what he did or did not do the papers found it significant: when he declined the post as minister to Mexico, this was interpreted as proof of his interest in the presidency; when he declined to go on tour through the Northwest, this was interpreted as a lack of interest in the presidency.

What actually caused the first real break in his resolution? she asked herself. Was it the information that President Monroe was supporting Secretary William Crawford? Was it the fact that the second of his personal adversaries, Henry Clay of Kentucky, was rapidly gaining adherents in such states as Ohio, Indiana and Illinois? Was it the disconcerting news that the man he was backing for the post, John Quincy Adams, was losing ground? Or was it, as she was coming more and more to suspect, that Andrew's interest had lain dormant simply because the election had been so far away?

Activity about the Hermitage increased: newspapermen, politicians, officers who had been disappointed at the cutting down of the army, oldtime friends and that little clique of Jacksonians, Overton, Lewis and Eaton, were constantly closeted with Andrew, analyzing for him the newest developments, building on their one sure foundation: that Adam's strength was failing and that the next president would be either William Crawford or Henry Clay; and how would he be able to live peaceably and happily at the Hermitage with either of these two men as Chief Executive?

"I know I don't have the proper training or temperament for the presidency," Andrew confided to her late one Sunday night, after she had gone to bed exhausted from entertaining almost a hundred guests; "but certainly I have greater honesty and integrity than either of those two adventurers."

"Perhaps if you went on a tour at election time, urging everyone to support Mr. Adams . . .?"

"Then I'd be in politics again, up to my scrawny neck. Either I am in . . . completely . . .or completely out."

The inevitable incident came in the fall after they had harvested their crop and then found there was no market whatever for the cotton. Perhaps if he had not been depressed over the lack of money he would not have reacted so volcanically to the attack unleashed against him by Senator Williams of Tennessee, a Crawford man who thought the moment ripe to eliminate Mr. Jackson permanently from the presidential scene. Senator Williams made his criticism of Andrew the major plank in his own platform for re-election. Andrew had endorsed his old friend Congressman Rhea for senator, and John Overton, John Eaton and William Lewis were at the capital fighting desperately to win votes for Rhea in the state legislature where the election was to be determined.

On the night before the senatorial election John Overton rode into the Hermitage weary and disheveled, accompanied by one of Andrew's former generals. Rachel saw by John's paleness and by the angularity of his movements that it was a moment of crisis. She got the two men a cool drink, then sat stiffly on a straight-backed chair listening to every word.

"Andrew, we're licked. Rhea can't make it. You are going to have to take his place and run for the Senate; that's the only way we can defeat Williams and his anti-Jackson platform. If we defeat Williams, and you go to the Senate, we are in a perfect position for next year's presidential campaign." John's gray eyes had bulked up dark. "Gather together a few things and come back with us. It's going to be a difficult battle, and your presence will help."

Rachel found herself unable to breathe. Andrew turned to gaze at her. After a moment he murmured, "Excuse me, I wish to talk to my wife."

He came to her side, put his hand under her arm and lifted her from the chair. They left Andrew's office, went through the hall and into the parlor. He closed the door behind them.

They stood in the center of the room facing each other, very close, very intent, their eyes boring deep, touching one another neither by hand nor thought. Her only positive feeling at the moment was the need within herself to find out what, under the layers of years, wounds, ambitions, accomplishments and failures, was the real truth about what Andrew wanted. He grinned at her sheepishly.

"Everything would be simple, my dear, if only I knew what I wanted. I've never been happier than during the last two years living quietly here at the Hermitage, being a gentleman planter, enjoying your companionship."

She tried to keep all emotion out of her voice.

"There's a time to lie fallow and there's a time to bear fruit. If you want the presidency, Andrew, and I can understand how greatly a man would feel honored . . .''

"No, no, it's not honor that I would be seeking, I've had all of that any man could want. It's the chance for service that intrigues me. I'd fight for this country every minute of the day, just as hard as I fought at New Orleans."

"And just as well, too. If this is the thing you want, Andrew, then you must do everything in your power to achieve it. You must go tonight with John and General Coleman."

He opened his arms to her and at last they were clinging to each other, lonely and a little forlorn.

"And what of you, Rachel? What of the consequences?"

She left his side, walked over to the big front window, her head lowered, caught somewhere in the mysterious space between thought and reverie. What precisely did Andrew mean? The fact that she would have to leave the Hermitage which she loved dearly and move to Washington City? That she too would become a public servant, be obliged to enter the world of protocol and society? Did she have the temperament for that kind of life after having sought seclusion these many years?

Her mind drifted backward, to New Orleans, and the birthday party she had given for Andrew when the peace with Britain had become official; to the letter from her cousin, John Stockly, which had said, "We are entitled to a President from the West," to the question she had asked herself then, If it all were to come to pass, would I make any effort to stop it? She had recognized the issue then; and nothing had changed. This could be the most important decision of her life, for the followers of neither Mr. Crawford nor Mr. Clay would hesitate to use her private affairs as the whipping post on which to flay the political aspirations of Andrew Jackson to death. The presidential campaign would be bloody and bitter.

Wasn't that what Andrew meant when he spoke of the consequences? Wasn't he asking for her permission to plunge her into this maelstrom?

They were so completely without cash that they would have to borrow money from John Overton to cover Andrew's expenses. She would have to remain at the Hermitage to get the cotton ginned, the foodstuffs stored, the tools and cabins repaired, the mill moved and the new gin house built. He would be gone for . . . how long . . .six months, a year? Once again she would be alone in a big house.

Our lives have come full circle, she thought. How impossible it is for any man to break out of his pattern. We have come through all these years and all this suffering only to be caught in the identical predicament at the end of our lives that we were in in the beginning.

She rose, walked to her husband, who had been standing awkwardly in the center of the room, trying not to intrude upon her decision. She reached up her face to be kissed, then said quietly:

"I will accept the consequences."

BOOK SEVEN

1

The hours clung stickily to her fingers; yet this long separation after Andrew had been elected and gone to the Senate was not unpleasant. Andy, who had opened his law office in Nashville, was taking full responsibility for affairs at the Hermitage. He was selling their cotton for a good price and, at his uncle's orders, putting the money away for the trip the family would take with Andrew to Washington City the following fall. Andy had his father's rich black hair and big warm sensitive brown eyes as well as his voice and gestures; it was like having Samuel at her side.

The house was filled with her young nieces: there were seldom fewer than five or six of them visiting at one time and that meant their admirers and suitors as well. The evenings and weekends were gay with music and singing and laughter. It seemed to Rachel that she was never alone; she did not discover until spring that this was no accident, but rather an express order from Andrew in Washington City to Andy at home:

"Keep your aunt's spirits up."

In the Senate Andrew sat next to Thomas Hart Benton, and the two men had become friends again; he extended the olive branch to General Winfield Scott, with whom he had quarreled over the powers of the War Department; Henry Clay had come to dinner with him several times at O'Neale's Tavern.

At Christmas she helped decorate Johnny's house for the big family party, festooning the walls and windows with holly and berries and clusters of mistletoe. Johnny told her that from everything he could sense in the papers and the wind, Andrew would be the next president; he then added in a bemused tone:

"Your husband is a very surprising man; his nearest and best friends never found him out."

A strange way, thought Rachel, of saying, We never fully appreciated him.

After the holidays she was able to fulfill a wish she had been nurturing for several years: to have a little church right on the Hermitage where their friends and relatives could come on Sunday morning for services, and one night a week for a good bout of preaching. She built it of brick, just a mile or so from the house; it looked like a New England schoolhouse, for it had no steeple or portico; on the inside there were forty unpainted pews standing on a brick floor. The building of the church and the hiring of a pastor absorbed most of her energies over the winter. In the spring she replanted her garden with hollyhocks, white and purple heliotrope, tiger lilies and white lilacs, many of the beds being edged with sage and thyme. At the entrance to the garden there was a rope tied to the limb of a hickory tree where the dozens of children who visited the Hermitage could swing. Some of the trees brought by friends from distant places were beginning to bloom now, the pink magnolia from Japan, the fig tree from the far South.

For years there had been twenty to thirty journals coming into the Hermitage, but Andrew had canceled all of these except the Nashville newspaper. How much more pleasant it was to follow the romance of the youngsters about her: for twenty-three-year-old Andy had been smitten by Johnny's youngest daughter, sixteen-year-old Emily, the red-haired, delicate-featured beauty of the Donelson crop. Her brother Johnny opposed this marriage because they were first cousins; Rachel gave them sanctuary at the Hermitage.

"I guess I'm a sentimentalist; I don't think love should be opposed."

One day late in March she perceived through a subtle change in the tone and manner of her family that something untoward had happened, She asked Andy to tell her what it was.

"Uncle has forbidden me to pass on any such information. It is not important."

"Darling, you never were any good at concealing, even as a child."

"But Aunt Rachel, Uncle says it is simply that the caucus people behind Crawford are growing desperate because they see his strength waning and so they are trying to arouse Uncle's anger." He hesitated, but there was no turning away from the command in her eyes. "John Overton has received a letter from Senator John Eaton asking for detailed information and proof about your marriage . . . so they can put an end to the rumors in Washington."

Rachel cried, "But surely John hasn't complied!"

"I don't know, Aunt Rachel. I haven't discussed it with him."

"Then I shall have to. Andy, have a horse saddled for me at once."

She did not bother to knock at the front door, for John was sure to be in his garden in this pleasant weather. She found him cultivating a new flower bed; to her precipitate question of what he had done about Eaton's letter he said:

"Nothing. These attacks should not be dignified with a reply."

She sat down abruptly on a log bench, begging his forgiveness for imagining that he could be indiscreet. He sat beside her, his arm about her shoulder, sharing her distress.

"Rachel, as your friend and family lawyer, I must counsel you not to pursue these matters. They should be no part of your life."

"John, isn't knowing better than conjuring up dragons?"

He walked a short distance from her and said in a voice so low she barely could hear:

"The truth is rarely as ugly as we imagine it."

"Then please, John, let me see Eaton's letter."

They entered his office through a side door. She could hear the sound of children playing in the upper rooms. He took the letter from a desk drawer and handed it to her. She read:

DEAR SIR:
   Today I have written to Mr. Crutcher with the request that he and you should give me information of the circumstances of General Jackson's marriage. Now seemingly a most prominent rival, they are bringing all their batteries to bear against him; and yesterday I was told by a friend that they were preparing to attack him on this ground. They will doubtless make a very varnished and false presentation of the facts, and delicate as it may be to go into a man's family concerns, necessity demands that we should at least be possessed of the facts, that we may act defensively.

Rachel rested the letter on the desk. Her chest rose and fell rapidly; she seemed unable to get enough air into her lungs. She felt considerable pain about her heart. John poured some water from the heavy silver pitcher on his desk, self-reproaches tumbling from his lips.

"No, John, it's still better this way. Could you take me home?"

She remained in bed for two days, provoked with herself for feeling ill; troubles worked themselves out, given time enough. This one would too.

Andrew returned in mid-June with the news that he had engaged a suite for them at O'Neale's Tavern. He had even investigated the college there for young Andrew and found that it was supervised by a Baptist clergyman of considerable ability. He looked well, his skin bronzed, his eyes clear and peaceable. Rachel was delighted to find that for the first time politics was agreeing with him. Although he had not missed a single day of the Senate session he had risen to speak only twice, and even where he had been involved in controversial issues, such as pleading for internal improvements and for a "judicious tariff," he had remained calm. Straw votes being taken at mass meetings and militia musters indicated him to be a favorite among the people, but when stories came in about the weakening of his chances he appeared to be unperturbed, maintaining that he was neither burning nor running after the office the way Clay and Crawford were.

"Andrew, I must ask you, so that I will know how to plan: in your own mind are you returning to Washington for another session of the Senate, or to move into the White House?"

"According to our best reports the vote is going to be split between Adams, Clay, Crawford and myself. I doubt if anyone of us will get a majority of the electoral votes. The election will therefore be thrown into the House."

"What happens if the House should select one of the others as president?"

He wandered through the implications of her straightforward question as though it were a forest, After a few moments he came out the other side in the clear sunlight and smiled at her with a slightly deprecatory shrug of his left shoulder.

"We remain to congratulate the president at his inauguration, then put our trunks on top of the carriage and come home."

"With no ill will, and no regrets?"

"None."

"Not even if it's William Crawford you must congratulate?"

He clenched his fists at his side.

"My dear, you would have made a good prosecuting attorney."

She saw that he was hurt. "I'm simply trying to find out how we stand for the future," she said gently. "If any of these men is elected, we will be back here by the end of March, to stay?"

"Forever," he said grimly.

"What do you intend to do about the election?"

"Remain home and watch it. Maybe write a few letters. My advisers want me to attend a number of musters and barbecues to meet the people. They say it's a new form of campaigning, because this is the first time the president is going to be elected by the voters instead of the Congress. I'm not going, of course. But could we have open house on July Fourth? It comes on a Sunday this year."

Barbecues being the new vogue, she had a great pit dug down by their old cabin for the roasting of venison, beef and lamb. Four hundred of their neighbors came, spicing the roasted meats with peppered speeches and the reading of editorials. The one that aroused the greatest shout of derision was from a Louisville newspaper which reported that at a military muster in Ohio, where Andrew had drubbed Henry Clay in a test vote. . ."the rowdies, the very dregs of the community, had won the day."

Each week brought its important development, good and bad: John Calhoun decided to content himself with the vice-presidency, and threw his weight behind Andrew; however Andrew's stand on the tariff was losing him votes in the South. William Crawford suffered a paralytic stroke and some of his supporters were talking of shifting to Jackson; while Jesse Benton, no whit placated by the fact that Andrew and his brother had become friends again, issued a pamphlet containing thirty-two charges against Andrew, all of them widely reprinted in the opposition press.

Toward the end of September the family assembled at Johnny Donelson's house, the Mansion, for the wedding of Emily and Andy. The night before, Rachel went into Andy's room to tell him that he and Emily could have a honeymoon trip to Washington City if they desired it; Andy would serve as his uncle's secretary while there, and the young couple could move into the White House if Andrew were elected. Andy hesitated; he was beginning to get a few clients and he did not want to abandon his practice if he would have to start all over again in six months. Rachel tucked the covers around his shoulders, then sat on the edge of the bed and said:

"Andy, we are all gambling. Don't you think you ought to throw in your lot with the family? Uncle Andrew needs you very much."

"Well, I'd like to be the President's secretary. . .and Emily's never been out of the Cumberland. All right. Thank Uncle Andrew for me. And don't tell him that I even thought there was any gamble involved."

They were scheduled to leave for Washington City during the first week in November. Rachel found herself with a packing problem. How long was she to be gone: four months or four years? Did she take only winter clothes, or summer clothes as well? Should she have Sarah Bentley make an inaugural gown in Nashville? Should she keep the house open and running so they could come back to it at the end of March, or cover the furniture and put away the silver, china and linens? Did she interrupt her son's term at school and take him with her, or did she leave him behind?

There was no use going to any of Andrew's friends for information: they had already moved her into the White House, even the usually levelheaded John Overton. But she had learned from experience that for the Jacksons fulfillment rarely came when anticipated; generally it was achieved later, when it had lost much of its meaning and savor. She recalled how eagerly Andrew had wanted to be appointed governor of Louisiana back in 1804, and how sure everyone was that President Jefferson would give him the appointment; she remembered how terribly he had wanted to be judge of the Mississippi Territory, and how certain he was that he would get it; she recalled how he had been kept out of Canada during the War of 1812 by an Administration that was desperate for commanding generals, only to be sent to Natchez and then dismissed without firing a shot.

When had he ever achieved anything the easy way? Why should they expect a smooth passage to this highest office in the land when even their simplest ambitions had taken years of disappointment, frustration and defeat?

2

They left the Hermitage on November 7, 1824, in the morocco-lined carriage they had taken to Florida with them three years before. Rachel and Emily rode in the carriage, with Andrew and Andy alongside on their saddle horses. It would be a hard trip in spite of the fact that they were taking the road through Harrodsburg and Lexington, then over the new National Turnpike through Ohio. Rachel dreaded the moment she would reach Harrodsburg; but perhaps it was fitting that she should go over the scene of her early trials on her way to Washington City, for was not Harrodsburg the omnipresent obstacle in the way of Andrew's progress to the White House?

She hardly recognized the town, which had grown from a few scattered cabins to a good-sized village with a comfortable inn. Supper was served before the fire, but she had little appetite and listened instead to Andy and Emily speak excitedly about the ball to be given for them at Lexington by Henry Clay's followers, who had assured them that if Clay could not have the presidency Kentucky would support Jackson.

Later, lying warm under a huge *federbett,* with Andrew sleeping peaceably at her side, apparently unconcerned about Harrodsburg or perhaps even having forgotten that as a young man of twenty-three he had ridden up the Kentucky Road to rescue her, she remembered the smallest details, reliving them as the night wore on: her arrival as a bride at the Robards home, her early attempts to understand Lewis's moodiness and unwillingness to assume responsibility, the later jealous quarrels and their culmination in his announcement that he was casting her out, that he had written to her family for someone to come and get her; and her trip home with Samuel. She remembered her return to Harrodsburg, her hope for her marriage almost completely dissipated, but not knowing what other way of life she could pursue; and Lewis's red-eyed, mean-tempered reception of her. She saw her mother-in-law's thin face on the pillow, telling her to return to Nashville, that she would not be able to live with Lewis; and finally that incredible sight of Andrew in buckskin trousers and leather hunting shirt coming up the road to the Robards door. How much heartache and disillusion she had suffered here! Her brother Samuel had been only twenty years old then, and now his son Andy was twenty-four and sleeping in the next room with his bride; and Andrew was on his way to Washington, perhaps to the presidency . . .

As dawn grayed the bedroom window she felt Andrew stirring beside her. They were in high spirits at breakfast, Emily because she was heading for a formal ball; her husband and nephew because they were reasoning that this reception tonight would be Kentucky's official declaration of support for Andrew; Rachel because she was leaving Harrodsburg behind. As she was handed into the carriage and settled into the comfortable leather cushions she realized that the very name of the town had haunted her . . . haunted? That was the word Lewis Robards had used. Lewis was dead ten full years now, buried in the little cemetery they were passing even then.

A few miles beyond, as they reached the top of a steep and rocky hill, there was heard a splintering sound, then a sharp rending crack. The carriage tongue had broken. Andrew lunged for the lead horse but it was too late; down the hill went carriage, horses and passengers. Several times they teetered on two wheels; once they barely missed going over into a ditch.

When they finally stopped at the bottom of the hill and the two Andrews had lifted their wives out, Rachel said with a wry smile:

"I never did have any luck in that town."

At eleven o'clock on December 7 they crossed the bridge which led into Washington from Virginia. Rachel pointed out to Emily the Bulfinch Dome of the Capitol. They made their way up a dirt road called Pennsylvania Avenue. When they passed the White House Rachel said to Emily, "That's where Mr. and Mrs. Monroe live." Emily leaned out the window, gazing rapturously at the structure.

"And where the four of us are going to live!"

O'Neale's Tavern at the corner of Pennsylvania Avenue and Twenty-first Street had changed hands and was now known as the Franklin House. Rachel and Andrew had a comfortable suite of bedroom and parlor, while Andy and Emily had a considerably smaller one. Rachel was concerned over the fact that these two suites cost them a hundred dollars a week, including their meals.

"I've just found a good reason to hope you are elected, Andrew. The rent at the White House should be somewhat cheaper than it is here."

Andrew shook his head, smiling ironically.

"Not really. Mr. Monroe tells me he is going out poor and dissatisfied."

"And that's the office for which you, Mr. Adams, Mr. Crawford and Mr. Clay are battling so furiously!"

"Maybe it's part of the genius of this form of government that men want to serve in the highest offices, knowing that they will come out impoverished and tender from the many beatings."

Their rooms were crowded with a host of neighbors from Tennessee, officers from the Creek and British wars, the ever-growing clique of president-makers and the many eastern friends Andrew had accumulated since his first trip to the Congress in 1796. It wasn't until midafternoon of the second day that she perceived their callers were men only. No woman had so much as left her card at the Franklin House. Though there was a written invitation from President and Mrs. Monroe to a reception at the White House, Washington society, dominated by the wives of the higher officials, was pointedly staying away. That evening when she went in to bid Emily good night she found her niece in tears. At her feet she saw a newspaper which had obviously been crumpled in high anger. She picked it up, smoothed out the page and saw that it was the Raleigh *Register*. The offending article read:

> *I make a solemn appeal to the reflecting part of the community, and beg of them to ponder well before they place their tickets in the box, how they can justify it to themselves and posterity to place such a woman as Mrs. Jackson! at the head of the female society of the United States.*

Emily sought refuge in her aunt's arms.

"Oh, Aunt Rachel, they're saying the most terrible things about us: that we are vulgar, ignorant and awkward frontierswomen without breeding or decorum. But they have never even met us!"

Rachel had never made any pretension about her education or culture. The imputations against her background she resented more for her parents' sake than for her own. She held Emily at arm's length.

"Wipe your eyes, child. This is all part of what your uncle would call 'the consequences of politics.' As for my lack of social polish, neither Mr. Madison nor Mr. Monroe seemed to notice it."

Late that afternoon they had their first callers: the wives of two senators. Rachel wore a dress of pale brown cambric finished at the bottom by two rows of "letting-in-lace," embroidered between with muslin leaves and touched off by an apron of cambric trimmed with two rows of quilted muslin. She had refused the elaborate hair styling with curls which Emily insisted was the newest thing, saying that she thought the height of her hair on top of her head made her face seem a little less round. She had tea served in her parlor. Her practiced eye perceived that it was curiosity that had helped overcome the ladies' prejudice. She thought, I'll not let them know what I see; but neither will I make a great effort. They must like us for what we are.

It did not prove to be a difficult task: at the end of an hour the women had become friends and were exchanging stories about the domestic problems in different parts of the country. Nor would they leave until Rachel had accepted their invitations to tea.

That, and Elizabeth Monroe's party for them at the White House, broke the ice; Emily was the happiest girl in the capital because there were invitations for each day. The December weather was springlike in its warmth; Rachel paid calls, and went with Andrew to dinner with friends, but they turned down the hundreds of invitations for the evenings to the theater, to parties and balls, content to remain in their hotel sitting room before the fire, smoking their pipes and receiving a few intimates. On Sunday mornings they went to the Presbyterian church to hear Mr. Baker preach, and one night a week they went to the Methodist church for Mr. Summerfield's prayer meeting.

On December 16, the results from the last state to vote, Louisiana, reached Washington. Andrew had the largest popular vote, 152,901; Mr. Adams came second with 114,023; Mr. Clay 47,217 and Mr. Crawford 46,979. In the electoral votes by states Andrew had a decisive lead also: 99 to Adams's 84, with Crawford showing a surprising 41 to eliminate Mr. Clay from the race. Because no one candidate had achieved a majority the election would go into the House. Andrew's supporters were certain he would be selected: after all, the most people had wanted him, and the most states: he had the electoral votes of eleven states and needed only two more for a majority. With Mr. Clay out, the Kentucky legislature adopted a resolution recommending that their representative in the House support Mr. Jackson; the Missouri representative declared that since the people of his state wanted Clay first and Jackson second, he contemplated casting his vote for General Jackson; Ohio should be his, too, for he had received only a few votes less than Clay, with Mr. Adams running an unpopular third.

In January there were blizzards and snowstorms which brought Rachel down with a cold. The Senate was in session and Andrew attended faithfully each day. Old friends came in for dinner. Though Andrew refused to let them join politics with their food, they were nevertheless surrounded by intrigue: if he would make certain promises, commit himself as to whom he would name Secretary of State, the presidency could be his. There were rumors to the effect that Henry Clay had made such a bargain with John Quincy Adams, Mr. Clay to throw all of his influence and votes to Mr. Adams in return for Mr. Adams's appointment of Mr. Clay as Secretary of State. John Eaton was disturbed, but Andrew did not take it seriously.

"Mr. Adams is an honest man and a good man. He would not engage in a corrupt bargain. If he gets the majority of votes in the House, I will be content. He was my first choice, anyway."

They awakened on the morning of February 9, the day of decision, to find snow falling heavily. Andrew donned a greatcoat and boots and left the hotel in time to reach the Capitol by noon, so that he might participate in the senatorial count which would name John Calhoun as vice-president. When Rachel asked if he were intending to remain after the Senate adjourned and the House took its seat to vote for president, he replied that he did not think it proper for him to be in the House while the members were being polled.

He was back shortly after one o'clock, ordering dinner sent up to their room so they could avoid the milling crowds below in the tavern. The first course had just been set on their parlor table when Andy came in, the expression on his face clearer than any marked ballot: Mr. Adams had been elected on the first count! By prodigious efforts and brilliant maneuvering Henry Clay, singlehanded, had swung Kentucky, Ohio and Missouri behind Adams.

John Eaton stormed in, his face black with disappointment and chagrin, and proceeded to give Henry Clay a thorough castigation. Andrew heard him out, then said quietly:

"That's not altogether fair to Mr. Clay, John. He has a right to throw his influence to the man he thinks best for the job. You remember he once accused me, right on the floor of the House, of being a 'military chieftain who would overthrow the liberties of the people.' "

That evening they attended the last of President Monroe's regular Wednesday levees. Andrew congratulated Mr. Adams cordially. While riding back to the hotel in the Jackson carriage, John Eaton commented on how quiet the city was: no bonfires, no victory celebrations or cheering crowds.

"They wanted you, General," Eaton concluded morosely. "They feel cheated."

But nothing could shake Andrew's calm acceptance. For her own part, Rachel was content. On the whole it had been a decent election; the predictions that the Republic would fall into ruin because its Chief Executive was to be chosen by popular vote had failed to materialize; and so had her own fears of being pilloried by the opposition.

Back in their suite with a log fire crackling on the hearth, they had a hot toddy with Andy and Emily.

"How much longer do you think we will be in Washington, Uncle Andrew?" asked Andy anxiously. "I must be getting back to Nashville and starting my practice. I've got a bride to support, you know."

"Your uncle and I have a wedding present for you that will make things a little easier," said Rachel, knowing how disappointed the two youngsters had been at Andrew's defeat. "We are going to give you the Sanders plantation."

There were expressions of joy and much embracing before the young couple left for their rooms. Despite the fire, the room was chilly; Andrew wrapped a blanket about Rachel's legs, tucking it under her feet.

"Well, Rachel, my dear, I tried to make you First Lady of the land. You are not too disappointed, are you?"

She smiled inwardly, ran her fingers over the bony ridge of his face.

"Whatever disappointment I may feel is for you."

"Well, then, I'll be happy to get back to the Hermitage."

"For how long?" she asked softly. ". . . until the next election?"

His eyes met hers. They were stern.

"I will be fifty-eight in a month. Mr. Adams is certain to serve the regular two terms. Surely you don't think at the age of sixty-six . . . ? This is *forever!*"

He used that word to me at home, thought Rachel, but this time he means it. Perhaps at long last he will be content to remain a gentleman planter.

Forever lasted five days. On February 14, President-elect Adams offered the post of Secretary of State to Henry Clay. All hell broke loose, in Washington and across the nation . . . and particularly in their two rooms in the Franklin House. People came and went continually, all passionately protesting against what now appeared to have been a swap of votes for office.

Every ounce of Andrew's calm and acceptance vanished. She knew from the sense of outrage that shook his long lean frame that nothing in his tumultuous career, always excepting the maraudings of the British, had ever made him so utterly determined to avenge a wrong. As he stood in the far corner of the room surrounded by his most ardent supporters, she heard him cry:

"So the Judas of the West has closed the contract and will receive the thirty pieces of silver? The end will be the same. Was there ever witnessed such a barefaced corruption before?"

A dozen voices answered him at once.

"But surely Mr. Clay will know that the whole country is outraged?" "He can't be so stupid as to accept . . ."

"What, refuse his part of the booty?" Andrew's voice, as it penetrated to her, was shrill and cold. "But he must go before the Senate for confirmation. By the Eternal, gentlemen, I still have a vote there, and I pledge you my word that I shall unbosom myself. This barter of votes is sheer bribery, and if allowed to continue will destroy our form of government."

Three weeks later, in a slanting rainstorm, the family left the capital, all four riding in the carriage with the extra horses tied behind. Andrew was silent, his head on his chest, his eyes closed; he was still smarting from his defeat in the Senate where he had been able to garner only fourteen votes against the appointment of Mr. Clay. She had persuaded him that, as a matter of form, he should attend the inauguration. He had complained to her that Mr. Adams "had been escorted to the Capitol with the pomp and ceremony of guns and drums, which is not consistent with the character of the occasion." However, he had been among the first to shake hand with Mr. Adams, and had administered the oath to Calhoun, the new Vice-President, in the Senate.

As the carriage passed the boundary of Washington City she felt him stiffen at her side. He turned in his seat, gazing long and hard at the capital. In his expression she saw the unshatterable resolve she had known so well during the years leading up to the Battle of New Orleans.

He brought his face around to hers.

"We'll be back."

3

They arrived at the Hermitage in the midst of a dry cold spring. The plantation had been well cared for, though both the corn and the cotton needed rain. She had brought home a lemon tree and a box of plants for her garden, and was eager to lay aside her city clothes, don her calico and get out onto the land. She pushed to the back of her mind the knowledge that this was an interlude, that she would have to go through the identical process yet again, enjoying the feel of the rich red earth between her fingers, the fragrance of the adjacent forest in her nostrils and the sight of the tree-covered rolling hills. But what a shame, she thought, that the contest could not have been settled permanently, one way or the other.

Their journey home had been more like a triumphal procession than the return of a defeated candidate; though Andrew had sent word ahead asking that there be no formal demonstrations, the crowds that assembled in every town to greet him were tremendous; at Louisville, in Mr. Clay's home state of Kentucky, they attended a banquet where toasts were drunk to General Jackson as the next president of the United States. It was abundantly clear that the election of 1824 was by no means over; every hour of the day and night between now and November of 1828 would be devoted to this struggle.

The Hermitage became not only the Jackson rallying point, with hundreds of people, letters, couriers, newspapers and broadsides arriving each day, but in actuality a frontier White House in which all elements of the opposition centered, where they looked for leadership. The dominating passion was hatred of Adams and Clay, and the conviction that the will of the people had been thwarted.

One evening, when a particularly torrid discussion filled her dining room and parlor, Rachel found herself unable to stand the intensity of feeling or the volume of noise. She went upstairs to the quiet of her bedroom, where the air was free of tobacco smoke, human odors and the restless movement of excited men. She pulled up a chair to the open window. The tempest in the downstairs of her house was no temporary reaction; the volume, the tone and intensity would rise with the passing weeks and months. Andrew was in deep now, up to the top of his bushy white hair; but would it not be the better part of wisdom for her to withdraw? To provide food and drink and beds for the travelers, and close her ears to what was going on? She had given her husband his freedom to pursue this ambition; was she also obliged to participate? Would it not be better to remove herself from the turbulence, to enjoy her garden, her ever-growing circle of nieces and nephews, to sit before her fire reading or working tranquilly at her loom?

The late summer rains revived the meadows. Their herds of cattle and sheep grew fat and sleek. The harvesting seemed to require more than its usual hard work, but now the cotton and corn were in the storehouse, and the market price was good.

In October of 1825 the Tennessee legislature formally nominated Andew Jackson for the presidency. He persuaded her to accompany him to the capital at Murfreesboro where he accepted the nomination and officially resigned his seat in the Senate. From here they swung west to visit Jane. The hurtleberries were still abundant in the swamps, and the sloes, serviceberries and grapes were heavy on the vines.

Jane's figure was trim, her hair had lost little of its blond light and her eyes were penetratingly clear. She too had taken to smoking a clay pipe. The two sisters sat before the fire talking nostalgically of the past, exclaiming at the vast extent of the Donelson clan throughout Tennessee, Kentucky, Mississippi and Louisiana.

When they passed through Nashville on their way home they found the town abuzz: someone by the name of Day, a seedy little man whose occupation was allegedly that of collecting bills for Baltimore and Pittsburgh merchants, had spent the past few days in Nashville asking endless questions about the Jackson marriage, and displaying a transcript of the Robards divorce records from Harrodsburg, legally copied out for him by the clerk.

On their return to the Hermitage John Overton told them that he believed the material was being collected to hold over Andrew's head in the hope of making him withdraw from the race. John Eaton thought the stories were being assembled for future publication in an effort to provoke Andrew to a violent outburst, perhaps even to a duel, thus reestablishing him as a man of uncontrollable temper.

Rachel went upstairs, undressed, got into bed and pulled the covers over her head. What good to withdraw from the turmoil of the politics about her when at any moment she could become the focus of its vehemence? They were still three years away from the election of 1828, but already some member of the opposition had sought her out as a potential weapon.

Actually there was only one way to avoid the torment: to go to Andrew and say, Andrew, I've made a mistake. I thought I could take the consequences, but I can't. I haven't the moral strength. You must release me. I've been a good and faithful wife to you for nearly forty years. I have given you everything in my power to give, and I've never asked that you forsake anything you wanted to do. I have aided you whenever I was able. We're going on fifty-nine. You know that I love you dearly, I know that you love me. Then, Andrew, sacrifice this last campaign. Fulfill your promise that we would live tranquilly at home and enjoy the companionship of our last years. This is no longer an ordinary political contest; it is war. Surely if you have to become president by placing me on the battlefield, you would refuse?

But several hours later, when Andrew came up to bed, she said nothing. Hadn't they undergone countless attacks since their difficulties in 1793; and hadn't they always managed to survive them?

By the spring of 1826 the Hermitage had become headquarters for an integrated political group which established its own newspaper, Duff Green's *Telegraph* in Washington City, and had enthusiastic organizations in nearly every state of the Union, its members comprising not only the westerners who were in favor of Andrew Jackson but also those who were left over from the now-defunct Crawford organization, those who hated Henry Clay, those who could find no sympathy for the temperamentally cold John Quincy Adams or his buffeted Administration, those who belonged to no party but felt that Jackson had been robbed; and lastly the masses of simple folk who never before had had the right to vote for their president and were convinced that General Jackson had earned them this right, that he alone would fight for their interests.

The New York *Courier* was pro-Jackson; nearly every major city had its pro-Jackson newspaper. When the results of the mid-term Congressional election of 1826 were tabulated it was found that most of the Henry Clay men who had helped put Adams into the presidency had been defeated; and that the Jackson supporters had been triumphant in New York, Ohio, Virginia, Georgia, Kentucky, Missouri and Illinois. Once again visitors to the Hermitage assured Rachel that her husband would be the next president.

Then, within a matter of weeks, a pamphlet reached the Hermitage, printed in East Tennessee by Thomas Arnold, who belonged in the camp of the defeated Senator Williams:

Andrew Jackson spent the prime of his life in gambling, in horse-racing; and to cap it all tore from a husband the wife of his bosom.

Anyone approving of Andrew Jackson must therefore declare in favor of the philosophy that any man wanting someone else's pretty wife has nothing to do but take his pistol in one hand and a horse-whip in another and possess her.

General Jackson has admitted that he boarded at the house of old Mrs. Donelson, and that Robards became jealous of him, but he omits the cause of that jealousy . . . that one day Robards surprised General Jackson and his wife exchanging most delicious kisses.

Her first reaction was one of shame: shame that this assault should have sprung from her home state and from one of her neighbors. She told herself that she would be calm, that she would not become upset over these scurrilous lines; yet she burned inwardly at the implication of an illicit carnality; of a vulgar, behind-the-back deception which debased her motives as well as her conduct. Andrew grew silent and grim, but no word of the pamphlet passed between them. She burned her copy, resolutely putting it out of her mind.

She had underestimated the power of the printed word. Shortly after, Colonel Charles Hammond, editor of a Cincinnati newspaper, emboldened by the fact that he now had a published precedent, wrote an article for his paper based on the Arnold pamphlet, adding to it the stories collected by Mr. Day. The clipping was sent to her anonymously through the mail:

If the President be a married man, his wife must share the distinction of the station he occupies. Her qualifications for the station, her character, and standing, her personal defects, or excellencies, must all be drawn out, and made subjects of remark, and will be commended, caricatured or ridiculed, as they may furnish occasion.

If she be weak and vulgar she cannot escape becoming a theme for ridicule, a portion of which, and its consequent contempt, must attach to her husband. . . . We must see a degraded female placed at the head of the female society of the nation, or we must proclaim and urge the fact as a ground for excluding her husband.

Wherever he was known, public rumor had circulated suspicions as to the correctness of his matrimonial alliance. . . . It was no case of mere surmise against an unmarried female, arising out of possible indiscretion, and resting upon a peculiar freedom of manners. On the contrary . . . it was an accusation of gross adultery, in which outrage upon the rights of the husband was urged against General Jackson, and desertion from her husband to the arms of a paramour, was charged against the wife.

In September, 1793, twelve men, constituting a jury, after hearing proof, declared . . . that Mrs. Robards was guilty of adultery. Ought a convicted adultress, and her paramour husband, to be placed in the highest offices?

Her arms fell wearily to her side. The Cincinnati newspaper dropped to the floor. There it was at last, the dread and awful word that had pursued her all of her married life, that had changed her from a gay and happy young woman into a wounded prisoner within her own walls:

Adulteress.

4

That night a group of tight-lipped, white-faced men sat in Andrew's study behind the closed door and spoke in voices so low that no sound escaped the room. The meeting lasted late, but she remained rigid and wide-eyed before the parlor fireplace, waiting for Andrew to come. It was in this very room he had sought her permission to run for the Senate and the presidency. He had asked, "And what about you, Rachel?" She had said, "I will accept the consequences."

It was midnight when he came into the room. He explained quietly:

"There is a cloud collecting and I must endeavor to burst it before it bursts upon us."

". . . yes . . . but by what means?"

"By making our position impregnable. We are going to get testimonials from the Reverend Craighead's widow, and Polly's mother, General Smith's widow. They've known us from the beginning."

"Testimonials . . .about what?" she asked numbly.

He leaned down, put his arms about her and raised her from the chair, kissing her cool cheeks and tired eyes.

"I know how hard it is on you, darling, but we must defend ourselves at every point where we are attacked. There's no part of my life that they are not trying to falsify and degrade, but we will meet them head on with documents and affidavits, and we will beat them every time."

She wanted to say, That is all right for public matters having to do with your work! How can it help me to prove that Colonel Hammond is a liar when he accuses me of "gross adultery"? To admit still more people into our private affairs, and spread the controversy ever wider?

The letters written by the Reverend Craighead's widow and General Daniel Smith's widow were loving tributes. They told the story of her difficulties with Lewis Robards, of her several attempts to reconcile with him, of his going before the Virginia legislature for a divorce. These testimonials would be enough to convince any man of good will; but word now arrived from their friend Sam Houston in Washington City that Hammond was in Henry Clay's service.

The testimonials were no sooner locked in her strongbox than Editor Hammond made his next move. He informed Senator John Eaton that Rachel and Andrew Jackson had never been married in Natchez! Rachel dropped her gardening tools, thrust her hands into the deep pockets of her earth-stained, heavy muslin apron. If she had married Andrew Jackson in 1791 when convinced that Robards had been granted his divorce by the Virginia legislature, then any sin or crime she had committed during the next two years of living with Andrew had been of a technical nature. Surely most people would understand her predicament, and would not hold that unfortunate situation against her. But if Editor Hammond convinced the country that she had not been married to Andrew Jackson in Natchez, that she had lived with him openly in an unwed state for more than two years until Lewis went into the Harrodsburg court and secured his divorce, then that would appear to have been bold concupiscence.

They had no written document of their marriage in Natchez. The ceremony performed at Springfield had been considered legal and binding by the Americans living in the Spanish territory, but to whom did they go for proof after thirty-six years? Old Thomas Green was long since dead, many of his descendants and friends also were dead, the rest widely scattered. Andrew dispatched William Lewis down the Mississippi to find and bring back any written record he could trace.

Taking this attack on a Tennessee woman as a personal affront, the members of the Culture Club, now known as the Nashville Ladies Club, went out of their way to express their vote of confidence. Many letters came through the mail to the Hermitage; three of the ladies came to call. Rachel received them in her parlor and served tea. It was a heartwarming hour for her.

By way of further buttressing their defenses a mass meeting was called by Andrew's closest friends at the Nashville courthouse. Andy attended and rode home to bring news of hundreds of people gathering in the square to pledge their support to the Jacksons, resolving:

"To detect and arrest falsehood and calumny by the publication of truth."

A committee of eighteen of the most respected citizens of the state, among them their former friend Judge John McNairy, Colonel Edward Ward, former Ambassador George W. Campbell, Thomas Claiborne, a relative of the governor of Louisiana, Justice John Catron of the United States Supreme Court, two members of the highest court of Tennessee and a number of others who had long disagreed politically with Andrew, was set up to examine all materials relative to the relationship and marriages of Rachel and Andrew Jackson. John Overton was to head the committee.

He came directly out from Nashville to the Hermitage, joining them for dinner. Andrew poured a drink from the sideboard, saying as they clinked glasses:

"John, this is one time I'm not going to ask you to stay out of my private affairs. I want you to get in just as deeply as you can and see that the committee obtains the full truth."

John picked up a spoon from the sideboard, using it to stir the sugar around in the bottom of his whisky glass.

"I'll be as strict and objective as I ever was as a member of the Tennessee Supreme Court. No material will be accepted that can't withstand the most relentless scrutiny; witnesses will state for the record only what they know; and we will publish only what we can prove. The language of the report will be kept calm and judicial; nothing will be allowed that won't hold up as the authentic truth when looked at a hundred years from today."

There was a moment of silence in the dining room. The men turned to Rachel. John's eyes bulked gun-metal gray. She gave him a quick nod of approbation, happy that he was undertaking to head up her defense; he had been her friend at the Robards house in Harrodsburg even before she had met Andrew.

"I haven't approved of any of these methods of defending ourselves, John, but I think this one is right. I know you will do a fine job. Let us publish our story to the world, once and for all, and then rest content."

The full report of the Overton committee, as well as the testimonial letters from Mrs. Craighead and Mrs. Smith, was published in the *United States Telegraph* on June 22, 1827, and widely reproduced throughout the country. Reluctant as Rachel had been to expose her intimate relationships to the eyes of thousands of strangers who had known nothing about them before, she found that the report had an immediate and salutary effect. Letters came to the Hermitage from Washington City, Philadelphia, New York and New Orleans offering congratulations "on the vindication of your innocence," and assuring her of continued friendship.

She locked away the newspapers, letters and reports, going through the automatic gesture of washing her hands of them. "I'll read no more charges and I'll participate in no more answers. They've done me all the harm they can. With God's help, I've risen above it."

She had reckoned without her own family. Emily called one morning when Rachel was in the dining room having breakfast. She pulled up a chair to the dining table and placed upon it a paper she held in her hand.

"Aunt Rachel," she began, straightening out the paper, "have you seen this copy of Hammond's latest pamphlet? We can't let them say this kind of thing about you. After all, we Donelsons have our pride!"

Rachel thought, She surely is Johnny's daughter!

"We've got to release our own statement," continued Emily. "The honor of our family is at stake! When you have read it, I'm certain you'll join with us in issuing a Donelson answer."

Filled with an almost ineluctable dread, Rachel's eyes went down the tight-packed column:

It is an insult to common sense to say that Overton's narrative does not place the seduction and adultery in as prominent and reprehensible a light as it is placed by the legislative and judicial proceedings themselves.

Mrs. Jackson was unfaithful to her marriage vow with Robards. No man of the world can believe that she would have been guilty of the great indiscretion of flying beyond the reach of her husband, with a man charged to be her paramour, were she innocent of the charge.

It would be as rational to give credit of innocence, had they been found at midnight, undressed, in the same bed.

When they assumed the open relation of husband and wife, it was an illegal and criminal act. They are the mere creatures of passion. General Jackson and Mrs. Robards . . . voluntarily, and for the gratification of their own appetites, placed themselves in a situation to render it necessary that Mrs. Robards should be convicted of desertion and adultery . . .

Those then, who believe that an adulteress, who has become, after a time, the legal wife of her paramour is not a suitable person to be placed at the head of the female society of the United States, cannot with propriety, vote for General Jackson . . .

The small print swam before her eyes. She dug her nails into her palms, then drank the last bitter dregs of the coffee in the bottom of her cup. When Emily left she sat frozen in the chair. Had the country gone insane, that the campaign should be waged on whether or not she had lived in adultery with Andrew? What had those two years so long ago got to do with his accomplishments or capacity for being President? He had been a lawyer, an attorney general, a congressman, a senator, a judge, a general, a governor; he had served his country long and well.

She did not hear him come into the room and stand behind her. When his hand touched her shoulder she turned, saw that his face was ashen. He held in his hand a copy of the same publication that had stirred Emily to action.

"Sit down, my dear. I'll get you a cup of hot coffee."

He sank into the chair Emily had used, staring at her with rout in his fierce blue eyes.

"Do you know that this is the most difficult task of my life, to be forced to sit here, impotent, while they call you foul names, debase our love and our marriage? I've never wanted anything so much in my life as to go to Cincinnati and shoot that slimy creature in his tracks. When I realize that I let myself get into a position where, no matter what they say about you, I cannot rise up in your defense . . ."

"Andrew, we knew this would happen. I fully expected it during the first campaign. It seemed to me a miracle that it didn't happen. But it was only a postponement, and the storm is doubly violent now because it's been so long in the making. Surely you knew that this would be part of what you called 'the consequences'?"

"No. I . . . didn't. . . . It's unprecedented! They've never attacked a defenseless woman . . ."

He stopped, sat in silence for a moment, his misery hovering about him like a cloak. Then he drew a letter from his pocket. It had just arrived from John Eaton, who was serving as senator in Washington and directing the Jackson campaign. "You hear what Eaton says? 'Be cautious, be still, be quiet. Avoid all issues and controversies. Weigh and bale your cotton and sell it; and if you see anything about yourself just throw the paper into the fire, and go on to weigh the cotton. All you have to do is remain quietly at the Hermitage and the people will sweep you into office.' "

He rose, went to the window and stared out moodily, his back to her.

". . . sweep you into office." He turned around abruptly. "I saw it as a chance for service. There's so much I thought I could contribute to the growth of our country. But now that they're crucifying you . . . is it worth it?"

To herself she murmured, It's too late for this kind of questioning.

5

She found herself living in two diametrically opposed worlds. The first concerned itself with the normal routine of her everyday life, and most of it was pleasant; the dining table she had bought in New Orleans was always set for its full capacity of thirty guests for dinner. There were acquaintances from Louisiana who were passing through Tennessee on their way north; a honeymoon couple whose family had known her family in Accomac County in Virginia; newly made friends from New York and Pennsylvania, traveling south: all roads appeared to lead through the Hermitage. The flow of visitors constituted a heavy drain on their purse; an obscure disease had hit their livestock and they had lost three thousand dollars' worth of horses in the last eighteen months. Although they had brought in a good cotton crop, the market was so low as to leave no measurable profit. In addition she had never found anyone to take the place of Jane Caffrey as a household manager, and so most of the unending duties fell upon her shoulders.

But these difficulties were supportable, for they represented a sane workaday world; and no matter how great the problem or disappointment, as when their young grandnephew, Andrew Jackson Hutchings, was expelled from Cumberland College, or her son got into some irresponsible scrape from which his father had to bail him out, she could cope with them because they were part of a normal pattern.

But there was a second world that engulfed her like a black, noxious cloud, a world filled with hysteria and insanity, with which she found herself unable to cope. There was no tiny segment of her husband's personal or professional life that was left unraked: he had tried to kill Governor Sevier in a public brawl, had murdered Charles Dickinson in cold blood, had conspired with Aaron Burr to destroy the Union, had executed loyal militiamen during the Creek wars, had robbed and maltreated the Indians, bullied and outraged the Spanish, had been in flight from the British when stopped by Monroe, had fought the Battle of New Orleans stupidly, stolen thousands of dollars of military funds, flouted the civil law and set himself up as a military dictator . . .

Andrew's advisers prevailed upon him to make the trip for the January 8, 1828, anniversary of the Battle of New Orleans on the grounds that such a celebration would receive national attention that would serve as an excellent starting point for the final push to the presidency. Andrew asked Rachel to go with him, assuring her that the steamboat *Pocahontas* could actually make its way up the Mississippi against the current.

They stood on the prow watching the snow-lined banks of the Tennessee give way to the semi-tropical verdure of the Mississippi, much of it country they knew so well. She had been reluctant to leave the Hermitage, but she enjoyed the sight at Natchez where the heights above the river were filled with spectators cheering their arrival. At New Orleans there was a picturesque forest of masts rising from the water as the fleet of steamboats came to escort them; and at ten in the morning the thick mist that covered the water began to rise, and the city with its many steeples became visible. They stood on the back gallery of the *Pocahontas,* while the thousands of people on the banks and in the boats cheered and the artillery kept up a constant fire.

They were met by Edward and Louise Livingston. When Andrew realized how much the two women liked each other he promised Rachel that if he were elected president, Edward Livingston would be given a position in the government and Rachel would have Louise by her side in Washington City to help with the arduous social life.

But even as they were returning to the Hermitage the opposition launched its answer to the victory celebration in the form of *Truth's Advocate, A Monthly Anti-Jackson Expositor* published in Cincinnati by Colonel Charles Hammond, the material being promptly reproduced in all of the Clay newspapers.

There was no respite. Each week saw deadlier charges hurled, elaborations on a theme that fed on itself, until Andrew Jackson had "torn her from her nuptial couch and seduced her"; they had "indulged their unbridled appetites" during all the time she was married to Robards; she had not gone down the river with Colonel Stark and his wife, but had followed in a second boat on which she and Andrew had lived alone. Her relations with Andrew had been a "standing jest for nearly thirty years"; she was even today an adulteress, for there never had been any marriage ceremony performed between Rachel and Andrew Jackson, not even that second time in 1794.

. . . adulteress . . . Adulteress . . . ADULTERESS . . .

The attack was so sharp and so virulent that the walls of the Hermitage were not thick enough to hold it out. It was mixed in the air she breathed and the food she ate; at night when she went upstairs while Andrew remained below at his desk frantically writing hundreds of letters of defense and justification during the dark hours, not even the act of locking her door and closing her windows could keep out the malignant wind. She lay rigidly in bed, every bone and muscle in her body aching, her eyes wide and staring, hearing the word reverberate hollowly about the room, encompassing her, possessing her.

The election approached; the tension mounted. The Adams press now joined the hunt, referring to her as "the woman they call Mrs. Jackson." They accused her of having caused the early death of Lewis Robards; and at long last, thirty-five years after she and Andrew had been forced to remain quiet and allow Lewis Robards to convict her of adultery, the record from the Harrodsburg court as copied out for Mr. Day was splashed across the press of the nation. Seventy thousand dollars of the government's contingent funds were used to print the anti-Jackson, anti-Rachel material; fifteen thousand pamphlets a month containing the charges against Rachel and Andrew Jackson were being franked by the Adams and Clay supporters in Congress and sent through the mails.

When she was the most soul-sick she went for comfort to her little church. She had been praying for a cessation of the attacks; now her clergyman, Dr. A. D. Campbell, taught her that instead of praying for herself she should be praying for her traducers, for they were the ones who would need her prayers on Judgment Day. That night she knelt by the side of the bed and prayed:

"Forgive them, O Lord, for they know not what they do."

Summer came on. Hundreds of test ballots were taken throughout the land. In most of them Andrew emerged triumphant by landslide proportions. She thought, Perhaps now, if not from compassion, then from fear of retribution, the vehemence will cease. But there were still several months before the official casting of the ballots; crude caricatures were being distributed showing her as an ignorant backwoodswoman, ribald songs were being chanted about her in the streets of the big cities, obscene poems were printed by the thousands.

William Lewis returned from Natchez, having been unable to locate a record of their first marriage. She listened to his report to Andrew with half an ear: there was nothing further they could say of her. Besides, it was growing increasingly difficult for her to breathe, and she was almost never without pain in her chest. Merely to get through her daily tasks was taking all of her energy and concentration.

She was no stranger to the insidious power of rumor and gossip; she had lived with it a very long time and knew its many faces. And so she was only mildly startled when John Eaton and William Lewis came to her and suggested that perhaps it would be better advised for her not to join the triumphal procession to Washington City, or the inaugural festivities, since tempers were high and any show of violence would necessarily endanger her. She knew that her friends truly believed her innocent of wrongdoing, nevertheless the opposition had at last succeeded in making even them consider her a liability and a burden. That night as she was preparing for bed she said to Andrew:

"My dear, if you should be elected I think it best that you go to Washington City alone. I'll come on later, after you've been installed in office, when the election hysteria has died down. Then I can slip in quietly, without causing comment."

He was both angry and hurt, though she could not judge which emotion predominated. He jumped to his feet and stood towering above her.

"Don't you see how wrong that would be! If you remain at home you admit that you are frightened. Even worse, you would make it look as though I didn't want you. Or that you are not qualified to serve as First Lady. This will be as much your triumph as mine; we'll go to Washington City together. You'll be by my side when I take the oath of office. And then God pity those wretches who have made life so miserable for you. I know you pray to God that He forgive your enemies; I never can."

On November 24, Governor Carroll of Tennessee rode up to the Hermitage in great excitement. Rachel received him in the parlor. The governor's face was shining. He bowed low, kissed Rachel's hand, exclaimed:

"I would let no one else bring the news. I wanted to be the first to tell you that Andrew Jackson has been elected president of the United States."

It was over. She had survived. She stood before the governor in silence, hearing only the tremendous pounding of her own heart, which felt as though it would burst through her chest. When Andrew came into the room she put her arms about his neck, kissed him on the lips and said:

"I'm happy for you, darling."

Nashville went wild with joy. A huge celebration banquet was planned for December 23. It seemed to Rachel as though the entire Cumberland Valley came to the front door of the Hermitage to shake Andrew's hand and then hers. The Nashville Ladies Club was having a beautiful and costly wardrobe prepared for her. Yet she observed that there was not much of rejoicing or exultation in Andrew. He seemed subdued. She asked herself, Is it because he has suffered so terribly these past two years, suffered for both himself and for me? As she watched him accept the congratulations of throngs that came out from Nashville, heard the crowds cheer him when they rode into town, the picture flashed into her mind of Andrew in New Orleans after his great triumph, when the Louisianians had lined the streets and the roads crying out his praises, and he had doffed his hat awkwardly as though his spirit were humbled and abashed.

Only now did she realize how much burden there was in every victory; Andrew would become Chief Executive of a torn, almost shattered country, with whole classes of its society loathing him and predicting that he would bring the mob, the canaille, into government, that the day he took office would mark the end of the great American Republic. She found herself pitying her husband for the terrifying task that lay ahead of him.

And what of herself? What of the vast responsibility that faced her as mistress of the White House? The scandalmongering would die down, but was it possible that these years of vituperation could ever wholly be forgotten? Where in all of Washington City would she find privacy from the probing eyes of strangers who wondered what part of the story might be true? She had no choice; she could not refuse to go to Washington City with Andrew. The law might question her Natchez marriage, but there was no question in her own heart. There, under Tom Green's glowing chandelier, she had inextricably tied her fate to Andrew's . . . and would today, if she had it to do all over again.

6

There was much work to be done. This time she did not have to ask her husband whether they were going for a few months or a few years. He told her that if they were fortunate they might get back to the Hermitage for a visit in the summer of 1830, but that she was not to count on it. The plantation would be well run; but what of the house itself? Should they cover the furnishings, batten down the blinds? Or should they leave it as it was with perhaps a niece or nephew installed so that their friends could continue to stop over? And for that matter, how completely furnished was the White House? Knowing Andrew's propensity for keeping his home full of guests, had she not better take along large quantities of silver, dishware, linens?

December was hectic; when she found herself growing increasingly tired and tense she called Dr. Samuel Hogg, their family physician, who bled her, relieving the pressure. Several times when she was supposed to go into Nashville for fittings or to buy what they needed for their trip she could not summon the energy to get out of bed. They were scheduled to leave the Hermitage for Washington City immediately after the holidays.

On Monday, December 17, she received an urgent message from Sarah Bentley: if she did not come in for the final fitting on her inaugural dress and reception gown she could not possibly have them ready by the time she left for Washington City. Rachel knew how disappointed Sarah would be, and Andrew too, if she did not take these clothes with her; digging deep into her reserves, she dressed and was driven in the carriage to Nashville.

The fittings were long and exhausting, for Sarah was determined that her gowns should reflect credit on Tennessee. When they were finished, Rachel said:

"Sarah, when my boy comes for me, please tell him I will be at the Nashville Inn: I'll rest there till time to go home."

She walked a block down the street, entered the inn, found the small back parlor deserted at this hour, and with a sigh of relief sank into a big comfortable chair in a corner hidden from the larger lounging room just beyond.

She had fallen into a half sleep when fragments of conversation drifting through the open doorway from the next parlor awakened her. Two women were talking; the voices sounded familiar . . . she had heard them before: loud, haughty, metallic; but there were differences too . . . she could not be sure . . .

Then she stopped listening to the intonations and began to hear the words. The women were discussing the election and the imminent departure of the Jacksons. The one with the deeper, chesty voice asked what would become of the country now that the lowest and most ignorant class of society had come into power, with a drinking, gambling bully and murderer sitting in the White House. The voice that was higher and shriller said she shuddered to think what Washington City's international society would make of his dumpy, pipe-smoking illiterate backwoodswoman who was now to become First Lady of the land.

"Lady?" exclaimed the first. "How can you call her a lady . . . ?"

Rachel gripped the arms of her chair and raised herself up. She knew what was coming next. She planted her feet firmly on the carpet, her legs a little apart, digging her toes into her shoes, her back arched, her arms rigidly outstretched to catch and hold the heavy weight.

". . . it's just as the newspapers kept asking: shall there be a *whore* in the White House?"

She was totally unprepared. A sharp, knifelike stab of almost unendurable pain went through her heart and down her left arm. She sagged, fell into the chair behind her. Had she thought it was over? It would never be over!

To her lips came a prayer:

No, no, dear God, not here . . . in a strange hotel parlor. Please let me get home . . . to my own roof . . . my own bed . . . my husband . . .

With an intense effort she dragged herself to her feet once again, walked stiffly to the entrance.

Her carriage was waiting. The boy helped her in. She leaned back against the cushions. Her left arm felt useless . . . paralyzed. Her head was heavy, her thoughts cloudy; there was only the one determination remaining: to hold on until she got back to the Hermitage.

Halfway home the road paralleled a creek. The sound of the clearly flowing water was refreshing. Perhaps if she bathed her face a little in the cold water it would revive her? She did not want to reach home in this state; Andrew would be so frightened and upset . . .

She asked the driver to stop, laboriously descended from the carriage, then pushed her way down the shallow bank to the water's edge. She took off her hat, loosened her coat, dipped her handkerchief into the stream, held it against her eyes and brow.

The coldness was good. She leaned farther over the water, cupping handfuls of it and patting it back through her hair. She felt relieved; the intense pain in her heart was lessening. Into her mind flashed another journey home, another stream where she had run water through her long black hair and cooled her fevered thoughts: she had been ordered out of the Robards house and had stopped by a little stream to make herself presentable before facing her family, resolved to hold her head high, secure in the knowledge that she had done no wrong.

How surely the end was implicit in the beginning!

Andrew was completely distraught. He sat by her bed clasping her hand in his, unable to speak. The neighborhood doctor bled her at once, saying to Andrew: "Spasmodic affection . . . muscles of chest and left shoulder . . . irregular action of heart . . ." Dr. Heiskell arrived from Nashville, found that the first bleeding had not caused an abatement of the symptoms, and bled her again. It was night before Dr. Hogg reached the Hermitage; he bled her a third time, and now all her pain seemed to vanish. Andrew placed a pillow behind her and raised her a little in the bed, then seated himself in a chair beside her.

She did not know how much time passed; at least twice it was night, then twice it was day. Andrew never left her side. Dimly she heard the doctors telling him that he must get some sleep or he would collapse: there was the celebration banquet in Nashville the next day which he must attend, and it was not right that he should receive this acclaim from his neighbors looking like a death's-head.

She raised herself slightly and managed a little smile. She felt no pain; in fact she could not feel her body at all.

"I'm so much . . . better," she said slowly. "Could you put me in that chair . . . in front of the fire? We'll visit for a little while . . . you'll have a night's sleep."

He put a fresh log on the fire, then lifted her out of the bed, covers and all. He sat on the floor before her, his long thin arms holding the blankets securely about her knees, his devotion carved deep in every line of his face.

"Andrew, you must prepare to go to Washington City without me. I'll follow in a few weeks . . . as soon as I am strong enough."

"No!" He rose to his knees. "I won't go without you! I can't face it . . . I can wait . . . I have time to wait. We've endured so much, we can conquer this too.

Your love is the most important thing in my life. I'll not set foot out of this house until you are able to stand by my side . . . as you always have.''

She took his thin, seamed face in her hands, remembering the first time she had seen him, when he had knocked on the door of the Donelson stockade and she had stood smiling as she gazed at the bushy red hair, the piercing blue eyes, the overly large mouth and the powerful chin. Well, his hair was snow-white now, his lips taut, his brow and cheeks deeply furrowed. But he had earned his age; and now he would go on to the highest position in the land. How richly his life had been fulfilled; and in the doing, how richly it had fulfilled hers!

She kissed him on the forehead, murmured:

''That's what I wanted to hear you say, my darling. Everything's all right now. Go to bed and get some sleep. I will be here in the morning. And I'll go to Washington City with you.''

He kissed her good night. She watched him go out the door, across the hall to the guest bedroom.

She sat watching the flames light up the fireplace and the room . . . then felt herself slipping . . .

She fell. In the distance she heard the sound of running feet. Someone picked her up. Was it . . . ? Yes, it was Andrew. That was good. That was the way it should be.

With the last of her consciousness she felt herself put into bed. Her head was on her own pillow. She felt Andrew's tear-stained cheek on hers, heard him say over and over:

''I love you, I love you.''

Somewhere within herself, at a great and receding distance, she smiled. And then she knew nothing more.

7

He left Gadsby's Hotel with a small group of friends and walked up Pennsylvania Avenue to the Capitol. There were patches of snow underfoot. Cannons boomed, the thousands of people lining the avenue cheered lustily; he heard neither. He entered the Capitol through a rear basement, made his way to a roped-off portico where Chief Justice Marshall administered the oath while the enormous assemblage roared its approval. His mind was back at the Hermitage; he had told Rachel that she would be by his side when he took this oath of office, but she lay buried in her beloved garden in the Cumberland Valley. The Reverend Hume had said, ''The righteous shall be in everlasting remembrance.'' And so it would be.

He mounted his horse and rode to the White House. Long tables had been set up in the beautiful East Room, laden with orange punch, ice cream and cakes. This was to be his first reception; yet he hated the thought of it, walking the horse slowly, his head lowered. Protocol had dictated who might be invited: the highest-ranking members of Washington society: the friends of John Quincy Adams and Henry Clay, who had branded him an ignoramus, a thief, a coward, a bully, a liar, a revolutionist who would destroy the Republic. Aside from a few personal friends and his adherents in Congress, there would be no one at the reception he wanted; none of his followers or the people who had elected him. No, the White House and the East Room would be filled with the bejeweled women and the socially and politically important men who had despised his wife, called her every foul name they could conjure up; and had ended by murdering his beloved Rachel. These were the people he must receive!

But he had reckoned without the mob of his followers who had come to Washington City from every part of the Union to witness his inauguration. They poured down Pennsylvania Avenue, streamed through the gates of the White House, fought their way into the East Room, devoured the ice cream and cakes and orange punch. They climbed on the furniture to catch a glimpse of Andrew, soiling the damask chairs with their muddy boots, staining the carpets, breaking glasses and china, shouting and surging and pushing, all thousands of them, wanting to reach Andrew, to embrace him.

He stood at the back of the room, imprisoned, yet feeling the first glint of happiness since Rachel's death. These were the people; they had stood by him. They had loved Rachel, they had vindicated her. For that, he loved them, and would fight for them the rest of his days.

The Agony and the Ecstasy

BOOK ONE

THE STUDIO

He sat before the mirror of the second-floor bedroom sketching his lean cheeks with their high bone ridges, the flat broad forehead, and ears too far back on the head, the dark hair curling forward in thatches, the amber-colored eyes wide-set but heavy-lidded.

"I'm not well designed," thought the thirteen-year-old with serious concentration. "My head is out of rule, with the forehead overweighing my mouth and chin. Someone should have used a plumb line."

He shifted his wiry body lightly so as not to waken his four brothers sleeping behind him, then cocked an ear toward the Via dell'Anguillara to catch the whistle of his friend Granacci. With rapid strokes of the crayon he began redrafting his features, widening the oval of the eyes, rounding the forehead, broadening the narrow cheeks, making the lips fuller, the chin larger. "There," he thought, "now I look better. Too bad a face can't be redrawn before it's delivered, like plans for the façade of the Duomo."

Notes of a bird's song came fluting through the ten-foot window, which he had opened to the cool morning air. He hid his drawing paper under the bolster at the head of his bed and went noiselessly down the circular stone stairs to the street.

His friend Francesco Granacci was a nineteen-year-old youth, a head taller than himself, with hay-colored hair and alert blue eyes. For a year Granacci had been providing him drawing materials and sanctuary in his parents' home across the Via dei Bentaccordi, as well as prints borrowed surreptitiously from Ghirlandaio's studio. Though the son of a wealthy family, Granacci had been apprenticed to Filippino Lippi at the age of ten, at thirteen had posed as the central figure of the resurrected youth in St. Peter Raising the Emperor's Nephew, in the Carmine, which Masaccio had left uncompleted, and was now apprenticed to Ghirlandaio. Granacci did not take his own painting seriously, but he had a sharp eye for talent in others.

"You're really coming with me this time?" Granacci demanded excitedly.

"It's my birthday present to myself."

"Good." He took the younger boy's arm, guiding him along the curving Via dei Bentaccordi which had been built on the oval site of the old Roman colosseum, past the high walls of the prison of the Stinche. "Remember what I told you about

Domenico Ghirlandaio. I've been apprenticed to him for five years, and I know him well. Be humble. He likes his apprentices to appreciate him.''

By now they had turned into the Via Ghibellina, just above the Ghibellina gate which marked the limits of the second wall of the city. On their left they passed the magnificent stone pile of the Bargello, with its colorful governor's courtyard, and then, after they had turned right on the Street of the Proconsul, the Pazzi palace. The younger boy ran his hand lovingly over the irregular roughhewn blocks of its walls.

"Let's hurry," urged Granacci. "This is the best moment of the day for Ghirlandaio, before he begins his drawing.''

They went with unmatched strides along the narrow streets, past the Street of the Old Irons with its stone palaces and exterior flights of carved stone stairs leading to jutting penthouses. They made their way along the Via del Corso and saw on their right through the narrow slit of the Via dei Tedaldini a segment of the red-tiled Duomo, and after another block, on their left, the Palazzo della Signoria with its arches, windows and crownings of its tan stone tower penetrating the faint sunrise blue of the Florentine sky. To reach Ghirlandaio's studio they had to cross the Square of the Old Market, where fresh beeves, cut down the backbone and opened wide, hung on pulleys in front of the butchers' stalls. From here it was but a short walk past the Street of the Painters to the corner of the Via dei Tavolini where they saw the open door of Ghirlandaio's studio.

Michelangelo stopped for a moment to gaze at Donatello's marble St. Mark standing in a tall niche of the Orsanmichele.

"Sculpture is the greatest art!'' he exclaimed, his voice ringing with emotion.

Granacci was surprised that his friend had concealed this feeling for sculpture during their two years of friendship.

"I don't agree with you," he said quietly. "But stop gaping, there's business to be done.''

The boy took a deep breath. Together they entered the Ghirlandaio workshop.

2

The studio was a large high-ceilinged room with a pungent smell of paint and charcoal. In the center was a rough plank table set up on horses around which half a dozen sleepy young apprentices crouched on stools. In a near corner a man was grinding colors in a mortar, while along the side walls were stacked color cartoons of completed frescoes, the Last Supper of the church of the Ognissanti and the Calling of the First Apostles for the Sistine Chapel in Rome.

In a protected rear corner on a raised platform sat a man of about forty, his wide-topped desk the only ordered spot in the studio, with its neat rows of pens, brushes, sketchbooks, its scissors and other implements hanging on hooks, and behind, on the wall shelves, volumes of illuminated manuscripts.

Granacci stopped below his master's desk.

"Signor Ghirlandaio, this is Michelangelo, about whom I told you.''

Michelangelo felt himself being spitted by a pair of eyes reputed to be able to see and record more with one thrust than any artist in Italy. But the boy too used his eyes as though they were silver-point pens, drawing for his mind's portfolio the artist sitting above him in an azure coat and red cloak thrown over the shoulders against the March chill and wearing a red cap, the sensitive face with its full purple lips, prominent bone formations beneath the eyes, deep cheek hollows, the opulent black hair parted in the center and worn down to his shoulders, the long supple fingers of his right hand clasped against his throat. He remembered Granacci telling him of Ghirlandaio's exclamation only a few days before:

"Now that I have begun to understand the ways of this art, it is a grief to me that I am not given the whole circumference of the walls of Florence to cover with fresco.''

"Who is your father?'' demanded Ghirlandaio.

"Lodovico di Lionardo Buonarroti-Simoni.''

"I have heard the name. How old are you?''

"Thirteen.''

"We start apprentices at ten. Where have you been for the past three years?''

"Wasting my time at Francesco da Urbino's school of grammar, studying Latin and Greek.''

A twitching at the corner of Ghirlandaio's dark wine lips showed that he liked the answer.

"Can you draw?''

"I have the capacity to learn.''

Granacci, wanting to help his friend but unable to reveal that he had been borrowing Ghirlandaio's prints for Michelangelo to copy, said:

"He has a good hand. He made drawings on the walls of his father's house in Settignano. There is one, a satyr . . .''

"Ah, a muralist,'' quipped Ghirlandaio. "Competition for my declining years.''

Michelangelo was so intense that he took Ghirlandaio seriously.

"I've never tried color. It's not my trade.''

Ghirlandaio started to answer, then checked himself.

"Whatever else you may lack for, it isn't modesty. You won't become my competitor, not because you haven't the talent to do so, but because you care nothing for color.''

Michelangelo felt rather than heard Granacci's groan beside him.

"I didn't mean it that way.''

"You're small for thirteen. You look too frail for the heavy work of this studio.''

"To draw one does not need big muscles.''

He realized that he had been baited into saying the wrong thing, and that in addition he had raised his voice. The apprentices had turned at this contretemps. After a moment Ghirlandaio's good nature asserted itself.

"Very well, suppose you sketch for me. What will it be?''

Michelangelo's eyes traveled over the workshop, swallowing impressions the way country youths break bunches of grapes in their mouths at autumn wine festivals.

"Why not the studio?''

Ghirlandaio gave a short disparaging laugh, as though he had been rescued from an awkward position.

"Granacci, give Buonarroti paper and charcoal. Now, if you have no objections, I will go back to my work.''

Michelangelo found a point of vantage near the door from which to see the workshop best, and sat down on a bench to sketch. Granacci lingered by his side.

"Why did you have to suggest such a difficult theme? Take plenty of time. He'll forget you're here . . .''

His eye and hand were good working partners, grasping the essentials of the large room: the worktable in the center with its apprentices on both sides, Ghirlandaio on his platform under the north window. For the first time since entering the studio his breathing was normal. He felt someone leaning over his shoulder.

"I'm not finished,'' he said.

"It is enough.'' Ghirlandaio took the paper, studied it for a moment. "You have worked at another studio! Was it Rosselli's?''

Michelangelo knew of Ghirlandaio's dislike of Rosselli, who conducted the only other painters' workshop in Florence. Seven years before Ghirlandaio, Botticelli and Rosselli had been called to Rome by Pope Sixtus IV to create wall panels for the newly completed Sistine Chapel. Rosselli had caught the pontiff's eye by using

the most garish reds and ultramarine blues and illuminating every cloud, drapery
and tree with gold, and won the coveted prize money.

The boy shook his head no.

"I've drawn in school when Master Urbino wasn't looking. And I've copied
after Giotto in Santa Croce, after Masaccio in the Carmine . . ."

Mollified, Ghirlandaio said, "Granacci was right. You have a strong fist."

Michelangelo held his hand in front of him, turning it from back to palm.

"It is a stonecutter's hand," he replied proudly.

"We have little need for stonecutters in a fresco studio. I'll start you as an
apprentice, but on the same terms as though you were ten. You must pay me six
florins for the first year . . ."

"I can pay you nothing."

Ghirlandaio looked at him sharply.

"The Buonarroti are not poor country people. Since your father wants you
apprenticed . . ."

"My father has beat me every time I mentioned painting."

"But I cannot take you unless he signs the Doctors and Apothecaries Guild
agreement. Why will he not beat you again when you tell him?"

"Because your willingness to accept me will be a defense. That, and the fact
that you will pay him six florins the first year, eight the second, and ten the third."

Ghirlandaio's eyelids flared.

"That's unheard of! Paying money for the privilege of teaching you!"

"Then I cannot come to work for you. It is the only way."

The color grinder was twirling his pestle idly in the air while he gazed over his
shoulder at the scene. The apprentices at the table made no pretense of working.
The master and would-be apprentice had reversed positions as though it were
Ghirlandaio who, needing and wanting Michelangelo, had sent for him. Michelangelo
could see the "No" beginning to take form on Ghirlandaio's lips. He stood his
ground, his manner respectful both to the older man and to himself, gazing straight
at Ghirlandaio as though to say:

"It is a thing you should do. I will be worth it to you."

Had he shown the slightest weakness Ghirlandaio would have turned his back
on him. But before this solid confrontation the artist felt a grudging admiration.
He lived up to his reputation of being a man "lovable and loved" by saying:

"It's obvious we shall never get the Tornabuoni choir finished without your
invaluable help. Bring your father in."

Out on the Via dei Tavolini once again, with the early morning merchants and
shoppers swirling about them, Granacci threw an arm affectionately about the
smaller boy's shoulder.

"You broke every rule. But you got in!"

Michelangelo flashed his friend one of his rare warming smiles, the amber-colored
eyes with their yellow and blue specks sparkling. The smile accomplished the
redesigning for which his crayon had groped earlier in front of the bedroom mirror:
when parted in a happy smile his lips were full, revealing strong white teeth, and
his chin thrusting forward achieved sculptural symmetry with the top half of his
face.

3

Walking past the family house of the poet Dante Alighieri and the stone church
of the Badia was for Michelangelo like walking through a gallery: for the Tuscan
treats stone with the tenderness that a lover reserves for his sweetheart. From the
time of their Etruscan ancestors the people of Fiesole, Settignano and Florence had

been quarrying stone from the mountains, hauling it by oxen to their land, cutting, edging, shaping and building it into homes and palaces, churches and loggias, forts and walls. Stone was one of the richest fruits of the Tuscan earth. From childhood they knew its feel and smell, the flavor of its outer shell as well as its inner meat; how it behaved in the hot sun, in the rain, in the full moonlight, in the icy *tramontana* wind. For fifteen hundred years their ancestors had worked the native *pietra serena,* serene stone, building a city of such breath-taking beauty that Michelangelo and generations before him cried:

"Never shall I live out of sight of the Duomo!"

They reached the carpenter shop which occupied the ground floor of the house the Buonarroti clan rented in the Via dell'Anguillara.

"*A rivederci,* as the fox said to the furrier," Granacci twitted.

"Oh, I'll take a skinning," he responded grimly, "but unlike the fox I shall come out alive."

He turned the sharp corner of Via dei Bentaccordi, waved to the two horses whose heads were sticking out of the open-top door of the stable across the street, and climbed the rear staircase to the family kitchen.

His stepmother was making her beloved *torta:* the chickens had been fried in oil earlier in the morning, ground into sausage with onions, parsley, eggs and saffron. Ham and pork had been made into *ravioli* with cheese, flour, clove, ginger, and laid with the chicken sausage between layers of pastry, dates and almonds. The whole dish had then been shaped into a pie and was being covered with dough, preparatory to being placed in the hot embers to bake.

"Good morning, *madre mia.*"

"Ah, Michelangelo. I have something special for you today: a salad that sings in the mouth."

Lucrezia di Antonio di Sandro Ubaldini da Gagliano's name was longer than the written list of her dowry; else why should so young a woman marry a forty-three-year-old graying widower with five sons, and cook for a household of nine Buonarroti?

Each morning she rose at four o'clock in order to reach the market square at the same time the *contadini* arrived through the cobbled streets with their pony carts filled with fresh fruits and vegetables, eggs and cheese, meats and poultry. If she did not actually help the peasants unload, at least she lightened their burden by selecting while the produce was still in the air and before it had a chance to settle in the stalls: the tenderest, slender green beans and *piselli,* peas, unblemished figs, peaches.

Michelangelo and his four brothers called her *Il Migliore,* The Best, because every ingredient that went into her cooking had to be The Best. By dawn she was home, her baskets piled high with capture. She cared little about her clothing, paid no attention to her plain dark face with its suggestion of sideburns and mustache, the lackluster hair pulled tightly back from her brow. But as Michelangelo gazed at her flushed cheeks, the excitement in her eyes as she watched her *torta* baking, moving with authority and grace from the fire to her majolica jars of spices to sprinkle a fine dust of cinnamon and nutmeg over the crust, knowing every second of the seven-hour morning precisely where she was on schedule, he saw that she exuded radiance.

He knew his stepmother to be a docile creature in every phase of her marriage except the kitchen; here she was a lioness in the best fighting tradition of the Marzocco, Florence's guardian lion. Wealthy Florence was supplied with exotic foods from all over the world: aloes, zedoary, cardamom, thyme, marjoram, mushrooms and truffles, powdered nuts, *galinga.* Alas! they cost money to buy. Michelangelo, who shared the bedroom with his four brothers next to his parents' room, often heard his parents' predawn debates while his stepmother dressed for marketing.

"Everyday you want a bale of herrings and a thousand oranges."

"Lodovico, stop cutting costs with a cheese parer. You are one who would keep money in the purse and hunger in the belly."

"Hunger! No Buonarroti has missed his dinner in three hundred years. Each week don't I bring you in a fresh veal from Settignano?"

"Why should we eat veal every day when the markets are full of suckling pig and pigeon?"

On those days that Lodovico lost he gloomed over the account books, certain that he would not be able to swallow a bite of the *bramangiere* of fowls, almonds, lard, sugar, cloves and expensive rice with which his young irresponsible wife was ruining him. But slowly, as the fragrances seeped under the door of the kitchen, through the family sitting room and into his study, it would eat away his fears, his anger, his frustration; and by eleven o'clock he would be ravenous.

Lodovico would devour a prodigious dinner, then push his chair back from the table, slap his bulging viscera with widespread fingers and exclaim the one sentence without which the Tuscan's day is drear and futile:

"Ho mangiato bene! I have eaten well!"

With this tribute Lucrezia put away the remains for a light evening supper, set her slavey to wash the dishes and pots, went upstairs and slept until dark, her day complete, her joy spent.

Not so Lodovico, who now went through the inverse process of the morning's seduction. As the hours passed and the food was digested, as the memory of the delicious flavors receded, the gnawing question of how much the elaborate dinner had cost began eating at him and he was angry all over again.

Michelangelo walked through the empty family room with its heavy oak bench facing the fireplace, the six-foot bellows propped against the stone, its wall chairs with leather backs and leather seats: all prodigal pieces that had been made by the family's founder. The next room, still overlooking the Via dei Bentaccordi and the stables, was his father's study, for which Lodovico had had built in the downstairs carpenter shop a triangular desk to fit into the forty-five-degree angle caused by the joining of the two streets at this end curve of the old colosseum. Here Lodovico sat cramped over his gray parchment account books. As long as Michelangelo could remember, his father's sole activity had been a concentration on how to avoid spending money, and how to retain the ragged remnants of the Buonarroti fortune, which had been founded in 1250 and had now shrunk to a ten-acre farm in Settignano and a house with a legally disputed title close by this one which they rented.

Lodovico heard his son come in and looked up. Nature had been opulent to him in only one gift, his hair: since it grew freely he sported a luxurious mustache which flowed into his beard, cut square four inches below his chin. The hair was streaked with gray; across the forehead were four deep straight lines, hard-earned from his years of poring over his account books and family records. His small brown eyes were melancholy with tracing the lost fortunes of the Buonarroti. Michelangelo knew his father as a cautious man who locked the door with three keys.

"Good morning, *messer padre.*"

Lodovico sighed:

"I was born too late. One hundred years ago the Buonarroti vines were tied with sausages."

Michelangelo watched his father as he sank into his work-reverie of the Buonarroti records, the Old Testament of his life. Lodovico knew to the last florin how much each Buonarroti generation had owned of land, houses, business, gold. This family history was his occupation, and each of his sons in turn had to memorize the legend.

"We are noble burghers," Lodovico told them. "Our family is as old as the Medici, Strozzi or Tornabuoni. The Buonarroti name has lasted three hundred years with us." His voice rose with energy and pride. "We have been paying taxes in Florence for three centuries."

Michelangelo was forbidden to sit in his father's presence without permission, had to bow when given an order. It had been duty rather than interest that led the boy to learn that when the Guelphs took over power in Florence in the middle of the thirteenth century their family rose rapidly: in 1260 a Buonarroti was councilor for the Guelph army; in 1392 a captain of the Guelph party; from 1343 to 1469 a Buonarroti had ten times been a member of the Florentine *Priori* or City Council, the most honored position in the city; between 1326 and 1475 eight Buonarroti had been *gonfaloniere* or mayor of the Santa Croce quarter; between 1375 and 1473 twelve had been among the *buonuomini* or Council of Santa Croce, including Lodovico and his brother Francesco, who were appointed in 1473. The last official recognition of the waning Buonarroti family had taken place thirteen years before, in 1474, when Lodovico had been appointed *podestà,* or outside visiting mayor, for the combined hamlets of Caprese and Chiusi di Verna, high in the rugged Apennines, where Michelangelo had been born in the town hall during the family's six months' residence.

Michelangelo had been taught by his father that labor was beneath a noble burgher; but it was the son's observation that Lodovico worked harder in figuring out ways not to spend money than he would have had to work in earning it. Within the Buonarroti fortress there had remained a few scattered resources, enough to let him eke out his life as a gentleman providing he spent nothing. Yet in spite of all the skill and dedication Lodovico brought to his task their capital had dribbled away.

Standing in the recessed wall of the eight-foot window, letting the thin March sun warm his bony shoulders, the boy's image went back to their home in Settignano, overlooking the valley of the Arno, when his mother had been alive. Then there had been love and laughter; but his mother had died when he was six, and his father had retreated in despair into the encampment of his study. For four years while his aunt Cassandra had taken over the care of the household, Michelangelo had been lonely and unwanted except by his grandmother, Monna Alessandra, who lived with them, and the stonecutter's family across the hill, the stonecutter's wife having suckled him when his own mother had been too ill to nourish her son.

For four years, until his father had remarried and Lucrezia had insisted that they move into Florence, he had fled at every opportunity to the Topolinos. He would make his way down the wheat fields among the silver-green olives, cross the brook which marked the division of the land, and climb the opposite hill through the vineyards to their yard. Here he would silently set to work cutting the *pietra serena* from the neighboring quarry into beveled building stones for a new Florentine palace, working out his unhappiness in the precision blows in which he had been trained in this stonecutter's yard since he was a child and, along with the stonecutter's own sons, had been given a small hammer and chisel to work scraps.

Michelangelo pulled himself back from the stonecutter's yard in Settignano to this stone house on the Via dell'Anguillara.

"Father, I have just come from Domenico Ghirlandaio's studio. Ghirlandaio has agreed to sign me as an apprentice."

4

During the silence that pulsed between them Michelangelo heard one of the horses neigh across the street and Lucrezia stir the embers of her fire in the kitchen. Lodovico used both hands to raise himself to a commanding position over the boy. This inexplicable desire of his son's to become an artisan could be the final push that would topple the shaky Buonarroti into the social abyss.

"Michelangelo, I apologize for being obliged to apprentice you to the Wool Guild and force you to become a merchant rather than a gentleman. But I sent you to an expensive school, paid out money I could ill afford so that you would be educated and rise in the Guild until you had your own mills and shops. That was how most of the great Florentine fortunes were started, even the Medici's.''

Lodovico's voice rose. ''Do you think that I will now allow you to waste your life as a painter? To bring disgrace to the family name! For three hundred years no Buonarroti has fallen so low as to work with his hands.''

''That is true. We have been usurers,'' angrily responded the boy.

''We belong to the Money Changers Guild, one of the most respectable in Florence. Moneylending is an honorable profession.''

Michelangelo sought refuge in humor.

''Have you ever watched Uncle Francesco fold up his counter outside Orsanmichele when it starts to rain? You never saw anyone work faster with his hands.''

At the mention of his name Uncle Francesco came running into the room. He was a larger man than Lodovico, with a brighter countenance; the working half of the Buonarroti partnership. Two years before he had broken away from Lodovico, made considerable money, bought houses and set himself up in style, only to be lured into a bad investment in foreign currencies, lose everything and have to move back into his brother's house. Now when it rained he scooped up his velvet covering from the folding table, grabbed his bag of coins from between his feet and ran through the wet streets to his friend, Amatore the cloth cutter, who allowed him to set up his table under cover.

Francesco said in a hoarse voice:

''Michelangelo, you couldn't see a crow in a bowlful of milk! What perverse pleasure can you derive from injuring the Buonarroti?''

The boy was furious at the accusation.

''I have as much pride in our name as anyone. Why can't I learn to do fine work that all Florence will be proud of, as they are of Ghiberti's doors and Donatello's sculptures and Ghirlandaio's frescoes? Florence is a good city for an artist.''

Lodovico put his hand on the boy's shoulder, calling him *Michelagnolo,* his pet name. This was his favorite of the five sons, for whom he had the highest hopes; it was this affection that had given him courage to spend money for three years of schooling at Urbino's. The master had been too proud to report to the father that his seemingly bright son had preferred drawing in his notebooks to learning his letters from the collection of Greek and Latin manuscripts. As for rhetoric, the boy had been bound by his own rules of logic which the persuasive Urbino had been unable to alter.

''Michelagnolo, the things you say about artists are as true as the word of a bench-talker. I've been too angry at your stupidity to do anything but beat you. But you're thirteen now; I've paid for your training in logic, so I should practice logic with you. Ghiberti and Donatello began as artisans and ended as artisans. So will Ghirlandaio. Their work never raised their social position one *braccio,* an arm's length, and Donatello was so destitute at the end of his life that Cosimo de' Medici had to give him a charity pension.''

The boy flared at this attack.

''That's because Donatello put all his money into a wire basket hung from the ceiling so his assistants and friends could help themselves when they needed. Ghirlandaio makes a fortune.''

''Art is like washing an ass's head with lye,'' observed Francesco, for the Tuscan's wisdom is a web of proverbs; ''you lose both the effort and the lye. Every man thinks that rubble will turn into gold in his hand! What kind of dreaming is that?''

''The only kind I know,'' cried Michelangelo. He turned back to Lodovico. ''Bleed me of art, and there won't be enough liquid left in me to spit.''

''I prophesied that my Michelangelo would recoup the Buonarroti fortune,'' cried Lodovico. ''I should have spoken with a smaller mouth! Now, I'll teach you to be vulgar.''

He started raining blows on the boy, his right elbow crooked stiffly so that he could use his arm as a club. Francesco, not wanting to fail his nephew in this critical moment of his youth, also began hitting the boy, boxing his ear with the heel of his palm.

Michelangelo lowered his head as dumb beasts do in a storm. There was no point in running away, for then the argument would have to be resumed later. Deep in his throat he sounded the words of his grandmother:

"*Pazienza!* Patience! No man is born into the world whose work is not born with him."

From the corner of his eye he saw his aunt Cassandra bulking in the doorway, a big-boned woman who seemed to put on flesh from the air she breathed. Cassandra of the enormous thighs, buttocks and bosom, with a voice that matched her weight, was an unhappy woman. Nor did she feel it her duty to dispense happiness.

"Happiness," said Aunt Cassandra, "is for the next world."

The boom of Aunt Cassandra's voice demanding to know what was going on now hurt his ear more than her husband's palm. Then, suddenly, all words and blows stopped and he knew that his grandmother had entered the room. She was a retiring woman in black, not beautiful but with a finely modeled head, who exercised her matriarchy only in moments of family crisis. Lodovico did not like to give his mother offense. He slumped into his chair.

"That's the end of the discussion!" he announced. "I have brought you up not to crave the whole world; it is enough to make money and serve the Buonarroti name. Never let me hear again about this being apprenticed to artists."

Michelangelo was glad that his stepmother was too deeply involved in her *torta* to permit her to leave the kitchen; the room was too crowded now for more spectators.

Monna Alessandra went to her son's side at the account desk.

"What difference does it make whether he joins the Wool Guild and twists wool or the Apothecaries Guild and mixes paints? You won't leave enough money to set up five geese, let alone sons." Her voice was without reproach; had it not been her husband, Lionardo Buonarroti, whose bad judgment and bad luck began the downfall of the family? "All five boys must look to their living; let Lionardo go into the monastery as he wishes, and Michelangelo into a studio. Since we can no longer help them, why hinder them?"

"I am going to be apprenticed to Ghirlandaio, Father. You must sign the papers. I'll do well by us all."

Lodovico stared at his son in disbelief. Was he possessed by an evil spirit? Should he take him to Arezzo and have him exorcised?

"Michelangelo, you are saying things that make me swell up a dozen times in anger." He shot his last and crushing bolt. "We have not a scudo to pay for any apprenticeship to Ghirlandaio."

This was the moment for which Michelangelo had been waiting. He said gently:

"There is no need for money, *padre*. Ghirlandaio has agreed to pay you for my apprenticeship."

"He will pay!" Lodovico lunged forward. "Why should he pay me for the privilege of teaching you?"

"Because he thinks I have a strong fist."

After a considerable silence Lodovico lowered himself slowly into his leather chair.

"Except God keep us, we shall be destroyed. Truthfully, I don't know where you come from. Certainly not from the Buonarroti. All this must be your mother's side, the Rucellai."

He spat out the name as though it were a mouthful of wormy apple. It was the first time Michelangelo could remember hearing the name spoken in the Buonarroti house. Lodovico crossed himself, more in perplexity than piety.

"Truly I have conquered myself in more battles than a saint!"

5

Domenico Ghirlandaio's was the most bustling and successful *bottega* in all Italy. In addition to the twenty-five frescoed panels and lunettes for the Tornabuoni choir at Santa Maria Novella, which had to be completed in the two years remaining of the five-year contract, he had also signed agreements to paint an Adoration of the Kings for the hospital of the Innocenti and to design a mosaic for over a portal of the cathedral. Every few days he made a trip on horseback to a neighboring town which wanted him to paint anything from a small altarpiece to the hall of a ducal palace. Ghirlandaio, who never sought a commission, could refuse none; on Michelangelo's first day in the studio he told him:

"If a peasant woman brings you a basket that she wants ornamented, do it as beautifully as you can, for in its modest way it is as important as a fresco on a palace wall."

Michelangelo found the place energetic but good-natured. Twenty-eight-year-old Sebastiano Mainardi, with long black hair cut to imitate Ghirlandaio's, a pale, narrow face with a jutting bony nose and protruding teeth, was in charge of the apprentices; he was Ghirlandaio's brother-in-law, though not, insisted Jacopo dell'Indaco, imp son of a baker, through any willing of his own.

"Ghirlandaio married him to his sister in order to keep him working for the family," Jacopo told Michelangelo. "So be on your guard."

Like most of Jacopo's deviltries, this one contained a kernel of truth: the Ghirlandaios were a family of artists, having been trained in the workshop of their father, an expert goldsmith who had originated a fashionable wreath, called a *ghirlanda,* which the Florentine women wore in their hair. Domenico's two younger brothers, David and Benedetto, were also painters. Benedetto, a miniaturist, wanted to paint only the minute and precise aspects of a woman's jewels or flowers; David, the youngest, had signed the contract for the Santa Maria Novella along with his brother.

Domenico Ghirlandaio had moved on from his father's studio to that of Baldovinetti, the master of mosaics, where he had remained until he was twenty-one, leaving reluctantly to open his own studio. "Painting is drawing, and the true eternal painting is mosaic," he declared, but since few wanted mosaics any more he had turned to fresco, becoming the greatest absorber and eclectic in Italy. He had learned everything that the earlier fresco painters, from the time of Cimabue, had to teach. In addition he added something peculiarly and brilliantly his own.

Ghirlandaio had in truth embraced young Mainardi as a brother-in-law after the younger apprentice had helped him paint his masterly frescoes in the church at San Gimignano, a neighboring town of seventy-six towers. Mainardi, who now took Michelangelo in tow, was amazingly like Ghirlandaio: good-natured, talented, well trained in the studio of Verrocchio, loving above all things to paint, and agreeing with Ghirlandaio that it was the beauty and charm of a fresco that was important. Paintings had to tell a story, either from the Bible, religious history or Greek mythology, but it was not the painter's function to look behind the meaning of that story, to search for its significance or judge its validity.

"The purpose of painting," explained Mainardi to his newest apprentice, "is to be decorative, to bring stories to life pictorially, to make people happy, yes, even with the sad pictures of the saints being martyred. Always remember that, Michelangelo, and you will become a successful painter."

If Mainardi was the major-domo of the apprentices, Michelangelo soon learned that sixteen-year-old Jacopo, with the monkey-like face, was the ringleader. He had a gift for appearing to be busy without doing a lick of work. He welcomed the thirteen-year-old boy to the studio by warning him gravely:

"Doing nothing else but hard work is not worthy of a good Christian." Turning to the table of apprentices, he added exultantly, "Here in Florence we average nine holidays every month. Add Sundays to that and it means we only have to work every other day.''

"I can't see that it makes any critical difference to you, Jacopo," commented Granacci with a rare burn of acid. "You don't work on workdays.''

The two weeks flew by until the magic day of his contract signing and first pay dawned. Michelangelo suddenly realized how little he had done to earn the two gold florins which would constitute his first advance. So far he had been used as an errand boy to pick up paints at the chemist's, to screen sand to give it a fine texture and wash it in a barrel with a running hose. Awakening while it was still dark outside, he climbed over his younger brother Buonarroto, sprang out of the bed, fumbled in the bed-bench for his long stockings and knee-length shirt. At the Bargello he passed under a body hanging from a hook in the cornice; this must be the man who, failing to die when hanged two weeks before, had uttered such vengeful words that the eight magistrates had decided to hang him all over again.

Ghirlandaio was surprised to find the boy on his doorstep so early and his *buon giorno,* good morning, was short. He had been working for days on a study of St. John Baptizing the Neophyte and was upset because he could not clarify his concept of Jesus. He was further annoyed when interrupted by his brother David with a batch of bills that needed paying. Domenico pushed the accounts aside with a brusque gesture of his left hand, continuing to draw irritatedly with his right.

"Why can't you manage this *bottega,* David, and leave me alone to do my painting?''

Michelangelo watched the scene with apprehension: would they forget what day it was? Granacci saw his friend's expression. He slipped off his bench, went to David, murmured something in his ear. David reached into the leather purse he kept hooked onto his wide belt, crossed the room to Michelangelo and handed him two florins and a contract book. Michelangelo quickly signed his name alongside the first payment, as stipulated in the Doctors and Apothecaries Agreement, then wrote the date:

April 16, 1488

Joy raced through his veins as he anticipated the moment when he would hand the florins to his father. Two florins were not the wealth of the Medici, but he hoped they would lighten the murky atmosphere around the Buonarroti house. Then he was aware of an enthusiastic hubbub among the apprentices and the voice of Jacopo saying:

"It's agreed, we draw from memory that gnome figure on the alley wall behind the *bottega.* The one who draws the most accurate reproduction wins and pays for dinner. Cieco, Baldinelli, Granacci, Bugiardini, Tedesco, are you ready?''

Michelangelo felt a dull pain in the chest; he was being left out. His had been a lonely childhood, he had had no intimate friend until Granacci recognized in his young neighbor a talent for drawing. So often he had been excluded from games. Why? Because he had been small and sickly? Because there was not enough laughter in him? Because he communicated with difficulty? He so desperately wanted to be included in the companionship of this young group; but it did not come easy. At the end of his first week Granacci had had to teach him a lesson in getting along with one's contemporaries.

Thirteen-year-old, heavy-boned Giuliano Bugiardini, a simple-natured lad who had been friendly to Michelangelo from the moment he entered the studio, had done a practice study of a group of women. Bugiardini could not draw the human figure and had no interest in it.

"What's the use?" he demanded. "We never show anything except the hands and face.''

Seeing the sacklike outlines, Michelangelo had impulsively picked up a stub pen and made a number of quick strokes which had put limbs under the heavy dresses of the women and infused them with a sense of movement. Bugiardini blinked his heavy eyelids a few times to see his figures spring to life. He was free of envy and did not resent the corrections. It was the thirteen-year-old Cieco, who had been apprenticed to Ghirlandaio at the conventional age of ten, who had taken offense. The sharp-tongued Cieco cried out:

"You've been studying from a female nude model!"

"But there's no such thing in Florence," protested Michelangelo.

Tedesco, rawboned redhead, fruit of an early invasion of Florence, asked in a voice edged with hostility, "Then how do you know about the movements of a woman's breasts and thighs, that you can put real people under their clothes?"

"I watch the women picking beans in the fields, or walking along the road with a basket of faggots on their head. What your eye sees, your hand can draw."

"Ghirlandaio is not going to like this!" crowed Jacopo joyously.

That evening Granacci said confidingly:

"Be careful about raising jealousies. Cieco and Tedesco have been apprenticed for a long time. How could they see any justice in your being able to draw better instinctively than they can after years of training? Praise their work. Keep your own to yourself."

Now, at the apprentices' table, Jacopo was completing the details of the game. "Time limit, ten minutes. The winner to be crowned champion and host."

"Why can't I compete, Jacopo?" Michelangelo cried.

Jacopo scowled. "You're just a beginner, you couldn't possibly win, and there would be no chance of your paying. It wouldn't be fair to the rest of us."

Stung, Michelangelo pleaded, "Let me join in, Jacopo. You'll see, I won't do too badly."

"All right," Jacopo agreed reluctantly. "But you can't have a longer time. Everyone ready?"

Excitedly, Michelangelo picked up charcoal and paper and began hammering down the outlines of the gnarled figure, half youth, half satyr, which he had seen several times on the rear stone wall. He could summon lines from his memory the way the students at Urbino's school had so miraculously brought forth verses of Homer's *Iliad* or Virgil's *Aeneid* when the master demanded them.

"Time limit!" cried Jacopo. "Line up your drawings, center of the table."

Michelangelo ran to the table, put his sketch in line, quickly scanned the other sheets. He was astonished at how unfamiliar, even incomplete they appeared. Jacopo stared at him with his mouth wide open.

"I can't believe it. Look, everyone, Michelangelo has won!"

There were cries of congratulation. Cieco and Tedesco smiled at him for the first time since their argument. He glowed with pride. He was the newest apprentice, yet he had won the right to buy everyone dinner. . . .

Buy everyone dinner! His stomach sank as though he had swallowed his two gold florins. He counted heads; there were seven of them. They would consume two liters of red wine, soup-of-the-country, roast veal, fruit . . . making a sizable hole in one of the gold pieces that he had waited for so eagerly to turn over to his father.

On the way to the *osteria,* with the others rushing ahead laughing heartily among themselves a loose thread began flapping in his mind. He ran the spool of his thoughts backward, fell in step beside Granacci.

"I was gulled, wasn't I?"

"Yes."

"Why didn't you warn me?"

"It's part of the initiation."

"What will I tell my father?"

"If you had known, would you have made yourself draw badly?"

Michelangelo broke into a sheepish grin.

"They couldn't lose!"

6

There was no formal method of teaching at Ghirlandaio's studio. Its basic philosophy was expressed in a plaque which Ghirlandaio had nailed to the wall alongside his desk:

THE MOST PERFECT GUIDE IS NATURE. CONTINUE WITHOUT FAIL
TO DRAW SOMETHING EVERY DAY.

Michelangelo had to learn from whatever task each man had at hand. No secrets were kept from him. Ghirlandaio created the over-all design, the composition within each panel and the harmonious relation of one panel to the many others. He did most of the important portraits, but the hundred others were distributed throughout the studio, sometimes several men working on a single figure and on a one-day spread of plaster. Where there was an excellent angle of visibility from the church, Ghirlandaio did the entire panel himself. Otherwise major portions were painted by Mainardi, Benedetto, Granacci and Bugiardini. On the lateral lunettes, which were hard to see, he let Cieco and Baldinelli, the other thirteen-year-old apprentice, practice.

Michelangelo moved from table to table, doing odd jobs. No one had time to stop work to teach him. He watched Ghirlandaio complete a portrait of Giovanna Tornabuoni, painted as a separate commission, and then draw it for the cartoon of the Visitation panel.

"Oil painting is for women," Ghirlandaio said sarcastically. "But this figure will go well in the fresco. Never try to invent human beings, Michelangelo; paint into your panels only those whom you have already drawn from life."

David and Benedetto shared with Mainardi a long table in the far corner of the studio. Benedetto never worked freehand. It seemed to Michelangelo that he paid more attention to the mathematical squares on the paper before him than to the individual character of the person portrayed. Nevertheless he was an expert with the instruments for squaring up. He told Michelangelo:

"Remember that the face is divided in three parts: first, the hair and forehead, then the nose, then the chin and mouth. Now take the proportions of a man. I omit those of a woman because there is not one of them perfectly proportioned. The arm with the hand extends to the middle of the thigh . . . so. The whole length of a man is eight faces; and equal to his width with the arms extended. Always remember that a man has on his left side one less rib than a woman . . ."

Michelangelo tried drawing to Benedetto's geometric plan, with its plumb line and compass half circles, but the restriction was a coffin into which he could squeeze only dead bodies.

Mainardi however had an accurate hand and a self-assurance that breathed life into his work. He had painted important parts of both lunettes and all the panels, and was working out a color pattern for the Adoration of the Magi. He showed Michelangelo how to tint flesh in tempera, going twice over the naked parts.

"This first bed of color, particularly for young people with fresh complexions, must be tempered with the yolk of an egg of a city hen; the red yolks of country hens are only fit to temper flesh colorings of old or dark persons."

From Mainardi, Michelangelo learned to let the green tint under the flesh colors be just visible; to put highlights over the eyebrows and on the top of the nose with a little pure white; to outline the eyelids and lashes with black.

From Jacopo he received not technical instruction but news of the city. Nothing nefarious was safe from Jacopo. He could pass by virtue all his life and never stumble over it, but his nose smelled out the nether side of human nature as instinctively as a bird smells manure. Jacopo was the town's gossip gatherer and crier; he made the daily rounds of the inns, the wine- and barbershops, the quarters

of the prostitutes, the groups of old men sitting on stone benches before the *palazzi*,
for they were the best purveyors of the town's yarns and scandal. Each morning
he walked to the workshop by a circuitous route which enabled him to tap all of
his sources; by the time he reached Ghirlandaio's he had a shopping basketful of
the night's news: who had been cuckolded, who was going to be commissioned
for what art project, who was about to be put in stocks with his back against the
Signoria wall.

Ghirlandaio had a manuscript copy of Cennini's treatise on painting; although
Jacopo could not read a word, he sat on the apprentices' table with his legs crossed
under him, pretending to spell out the passages he had memorized:

"As an artist your manner of living should always be regulated as if you were
studying theology, philosophy, or any other science; that is to say, eating and
drinking temperately at least twice a day . . . ; sparing and reserving your hand,
saving it from fatigue caused by throwing stones or iron bars. There is still another
cause, the occurrence of which may render your hand so unsteady that it will
tremble and flutter more than leaves shaken by the wind, and this is frequenting
too much the company of women."

Jacopo threw back his head and laughed froth bubbles at the ceiling, then turned
upon the quite astonished Michelangelo, who knew less about women than he did
of Ptolemy's astronomy.

"Now you know, Michelangelo, why I don't paint more: I don't want the
Ghirlandaio frescoes to tremble and flutter like leaves in the wind!"

Amiable, easygoing David had been well trained in enlarging to scale the individual
sections and transferring them to the cartoon itself, which was the dimension of
the church panel. This was not creative work, but it took skill. He demonstrated
how to divide the small painting into squares and the cartoon into the same number
of larger squares, how to copy the content of each small square into the corresponding
square of the cartoon, pointing out how mistakes that were almost unnoticeable in
the small drawing became obvious when blown up to cartoon size.

Bugiardini, whose clumsy body made it appear that he would have trouble
whitewashing his father's barn, nevertheless managed to get a spiritual tension into
his figures for the Visitation, even though they were not accurate anatomically. He
made Michelangelo spend one whole dinner period sitting for a sketch. After two
hours Bugiardini said, "Have a look at your portrait. I have already caught the
expression of your face."

Michelangelo broke into laughter.

"Bugiardini, you have painted me with one of my eyes on my temple! Look at
it!"

Bugiardini studied Michelangelo's face, then his sketch.

"It seems to me that your eye is exactly as I painted it, and so is your face."

"Then it must be a defect of nature," responded the boy.

Taking an indirect route home, Michelangelo and Granacci entered the Piazza
della Signoria where a large crowd was gathered, and climbed the steps of the
Loggia della Signoria. From here they could see into the *rin-ghiera* of the palace
where an ambassador of the Turkish sultan, garbed in eggshell turban and flowing
green robes, was presenting a giraffe to the councilmen of the Signoria. Michelangelo
wished he could sketch the scene but, knowing that he could capture only a small
part of its complexity, he complained to Granacci that he felt like a chessboard,
with alternating black and white squares of information and ignorance.

The next noon he ate sparingly of Lucrezia's veal roast and returned to the studio,
empty now because the others were taking their *riposo*, afternoon nap. He had
decided that he must study the drawing of his master. Under Ghirlandaio's desk
he found a bundle labeled Slaughter of the Innocents, took it to the apprentices'
table and spread out the dozens of sheets for the fresco. It seemed to him, poring
over the finished fresco, that Ghirlandaio could not portray motion, for the soldiers

with their swords up-raised, the mothers and children running, created confusion and an emotional chaos in him. Yet these rough studies had simplicity and authority. He began copying the drawings and had made a half dozen sketches in quick succession when he felt someone standing behind him. He turned to find a disapproving frown on Ghirlandaio's face.

"Why are you prying into that bundle? Who gave you permission?"

Michelangelo put down his charcoal, frightened.

"I didn't think there was any secret about it. I want to learn." He regained his composure. "The quicker I learn, the quicker I can help. I want to earn those gold florins."

The appeal to his logic served less to banish Ghirlandaio's anger than the intensity in the boy's eyes.

"Very well. I'll take some time with you now."

"Then teach me how to use a pen."

Ghirlandaio took his newest apprentice to his desk, cleared it and set up two corresponding sheets of paper. He handed Michelangelo a fine-nibbed pen, picked up another for himself, started crosshatching.

"Here's my calligraphy: circles for the eyes, angular tips for the nose, like this; use the short nib to render a mouth and score the underlip."

Michelangelo followed the older man with quick movements of the hand, noting how Ghirlandaio in sketching a figure never bothered to finish the legs but tapered them down to nothing. Ghirlandaio could hang a convincing drapery on a figure with a few rapid strokes, do a woman holding up her dress with delicate grace, achieve a lyrical flow of the body lines and at the same time give the figures individuality and character.

A look of rapture came over Michelangelo's face. This was the happiest he had been. With pen in hand he was an artist, thinking out loud, probing his mind, searching his heart for what he felt and his hand for what it could discern about the object before him. He wanted to spend hours at this work desk, redrawing models from a hundred different angles.

Ghirlandaio was aware of the eagerness in the boy's face, the excitement in his hand.

"Michelangelo, you must not draw for its own sake. This figure is not usable in a fresco."

Seeing how well his apprentice followed him, Ghirlandaio took from his desk two more of his drawings, an almost life-size study of the head of a smooth-cheeked, full-faced, wide-eyed and thoughtful man under thirty, with robust modeling, the drawing of the hair finely decorative; the second, the baptism of a man within the choir of a Roman basilica, done with a beauty of composition.

"Magnificent!" breathed Michelangelo, reaching for the sheets. "You've learned everything that Masaccio has to teach."

The blood drained from Ghirlandaio's dark face; had he been insulted, judged a copier? But the boy's voice was full of pride. Ghirlandaio was amused: the rawest apprentice was complimenting the master. He took the drawings from him.

"Sketches are nothing, only the finished fresco counts. I shall destroy these."

They heard the voices of Cieco and Baldinelli outside the studio. Ghirlandaio got up from the desk, Michelangelo picked up his paper and new pen, quickly reassembled the bundle of the Slaughter of the Innocents, had it tied and back in its corner by the time the boys came into the room.

Locked in the big drawer of his desk, Ghirlandaio kept a folio from which he studied and sketched while he was conceiving a new panel. Granacci told Michelangelo that it had taken Ghirlandaio years to assemble these drawings of men he considered masters: Taddeo Gaddi, Lorenzo Monaco, Fra Angelico, Paolo Uccello, Pollaiuolo, Fra Filippo Lippi and many others. Michelangelo had spent enthralled hours gazing at their altars and frescoes with which the city was lavishly endowed, but he had never seen any of the working studies.

"Certainly not," replied Ghirlandaio brusquely when Michelangelo asked him if he might see the portfolio.

"But why not?" cried Michelangelo desperately. Here was a golden opportunity to study the thinking and techniques of Florence's finest draftsmen.

"Every artist assembles his own portfolio," said Ghirlandaio, "according to his own tastes and judgment. I have made my collection over a period of twenty-five years. You build your own."

A few days later Ghirlandaio was studying a sketch by Benozzo Gozzoli of a nude youth with a spear, when a committee of three men called for him to accompany them to a neighboring town. He failed to put the drawing back into the locked drawer.

Waiting until the others had left for dinner, Michelangelo went to the desk, took up the Benozzo Gozzoli sketch. After a dozen attempts he made what he considered a faithful copy; and an errant idea popped into his mind. Could he fool Ghirlandaio with it? The sketch was thirty years old, the paper soiled and yellowing with age. He took some scraps into the back yard, ran his finger over the earth, experimented with rubbing the dirt along the grain of the paper. After a while he brought his copy out to the yard, and slowly began discoloring his own sheet.

Old drawing paper had a smoky quality around the edges. He returned to the studio where a fire burned in the hearth, held his discolored scraps over the smoke for testing, and after a moment his copy of the youth. Then he put the imitation on Ghirlandaio's desk and secreted the original.

During the weeks he watched Ghirlandaio's every move; whenever the teacher failed to return a sketch to the portfolio, a Castagno, Signorelli or Verrocchio, the boy remained behind to make a reproduction. If it was late afternoon he would take the sheet home and, when the rest of the family was asleep, make a fire in the downstairs hearth and stain the paper the proper color. At the end of a month he had assembled a portfolio of a dozen fine sketches. At this rate his folio of master sketches would become as thick as Ghirlandaio's.

Ghirlandaio still came in early from dinner occasionally to give his apprentice an hour of instruction: in the use of black chalk; how to work in silver point, and then to intensify the effect with white chalk. Michelangelo asked if they might sometimes draw from nude models.

"Why should you want to learn to draw the nude when we must always paint it under drapes?" demanded Ghirlandaio. "There aren't enough nudes in the Bible to make it profitable."

"There are the saints," replied the boy; "they have to be nude, nearly, when they are being shot with arrows or burned on a grill."

"True, but who wants anatomy in saints? It gets in the way of spirit."

"Couldn't it help portray character?"

"No. All of character that's necessary to show can be done through the face . . . and perhaps the hands. No one has worked in nudes since the pagan Greeks. We have to paint for Christians. Besides, our bodies are ugly, misproportioned, full of boils, fever and excrement. A garden of palms and cypresses, oranges in bloom, an architectural design of a straight stone wall with steps running down to the sea . . . that is beauty. And non-controversial. Painting should be charming, refreshing, lovely. Who can say that the human body is any of these things? I like to draw figures walking delicately under their gowns . . ."

". . . and I would like to draw them the way God made Adam."

7

With June the summer heat clamped down on Florence. The boy packed away his *calzoni*, long hose, and stuck his bare feet into sandals. He wore a light cotton shirt. The back doors of the studio were thrown open and the tables moved into the yard under the green-leafed trees.

For the festival of San Giovanni the *bottega* was locked tight. Michelangelo rose early, and with his brothers walked down to the Arno, the river which flowed through the city, to swim and play in the mud-brown waters before he met his fellow apprentices at the rear of the Duomo.

The piazza was covered by a broad blue awning sown with golden lilies to represent heaven. Each Guild had built its own cloud, high up in which sat its patron saint on a wooden frame thickly covered by wool, surrounded by lights and cherubs and sprinkled with tinsel stars. On lower iron branches were children dressed as angels, strapped on by waistbands.

At the head of the procession came the cross of Santa Maria del Fiore, and behind it singing companies of wool shearers, shoemakers, bands of boys dressed in white, then giants on stilts six cubits high, hooded with fantastic masks, then twenty-two Towers mounted on carts and carrying actors who gave tableaux out of Scripture: the Tower of St. Michael depicting the Battle of the Angels showed Lucifer being cast out of heaven; the Tower of Adam presented God Creating Adam and Eve, with the serpent making its entrance; the Tower of Moses acted out the Delivery of the Law.

To Michelangelo the tableaux seemed endless. He had never liked biblical plays and wanted to leave. Granacci, enchanted with the painted scenery, insisted on staying to the very end. Just as high mass was beginning in the Duomo a Bolognese was caught stealing purses and gold belt buckles from the worshipers jammed before the pulpit. The crowd in the church and piazza turned into an angry mob shouting, "Hang him! Hang him!" carrying the apprentices along with them to the quarters of the captain of the guard, where the thief was promptly hanged from a window.

Later that day a tremendous wind and hailstorm struck the city, destroying the colorful tents, turning the racecourse for the *palio* into a marsh. Bugiardini, Cieco, Baldinelli, Michelangelo huddled inside the Baptistery doors.

"This storm came because that wretched Bolognese stole in the Duomo on a holy day," cried Cieco.

"No, no, it's the other way round," protested Bugiardini. "God sent the storm as punishment for our hanging a man on a religious holiday."

They turned to Michelangelo, who was studying the gilt bronze sculptures of Ghiberti's second set of doors, their ten glorious panels populated layer upon layer by all the peoples, animals, cities, mountains, palaces of the Old Testament.

"What do I think?" Michelangelo said. "I think these doors are the gates of paradise."

At Ghirlandaio's the Birth of St. John was ready to be transferred to the wall of Santa Maria Novella. Early as he arrived at the studio, Michelangelo found himself to be the last. His eyes opened wide at the excitement, with everyone bustling about, collecting cartoons, bundles of sketches, brushes, pots and bottles of color, buckets, sacks of sand and lime, charcoal bags. The materials were loaded on a small cart behind an even smaller donkey, and off went the entire studio with Ghirlandaio at its head like a commanding general and Michelangelo, as the newest apprentice, driving the cart through the Via del Sole to the Sign of the Sun, which meant they were entering the Santa Maria Novella parish. He guided the donkey to the right and found himself in the Piazza Santa Maria Novella, one of the oldest and most beautiful in the city.

He pulled the donkey up short: in front of him loomed the church, which had stood uncompleted in its rustic brick from 1348 until Giovanni Rucellai, whom Michelangelo counted as an uncle, had had the good judgment to choose Leon Battista Alberti to design this façade of magnificent black and white marble.

Michelangelo felt a quickening at the thought of the Rucellai family, the more so because he was not permitted to mention the name in the Buonarroti house. Though he had never been inside their palace on the Via della Vigna Nuova, when passing by he always slowed his pace a little to see into the spacious gardens with their antique Greek and Roman sculptures, and to study the architecture of Alberti, who had designed the stately building.

Gangling Tedesco was the unloading foreman, gustily bossing the thirteen-year-olds in his moment of command. Michelangelo entered the bronze doors, a roll of sketches in his arms, and stood breathing the cool incense-heavy air. The church stretched before him in the form of an Egyptian cross over three hundred feet long, its three pointed ogive arches and rows of majestic pillars gradually decreasing in distance from each other as they approached the main altar behind which the Ghirlandaio studio had been working for three years. Its lateral walls were covered with bright murals; immediately over Michelangelo's head stood Giotto's wooden crucifix.

He walked slowly up the main aisle, savoring every step, for it was like a journey through Italian art: Giotto, painter, sculptor, architect, who legend said had been discovered by Cimabue as a shepherd boy drawing on a rock, and brought into his studio to become the liberator of painting from its dark Byzantine lifelessness. Giotto was followed by ninety years of imitators until—and here on the left of the church Michelangelo saw the living, glowing evidence of his Trinity—Masaccio, arising from God alone knew where, began to paint and Florentine art was reborn.

Across the nave to the left he saw a Brunelleschi crucifix; the Strozzi family chapel with frescoes and sculptures by the Orcagna brothers; the front of the major altar with its Ghiberti bronzes; and then, as the epitome of all this magnificence, the Rucellai chapel, built by his own mother's family in the middle of the thirteenth century when they had come into their fortune through a member of the family who had discovered in the Orient how to produce a beautiful red dye.

Michelangelo had never been able to get himself to mount the few stairs leading to the Rucellai chapel, even though it contained the supreme art treasures of Santa Maria Novella. A grudging family loyalty had kept him out. Now that he had made his break from the family and was going to work here in Santa Maria Novella, had he not earned the right to enter? Enter without feeling an intruder on that side of the family which after his mother's death had cut all communication, caring nothing of what happened to the five sons of Francesca Rucellai del Sera, daughter of Maria Bonda Rucellai?

He put down the package he was carrying and walked up the stairs, slowly. Once inside the chapel with its Cimabue Madonna before him, he fell to his knees; for this was the very chapel where his mother's mother had worshiped all through her youth, and where his mother had worshiped on those feast days of family reunion.

Tears burned, then overflooded his eyes. He had been taught prayers but he had only mouthed the words. Now they sprang to his lips unbidden. Was he praying to the beautiful Madonna or to his mother? Was there truly a difference? Had she not been very like the Madonna above him? Whatever vague memories he had of her melted into those of the Lady.

He rose, walked to a sculptured Virgin and ran his long bony fingers sentiently over the marble drapery. Then he turned and left the chapel. For a moment he stood on top of the stairs thinking of the contrast between his two families. The Rucellai had built this chapel around 1265, at the same time that the Buonarroti had come into their wealth. The Rucellai had recognized the finest practitioners, almost the creators of their arts: Cimabue in painting, somewhere around the close of the thirteenth century, and Nino Pisano in 1365. Even now they were in friendly competition with the Medici for the marble sculptures being dug up in Greece, Sicily and Rome.

The Buonarroti had never commissioned a chapel. Every family of similar wealth had done so. Why not they?

Behind the choir he could see his comrades loading supplies up on the scaffolding.

Was it enough to say that it had happened because the Buonarroti were not and never had been religious? Lodovico's conversation was interlarded with religious expressions, but Monna Alessandra had said of her son:

"Lodovico approves all the Church's laws even when he doesn't obey them."

The Buonarroti had always been hard men with a florin, sharing the native shrewdness about money and the fierce concentration in guarding it. Had the willingness to invest solely in houses and land, the only true source of wealth to a Tuscan, kept the Buonarroti from ever wasting a scudo on art? Michelangelo could not remember having seen a painting or sculpture of the simplest nature in a Buonarroti house. This took considerable doing for a family of wealth living for three hundred years in the most creative city in the world, where even homes of modest means had religious works that had come down through the generations.

He turned back for a last look at the frescoed walls of the Rucellai chapel, realizing with a sinking heart that the Buonarroti were not only stingy, they were enemies of art because they despised the men who created it.

A shout from Bugiardini on the scaffolding called him. He found the entire studio moving in harmony. Bugiardini had put a heavy coat of intonaco on the panel the day before, hatching a rough surface on which he was now plastering the precise area to be painted that day. With Cieco, Baldinelli and Tedesco he took up the cartoon, which they held over the wet panel. Ghirlandaio pounced the lines of the figures onto the fresh intonaco with his bag of charcoal, then gave the signal for it to be taken away. The young apprentices scrambled down the scaffolding, but Michelangelo remained to watch Ghirlandaio mix his mineral earth colors in little jars of water, squeeze his brush between his fingers and commence his painting.

He had to work surely and swiftly, for his task had to be completed before the plaster dried that night. If he delayed, the unpainted plaster formed a crust from the air currents blowing through the church, and these portions would stain and grow moldy. If he had failed to gauge accurately how much he could do that day, the remaining dry plaster would have to be cut away the following morning, leaving a discernible seam. Retouching was forbidden; colors added later needed to contain size, which would discolor the fresco, turn it black.

Michelangelo stood on the scaffolding with a bucket of water, sprinkling the area just ahead of Ghirlandaio's flying brush to keep it moist. He understood for the first time the truth of the saying that no coward ever attempted fresco. He watched Ghirlandaio moving boldly forward, painting the girl with the basket of ripe fruits on her head, the billowing gown then in fashion which made the Florentine girls look like carrying matrons. Next to him stood Mainardi, painting the two older, sedate aunts of the Tornabuoni family, come to visit Elisabeth.

Benedetto was highest on the scaffold, painting the elaborate cross-beamed ceiling. Granacci had been assigned the serving girl in the center of the background, bringing in a tray to Elisabeth. David was working on Elisabeth reclining against the richly carved wooden bedboard. Bugiardini, who had been allotted the window and door frames, summoned Michelangelo to his side, flicking his fingers for him to sprinkle some water, then stepped back in admiration from the tiny window he had just painted above Elisabeth's head.

"Have you ever seen a more beautiful window?" he demanded.

"Brilliant, Bugiardini," replied Michelangelo. "Particularly the open space that we see through."

Bugiardini studied his work, puzzled but proud.

"You like that part too? Funny, I haven't painted it yet."

The climax of the panel was reached when Ghirlandaio, with Mainardi assisting, painted the exquisite young Giovanna Tornabuoni, elaborately robed with the richest of Florentine silks and jewels, gazing straight out at Ghirlandaio, not in the least interested in either Elisabeth, sitting up in her high-backed bed or John, suckling at the breast of another Tornabuoni beauty sitting on the bed-bench.

The panel took five days of concentrated work. Michelangelo alone was not permitted to apply paint. He was torn: part of him felt that though he had been in the studio for only three months he was as qualified to work the wall as the other thirteen-year-olds. At the same time an inner voice kept telling him that all of this feverish activity had nothing to do with him. Even when he felt most unhappy about being excluded, he wanted to run out of the choir and the studio to a world of his own.

Toward the end of the week the plaster began to dry. The burnt lime recovered its carbonic acid from the air, fixing the colors. Michelangelo saw that his belief that the pigments sank into the wet plaster was a mistake; they remained on the surface, covered by a crystalline coating of carbonate of lime which fitted them the way the skin of a young athlete contains his flesh and blood. The entire panel now had a metallic luster which would protect the colors from heat, cold and moisture. But the amazing fact was that each day's segment was drying slowly to the very colors Ghirlandaio had created in his studio.

And yet, when he went alone to Santa Maria Novella the following Sunday during mass, weaving his way through the worshiping Florentines in their short velvet *farsetti,* doublets, voluminous cloaks of camlet trimmed in miniver, and high-crowned hats, he felt let down: so much of the freshness and vigor had leaked out from the drawings. The eight women were still lifes in mosaic, as if made of hard bits of colored stone. And certainly it was not the birth of John to the modest family of Elisabeth and Zacharias; it was a social gathering in the home of a merchant prince of Italy, utterly devoid of religious spirit or content.

Standing before the brilliant panel, the boy realized that Ghirlandaio loved Florence. The city was his religion. He was spending his life painting its people, its palaces, its exquisitely decorated rooms, its architecture and streets thronging with life, its religious and political pageants. And what an eye he had! Nothing escaped him. Since no one would commission him to paint Florence he had made Florence Jerusalem; the desert of Palestine was Tuscany, and all the biblical people modern Florentines. Because Florence was more pagan than Christian, everyone was pleased with Ghirlandaio's sophisticated portraits.

Michelangelo walked out of the church feeling depressed. The forms were superb; but where was the substance? His eyes hazed over as he tried to formulate words to shape the thoughts pushing against each other inside his head.

He too wanted to learn how to set down accurately what he saw. But what he felt about what he saw would always be more important.

8

He drifted over to the Duomo, where young men gathered on the cool marble steps to make laughter and view the passing pageant. Every day in Florence was a fair; on Sundays this richest city in Italy, which had supplanted Venice in its trade with the Orient, was out to prove that its thirty-three banking palaces were providing wealth for all. The Florentine girls were blond, slender, they carried their heads high, wore colorful coverings on their hair and long-sleeved gowns, high-necked, with overlapping skirts pleated and full, their breasts outlined in filmier fabric and color. The older men were in somber cloaks, but the young men of the prominent families created the great splash between the Duomo steps and the Baptistery by wearing their *calzoni* with each leg dyed differently and patterned according to the family blazon. Their suite of attendants followed in identical dress.

Jacopo was sitting on top of an old Roman sarcophagus, one of several that stood against the jagged tan brick face of the cathedral. From here he kept up a running comment about the passing girls while his scandalous eye sought out the ones to whom he awarded his highest accolade:

"Ah, how mattressable."

Michelangelo went to Jacopo's side, ran his hand caressingly over the sarcophagus, his fingers tracing out in its low relief the funeral procession of fighting men and horses.

"Feel how these marble figures are still alive and breathing!"

His voice carried such exultation that his friends turned to stare at him. Now his secret had burst into the open of the Florentine dusk, with the sinking sun setting the domes of the Baptistery and cathedral on fire. His hunger had gotten the better of him.

"God was the first sculptor; He made the first figure: man. And when He wanted to give His laws, what material did He use? Stone. The Ten Commandments engraved on a stone tablet for Moses. What were the first tools that men carved for themselves? Stone. Look at all us painters lolling on the Duomo steps. How many sculptors are there?"

His fellow apprentices were stunned by the outburst. Even Jacopo stopped searching for girls. They had never heard him speak with such urgency, his eyes glowing like amber coals in the fading light. He told them why he thought there were no more sculptors: the strength expended in carving with hammer and chisel exhausted mind and body alike, in contrast to the brushes, pens and charcoal which the painter used so lightly.

Jacopo hooted. Granacci answered his young friend.

"If extreme fatigue is the criterion of art, then the quarryman taking the marble out of the mountain with his wedges and heavy levers has to be considered nobler than the sculptor, the blacksmith greater than the goldsmith and the mason more important than the architect."

Michelangelo flushed. He had made a bad start. He studied the grinning faces of Jacopo, Tedesco and the two thirteen-year-olds.

"But you have to agree that the work of art becomes noble in the degree to which it represents the truth? Then sculpture will come closer to true form, for when you work the marble the figure emerges on all four sides. . . ."

His words, usually so sparse, spilled over each other: the painter laid his paint on a flat surface and by use of perspective tried to persuade people that they were seeing the whole of a scene. But just try to walk around a person in a painting, or around a tree! It was an illusion, a magician's trick. Now the sculptor, ah! he carved the full reality. That was why sculpture bore the same relationship to painting that truth did to falsehood. And if a painter blundered, what did he do? He patched and repaired and covered over with another layer of paint. The sculptor on the contrary had to see within the marble the form that it held. He could not glue back broken parts. That was why there were no more sculptors today, because it took a thousand times more accuracy of judgment and vision.

He stopped abruptly, breathing hard.

Jacopo jumped down from his perch on the lid of the sarcophagus, extended his two arms to indicate that he had taken over. He was bright; he liked painting and understood it even though he was too lazy to work at it.

"Sculpture is a bore. What can they make? A man, a woman, a lion, a horse. Then all over again. Monotonous. But the painter can portray the whole universe: the sky, the sun, the moon and the stars, clouds and rain, mountains, trees, rivers, seas. The sculptors have all perished of boredom."

Sebastiano Mainardi joined the group and stood listening. He had taken his wife for her weekly walk, then returned to the Duomo steps and the company of his young men friends which, like all Florentines, he enjoyed more than that of women. There were spots of color on his usually pale cheeks.

"That's true! The sculptor needs only a strong arm and an empty mind. Yes, empty; after a sculptor draws his simple design, what goes on inside his head during the hundreds of hours that he has to pound these chisels and points with a hammer? Nothing! But the painter has to think of a thousand things every moment, to relate all the integral parts of a painting. Creating the illusion of a third dimension is craftsmanship. That's why a painter's life is exciting, and a sculptor's dull."

Tears of frustration welled in Michelangelo's eyes. He cursed himself for his inability to carve out in words the stone forms that he felt in his innards.

"Painting is perishable: a fire in the chapel, too much cold, and the paint begins to fade, crack. But stone is eternal! Nothing can destroy it. When the Florentines tore down the colosseum, what did they do with the blocks? Built them into new walls. And think of the Greek sculpture that is being dug up, two, three thousand years old. Show me a painting that's two thousand years old. Look at this Roman marble sarcophagus; as clear and strong as the day it was carved . . . ."

"And as cold!" cried Tedesco.

Mainardi raised his arm for attention.

"Michelangelo," he began gently, "has it ever occurred to you that the reason there are no sculptors left is because of the cost of material? A sculptor needs a rich man or organization to give him a supply of marble and bronze. The Wool Guild of Florence financed Ghiberti for fifty years to make the doors of the Baptistery. Cosimo de' Medici supplied Donatello with the resources he needed. Who would provide you with the stone, who would support you while you practiced on it? Paint is cheap, commissions are abundant; that's why we take on apprentices. And as for the danger of working in sculpture and making the fatal mistake, what about the painter working in fresco? If the sculptor must see the form inherent in the stone, must not the painter foresee the final result of his color in the fresh wet plaster and know precisely how it will turn out when dry?"

Michelangelo numbly had to agree that this was true.

"Besides," continued Mainardi, "everything that can ever be accomplished in sculpture has already been created by the Pisanos, by Ghiberti, Orcagna, Donatello. Take Desiderio da Settignano or Mino da Fiesole; they made pretty, charming copies of Donatello. And Bertoldo, who helped Donatello cast his figures, and was there to learn the secrets that Donatello learned from Ghiberti: what has Bertoldo created except a few miniatures reduced from Donatello's great concepts? And now he's sick and dying, his work done. No, the sculptor can do little more than copy, since the range of sculpture is so narrow."

Michelangelo turned away. If only he knew more! Then he could convince them of the magnificence of fashioning figures in space.

Granacci touched the boy's shoulder comfortingly.

"Have you forgotten, Michelagnolo, what Praxiteles said? 'Painting and sculpture have the same parents; they are sister arts.'"

But Michelangelo refused to compromise. Without another word he walked down the cool marble steps, away from the Duomo, over the cobbled streets to home.

9

The night was sleepless. He rolled and tossed. The room was hot, for Lodovico said that air coming in a window was as bad as a crossbow shot. Buonarroto, who shared the bed, was placid in sleep as in all other things. Though two years younger than Michelangelo, he was the manager of the five boys.

In the bed closer to the door, with the curtains drawn around it, slept the good and evil of the Buonarroti progeny: Lionardo, a year and a half older than Michelangelo, who spent his days yearning to be a saint; and Giovansimone, four years younger, lazy, rude to his parents, who had once set fire to Lucrezia's kitchen because she had disciplined him. Sigismondo, the youngest, still slept in a trundle at the foot of Michelangelo's bed. Michelangelo suspected that the boy would never be anything but a simpleton, since he lacked all capacity to learn.

Quietly he sprang out of bed, slipped into his loincloth *brache,* short drawers, shirt and sandals, and left the house. He walked down the Via dell'Anguillara, the streets freshly washed and the stoops scrubbed, to Piazza Santa Croce, where the Franciscan church stood rough and dark in its unfinished brick. As he passed the open-sided gallery his eyes sought the outline of the Nino Pisano sarcophagus, held up by its four carved allegorical figures. He turned left on the Via del Fosso, built at the second limit of the city walls, passed the prison, then the house belonging to the nephew of St. Catherine of Siena, and at the end of the street, at the corner of the Swallows, the city's famous chemist shop. From here he turned into Via Pietrapiana, Street of the Flat Stones, which led through Piazza Sant'Ambrogio, in the church of which were buried the sculptors Verrocchio and Mino da Fiesole.

From the piazza he followed the Borgo la Croce until it led to a country road called Via Pontassieve, at the end of which he came to the Affrico River, an affluent of the Arno, its green banks covered with trees and luxuriant vegetation. After crossing the Via Piagentina he reached Varlungo, a little cluster of houses at what had been a Roman ford, then turned once again to the left and made his way up the slope toward Settignano.

He had been walking for an hour. Dawn flashed hot and bright. He paused on the hillside to watch the mammal hills of Tuscany emerge from their dark sleep. He cared little about the beauties of nature that so moved painters: the red poppies in the growing green wheat, the stands of almost black cypresses.

No, he loved the valley of the Arno because it was a sculptured landscape. God was the supreme carver: the lyrical hills, each range composed by a draftsman's hand, complementing the succeeding ranges as they rolled back, with nothing the eye could see that was carelessly conceived. In the clarity of its air distant peaks, rolling ridges, villas, trees though miles away, stood out to be touched, their form tactile. Here nature's perspective worked in reverse: the more distant the object, the nearer at hand it seemed.

The Tuscan was a natural sculptor. When he took over the landscape he built his stone terraces, planted his vineyards and olive orchards in harmony with the hills. No two haycocks were shaped the same; each family inherited a sculptural form: circular, oblong, umbrella, tent, which stood as a sign for the farm.

He climbed the cart road into the hills, closed in by the walls that are the buttress of the Tuscan's life, giving him privacy and security and at the same time sustaining his land and his sovereignty; standing as much as thirteen feet high to hold the descending slopes, and built to last a hundred generations. Stone was the dominant factor: with it he built his farms and villas, enclosed his fields, terraced his slopes to retain his soil. Nature had been bountiful with stone; every hill was an undeveloped quarry. If the Tuscan scratched deep with his fingernail he struck building materials sufficient for a city. And when he built of dry rock, his walls stood as though masoned.

"The skill with which men handle stone tells how civilized they are."

He left the road where it turned off for the quarry at Maiano. For four years after his mother died he had been left to roam this countryside, though it was the proper age for him to be in school. There was no master at Settignano, and his father had been too withdrawn to care. Now he climbed through land of which he knew every jutting boulder and tree and furrow.

His upward push brought him to the settlement of Settignano, a dozen houses collected around a gray stone church. This was the heart of the stonemason country, having bred the greatest *scalpellini* in the world, the generations that had built Florence. It was only two miles from the city, on the first rise above the valley floor, and an easy haul to town.

It was said of Settignano that its surrounding hills had a stone heart and velvet breasts.

As he walked through the tiny settlement toward the Buonarroti home he passed a dozen stoneyards scattered among the *poderi* or farms. Shortly, he came to the big yard that had produced Desiderio da Settignano. Death had caused him to drop his hammer and chisel at the age of thirty-six, but even by that time he was famous. Michelangelo knew well his marble tombs in Santa Croce and Santa Maria Novella, with their exquisite angels, and the Virgin carved so tenderly that she appeared asleep rather than dead. Desiderio had taken in Mino da Fiesole, who was just a young hewer of stones, and taught him the art of carving marble. Mino had wandered off to Rome in grief over the loss of his master.

Now there was no sculptor left in Florence. Ghiberti, who had trained Donatello and the Pollaiuolo brothers, had died some thirty-three years before. Donatello, who had died twenty-two years ago, had operated a studio for half a century, but of his followers Antonio Rossellino had been dead nine years, Luca della Robbia six, Verrocchio had just died. The Pollaiuolo brothers had moved to Rome four years ago, and Bertoldo, Donatello's favorite and heir to his vast knowledge and workshop, was fatally ill. Andrea and Giovanni della Robbia, trained by Luca, had abandoned stone sculpture for enameled terra-cotta reliefs.

Yes, sculpture was dead. Unlike his father who wished he had been born a hundred years before, Michelangelo asked only that he could have been born forty years ago so that he could have been trained under Ghiberti; or thirty years, so he could have been apprenticed to Donatello; or even twenty or ten or five years sooner, so that he could have been taught to work the marble by the Pollaiuolo brothers, by Verrocchio or Luca della Robbia.

He had been born too late, into a country where for two hundred and fifty years, since Nicola Pisano had unearthed some Greek and Roman marbles and begun carving, there had been created in Florence and the valley of the Arno the greatest wealth of sculpture since Phidias completed his work on the Greek Parthenon. A mysterious plague which affected Tuscan sculptors had wiped out the very last of them; the species, after having flourished so gloriously, was now extinct.

Sick at heart, he moved on.

10

Down the winding road a few hundred yards was the Buonarroti villa in the midst of a five-acre farm, leased to strangers on a long-term agreement. He had not been here for months. As always he was surprised by the beauty and spaciousness of the house, hewn two hundred years before of the best Maiano *pietra serena,* graceful in its austere lines, and with broad porches overlooking the valley, the river gleaming below like a silversmith's decoration.

He could remember his mother moving in the rooms, weaving on the broad downstairs porch, kissing him good night in his big corner room overlooking the Buonarroti fields, the creek at the bottom, and the Topolino family of stonemasons on the opposite ridge.

He crossed the back yard and the bone-textured stone walk past the stone cistern with its intricate hatching and crosshatching from which he had taken his first drawing lesson. He then scampered down the hill between the wheat on one side and the ripening grapes on the other, to the deep creek at the bottom, shaded by lush foliage. He slipped out of his shirt, short drawers and sandals and rolled over and over in the cool water, enjoying its wetness on his anxious tired body. Then he crouched in the hot sun for a few moments to dry, put on his clothes and climbed refreshed to the opposite ridge.

He paused when he came in sight of the yard. This was the picture he loved, one which meant home and security for him: the father working with tempered iron chisels to round a fluted column, the youngest son beveling a set of steps, one of the older two carving a delicate window frame, the other graining a door panel, the grandfather polishing a column on a pumice wheelstone with thin river sand. Behind them were three arches, and under them scurrying chickens, ducks, pigs.

In the boy's mind there was no difference between a *scalpellino* and a *scultore,* a stonecutter and a sculptor, for the *scalpellini* were fine craftsmen, bringing out the color and grain of the *pietra serena*. There might be a difference in the degree of artistry, but not in kind: every stone of the Pazzi, Pitti and Medici palaces was cut, beveled, given a textured surface as if it were a piece of sculpture: which to the Settignano *scalpellino* it was. Lesser craftsmen were confined to making routine blocks for smaller houses and paving stones for the streets. Yet so proud were all Florentines of their simplest paving blocks that the whole town bragged of the wretch who, being jostled in the cart that was taking him to the Palazzo della Signoria for hanging, cried out in protest:

"What idiots were these, who cut such clumsy blocks?"

The father heard Michelangelo's footsteps.

"*Buon dì,* Michelangelo."

"*Buon dì,* Topolino."

"*Come va?* How goes it?"

"*Non c'è male.* Not bad. *E te?* And you?"

"*Non c'è male.* The honorable Lodovico?"

"He goes well."

Topolino did not really care how things went with Lodovico: he had forbidden Michelangelo to come here. No one got up, for the stonemason rarely breaks his rhythm; the two older boys and the one exactly Michelangelo's age called out with welcoming warmth.

"*Ben venuto,* Michelangelo. Welcome."

"*Salve,* good health, Bruno. *Salve,* Gilberto. *Salve,* Enrico."

The *scalpellino's* words are few and simple, matching in length the single blow of the hammer. When he chips at the stone he does not speak at all: one, two, three, four, five, six, seven: no word from the lips, only the rhythm of the shoulder and the moving hand with the chisel. Then he speaks, in the period of pause: one, two, three, four. The sentence must fit the rest count of four or it remains unsaid or incomplete. If the thought must be involved it will be spaced between several work counts of seven, filling two or three counts of four. But the *scalpellino* has learned to confine his thinking to what can be expressed in the single four-count pause.

There was no schooling for the stoneman. Topolino figured his contracts on his fingers. The sons were given a hammer and chisel at six, as Michelangelo had been, and by ten they were working full time on the stone. There was no marriage outside the stone ring. Agreements with builders and architects were handed down from generation to generation, as were the quarrying jobs at Maiano, where no outsider could find work. Between the arches hung an oblong piece of *pietra serena* with examples of the classic treatments of the stone: herringbone, *subbia* punch-hole, rustic, crosshatch, linear, bevel, centered right angle, receding step: the first alphabet Michelangelo had been given, and still the one he used more comfortably than the lettered alphabet with which he had been taught to read the Bible and Dante.

Topolino spoke. "You're apprenticed to Ghirlandaio?"
"Yes."
"You do not like it?"
"Not greatly."
"Peccato. Too bad."
"Who does somebody else's trade makes soup in a basket," said the old grandfather.
"Why do you stay?" It was the middle brother asking.
"Where else is there to go?"
"We could use a cutter." This was from Bruno.
Michelangelo looked from the oldest son to the father.
"Davvero? It is true?"
"Davvero."
"You will take me as apprentice?"
"With stone you're no apprentice. You earn a share."
His heart leaped. Everyone chipped in silence while Michelangelo stood above the father who had just offered him a portion of the food that went into the family belly.
"My father . . ."
"Ecco! There you are!"
"Can I cut?"
The grandfather, turning his wheel, replied: " 'Every little bit helps,' said the father who peed into the Arno because his son's boat was beached at Pisa."
Michelangelo sat before a roughed-out column, a hammer in one hand, a chisel in the other. He liked the heft of them. Stone was concrete, not abstract. One could not argue it from every point of the compass, like love or theology. No theorist had ever separated stone from its quarry bed.
He had a natural skill, unrusted after the months of being away. Under his blows the *pietra serena* cut like cake. There was a natural rhythm between the inward and outward movement of his breath and the up-and-down movement of his hammer arm as he slid the chisel across a cutting groove. The tactile contact with the stone made him feel that the world was right again, and the impact of the blows sent waves of strength up his skinny arms to his shoulders, torso, down through his diaphragm and legs into his feet.
The *pietra serena* they were working was warm, an alive blue-gray, a reflector of changing lights, refreshing to look at. The stone had durability, yet it was manageable, resilient, as joyous in character as in color, bringing an Italian blue-sky serenity to all who worked it.
The Topolinos had taught him to work the stone with friendliness, to seek its natural forms, its mountains and valleys, even though it might seem solid; never to grow angry or unsympathetic toward the material.
"Stone works with you. It reveals itself. But you must strike it right. Stone does not resent the chisel. It is not being violated. Its nature is to change. Each stone has its own character. It must be understood. Handle it carefully, or it will shatter. Never let stone destroy itself.
"Stone gives itself to skill and to love."
His first lesson had been that the power and the durability lay in the stone, not in the arms or tools. The stone was master; not the mason. If ever a mason came to think he was master, the stone would oppose and thwart him. And if a mason beat his stone as an ignorant *contadino* might beat his beasts, the rich warm glowing breathing material became dull, colorless, ugly; died under his hand. To kicks and curses, to hurry and dislike, it closed a hard stone veil around its soft inner nature. It could be smashed by violence but never forced to fulfill. To sympathy, it yielded: grew even more luminous and sparkling, achieved fluid forms and symmetry.
From the beginning he had been taught that stone had a mystic: it had to be covered at night because it would crack if the full moon got on it. Each block had

areas inside where it was hollow and bent. In order for it to remain docile it had to be kept warm in sacks, and the sacks kept damp. Heat gave the stone the same undulations it had in its original mountain home. Ice was its enemy.

"Stone will speak to you. Listen as you strike with the side of your hammer." Stone was called after the most precious of foods: *carne,* meat.

The *scalpellini* respected this stone. To them it was the most enduring material in the world: it had not only built their homes, farms, churches, town, but for a thousand years had given them a trade, a skill, a pride of workmanship, a living. Stone was not king but god. They worshiped it as did their pagan Etruscan ancestors. They handled it with reverence.

Michelangelo knew them as men of pride: to care for their cattle, pigs, vines, olives, wheat, this was ordinary work; they did it well in order to eat well. But working the stone, ah! that was where a man lived. Had not the Settignanese quarried, shaped and built the most enchanting city in all Europe: Florence? Jewel of the stonecarver's art, its beauty created not by the architect and sculptor alone but by the *scalpellino* without whom there would have been no infinite variety of shape and decoration.

Monna Margherita, a formless woman who worked the animals and fields as well as the stove and tub, had come out of the house and stood under the arch, listening. She was the one about whom Lodovico had said bitterly, when Michelangelo wished to work with his hands:

"A child sent out to nurse will take on the condition of the woman who feeds him."

She had suckled him with her own son for two years, and the day her breast ran dry she put both boys on wine. Water was for bathing before mass. Michelangelo felt for Monna Margherita much as he did for Monna Alessandra, his grandmother: affection and security.

He kissed her on both cheeks.

"*Buon giorno, figlio mio.*"

"*Buon giorno, madre mia.*"

"*Pazienza,*" she counciled. "Ghirlandaio is a good master. Who has an art, has always a part."

The father had risen.

"I must choose at Cave Maiano. Will you help load?"

"Willingly. *A rivederci, nonno,* grandfather. *A rivederci,* Bruno. *Addio,* Gilberto. *Addio,* Enrico."

"*Addio,* Michelangelo."

They rode side by side on the high seat behind the two beautiful-faced white oxen. In the fields the olive pickers were mounted on ladders made of slender tree stalks, notched to take the light crossbar branches. Baskets were tied around their waists with rope, flat against the stomach and crotch. They held the branches with their left hand, stripping down the little black olives with a milking movement of the right. Pickers are talkers; two to a tree, they speak their phrases to each other through the branches, for to the *contadino* not to talk is to be dead a little. Topolino said under his breath:

"Daws love another's prattle."

The road, winding along the contour of the range, dipped into a valley and then slowly climbed Mount Ceceri to the quarry. As they rounded the bend of Maiano, Michelangelo saw the gorge in the mountain with its alternating blue and gray *serena* and iron-stained streaks. The *pietra serena* had been buried in horizontal layers. From this quarry Brunelleschi had chosen the stones for his exquisite churches of San Lorenzo and Santo Spirito. High on the cliff several men were outlining a block to be quarried with a *scribbus,* a point driven against the grain to loosen the hold from the main mass. He could see the point marks in successive layers through the stone formation, layers of stone peeled off as though stripped from a pile of parchment sheets.

The level work area where the strata fell after they were loosed was shimmering with heat and dust from the cutting, splitting, shaping: by men wet with perspiration, small, lean, sinewy men who worked the rock from dawn to dark without fatigue and who could cut as straight a line with hammer and chisel as a draftsman with pen and ruler: as concentrated in their hardness and durability as the rock itself. He had known these men since he was six and began riding behind the white oxen with Topolino. They greeted him, asked how things went: a primordial people, spending their lives with the simplest and most rudimentary force on earth: stone of the mountain, thrown up on the third day of Genesis.

Topolino inspected the newly quarried stone with the running commentary Michelangelo knew so well:

"That one has knots. Too much iron in this. Shale; it'll crumble into crystals like sugar on a bun. This one will be hollow."

Until finally, climbing over the rocks and making his way toward the cliff, he let out his breath sharply:

"Ah! Here is a beautiful piece of meat."

There is a way of making stone lift itself by distributing the tension. Michelangelo had been shown how to handle the density of the material without pulling his arms out of their sockets. He planted his legs wide, swung his weight from the hips; Topolino opened the first crack between the stone and the ground with an iron bar. They moved the stone over the boulders to open ground, then with the help of the quarrymen the block was fulcrumed upward through the open tail of the cart.

Michelangelo wiped the sweat from his face with his shirt. Rain clouds swept down the Arno from the mountains to the north. He bade Topolino good-by.

"A domani," replied Topolino, flicking the lines for the oxen to move off.

Until tomorrow, Michelangelo thought, tomorrow being the next time I take my place with the family, be it a week or a year.

He left the quarry, stood on the hill below Fiesole. Warm rain fell on his upturned face. The dark clumps of leaves on the olives were silver green. In the wheat the peasant women were cutting with colored kerchiefs over their hair. Below him Florence looked as though someone were sprinkling it with gray powdered dust, blotting out the carpet of red tile roofs. Only the mammal dome of the cathedral stood out, and the straight proud upward thrust of the tower of the Signoria, complementary symbols under which Florence flourished and multiplied.

He made his way down the mountain, feeling fifteen feet tall.

11

Having taken a day off without permission, Michelangelo was at the studio early. Ghirlandaio had been there all night, drawing by candlelight. He was unshaven, his blue beard and hollow cheeks in the flickering light giving him the appearance of an anchorite.

Michelangelo went to the side of the platform on which the desk stood majestically in command of its *bottega*, waited for Ghirlandaio to look up, then asked:

"Is something wrong?"

Ghirlandaio rose, raised his hands wearily to breast height, then shook his fingers up and down loosely, as though trying to shed his troubles. The boy stepped onto the platform and stood gazing down at the dozens of incomplete sketches of the Christ whom John was to baptize. The figures were slight to the point of delicacy.

"I'm intimidated because of the subject," Ghirlandaio growled to himself. "I've been afraid to use a recognizable Florentine . . ."

He picked up a pen and flicked it swiftly over a sheet. What emerged was an irresolute figure, dwarfed by the bold John whom Ghirlandaio had already completed, and who was waiting, bowl of water in hand. He flung down the pen in disgust, muttered that he was going home for some sleep. Michelangelo went into the cool back yard and began sketching in the clear light that broke open Florence's summer days.

For a week he drew experimentally. Then he took a fresh paper and set down a figure with powerful shoulders, muscularly developed chest, broad hips, a full oval stomach, and a robust pair of thighs rooted firmly in big solid feet: a man who could split a block of *pietra serena* with one blow of the hammer.

Ghirlandaio was shocked when Michelangelo showed him his Christ.

"You used a model?"

"The stonemason in Settignano who helped raise me."

"Christ a stonemason!"

"He was a carpenter."

"Florence won't accept a working-class Christ, Michelangelo. They're used to having him genteel."

Michelangelo suppressed a tiny smile.

"When I was first apprenticed you said, 'The true eternal painting is mosaic,' and sent me up to San Miniato to see the Christ Baldovinetti restored from the tenth century. That Christ is no wool merchant from Prato."

"It's a matter of crudity, not strength," replied Ghirlandaio, "easy for the young to confuse. I will tell you a story. When Donatello was very young he once spent a lot of time making a wooden crucifix for Santa Croce, and when it was finished he took it to his friend Brunelleschi. 'It seems to me,' said Brunelleschi, 'that you have put a plowman on the cross, rather than the body of Jesus Christ, which was most delicate in all its parts.' Donatello, upset at the unexpected criticism from the older man, cried, 'If it were as easy to make this figure as to judge it . . . Try to make one yourself!'

"That very day Brunelleschi set to work. Then he invited Donatello to dinner, but first the two friends bought some eggs and fresh cheese. When Donatello saw the crucifix in Brunelleschi's hall he was so amazed that he threw up his arms in resignation, the eggs and the cheese that he had been holding in his apron falling to the floor. Brunelleschi said laughingly:

" 'What are we to have for dinner, Donato, now that you have broken the eggs?'

"Donatello, who could not take his eyes off the beautiful Christ, answered 'It is your work to make Christs, and mine to make plowmen.' "

Michelangelo knew both crucifixes, the one of Brunelleschi being in Santa Maria Novella. Stumblingly he explained that he preferred Donatello's plowman to Brunelleschi's ethereal Christ, which was so slight that it looked as though it had been created to be crucified. With Donatello's figure the crucifixion had come as a horrifying surprise, even as it had to Mary and the others at the foot of the cross. He suggested that perhaps Christ's spirituality did not depend on his bodily delicacy but rather on the indestructibility of his message.

Abstract theology held no interest for Ghirlandaio. He turned back to his work, the automatic gesture of dismissal for an apprentice. Michelangelo went into the yard and sat in the baking sun with his chin resting on his chest. He had made a nuisance of himself.

A few days later the studio was buzzing. Ghirlandaio had completed his Christ and was blowing it up to full size with color for the cartoon. When Michelangelo was permitted to see the finished figure he stood stunned: it was his Christ! The legs twisted in an angular position, a little knock-kneed; the chest, shoulders and arms those of a man who had carried logs and built houses; with a rounded, protruding stomach that had absorbed its quantity of food: in its power and reality far outdistancing any of the still-life set figures that Ghirlandaio had as yet painted for the Tornabuoni choir.

If Michelangelo expected Ghirlandaio to acknowledge him, he was disappointed. Ghirlandaio apparently had forgotten the discussion and the boy's drawing.

The following week the studio moved *en masse* to Santa Maria Novella to start the Death of the Virgin in the crescent-shaped lunette topping the left side of the choir. Granacci was pleased because Ghirlandaio had given him a number of the apostles to paint, and he climbed the scaffolding singing a tune about how passionately he loved his sweetheart, Florence, the object of all Florentines' romantic ballads. Up the scaffold went Mainardi to do the figure kneeling to the left of the recumbent Mary, and David on the extreme right, doing his favorite subject, a Tuscan road winding up a mountainside to a white villa.

Santa Maria Novella was empty at this early hour except for a few old women in their black shawls praying before the Madonnas. The canvas screen had been taken down to let fresh air into the choir. Michelangelo stood irresolutely beneath the scaffolding, unnoticed, then began to walk the long center nave toward the bright sunlight. He turned to take a final look at the scaffolding rising tier upon tier in front of the stained-glass windows, dark now in the slight western light; at the glowing colors of the several completed panels; the Ghirlandaio artists, tiny figures weaving across the lunette; at the wooden stalls at the base of the choir covered with canvas, the sacks of plaster and sand, the plank table of painting materials, all bathed in a soft glow.

At the center of the church were a few wooden benches. He pulled one in place, took drawing paper and charcoal out of his shirt and began drawing the scene before him.

He was surprised to see shadows climbing down the scaffolding.

"It's time for dinner," announced Granacci. "Funny how painting spiritual subjects can give a man a carnal appetite."

Michelangelo commented: "Today is Friday and you'll have fish instead of *bistecca*. Go along with you, I'm not hungry."

The empty church gave him the chance to draw the architecture of the choir. Long before he would have imagined it his comrades were climbing back up the scaffolding. The sun arched to the west and filled the choir with rich color. He felt someone staring holes through him from behind, turned to find Ghirlandaio standing there. Michelangelo remained silent.

Ghirlandaio whispered hoarsely, "I can't believe that a boy of such tender years can have received such a gift. There are some things you know more about than I do, and I have been working for over thirty years! Come to the studio early tomorrow. Perhaps we can make things more interesting for you from now on."

Michelangelo walked home, his face suffused with ecstasy. Granacci teased:

"You look like a beatified Fra Angelico saint floating above the paving stones."

Michelangelo looked at his friend mischievously.

"With wings?"

"No one could call you a saint, not with your crusty disposition. But all honest effort to re-create that which God created originally . . ."

". . . is a form of worship?"

"Has in it a love of God's universe. Else why would the artist bother?"

"I have always loved God," replied Michelangelo simply.

The next morning he waited impatiently for the first gray ash to sift into the narrow strip of sky over the Via dei Bentaccordi. In the Via Larga the country people were dozing in their carts as the donkeys and oxen clop-clopped over the stones with their produce for the Old Market. He saw Giotto's Campanile standing pink and white in the first streaked dawn. Even in his eager rush through the streets he had time to marvel at the dome which Brunelleschi had had the genius to build after the vast space had stood open to the skies and the elements for more than a hundred years, because no one knew how to close it without the use of traverse beams.

Ghirlandaio was at his table when Michelangelo arrived.

"Sleep is the greatest of all bores. Draw up a stool."

The boy sat before Ghirlandaio, who pulled aside the curtain behind him so that the north light fell on them.

"Turn your head. A little more. I'm going to sketch you as young John leaving the city to go to the desert. I hadn't found a satisfactory model until I saw you working in Santa Maria Novella yesterday. . . ."

Michelangelo swallowed hard. After his sleepless night's dream of originating whole cartoons with which to fill the still empty panels . . . !

12

Ghirlandaio had not meant to deceive his apprentice. He summoned Michelangelo, showed him the over-all plan for the Death of the Virgin, added casually:

"I want you to collaborate with Granacci in this scene of the apostles. Then we'll let you try your hand at the figures on the left, together with the little angel beside them."

Granacci had not a jealous bone in him. Together they sketched the apostles, the one bald-headed, the other supporting the weeping John.

"Tomorrow morning after mass," said Granacci, "let's come back to the studio and I'll start you at bedrock."

Granacci had been speaking literally: he put Michelangelo to work on the rock wall at the back of the studio yard.

"Your wall has to be sound; if it crumbles your fresco goes with it. Check for saltpeter; the slightest patch and your paint will be eaten up. Avoid the sand that has been taken from too near the sea. Your lime should be old. I'll show you how to use a trowel to get a full smooth surface. Remember, plaster has to be beaten with the least possible amount of water, to the consistency of butter."

Michelangelo did as he had been instructed, but complained:

"Granacci, I want to draw with a pen, not a trowel!"

Granacci replied sharply:

"An artist has to be master of the grubbiest detail of his craft. If you don't know how to do the job how can you expect a plasterer to get you a perfect surface?"

"You're right. I'll beat it some more."

When the mixture was right Granacci handed Michelangelo a square board to be held in one hand, and a flexible five-inch trowel with which to apply the plaster. Michelangelo soon had the feel of it. When the plaster had dried sufficiently Granacci held an old studio cartoon against the wall while Michelangelo pierced holes with a needle to outline several figures, then with Granacci still holding took up the little bag of charcoal to fill the holes, Granacci removed the cartoon, the boy drew a connecting outline with red ochre and, when this had dried, dusted off the charcoal with a feather.

Mainardi came into the studio, saw what was going on and forcibly turned Michelangelo to him.

"You must remember that fresh plaster changes its consistency. In the morning you have to keep your colors liquid so that you don't choke up its pores. Toward sundown they have to be kept liquid because the plaster will absorb less. The best time for painting is the middle of the day. But before you can apply colors you have to learn how to grind them. You know there are only seven natural colors. Let's start with black."

The colors came from the apothecary in walnut-sized pieces of pigment. A piece of porphyry stone was used as a base, a porphyry pestle to grind with. Though the minimum grinding time was a half hour, no paint was allowed on a Ghirlandaio panel that had been ground hard for less than two hours.

"My father was right," commented Michelangelo, his hands and arms blackened with the pigment: "to be an artist is first to be a manual laborer."

Ghirlandaio had entered the studio.

"Hold on there," he exclaimed. "Michelangelo, if you want a real mineral black, use this black chalk; if you want a slag black you'll need to mix in a little mineral green, about this much on your knife." Warming to the situation, he threw off his cape. "For the flesh colors you have to mix two parts of the finest sinopia with one part white well-slaked lime. Let me show you the proportions."

David appeared in the open door, one hand clutching a sheaf of bills, under his other arm an account book.

"What's the good of teaching him about colors," he exclaimed, "if he doesn't know how to make his own brushes? Good ones are not always available. Look here, Michelangelo, these hog bristles are taken from white pigs; but be sure they're domestic. Use a pound of bristles to a brush. Bind them to a large stick like this . . ."

Michelangelo threw his stained arms ceilingward in mock despair.

"Help! You're crowding my whole three years of apprenticeship into one Sunday morning!"

When Granacci's fresco was ready Michelangelo went up onto the scaffold to serve as his assistant. Ghirlandaio had not yet given him permission to handle a brush, but he worked for a week applying the intonaco and mixing colors.

It was autumn by the time he completed his own drawings for the Death of the Virgin and was ready to create his first fresco. The early October air was crisp and lucid. The crops were in, the wine pressed, the olive oil secure in big jars; the *contadini* were cutting back the trees and hauling home the branches for winter warmth, the fields were lying fallow as the foliage turned a russet brown to match the warm tan stones of the crenelated Signoria tower.

The two friends climbed the scaffolding loaded with buckets of plaster, water, brushes, mixing spoons, the cartoon and colored sketches. Michelangelo laid a modest area of intonaco, then fixed the cartoon of the white-haired and bearded near saint with the enormous eyes onto the wall. He used the charcoal bag, the red ochre connecting line, the feather duster. Then he mixed his paints for the *verdaccio*, which he applied with a soft brush to get a thin base. He picked up a finely pointed brush and with terra verde sketched the outstanding features: the powerful Roman nose, the deep-set eyes, the shoulder-long waving white hair and mustache flowing gracefully into the full-face beard. Freehand, glancing only once at his sketch, he put in the old man's neck, shoulder and arm.

Now ready to apply paint in earnest, he turned to Granacci with big eyes.

"I can't be of any more help to you, *Michelagnolo mio*," responded Granacci; "the rest is between you and God. *Buona fortuna*. Good luck."

With which he scrambled down the scaffolding.

Michelangelo found himself alone at the top of the choir, alone on his perch above the church and the world. For a moment he suffered vertigo. How different the church looked from up here; so vastly hollow and empty. In his nostrils was the dampness of the fresh plaster and the pungence of paint. His hand clamped the brush. He squeezed it between the fingers and thumb of his left hand, remembered that in the early morning he would have to keep his colors liquid, took a little terra verde and began to shade all those parts of the face that would be darkest: under the chin, the nose, the lips, the corners of the mouth and the eyebrows.

Only once did he go to the master of the studio for help.

"How do I mix the exact shade I had yesterday?"

"By the weight on your knife of the amount you cut off the pigment cake. The hand can judge more accurately than the eye."

For a week he worked alone. The studio stood by to assist if called, but no one intruded. This was his baptism.

By the third day everyone knew he was not following the rules. He was drawing anatomical nude bodies of male figures, using for models two men he had sketched unloading in the Old Market, then draping them with robes, the reverse of the practice of suggesting a man's bones by the folds of a cloak.

Ghirlandaio made no effort to stop or correct him, contenting himself with a sotto voce:

". . . I'll draw them the way God made Adam."

Michelangelo had never seen an angel, and so he did not know how to draw one. Even more perplexing was what to do about the wings, for no one could tell him whether they were made of flesh or some diaphanous material out of the Wool or Silk Guild. Nor could anyone give him any information about the halo: was it solid, like a metal, or atmospheric like a rainbow?

The youngsters ragged him mercilessly.

"You're a fake," cried Cieco. "Those are no wings at all."

"And a fraud," added Baldinelli. "They fade into the robe so no one can see them."

"That halo could be taken for an accidental marking on the wall," contributed Tedesco. "What's the matter, aren't you a Christian?"

"Haven't you any faith?"

Michelangelo grinned in sickly fashion.

"My angel is the carpenter's son downstairs of us. I asked his father to carve a pair of wings for him . . ."

His two figures were a distinct picture by themselves, located in the bottom corner of the lunette under a cone-shaped mountain crowned by a castle. The rest of the lunette was crowded with more than twenty figures surrounding the Virgin's high-pillowed bier, the saints' and apostles' apocryphal faces set at slightly different angles of anguish. It was even difficult to find Mary.

When Michelangelo came down from the scaffold the last time, Jacopo passed David's little black hat and everybody contributed a few scudi to buy wine. Jacopo raised the first toast:

"To our new comrade . . . who will soon be apprenticed to Rosselli."

Michelangelo was hurt.

"Why do you say that?"

"Because you've stolen the lunette."

Michelangelo never had liked wine, but this cup of Chianti seemed particularly galling.

"Shut up with you now, Jacopo. I want no trouble."

Late that afternoon Ghirlandaio called him aside. He had said no word to Michelangelo about his fresco, either of praise or criticism; it was as though he had never mounted the scaffold at all. He looked up from his desk, his eyes dark.

"They are saying I am jealous. It is true. Oh, not of those two figures, they're immature and crude. If they stand out, it's not because they are better drawn but because they don't fit into our studio style. My six-year-old Ridolfo comes closer to copying the *bottega* method than you do. But let there be no mistake, I am jealous of what will ultimately be your ability to draw."

Michelangelo suffered a rare moment of humility.

"Now what am I going to do with you? Release you to Rosselli? Assuredly not! There is plenty of work ahead in these remaining panels. Prepare the cartoon for the figures of the assistants on the right. And try not to make them stand out like bandaged toes."

Michelangelo returned to the studio late that night, took his copies of Ghirlandaio's drawings out of the desk and put back the originals. The next morning Ghirlandaio murmured as Michelangelo went by:

"Thank you for returning my drawings, I hope they have been helpful."

13

The valley of the Arno had the worst winter weather in Italy. The skies overhead were leaden, the cold had a creeping quality that permeated stone and wool and bit at the flesh within. After the cold came the rain and the cobbled streets were running rivers. Anything not cobbled was a bog of mud. The only bright spot was the arrival of Isabella d'Aragona on her way north to marry the Duke of Milan, with her large train of ladies and gentlemen sumptuously gowned by her father, the Duke of Calabria.

Ghirlandaio's studio had but one fireplace. Here the men sat at a semicircular table facing the flames, crowded together for warmth, their backs cold but their fingers getting enough heat to enable them to work. Santa Maria Novella was even worse. The choir was as icy as an underground cave. Drafts that blew through the church rattled the planks and leather thongs of the scaffolding. It was like trying to paint in a high wind, with one's nostrils breathing ice water.

But if the winter was intense, it was brief. By March the *tramontana* had stopped blowing, the sun's rays had a little warmth in them again, and the skies were powdered with a touch of blue. On the second of these days Granacci burst into the studio, his usually placid eyes blinking hard. Michelangelo had rarely seen his friend so keyed up.

"Come with me. I have something to show you."

Granacci secured David's permission and in a moment the two boys were in the street. Granacci guided Michelangelo across town toward the Piazza San Marco. They paused a moment as a procession passed carrying relics of San Girolamo, a jaw and an armbone richly bound in silver and gold, from the altar of Santa Maria del Fiore. On the Via Larga, opposite one side of the church, was a gate.

"We go in here."

He pushed the gate open. Michelangelo entered, stood confounded.

It was an enormous oblong garden, with a small building, or casino, in the center; in front, and directly at the end of a straight path, was a pool, a fountain, and on a pedestal a marble statue of a boy removing a thorn from his foot. On the wide porch of the casino a group of young men were working at tables.

All four walls of the garden were open loggias displaying antique marble busts: of the Emperor Hadrian, of Scipio, the Emperor Augustus, Agrippina, Nero's mother, and numerous sleeping cupids. There was a straight path leading to the casino, lined with cypresses. Coming from each corner of the quadrangle and centering on the casino were other tree-lined paths curving through green lawns as big as meadows.

Michelangelo could not take his eyes from the loggia of the casino where two young men were working over a piece of stone, measuring and marking, while several others were carving with toothed chisels.

He turned to Granacci, stuttered:

"Who . . . what . . . is this?"

"A sculpture garden."

"But . . . what for?"

"A school."

". . . school?"

"To train sculptors."

His knees sagged.

"What sculptors . . . ?"

"This garden belonged to Clarice de' Medici. Lorenzo bought it for her, to be her home in case of his death. Clarice died last July, and Lorenzo has started a school for sculptors. He has brought in Bertoldo to teach."

"But Bertoldo is dead!"

"No, he was only dying. Lorenzo had him carried here on a litter from Santo Spirito hospital, showed him the garden, and told Bertoldo he must restore Florence to its days of greatness in sculpture. Bertoldo got off the litter and promised Lorenzo that the era of Ghiberti and Donatello would be re-created."

Michelangelo's eyes devoured the garden, moving around the long loggias, consuming statues, Grecian urns, vases, the bust of Plato beside the gate.

"That's Bertoldo now on the porch," said Granacci. "I met him once. Shall I present you?"

Michelangelo shook his head up and down savagely.

They walked down the gravel path, circled the pool and fountain. Half a dozen men from fifteen to thirty years old were working at board tables. Bertoldo, a figure so slight as to seem all spirit and no body, had his long white hair wrapped in a turban. His red cheeks glowed as he instructed two boys in roughing a piece of marble.

"Maestro Bertoldo, may I present my friend Michelangelo."

Bertoldo looked up. He had light blue eyes and a soft voice that strangely carried over the blows of the hammer. He looked at Michelangelo.

"Who is your father?"

"Lodovico di Lionardo Buonarroti-Simoni."

"I have heard the name. Do you work stone?"

Michelangelo's brain stood numb. Someone called to Bertoldo. He excused himself and went to the other end of the loggia. Granacci took Michelangelo's hand and led him through the rooms of the casino, one displaying Lorenzo's collection of cameos, coins and medals, another examples from all the artists who had worked for the Medici family: Ghiberti, who won Lorenzo de' Medici's great-grandfather's contest for the Baptistery doors; Donatello, who was Cosimo de' Medici's protégé; Benozzo Gozzoli, who had frescoed the chapel in their palace with portraits of the Medici in his Journey of the Wise men to Bethlehem. Here were Brunelleschi's models for the Duomo, Fra Angelico's drawings of saints for San Marco, Masaccio's sketches for the church of the Carmine, a trove that staggered the boy.

Granacci again took him by the hand, led him down the path to the gate and out into the Via Larga. Michelangelo sat on a bench in the Piazza San Marco with pigeons thronging about his feet and the heel of his palm pressing his forehead bruisingly. When he looked up at Granacci his eyes were feverish.

"Who are the apprentices? How did they get in?"

"Lorenzo and Bertoldo chose them."

Michelangelo groaned.

"And I have more than two years left at Ghirlandaio's. *Mamma mia,* I have destroyed myself!"

"*Pazienza!*" consoled Granacci. "You are not an old man yet. When you've completed your apprenticeship . . ."

"Patience!" exploded Michelangelo. "Granacci, I've got to get in! Now! I don't want to be a painter, I want to be a marble carver. Now! How can I get admitted?"

"You have to be invited."

"How do I get invited?"

"I don't know."

"Then who does? Someone must!"

"Stop pushing. You'll shove me clear off this bench."

Michelangelo quieted. Tears of frustration came to his eyes.

"Oh, Granacci, have you ever wanted anything so hard you couldn't bear it?"
". . . no. Everything has always been there."
"How fortunate you are."
Granacci gazed at the naked longing on his friend's face.
"Perhaps."

BOOK TWO

THE SCULPTURE GARDEN

He was drawn to the garden on the Piazza San Marco as though the ancient stone statues had magnets buried within them. Sometimes he did not know that his feet were carrying him there. He would find himself inside the gate, lurking in the shadow of the loggia. He did not speak to anyone, did not venture down the path through the meadow to the casino where Bertoldo and the apprentices were working. He just stood motionless, a hunger in his eyes.

Thrashing deep into the night, as his brothers lay sleeping around him, he thought, "There must be some way. Lorenzo de' Medici's sister Nannina is married to Bernardo Rucellai. If I went to him, told him I was Francesca's son, asked him to speak to *Il Magnifico* for me . . ."

But a Buonarroti could not go to a Rucellai, hat in hand.

Ghirlandaio was patient.

"We must finish the Baptism panel in a matter of weeks and pull our scaffolding down to the lower panel, Zacharias Writing the Name of His Son. Time is growing short now. Suppose you start drawing instead of running the streets?"

"May I bring in a model for the neophyte? I saw one in the Old Market, unloading his cart."

"Agreed."

The boy sketched his roughhewn young *contadino* just in from the fields, naked except for his *brache,* kneeling to take off his clodhoppers; the flesh tones a sunburned amber, the figure clumsy, with graceless bumpkin muscles; but the face transfused with light as the young lad gazed up at John. Behind him he did two white-bearded assistants to John, with beauty in their faces and a rugged power in their figures.

Granacci hovered over him uneasily as the figures emerged.

"Ghirlandaio is incapable of drawing such figures."

"Bandaged toes, eh?"

Ghirlandaio was too swamped in designing the remaining half dozen panels to interfere. This time when Michelangelo mounted the scaffold he no longer felt timorous before the wet plaster. He experimented with flesh tones from his paint pots, enjoyed this culminating physical effort of bringing his figures to life, clothing

511

them in warm-colored lemon-yellow and rose robes. Yet always at the back of his mind he was crying:

"Two whole years? How will I endure it?"

Ghirlandaio was working him hard.

"We'll move you over to the other side of the choir now for the Adoration of the Magi. Prepare the cartoon for the last two standing figures here on the right."

The Adoration cartoon was already so crowded with figures that he derived little pleasure from adding two more. Returning from dinner, Granacci announced to the apprentices' table:

"It's just a year ago today that Michelangelo started. I've ordered a *damigiana* of wine brought in at sundown; we'll have a celebration."

Silence greeted him; the studio was crackling with tension. At the center table the apprentices had their heads down over their work. Ghirlandaio was sitting at his desk as rigid as one of his master's mosaics, his scowl blacker than the base of his beard.

"*Il Magnifico* has summoned me and asked if I would like to send my two best apprentices to his new Medici school," he declared.

Michelangelo stood riveted to the planks of the studio floor.

"No, I would not like to send my two best apprentices," cried Ghirlandaio, "To have my *bottega* raided. And certainly not on the day that Benedetto is invited to Paris to paint for the King of France. I have half a dozen panels to complete!" He glared down at the assemblage. "But who dares say 'No' to *Il Magnifico*? You, Buonarroti. You would like to go?"

"I have been hanging around that garden like a starved dog in front of a butcher stall," pleaded Michelangelo.

"*Basta!* Enough!" It was the angriest Michelangelo had ever seen him. "Granacci, you and Buonarroti are released from your apprenticeship. I'll sign the papers at the Guild this evening. Now back to work, all of you! Do you think I am Ghirlandaio *Il Magnifico*, with millions to support an academy?"

Joy drenched Michelangelo to the skin like a *tramontana* rain. Granacci stood glum.

"Granacci, *caro mio*, what is it?"

"I like paint. I can't work with stone. It's too hard."

"No, no, my friend, you will be a fine sculptor. I will help you. Just wait and see."

Granacci achieved a wistful smile.

"Oh, I will come with you, Michelangelo. But whatever will I do with a hammer and chisel? I'll cut myself off at the knees!"

Michelangelo could not concentrate. After a little time he left the big table and went to Ghirlandaio's desk. He wanted to thank the man who only a year ago had taken him in; but he stood below the desk, stars in his eyes and silence in his mouth: how do you express gratitude to a man for letting you abandon him?

Ghirlandaio saw the conflict on the boy's face. When he spoke, it was softly, so no one else might hear.

"You were right, Buonarroti: fresco is not your trade. That neophyte you did for me looks as though it were carved out of rock. You have talent as a draftsman; with years of training perhaps you can transfer it to stone. But never forget that Domenico Ghirlandaio was your first master."

In front of the Buonarroti house that evening Michelangelo muttered to Granacci:

"You'd better come in with me. With two of us in the same sack he's not so likely to drop it off the Ponte Vecchio."

They climbed the main stairway to avoid the kitchen and Michelangelo's stepmother, went quietly into the family room where his father sat hunched over the angular corner desk, dwarfed by the fourteen-foot ceiling. The room was cold; it took the Florentine sun the better part of spring to permeate the stone.

"Father, there is news. I am leaving Ghirlandaio's."

"Ah, splendid! I knew you would come to your senses. You will join the Wool Guild . . ."

"I'm leaving to become a student at the Medici sculpture garden."

Lodovico was caught between joy and befuddlement.

". . . Medici garden . . . what garden?"

"I'm going too, Messer Buonarroti," added Granacci; "we are to be apprenticed to Bertoldo, under the guidance of *Il Magnifico*."

"A stonecutter!" Lodovico threw anguished arms ceilingward.

"To be a sculptor, Father. Bertoldo is the last master left."

"One never knows the end of a piece of bad luck: it has more turns than a snake. If your mother hadn't been thrown from her horse you would not have been sent to the Topolinos to nurse; you would have known nothing of stonecutting."

Michelangelo did not risk an answer. Granacci spoke.

"Messer Buonarroti, a dozen other children might have been placed with the Topolinos and never got stone dust in their lungs. Your son has an affinity for sculpture."

"What is a sculptor? Lower than a painter. Not even a member of the Twelve Guilds. A laborer, like a woodchopper. Or an olive picker."

"With one big difference," Granacci persisted courteously; "the olives are pressed for oil, the wood is burned cooking soup. Both are consumed. Art has a magic quality: the more minds that digest it, the longer it lives."

"Poetry!" screamed Lodovico. "I'm talking hard common sense to save the life of my family, and you recite poetry."

Monna Alessandra, his grandmother, had come into the room.

"Tell your father what Lorenzo, *Il Magnifico,* is offering, Michelagnolo. He is the richest man in Italy, and known to be generous. How long is the apprenticeship? How large the wage?"

"I don't know. I didn't ask."

"You didn't ask!" sneered Lodovico. "Do you think we have the wealth of the Granacci, that we can support you in your follies?"

A flush mottled Francesco Granacci's blond cheeks. He spoke with unaccustomed bluntness.

"I asked. Nothing is promised. No contract. No pay. Just free instruction."

Michelangelo shifted his legs and torso to receive Lodovico's culminating burst of rage. Instead Lodovico collapsed onto a hard leather chair with a heavy plop, tears coming to his eyes. Detachedly Michelangelo thought:

"It's funny about us Florentines: not one drop of our blood is salted with sentiment, yet we cry so easily." He went to his father's side, put a hand on his shoulder. "Father, give me a chance. Lorenzo de' Medici wants to create a new generation of sculptors for Florence. I want to become one of them."

Lodovico looked up at his most promising son.

"Lorenzo has asked specifically for you? Because he thinks you have talent?"

The boy thought how much easier it would be for everyone if he could tell a few simple lies.

"Lorenzo asked Ghirlandaio for his two best apprentices. Granacci and I were chosen."

His stepmother had been listening at the kitchen door. She came into the room. Her face was pale, the dark side hairs standing out in stark relief. To Michelangelo she said:

"I have nothing against you, Michelangelo. You are a good boy. You eat well." She turned to Lodovico. "But I must speak for my people. My father thought it would be an honor for us to be connected with the Buonarroti. What do I have left if you let this boy destroy our position?"

Lodovico gripped the sides of his chair. He looked weary. "I will never give my consent."

Then he walked out of the room, taking his wife and mother with him. In the lacerated silence Granacci said:

"He's only trying to do his duty by you. How can he conceive that a fourteen-year-old's judgment is better than his? It's asking too much."

"Should I lose my opportunity?" flared Michelangelo angrily.

"No. But remember he's doing the best he can, with a bullheaded son forcing him into a situation which he has not, forgive me, the intellect to understand."

Michelangelo blinked in silence.

"You love your father, don't you, Granacci?"

"Yes."

"I envy you."

"Then you should be kind to your father."

"Kind?"

"Yes, since you have no intention of being hurt by him."

2

The Medici sculpture garden was unlike Ghirlandaio's *bottega;* it did not have to earn its living. Domenico Ghirlandaio was always rushed, not only to earn money for a large family but because he signed so many contracts with completion dates.

Nothing could be further from pressure than the atmosphere into which Michelangelo stepped on the warm April day when he began his apprenticeship to Lorenzo the Magnificent and Bertoldo. The feel of the garden was:

"Take your time. Don't make haste. We have only one mission here: to learn. We have nothing to sell but training, nothing to push to completion but your own skill and artistry. You have only to grow. *Calma!* Prepare yourself for a lifetime of sculpturing."

The first person to greet him was Pietro Torrigiani, a powerfully built blond green-eyed beauty. He said with a flashing white-toothed smile:

"So you're the lurker. The Ghost of the Garden. You haunted these porticoes."

"I didn't think you noticed me."

"Noticed!" replied Torrigiani. "We were devoured by your eyes."

Bertoldo loved only two things as well as sculpture: laughter and cooking. His humor had in it more spice than his chicken *alla cacciatora*. He had written a cookbook, and his one complaint at having moved into the Medici palace was that he had no chance to celebrate his recipes.

But sculpture he could and did celebrate: for this frail person with the snow-white hair, red-cheeked face and pale blue eyes was the inheritor of all the communicable knowledge of the Golden Age of Tuscan sculpture.

He linked his thin arms through those of the new apprentices.

"True, not all skill is communicable," he explained. "Donatello made me his heir, but he could never make me his peer. He poured his experience and craftsmanship into me the way molten bronze is poured into a cast. No man can do more. Without Donato, I would have been a maker of gold jewelry; after more than half a century with him, I remained only a miniaturist. Try as he would he couldn't put his finger on my fist, nor his passion in my bowels. We all are as God made us. I will show you everything Ghiberti taught Donatello, and Donatello taught me; how much you absorb depends on your capacity. A teacher is like a cook; give him a stringy chicken or a tough piece of veal, and not even his most delicious sauce can make it tender."

Michelangelo laughed out loud. Bertoldo, pleased with his own humor, turned them toward the casino.

"And now to work. If you have any talent, it will come out."

Michelangelo thought, "Just let them put a hammer and *subbia* in my hands and they will see the chips fly!"

Bertoldo had no intention of putting these tools into the hands of a beginner. He assigned Michelangelo a drawing desk on the portico between seventeen-year-old Torrigiani and twenty-nine-year-old Andrea Sansovino, who had been apprenticed to Antonio Pollaiuolo and whose commissioned work was to be seen in Santo Spirito.

Supplying him with materials from the inner rooms, Bertoldo said:

"Drawing is a different medium for the sculptor. A man and a block of stone are three-dimensional, which immediately gives them more in common than a man and a wall or a panel of wood to be painted."

Michelangelo found the apprentices in the garden akin to those at Ghirlandaio's. Sansovino was the counterpart of Mainardi: already a professional artist who had earned his living for years at terra cotta; with Mainardi's sweet disposition, giving generously of his time and patience to the beginners. At the other end of the scale was Soggi, a fourteen-year-old like Cieco, who had stumbled into sculpture and to Michelangelo's rigorous eye was totally without talent.

And there was the inevitable Jacopo, in this case twenty-year-old Baccio da Montelupo, as thoughtless as a wren and, like Jacopo, an amoral, carnal Tuscan who scavenged each night's scandal for the morning's tall tale. On Michelangelo's first morning of work Baccio burst in late with the day's most exciting news: a monster had been born in Venice, with one eye behind each ear; in neighboring Padua another monster had been born with two heads, and two hands for each arm. The next morning he told of the Florentine who consorted with bad females "so as to save as much as possible his wife's virtue."

He was particularly good with *contadini* humor; he told of the patrician Florentine lady, elaborately gowned in silk and pearls, who asked a peasant coming out of Santo Spirito: "Is the mass for the *villani,* ill bred, over?" "Yes, madam," replied the peasant, "and the mass for the *puttane,* whores, is about to begin, so hurry!"

Bertoldo clapped his hands in delight.

The counterpart of Granacci was Rustici, fifteen-year-old son of a wealthy Tuscan nobleman, who worked for his own pleasure and the honor of creating art. Lorenzo had wanted Rustici to live in the Medici palace, but the young man preferred to stay by himself in rooms in the Via de' Martelli. Michelangelo had been at the garden only a week when Rustici invited him to dinner.

"Like Bertoldo, I enjoy the homely details of cooking. I'll put a goose in the oven to bake in the morning."

Michelangelo found Rustici, rustic, living up to his name, for the apartment was filled with animals: three dogs, an eagle chained to a perch, a mynah bird trained by the *contadini* of his father's estate who kept screeching: *"Va' all' inferno!* Go to hell!" Even more distracting was the porcupine Rustici had trained to be a pet, who moved restlessly under the dinner table pricking Michelangelo's legs with his quills.

After dinner they entered a quiet room with family paintings on the walls. Against this aristocratic background, the rustic became the cultured young man.

"You can draw, Michelangelo. From this perhaps you will evolve into a sculptor. Then let me warn you: do not go to live in the luxuriousness of the palace."

Michelangelo gave a repudiatory snort.

"Little danger of that."

"Listen, my friend: it's pleasant to get used to the expensive, the soft, the comfortable. Once you're addicted, it's so easy to become a sycophant, to trim the sails of your judgment in order to be kept on. The next step is to change your work to please those in power, and that is death to the sculptor."

"I'm plain, Rustici."

The apprentice to whom he became closest was Torrigiani, who looked to Michelangelo more like a soldier than a sculptor. Torrigiani fascinated Michelangelo; he also terrified him when he knitted his brows and spoke in his deeply resonant voice. Torrigiani came from an ancient family of wine merchants, long since noble, and was the most audacious of the apprentices in handling Bertoldo. He could also be quarrelsome, having alienated several of his fellow apprentices. He gave Michelangelo a quick, warm friendship, talking to him constantly from the adjoining worktable. Michelangelo had never known anyone as handsome as Torrigiani; this kind of physical beauty, almost of human perfection, left him weak in the face of his own lack of fine features and smallness of stature.

Granacci watched the relationship with Torrigiani grow. To Michelangelo's question whether Granacci did not think Torrigiani magnificent, Granacci replied guardedly:

"I have known him all my life. Our families are associated."

"You haven't answered my question, Granacci."

"Before you make a friend, eat a peck of salt with him."

He had been in the garden for a week when Lorenzo de' Medici entered with a young girl. Michelangelo now saw close up for the first time the man who, without office or rank, ruled Florence and had made her a mighty republic, wealthy not only in trade but in art, literature, scholarship. Lorenzo de' Medici, forty years old, had a roughhewn face that appeared to have been carved out of dark mountain rock; it was an irregular countenance, not at all handsome, with muddy skin, a jutting jaw, lower lip which protruded beyond the upper, a turned-up nose, the up-tilting end of which bulked larger than the bony bridge; large dark eyes, cheeks showing dark hollows beyond the corners of the mouth; and a mass of dark hair parted in the center, then combed down to the middle of each eyebrow. He was dressed in a long sienna-colored robe, with purple sleeves, the tip of a white collar showing at the neck. He was just over medium height, with a sturdy physique which he kept in condition by days of hard riding, and hawking.

He was also a trained classical student, an omnivorous reader of Greek and Latin manuscripts, a poet whom the Plato Academy likened to Petrarch and Dante, the builder of Europe's first public library for which he had assembled ten thousand manuscripts and books, the largest collection since Alexandria. He was acknowledged to be "the greatest patron of literature and art that any prince has ever been," with a collection of sculptures, paintings, drawings, carved gems, open to all artists and students for study and inspiration. For the scholars who had gathered in Florence to make it the scholastic heart of Europe, he had provided villas on the slope of Fiesole, where Pico della Mirandola, Angelo Poliziano, Marsilio Ficino and Cristoforo Landino translated newly found Greek and Hebraic manuscripts, wrote poetry, philosophic and religious books, helped create what Lorenzo called "the revolution of humanism."

Michelangelo had heard the stories about Lorenzo, the single favorite topic of conversation in Florence: of how he had weak eyes, and had been born without a sense of smell. Now, as he listened to Lorenzo speaking to Bertoldo, he realized that the voice had a harsh, unpleasing quality.

Yet this would appear to be Lorenzo's only unpleasing quality, just as the weakness of his eyes was his only weakness, and the lack of a sense of smell the only lack with which he had been born. For Lorenzo, single richest man in the world, courted by rulers of the Italian city-states, as well as dynasties as powerful as Turkey and China, had an open, lovable nature and a total lack of arrogance. Ruler of the Republic, in the same sense that the *gonfalonieri di giustizia* and the Signoria were governors of the law and ordinance of the city, he had no army, no guard, walked the streets of Florence unattended, speaking to all citizens as true equals, living a simple family life, romping on the floor with his children and holding open house to the artists, literary men and scholars of the world.

Therein lay his genius. He exercised absolute authority in matters of policy, yet governed Florence with such good judgment and inherent courtesy and dignity that people who might otherwise be enemies worked together harmoniously. Not even his able father, Piero, or his genius grandfather, Cosimo, called *Pater Patriae,* Father of his Country, by all Tuscany for creating a republic out of Florence's several hundred years of bloody civil war between the opposing factions of Guelphs and Ghibellines, had obtained such happy results. Florence could sack Lorenzo, *Il Magnifico,* and his palace, on an hour's notice and drive him out. He knew it, the people knew it, and this knowledge made Lorenzo's untitled governing work. For just as there was no arrogance in him, there was no cowardice: he had saved his father's life in a dashing military coup while only seventeen and had risked his own life by invading the camp of Ferrante in Naples with no more personal protection than he used on the streets of Florence, to save his city from invasion.

This was the man who stood just a few feet from Michelangelo, talking affectionately to Bertoldo about some antique sculptures that had just arrived from Asia Minor that day: for sculpture was as important to Lorenzo as his fleets of ships sailing the world's seas, his chains of banks throughout Europe and the Mediterranean, his millions of golden florins' worth of produce and trade each year in every commodity from Florence's wool, oil, wine to the exotic perfumes, flavorings and silks of the Orient. From some Lorenzo commanded respect because of his wealth, from others because of his power; but by the scholar and artist he was respected and loved for his passion for knowledge; for the freedom of the mind, imprisoned more than a thousand years in dark dank dungeons, which Lorenzo de' Medici had pledged himself to liberate.

Now Lorenzo stopped to chat with the apprentices. Michelangelo turned his gaze to the girl walking beside him. She was a slight thing, younger than himself, dressed in a long-sleeved gown of rose-colored wool, a *gamurra* with its full skirt falling in soft, loose pleats, and a tight-laced bodice under which she wore a pale yellow blouse with a high rounded neck. Her slippers were of brocaded yellow and on her thick dark hair was a rose satin cap encrusted in pearls. She was so pale that not even the rose-colored cap and gown could throw color into her thin cheeks.

As Lorenzo passed his table with an imperceptible nod, suddenly Michelangelo's eyes met those of the girl.

He stopped in his work. She stopped in her walk. He could not take his gaze from this slender, piquant-faced girl. She was startled by the ferocity of expression in his face from the pouring of his energies into the drawing before him. Color pulsated upward in her ivory cheeks.

Michelangelo felt this awakening between them in quickened breath. For a moment he thought she was going to speak to him, for she moistened her pale lips. Then with a quivering movement she removed her gaze and rejoined her father.

Lorenzo put his arm about the girl's tiny waist. They strolled past the fountain, made their way to the gate and out into the piazza.

Michelangelo turned to Torrigiani.

"Who was that?"

"The Magnificent One, you idiot."

"No, no, the girl."

". . . girl? Oh, Contessina. His daughter. Last one left in the palace."

"Contessina? *Little countess?*"

"Yes. Lorenzo used to call his other daughters 'Contessina' as a nickname. When this puny one was born he had her baptized Contessina. Why do you ask?"

"No reason."

3

Lodovico had never given his consent to Michelangelo's entering the garden. Although the family knew that he had left the Ghirlandaio studio, they were avoiding the descent into sculpture by declining to acknowledge it. They rarely saw him; he left at dawn when all were asleep, except his stepmother, already out marketing, came home promptly at twelve when Lucrezia brought in the roast or fowl, and worked at the garden until dark, loitering as long as possible on the way home so the family would be in bed and there would be only his brother Buonarroto lying awake to ask the news of the day, or his grandmother waiting in the kitchen to give him a light supper.

"You're outgrowing your shirts, Michelagnolo," Monna Alessandra said, "and your stockings are shabby. Your father feels that since you chose not to earn . . . but no matter. I've had this money put away. Buy yourself what you need."

He pecked at her leathery cheek; theirs was the abiding love in the family, and they knew only sketchily how to communicate it.

He was austere by nature, and had no desire for things.

"I'll be carving soon and covered from head to foot with stone dust. No one will notice the clothes."

She respected his pride, put the few coins back in a pouch.

"As you will. The money is here for you."

Granacci saw no need to rise so early each morning or to return so late at night; only at midday did the boys come and go together. Granacci was growing more depressed each day, his hunched-over shoulders seemed only an inch or two above Michelangelo's.

"It's that cold clammy clay," he complained. "I hate it. I try to model as badly as possible so Bertoldo won't tell me I'm ready for carving. I've tried *pietra dura,* hard stone, a dozen times and every blow of the hammer goes through me instead of the stone."

"But, Granacci, *carissimo,* marble has resonance," Michelangelo pleaded. "It's receptive. *Pietra dura* is like stale bread. Wait until you work marble, that's like sinking your fingers into fresh dough."

Granacci searched his friend's features, puzzled.

"You're so flinty about everything, but put marble in your mouth and you're a poet."

He found himself plunged into a cauldron of drawing. Almost the first sentence Bertoldo uttered to him was: "Here in the garden drawing is the *sine qua non;* when you arrive in the morning draw your left hand, then take off your shoes and draw your feet; it's good practice in foreshortening."

"How about drawing my right hand as well?"

"Another humorist in our midst," groaned Bertoldo with delight.

Even when he had worked the *pietra serena* for the Topolinos Michelangelo had shifted the hammer from right hand to left, feeling no difference in precision or balance. When he had drawn his left hand from a number of positions he shifted the pen and drew his right, first gazing at his palm, then turning it over with the fingers stretched rigidly outward.

Bertoldo came by, picked up the sheet with the half dozen drawings crowding each other on the paper.

"The hogshead gives the wine it contains," he murmured softly.

"I took no offense. My right and left, they are the same."

Live models were drawn from every quarter of Florence, provided through Lorenzo: scholars in black velvet; soldiers with bullnecks, square heads and thick arching eyebrows; swashbuckling toughs; *contadini* off their carts; bald-headed old men with hooked noses and nutcracker chins; monks in black cloaks, black caps with their flaps turned up over their gray hair; the gay blades of Florence, handsome, with Greek noses running straight from the brow, curly hair worn low on their necks, round empty eyes; the wool dyers with stained arms; the callused ironmongers; the burly porters; plump house servants; nobles in red and white silk hemmed with pearls; slender boys in violet; chubby children to serve as models for *putti*.

Michelangelo grumbled at Bertoldo's harsh criticism of a torso he had drawn:

"How can we draw only from the outside? All we see is what pushes against the skin. If we could follow the inside of a body: the bone, muscle . . . To know a man we must know his *budelli e sangue*, guts and blood. Never have I seen the inside of a man."

"*Dio fottuto!*" swore Bertoldo softly. "God is scuttled! Doctors are allowed to dissect one body on a special day of the year, in front of the City Council. Other than this it is the worst crime in Florence. Put it out of your mind."

"My mouth, yes; my mind, no. I'll never sculpture accurately until I can see how a human body works."

"Not even the Greeks dissected, and they were a pagan people without a Church to forbid. Nor did Donatello need to cut into a human body for his marvelous knowledge. Do you need to be better than Phidias and Donatello?"

"Better, no. Different, yes."

Michelangelo had never seen Bertoldo so agitated. He reached a hand to the old man's thin arm, patted it quietingly.

In spite of these daily shocks, they became friends. While the others were modeling in clay or carving stone, Bertoldo took the boy into the casino and stood over him for hours while Michelangelo copied Egyptian amulets, Greek medallions, Roman coins, holding each precious work of art in his hand while he explained what the ancient artist had tried to achieve.

To his surprise Michelangelo also acquired the devotion of Torrigiani, who now moved his workbench closer to Michelangelo's. Torrigiani had an overwhelming personality; he swept Michelangelo off his feet with his charm, his attentions, his vivacity. He was a dandy who garbed himself in colorful silk shirts and a broad belt with gold buckles; he stopped at the barber in the straw market every morning before coming to work to be shaved and have his hair combed with a perfumed oil. Michelangelo was a messy worker: he got charcoal on his hands, which he then forgetfully rubbed into his face; he spilled paint on his shirt, ink on his stockings.

Torrigiani turned in a good day's work yet managed to keep immaculate his bright yellow linen *camicia*, a waist-length shirt with puffed sleeves, the green tunic with a "T" embroidered on the shoulder in yellow silk, the dark blue jersey *calzoni*. He had evolved a sculpturing stance which kept the stone dust and chips out of his clothes and hair, unheard of for stonecarvers, who emerge at the end of a day's work looking like monoliths. He was an object of wonder to Michelangelo, who was flattered when Torrigiani put a powerful arm around his shoulders, held his handsome face close to his and exclaimed about his latest design.

"Michelangelo *mio,* you do the cleanest work and get dirtier doing it than anyone I know."

Torrigiani was always in motion, laughing, posturing, talking good sense and nonsense, but never still, never quiet, waving his hands with their emerald and pearl rings, needing to dominate the air about him. His robust singing voice rang out over the lush spring meadow with its wild flowers, and the *scalpellini* in the far corner of the garden who were building a library to house Lorenzo's manuscripts and books stopped for a moment to listen.

When the apprentices walked in the morning to study the early sun on the Giottos in Santa Croce, or the afternoon rays on Filippino Lippi's Young St. John and Two Saints in Santo Spirito, or to catch the sunset glow on the sculptured figures on the Campanile, designed by Giotto and executed by his pupil, Andrea Pisano,

Torrigiani slipped his arm through Michelangelo's, wooed him, kept him a captive though enchanted audience.

"Ah, to be a soldier, Michelangelo. To fight in mortal combat, to kill the enemy with sword and lance, conquer new lands and all their women. That is the life! An artist? Bah! It is work for the sultan's eunuchs. You and I must travel the world together, *amico mio,* find combat and danger and treasure."

Michelangelo felt a deep affection for Torrigiani, a love almost. He felt himself to be simple; to have won the admiration of so beautiful and desirable a youth as Torrigiani . . . it was heady wine to one who never drank.

4

He now had to unlearn much that he had accumulated at Ghirlandaio's studio because of the differences in drawing for fresco and for sculpture.

"This is drawing for its own sake," Bertoldo cautioned him, in precisely the words Ghirlandaio had used to caution him against it, "to achieve authority of eye and hand."

Bertoldo drummed the differences into him. The sculptor is after three-dimensional figures, not only height and width, but *depth.* The painter draws to *occupy* space, the sculptor to *displace* it. The painter draws still life within a frame; the sculptor draws to surprise movement, to discover the tensions and torsions striving within the human figure.

"The painter draws to reveal the particular, the sculptor draws to unearth the universal. *Comprendi?* Understand?" he demanded.

Michelangelo was silent.

"Most important of all, the painter draws to externalize, to wrench a shape out of himself and set it down on paper; the sculptor draws to *internalize,* to pull a shape out of the world and solidify it within himself."

Some of this Michelangelo had sensed, but much of it he recognized as the hard wisdom of experience.

"I am a *stufato,* a stew," apologized Bertoldo. "Everything that every sculptor in Tuscany has believed for two centuries has been poured into my head. You must forgive me if it leaks *obiter dicta.*"

Bertoldo, burdened with the task of rearing a new generation of sculptors, was a dedicated teacher, unlike Ghirlandaio, who simply did not have the time. Sculptors are at best monosyllabic men, the sounds of the hammer and chisel their overlanguage and their true speech, drowning out small voices and smaller worlds. Bertoldo was the exception.

"Michelangelo, you draw well. But it is also important to know why one must draw well. Drawing is a candle that can be lighted so that the sculptor does not have to grope in the dark; a plan for understanding the structure you are gazing at. To try to understand another human being, to grapple for his ultimate depths, that is the most dangerous of human endeavors. And all this the artist essays with no weapon but a pen or charcoal." He shrugged. "That romantic Torrigiani talks about going off to the wars. Child's play! There is no thrill of mortal danger to surpass that of a lone man trying to create something that never existed before."

Michelangelo held his day's work in his hand, searching it as though to understand better what Bertoldo was saying, seeking to find in it some part of what Bertoldo wanted there.

"Drawing is the supreme way of blotting out your ignorance of a subject," the old man exhorted, "establishing wisdom in its place, just as Dante did when he wrote the lines of the *Purgatorio*. Yes, yes, drawing is like reading: like reading

Homer so that you will know about Priam and Helen of Troy; Suetonius so that you may learn about the Caesars.''

Michelangelo lowered his head.

"I am ignorant. I do not read Greek or Latin. Urbino tried for three years to teach me, but I was stubborn, I would not learn. I wanted only to draw.''

"*Stupido!* You have missed my point. No wonder Urbino had trouble teaching you. Drawing is learning. It is discipline, a measuring stick with which to see if there is honesty in you. It's a confessional; it will reveal everything about you while you imagine you are revealing someone else. Drawing is the poet's written line, set down to see if there be a story worth telling, a truth worth revealing.''

The old man's voice became soft, affectionate.

"Remember this, *figlio mio:* to draw is to be like God when He put breath into Adam; it is the outer breathing of the artist and the inner breathing of the model that creates a new third life on paper. The act of love, Michelagnolo, the act of love: through which everything on earth is born.''

Yes, drawing was the breath of life, he had known that; yet for him it was not an end but a means.

He began remaining behind at night, unknown to anyone, picking up tools and working the scraps of stone lying about: yellowish-white travertines from the quarries of Rome, *pietra forte* from Lombrellino, conglomerate *breccia* from Impruneta, dark green marble from Prato, mottled reddish-yellow marble from Siena, pink marble from Gavorrano, transparent *cipollino* marble, blue and white flowered *bardiglio.* But his greatest joy came when someone left behind a fragment of pure white Carrara. As a child he had stood before the marble cutters, hungering to get his hands on this precious stone. It had never been possible; white marble was rare and costly, only enough was brought in from Carrara and Seravezza to fulfill commissions.

Now surreptitiously he began to experiment with the point, the toothed and flat chisels, working surface textures on the marble as he had on the *pietra serena* at the Topolinos'. It was the finest hour of the day for him, alone in the garden, with only the statues for company. Soon, soon, he must have these tools in his hand for good; he must be able to pick them up first thing in the morning because they were his natural appendages, like arms and legs. He always remembered, when dark fell, to chisel off the contours he had worked so no one would know, to clear away his chips, throwing them into the stone pile in the far end of the garden.

Inevitably he was caught; but by the last person he would have expected to surprise him. Contessina de' Medici came to the garden nearly every day now, if not with Lorenzo, then with Poliziano or Ficino or Pico della Mirandola, her father's Platonic scholars. She spoke with Granacci, with Sansovino and Rustici, whom she apparently had known a long time; but no one introduced Michelangelo. She never spoke to him.

He knew instantly, without catching sight of the quick-moving figure or the face that was all eyes, when she entered the gate. He felt a heightened consciousness, as though all movement around him, even of the sun and air, had been speeded up.

It was Contessina who freed Granacci from the drudgery of stone. He spoke to her of his feelings; she told her father. One day Lorenzo came into the garden and said:

"Granacci, I'd like a big panel, a Triumph of Paul Emilius. Would you undertake to paint it?''

"Would I! When need is highest, help is nighest.''

When Lorenzo turned aside, Granacci pressed his left hand to his lips and fluttered the fingers to Contessina in gratitude.

She never paused to look at Michelangelo's work. Always she stopped at Torrigiani's table, standing at the far side of the desk so that she was facing Michelangelo, and he could see her every gesture, hear her laughter as Torrigiani amused her. Though he watched, fascinated, their eyes never met.

When at length she left he found himself emotionally exhausted. He could not understand this. He cared nothing for girls. Not even a year of Jacopo's tutelage had led him to discern which were "mattressable." There were no girls in his family, none in their small circle of friends. He could hardly remember having talked to one. He had never even wanted to sketch one! They were alien to him. Then why was it painful when he saw her laughing in comradeship with Torrigiani, only a few feet away? Why did he become furious with Torrigiani, and with her? What could she mean to him, this princess of the noble Medici blood?

It was a kind of mysterious malady. He wished she would stay away from the garden, leave him in peace. Rustici said she seldom used to come. Why now, every day, staying for an hour or more? The more passionately he threw himself at the blank pages the more conscious he was of her standing shivering at Torrigiani's workbench, flirting with the beautiful muscular athlete while somehow seeing and absorbing his own every stroke of the charcoal like a personal affront.

It was a long time, deep into the heat of summer, with the wild flowers dead and the garden meadows burned brown, before he realized that he was jealous. Jealous of Torrigiani. Jealous of Contessina. Jealous of the two of them together. Jealous of each of them separately, apart.

And he was appalled.

And now she had discovered him in the garden after the others had left. She was with her brother Giovanni, the fat one with the cast in his eye, about his own age, fourteen, Michelangelo would have guessed, already a cardinal-elect; and her cousin, the illegitimate son of Lorenzo's beloved brother Giuliano, stabbed to death in the Duomo by Pazzi conspirators. Michelangelo had been only three at the time, but Florentines still talked of the sight of the conspirators hanging from the windows of the Signoria.

The first words slipped out unannounced.

"*Buona sera.*"

"*Buona sera.*"

"Michelangelo."

"Contessina."

"*Come va?*" This was Contessina.

"*Non c'è male.*" Like a Settignano stonemason.

He had been carving a herringbone pattern on a piece of *pietra serena*. He did not stop working.

"The stone has a smell."

"Of freshly picked figs."

"And this?" She pointed to a piece of marble on the bench beside him. "Does it smell of freshly picked plums?"

"No, it has hardly any." He chipped a piece. "Here, smell for yourself."

She crinkled her nose, laughing at him. He set himself before the marble, began raining blows with the chisel that sent the chips flying.

"Why do you work so . . . so furiously? Doesn't it exhaust you? It would me."

He knew of her frailty, the consumption in her family that had taken her mother and sister within the past year. That was why Lorenzo was so devoted to her, Rustici said, because she was not long for this world.

"No, no, cutting stone does not take strength out of you, it puts it back in. Here, try working this white marble. You'll be amazed at how alive it comes under your hands."

"Under your hands, Michelangelo. Will you finish that design on the *pietra serena* for me?"

"But it is nothing, just herringbones, such as we carve for garden walks or cistern covers."

"I like it."

"Then I will finish."

She stood still, just above him, as he crouched over the stone. When he came to a hard spot he looked around for a bucket of water, saw none, spat precisely on the area he wanted to soften, then continued the sweep of the chisel over the stone.

Amused, she asked, "What do you do when you run dry?"

He gazed up at her, his face flushed.

"No good *scalpellino* ever ran out of spit."

5

With the first intense locked-in heat of the garden came the first casualty: Soggi. His enthusiasm had been withering like the grass of the meadow. He had won no prizes or commissions, and although Bertoldo had been paying him a few coins, his earnings were higher only than Michelangelo's, which were non-existent. For this reason Soggi thought that Michelangelo might join with him.

One breathless evening late in August he waited until everyone had left, then flung down his tools and came to the newest apprentice.

"Michelangelo, let's you and I get out of here. All this stuff is so . . . so impractical. Let's save ourselves while there is still time."

"Save ourselves, Soggi? From what?"

"Look, don't be blind. They're never going to give us any commissions or money. Who really needs sculpture in order to live?"

"I do."

The emotions of disgust, renunciation and even fear carved on Soggi's face were more eloquent than anything the lad had been able to work into his wax or clay models.

"Where are we going to find work? If Lorenzo should die . . ."

"But he's a young man, only forty."

". . . then we would have no more patron, no more garden. Are we to wander about Italy like beggars with hats in our hands? Do you need a marble cutter? Could you use a Madonna? A Pietà? I can make you one, if only you'll give me a roof and victuals."

Soggi swept his few personal possessions into a bag.

"*Ma che!* I want to be in a trade where folks come to me. Every day! For *pasta* or pork, for wine or *calzoni*. People can't live without these things, every day they must buy. So every day I must sell. On what I sell, I will live. I have a practical nature, I have to know that each day I will earn so many soldi. Sculpture is the last of the luxuries, on the very bottom of the list. I want to trade in something on top of the list. What do you say, Michelangelo? They haven't paid you a single scudo. Look how ragged your clothes are. Do you want to live like a pauper all your life? Quit now, with me. We'll find jobs together . . ."

Soggi's outburst was deeply felt; it had been building up for weeks, perhaps months. Yet at the back of his mind Michelangelo was a little amused.

"Sculpture is at the top of my list, Soggi. In fact, there is no list. I say, 'Sculpture,' and I'm finished."

"Finished is right!" agreed Soggi. "My father knows a butcher on the Ponte Vecchio who is looking for help. The chisel, it's just like a knife. . . ."

The next morning when Bertoldo heard of Soggi's departure he shrugged.

"The casualties of sculpture. Everyone is born with a little talent; but with most people, how quickly the flame flickers out."

He ran a hand resignedly through his thin white hair.

"We always had this in the studios. You start out knowing that a certain amount of teaching will be wasted; but you can't withhold for that reason, or all your apprentices will suffer. These Soggi, their prompting is not love or affinity for sculpture, but the exuberance of youth. As soon as this first flush begins to fade they say to themselves, 'Stop dreaming. Look for a reliable way of life.' When you are the master of a *bottega* you will find this to be true. Sculpture is hard, brutal labor. One should not become an artist because he can, but because he must. It is only for those who would be miserable without it."

The next morning moonfaced Bugiardini, no taller, but plumper, arrived as the new apprentice for the garden. Michelangelo and Granacci embraced him warmly.

Granacci, having completed his painting for Lorenzo, had shown so much talent at organization that Lorenzo had asked him to become the manager of the garden. He enjoyed being an executive, spending his days making sure that the proper stone, iron or bronze arrived, setting up contests for the apprentices, getting modest commissions from the Guilds.

"Granacci, you mustn't," protested Michelangelo. "You have as much talent as anybody in this garden."

"But I enjoy it," replied Granacci mildly.

"Then stop enjoying it. If we need charcoal, or a model, let us get them for ourselves. Why should you give up your work to help us get ours done?"

Granacci was not insensible to the compliment embedded in Michelangelo's fury.

"There's time for everything, *caro mio,*" he replied. "I have painted. I will paint again."

But when Granacci returned to painting Michelangelo was angrier than ever: for Lorenzo had pressed him into service to design stage settings for a morality play, banners and arches for a pageant.

"Granacci, *idiota,* how can you stand here singing so happily, painting carnival decorations that will be thrown out the day after the pageant?"

"But I like doing what you call trivia. Everything doesn't have to be profound and eternal. A pageant or a party are important because people get pleasure from them, and pleasure is one of the most important things in life, as important as food or drink or art."

"You . . . you . . . Florentine!"

6

As the days of fall deepened, so did Michelangelo's friendships. On feast days or church holidays, when the garden was locked tight, Rustici invited him for dinner, then took him through the countryside looking for horses, paying farmers, stablemen, grooms for the privilege of drawing in their barns and fields.

"Horses are the most beautiful of God's creatures," exclaimed Rustici. "You must draw them over and over again, every horse you can find."

"But, Rustici, I never intend to sculpture a horse. Only men."

"Once you know a horse, you know the world."

Sansovino, the *contadino* from Arezzo, twice Michelangelo's age, had his own philosophy.

"An artist must return frequently to the soil; he must plow it, sow it, weed it, harvest the grain. The contact with the earth renews us. To be only an artist is to feed on oneself, and go barren. That is why I ride my mule home to Arezzo every few weeks. You must come with me, Michelangelo, and feel the tilled earth under your feet."

"I'd like to visit Arezzo with you, Sansovino, if there's any marble I can plow a furrow through."

It was only at home that he was unhappy. Lodovico had managed to keep a rough check on how much each of the apprentices at the garden was receiving of prize money, awards and commissions; he knew that Sansovino, Torrigiani and Granacci were earning good sums.

"But not you?" Lodovico demanded. "Not one single scudo."

"Not yet."

"After a full eight months. Why? Why the others and not you?"

"I don't know."

"I can only come to one conclusion: that you can't compete with the others."

"I have not."

"Wouldn't Lorenzo know if you had any talent as a sculptor?"

"Undoubtedly."

"But he has never noticed you?"

"Never."

"*Allora!* I'll give you another four months to make it a full year. Then if Lorenzo still thinks you're dry fruit, you'll go to work."

But Lodovico's patience lasted only four weeks. He cornered Michelangelo in his bedroom of a Sunday morning.

"Does Bertoldo praise your work?"

"No."

"Does he say you have talent?"

"No."

"He gives no encouragement?"

"He gives me instruction."

"It is not the same thing."

"*Ammesso.* Admitted."

'Does he praise the others?"

"Sometimes."

"Could it be you have the least promise?"

"It could not be."

"Why not?"

"I draw better than they."

"Draw. What does that mean? If they are training you to be a sculptor why don't you sculpture?"

"Bertoldo won't let me."

"Why not?"

"He says I'm not ready."

"But the others sculpture?"

"Yes."

"Can't you see what that means?"

"No."

"It means that you have less ability than they."

"That will be proved when I get my hands on stone."

"When will that be?"

"I don't know."

"Until you work the stone, you can earn no return."

"No."

"And they show no sign of letting you start on the stone?"

"None."

"Doesn't it look hopeless to you?"

"No."

"Then how does it look?"

"Puzzling."

"And how long can you remain there puzzled?"

"As long as Bertoldo thinks I should."

"What has happened to your pride?"

"Nothing."

"The same as has happened to you in the garden: nothing."

"One does not lose pride while learning."

"You are almost fifteen now. Are you to earn nothing forever?"

"I will earn."

"When? How?"

"I don't know."

"Two dozen times you have said 'No,' or 'I don't know.' When will you know?"

"I don't know."

Exhausted, Lodovico cried, "I should beat you with a stick. When will you get some sense in your head?"

"I'm doing what I must. That is sense."

Lodovico slumped into a chair.

"Lionardo wants to become a monk. Whoever heard of a Buonarroti a monk? You want to become an artist. Whoever heard of a Buonarroti an artist? Giovansimone wants to become a street rowdy, stoning passers-by. Whoever heard of a Buonarroti as a *malandrino?* Urbino has sent Sigismondo back saying I am wasting my money, he cannot learn his letters. Whoever heard of a Buonarroti as illiterate? I don't know any more what a man has sons for!"

Michelangelo walked over to Lodovico's chair and put a finger lightly on his father's shoulder.

"Trust me, Father. I am not looking for wool on an ass."

Affairs grew no better for him at the garden; they seemed indeed to become worse. Bertoldo was pushing him hard, never pleased with anything he did, jumping from one foot to the other crying: "No, no, you can do it better. Again! Again." Making him redraw models from a ladder above them, the floor beneath, and at the end of a week obliging him to come in on a holiday to create a theme that would embrace all the figures he had sketched during the week.

Walking home with Granacci at night, Michelangelo cried in anguish:

"Why am I discriminated against?"

"You're not," replied Granacci.

"But anyone can see it. I am not permitted to enter any of the competitions for Lorenzo's prize money, or work on any of the commissions. I'm not permitted to visit the palace and see the art works. You're manager of the garden now. Speak to Bertoldo. Help me!"

"When Bertoldo considers you ready to enter contests, he'll say so. Until then . . . ."

"0 Dio!" swore Michelangelo under his breath. "Until then I'll be sleeping in the Loggia della Signoria where my father can't get at me with a stick."

There was something else he was unhappy about but could not mention to Granacci: with the wet weather Lorenzo had forbidden Contessina to leave the palace. To Michelangelo she did not seem frail. He felt a flame in her, a flame strong enough to consume death. Now that she no longer came, the garden seemed strangely empty, the days long and unbroken without the excitement of waiting.

In his loneliness he turned to Torrigiani. They became inseparable. Michelangelo raved about Torrigiani: of his wit, his flair, his physique . . .

Granacci raised an eyebrow.

"Michelangelo, I am in a difficult position: I can't say too much without appearing jealous and hurt. But I must warn you. Torrigiani has done this before."

"Done what?"

"Lavished his affection, won someone over completely, only to fly into a rage and break off the relationship when there is someone new to romance. Torrigiani needs an audience; you are providing him with that audience. Do not confuse this use with loving you."

Bertoldo was not so gentle. When he saw a drawing of Michelangelo's in which he had imitated one that Torrigiani had just completed, he tore it into a hundred shreds.

"Walk with a cripple for a year and at the end you will limp. Move your desk back where it belongs!"

7

Bertoldo knew that Michelangelo had reached a boundary of patience. He put an arm as brittle as an autumnal leaf about the boy's shoulder.

"And so: on to sculpture."

Michelangelo buried his head in his hands; his amber-colored eyes were intense with feeling, sweat broke out on his forehead. Relief, joy, misery were mixed together, making his heart pound and hands tremble.

"Now what is sculpture?" demanded Bertoldo in a mentor's tone. "It is the art which, by removing all that is superfluous from the material under treatment, reduces it to that form designed in the artist's mind . . ."

"With hammer and chisel," exclaimed Michelangelo, recovering his calm.

". . . or by successive additions," persisted Bertoldo, "as in modeling in clay or wax, which is by the method of putting on."

Michelangelo shook his head vigorously.

"Not for me. I want to work directly on the marble. I want to work as the Greeks did, carving straight from the stone."

Bertoldo smiled wryly.

"A noble ambition. But it takes a long time for an Italian to reach back to the Greeks. First you must learn to model in clay and wax. Not until you have mastered the putting-on method can you dare the method of removing."

"No stone?"

"No stone. Your wax models should be about a foot high. I had Granacci buy a supply of wax for you. To render it supple we use a little of this animal fat. So. If on the other hand you need more tenacity, you add turpentine. *Va bene?*"

While the wax was melting Bertoldo showed him how to make an armature, using sticks of wood or iron wires, and after the wax had cooled, how to make it into rolls. Once the framework was up, Michelangelo started applying the wax to see how close he could come to creating a three-dimensional figure from a two-dimensional drawing.

This then was the miracle he had cried about on the steps of the Duomo. For this he had argued the virtues of sculpture over painting. The real task of the sculptor: depth, the round, the dimension that the painter could only suggest by the illusion of perspective. His was the harsh world of reality; no one could walk around his drawing, but anyone could walk around his sculpture, and judge it from every side.

"And so it must be perfect, not only from the front but from every angle," said Bertoldo. "Which means that every piece has to be sculptured not once but three hundred and sixty times, because at each change of degree it becomes a different piece."

Michelangelo was fascinated; Bertoldo's voice swept through him like a flame.

"*Capisco.* I understand."

He took the wax, felt the warmth against his palms; for hands hungry for stone, the roll of wax could not be pleasant. But Bertoldo's words gave him impetus to see if he could build a head, torso, full figure that in some measure captured the drawing. It was not easy.

"But the sooner begun," he cried, "the sooner ended."

After he had massed his wax on the skeletal frame he followed Bertoldo's orders to work it with tools of iron and bone. After achieving the roughest approximation, he refined it with his strong fingers. The results had a touch of verisimilitude, some raw power.

"But no grace whatever," criticized Bertoldo; "and not the slightest facial resemblance."

"I'm not doing portraiture," growled Michelangelo, who absorbed instruction like a dehydrated sponge thrown into the Arno, but bridled at criticism.

"You will."

"May I speak plainly?"

"Have you any other way?"

"The devil with portraiture. I never will like it."

"Never is longer at your age than mine. When you're hungry and the Duke of Milan asks you to do his portrait in a bronze medallion . . ."

Michelangelo glowered. "I don't get that hungry."

Bertoldo held his ground. He talked of expression and grace and balance. Of the interrelation of the body to the head: if the figure had the face of an old man, it had to have the arms, body, legs, hands and feet of an old man. If it had the face of a youth, it had in like manner to be round, soft and sweet in expression, the flow of the drapery had to be turned so it suggested a young nude beneath. The hair and beard had to be worked with delicacy.

Baccio was the leaven. On those days when Torrigiani had the vapors and sulks; or Sansovino was suddenly homesick for Arezzo; or Michelangelo cried to move ahead to clay; when Bertoldo reproved Rustici for drawing horses while sketching from a male model; when Granacci developed a splitting headache from the constant noise of hammer on chisel; when Bertoldo, racked with cough, moaned that he could have saved himself a lot of trouble by dying from his last attack; this was the moment that Baccio rushed to the rescue, bringing with him the humor of the wineshops and brothels.

"Maestro, did you hear about the merchant who complained of his wife's expensive dress: 'Every time I go to bed with you it costs me a golden scudo.' 'If you went to bed with me more often,' replied the young wife tartly, 'it would cost you only a penny each time.' "

"No, I don't keep him on as the garden clown," explained Bertoldo. "He has a promise of talent and is never unperceptive. Baccio as much as anyone in this garden has the will to dedication. He doesn't like to study, he's absorbed by pleasure. But he'll wear these things out. His brother, the Dominican monk, is dedicated to purity; perhaps that's why Baccio is devoted to lasciviousness."

The weeks passed. Bertoldo insisted that Michelangelo perfect himself in the transcription from charcoal to wax. When Michelangelo could stand no more he threw down his bone tools, walked to the far end of the garden, picked up hammer and chisel, and worked out his fury cutting building blocks for Lorenzo's library. The foreman, not sure he should permit this uprising, asked the first time:

"Why do you come to us?"

"I must wear this wax off my fingers."

"Where did you learn to chip stone?"

"In Settignano."

"Ah!"

Each day for an hour or two he worked with the *scalpellini*. The *pietra serena* blocks between his legs and under his hand lent him durity.

Bertoldo capitulated.

" '*Alla guerra di amor vince chi fugge*,' " he said. " 'In a love fight, he who flees is the winner.' We will go on to clay . . . . Remember that clay worked in a damp state shrinks. Build up your clay bit by bit. Mix in soft cuttings and horsehair to make sure your large models don't split. To clothe your figure, wet a drapery cloth to the consistency of thick mud, then arrange it around your figure in folds. Later you'll learn how to expand the model into the size you intend to carve.''

"You've used the word," grinned Michelangelo. "I must be getting closer.''

February closed in, with fogs down from the mountains and rain enveloping the walled city until every street became a river. There were few hours of gray light to work by, the churches and palaces were too damp to visit for copying. They were confined to the inner rooms of the casino, with each apprentice sitting on a high stool over a brazier of hot coals. Bertoldo was forced to remain in bed for days at a time. The wet clay seemed clammier and colder than ever. Frequently Michelangelo worked by oil light, frequently alone in the icy casino, not happy, but more content to be here than anywhere else.

April was only a couple of months away. And so was Lodovico's decision to take him out of the garden if he had not reached some paid capacity. Bertoldo, when he came wrapped in heavy robes, was a pale wraith; but Michelangelo knew that he must speak. He showed Bertoldo the clay figures he had been modeling, asked permission to copy them in stone.

"No, *figlio mio*," croaked Bertoldo hoarsely, "you are not ready.''

"The others are; I am not?''

"You have much to learn.''

"Admitted.''

"*Pazienza*," exclaimed Granacci. "God shapes the back to the burden.''

8

There were several thorns festering. Bertoldo drove him the hardest, accompanied by a constant stream of criticism; try as he might, Michelangelo could earn no word of praise. Another sore spot was that he still had not been invited to the palace. Bertoldo would cry:

"No, no, this modeling is overcaressed; when you see the sculpture in the palace you will understand that marble wants to express only the most intense and profound of sentiments.''

Michelangelo thought, "Well then, invite me, and I will see!''

When Lorenzo invited Bugiardini to the palace Michelangelo grew angry. At whom: Bertoldo? Lorenzo? Himself? He could not tell. The exclusion implied rejection. He felt like the ass who carries gold and eats thistles.

Then, on a cold but sharply bright end-of-March day, Bertoldo stood over a clay model Michelangelo had just completed from studies of ancient demigods, half human, half animal.

"There's a newly discovered Faun at the palace," said Bertoldo. "We unpacked it last night. Pagan Greek, beyond doubt. Ficino and Landino think about the fifth century before Christ. You must see it.''

Michelangelo held his breath.

"Right now would be the best time. Come along.''

They crossed the Piazza San Marco and turned down the Via Larga. Bertoldo raised one layer of the heavy wool scarf wound double around his neck, placed it across the lower half of his face to protect his mouth from the piercing cold. On the Via de' Gori side the Medici palace had used the wall of the second city limit as a foundation. The architect Michelozzo had completed it thirty years before for Cosimo. It was large enough to house a numerous family of three generations, the government of a republic, the management of a world-wide business, a center for artists and scholars who traveled to Florence: a combined home, office, shop, university, *bottega*, art gallery, theater and library: austere, with a majestic simplicity that characterized the taste of the Medici.

"There is no bad art in the palace," said Bertoldo.

The stonework thrilled Michelangelo as he paused on the Via Larga for a moment to gaze in admiration. Though he had seen the palace a hundred times it always seemed fresh and new. What superb craftsmen these *scalpellini* were. Each rough protruding block of the rustic ground floor was chiseled with the authority of a piece of sculpture: the surface resourcefully textured by the *calcagnolo*, the edges beveled with a lyrical "curve-out-of-mass" that made the huge blocks sing; and no two stones any more duplicates than two marble statues by Donatello.

Inserted in the heavy blocks was a row of iron rings to which visitors' horses were fastened; at the corners were large bronze holders in which the night torches were placed. Around the palace on both streets ran a high stone bench on which the convivial Florentines could chat and sun themselves.

"Each stone of the rustic is so good," said Michelangelo, breaking the silence, "it could be set up on a pedestal and placed in the loggia."

"Perhaps," agreed Bertoldo, "but for me, too ponderous. They make a building look too much like a fort. I prefer those flat regular stone panels of the second floor, and even better the miniature stones of the third floor, each carved like a gem. That's what makes the palace grow lighter as it rises in space."

"I have never realized," said Michelangelo, "architecture is almost as great an art as sculpture."

Bertoldo smiled indulgently.

"Giuliano da Sangallo, the finest architect in Tuscany, would tell you that architecture *is* sculpture: the designing of forms to occupy space. If the architect is not a sculptor all he gets is enclosed walls. If you need work, you will design a palace instead of a Pietà."

The corner of the Via Larga and Via de' Gori was an open loggia which the Medici family used for their feasts and festivities, considered as entertainments by the Florentines, who insisted on seeing what was going on. The loggia had magnificent thirty-foot arches carved out of *pietra forte,* strong stone; it was here that citizens, merchants and politicos came to confer with Lorenzo, artists and students to discuss their projects. For all there was a glass of sweet white Greco wine, "the perfect drink for gentlemen," and a cake of welcome.

They entered through the massive gate and came into the square courtyard with its three complete arches on each side held up by twelve heroic columns with decorated capitals. Bertoldo pointed proudly to a series of eight sculptured classical figures between the tops of the arches and the window sills.

"They're mine. I copied them from antique gems. You'll see the originals in Lorenzo's collection in his *studiolo*. They're so good people mistake them for Donatellos!"

Michelangelo frowned: how could Bertoldo be content to run so far behind his master? Then his eye moved to two of the great sculptures of the city: the Davids of Donatello and of Verrocchio. He rushed with a cry of joy to touch the pieces.

Bertoldo came to stand by him, running his practiced hand over the magnificent bronze surfaces.

"I helped cast this piece for Cosimo. It was intended to stand right here in this courtyard, to be looked at from every side. How excited we were! For centuries we had had only the relief, or figures attached to their background. This was the first isolated bronze to be cast in more than a thousand years. Before Donatello, sculpture was used to ornament architecture: in niches, doors, choir stalls and pulpits. Donato was the first sculptor in the round since the Romans."

Michelangelo gazed openmouthed at Donatello's David, so young and soft, with long curls of hair and high-nippled breasts, the slender arm holding a gigantic sword, the left leg curved so gracefully to put the open-sandaled foot on Goliath's decapitated head. It was a double miracle, Michelangelo thought: that the bronze casting had come out with such a satin-smooth perfection; for this he knew Bertoldo shared the credit; and that so delicate a figure, almost as slight as Contessina's, could have killed Goliath.

He had only another moment to study three Roman sarcophagi under the arches, and two restored statues of Marsyas, before Bertoldo started up the great staircase to the chapel above, with its Gozzoli frescoes so brilliant in color that Michelangelo cried out in astonishment.

Then as Bertoldo led him from room to room his head began to spin: for here was a veritable forest of sculptures and gallery of paintings. He did not have enough eyes in his head or strength in his legs to move from piece to piece, or to carry his emotional excitement. No good Italian artist since Giotto or Nicola Pisano was unrepresented. Marbles by Donatello and Desiderio da Settignano, by Luca della Robbia and Verrocchio, bronzes by Bertoldo. Paintings hung in every anteroom, hallway, salon, family room, office, bedroom: Masaccio's St. Paul, Piazza della Signoria; Paolo Uccello's Battle of San Romano, Fight of Dragons and Lions; Giotto's Crucifixion on a wooden table; Fra Angelico's Madonna, Adoration of the Magi; Botticelli's Birth of Venus, Spring, Madonna of the Magnificat. There were Castagnos, Filippo Lippis, Pollaiuolos and a hundred others from Venice and Bruges.

They reached Lorenzo's *studiolo,* the last of a suite of beautiful rooms on what was called "the noble floor of the palace," not Lorenzo's office but his small writing room, its vault sculptured by Luca della Robbia, Lorenzo's desk against the back wall under the shelves that held his treasures: jewels, cameos, small marble bas-reliefs, ancient illuminated manuscripts: a cozy, crowded room intended more for pleasure than work, with small painted tables by Giotto and Van Eyck, antique bronzes and a nude Hercules above the fireplace, small bronze heads on the lintels above the doors, glass vases designed by Ghirlandaio.

"What do you think?" Bertoldo demanded.

"Nothing. Everything. My brain is paralyzed."

"I'm not surprised. Here is the Faun that arrived from Asia Minor yesterday. His eyes are telling you how much he has reveled in the carnal joys. Must have been the first Florentine! Now I will leave you for a few minutes while I get something from my room."

Michelangelo went close to the Faun. He found himself looking into gleaming, gloating eyes. The long beard was stained as though red wine had been spilled in merriment. It seemed so intensely alive that Michelangelo felt it was about to speak, yet inside the wicked smile the lips and teeth were no longer visible. He ran his finger tips over the gaping hole, searching for the carving, but it was gone. He threw back his head and laughed, the stone room echoing the sound. The blood had begun to circulate again in his veins.

"Have you lost your mouth by boasting of your droll adventures?" he cried out to the Faun.

Then he took drawing paper and red crayon from inside his shirt, sat at the far side of the room and sketched the Faun, giving it lips, teeth and an impudent tongue, as he imagined they would have appeared when the Greek sculptor carved them two thousand years before.

He felt someone at his shoulder, then a faint perfume came to his nostrils. He whirled about abruptly.

Many weeks had passed since he had seen her. She was so slight a little body, displacing such a modest amount of space. Her eyes were omnivorous, consuming the rest of her pale sensitive features by dissolving them in the warm brown liquid of her pupils. She was dressed in a blue *gamurra* trimmed in brown fur. White stars were appliquéd on shirt and sleeves. In her hand was a Greek parchment copy of Isocrates' *Orations*.

He sat motionless, consumed like herself in her eyes.

"Michelangelo."

How could there be so much joy from this mere pronouncing of a name which one heard all day without emotion?

"Contessina."

"I was studying in my room. Then I knew someone was here."

"I did not dare hope I would see you. Bertoldo brought me to see the art."

"Father won't let me come with him to the garden until spring. You do not think I will die?"

"You will live to bear many sons."

Color flooded her cheeks.

"I have not offended you?" he asked apologetically.

She shook her head. "They told me you were blunt." She took a step or two closer to his chair. "When I am near you I feel strong. Why?"

"When I am near you I feel confused. Why?"

She laughed, a gay, light sound.

"I miss the garden."

"The garden misses you."

"I should not have thought it noticed."

"It noticed."

She turned from the intensity in his voice.

"Your work, it goes well?"

"Non c'è male."

"You're not very communicative."

"I do not aspire to be a talker."

"Then you should mask your eyes."

"What do they say?"

"Things that please me."

"Then tell me. I carry no mirror."

"What we know of others is our personal secret."

He felt exposed, humiliated for showing any emotion which he could not name. He picked up his sketching paper.

"I must work now."

She stamped her foot. "One does not dismiss a Medici." Anger flared into her eyes, darkening their translucence to opaque, then a tiny smile moved in. "You will not hear such stupid words from me again."

"Non importa. I have a variety of my own."

She put out her hand. It was small, the fingers as fragile as birds in his rough, powerful paw. He knew enough not to squeeze. Then after an instant he felt a stirring, a warmth, a robust shaking of his hand in her strong grasp.

"Addio, Michelangelo."

"Addio, Contessina."

"Work well."

"Grazie mille."

She was gone, out the door of her father's study, leaving behind a faint perfume in his nostrils, a forging of the blood in his hand as though he had been working with a perfectly balanced Swedish iron chisel.

He applied the red crayon to the paper.

9

That night he tossed and turned, sleepless. His first year in the garden was almost up. Suppose that Lodovico should go to Lorenzo, as he had threatened, and demand that his son be released? Would Lorenzo be willing to antagonize a good Florentine family? For an apprentice whom he had never even noticed?

Yet he simply could not go away without once having got his hands on a piece of stone.

He could stand the empty-handed hunger no longer. He leaped out of bed, hurtled into his clothes in the moonlight, bent on reaching Settignano by dawn and spending the day cutting *pietra serena* blocks and columns. But when he had run noiselessly down the circular staircase to the Via dei Bentaccordi he stopped short. Into his mind there flashed the picture of himself working with the *scalpellini* at the rear of the garden where all stones were stored. He saw one in particular, a modest-sized piece of white marble, lying in the grass a short distance from the building blocks. It came to his mind that this block was exactly the right size for the piece of sculpture he envisioned: a Faun like the one in Lorenzo's *studiolo*, but his own!

Instead of turning to his left and following the street of the ditch toward the open country, he turned to his right, walked the Via dei Benci with its handsome, sleeping Bardi palaces to the high wooden gate in the city wall, identified himself to a guard, crossed the Ponte alle Grazie and climbed up to the ruins of the Belvedere fort, and sat on a parapet with the shimmering Arno at his feet.

Florence, luminous in the full moonlight, so close that he felt he could touch the Signoria or Duomo with his fingers, was a sight of such incredible beauty that he drew in his breath sharply. No wonder the young men of the city sang their romantic ballads to their town, with whom no girl could compete. All true Florentines said, "I will not live out of sight of the Duomo." For him the city was a compact mass of *pietra serena*, the streets cut through with a mason's chisel, looking like dark rivers, the cobbled piazzas gleaming white in the moonlight. The palaces stood sentinel, a couple of ranges higher than the modest houses clustered so tightly about them; and piercing the creamy gold sky the spires of Santa Croce, Santa Maria Novella, the magnificent three-hundred-foot thrust of the Signoria. Making a little group of its own were the great red dome of the cathedral, the glistening small white dome of the Baptistery, the noble flesh pink of the Campanile. Around all was the turreted, tower-studded city wall.

And sitting there, above his beloved city, he knew what he must do.

The moon was beginning to sink beyond the hills; the last of the mist of luminous gray powder settled down on the housetops and was absorbed. Light subtly suggested itself in the east, then flared as though the sun had been hovering jealously below the horizon waiting only a signal to precipitate itself upon the stage of the Arno Valley and rout the magical mystical moonlight with fierce proof of its own greater power to light, to heat, to make everything known. Cocks began to crow in the farms upriver, bordering the marsh lake; the guards at the gate gave the cries to open the heavy barred doors.

He made his way down the hill, walked along the river to the Ponte Vecchio, the bridge with its meat stalls just being opened by sleepy apprentices, and continued down to the Piazza San Marco and the garden. He went directly to the marble block in the grass beyond the new building site, picked it up in his arms and struggled under its weight down the path to the rear. Here he righted a sawed tree trunk, set the marble block securely upon it.

He knew he had no right to touch this marble, that at least by implication he had rebelled against the authority of the garden, overthrown Bertoldo's iron-edged discipline. Well, he was on his way out anyway if his father had his say; and if Bertoldo was going to sack him, let it be done in front of a piece of sculpture for which he had been brought here in the first place.

His hands caressed the stone, searched out its more intimate contours. During the entire year he had never once touched a block of white statuary marble.

"Why," he asked himself, trembling, "do I feel this way?"

For him the milky white marble was a living, breathing substance that felt, sensed, *judged*. He could not permit himself to be found wanting. It was not fear but reverence. In the back of his mind a voice said:

"This is love."

He was not frightened, or even startled. He recognized it for the simple truth. It was his primary need that his love be reciprocated. Marble was the hero of his life; and his fate. Not until this very moment, with his hands tenderly, lovingly on the marble, had he come fully alive.

For this was what he wanted to be all his life: a white-marble sculptor, nothing more, nothing less.

He picked up Torrigiani's tools and set to work: without drawing, without wax or clay model, without even charcoal markings on the tough outer skin of the marble. All he had to go on, beyond impulse and instinct, was the clearly etched image of the Faun in the palace: mischievous, pleasure-sated, wily, wicked and thoroughly enchanting.

He placed his chisel on the block, struck the first blow with his hammer. This was where he belonged. He, the marble, the hammer and chisel, were one.

10

The Faun was completed. For three nights he had worked behind the casino; for three days he had hidden it beneath a wool cloth. Now he carried it to his workbench. Now he was willing for Bertoldo to see it: his own Faun, with full sensual lips, set of saucy white teeth, insouciant tongue barely peeping through. He was polishing the top of the head with *pietra ardita* and water to grind away the tool markings and white dots when the apprentices arrived and Lorenzo came down the walk. He stopped in front of the workbench.

"Ah, the Faun from my *studiolo*," said Lorenzo.

"Yes."

"You left out his beard."

"I did not feel it necessary."

"Isn't the job of the copyist to copy?"

"The sculptor is not a copyist."

"Not even an apprentice?"

"No. The student must create something new from something old."

"And where does the new come from?"

"From where all art comes. Inside himself."

He thought he saw a flicker in Lorenzo's eye. It was quickly suppressed.

"Your Faun is old."

"Shouldn't he be?"

"I wasn't questioning his age. It's just that you left him all his teeth."

Michelangelo gazed at his statue.

"I was making amends for the other mouth that decayed."

"You should have known that there are always some wanting in fellows of his age."

"In a man, yes. But in fauns?" He could not resist an impish grin. "Fauns are supposed to be half goat. Do goats lose teeth?"

Lorenzo laughed good-naturedly.

"I've never looked!"

When he left, Michelangelo took up his chisel and went to work on the Faun's mouth. Lorenzo returned to the garden the next day. Today it was warmer, and Bertoldo was with him. Lorenzo stopped in front of the workbench.

"Your Faun seems to have matured twenty years in a day."

"The sculptor is master of time: he can age his subjects forward or back."

Lorenzo seemed pleased.

"I see you have removed an upper tooth. And two lower ones in the other corner."

"For balance."

"You have also closed his gums where the teeth had been."

Michelangelo's eyes danced.

"It was perceptive of you to rework the entire mouth. Someone else might have been content just to hammer out the few teeth."

"It followed logically."

Lorenzo stared at him for a moment in silence, his deep brown eyes somber. Then he said, "I'm pleased to see that we have not been making soup in a basket."

He departed. Michelangelo turned to Bertoldo, who was pale and trembling a little. Bertoldo said nothing. Then he too left.

The next morning a page in varicolored stockings and scarlet coat appeared in the garden. Bertoldo called out:

"Michelangelo, you are wanted at the palace. Accompany the page."

"You've gotten yourself sacked!" exclaimed Baccio. "For stealing that marble."

Michelangelo looked at Bertoldo, then Granacci. Their expressions told him nothing. He went with the page, entered the rear garden through an old battlemented wall, stared with bulging eyes at the box trees cut into the shape of elephants, stags, ships under full sail. He stopped short in front of a fountain with a granite basin on which stood Donatello's bronze Judith.

"If you please, sir," cried the page, "*Il Magnifico* must not be kept waiting."

It took an act of violence to tear his eyes and body away from the powerful yet defeated figure of Holofernes, about to have his head cut off by Judith's upraised sword. The page led him down a wooden carriage ramp to the basement, then up two flights of narrow back stairs.

Lorenzo was seated behind his desk in the library, a large shelf-lined room housing the books which his grandfather had begun assembling fifty years before. There were only two pieces of sculpture in the room, marble busts of Lorenzo's father and uncle by Mino da Fiesole.

Michelangelo walked quickly to the bust of Piero, Lorenzo's father, his face flushed.

"See this high polish: as though a thousand candles were burning within."

Lorenzo rose, stood by Michelangelo's side to study the sculpture.

"That was Mino's special gift: he could make white marble appear like warm flesh."

"He used a full-rounded chisel to shape the hair. But see how gently the chisel penetrated the marble."

Michelangelo ran his finger over the flowing waves.

"Yet the lines are sharply incised," said Lorenzo. "That's called *ferrata;* where the tool spontaneously describes a movement of the hair."

"What the stonemasons call 'the long drive,' " added the boy.

"Mino was an exquisite," said Lorenzo. "He substituted sentimentality for technique. Yet this bust of my father is the first full marble portrait ever carved in Florence."

"The first! Then Mino had courage."

In the silence that followed Michelangelo's face suddenly went crimson. He bowed stiffly from the waist.

"I did not present my greetings, *messere*. I became excited about the sculpture and began talking."

Lorenzo waved this aside.

"I forgive you. How old are you, Michelangelo?"

"Fifteen."

"Who is your father?"

"Lodovico di Lionardo Buonarroti-Simoni."

"I have heard the name."

He opened his desk took out a parchment folio. From it he spread out dozens of drawings. Michelangelo could not believe what he saw.

"But . . . those are mine . . . ."

"Just so."

"Bertoldo told me he destroyed them."

Lorenzo leaned over his desk toward him. "We have put many obstacles in your path, Michelangelo. Bertoldo has borne down hard, with harsh criticism and little praise or promise of reward. We wanted to make sure you had . . . stamina. We knew you had a real talent but did not know your character. If you had left us for lack of praise or money awards . . ."

There was a silence in the beautiful room, permeated with the delicious aromas of parchment pages, leather bindings and freshly printed sheets. Michelangelo's eyes roamed the walls, seeing titles in a dozen different languages of which he could make out not a letter. His back teeth had so locked that his tongue had no room to move or speak.

Lorenzo came around to the boy's side.

"Michelangelo, you have the makings of a sculptor. Bertoldo and I are convinced that you could become heir to Orcagna, Ghiberti, Donatello."

Michelangelo remained tautly silent.

"I should like you to come and live in the palace. As a member of my family. From now on you need concern yourself only with sculpture."

"I like best to work in marble."

Lorenzo chuckled.

"No thanks, no expression of pleasure at coming to live in the palace of a Medici. Only your feeling for marble."

"Isn't that why you invited me?"

"*Senz'altro.* Will you bring your father to me?"

"Tomorrow. What must I call you?"

"What you will."

"Not *Magnifico.*"

"Why not?"

"What meaning has a compliment if one hears it night and day . . ."

". . . from the lips of sycophants?"

"I did not say that."

"With what name do you think of me?"

"Lorenzo."

"You speak it with affection,"

"So I feel."

"Do not in the future ask me what you must do. I have come to expect the unexpected from you."

Once again Granacci offered to plead for him with Lodovico. Lodovico could make no sense out of what Granacci was telling him.

"Granacci, you are leading my son astray."

"The Medici palace is not really astray, Messer Buonarroti; they say it is the finest palace in Europe."

"But what does it mean, a stonecutter in a fine palace? It is the same as a groom."

"Michelangelo is not a stonecutter. He is a sculptor."

"*Non importa.* Under what terms does he go into the palace?"

"You do not understand, *messere:* he is not to be paid."

"Not to be paid! Another year of waste!"

"*Il Magnifico* has asked Michelangelo to come to live in the palace. He will be as a member of the family. He will eat at table with the great of the world . . ."

"Who eats with the powerful will have his eyes squirted out with cherry stones."

"He will learn from the Plato Academy, the finest scholars of Italy," continued Granacci stolidly. "And he will have marble to carve."

"Marble," groaned Lodovico, as though the word were anathema.

"You cannot refuse to speak to *Il Magnifico*."

"I will go," mumbled Lodovico. "What else can I do? But I don't like it, not at all."

In the palace, standing before Lorenzo in the *studiolo*, with Michelangelo at his side, the son found the father humble, almost pathetic. And he felt sorry for him.

"Buonarroti-Simoni, we would like Michelangelo to live with us here, and become a sculptor. Everything will be provided for him. Will you concede the boy?"

"*Magnifico messere*, I know not how to deny you," replied Lodovico, bowing deeply. "Not only Michelangelo, but all of us, with our lives and wits, are at the pleasure of Your Magnificence."

"Good. What do you do?"

"I have never followed any craft or trade. I have lived on my meager income, attending to the few possessions left to me by my ancestors."

"Then make use of me. See if there is in Florence something I can do for you. I will favor your interest to the utmost of my power."

Lodovico glanced at his son, then looked away.

"I know not how to do anything but read and write. The companion of Marco Pucci in the customhouse has just died, and I should be pleased to have his place."

"The customhouse! It pays only eight scudi a month."

"It seems to me I could fitly discharge that office."

Lorenzo raised both hands to elbow height, shook his fingers as though to rid them of water.

"I had expected you would request something much grander. But if you desire to become the companion of Pucci, you can do so."

He turned back to Michelangelo standing tight-lipped before him. A warm smile lighted the dark homely face.

"It is sixty years since my grandfather Cosimo invited Donatello into his home to execute the bronze statue of David."

BOOK THREE

THE PALACE

A page escorted him up the grand staircase and along the corridor to an apartment opposite the central courtyard. The page knocked. Bertoldo opened the door.

"Welcome, Michelangelo, to my home. *Il Magnifico* thinks I have so little time left, he wants me to teach you in my sleep."

Michelangelo found himself in an L-shaped interior dividing into separate rooms. There were two wooden beds covered with white blankets and red coverlets, each with a coffer at its foot. Bertoldo had his bed on the inside of the L; covering a wall above his head was a painted tapestry representing the Palazzo della Signoria. There was a big cupboard turned catercorner against the inside angle of the L, filled with Bertoldo's books, including the pigskin-bound manuscript of his cookbook, bronze candlesticks which he had designed for Donatello; and on the various levels the wax or clay models of most of his sculptures.

Michelangelo's bed was in the door half of the L, from which he could see the sculptures on the cupboard but nothing of Bertoldo's bed area. On the wall opposite the bed was a wooden tablet with the Baptistery painted on it, and next to a window overlooking the Via de' Gori a hatrack and a table with a vase and pitcher of water.

"This arrangement will give us privacy," said Bertoldo. "Put your things in the coffer at the foot of your bed. If you have any valuables I'll lock them in this antique chest."

Michelangelo glanced at his small bundle of clothes and darned stockings.

"My only valuables are my two hands: I like to keep them by my side."

"They'll take you farther than your feet will."

They retired early, Bertoldo lighting the candles in the bronze holders which sent flickering fingers of light into both wings. They could not see each other, yet their beds were only a few feet apart and they could talk in a quiet tone. The one thing they could both see was the catercornered cupboard, with the models of Bertoldo's work.

"Your sculptures look beautiful in the candlelight."

Bertoldo was silent for a moment. "Poliziano says, 'Bertoldo is not a sculptor of miniatures, he is a miniature sculptor.' "

Michelangelo drew in his breath sharply. Bertoldo heard the sound of protest, said softly:

"There is an element of truth in that cruel witticism. Isn't it a bit pathetic that from your pillow you can take in with one glance my whole lifetime of work?"

"But, Bertoldo, sculpture isn't measured by how many pounds it weighs."

"By any measurement it is a modest contribution. Talent is cheap; dedication is expensive. It will cost you your life."

"What else is life for?"

Bertoldo sighed.

"Alas, I thought it was for many things: falconing, testing recipes, pursuing pretty girls. You know the Florentine adage, 'Life is to be enjoyed.' The sculptor must create a *body of work*. He must produce for fifty to sixty years, as Ghiberti and Donatello did. He must produce enough to permeate the whole world."

The old man was tired. Michelangelo heard him sigh into sleep. He himself lay awake, his hands locked behind his head. He could think of no difference between "Life is to be enjoyed" and "Life is work." Here he was, living in the Medici palace, enjoying the contemplation of unlimited art works to study, and a corner of the sculpture garden full of beautiful marble to carve. He fell asleep with a smile on his lips.

He woke with the first sunlight, quietly dressed and went out into the halls of the palace. He ran his hands over the antique marble of Marsyas, the figures of Faustina and Africanus; studied the richly colored Venetian paintings in what appeared to be a withdrawing room; contrasted portraits in paint by Pollaiuolo with portraits in marble by Mino da Fiesole; spent an hour in the chapel glorying in the Benozzo Gozzoli frescoes of the Three Wise Men of the East coming down the hill from Fiesole; knocked on doors and entered to find himself gazing in wide-eyed wonder and awe at Donatello's Ascension, Masaccio's St. Paul, Uccello's Battle of San Romano . . . until he became so lightheaded he thought he must be in a dream.

At eleven he returned to his room to find that the palace tailor had left a new outfit on his bed. In a festive mood he slipped on the colorful silks, then stood before the mirror surveying himself with satisfaction. It was amazing how much more attractive the new clothes made him look, the crimson *berretto* sending color into his cheeks, the cowl collar of the violet cloak making his head seem better proportioned, the golden shirt and stockings adding a sheen of gaiety. He remembered the day, two years before, when he had sat on his bed redrafting his features with a crayon while awaiting Granacci's summoning whistle.

As he postured before the mirror he was delighted at the changes in himself. He had not only added a couple of inches of height, now standing five feet four, but he had put on some weight. The high bone ridges of his cheeks no longer seemed skeletal; and with the growth of his mouth and chin it was not so noticeable that his ears were placed too far back on his head. He combed his curly hair forward to cover part of the too broad forehead. His small, heavy-lidded eyes seemed more widely open, their secure expression reflected his having found a place for himself in the world. People need no longer think his face out of plumb.

He worshiped beauty in others; and had so little himself. At thirteen he had reconciled himself to being small, burdened with an insignificant figure. Having the deepest admiration for the magnificent strength and proportion of the male body, his own mediocre limbs and torso had seemed a tattered cloak. Now he no longer cut so dull a figure.

In his absorption, he did not see Bertoldo enter.

"Oh, Bertoldo . . . I was just . . ."

"You fancy yourself in that raiment?"

"I didn't know I could look like this."

"You can't. They're for *festa* only."

"Isn't Sunday dinner a holiday?"

"Put on this blouse and tunic. Come the Day of the Virgin, you can show off."

Michelangelo sighed, took off the violet cloak and unlaced the fine yellow linen blouse, then glanced mischievously at his teacher.

"Ah well, put not an embroidered crupper on a plow horse."

They made their way up the broad staircase from the entresol to the long foyer, then turned sharply to their right into the dining room. He was surprised to find himself in a severe room without a single work of art. The panel frames and lintels were done in gold leaf, the walls in a cool cream color, quiet and restrained. There was a table across the end, seating a dozen, and coming down both sides at right angles to it two more tables formed a U, seating another dozen inside and out, so that no one was more than a few slender gilt chairs from Lorenzo, and sixty could dine in intimacy.

They were early. Michelangelo held back in the doorway. Lorenzo, who had Contessina on his right and a Florentine merchant on his left, saw them.

"Ah, Michelangelo, come sit near us. We have no prearranged places; whoever comes first takes the nearest empty seat."

Contessina put her hand on the chair next to hers, inviting him to join her. As he sat down he noticed the beautiful table settings: square-shaped crystal glasses with gold trim, silver plates with the Florentine *giglio*, lily, inlaid in gold, silver knives, spoons with the Medici crest of six raised balls: three, two and one. As he presented his compliments to Lorenzo, palace pages were removing green plants to reveal the palace orchestra in a shell-shaped niche behind him: a harpsichord with a double keyboard, a harp, three big violas, a large lute.

"Welcome to the palace, Michelangelo," said Contessina. "Father says you are to be one of the family. Am I to call you 'brother'?"

He knew he was being teased, asked himself, "Why was I born with a heavy tongue?" After a moment he replied:

"Perhaps 'cousin' would be better?"

Contessina chuckled. "It's pleasant for me that your first dinner is on a Sunday. Other days women are not permitted at table. We have our meals in the upper loggia."

"Then I am not to see you during the week?" he blurted out.

Her eyes were as round as Giotto's O.

"The palace is not that large."

He watched the colorful array of diners as they entered as though into the court of a king, while the musicians played *Un Cavaliere di Spagna:* Lorenzo's daughter Lucrezia and her husband Jacopo Salviati; Lorenzo's second cousins Giovanni and Lorenzo de' Medici, whom Lorenzo had raised and educated after they were orphaned; Prior Bichiellini, brilliant and bespectacled head of the Augustinian Order at the church of Santo Spirito which housed the libraries of Petrarch and Boccaccio; Giuliano da Sangallo, who had designed the exquisite villa at Poggio a Caiano; the Duke of Milan en route to Rome with his retinue; the ambassador from the Sultan of Turkey; two cardinals from Spain; reigning families from Bologna, Ferrara, Arezzo; scholars from Paris and Berlin bringing manuscripts, treatises, works of art; members of the Signoria of Florence; bland, homely Piero Soderini, whom Lorenzo was training to become chief magistrate of Florence; an emissary from the Doge of Venice; visiting professors from the university of Bologna; prosperous city merchants and their wives; visiting businessmen from Athens, Pekin, Alexandria, London. All came to pay their respects to their host.

Contessina kept up a running identification. Here were Demetrius Chalcondyles, head of Lorenzo's public Academy of Greek and co-publisher of the first printed edition of Homer; Vespasiano da Bisticci, leading bibliophile and dealer in rare manuscripts who supplied the libraries of the late Pope Nicolas V, Alessandro Sforza, the Earl of Worcester, and the Medici; the English scholars Thomas Linacre and William Grocyn, who were studying under Poliziano and Chalcondyles of

Lorenzo's Platonic Academy; Johann Reuchlin, the German humanist and disciple of Pico della Mirandola; the monk Fra Mariano, for whom Lorenzo had built a monastery outside the Porta San Gallo designed by Giuliano da Sangallo; an emissary bearing news of the sudden death of Matthias of Hungary, who had admired "the philosopher-prince Lorenzo."

Piero de' Medici, oldest son of Lorenzo, and his elegantly gowned wife Alfonsina Orsini, came in late and had to take places at the foot of one of the long tables. Michelangelo saw that they were offended.

"Piero and Alfonsina don't approve of all this republicanism," Contessina whispered. "They think we should hold court, with only Medici allowed at the head table, and the plebeians seated below us."

Giovanni, Lorenzo's second son, and his cousin Giulio entered, Giovanni with his tonsure fresh-shaved, the eye with the cast involuntarily blinking. He had his mother's light brown hair and fair complexion, was tall and corpulent, with a heavy face and plump underchin. Giulio, illegitimate son of Lorenzo's dead brother, was dark, handsome, saturnine. His eyes slashed through the assemblage, separating every personage and relationship. He missed nothing that could be useful to him.

The last to enter was Nannina de' Medici on the arm of a handsome, brilliantly dressed man.

"My aunt Nannina," murmured Contessina, "and her husband Bernardo Rucellai. He's a good poet, Father says; he writes plays. Sometimes the Plato Academy meets in his garden."

Michelangelo's eyes studied every aspect of this cousin of his mother. He said nothing to Contessina of the relationship.

The musicians began to play *Corinto,* the music of which had been set to one of Lorenzo's poems. Two servingmen who stood at the lifts began hauling up the food. As the waiters passed among the diners with heavy silver trays *of* fresh-water fish, Michelangelo was staggered to see a youngish man in a multicolored shirt pick up a small fish, put it to his ear, then to his mouth as though talking to it, and after a moment burst into tears. All eyes were centered on him. Michelangelo turned his perplexed gaze on Contessina.

"Jacquo, the palace buffoon. 'Laugh. Be a Florentine.' "

"Why are you crying, Jacquo?" asked Lorenzo.

"My father was drowned some years ago. I asked this little fish whether he ever saw him anywhere. He said he was too young to have met him and suggested that I ask those bigger fish who may know more about the matter."

Lorenzo, amused, said, "Give Jacquo some of the big fishes so that he may interrogate them."

The laughter had an annealing quality; strangers at Lorenzo's table who had never met and perhaps came from diametrically opposed ways of life began talking with the people around them. Michelangelo, who knew not the nature of fun and had been shocked to find a buffoon at Lorenzo's table, felt his disapproving scowl soften. Contessina had been watching him.

"Don't you like to laugh?"

"I am unpracticed. No one laughs in my house."

"You are what my French tutor calls *un homme sérieux.* But my father is a serious man too; it's just that he believes laughter can be useful. You will see when you have lived with us for a time."

The fish dish was removed and he was served with *fritto misto.* Michelangelo was too fascinated watching Lorenzo as he spoke in turn to some thirty or forty guests to more than taste the food.

"*Il Magnifico,* does he work through the entire meal?"

"He enjoys all these people, the noise and talk and fun. Yet at the same time he sits down with a hundred purposes in mind, and rises with them all accomplished."

The servants at the lift took off young suckling pigs roasted on a spit, with rosemary in their mouths. *Il Cardiere,* an improviser upon the lyre, entertained by singing the news and gossip of the week accompanied by satiric comments in rhymed and cadenced verse.

After dessert the guests promenaded in the wide foyer. Contessina slipped her arm through his.

"Do you know what it means to be a friend?" she asked.

"Granacci has tried to teach me."

"Everyone is a friend to the Medici," she said quietly, ". . . and no one."

2

The following morning he and Bertoldo walked through the sentient air of early spring, the sky a cerulean blue, the stones of Florence fire-gold as they absorbed the sun. Above them on the hills of Fiesole each cypress, villa and monastery stood out from the green-gray background of olives and vines. They went to the far end of the garden, to the collection of marble blocks. It was as though they were standing in an ancient cemetery whose tumbled headstones had been bleached by the sun.

Bertoldo turned to his protégé with a shy expression in his pale blue eyes.

"Admittedly, I am not a great marble carver. But with you perhaps I can become a great teacher."

"Here's a beautiful piece of meat," Michelangelo cried impetuously.

Bertoldo smiled at this use of the quarryman's vernacular.

"The figure you want to carve must run with the block. You will know whether you're going with the grain by the way it chips when you hit it. To see how the veins run, pour water on the block. The tiny black marks, even in good marble, are iron stains. Sometimes they can be chipped off. If you hit an iron vein you will feel it because it is much harder than marble, and it will be your metal on the metal of the stone."

"Makes my teeth grind to think of it."

"Every time you hit the marble with a chisel you mash crystals. A mashed crystal is a dead crystal. Dead crystals ruin sculpture. You must learn to carve great blocks without crushing the crystals."

"When?"

"Later."

Bertoldo told him about air bubbles, the spots in the marble that fall out or become hollow after weathering. They cannot be seen from the outside, and one must learn to know when they are inside. It was like selecting an apple; one could tell it was wholesome because it bulged forth in healthy form into space while a rotting apple tended to become concave, as if being subdued by space.

"Marble is like man: you have to know everything that is in it before you start. If there are concealed air bubbles in you, I'm wasting my time."

Michelangelo made a childish joke which Bertoldo ignored, going instead for a set of tools from the shed.

"Here is a punch. It is a tool to remove. Here are an *ugnetto* and a *scarpello.* They are the tools to form."

Bertoldo demonstrated that even when he was tearing out marble to get rid of what he did not want he must work with rhythmical strokes so that he achieved circular lines around the block. He was never to complete any one part, but work on all parts, balancing relationships. Did he understand?

"I will, after you turn me loose among these marbles. I learn through my hands, not my ears."

"Then take the wax out! That Faun wasn't too bad, but you arrived at your results through blind intuition. For consistent results you have to know why you are doing what."

The outdoor sculpture workshop was a combination forge, carpenter's and blacksmith's shop. There was on hand a supply of beams, wedges, wooden horses, saws, bevels, hammers, wood chisels to repair the handles of hammers. The floor was cement to allow for solid footing. Standing alongside the forge were newly arrived rods of Swedish iron that Granacci had bought the day before so that Michelangelo could make himself a full set of nine chisels.

Bertoldo told him to start a fire in the forge; chestnut wood made the best charcoal and produced a slow, intense, even heat.

"I already know how to temper tools for *pietra serena,*" said Michelangelo. "The Topolinos taught me."

With the fire started, he reached for the blower, an enclosed wheel with metal slabs about its circumference, to feed it a good draft.

"*Basta,*" exclaimed Bertoldo. "Tap these iron rods together and see if they ring like bells."

The rods were good grade iron, all except one, which was discarded. When the fire was hot enough he became immersed in making his first set of tools. He knew that "the man who does not make his own tools does not make his own sculpture." The hours passed. They did not stop for dinner. Dusk was falling when the old man became faint, his skin ashen gray. He would have fallen if Michelangelo had not caught him in his arms. He carried him to the casino, marveling that Bertoldo could weigh so little, less than a rod of Swedish ore. He put his teacher down gently on a chair.

"How could I have let you work so long?" he groaned.

A little color spread over the brittle bones of Bertoldo's cheeks. "It is not enough to handle marble; you must also have iron in your blood."

The next morning Michelangelo rose in the dark, quietly so that he would not waken Bertoldo, walked through the sleeping streets in order to be in the garden at dawn. He knew that it was the first rays of the sun that revealed the truth about marble. Under these piercing rays marble was almost translucent; all veins, faults, hollows were mercilessly exposed. Quality that could survive the earliest sun would be intact when night fell.

He went from block to block tapping with his hammer. The solid blocks gave out a bell-like sound, the defective ones a dull thud. One small piece that had been exposed to the weather for a long time had developed a tough skin. With hammer and chisel he cut away the membranous coating to get to the pure milky substance below. Wanting to learn the direction of the vein, he held his hammer tightly and fractured off the high corners.

He liked what he saw; took a piece of charcoal and drew the head and beard of an old man on the marble. Then he pulled up a bench, straddled the block, gripping it with both knees, picked up hammer and chisel. His body settled down with a soughing movement. Tensions within him fell away with each falling chip. Stone filled him out, gave him body; he felt implemented and whole. His arm grew lighter and stronger with the passing of the hours. These metal tools clothed him in their own armor. They made him robust.

He thought, "As Torrigiani loves the feel of a gun in his hand, Sansovino the plow, Rustici the rough coat of a dog, and Baccio a woman, just so am I happiest with a block of marble between my legs and a hammer and chisel in my hands."

White marble was the heart of the universe, the purest substance created by God; not merely a symbol of God but a portrait, God's way of manifesting Himself. Only a divine hand could create such noble beauty. He felt himself a part of the white purity before him, felt its integrity as though it were his own.

He remembered Bertoldo quoting Donatello: "Sculpture is an art which, by removing all that is superfluous from the material under treatment, reduces it to that form designed in the artist's mind."

Was it not equally true that the sculptor could never force any design on the marble which was not indigenous to its own nature? He had the impression that, no matter how honestly a sculptor designed, it would come to nothing if it did not agree with the basic nature of the block. In this sense a sculptor could never be completely master of his fate, as a painter could be. Paint was fluid, it could bend around corners. Marble was solidity itself. The marble sculptor had to accept the rigorous discipline of a partnership. The marble and he were one. They spoke to each other. And for him, the feel of marble was the supreme sensation. No gratification of any other sense, taste, sight, sound, smell, could approach it.

He had removed the outer shell. Now he dug into the mass, entered in the biblical sense. In this act of creation there was needed the thrust, the penetration, the beating and pulsating upward to a mighty climax, the total possession. It was not merely an act of love, it was the act of love: the mating of his own inner patterns to the inherent forms of the marble; an insemination in which he planted seed, created the living work of art.

Bertoldo entered the shop, saw Michelangelo at work, cried out, "No, no, that's wrong. Stop! That's the amateur way to carve."

Michelangelo heard the voice over the pounding of his hammer, turned to flash recognition, but without ceasing the gouging-out movement of his *ugnetto*.

"Michelangelo! You're beginning at the wrong end."

Michelangelo did not hear him. Bertoldo turned away from the sight of his apprentice cutting a furrow through the stone as though it were quince jelly. He shook his head in amused despair.

"As well try to keep Vesuvius from erupting."

3

That evening he bathed in a tub of hot water placed for him in a small room at the end of his hallway, put on a dark blue shirt and hose and accompanied Bertoldo to Lorenzo's *studiolo* for supper. He was nervous. What would he say? The Plato Academy was reported to be the intellectual heart of Europe, a university and a printing press, a fount of literature and a world-exploring expedition which had for its purpose the turning of Florence into a second Athens. If only he had listened to Urbino when his teacher had been reading from the old Greek manuscripts.

There was a fire crackling in the hearth, warm light in the brass lamps on Lorenzo's writing desk, a pleasant air of camaraderie. Seven chairs were drawn up to a low table. The shelves of books, Greek reliefs, cases of cameos and amulets made the room intimate and cozy. The Plato group received him casually, then returned to their discussion of the comparative worth of medicine and astrology as sciences, giving Michelangelo an opportunity to sort out the faces and personalities of the four scholars who were reputed to be the outstanding brains of Italy.

Marsilio Ficino, fifty-seven, had founded the Plato Academy for Cosimo, Lorenzo's grandfather. He was a tiny man, under five feet, and though suffering the continuing ills of the hypochondriac he had translated all of Plato and become a living dictionary of ancient philosophies by translating the body of Egyptian wisdom before devouring the work of the sages from Aristotle through the Alexandrians, Confucianists, Zoroastrians. Trained by his father to be a doctor, he was well acquainted with the natural sciences as well. He had helped introduce the printing of books in Florence. His own writings attracted scholars from all over Europe who came to listen to his lectures. In his beautiful villa in Careggi, which Cosimo had had Michelozzo design for him, and which was managed by his nieces, he burned an undying lamp in front of a statue of Plato, whom he was trying to have canonized as the "dearest of Christ's disciples," an act of heresy as well as inverted history for which Rome had very nearly excommunicated him. His nieces quipped:

"He can recite the whole of a Plato dialogue but he can never remember where he left his slippers."

Michelangelo next turned his attention to Cristoforo Landino, about sixty-six, tutor of Lorenzo's father, Piero the Gouty, and of Lorenzo himself, brilliant writer and lecturer, training the Florentine mind to free itself from dogma and to apply the findings of science to nature. He had served as confidential secretary to the Signoria, was experienced in politics, and a leader of the Medici circle for three generations. He was the Dante authority, having published his commentary in the first version of *The Divine Comedy* printed in Florence. His lifetime work centered around the Italian language, the *volgare,* which almost singlehanded he was turning from a despised argot into a respected language by translating into it Pliny, Horace, Virgil.

He was known in Florence for his revolutionary credo: "The deepest basis for action is the clear supremacy of contemplation and knowledge." In Lorenzo he had found the hero of Plato's *Republic:* "The ideal ruler of a city is the scholar."

Perched on the edge of a stiff leather chair was Angelo Poliziano, thirty-six years of age, who was said by opponents of the Medici to be kept close at hand because by contrast he made Lorenzo appear attractive. Yet he was acknowledged to be the most fantastic scholar there: publishing in Latin at the age of ten, invited into the Florentine *Compagnia di Dottrina* at twelve to be trained by Ficino, Landino and the Greek scholars brought to Florence by the Medici. He had translated the first books of Homer's *Iliad* by sixteen and been taken into the palace by Lorenzo to become tutor to his sons. One of the ugliest of men, he was possessed of as lucid and limpid a style as any poet since Petrarch; his *Stanza per la Giostra di Giuliano,* a book-length poem celebrating the tournament of Giuliano de' Medici, Lorenzo's younger brother, killed by the Pazzi, had become a model for Italian poetry.

Michelangelo's eyes now went to the youngest and most attractive of the group, twenty-seven-year-old Pico della Mirandola, who read and wrote in twenty-two languages. The other members of the group teased him by saying, "The only reason Pico doesn't know a twenty-third is that he can't find one." Known as the "great lord of Italy," with a sweet and sincere nature, unspoiled by his soft golden hair, deep blue eyes, flawless blond skin, slender figure, Florentines called him "beautiful and beloved." His intellectual concept was the unity of knowledge; his ambition, to reconcile all religions and philosophies since the beginning of time. Like Ficino, he aspired to hold in his mind the totality of human learning. To this end he read Chinese philosophers in Chinese, Arabic in Arabic, Hebrew in Hebrew believing that all languages were rational divisions of one universal language. Of all Italians the most divinely gifted, he yet made no enemies, even as ugly Poliziano could make no friends.

The door opened. Lorenzo entered, limping from an attack of his recurrent gout. He nodded to the others, turned to Michelangelo.

"This is the *sancta sanctorum:* most of what Florence learns is started in this room. When we are in the palace, and you are free, join us."

Lorenzo moved an ornamented screen and knocked on the dumb-waiter behind, from which Michelangelo assumed that the *studiolo* was directly below the dining room. He heard the platform moving inside the shaft, and within a few moments the academicians were taking plates of cheese, fruit, bread, honey, nuts and setting them on the low table in the center of the room. There were no servants about; nor was there anything but milk to drink. Though the talk was light, Michelangelo perceived that the group met for work; and after supper "wine made the hair swell."

The table was cleared, the plates, fruit rinds and nutshells dispatched down the lift. At once the conversation became serious. Sitting on a low stool beside Bertoldo, Michelangelo heard the case against the Church, which the scholars in this room no longer considered synonymous with their religion. Florence in particular was a seat of disaffection because Lorenzo and the majority of his fellow townsmen agreed that Pope Sixtus of Rome had been behind the Pazzi conspiracy which had resulted in the murder of Giuliano and the almost fatal stabbing of Lorenzo. The Pope had excommunicated Florence, forbidding the clergy to fulfill the duties of their office. Florence in turn had excommunicated the Pope, declaring the papal claims to power were based on such eighth-century forgeries as the Donation of Constantine. The Pope in an effort to crush Lorenzo had sent troops into Tuscany, which had burned and pillaged as close as the neighboring town of Poggibonsi. . . .

With the advent of Innocent VIII in 1484, peace had been re-established between Florence and Rome; but as Michelangelo heard the evidence summarized by the men around the table, it appeared that much of the Tuscan clergy had become increasingly immoral in personal conduct as well as in clerical practice. The outstanding exception was the Augustinian Order at Santo Spirito, living in flawless self-discipline under Prior Bichiellini.

Pico della Mirandola put his elbows on the low table, resting his chin on his clasped hands.

"I think I may have come upon an answer to our dilemma over the Church: in the form of a Dominican monk from Ferrara. I've heard him preach there. He shakes the ribs of the cathedral."

Landino, whose white hair was worn long in back, with tufts coming over his forehead, leaned across the table, so that Michelangelo could see the fine network of wrinkles circling his eyes.

"This monk, is he all volume?"

"On the contrary, Landino," replied Pico, "he's a brilliant student of the Bible and St. Augustine. He feels even more strongly about the corruption of the clergy than we do."

Angelo Poliziano, of the heavy features and coarse black hair worn string-like down over his ears and covering part of the rough skin, moistened his overly red, projecting underlip.

"It's not only the corruption, it's the ignorance that appalls me."

Ficino, light-complected, with a bright, perceptive face and tiny nose and mouth, cried out eagerly:

"It's been a long time since we've had a scholar in a Florentine pulpit. We have only Fra Mariano and Prior Bichiellini."

"Girolamo Savonarola has given himself over to years of study," Pico assured them. "Plato and Aristotle as well as Church doctrine."

"What are his ambitions?" asked Lorenzo.

"To purify the Church."

"Nothing more? What about power?"

"Only the power within him."

"If this monk would work with us . . . " proffered Lorenzo.

"If Your Excellency will request his transfer of the Lombard Fathers?"

"I'll attend to it."

The subject settled, the oldest, Landino, and the youngest, Pico, now turned their attention to Michelangelo. Landino asked if he had read what Pliny wrote about the famous Greek statue of the Laocoön.

"I know nothing of Pliny."

"Then I shall read it to you."

He took a book down from the shelf, quickly thumbed through it and read the story of the statue in the palace of Emperor Titus, "a work that may be looked upon as preferable to any other production of the art of painting or of statuary. It is sculptured from a single block, both the main figures as well as the children, and the serpents with their marvelous folds.''

Poliziano followed with a description of the Venus of Cnidos from Lucian, which represented Venus standing before Paris when he awarded her the prize of beauty. Pico then remembered the Pentelic marble statue at the tomb of Xenophon.

"Michelangelo will want to read Pausanias in the original," said Pico. "I will bring you my manuscript."

"I don't read Greek," said Michelangelo a bit ashamedly.

"I will teach you."

"I do not have the gift for languages."

"No matter," interceded Poliziano, "in a year you will be writing sonnets in Latin as well as Greek."

To himself, Michelangelo murmured, "Permit me to doubt." But it would be bad manners to kill the enthusiasm of these new friends who were now arguing among themselves as to which books he should be taught from.

". . . Homer. For Greek, he is the purest."

"Aristophanes is more fun. To laugh while learning . . ."

He was relieved when the group turned its attention away from him. The most important idea he gleaned from the swift, learned talk was that religion and knowledge could exist side by side, enriching each other. Greece and Rome, before the dawn of Christianity, had built gloriously in the arts, humanities, sciences, philosophy. Then for a thousand years all such wisdom and beauty had been crushed, declared anathema, buried in darkness. Now this little group of men, the sensual Poliziano, the lined Landino, the tiny Ficino, the golden-haired Pico della Mirandola, these few fragile men, led and aided by Lorenzo de' Medici, were attempting to create a new intellect under the banner of a word Michelangelo had never heard before: *Humanism*.

What did it mean?

As the hours wore on he found himself caught up in interest. So much so that when Bertoldo signaled that he was leaving, slipping out quietly, Michelangelo remained. And as each of the Platonists poured out his thoughts he slowly gathered the sense of what they meant:

We are giving the world back to man, and man back to himself. Man shall no longer be vile, but noble. We shall not destroy his mind in return for an immortal soul. Without a free, vigorous and creative mind, man is but an animal, and he will die like an animal, without any shred of a soul. We return to man his arts, his literature, his sciences, his independence to think and feel as an individual, not to be bound to dogma like a slave, to rot in his chains.

At the end of the evening when he returned to his room and found Bertoldo still awake, he blurted out:

"They make me feel so stupid."

"They are the best minds in Europe. They can give you heroic themes to ponder on." Then to console the tired youth, he added, "But they cannot carve marble, and that is a language as eloquent as any."

The next morning he reached the garden early. Torrigiani sought him out in the workshed where he had set up his bearded old man to practice on.

"I'm consumed by curiosity," cried Torrigiani. "Tell me about life in the palace."

Michelangelo told his friend of the room he shared with Bertoldo, how he had wandered down the long halls, free to handle the art treasures, of the guests at the Sunday dinner and his exciting supper in Lorenzo's *studiolo* with the Platonists. Torrigiani was interested only in personalities.

"What are Poliziano and Pico della Mirandola like?"

"Well, Poliziano is ugly until he starts to speak, then his words make him beautiful. Pico della Mirandola is the best-looking man I've ever seen, and brilliant."

"You're very impressionable," said Torrigiani tartly. "A new pair of bright blue eyes, long wavy golden hair, and your eyes pop out of their sockets."

"But, Torrigiani, think of being able to read and write in twenty-two languages! When we can barely express ourselves in one."

"Speak for yourself," retorted Torrigiani. "I have a nobleman's education, and I can discuss with the best of them. It is not my fault if you are ignorant."

Michelangelo realized that his friend had become quarrelsome.

"I meant no criticism of you, Torrigiani."

"One night in the Medici palace and already the rest of Florence seems ignorant to you."

"I was merely . . ."

". . . you were merely bragging about your new friends," interrupted Torrigiani, "men who are so much more attractive and intelligent than your old, grubby friends with whom you have been imprisoned in these garden walls."

"I had no such thought. Why do you say such things?"

But Torrigiani had turned away.

Michelangelo sighed, returned to his marble.

4

Palm Sunday was a warm spring day. On his washstand he found three gold florins which Bertoldo said would be left for him each week by Lorenzo's secretary, Ser Piero da Bibbiena. He could not resist the temptation of showing off to his family. On his bed he laid out another new outfit, the white blouse embroidered with grapes and leaves, the short surcoat with cape sleeves belted in front with silver buckles, the wine-colored stockings. He smiled to himself as he pictured Granacci's expression when he met him in the Piazza San Marco so they could walk home together.

Rustici stared at him as he came down the path and, when Michelangelo was close enough, mimicked:

"I'm plain." Then, more acidly, "Spread your tail."

"My tail?"

"All peacocks have colorful tails."

"Oh, now, Rustici," he wailed, "can't I wear them even once?"

"Can't I wear this jewelry just once? Can't I drink this rare wine just once? Order these servants around just once? Squander some gold coins just once? Sleep with this pretty girl just once? . . ."

"All the temptations of the flesh in one sonnet. Truly, Rustici, I feel as though I were dressed up in a costume for a pageant. But I would like to impress my family."

"Vai via," growled Rustici. "Go your way."

Torrigiani came stalking down the path, his flame-colored cloak and orange plumes on his black velvet hat flying. He hauled up short in front of Michelangelo.

"I want to talk to you, alone."

Torrigiani seized his arm. Michelangelo held back.

"Why alone? We have no secrets."

"We shared confidences. Until you moved into the palace and became so important."

There was no mistaking the emotion behind Torrigiani's outburst. Michelangelo spoke gently, hoping to placate him.

"But you live in your own palace, Torrigiani."

"Yes, and I don't have to play cheap little tricks like knocking out a faun's teeth to ingratiate myself with the Medici."

"You sound jealous."

"Of what! Of an insufferable prig?"

"Why a prig? What's the connection?"

"Because you know nothing about happiness or comradeship."

"I've never been happier."

"Yes, setting down charcoal lines with your grimy hands."

"But good charcoal lines," protested Michelangelo, refusing to take Torrigiani seriously.

Torrigiani went purple in the face.

"Are you implying that mine are not?"

"Why do you always bring a discussion back to yourself? You're not the center of the universe."

"To myself, I am. And I was to you too, until your head got swollen."

Michelangelo stared at him in amazement.

"You were never the center of my universe."

"Then you deceived me. You're sucking up for your commissions an awful long time in advance."

The sun went cold on Michelangelo's face. He turned and ran as hard as he could, out of the garden and down the Street of the Cuirass Makers.

The carpenter and grocer sitting in the sun before their shops pulled at their caps respectfully; otherwise his new clothes were no more of a success at home than they had been with Rustici. His father felt hurt, as though the finery was in some way a reproach to him.

Michelangelo took the three gold florins from the purse on his belt and put them on Lodovico's desk. Lodovico gazed at them without comment, but his stepmother Lucrezia bussed him happily on both cheeks, her eyes bright with excitement.

"Now tell me! What sauces do they use on the *pasta?*"

Michelangelo racked his brains, wanting to please.

"I can't remember."

"Then the meats. Do the palace cooks use zedoary? What of their famous sole cooked with banana strips and pine nuts?"

"Forgive me, *madre mia,* I don't know."

She shook her head in despair.

"Don't you remember what you chew? Then make friends with the cooks. Write down the recipes for my sake."

Now the full family had assembled in Lodovico's combination office and sitting room. His grandmother was happy because he was meeting the great men of Florence. His brother Giovansimone was interested in the parties. His aunt and uncle were pleased because of the gold coins he had brought home. Buonarroto wanted to know about the business arrangement: was he to receive three gold coins every week? Were the stone and materials taken out of his salary?

His father called for attention.

"How do the Medici treat you? *Il Magnifico?*"

"Well."

"Piero?"

"He is arrogant; it is his nature."

"Giovanni, the cardinal-to-be?"

"He treats all alike. As though each meeting were the first."

"Giuliano?"

Michelangelo smiled. "The whole palace loves him."

Lodovico cogitated a moment, then announced:

"Piero's attitude will prevail: you are in the palace as a humble workman." He eyed the three gold coins gleaming on the desk. "What are they? A gift? A wage?"

"I am to have three florins each week."

"What did they say when they delivered the money?"

"It was on my wash table. When I asked Bertoldo, he said that it was a weekly allowance."

His uncle Francesco could not contain his delight.

"Splendid. With this steady money we can rent a stall. Michelangelo, you will be a partner, you will share in the profits . . ."

"Imagine," his aunt Cassandra chimed in with a newborn respect, "that Michelangelo should be the one to put us back in commerce."

"No!" It was Lodovico, his face a deep red. "We are not the bashful poor."

"But they were given to Michelangelo as a member of the Medici family," answered his young wife.

"Humpf!" snorted Lodovico. "What makes him a Medici? Three gold coins?"

"It is not charity." Michelangelo was indignant. "I work from light to dark."

"Are you legally apprenticed? Did I sign a Guild agreement?" He turned on his brother Francesco. "A gift is a whim. Next week there may be nothing!"

Michelangelo thought his father was going to throw the money at his head. He had meant only to bring home his earnings like a dutiful son . . . perhaps bragging a little. But the three gold florins were more than Lodovico would earn in months at the customs. Michelangelo realized that he had been indelicate, for now, with his head on his chest, Lodovico commented, "Think how many millions of florins the Medici must have if they can give a fifteen-year-old student three of them each week." Then, with a quick movement of his hand, he swept them into the top drawer of his desk.

Lucrezia seized the moment to summon them to table. After dinner the family reassembled in the sitting room. Lionardo, silent during the earlier discussion, placed himself in front of Michelangelo to proclaim in a pontifical voice:

"Art is a vice."

"Art, a vice!" Michelangelo was amazed at his brother. "How . . . why?"

"Because it is self-indulgence, concentration on your own lust to create instead of contemplating the glories of what God has created."

"But, Lionardo, our churches are plastered with art."

"We have been led astray by the devil. A church is not a fair; people must go to pray on their knees, not to see a play painted on the walls."

"Then there is no place for a sculptor in your world?"

Lionardo clasped his hands, gazing devoutly through the ceiling.

"My world is the next world, where we will sit at the right hand of God."

Lodovico rose from his seat, exclaimed: "Now I have two fanatics on my hands."

He left for his midday nap, followed by the rest of the family. Only Monna Alessandra remained sitting quietly in a corner. Michelangelo too wanted to leave; he was feeling tired. The whole day had been a disappointment.

Lionardo would not let him go. He moved into a frontal attack on Lorenzo and the Plato Academy as pagans, atheists, enemies of the Church, antichrists.

"I promise you, Lionardo," began Michelangelo placatingly, "I have heard no sacrilege, irreverence, at least not to religion itself. Only to the abuses. Lorenzo is a reformer; he wants to cleanse the Church."

"Cleanse! A word that infidels use when they mean destroy. An attack on the Church is an attack on Christianity."

Now in a high rage Lionardo accused Lorenzo de' Medici of carnality, debauchery, of leaving the palace at midnight to ride out with his cronies to nights of revelry and seduction of young women.

"Of these charges, I know nothing," said Michelangelo quietly, " but he is a widower. Should he not love?"

"He was a philanderer before the death of his wife. It is common knowledge. His lust has already enfeebled his body."

He wondered how his brother came into possession of such charges. He did not think of Lorenzo as a saint; he had heard him say laughingly to Landino, "I do not err through wickedness, but rather through some part of my nature that loves pleasure," and he remembered Lorenzo's reply to Ficino, "I cannot regret that I love the pleasures of the flesh; for the love of painting, sculpture and literature are also sensual in nature." All this seemed to him to be the private affair of a virile, effective man.

"Only a toady like yourself would be unable to see that Lorenzo is a tyrant," continued Lionardo.

Michelangelo thought, "This is the second time today I have been called a toady!" He became increasingly miserable, his clothes felt tight and ridiculous.

"He has destroyed the freedom of Florence," cried Lionardo. "He has made things soft and easy for the people. He gives them bread and circuses. . . . The only reason he has failed to take a crown and become king is that he is too devious; he likes to work behind the scenes, controlling every move while the Tuscans are reduced to pawns . . ."

Before Michelangelo could reply, Monna Alessandra said, "Yes, Lionardo, he is softening us. He has kept us from civil war! For years we destroyed each other, family against family, neighborhood against neighborhood, with blood flowing in the streets. Now we are a unified people. Only the Medici can keep us from each other's throats."

Lionardo refused to answer his grandmother.

"Michelangelo, I wish one last word with you."

Michelangelo faced his brother across a heavy mahogany table. He had never been able to talk to this strange boy, or enjoy any companionship with him.

"This is my farewell to you. I leave the house tonight, to join Girolamo Savonarola in San Marco."

"Then Savonarola has arrived? Lorenzo invited him. I was in the *studiolo* when Pico della Mirandola suggested it, and Lorenzo agreed to write to Lombardy."

"A Medici lie! Why should Lorenzo summon him, when it is Savonarola's intention to destroy the Medici? I leave this house as Fra Savonarola left his family in Ferrara: with only a shirt on my back. Forever. I shall pray for you on the floor of my cell until there is no skin left on my knees and the blood comes. Perhaps in that blood you can be redeemed."

Michelangelo could see from Lionardo's burning eyes that there was no use in answering. He shook his head in mock despair, thought: "Father is right. How did this sane, sensible, money-changing Buonarroti family, who have had nothing but conformists for two hundred years, hatch two fanatics in one generation?"

He murmured to Lionardo, "We shall not be too far apart, only a few hundred feet across the Piazza San Marco. If you lean out the window of your monastery cell you will hear me cutting stone in the garden."

5

The following week, when he again found three gold coins on his washstand, he decided not to take them home. He went looking for Contessina, found her in the library.

"I must buy a gift."

"For a lady?"

"For a woman."

"Jewels, perhaps?"

"No." Sullenly. "She is the mother of my friends, the stonecutters."

"How about a linen tablecloth bordered with openwork?"

"They have a tablecloth."

"Has she many dresses?"

"The one she was married in."

"A black dress for mass, then?"

"Excellent."

"How big is she?"

He looked bewildered.

"Draw me her picture."

He grinned. "With a pen I know everything: even a woman's proportions."

"I will ask my nurse to take me to the shop to buy a length of black wool. My *sarta* will cut it to fit your drawing."

"You are kind, Contessina."

She wanted no gratitude. "It is nothing."

He went to the outdoor market in the Piazza Santo Spirito and purchased gifts for the other Topolinos, then arranged with one of the grooms in the basement of the palace to borrow a horse and saddlebag. Sunday morning after attending mass in the palace chapel he packed the bag and set out for Settignano, with the sun burning warmly on his bare head. At first he had thought he would change to his old clothes so that the Topolinos would not think he was putting on airs, but quickly realized that this would be an affectation. Besides he fancied himself in the dark blue shirt and hose which he was already wearing.

The Topolinos were sitting on the terrace overlooking the valley and the Buonarroti house on the ridge opposite, enjoying their weekly hour of idleness after returning from mass in the little village church. They were so surprised to see him come riding up the road on a silver-gray stallion, sitting on a silver saddle, that they forgot to say hello. Michelangelo too was silent. He got down from the horse, tied him to a tree, took off the saddlebag and emptied it onto the rough board table. After a moment of silence the father asked what the packages were. Michelangelo replied: "Gifts."

"Gifts?" The father gazed at his three sons in turn, for except to children, Tuscans do not give presents. "Are you late for the last Befana, or early for the next?"

"Both. For four years I ate your bread and drank your wine."

The father replied roughly, "You cut stone for your soup."

"I took my first money home to the Buonarroti. Today, for the Topolinos, I bring the second."

"You have a commission!" cried the grandfather.

"No. Each week Lorenzo gives me spending money."

The Topolinos scrutinized one another's faces.

"Spending money?" asked the father. "You mean wages."

"I receive no wages."

"Oh, it is keep money: for your room and food?"

"I do not pay for room and food."

"It is purchase money? For your *calze,* or for marble?"

"Everything is provided."

"Then what is it for?"

"To spend on whatever comes to mind."

"If you have food, bed, marble, what would come to mind?"

"Pleasure."

"Pleasure?" The family rolled this word on their tongues as though it were a new fruit. "What manner of pleasure?"

Michelangelo thought about that.

"Well, gambling at seed cards, for example."

"Do you gamble?"

"No."

"What else?"

After a moment: "To be shaved in the straw market."

"Do you have a beard?"

"Not yet. But I could have oil put in my hair like Torrigiani does."

"Do you want oil in your hair?"

"No."

"Then it is not a pleasure. What other?"

In desperation: "Well, the women who wear a cowl with a bell on their heads when they walk on Saturday afternoons."

"Do you want these women?"

"I use it as an illustration. I could buy candles to burn before the Virgin."

"That is a duty."

"A glass of wine of a Sunday afternoon?"

"That is a custom."

He walked to the table.

"It is to bring things to your friends."

Slowly amidst a deep silence, he began distributing his gifts.

"To *mia madre*, for mass. For Bruno, a leather belt with silver buckle. For Gilberto a yellow shirt and stockings. A *nonno*, a wool scarf for your throat in winter. For Father Topolino, high boots for when you work in Cave Maiano. Enrico, you said that when you grew up you would own a gold ring. *Eccolo.*"

For a long moment they gazed at him, speechless. Then the mother went into the house to put on the dress; the father pulled on the high boots; Bruno clasped the belt about his waist; Gilberto donned the new gold shirt; the grandfather stood wrapping and unwrapping the soft wool scarf around his neck. Enrico mounted the horse, the better to admire his ring in privacy.

Then the father spoke.

"All of these . . . these gifts: they are from spending money?"

"All."

"And Lorenzo, he gives you this money to buy us gifts."

"Yes."

"He is truly The Magnificent One."

Michelangelo noticed another package on the table. Perplexed, he opened it, pulled out a linen tablecloth. He remembered Contessina saying, "How about a linen tablecloth?" Contessina had put this gift in the saddlebag as her contribution. The color rose to his cheeks. *Dio mio!* How could he explain it? He thrust the cloth into the hands of Mother Topolino.

"This is a gift from Contessina de' Medici. For you."

The Topolinos were stupefied.

"Contessina de' Medici! How would she send us a tablecloth? She does not know we live."

"Yes, she does. I told her about you. Her *sarta* sewed your dress."

The *nonno* crossed himself. "It is a miracle."

Michelangelo thought, "Amen. It is true."

6

Each of the Plato Four had his own villa in the country around Florence. They came in several times a week to lecture and work with Lorenzo in the *studiolo*. Lorenzo seemed eager that Michelangelo take advantage of these opportunities, and so he attended faithfully.

The Platonists tried to interest him in Latin and Greek, working up charts to show him that the calligraphy of the two languages was a drawing similar in nature to his figure drawing. He took their manuscripts and assignments to his room, pored over them for hours . . . and learned little.

"Nothing sticks!" he wailed to Bertoldo.

Stopped, the men taught him to read aloud, poetry in the vulgate: Dante, Petrarch Horace, Virgil. This he enjoyed, particularly the discussions that followed his reading of *The Divine Comedy,* with the interpretation of its philosophy. The Platonists complimented him on his growing clarity of diction, then brought in Girolamo Benivieni, whom they described as "the most fervent partisan of poetry in the *volgare,"* to teach Michelangelo how to write his own verse. When he demurred on the grounds that he wanted to become a sculptor, not a poet, Pico said:

"The structure of a sonnet is as rigorous a discipline as the structure of a marble relief. When Benivieni teaches you to write sonnets he trains your mind in the rules of logic and composition of thought. You simply must take advantage of his talent!"

Landino reassured him, "We will not try to weaken your carving arm by replacing hammer and chisel with pen and ink!"

Poliziano added, "You must not give up studying poetry. You must continue to read aloud. To be a complete artist it is not enough to be a painter, sculptor or architect. One must also be a poet, if one is to attain full expression."

"I do so poorly," Michelangelo complained one night to Benivieni when he had tried to make the lines scan; "how can you bear to read my clumsy attempts?"

Benivieni, also a talented musician, clucked at Michelangelo's despair, sang a gay song of his own composition, then replied, "My early efforts were no better; worse, if anything. You will think you are a bad poet until the day comes when you have a need to express something; then you'll have the tools of poetry at hand, meter and rhyme, just as you have hammer and chisel on your workbench."

On religious holidays when Lorenzo closed the garden, Michelangelo would ride horseback to Landino's villa on the hill in the Casentino, which had been given to him by the Florentine Republic for his commentaries on Dante; to Ficino's villa at Careggi, a castle with battlements and covered galleries; to Pico's The Oak or Poliziano's Villa Diana, both on the slopes of Fiesole. At the Villa Diana they would settle down in a garden pavilion like the one in which the characters from Boccaccio's *Decameron* spun their tales, and listen to Poliziano read his newest poem:

> Come where green the grass is,
> Green the trees are turning.
> Have no fear, fair lasses,
> Every lad is yearning;
> Beasts and birds are burning
> All with love the May. . . .
>
> Youth's a brittle jewel.
> Grass again is greening,
> Age knows no renewal.
> Fair ones, be not cruel
> To your loves the May.

An idea began to shape in Michelangelo's mind: he too would one day have a house like the Villa Diana, with a sculpture workshop and an annual stipend from Lorenzo which would enable him to buy Carrara marbles from which to carve great statues. Was there any reason why he should not be so treated? He was in no hurry, but when Lorenzo did give him one he would like it to be in Settignano, among stonecarvers.

The days and the weeks passed, drawing from live models, transferring the figures to clay, experimenting with scraps of stone to bring forth a knee joint, a hip movement, the turn of a head on its neck, learning how to avoid a welt when the point of his punch broke, studying Lorenzo's Greek sculptures for techniques.

Lorenzo also pushed his education. One Sunday morning he asked Michelangelo to accompany the Medici family to the church of San Gallo where they would hear Fra Mariano, to whose cloister Lorenzo went when he wanted a serious discussion on theology. "Fra Mariano is my ideal," said Lorenzo, "he has graceful austerity, elegant asceticism, and the liberal religion of enlightened common sense. You will hear."

Fra Mariano preached in a mellow voice, harmonious cadences and apt words. He complimented Christianity on its resemblance to Platonism, quoted from the Greeks, declaimed lines from the Latin poets with polished eloquence. Michelangelo was captivated; he had not heard this manner of priest before. When Fra Mariano modulated his voice he was charmed; when Mariano unfolded his argument he was convinced; when Mariano illustrated with a funny anecdote he smiled; when he pressed with serious truths he yielded to their force.

To Lorenzo he said, "I understand better now what the Academy means by modern religion."

One of Piero's grooms knocked on the door of his apartment and entered.

"His Excellency, Piero de' Medici, commands Michelangelo Buonarroti to present himself in His Excellency's anteroom at the hour before sunset."

Michelangelo thought, "How different from his father, who asks if it would give me pleasure to join him." To the groom he replied courteously, "Inform His Excellency that I shall be present."

There was ample time for a soak in a round wooden tub in the bathing closet at the end of the hall, sitting with his knees clasped under his chin, wondering what the crown prince of the Medici dynasty, who had never favored him with anything more than a formal bow, could want of him. Some instinct told him that his peacock outfit of embroidered shirt and violet cloak was precisely what Piero would approve.

Piero's suite was on the first floor of the palace, just over the open loggia in the corner of the Via de' Gori and Via Larga. Michelangelo had never been in this wing of the palace, not even to see the art works he had heard discussed, because of Piero's coolness. Now his feet dragged along the corridor leading to Piero's suite, for on the walls there was a brilliant painting by Fra Angelico and a delicate marble relief by Desiderio da Settignano.

The groom was waiting outside Piero's anteroom. He admitted Michelangelo. Madonna Alfonsina, Piero's wife, gowned in gray damask embroidered with jewels, was sitting motionless in a high-backed purple throne chair. Covering the wall behind was a tapestry of leaves and flowers, and on the wall to her left, a large oil portrait of her, the cheeks a pale alabaster. Piero pretended he had not heard Michelangelo enter. He stood on a multi-colored Persian carpet with his back to his guest, studying a bone tabernacle with glass panels, inside which were painted stories of Christ.

Alfonsina stared at Michelangelo imperiously, giving no sign of recognition but sniffing slightly as she always did, as though Florence and the Florentines smelled bad. She had from the beginning made no attempt to conceal her contempt for the Florentines. To the Tuscans, who had hated Rome and everything Roman for centuries, this was infuriating. And Piero de' Medici, half Orsini by inheritance, was now having the other half of his heritage usurped by this second Orsini.

Piero wheeled around, his long thick hair waving down to his shoulders, the face handsome despite the askew cleft in the chin. Without any formal greeting he announced:

"We instruct you, Michelangelo Buonarroti, that we wish Madonna Alfonsina's portrait sculptured in marble."

"Thank you, Excellency," replied Michelangelo, "but I cannot carve portraits."

"Why not?"

Michelangelo attempted to explain that his purpose was not to create any one person. "I could not capture a likeness, as this painter has, that would satisfy you."

"Twaddle! I order you to carve my wife in marble!"

Michelangelo gazed at Piero's contemptuous expression, heard his father's voice saying, "What is it, to be a stonecutter in the Medici palace? The same as a groom."

Madonna Alfonsina spoke for the first time.

"Kindly remove this discussion to your own room."

Piero angrily opened a door and stalked through. Michelangelo surmised that he had best follow. He closed the door behind him and was surprised to find that, among Piero's silver prizes of helmets and cups won in tournaments, were many fine works of art: Botticelli's Pallas, Bertoldo's Bellerophon, and in niches, ancient painted wood sculptures against a golden ground. Involuntarily he exclaimed:

"Your Excellency has superb taste in the arts."

Piero was not propitiated.

"When I want your opinion I will ask for it. In the meanwhile you will explain why you think you are better than any other of our hirelings."

Michelangelo clenched his anger with his back teeth, forcing himself to reply politely.

"I am a sculptor. Resident in this palace at your father's request."

"We have a hundred tradesmen living off this palace. What they are told to do, they do. You will commence tomorrow morning. And see that you make Her Excellency into a beautiful statue."

"Not even Mino da Fiesole could do that."

Piero's eyes flashed.

"You . . . you . . . contadino! Pack your rags and get out of our presence."

Michelangelo went to his room, began throwing clothing from the chest onto the bed. There was a knock. Contessina entered with her nurse.

"I hear you have been feuding with my brother."

He leaned down to take something from the bottom of the chest.

"Stand up here and talk to me!" Imperiously.

He rose, went close to her.

"I have nothing to say."

"Is it true that you refused to carve Alfonsina's portrait?"

"I refused."

"Would you refuse if my father asked you to do his portrait?"

Michelangelo was silent. Would he refuse Lorenzo, for whom he felt so deep an affection?

"Would you refuse if I asked?"

Again he was trapped.

"Piero did not ask me," he replied quietly. "He ordered me."

There were hurried footsteps in the corridor. Lorenzo came into the room, his skin unusually dark, his eyes snapping. The nurse stammered:

"Excellency . . . . I tried to stop her . . . ."

Lorenzo waved her away.

"I will not have this happen in my home."

Michelangelo's eyes blazed.

"I asked your father to cede you to me, did I not?"

"Yes."

"Then I am responsible for you."

"I have no apologies to offer."

"I am not asking for apologies. You came in here as one of the family. No one will treat you as . . . as an entertainer . . . or order you out of your own home."

Michelangelo's knees went weak. He sat down on his bed. Lorenzo spoke more gently.

"But you, too, have much to learn . . ."

"Admitted. My manners . . ."

". . . that you do not rush back here every time you are offended, and start packing your possessions. That is poor loyalty to me. Is that understood?"

Michelangelo rose, trying to hold back the tears.

"I owe Piero an apology. I said something unkind about his wife."

"He owes you one. What you wish to say to him in return is your own business."

Contessina lagged behind to whisper over her shoulder:

"Make it up with Piero. He can cause a lot of trouble."

7

The time had arrived to try a theme. What was a theme? And which themes interested him?

"It must be a Greek theme," decreed the Plato Four. "It should come out of the legends: Hercules and Antaeus, the Battle of Amazons, the Trojan War," proffered Poliziano, with particles of cantaloupe clinging to his enormous dark lips. "It would be in the mood of the frieze on the Parthenon at Athens."

Michelangelo said, "But I know little of such matters."

Landino, his face grave, replied:

"That, my dear Michelangelo, is what we have been trying to suggest for the past months: that as your *ex officio* tutors we teach you about the Greek world and its culture."

Pico della Mirandola laughed, and the *studiolo* was filled with the music of violas and clavichords.

"What I think our friends are trying to say is that they would like to guide you back to the golden age of paganism."

They told him stories of the twelve tasks of Hercules, Niobe suffering for her dying children, of the Athenian Minerva, the Dying Gladiator. Lorenzo moderated the discussion in his slightly unpleasant voice.

"Do not issue edicts to our young friend. He must come to a theme of his own free will."

Michelangelo pulled back into his seat and sat with his head resting on the back of the chair, his eyes gleaming amber in the candlelight that brought whorls of red to his chestnut hair. He listened to his own voices. One thing he knew for certain: his first theme could not come from Athens or Cairo or Rome or even Florence. It had to come from him, something he knew and felt and understood. Otherwise he would be lost. A work of art was not like a work of scholarship; it was personal, subjective. It had to be born within.

Lorenzo had asked, "What do you want to say?" To himself he replied, "Something simple, about which I can feel deeply. But what do I know? Even about myself? That I want to become a sculptor, and that I love marble? I can carve no sculpture out of these sentiments."

Then, against the murmur of voices, he saw himself standing on the steps of the Rucellai chapel the day he had first gone with the Ghirlandaio studio to Santa Maria Novella. He saw the chapel vividly before him, the Cimabue and Nino Pisano Madonnas, and felt again his love for his mother, his sense of loss when she was gone, his aloneness, the hunger for love.

It had grown late. The meeting broke up. Lorenzo remained. Though at times his tongue was said to have a rough edge, he spoke with naturalness and clarity.

"You must forgive our Platonists their enthusiasm," he said. "Ficino burns a lamp before Plato's bust. Landino gives the finest literary banquet of the year on Plato's anniversary. For us, Plato and the Greeks are the key that has let us escape from a dungeon of religious prejudices. We are trying to establish here in Florence another age of Pericles. In the light of our ambition, you must understand the excesses of our zeal."

"If you are not tired, Lorenzo," said Michelangelo, "could we make a little tour of the palace and look at the Madonnas and Child?"

Lorenzo took up the highly polished bronze lamp. They went down the corridor until they came to the anteroom of Lorenzo's office, in which there was a Donatello marble relief, so remote and impersonal, Michelangelo thought, as to prevent identification. From here they went to Giuliano's bedroom. The youngest Medici continued to sleep, the covers pulled up over his face, while Michelangelo and Lorenzo discussed Pesellino's Madonna and Child with Two Little Angels, painted on a wooden table. They trod the corridors examining the Fra Filippo Lippi Virgin Adoring Child on the altar of the chapel, about which Lorenzo explained that the models were the nun, Lucrezia Buti, with whom Fra Filippo had fallen in love, and the child of their mating, Filippino Lippi, now a painter who had been trained by Botticelli, even as Botticelli had been trained by Fra Filippo. They examined the Neri di Bicci Madonna; then went on to Luca della Robbia's Madonna and Child with the Medici crest, all in high glowing color; and finally to Lorenzo's bedroom to see the Botticelli Madonna of the Magnificat, painted for Lorenzo's father and mother some twenty years before.

"Those two angels kneeling before the Virgin and Child are my brother Giuliano and myself. When the Pazzi murdered him, the brightest light went out of my life . . . . The portrait of me is an idealization, as you can see. I am a homely man, and not ashamed of it; but all painters think I want to be flattered. Benozzo Gozzoli did so in our chapel, as well; they make my dark skin light, my turned-up nose straight, my scraggly hair as beautiful as Pico's."

Lorenzo shot him a piercing look, lips compressed, brow stern.

"You appear to know I don't need flattery."

"Granacci says I'm crusty," said Michelangelo, embarrassed.

"You are armed in adamant," declared Lorenzo. "Stay that way."

Lorenzo told him the legend of Simonetta Vespucci, original of Botticelli's Madonna of the Magnificat, "the purest beauty Europe has known," said Lorenzo. "It is not true that Simonetta was my brother Giuliano's mistress. He was in love with her, as was all Florence, but platonically. He wrote long sentimental poems to her . . . but had my nephew Giulio by his real mistress, Antonia Gorini. It was Sandro Botticelli who truly loved Simonetta; though I doubt if he ever spoke to her in person. She is the woman in all his paintings: Primavera, Venus, Pallas. No man has ever painted such exquisite female beauty."

Michelangelo was silent. When he thought of his mother he saw her too as a beautiful young woman; yet it was a different beauty he felt, one coming from within. Not a woman desirable to all men, as was Botticelli's love; but one who would love a son and be loved by him. He turned his face up to Lorenzo, speaking in full confidence.

"I feel close to the Madonna. She is the only image I have of my mother. Since I still have to search for my technique, wouldn't it be best to know what I'm trying to say?"

"It could be best," replied Lorenzo gravely.

"Perhaps what I feel about my mother will be true of what she felt about me."

He haunted the rooms of the palace, drawing after the masters, sometimes with Contessina or Giuliano keeping him company. Then he grew impatient with other men's ideas and went into the poorer parts of town where the women worked on the sidewalks before their houses, weaving cane chair seats or demijohn covers, with their babes on their laps or at the breast. He went into the countryside to the *contadini* around Settignano who had known him since he was a child, and who gave no second thought to his drawing them while they bathed or suckled their young.

He was not looking for portraiture but for the spirit of motherhood. He drew the mother and child in every position he found, seeing the true relation between them through his charcoal and paper; and then, for a few scudi, persuaded the women to move, change, shift themselves and the child to give him more angles of approach, to search for . . . he knew not what.

With Granacci, Torrigiani, Sansovino and Rustici he went out to the art of Florence, drawing concentratedly on the Madonna and Child theme, listening to Bertoldo dissect each piece as they spent their hours trying to learn how their predecessors had achieved their results.

The Bernardo Rossellino in his home church of Santa Croce, Michelangelo found to be a fat expressionless mother and child; and in the same church a Desiderio da Settignano, a *contadina* and *bambino* wrapped in Tuscan swaddling clothes, ordinary folk in from the country for a *festa*. They went to Orsanmichele to see the Orcagna Virgin of the Nativity, which was tender and loving and had power, but to Michelangelo seemed primitive and wooden. The free-standing Nino Pisano in Santa Maria Novella appeared to be the best carved, but the well-groomed Pisan merchant's wife holding her expensively clothed earthling son was poorly proportioned and without spirituality. A Verrocchio terra-cotta Virgin and Child presented a middle-aged Madonna gazing in perplexity at this son who was already standing up and blessing the world. On they moved to Agostino di Duccio's Virgin and Child, richly garbed young elegants with blank coy faces.

The next morning he went for a walk alone up the Arno toward Pontassieve. The sun was biting hot. He took off his shirt, exposing his chest to its germinal heat. The blue Tuscan hills blurred and faded back in serried ranges. He loved these mountains.

Striking off into the hills, with the feel of the steep slope under him, he realized that he had not yet come to grips with what he wanted to convey about Mary and her child. He knew only that he wanted to attain something fresh and vital. He fell to musing about the character and fate of Mary. The Annunciation was a favorite theme of Florentine painters: the Archangel Gabriel come down from heaven to announce to Mary that she was to bear the Son of God. In all the paintings he remembered, the news seemed to come to her as a complete surprise, and apparently she had been given no choice.

But could that be? Could so important a task, the most important assigned to any human since Moses, have been forced on Mary without her knowledge or consent? Surely God must have loved Mary above all women on earth to choose her for this divine task? Must He not have told her the plan, related every step of the way from Bethlehem to Calvary? And in His wisdom and mercy have allowed her the opportunity to reject it?

And if Mary did have freedom of choice, when would she be likely to exercise it? At the Annunciation? When she had borne her child? At a moment of suckling, while Jesus was still an infant? Once she accepted, must she not carry her burden from that moment until the day that her child was crucified? Knowing the future, how could she subject her son to such agony? Might she not have said, "No, not my son. I will not consent. I will not let it happen"? But could she go against the wish of God? When He had appealed to her to help Him? Was ever mortal woman cast in so pain-fraught a dilemma?

He decided that he would carve Mary at the moment of decision, while suckling her infant, when, knowing all, she must determine the future: for herself; for her child; for the world.

Now that he understood what he was about, he was able to draw with a purpose. Mary would dominate the marble. She would be the center of the composition. She would be heroic in stature, a woman not only given the freedom to come to her own decision but with the inner force and intelligence to make it. The child would be secondary; present, vitally alive, but in no way distracting.

He would place the child on his mother's lap, his face buried in his mother's breast, but his back fully turned on his viewers. This would give the child his natural place, caught at the most urgent activity of his day; and by the same symbolism this could be the moment when Mary would feel most urgently that her decision had to be made.

As far as he knew, no one had sculptured or painted Jesus with his back turned. Yet his drama would not be begun for some thirty years. This was the mother's time, and the mother's portrait.

He reviewed the hundreds of sketches of mother and child he had made in the past months, extracting those that would fit his new concept, and with the sketches on a table before him began his search for the background of the theme. Where was Mary at the time? Here was a drawing showing a mother sitting on a bench at the bottom of a flight of stairs. Who besides her child was with her? Here were any number of young children in attitudes of play. The figure of Mary could be a composite of these strong Tuscan mothers. But how did one portray the face of the Madonna? His memory of his own mother's appearance was nearly ten years old now, and had a vague dreamlike quality.

He put the drawings aside. Was it possible to conceive a piece of sculpture without knowing the marble from which it would draw its sustenance?

He sought out Granacci, who had been given one of the largest rooms in the casino as his painting studio, and asked if they could visit the stone shops of the city.

"I'll work better if I have the marble at hand so I can see and feel it, and learn about its inner structure."

"Bertoldo says marble shouldn't be bought until the drawings and models are completed; then you can be sure you will choose an adequate block."

"It could work the other way round," he answered thoughtfully. "I think it's a kind of wedding . . ."

"All right, I'll tell Bertoldo some fancy yarn, and we'll go tomorrow."

Florence had dozens of stone stores scattered through the Proconsul section, with all sizes and shapes of granite, travertine, colored marbles, as well as ready-cut building stones, doorframes, window seats, columns. But they failed to turn up the Carrara block for which Michelangelo was searching.

"Let's walk up to the Settignano yards. We'll have a better chance there," he suggested.

In the old yard where Desiderio had trained Mino da Fiesole, he saw a piece that captivated him at once. It was of modest size, but its crystals were gleaming white. He poured water on it to look for cracks, struck its ends with a hammer to listen for its sounds, tested for flaws, bubbles, stains.

"This is the one, Granacci," he cried with glee. "It will hold the Madonna and Child. But I'll have to see it by the first rays of sunlight. Then I'll know for sure it's perfect."

"If you think I'm going to sit on the ground worshiping your marble until dawn . . ."

"No, no, you settle the price. I'll borrow a horse from the Topolinos for you so you reach home alive."

"You know, amico, I don't believe a word of this 'sunrise tells all' nonsense. What can you conceivably see at sunrise that you don't see better right now in a strong light? I think it's a kind of pagan worship: fertility rites you have to perform at dawn to make sure the gods of the mountains are propitiated."

Michelangelo slept on a blanket under the Topolino arches, left before the first morning light and was standing over his marble when the fingers of dawn came over the hills. The block was as though translucent. His eyes could pierce through its width and height and breadth; through the built-up layers of crystals compounded within its structural unity. There was no perceptible flaw: no crack or hollow, no discoloration, the crystals flickering brilliantly on its surface.

"You are a noble block," he said aloud.

He paid the owner Granacci's gold coins, loaded the marble onto the Topolino cart and rode off behind the pair of undulating white oxen as he had ridden from the Cave Maiano since he was six. He drove down the hill, turned right at Varlungo, went along the shore of the Affrico River, past the ancient Porta alla Croce marking the fourth limit of the city, along the Borgo la Croce, past the hospital of Santa Maria Nuova, turned right at Via Larga in front of the Medici palace, through the Piazza San Marco to the garden gate, as proud as though he were carrying home his bride.

One of the stonemasons helped take the block to the shed. He then moved his drawing table and working equipment from the casino. Bertoldo came to the back of the garden, puzzled.

"You are ready to begin carving?"

"No. I'm a long way yet."

"Then why move from the casino?"

"Because I would like to work in quiet."

"Quiet? You won't be out of sound of those hammers of the *scalpellini* all day."

"That is a good sound. I was raised with it."

"But I must spend some time at the casino with the others. If you're near me, I can suggest and correct when you need help."

Michelangelo thought for a moment, then said, "Bertoldo, I feel the need to be solitary, to work beyond all eyes; even yours. I could have instruction when I came to ask."

Bertoldo's lips trembled. "You will make more mistakes that way, *caro,* and continue in them longer."

"Isn't that the best way to learn? To carry one's mistakes to their logical conclusion?"

"A word of advice can save you time."

"I have time."

Bertoldo withdrew behind his tired pale eyes. Then he smiled.

"*Davvero.* You have time. When you want help come to me."

Late that afternoon when the others had left the garden, Michelangelo turned to find Torrigiani glaring at him.

"Now you're too good even to draw next to me."

"Oh, Torrigiani! It's just that I want a little privacy . . ."

"Privacy! From me? Your best friend? You didn't want privacy all that first year while you needed help and company. Now that *Il Magnifico* has selected you . . ."

"Torrigiani, please believe me, nothing has changed. I've only moved a hundred and fifty feet . . ."

"It's the same as moving fifty miles. I told you that when you were ready I would set up a sculptor's bench next to mine."

"I want to make my mistakes by myself."

"Or is it that you're afraid we'll steal your secrets?"

"Secrets!" Michelangelo was growing angry. "What secrets can a beginning carver have? This is my first theme. You've already done half a dozen."

Torrigiani insisted, "It's me you're rejecting."

Michelangelo fell silent. Was there an element of truth in the accusation? He had admired Torrigiani's physical beauty, stories, songs . . . but he no longer wanted to talk and listen to anecdotes with the block of marble standing challengingly by.

"You spoiled fast!" declared Torrigiani. "I've been patronized before. But the ones who do it always come a cropper."

A few minutes later Granacci arrived, looking dour. He inspected the anvil, rough board table on horses, workbenches and drawing desk on a platform raised off the ground.

"What's wrong, Granacci?"

"It's Torrigiani. He came back to the casino in a black funk. Said some unpleasant things about you."

"I heard them first."

"Look, Michelangelo, I'm now on the other side of the *calcio* field. A year ago I warned you against paying too much attention to Torrigiani. Now I have to warn you that you're not being fair. Don't cut him off . . . . I know of your growing preoccupation with marble, but Torrigiani doesn't see anything so magical about marble, and quite justifiably thinks it results from your life in the palace. If we threw over our friends because we grew fatigued with them, how many of our friendships would last?"

Michelangelo ran his thumb in a silhouetting line over the block.

"I'll try to make it up to him."

8

"Marble" was derived from the Greek word meaning "shining stone." How his block glistened in the early morning sunlight as he set it up vertically on the wooden bench, gazing at the luster produced by the light penetrating a short way and being reflected at the surfaces of the deeper-lying crystals. He had lived with this block for several months now, studied it in every light, from every angle, in every degree of heat and cold. He had slowly come to understand its nature, not by cutting into it with a chisel but by force of perception, until he believed he knew every layer, every crystal, and precisely how the marble could be persuaded to yield the forms he needed. Bertoldo said that the forms had first to be released before they could be exalted. Yet a marble contained a myriad of forms; had this not been so, all sculptors would carve identically.

He picked up his hammer and *subbia* and began cutting with the *colpo vivo,* the live blow, his passage handled in one "Go!", the chisel continuing in an uninterrupted direction as he used the point, a finger that dug delicately into the marble and threw out substance; the toothed chisel, a hand that refined the textures left by the point; the flat chisel, which was as a fist, knocking down the grooves of the toothed chisel. He had been right about this marble block. It obeyed every sensitivity he hoped to impart to it as he worked downward toward his figures through the successive layers.

The marble turned light into the dark unexplored corners of his mind, opening him up to the seeds of new conceptions. He was not working from his drawings or clay models; they had all been put away. He was carving from the images in his mind. His eyes and hands knew where every line, curve, mass must emerge, and at what depth in the heart of the stone to create the low relief; for only a quarter of the figure would emerge.

He was at work in his shed when he received a visit from Giovanni, the first time the fifteen-year-old near-cardinal had come to see him since he had been brought to the garden by Contessina a year before. In spite of the fact that he was totally unblessed with looks, Michelangelo found his expression intelligent and alert. Florence said that the easygoing, pleasure-loving second son of Lorenzo had ability but that he would never use it because the obsession of his life was to avoid trouble. He was flanked by his saturnine shadow, his fifteen-year-old cousin Giulio, in whom nature had undertaken the task of creating Giovanni's opposite: tall, spare, with an angular face, straight nose and cleft chin, arched dark eyebrows, large eyes: handsome, graceful, efficient, loving trouble as his natural métier, but as cold and hard as a corpse. Recognized as a Medici by Lorenzo, but despised by Piero and Alfonsina because of his illegitimacy, Giulio could make a place for himself only through one of his cousins. He had attached himself to fat, good-natured Giovanni and had craftily insinuated himself into the position where he did all of Giovanni's work, took care of his unpleasantnesses, provided his pleasures and made decisions as Giovanni would have wanted them. When Giovanni became a full cardinal and moved to Rome, Giulio would accompany him.

"Giovanni, how kind of you to visit," said Michelangelo.

"It's not really a visit," replied Giovanni in his plump voice. "I came to invite you to join my big hunt. It is the most exciting day of the year for the whole palace."

Michelangelo had heard about the hunt: how Lorenzo's hunters, horsemen and grooms had been sent to a spot in the mountains which abounded with hares and porcupines, stags and wild boar; how the entire area had been enclosed by sailcloth and was guarded by the *contadini* of the neighborhood to keep the stags from jumping the cloth fence or the boars from tearing holes through it, which would let out the sea of game. He had never seen the phlegmatic Giovanni so buoyed with enthusiasm.

"Forgive me, but as you can see I am in the marble, and I cannot leave off."

Giovanni looked crestfallen. "You are not a laborer. You can work when you wish. You are free."

Michelangelo clenched and unclenched his fist around the chisel which he had shaped octagonally so that it would not slip in his fingers.

"That is debatable, Giovanni."

"But who would hold you?"

"Me."

"You would really prefer your work to my hunt?"

"Since you give me a choice, yes."

"How very odd. I wouldn't have believed it. You want only to work? You have no room for diversion?"

That word was a stickler to Michelangelo, even as the word "pleasure" had been to the Topolinos. He wiped the matted marble dust off his perspiring upper lip.

"Doesn't everyone have his own definition of diversion? For me, marble has the excitement of the hunt."

Giulio said in an undertone to his cousin, "May we be spared from zealots."

In his first sentence directed to Giulio, Michelangelo asked, "Why am I a zealot?"

Giovanni replied, "Because you are interested in only one thing."

Giulio spoke again in an undertone to Giovanni. Giovanni replied, "You are entirely right," and the two young men moved off without a further word.

Michelangelo returned to his carving, the incident going out of his mind. But not for long. In the cool of dusk Contessina entered the garden. Coming close to Michelangelo's marble and speaking softly, she said, "My brother Giovanni says you frighten him."

". . . frighten him? But I haven't done anything."

"Giovanni says you have a kind of . . . ferociousness."

"Tell your brother not to despair of me. Perhaps I am too young to be broken to pleasure."

Contessina threw him a searching look.

"Giovanni's hunt is his supreme effort of the year. For those few hours he is the head of the Medici family, and even my father takes orders from him. If you reject his hunt it is as though you were rejecting Giovanni, setting yourself up as superior to him. He is kind, he never wants to hurt anyone. Why should you want to hurt him?''

"I don't want to hurt him, Contessina. It's just that I don't want to break the mood. I want to carve all day and every day until I'm finished.''

She cried, "You've already made an enemy of Piero! Must you do the same to Giovanni?''

He could think of nothing to answer. Then, the mood broken, he put down his three-toothed chisel, dampened a large white cloth in water at the fountain, covered his piece. The day would come when he would let no one stop him at his work!

"All right, Contessina . I'll go.''

For a rhythmical movement he had learned to pick up hammer and chisel at the same instant, the point held loosely so that it could move freely without restricting the hammer force, his thumb curling over the tool and holding it by his four fingers, automatically shutting his eyes against chips at the moment of the impact. Working in low relief, he could cut away but little, and had to chain the physical force within himself. His point entered the marble at a near-perpendicular angle, but as he approached the forms with the highest projections, the Madonna's face and the back of Jesus, he had to change his position.

There were so many things to think of at one time. His strokes had to hit toward the main mass, strike the marble toward the block it came out of, so that it could sustain the blow. He had designed his figures and stairs in a vertical position to lessen the possibility of cracking the block, but found that the marble would not yield to exterior force without accenting its own essence: stoniness. He had not realized to what extent marble had to be battled. His respect for his material grew blow by blow.

Bringing out the live figures involved long hours and longer days, a slow peeling off, layer by layer. Nor could the birth of substance be hastened. After each series of blows he stepped back to inspect his progress.

On the left-hand side of his design there descended the flight of heavy stone steps. Mary was seated in profile on a bench to the right, the broad stone balustrade giving the illusion of ending in her lap, just under her child's knee. He saw that if Mary's strong left hand, holding the child's legs securely, were to open more widely, be moved out a little on a flat plane, it could be holding firmly not only her son but also the bottom of the balustrade, which would become an upright beam. Mary would then be supporting on her lap both the weight of Jesus and, if she made the choice to serve God as He had asked, the cross on which her son would be crucified.

He would not force the symbolism on the viewer, yet it would be there for anyone to see who might feel it.

Now he had the upright, but where was the transverse bar? He studied his drawings to find a way to complete the imagery. He looked at the boy, John, playing on top of the steps. If he threw the plump arm across the balustrade at a right angle . . .

He drew a fresh charcoal sketch, then began digging deeper into the crystalline flesh of the marble. Slowly, as he penetrated the block, the boy's body and right arm formed the living, pulsating crossbeam. As it should have, since John was to baptize his cousin Jesus and become an integral part of the passion.

With the carving of images of two other small children playing above the stairs, his Madonna and Child was finished. He began under Bertoldo's rigorous instruction the one task in which he had no training: polishing. Bertoldo hammered into him the evils of "overlicking," which rendered a piece sweetly sentimental. Since he had worked the block on the south wall of his shed he now asked Bugiardini to help him stand the sixteen-by-twenty-two-inch plaque against the west wall so that he could polish it in the indirect north light.

First he used a rasp to bring down the rough surfaces, then he washed away the fine marble dust. He found holes which Bertoldo explained had been made at an early stage of his work when the chisel had penetrated too deeply, mashing crystals beneath the surface.

"Use a fine-grain emery stone with water," Bertoldo instructed. "But with a light hand."

This accomplished, he once again washed his block with water. Now his work had a tactile quality similar to that of mat paper. Next he used light weight pumice stones to refine the surface and expose fresh, sparkling crystals, running his fingers over the surface to feel the new silklike texture. When he found himself needing better lighting to observe the subtle surface changes he took down the planks of the north and east walls. In the new intense light the values changed. He felt obliged to wash down the carving, sponge it, let it dry . . . start all over with emery stone and pumice.

Slowly the highlights emerged: sunlight on the Madonna's face, on the curls, left cheek and shoulder of the child. On the foredrapery covering the Madonna's leg, on the back of John as he straddled the balustrade, on the inside of the balustrade itself to accent its importance in the structure. All the rest, the block-seat, stairs, walls were in quiet shadow. Now, he thought, one saw and felt the crisis, the intense emotional thinking reflected on Mary's face as she felt the tug of Jesus at her breast and the weight of the cross in her hand.

Lorenzo summoned the Plato Four. When Michelangelo entered the room with Bertoldo they found that the block had been mounted on a high flat altar covered with black velvet.

The Plato group was hilarious.

"You have carved a Greek figure, after all!" cried Poliziano exultantly.

Pico said with an intensity unusual for him, "When I look at your carving I am outside Christianity. Your heroic figure has the impenetrable divinity of ancient Greek art."

"I agree," added white-haired Landino; "the carving has a tranquillity, a beauty and superhuman aspect that can only be described as Attic."

"But why should it be?" asked Michelangelo numbly.

"Why? Because you fell right off the Acropolis into Florence," exclaimed Ficino. "You're pagan at heart, the same as we are. *Magnifico,* could we have that ancient stele brought from your office, the seated woman on a grave relief?"

Within a matter of moments the palace groom had brought to the studio not only the ancient stele but several of the more portable Madonnas and Child, with which the Platonists attempted to prove that Michelangelo's carving bore no relationship to Christian carvings.

"It was not supposed to," he replied a little heatedly. "I set out to create something original."

Lorenzo had been enjoying the scene.

"Michelangelo has achieved a synthesis: his work is both Greek and Christian, beautifully fused, presenting the best of both philosophies. That should be particularly apparent to you who have spent your lives trying to achieve a unity of Plato and Christ."

Michelangelo thought, "Not one word have they said about Mary and her moment of decision. Is the meaning buried too deep? Or is that the part they find Greek? Because the child is not yet committed?"

Bertoldo, who had remained silent, growled, "*Allora,* let us speak of sculpture. Is it good? Is it bad?"

Michelangelo was ignored as though he were not in the room. He gathered that they liked his first major work because they considered it a child of humanism. They were delighted at the revolutionary idea of the Christ child with his back toward the viewer; of Mary's noble knowledgeability. They were enthusiastic about his achievement in perspective, which was just beginning to be understood in marble; not even Donatello had attempted it in his Madonnas, being content to suggest that angels and cherubs were vaguely behind the main figures. They were impressed with the projecting power of the three main figures, bursting with tension, one of the most vitalic low reliefs they had seen.

There were also things they did not like. They told him without mincing words that they found the Madonna's face to be overstylized, her super-abundance of draperies diverting. The figure of the child was too muscular, the position of its arm and hand awkward; the figure of John so oversized as to be brutalized . . .

Lorenzo cried, "Stop, stop, our young friend has worked a half a year on this project . . ."

" . . . and thought it through entirely by himself," interjected Bertoldo; "any help I gave was purely academic."

Michelangelo stood up to draw their attention.

"First, I hate draperies, I want to work only in the nude; and I simply failed to control them. As for the Madonna's face, I could never find it. In my own mind, I mean, and that is why I could never draw or carve it with more . . . reality. But I would like to tell you, now that it is finished, what I hoped to accomplish."

"The room is full of ears," quipped Poliziano.

"I wanted the figures to be real and believable so that you would feel that with their very next breath would begin life itself."

Then, shyly, he explained his thinking about Mary and her child, and her moment of decision. Lorenzo and the Plato Four fell silent, studying the marble. He felt them searching, pondering. Then, slowly, one by one, they turned back to him; pride was in their eyes.

When he returned to his apartment he found a leather pouch on his washstand. It was filled with bright gold florins, just how many he could not imagine.

"What is this?" he asked Bertoldo.

"A purse from Lorenzo."

Michelangelo picked up the pouch and walked to the staircase adjoining the apartment, up to the first floor and down the corridor to Lorenzo's bedroom. Lorenzo was sitting at a small table, before an oil lamp, writing letters. He turned in his chair as his valet announced Michelangelo.

"Lorenzo, I can't understand why . . ."

"Gently, gently. Sit down here. Now, start at the beginning."

Michelangelo gulped, quieted himself.

"It's this purse of money. You should not have to buy the marble. It is yours already, I've lived in the palace while carving it, you've given me everything . . ."

"I was not buying the piece, Michelangelo. It belongs to you. The purse is a kind of completion prize, similar to the one I gave Giovanni when he completed his ecclesiastical studies at Pisa. I thought you might like to travel and see other art works. North through Bologna, Ferrara and Padua to Venice? South through Siena to Rome and Naples? I will give you letters of introduction."

Despite the lateness of the hour Michelangelo rushed home to the Via dei Bentaccordi. Everyone was asleep, but they quickly gathered in the family room, each carrying a candle, their nightcaps askew. Michelangelo spilled out the golden coins in a dramatic sweep across his father's desk.

"But . . . what . . . what. . . ?" Lodovico stumbled.

"My prize money. For completing the Madonna and Child."

"It's a lot," exclaimed his uncle. "How much?"

"I haven't stopped to count," replied Michelangelo loftily.

" . . . thirty, forty, fifty," counted his father. "Enough to support a family in ease for half a year."

As long as he was showing off Michelangelo decided he should do a thorough job, and so he asked, "Why should not six months of my work support a family for half a year? That is simple justice."

Lodovico was jubilant.

"I haven't had my hands on fifty gold florins for a long time. Michelangelo, you must start on another piece immediately, tomorrow morning, since they are so well paid."

Michelangelo was amused. No word of thanks. Only undisguised joy at running his hands through this pile of gold pieces shimmering in the candlelight. Ironically, he remembered his own cry for marble when Lorenzo first invited him into the palace!

"We're going to look for another farm," cried Lodovico. "Land is the only safe investment. Then with the extra income . . ."

"I'm not sure I can let you do that, Father. *Il Magnifco* says he is giving me the florins for travel: to Venice or Naples, to see all the sculptures . . ."

"Travel to see sculptures!" Lodovico was aghast, his new acres disappearing before his eyes. "What purpose will it serve to look at sculptures? You look, you leave, the money is gone. But with new farms . . ."

His brother Buonarroto asked, "Are you really going traveling, Michelangelo?"

"No," said Michelangelo laughingly, "I want only to work." He turned to Lodovico. "They're yours, Father."

9

Several times a week Bertoldo insisted that they go to the churches to continue drawing from the masters. They carried wooden stools with them so they could move with the changing light. They were sketching in the Brancacci chapel in the Carmine. Torrigiani set his stool so close to Michelangelo's that his shoulder pressed against Michelangelo's arm. Michelangelo moved his stool a little. Torrigiani was offended.

"I can't draw without a free arm," explained Michelangelo.

"What are you so cranky about? All I wanted to do was amuse us while we work. I heard a bawdy new ballad last night . . ."

"I want to concentrate."

"I'm bored. We've drawn these frescoes fifty times. What more is there to learn?"

"How to draw like Masaccio."

"I want to draw like Torrigiani. That's good enough for me."

Without looking up Michelangelo barked impatiently, "But not good enough for me."

"Look who's talking! I won three drawing prizes last year. How many did you win?"

"None. That's why you'd better let me learn."

Torrigiani felt he had been scored against. He said with a crooked smile, "I'm surprised the favorite student still has to submit to these schoolboy exercises."

"Copying Masaccio is not a schoolboy exercise, except to a schoolboy mind."

"Oh, so now your mind is better than mine." Flaring, "I thought it was only your drawing hand?"

"If you could draw, you would know there is no difference."

"And if you could do anything else but draw, you would know how little you are alive. It's as they say: little man, little life; big man, big life."

"Big man, big wind."

Torrigiani was furious. Michelangelo swiveled on his stool to face the painting by Filippino Lippi of the emperor's son whom St. Peter had raised from the dead, the one for which Granacci had posed when he was thirteen. Torrigiani pushed his stool around so that he could stare head on at Michelangelo.

"You meant that as an insult!"

He sprang up from his stool, put his massive hand on Michelangelo's shoulder and yanked him to his feet. Michelangelo had time to see the grim set of Torrigiani's expression, which told him that Torrigiani was striking with all his might; but he had no chance to duck or avoid the blow. Torrigiani's fist exploded on the bridge of his nose with the sound of powder exploding behind a cut of *pietra serena* in the Maiano quarry. He tasted blood and crushed bone in his mouth; and then, as from a distance, heard Bertoldo's anguished cry.

"What have you done?"

While stars burst in a black heaven, Michelangelo heard Torrigiani reply:

"I felt his bone and cartilage crumble like biscuit beneath my knuckles. . . ."

Michelangelo slipped angularly to his knees, the blue stars circling the painted chapel. He felt the hard cold cement against his cheek, saw the dead-green Granacci on the fresco, then lost consciousness.

He awakened in his bed in the palace. There were wet cloths over his eyes and nose. His head was a mass of pain. As he stirred, someone removed the cloths. He tried to open his eyes but could achieve only the slightest slit. Bending over him was Pier Leoni, Lorenzo's physician, Lorenzo and Bertoldo. There was a knock on the door. He heard someone enter, say:

"Torrigiani has fled the city, Excellency. Through the Porta Romana."

"Send our fastest riders after him. I'll lock him in the stocks with his back against the Signoria wall . . ."

Michelangelo let his lids fall again. The doctor resettled him on the pillow, wiped his mouth, then began exploring his face with his fingers.

"The bridge of his nose is crushed. The bone splinters may take as long as a year to work their way out. The passage is completely closed now. Later, if he's lucky, he'll be able to breath through it again."

He slipped an arm under Michelangelo's shoulder, raised him slightly and pressed a cup to his lips.

"Drink. It will put you to sleep. When you wake the pain will be less."

It was torture to open his lips, but he gulped down the warm herb tea. The voice above him receded. Once again he slipped off, heard Torrigiani's jeering words in his ears, saw the spinning blue stars and felt the cold paving on his cheek.

When he awakened he was alone in the room. The pain had localized now, and he felt the throbbing behind his eyes and nose. There was light out the window.

He pushed aside the covers, got out of bed, reeled, caught the side of the wash table to steady himself. Then, summoning courage, looked up into the mirror. Once again he had to grip the edge of the table to keep from fainting: for he could barely recognize his own face in the glass. Both of his eyes were swollen the size of blue goose eggs. He struggled to get the lids opened a trifle more, saw a wild palette of discoloration: purples and lavenders, orange and burnt sienna.

He would not be able to know the full consequence of Torrigiani's blow until the swelling went down. It would be weeks, perhaps months before he could see how completely his erstwhile friend had accomplished, in reverse, the redrafting job on his face for which he had longed. That one powerful blow from Torrigiani's big fist had thrown his face out of focus as surely as though Torrigiani had been shaping soft wax.

Shivering with fever, he crawled on hands and knees back into his bed, pulled the covers over his head as though to wipe out the world and reality. And he was sick at heart. His pride had brought him to this low, beaten state.

He heard the door open. Unwilling to see anyone, he remained motionless. A hand pulled back the cover from his head. He found himself gazing up at Contessina.

"Michelangelo *mio*."

"Contessina ."

"I'm sorry it happened."

"Not so sorry as I."

"Torrigiani got away. But Father swears he'll catch him."

Michelangelo moved his head painfully on the pillow.

"It would do no good. I blame myself. I taunted him . . . beyond his powers of endurance."

"He began it. We've heard the story."

He felt hot tears stinging his eyes as he forced himself to say the cruelest words that could escape his lips:

"I'm ugly."

Her face had been close to his as they spoke, almost in whispers to insure their privacy from her nurse, who lolled uncertainly at the open door. Without moving she placed her lips on the swollen distorted bridge of his nose; and he felt their faint warm moisture like an annealing balm. Then she was gone from the room.

The days passed. He could not bring himself to leave the palace, even though the swelling and pain continued to recede. His father heard the news, came to assess the damage. Lodovico seemed happier to be vindicated in his judgment on art and artists than saddened at what had happened to his son's face. He was also concerned that the three gold florins might not show up while Michelangelo was confined to his room.

"Will Lorenzo stop your wage?"

Michelangelo was furious,

"It isn't a wage. And it won't be stopped because I'm not working. Perhaps nobody will think I have use for the money while I am locked up here."

Lodovico grumbled, "I counted on it," and left.

"He has no right to reproach me," sighed Michelangelo to Buonarroto when he came to visit, bringing a bowl of chicken soup with toasted almonds from Lucrezia. Buonarroto was now apprenticed to the Strozzi in the cloth trade. His expression was serious.

"Michelangelo, men need a little money of their own. This is a good time for you to put aside some florins. Let me come for a few weeks and mind the money for you."

Michelangelo was touched at his brother's sympathetic concern, and amused at his new-found business acumen.

Lorenzo visited for a few moments each afternoon, bringing a new cameo or ancient coin for them to discuss. *Il Cardiere* wandered by with his lyre to sing a salty version of the goings-on in Florence, including Michelangelo's mishap in rhymed couplets. Landino came to read Dante; Pico to show him some new findings on Egyptian stone carvings which indicated that the Greeks learned their main sculpture principles from the Egyptians. Contessina came with her nurse for the hour before dark, to study and chat. Even Giovanni and Giulio stopped by for a moment. Piero sent condolences.

Jacopo of the implike face and Tedesco the redhead came over from Ghirlandaio's to assure him that if they saw Torrigiani on the streets of Florence they would stone him clear out of the Porta Prato. Granacci spent hours in the apartment, bringing drawing materials and folios. The doctor came to probe his nose with sticks, and finally assure him that he would breathe through one nostril at least. Bertoldo was charming about having his privacy invaded. He tried to comfort Michelangelo.

"Torrigiani thought to flatten your talent with his fist so it would reach his own level."

Michelangelo shook his head. "Granacci warned me."

"Still, it is true: people who are jealous of talent want to destroy it in others. You must come back to work now. We miss you in the garden."

Michelangelo studied himself in the mirror over the washbasin. The bridge of his nose had been caved in permanently. With a massive hump in the middle, the nose careened from the corner of his right eye toward the left corner of his mouth, wiping out whatever symmetry it had had before. He winced.

"What a botched-up piece of sculpture! The stone was soft and filled with holes. It shattered at the first blow of the hammer. Now it is spoiled, without balance or design, scarred like an abandoned quarry in a mountainside. I was never much to look at; but how I loathe this crushed-in view of myself."

He was filled with a bitter despair. Now he would truly be the ugly sculptor trying to create beautiful marbles.

10

The swelling receded, the discoloration faded; but he was still unable to present himself to the world in this changed, mutilated form. If he could not face Florence in the light, he slipped out late at night and walked the silent streets for hours, working off his caged energies. How different the city looked with the oil lamps lighted high on the palaces, how much larger the slumbering stone buildings seemed in the starlight.

Poliziano came to the apartment one day, ignoring Bertoldo, and asked:

"May I sit down? Michelangelo, I have just completed my translation of Ovid's *Metamorphoses* into Italian. While I was translating Nestor's tale of the centaurs I thought of what a fine carving you could make of the battle between the centaurs and the Thessalians."

Michelangelo sat on the bed watching Poliziano intently, comparing their uglinesses as Poliziano crouched forward in the chair, his beady eyes and oily black hair seeming to Michelangelo as moist as the purple, repulsively carnal lips. Yet ugly as Poliziano was, his face was lighted by an inner glow as he spoke of Ovid and his poetic recounting of the Greek tales.

"The opening lines will set the stage:

> Pirithous took as bride young Hippodame;
> To celebrate the day, tables were set up
> And couches placed for greater luxury
> Beside them in a green, well-arboured grotto.
> Among the guests were centaurs, rugged creatures
> (Half horse, half man, conceived in clouds, they say),
> Myself, and noblemen of Thessaly . . ."

In his soft, modulated voice Poliziano went on to tell of the gaiety of the palace:

> ". . . Oh the bride was lovely!
> Then we began to say how sweet the bride was
> But our intentions began to bring ill fortune to the wedding.
> Eurytus, craziest of rough-hewn centaurs,
> Grew hot with wine, but when he saw the bride
> Was that much hotter: tables were rocked,
> Turned upside down, then tossed away.
> Someone had seized the bride and mounted her.
> It was Eurytus, while the other centaurs
> Took women as they pleased, first come, first taken,
> The scene was like the looting of a city . . ."

Vividly he projected the scenes into the room: Theseus swinging an ancient urn full of wine across Eurytus' face, until the creature's brains burst forth from the broken skull; Gryneus throwing the altar on the heads of two men; Rhoetus killing his man "by thrusting torch and fire down his throat."

Michelangelo's eyes went to the cupboard on which stood the model for Bertoldo's Battle of the Romans and Barbarians. Poliziano followed his gaze.

"No, no," he said, "Bertoldo's Battle is a copy of the sarcophagus at Pisa, a reproduction, actually. Yours would be original."

Bertoldo was furious.

"You are lying! Michelangelo, I'll take you to Pisa and show you. Tomorrow! You will see that in the center of the sarcophagus there are no figures at all, I had to re-create them. I introduced whole new themes for narrative, like my riding warrior . . ."

Poliziano put his manuscript into Michelangelo's hands.

"Read it at your leisure. I thought of you carving the scenes even while I translated them. You could not find a more powerful theme."

Bertoldo ordered horses that night. At dawn they were riding down the Arno to the sea past Empoli, until the dome and leaning Campanile of Pisa stood against the powder-blue sky. Bertoldo led Michelangelo directly into the Camposanto, a rectangular cemetery surrounded by a wall begun in 1278; its galleries were lined by some six hundred tombs and ancient sarcophagi. Bertoldo made for the Roman battle scene and, coveting his pupil's good opinion, elaborately explained the differences between this sarcophagus and his own Battle. The more he pointed out the differences the more Michelangelo saw the similarities. Placatingly, he murmured:

"You told me that even in art we all have to have a father and a mother. Nicola Pisano, starting modern sculpture right on this spot, was able to do so because he saw these Roman sarcophagi that had been hidden for a thousand years."

Mollified, Bertoldo took them to an *osteria* behind a grocery store, where they ate tunny fish and beans, and while the old man slept for a couple of hours Michelangelo returned to the Duomo, and then to the Baptistery, much of it designed by Nicola and Giovanni Pisano, containing Nicola Pisano's masterpiece, a marble pulpit with five high reliefs.

Outside once again, he looked at the Campanile leaning dizzily against the brilliant Pisan sky. He thought, "Bertoldo was only partly right: it is not enough to be an architect and sculptor; one must also be an engineer!"

Riding home in the cool dusk with the soft, modeled hills gliding past, the horses' hoofs rhythmic on the hard-packed dirt road, Michelangelo began to see pictures in his mind: of struggles between men, of the rescue of women, of the wounded, the dying. When they had reached the palace and Bertoldo had fallen into a fast sleep, he lit a lamp and began reading Poliziano's translation.

He had read only a few pages when he asked himself, "But how could one carve this legend? It would require a piece of marble the size of a Ghirlandaio fresco." Nor could a sculptor use all the weapons employed in the mythological battle: altars, torches, spears, antlers, javelins, tree trunks. The marble would turn out to be a jumble.

He recalled an earlier line and leafed back through the pages until he found it: "Aphareus lifted a sheet of rock ripped from the mountainside . . ."

The image was vivid for him. He became excited. Here could be a unifying theme, and unifying force. His theme! Since one could not portray all weapons he would use only one, the earliest and the most universal: stone.

He pulled off his shirt and *brache* and stretched himself under the red coverlet, his hands behind his head. He realized that he had been out all day, among people, and had not once thought of his nose. Equally important, images began crowding through his mind: not of the Camposanto or the Pisano Baptistery; but of the Battle of the Centaurs.

"Glory be to God," he thought, "I'm cured."

Rustici was overjoyed. "Didn't I tell you to sketch horses? A work of art without a horse is nothing."

Amused, Michelangelo replied, "Now if you can show me where to find some centaurs . . ."

The tension was gone from the garden. No one mentioned Torrigiani's name or referred to the quarrel: Torrigiani had not been caught, and probably never would be. Excited by his new project, Michelangelo concentrated on the resolving of his theme. Poliziano, flushed with pleasure, gave a summary of the centaur's role in mythology while Michelangelo sketched rapidly, drawing what he imagined it might be like: the whole of the horse except the shoulders, neck and head; and emerging from the body of the horse, the torso and head of a man.

He cared little for mythological legends, they were foreign to his nature. He was drawn to reality, as much of it as he could grasp; for him, the truest, most significant reality was the male figure, containing within itself the prototype of all other forms and designs.

He began searching within himself for an over-all design into which he could fit some twenty figures. How many separate scenes of action could there be? What would be the central focus, from which the eye would move in orderly, perceptive manner as he, the sculptor, wanted?

In the Roman Battle sarcophagus in Pisa and Bertoldo's Battle relief the warriors and women were clothed. As long as he was going back to Greek legend he felt he had the right to carve nudes, unencumbered by helmets, robes, loincloths which in his opinion cluttered Bertoldo's bronze. Hoping to achieve simplicity and control, he eliminated clothing as he had ruled out horses and the multiplicity of centaurs and weapons.

With this decision he got nowhere. Even Granacci could not help him.

"It was never possible to get nude models."

"Couldn't I rent a small studio somewhere, work alone?"

Granacci shook his head angrily. "You are Lorenzo's protégé, everything you do reflects on him."

"Then there's only one thing left to do. I'll work up at the Cave Maiano."

He walked up to Settignano in the cool of evening. As he came across the dark fields and forded the creek at the bottom of the ravine, he had a moment of apprehension. The Topolinos had heard about the fight with Torrigiani; but they would make no such scene as had occurred in the Buonarroti home the first time he returned, with his stepmother and aunt weeping, his uncle cursing, and his grandmother standing silent, her eyes dry, but suffering for him as he had suffered for himself.

The Topolinos greeted him casually. They were pleased that he was spending the night. If they noted the damage to his face, or even peered through the dark evening to gauge its extent, he could not tell it.

He washed in the creek at dawn, then made his way over the ox roads rutted along the contour of the hills to the quarries, where the stonemasons began work an hour after sunrise. From the top of the mountain he looked down on a castle surrounded by parallel lines of olives and grapevines. In the quarry the *pietra serena* cut the afternoon before was a turquoise blue while the older blocks were taking on a beige tone. Ten columns had been completed, and a huge panther blocked out, surrounded by a sea of chips. The quarrymen and masons were already forging and tempering their tools; each used twenty-five points in a day, so quickly did the *pietra serena* wear them down.

The masons were in good humor, greeting Michelangelo jovially.

"Come back to the quarries to do an honest day's work, eh? Once a stonemason always a stonemason."

"In this weather?" quipped Michelangelo. "I'm going to sit under a cool tree and never pick up anything heavier than a stick of charcoal."

They needed no further explanation.

The *pietra serena* threw off tremendous heat. The masons removed their clothes, everything except breechclout, straw hat and leather sandals. Michelangelo sat watching them. They could not pose, they had their day's stone to cut; and their small bodies, lean, wiry, bumpy, were a long way from the ideal of Greek beauty that he had seen in early statues. But in the warm sun the sweat on their skin caused them to shine and glisten like polished marble. They used every muscle of back and shoulder and leg to cut and lift the stone. They were completely unselfconscious as he sketched them, seeking the strength that lay buried in the indestructible bodies of these skilled craftsmen.

When the morning was half spent the masons gathered in their "hall," a cave cut out of the *pietra serena* at the base of the mountain which remained the same temperature the year round. Here they ate their breakfast of herring and onion, bread and red Chianti wine. Michelangelo told them of his proposed Battle of the Centaurs.

"It's time this ridge of stone under Mount Ceceri produced another sculptor," said a young, hard-bodied quarryman. "We have always had one: Mino da Fiesole, Desiderio da Settignano, Benedetto da Maiano."

In a few minutes they returned to work and Michelangelo to his drawing, working close up now, catching the tensions of the hands, the protrusion about the second phalanges, where the skin was stretched from holding hammer and chisel. How much there was to learn about the human body! How many thousands of intricate parts, each different, each with its fascinating detail. An artist could draw the human figure all his life and still catch only a fraction of its changing forms.

When the sun was high overhead several young boys appeared, carrying on their shoulders long branches with a row of nails in them, and hanging from each nail a basket with a man's dinner. Once again they gathered in the cool "hall." The quarrymen shared their vegetable soup, boiled meat, bread, cheese and wine with Michelangelo, then lay down for an hour's sleep.

While they slept he drew them: sprawled out on the ground, hats over their faces, their bodies quiet, recuperative, the lines tranquil, the forms somnolent. By the time they awakened the children had returned bringing fresh water to drink and for the forge; turning the wheels, sharpening the tools, using their hammers and chisels to help. Michelangelo sketched their supple limbs in action.

The next morning as he left the palace he was surprised to have a monk stop him, ask his name, take a letter from the folds of his black robe, and disappear as soundlessly as he had appeared. Michelangelo unfolded the note, saw his brother's signature, began to read. It was a plea to Michelangelo to abandon the pagan, godless theme which could only put his soul in jeopardy; and if he must persist in carving graven images, to do only those sanctified by the Church.

"The Battle of the Centaurs is an evil story," Lionardo concluded, "told to you by a perverted man. Renounce it and return to the bosom of Christ."

Michelangelo reread the letter, shaking his head with disbelief. How could Lionardo, buried within the monastery walls, know what theme he was carving? And that it had been inspired by Poliziano? He was only an apprentice. How could anyone consider a learning-theme important enough to tattle about? He was a little frightened at how much the monks inside San Marco knew of everyone's business.

He took the letter to the *studiolo,* showed it to Lorenzo.

"If I am doing you harm by carving this theme," he said quietly, "perhaps I ought to change?"

Lorenzo seemed weary. Bringing Savonarola to Florence had been a mistake and a disappointment. "That is precisely what Fra Savonarola is trying to accomplish: to cow us all, to impose his rigid censorship. We are not going to help him convert the Duomo into the Stinche. If we give in on the smallest detail it will be easier for him to win the next one. Continue your work."

Michelangelo threw his brother's letter into a bronze Etruscan pot under Lorenzo's desk.

11

He used pure beeswax which came in cakes, placing a container over his charcoal fire and breaking the wax into small bits. When it had cooled he kneaded it with his fingers into strips. In the morning he poured a little *trementina* onto his fingers to make the wax more pliable. Since this sculpture was to be in high relief, the outer half of the figures would emerge from the marble.

Moonfaced Bugiardini, who was growing to hate stone carving with a ferocity deep as Granacci's, began spending his days at the shed, gradually taking on manual tasks and becoming Michelangelo's assistant. Michelangelo had him chop a wooden block the size of the marble block he intended to use, and drive wires through it for an armature. Then from his exploratory drawings he began modeling the wax figures, attaching them to the armature, balancing the intertwined arms, torsos, legs, heads and stones as they would tumble backward in the final marble.

He found the block he wanted in the palace yard. Bugiardini helped him bring the stone into his shed and set it up on round wooden beams to protect its corners. Just to stand and gaze at it gave Michelangelo a sense of intense power. When he began roughing out he worked with his whole body, planting both feet wide apart for support, throwing all his weight into the arm holding the hammer, achieving the sculptor's equilibrium: the force to remove must be equal to the marble to be taken away. He remembered having scraped a pan with a piece of metal and having felt the metal in his teeth; now he felt the marble in his veins.

It was his desire to communicate his existence in space. That was one reason he had known that he must be a sculptor: to fill the void of emptiness with magnificent statues, statues of noble marble, expressing the richest, most profound feelings.

In its formation his four-foot block had a veining like wood, angling off to where the sun rises. He checked for due east and rolled the block into the same position in which it had lain in its mountain bed. He would have to cut across the grain, north and south, otherwise his marble would peel in fragmented layers.

He drew a deep breath, raised his hammer and chisel for the opening assault. Marble dust began to cover his hands and face, penetrating his clothes. It was good to touch his face and feel its dust, it was the same as touching the marble he was working on; he had the sensation of becoming one with his medium.

Saturday nights the palace emptied. Piero and Alfonsina visited with the noble families of Florence, Giovanni and Giulio began a social round, Lorenzo sought pleasure with his group of young bloods, according to rumor, participating in orgies of drinking and love-making. Michelangelo never knew whether these tales were true; but the next day Lorenzo would be wan and listless. His gout, inherited from his father, would keep him in bed or hobbling about the palace with a heavy cane.

On such evenings Michelangelo was free to have supper with Contessina and Giuliano on the open loggia of the top floor, in the soft night air. As they ate cold watermelon and chatted over candlelight, Contessina told him of having read the Boccaccio comments on the centaurs.

"Oh, I've already left the original battle far behind," he laughed.

He took paper from inside his shirt, a piece of charcoal from his purse, and moving the charcoal rapidly over the paper, he told Contessina what he was after. Man lived and died by stone. To suggest the unity of man and marble, the heads and the blocks being thrown would be indistinguishable. All twenty men, women and centaurs would be but one, each figure a facet of man's many-sided nature, animal as well as human, female as well as male, each attempting to destroy the other parts. He indicated with swift strokes some of the sculptural goals he was trying to achieve: the three receding levels of figures, each level in lower relief but not lower in vitality, the half-released forms appearing to be free-standing, each figure radiating its own force.

"I once heard you say that behind a carving there must be worship. What will there be to worship in your version of man's battle?"

"The supreme work of art: the male body, infinite in its expressiveness and beauty."

Contessina unconsciously looked down at her thin legs, the barely beginning-to-blossom bosom, then met his eyes amusedly.

"I can blackmail you for your pagan worship of the body of man. Plato might agree with you, but Savonarola would have you burned as a heretic."

"No, Contessina. I admire man, but I worship God for being able to create him."

They laughed, their heads close. Seeing Contessina's eyes move to the door and her head come up sharply, a mottled flush come to her cheeks, he turned and could tell from Lorenzo's posture that he had been standing there for a considerable time. Their intimacy had permeated the room, irradiating the atmosphere. Michelangelo had not been conscious of it. But interrupted at its height, it provided an aura that neither he nor Contessina nor Lorenzo could miss. Lorenzo stood silent, his lips compressed.

". . . we were . . . discussing . . . I had made some drawings . . ."

The harshness receded from Lorenzo's brow. He came forward to look at the drawings.

"Giulio reports your meetings to me. Your friendship is good. It can hurt neither of you. It is important that artists have friends. And Medici as well."

A few nights later when the moon was full and the air stirring with wild scents, they sat together in a library window seat overlooking the Via Larga and the enclosing hills.

"Florence is full of magic in the moonlight," sighed Contessina. "I wish I could look down from a height and see it all."

"I know a place," he exclaimed. "Just across the river. It's as though you could reach out your arms and embrace the city."

"Could we go? Now, I mean? We could slip out the back garden, separately. I'll put on a full head cape."

They walked the way he always went, at a sharp angle toward the Ponte alle Grazie, crossing the Arno and climbing up to the ancient fort. Sitting on the stone parapet, it was as though they were dangling their feet in the gray stone waters of the city. Michelangelo pointed out her father's villa in Fiesole, the Badia just below it; the wall of eight towers guarding the city at the foot of the Fiesole hills; the glistening white cluster of Baptistery, Duomo and Campanile; the golden-stoned, high-towered Signoria; the tight oval city enclosed by its walls and river; and on their side of the river the moonlit Pitti palace built of stone from its own quarry in the Boboli gardens just behind the parapet.

They sat a little apart, touched by the moon, caught up in the beauty of the city and the ranges of hills that embraced them as fondly as was Florence by her walls. Their fingers fumbled slowly toward each other on the rough surface of the stone; touched and interlocked.

The repercussion came quickly. Lorenzo, who had been taking the baths at Vignone for several days, summoned him from the garden. He was seated at the big desk in his office, its walls covered with a map of Italy, a map of the world, the Sforza castle in Milan; the tables and shelves bearing a collection of hard stone vases, ivories, purple leather volumes of Dante and Petrarch, a Bible bound in purple velvet with silver ornaments. Standing beside him was his secretary, Ser Piero da Bibbiena. Michelangelo did not need to be told why he had been sent for.

"She was safe, Excellency. By my side the whole time."

"So I gather. Did you really think you would not be observed? Giulio saw her going out the rear gate."

Miserable now, Michelangelo replied, "It was indiscreet." He lifted his eyes from the richly patterned Persian rug, cried, "It was so beautiful up there; as though Florence were a marble quarry, with its churches and towers cut out of a single stratum of stone."

"I am not questioning your conduct, Michelangelo. But Ser Piero does question its wisdom. You know that Florence is a city of wicked tongues."

"They would not speak evil of a little girl."

Lorenzo studied Michelangelo's face for a moment.

" 'Contessina' can no longer be interpreted as 'little girl.' She is growing up. I had not fully realized it before, That is all, Michelangelo, you can return to work now, as I know you are impatient to do."

Michelangelo did not move, even though he had been dismissed.

"Is there not something I can do to make amends?"

"I have already made them." Lorenzo came from behind his desk, put both hands on the boy's trembling shoulders. "Do not be unhappy. You meant no wrong. Change for dinner, there is someone you should meet."

The last thing Michelangelo wanted in his wretched state was to eat with sixty guests; but this was no time to disobey. He washed splashingly out of his bowl, donned a russet silk tunic, and went up to the dining hall where a groom took him to a seat Lorenzo had saved next to Gianfrancesco Aldovrandi, of one of the leading families of Bologna. Lorenzo had named Aldovrandi *podestà* or visiting mayor of Florence for the year 1488. Michelangelo's concentration was not very good, his mind and stomach were in a turmoil. Aldovrandi turned his full attention on him.

"His Excellency was so kind as to show me your drawings and the marble Madonna and Child. I was greatly stimulated."

"Thank you."

"I am not indulging in compliments. I speak because I am a sculpture enthusiast myself, and I have grown up with the magnificent work of Jacopo della Quercia."

Michelangelo numbly asked who he might be.

"Ah, that is why I asked *Il Magnifico* if I could speak to you. Jacopo della Quercia is not known in Florence, yet he is one of the greatest sculptors that Italy has produced. He was the dramatist in stone, as Donatello was the poet. It is my hope that you will come to Bologna and permit me to show you his work. It could have a profound influence on you."

Michelangelo wanted to reply that profound influences were precisely what he wished to avoid; yet Aldovrandi would prove to be a prophet.

During the ensuing days Michelangelo heard that Piero and Alfonsina had several times protested against "a commoner being allowed to associate on such intimate terms with a Medici"; and Ser Piero da Bibbiena had written to Lorenzo at the baths, a veiled but strong note saying, "If some decision is not taken about Contessina, we may regret it."

It was not until several nights later that he learned what Lorenzo meant by amends. Contessina had been sent for a visit to the Ridolfi villa in the country.

12

He received a message from his father. The family was concerned about Lionardo, who had been reported ill in the monastery at San Marco.

"Could you use your Medici connections to get in to see Lionardo?" asked Lodovico, when he went to see them.

"No outsider is allowed in the monks' quarters."

"San Marco is a Medici church and monastery," said his grandmother, "built by Cosimo and supported by Lorenzo."

After a number of days he found that his requests were being ignored. Then he learned that Savonarola would preach in San Marco the following Sunday.

"The monks will all be there," Bertoldo told him. "You will get a look at your brother. You might even exchange a few words. Bring us back a report on the friar."

San Marco was delightfully cool in the early morning. His plan to take up a position at the side door leading in from the cloister, so that Lionardo would have to pass close to him, was spoiled by the presence of the tight knot of monks in their black habits who had been praying and chanting in the choir since before morning light. Their cowls were pulled so far forward that their faces were buried. It was impossible for Michelangelo to see whether Lionardo was in the group.

The church was by no means full. When a murmur announced the entrance of Savonarola, he slipped into a pew close to the pulpit and sat on the edge of the hard bench.

There was little to mark a difference between Savonarola and the other fifty-odd monks as he slowly climbed the pulpit stairs. His head and face were deep in his Dominican cowl, a slight figure under the robe. Michelangelo could see little but the tip of his nose and a pair of dark veiled eyes. His voice had harsh northern accents; at first it was quiet, but soon it took on a commanding tone as he expounded his thesis on the corruption of the priesthood. Never, even in the most heated attacks in the palace, had Michelangelo heard the slightest part of the charges Savonarola now levied against the clergy: the priests were political rather than spiritual, put into the Church by their families for worldly gain; they were careerists and opportunists seeking only wealth and power; guilty of simony, nepotism, bribery, selling of relics, accumulation of benefices: "The adulteries of the Church have filled the world."

Warming to his task, Savonarola pushed back the cowl and Michelangelo got his first view of the friar's face. He found it as emotionally disturbing as the words that were coming with accelerating heat and rapidity from the contradictory mouth, the upper lip thin and ascetic as the material of a hair shirt, the lower lip more fleshy and voluptuous than Poliziano's. The black eyes flashing to the farthest corner of the church were sunken under high-boned, hollowed-out cheeks, obviously the victims of fasting; his nose jutted outward in a massive ridge with wide, flaring nostrils. It was a dramatic face that could have been invented by no artist save Savonarola himself. The bone structure fascinated Michelangelo as a sculptor, for the dark marblelike chin was carved from the same flesh as the passionate hanging underlip, polished with pumice and emery stone.

Michelangelo tore his eyes from Savonarola's face so that he might better hear the words that were now pouring like molten bronze, the voice filling the church, reverberating off the hollow chapels, returning to invade the left ear after it had boxed and reddened the right.

"I have beheld proud ambition invade Rome and contaminate all things, until she has become a false, proud harlot. O Italy, O Rome, O Florence, your villainies, your impieties, your fornications, your usuries, your cruelties are bringing us tribulations. Give up your pomps and shows. Give up, I tell you, your mistresses and your love boys. The earth is covered with blood, but the clergy cares not a rap.

They are far indeed from God, those priests whose worship is to spend the night with harlots, the days gossiping together in the sacristies. The altar itself has been turned into a clerical shop. The sacraments are the counters of your simony. Your lust has made of you a brazen-faced whore. Once you were at least ashamed of your sins; once priests had the grace to call their sons nephews. They no longer bother now. 'I will descend on you in your scurrility and your wickedness,' says the Lord, 'upon your whores and your palaces.' "

He scourged the people of Florence, cried out that Dante had used Florence as his model for the City of Dis:

> "Within the second circle are confined
> Hypocrisy and flattery, and those
> Who practice witchcraft, sorcery and theft,
> Falsehood and Simony and suchlike filth."

Summoning his will, for Savonarola's voice was a paralyzing agent, Michelangelo looked around and saw that the congregation was sitting as one individual, soldered together.

"The whole of Italy will feel God's wrath. Her cities will fall prey to foes. Blood will run in the streets. Murder will be the order of the day. Unless ye repent! repent! repent!"

The cry of "Repent!" echoed around the church a hundredfold while Savonarola pulled his hood forward, masking his face, prayed long and silently, then came down the pulpit stairs and out the cloister door, leaving Michelangelo deeply moved, a little exalted, a little sick. When he was again out in the hot glaring sunshine of the piazza he stood blindly blinking, unwilling to go to his home or to the palace, not knowing what to say. Finally he sent word to his father that he had been unable to see Lionardo.

The emotional upheaval had faded when he received a note from Lionardo asking him to come to San Marco at vespers. The cloister was beautiful at dusk, the grass freshly cut, the hedges trimmed, jasmine and sunflowers growing in the shade of the arches, the atmosphere tranquil and secluded from the world.

Lionardo seemed to Michelangelo as cadaverous as Savonarola.

"The family has been worried about your health."

Lionardo's head shrank deeper into the cowl. "My family is the family of God."

"Don't be sanctimonious."

When Lionardo spoke again Michelangelo detected a touch of affection.

"I called for you because I know you are not evil. You have not been corrupted by the palace. Even in the midst of Sodom and Gomorrah, you have not been debauched, you have lived like an anchorite."

Amused, Michelangelo asked, "How do you know these things?"

"We know everything that goes on in Florence." Lionardo took a step forward, held out his bony hands. "Fra Savonarola has had a vision. The Medici, the palace, all the obscene, godless art works within its walls will be destroyed. They cannot save themselves; but you can, for your soul is not yet lost. Repent, and forsake them while there is still time."

"Savonarola attacked the clergy, I heard his sermon, but he did not attack Lorenzo."

"There are to be nineteen sermons, starting on All Saints' Day, through to Epiphany. By the end of them, Florence and the Medici will be in flames."

They stood side by side in the airless corridor along one side of the cloister. Michelangelo was shocked into silence.

"You won't save yourself?" implored Lionardo.

"We have different ideas. All of us can't be the same."

"We can. The world must be a monastery such as this, where all souls are saved."

"If my soul is to be saved, it can only be through sculpture. That is my faith, and my discipline. You said that I live like an anchorite; it's my work that keeps me that way. Then how can that work be bad? Wouldn't God give me a choice, as long as we both serve Him equally?"

Lionardo's eyes burned into Michelangelo's for a moment. Then he was gone, through a door and up a flight of stairs.

"Into a cell decorated by Fra Angelico, I hope," said Michelangelo to himself, a little bitterly.

He felt he owed it to Lorenzo to attend the All Saints' Day sermon. This time the church was full. Again Savonarola began in a quiet, expository manner, explaining the mysteries of mass and the wholeness of the divine word. The newcomers seemed disappointed. But the friar was just working up warmth; soon he had moved into oratory, and then into crescendo, his mighty voice whipping the congregation with its impassioned eloquence.

He attacked the clergy: "Ye hear it said, 'Blessed the house that owns a fat cure.' But a time will come when rather it will be said, 'Woe to that house.' Ye will feel the edge of the sword upon ye. Affliction shall smite ye. This shall no more be called Florence, but a den of thieves, of turpitude and bloodshed."

He attacked the moneylenders: "Ye are guilty of avarice, ye have corrupted the magistrates and their functions. None can persuade ye that it is sinful to lend at usury, but rather ye hold them to be fools that refrain from it."

He attacked the morals of Florence: "Ye have fulfilled the saying of Isaiah: 'They declare their sin as Sodom, for they hide it not,' and that of Jeremiah: 'Thou hadst a whore's forehead, thou refusedst to be ashamed.' "

He declared: "I vowed not to prophesy, but a voice in the night said, 'Fool, dost thou not see that it is God's will that thou shouldst continue?' That is why I cannot stop prophesying. And I say unto ye: know that unheard-of times are at hand!"

There was a deepening murmur in the church. Many of the women were weeping.

Michelangelo rose, made his way up a side aisle, the angry voice following through the door. He crossed the Piazza San Marco, entered the garden and retreated to his shed, shaking as though with ague. He resolved not to return to the church: for what had this recital of lust and avarice to do with him?

13

Contessina found him in the library where he was sketching from the illustrations in an ancient manuscript. She had been away for several weeks. Her face was ashen. He jumped up.

"Contessina, have you been ill? Sit down here."

"I have something to tell you." She sank into the chair, leaned forward to the cold hearth as though to warm her hands. ". . . the contracts have been drawn."

"Contracts?"

"For my marriage . . . to Piero Ridolfi. I did not want you to hear of it from the palace gossip."

After an instant he asked brusquely, "Why should it affect me? Everyone knows that Medici daughters are given in political marriages: Maddalena to Franceschetto Cibo, the Pope's son; Lucrezia to Jacopo Salviati . . ."

"I don't know why it should affect you, Michelangelo, any more than it should affect me."

He met her eyes squarely, for the first time.

"And does it?"

"How could it? Everyone knows that Medici daughters are given in political marriage."

"Forgive me, Contessina. I was hurt."

"It's all right," she smiled wistfully. "I know you by now."

"And the marriage . . . when?"

"Not for a while. I am too young. I asked for another year."

"Yet everything has changed."

"Not for us. We are still friends in the palace."

After a silence, Michelangelo asked, "Piero Ridolfi, he will not make you unhappy? He is fond of you?"

Contessina looked up at him with her head bowed.

"We do not discuss such matters. I will do what I must. But my feelings are my own."

She rose, went close to him. He hung his head like a dumb beast in a storm. When at last he looked up he saw tears sparkling in her eyes. He reached out his hand, tentatively, and slowly she placed her fingers into his until they were locked together quite hard. Then she withdrew, leaving behind only her faint mimosa scent, and a hot dryness in his throat.

There was no way to keep Savonarola's ringing voice out of his ears, for Lionardo's warning became a reality. In the midst of his second sermon against vice in Florence, Savonarola suddenly cried out against the Medici, blamed Lorenzo for the evil of the city, predicted the downfall of the ruling family and, as a climax, the Pope in the Vatican.

The Plato Academy assembled hastily in the *studiolo*. Michelangelo reported the first two sermons, then told of Lionardo's warning. Though Lorenzo had had his monumental battles with the Vatican, at this moment he wanted to keep the peace with Pope Innocent VIII because of Giovanni, who had only a few months to wait before he was invested a full cardinal and would leave for Rome to represent the Medici. The Pope might well imagine that since Lorenzo had summoned Savonarola to Florence, and Savonarola was preaching in a Medici church, he was attacking the papacy with Lorenzo's knowledge and consent.

"It is a good thing he is attacking me at the same time," he murmured ruefully.

"We'll simply have to shut him up," growled Poliziano.

"We need only to put an end to his prophecies," said Lorenzo. "They are no part of our religion or of his office. Pico, that much you will have to undertake."

The first defection came from the sculpture garden. Granacci reported that the fun-loving Baccio fell silent for hours on end, then took to disappearing for a day or two at a time. Soon he began making derogatory remarks about the Medici; then he began extolling the virtues of Savonarola and the spiritual life of the cloister. One day he deserted to the Dominicans.

Savonarola's sermons in San Marco were now attracting such large crowds that late in March, for the second Sunday in Lent, he transferred his activities to the cathedral. Ten thousand Florentines stood packed together, yet dwarfed by the enormousness of space around them. In the few months that had passed since Michelangelo had heard him preach in San Marco, several changes had come over the friar. Because of his rigid fasting, the penance on his knees in the cells of San Marco, he could barely summon the strength to mount the pulpit stairs. He had assumed a complete identification of himself with Christ.

"As ye can see and hear, I do not speak with my own tongue but that of God. I am His voice on earth."

A cold shiver ran through the congregation. Savonarola was no less moved than his admirers.

Michelangelo timed his arrival at the Duomo to meet his father and the rest of the family, deserters from Santa Croce to hear the new prophet, with the end of the service. He stood inside the door and gazed up at the Donatello and Luca della Robbia choir stalls high on either side of the central altar: marble carvings of children at play, singing, dancing, laughing, serenading with musical instruments, pure Greek in their joyous love of life, in their testament to the beauty of their young bodies. For Michelangelo, the marbles cried out, "People are good!" while Savonarola was thundering, "Humanity is evil!"

Who was right? Donatello and Della Robbia? Or Savonarola?

The gloom of the church sat heavily around the Buonarroti dinner table. Lucrezia was in tears.

"That wicked man. He has ruined my beautiful white veal. From now on, Lodovico, if you wish to hear Savonarola preach it must be after dinner and not before."

Though the city was shaking in a religious upheaval, Michelangelo kept working calmly. Unlike Savonarola, he could not persuade himself that God was speaking through him, but he did feel that if God saw He would approve the work.

He felt a grudging admiration for Savonarola. Was he not an idealist? As for his fanaticism, had not Rustici said, "You're like Savonarola, you fast because you can't bring yourself to stop work in the middle of the day"?

Michelangelo grimaced at the accusation. Yet did he not feel a dedication to the task of revolutionizing marble sculpture even as Phidias had taken death-worshiping Egyptian sculpture and rendered it Greek-human? Would he not have been willing to fast and pray until he barely had the strength to drag himself through the garden to his workshop, if that were necessary?

And what was wrong with God speaking to His children? Surely He had the right? The power? He believed in God. If God could create the earth and man, could He not create a prophet . . . or a sculptor?

The Signoria invited Savonarola to address them in the great hall of the Palazzo della Signoria. Lorenzo, the Plato Four, the important Medici hierarchy throughout the city announced its intention of going. Michelangelo took his place on a long bench between Contessina and Giovanni, facing the platform on which Savonarola stood before a wooden lectern, with the city government banked behind.

When Savonarola first mentioned Lorenzo de' Medici as a tyrant, Michelangelo saw Lorenzo's lips lift in a faint smile. He himself barely heard the words, for he was gazing about the great hall with its long side panels of pure white plaster and thinking what magnificent frescoes could be painted there.

Lorenzo's smile vanished as Savonarola mounted his attack: All the evil and all the good of the city depend from its head, and therefore great is his responsibility. If he followed the right path, the whole city would be sanctified. Tyrants are incorrigible because they are proud. They leave all in the hands of bad ministers. They hearken not unto the poor, and neither do they condemn the rich. They corrupt voters and aggravate the burdens of the people.

Now Michelangelo began listening intently, for Savonarola charged that Lorenzo had confiscated the Florentine Dower Fund, monies paid into the city treasury by poorer families as guarantee that they would have the eventual dowry without which no Tuscan girl could hope to marry; that Lorenzo had used the money to buy sacrilegious manuscripts and evil works of art; to stage bacchanals through which he rendered the people of Florence prey to the devil.

Lorenzo's dark skin turned green.

Savonarola was not through: Lorenzo, the corrupt tyrant, must go. The dishonest Signoria sitting behind him must go. The judges, the officials, must go. An entirely new government, ruled by a completely new and rigorous set of laws, must be installed to render Florence a City of God.

Who was to govern Florence? Revise its laws and execute them?

Savonarola.
God had ordered it.

14

When Michelangelo reached the *studiolo* he found Fra Mariano there. The humanist preacher of San Gallo had been losing his congregation to Savonarola. Michelangelo drew his usual chair to the low table, put an apple on his plate, and then sat back.

"We will not attempt to refute Savonarola's personal slanders," Lorenzo was saying. "The facts of such matters as the Dower Fund are clear for all Florentines to see. But his prophesying of doom is causing a mounting hysteria in Florence. Fra Mariano, I have been thinking that you are the one to answer Savonarola. Could I suggest that you preach a sermon on Acts 1:7, 'It is not for you to know the times and seasons which the Father has fixed by his own authority'?"

Fra Mariano's face lighted.

"I could review the history of prophecy, the ways in which God speaks to His people, and show that all Savonarola lacks is a witch's cauldron . . ."

"Gently," said Lorenzo. "Your sermon must be quiet and irrefutable, in fact as well as logic, so that our people will see the difference between revelation and witchcraft."

The discussion centered around what biblical and literary materials Fra Mariano should use. Michelangelo ate a little of the fruit, slipped out unnoticed.

There followed a month of tranquillity and steady work. He locked out all contact with the world, eating and sleeping little, tackling the twenty intertwined entities of his marble block.

The palace spread the word that the faithful should go to San Gallo on Holy Thursday to hear Fra Mariano demolish Fra Savonarola. When Michelangelo walked into the church he found there every important family in Tuscany: nobles, landowners, merchants, scholars, travelers from Europe and England, the Signoria, judges and councilors from the four quarters of Florence.

Fra Mariano mounted the pulpit and began in his cultivated, scholarly voice by quoting from Cosimo de' Medici: "States are not ruled by *pater-nosters,*" which brought a ripple of laughter. He then spoke learnedly on the need for separation of Church and State, and the·dangers to human freedom when, as in the past, they had been combined.

It was a good beginning. Lorenzo sat relaxed on his bench. The congregation listened intently with growing satisfaction, as Mariano proceeded by logical steps, quoting from Scripture, to show the true role of the Church and its position in the spiritual life of its people.

Then something went wrong. Fra Mariano's face grew red, his arms were thrown up to the heavens in as violent a gesture as any of Savonarola's. His voice changed as he mentioned for the first time the name of Girolamo Savonarola, spitting it out as something diseased. He threw away his carefully prepared argument, called the friar a "disseminator of scandal and disorder," and a series of evil epithets.

Michelangelo could think of only one answer: Fra Mariano had allowed his jealousy of Savonarola to conquer his judgment. He was still shouting from the pulpit when Lorenzo gathered his family about him and limped down the center aisle and out of the church.

Now for the first time Michelangelo found the palace soaked in gloom. Lorenzo suffered an acute attack of the gout and could barely hobble about the halls. Poliziano, visibly shaken, clung to Lorenzo like a child, his wit and profundity vanished. Ficino and Landino were apprehensive about their lifetime work, for Savonarola was threatening to burn all the books in Florence except the approved

Christian commentaries. Pico was the hardest hit; not only had he recommended bringing the friar to Florence, he was still sympathetic to most of Savonarola's program, and too honest to conceal it from Lorenzo.

Lorenzo rallied to make another frontal attack by asking Prior Bichiellini of Santo Spirito to join them in the *studiolo*. Michelangelo had become acquainted with the prior at Sunday dinners in the palace, and sometimes returned with him to the church to sketch in the afternoon from such familiar frescoes as the Young St. John. The prior, an energetic man of fifty, was famous in Florence as the only one who wore his spectacles on the street.

"The faces of people as they hurry by," he once explained to Michelangelo, "are like the pages of a book fluttering past. Through these magnifying lenses I study their expressions and character."

Now the prior sat before the low table in the *studiolo* while Lorenzo asked if he would send to Rome for the Augustinians' most brilliant preacher "to spell some sense into the Florentines."

"I think I know our man. I shall write at once."

Florence turned out to hear the visiting Augustinian monk expose, intellectually, the extremities and danger of Savonarola's preaching; came to Santo Spirito, listened politely to his words, and went away unheeding.

Michelangelo again tried to lock himself in his shed, but the walls were too thin to keep out each day's ration of bad news: Pico tried to dissuade Lorenzo from setting spies on Savonarola on the grounds that he was too dedicated to commit the kind of "sin of the flesh" in which Lorenzo hoped to catch him. Savonarola's espionage system caught Lorenzo's spies and exposed them. Fra Mariano had deserted Lorenzo and gone on his knees to Savonarola to implore forgiveness. Only a handful of students had attended the last lectures of the Plato Academy. Florence's printers were refusing to print anything the friar did not approve. Sandro Botticelli had deserted to Savonarola, publicly declaring his female nudes to be lewd, lascivious and immoral.

Michelangelo still approved Savonarola's crusade for reform; he disapproved only of the attacks on the Medici and the arts. When he tried to explain this dilemma, Bertoldo grew querulous and, when Michelangelo next showed him his work, exclaimed that Michelangelo had missed the whole point of the Battle of the Centaurs.

"It's too bare. You haven't learned anything from my Battle or the one in Pisa. You've designed out all the richness. Savonarola's influence, I would guess. You need the horses, the flowing robes, the weapons, else what have you left to carve?"

"People," muttered Michelangelo under his breath.

"Your marble is poverty-stricken. If you want my opinion you'll throw away this block as an exercise that went wrong, and ask Granacci to find you a new one."

Bertoldo did not come to the rear of the garden for several days. Michelangelo had a visitor in his place, his brother Lionardo, in cloak and cowl, sunken-cheeked.

"Welcome to my workshop, Lionardo."

Lionardo gazed with set jaw at the Battle.

"It is your sculpture I have come about. We want you to offer it up to God."

"How do I do that?"

"By destroying it. Along with the drawings Botticelli has brought in, and other art obscenities that the congregation has volunteered. It is to be Savonarola's first fire in the purifying of Florence."

This was the second invitation to destroy his work. "You consider my marble obscene?"

"It is sacrilegious. Bring it to San Marco and fling it on the flames yourself."

Lionardo's voice had an intensity of emotional fervor that set Michelangelo on edge. He took him by the elbow, even in his anger able to feel that there was no flesh whatever on his brother's bones, escorted him to the rear gate and put him into the street.

He had planned to do weeks of polishing to bring out the highlights of his figures. Instead he asked Granacci to help him move the block into the palace that night. Granacci borrowed a wheelbarrow which Bugiardini pushed through the Piazza San Marco and down the Via Larga.

With Bugiardini and Granacci helping, he carried the block to Lorenzo's sitting room. Lorenzo had not seen the piece for a month, not since Fra Mariano's sermon. He came into the room, face sallow, eyes lackluster, hobbling painfully with the aid of a cane, and was taken completely by surprise. "Ah!" he exclaimed, and dropped into a chair. He sat for a long time in silence, his gaze riveted on the sculpture, studying it section by section, figure by figure, the color rising in his cheeks. Vitality seemed to return to his limbs. Michelangelo remained standing behind him, also studying the marble. Finally Lorenzo turned and looked up at him, his eyes gleaming.

"You were right not to polish. The chisel textures help bring out the anatomy."

"Then you approve the carving, Excellency?"

"What is there to approve? I can feel every body, every stone, every crushed bone, the fingers of the injured youth in the corner, pressed into his hair and skull, his arm sheltering the stones he will never throw. It's unlike any marble I've seen."

"We've already had an offer for the piece."

"A patron? Someone wants to buy?"

"Not exactly. They want it as a contribution. From Savonarola, through my brother Lionardo, to offer it up to God on their bonfire."

There was an almost imperceptible pause before Lorenzo said, "And you answered?"

"That I was not free to give it. The piece belonged to Lorenzo de' Medici."

"The marble is yours."

"Even to give to Savonarola for burning?"

"If that is your wish."

"But suppose, Excellency, that I had already offered the piece to God? The God who created man in His own image of goodness and strength and beauty? Savonarola says that man is vile. Would God have created us in hate?"

Lorenzo rose abruptly, walked about the room with only the barest indication of a limp. A groom came in, set a small table with two places.

"Sit down and eat while I talk to you. I too will eat, though I had no appetite before you came." He reached for a crisp crust of bread. "Michelangelo, the forces of destruction march on the heels of creativity. The arts, finest flowering of each age, are torn down, broken, burned by the next. Sometimes, as you see here in Florence today, by erstwhile friends and neighbors in the same city in the same year. Savonarola is not only after what he calls the non-religious works and the 'lascivious' nudes; he also means to destroy the painting and sculpture that does not fit into his pattern: the frescoes of Masaccio, Filippo Lippi, the Benozzo Gozzolis here in the palace chapel, the Ghirlandaios, all of the Greek and Roman statuary, most of our Florentine marbles.

"Little will remain but the Fra Angelico angels in the San Marco cells. If he has his way, and his power is growing, Florence will be ravished, as was Athens by Sparta. The Florentines are a fickle people; if they follow Savonarola to the end of his announced road, everything that has been accomplished since my great-grandfather offered his prize for the Baptistery doors will be wiped out. Florence will slip back into darkness."

Shaken by the intensity of Lorenzo's emotion, Michelangelo cried:

"How wrong I was to think that Savonarola would reform only what was evil in Florentine life. He will destroy everything that is good as well. As a sculptor I would be a slave, with both hands cut off."

"Nobody misses the loss of another man's freedom," replied Lorenzo sadly. Then he pushed aside his plate. "I want you to take a walk with me. There is something I must show you."

They went to the rear of the palace and across a small enclosed square to the front of San Lorenzo, the family church of the Medici. Inside was buried Cosimo, Lorenzo's grandfather, near one of the bronze pulpits designed by Donatello and executed by Bertoldo; in the Old Sacristy, designed by Brunelleschi, was a sarcophagus containing Cosimo's parents, Giovanni di Bicci and his wife; and a porphyry sarcophagus of Piero the Gouty, Lorenzo's father, created by Verrocchio. But the principal face of the church remained of rough, unevenly spaced, earth-colored brick, obviously uncompleted.

"Michelangelo, this is the last great work of art I must complete for my family, a marble façade with some twenty sculptured figures standing in its niches."

"Twenty sculptures! That's as many as stand in the façade of the Duomo."

"But not too many for you. One full-size statue for every figure suggested in your Battle. We must create something over which all Italy will rejoice."

Michelangelo wondered whether the sinking feeling in his diaphragm was joy or dismay. Impetuously he cried, "I will do it, Lorenzo, I promise. But I will need time. I still have so much to learn. . . . I have not yet tried my first free-standing figure."

When he reached his apartment he found Bertoldo wrapped in a blanket, sitting over a live-coal brazier in his half of the L, his eyes red and his face a pasty white. Michelangelo went quickly to his side.

"Are you all right, Bertoldo?"

"No, I'm not all right! I'm a stupid, blind, ridiculous old man who has outworn his time."

"What leads you to this harsh conclusion?" asked Michelangelo lightly, trying to cheer him.

"Looking at your Battle in Lorenzo's room, and remembering the things I said about it. I was wrong, terribly wrong. I was trying to turn it into a cast bronze piece; your marble would have been spoiled. You must forgive me."

"Let me put you to bed."

He settled Bertoldo under the feather-bed quilt, went down to the basement kitchen and ordered a mug of wine heated on the dying embers. He held the silver cup to Bertoldo's lips, feeding consolation with the hot liquid.

"If the Battle is good, it's because you taught me how to make it good. If I couldn't make it like bronze, it was because you made me aware of the differences between solid marble and fluid metal. So be content. Tomorrow we will start a new piece, and you will teach me more."

"Yes, tomorrow," sighed Bertoldo. He closed his eyes, opened them again briefly, asked, "Are you sure, Michelangelo, there is a tomorrow?" and dropped off to sleep.

In a few moments there was a change in his breathing. It seemed to become heavy, labored. Michelangelo went to wake Ser Piero, who sent a groom for Lorenzo's doctor.

Michelangelo spent the night holding Bertoldo so that he could breathe a little more easily. The doctor confessed that he could think of nothing to do. At first light Bertoldo opened his eyes, gazed at Michelangelo, the doctor and Ser Piero, understood his plight, and whispered:

". . . take me to Poggio . . . it's so beautiful . . ."

When a groom came to announce that the carriage was ready, Michelangelo picked Bertoldo up, blankets and all, and held him on his lap for the drive out toward Pistoia to the most exquisite of the Medici villas, formerly owned by Michelangelo's cousins, the Rucellai, and remodeled with magnificent open galleries by Giuliano da Sangallo. Rain lashed at their carriage all the way, but once Bertoldo was installed in the high bed in his favorite room, overlooking the Ombrone River, the sun emerged and lighted the lush green Tuscan landscape. Lorenzo rode out to comfort his old friend, bringing Maestro Stefano da Prato to try some new medicines.

Bertoldo died in the late afternoon of the second day. After the priest had given him extreme unction, he uttered his last words with a little smile, as though trying to make his exit as a wit rather than a sculptor.

"Michelangelo . . . you are my heir . . . as I was Donatello's."

"Yes, Bertoldo. And I am proud."

"I want you to have my estate . . ."

"If you wish."

"It will make you . . . rich . . . famous. My cookbook."

"I shall always treasure it."

Bertoldo smiled again, as though they shared a secret joke, and closed his eyes for the last time. Michelangelo said his good-bys silently, turned away. He had lost his master. There would never be another.

15

The disorganization of the garden was now complete. All work stopped. Granacci gave up the painting of a street festival scene that he had almost completed and spent his time feverishly supplying models, finding marble blocks, scaring up small commissions for a sarcophagus, a Madonna.

Michelangelo cornered his friend late one afternoon.

"It's no good, Granacci. School is over."

"Don't say that. We have only to find a new master. Lorenzo said last night I could go to Siena to seek one . . ."

Sansovino and Rustici drifted into the studio.

"Michelangelo is right," said Sansovino. "I'm going to accept the invitation from the King of Portugal, and go there to work."

"I think we've learned all we can as students," agreed Rustici.

"I was never intended for cutting stone," said Bugiardini. "My nature is too soft, it's made for mixing oil and pigment. I'm going to ask Ghirlandaio to take me back."

Granacci snapped at Michelangelo, "Don't tell me you're leaving too!"

"Me? Where would I go?"

The group broke up. Michelangelo walked home with Granacci to report the death of Bertoldo to the family. Lucrezia was excited by the cookbook, reading several of the recipes aloud. Lodovico showed no interest.

"Michelangelo, it is finished, your new sculpture?"

"Sort of."

"*Il Magnifico,* he has seen it?"

"Yes, I took it to him."

"Did he like it?"

"Yes."

"That's all, just yes? Didn't he show pleasure, approval?"

"Yes, Father, he did."

"Then where is the money?"

"What money?"

"The fifty florins."

"I don't know what . . ."

"Come now. *Il Magnifico* gave you fifty florins when you finished the Madonna and Child. Hand over the purse."

"There is no purse."

"No purse? You worked for a whole year. You're entitled to your money."

"I'm not entitled to anything, Father, beyond what I have had."

"*Il Magnifico* paid you for the other and not for this one." Lodovico was emphatic. "That can only mean that he does not like this one."

"It can also mean that he is ill, worried about many things . . ."

"Then there is still a chance that he will pay you?"

"I have no idea."

"You must remind him."

Michelangelo shook his head in despair; returned slowly through the cold wet streets.

An artist without ideas is a mendicant; barren, he goes begging among the hours. For the first time since he had entered Urbino's school seven years before, he had no desire to draw. He avoided the formation of the word "marble" in his mind. His broken nose, which had given him no trouble while he was working, began to pain him; one nostril was closed completely, making it difficult for him to breathe. Again he became conscious of his ugliness.

The garden was lonely. Lorenzo had suspended work on the library. The stonemasons were gone, and with them the rhythmical chipping of building blocks that was the most natural *ambiente* for his work. There was a feeling of transition in the air. The Plato group rarely came in to Florence to lecture. There were no more evenings in the *studiolo*. Lorenzo decided that he must take a complete cure in one of his villas, with six months away from the palace and its duties. There he could not only eradicate his gout but lay his plans to come to grips with Savonarola. This was to be a battle to the death, he said, and he would need his full vitality. Though all the weapons were in his hands: wealth, power, control of the local government, treaties with outside city-states and nations, firm friends in all the neighboring dynasties; and Savonarola had nothing but the cloak on his back; yet Savonarola, living the life of a saint, dedicated, uncorruptible, a brilliant teacher, an executive who had already effected serious reforms in the personal life of the Tuscan clergy as well as the indulgent life of the rich Florentines who were flocking to his side to renounce the pamperings of the flesh, Fra Savonarola seemed to have the upper hand.

As part of his plan to put his affairs in order, Lorenzo made arrangements for Giovanni to be invested as cardinal, worried lest Pope Innocent VIII, an old man, should die before fulfilling his promise, and the succeeding Pope, perhaps hostile to the Medici as former ones had been, refuse to accept the sixteen-year-old youth into the ruling hierarchy of the Church. Lorenzo also knew that it would be a strategic victory with the people of Florence.

Michelangelo was troubled by Lorenzo's preparations for his departure to Careggi, for he had begun to hand over important business and governmental matters to Piero. If Piero were to be in command, what would life be like for him here? Piero could order him out of the palace. For that matter, what was his status, now that the sculpture garden had virtually closed down?

Nothing had been said about completion money for the Battle, so he could not go home. The three florins spending money was no longer being deposited on his washstand. He had no need for the money, but its sudden disappearance unnerved him. Who had ordered this? Lorenzo? Ser Piero da Bibbiena, perhaps thinking that it was no longer necessary since the garden was not functioning? Or was it Piero?

In his irresolution, Michelangelo turned to Contessina, seeking out her company, spending hours talking to her; picking up *The Divine Comedy* and reading aloud to her the passages he liked best, such as the one in Canto XI of the *Inferno:*

"Art, as best it can, doth follow nature,
  As pupil follows master; industry

> Or Art is, so to speak, grandchild to God.
> From these two sources (if you will call to mind
> That passage in the Book of Genesis)
> Mankind must take its sustenance and progress.''

The Platonists had urged him to write sonnets as the highest expression of man's literary thought, and had read from their own poetry in the hope of giving him insight into the art. While he was expressing himself fully in drawing, modeling and carving, he had had no need for a supplementary voice. Now in his solitude and confusion he began putting down his first stumbling lines . . . to Contessina.

> Heavenwards I am borne by an enchanting face,
> Nought else on earth can yield me such delight.

And later:

> A soul none sees but I,
> Most exquisite, my spirit sees . . .

He tore up the fragments, knowing them to be high-flown and adolescent; went back to the deserted garden to wander along the paths, visit the casino from which Piero had ordered all the cameos, ivories and folios of drawings to be returned to the palace. He was aching to work, but felt so empty he did not know what to work at. Sitting at his drawing board in the shed, hearing only the buzzing of insects in the wild-growing flowers, there welled up in him a sadness and sense of being alone in the world.

At last Lorenzo sent for him.

''Would you like to come to Fiesole with us? We are spending the night in the villa. In the morning Giovanni is to be invested in the Badia Fiesolana. It would be well for you to witness the ceremony. Later, in Rome, Giovanni will remember that you attended.''

He rode to Fiesole in a carriage with Contessina, young Giuliano and the nurse. Contessina asked to get off at San Domenico, halfway up the hill, for she wanted to see the Badia to which, as a woman, she would be denied admittance to her brother's investiture.

Michelangelo knew the little church intimately, having stopped off to visit it during his walks to Fiesole and the Cave Maiano. The Romanesque lower part of the façade dated back to 1050, but for Michelangelo its great beauty was in the interior, remodeled in the style of Brunelleschi, every tiny detail of stonework: the walls, pillars, windows, altars, flawless works of art of the stonecutters of Fiesole and Settignano, including his own Topolinos. When he exclaimed over this perfection, Contessina retorted laughingly:

''You're a heretic, Michelangelo; you think the importance of a church is in its art works.''

''Isn't it?''

He was awakened two hours before morning light, dressed himself and joined the procession going down the hill to the Badia, where Giovanni had spent his night in prayer. His heart sank when he saw that Lorenzo was being carried on a litter.

The little church sparkled in the light of a hundred candles. Its walls were covered with the emblems of Giovanni's Medici ancestors. Michelangelo stood by the open door, watching the sun come up over the valley of the Mugnone. With the first streaks of dawn Pico della Mirandola passed him with a solemn nod, followed by the public notary from Florence. Giovanni knelt before the altar to receive the sacrament. High mass was sung, the superior of the abbey blessed the insignia of

Giovanni's new rank: his mantle, broad-brimmed hat with the long tassle. The Papal Brief was read, ordering the investment, after which a sapphire ring, emblematic of the Church's celestial foundation, was slipped onto Giovanni's finger by Canon Bosso.

Michelangelo left the Badia and began walking down the road to Florence. In the early spring sunlight the red roofs of the city formed a tightly interwoven pattern beneath him. At the Ponte di Mugnone he met a gaily clad deputation of the most prominent Florentine citizens, some of whom he recognized from Lorenzo's dinner table, followed by a throng of plain citizens and, as a sign that the worst of Lorenzo's troubles might be over, a large portion of Florence's clergymen, some of whom, he knew, had sworn allegiance to Savonarola, coming up to the Badia with songs and cheers to ask for a blessing from the new Cardinal Giovanni de' Medici.

That night at the palace there was music and dancing and pageantry and song. That night, too, the whole of Florence was fed, supplied with wine and lavish entertainment by the Medici.

Two days later Michelangelo stood in a reception line to bid farewell to the cardinal and his cousin Giulio, who was accompanying him. Giovanni blessed Michelangelo and invited him to visit if he should ever come to Rome.

All gaiety left the palace with the cardinal. Lorenzo announced his departure for Careggi. During his absence his son Piero would be in charge.

16

It was two weeks since Lorenzo had left the palace. Michelangelo was sitting alone in his bedroom when he heard voices in the corridor. A thunderbolt had struck the lantern atop the Duomo and it had fallen in the direction of the Medici palace. The city went out into the streets to gaze at the smashed lantern, then turn sorrowfully toward the palace as though in mourning. The following day Savonarola seized the opportunity to preach a sermon presaging such calamities for Florence as destruction from invasion, from earthquake, fire and flood. Michelangelo stood in the dense throng listening, dug his nails into Granacci's arm.

That night a rumor came to him in the palace, brought by the groom of Lorenzo's secretary: instead of getting better, Lorenzo was failing. A new doctor had been sent for, Lazzaro of Pavia, who had administered to Lorenzo a pulverized mixture of diamonds and pearls. This hitherto infallible medicine had failed to help. Lorenzo had sent for Pico and Poliziano to read from his favorite authors to ease his pain.

Michelangelo paced the corridors for the rest of the night in an agony of apprehension. Piero had already left for Careggi, taking Contessina and Giuliano with him. At daylight he rushed down to the basement, threw a saddle over a horse, and rode the four miles into the foothills to Lorenzo's beautiful villa, with its high tower, pigeon house and vegetable gardens running down the slope toward the valley.

He went around the far side of the estate, slipped through the walls and made his way to the courtyard. There was a wailing coming from the kitchen. He climbed the broad staircase silently, for fear someone would hear him. At the head of the stairs he turned to his left, stood for an irresolute moment before Lorenzo's bedchamber, then slowly turned the heavy knob.

The bedchamber was a large high-ceilinged room with heavy draperies covering the walls on either side of the door, the better to keep in the heat from the massive fireplace, now burning a tree trunk. At one end Michelangelo saw Lorenzo in his high-bolstered bed, propped up with many pillows, being bled from the forearm by Dr. Pier Leoni. At the foot of the bed sat Poliziano, the tears streaming down his face, and Pico, reading from his book *The Being and the One*. He slipped behind the hanging next to the door, even as Lorenzo's confessor, standing nearby, motioned Dr. Leoni to stop the bleeding and banish everyone from the bedside. He took Lorenzo's confession, gave him absolution.

Michelangelo remained motionless as Pico and Poliziano returned to Lorenzo's side. After a moment he heard Lorenzo in a weak voice ask that Piero be summoned from the library. A servant entered, fed Lorenzo a hot broth. Poliziano asked:

"How are you relishing your food, *Magnifico* Lorenzo?"

Michelangelo saw a smile light Lorenzo's tired features.

"As a dying man always does," he replied cheerfully. "I need strength to give Piero his lecture."

Piero came in, his head bowed, humble in the face of death. The servants left the room. Lorenzo began to speak.

"Piero, my son, you will possess the same authority in the state that I have had. But as Florence is a republic, you must realize that it has many heads. It will not be possible for you to conduct yourself on every occasion so as to please everyone. Pursue that course of conduct which strict integrity prescribes. Consult the interests of the whole community rather than the gratification of any one part. If you will do so, you will protect Florence and the Medici."

Piero kissed his father on the forehead. Lorenzo motioned to Pico and Poliziano to come near.

"Pico, I only regret that I was not able to finish our library in the sculpture garden, for I wished you to have charge of it."

There was a hurried movement from the outside hall. To Michelangelo's amazement Savonarola brushed past him, so close that he could have seized his arm. Savonarola went to Lorenzo, dropped his hood so that Lorenzo could see his face. The others fell back.

"You sent for me, Lorenzo de' Medici?"

"I did, Fra Savonarola."

"How can I serve you?"

"I wish to die in charity with all men."

"Then I exhort you to hold the faith."

"I have always held it firmly."

"If you live, I exhort you to amend your life."

"I shall do so, Father."

"Finally I urge you to endure death, if need be, with fortitude."

"Nothing could please me more," replied Lorenzo with a weakening voice.

Savonarola bowed formally, turned and started for the door. Lorenzo leaned up on his pillows, called out hoarsely, "Give me your blessing, Father, before you go."

Savonarola returned, lowered his head, recited the prayers for the dying. Lorenzo, his face grave now, and pious, repeated phrases and snatches as the friar went along. Poliziano and Pico gave way to uncontrollable grief. Savonarola pulled his cowl over his head, blessed Lorenzo, and departed.

Lorenzo lay quietly, recouping his strength, then sent for his servants. When they surrounded his bed he bade them farewell, asking their forgiveness if he had ever offended them.

Michelangelo strove with all his might not to push aside the heavy hanging, run to Lorenzo's side, drop to his knees and cry out, "I, too, have loved you! Bid me farewell." He had not been summoned here. He was an intruder, his presence unknown. And so he buried his face in the rough undersurface of the velvet, even as Lorenzo fell back on his pillow.

Dr. Leoni leaned over the bed, closed Lorenzo's eyes and lifted the sheet over Lorenzo's face.

Michelangelo slipped out of the open door, ran down the stairs and into the vegetable garden. His heart felt swollen in his chest. He wondered how the others found it so easy to weep. His own tears were a hot burning blindness behind his eyes as he stumbled from one furrow to another.

Lorenzo was dead! He could not believe it. The truly Magnificent One. How could all that great spirit and brain and talent, so alive and robust only a few months before, be gone forever? For what reason had he summoned Savonarola, his avowed destroyer, to give him this final satisfaction of seeing his threats and predictions come true? All of Florence would say that Savonarola had defeated Lorenzo, that it must have been God's will for it to have been accomplished so quickly and easily.

He sat at the far end of the garden, his world smashed. With Lorenzo lying up there in his bedroom, dead, he had lost his greatest friend, the one who had taken the place in his loyalty and devotion that should have been occupied by Lodovico Buonarroti.

After a time he lurched to his feet. His throat was locked, dry. He made his way slowly back toward the palace. Coming to a well, he dropped the bucket on its rope, looked down to watch it fill.

There, lying face up, was a man. Almost paralyzed with shock and fear, Michelangelo stared down into the wet darkness. Then he recognized the face. It was Dr. Pier Leoni. He had killed himself.

He stifled the scream in his throat. Wrenching himself away, he ran until he was exhausted and fell. The tears came now, hot and racking, mixing with the Tuscan earth beneath him.

BOOK FOUR

THE FLIGHT

He shared his former bed with Buonarroto. Under it he put his two marble reliefs, wrapped in soft wool cloth. Lorenzo had said that the sculptures were his. Assuredly, he thought with a wry smile, Piero would not want them. After two years of having a comfortable apartment and freedom of movement in the palace, it was not easy for him to live in this small room with his three brothers.

"Why can't you go back and work for Piero de' Medici?" his father asked.

"I would not be wanted."

"But Piero never said in plain words that he didn't want you?"

"Piero has only fancy words."

Lodovico ran both hands through his luxuriant hair.

"You can't afford pride. You haven't the price in your purse."

Michelangelo replied humbly, "Pride is all I have left at the moment, Father."

Out of kindness, Lodovico desisted.

This three months was the longest stretch he could remember having gone without drawing. The idleness made him cranky. Lodovico too was upset, the more so because Giovansimone, now thirteen, was in trouble with the Signoria because of acts of vandalism. When the heat of July came on and Michelangelo was still too distracted to work, Lodovico lost patience.

"The last thing I thought I would say about you, Michelagnolo, was that you were lazy. I can't allow you to mope around the house any longer. I've asked your uncle Francesco to get you into the Money Changers Guild. You had two years of education with those professors in the palace . . ."

Michelangelo smiled ruefully as he thought of the Plato Four sitting around the low table in the *studiolo* analyzing the Hebraic sources of Christianity.

"Nothing that would help me turn a profit."

". . . and someday you'll form a partnership with Buonarroto. He is going to be a shrewd businessman. You will prosper."

He walked upstream along the Arno to a willow-covered bank where he submerged his hot body in the muddy waters. When his head cooled, he asked himself, "What are my alternatives?" He could go to live and work with the Topolinos. He had walked up the hills several times and sat in silence in the yard, hewing building stone; it was a relief, but not a solution. Should he seek out a sculpture commission

592

by going from palace to palace, church to church, Tuscan village to village like an itinerant knife grinder, singing out, "Any marble to carve today?"

Unlike the Plato Four, he had not been given a villa and the resources to continue his work. Lorenzo had asked Lodovico, "Will you cede him?" yet had not made him a member of the family. Lorenzo had in effect commissioned him to do a whole façade for the unfinished front of the Medici church, with twenty marble statues, but had made no provision for the work.

He put his shirt on over his wet body, as tawny now as a Maiano quarryman's from his flights along the river. When he reached home he found Granacci waiting for him. Granacci had returned to Ghirlandaio's *bottega* with Bugiardini a few days after Lorenzo's funeral.

"*Salve,* Granacci. How go things at Ghirlandaio's?"

"*Salve,* Michelangelo. Quite good. Two panels for the abbey of San Giusto at Volterra, the Salutation for the church of Castello. Ghirlandaio wants to see you."

The studio smelled as he remembered it: of fresh ground charcoal, paint pigments in chemists' sacks, bags of fresh plaster. Bugiardini embraced him joyfully. Tedesco pounded him on the shoulder. Cieco and Baldinelli got off their stools to ask the news. Mainardi kissed him affectionately on both cheeks. David and Benedetto shook his hand. Domenico Ghirlandaio sat at his fastidious desk at the rear of the studio observing the scene with a warm smile. Michelangelo gazed up at his first master, thinking how much had happened in the four years since he had first stood here.

"Why not finish out your apprenticeship?" asked Ghirlandaio. "I'll double the contract money. If you need more later, we can discuss it as friends."

Michelangelo stood numb.

"We have much work on hand, as you can see. And don't tell me again that fresco is not for you. If you can't paint the wet wall, you certainly will be valuable in working up the figures and cartoons."

He left the studio, walked into the Piazza della Signoria and stood in the burning sun gazing sightlessly at the statues in the loggia. The offer was timely, it would get him out of the house during the day, the offer of double pay would placate Lodovico. He had been lonely since the garden broke up. The studio would give him companionship. It would also put him under a professional roof again, and at seventeen that was proper. He had no incentive to work, but Ghirlandaio would plunge him into a cauldron of activity and assignments. Perhaps this would shake him out of his lethargy.

Unmindful of the intense heat, he took the road up to Settignano, trudged through the ripe wheat fields, cooled himself in the slow-running creek at the bottom. Refreshed, he continued on to the Topolinos', took a seat under the arches and began chipping stone.

He stayed for several days, working steadily, sleeping in the open with the boys on straw mattresses spread under the arches. The Topolinos knew he was troubled. They asked no questions and proffered no advice. He would have to pound out his answer for himself. His hands groped open and shut for the hammer and chisel; he felt the familiar solidity of them grasped in his clenched palms and fingers; felt the rhythmical movements of his wrist and arm and shoulder as he chipped away, bringing outline and form to the *pietra serena*. Strange how his heart could stand empty because his hands were empty.

In Settignano it was said, "Who works stone must share its nature: rough on the outside, serene within."

As he worked the stone he worked his thoughts: one two three four five six seven for work and no thought; one two three four during the rest to formulate a fragment. Here he could achieve emotional tranquillity and clarity; here his inner strength could resolve itself. As the stones took shape under his hands, so his thoughts matured in his mind; and he knew that he could not go back to Ghirlandaio's. For that was what it would be, a going backward: to an art and a trade that he had never wanted, and had taken only because there was no sculpture studio in Florence. The demands of the frescoes would change his drawing and design and he would lose all that he had learned of sculpture over the past three years. It would be a continuous contest, unfair to Ghirlandaio. It simply would not work. He had to move forward even if he could not see where or how.

He bade the Topolinos good-by, walked down the hill to the city.

In the Via de' Bardi he met bespectacled Father Nicola Bichiellini, tall, solidly built prior of the Order of Hermits of Santo Spirito. The prior had grown up in Michelangelo's neighborhood, the best football player on the broad earthen square before Santa Croce. At fifty his close-cropped black hair was shot with gray, but his body under the black woolen tunic and leather belt was still so charged with vitality that he welcomed each twenty-four-hour workday in which he governed his self-sustaining monastery-village of church, hospital, guesthouse, bakehouse, library, school and four hundred silent monks.

He greeted Michelangelo heartily, his sparkling blue eyes enormous behind the magnifying lenses.

"Michelangelo Buonarroti, what pleasure! I have not seen you since Lorenzo's funeral."

"I guess I haven't seen anybody, Father."

"I can remember you drawing in Santo Spirito before you ever went into the Medici garden. You stayed away from Master Urbino's school to copy those frescoes of Fiorentini's. Did you know that Urbino complained to me?"

Michelangelo began to feel warm inside himself.

"How flattering that you should remember, Father."

Suddenly there came into his mind the picture of the beautifully bound volumes and manuscripts in Lorenzo's *studiolo* and library, books from which he had now locked himself out.

"May I read in your library, Father? I no longer have access to books."

"But of course. Ours is a public library. If you will forgive me the sin of bragging, it is also the oldest library in Florence. Boccaccio willed us his manuscripts and books. And Petrarch as well. Drop into my office."

Michelangelo felt happy for the first time in months.

"Thank you, Father. I'll bring my sketching materials."

Early the next morning he crossed Ponte Santa Trinita to the church of Santo Spirito. He copied for a while before a fresco of Filippino Lippi and a sarcophagus of Bernardo Rossellino. It was the first work he had done since Lorenzo's death. He felt his vitality rise, his breathing become deep and natural without the obstacle of unhappiness breaking its rhythm.

Then he walked at an angle across the square to the monastery which occupied the entire area behind Piazza Santo Spirito. Here the prior had his office. He had to meet the world, and his door was open to all; but the rest of the monastery maintained complete seclusion. No one was allowed into the monastery itself; the monks were confined to the specific paths of their duties. Prior Bichiellini looked at his drawings, exclaimed, "Good! Good! You know, Michelangelo, we have much older and better works inside the monastery. Frescoes by the Gaddi family in the Cloister of the Masters. Our chapter house walls have fine scenes by Simone Martini . . ."

Michelangelo's amber eyes sparkled with the magnified intensity of the prior's behind his spectacles.

"But no one is allowed inside . . . ."

"We can arrange it. I'll draw up a schedule for you when there will be no one in the cloisters or chapter house. I've long felt these art works should be used by other artists. But it was the library you wanted. Come along."

Prior Bichiellini led the way to the library rooms. Here half a dozen Florentine laymen were studying from ancient tomes, while in the alcoves specially trained monks were making copies of valuable volumes that had been loaned to Santo Spirito from all over Europe. The prior led Michelangelo to the full sets of Plato, Aristotle, the Greek poets and dramatists, the Roman historians. He explained in an academic tone, "We are a school. We have no censors here in Santo Spirito. There are no forbidden books. We insist that our students remain free to think, inquire, doubt. We do not fear that Catholicism will suffer from our liberality; our religion is strengthened as the minds of our students grow mature."

"Shades of Fra Savonarola," said Michelangelo ironically.

The prior's hearty, warm-cheeked face went dark at the mention of Savonarola's name.

"You will want to see Boccaccio's manuscripts. They are fascinating. Most people think he was an enemy of the Church. On the contrary, he loved the Church. He hated its abuses, as did St. Augustine. We eat frugally, own nothing but the habit on our backs, and our vows of chastity are as precious to us as our love of God."

"I know that, Father. Santo Spirito is the most respected order in Florence."

"And could we be respected if we were afraid of learning? We believe that the human brain is one of God's most magnificent creations. We also believe that art is religious, because it is one of man's highest aspirations. There is no such thing as pagan art, only good and bad art." He paused for a moment to look about with pride at his library. "Come back to the office when you have finished reading. My secretary will draw a map of the buildings for you, and a schedule of hours when you may work in each cloister."

In the weeks that followed he saw no one whose daily work route did not carry him through the Cloister of the Dead, or through the Second Cloister with its three generations of Gaddi frescoes, or the chapter house where the Sienese painter, Martini, had done the Passion of Christ. The occasional monk or lay brother who passed gave no indication that he was there. The silence he found annealing, as though he were alone in the universe: just he, his drawing materials, the tombs he was copying, or the Cimabue frescoes under the arches. When he was not copying he spent his time in the library reading: Ovid, Homer, Horace, Virgil.

The prior was pleased that he was using all the hours vouchsafed him by the schedule. He would discuss with him the developments of the day. Michelangelo never had had much interest in politics. Under the hand of Lorenzo the domestic government worked so smoothly and the international alliances were so strong that there were few strictly political discussions in the palace, the streets, Ghirlandaio's, on the Duomo steps. Now he desperately needed someone to talk to; the prior, sensing the need, gave freely of his time.

With Lorenzo's death everything had changed. Where Lorenzo had met continually with his Signoria, gaining their agreement through the powers of persuasion, Piero ignored the elected Councils, made arbitrary decisions. Where his father had walked through the street with a friend or two, nodding and speaking to all, Piero never appeared except on horseback, surrounded by hired guards, recognizing no one as he scattered people, carts, donkeys, produce, on his majestic way in and out of the city to his villas.

"Even this might be forgiven," Prior Bichiellini observed, "if he were good at his job. But he is the poorest ruler Florence has had since our disastrous Guelph and Ghibelline civil wars. Visiting Italian princes from the city-states who come to renew their alliances do not like him, judge him without talent. All he can do is give orders. If only he had the good sense to hold open discussions with the Signoria . . ."

"That is not in his character, Father."

"Then he had better start to learn. The opposition is beginning to join hands: Savonarola and his followers, the Medici cousins, Lorenzo and Giovanni, and their followers; the old families whom he is excluding; the disgruntled members of the City Council; the citizens who accuse him of neglecting the most pressing affairs of state to stage athletic contests, and arranging his tournaments so that he alone can win. We are in for troubled times. . . .''

2

"Buonarroto, how much money are you holding for me?" demanded Michelangelo that evening.

Buonarroto consulted his account book, told his brother how many florins were left from the palace savings.

"Good. It is enough to buy a piece of marble, and leave some over for rent."

"Then you have a project?"

"No, I have only the need. You must back me in my lie to Father. I shall tell him that I have a modest commission, and that they are paying for the marble plus a few scudi a month while I work. We'll pay this money to Lodovico from the savings."

Buonarroto shook his head sadly.

"I shall say that the one commissioning has the right of rejection. In that way I'll protect myself if I can't sell it."

With this Lodovico had to be content.

Michelangelo then moved on to the next problem. What did he want to carve? He felt that the time had arrived to work his first statue in the round. But what figure? What was it to be about? The question was seminal; everything that emerged grew out of the original concept. No concept, no work of art; it was as simple, and as agonizingly complex, as that.

The single desire of his heart rose out of love and sorrow: to do something about Lorenzo, a theme that would express the totality of talent, courage, width and depth of knowledge; the human understanding of this man who had undertaken to lead the world into an intellectual and artistic revolution.

An answer was slow in coming; answers always were. Yet it was only by sticking doggedly to the task that he could arrive at a conception that would swing open the doors of his creative force. His thoughts kept returning to the fact that Lorenzo had often spoken of Hercules, suggesting that the Greek legend did not mean that his twelve labors were to be taken literally: the capture of the Erymanthian boar, the defeating of the Nemean lion, the cleaning of the Augean stables by running a river through. These feats perhaps were meant as symbols for all the varied and near-impossible tasks with which each new generation of man was faced.

Was not Lorenzo the incarnation of Hercules? Had he not gone forth on twelve labors against ignorance, prejudice, bigotry, narrowness, intolerance? Surely he had set a Herculean pattern in founding universities, academies, art and manuscript collections, printing presses, in encouraging artists, scholars, poets, philosophers and scientists to reinterpret the world in vigorous modern terms, and to extend man's reach to all the fruits of the human intellect and spirit.

Lorenzo had said, "Hercules was half man and half god, sprung from Zeus and the mortal Alcmene. He is the everlasting symbol that all of us are half man and half god. If we use that which is half god in us, we can perform the twelve labors every day of our lives."

He must find a way to represent Hercules so that he became Lorenzo as well; not solely the physical giant of Greek legend as depicted on Giotto's Campanile, or in Pollaiuolo's nine-foot painting, but as poet, statesman, world merchant, patron, revolutionist.

In the meanwhile he had to get out of the house, into his own workshop.

Just as he had left bas-relief behind him, so he had outgrown Bertoldo's art of the miniature. Moreover he could not conceive of sculpturing the Hercules, or Lorenzo, in less than life size. By rights it should be half again as large as man, for they were demigods who needed heroic marble from which to be born. But where to find such marble? And how to pay for it? His savings contained but a tithe of such a cost.

He remembered the workshop of the Duomo behind the vast cathedral which had been the headquarters for the workmen and materials while the cathedral was being built, and which was subsequently used by the foreman and his maintenance crew. In passing the gates, while materials were being moved in or out, he recalled having seen several large blocks of marble lying about. He walked to the workshop, made a tour of the yard. The foreman, bald as a slab of pink marble, and with a nose that stuck straight out like a leveled finger from his face, came up to ask if he could be of service. Michelangelo introduced himself.

"I was an apprentice in the Medici garden. Now I must work alone. I need a large marble, but I have little money. I thought the city might be willing to sell something it did not need."

The foreman, a stonemason by trade, closed his eyes to the narrow protective slits against flying chips.

"Call me Beppe. What interests you?"

Michelangelo took a deep breath.

"First, Beppe, this big column. The one that has been worked on."

"That's called the 'Duccio block.' Comes from Carrara. Stands seventeen, eighteen feet high. Board of Works of the Duomo bought it for Duccio to carve a Hercules. To save labor Duccio ordered it blocked out in the quarry. It reached here ruined. I was twelve then, apprenticed." Beppe scratched his behind vigorously with his six-toothed chisel. "Duccio cut for a week. He could find no figure in it, big or small.".

Michelangelo walked around the enormous block. He ran his fingers exploringly over it.

"Beppe, was this block really ruined in the quarry? It's awkwardly shaped, yes, but maybe Duccio spoiled it himself by these cuts, like here, where he gouged too deeply around the middle. Would the Board of Works sell it?"

"Not possible. They speak of using it one day."

"Then what about this smaller one? It also has been worked on, though not so badly."

Beppe examined the nine-foot block Michelangelo indicated.

"I could ask. Come back tomorrow."

"And would you plead price for me?"

The foreman opened his mouth in a toothless grin.

"I never yet knew a stonecarver who had tomorrow's *pasta* money in today's purse."

The answer was several days in coming, but Beppe had done a job for him.

"She's yours. I told them it was an ugly piece of meat and we'd be glad for the room. They told me to set a fair price. How about five florins?"

"Beppe! I could embrace you. I'll be back tonight with the money. Don't let it get away."

Beppe scratched his bald scalp with the end of an *ugnetto*.

Now that he had his marble he had to find a workshop. Nostalgia drew him to the Medici garden. It was unused since Lorenzo's death, the summer grass high, uncut, turning brown, the little casino in the center stripped bare, only the piles of stones at the far end, where work on Lorenzo's library had been abandoned, remaining the same. He wondered, "Could I work in my old shed? It wouldn't hurt anything, or cost Piero anything. Perhaps he would let me if I told him what I was carving."

He could not make himself go to Piero.

As he turned to leave through the rear gate, the corner of his eye caught two figures coming through the main door from the Piazza San Marco: Contessina and Giuliano. They had not seen each other since Lorenzo's death. On the porch of the casino they came together. Contessina seemed to have shrunk in size; even in the bright July sun her face was sallow. All that was visible under the wide protective hat were her brown eyes, enormously alive.

Giuliano spoke first.

"Why have you not come to see us? We have missed you."

Contessina's voice was reproachful. "You could have called."

". . . but Piero . . ."

"I too am a Medici. So is Giuliano." She was angry. "The palace is our home. Our friends are welcome."

"I asked Contessina why you did not come," said the boy.

"I have not been invited."

"I invite you" she cried impulsively. "Giovanni must go back to Rome tomorrow, then we will be all alone, except for Piero and Alfonsina, and we never see them."

Contessina continued: "Pope Innocent is dying. Giovanni must be on hand to protect us against a Borgia being elected Pope."

She looked out at the garden.

"Giuliano and I walked over here nearly every day. We thought you would work, and where should you work but here?"

"No, Contessina, I have not worked. But today I bought a piece of marble."

"Then we can come and visit you," said Giuliano eagerly.

Michelangelo stood blinking hard at Contessina.

"I have not the permission . . ."

"And if I secure it for you?"

He straightened up.

"It is a nine-foot column, Contessina. Very old. Badly used. But good inside. I'm going to carve a Hercules. He was your father's favorite."

He reached out his hand for hers. Her fingers were surprisingly cold for a hot summer day.

He waited patiently, one day, two, three, four, returning at the sunset hour. But she did not come. Then, on the fifth day, as he sat on the steps of the casino chewing on a handful of hay-brown grass, he saw her walk through the main gate. His heart leaped. Her old nurse was with her. He rushed down the path to meet her.

Her eyes were red.

"Piero has refused!" he cried.

"He has not answered. A hundred times I have asked him. He stands in silence. That is his way. Then it can never be said that he refused."

High bright hope of continuing in the garden crashed.

"I was afraid it would be so, Contessina. That is why I left the palace. And have not come back. Even to see you."

She took a step closer. They now stood with their lips only an inch apart. The nurse turned away.

"Piero says the Ridolfi family will be displeased if we see each other again. . . . Not until after my marriage, at least."

Neither of them moved closer, their lips did not meet, their slight young bodies did not touch; yet he felt himself held and holding in a beloved embrace.

Contessina walked slowly down the center path, past the little bronze boy taking a thorn out of his foot in the now still fountain. Together she and the nurse disappeared into the piazza.

3

Beppe of the blue-veined, red cheeks, as ugly a man as the original Etruscans had left behind them, Beppe came to his rescue.

"I tell the Board I can use part-time man, that you offer to work for no pay. For free a good Tuscan refuses nothing. Set up your shop along the far wall."

The Florentines, who carried half a dozen family names and believed that a short name meant a short life and fortune, had named this workyard the Opera di Santa Maria del Fiore del Duomo. It was an establishment that could carry its compounded title, for it occupied a full square behind a half-moon fringe of houses, studios and offices that lined the street behind the cathedral. In this front line of buildings Donatello, Della Robbia and Orcagna had carved their marbles, had cast their bronze pieces in the Opera furnaces.

The wooden wall of the yard, semicircular in shape, had an overhang under which the workmen found protection from the beating sun in summer and the rain being driven down the valley of the Arno from the mountains in winter. Here Michelangelo set up a forge, brought sacks of chestnut wood and Swedish iron rods, fashioned himself a set of nine chisels and two hammers, made a drawing desk from pieces of lumber that looked as though they had been lying about the yard since Brunelleschi finished the dome.

Now he had a workshop where he could make his headquarters from first light to dark. Once again he could work within the sound of the hammers of the *scalpellini*. Then, settled in with drawing paper, charcoal, pens and colored inks, he was ready to begin.

He asked himself questions, for his final result would depend on the ever widening and deepening circles of questions asked and answered. How old was Hercules at the moment of emerging from the marble? Were all twelve of the labors behind him, or was he halfway on his journey? Was he wearing the token of his triumph, the Nemean lion skin, or was he naked to the world? Would he have a sense of grandeur at how much he had been able to accomplish as a half god, or a sense of fatality that as a half human he would die poisoned by the blood of the centaur Nessus?

He learned with the passing months that most of the charges against Lorenzo of debauching the morals and freedom of the Florentines were untrue, that he was perhaps the greatest human being since Pericles had brought in the golden age of Greece two thousand years before. How to convey that Lorenzo's accomplishments were as great as those of Hercules?

First, Lorenzo was a man. As a man he would have to be re-created, brought to glowing life out of this weather-stained block of marble propped up by beams before him. He had to conceive of the strongest male that ever walked the earth, overwhelming in all his aspects. Where in Tuscany, land of small, lean, unheroically designed men, would he find such a model?

He scoured Florence looking at coopers with their heavy wooden hammers, the wool dyers with their arms stained blue and green, the ironmongers, blacksmiths, rustic stone bevelers working the Strozzi palace; the porters running the streets bent double under their packs, the young athletes wrestling in the park, the near-naked sand dredgers in their flat boats pulling up spoons of Arno mud. He spent weeks in the countryside watching the farmers take in their grain and grapes, loading heavy sacks and boxes on carts, flailing the wheat, rolling the granite wheels of the olive crusher, chopping down old trees, building rock walls. Then he returned to the Duomo workshop where he doggedly drew every feature, limb, torso, back under tension, shoulder muscle lifting, arm pushing, thigh straining, until he had a folio of hundreds of fragments. He set up an armature, bought a supply of pure beeswax, began modeling . . . and was dissatisfied.

"How can I establish a figure, even the crudest outline, if I don't know what I'm doing? How can I achieve anything but surface skin sculpture, exterior curves, outlines of bones, a few muscles brought into play? Effects. What do I know of the causes? The vital structure of a man that lies beneath the surface, and that my eye can't see? How can I know what creates, from within, the shapes I see from without?"

These questions he had already asked Bertoldo. Now he knew the answer. It had been buried within him for a long time. He came to grips with its necessity. There was no escape. He could never become any part of the sculptor he planned to be until he had trained himself through dissection; until he knew the workings of every last component within the human body, precisely what function it served and how it accomplished its end; the interrelation of all the parts, bone, blood, brain, muscle, tendon, skin, guts.

Figures in the round had to be complete, seen from every angle. A sculptor could not create movement without perceiving what caused the propulsion; could not portray tension, conflict, drama, strain, force unless he saw every fiber and substance at work within the body that was shaping the power and drive; unless he knew what a movement in front did to the corresponding muscles behind; until he grasped the whole of the human body itself.

Learn anatomy he must! But how? Become a surgeon? That would take years. Even if he could follow that unlikely train, what good would it do to dissect two male corpses a year, in a group effort in the Piazza della Signoria?

There must be some way that he could see a dissection.

He remembered that Marsilio Ficino was the son of Cosimo de' Medici's doctor. He had been trained by his father until Cosimo had suggested that he was "born to doctor men's minds, not their bodies."

He set out on foot for Careggi and Ficino's villa to lay his problem before the near sixty-year-old who was working night and day in his manuscript-strewn library in hopes of completing his commentary on Dionysius the Areopagite. He was admitted to the villa by Ficino's two pretty nieces and escorted into the library. The tiny founder of the Plato Academy sat beneath a bust of Plato, pen in inky fingers, deep furrows in his tight-skinned face.

Michelangelo made it clear at once why he had come. Then added:

"As the son of a doctor, trained to be a doctor yourself, you must know what the insides of a man is like."

"I did not complete my medical studies."

"Do you know if anyone is dissecting now?"

"Assuredly not! Don't you know the penalty for violating a corpse?"

"Banishment for life?"

"Death."

After a silence, Michelangelo asked, "And if one were willing to risk it? How could it be gone about? Watch the poverty fields for burials?"

Aghast, Ficino cried, "My dear young friend, you cannot conceive of yourself as a grave robber. How many times do you think you would succeed? You would be caught with the mutilated corpse and hanged from the third-floor window of the Palazzo della Signoria. Let's talk of other, more pleasant things. How does your sculpture go?"

"That's what we have been talking about, dear Ficino."

He stuck to his problem. Where to find available corpses? The dead of the rich were buried in the family tombs; those of the middle class were surrounded with religious ritual. Which dead in Florence were unwatched and unwanted? Only the very poor, the familyless, the mendicants who filled the roads of Italy. These people were taken to hospitals when they were sick. Which hospitals? Those attached to churches, with free beds. And the church with the largest charity hospital was the one that had the largest and best known free guesthouse.

Santo Spirito!

He could feel his hair crackle on his forehead. Santo Spirito, of which he knew not only the prior but every corridor, the library, guesthouse, gardens, hospital, cloisters.

Could he ask Prior Bichiellini for his unclaimed corpses? If the prior were caught, something worse would happen to him than death: he would be put out of his order, excommunicated. Yet this was a courageous man who feared no force on earth so long as he did not personally offend God. How proud he was that a former prior of the order had befriended Boccaccio, the most hated and reviled man of his age: taken him in, protected him, used Boccaccio's library for the furthering of human knowledge. These Augustinians, when they thought they were right, knew not fear.

And what was ever accomplished without risk? Had not an Italian from Genoa that very year sailed three little ships over the flat Atlantic Ocean from which he was told he would fall off, seeking for a new route to India?

If the prior were willing to take the awful risk, could he, Michelangelo, be so selfish as to ask it? Would the ends warrant that risk?

He spent agitated days and sleepless nights coming to his decision. He would approach Prior Bichiellini with an honest, straightforward request, telling precisely what he wanted and needed. He would not insult the prior by being subtle; there was nothing subtle about excommunication or a hangman's noose.

But before he was willing to talk to the prior he had to know precisely how the plan could operate. Step by step he groped his way forward. With trepidation he moved in the stonemason's rhythm of no thought for the seven count of the chisel hammering on the stone, and only the few words that could be formulated during the one two three four rest period between chipping. He wandered through Santo Spirito, the cloisters, the outside vegetable gardens, the streets and little alleys that surrounded the section, checking entrances, observation points, approaches to the burial chapel, and within the monastery itself the location of the dead room where the bodies were kept overnight until burial in the morning.

He drew up diagrams, accurate and in scale, of the juxtaposition of the guesthouse to the hospital, the monks' quarters. He traced the route by which he could enter from the back gate on the Via Maffia without being seen, make his way through the gardens and corridors to the dead room. He would come late at night and leave before morning light.

He had to decide when to state his case, the right moment and place, both to increase his chances and to achieve clarity. The place to face up to the prior was in his writing study, amidst his books and manuscripts.

The prior let him recite only a part of his proposal, took a quick look at the diagrams spread out on the desk before him, then stopped him cold.

"Enough! I comprehend fully. Let us never mention this subject again. You have not brought it up. It has vanished like smoke, leaving no trace."

Stunned by the rapidity of the rejection, Michelangelo gathered his maps and found himself standing out in the Piazza Santo Spirito, suddenly cold under an overcast autumnal sky, blind to the market bustling about him in the piazza, aware only that he had put the prior in an intolerable situation. The prior would never want to see him again. The church he could go into; it belonged to everybody, but not the cloisters. He had lost his privileges.

He walked through the blustery streets, sat numbly in front of his Hercules block. What right had he to carve a Hercules, to attempt to interpret Lorenzo's favorite figure? He rubbed his fingers over the bones of his nose as though it were hurting for the first time.

He was desolate.

4

He was sitting on a bench before a large fresco. Santo Spirito was quiet after the early morning service. An occasional woman, her head covered with a black handkerchief, knelt before the altars. A man entered, genuflected, and hurried out. A heavy scent of incense was suspended in the sun's rays.

Prior Bichiellini came out from the sacristy, saw Michelangelo and walked toward him. He stood for a moment studying the few hesitant lines of the drawing, then asked:

"Where have you been these past weeks, Michelangelo?"

"I . . . I . . ."

"How is the sculpture going?"

There was no change in his manner, it showed the same interest and affection.

"It's . . . sitting there. . . ."

"I thought of you when we received a new illuminated manuscript. There are some figure drawings from the fourth century that might interest you. Would you like to see them?"

Michelangelo rose timidly and followed the prior through the sacristy, across the cloister and into his study. On the desk was a beautiful parchment manuscript illustrated in blue and gold. The prior reached into his desk and took out a long key which he laid across the binding to keep the leaves spread. They talked for a few moments, then the prior said:

"*Allora,* we both have work to do. Come back again soon."

Michelangelo returned to the church, enveloped in a warm glow. He had not lost the prior's friendship. He had been forgiven, the incident forgotten. If he were no farther along on his search for anatomy, at least he had done no irreparable damage.

But he had no intention of abandoning the search. He sat on the hard bench, unable to work, wondering whether grave robbing was not the most workable solution, since it involved no one else. Yet how was he to dig up a corpse, refill the grave against passers-by, carry the cadaver to a nearby house, return it to the cemetery when he had completed his explorations? It seemed physically impossible.

He returned to the library of Santo Spirito to look among its books for new clues on how the ancients had conceived of Hercules. At the same time he found one illustrated medical manuscript showing how patients were tied to rope mattresses before being operated on; but no illustration of what the surgeon had found after the cutting.

Again the prior offered his assistance, finding him a heavy leather volume on one of the higher shelves, scanning through it, exclaiming, "Ah yes, here is some material," laying the heavy bronze key across the pages.

It was not until the fourth or fifth session that Michelangelo began to notice the key, of and by itself. The prior used it not only to keep books open but as a place marker when he closed a volume, a pointer when he was underscoring lines.

Always the key. Always the same key. But never when he was in the study with others, either monks or lay friends.

Why?

He went back a dozen times in the following weeks. If he set about his drawing for an hour or two the prior would come through the church, greet him cheerily, invite him into the study. And invariably the big bronze key came out of the desk.

At night Michelangelo lay awake, seeing the key before him. During the day he went for long walks in the fall rain up to the Maiano quarry, holding dialogues with himself.

"It must mean something. But what? What are keys for? Obviously to open doors. How many doors are there in which I am interested? Only one. The dead-room door."

He would have to take a gamble. If the prior meant for him to have it, well and good; if he did not, then he would simply carry it off by accident, forgetfully, and return it the next day. During the night he would let himself in through the rear garden gate of the monastery, make his way to the dead room. If the key fitted the door, then his assumption would be correct. If it did not . . .

It was midnight when he reached the monastery, having slipped out of his house noiselessly so as to waken no one, and taken a circuitous route to the hospital from Santa Croce across the Ponte Vecchio, past the Pitti palace, through a maze of side streets. In this way he missed the night guards who followed a prescribed route with their lanterns and could be seen a piazza away.

He hugged the walls of the infirmary on the Via Sant'Agostino, turned into the Via Maffia to the little gate in the center of the block above which the fresco of Our Lady with the Child by Agnolo Gaddi gleamed softly in the darkness. All Santo Spirito keys opened this gate; he admitted himself, slipped past the stables on his left, avoided the main walk because the next building was the dormitory for lay brothers, skirted the walls of the dark kitchen, his breath coming a little faster now, made an angular dart to the inner wall of the infirmary.

He found the open, central arch, slipped into the corridor admitting to the cells for patients, the doors of which were closed, and turned toward the dead room. An oil lamp stood in a niche. He took a candle out of the green canvas bag he carried, lighted the wick, shielded it under his cape.

His only serious danger was from the chief of the infirmary; but since the monk was also encharged with the administration of the properties of the order, working from dawn to dark supplying the needs of the infirmary, guesthouse and monastery, he was not likely to venture out of his cell on nocturnal inspections. Once the five o'clock supper was served the patients were made ready for sleep and the doors of their cells closed. There was no resident doctor; the patients were not expected to grow sicker or ask for help during the night. They docilely did what was expected of them.

He stood for a moment rigid, before the door of the dead room. He inserted the big key, made a slow movement to the right, then left, felt the lock slip. In an instant he had opened the door, darted into the room, closed and locked the door behind him. And at this moment of commitment he did not know whether he dared face the task ahead.

The dead room was small, about eight feet by ten, windowless. The stone walls were whitewashed, the floor of rough blocks. In the center of the room, on narrow planks mounted on two wooden horses, and wrapped from head to foot in a burial sheet, was a corpse.

He stood leaning against the door, breathing hard, the candle shaking in his hand like trees in a *tramontana*. It was the first time he had been alone in a room with death, let alone locked in, and on a sacrilegious errand. His flesh felt as though it were creeping along his bones; he was more frightened than he had ever been in his life.

Who lay wrapped in that sheet? What would he find when he unrolled the body and dropped the winding cloth to the floor? What had this unfortunate creature done that he should now, without his knowledge or consent, be mutilated?

"What kind of nonsense is this?" he demanded of himself. "What difference could it make to a man already dead? His body does not get into the kingdom of heaven, only his soul. I have no intention of dissecting this poor fellow's soul, even if I should stumble across it."

Reassured by his own grim humor, he put down his bag and looked for a place to set his candle, of importance to him not only for light but as a clock as well: for he had to be safely out of here before three in the morning when the monks who operated the large bakehouse on the corner of the Via Sant'Agostino and Piazza

Santo Spirito rose to make the day's bread for the monastery, the deserving poor and the relatives of all who lived here. It had taken much experimenting to ascertain with accuracy how long each type of candle would burn. This one, for which he was now searching for a resting place, was the three-hour variety; when it began its first sputtering he would have to leave. He must also exercise care that no drippings could be discovered the next morning.

He emptied his bag of its scissors and kitchen knife, flattened it on the floor, held the candle upside down for a moment, then secured it in the soft wax. He took off his cape, for he was already sweating in the cold room, laid it in a corner, uttered a jumbled prayer which sounded like, "Lord forgive me, for I know not what I do," and approached the corpse.

First he would have to unroll it from its winding sheet. The trestle bench was narrow. He had not known that he could be so clumsy. Slowly he wrestled the stiff body, first raising the legs until the sheet pulled out from under the lower half, then lifting it from the waist and holding it in his left arm, against his chest, until he could maneuver the cloth from around the torso and head. The winding sheet was long, he had to go through the tortuous process five times before he finally divested the cadaver of its protective wrapping.

He picked up his candle from the floor, held it aloft in his left hand to study the body. His first feeling was one of pity for this dead man. His second was one of fear:

"This is how I shall end up!"

Suddenly all the differences between life and death became apparent.

The face was expressionless; the mouth semi-open, the skin green from gangrene. The man had been strongly built and was in mid-life when apparently he had received a stab wound in the chest. The cadaver had been here long enough to sink to the temperature of this freezing room.

His nostrils picked up an odor, something like very old flowers dying in water. It was not strong, it fell away when he backed to the wall to get a moment of relief; but it came to him again as he approached the cadaver, and from that point remained in his nostrils inescapably.

Where to begin? He raised the arm on the side closest to him and felt a cold such as he had never felt before. Not colder than anything else, but different. It was a cold filled with emotional content, a hard cold, not the skin, but the muscle under it. The skin was soft, like velvet. He felt disgust, as though an iron hand were squeezing his stomach. All his memories of warm arms and shoulders recurred to him. He withdrew.

It was a considerable time before he could pick up the knife from the floor, recall what he had read about the human body, the few illustrations he had seen. He poised over the cadaver, frozen himself, swallowing hard. Then he brought the knife down and made his first incision: from the chestbone down to the groin. But he had not exerted enough pressure. The skin was surprisingly tough.

He started over. Now applying strength behind the knife, he found the substance under the skin quite soft. The skin opened about two inches. He asked himself, "Where is the blood?" for it did not flow. This increased his impression of cold and death. Then he saw the fat, a soft, deep yellow. He knew what it was, for he had seen fat cut from animals in the markets. He made a deeper cut to reach the muscle, which was different in color from the skin and the fat, and harder to cut. He studied the dark red columns of fibers. He cut again and saw the bowel.

The smell was growing heavier. A nausea started within him. At the first cut he had summoned all his strength to proceed; now all sensations came together: the cold, fear, smell, reaction to death. He was repulsed by the slippery feeling of the tissue, the fat fluidifying on his fingers like oil. He wanted to put his hands in hot water and wash them.

"What do I do now?"

He trembled, hearing his voice echo off the stone walls. He was in little danger of being heard, for he was bound at his back by the solid wall beyond which lay the garden, to his side by the chapel reserved for the death services, on the infirmary side by stone through which no sound could penetrate.

It was dark inside the cavity. He picked up the candle, secured the canvas bag under the foot of the cadaver, placed his candle at body height.

All of his senses were heightened. The intestines that he now began to handle were cold, slippery, moving. A pain ricocheted through his own bowels. He took one side of the flap in one of his hands, the other side in the other, held them apart to have a careful look. He saw a pale gray transparent snake, long, going round and round in coils. It had a superficial aspect of mother-of-pearl, shining because humidified, filled up with something that moved and emptied when he touched it.

His initial emotion of disgust was overcome by excitement. He picked up his knife and started to cut upwards from the bottom of the rib cage. The knife was not strong enough. He tried his scissors but had to angle along the ribs, one at a time. The rib bones were hard; it was like cutting wire.

Suddenly the candle began to splutter. Three hours already! He could not believe it. Yet he did not dare ignore the warning. He set his green bag and candle on the floor, picked up the winding sheet from the corner. The wrapping process was a thousandfold more difficult than the unwrapping because he could no longer turn the corpse on its side or the whole of its guts would spill out onto the floor.

The perspiration ran down into his eyes, his heart pounded so loud he thought it would wake the monastery as he used the last vestige of his strength to lift the corpse from the table with one arm while he pulled the winding sheet under and around the necessary five times. He barely had a moment to make sure that the corpse was stretched out upon the planks as he had found it, to check the floor for possible stains or wax, before the candle gave its last flickering sputter and went out.

He had enough control to take a wandering route home, stopping a dozen times to retch against the corners of buildings and in the darkness of open ground. The smell of the corpse was in his nostrils with every breath he took. When he reached home he was afraid to boil water on Lucrezia's glowing embers for fear the noise would wake the family; yet he could not live without getting the feel of that fat off his fingers. He hunted quietly for some harsh lye soap to use in the cold water.

His body, as he got into bed, was icy. He huddled against his brother, but not even Buonarroto's warmth could help him. Several times he had to rise and retch into a pail. He heard Lucrezia get out of bed, dress and make her way through the kitchen and down the circular stairway to the street as the faintest tinge of pearl gray touched his window overlooking the stables on the Via dei Bentaccordi.

He had chills and fever all day. Lucrezia made him a chicken broth, but he could not hold it down. The family came one by one into the bedroom to find out what was the matter with him. He lay there feeling as clammy as the corpse. Nothing was able to remove the smell of death from his nostrils. After he had assured Lucrezia that it was not her supper which had upset him, she returned to the kitchen to boil up an herb bouquet to cure him. Monna Alessandra examined him for spots. By late afternoon he was able to retain a little of the herb tea, for which he thanked Lucrezia most gratefully.

About eleven o'clock he rose, slipped into his shoes, *calze*, warm shirt and cloak, and with his legs rickety beneath him, made his way to Santo Spirito.

There was no corpse in the dead room. Neither was there one on the following night. The two days gave him a chance to recover. On the third night he again found a body in its winding sheet on the planked table.

The second cadaver was older, with white beard patches on a big red face, the skin tight, the fluid under the skin marbleized. This time he used his knife with more authority, opening the abdomen with a clean cut, then using his left hand to pry apart the rib cage, which made a noise like crackling wood. It remained attached at the collarbone.

He picked up his candle and held the light close to the innards, for this was his first complete view. He saw something pale red, netlike in design, and of solid tissue, which he deduced was the lungs. This network had a black covering, something that he had heard happened to wool workers.

Experimentally, he pressed the lung; a hissing noise came out of the mouth of the corpse. He dropped the candle in fright. Fortunately it did not go out. When he regained his calm and had picked up the candle, he realized that in touching the lung he had forced out the residual air; and for the first time he understood what breathing was, because he could see and feel and hear the communication between the lungs and the mouth, realized what it did to the whole figure.

After he had moved aside the lung he noticed a dark red mass; this must be the heart. It was covered by a shining membrane. Probing, he found that all of the tissue was connected to a form shaped something like an apple, almost free in the chest, attached only at the top of the pyramid.

"Shall I take it out?"

He hesitated a moment, then picked up his scissors, cut across the pyramidal membrane. Substituting his knife, he peeled away the membrane as though he were opening a banana. Now he had the heart in his two hands. Unexpectedly, he was hit by an emotional impact as strong as Hercules' club. If the soul and heart were one, what happened to this unfortunate cadaver's soul now that he had cut out its heart?

As quickly as it had come, the fear departed. In its place came a sense of triumph. He was holding a human heart in his hands! He felt the happiness that arises out of knowledge, for now he knew about the most vital organ of the body, what it looked like, how it felt. He opened the heart with his knife, was shocked to find that there was nothing inside. He replaced it in its cavity, put back the chest's rib structure, which artists had observed so well from the lean Tuscans around them. But now he knew precisely where the heart beat beneath it.

He did not have the faintest idea of how to start work on the snake of the intestine. He picked up a piece, pulled. It came easily for a time, about five feet of it; the bowels were attached loosely to the posterior wall, and came away. Then he began to feel resistance. The upper part was enlarged, a sort of bag was attached, which he deduced was the stomach. He had to use his knife to cut it loose.

He freed some twenty-five feet of bowel, fingered it, feeling the differences of size and content. Some places had fluid in them, some solid; he learned that it was a continuous channel, with no opening from the beginning to the end. To get a concept of its interior aspect he cut into it with his knife at several points. The lower bowel contained stools. The smell was terrible.

Tonight he had a four-hour candle, but already it began to splutter. He bundled the viscera back into the abdominal cavity, and with great difficulty got the corpse rewrapped.

He ran to the fountain in the Piazza Santo Spirito and scrubbed his hands, but he could not get the feeling of dirt off his fingers. He stuck his head into the icy water to wash away the sense of guilt, standing for a moment with his hair and face dripping water; then ran all the way home, shaking as though with ague.

He was emotionally exhausted.

He awoke to find his father standing over him, a displeased look on his face.

"Michelangelo, get up. It's noon. Lucrezia is putting food on the table. What kind of new nonsense is this, that you sleep until dinner? Where were you last night?"

Michelangelo lay staring up at Lodovico.

"I'm sorry, Father. I'm not feeling well."

He washed carefully, combed his hair, put on fresh clothing and went to the table. He thought he was going to be all right. When Lucrezia brought in a bowl of beef stew, he rushed back into his bedroom and retched into the chamber pot until his insides were sore.

But that night he was back in the dead room.

Before he had the door locked behind him he was drenched in the smell of putrefaction. He unwound the sheet, saw that the left leg of the corpse was of a brown color with a green secretion coming out from under the skin, the leg swollen half again its size. The rest of the body was ash gray, the face completely sunken.

He began to work where he had left off the night before, cutting directly to the bowel, and unraveled it piece by piece. He placed it on the floor and raised his candle close to the cavity. There were a number of the organs he had been searching for: the spleen on the left side, the liver on the right. He recognized the liver from the beeves and lambs cut up in the markets; bilaterally, just aside of the bone column, were the kidneys.

He picked them up carefully and perceived that they were connected with the bladder by small tubes, like wires. He went on to where the liver was attached, posteriorly; cut the ligaments with his scissors and removed it from the cavity. He studied the shape in his hands, examining the small bladder attached to its lower side, opened it with his knife. A dark green fluid came out.

He moved his candle closer, saw something that he had missed before: the abdominal cavity was separated from the chest cavity by a dome-shaped muscle. In the center of this dome were two holes through which passed tubes connecting the stomach with the mouth. The second big channel, alongside the backbone, went up into the chest. He now realized that from the chest to the abdomen there were only two means of communication, one bringing food and liquids. The other baffled him. He lifted the bone structure of the chest but could not determine what the second channel was used for. The candle spluttered.

As he crept silently up the stairs of his house he found his father waiting for him. "Where have you been? What is that horrible odor about you? You smell like death."

Michelangelo mumbled an excuse with eyes cast down, brushed past Lodovico to the security of his bedroom.

He could not sleep.

"Will I never get used to this?" he groaned.

The next night there was no corpse in the dead room. He had an uneasy feeling of impending danger as he noticed that the section of floor where he had allowed the bowels to rest had been scrubbed, and was brighter than the stones around it. A bit of wax from his candle had been left untouched at the foot of the plank table. Yet even if his activities had been noticed, he was protected by the vow of silence in the monastery.

The following night he found a boy of about fifteen who showed no external evidence of disease. The pale skin, almost completely white, was soft to the touch. The eyes were blue when he raised the lids, deep in color, contrasting with the pale white of the eyelids. Even in death he was attractive.

"Surely he will wake up," he murmured.

He saw that the boy was still without hair on his chest, and felt a pity deeper than he had known since he had viewed his first corpse.

He turned away; he'd wait until another night. Then, facing the corner of the whitewashed walls, he stopped. By the next morning this lad would be buried under four feet of earth in the Santo Spirito cemetery. He touched the boy, found him as cold as winter; beautiful, but as dead as all the others.

He made his incisions expertly now, put his hand under the chestbone. It came away easily. Up toward the neck he felt a tubelike appendage, about an inch in diameter, that gave the impression of a series of hard rings; among these rings he found a soft membranous tube that came down from the neck. He could not find where this tube ended and the lung began, but when he pulled on it the boy's neck and mouth moved. He took his hand out swiftly and shuddered away from the table.

A moment later he cut the tube blindly, not being able to see it, then lifted the lungs out separately. They were light in weight and when he squeezed them he found that the sensation was rather like squeezing snow. He tried to cut the lung open with his knife, put it on the table and, with a hard surface under him, found that it was like cutting through dry sponge. In one of the lungs he found a pale yellow-white mucus which kept the lung moist, in the other a pink-red mucus. He wanted to get his hand down the boy's mouth in order to search out the throat and neck, but the feel of the teeth and tongue repelled him.

Suddenly he felt as though someone were in the room with him, though he knew it was impossible because he had locked the door from the inside. Tonight was just too difficult.

He wrapped up the corpse easily, for it weighed so little, put it back on the table, and let himself out.

5

He could not risk his father's again detecting the odor of death, so he walked the streets until he found a wineshop in the workmen's quarter that was open. He drank a little of the Chianti. When the proprietor turned his back, he sprinkled the rest of the wine over his shirt.

Lodovico was outraged when he smelled the strong wine.

"It is not enough that you wander the streets all night doing God alone knows what, associating with what manner of loose women, but now you come home smelling like a cheap tavern. I can't understand you. What is driving you to these evil ways?"

The only protection he could give his family was to keep them in ignorance. It was best for his father to believe that he was carousing, about which Lodovico was learning a great deal from Giovansimone, who frequently came in with his face bloodied and clothes torn. But as the days passed, and Michelangelo stumbled into the house every morning toward dawn, the family rose in arms. Each was outraged for his own special reason. Lucrezia because he was not eating, his uncle Francesco because he was afraid Michelangelo would run into debt, his aunt Cassandra on moral grounds. Only Buonarroto brought a smile to his brother's lips.

"I know you are not carousing," he said.

"How could you know that?"

"Simple: you haven't asked me for a scudo since you bought those candles. Without money you do not buy women in Florence."

He realized that he would have to find somewhere else for his daily rest. The Topolinos would never ask questions, he could stay there, but Settignano was so far away; he would lose valuable hours coming and going. In the morning he went to the Duomo workshop and mounted the stool before his drawing table. Beppe came over to greet him, a puzzled expression on his homely old face.

"My young friend, you look like a cadaver. What have you been making with yourself?"

Michelangelo looked up sharply.

"I've been . . . working, Beppe."

Beppe cackled toothlessly.

"Ah, that I were young enough for that kind of work! Well, do not try to raise Hercules' club every night. Remember, what you put into the ladies at night you don't have left to spend on marble in the morning."

That night he came across his first ugly corpse, one that made him shiver as he observed what could happen to God's handiwork. The man was about forty, with a big dark red face, swollen near the neck. The mouth was open, the lips blue, the whites of the eyes full of red spots. Through the yellow teeth he could see the dark red tongue, swollen, filling almost the whole mouth.

He put his hand on the man's face. The cheeks felt like uncooked dough. Now seemed a good time to get at the structure of the human face. He picked up the smaller of his knives and cut from the hairline to the bridge of the nose. He tried to peel the skin off the forehead but he could not, it was too closely attached to the bone. He cut on top of each eyebrow to the edge of the eye, stripped the skin from the corner of the eye outward, continued from the eye to the ear, then down along the cheekbone.

The effect of this mutilation was so ghastly that he could not work on it. He picked up the winding sheet from the corner, covered the man's head, and turned his attention to the hipbone, to the fibered muscles of the heavy thigh.

A couple of nights later when there was a new corpse, he cut lightly into the skin of the face, peeling it off with his scissors. Under the thin yellow tissue of fat he discovered a large membrane of red muscular tissue which went continuously from the ear around the lips to the other ear. Now he had his first understanding of how these muscles could move the face to laughter, smiles, tears, grief.

Under it was a thicker tissue extending from the corner of the jaw to the base of the skull. Putting his finger under this second layer, he pushed the tissue a little and saw the jaw move. He worked it up and down to simulate the chewing movement, then searched for the muscle that would move the eyelid. He had to see inside the cavity of the eye to know what made it move. Trying to push his finger inside, he exerted too much pressure. The eye globe broke. A white mucus poured out over his fingers, leaving the cavity empty.

He turned away terror-stricken, walked to a corner of the whitewashed wall and crushed his forehead against its coldness, fighting desperately the desire to retch. When he had regained control of himself he went back to the corpse, cut the tissue from around the second eye, found where it was attached at the bottom of the cavity. Then putting his finger in above the eye and moving it slowly inside, he plucked it out. He turned it around and around in his hand, trying to find out how it moved. He held his candle close, peered into the empty cavity. On the bottom he could perceive a hole through which gray soft tissuelike wires went up into the skull. Until he could remove the top of the skull and expose the brain, he could learn nothing about how an eye sees.

His candle had only a bit of tallow. He cut the flesh away from the bridge of the nose, saw clearly what had happened to his own under Torrigiani's fist.

The candle spluttered.

Where to go? He dragged himself away from Santo Spirito. His body ached with tiredness, his eyes smarted, his stomach and spirits were in a state of revulsion. He could not face Lodovico, who would surely be waiting for him at the top of the stairs, screaming that he was going straight to the Stinche.

He made his way to the workshop of the Duomo. It was easy to throw his bag over the gate, then hoist himself over. In the moonlight the blocks of white marble glistened with white luminosity, the chips around the semifinished columns were like snow, clean and refreshing. The cold air settled his stomach. He went toward his workbench, cleared a place under it, stretched out, covered himself with a heavy piece of canvas and fell asleep.

He woke a few hours later; the sun had risen. In the piazza he could hear the noise of the *contadini* setting up their stalls. He walked to the fountain, washed, bought himself a slice of *parmigiano,* two thick-crusted *panini,* and returned to the workyard.

He tried to cut marble around the edges of the Hercules block, thinking that the feel of the iron instruments would bring him enjoyment. He soon set them down, climbed up on his stool and began to draw: the arm, muscles and joints, the jaw, the heart, the head. When Beppe arrived, came close to give him a *buon giorno*, he spread a concealing hand over the sheet before him. Beppe stopped short; but not before he got a look at an empty eye socket and exposed viscera. He shook his head grimly, turned and walked away.

At noon Michelangelo went home to dinner, to allay Lodovico's fears about his absence.

It took him several days to work up the courage to return to the dead room and crack a man's skull. Once there he began working rapidly with hammer and chisel, cutting backward from the bridge of the nose. It was a nerve-racking experience, for the head moved each time he made a stroke. Nor did he know how much force to exert to break the bone. He could not get the skull open. He covered the head, turned the man over, spent the rest of the night studying the structure of the spinal column.

With the next cadaver he did not make the mistake of cutting backward on the skull, but instead cut around the head, from the tip of the left ear along the hairline, taking three or four hard blows of the hammer to penetrate the half inch of bone. There was now room enough to keep his scalpel under the skull and cut all the way around. A white-yellow cream escaped; the fissure opened wider. When he had cut the bone more than halfway, he used his scalpel as a lever and ripped. The skull lifted off in his hands.

It was like dry wood. He was so shaken he barely prevented its dropping onto the floor. He shifted his eyes from the skull to the corpse. He was horrified, for with the top of the head off, the face was absolutely destroyed.

Again he was overcome by a sense of guilt; but with the skull lifted off he had his first look at a human brain. As an artist he had been fascinated by what created expression; what was it in the brain that enabled the face to convey emotion? Holding his candle close to the brainpan, he saw that the mass inside was yellow-white, with red-blue lines on the surface, the arteries and veins going in all directions. He could see that the mass of the brain was divided in the middle, exactly corresponding to the divided line of the skull. He could detect no odor, but to his first touch it was wet, very soft and even, like the skin of a soft fish.

He put the skull back on top of the head, wrapping the sheet tightly at the top to hold it in place. He was neither ill nor distressed as he had been on most other nights, but could hardly wait to get back to his next corpse and open the brain itself.

When he took off his next skull he was astonished to think that men could be so different when their brains looked and felt so much alike. From this he deduced that there must be a physical substance inside the brain which differed with each man. Using his index finger, he moved around the base of the skull, learned that the brain was completely detached and free from the bone. Putting his fingers in on both sides, he tried to take it out whole. It would not lift.

Where his fingers came together the mass was attached by something like a series of wires to the bottom of the skull basin. He cut the wires, pulled out the mass. It was so soft, and at the same time so slippery, he had to concentrate tremendously just to hold it together. He looked at it in wonderment and admiration: from this relatively small substance, which could weigh no more than a couple of pounds, emerged all the greatness of the human race: art, science, philosophy, government, all that men had become for good as well as evil.

When he cut the brain down the line of division it was similar to cutting very soft cheese; there was no noise, no spoilage, no odor. The two halves were exactly alike. No matter where he cut, it was all the same, gray in color, a little yellowish. He pushed the corpse over on the table to make enough space to lay the brain out on the wooden plank, and was amazed to see that in and by itself it had no structure, that it slowly collapsed over the wooden boards.

The holes in the skull he found filled with the same wirelike substance he had had to break in order to detach the brain. Following these strands down through the neck, he surmised that this substance was the sole connection between the brain and the body. The front holes he discerned were between the brain and the eyes; the other two holes corresponded to the ears. He pushed through the inch-and-a-half hole at the back base of the skull, connecting to the vertebrae; this was the connection between the brain and the back.

He was exhausted now, for he had worked for five hours and was glad when his candle burned out.

He sat on the edge of the fountain in the Piazza Santo Spirito throwing cold water at his face and asking himself:

"Am I obsessed to be doing these things? Have I the right to do this just because I say it is for sculpture? What price might I have to pay for this precious knowledge?"

Spring arrived, the air warmed. Beppe told him of some sculpture that needed doing for the new vault of the vestibule of Santo Spirito: carved capitals and a number of worked stones to decorate the vault and the doors. It never occurred to him to ask Prior Bichiellini to intervene. He went directly to the foreman in charge of constructing the square stone vault and asked for the job. The foreman did not want a student. Michelangelo offered to bring his Madonna and Child and Centaurs to prove that he could do the work. The foreman reluctantly agreed to look. Bugiardini borrowed one of Ghirlandaio's carts, came to the Buonarroti house, helped him wrap and carry the marbles down the stairs. They stowed them safely on a bed of straw, then wheeled the cart through the streets, across the Ponte Santa Trinita to Santo Spirito.

The foreman was unimpressed. The pieces were not suited to what he had to do. "Besides, I already hired my two men."

"Sculptors?" Michelangelo was surprised.

"What then?"

"What are their names?"

"Giovanni di Betto and Simone del Caprina."

"Never heard of them. Where were they trained?"

"In a silversmith's shop."

"Are you ornamenting the stones with silver?"

"They worked at Prato on a similar job. They are experienced."

"And I am not? After three years in Lorenzo's sculpture garden, under Bertoldo?"

"Don't take it so hard, son. These are older men with families to support. You know how little marble work there is. But of course if you brought an order from Piero de' Medici, since you are a Medici protégé, and Piero is paying for the work . . ."

Michelangelo and Bugiardini wheeled the reliefs through the cobbled streets, put them back under the bed.

Lodovico waited resignedly for his son to reform. Michelangelo continued to come in at dawn, after having dissected the knee and ankle bone, the corresponding elbow and wrist bone, the hip and pelvis, the private parts. He studied the muscular structure again and again, the shoulders and forearms, the thighs and calves. Lodovico cornered him.

"I order you to give up this dissolute life at once, to go back to work during the day and to bed after supper at night."

"Give me a little more time, Father."

Giovansimone was delighted that Michelangelo had taken off on the wild life. Florence was agog over its latest scandal: Piero had interceded with the Dominican authorities and had Savonarola banished to Bologna as "too great a partisan of the people." But for Giovansimone there had been no change in activity.

"How about coming with me tonight? I'm going where there's good gambling and whoring."

"No, thank you."

"Why not? Are you too good to go out with me?"

"Everyone to his own evil, Giovansimone."

6

An unexpected death put an end to his dissecting.

Working in robust good health, Domenico Ghirlandaio contracted a pestilence and in two days was dead. Michelangelo went to the *bottega* to take his place with Granacci, Bugiardini, Cieco, Baldinelli, Tedesco and Jacopo on one side of the coffin, while the son, brothers and brother-in-law stood on the other, and the friends came to say good-by. Together they all walked behind the funeral procession, over the route on which Michelangelo had driven the cart for his first day of frescoing in Santa Maria Novella, to attend the mass, and then the burial.

That afternoon he went to visit Prior Bichiellini, casually laid the long bronze key over the pages of the book the prior was reading, and said, "I should like to carve something for the church."

The prior showed pleasure but not surprise.

"I have long felt the need of a crucifix for the central altar. I've always envisioned it in wood."

"Wood? I wonder if I can?"

For once he had the good sense not to say, "Wood is not my trade." If the prior wanted a Crucifixion in wood, then wood it must be, though he had never even whittled. There was no material of sculpture that Bertoldo had not obliged him to handle: wax, clay, the varying stones. But never wood; probably because Donatello had not touched wood for the last thirty-five years of his life, after he had completed his Crucifixion for Santa Croce.

He accompanied the prior through the sacristy. The prior stopped and pointed out the arch behind the main altar, which formed one of the two entries to the chancel, then asked:

"Could it carry a life-size figure?"

"I will have to draw the arches and the altar to scale to be sure; but I should think it could be almost life size. May I work in the monastery carpenter shop?"

"The brothers would be pleased to have you."

The lay brothers in the carpenter shop worked with sunlight streaming on their shoulders from overhead windows. In the relaxed atmosphere of the workbenches he was treated as another carpenter come to make still one more useful article among the hundreds needed for Santo Spirito. Though there was no order of silence in the busy shop, no one who liked to gab ever came close to an Augustinian monastery.

This suited Michelangelo; he felt at home working in the comfortable silence framed by the pleasant sounds of saw, plane and hammer. The smell of sawdust was salutary. He worked on the various woods the monastery had to offer to get the knack of carving in this material which he found so unlike marble. The wood did not seem to fight back.

He took to reading the New Testament, the story of Christ as related by Matthew and Mark. The more he read, the more the terror-laden, agony-infused Crucifixion of previous centuries to be seen in the chapels of Florence, receded from his mind, and into it came the image of Prior Bichiellini: cheerful, hearty, dedicated, serving all humanity in God's name, with a great mind and noble spirit that gloried in living.

It was a need of his nature to be original. But what could one say about Christ on the cross that had not been carved and painted before? Though the theme of the Crucifixion would not have occurred to him, he was eager to do something particularly fine to justify the prior's faith in him. The finished work would have to be intensely spiritual, lest the prior wonder if he had made a mistake in letting him dissect.

He started drawing in front of the earliest Crucifixions, those of the thirteenth century, carved with the head and knees of Christ turned in the same direction, perhaps because this was the simplest form for the sculptor and because the design evoked, in terms of emotion, the simplicity of unquestioning acceptance. By the fourteenth century the sculptors were showing Christ in full face, with all parts of the body symmetrically disposed on either side of a central, structural line.

He spent time in front of Donatello's Santa Croce Crucifixion, marveling at the magnificence of its conception. Whatever emotion Donatello had set out to achieve, strength combined with idyllic fulfillment, power to forgive as well as subdue, the ability to be destroyed as well as resurrected, all these emotions he had succeeded in conveying. Yet Michelangelo did not feel within himself any of the things that Donatello felt. He had never been altogether clear in his own mind why God could not accomplish by Himself all the things He sent His son down on earth to do. Why did God need a son? The exquisitely balanced Donatello Christ said to him:

"This is how God wanted it to be, exactly the way it was planned. It is not hard to accept one's fate when it has been preordained. I have anticipated this pain."

This was not acceptable to Michelangelo's temperament.

What had the violent end to do with God's message of love? Why did He permit violence to take place, when its very form would create hatred, fear, retribution and continuing violence? If He were omnipotent, why had He not devised a more peaceable way to bring His message to the world? His impotence to stop this barbarism was a terrifying thought to Michelangelo . . . and perhaps to Christ as well.

As he stood in the bright sunlight on the steps of Santa Croce, watching the boys play football on the hard earth of the square, then walked slowly past the palaces of the Via de' Bardi, patting affectionately the carved stones of the buildings as he went by, he thought:

"What went through the mind of Christ between the sunset hour when the Roman soldier drove the first nail through his flesh, and the hour when he died? For these thoughts would determine not only how he accepted his fate, but also the position of his body on the cross. Donatello's Christ accepted in serenity, and thought nothing. Brunelleschi's Christ was so ethereal that he died at the first touch of the nail, and had no time to think."

He returned to his workbench, began exploring his mind with charcoal and ink. On Christ's face appeared the expression, "I am in agony, not from the iron nails, but from the rust of doubt." He could not bring himself to convey Christ's divinity by anything so obvious as a halo; it had to be portrayed through an inner force, strong enough to conquer his misgivings at this hour of severest trial.

It was inevitable that his Christ would be closer to man than to God. He did not know that he was to be crucified. He neither wanted it nor liked it. And as a result his body was twisted in conflict, torn, like all men, by inner questioning.

When he was ready to begin carving he had before him a new concept: he turned Christ's head and knees in opposite directions, establishing through this contrapuntal design a graphic tension, the intense physical and spiritual inner conflict of a man who is being pulled two ways.

He carved his figure in the hardest wood available in Tuscany, walnut, and when he had finished with hammer and chisel, sandpapered it down, and rubbed the surface with stainless oil and wax. His fellow carpenters made no comment, but they stopped by his bench to observe progress. Nor, for that matter, did the prior enter into a discussion of its message. He said simply:

"Every artist's Crucifixion is a self-portrait. It is what I envisioned for the altar. Thank you."

On Sunday morning Michelangelo brought his family to Santo Spirito. He led them to a bench close to the altar. His Christ loomed above them. His grandmother whispered:

"You make me feel compassion for him. Always before I thought Christ was feeling compassion for me."

Lodovico was not feeling compassion for anybody. He asked, "How large was the commission?"

"It wasn't a commission. I volunteered."

"You mean you're not getting paid?"

"The prior has been good to me. I wanted to repay my debt."

"Good to you in what way?"

". . . well . . . he let me copy the works of art . . ."

"The church is open to everybody."

"In the monastery. And to use his library."

"It is a public library. Are you *pazzo,* crazy, that a penniless lad should work free for a rich monastery?"

A heavy snowstorm that lasted for two days and nights left Florence a white city. Sunday dawned clear, crisp and cold. He was alone in the enclosed Duomo workshop, huddled over a brazier while trying to make the first of the Hercules drawings, when Piero's groom came looking for him.

"His Excellency, Piero de' Medici, asks if you could come to the palace."

He made his way to the barber in the straw market, where he had his hair cut, the patches of beard down the sides of his cheek and chin shaved, then returned home, boiled himself a tub of hot water, bathed, put on his blue wool tunic and set out for the first time in over a year and a half for the palace. The statues in the courtyard, as he came through, were piled high with snow. He found the Medici children and grandchildren assembled in Lorenzo's *studiolo,* a bright fire burning.

It was Giuliano's birthday. Cardinal Giovanni, who had settled in a small but exquisite palace in the quarter of Sant'Antonio when a hostile Borgia had been elected Pope, looked plumper than ever sitting in Lorenzo's chair, hovered over by his cousin Giulio. Their sister Maddalena, married to the former Pope Innocent VIII's son, Franceschetto Cibo, was back with their two children; so was Lucrezia, married to Jacopo Salviati of the Florentine banking family, who owned the home of Dante's Beatrice; their aunt Nannina and her husband, Bernardo Rucellai; Piero and Alfonsina with their oldest son. They were dressed in their gayest brocades, jeweled satins and cut velvets.

And Contessina was there, elegantly gowned in aquamarine silk interwoven with silver thread. Michelangelo noted with surprise that she was taller, that her arms and shoulders had filled out a little, and her bosom, propped by stays under the embroidery, was approaching maturity. Her eyes, when they met his, sparkled as brightly as the silver jewels with which her dress was ornamented.

A servant handed him a glass of hot mulled wine. The drink, combined with the warmth of the reception, the sharp nostalgia the room evoked, and Contessina's bemused smile, all went to his head.

Piero stood with his back to the fire. He smiled, and seemed to have forgotten their quarrel. "Michelangelo, it is our pleasure to welcome you back to the palace. Today we must do everything that pleases Giuliano."

"I should like to help make Giuliano happy today."

"Good. The first thing he said this morning was, 'I should like to have the greatest snowman ever made.' And since you were our father's favorite sculptor, what would be more natural than that we should think of you?"

Something within him sank like a stone. While the Medici children turned their faces toward him, he remembered the two tubes in the cadaver that extended downward from the mouth, one to carry air, the other food. Should there not be a third, to swallow crushed hopes?

"Please do it for me, Michelangelo," cried Giuliano. "It would be the most wonderful snowman ever made."

His acrid impression of having been summoned as an entertainer passed with Giuliano's plea. Was he to reply, "Snow is not my trade?"

"Do help us, Michelangelo." It was Contessina, who had come close to him. "We'll all serve as your assistants."

And he knew it was all right.

Late that afternoon, when the last of the Florentine crowds had thronged through the palace grounds to see the hilariously grotesque, giant snowman, Piero sat at his father's desk in the big office, under the maps of Italy.

"Why not move back into the palace, Michelangelo? We would like to bring together again my father's circle."

"Could I ask under what conditions I would return?"

"You would have the same privileges as when my father was alive."

Michelangelo gulped; he was fifteen when he had come to live in this palace. He was almost eighteen now. Hardly an age to receive spending money left on his washstand. Yet it was a chance to get out of the drear Buonarroti house, the nagging domination of Lodovico, to earn some money, perhaps to carve something good for the Medici.

7

A groom moved him back into his old apartment, with Bertoldo's sculptures still untouched on the catercornered shelves. A palace tailor came with fabrics and measuring tapes; and on the following Sunday Piero's secretary, Ser Bernardo da Bibbiena, deposited three gold florins on the washstand.

Everything was the same; yet everything was different. The scholars of Italy and Europe no longer came to the palace. The Plato Academy preferred to hold its meetings in the Rucellai gardens. At Sunday dinner only those noble families with pleasure-loving sons were at table. The great families from the Italian city-states were not present on the pleasant duties of treaty making, nor were the merchant princes who had prospered with the Medici, nor yet the *gonfalonieri, buonuomini* or councilmen from the Florentine districts whom Lorenzo had kept close to him in bonds of intimacy. All these were replaced by entertainers and Piero's young sporting friends.

The Topolinos rode into the city behind their white oxen on Sunday after mass and hoisted the Hercules block onto their cart. The grandfather drove, while the father, three sons and Michelangelo walked through the quiet streets that had been hosed and swept immaculately clean at sunrise, each holding an end of the lashing ropes. They drove in through the back entrance of the garden, unloaded and propped the marble next to his old sculpture shed.

Comfortably settled, he returned to his drawings, made one in red chalk of the youth pulling apart the jaws of the Nemean lion with his bare hands; the man in his middle years wrestling Antaeus to death; the old man fighting the hundred-headed hydra; all of which he found too pictorial. Finally rejecting the outspread figure of earlier Florence Herculeses, the legs wide apart, arm on the hip, he designed a closed, compact figure closer to the Greek concept, in which all of Hercules' bursting power was held in a unifying force between torso and limbs.

What concession must he make to the conventional? First, the huge club: this he designed as a tree trunk upon which Hercules leaned. The inevitable lion's pelt, which had always formed a frame for the figure, he knotted far out on one shoulder, letting the barest suggestion fall across the chest, concealing nothing of the heroic torso. He extended one arm only a little, patently enclosing the round firm apples of the Hesperides. The club, the long lion skin, the apples had been used by former sculptors to depict fortitude; his Hercules, naked before the world, would carry within its own structure everything that mankind needed of fortitude and resolution.

He was not daunted by the fact that his would be the largest Hercules ever carved in Florence. As he marked out the proportions of the great figure, seven feet seven inches in height, with a foot-and-a-half base and five inches of safety marble above the head from which he would carve downward, he recalled that Hercules had been the national hero of Greece, as Lorenzo had been of Florence. Why then portray him in small, exquisite bronzes? Both Hercules and Lorenzo had failed, but oh! how much they had accomplished in the trying! How richly they deserved to be carved bigger than life.

He built a rough clay model, working out the shifts of weight and stance, the movements of the back muscles because of the extended arm, the muscle distribution because the figure was leaning, the straining of tendon and ligament, the swivel of hip and shoulder, all of which he now knew and could project with conviction. Yet some instinct kept him from using measuring cords and iron pegs to enlarge the model to scale. For his first life-size figure in the round, which was also the first work he was creating in absolute independence, he wanted to see how far and faithfully his hand could follow his eye.

He forged his tools for the initial massing, pounded the rods to increase their length, giving them a stubbier end to withstand the greater hammer blows, and once more, with the handling of the metal, achieved in himself a feeling of hardness, durability. He squatted on his haunches before the marble. Looking at the huge block gave him a sense of power. He removed the edges with heavy point and heavy hammer, thought with satisfaction that by this very act he was already adding to the stature of the block before him. He had no wish to conquer the nine-foot slab, only to persuade it to express his creative ideas.

This was Seravezza marble, quarried high in the Apuan Alps. After he had penetrated its weathered outer skin it behaved like a lump of sugar under his dog's-tooth chisel, its pure milky-white slivers crumbling between his fingers. He used a flat stick to gauge approximately how deep he had to cut to get down to neck depth, armpit depth, torso depth, the bended knee. Then he went back to the forge, made a *calcagnolo*, and attacked the marble with fury, the chisel hugging close to the surface like a plow through the earth. And now the Seravezza marble suddenly became hard as iron, and he had to struggle with all his strength to achieve his forms.

Ignoring the instructions of Bertoldo, he did not attempt to work his block all around, develop it as a whole, but went after the head, shoulders, arms, hips, using his flat stick and naked eye to measure his high points as he dug deeper. Then he almost ruined his block. He had cut too deeply to free the neck and head, and now his strong chisel strokes on the emerging shoulder muscles caused intense vibrations to run up through the neck into the head. The shivering marble looked for an instant as though it would crack at the narrow point; his Hercules would lose his head, and he would have to begin again on a reduced scale. Then the trembling ceased.

He sat down on a nearby box to wipe the perspiration from his face.

He forged new fine-edged tools, making sure every point was symmetrical. Now each blow of his hammer was transferred directly to the carving end of the tool, as though it were his fingers rather than the chisels that were cutting through the crystals. Every few moments he stepped back and circled the block because, no matter how deep he cut, a fog of texture obscured the contour of knee socket, rib cage. He used a brush to clear away the dust.

He made a second series of mistakes; his eye failed to measure accurately the receding planes, and he delivered some hard blows which spoiled the frontal harmony. But he had left himself spare marble at the back, and so he was able to push the entire figure deeper into the block than he had intended.

His progress became swifter as he stepped inside the marble, so passionately tearing out deepening layers that he felt as though he were standing in the midst of a snowstorm, breathing its flurries, closing his eyes at the moment of the hammer impact.

The anatomy of the marble began matching the anatomy of his clay model: the powerful chest, magnificently rounded forearms, the thighs like the white meat under the bark of giant trees, the head focusing enormous power within its limited area. Hammer and chisel in hand, he stood back from the galvanic male figure before him, still faceless, standing on a rough-gouged base to show the material from which it had emerged, thinking that from the very beginning the marble had yielded to love: pliable, vulvar. With marble he was the dominant male; his was the choice, his the conquest. Yet coming together with the object of his love, he had been all tenderness. The block had been virginal but not frigid; it had been set on fire by his own white heat. Statues came out of the marble, but not until the tool had penetrated and seeded its female form. From love came all of life.

He finished the surface with a good pumicing, but gave it no polish, afraid that to do so would diminish its virility. He left the hair and beard in a crude state, with just a suggestion of curls, angling the small three-toothed chisel so that he could dig in with the last tooth for accent.

Monna Alessandra went to bed feeling tired one night, and never awoke. Lodovico took the loss hard; like most Tuscans, he was deeply attached to his mother, and had for her a gentleness he showed no one else in the family. For Michelangelo the loss was poignant; since the death of his own mother thirteen years before, Monna Alessandra had been the only woman to whom he could turn for love or understanding. Without his grandmother the Buonarroti house seemed gloomier to him than ever.

The palace, by contrast, was in an uproar over Contessina's marriage, which was to take place late in May. Since Contessina was the last of the Medici daughters, Piero was ignoring all of the sumptuary laws and preparing to spend fifty thousand florins to give Florence the greatest celebration in its history. Contessina went her busy way, whirling from *sarta* to *sarta* for her gowns, commissioning dowry chests to be painted, interviewing merchants from all over the world to select her linens, brocades, jewelry, silver and goldware, dishes, blankets, furnishings that were her rightful and imperative dowry as a Medici.

Then one evening they met by accident in the *studiolo*. It was so like old times, with Lorenzo's books and art works about them, that they forgot for the moment the impending ceremonies and linked arms affectionately.

"I hardly see you any more, Michelangelo. You are not to be unhappy at my wedding."

"Am I to be invited?"

"The wedding takes place here. How could you not attend?"

"The invitation must come from Piero."

"Stop being difficult!" Her eyes flashed with the anger he remembered flaring up at his other obstinacies. "You will celebrate for three days, just as I will."

"Not quite," he replied; and they both blushed.

Granacci was commissioned by Piero to take charge of the scenery for the wedding pageant, ball, banquet, theatricals. The palace was full of singing, dancing, drinking, revelry. Yet Michelangelo was lonely. He spent most of his time in the garden.

Piero was polite but distant, as though having his father's sculptor under his roof was all he had been after. The feeling of being an exhibit was strengthened when he heard Piero boast that he had two extraordinary persons in the palace: Michelangelo, who made great snowmen, and a Spanish footman who ran so fast that Piero, riding his best horse at a gallop, could not outrun him.

"Excellency, could we speak seriously about my carving marbles? I wish to earn my keep."

There was incredulity in Piero's expression.

"A couple of years ago you were offended because I treated you as a tradesman. Now you are offended because I do not. How is one to keep you artists happy?"

"I need a goal such as your father outlined to me."

"What was that?"

"To build a façade for San Lorenzo with niches for twenty life-size marble figures."

"He never mentioned it to me."

"It was before he went out to Careggi the last time."

"Ah well, the fleeting dreams of a dying man. Not very practical, are they? You just keep yourself busy as best you can, Buonarroti, and someday I'll think of something for you to do."

He watched the wedding gifts roll in from all over Italy, Europe and the Near East, from Lorenzo's friends, from business associates of the Medici: rare jewels, carved ivories, perfumes, costly satins from Asia; goblets and bowls of gold from the Orient, carved furniture. He too wanted to give Contessina a gift. But what?

The Hercules! Why not? He had bought the marble with his own money. He was a sculptor, he should give her sculpture for her wedding. The Hercules for the garden of the Ridolfi palace! He would not tell her about it, he would simply ask the Topolinos to help him move it there.

Now for the first time he came to grips with Hercules' face. It would be a portrait of *Il Magnifico:* not of his upturned nose, muddy skin, scraggly hair; but of the inner man and mind of Lorenzo de' Medici. The expression would convey intense pride, coupled with humility. It would have not only the power but the desire to communicate. Matching the devastating strength of the body would be a gentleness that would yet convey the fighter who would do battle for mankind, be concerned with remolding man's treacherous world.

His drawings finished, he started carving excitedly, using the hand drill to bring out the nostrils and ears, the profusion of hair falling about the face, the finest edged chisel to round the cheekbones, the hand-twirling bore to touch ever so lightly the eyes to achieve the clear, piercing communication with every soul who looked upon him. He worked from dawn to dark, not bothering to eat at midday, and falling into bed at night like a dead man.

Granacci praised him for his completion of so complex a task, then added quietly:

"*Amico mio,* you can't give it to Contessina. It wouldn't be right."

"Why not?"

"It's too . . . too big."

"The Hercules is too big?"

"No, the gift. The Ridolfi might not think it proper."

"For me to give Contessina a gift?"

"So large a gift."

"Are you speaking of size? Or value?"

"Both. You are not a Medici, nor a member of a ruling house of Tuscany. It might be considered in bad taste."

"But it has no value. I couldn't sell it."

"It has value. You can sell it."

"To whom?"

"The Strozzi. For the courtyard of their new palace. I brought them here last Sunday. They authorized me to offer you a hundred large gold florins. It will enjoy a place of honor in the courtyard. It is your first sale!"

Tears of frustration smarted behind his lids, but he was older now, he could blink them back.

"Piero and my father are right: no matter how an artist may strive, he ends up as a hireling, with something to market."

There was no way to escape the excitement of the three thousand wedding guests pouring into the city and filling Florence's palaces to capacity. On the morning of May 24 he donned his green silk tunic with velvet sleeves, the violet cloak. In front of the palace was a fountain garlanded with fruits, in its center two figures designed by Granacci from which red and white wine flowed so abundantly that it ran down the Via de' Gori.

He walked with Granacci behind the wedding party as Contessina and Ridolfi paraded through streets decorated with flags, preceded by trumpeters. At the entrance to the Piazza del Duomo was a replica of a Roman triumphal arch festooned with garlands. On the steps of the cathedral a notary read aloud the marriage contract to the thousands who jammed the piazza. When Michelangelo heard the extent of Contessina's dowry, he blanched.

At the family church of San Lorenzo, Piero formally presented Contessina to Ridolfi, who placed the betrothal ring on her finger. Michelangelo remained at the back of the church and slipped out a side door in the middle of the nuptial mass. A wooden stand filled one side of the square, to accommodate the crowds, while in the center there was a fifty-foot tree supporting a white pavilion in which musicians played. The surrounding houses were hung with tapestries.

The wedding party emerged from the church, Ridolfi tall in his white satin cloak, jet-black hair framing his thin, pale face. Michelangelo stood on the steps watching Contessina in her crimson samite gown with its long train and collar of white ermine, on her head an elaborate headdress mounted on a crimson support and adorned with carved gilt beads. As soon as she was seated in the bedecked stands the entertainment began: a play depicting "A Fight Between Chastity and Marriage," a tournament in which Piero jousted; and as the climax, a contest of the "Knights of the She-Cat" in which a man, naked to the waist and with shaven head, entered a cage on a wooden platform where he had to kill a cat with his teeth, without using his hands.

A seat had been reserved for him in the dining salon. The finest produce of Tuscany had been brought to the palace for the feast: eight hundred barrels of wine, a thousand pounds of flour, of meat, of game, of marzipan. He watched the ceremonial acts of a child being placed in Contessina's arms and a gold florin in her shoe to bring fertility and riches. Then, after the nuptial feast, when the guests went into the ballroom which Granacci had converted into ancient Bagdad, he left the palace and walked from piazza to piazza, where Piero had set up prodigal tables of food and wine for all of Florence to participate. But the people seemed glum.

He did not return to the palace where there were to be two more days of feasting and celebration before Contessina would be escorted to the Ridolfi palace. Instead, in the dark of night, he walked slowly up to Settignano, spread an old blanket under the Topolino arches and, his hands locked behind his head, watched the sun emerge over the hills to light the roof of the Buonarroti house across the ravine.

8

Contessina's marriage proved to be a turning point: for himself; for Florence. He had witnessed the resentment of the people on the first night of the feasts, heard the general murmurings against Piero. There was little need for the fiery sermons preached against him by Savonarola, returned to the city with more power than ever in his Dominican Order, demanding that Piero be prosecuted by the Signoria for violation of the city's sumptuary laws.

Puzzled at the intensity of the reaction, Michelangelo went to visit Prior Bichiellini.

"Were the marriages of the other Medici daughters less sumptuous?" he asked.

"Not particularly. But with Lorenzo, the people of Florence felt he was sharing; with Piero, they felt he was giving. It made the wedding wine turn sour in their mouths."

The completion of Contessina's wedding celebration was a signal to the Medici cousins to begin their political campaign against Piero. Within a few days the city was awash with scandal: at a party the night before Piero and his cousin Lorenzo had fought over a young woman. Piero struck Lorenzo a blow on the ear; the first time one Medici had ever struck another. They had both pulled their knives and there would have been a killing if friends had not stepped in. When Michelangelo went in to midday dinner he found a few more of the older friends missing. The laughter of Piero and his comrades sounded a trifle hysterical.

Granacci came into the garden at dusk to tell him that someone had seen his Hercules in the Strozzi courtyard, was waiting for him there, and would like to speak to him about a commission. Michelangelo hid his surprise when he found the new patrons to be the Medici cousins, Lorenzo and Giovanni. He had met them many times in the palace while Lorenzo was alive, for they had loved him as a father, and the Magnificent One had given them the highest of diplomatic posts, even sending them to France eleven years before to congratulate Charles VIII on ascending the throne. Piero had always condescended to them as coming down through the lesser branch of the family.

The Medici cousins were standing on either side of his Hercules. Lorenzo, who was twelve years older than Michelangelo, had regular features full of expression, though his skin was pockmarked; he was a powerfully built man with a strong neck, shoulders and chest. He lived like a great lord in the family palace on Piazza San Marco, with villas on the declivity of the hill below Fiesole and at Castello. Even now Botticelli was living on his commission to illustrate Dante's *Divine Comedy*. He himself was a respected poet and dramatist. Giovanni, the younger brother, twenty-seven, was called "The Handsome" by Florentines.

They greeted him heartily, spoke highly of the Hercules, then got to the point. Lorenzo was the spokesman.

"Michelangelo, we saw the two marble pieces you sculptured for our uncle Lorenzo, and we have often said, my brother and I, that one day we should like you to carve a piece for us."

Michelangelo remained silent. The younger brother continued.

"We've always yearned for a young St. John. In white marble. As the patron saint of our home. Would the theme interest you?"

Michelangelo shifted awkwardly from foot to foot, gazing out the main gate of the Strozzi palace to the intense pool of sunlight lying in the Via Tornabuoni. He needed work, not merely because of the money involved but because he was growing restless. It would put marble in his hands.

"We are prepared to pay a good price," said Lorenzo, while his brother added, "And there is a place at the back of our garden for a workshop. What do you say?"

"To be wanted is always good. May I think it over?"

"Of course," replied Lorenzo heartily. "We have no desire to rush you. Give us the pleasure of your company at Sunday dinner."

He walked home in silence, his head down. Granacci profered no word or suggestion until they parted at the corner of the Via dei Bentaccordi and Via dell'Anguillara.

"I was asked to bring you. I brought you. That does not mean that I necessarily think you should accept."

"Thank you, Granacci. I understand."

His family had no such tolerance.

"Of course you'll take the commission!" boomed Lodovico, pushing masses of his gray-black hair back out of his eyes. "Only this time you can dictate the fee because they came to you."

"Why did they come to me?" persisted Michelangelo.

"Because they want a St. John," replied his aunt Cassandra.

"But why at this moment, when they are setting up an opposition party to Piero? Why didn't they ask me at any time during the past two years?

"What business is that of yours?" demanded his uncle Francesco. "Who is crazy enough to look a sculpture commission in the mouth?"

"But something more is true, Uncle Francesco. Prior Bichiellini says the aim of the cousins is to drive Piero out of Florence. I think they want to strike another blow at Piero."

"And you are a blow?" Lucrezia's face was puzzled.

"A modest one, *madre mia*." Michelangelo's whimsical smile offset the ugliness of his flattened nose.

"Let's get out of politics," commanded Lodovico, "and back into business. Are times so good for the Buonarroti that you can afford to turn down a commission?"

"No, Father, but I can't be disloyal to Lorenzo."

"The dead don't need loyalty."

"They do. As much as the living. I just gave you the hundred florins from the Hercules."

The cousins reserved him a place of honor at their festive Sunday dinner, spoke of everything but Piero and the St. John. When, after dinner, Michelangelo stammered that he appreciated their offer but could not at the moment accept, Lorenzo replied easily:

"We are in no hurry. The offer stands."

There was no real place for him in the palace. He served no purpose and was valuable to no one except Giuliano, who needed the affection. He went looking for jobs to justify his presence: sorting Lorenzo's collection of drawings, adding Piero's occasional acquisition of an ancient medallion or carved gem to its proper place in the cabinets. Lodovico had told him that he did not have the price of pride; but sometimes a man's nature did not give him the choice of deciding whether he could afford a trait of character with which he had been born.

Piero too was unhappy, sitting at table pale, cold, as he asked his few remaining friends:

"Why can't I get the Signoria to see things my way? Why do I have trouble with everything, when my father had life so smooth?"

Michelangelo posed the question to Prior Bichiellini, who sat back in his black tunic with the white shirt showing crisp and clean at the throat. His eyes snapped with anger.

"His four Medici ancestors considered the *act* of governing as the *art* of governing. They loved Florence first, themselves second. Piero . . ."

Michelangelo was surprised at the denunciatory edge to the prior's voice.

"I have not heard you bitter before, Father."

". . . Piero won't listen to counsel. A weak man at the helm, and a power-hungry priest working to replace him . . . These are sad days for Florence, my son."

"I have heard some of Savonarola's 'plank by plank' sermons on the coming Flood. Half the people of the city believe Judgment Day is the next rain away. What is his purpose in terrorizing Florence?"

The prior took off his spectacles.

"He wants to become Pope. But his ambition doesn't end there: he has plans to conquer the Near East, then the Orient."

Michelangelo asked banteringly, "You have no passion for converting the heathen?"

The prior was quiet for a moment. "Would I like to see an all-Catholic world? Only if the world wished to be converted. And certainly not by a tyrant who would burn down the humanities and destroy the world's mind to save its soul. No true Christian would want that."

At the palace he found an urgent message from his father. Lodovico led him into the boys' bedroom, lifted a pile of clothing from the top of Giovansimone's locker, and scooped out a pile of jewelry, gold and silver buckles, medallions.

"What does this mean?" he asked Michelangelo. "Has Giovansimone been burglarizing people's homes at night?"

"Nothing quite so illegal, Father. Giovansimone is a captain in Savonarola's Army of Boys. They strip women in the streets who violate the padre's orders against wearing jewelry in public; they knock on doors, twenty or thirty of them, if they hear of a family violating the sumptuary laws and strip it bare. If they meet opposition, they stone people half to death."

"But is Giovansimone allowed to keep these things? They must be worth hundreds of florins."

"He is supposed to bring them all to San Marco. Most of the children do. But Giovansimone has converted his old gang of hoodlums into what Savonarola calls his 'white-shirted angels.' The Council is powerless to stop them."

Lionardo chose this time to summon Michelangelo to San Marco to show him the school for painters, sculptors and illuminators Fra Savonarola had set up in the cells off the cloister garden.

"You see, Michelangelo. Savonarola is not against art, only obscene art. Now is your chance to join us and become the sculptor for our order. You'll never want for marble or commissions."

"What will I sculpture?"

"What does it matter to you what you sculpture, as long as you are working?"

"Who will tell me what to carve?"

"Fra Savonarola."

"And if I don't want to carve what he wants?"

"As a monk you will not question. You will have no personal desires. . . ."

He went back to his workbench in the abandoned casino. Here at least he was free to draw from memory anatomical pictures of the things he had learned during his months of dissection. He burned the crowded, over-scrawled papers, yet it was hardly necessary since no one came to the garden any more except the fifteen-year-old Giuliano, who sometimes walked over, books under his arm, to study in companionable silence at Torrigiani's old worktable on the casino porch. They would walk back to the palace through the summer dusk that sifted downward like gray powder on the city, quenching the serene blue and golden-tan light of the building stones.

9

With the fall, Florence became embroiled in an international dispute that could lead to the city-state's destruction. It was all happening, Michelangelo gathered, because Charles VIII, King of France, had built the first permanent army since Caesar's legions, consisting of some twenty thousand trained and heavily armed men. He was now bringing that army across the Alps and into Italy to claim the Kingdom of Naples through inheritance. During Lorenzo's lifetime Charles VIII would have been too friendly to the Medici to threaten a march across Tuscany; if he had, Lorenzo's allies, the city-states of Milan, Venice, Genoa, Padua, Ferrara, would have closed ranks to keep him out. But Piero had lost these allies. The Duke of Milan had sent emissaries to Charles, inviting him to Italy. The Medici cousins, who had been at Versailles for his coronation, assured the king that Florence awaited his triumphal entry.

Because of the alliance of the Orsini, his mother's and wife's family, with Naples, Piero refused Charles safe passage. Yet during the months from spring to autumn he did nothing to assemble soldiers or arms to stop the French king if he did invade. The citizens of Florence who would have fought for Lorenzo were ready to welcome the French because they would help drive out Piero. Savonarola too invited Charles to enter Florence.

By the middle of September Charles VIII had brought his army across the Alps, been welcomed by the Duke of Milan, and sacked the town of Rapallo. The news threw Florence into a fever. All normal business was suspended, yet when Charles again sent his emissaries to ask for safe passage, Piero turned them away without a definite answer. The French king vowed to storm through Tuscany and conquer the city.

Michelangelo now had a new neighbor in the palace. Piero imported Alfonsina's brother, Paolo Orsini, to lead one hundred mercenaries . . . to stop Charles's army of twenty thousand. A dozen times Michelangelo vowed he would flee the palace, travel to Venice as Lorenzo had suggested. Loyal to Lorenzo, to Contessina, Giuliano, and even to Cardinal Giovanni, he had no feeling whatever for Piero, who had given him a home, a place to work and a salary. But he could not bring himself to join the deserters.

His three years under Lorenzo in the garden and palace had been years of excitement, growth, learning, mastery of his tools and trade, every day a precious jewel to be valued, cherished; every day like a year of maturing. And now, for the better part of these last two and a half years since Lorenzo's death, he had been stopped in his tracks. He was a better draftsman, yes, thanks to Prior Bichiellini and his months of dissection, but he felt less alive, less knowledgeable, less creative than he had in the flush of his training by Bertoldo, *Il Magnifico,* Pico, Poliziano, Landino, Ficino, Benivieni. For a long time he had been traversing the bottom half of a circle. How did he get into an upward swing again? How did he rise above the tumult, fears, paralysis of Florence, start his mind and hands working again as a sculptor?

How indeed, with even Poliziano going to Savonarola for absolution, begging in his last words to be taken into the Dominican Order so that he could be buried in a monk's habit inside the walls of San Marco?

Granacci would give him no council. Bugiardini said simply, "If you go to Venice, I go along." When Jacopo heard that Michelangelo was thinking of the journey he sought him out and cried:

"I always wanted to see Venice. On somebody else's florins. Take me along. I will protect you on the road from assassins. . . ."

"By telling them jokes?"

Jacopo screwed up his face, said, "Laughter is a lance. What do you say?"

"Agreed, Jacopo. When I leave for Venice, I'll take you with me."

On September 21, Fra Savonarola, in a final effort to drive Piero out, preached a climactic sermon in the Duomo. Florentines jammed the cathedral. Never before had the friar had such power, and never had his voice rung out with such a clap of doom. The hair of the Florentines stood on end as they cried and lamented while Savonarola portrayed the destruction of Florence and every living creature in it.

"Now the earth was corrupt in God's sight, and the earth was filled with violence. And God saw the earth, and behold, it was corrupt; for all flesh had corrupted their way upon the earth.

" 'For behold, I will bring a flood of waters upon the earth, to destroy all flesh in which is the breath of life from under heaven; everything that is on the earth shall die . . .' "

The friar's faintest whisper pierced the remotest corners of the vast cathedral. Each stone served as a rebounding wall. Michelangelo, standing just inside the doors, felt closed in on every side by a sea of sound, drowning him like rising waters. He returned to the street surrounded by a mass of people half dead with fright, speechless, their eyes glassy.

Only Prior Bichiellini was calm.

"But, Michelangelo, that is necromancy. From the darkest ages of man. God himself promised Noah and his sons, in Genesis 9:9–11, that there would never be a second Deluge: 'Here is a covenant I will observe with you and with your children after you. . . . Never more will the living creation be destroyed by the waters of a flood; never again a flood to devastate the world.' Now tell me, by what right does Savonarola rewrite the Bible? One day Florence is going to find out it has been made a fool of. . . ."

The prior's soft voice dispelled Savonarola's spell.

"At that time you can open the gates of Santo Spirito to him, to save him from the mob," suggested Michelangelo.

The prior smiled wryly.

"Can't you imagine Savonarola taking the vow of silence? He'd sooner burn at the stake."

The web closed tighter each day: Venice declared herself neutral, Rome declined to provide troops. Charles attacked the frontier fortresses of Tuscany, a few of them fell, Pietrasanta's marble quarrymen put up a good fight; but it could be only a few days before the French army entered Florence.

He had little opportunity for rational thought. Alternating hysterias of fear and relief swept the populace, with all of the city in the streets, summoned to the Piazza della Signoria by the ringing of the great bell in the tower, to hear the news. Was the city to be sacked? The Republic overthrown? Was the wealth, art, trade, security, prosperity to be gobbled up by an invading monarch with a powerful army, after Florence had lived at peace with the world for so long that it had no more army, weapons, no will to fight? Had the second Deluge begun?

One morning Michelangelo rose to find the palace abandoned. Piero, Orsini and their staffs had rushed out to treat with Charles. Alfonsina had left with her children and Giuliano for refuge in a hillside villa. Aside from a few old servants, Michelangelo seemed alone. The magnificent palace was frightening in its hollow silence. Lorenzo's body had died in Careggi, and now the great spirit of the man, represented by his magnificent library and art works, seemed to be dying as well. As he walked the echoing corridors and looked into the big empty rooms, something of the dread odor of death pervaded them. He ought to know, he who had become an expert in the Santo Spirito dead room.

Chaos continued. Piero prostrated himself before Charles, offered the conqueror the coast fortresses, Pisa and Leghorn and two hundred thousand florins if he "would continue down the coast and avoid Florence." Outraged at this humiliating capitulation, the City Council rang the bell on top of the Signoria, summoned the people, and castigated Piero for his "cowardice, foolishness, ineptitude, surrender."

A delegation, including Fra Savonarola, was sent to Charles. It ignored Piero. Piero dashed back to Florence to reassert his rights. The city was wild in its rage against him. He demanded to be heard. The crowd yelled, "Go away! Do not disturb the Signoria!" Piero turned away in contempt. The crowd in the piazza wagged their hoods in denunciation, small gangs of boys hissed and threw stones. Piero drew his sword. The crowds chased him through the streets. He disappeared into the palace and diverted the throngs momentarily by having the remaining servants bring out wine and cake.

Then couriers came down the street crying, "The Signoria has banished the Medici! For life! There is a price of four thousand florins on Piero's head. Down with Piero!"

Entering the palace, Michelangelo found that Piero had escaped through the rear garden, joined Orsini's band of mercenaries at the Porta San Gallo and fled. Cardinal Giovanni, his fat face red with perspiration from the armload of manuscripts he was carrying, behind him two of his house servants also loaded down with fine bindings, was cutting through the garden and out the rear gate to safety. His apprehensive face lit up when he saw Michelangelo.

"Buonarroti! I've saved some of Father's rarest manuscripts, the ones he loved best."

Florence was only a moment behind.

Into the courtyard surged the mob. Cries of "The Medici are banished!" were followed with "Everything in the palace is ours!" Rioters poured down into the wine cellars, broke open bins, and when they could not edge out the corks, smashed the bottles against the walls. Hundreds of bottles and demijohns passed from hand to hand and mouth to mouth, were drunk from blindly in long untasting gurgles, the wine spilling so freely it flooded the cellar. Now, brutally, this first contingent mounted the stairs, passing those pressing their way down, to sack the palace.

Michelangelo stood defensively before the Donatello David. The crowd still poured through the main gate, jamming the courtyard, individual faces that he had seen all his life on the streets and in the piazzas, quiet, good-natured people, suddenly inflamed, bent on destruction, with the faceless irresponsibility of the mob. What had caused the change? Was it the sense of being within the Medici palace for the first time as masters rather than outsiders?

He was knocked very hard against the David and a lump was raised on his head. The Donatello Judith and Holofernes standing nearby was picked up base and all, and with a roar of approval carried out through the rear garden. What was too big to move, Roman portraits and marble busts, was shattered with smashes of pikes and poles.

He edged along the wall, raced up the main staircase, ran at top speed down the corridor to the *studiolo,* slammed the door behind him, searched for the bolt. There was none. He looked about at the priceless manuscripts, cases of rare cameos, amulets, carved jewels, old coins, the Greek bas-reliefs above the door, the marble and bronze reliefs by Donatello, the painted wooden tables with Giotto's Deposition of Christ. Van Eyck's St. Jerome. What could be done to protect them?

His eyes fell upon the dumbwaiter. He opened the door, pulled on the ropes and, when the lift was level, began piling in the small paintings, enameled and mosaic tablets, cups of jasper, sardonyx and amethyst, a small statue of Plato, a crystal clock mounted on gilt silver, glass vases by Ghirlandaio, manuscripts, rings and brooches. The old toothless Faun that he had copied for his own first piece of sculpture he stuffed inside his shirt. Then he pulled the opposite rope, sent the box down a way and closed the door. A mass of humanity reached the *studiolo* at that moment and began looting the room like locusts. He fought his way to his own apartment, where he threw Bertoldo's models and a few of the bronzes under the beds.

It was the end of his usefulness. Hundreds of rioters were sweeping through the palace and into the great rooms, pilfering the family plate in the dining room, smashing the dishes and glassware, fighting and screaming with joy over the Medici collections of medals of gold and silver, taking from Piero's rooms his cups and trophies, throwing half-full bottles of wine at Pollaiuolo's Hercules and the Lion. In Lorenzo's room he watched helplessly as they grabbed up the four jasper vases with *Il Magnifico's* name inscribed, carried out the painted tables of Masaccio, Veneziano, cut paintings out of their frames, ripped sculptures off their bases, smashing the chairs and tables, what was too large to be moved, destroying chests. In the library, rare books and manuscripts had been pulled down from the shelves, the volumes trampled on.

Were these Florentines revenging themselves on Piero? But these magnificent collections were not Piero's. Watching the men brutally rip velvet hangings and slash silk upholsteries, he shook his head in despair. "Who can look into the mind of a mob?"

He recognized only one of the Medici faithful, his cousin Bernardo Rucellai, Nannina de' Medici's husband, standing before Botticelli's Pallas Subduing the Centaur in the anteroom adjoining a parlor. He was crying out:

"You are Florentine citizens! Why are you ravaging your own treasures? Stop, I implore you."

To Michelangelo he appeared a heroic figure, his eyes blazing and arms outstretched to protect the canvas. Then Rucellai was knocked down. Michelangelo struggled to the prostrate form, picked the man up in his arms and carried him, bleeding, into a small storage room next door. He thought, ironically:

"This is the most intimate contact I have had with my mother's side of the family."

The palace was a shambles. Then, in Lorenzo's office, after tearing the maps and tapestries from the walls, some burly porters succeeded in smashing open the safe. Out came a rain of twenty thousand florins which sent the mob into a final paroxysm of joy as they fought each other for the gold coins.

He made his way down the rear staircase and out through the garden, then through back alleys to the Ridolfi palace. He asked a groom for pen and ink, wrote Contessina a brief note: When it is safe . . . send someone to your father's studiolo. . . .I loaded the food lift as full as I could. He signed it M.B.

He made two stops on his way home: at Bugiardini's and Jacopo's, leaving word for them to meet him at the Porta San Gallo at midnight. When the city at last slept he slipped past the quiet houses to the Medici stables. Two of the grooms had stayed with the horses, keeping them quiet during the pandemonium around them. They knew that he had the right to take out horses whenever he desired. They helped him saddle up three. He rode one, led the other two.

There was no guard at the gate. Bugiardini was waiting, complacently standing in the dark cutting his long fingernails with a knife. Jacopo arrived shortly after. They started out for Venice.

10

By afternoon of the second day they had crossed the Apennines and dropped down out of the Futa Pass into Bologna, enclosed by orange brick walls, its turrets and almost two hundred towers, several of them leaning more crazily than the one at Pisa, puncturing the pellucid Emilian skies. They entered the city toward the river side, through the littered remains of a produce market which a bevy of old women in black were sweeping with brooms made of twigs tied to small branches. They asked one of the crones for a direction, and made for the Piazza Comunale.

The narrow tortuous streets, covered over by the protruding second floor of the houses, were suffocatingly airless. Each Bolognese family had built a tower for protection against its neighbors, a Florentine custom that had been abolished by Cosimo, who had obliged the Florentines to saw off their towers at roof height. The wider streets and the piazzas were lined with arches of orange brick to protect the people from snow, rain and the intense summer heat, so that the Bolognese could traverse his town from any direction and never be exposed.

They reached the main square with its majestic church of San Petronio at one end, and the Communal Palace covering an entire side; dismounted, and were promptly surrounded by Bolognese police.

"You are strangers in Bologna?"

"Florentines," Michelangelo replied.

"Your thumbs, if you please."

"Thumbs? What do you want with thumbs?"

"To see the mark of the red wax."

"We don't carry red wax."

"Then you will have to come with us. You are under arrest."

They were led to the customs office, a series of rooms buried behind porticoes, where the officer in charge explained that every stranger coming into Bologna had to register and be thumbprinted as he came through one of the city's sixteen gates.

"How could we know?" demanded Michelangelo. "We've never been here before."

"Ignorance of the law excuses no one. You are fined fifty Bolognese pounds."

"Fifty Bolognese . . . We don't have that much money."

"Too bad. Fifty days in jail."

Michelangelo stared with openmouthed speechlessness at Bugiardini and Jacopo. Before they could recover their wits a man stepped forward.

"May I speak with the young men, Officer?"

"Certainly, Excellency."

To Michelangelo the man said, "Is not your name Buonarroti?"

"It is."

"Is not your father an officer of the Florentine customs?"

"Yes, sir."

The Bolognese turned to the customs official.

"Our young man here comes of a fine Florentine family; his father has charge of a branch of their customs office, as you have. Do you not think our two sister cities might exchange hospitality with its important families?"

Flattered, the officer replied, "Assuredly, Excellency."

"I will guarantee their conduct."

Back in the brittle winter sun of the piazza, Michelangelo studied his benefactor. He had a broad pleasant face, without a vestige of strain. Though a touch of gray indicated that he might be in his mid-forties, he had the smooth skin, high coloring and beardless face of a younger man, with small, perfect white teeth and small mouth held almost prisoner between a strong nose and chin. His brows came only halfway across his eyes from the bridge of his nose, then pointed upward quizzically. He was wearing a soft black wool robe with a white ruffled collar.

"You are most kind, and I am stupid: you remembered my unmemorable face, while I, though I knew we had met . . . ?"

"We sat next to each other at one of Lorenzo de' Medici's dinners," explained the man.

"Of course! You are Signor Aldovrandi. You were *podestà* of Florence. You told me about the work of a great sculptor which is here in Bologna."

"Jacopo della Quercia. Now I will have an opportunity to show it to you. Won't you and your friends give me the pleasure of your company at supper?"

"The pleasure will be ours," grinned Jacopo. "We haven't delighted our stomachs since we lost sight of the Duomo."

"Then you have come to the right city," replied Aldovrandi. "Bologna is known as *La Grassa,* The Fat. Here we eat better than anywhere in Europe."

They left the piazza, walked to the north, with the church of San Pietro on their right, the connecting seminary on the left, then turned onto the Via Galliera. The Aldovrandi palace was number 8 on the left side of the street, a gracefully proportioned building of brick, three stories high. There was an ogive door framed by a colored terra-cotta frieze with the family coat of arms; the windows were arched and divided by marble columns.

Bugiardini and Jacopo arranged the care of the horses while Aldovrandi took Michelangelo to see his wood-paneled library, of which he was enormously proud.

"Lorenzo de' Medici helped me assemble the volumes."

He had a copy of Poliziano's *Stanze per la Giostra* inscribed by Poliziano. Michelangelo picked up the leather-bound manuscript.

"You know, Messer Aldovrandi, that Poliziano died a few weeks ago."

"I was heartbroken. For such a great mind not to exist any longer. And Pico too: on his deathbed. How bleak the world will be without them."

"Pico?" Michelangelo swallowed brine. "I did not know. But Pico is young. . . ."

"Thirty-one. When Lorenzo died it was the end of an era. Nothing will be the same again."

Michelangelo held the poem in his hand, began reading aloud, hearing the voices of the Plato Four instructing him. Aldovrandi said with respect:

"You read well, my young friend. Your diction is clear and you have a way of phrasing a line . . ."

"I had good teachers."

"You like to read aloud? I have all of the great poets: Dante, Petrarch, Pliny, Ovid."

"I had not thought I liked it."

"Tell me, Michelangelo, what brings you to Bologna?"

Aldovrandi already knew about Piero's fate, for the Medici party had passed through Bologna the day before. Michelangelo explained that he was on his way to Venice.

"How does it happen that you do not have fifty Bolognese pounds between the three of you if you are traveling so far?"

"Bugiardini and Jacopo haven't a soldo. I'm paying the expenses."

Aldovrandi smiled. "I too should like to travel the world if you will pay my costs."

"We hope to find work in Venice."

"Then why not remain in Bologna? There is Della Quercia to study from; we may even discover a sculpture commission for you."

Michelangelo's eyes gleamed.

"After supper I will speak to my two companions."

The brush with the Bolognese police had been enough to take the wanderlust out of Jacopo and Bugiardini. Neither were they interested in the sculpture of Della Quercia. They decided they would prefer to return to Florence. Michelangelo gave them the money for the journey and asked them to lead back his Medici horse. He then told Aldovrandi he would remain in Bologna and find lodgings.

"Unthinkable!" replied Aldovrandi. "No friend and protégé of Lorenzo de' Medici may live in a Bolognese inn. A Florentine trained by the Plato Four is a rare treat for us. You will be our guest."

He awakened to the orange Bolognese sun streaming into his room, lighting the tapestry behind him and the bright-colored boxed ceiling. In a painted coffer at the foot of the bed he found a linen towel, then washed himself in a silver bowl on a chest under the window, his naked feet warm on the Persian rug. He had been invited into a joyful house. He heard voices and laughter ringing through this wing of the palace which housed Aldovrandi's six sons. Signora Aldovrandi, an attractive young second wife who had contributed her quota of sons, was a pleasant woman who enjoyed all six of the boys equally, and welcomed Michelangelo as warmly as though he were a seventh son. His host, Gianfrancesco, belonged to the branch of the Aldovrandi which had split off from the ancient parental palace, applied itself to trade and money changing, and prospered so greatly that Gianfrancesco, graduated from the university as a notary, and an able banker in his younger years, was now free to spend his time in the arts. An enthusiast of poetry, he was also an able versifier in the vulgate. He had risen rapidly in the political life of the city-state: senator, *gonfaloniere* of justice, member of the ruling Sixteen Reformers of the Free State which governed Bologna, an intimate of the ruling Bentivoglio family.

"It is the one regret of my life that I cannot write in Greek and Latin," he told Michelangelo over a sweet bun and hot water flavored with spice as they sat at the end of the forty-place walnut dining table with its coat of arms inlaid in the center. "I read them, of course, but in my youth I spent too much time changing money instead of meters."

He was an avid collector. He escorted Michelangelo through the palace to show him painted diptychs, carved wooden tablets, silver and gold bowls, coins, terracotta heads, ivories, bronzes and small carved marbles.

"But no important local art, as you can see," he explained ruefully. "It is a mystery to me: why Florence and not Bologna? We are as rich a city as you, our people are as vigorous and courageous. We have a fine history in music, scholarship; but we have never been able to create great painting or sculpture. Why?"

"With all respect, why are you called 'Bologna, the Fat'?"

"Because we are gourmets, and have been famous since Petrarch's time for the pleasures of the flesh. We are a self-avowed carnal city."

"Could that be the answer?"

"That when all wants are satisfied there is no need for art? Yet Florence is rich, it lives well . . ."

"The Medici, the Strozzi, a few families. Tuscans are lean by nature. And frugal. We don't derive pleasure from spending. I don't ever remember another family eating in our house; or our family eating with friends. I don't remember the Buonarroti giving or receiving a gift. We like to earn money, but not to spend it."

"And we Bolognese think money is made only to be spent. Our whole genius has gone into the refinement of our pleasures. Did you know that we have created an *amore bolognese?* That our women will not wear Italian patterns, but only French? That they must use several different materials in a single dress? That our sausages are so special, we guard the recipe as though it were a state secret?"

At the midday dinner there was the full component of forty at the table: Aldovrandi's brothers and nephews, professors from the University of Bologna, reigning families from Ferrara and Ravenna passing through, princes of the Church, members of Bologna's ruling Sixteen. Aldovrandi was a charming host but, unlike Lorenzo, he made no effort to hold his guests together, to transact business or accomplish any purpose other than enjoyment of the superb fishes, sausages, meats, wines, storytelling and camaraderie.

After the *riposo* Aldovrandi invited Michelangelo for a tour of the city.

They walked under the arches where the shops displayed the most delicious foods of Italy: exquisite cheeses, the whitest of breads, rarest of wines, the rows of butcher shops in the Borgo Galliera displaying more meat than Michelangelo had seen in a year in Florence; then the Old Fish Market, with the sweet produce of the marshy valleys around Ferrara: sturgeon, crawfish, mullet. The hundreds of game sheds were selling the fruit of yesterday's hunt: roe deer, quail, hare, pheasant; and in every block of the city their world-famous *salame*. Everywhere Michelangelo passed students from the university, who did their studying at the little cafés under the orange-colored porticoes, playing dice and cards between pages of their assignments.

"There is one thing I miss, Messer Aldovrandi. I have seen no stone sculpture."

"Because we have no stone quarries. A simple equation, eh? But we have always brought in the best marble carvers who would come: Nicola Pisano, Andrea from Fiesole near you, Della Quercia from Siena, Dell'Arca from Bari. Our own sculpture is of terra cotta."

It was not until they reached Santa Maria della Vita, where Aldovrandi showed him Dell'Arca's Lamentation over the Dead Christ, that Michelangelo found himself excited. This large terra-cotta group was melodramatic and profoundly disquieting, for Dell'Arca had caught his people in fully expressed agony and lamentation.

A few moments later they came upon a young man making terra-cotta busts to be placed above the capitals of the Palazzo Amorini in the Via Santo Stefano. He was powerfully built, with enormous shoulders and biceps, but with an egg-shaped head that was narrower at the top than at its base; his skin was burnt the precise orange of Bologna's brick. Aldovrandi called him Vincenzo.

"This is my friend Buonarroti," he said, "the best young sculptor in Florence."

"Ah, then it is proper that we meet," replied Vincenzo, "for I am Bologna's best young sculptor. I am Dell'Arca's successor. I am to finish the great Pisano tomb in San Domenico."

"You have received the commission?" asked Aldovrandi sharply.

"Not yet, Excellency, but it must come to me. After all, I am Bolognese. I am sculptor. What could be more natural?" He turned to Michelangelo. "If you need help in Bologna, I show you everything."

As they walked on Aldovrandi said:

"Successor to Dell'Arca indeed! He is the successor to his grandfather and father, who are the finest brickmakers in Bologna. Let him stick to his trade."

They made their way to the church of San Domenico, built in 1218 by the Dominican brothers. The interior had three naves, more ornate than most Florentine churches, with a sarcophagus of St. Dominic by Nicola Pisano to which Aldovrandi led him. He pointed out the marble carvings that had been done in 1267, and then the work that had been continued by Niccolò dell'Arca.

"Dell'Arca died eight months ago. There are three figures left to be sculptured: an angel here on the right, St. Petronius holding the model of the city of Bologna; and a St. Proculus. These are the marbles that Vincenzo said he was going to carve."

Michelangelo looked hard at Aldovrandi. The man added nothing more, merely led him out of the church and to the Piazza Maggiore to see the work of Jacopo della Quercia over the main portal of San Petronio. He held back, letting Michelangelo go forward alone.

Michelangelo stood transfixed, gasping in astonishment and delight. Aldovrandi came forward.

"Did you know that Della Quercia competed for the bronze doors of the Baptistery in Florence? Back in 1400? Ghiberti beat him out. These five scenes on either side of the lateral supports, and the five above, are his answer to the rejection. Here in Bologna we think they are as good as Ghiberti's."

Michelangelo stood before the stone panels shaking his head in disbelief. This could be the single greatest sculpture he had ever laid eyes on.

"Perhaps as good, perhaps better, certainly different," he replied. "Della Quercia was as much an innovator as Ghiberti. Look at how alive he makes his human figures, how they pulsate with inner vitality." Raising and lowering his arms, he indicated first one then another of the panels, exclaiming, "That carving of God. Of Adam and Eve. Of Cain and Abel. Of Noah drunk. Of the Expulsion from the Garden. See the strength and depth in the design. I'm stunned."

He turned to his friend, added hoarsely,

"Signor Aldovrandi, this is the kind of human figure I've dreamed of carving."

<h1 style="text-align:center">11</h1>

He found another excitement in Bologna, one he had not dreamed of.

He went everywhere with Aldovrandi: to the palaces of the brothers for family dinner, to friends' for intimate suppers. The Bolognese were a naturally hospitable people who loved to entertain. It was at a supper given by Marco Aldovrandi, his host's nephew, that he met Clarissa Saffi, in Marco's villa in the hills where she was serving as his hostess. There were no other women present, just Marco's men friends.

She was slender, golden-haired, the hair plucked back from the natural hairline of the brow in the fashion of the day. A lithe, willowy figure that moved with a delicate sensuousness; every slight rhythm of the arm and shoulder and leg as smooth as music, and as pleasurable. She appeared to be one of those rare creatures whose every breath was made for love. Sketching her figure in his mind, he found a wholeness here, an undulant softness of manner, voice, gesture, motion.

From the beauty of neck and shoulder and bosom he thought of Botticelli's passion for the perfect female nude: not to love, but to paint. Clarissa had much of the golden loveliness of Simonetta, without the sad innocence Botticelli had given her.

She was unlike any woman he had ever seen. He was aware of her not merely through his eyes but through every pore and part of his body. Her very presence in Marco's drawing room, before she moved or said a word, sent the blood pounding through his veins, shot his back and shoulders involuntarily upward, thrust his pelvic structure forward alive with new life. Jacopo would have cried as she passed the Duomo steps, "How mattressable!" but Clarissa, he perceived, was more than that. She was love in its ultimate female form.

Clarissa's welcoming smile for him was embracing; she liked all men, had a natural affinity for them. Her movements had a captivating grace that was a delight to his senses. The long braids of burnished golden hair seemed to have the hot Italian sun on them, even in this cool room, and warmed him as thoroughly. Though an inner drum was pounding in his ears, he heard the soft, sibilant music of her voice that shocked him to intense awareness.

She had been Marco's mistress for three years, since he had stumbled across her cleaning her father's cobbler shop. The first to recognize her beauty, he had set her up in a secluded villa, taught her how to wear rich gowns and jewels, had brought in a tutor to teach her to read and write.

After supper, while the old friends were involved in a discussion of politics, Michelangelo and Clarissa found themselves alone in a little French music room. In spite of his protestations that he had no interest in the female form, that he found no excitement worthy of sculpturing, he could not tear his eyes away from Clarissa's bodice, clothed in a net of fine woven gold which accomplished the harrowing miracle of seeming to expose her breasts while at the same time keeping them under cover. The harder he looked, the less he could actually see: for he was confronted by a masterpiece of the dressmaker's art, designed to excite and intrigue, yet reveal nothing beyond a suspicion of white doves nestling.

Clarissa was amused at his gaucherie.

"You are an artist, Buonarroti?"

It was an effort to meet her gaze, for her eyes too were soft and rounded, now concealing, now revealing their intimacies.

"I am a sculptor."

"Could you carve me in marble?"

"You're already carved," he blurted out. "Flawlessly!"

A touch of color rode the high cheekbones of her slender, creamy cheeks.

They laughed together, leaning a little toward each other. Marco had trained her well, and she spoke with a good inflection. Michelangelo was also aware of a quick and intuitive perception.

"Will I see you again?" he asked.

"If Signor Aldovrandi brings you."

"Not otherwise?"

Her lips parted in a smile.

"Is it that you wish me to pose for you?"

IRVING STONE

"No. Yes. I don't know. I don't even know what I am saying, let alone what I mean."

She laughed heartily. Her movements tightened the net over her bosom, and once again he found himself watching the lovely forms take discernible shape beneath the gold bodice. To himself he said:

"This is *pazzesco*, crazy! What has happened to me?"

It was his friend Aldovrandi who saw the naked longing in his eyes. He slapped him smartly on the shoulder and cried:

"Well, Michelangelo, you have too much sense to get involved in our local political talk. We will have some music now. You knew that we are one of the great music centers of Europe?"

On the way home, as they rode their horses side by side down the sleeping orange streets, Aldovrandi asked:

"You were taken with Clarissa?"

Michelangelo saw that he could be honest, replied, "She makes my flesh crawl; I mean the flesh inside my flesh."

"Our Bolognese beauties can do that. To cool you down a trifle, can you guess how expensive she is?"

"I see that her gowns and jewels are costly."

"Only the beginning: she also has an exquisite box of a palace, with servants, a stable of carriages . . ."

"Enough!" cried Michelangelo, with a wry grin. "But I have never seen a woman like her. If ever I was to carve a·Venus . . ."

"Don't! My nephew has the quickest temper and rapier in Bologna."

That night he writhed in fever. When he found himself turning and twisting in an effort to bury his face between her breasts he realized what had happened to him, but he was as incapable of stopping the burrowing in the soft warm pillows as he had been of stopping his search for them under the gold net.

The next day he passed her in the Via Drapperie, the street of cloths and drapes, accompanied by an older woman. She was wearing a wreath of flowers through her hair and moved through the street with the same effortless magic under her silken gown with its gold belt encrusted with precious stones, woolen cape over her shoulders. She bowed, smiled slightly, and walked on, leaving him standing there rooted to the brick pavement.

That night, when again he could not sleep, he went down to Aldovrandi's library, lit a lamp, took up his host's pen, and after many false starts, wrote:

The Garland and the Girdle

What joy hath yon glad wreath of flowers that is
Around her golden hair so deftly twined,
Each blossom pressing forward from behind,
As though to be the first her brows to kiss!

The livelong day her dress hath perfect bliss,
That now reveals her breast, now seems to bind:
And that fair woven net of gold refined
Rests on her cheek and throat in happiness!

Yet still more blissful seems to me the band,
Gilt at the tips, so sweetly doth it ring,
And clasp the bosom that it serves to lace:

Yea, and the belt, to such as understand,
Bound round her waist, saith: Here I'd ever cling!
What would my arms do in that girdle's place?

He suspected that this was not exactly the kind of sonnet for which Benivieni had spent the hours training him. Yet the writing had, in Aldovrandi's expression, "cooled him down." He returned to his bedroom and slept.

A few Sundays later Aldovrandi invited him for the evening to Clarissa's villa, where a group of Marco's intimates were gathering for their favorite game, *tarocchino di Bologna*, played with sixty oversized cards. Michelangelo knew nothing of such games, nor had he any money with which to gamble. After Clarissa had seen to it that Marco's friends were supplied with food and drink, she sat with Michelangelo before a crackling log fire in a side parlor with a handsome terra-cotta frieze. He watched her face in the firelight, the features so fragile, yet with such implicit passion.

'It's pleasant to have someone my own age to talk to," Clarissa confided. "All of Marco's friends are older."

"You do not have young friends?"

"Not any more. But I am happy. Is it not odd, Buonarroti, that a girl can grow up in utter poverty yet fit so naturally into all this elegance?"

"I don't know, Madonna, you are out of my quarter."

"Just what is your quarter? Beside sculpture, that is."

"Poetry." He tendered her a wan smile. "You cost me two nights' sleep before I could get the sonnet down on paper."

"You wrote a sonnet to me?" She was amazed. "It is the first. Could I hear it?"

He flushed.

"I think not. But I will bring a copy sometime. You can read it in privacy."

"Why are you embarrassed? It is good to be desired. I accept it as a compliment."

He cast his eyes down. How could he confess that he was as new at this game as he would have been at *tarocchino?* How could he acknowledge the fire burning in his loins?

He looked up suddenly, found her eyes on him. She had read his feelings. She put her hand in his, studied his bashed-in face. These minutes of perception changed the relationship.

"What fell on your nose, Michelangelo?"

"A ham."

"From a butcher's rack? Did you forget to duck?"

"The way the people on Vesuvius forgot to run from the lava: it had covered them before they knew it was coming."

"Have you ever been in love?"

". . . in a way."

"It's always 'in a way.' "

"Is love never whole?"

"Not that I know of. It's political, like the marriage of Violante Bentivoglio to Pandolfo Malatesta in Rimini, in which your friend Aldovrandi headed the wedding party; or to get the children born and scrubbing done, as with the *contadini;* or for the pleasure of pearls and palace . . . as with myself. . . ."

"Also what we feel for each other?"

Her body stirred in its gown, causing a sibilance of the silk. Her fashionably shod foot rested lightly against his calf. His insides somersaulted.

"We are young people together. Why should we not want each other?"

Again he thrashed the night through, his feverish body no longer content to nestle its face between her breasts; now he was pulsating to enter whole. He kept hearing her words over and over again in the darkness of his room while he throbbed with an unbearable urgency.

"Why should we not want each other?"

He rose, went down to Aldovrandi's library, began writing scraps, phrases, lines, as they came tumbling into his head:

> Kind to the world, but to itself unkind,
> A worm is born, that, dying noiselessly,
> Despoils itself to clothe fair limbs, and be
> In its true worth by death alone divined.
>
> Oh, would that I might die, for her to find
> Raiment in my outworn mortality!
> That, changing like the snake, I might be free
> To cast the slough wherein I dwell confined!
>
> Nay, were it mine, that shaggy fleece that stays,
> Woven and wrought into a vestment fair,
> Around her beauteous bosom in such bliss!
>
> All through the day she'd clasp me; would I were
> The shoes that bear her burden! When the ways
> Were wet with rain, her feet I then should kiss!

It was during the Christmas festivities, with the symbolic "good wish" log burning in the drawing-room fireplace, and the poor children of the town singing carols outside for their gifts, with Signora Aldovrandi presiding over the annual appearance of the servants for the game of "fortune extracting" from a sack, that Michelangelo was rescued from his turmoil.

When the servants had drunk their toasts and departed, and the Aldovrandi family, some thirty strong, had "extracted" their gifts, Aldovrandi turned to Michelangelo: "Now you must try your fortune."

He put his hand into the hemp bag. There was one package left. From the broad smiles all about him it was apparent that everyone was in on the joke. He pulled, and out came a terra-cotta replica of the Dell'Arca San Domenico tomb. In the three empty places, where the angel, St. Petronius and St. Proculus were missing, were oversized caricatures of himself, broken nose and all.

"I . . . I have the commission?"

Aldovrandi smiled at him happily. "The Council awarded it to you last week."

When the guests had departed Aldovrandi and Michelangelo went into the library. Aldovrandi explained that he would send to Carrara for the marble when the drawings were ready and the dimensions established. Michelangelo was sure that his host had not only secured him this commission, which would pay him thirty gold ducats, but would be paying for the marble as well, and the haul over the Apennines by oxcart. His heart was too full to know how to thank him. Impulsively he opened a copy of Dante, leafed through. He picked up a pen and at the top of the page, in the margin and below, quickly sketched scenes from Florence: the Duomo and Baptistery, the Palazzo della Signoria and the Ponte Vecchio over the Arno, stone Florence lying in the womb of its walls.

"By your leave, each day I shall illustrate another page of Dante."

Aldovrandi stood over him, studying the rough-hatched pen sketches, his eyes shining.

He went with Aldovrandi to Dell'Arca's workshop at the rear of San Petronio, part of an enclosed courtyard admitting to the vestment room of the church, partly covered by a portico, with workstalls for the maintenance crew similar to those in the Duomo, though smaller than the one in which he had worked his Hercules. The shop had been left untouched since Dell'Arca's sudden death some ten months before. On his workbench were his chisels, hammers, dried wax and clay improvisations, miniatures, folios of sketches for the remaining figures of the tomb, stubs of charcoal: a portrait of a man interrupted in the midst of life and work.

It was cold in the raw January manner of Emilia, but two capacious braziers kept the open-faced shed warm. After two months of copying in the churches of Bologna, and drawing from the Della Quercias, he was desperately eager to get back to work: to the early modeling in clay, the firing of the forge and making of tools, the setting up of the marble on its wooden blocks and the first fastidious knocking off of the corners to begin searching for the figures in the round. It was half a year since he had finished the Hercules.

He had been working only a few days, crouched over his drawing table, heavy wool hat covering his head and ears, when a massive shape loomed before him. He looked up, saw that it was Vincenzo, the terra-cotta sculptor. His face was a raw umber from the cold, his eyes were intense.

"Buonarroti, you got the work I been after."

Michelangelo remained silent for a moment, then murmured: "I'm sorry."

"No, you're not. You're a stranger. I'm Bolognese. You take bread out of the mouths of us native sculptors."

Placatingly, Michelangelo replied, "I understand. I lost some carving at Santo Spirito last year to silver workers."

"It's good you understand. Go to the Council, tell them you decide against it. Then the commission comes to me."

"But, Vincenzo, if it hasn't come to you since Dell'Arca died . . .?"

Vincenzo brushed this aside with a sweep of his powerful brickmaker's arms.

"You stole the commission with Aldovrandi influence. No one even knows you sculpt."

Michelangelo sympathized with the big fellow standing before him, sick with frustration.

"I'll speak to Messer Aldovrandi."

"You better. Or I make you sorry you came to Bologna."

When Michelangelo told Aldovrandi of the encounter, he replied:

"It is true he is Bolognese. He watched Dell'Arca work. He knows what our people like. He has only one shortcoming: he can't carve marble. He should be making our fine Bolognese brick if he wishes to immortalize himself."

"Shall I offer him a job as my assistant?"

"Do you need one?"

"I'm being a diplomat."

"Be a sculptor instead. Forget him."

"I'll never let you forget me," said Vincenzo the following day when Michelangelo reported that there was nothing he could do to help him..

Michelangelo looked at the enormous bony hands of Vincenzo, twice the size of his own. Vincenzo was his own age, about nineteen, but probably weighed twice as much as his own one hundred and twenty pounds, and loomed a head taller than his own five feet four inches. He thought of Torrigiani, could see Torrigiani's powerful fist coming through the air, hitting him, could taste the blood and feel the crushed bone. He became a little faint.

"What's the matter, Buonarroti? You don't look good. Afraid I make life miserable for you?"

"You already have."

But no more miserable than he would be to have to relinquish the opportunity to carve three beautiful blocks of white Carrara marble. If this were the price . . .

12

He did not write to his family, nor did he receive letters from home, but once a week business associates of Aldovrandi made the trip over the Futa Pass to

Florence. They took news of Michelangelo to the Buonarroti, and brought it back in turn.

A week after Michelangelo had fled, Charles VIII had entered the city with his lance leveled to indicate that he was a conqueror, though no shots had been fired. He was welcomed through streets draped with tapestries and awnings and oil lamps. The Ponte Vecchio had been festively decorated; he was graciously received by the Signoria for prayers in the Duomo. He was given the Medici palace as his headquarters. But when it came to the peace treaty, Charles had acted haughtily, threatened to recall Piero, demanded an emperor's ransom. Fighting had broken out in the streets, French soldiers and Florentines had attacked each other, the Florentines had shut down their city and prepared to evict the French. Charles grew more reasonable, settled for a hundred and twenty thousand florins, the right to maintain two fortresses in Florence until his war with Naples was over, and took his army out of Florence. The city was proud of having faced up to the leader of twenty thousand armed soldiers, of having replied, when he threatened, "We shall sound our trumpets!" with "And we will ring our bells!"

Yet the wheels of the city-state had creaked to a painful halt. Ruled for so long by the Medici, the governmental structure did not work without an executive. Former councilors had been Medici adherents who had developed a *modus vivendi* for working together. Now the city was torn by factions. One group wished to install the Venetian form of government; another wanted one Council of the People to pass the laws and elect magistrates, a second Council, smaller, of experienced men to establish domestic and international policy. Guidantonio Vespucci, spokesman for the wealthy nobles, called these measures dangerously democratic, fought to keep all power in a few hands.

By mid-December news reached Bologna that Savonarola had stepped into the crisis with a series of Haggai sermons in which he backed the proposed democratic structure. Visitors to the Aldovrandi palace outlined the priest's concept of elected councils: only real property was to be taxed; every Florentine was to have a vote; all over twenty-nine years of age, who had paid their taxes, were to be eligible to the Grand Council. By the end of the sermons, Vespucci and his nobles had been defeated, Savonarola's plan had been adopted. From Bologna it appeared that Savonarola had become political as well as religious leader of Florence. His victory over *Il Magnifico* was complete.

With the coming of the New Year, Piero de' Medici returned to Bologna to set up headquarters. Coming home from his workshop, Michelangelo found a group of Piero's professional soldiers in the street before the Aldovrandi palace. Piero was inside with Giuliano. Though Charles, when he made the peace with Florence, had insisted that the price on Piero's head and on Giuliano's be revoked, all Medici estates had been confiscated, and Piero himself banished to two hundred miles from the Tuscan border.

When they met at the entrance to the dining room, Michelangelo exclaimed, "Excellency, how good to see you again. Though I could wish it were at the Medici palace."

"We'll be back there soon enough," growled Piero. "The Signoria drove me out by force. I am assembling an army and shall drive them out by force."

Giuliano, now grown as tall as Michelangelo, had bowed formally to Michelangelo, but when Piero took Signora Aldovrandi in to dinner, the two young men hugged each other.

There was little pleasure at the usually gay Aldovrandi table, for Piero immediately outlined his plan for the reconquest of Florence. All he required was sufficient money, hired mercenaries, weapons, horses. Piero expected Aldovrandi to contribute two thousand florins to his campaign.

"Excellency, are you sure this is the best way?" asked Aldovrandi respectfully. "When your great-grandfather Cosimo was exiled he waited until the city found it needed him and called him back. Wait for that hour, Excellency."

"I am not as forgiving as my grandfather. Florence wants me back right now. It is just Savonarola and my cousins who have schemed against me."

He turned to Michelangelo.

"You shall enter my army as an engineer, help design the wall fortifications after we have conquered the city."

Michelangelo sat with his head bowed. "Would you wage war on Florence, Excellency?" he murmured after a moment.

"I would, and I shall. As soon as I have a force strong enough to batter down the walls."

"But if the city were bombarded it could be destroyed . . ."

"What then? Florence is a pile of stones. If we knock them down, we will put them together again."

"But the art . . ."

"What is art? We can replace all the paint and marble in a year. And it will be a Florence that I will command!"

No one touched a bite of food. Aldovrandi turned to Piero.

"In the name of my friend, *Il Magnifico,* I must decline. The money you ask for is yours, but not for purposes of war. Lorenzo would have been the first to stop you, were he alive."

Piero turned to Michelangelo.

"And you, Buonarroti?"

"I too, Excellency, must decline. I will serve you in any way you ask, but not to wage war against Florence."

Piero pushed his chair back, rose to his feet.

"The kind of people I inherited from my father! Poliziano and Pico, who preferred dying to fighting. You, Aldovrandi, who were my father's *podestà* of Florence. And you, Michelangelo, who have lived under our roof for four years. What kind of men are you that you will not fight back?"

He swept out of the room. Michelangelo said with tears in his eyes: "Forgive me, Giuliano."

Giuliano had also risen, turned to leave the room.

"I too shall refuse to wage war. That would only make Florence hate us the more. *A rivederci,* Michelangelo, I shall write Contessina that I have seen you."

He was still skittish about angels. He remembered the first one he had done for the Ghirlandaio fresco, using the son of the carpenter downstairs of the Buonarroti house. The other apprentices had called him a fraud because he had cheated on the halo, making it fade into the background. What was an angel: male or female, human or divine? Prior Bichiellini had once called it "a spiritual being attendant on God."

His embarrassment as he drew hundreds of angels was the more acute after his months of dissection. Now that he knew the tissue and function of human anatomy he could hardly refrain from using that knowledge. But did an angel have a twenty-five-foot snake of bowel? He must also carve his angel fully clothed to match the one on the other end of the Ark. With the angel and the two saints he was right back where Ghirlandaio had told him he would stay all his life: able to portray hands, feet, perhaps a little of the neck and throat. For the rest, all his hard-earned knowledge would be hidden under flowing robes.

For his "spiritual being attendant on God," he chose a *contadino* boy, in from the farm with his family to attend church, looking a little like Bugiardini, with a wide, fleshy face but the features cut square in the Greek tradition. He had well-developed arms and shoulders, built by guiding a plow behind oxen. This powerful young male held high a candelabrum that would have required a giant to lift. Instead of compensating with delicate, diaphanous wings, as he knew he ought, he rubbed salt into the wound of his own befuddlement by designing the two wings of an eagle, about to take off, coming all the way down the boy's back. These he carved out of wood to attach to his clay model, wings so heavy they would have floored the delicate Dell'Arca angel on the opposite side.

He invited Aldovrandi to visit the workshed. Aldovrandi was not at all upset by the vigor of the model.

"We Bolognese are not spiritual beings. Carve a lusty angel."

And so he did, setting up the thickest of Aldovrandi's three Carrara blocks. He felt complete again with the hammer and chisel in his hands, the dry caking marble dust in his nostrils, the white chips and powder covering his hair and clothes. When he worked stone he was a man of substance. Now he did not need the braziers, for he created his own warmth, moving the workbench out into the open courtyard when there was any winter sun, to feel the space around him.

In the evenings, after he had read aloud to Aldovrandi and illustrated a page of Dante, he would do his exploratory drawing for the St. Petronius, patron saint of Bologna, convert to Christianity from a noble Roman family, and builder of San Petronio. He used as his models the older guests in the Aldovrandi palace: members of the Sixteen, professors from the university, justices, sketching their faces and figures in his mind while he sat with them at table, then retiring to his room to hammer down on paper the lines, forms, interrelation of feature and expression that makes every human being different from another.

There was little he could do with St. Petronius that could be original. The Dominicans of San Domenico and the Bolognese government officials were set on what they wanted: St. Petronius must be no less than sixty. He must be fully gowned in luxuriant robes, an archbishop's crown on his head. He must hold in his arms a model of the city of Bologna with its towers and palaces piled high above its protecting walls.

He acquired a neighbor in the stall opposite. It was Vincenzo, whose father had secured a contract for making new brick and tile for a cathedral repair job. A crew of mechanics came in to fill the stalls for the repairs, and the enclosed courtyard rang with the noise of materials being unloaded. Vincenzo afforded the workyard running entertainment by taunting Michelangelo throughout the workday.

"Our brick lasts for a thousand years. It's harder than your Florentine stone."

"It's true you make durable brick, Vincenzo."

"Don't patronize me," said Vincenzo. "You Florentines think you are the only artists in Italy."

Michelangelo blushed. Vincenzo cried to the workmen, "Look at his face. I caught him out."

When Vincenzo arrived with a wagonload of fresh tiles, he badgered Michelangelo with: "I made a hundred durable stones yesterday. What did you make? Charcoal scratches on a paper?" Encouraged by the laughter of his townsmen, the brickmaker continued, "That makes you a sculptor? Why don't you go home and leave Bologna to its natives?"

"I intend to, when I have finished my three pieces."

"Nothing can hurt my brick. Think how easy it's going to be for an accident to happen to one of your statues."

The workmen stopped in their tasks. Silence filled the yard. Vincenzo, who made words much as he did brick, with shaping movements of his hands, continued with a crafty smile:

"Somebody brushes too close to the Ark. Smasho! Your angel is in a dozen pieces."

Michelangelo felt anger rise in his throat.

"You wouldn't dare!"

"No, no, Buonarroti, not I. I am too graceful. But someone clumsy might stumble."

The laughter of the workmen as they picked up their tools made him a little ill: the forces of destruction always one short step behind creation! He suffered through the days and weeks.

St. Petronius emerged with a sad and deeply furrowed face; but there was inherent power in the body. The set of the head on the shoulders, the gripping strength of the feet in the thin-soled sandals, the puissant stance of the knees, hips, shoulders under the rich robe, the arms in which he firmly held Bologna, this vigor he could convey. As a craftsman he knew he had done a good job. It was as a creative artist that he felt he had contributed little.

"It is very fine," said Aldovrandi when he saw the polished piece. "Dell'Arca could not have surpassed it."

"But I am determined to give you something more," said Michelangelo doggedly. "I must not leave Bologna without carving something exciting and original."

"Very well, you disciplined yourself to give us the St. Petronius we wanted. I will discipline Bologna to accept the St. Proculus that you want."

Bologna the Fat became Bologna the Lean for him. He did not return home for the big midday dinner. When an Aldovrandi groom brought him hot food he let it grow cold if it was not a moment when he wanted to stop. Now that spring was approaching he was able to work longer each day, and frequently did not reach the Aldovrandi palace until after dark, dirty, sweaty, charcoal- or chip-covered, ready to fall into bed of exhaustion. But the Aldovrandi servants brought him a big wooden tub filled with hot water, and laid out his clean clothes. He knew he was expected to join his patron in the library for a few hours of companionable talk.

Clarissa he saw rarely, since he was attending few parties. But when he did see her the delight and the torment racked him for nights, obliterating his sleep and permeating his mind for days while he tried to create the figure of St. Proculus, and drew instead Clarissa nude under her silks.

He preferred not to see her. It was too painful.

On the first of May, Aldovrandi told him he might not work. This was the happiest day in the year for Bologna, when the Countess of Love reigned, people gathered wild flowers in the country for their relatives and friends, romantic young courtiers planted leafy trees with colored silk ribbons under the windows of their beloved while their friends serenaded her.

Michelangelo accompanied the Aldovrandi outside the main gate of town where a platform had been erected, covered with damask and festoons of flowers. Here the Countess of Love was crowned, with all Bologna gathered to pay homage.

Michelangelo too wanted to pay homage to love, or whatever it was that had been started boiling in his blood by the intoxicating air of the wild spring morning, the fragrance of the thousands of blossoms, the perfumes of the Bolognese women, beautiful on this ritual day, gowned in silks and jewels.

But he did not see Clarissa. He saw Marco in the midst of his family with two young maidens, apparently the family choices for marriage, hanging on either arm. He saw the older woman who had accompanied her on her shopping trips to the city, saw her maid and several other of the servants picnicking in the fields beyond the platform where the ceremonies took place. But no Clarissa. Search as he might.

And then he found he was no longer before the May platform, or in the celebrating Bolognese crowds. His feet were carrying him swiftly up the road to Clarissa's villa. He did not know what he would do when he got there. What he would say, how he would explain when someone opened the gate to him. Trembling all over, he half walked, half ran up the foothill road.

The front gate was unbolted. He went to the front door, pushed on the clapper, knocked again and again. Just as he was beginning to think that no one was at home, and that he had acted stupidly, the door was opened a crack. There stood

Clarissa, in a peignoir, her golden hair hanging loosely down her back, almost to her knees, without cosmetics or jewels, smelling aseptically of soap; and her face, to Michelangelo, more beautiful, her whole body more desirable because it was unornamented.

He stepped inside the door. There was no sound in the house. She threw the bolt. Then they were in a passionate embrace, their bodies merging, knee and crotch, breasts and chest, their mouths moist and sweet and glued and drinking deep, their arms with all the power of an unquenchable life force crushing each to the other in a total pulsating time- and place- and sense-annihilating embrace.

She led him to her bedroom. She had nothing on beneath the robe. The slender body, the red pointed breasts, the golden Mount of Venus were as his draftsman's eye had known them all along: a female beauty, made for love.

It was like penetrating deep into white marble with the pounding live thrust of his chisel beating upward through the warm living marble with one "Go!", his whole body behind the heavy hammer, penetrating through ever deeper and deeper furrows of soft yielding living substance until he had reached the explosive climax, and all of his fluid strength, love, passion, desire had been poured into the nascent form, and the marble block, made to love the hand of the true sculptor, had responded, giving of its inner heat and substance and fluid form, until at last the sculptor and the marble had totally coalesced, so deeply penetrating and infusing each other that they had become one, marble and man an organic unity, each fulfilling the other in the greatest act of art and of love known to the human species.

After May Day he completed the drawing of his virile St. Proculus, who had been martyred before the gates of Bologna in 303, while in the full flower of his youth and strength. He clothed him in a belted tunic which did nothing to conceal the vigorous torso and hips and bare legs. It was anatomically true and convincing. As he made his clay model his experience with the Hercules bore fruit, for he was able to achieve the corded, driving thighs, the bulging stamina-packed calves: truly the torso and legs of a heroic warrior and deliverer, powerful, indestructible.

Then, quite unabashedly, he modeled his own portrait from a mirror of his bedroom: the punched-in bridge of the nose, the flat spread of the cheekbones and wide spread of the eyes, the thatch of hair worn halfway down his forehead, the steadfast gaze, resolved to triumph: against the enemies of Bologna? The enemies of art? Of life? Was it not all the same?

Carving in marble, feeling the blow of his chisel, Vincenzo was blotted out, the orange-earth figure and the heavy sound of his voice. With his eyes slitted against the flying chips, with the emergence of form from the block, he again felt himself to be fifteen feet tall. Vincenzo began to shrink in size, then fade; until finally he stopped coming to the courtyard.

When the early afternoon sun made it too hot to work in the enclosed courtyard, he took crayon and paper to the front of the church, sat on the cool stone before Della Quercia's carvings and each day refreshed himself by copying a different figure: God, Noah, Adam, Eve, trying to capture some part of Della Quercia's power of imparting emotion, drama, conflict and reality through his half-released Istrian stone figures.

The hot summer months passed in fulfillment: up before first light, working the marble by dawn, carving for six hours before he ate from his basket of cold sliced *salame* and bread. At night when the light had begun to hide the planes and surfaces of the figure, he would drape it in moist cloth, put it back in his shed, lock the doors securely behind him; walk to the wide, shallow Reno River for a cool soak and swim, then to the Aldovrandi's, watching the stars be born in the deep blue canopy of the Emilian plain.

Vincenzo had disappeared, and so had Clarissa. He learned from a passing remark of Aldovrandi's that Marco had taken her to his hunting lodge in the Apennines for the hot summer months. The Aldovrandi family too departed for their summer villa in the mountains. For most of July and all of August, Bologna was shut down as though decimated by the plague, its shops locked behind iron, roll-down shutters. He stayed alone in the palace with a pair of servants who considered themselves too old to travel, and saw his host only when Aldovrandi rode in for a day to take care of his affairs, his face tanned by the mountain sun. Once he brought startling news from Florence. His short, quizzical eyebrows pointed almost vertically as he exclaimed:

"Your Fra Savonarola has come out into the open. He has declared war on the Pope!"

"You mean the way Lorenzo did when Rome excommunicated Florence?"

"Ah, no. This is personal and punitive."

Aldovrandi read from a report of Savonarola's latest Duomo sermon: "When you see a head which is healthy, you can say that the body is healthy also; but when the head is bad, look out for the body. And so when the head of the administration happens to be ambitious, lustful, and in other ways vicious, be sure that the scourge is near. . . . When you see therefore that God allows the head of the Church to wallow in crime and simony, then I say that the scourge of the people approaches. . . ."

Michelangelo was not as shocked as Aldovrandi expected, for Prior Bichiellini had predicted long ago that the Pope was Savonarola's ultimate target.

"How has the Pope replied?"

"He summoned Savonarola to Rome to explain his divine revelations. But Savonarola has declined, declaring, 'All good and wise citizens judge that my departure from this place would be to the great detriment of the people, yet of little use to you in Rome. . . . Because of the furtherance of this work I am quite sure these difficulties in the way of my going spring from God's will. Therefore it is not the will of God that I should leave this place at present.' " Aldovrandi chuckled. "An infallible system, don't you think?"

Michelangelo too declined to leave "this place" when Aldovrandi suggested he spend a cool holiday in the mountains with him.

"Thank you, but I'm moving along rapidly with the St. Proculus. At this rate I shall finish by fall."

The summer was over, Bologna rolled up its shutters and became a living city. Fall set in, and the St. Proculus was finished. Michelangelo and Aldovrandi stood before the figure. Michelangelo ran his hand caressingly over the high polish. He was exhausted, but happy with it. So was Aldovrandi.

"I will ask the fathers to set an unveiling date. Perhaps during the Christmas holidays?"

Michelangelo was silent; it was the sculptor's job to carve and the patron's to unveil.

"We could honor you in San Domenico."

"My work is done, and I have grown homesick for Florence," said Michelangelo quietly. "You have been a good friend."

Aldovrandi smiled. "For a year of bed and board I have extracted from you countless hours of reading poetry, and an illustrated copy of *The Divine Comedy!* What Aldovrandi ever drove a shrewder bargain?"

He could not go without saying good-by to Clarissa. That took a little waiting. Finally Aldovrandi invited him to a party at a secluded villa in the hills where the wealthy young Bolognese felt free to bring their mistresses for feasting and dancing. Michelangelo saw that there would be no chance for even a moment of privacy in a quiet library or music room. They would have to say good-by in the middle of a drawing room surrounded by twenty couples; and on their faces they would have to wear the bantering Bolognese smile which meant that charming pleasantries were being exchanged.

"I have waited to say good-by, Clarissa. I am going back to Florence."
Her eyebrows came together for a moment, but the fixed smile never wavered.
"I'm sorry. It has been pleasant to know you were here."
"Pleasant? A torture, pleasant?"
"In a way. When will you return?"
"I don't know. Perhaps never."
"Everyone returns to Bologna. It's on the road to everywhere."
"Then I'll be back."

13

The family was genuinely glad to have him home, kissing him on both cheeks and exclaiming at his stubble of beard. Lodovico was delighted with the twenty-five ducats Michelangelo brought him. Buonarroto seemed to have grown a full foot; Sigismondo, no longer a child, was apprenticed to the Wine Guild; and Giovansimone had left the house entirely, maintaining himself regally in a flat across the Arno as one of the leaders in Savonarola's Army of Boys.

"He does not come home any more," sighed Lodovico; "we ask too many embarrassing questions."

Granacci was working in deadly earnest from first light to dark at Ghirlandaio's in an effort to keep the *bottega* afloat. When Michelangelo visited the studio he saw the cartoons being drawn for the new frescoes for the chapel of San Zanobi by David and Benedetto Ghirlandaio, by Mainardi, Bugiardini, Tedesco. They seemed well done.

"Yes," agreed David, "but always we face the same criticism: 'With Domenico dead, the studio is finished.' "

"We work twice as hard as before," sighed Mainardi, "but none of us has Domenico's genius. Except his son Ridolfo here; but he's only twelve, it will be ten years before he can take his father's place."

On the walk home Granacci reported, "The Popolano family wants you to sculpture something for them."

"Popolano? I don't know any Popolanos."

"Yes, you do." Granacci's usually bland voice had an edge to it. "It's the Medici cousins, Lorenzo and Giovanni. They have changed their names to coincide with the People's party, and are now helping to rule Florence. They asked me to bring you around when you returned."

The brothers Lorenzo and Giovanni Popolano received him in a drawing room filled with precious art works from Lorenzo's palace. Michelangelo glanced from a Botticelli to a Gozzoli to a Donatello stupefied.

"We did not steal them," said Giovanni easily; "the city auctioned them off in public sale. We bought them."

Michelangelo sat down, uninvited. Granacci came to the defense of the cousins.

"This way the paintings and sculptures are safe. Some of the best pieces are being sold outside Florence."

Michelangelo rose to his feet. "I was taken by surprise . . . so many memories flooded over me."

Giovanni Popolano ordered sweet wine and cake. Lorenzo then said they were still interested in having a young St. John. If he cared to move into the palace, for convenience' sake, he would be welcome.

That evening when all the bells of the city were ringing loud enough to remind him of the Tuscan adage, "Bells ring to summon others, but never go to church themselves," he crisscrossed the narrow streets of the city to the Ridolfi palace.

He had been shaved and had his hair cut by Torrigiani's barber in the Straw Market; had bathed and donned his best blue woolen shirt and stockings for the visit.

The Ridolfi had been members of the *Bigi,* or Gray party, which had been pardoned by the Council for being followers of the Medici, and were now ostensibly members of the *Frateschi,* or Republicans. Contessina received him in the drawing room, still attended by her old nurse. She was heavy with child.

"Michelangelo."

"Contessina. *Come va?*"

"You said I would bear many sons."

He gazed at her pale cheeks, burning eyes, the upturned nose of her father. And he remembered Clarissa, felt her standing in this room beside Contessina. "All love is 'in a way.' "

"I have come to tell you that your cousins have offered me a commission. I could not join Piero's army, but I want no other disloyalty on my conscience."

"I heard of their interest. You proved your loyalty, Michelangelo, when they first made the offer. There is no need for you to continue demonstrations. If you wish to accept, do so."

"I shall."

"As for Piero . . . at the moment my sister and I live under the protection of our husbands' families. If Piero ever attacks with a strong force, and the city is in real danger, who knows what will happen to us?"

The major change had taken place in the city itself. As he walked the familiar streets he felt an air of hostility and suspicion. Florentines who had lived at peace with each other since Cosimo de' Medici had ordered their defense towers cut down to roof level had now split into three antagonistic party factions, shouting imprecations at each other. He learned to recognize them by their symbols. The *Arrabbiati,* or Maddened, were the men of wealth and experience who now hated Piero and Savonarola both, calling the friar's followers Snivelers and Prayer-mumblers. Next he distinguished the Whites, or *Frateschi* which included the Popolanos, who liked Savonarola no better than the Maddened, but had to support him because he was on the side of popular government. Lastly there was Piero de' Medici's group, the Grays, who were intriguing for Piero's return.

When he met Granacci in the Piazza della Signoria, Michelangelo was shocked to see Donatello's bronze Judith, which had been stolen out of the Medici courtyard, standing in front of the Signoria, and the David from the Medici courtyard installed in the Signoria courtyard.

"What is the Judith doing here?" he asked.

"She's now the reigning goddess of Florence."

"Stolen by the city. And the David too?"

"Harsh words, my friend. Confiscated."

"What does that plaque say?"

"That citizens placed this statue here *as a warning to all who should think to tyrannize over Florence.* Judith with that sword in her hand is us, the valiant citizens of Florence. Holofernes, about to have his head cut off, represents the party one doesn't belong to."

"So that a lot of heads will be rolling in the piazza? Are we at war with ourselves?"

Granacci did not answer; but Prior Bichiellini said:

"I am afraid so."

Michelangelo sat in his study surrounded by the shelves of leather-bound manuscripts and the desk piled high with records and sheets of an essay the prior was writing. The prior folded his hands into his black Augustinian sleeves to warm them.

"We have achieved some reform in taxes and morals. We have a more democratic government, more people can participate. But the government is paralyzed unless Fra Savonarola approves its acts."

With the exception of the dedicated group at Ghirlandaio's studio, art and artists had vanished in Florence. Rosselli had fallen ill, and his studio was not working. Two of the Della Robbia family, who had inherited Luca's sculpture processes, had become priests. Botticelli would paint only subjects which his mind could shape from Savonarola's sermons. Lorenzo di Credi, trained by Verrocchio, was reduced to restoring Fra Angelico and Uccello, and had entered a monastery.

"I thought of you," observed the prior, "when the friar announced a sermon for artists. I have some notes I jotted down . . . accurately, I assure you: 'In what does beauty consist? In color? No. In form? No! God is beauty itself. Young artists go about saying of this woman or man, Here is a Magdalene, here a Virgin, there a St. John; and then ye paint their faces in the churches, a great profanation of divine things. Ye artists do very ill, ye fill the churches with vain things. . . .' "

"I've heard it all from my brother. But if Savonarola prevails . . ."

"He prevails."

". . . then perhaps I should not have returned. What place is there for me here?"

"Where would you go, my son?"

Michelangelo was silent. Where indeed?

On New Year's Day of 1496 a large group of men converged on the monastery in Piazza San Marco carrying lighted torches and chanting:

"Burn down his house! Burn down San Marco! Burn down this dirty fellow of a friar!"

Michelangelo stood quietly in the shadow of the Popolano palace. The San Marco monks came out in their habits and cowls, stood shoulder to shoulder in a line across the front of the church and monastery, arms linked in a solid phalanx. The crowd continued to shout imprecations against Savonarola, but the monks stolidly held their ground; and after a time the torch carriers began to drift out of the piazza, their fires vanishing down the half dozen streets facing into the square.

Leaning against the cold stone wall, Michelangelo felt a chill sweep through him. Into his mind came Donatello's Judith, standing with sword raised, ready to cut off . . . whose head? Savonarola's? Prior Bichiellini's? Piero's? Florence's?

His own?

14

He went to see Beppe in the Duomo workyard and heard of a small, quite good piece of marble in a neighboring yard which he could buy at a reasonable price. The rest of the money advanced to him for the St. John he turned over to Lodovico.

He could not bring himself to live in the renamed "Popolano palace," but he did set up his workbench in the garden. The cousins treated him as a friend, frequently inviting him inside, work clothes and all, to see a new piece of art or illuminated manuscript. At home there were only three in the boys' bedroom now, but since Buonarroto had volunteered to share with Sigismondo, Michelangelo was able to continue in the luxury to which he had grown accustomed: a bed to himself. The weather was cold and he ate and drank nothing until midday, so he brought home a substantial appetite which kept Lucrezia happy. Even Lodovico seemed pleased with him.

The Popolano garden was formal, enclosed by a high protecting wall, with a covered three-sided porch under which he worked for warmth. Yet he could find little joy, and no creative surge. He kept asking himself, "Why?"

It was a sympathetic subject: young St. John setting out for the desert to preach in the wilderness, "a garment of camel's hair and a leather girdle about his loins, and locusts and wild honey were his food." Florence had many St. Johns: Andrea Pisano's St. John Baptizing on the Baptistery door, Ghiberti's bronze statue at

Orsanmichele. Donatello's marble on the Campanile, Ghirlandaio's fresco in Santa Maria Novella, Verrocchio's Baptism of Christ painted for San Salvi with the assistance of Leonardo da Vinci.

As he read his Bible, Michelangelo gathered that John would have been fifteen years old when he set out for the desert, Palestine, to preach to the Samaritans. Most of the representations showed him as a small boy, slight in figure, with a childlike face. But that did not need to be. At fifteen many Italian youths were already men. Why could not the young St. John be a robust, healthy, hearty creature, well equipped to endure the rigors to which he was about to expose himself? The kind of figure he found it exciting to carve?

Was it the anxious confusion of the city that depleted his enthusiasm, that caused him concern about his place in his own home? The stories going the rounds included all manner of fantastic rumors and fears: Savonarola would rule the city completely. Florence, having refused to join an Italian City-State League, frightened that the League would put Piero back in power, was again in danger of being conquered. Venice, the Duke of Sforza in Milan, the Borgia Pope in Rome, finding Piero a convenient ally against Savonarola, had helped Piero accumulate ten thousand ducats for the hiring of troops.

But art had been threatened before. Artists had worked in a troubled world. In truth would there ever again be any other kind?

Or was the difficulty of his approach to the St. John the old disturbing question, the elusiveness of John's meaning? Why should God have had to send someone to prepare the world for Jesus? Since he had God's capacity to set aside the laws of nature and perform miracles with which to convince the skeptical, why would the ground have to be plowed in advance for him?

Michelangelo's mind was an inquiring one. He needed to know the reasons behind things; the motivating philosophic principles. He read the story of John in Matthew:

"In those days John the Baptist appeared, preaching in the wilderness of Judaea; Repent, he said, the kingdom of heaven is at hand. It was of him that the prophet Isaiah spoke, when he said, There is a voice of one crying in the wilderness, Prepare the way of the Lord, straighten out his paths."

But the boy of fifteen first going out to preach was not the older man who later baptized Jesus. What was he like then? What was his importance to Christianity? Was his story imperative, or was it merely a fulfillment of the Old Testament prophecy, because the first Christians felt that the more strongly they based their religion on the Old Testament the better chance it would have to survive?

If he was not a trained theologian, he was a good craftsman. He spent weeks sketching throughout the city, every youth he could detain for a few moments. Though he was not intending to create a massive John, neither would he have anything to do with the fragile, elegant St. John with which Florence was adorned. And so he designed, and then carved into the block, the suppleness of limb of a fifteen-year-old, using only the loincloth as a cover. He refused to carve a halo for the boy or give him the traditional tall cross to carry, as Donatello had, since he did not think that the young John carried a cross that many years before the cross came into Christ's life. It turned out to be a vital portrait of a youth; but when he finished polishing the piece, he still did not know what he meant by it.

The Medici cousins needed less meaning. They were well pleased, placing the statue in a protective niche in the far garden wall where it could be seen from the rear windows of the palace. They paid him the balance of the florins and told him he was welcome to continue using their garden as his workshop.

But not a word about another commission.

"Nor can I blame them," Michelangelo commented to Granacci with a melancholy air. "It is nothing very special."

A despair enveloped him. "I've learned to carve in the round; but when do I carve something extraordinary in the round? I feel that I know less now, with my twenty-first birthday coming, then I did at seventeen. How can that be possible?"

"It isn't."

"Bertoldo told me, 'Create a body of work.' I have carved six pieces in these four years: the Hercules, the wood Crucifixion, the Angel, St. Petronius and St. Proculus in Bologna, and now this St. John. But only the St. Proculus has something original in it."

On his birthday he walked disconsolately into the workshop in the Popolano garden. He found a block of white marble sitting on his workbench. Across it, scrawled in charcoal in Granacci's handwriting, was the greeting:

"Try again!"

He did, immediately, without sketching or going into wax or clay, an infant that had half formulated itself in his mind while he was slogging away at the St. John: robust, lusty, pagan, carved in the Roman tradition. He never imagined he was doing a serious piece, it was an exercise really, something he got fun out of, an antidote to the confusions and tensions of the St. John. And so the marble flowed freely, and out of the block emerged a delightful child of six, sleeping with his right arm under his head, his legs spread comfortably apart.

The piece took him only a few weeks to carve and polish; he was neither attempting perfection nor hopeful of selling it. The whole project was a lark, designed to cheer him up; and now that it was finished he intended to return the marble to Granacci with a note which would read:

"Only a little the worse for wear."

It was Lorenzo Popolano who changed his mind. When he saw the completed piece his face flushed with pleasure.

"If you were to treat it so that it seemed to have been buried in the earth, I would send it to Rome, and it would pass for an antique Cupid. Would you know how to do that?"

"I think so. I antiqued a whole folio of drawings once."

"You would sell it for a far better price. I have a shrewd dealer there, Baldassare del Milanese. He will handle it."

He had seen enough Greek and Roman statues to know how his marble should look. He worked first with the scraps left from the Bambino, rubbing the dirt of the garden into the crystals with his fingers, then sandpapering lightly before applying another layer, staining the outside edges heavily with earth tans and rust, using a hard bristle brush to bury the discoloration.

When he was satisfied that he had a good process, he began on the Bambino, working carefully, as amused at the idea of the impending fraud as he had been at the carving itself.

Lorenzo liked the result.

"It is convincing. Baldassare will get you a good price. I have packets going to Rome in a few days, and I'll include your little statue."

Lorenzo had guessed rightly: the Bambino was sold to the first customer to whom Baldassare offered it: Cardinal Riario di San Giorgio, grand-nephew of Pope Sixtus IV. Lorenzo poured a pouch of gold florins into Michelangelo's hands, thirty of them. Michelangelo had thought an antique Cupid in Rome would bring at least a hundred florins. Even so, it was twice what it would have brought in Florence; if indeed anyone would have wanted it, with Savonarola's Army of Boys forcibly sequestering all such pagan images from private homes.

Just before Lent Michelangelo saw his brother Giovansimone hurrying down the Via Larga at the head of a group of white-robed boys, their arms laden with mirrors, gowns of silk and satin, oil paintings, statuary, jewel boxes. Michelangelo grabbed his brother, almost toppling his load of loot.

"Giovansimone! I have been home for four months and haven't laid eyes on you."

Giovansimone shook his arm loose with a broad grin, exclaimed:

"Haven't time to talk to you now. Be sure to be in the Piazza della Signoria tomorrow at dusk."

It would not have been possible for Michelangelo or anyone else in Florence to miss the giant spectacle the following evening. In the four main quarters of Florence the Army of Boys in their white robes were shaped into military formations and, preceded by drummers, pipers and mace bearers carrying olive branches in their hands and chanting, "Long live Christ, the King of Florence! Long live Mary, the Queen!" they marched on the Piazza della Signoria. Here, in front of the tower, a huge tree had been erected. Built around it was a pyramidal scaffold. The citizens of Florence and the outlying villages poured into the square. The section for the burning was roped off by the monks of San Marco standing arm in arm, with Savonarola in commanding position.

The boys built their pyre. At the base they threw bundles of false hair, rouge pots, perfumes, mirrors, bolts of silk from France, boxes of beads, earrings, bracelets, fancy buttons. Then came all the paraphernalia of gambling, a shower of playing cards dancing for a moment in the air, dice and checkered boards with their pawns and characters.

On the next layer of the pyramid were piled books, leather-bound manuscripts, hundreds of drawings, oil paintings, every piece of ancient sculpture the boys had been able to lay their hands on. Thrown onto the highest tier were violas, lutes and barrel organs, their beautiful shapes and glistening woods converting the mad heap to a scene of bacchanalia; then came masks, costumes from pageants, carved ivories and oriental art works; rings, brooches, necklaces sparkled as they landed. Michelangelo recognized Botticelli as he ran up to the pyre and threw onto it sketches of Simonetta. Fra Bartolommeo followed with his studies, the Della Robbia monks, with frenzied motion, added their varicolored terra-cotta sculptures. It was difficult to tell from the alternating outbursts of the crowd whether they greeted the sacrifices with fear or ecstasy.

On the balcony of the tower stood the members of the Signoria watching the spectacle. The Army of Boys had gone from house to house asking for "all art works inappropriate to the faith," all ornaments, fineries and decorations not permitted by the sumptuary laws; if they had not been given what they considered a sufficient contribution, they had brushed past the owners of the house and looted it. The Signoria had done nothing to protect the city against these "white-robed angels."

Savonarola raised his arms for silence. The guarding line of monks unlocked their arms and raised them to the heavens. A monk appeared with a lighted torch and handed it to Savonarola. Savonarola held the torch high while he gazed around the square. Then he walked around the pyre, touching it in one place after another until the entire scaffolding was one huge mass of flames.

The Army of Boys marched about the burning pyre chanting, "Long live Christ! Long live the Virgin!" Great answering shouts went up from the packed mass. "Long live Christ! Long live the Virgin!"

Tears came to Michelangelo's eyes. He wiped them away as a child would, first with the back of his left hand and then with his right. But they continued to well up, as the flames mounted higher and higher and the wild singing and crying reached an ever greater crescendo, until they rolled down his cheeks and he felt their saltiness on his lips.

He wished with all his heart that he could go away, as far from the sight of the Duomo as he could get.

15

In June a groom came with a message from Giovanni Popolano asking Michelangelo if he would come to the palace to meet a Roman nobleman interested in sculpture. Leo Baglioni, the Popolanos' guest, was a man of about thirty, blond, well spoken. He walked with Michelangelo out to the workshop.

"My hosts tell me you are an excellent sculptor. Could I see something of your work?"

"I have nothing here, only the St. John in the garden."

"And drawings? I am particularly interested in drawings."

"Then you are a rarity among connoisseurs, sir. I should welcome your seeing my folio."

Leo Baglioni pored over the hundreds of sketches.

"Would you be so kind as to make a simple drawing for me? A child's hand, for example."

Michelangelo drew rapidly, a number of memories of children in various poses. After a time Baglioni said:

"There can be no question about it. You are the one."

"The one?"

"Yes. Who carved the Cupid."

"Ah!"

"Forgive me for dissembling, but I was sent to Florence by my principal, Cardinal Riario di San Giorgio, to see if I could find the sculptor of the Cupid."

"It was I. Baldassare del Milanese sent me thirty florins for the piece."

"Thirty! But the cardinal paid two hundred . . ."

"Two hundred! Why, that . . . that thief . . ."

"Precisely what the cardinal said," declared Leo Baglioni with a mischievous gleam in his eye. "He suspected it was a fraud. Why not return to Rome with me? You can settle your account with Baldassare. I believe the cardinal would be pleased to offer you hospitality. He said that anyone who could make such an excellent fake should be able to make even better authentic carvings."

Michelangelo shook his head in perplexity over the series of events; but there was no faltering in his decision.

"A few articles of clothing from my home, sir, and I shall be ready for the journey."

BOOK FIVE

THE CITY

He stood on a rise just north of the city. Rome lay below in its bed of hills, destroyed, as though sacked by vandals. Leo Baglioni traced the outlines of the Leonine Wall, the fortress of Sant'Angelo.

They got back on their horses and descended to the Porta del Popolo, passing the tomb of Nero's mother to enter the small piazza. It stank from piled garbage. Above them to the left was the Pincio hill covered with vineyards. The streets they followed were narrow lanes with broken cobbles underfoot. The noise of carts passing over the stones was so deafening that Michelangelo could barely hear Baglioni identifying the dilapidated tomb of the Roman emperor Augustus, now a grazing field for cows; the Campo Marzio, a plain near the Tiber inhabited by the poorer artisans whose shops were huddled between ancient palaces that looked as though they would topple at any moment.

More than half of the buildings he passed were gutted. Goats wandered among the fallen stones. Baglioni explained that the previous December the Tiber had flooded and the people had had to flee for three days to the surrounding hills, returning to a dank, decaying city in which the plague struck and one hundred and fifty corpses were buried each morning on the island in the river.

Michelangelo felt sick to his stomach: the Mother City of Christendom was a waste heap and a dunghill. Dead animals lay under the feet of their horses. Wrecking crews were breaking out walls of building stone for use elsewhere, burning marble slabs and columns for their lime content. He guided his horse around a piece of ancient statuary sticking up through the dirt of the road, passed rows of abandoned houses, salt and vines growing in their crumbling mortar. Skirting a Grecian temple, he saw pigs penned between its columns. In a block-square subterranean vault with broken columns half emerging from an ancient forum there was a horrendous odor, rising from hundreds of years of dumped refuse, and generations of men whose descendants even now were squatting over its void, defecating into its depth.

His host led him through a series of dark, winding streets where two horses could barely pass each other, past the theater of Pompey with hundreds of families living in its yawning vault; and then at last into the Campo dei Fiori where he saw his first signs of recognizable life: a vegetable, flower, cheese, fish and meat market, crowded with row upon row of clean colorful stalls, the cooks and housewives of

Rome shopping for their dinner. For the first time since they had descended into
Rome he was able to look at his host and tender him a wisp of a smile.

"Frightened?" Leo Baglioni asked. "Or revulsed?"

"Both. Several times I almost turned my horse and made a run for Florence."

"Rome is pitiful. You should see the pilgrims who come from all over Europe.
They are robbed, beaten, ridden down by our princely processions, bitten half to
death by vermin in the inns, then separated from their last denaro in the churches.
Bracciolini wrote some sixty years ago, 'The public and private buildings lie prostrate,
nude and broken like the limbs of a giant. Rome is a decaying corpse.' Pope Sixtus
IV made a real effort to widen the streets and repair some of the buildings; but
under the Borgias the city has fallen into a worse condition than that of which
Bracciolini wrote. Here's my home."

Standing on a corner overlooking the market was a well-designed house of three
floors. Inside, the rooms were small and sparsely furnished with walnut tables and
chairs, but richly carpeted, with tapestries and precious cloths on the walls, and
decorated with painted wooden cupboards, gold mirrors and red leather ornaments.

Michelangelo's sailcloth bag was carried up to the third floor. He was given a
corner room overlooking the market and a staggeringly huge, new stone palace
which his host told him was just being completed by Cardinal Riario, who had
bought his Bambino.

They had an excellent dinner in a dining room that was protected from the noises
of the street. Late in the afternoon they strolled to the cardinal's old villa, through
the Piazza Navona, former site of the long stadium of Domitian, where Michelangelo
was fascinated by a half-buried, half-excavated marble torso, brilliantly carved,
standing before the house of one of the Orsini, a relative of Piero's wife Alfonsina,
and which Leo thought might be Menelaus Carrying Patroclus.

They continued on to the Piazza Fiammetta, named after the mistress of Caesar
Borgia, son of the Pope, and then to the Riario palace facing the Via Sistina and
the city's cleanest inn, the Hostaria dell'Orso, Inn of the Bear. Baglioni filled in
his background on Raffaelle Riario di San Giorgio, a grandnephew of Pope Sixtus
IV who had been made a cardinal when an eighteen-year-old student at the University
of Pisa. The young cardinal had gone for a visit to the Medici palace in Florence,
and had been worshiping at the altar in the Duomo when assassins killed Giuliano
de' Medici and stabbed Lorenzo. Though Lorenzo and the Florentines had been
convinced that it was Pope Sixtus and his nephews who had connived with the
Pazzi to murder both Medici, Lorenzo had absolved the cardinal of knowledge of
the plot.

Cardinal Riario received Michelangelo amidst piles of boxes and half-packed
trunks that were being readied for moving. He read Lorenzo Popolano's letter of
introduction, bade Michelangelo welcome to Rome.

"Your Bambino was well sculptured, Buonarroti, even though it was not an
antique. I have the impression that you can carve something quite fine for us."

"Thank you, Excellency."

"I should like you to go out this afternoon and see our best marble statues. Start
with the arch of Domitian on the Corso, then go to the column of Trajan, after that
see the Capitoline collection of bronzes that my grand-uncle, Sixtus IV, started . . ."

By the time the cardinal finished he had named some twenty pieces of sculpture
in a dozen different collections and parts of the city. Leo Baglioni guided him first
to see the river god Marforio, a monstrous-sized statue lying in the street between
the Roman forum and the forum of Augustus, which was supposed to have been
in the temple of Mars. From here they moved on to the column of Trajan, where
Michelangelo exclaimed over the carving of the Lion Devouring the Horse. They
walked up the winding Quirinal hill where he was stunned by the size and brute
force of the eighteen-foot-high marble Horse Tamers and the gods of the Nile and
the Tiber, the Nile resting an arm on a sphinx, the Tiber leaning on a tiger, which

Leo thought came out of the baths of Constantine. Near them was a nude goddess of breath-taking beauty, "probably a Venus," proffered Leo.

They continued on to the garden of Cardinal Rovere at San Pietro in Vincoli, Leo explaining that this nephew of Sixtus IV was the founder of the first public library and museum of bronzes in Rome, had accumulated the finest collection of antique marbles in Italy, and had been Sixtus' inspiring force in the project to fresco the walls of the Sistine Chapel.

Michelangelo stood breathless when he entered the little iron gate of Cardinal Rovere's garden, for here was an Apollo, just the torso remaining, that was the most staggering piece of human projection he had ever seen. As he had in the Medici palace on his first visit with Bertoldo, he moved half stunned in a forest of sculpture, from a Venus to an Antaeus to a Mercury, his mind captivated, only dimly hearing Leo's voice telling him which pieces had been stolen from Greece, which had been bought by Emperor Hadrian and sent to Rome by the shipload. If Florence were the richest center in the world for the creation of art, surely this miserably dirty, decaying city must hold the greatest collection of antique art? And here was the proof of what he had tried to tell his fellow Ghirlandaio apprentices on the steps of the Duomo: here were marble carvings as alive and beautiful as the day they were carved, two thousand years ago.

"Now we shall go to see the bronze Marcus Aurelius before the Lateran," continued Leo. "Then perhaps . . . ."

"Please, no more. I'm quivering inside. I must lock myself in my room and try to digest what I've already seen."

He could eat no supper that night. The next morning, Sunday, Leo took him to mass in the little church of San Lorenzo in Damaso, next to Cardinal Riario's new palace, and attached to it by a break-through in one of its walls. Michelangelo was staggered to find himself surrounded by a hundred marble and granite columns, no two alike, carved by expert stonemasons, each with a differently sculptured capital, "eclectically borrowed from all over Rome," Leo explained, "but mainly from the front of the portico of the theater of Pompey. . . ."

The cardinal wished Michelangelo to come to the new palace. The vast stone edifice, twice the size of the Medici palace, was finished except for the central courtyard. Michelangelo climbed a broad flight of stairs, went through the audience chamber with rich tapestry curtains and mirrors framed in jasper, the drawing room with oriental carpets and carved walnut chairs, the music room with a beautiful harpsichord, until he came upon the cardinal in his red hat and vestments, sitting in his antique sculpture room, with a dozen pieces lying in open boxes filled with sawdust.

"Tell me, Buonarroti, what do you think of the marbles you have seen? Can you do something equally beautiful?"

"I may not carve anything as beautiful. But we will see what I can do."

"I like that answer, Buonarroti, it shows humility."

He did not feel humble, all he had meant was that his pieces would be different from anything he had seen.

"We had best start at once," continued Riario. "My carriage is outside. It can take us to the stoneyard."

As the cardinal's groom drove them across the Sisto bridge and through the Settimiana gate to the Trastevere stoneyards, Michelangelo studied the face of his new patron. It was said that Riario had been so shocked at the Medici stabbings that his face had turned purple; in fact it remained so to this day. He had a long, hooked nose that clamped down on a tight-lipped mouth.

Once in the stoneyard Cardinal Riario seemed impatient. Michelangelo wandered among the blocks wondering how large a piece he dared select. Finally he stopped before a white Carrara column over seven feet tall and four feet thick. His eyes lighted with excitement. He assured the cardinal that there could be a fine statue contained in it. Cardinal Riario quickly paid out thirty-seven ducats from the purse on his belt.

The next morning Michelangelo rose at first light, made his way downstream to the Florentine bridge and crossed the Tiber to Trastevere, densely inhabited section of Rome, home of the potters, tanners, millers, ropemakers, metalworkers, fishermen, boatmen, gardeners, a brawling, sprawling population descended from the original Romans, self-contained within high walls and the Tiber, their crowded quarters unchanged for hundreds of years. He wound through a labyrinth of narrow streets, watched workmen handling raw materials in dark shops, all light cut off by projecting upper stories, the narrow houses jammed together, while above them the roofs pitched angularly, surmounted by bristling square towers. Peddlers were calling their wares, women and children brawling, open fish, cheese and meat marketeers crying out bargains, the whole of the tumultuous noise and smell locked in to overwhelm one's ears and eyes and nose.

He walked along the Via della Lungara to the stoneyard just outside the Vatican wall and Santo Spirito hospital. Not a soul was stirring. He listened through a cacophony of cockcrows before the owner showed up.

"What are you doing here?" he demanded, still half asleep and sullen. "We say we deliver today. What we say, we do."

"I wasn't worried about your failure to deliver. I just thought I'd help load . . ."

"You telling me we don't know how to load?" Now the owner was insulted. "We been carting marble in Rome for five generations, and we need a Florentine statue maker to teach us our business?"

"My family trained me in the Maiano quarries. I'm a pretty good hand with a crowbar."

Mollified, the owner replied, "Quarryman, eh? That's different. We quarry travertine in our family. Guffatti is our name."

Michelangelo made sure there was a sufficient bed of sawdust and that the block was securely lashed before the open-end wagon started on its journey through streets rutted to the hubs of the wheels. He walked behind, patting the end of the column while praying that the rickety farm wagon, in the family for the five generations, would not collapse in a pile of splinters and leave the marble block in the roadbed.

Arriving at the palace, Guffatti asked, "Where do we unload?"

Michelangelo suddenly realized that he had not been told where he would work. He cried, "Wait right here!" ran through the courtyard and up the broad staircase to the reception room . . . to come head on against one of the palace secretaries, who glanced disapprovingly at this bundle of work clothes dashing into the main foyer of the newest palace in Rome.

"I have to see the cardinal immediately. It's urgent."

"Urgent for the cardinal, or you?"

The cool tone slowed Michelangelo down.

"It's the marble block . . . we bought it yesterday . . . it's arrived and I have no place . . ."

He stopped, watching the secretary thumb through an appointment calendar.

"His Excellency has no time available until next week."

Michelangelo stood with his mouth open.

"But . . . we can't wait."

"I'll take the matter up with His Eminence. If you would care to return tomorrow."

He ran back down the central staircase at full speed, out the palace, to the corner and across the street to Leo Baglioni's house. Leo was being barbered, a towel over his shoulders to catch the clipped locks. His eyes danced while he listened to Michelangelo's outburst. He told the barber to wait, removed the towel, rose from the only cushioned chair in the house.

"Come, we'll find a space for you."

Leo located a shed behind the cupola of San Lorenzo in Damaso, in which the workmen who built the palace had left their tools at night. Michelangelo removed the doors from their hinges. Leo returned to his barber. The Guffatti unloaded the marble.

Michelangelo sat on the earthen floor before the block, holding his knees under his chin. "You are a beautiful piece of meat," he said fondly; and fell to musing about the kind of theme a prince of the Church might choose for a life-size figure. Would it not have to be a religious subject? Yet the cardinal had a liking for ancient Greek and Roman carvings.

That afternoon the cardinal sent for him. He was received in an austere room bare of all furniture. There was a small altar at one end, and a doorway beside it. Riario was wearing a severely tailored red cassock and skullcap.

"Now that you are about to undertake a prolonged piece of work, you had better move into the palace. Signor Baglioni's guestroom has a long list of lovely ladies waiting to share it."

"On what terms am I to live in the palace, Excellency?"

"Let us just say that your address is the palace of the Cardinal Riario. And now we must leave you."

No word about what the cardinal wanted sculptured. Or what the price would be. Or whether he was to have regular payments during his year of work. The palace would be his address; he knew nothing more.

But he learned. He was not to live here as a son, as he had in the Medici palace, nor as a close friend as in the Aldovrandi home in Bologna. A chamberlain directed him to a narrow cell at the rear of the ground floor, one of perhaps twenty such rooms, where he unpacked his few possessions. When he went looking for his first meal he found himself relegated to what was known as the "third category" dining room, in which he found his companions to be the cardinal's scriveners, the head bookkeeper, the purchasing agent for the palace, the managers of his far-flung farm lands, timber stands, ships, benefices all over Italy.

The Cardinal Riario had made himself clear; Michelangelo Buonarroti was to live in the palace as one of the crew of skilled workmen. Nothing more, and nothing less.

2

Early the next morning he went to see Baldassare the art dealer, who had just been obliged to return Cardinal Riario's two hundred ducats for the Bambino. Baldassare was a swarthy fat man with three jowls and an enormous stomach which he pushed ahead of him as he came from the back of his open sculpture yard, just off the forum of Julius Caesar. Michelangelo's progress was slow in coming down the yard, for the dealer had a number of antiques mounted on bases.

"I am Michelangelo Buonarroti, sculptor of Florence."

Baldassare made an obscene noise with his lips.

"I want you to return my Bambino. I will repay the thirty florins you sent me."

"Certainly not!" the dealer cried.

"You defrauded me. All you were entitled to was your commission. You sold the marble for two hundred ducats and kept one hundred and seventy."

"On the contrary, it is you and your friend Popolano who are the frauds. You sent me a false antique. I could have lost the cardinal's patronage."

Michelangelo walked fuming out of the yard, half ran down the Via Santa. He crossed the street, stood gazing at Trajan's column until his head cleared. Then he burst into laughter.

"Baldassare is right. It is I who was the cheat. I falsified the Bambino."

He heard someone behind him exclaim:

"Michelangelo Buonarroti! Do you always talk to yourself?"

He turned, recognized a chap of his own age who had been apprenticed to the Money Changers Guild and worked briefly for his uncle Francesco in an early period of prosperity. They might have known each other for a hundred years in Florence and never become friends, but here they fell on each other's necks.

"Balducci. What are you doing in Rome?"

"Working for Jacopo Galli's bank. Head bookkeeper. The dumbest Florentine is smarter than the smartest Roman. That's why I'm moving up so fast. How about having dinner together? I'll take you to a Tuscan restaurant in the Florentine section. I can't stand this Roman food. Wait till you taste the *tortellini* and beefsteak, you'll think you're back in sight of the Duomo."

"There is time before noon. Come with me to the Sistine Chapel, I want to see the Florentine frescoes."

The Sistine Chapel, built between 1473 and 1481, was a mammoth barrel-roofed structure with high windows toward the ceiling and a railed balcony-walk beneath them. The rectangular dome was painted blue with gold stars scattered about. At the far end was the altar, and dividing the sanctuary and the nave, a marble screen by Mino da Fiesole. What would have appeared a clumsily proportioned and graceless building was saved by a magnificent frieze of frescoed panels on both sides of the chapel, running full length to the altar.

Michelangelo went excitedly to the Ghirlandaio frescoes which he remembered from the cartoons in the studio: the Resurrection and the Calling of Peter and Andrew. His admiration for Ghirlandaio's pictorial skill was renewed. Next he went to Rosselli's Last Supper, which he did not find as garish as Ghirlandaio had charged; then turned his gaze raptly to the Botticelli Moses Before the Burning Bush, and to the Umbrian masters, Perugino, Pinturicchio and Signorelli. As he moved about the chapel he sensed that under this awkward, unbalanced roof there had been assembled the greatest combination of masters to be found in Italy. He decided that Perugino's Christ Giving the Keys to St. Peter stood up with the finest of the Florentine tradition, the highest compliment he could pay any artist. He remarked to Balducci how strange it was that this topheavy, cavernous chapel, as inept and arid a piece of architecture as he had yet seen, could have called forth the painters' richest creative efforts.

Balducci had not even glanced at the frescoes.

"Let's get to the *trattoria*. I'm famished."

While eating, Michelangelo learned that Torrigiani was in Rome.

"But you won't see much of him," said Balducci. "He consorts with the Borgias so the Florentines don't receive him. He's doing stuccos for the tower of the Borgia palace, also a bust of the Pope. He has all the sculpture work he wants. He also says he is going to join Caesar Borgia's army to conquer Italy."

That evening Balducci took him to the home of Paolo Rucellai, a cousin of the Rucellai in Florence and hence a distant cousin of his own. Rucellai lived in the district of Ponte, known as "a little Florence, walled within itself." Here, centered around the Florentine consul's house and the Tuscan banks, the Florentines in Rome lived close together, with their own markets, which imported their *pasta,* meats, vegetables, fruits and sweets from Tuscany. They had acquired land on which to build a Florentine church, and had bought the few remaining houses on the Via Canale so that no Romans could move in. The hatred was mutual. The Romans said:

"Better a corpse in the house than a Florentine at the door."

The Florentines reinterpreted the S.P.Q.R. of the Roman's *Senatus Populus Que Romanus* to read, *"Sono Porci, Questi Romani.* They are pigs, these Romans."

The Florentine section of Ponte was the area held within a wide bend of the river, in the center of which was the Florentine bridge leading to Trastevere. In the area were fine palaces, two streets of solidly built houses, with flower and vegetable gardens interspersed. The Florentine banks were on the Via Canale, adjoining the Camera Apostolica, the official bank of the Vatican. At the extreme end of the colony, near the bridge of Sant'Angelo, were the Pazzi and Altoviti palaces. Near the riverbank was an open space filled with flowers and vegetables which became a lake when the Tiber overflowed, as it had the year before.

In the midst of the chaos and filth of Rome the prosperous Florentines swept and washed down their streets every day at dawn, replaced the cobblestones to make a smooth and quiet roadbed, put their houses in a good state of repair, sold or leased only to Florentines. There were prohibitive fines against dumping refuse in the streets or hanging laundry from the front windows instead of the back. Armed guards policed the quarter at night; it was the only section where one was sure not to stumble over a corpse on one's stoop at daybreak.

At the Rucellai house he was presented to the leading families of the community: the Tornabuoni, Strozzi, Pazzi, Altoviti, Bracci, Olivieri, Ranfredini and Cavalcanti, to whom he was carrying a letter of introduction.

Some of the Florentines were bankers, others were silk and wool merchants, jewelers, importers of wheat, gold- and silversmiths, shipowners and shipbuilders who had thriving ports at Ripa Grande and Ripetta, where boats came up the Tiber from the sea carrying luxuries from the Near East, wines and oil from Tuscany, marble from Carrara, timber from across the Adriatic.

A number of the men asked, "Who is your father?" When he replied, "Lodovico Buonarroti-Simoni," they nodded their heads, said, "I know the name," accepting him forthwith.

The Rucellai had converted their Roman house into pure Florentine, with a recessed fireplace surrounded by *pietra serena,* the floor of the dining room tiled in the tradition of Luca della Robbia, and the familiar inlaid furniture so beloved of his countrymen. He did not tell handsome affable Paolo that he too was a Rucellai. The Rucellai had terminated the family relationship with the Buonarroti. His pride would never let him be the first to speak.

He set up his seven-foot block on beams braced from behind so that he could move around it. His disappointment that the cardinal did not immediately present him with a specific subject gave way to the realization that it would be better if he himself knew what he wanted to carve. Then he would not have to ask humbly, "What would Your Excellency like me to make out of this marble?"

"Exercise extreme care," Leo warned him, "not to touch that column until Cardinal Riario gives you permission to do so. He is adamant about his properties."

"I could not hurt the marble, Leo, by rounding the edges and exploring a little. . . ."

He was humiliated at being cautioned like a laborer not to manhandle the property of his *padrone.* Yet he had to promise not to chip a single crystal off the block.

"You can use your time profitably," said Leo placatingly. "There are wonderful things in Rome to study."

"Yes, I know," said Michelangelo. Why try to explain his marble fever? He changed the subject. "Can one secure nude models in Rome? It is not allowed in Florence."

Leo replied mischievously, "That's because we Romans are a clean and moral people. But you Florentines . . . !" He laughed as Michelangelo flushed. "I suppose it's because we have never suffered from the Greek sickness, and Florence has been famous, or should I say infamous?, for it. Here our men have been making business deals, arranging political alignments and marriages while they take their leisure and exercise in the nude."

"Could you arrange for me to have models?"

"Tell me what kind you want."

"All kinds: short, tall, skinny, fat, young and old, dark and light, laborers and idlers, traders."

He set up a low screen to give him a modicum of privacy. The next morning Leo's first nominee arrived, a burly middle-aged cooper who shed his stinking shirt and sandals and moved about unconcernedly as Michelangelo directed him to a variety of poses. Each morning at sunrise he went out to his workshop to prepare his paper, chalk, ink, charcoal, colored crayons, not knowing what new task the day's model would bring: Corsicans who formed the papal bodyguard, German typographers, French perfumers and glovemakers, Teutonic bakers, Spanish booksellers, Lombard carpenters from the Campo Marzio, Dalmatian boatbuilders, Greek copyists, Portuguese trunkmakers from the Via dei Baullari, goldsmiths from beside San Giorgio. Sometimes they were superb figures whom he drew in full frontal or rear positions, posed straining, turning, lifting, pushing, twisting, battling with an army of work tools, clubs, stones. More often the whole figure would not be interesting, only a specially knotted shoulder, the shape of a skull, an iron-corded calf, a barrel chest, and then he would spend the entire day drawing only that one segment, seen from a dozen angles and in differing postures.

His years of training were coming into focus. The months of dissection had given his drawing an authority, an inner truth that had changed the projection of his work. Even the urbane and sophisticated Leo commented on the propulsive force of these figures.

"Each morning you come out to a different model as though you were going on an exciting adventure. Don't you get tired drawing the same thing over and over again: head, arms, torso, legs . . ."

"But, Leo, they are never the same! Every arm and leg and neck and hip in the world is different, with a true character of its own. Listen, my friend, all forms that exist in God's universe can be found in the human figure. A man's body and face can tell everything he represents. So how could I ever exhaust my interest in it?"

Baglioni was entertained by Michelangelo's intensity. He glanced at the batch of sketches under Michelangelo's arm, shook his head unbelievingly.

"What about the inner qualities? In Rome we conceal rather than reveal what we are."

"That is a measure of the sculptor: how deeply can he penetrate the shell? With every subject I say to myself, 'What are you, truly, as you stand naked before the world?' "

Leo pondered on this for a moment. "Then, for you, sculpture is a search."

Michelangelo smiled shyly.

"Isn't it, for all artists? Every man sees truth through his own funnel. I feel about each new figure the way an astronomer does each time he discovers a new star: one more fragment of the universe has been filled in. Perhaps if I could draw every male on earth I could accumulate the whole truth about man."

"Well then," said Leo, "I would recommend that you come with me to the baths. There you can do a hundred in a sitting."

He took Michelangelo on a tour of the staggeringly vast and ornate ruins of the ancient baths of Caracalla, Trajan, Constantine, Diocletian, telling him of how the early Romans had used the baths as clubs, meeting halls, spending every afternoon of their lives in them.

"You have heard the line attributed to Caesar, 'Give the populace bread and circuses.' Several of the emperors felt it equally important to give them water, believing their popularity depended on how beautiful they made their public baths."

Now that the baths were run for profit they were far less lavish, but they had several pools for swimming, steam and massage rooms, courts where the clients entertained each other with the day's gossip while musicians and jugglers made the rounds, food vendors came through hawking their wares, the younger men played a variety of ballgames.

Leo was well known in the bath on the Piazza Scossacavalli which belonged to the Cardinal Riario. After they had had their warm bath and a swim in a cold pool, they sat on a bench at the far end of the area where knots of men were sitting and standing, arguing, laughing, telling anecdotes, while Michelangelo composed scene after scene in a fever of composition, so superb were the modeled planes, curves and masses of the figures against each other.

"I've never seen anything like it. In Florence public baths are for the poor," he exclaimed.

"I will spread the word that you are in Rome on the cardinal's invitation. Then you'll be able to sketch here to your heart's content."

In the weeks that followed he took Michelangelo to the baths connected with the hostels, monasteries, old palaces, to the one in the Via dei Pastini, to Sant'Angelo in the Pescheria. Everywhere Leo introduced Michelangelo so that he could come back alone; and in each new setting of light, wall color, reflection of sun and water on the bodies, he found fresh truths and ways of expressing them in simple bold lines.

But he never quite got used to sketching while he himself was naked. "Once a Florentine . . . !" he muttered to himself.

One afternoon Leo asked, "Wouldn't you like to sketch some women? There are several baths for both sexes within the city walls, run by prostitutes, but with quite respectable clienteles."

"I have no interest in the female form."

"You're summarily dismissing half the figures in the world."

"Roughly, yes." They laughed together. "But I find all beauty and structural power in the male. Take a man in any action, jumping, wrestling, throwing a spear, plowing, bend him into any position and the muscles, the distribution of weight and tension, have their symmetry. For me, a woman to be beautiful or exciting must be absolutely still."

"Perhaps you just haven't put them into the proper positions."

Michelangelo smiled. "Yes, I have. I find it a sight for love, but not for sculpture."

3

He disliked Rome as a city; but then it was not one city but many, the Germans, French, Portuguese, Greeks, Corsicans, Sicilians, Arabs, Levantines, Jews all compacted within their own areas, welcoming outsiders no more than did the Florentines. Balducci had said to him, "These Romans are an ugly race. Or, I should say, a hundred ugly races." He had found it a heterogeneous gathering of peoples who wore different clothes, spoke different languages, ate different foods, cherished different values. Everybody appeared to have come from somewhere else, habitually calling down a pox on the city for its decay, floods, pestilences, lawlessness, filth and corruption. Since there was no government, no laws or police courts or councils for protection, each section governed itself as best it could. The convenient cemetery of crimes was the Tiber, where floating corpses regularly greeted the early morning risers. There was no equitable distribution of wealth, justice, learning, art.

As he walked for hours about Rome he found it a shambles, its widespread walls, which had protected half a million people in the days of the Empire, now enclosing less than seventy thousand. Whole areas that had been populated were neglected ruins. There was hardly a block, even in the heavily populated sections, without black gaping holes between buildings, like missing teeth in an old crone's mouth. Its architecture was a hodgepodge of crude dung-colored brick, black tufa stone, tan travertine, blocks of gray granite, pink and green marble stolen from other eras. The manners of the people were execrable: they ate in the streets, even the well-dressed wives emerging from bakery shops to walk along munching on fresh sugar rolls, chewing pieces of hot tripe and other specialties from the vendors' carts and street cookstoves, consuming dinner piecemeal in public.

The residents had no pride in their city, no desire to improve it or provide rudimentary care. They told him, "Rome is not a city, it's a church. We have no power to control or change it." When he asked, "Then why do people stay?" he was answered, "Because there is money to be made." Rome had the most unsavory reputation in Europe.

The contrasts with homogeneous Florence, compact within its walls, immaculately clean, a self-governing Republic, inspired of art and architecture, growing rapidly without poverty, proud of its tradition, revered throughout Europe for its learning and justice, were for him sharp and painful. Most personally painful was the atrocious stonework of the buildings he passed each day. In Florence he had rarely been able to resist running his fingers over the beautifully carved and fitted *pietra serena* of the edifices; here he winced as his practiced eye picked out the crude strokes of the chisel, the gouged and blemished surfaces, the unmatched beveling. Florence would not have paved its streets with these botched building stones!

He stopped in front of a construction in the Piazza del Pantheon, with its wood and iron-pipe scaffolding held together at the joints by leather thongs. Masons putting up a wall of a house were pounding large blocks of travertine, bruising the substance because they did not know how to split it. He picked up a sledge, turned to the foreman and cried:

"Permettete?"

"Permit you what?"

He tapped the end of a block, found its point of stratification, with a swift authoritative blow split it longways. Taking a hammer and chisel from a workman's hands, he shaped and beveled blocks out of the two layers, tooling the surfaces with long rhythmic strokes until the stone changed color as well as form, and glowed beneath his hand.

He looked up to find himself surrounded by resentful eyes. One of the masons growled, "Stonework is for beasts. Do you think we would be here if we didn't have to eat?"

Michelangelo apologized for intruding. He walked down the Via Pellicciaria feeling a fool; yet for a Florentine stonemason the surfacing of a block constituted his self-expression. He was respected by his friends according to his skill and resourcefulness in modeling the stones to bring out their individual character. Working the stone was considered the most venerable of crafts, an inherent part of the elemental faith that man and stone had natural affinities.

When he returned to the palace he found an invitation from Paolo Rucellai to attend a reception for Piero de' Medici, who was in Rome attempting to gather an army, and Cardinal Giovanni de' Medici, who had taken a small house near the Via Florida. Michelangelo was touched to have been included, happy to leave his own dull room and board, to see Medici again.

Saturday morning at eleven, as he finished shaving and combing his hair, forming deep curls on his forehead, he heard the sound of trumpets and ran out to see the spectacle, excited to lay eyes at last on this Borgia Pope whom the Medici had feared and Savonarola had picked as his special target. Preceded by red-robed cardinals and the cross, and followed by purple-cloaked princes, Pope Alexander VI, born Rodrigo Borgia in Spain, dressed all in white, white stole and precious pearls, white robe on a white horse, was leading a procession through the Campo dei Fiori on his way to the Franciscan convent in Trastevere.

Sixty-four-year-old Alexander VI appeared to be a man of enormous virility, built big of bone and flesh, with a widely arced nose, swarthy complexion and fleshy cheeks. Though he was called a theater actor in Rome, he possessed many attributes besides the "brilliant insolence" for which he was known. As Cardinal Rodrigo Borgia he had won the reputation of amassing more beautiful women and vaster sums of wealth than anyone preceding him. As early as 1460 he had been reproved by Pope Pius II for "unseemly gallantry," a euphemism that covered his six known children of varying mothers, of whom his three favorites were Juan, playboy, exhibitionist, prodigious spender of the vast fortunes his father had absorbed from the Roman clergy and barons; Caesar, handsome sensualist, sadist and warrior, accused of clogging the Tiber with corpses; and the beautiful Lucrezia, accused by Rome of having informal love affairs between her growing list of official marriages.

The high walls around the Vatican were guarded by three thousand armed guards, but Rome had developed a communications system that spread news of the happenings therein to the seven hills. If good things occurred, little of it leaked out.

The full panoplied procession having passed, Michelangelo walked up the Via Florida to the Ponte. Because he had arrived too early, Paolo Rucellai received him in his study, a room with dark wood paneling, containing bound manuscripts, marble bas-reliefs, oil paintings on wood, a Florentine carved desk and leather chairs. Paolo's handsome face resembled Bernardo Rucellai's, with its strong regular features, large expressive eyes and light skin, none of which, Michelangelo mourned, had he inherited from his mother's family.

"We Florentines are a tightly knit colony here," Paolo was saying. "As you know by now we have our own government, treasury, laws . . . and means of enforcing them. Otherwise we could not exist in this morass. If you need help, come to us. Never go to a Roman. Their idea of a square deal is one in which they are protected on five sides."

In the drawing room he met the rest of the Florentine colony. He bowed to Piero, who was cool and formal after their quarrel in Bologna. Cardinal Giovanni, despised by the Pope and frozen out of all church activity, seemed genuinely happy to see him, though Giulio was frigid. Michelangelo learned that Contessina had been brought to bed with a son, Luigi, and was again *incinta*. To his eager question about whether Giuliano was also in Rome, Giovanni replied:

"Giuliano is at the court of Elisabetta Gonzaga and Guidobaldo Montefeltro in Urbino. He will complete his education there." The court of Urbino, high in the Apennines, was one of the most cultured in Italy. Giuliano would thrive.

Thirty Florentines sat down to dinner, eating *cannelloni* stuffed with fine chopped beef and mushrooms, veal in milk, tender green beans, drinking Broglio wines and talking animatedly. They never referred to their adversary as the Pope, or Alexander VI, but only as "the Borgia," striving to preserve their reverence for the papacy while expressing their utter contempt for the Spanish adventurer who through a series of calamitous mishaps had seized the Vatican and was ruling on the premise, according to Cavalcanti, that:

"All the wealth of Christendom belongs to the papacy. And we shall have it!"

The Florentines in turn were not popular with the Pope. He knew them to be adversaries, but he needed their banks, world trade, the high import duties they paid on products brought into Rome, their stability. Unlike the Roman barons, they did not wage war against him, they just prayed fervently for his demise. For this reason they favored Savonarola in his struggle against the Pope, and found Piero's mission embarrassing.

Over their port the guests grew nostalgic, spoke of Florence as though they were only a few minutes from the Piazza della Signoria. It was a moment for which Michelangelo had been waiting.

"What about art commissions in Rome?" he asked. "The Popes have always called in painters and sculptors."

"The Borgia summoned Pinturicchio from Perugia to decorate his apartments in the Vatican," said Cavalcanti, "and several rooms in Sant'Angelo. Pinturicchio finished last year and left Rome. Perugino has frescoed the Borgia's sitting room, as well as the tower in the papal palace. Perugino is gone now too.''

"What of marble?''

"My friend Andrea Bregno is the most respected sculptor in Rome; he seems to have a monopoly on tomb carving. Runs a big shop with a number of apprentices.''

"I should like to meet him.''

"You'll find him an able man, a lightninglike worker who has decorated most of the churches. I'll tell him that you are coming in to see him.''

Balducci shared his countrymen's detestation of Rome, yet there was one phase of Roman life that he relished: the seven thousand public women, assembled from all parts of the world. The next Sunday, following their midday dinner at the Trattoria Toscana, Balducci took Michelangelo for a tour. He knew Rome's piazzas, fountains, forums, triumphal arches, temples, not for their historical background but for the nationality of the women who made these areas their headquarters. They walked the streets for hours peering into the faces, adjudging the figures beneath the *gamurre,* while Balducci kept up a running fire of commentary on the virtues, drawbacks, pleasurable qualities of each. The Roman women, carrying parrots or monkeys on their shoulders, covered with jewelry and perfume and followed by their shiny black servants, arrogantly lorded it over the foreigners: the Spanish girls, with their jet-black hair and eyes of great clarity; the tall Greek girls dressed in their native white robes buckled at slender waists; the dark-skinned Egyptian women in cloaks hanging straight down from the shoulders; the blue-eyed blondes from the north of Europe, with flowers twined through their braids; the straight-haired Turkish women, peering from behind veils; the sloe-eyed Orientals swathed in yards of brightly colored silks . . .

"I never take the same one twice,'' Balducci explained. "I like variety, contrast, different colors, shapes, personalities. That's the interesting part for me, like traveling around the world.''

"How can you tell, Balducci, that the first one you pass won't be the most attractive of the day?''

"My innocent friend: it's the hunt that counts. That's why I prolong the search, until late at night sometimes. The externals are different: size, shape, mannerism. But the act? The same, largely the same: routine. It's the hunt that counts. . . .''

Michelangelo was amused. His experience with Clarissa had given him no desire for a simulation of love with some strange hired woman, only a desire for Clarissa.

"I'll wait for something better than routine.''

"For love?''

"In a way.''

"*Che rigorista!* I'm surprised to find an artist so conventional.''

"I save all my unconventionality for my carving.''

He could go without carving so long as he was drawing with a sculpture in mind. But the weeks passed and no word came from Cardinal Riario. He applied to the appointment secretaries several times, only to be put off. He understood that the cardinal was busy, for next to the Pope he was said to be the richest man in Europe, running a banking and commercial empire comparable to Lorenzo de' Medici's. Michelangelo never saw the man perform a religious service, but Leo volunteered that he said his offices in the palace chapel early in the morning.

Finally Leo arranged an appointment. Michelangelo carried a folio of sketches. Cardinal Riario appeared pleased to see him, though mildly surprised that he was still in Rome. He was in his office, surrounded by ledgers, the bookkeepers and scriveners with whom Michelangelo had been eating several times a week, but with whom he had not become friends. They stood at tall desks and did not look up from their work. When Michelangelo asked if the cardinal had decided what he might like to see sculptured from the seven-foot block, Riario replied:

"We will think about it. All in good time. In the meanwhile, Rome is a wonderful place for a young man. There are few pleasures of the world that we have not developed here. And now we must be excused."

Michelangelo walked slowly down the broad staircase to the unfinished courtyard, his chin burrowing into his chest. Apparently he was in the same position as he had been with Piero de' Medici: once one was under the roof of these gentlemen they were content; nothing further needed to be done.

Waiting for him in his room was a gaunt figure in black mantle over a white habit, eyes sunken, looking hungry and exhausted.

"Lionardo! What are you doing in Rome? How did you leave our family?"

"I have seen no one," said Lionardo coldly. "I was sent on a mission by Savonarola to Arezzo and Perugia. Now I go back to Viterbo to discipline a monastery there."

"When did you eat last?"

"You may give me a florin to take me to Viterbo."

Michelangelo dug into his money pouch, handed Lionardo a gold coin. He took it without change of expression.

"Don't you say thank you?" Michelangelo asked, nettled.

"For money you give to God? You are helping in His work. In return you will have a chance for salvation."

He had barely recovered from his surprise at seeing Lionardo when a letter arrived from his father, brought in by the weekly mail courier from Florence. Lodovico was writing in a high state of perturbation, for he had fallen into debt over a supply of textiles and the mercer was threatening to take him into court. Michelangelo turned the sheet over several times, searching amidst the news of his stepmother, brothers, aunt and uncle for some clue as to how much the mercer was demanding, and how Lodovico had fallen into debt to him in the first place. There was no clue. Only the entreaty, "Send me some money."

He had been anxious to settle down to a steady project because of his need for a consuming work. Now the time had come to face his money situation. He still did not know how much Cardinal Riario was going to pay him for his sculpture.

"How could His Eminence decide," Leo replied tartly to his question, "when he doesn't know what you are going to carve or how good it will be?"

He had been provided with drawing material and models, and it had cost him nothing to live in the palace; yet the few florins he had saved out from the Popolanos' payment for the St. John were gone. He had been eating with Balducci several times a week at the Florentine restaurant, and had had to buy an occasional shirt or pair of stockings for his visits to the Florentine homes, as well as a warm robe for the coming winter. The thirty florins he had brought to Rome to buy back his Bambino were lightening in his pouch. It appeared that he would have no cash payment from the cardinal until his sculpture was completed; and that would be many months away.

He counted his florins. There were twenty-six. He took thirteen of them to Jacopo Galli's bank, asked Balducci to send a credit draft to Galli's correspondent in Florence. He then returned to his workshop and sat down in deadly earnest to conceive a theme that would compel Cardinal Riario to order. Not knowing whether the man would prefer a religious or antique subject, he planned to prepare one of each.

It took a month to evolve, in rough wax, a full-bodied Apollo, inspired by the magnificent torso in the Cardinal Rovere's garden; and a Pietà which was a projection of his earlier Madonna and Child, at the end of the journey rather than the beginning.

He wrote the cardinal a note, telling him that he had two models ready for His Eminence to choose from. There was no reply. He wrote again, this time asking for an appointment. No answer came. He walked to Leo's house, interrupted his friend at supper with a beautiful woman, and was unceremoniously thrown out.

Leo came by the next morning, urbane as usual, promised to speak to Riario.

The days passed, and the weeks, while Michelangelo sat by, staring at the marble block, aching to get his hands on it.

"What reason does he give?" he stormed at Leo. "I need only one minute to let him choose between the themes."

"Cardinals don't have to give reasons," replied Leo. "Patience."

"The days of my life are going by," groaned Michelangelo, "and all I get to carve out of time is a block of 'Patience.' "

4

He could get no appointment with the cardinal. Leo explained that Riario was worried about a fleet of ships long overdue from the Orient and "had no stomach for art." All he could do, according to Leo, was pray that the cardinal's ships would come up the Tiber. . . .

From the sheer hunger to carve he went to see Andrea Bregno. Bregno was from Como, in northern Italy, a vitalic man of seventy-five. He stood in the middle of a large stable belonging to an ancient palace which he had converted into the most active sculpture studio in Rome by ripping out two of every three stalls, erecting workbenches, and putting a northern Italian apprentice into each of the expanded stalls.

Before going to the studio Michelangelo had stopped to see Bregno's altars and sarcophagi in Santa Maria del Popolo and Santa Maria sopra Minerva. Bregno was prolific, had taste, proficiency in the classical style, and was good at carving decorative reliefs. But he had no more inventiveness than a cat; no idea of creating illusion in carving, perspective, the dimension of depth. He could do anything he thought of with hammer and chisel; but he never carved anything that he had not already seen carved. When he needed new themes he searched for old Roman tombs and copied the patterns.

Bregno welcomed him cordially when Michelangelo told him that he was from Settignano. The old man's speech and manner were staccato, the only evidence of age the maze of wrinkles on his parchmentlike face.

"I did the earliest Riario tomb with Mino da Fiesole. He was an exquisite carver, made the loveliest cherubs. Since you come from his neighborhood, you are as good as Mino?"

"Perhaps."

"I can always use helpers. You see here, I have just finished this tabernacle for Santa Maria della Quercia in Viterbo. Now we are working on this Savelli monument for Santa Maria in Aracoeli. I did my apprenticeship for a silversmith, so we are never rushed and never late because I know within a matter of minutes how long each panel of fruit or spray of leaves will take to carve. I run my *bottega* like a silversmith's shop."

"But suppose you run into something new, Messer Bregno, an idea not carved before?"

Bregno stopped short, wagged his left hand back and forth in front of him.

"Sculpture is not an inventing art, it is reproductive. If I tried to make up designs, this studio would be in chaos. We carve here what others have carved before us."

"You carve it well," said Michelangelo, glancing about at the many projects in work.

"Superbly! I have never had a rejection in half a century. Very early in my career I learned to accept the convention, 'What is, must continue to be.' This wisdom of mine, Buonarroti, has paid me a fortune. If you want to be successful in Rome you must give the people exactly what they have grown up with."

"What would happen to a sculptor who said to himself, 'What is, must be changed'?"

"Changed? For the sake of change?"

"No, because he felt that each new piece he carved had to break through the existing conventions, achieve something fresh and different."

Bregno moved his jaws in a chewing movement, as though trying to pulverize this concept with his teeth. After a moment he spat into the sawdust underfoot, put a paternal hand on Michelangelo's shoulder.

"That is your youth speaking, my boy. A few months under my tutelage and you would lose such foolish notions. I might be willing to apprentice you for two years: five ducats the first, ten the second."

"Messer Bregno, I have already served a three-year apprenticeship under Bertoldo, in the Medici sculpture garden of Florence . . ."

"Bertoldo, who worked for Donatello?"

"The same."

"Too bad. Donatello has ruined sculpture for all you Florentines. However . . . We have quantities of angels to be carved on the tombs. . . ."

The wind-swept rains of November brought with them the departure of Piero de' Medici with troops to reconquer his empire; and Buonarroto's arrival. The rain had driven Michelangelo indoors to his bedroom, where he was drawing by lamplight on an ash-gray afternoon, when his brother appeared, drenched but with a happy smile lighting his small dark features. He embraced Michelangelo.

"I finished my apprenticeship and just couldn't bear Florence without you. I have come to look for work at the Wool Guild here."

Michelangelo was warmed by Buonarroto's affection.

"Come, get into dry clothes. When the rain stops I'll take you over to the Bear Hotel."

"I can't stay here?" asked Buonarroto wistfully.

Michelangelo glanced at the narrow monklike cot, the single chair. "I'm only a . . . guest. The Bear Inn is comfortable. Tell me quickly about Father and the mercer's suit."

"Quiet for the moment, thanks to your thirteen florins. But Consiglio claims that Father owes him much more money. Father ordered the textiles, all right, but what he intended to do with them, not even Lucrezia can find out."

While Buonarroto changed into Michelangelo's dry shirt, drawers and warm wool stockings he related the happenings of the last five months: Uncle Francesco had been ill; Lucrezia too had been bedded, apparently with a miscarriage. With nothing coming in except the rent from the Settignano farm, Lodovico could not meet his bills. He worried about finances night and day. Giovansimone had refused Lodovico's entreaties to contribute to the family coffers.

Buonarroto rented a bed at the Bear Inn; the brothers ate their suppers together at the *trattoria*. By the end of a week it was plain that there was no work for Buonarroto in Rome; the Florentines had no Wool Guild here, and the Romans would not hire a Florentine.

"I think you must return home," said Michelangelo regretfully. "If his four oldest sons are away, contributing nothing, how will Father manage?"

Buonarroto departed amidst a downpour; Piero de' Medici arrived back in Rome equally rain-soaked. The last remnants of his army were scattered, he was without funds, deserted even by the Orsini. He carried on his person a list of the families in Florence he was going to crush once he had regained power. Alfonsina had settled with her children in one of her ancestral homes; from here Piero scandalized Rome by his heavy gambling losses and violent quarrels in public with his brother Giovanni. He spent his mornings at the San Severino palace, then passed the hours until dark with his favorite courtesan of the moment. At night he went into the streets of Rome to take part in every evil the city offered, crawling back at daybreak to Alfonsina's palace. Equally bad, from the viewpoint of the Florentine colony, was his arrogance and tyranny. He announced that he would govern Florence by himself, without the help of any Council, because "I prefer to manage badly on my own account than well by others' help."

Michelangelo was surprised to have delivered to him an invitation written by Piero to attend Christmas dinner at Cardinal Giovanni's. The party was a lavish one. Giovanni's house was beautiful with the objects he had brought from Florence on his first trip: Medici paintings, bronzes, tapestries and silverplate . . . all pledged, at twenty per cent interest, to cover Piero's debts; so that now, as the Florentine bankers commented, "every florin the Medici spend costs them eight lire." Michelangelo was shocked to see the ravages of Piero's life: his left eyelid was almost closed, white patches of scalp showed through where clumps of hair had fallen out. The once handsome face was bloated and red-veined.

"Buonarroti," cried Piero. "I felt in Bologna that you were disloyal to the Medici. But I have learned from my sister Contessina that you saved many valuable gems and works of art at the palace."

"I was fortunate to have the opportunity, Excellency."

Piero imperiously raised his right arm. His voice was loud enough for everyone in the drawing room to hear.

"In return for your loyalty, Buonarroti, I commission you to do me a marble."

"That would make me happy, Excellency," replied Michelangelo quietly.

"A large statue," continued Piero loftily.

"Better make it small," contributed Giovanni, his plump face twisted in a deprecatory smile. "My brother seems to be moving around a lot, and he couldn't carry a life-size Hercules under his arm."

Piero waved his brother's words aside.

"I will send for you shortly. At that time, I shall give you my orders."

"I will await word."

On the way home from the tension-filled evening he caught his first glimpse of Torrigiani. He was with a group of young Romans, richly dressed in camlet with gold braid, his handsome face wreathed in laughter as he walked down the street, arms thrown affectionately about the shoulders of his companions, all of them full of wine and good cheer, roaring with laughter at Torrigiani's performance.

Michelangelo felt ill. He asked himself if what he was feeling was fear. Yet he knew that it was something more, something in his experience akin to the sacking of the Medici palace, the deterioration of Piero, an awareness of the senseless destructiveness that lay inherent in time and space, ready to lash out and destroy.

Cardinal Riario's ships at last reached the Ripetta docks. Leo wangled an invitation for Michelangelo to a New Year's reception.

"I'll get a couple of collapsible black boxes lined with velvet," he explained, "the kind the jewelry people use to display tiaras and crowns. We will put in your two clay models. When the cardinal is surrounded by people he likes to impress, I'll give you the signal."

And so he did. Cardinal Riario was surrounded by the princes of the Church, the Pope, his sons Juan and Caesar, Lucrezia and her husband, cardinals, bishops, the noble families of Rome, the women in gowns of silk and velvet with lavish jewelry.

Leo turned to Riario and said, "Buonarroti has been making sculpture models for you to choose between, Your Grace."

Michelangelo set the black boxes on a table, released the springs and let the sides fall away. He took one of his models in the palm of each hand, extending them for the cardinal to see. There was a murmur of pleasure from the men, while the women clapped their gloved hands discreetly.

"Excellent! Excellent!" cried the cardinal, looking at the models. "Keep working, my dear boy, and soon we'll have the one we want."

Michelangelo asked hoarsely, "Then Your Grace would not have me carve either of these in marble?"

Cardinal Riario turned to Leo. "Bring your friend to me as soon as he has new models. I'm sure they will be exquisite."

Outside the reception room, Michelangelo's anger stormed in torrential words.

"What kind of man is that? He's the one who asked me to carve something, who bought the marble for me. . . . I have a living to make. I could be here for months, for years, and not be allowed to touch that block."

Leo was despondent. "I thought he might like to flatter his guests by letting them choose. . . ."

"That's a fine way to decide what is to be carved out of a seven-foot column of Carrara marble!"

"But better than no decision at all! I'm sorry."

Michelangelo became contrite.

"Forgive my bitterness. I've spoiled your day. Go back to the reception."

Alone, he walked the streets, crowded now with families and children out to celebrate the holiday. From the Pincio hill fireworks of radiating rockets and revolving wheels burst into the air. Soggi was right! Sculpture was on the bottom of everybody's list. He would wander like a peddler singing, "Who wants an Apollo? A Pietà?"

"Time," he muttered to himself. "Everybody wants me to give them time. But time is as empty as space unless I can fill it with figures."

He went into a black funk, unable to speak civilly to anyone. Balducci found a golden-haired Florentine girl to help bring him out of his melancholy. Michelangelo smiled for the first time since he had left Cardinal Riario's reception.

"Ah, Balducci, if life were as simple as you conceive it."

In the Trattoria Toscana they came upon Giuliano da Sangallo, the Florentine architect, friend of Lorenzo, and the first man to instruct Michelangelo in the art of architecture. The luxuriant long golden mustaches still rolled down the sides of his mouth, but he looked lonely. He had had to leave his wife and son behind in Florence while he lived in rented rooms in Rome, waiting for better commissions than his present job of building a wooden ceiling for Santa Maria Maggiore, overlaying it with the first gold brought from America by Columbus. He invited Michelangelo and Balducci to join him, asked Michelangelo how things were going for him here in Rome, listening intently while the younger man spilled out his frustration.

"You are in the service of the wrong cardinal," Sangallo concluded. "It was Cardinal Rovere who came to Florence in 1481 to commission Ghirlandaio, Botticelli and Rosselli to paint murals for his uncle Sixtus IV's chapel. It was he who persuaded Sixtus to start the first public library in Rome, and to assemble the Capitoline Museum of bronzes. When Cardinal Rovere returns to Rome, I shall introduce you."

Heartened, Michelangelo asked, "When does he return?"

"He is in Paris now. He is bitter about the Borgia, and has stayed away for several years. But there is every indication that he will be the next Pope. Tomorrow I will come for you and show you the Rome I like best; not this stinking shambles of today, but the Rome of grandeur, when the world's greatest architects built here; the Rome I shall re-create stone upon stone once Cardinal Rovere becomes Pope. By tomorrow night you'll forget you wanted to sculpture, and give yourself over to architecture."

It was a needed diversion.

Sangallo wanted them to start first with the Pantheon because it was to the top of this magnificent Roman vaulted structure that Brunelleschi had climbed to learn an architectural secret forgotten for fifteen hundred years: that this was not one dome, but two, built one inside the other, the two domes interlaced structurally. With this revelation of Roman genius from 27 B.C., Brunelleschi had been able to return to Florence and apply the idea to closing the dome of the cathedral, which had stood open for more than a hundred years.

Sangallo handed Michelangelo a block of architectural paper, exclaimed, "Very well, now we re-create the Pantheon as the Romans of the time of Augustus saw it."

First they sketched inside, re-establishing the marble-faced interior, with the opening to the sky at the center of the dome. They moved outside, drew the sixteen red and gray granite columns holding up the portico, the giant bronze doors, the dome covered with bronze tiles, the vast brick circular structure as the historians had described it.

Then with paper pads under their arms they made their way to the Via delle Botteghe Oscure, and climbed up the Capitoline hill. Here, overlooking the great Roman forum, they were at the heart of the early Roman capital. Now it was a rubble heap with rough earthen mounds on which goats and swine were grazing, yet here on the two summits had been the temple of Jupiter and the temple of Juno Moneta, from the sixth century B.C.

While Sangallo talked about the roof of the temple of Jupiter, bronze overlaid thickly with gold, as described by Dionysius of Halicarnassus, then about the three rows of columns on the front, the single row on each side, the inside consisting of three parallel shrines to Jupiter, Juno and Minerva, they brought the structure to life on their paper. Plutarch had described the fourth temple of Domitian: slender pillars of Pentelic marble, the buildings of tremendous rustic stone, on the portico enthroned statues before which the emperors and magistrates had made their sacrifices to the gods; all this they sketched.

They scrambled down the side of the hill to the Roman forum, spent the remainder of their hours here, drawing the buildings as they had been in the days of their greatness: the temples of Saturn and Vespasian, the senate house of Julius Caesar, built of severely plain yellow brick; the great columned Castor's temple with its rich Corinthian capitals; then on through the arch of Titus to the colosseum . . . Michelangelo's hands flying faster than they ever had in his life, trying to keep up with Sangallo, who was pouring out a stream of sketches and verbal descriptions.

Night fell. Michelangelo was exhausted, Sangallo triumphant.

"Now you have uncovered the glory that was Rome. Work in it every day. Go up to the Palatine and reconstruct the baths of Severus, Flavian's palace. Go to the Circus Maximus, the basilica of Constantine, the golden house of Nero at the bottom of the Esquiline. The Romans were the greatest architects the world has known."

Michelangelo glanced at Sangallo's mobile, attractive face, the excitement glowing in his eyes.

"Sangallo has old Roman architecture to make his days important, Balducci his girls. And I could use a sculpture commission," he murmured to himself.

5

Deep in his bosom was the growing doubt that he would ever get Cardinal Riario's approval to carve the seven-foot block. In desperation he sought out Piero at the Orsini palace. He would suggest only a small, attractive piece to increase his chance of acceptance. Piero was in the midst of an uproarious quarrel with the servants over the way they had cooked his dinner. Alfonsina sat opposite him at the huge oak table. Her tired eyes gave him a brief flash of recognition.

"Excellency, I have the time now to make you a beautiful sculpture, if you would give me the order to commence."

Piero was half awake.

"Do you not recall? At your Christmas reception you ordered . . ."

"What about it?"

"I have a design for a Cupid, if you think that would please you."

"A Cupid? Well, why not?"

"I only needed your approval."

Piero had started shouting again. Michelangelo knew that he had been dismissed; but he had also been told to go ahead. He walked along the riverbank to the stoneyards by the docks on the Tiber, saw a small block, paid five florins from his dwindling supply, and trudged behind the barrow as a boy wheeled it home for him.

It took him two days to find out that the marble was bad. He had acted stupidly, walked into a yard and bought the first block that looked good to him. He never would have done such a thing in Florence. But here in Rome he had behaved like a novice. His five florins were thrown away.

The next morning at dawn he was in the yard of the Guffatti, from whom Cardinal Riario had bought the seven-foot column. Now he tested the blocks, at length found a white marble that looked translucent in the early rays of the sun, that showed no gullies or fissures when under water. This time he had invested his five florins well; but his purse was reduced to a last three florins.

He sketched for a morning in the workingmen's quarter in Trastevere, children playing in the streets, lying on pallets in front of the clanging metal shops. It was only a matter of days before he had his hammer and chisel raised for the first blows. Balducci asked:

"Hadn't you better get a signed commitment from Piero? He's pouring every florin he can commandeer into mercenaries to mount another attack on Florence."

Piero was not having any contracts.

"My dear Buonarroti, I'll be leaving Rome before you can finish this Cupid. In all likelihood I'll never be back. . . ."

"Are you telling me, Excellency, that you have changed your mind?" His need had put a sharp edge to his tongue.

"A Medici never changes his mind," said Piero coldly. "It's just that I'm preoccupied. Postpone the matter for a year . . ."

Out in the freezing Piazza Sant'Apollinare, Michelangelo cried, "It serves me right!" He had said it out loud, his voice bitter, his face contorted with disgust. Only his eagerness to begin a piece for someone could have considered Piero's flimsy agreement a commitment.

He carved the Cupid anyway, for the joy of working in the white marble and breathing its dust.

Two frustrating months passed before he could get another appointment with Cardinal Riario.

"What have you got for me today?" he asked in good humor. "Something vigorously pagan, to match those fine antiques in the Cardinal Rovere's garden?"

Michelangelo lied quickly. "Yes, Your Grace."

He sat on the bed in his narrow room with the sweat pouring off him as though he had a fever, searching his mind for the most totally joyous, pleasure-giving Greek god he could find. In the Florentine quarter one night, Altoviti had asked:

"Have you ever thought of doing a Bacchus?"

"No, I rarely drink wine."

"Bacchus is also Dionysus, a nature god, symbolizing fruitfulness. He is the god who brought strange and wondrous gifts to man, enabling him to forget his misery, drudgery, the brute tragedy of life. If it is good for man to have pleasure, to laugh, sing, be happy, then we owe much to Bacchus."

Into his memory came a youth he had seen at the baths, with the proportioned body of an athlete: slim legs and waist, powerfully muscled chest and arms, pantherlike.

His work was his only reward: on Good Friday violence broke out in Rome, the cobblestones of the city running with blood. It started with a riot incited by the Pope's Spanish mercenaries, who were so bitterly hated by the Romans that they fought the armed soldiers with clubs and stones; moved on to Lucrezia Borgia's husband, a Sforza, fleeing Rome after announcing that the Borgias were about to murder him because they wanted a Spanish alliance for Lucrezia; moved on to another departure of Piero de' Medici at the head of an army of thirteen hundred mercenaries to storm Florence; moved on to revolt in the Florentine quarter when the Pope excommunicated Savonarola; and ended in the grisly murder of Juan Borgia. Fishermen angling in the Tiber found Juan Borgia's body and brought it ashore, still dressed in velvet coat and mantle, boots and spurs, slashed with nine knife wounds, the hands tied. The Romans did little to conceal their joy.

A reign of terror settled over Rome. The Vatican and the city were paralyzed. The Pope's police forced their way into every house Juan had ever visited, tortured servants in their search for clues, ransacked the homes of the Florentines to prove a conspiracy, accused Lucrezia's rejected husband of the murder, then every noble Roman family that had ever fought the papacy . . . until word got around that the Pope, along with the rest of Rome, was convinced that Caesar had killed his older brother to get him out of the way of his own career.

Cardinal Riario went into mourning with his Pope. The palace was closed to all but the most compelling business. Sculpture was far from compelling business. It was a luxury to be abandoned the moment anything went wrong.

"The cardinal won't talk sculpture for a long time," said Leo Baglioni. "I would advise you to look for another patron."

"In Rome? Won't Cardinal Riario's attitude be reflected all over the city?"

"Unfortunately, yes. But is Florence any better under Savonarola?"

"No. But it's home. Could you arrange one last appointment? So that I can get paid."

"Paid? You haven't made a sculpture."

"I've worked. I've made drawings, models. But you wouldn't let me begin carving. The cardinal's a rich man, and I'm down to my last denari."

He tossed on his bed through the night, was cranky when Balducci insisted that he come with him to hunt ducks in the marshes:

"The air will be good for you. Make a man of you. I spend every spare hour tramping and shooting to keep up my manhood."

Michelangelo knew what Balducci meant by his manhood. He said satirically, "Building up your coin of the realm to spend on the women."

"But of course!" cried Balducci. "Every man builds up his fortune to spend somewhere."

Troubles all come ripe at the same time, like tomatoes. Lionardo showed up again, his habit torn, blood on his face. From his incoherent story, Michelangelo gathered that the monks at Viterbo had turned on him, beaten him and ejected him from the monastery for his championing of the excommunicated Savonarola.

"I want to get home to San Marco," he said hoarsely, licking his cracked lips. "Give me money for the journey."

Michelangelo took his last coins out of the leather pouch.

"I, too, feel badly beaten. My hope is also to get home. But stay here with me for a few days, until you feel better."

"Thank you, no, Michelagnolo. And thank you for the money."

It was the first softness Michelangelo had heard in his brother's voice in years.

The second blow was the news of his stepmother Lucrezia's death, written in a few broken sentences by his father. *"Il Migliore,"* he thought with affection, "The Best." She had bought only the best, and given of her best to all of them, the nine Buonarroti she had undertaken to feed. Had Lodovico loved her? It was hard to say. Had she loved them? This big family into which she had moved as a second wife? Yes, she had. It was not her fault if her only talent or excitement was for cooking. She had given unstintingly of what she had; and her stepson shed a tear for her passing.

A few days later a hotel groom brought a note from the Bear Inn announcing that Buonarroto was back. He hurried over, past the city market in Piazza Navona, the factories and shops between the ruined theater of Pompey and stadium of Domitian, the vegetable gardens leading to Piazza Sant'Apollinare.

"What of Father?" demanded Michelangelo. "How has he taken Lucrezia's death?"

"Badly. Locks himself in his bedroom."

"We must find him another wife."

"He says he would rather live alone than go through another death." He paused, then added, "The mercer is about to have him arrested for the bad debt. Consiglio can prove that Father took the goods, and since we have only a few florins left it could mean prison."

"Prison! *Dio mio!* He must sell the Settignano villa and farm."

"He can't. It's under long-term lease. Besides, he says he would rather go to the Stinche than deprive us of our last inheritance."

Michelangelo was furious.

"Our last inheritance, a house? Our last inheritance is the Buonarroti name. We've got to protect it."

"But what to do? I earn only a few scudi a month . . ."

"And I earn nothing. But I will! I'll make Cardinal Riario see the justice of my position."

The cardinal listened, playing quietly with the long gold chain around his neck.

"I would not expect you to have given this time for nothing."

"Thank you, Excellency; I knew you would be generous."

"Indeed I shall. I relinquish all right and title to the marble block and the thirty-seven ducats it cost me. The marble is yours, in return for patient waiting."

He had only one recourse: the Florentine bankers, Rucellai and Cavalcanti. He would go into debt. He sat down and wrote his father a letter telling him, "I shall send you whatever you ask me, even if I should have to sell myself as a slave," then went to Paolo Rucellai to explain his plight.

"A loan from the bank? No; it is too expensive for you at twenty per cent interest. From me, yes, as a personal loan without interest. Will twenty-five florins help?"

"I will pay it back; you will see."

"You are to forget about it until you have money in your belt."

He ran through the labyrinth of unpaved streets crowded with heavy traffic and clogged with sand from the river, gave Buonarroto the credit slip signed by Rucellai, added to it a note to Consiglio stating that he would take responsibility for the balance of the debt, guaranteeing to pay it within the year.

"That's what Father wanted, of course," Buonarroto said thoughtfully, fingering the two notes. "He's not going to earn anything more; nor is Uncle Francesco. You and me, we are the Buonarroti now. We can expect no help from Lionardo or Giovansimone. And the little one, Sigismondo . . . the Wine Guild has released him. Once Father sees these papers you will have the support of the Buonarroti family on your hands."

Good fortune comes in bunches, as do peaches when the trees turn ripe. Michelangelo finished polishing his Cupid, a lovely child just awakened from sleep and holding up its arms to be taken by his mother. Balducci was enchanted with its lighthearted warmth, the beautiful satiny texture. He asked if they could carry it to the Galli house to show his boss, Jacopo Galli.

There was no Bugiardini to wheel the marble through the streets. Balducci rented a mule with a large saddlebag. Michelangelo wrapped his Cupid in a blanket, led the animal past San Lorenzo in Damaso, through the lane of Lentari in Parione.

The Casa Galli had been built by one of Jacopo Galli's ancestors. Galli was grateful to this predecessor because he had begun, at the same time, a collection of ancient sculptures that was second only to the Cardinal Rovere's.

Balducci tied the mule while Michelangelo unwrapped the Cupid. After descending a broad flight of stone stairs, Michelangelo found himself in an atrium, closed on three sides by the house, and on the fourth by the flight of steps, giving the area the illusion of being a sunken garden; or, Michelangelo thought as he glanced hastily about him, a sunken wilderness of statues, marble friezes, crouching animals.

Jacopo Galli, who had been educated at the university in Rome, and had been reading every day of his life since, put down a copy of Aristophanes' *Frogs*, began pulling himself out of a low-lying chaise. He seemed never to stop getting up as he unfolded: six feet, six and a half, surely not seven? The tallest man Michelangelo had ever seen, hunched over at the shoulders from a lifetime of stooping to the short-statured Romans. Michelangelo was as a child before him.

"Ah, you come with a marble in your arms. That is the sight I like best in my garden."

Michelangelo set the Cupid down on the table next to Galli's book, turned to look up into the man's blue eyes.

"I'm afraid I've brought my Cupid into a rough arena."

"I think not," murmured Galli in a voice that he made an effort to keep reasonable-sized. "Balducci, take your friend Buonarroti into the house for a slice of cold watermelon."

When they returned to the garden a few minutes later they found that Galli had removed a torso from a pedestal on the low wall next to the steps and replaced it with the Cupid. He had settled back into the chaise. Standing behind his host, Michelangelo had an opportunity to study the three Greek torsos, Roman sarcophagus, temple frieze, wall slab with huge seated griffin, Egyptian lion with near-human head.

Galli's eyes were twinkling. "I feel as though your Cupid has been sitting there since the day I was born, a lineal descendant of any of these carvings. Would you sell it to me? What price shall we set?"

Humbly, Michelangelo murmured, "That is up to you."

"First, tell me your circumstances."

Michelangelo related the story of his year with Riario.

"So you end up without a scudo of pay, and a seven-foot marble block? Shall we say the Cupid is worth fifty ducats? Because I know you need money I will allow my cupidity to knock the price down to twenty-five ducats. Then, because I detest shrewdness in dealing with the arts, I will take the twenty-five ducats I was going to underpay you, and add them to my original estimate. Do you approve my formula?"

Michelangelo's amber eyes shone.

"Signor Galli, for a year I have been thinking bad things about the Romans. In your name, I apologize to the whole city."

Galli bowed while sitting down. "Now tell me about this seven-foot marble block. What do you think might be carved from that?"

Michelangelo told him about his drawings for an Apollo, for a Pietà, for a Bacchus. Galli was intrigued.

"I've never heard of a Bacchus unearthed hereabouts, though there are one or two that were brought from Greece, figures of old men with beards, rather dull."

"No, no, my Bacchus would be young, as befits a god of joy and fertility."

"Bring me the drawings tomorrow at nine."

Galli brought a purse from the house and handed Michelangelo seventy-five ducats. Michelangelo led the mule through the darkening streets to the stable where he paid for his hire, then walked to Rucellai's to return the twenty-five florins he had borrowed.

The next evening he presented himself in the Galli garden at the appointed time. No one was present. It seemed as though hours passed. He saw himself abandoning his marble, or reselling it to Guffatti for a fraction of its cost and returning to Florence with the next pack train. Then Galli came into the garden, welcomed him, poured them an apéritif, and settled down to study the drawings. Soon Signora Galli, a tall, lithe woman, no longer young but preserving a patrician beauty, joined them for supper over candlelight. A cool breeze stirred the summer heat. When supper was over, Galli asked:

"Would you be willing to move your block here, and carve this Bacchus for me? You could have a room to live in. I would pay you three hundred ducats for the completed statue."

Michelangelo bowed his head so that the candle gleam would not betray him. He had been saved from an ignominious return to Florence, from defeat.

Yet the next morning when he walked alongside the Guffatti wagon carrying his marble column from the Riario palace to Galli's, with his small bag of clothes under his arm, he felt like a mendicant. Was he to spend his years moving from one charitable bedroom to another? He knew that many artists traveled from court to court, from patron to patron, for the most part well housed, fed and entertained; but he also knew he would not be content to do so. He promised himself that one day soon he must become his own man, inside his own walls.

6

He was shown into a bedroom on the wing of the U opposite from the one occupied by the Galli, a pleasant room warm with sunlight. A door on the far side admitted to a fig orchard. At the edge of the orchard was a storage shed with a hard earthen floor. Michelangelo took off the plank roof, letting the fig trees close it over in shade. The building backed onto a rear lane, through which friends could come and visit him and materials be delivered. He could not see the house through the trees, and he was far enough away so that they could not hear his hammering. On the outside he rigged up a barrel so that he could bring water from the well and shower at night before putting on clean clothes and joining the Galli for supper in the garden. Jacopo Galli did not leave his bank at midday; no dinner was served except on Sundays and religious holidays. A servant brought Michelangelo a light meal on a tray, which he ate off his drafting board. He was grateful not to have to change clothes at midday, or be sociable.

He had a letter from his father, acknowledging the twenty-five florins. The mercer had accepted Michelangelo's assurance of payment, but he wanted half of the fifty florins still owed him. Could he possibly send another twenty-five florins by the Saturday post?

Michelangelo sighed, donned a lightweight blouse, took twenty-five ducats to Jacopo Galli's bank in the Piazza San Celso next to the bank of the Chigi family. Balducci was not in, so he went to Jacopo Galli's desk. Galli looked up, gave no sign of recognition. Nor did Michelangelo recognize Jacopo Galli; the face was stern, cold, expressionless. He asked in an impersonal tone what Michelangelo desired.

"A credit . . . for twenty-five florins. To send to Florence."

He put his coins on the desk. Galli spoke to a clerk nearby. The transaction was swiftly made. Galli returned his masked eyes and hard-set mouth to his papers.

Michelangelo was staggered. "What have I done to offend?" he demanded of himself.

It was dark before he could bring himself to return to the house. From his room he saw lights in the garden. He opened the door gingerly.

"Ah, there you are!" cried Galli. "Come have a glass of this fine Madeira."

Jacopo Galli was sprawled relaxedly in his chaise. He asked whether Michelangelo had set up his shop, what more he would need. His change of manner was simply explained. Jacopo Galli apparently could not, or would not, establish a bridge between the halves of his life. At his bank he held himself rigid, brusque. His business associates admired the way in which he dispatched their affairs and brought them the most profitable result, but did not like him as a person. They said he was not human. When he reached home Galli shed this skin as though he were a lizard, was gay, indulgent, humorous. No word of business ever passed his lips. Here in the garden he talked art, literature, history, philosophy. The friends who dropped in each evening loved him, considered him overgenerous with his family and household.

For the first time since he reached Rome, Michelangelo began to meet interesting Romans: Peter Sabinus, professor of Eloquence at the university, who cared little for Galli's sculptures but who had what Galli described as "an incredible number of early Christian inscriptions"; the collector Giovanni Capocci, one of the first Romans to attempt disciplined excavating at the catacombs; Pomponius Laetus, one of Galli's old professors, an illegitimate son of the powerful Sanseverino family, who could have dawdled in idle elegance but lived only for learning, ill clad in buckskins and housed in a shack.

"I used to go to his lecture hall at midnight to get a seat," Galli told Michelangelo. "Then we'd wait for dawn, until we saw him coming down the hill, lantern in one hand, old manuscript in the other. He was tortured by the Inquisition because our Academy, like your Plato Academy in Florence, was suspected of heresy, paganism, republicanism." Galli chuckled. "All perfectly true charges. Pomponius is so steeped in paganism that the sight of an antique monument can move him to tears."

Michelangelo suspected that Galli too was "steeped in paganism," for he never saw a man of the Church at Galli's, with the exception of the blind brothers, Aurelius and Raffaelle Lippus, Augustinians from Santo Spirito in Florence, who improvised Latin songs and poetic hymns on their lyres; and the French Jean Villiers de la Groslaye, Cardinal of San Dionigi, a wisp of a man in an elegantly trimmed white beard and scarlet cassock who had begun his religious life as a Benedictine monk and, beloved by Charles VIII for his devoutness and learning, had been made a cardinal through the king's intervention. He had nothing to do with the corruption of the Borgias, living the same devout life in Rome that he had in the Benedictine monasteries, continuing his studies of the Church Fathers, on whom he was an authority.

Not all the scholars were aged. He made friends with Jacopo Sadoleto from Ferrara, twenty years old, a fine poet and Latinist; Serafino, an idolized poet in the court of Lucrezia Borgia, who never mentioned the Borgias or the Vatican when he visited at Galli's, but read his historical poems while he accompanied himself on the lute; Sannazaro, forty, but seeming thirty, who mingled pagan and Christian images in his verse.

The Galli made the minimum number of gestures of conformity; they went to mass most Sundays and on the important holy days. Jacopo Galli confided that his anti-clericalism was the only gesture he could make against the corruption of the Borgias and their followers.

"From my reading, Michelangelo, I have been able to follow the rise, fulfillment, decay and disappearance of many religions. That is what is happening to our religion today. Christianity has had fifteen hundred years to prove itself, and has ended in . . . what? Borgia murders, greed, incest, perversion of every tenet of our faith. Rome is more evil today than Sodom and Gomorrah when they were destroyed by fire."

"Even as Savonarola has said?"

"As Savonarola has said. A hundred years of Borgias and there will be nothing left here but a historic pile of stones."

"The Borgias can't rule for a hundred years, can they?"

Galli's big, open face was creased by furrows.

"Caesar Borgia has just crowned Federigo as King of Naples, returned to Rome in triumph, and been consigned his brother Juan's estate by the Pope. An archbishop has been caught forging dispensations. A bishop was caught with ten thousand ducats from the sale of offices in the Curia. And so it goes."

Now all the drawings he had made for the Bacchus, the Greek god of joy, seemed superficial and cynical. He had tried to project himself backward into an Elysian age; but he was playing with a myth as a child plays with toys. His present reality was Rome: the Pope, Vatican, cardinals, bishops, the city plunged deep into corruption and decadence because the hierarchy battened off it. He felt a total revulsion for this Rome. But could he sculpture from hate? Could he use his pure white marble, which he loved, to depict the evil and smell of death that were destroying what had once been the capital of the world? Was there not the danger that his marble too would become hateful? He could not bring himself to abandon the Greek ideal of beauty-out-of-marble.

He slept fitfully. Often he went to Galli's library, lit a lamp and took up writing materials, as he had at Aldovrandi's after he had met Clarissa. It had been love that churned him then, made him pour out lines to "cool himself off." Now it was hate, as searing an emotion as love, that caused him to pour out hundreds of lines until, at dawn, he had had his say.

> Here helms and swords are made of chalices:
> The blood of Christ is sold so much the quart:
> His cross and thorns are spears and shields;
>   and short
> Must be the time ere even his patience cease.
>
> Nay, let him come no more to raise the fees
> Of this foul sacrilege beyond report!
> For Rome still flays and sells him at the court
> Where paths are closed to virtue's fair increase. . . .
>
> God welcomes poverty perchance with pleasure:
> But of that better life what hope have we,
> When the blessed banner leads to nought but ill?

He went searching through the collections in Rome for ancient carvings. The only young Bacchus he could find was about fifteen years old, dead sober. From the way he held a bunch of grapes, negligently, he seemed bored with the fact that he had conceived this strangest of fruits.

His sculpture would have joy in it, try to capture the sense of fertility of Dionysus, the nature god, the power of the intoxicating drink that enabled a man to laugh and sing and forget for a while the sorrow of his earthly miseries. And then, perhaps, at the same time he could portray the decay that came with too much forgetfulness, that he saw all around him, when man surrendered his moral and spiritual values for the pleasures of the flesh. The Bacchus would be the central figure of his theme, a human being rather than a demigod; then there would be a child of about seven, sweet-faced, lovable, nibbling from a bunch of grapes. His composition would have death in it too: the tiger, who liked wine and was loved by Bacchus, with the deadest, dead skin and head conceivable.

He went to the baths to look for models, thinking he might put together a composite Bacchus as he had his Hercules from hundreds of Tuscans: a throat here, a forearm there, a belly in the next place. But when after a few weeks he welded his features together with hard silver pen, his composite portrait was not convincing. He took himself to Leo Baglioni.

"I need a model. Young. Under thirty. Of a high family."

"And a beautiful body?"

"That once was, but is no longer. A figure that has been corrupted."

"By what?"

"Wine. Sensuousness. Self-indulgence."

Leo thought for a moment, flicking over in his mind the figures and features of the Roman youths he knew.

"I may know your man. The Count Ghinazzo. But he's wealthy, of a noble family. What can we offer him by way of inducement?"

"Flattery. That he is to be immortalized as the great Greek god Bacchus. Or Dionysus, if he prefers."

"That might work. He's idle and can give you his days . . . or what's left of them after he awakens from his bacchanals of the night before."

The count was delighted with his new role. When he had walked through the orchard with Michelangelo, stripped off his clothes and taken the pose Michelangelo requested, he said:

"You know, it's a coincidence my being selected for this. I've always thought of myself as a kind of god."

Michelangelo went to his drawing board, sucked in his breath with pleasure. If he had searched all of Italy he could not have found a more fitting subject than Leo had selected for him: the head a bit too small for the body, the belly soft and fleshy, the buttocks too large for the torso, the upper arm a touch flaccid, the legs as straight and firmly molded as a Greek wrestler's. It was a figure desexed, the eyes unfocused from too much wine at dinner, the mouth dazedly half open; yet the arm that held the wine cup aloft flexed with muscular power, and over all a flawless satin-smooth skin glistened in the strong frontal sunlight that made him appear illumined from within.

"You're perfect!" Michelangelo cried impulsively. "Bacchus to the very life."

"Delighted you think so," said Count Ghinazzo without turning his head. "When Leo first proposed serving as a model I told him not to be a bore. But this may prove to be interesting."

"What time can I expect you tomorrow? And don't hesitate to bring your wine with you."

"That makes everything splendid. I can remain the entire afternoon. Without wine, the day is so dull."

"You will never appear dull to me, *messere*. I will see you in a new light every minute."

He cast the man in a hundred poses, his right leg bent sharply at the knee, toes barely touching the rough wooden base; the body slumped over on one leg, striving to stand up, the torso leaning backward; the small head thrust forward, turned one way and another, moving slightly, satiated with pleasure. And in the late afternoons, when Ghinazzo had drunk much wine, Michelangelo wound bunches of grapes through his hair, sketching him as though the grapes were growing there . . . which amused the Roman inordinately. Until one afternoon he drank too much of the wine, began to sway dizzily, fell off the wood block and hit his chin on the hard earth, knocking himself out. Michelangelo revived him by throwing a bucket of water over him. Count Ghinazzo shivered into his clothes, disappeared through the orchard and from Michelangelo's life.

Jacopo Galli found him a lively boy of seven, with curling golden hair and large tender eyes, a delightful lad with whom Michelangelo made friends as he sketched. His only problem was to get the boy to maintain the difficult pose of holding his left arm in a *contrapposto* position against his chest, so that he could crush the bunch of grapes in his mouth. Next he went into the countryside, spending a whole day drawing the legs, hoofs and curling fur of the goats cropping the hillsides.

That was how his pen finally designed his sculpture: in the center the weak, confused, arrogant, soon to be destroyed young man holding cup aloft, behind him the idyllic child, clear-eyed, munching his grapes, symbol of joy; between them the tiger skin. The Bacchus, hollow within himself, flabby, reeling, already old; the Satyr, eternally young and gay, symbol of man's childhood and naughty innocence.

Sunday morning he invited Galli to the workshop to show him his drawing: the bowl held high in Bacchus' hand, the intertwined grapes and leaves that made up his hair, the long, curving bunch of grapes that formed a structural bond between the Bacchus and the Satyr, the tree trunk on which the Bacchus leaned and the Satyr would be sitting, and lastly the tiger skin held in the Bacchus' falling hand, winding down through the Satyr's arm, its head hanging between the Satyr's open-stanced goat's hoofs, the hollow tiger head a picturization of what would happen to the Bacchus' head, ere long.

Galli asked countless questions. Michelangelo explained that he would do some wax or clay modeling, some carving on scrap marble to test the component parts, "the way the Satyr's head rests against the Bacchus' arm, for instance."

"And the way the boy's thigh melts into the furry leg of the Satyr."

"Exactly."

Galli was fascinated. "I don't know how to thank you."

Michelangelo laughed a little embarrassedly.

"There is one way. Could you send some florins to Florence?"

Galli hunched his huge shoulders over Michelangelo protectively.

"Would you like our correspondent in Florence to deliver a few florins each month to your father, I mean regularly? Then you won't be distressed each time a packet of mail arrives. It will cost you no more that way; and we'll keep a record for you against the commission price."

". . . it isn't his fault, really," Michelangelo proffered, his pride hurt. "My uncle is ill, there are some debts . . ."

7

He lowered his column to a horizontal position on the ground, secured it on tightly wedged beams, then, using a point, bit into the corner where the wine cup would emerge. He concentrated on the frontal view, then started to join up the two sides to establish the visual flow. After heading for the high points of the fingers of the hand holding the cup, and the extended right kneecap, he struck in between to find the stomach, to establish the relationship between the highest projections and the deepest penetration. The intermediary forms would follow in natural sequence, as the forms of the side and back would take their cue from the front. He massed about the upper torso to indicate the reeling position of the upright figure, then turned the block over clockwise so that he could work on the width-plane, roughing out the cup-arm which was in the key position.

He summoned one of the Guffatti to help him set the column vertical again. Now the marble presented its personality: its size, proportion, weight. He sat in front of the block, studied it concentratedly, allowed it to speak, to establish its own demands. Now he felt fear, as though he were meeting an unknown person. To sculpture is to remove marble; it is also to probe, dig, sweat, think, feel and live with it until it is completed. Half the original weight of this block would remain in the finished statue; the rest would lie out in the orchard in chips and dust. His one regret was that he would sometimes have to eat and sleep, painful breaks when his work must stop.

The weeks and months of uninterrupted carving flowed by in a continuous stream. The winter was mild, he did not have to put back the roof of the shed; when the weather was sharp he wore his wool hat with its earmuffs, and a warm tunic. Thoughts, feelings, perceptions often came in a flash as the Bacchus and Satyr began to emerge, but to express these ideas in marble took days and weeks. Inside himself he had to grow as his sculpture grew and matured. The unfinished block haunted him at every hour of the night and day. It would be dangerous to release the bowl and the flexed knee in space; he would have to keep a webbing of marble between the out-stretched bowl and forearm, between the knee and elbow, between the base and knee to give them support while he dug deeper. Now he was chiseling the side plane, the face and head, part of the neck and curls of grapes, now the depth of the left shoulder, thigh and calf. At the rear he evolved the Satyr, the stump he was sitting on, the grapes he was eating, the tiger cloth tying the two figures together. It was the most complicated piece he had yet attempted. He turned the Satyr's head, arms and grapes adroitly to the Bacchus' arm, yet ran out of marble.

His real battle began the moment a muscle became defined or a structural element began to emerge. Standing out from the rough blocking, he felt a thumping in his heart to shed away quickly the rest of the marble skin to reveal the human form below. The marble was tenacious; he was equally tenacious to achieve the delicate play of muscle under the fleshy stomach, the soft, claylike trunk of the tree, the spiral torsion of the Satyr, the grapes on the Bacchus' head which seemed to be part of the vine of his hair. Each completed detail brought peacefulness to all of the faculties he had used in its creation; not only to his eyes and mind and bosom, but to his shoulders, hips and groin.

When unable to formulate a detail he dropped his tools, walked outside and gazed up through the trees to the skies. When he returned he approached the marble from a distance, saw its contours and masses, felt its continuity. The detail became part of the whole. He grabbed his tools again and worked furiously: one two three four five six seven strokes; then one two three four of rest, every few cycles stepping back to see what he had accomplished. His feelings were always ahead of his physical capacity to carve. If only he could work the four sides of the block at once!

When he was releasing a rounded kneecap, the hairy leg and hoof of the Satyr, the tiger skin, he strove to pull out as much wholeness as possible in one "Go." Each day had to be fruitful, he had to find a handful of form for each session of carving before he could put aside his hammer and chisel. Upon awakening he was heavily charged with nervous energy and his hours were one long drive. He could not leave one finger of a hand in a more advanced state than the others, for he worked in units. Each day's work was a full unit. It was these small bundles of intense entities throughout his sculpture that characterized his potency as a sculptor.

Just before retiring he looked over his work, spotted what had to be done the next day. During the evening, when he wrote to his family, he proudly signed the letters:

Michelangelo, Sculptor in Rome.

Because he would take no time off for friends or rest or social life, Balducci accused him of trying to escape the world by fleeing into marble. He admitted to his friend that he was half right: the sculptor carries into the marble the vision of a more luminous world than the one that surrounds him. But the artist was not in flight; he was in pursuit. He was trying with all his might to overtake a vision. Did God really rest on the seventh day? In the cool of that long afternoon, when He was refreshed, might He not have asked Himself, "Whom have I on earth to speak for Me? I had best create another species, one apart. I will call him 'artist,' His will be the task to bring meaning and beauty to the world.''

Nevertheless Balducci arrived faithfully every Sunday afternoon in the hope of seducing him out of the shed. He found for Michelangelo a girl so like Clarissa that Michelangelo was tempted. But the marble was exhausting. Between the two there could be no choice.

"When I have completed the Bacchus, I'll go out with you,'' he promised Balducci.

Balducci shook his head in despair.

"Just think of putting off the good things of life for so long. It's throwing time into the Tiber!''

Keyed up with his own fulfillment, Michelangelo threw back his head and laughed heartily with his friend.

His deepest emotional reaction came when breaking through a supporting web, noting the translucent quality of the marble where the breakthrough was to take place, aware that space would shortly be pouring through, the space that gave the limbs their freedom of movement, their independence, that permitted his forms to breathe air the moment his point felt no resistance.

His most delicate task was carving away the marble between the arm that held the lovely, ornamented wine cup and the side of the tilted head. He worked with infinite gentleness until he reached the sloping shoulder line. He did not yet feel secure enough to hammer away the web supporting the upheld arm and outstretched knee.

Balducci ragged him mercilessly.

"This is sheer prejudice. How come you didn't keep a column to hold up the poor fellow's privates? Suppose they fell off? That would be worse than his dropping that bowl you're so frightened of losing.''

Michelangelo reached for a handful of marble dust and threw it at him.

"Have you never had a thought that didn't originate in the erogenous zone?''

"Does anyone?''

He finally acceded to Balducci's importuning that he watch some of the Roman spectacles, and went with him to Mount Testaccio to see Rome celebrate carnival before Lent. They stood on a hillside while four young pigs, combed and tied with ribbons by special barbers, were bound into beflagged carts. At a signal from the trumpeters the carts were rolled down the hill toward the Aventine, with the populace rushing after them, armed with knives, yelling, *"Al porco! Al porco!"* At the bottom of the hill the carts smashed, the people fell upon the animals, fighting each other to see who could slice off the best pieces of meat.

When Michelangelo returned to the house he found the French Cardinal Groslaye of San Dionigi there. Galli broke a self-imposed rule by asking if they might take the cardinal out to the workshop to see the Bacchus. Michelangelo could not refuse.

In the lamplighted shed Michelangelo explained that he was working all around the figure simultaneously, to keep the forms advancing in the same stage of development. He showed how, in order to open the space between the two legs, and between the left arm and torso, he worked the front and then the back of the block, continuously making the marble web thinner and thinner. As the Cardinal of San Dionigi watched, he picked up a point and demonstrated the extremely light tapping required for the breakthrough, then used an *ugnetto* to remove the rest of the web, freeing the limbs.

"But how do you achieve in a half-finished figure this sense of throbbing vitality? I can feel the blood and muscle under your marble skin. It is good to see new marble masters arising.''

A few days later a servant brought a note to the workshed from Galli. *"Won't you join Groslaye and myself for supper tonight?"*

Michelangelo quit work at sundown, went to the baths close by, steamed the marble dust out of his pores, put on a fresh shirt and hose, brushed his hair forward over his brow. Signora Galli served a light supper, for the cardinal still followed the disciplines of his early years, ate no meat, and touched all foods sparingly. His fading eyes gleamed in the candlelight as he turned to Michelangelo.

"You know, my son, I am growing old. I must leave something behind me, something of singular beauty to add to the beauties of Rome. A tribute from France, from Charles VIII and my humble self. I have secured permission from the Pope to dedicate a sculpture in the Chapel of the Kings of France in St. Peter's. There is a niche that will take a life-size sculpture."

Michelangelo had not touched any of Galli's excellent Trebbiano wine, but he felt as though he had drunk more than Count Ghinazzo on a warm afternoon. A sculpture for St. Peter's, the oldest and most sacred basilica in Christendom, built over the tomb of St. Peter! Could it be possible that the French cardinal would choose him? But from what? The little Cupid? The still nascent Bacchus in his workshed?

By the time he brought his senses back to the table, the conversation had changed. The cardinal was telling Jacopo Galli of the writings of two unorthodox post-Nicene Fathers. Then the cardinal's carriage came for him. He bade Michelangelo a pleasant good night.

That Sunday Michelangelo went to mass in St. Peter's to see the Chapel of the Kings of France and the niche about which the Cardinal of San Dionigi had talked. He climbed the thirty-five stairs of marble and porphyry leading up to the basilica, crossed the atrium, passed the center fountain surrounded by porphyry columns and stood at the base of the Carlovingian bell tower, aghast at the dilapidated condition of St. Peter's, which was leaning sharply to the left. Inside he found the Chapel of the Kings of France to be of modest size, dark, the main light coming from small windows up near the roof, the only ornamentation some sarcophagi borrowed from pagan and early Christian tombs, and a wooden crucifix in a niche on the side. He measured with his eye the vacant niche on the opposite wall, disappointed to find it so deep that a statue would be seen only from the front.

It was seven days before Galli brought up the subject again.

"You know, Michelangelo, this commission of the Cardinal of San Dionigi's could be the most important since Pollaiuolo was assigned to do a tomb for Sixtus IV."

Michelangelo's heart began to pound. "What are my chances?"

Galli counted on his long supple fingers as on an abacus that reckoned artistic probability.

"First, I must convince the cardinal that you are the best sculptor in Rome. Second, you must conceive a theme that will inspire him. Third, we must secure a signed contract."

"It would have to be a spiritual theme?"

"Not because Groslaye is a member of the Church, but because he is a deeply spiritual man. He has lived in Rome for three years in such a state of grace that he literally has not seen and does not know that Rome is rotten at its core."

"Is it innocence? Or blindness?"

"Could we say that it is faith? If a man is as pure in heart as the Cardinal of San Dionigi, he walks with God's hand on his shoulder; he sees beyond present evil to the Church Eternal."

"Can I create a marble that would have the hand of God on it?"

Galli shook his leonine head.

"That is a problem you must wrestle with yourself."

To carve decay all day, and at the same time conceive a devout theme, seemed an impossible undertaking. Yet he knew very soon that his theme would be a Pietà: Pity, Sorrow. He had wanted to do a Pietà ever since he had completed his Madonna and Child: for just as the Madonna and Child was the beginning, the Pietà was the end, the preordained conclusion of everything that Mary had decided in that fateful hour God had allotted to her. Now, thirty-three years later, her son was again on her lap, having completed his journey.

Galli was intrigued with his thinking, took him to the Cardinal of San Dionigi's palace, where they waited for the cardinal to complete the five daily hours of prayer and offices required of every Benedictine. The three men sat in the open loggia, facing the Via Recta, with a painted Annunciation behind them. The cardinal was ashen after his long devotions. Michelangelo's practiced eye could perceive almost no body lines beneath his robe. But when the cardinal heard about the Pietà his eyes sparkled.

"What about the marble, Michelangelo? Could you find such a perfect piece as you speak of, here in Rome?"

"I think not, Your Grace. A column, yes; but an oblong block that is wider than it is tall, and cut deep, that I have not seen."

"Then we must turn to Carrara. I shall write to the brothers in Lucca, asking for aid. If they cannot find what we need you must go yourself to the quarries and find our marble."

Michelangelo bounded out of his chair.

"Did you know, Father, that the higher one quarries the purer white the marble becomes? No earth stains, no pressure to make holes or hollows. If we could quarry at the peak of Monte Sagro, there we would find the supreme block."

On the way home Galli said, "You must go to Carrara at once. I will advance the expenses for your trip."

"I can't."

"Why not?"

"I must finish the Bacchus," he replied.

"The Bacchus can wait. The cardinal can't. One day soon God will rest His hand just a trifle more heavily on his shoulder, and Groslaye will go to heaven. From heaven he cannot commission a Pietà."

"That is true. But I cannot stop work now," Michelangelo insisted stubbornly.

"I release you from our agreement. When you have finished the Pietà you will come back to the Bacchus."

"For me there is no coming back. The sculpture is growing complete in my mind. I must finish it now to get it perfect."

"I'm always amazed to find a romantic in affairs of practical business." Galli sighed. "I shan't burden the cardinal with the details of your orthodoxy."

"Until the Bacchus is completed the Pietà cannot begin. I behave virtuously because I must."

8

He removed the short column between the base and the heel of the Bacchus, and the right foot which was half suspended in the air, poised on its toes. Then he raised his drill to release the web between the elbow and the cup, drilling a series of holes close to the arm, delicately filing away the remaining marble. Finally he cut away the right-hand corner under the cup, to free the hand and cup now extending high into space. The Satyr in the lower left-hand corner and the cup at the upper right completed each other. His whole figure in the round was balanced superbly. He walked about it, satisfaction in his face and shoulders as his eye reviewed the line from the thrust of the right knee to the tip of the opposite shoulder; the tension from the edge of the bowl through the crotch to the corner of the Satyr's hoof.

The emphasis of his figure was in its weight masses. In the head projecting forward, the hard torso projecting outward, then flowing into the stomach, which pulled the whole body downward toward the loins. In the rear the *too* heavy buttocks served as a steadying weight, the balance held by the beautiful legs, though not too securely because the body was reeling; the left foot planted solidly, the right on tiptoe increased the sense of vertigo.

"You're like an engineer," said Galli when he saw it, his expression rapt as he traced Michelangelo's design.

"That's what I told Bertoldo a sculptor had to be."

"In the days of the emperors you would have been designing colosseums, baths and reservoirs. Instead, you've created a soul."

Michelangelo's eyes glowed yellow at the compliment.

"No soul, no sculpture."

"Many of my ancient pieces were found broken in several places, yet when we put them together their spirit persisted."

"That was the sculptor still alive in the marble."

The following Sunday he went to dine with the Rucellai, eager to hear news of Florence. Savonarola was at the heart of most of the happenings. The Florentine colony had been delighted with him for defying the Pope, for advising the Borgia that unjust excommunications were invalid, and for celebrating three forbidden masses in San Marco at Christmas. Savonarola had then written to kings, statesmen and churchmen all over Europe urging that a council be called to purge the Borgia, and to institute sweeping reforms that would rid the Church of simony, the purchase not only of cardinalates but of the papacy itself. On February 11, 1498, he had again preached in the Duomo against the Pope, and two weeks later had walked outside the cathedral with the host in his hand, before thousands of Florentines packed into the piazza, and beseeched God to strike him dead if he deserved excommunication. When God refrained, Savonarola celebrated his vindication by ordering another Burning of the Vanities. Florence was once again looted by the Army of Boys.

Savonarola's letters calling for a reformation were circulated secretly by the Florentines in Rome, to whom he had become an idol. When Michelangelo described to them the Burning of the Vanities that he had witnessed, the hundreds of irreplaceable manuscripts, books, paintings, sculptures that had been destroyed, they were not distressed.

"Any price is cheap in a famine," cried Cavalcanti. "We must destroy the Borgia at any cost."

Michelangelo was thoughtful.

"What will you think of this price in a few years when the Pope and Botticelli are both dead? There will be another Pope, but there can never be another Botticelli. All the works he threw on that fire are gone forever. It seems to me you are approving lawlessness in Florence to rid yourselves of lawlessness here in Rome."

If he could not touch them with his reasoning, the Pope touched them where it hurt: he promised to confiscate all business properties of the Florentines and to turn them out of the city penniless unless the Signoria of Florence sent Savonarola to Rome to stand trial. From what Michelangelo could gather, the colony made a complete capitulation: Savonarola had to be silenced; he had to honor his excommunication, to seek absolution from the Pope. They petitioned the Signoria to act in their behalf and to send Savonarola under guard to Rome. All the Pope asked, they explained, was that Savonarola come to Rome and receive absolution. Then he could return to Florence to save souls.

Before the end of March a rumor spread through Rome that sent Michelangelo racing to the Ponte: Savonarola's second in command, Fra Domenico, had committed himself to an ordeal by fire. The colony assembled at the home of the patriarch,

Cavalcanti. When Michelangelo entered the house he was plunged into a hubbub that tumbled down the stairs from the drawing room.

"What does it mean ordeal by fire?" he asked. "Is it what Savonarola tried before carnival, asking to be struck dead if his words were not inspired by God?"

"Similar. Except that fire burns."

This last development had been originated either by Fra Domenico himself or by the Dominicans' enemy in the struggle for power, the Franciscans, led by Francesco di Puglia. In a fiery sermon in defense of their leader, Fra Domenico had declared that he would enter fire to prove that everything Savonarola taught was inspired by God; and he challenged a Franciscan to enter with him. The next day Fra Francesco di Puglia accepted the challenge, but insisted that Savonarola himself must enter the fire, saying that only if Savonarola came through the fire alive could Florence believe him to be a true prophet. Meeting for supper at the Pitti palace, a young group of *Arrabbiati* assured Fra Francesco and the Franciscans that Savonarola would never accept; that by his refusal he would prove to Florence that he had no true faith in God's saving him.

At this point the voters of Florence turned against Savonarola politically. They had already endured seven years of wrangling, the Pope's threat to put an interdict on the entire population, which amounted to an excommunication that could paralyze trade and cause bitter turmoil. The city needed a three per cent tax on church property which the Pope now agreed to allow, once Savonarola was quieted. They defeated the Signoria pledged to Savonarola and elected a new Council which was against him. Florence was threatened with another Guelph and Ghibelline-like civil war.

On April 7 a platform was erected in the Piazza della Signoria, the logs smeared with pitch. A vast crowd assembled to watch the show. The Franciscans refused to enter the piazza until Fra Domenico agreed not to take the host into the fire. After a number of hours of waiting, a fierce winter rainstorm drenched the platform, scattering the crowd and putting an end to any burning.

The following night the *Arrabbiati* mobbed the monastery of San Marco, killing a number of Savonarola's followers. The Signoria moved in, arrested Savonarola, Fra Domenico and Fra Silvestro, the third in command, and jailed them in the bell tower of the Palazzo della Signoria. The Pope sent a courier to Florence demanding that Savonarola be delivered to him in Rome. The Signoria refused, but appointed a Commission of Seventeen to examine Savonarola and secure a confession that his words were not divinely inspired.

Savonarola refused to recant. The commission tortured him; first using the rack and the screw, then roping him to a pulley, raising him in the air, dropping him with a sudden jerk of the rope. Savonarola became delirious, agreed to write a confession. He was released to his cell. What he wrote was not satisfactory to the Signoria. He was tortured again. Weak from fasting and all-night prayers, Savonarola again succumbed, signed a confession written by a notary; but not before he rejected the paper and had to be tortured a third time.

The commission declared Savonarola guilty of heresy. The special advisory council called by the Signoria sentenced him to death. At the same time the Pope granted the city its long-desired three per cent tax on all church property in Tuscany.

Three platforms were built from the steps of the Palazzo della Signoria into the square. The throng began filling the piazza during the night, pushing up against the gibbet. By dawn the square and all the streets leading into it were a seething mass.

Savonarola, Fra Domenico and Fra Silvestro were led out onto the Signoria steps, stripped of their vestments, their tonsures scraped. They mounted the scaffold, praying silently. They climbed a steep ladder to the top of the gibbet. Ropes and chains were put about their necks. Within an instant, all three were dangling, their necks broken.

The pyre under the gibbet was lighted. The flames rose. The three bodies were held aloft by the chains after the ropes had burned. The *Arrabbiati* stoned the half-consumed corpses. The ashes were collected, carried in carts to the Old Bridge, and dumped into the Arno.

The martyrdom of Savonarola shook Michelangelo profoundly. He had sat as a boy and listened to Pico della Mirandola recommend to Lorenzo that the friar be invited to Florence. Savonarola had contributed to the deaths of Lorenzo, Pico, Poliziano, and now he too was dead. He hardly knew what to think or feel: except pity.

He turned to his work. Marble was dependable in a chaotic world. It had its own will and intelligence and stability. With marble in his hands, the world was good.

He became impatient to be finished with the Bacchus. He had only indicated the position of the forehead, nose, mouth, wanting to let the rest of the figure suggest the expression on the face. Now he completed the features, the expression dazed as the Bacchus stared at the cup of wine; the eyes bulging, the mouth opened greedily. For the grapes he used a drill, making each one round and juice-laden. To achieve the hair on the Satyr's goat legs he sliced the rough-edged marble with a fully rounded chisel which brought out the rhythmic play of curls, each tuft designed separately.

There was left two months of polishing to get the glowing flesh effects he wanted. Though this work involved infinite care and precision, it was technical in nature and used only that part of him which was the craftsman. It left his mind free during the warm spring hours to reflect on the Pietà and its meaning. In the cool of the evenings he began searching for this last moment that mother and son would spend together.

He asked Jacopo Galli if he could now complete a contract with the Cardinal of San Dionigi. Galli explained that the cardinal's monastery in Lucca had already ordered a block to Michelangelo's dimensions. The block had been cut, but the quarry at Carrara had refused to ship it to Rome before being paid. The monastery at Lucca had in turn refused to pay until the cardinal approved the block. The quarry had grown tired of holding it and had sold it to a buying agent.

That night Michelangelo wrote an agreement which he thought would be fair to himself and to the Cardinal of San Dionigi. Galli read it without expression, said he would take it to his bank and put it in a safe place.

By the end of summer the Bacchus was finished. Galli was overjoyed with his statue.

"I feel as though Bacchus is fully alive, and will drop his cup at any moment. The Satyr is innocent and naughty at the same time. You have made for me the finest sculpture in all Italy. We must place it in the garden and give it a party."

The blind Augustinians, Aurelius and Raffaelle Lippus, studied the Bacchus with their sensitive fingers, running them over every detail and saying they had never "seen" a male figure so powerful in projecting its inner life force. Professor Pomponius Laetus, who had been tortured by the Inquisition for paganism, was moved to tears, avowing that the statue was pure Greek in its structure and its gleaming white satiny finish. Serafino, the poet from Lucrezia Borgia's court, hated it on sight, declaring it "ugly, wanton, without any sense of loveliness." Sannazaro, the poet who mixed Christian and pagan images in his verses, declared it "a complete synthesis, Greek in carving, Christian in emotion, combining the best of both," even as the Plato Four had commented on his Madonna and Child. Peter Sabinus, professor of Eloquence at the university, collector of Christian inscriptions, and his friend Giovanni Capocci, who was excavating the catacombs, came back three times to debate the statue's virtues between themselves, finally concluding that, although they did not care for antique themes, this Bacchus was something new in the art of sculpture.

It was Giuliano da Sangallo's opinion Michelangelo valued most. Sangallo gleefully traced the intricate structural design. "You've built this Bacchus the way we build a temple or a palace. It was a dangerous, and courageous, experiment in construction. You could easily have suffered a collapse of material. This fellow will stand erect as long as there is space for him to displace."

The following night Galli brought home a contract he himself had written between Michelangelo and the Cardinal of San Dionigi, and which the cardinal had signed. In it Michelangelo found himself called *maestro* for the first time; but he was also described as *statuario,* statue maker, which was deflating. For the sum of four hundred and fifty ducats in papal gold he agreed to make a Pietà of marble, one hundred and fifty ducats to be paid as he began, and a hundred ducats every fourth month. By the end of a year the statue was to be completed. In addition to guaranteeing the cardinal's payments to Michelangelo, Galli had written:

> I, Jacopo Galli, do promise that the work will be more beautiful
> than any work in marble to be seen in Rome today, and such that
> no master of our own time will be able to produce a better.

Michelangelo gazed at Galli with affection.

"You must have written this contract at home, rather than the bank."

"Why?"

"Because you have taken quite a gamble. Suppose when I finish the cardinal says, 'I have seen better marbles in Rome.' What happens then?"

"I give His Grace back his papal ducats."

"And you are stuck with the carving!"

Galli's eyes twinkled. "I could endure it."

He went searching the stoneyards of Trastevere and the ports for the kind of block he needed; but a seven-foot-wide, six-foot-tall, three-foot-deep cut of marble was rarely quarried on the chance of sale. It took him only two days to complete the rounds; there was nothing even faintly resembling the massive block he needed. The next day, when he had decided that he would have to go to Carrara at his own expense, Guffatti came running up the rear alley to his workshed, crying out:

". . . just unloaded a barge . . . the very size you're looking for. It was cut for some order in Lucca. The quarry never got paid, so they sold it."

He dog-trotted down to the Ripetta dock. There it stood, gleaming pure and white in the summer sun, beautifully cut by the quarrymen high in the mountains of Carrara. It tested out perfect against the hammer, against water, its crystals soft and compacted with fine graining. He came back before dawn the next morning, watched the rays of the rising sun strike the block and make it as transparent as pink albaster, with not a hole or hollow or crack or knot to be seen in all its massive white weight.

His Pietà block had come home.

9

He removed the last reminders of the Bacchus, settled down to the Pietà. But the Bacchus had become a controversial figure. Many people came to see it. Galli brought the visitors to the workshop or sent a servant to the shed to ask if Michelangelo would mind coming to the garden. He found himself plunged into explanations and defenses, particularly from the Bregno enthusiasts, who attacked it as "a perversion of the Dionysus legend." When there were admirers he found himself involved in describing his concept and technique. Galli wanted him for supper every night now, and Sundays, so that he could make as many friends as possible, open the way to more commissions.

The Rucellai, Cavalcanti, Altoviti were proud of him. They gave parties in his honor, from which he awoke the next morning feeling tired. He yearned to put the Bacchus behind him, to wipe the slate of his mind clean of the pagan carving and make the transition to the spirituality he needed to think about the Pietà. After a month of festivities it became clear that he was not going to be able to conceive or carve a Pietà under these diverting conditions; that with his emergence as a professional sculptor had come the time to establish his own quarters and workshop where he could live quietly, secluded, work night and day if he wished, dedicate himself to abstemiousness. He had grown up, he was on his own. He could see no other way.

Perceptive Jacopo Galli asked, "Something is troubling you, Michelangelo?"

"Yes."

"It sounds serious."

"Just ungrateful."

"You owe me nothing."

"The men to whom I owe the most have all said that: Lorenzo de' Medici, Bertoldo, Aldovrandi, and now you."

"Tell me what you want to do."

"To move out!" he blurted. "Life with the Galli family is too pleasant. . . ." He paused. "I feel the need to work in my own household. As a man, rather than a boy, and perennial guest. Does this sound foolish?"

Galli gazed at him wistfully. "I want only that you be happy, and that you carve the most beautiful marbles in Italy."

"For me they are one and the same."

He was directed to several houses in which the ground floor was available, one recommended by Altoviti in the Florentine quarter, another near the Piazza del Quirinale, with a fine view of Rome. They were too elaborate and expensive. On the third day, on the Via Sistina, across from the Bear Inn and on the edge of the Campo Marzio lying below the embankment of the Tiber, he found a big corner room with two windows, one facing north for steady light, the other east for the sharp sunlight he sometimes needed. At the rear was a smaller room with a fireplace. He paid a few scudi for two months' rent, drew up the oiled linen on wooden frames that served as window covering, and studied the shabby space: the wooden floor, thin in spots, broken in others, cement crumbling between the stones of the walls, the ceiling plaster falling in patches, exposing variegated colors of decay where the rain had leaked through. He put the key in his pocket and returned to the Galli's.

He found Buonarroto waiting for him. His brother was jubilant. He had come as a guard on a mule train, and so the trip had cost him nothing. He was going back the same way. Michelangelo gazed with pleasure at the stubby features, the hair combed over Buonarroto's brow in imitation of his own. It had been a year since they had seen each other.

"You couldn't have come at a better time," he cried. "I need help in setting up my new home."

"You have taken a place? Good, then I can stay with you."

"Wait till you see my palatial quarters before you settle in," said Michelangelo, smiling. "Come with me to Trastevere, I need a supply of plaster, whitewash and lye. But first I will show you my Bacchus."

Buonarroto stood gazing at the statue a long time. Then he asked:

"Did people like it?"

"Most did."

"I'm glad."

That was all. Michelangelo observed to himself, "He doesn't have the faintest notion of what sculpture is about. His only interest is that people approve what I've done, so that I can be happy, and get more work . . . none of which he will ever understand. He's a true Buonarroti, blind to the meaning of art. But he loves me."

They bought the supplies, had dinner at the Trattoria Toscana, then Michelangelo took his brother to the Via Sistina. When Buonarroto entered the room he whistled sharply.

"Michelangelo, surely you're not thinking of living in this . . . this hole? The place is falling apart."

"You and I are going to put it back together," replied Michelangelo grimly. "It is adequate work space."

"Father would be distressed."

Michelangelo smiled. "Don't tell him." He set a tall ladder in the center of the room. "Let's scrape this ceiling."

When they had scraped and given the ceiling a coat of plaster, they began on the walls, then set to work patching the broken floor with odd-sized pieces of wood. Next they turned their attention to the private courtyard. The only door to it was from the side of his room, but the other tenants had access from their windows, as a result of which it was covered with a thick compost of garbage and debris. The odor was as thick as the enclosing walls. It took two days to shovel the refuse into sacks and carry it through his own room to a vacant lot below the Tiber.

Balducci, who held all physical labor in abhorrence, showed up after Michelangelo and Buonarroto had finished their repairs. He knew a second-hand furniture dealer in Trastevere, where he bargained shrilly for the best prices on a bed, rope mattress, kitchen table, two cane chairs, chest of drawers, a few pots, dishes and knives. When the donkey cart arrived a few hours later, the brothers set up the bed under the window to the east, where Michelangelo would be waked at first light. The chest of drawers went on the back wall, next to the opening to the kitchen. Under the front north window he placed a table of four planks on horses, for his drawing, wax and clay modeling. The center of the big room he kept clear for his marble. In the rear cubicle they installed the kitchen table, two chairs, pots and dishes.

Balducci returned, having explored the neighborhood.

"There's a plump little partridge lives just behind your rooms: blond, about fifteen, beautifully made, French, I think. I could persuade her to become your servant. Think how pleasant it would be to finish work at noon and find her in your kitchen over a pot of hot soup." Balducci did a little dance. ". . . and at night, to find her in your bed. It's part of their job; and you're going to need a little natural warmth in this cave."

Michelangelo and Buonarroto chuckled at Balducci's ebullience. In another minute he would be out the front door and down the street after the girl.

"Look, Balducci," cried Michelangelo. "I want no entanglements, and have no money for a servant. If I need anyone, I'll stick to the artist's custom of taking in a young apprentice and training him in return for services."

Buonarroto agreed. "I'll keep my eyes open in Florence for a bright young lad."

Buonarroto settled Michelangelo in, shopped and cooked the food, cleaned the rooms. The housekeeping went downhill the moment he left. Immersed in his work, Michelangelo took no time off to cook, to go out to a restaurant or eat in the streets. He lost weight, even as his rooms lost their tidy appearance. He saw nothing about him but his workbench and the huge white block sitting on beams in the center of the floor. He never bothered to make his bed or to wash the dishes he left on the kitchen table. The rooms became covered with dust from the street, ashes from the kitchen fire where he boiled water for an occasional hot drink. He knew by the end of a month that this system was not going to work. He even began to eye

Balducci's little French girl, who passed his door more frequently than he thought strictly necessary.

Buonarroto solved his problem. Michelangelo answered to a knock late one afternoon to see standing in the street a plain-faced, olive-complected lad of about thirteen, travel-stained, holding out a letter on which Michelangelo recognized his brother's handwriting. The note introduced Piero Argiento, who had come to Florence looking for a sculptor to whom he could be apprenticed. He had been sent by someone to the Buonarroti house, then made the long trip on foot to Rome.

Michelangelo invited him in, studied the boy while he told of his family and their farm near Ferrara. His manner was quiet, his voice plain.

"Can you read and write, Argiento?"

"The Gesuati fathers in Ferrara taught me to write. Now I need to learn a trade."

"And you think sculpture might be a good one?"

"I want a three-year apprenticeship. With a Guild contract."

Michelangelo was impressed by the forthrightness. He gazed into the muddy brown eyes of the stringy lad before him, at the soiled shirt, worn-out sandals, the thin, hungry cheeks.

"You have no friends in Rome? No place to go?"

"I came to see you." Stubbornly.

"I live simply, Argiento. You can expect no luxury."

"I am of *contadini*. What is to eat, we eat."

"Since you need a home, and I need a helper, suppose we try it for a few days? If it doesn't work out, we part as friends. I'll pay your way back to Florence."

"Agreed. *Grazie.*"

"Take this coin, and go to the baths near Santa Maria dell'Anima. On the way back, stop at the market for food to cook."

"I make a good soup-of-the-country. My mother taught me before she died."

The fathers had taught Argiento not only to count but also to be doggedly honest. He left the house before dawn for the markets, carrying with him a scrap of crayon and paper. Michelangelo was touched by the way he painfully kept his accounts written down: so many denari for vegetables, so many for meat, for fruit, for bread and *pasta,* with every coin accounted for. Michelangelo put a modest amount in a cooking pot as their weekly allowance. Argiento was a relentless pursuer of bargains. Within a week he knew every stall selling produce. His shopping took him the better part of the morning, which suited Michelangelo because it gave him the solitariness he sought.

They established a simple routine. After their one-dish midday dinner, Argiento cleaned the rooms while Michelangelo took an hour's walk along the Tiber to the docks to listen to the Sicilians sing as they unloaded the boats. By the time he returned home Argiento was taking his *riposo* on the truckle bed in the kitchen under the wooden sink. Michelangelo had two more hours of quiet at his workbench before Argiento woke, washed his face noisily in a basin, and came to the worktable for his daily instruction. These few hours in the afternoon appeared to be all the teaching Argiento wanted. At dusk he was back in the kitchen, boiling water. By the time dark settled in he was asleep on his truckle bed, a blanket drawn securely over his head. Michelangelo then lit his oil lamps and returned to his workbench. He was grateful to Buonarroto for sending Argiento to him; the arrangement looked as though it would be satisfactory, despite the fact that Argiento showed not a shred of talent for drawing. Later, when he began working the marble, he would teach the boy how to use a hammer and chisel.

In the Bible he read from John 19:38–40:

> After this Joseph of Arimathea, who was a disciple of Jesus
> . . . asked Pilate to let him take away the body of Jesus . . . so

> he came and took Jesus's body away; and with him was Nico-
> demus . . . he brought with him a mixture of myrrh and aloes,
> of about a hundred pounds' weight. They took Jesus's body, then,
> and wrapped it in winding-clothes with the spices; that is how the
> Jews prepare a body for burial.

Listed as present at the Descent were Mary, Mary's sister, Mary Magdalene, John, Joseph of Arimathea, Nicodemus. Search as he might, he could find no place where the Bible spoke of a moment when Mary could have been alone with Jesus. Mostly the scene was crowded with mourners, such as the dramatic Dell'Arca Lamentation in Bologna, where the grief-stricken spectators had usurped Mary's last poignant moment.

In his concept there could be no one else present.

His first desire was to create a mother and son alone in the universe. When might Mary have had that moment to hold her child on her lap? Perhaps after the soldiers had laid him on the ground, while Joseph of Arimathea was at Pontius Pilate's asking for Christ's body, Nicodemus was gathering his mixture of myrrh and aloes, and the others had gone home to mourn. Those who saw his finished Pietà would take the place of the biblical witnesses. They would feel what Mary was undergoing. There would be no halos, no angels. These would be two human beings, whom God had chosen.

He felt close to Mary, having spent so long concentrating on the beginning of her journey. Now she was intensely alive, anguished; her son was dead. Even though he would later be resurrected, he was at this moment dead indeed, the expression on his face reflecting what he had gone through on the cross. In his sculpture therefore it would not be possible for him to project anything of what Jesus felt for his mother; only what Mary felt for her son. Jesus' inert body would be passive, his eyes closed. Mary would have to carry the human communication. This seemed right to him.

It was a relief to shift in his mind to technical problems. Since his Christ was to be life size, how was Mary to hold him on her lap without the relationship seeming ungainly? His Mary would be slender of limb and delicate of proportion, yet she must hold this full-grown man as securely and convincingly as she would a child.

There was only one way to accomplish this: by design, by drawing diagrams and sketches in which he probed the remotest corner of his mind for creative ideas to carry his concept.

He started by making free sketches to loosen up his thinking so that images would appear on paper, Visually, these approximated what he was feeling within himself. At the same time he started walking the streets, peering at the people passing or shopping at the stalls, storing up fresh impressions of what they looked like, how they moved. In particular he sought the gentle, sweet-faced nuns, with head coverings and veils coming to the middle of their foreheads, remembering their expressions until he reached home and set them down on paper.

Discovering that draperies could be designed to serve structural purposes, he began a study of the anatomy of folds. He improvised as he went along, completing a life-size clay figure, then bought yards of an inexpensive material from a draper, wet the lightweight cloth in a basin and covered it over with clay that Argiento brought from the bank of the Tiber, to the consistency of thick mud. No fold could be accidental, each turn of the drapery had to serve organically, to cover the Madonna's slender legs and feet so that they would give substantive support to Christ's body, to intensify her inner turmoil. When the cloth dried and stiffened, he saw what adjustments had to be made.

"So that's sculpture," commented Argiento wryly, when he had sluiced down the floor for a week, "making mud pies."

Michelangelo grinned. "See, Argiento, if you control the way these folds are bunched, like this, or made to flow, you can enrich the body attitudes. They can have as much tactile appeal as flesh and bone."

He went into the Jewish quarter, wanting to draw Hebraic faces so that he could reach a visual understanding of how Christ might have looked. The Jewish section was in Trastevere, near the Tiber at the church of San Francesco a Ripa. The colony had been small until the Spanish Inquisition of 1492 drove many Jews into Rome. Here, for the most part, they were well treated, as a "reminder of the Old Testament heritage of Christianity"; many of their gifted members were prominent in the Vatican as physicians, musicians, bankers.

The men did not object to his sketching them while they went about their work, but no one could be persuaded to come to his studio to pose. He was told to ask for Rabbi Melzi at the synagogue on Saturday afternoon. Michelangelo found the rabbi in the room of study, a gentle old man with a white beard and luminous gray eyes, robed in black gabardine with a skullcap on his head. He was reading from the Talmud with a group of men from his congregation. When Michelangelo explained why he had come, Rabbi Melzi replied gravely:

"The Bible forbids us to bow down to or to make graven images. That is why our creative people give their time to literature, not to painting or sculpture."

"But, Rabbi Melzi, you don't object to others creating works of art?"

"Not at all. Each religion has its own tenets."

"I am carving a Pietà from white Carrara marble. I wish to make Jesus an authentic Jew. I cannot accomplish this if you will not help me."

The rabbi said thoughtfully, "I would not want my people to get in trouble with the Church."

"I am working for the Cardinal of San Dionigi. I'm sure he would approve."

"What kind of models would you prefer?"

"Workmen. In their mid-thirties. Not bulky laborers, but sinewy men. With intelligence. And sensitivity."

Rabbi Melzi smiled at him with infinitely old but merry eyes.

"Leave me your address. I will send you the best the quarter has to offer."

Michelangelo hurried to Sangallo's solitary bachelor room with his sketches, asked the architect to design a stand which would simulate the seated Madonna. Sangallo studied the drawings and improvised a trestle couch. Michelangelo bought some scrap lumber. Together he and Argiento built the stand, covering it with blankets.

His first model arrived at dusk. He hesitated for a moment when Michelangelo asked him to disrobe, so Michelangelo gave him a piece of toweling to wrap around his loins, led him to the kitchen to take off his clothes. He then draped him over the rough stand, explained that he was supposed to be recently dead, and was being held on his mother's lap. The model quite plainly thought Michelangelo crazy; only the instructions from his rabbi kept him from bolting. But at the end of the sitting, when Michelangelo showed him the quick, free drawings, with the mother roughed in, holding her son, the model grasped what Michelangelo was after, and promised to speak to his friends. . . . He worked for two hours a day with each model sent by the rabbi.

Mary presented quite a different problem. Though this sculpture must take place thirty-three years after her moment of decision, he could not conceive of her as a woman in her mid-fifties, old, wrinkled, broken in body and face by labor or worry. His image of the Virgin had always been that of a young woman, even as had his memory of his mother.

Jacopo Galli introduced him into several Roman homes. Here he sketched, sitting in their flowing gowns of linen and silk, young girls not yet twenty, some about to be married, some married a year or two. Since the Santo Spirito hospital had taken only men, he had had no experience in the study of female anatomy; but he had sketched the women of Tuscany in their fields and homes. He was able to discern the body lines of the Roman women under their robes.

He spent concentrated weeks putting his two figures together: a Mary who would be young and sensitive, yet strong enough to hold her son on her lap; and a Jesus who, though lean, was strong even in death . . . a look he remembered well from his experience in the dead room of Santo Spirito. He drew toward the composite design from his meticulously accurate memory, without need to consult his sketches.

Soon he was ready to go into a three-dimensional figure in clay. Here he would have free expression because the material could be moved to distort forms. When he wanted to emphasize, or get greater intensity, he added or subtracted clay. Next he turned to wax because there was a similarity of wax to marble in tactile quality and translucence. He respected each of these approach techniques, and kept them in character: his quill drawings had a scratchiness, suggesting skin texture; the clay he used plastically to suggest soft moving flesh, as in an abdomen, in a reclining torso; the wax he smoothed over to give the body surface an elastic pull. Yet he never allowed these models to become fixed in his mind; they remained rough starting points. When carving he was charged with spontaneous energy; too careful or detailed studies in clay and wax would have glued him down to a mere enlarging of his model.

The true surge had to be inside the marble itself. Drawing and models were his thinking. Carving was action.

10

The arrangement with Argiento was working well, except that sometimes Michelangelo could not figure who was master and who apprentice. Argiento had been trained so rigorously by the Jesuits that Michelangelo was unable to change his habits: up before dawn to scrub the floors, whether they were dirty or not; water boiling on the fire for washing laundry every day, the pots scoured with river sand after each meal.

"Argiento, this is senseless," he complained, not liking to work on the wet floors, particularly in cold weather. "You're too clean. Scrub the studio once a week. That's enough."

"No," said Argiento stolidly. "Every day. Before dawn. I was taught."

"And God help anyone who tries to unteach you!" grumbled Michelangelo; yet he knew that he had nothing to grumble about, for Argiento made few demands on him. The boy was becoming acquainted with the *contadini* families that brought produce into Rome. On Sundays he would walk miles into the *campagna* to visit with them, and in particular to see their horses. The one thing he missed from his farm in the Po Valley was the animals; frequently he would take his leave of Michelangelo by announcing:

"Today I go see the horses."

It took a piece of bad luck to show Michelangelo that the boy was devoted to him. He was crouched over his anvil in the courtyard getting his chisels into trim, when a splinter of steel flew into his eye and imbedded itself in his pupil. He stumbled into the house, eyes burning like fire. Argiento made him lie down on the bed, brought a pan of hot water, dipped some clean white linen cloth and applied it to extract the splinter. Though the pain was considerable Michelangelo was not too concerned. He assumed he could blink the splinter out. But it would not come. Argiento never left his side, keeping the water boiled, applying hot compresses throughout the night.

By the second day Michelangelo began to worry; and by the second night he was in a state of panic: he could see nothing out of the afflicted eye. At dawn

Argiento went to Jacopo Galli. Galli arrived with his family surgeon, Maestro Lippi. The surgeon carried a cage of live pigeons. He told Argiento to take a bird out of the cage, cut a large vein under its wing, let the blood gush into Michelangelo's injured eye.

The surgeon came back at dusk, cut the vein of a second pigeon, again washed out the eye. All the next day Michelangelo could feel the splinter moving, pushing. By nightfall it was out.

Argiento had not slept for some seventy hours.

"You're tired," said Michelangelo. "Why don't you take a few days off?"

Argiento's stubborn features lit up with pleasure. "I go visit the horses."

At first Michelangelo had been bothered by the people going in and out of the Bear Hotel across the street, the noise of their horses and carts on the cobbles, the cries of the grooms and babble of a dozen dialects. By now he had grown to enjoy the interesting characters who came from all over Europe for their pilgrimage, some wearing long gowns, others short tunics of brilliant greens and purples, others stiff hats. They served as an unending source of models for him to sketch at his worktable as he saw them through the open window. Soon he came to know the clients; as a guest reappeared he quickly pulled out his drawing, made corrections or additions, caught the bodies in a variety of movements: unloading carriages, carrying valises, unshouldering packs, getting on and off mules.

The noise in the street, the voices, the welcomes, the departures gave him company without intruding upon his privacy. Living in isolation as he was, this sense of other people in the world was companionable. It was all he needed, for with marble in his hands he would never stand on the periphery looking in; he would stand at the focal core looking out.

In his pen and ink sketches for the Pietà he had crosshatched the negative spaces, those parts of the block that had to be thrown away, indicating the tool strokes that should be used. Now, with hammer and chisel in hand, he found this roughing out unpleasing, impatient for that first moment when a flicker of a buried image shone through, when the block became a source of life that communicated with him. Then, from the space outside the block, he entered into his composition. After he had completed the sculpture, life would vibrate outward from the figures. But at this beginning moment the action was in reverse: the point of entry must be a force that sucked in space, pulling inward his gaze and attention. He had envisaged so big a block because he wanted to sculpture with an abundance of marble. He did not want to have to compress any portion of his forms, as he had had to compact the Satyr close to the Bacchus.

He broke into his marble block at the left side of the Madonna's head, worked to the left of the block, the north light behind him. By getting Argiento to help him turn the block on its beams he was able to have the shadows fall exactly where the cavities were to be carved, a play of light and shadow to show him where he must cast out stone; for the marble he took away was also sculpture, creating its own effects.

Now he had to plunge in boldly to find his principal features. The weight of the material of the Madonna's head covering, forcing her head downward to the inner hand of Christ that crossed her heart, compelled attention to the body stretched across her lap. The tight band which ran between the Virgin's breasts was like a tight hand constricting and crushing a palpitating heart. The lines of the drapery led to the Madonna's hand, with which she held her son, securely, under his arm, then to the human aspects of Christ's body, to his face, the eyes closed serenely in deep sleep, the nose straight but full, the skin clear and firm, the soft mustache and delicate curling chin whiskers, the mouth filled with anguish.

Because the Madonna was gazing down on her son, all who looked must turn to her face, to see the sadness, the compassion for all men's sons, asking with tender despair: "What could I have done to save him?" And from the depth of her love, "What purpose has all this served, if man cannot be saved?"

All who saw would feel how insupportably heavy was her son's dead body on her lap, how much heavier was the burden in her heart.

It was unusual to combine two life-size figures in the same sculpture, revolutionary to put a full-grown man onto the lap of a woman. From this point of departure he left behind all conventional concepts of the Pietà. Once again, even as Ficino had believed that Plato could have been Christ's most loving disciple, it was Michelangelo's desire to blend the classical Greek concept of the beauty of the human body with the Christian ideal of the immortality of the human soul. He banished the lugubrious death throes of the earlier Pietàs, bathed his two figures in tranquillity. Human beauty could reveal sacredness as clearly as could pain. At the same time, it could exalt.

All of this, and much more, the marble must be persuaded to say. If the end result were tragic, then doubly must they walk in beauty; beauty that his own love and dedication could match in this flawless white block. He would make mistakes, but the mistakes would be made with loving hands.

Winter came down like a clap of thunder: cold, wet, raw. As Buonarroto had predicted, there were leaks. Michelangelo and Argiento moved his workbench and bed to dry sections of the room, brought the forge in from the courtyard. He wore his Bologna cap over his head and ears. His nostrils swelled, giving him constant pain, making breathing difficult.

He bought a black iron brazier to put under his work stool, which warmed him posteriorly; but the moment he moved to another section of the room his blood froze. He had to send Argiento out for two more braziers, and baskets of coal, which they could hardly afford. When his fingers were blue he tried to carve while wearing woolen mittens. Within the hour he had an accident, some marble fell away and he felt his heart go down to his feet as the chunk hit the floor.

One Sunday Argiento returned from an outing feeling hot and strange. By midnight he had a high fever. Michelangelo picked him up off his truckle bed and put him into his own. By morning Argiento was in a delirium, sweating profusely, crying out names of relatives, fragments of stories, of beatings, accidents. Michelangelo wiped him dry, and a number of times had to restrain him from jumping out of bed.

At dawn he summoned a passer-by and sent him for a doctor. The doctor stood in the doorway, cried, "It's the plague! Burn everything he has touched since he came in here!" and fled.

Michelangelo sent a message to Galli. Maestro Lippi took one look, said scoffingly:

"Nonsense, it is not the plague. Quartan fever. Has he been around the Vatican lately?"

"He walked there on Sunday."

"And probably drank some stagnant water in the ditch beneath the walls. Go to the French monks on the Esquiline, they make a glutinous pill of sagepen, salt, coloquint . . ."

Michelangelo begged a neighbor to sit with Argiento. It took him almost an hour in the pelting rain to cross the city, go down the long street from Trajan's forum, past Augustus' forum and the basilica of Constantine, the colosseum, then up the Esquiline hill to the monastery. The pills lessened Argiento's headache, and Michelangelo thought he was making good progress during two quiet days; then the delirium returned.

At the end of the week Michelangelo was exhausted. He had brought Argiento's bed into the big room, and was catching a few moments of sleep while Argiento dozed, but worse than the lack of sleep was the problem of food, for he was unwilling to leave the boy alone.

Balducci knocked on the door.

"I told you to take that French girl at the rear. Then when she got sick, her family would have nursed her."

"Let's not go backward," said Michelangelo wearily. "Forward is hard enough."

"You can't keep him here. You look like a skeleton. Take him to the Santo Spirito hospital."

"And let him die?"

"Why should he die any faster at a hospital?"

"Because they don't get any care."

"What kind of care are you giving him, Dr. Buonarroti?"

"I keep him clean, watch over him. . . . He took care of me when I hurt my eye. How can I abandon him to a ward? That's not Christian."

"If you insist on committing suicide, I'll bring you food each morning before I go to the bank."

Michelangelo's eyes filled with gratitude. "Balducci, you just play at being cynical. Here's some money, buy me towels, and a sheet or two."

Michelangelo turned to find Argiento watching him.

"I'm going to die."

"No, you're not, Argiento. Nothing kills a countryman but a falling cliff."

The illness took three weeks to pass. What hurt most was the loss of almost a month of work; he began to worry that he could not finish his statue within the stipulated year's time.

Winter was mercifully short in Rome. By March the *campagna* was flooded with a bright, brittle sunlight. The stones of the workshop began to thaw. And with the warmer weather came the Cardinal of San Dionigi to see how his Pietà was faring. Each time Michelangelo saw him there appeared to be more material and less body in his robes. He asked Michelangelo if he had been receiving his payments regularly. Michelangelo assured him that he had. They stood in front of the massive white block in the middle of the room. The figures were still rough, with much webbing left for support; but he had done considerable carving on the two faces, and that was what interested the cardinal most.

"Tell me, my son," he said softly, "how does the Madonna's face remain so young, younger than her son's?"

"Your Grace, it seemed to me that the Virgin Mary would not age. She was pure; and so she would have kept her freshness of youth."

The answer was satisfactory to the cardinal.

"I hope you will finish in August. It is my dearest wish to hold services in St. Peter's for the installation."

11

He carved in a fury from first light to dark, then threw himself across his bed, without supper and fully clothed, like a dead man. He awoke around midnight, refreshed, his mind seething with sculptural ideas, craving to get at the marble. He got up, nibbled at a heel of bread, lit the brass lamp in which he burned the dregs of the olive oil, and tried to set it at an angle that would throw light on the area he was carving. The light was too diffused. It was not safe to use a chisel.

He bought some heavy paper, made a hat with a peak, tied a wire around the outside and in the center fashioned a loop big enough to hold a candle. The light, as he held his face a few inches from the marble, was bright and steady. Nor did his pounding waken Argiento under the kitchen sink, blanket over his head. The candles burned quickly, the soft wax running over the peak of his paper cap and onto his forehead, but he was delighted with his invention.

Late one night there was a sharp rap at the door. He opened it to find Leo Baglioni, dressed in an indigo velvet cloak, surrounded by a group of his young friends who were holding horn lanterns or wax torches on long poles.

"I saw the light and came to see what you were doing at this ungodly hour. You're working! What's that stuff all over your eyebrows?"

Michelangelo proudly showed them his cap and candle. Leo and his friends burst into a paroxysm of laughter.

"Why don't you use goat's tallow, it's harder, you won't be eating it all night," exclaimed Leo, when he caught his breath.

Argiento disappeared the next day after supper, came back at the second hour of evening weighed down with four heavy bundles which he dumped on the bed.

"Signor Baglioni sent for me. These are a present."

Michelangelo extracted a hard yellow taper.

"I don't need his assistance!" he cried. "Take them back."

"They have broken my arm from the Campo dei Fiori. I won't carry them back. I'll set them in front of the door and burn them all at once."

"Very well, let me see if they are better than wax. But first I'll have to widen this wire loop."

Leo had known what he was talking about: the goat's tallow melted more slowly and remained in a pool where it fell.

He divided the night into two halves, one for sleep, the other for work, and made rapid progress carving the voluminous outer folds of Mary's robe, Christ's lower torso, his legs, the inner one raised so that it would be visible from the front, leaving a webbing connecting it with Mary's outstretched hand to protect it.

He refused all invitations, saw few of his friends though Balducci kept bringing the news: Cardinal Giovanni, unwanted and unnoticed by the Borgia, had left to travel in Europe; Piero, trying to raise an army for a third attack on Florence, had been ostracized by the colony; Florence's intermittent war with Pisa had flared again; Torrigiani had joined Caesar Borgia's troops as an officer to help conquer the Romagna for the Vatican. The Borgia was excommunicating lords and churchmen, appropriating their lands; no Florentine knew when his turn would be next.

It was on a glorious summer morning with the air so translucent that the Alban hills seemed only a piazza away, that Paolo Rucellai sent for him to come as soon as possible. Michelangelo wondered what news it could be that Paolo considered urgent.

"Michelangelo, you look so thin."

"The sculpture grows fat, I grow thin. That is the natural order of things."

Rucellai regarded him in wonderment. "I had to tell you that on yesterday's post I received a letter from my cousin Bernardo. Florence is planning a sculpture competition."

Michelangelo's right hand began to tremble; he put his left hand over it to quiet it.

"To compete for what . . . ?"

"Bernardo's letter says: *To bring to perfection the marble column already blocked out by Agostino di Duccio and now stored in the workshop of the cathedral.*"

"The Duccio block!"

"You know it?"

"I tried to buy it from the Signoria for my Hercules."

"That could be an advantage, if you remember it well."

"I can see it before my eyes as though it were lying at our feet in this room."

"Can you make something good of it?"

Michelangelo's eyes shone. *"Dio mio."*

"My letter says the Council described the marble as 'badly blocked.' "

"No, no, it is a noble block. The original massing in the quarry was badly done, and Duccio dug in too deeply at the center . . ."

"Then you want to try for the competition?"

"More than anything in my whole life! Tell me, what must the theme be: political, religious? Is it for Florentine sculptors only? Must I be there to compete? Will they . . ."

"Whoa, whoa," cried Rucellai, "I have no further information. But I will ask Bernardo to send me full particulars."

"I'll come next Sunday to hear the news."

Rucellai laughed. "There won't be time for a reply, but come to dinner and we'll fatten you up for the competition."

"May I wait until you receive an answer?"

It took three weeks for Rucellai to summon him. Michelangelo sprinted up the steps to the library.

"Some news, not much. The date of the competition has not been set. It won't be until next year at the earliest. Themes can be submitted only by sculptors in Florence. . . ."

"I shall have to be back there."

"But the nature of the work has not yet been determined by the Council of the Wool Guild and the overseers of the cathedral."

"The cathedral? Then it will have to be a religious marble. After the Pietà, I was hoping to carve something different."

"The Wool Guild is paying, so I imagine the choice will be theirs. If I know these gentry, it will be a Florentine sculpture."

"Florentine? Like Marzocco?"

Rucellai chuckled at Michelangelo's dismay.

"No, not another lion. A symbol representing the new Republic, perhaps. . . ."

Michelangelo scratched his scalp in perplexity, using his fingers like a toothed chisel.

"What kind of statue would represent the Republic?"

"Perhaps that will be part of the competition? For the artist to tell them."

Paolo kept feeding him the news as it arrived over the Sabatini mountains from Florence: the competition would take place in 1500, to celebrate the hundredth anniversary of the competition for the Baptistery doors. The Wool Guild hoped that, like the Ghiberti, Brunelleschi and Della Quercia competition a century before, the Duccio block would attract sculptors from all over Italy.

"But this is already summer of '99. I have so much work left on the Pietà." His face was anguished. "I cannot rush, it is too important, too dear to me. Suppose I don't finish in time . . ."

Paolo put an arm about his trembling shoulders.

"I will bring you information steadily. The Wool Guild will debate through many meetings and many months before they set the terms."

It was the Cardinal of San Dionigi who lost the race with time. His Grace never did get to see his sculpture completed, though he sent the last hundred ducats to Galli's bank at the beginning of August, when the sculpture was to have been installed. The cardinal died quietly in the midst of his offices. Jacopo Galli attended the funeral with Michelangelo, standing below a catafalque sixteen feet long between the columns of the church, and nine feet wide, with singers behind the main altar. Returning to the Galli home, Michelangelo asked:

"Who decides whether or not the Pietà is 'more beautiful than any work in marble to be seen in Rome today'?"

"The cardinal already decided that. After his visit with you in May. He said you were fulfilling the contract. That's good enough for me. When do you think it will be finished?"

"I have still six to eight months of work."

"In time for the Centennial Year, then. That will give you an audience from all over Europe."

Michelangelo shifted uneasily in his seat.

"Would you send that last hundred ducats to my family? They are in some kind of trouble again."

Galli looked at him sharply. "That was your last payment. You say you have six to eight months of work left, and I have sent almost all of the cardinal's ducats to Florence. It begins to look like a bottomless well."

"This money I want to invest in buying a shop for my brothers, Buonarroto and Giovansimone. Buonarroto cannot seem to find a place for himself. Giovansimone, since Savonarola's death, takes jobs, then disappears for days. If they could find a good shop, and I shared in the profits . . ."

"Michelangelo, if neither of them is a good businessman, how are they going to make a profit?" Galli was exasperated; but when he spoke again his voice was solicitous. "I can't let you pour your last money down a hole. You must be practical and protect yourself against the future. Eighty per cent of your money from the Bacchus and the Pietà has gone to your family. I ought to know, I'm your banker."

Michelangelo hung his head, whispered, "Buonarroto won't work for anyone else, so I must set him up in business. And if I don't get Giovansimone in a straight path now, I may never have another chance."

The money was transferred to Florence, Michelangelo keeping a few ducats for himself. At once, he began to need things: equipment for his carving, utensils for the house, clothes for himself and Argiento. He went on short rations, gave Argiento money for nothing but the simplest foods. Their clothing became ragged. It took a letter from Lodovico to bring him to his senses.

Dearest Son:
   Buonarroto tells me that you live there in great misery. Misery is bad, since it is a vice displeasing to God and to one's fellow man, and also will hurt the soul and the body. . . . Live moderately and mind not to be in need, and abstain from discomfort. . . . Above all, take care of your head, keep it moderately warm and never wash yourself. Allow yourself to be rubbed, but do not wash yourself.

He went to Paolo Rucellai, borrowed the twenty-five florins he had returned two years before, took Argiento to the Trattoria Toscana for *bistecca alla fiorentina*. On the way home he bought himself and Argiento each a new shirt, a pair of long hose and sandals.

The next morning Sangallo arrived at the studio in a state of agitation, his golden mustaches bristling.

"Your favorite church, San Lorenzo in Damaso, is being destroyed. The hundred carved pillars are being pulled out."

Michelangelo was unable to follow his friend.

"Here, sit down. Now start over. What is happening to San Lorenzo?"

"Bramante, the new architect from Urbino. He has ingratiated himself with Cardinal Riario . . . sold him the idea of removing the pillars from the church and using them to complete his palace courtyard." Sangallo wrung his hands, as though wailing manually. "Do you think you could stop Bramante?"

"Me? But how? I have no influence with the cardinal, I have not seen him for almost two years . . ."

"Leo Baglioni. He has the cardinal's ear."

"I will go at once."

As he made his way to the Campo dei Fiori he tried to recall what he had been told about Bramante: fifty-five years old, from Urbino, he had worked as an architect for the Duke of Milan, and had come to Rome early in the year, intent upon living on his Lombard savings until he had studied and mastered the architectural genius of the ancient Romans; somewhat, thought Michelangelo, as Sangallo had.

He had to wait several hours for Baglioni. Leo listened with his features still, as he always did to other people's outbursts, then said quietly:

"Come, we'll go to see Bramante. It's his first commission in Rome. Since he's ambitious, I doubt if you'll be able to get him to relinquish it."

On the short walk to the palace courtyard Leo described Bramante as "a quite amiable man, really, delightful to be with, always gay and cheerful, and a magnificent teller of jokes and riddles. I've never seen him lose his good nature. Bramante is making a lot of friends in Rome." He glanced sidewise at Michelangelo. "I can't say as much for you!"

They approached the palace. Leo said, "There he is now, measuring off the bases for the columns."

Michelangelo stood at the opening to the court, gazing at Bramante, disliking intensely at first sight the big-skulled head, bald, a few remaining curls at the nape, the big-boned forehead and eyebrows, the pale green eyes; a snubbed nose and rosebud-like mouth lost in the hugeness of the head. As Michelangelo watched, Bramante moved some stones aside, his bullneck and muscled shoulders showing the power of an athlete.

Leo introduced them. Bramante greeted Michelangelo jovially, told them a humorous anecdote. Leo laughed heartily. Michelangelo was not amused.

"You do not like to laugh, Buonarroti?" asked Bramante.

"Reducing San Lorenzo to a shambles doesn't strike me as funny."

Bramante hunched his shoulders up around his jowl, as though he were a boxer protecting himself. Both men looked to Leo. Baglioni was remaining neutral.

"What business of yours are those columns?" asked Bramante, still courteous. "Are you Cardinal Riario's architect?"

"No, I'm not even his sculptor. But I happen to think this church one of the most beautiful in Italy. To destroy it is pure vandalism."

"On the contrary, those columns are coin of the realm. You know they were taken from the theater of Pompey in 384 to put in the church? All of Rome is quarry for those who know how to use its stone. There is nothing I would not tear down if I had the opportunity to build something more beautiful in its place."

"Stone belongs in the place for which it was designed and carved."

"That's an old-fashioned idea, Buonarroti; stone belongs wherever an architect has need for it. What is old, dies."

"And a lot of new things are born dead!"

Bramante's good temper was exhausted.

"You do not know me. You cannot have come here of your own accord. Someone has put you up to it. Tell me, who is my adversary?"

"Your critic is the finest architect in all Italy, builder of Lorenzo de' Medici's Poggio a Caiano villa, designer of the palace of the Duke of Milan: Giuliano da Sangallo."

Bramante burst into sneering laughter.

"Giuliano da Sangallo! What has he been doing in Rome? Restoring the ceiling of a church! That's what the old fossil is good for. Within a year I shall chase him out of Rome forever. Now if you will take yourself out of my way, I'll continue with the work of creating the most beautiful courtyard in all the world. Come back sometime and see how Bramante builds."

Walking to Baglioni's house, Leo said, "If I know Rome, he will make his way to the top. A bad man to have as an enemy."

"Something tells me I've got him," said Michelangelo grimly.

12

It was his task to impregnate the marble with manifest spirit; yet even in a religious theme he felt deeply for the whole man, alive to every nerve, muscle, vein, bone, to the skin and hair, fingers, eyes and mouth. All must come alive if he were to create power and monumentality by incorporating into the marble the strength of man. He carved upward, using his knowledge of the forms already released below, and an intuition as old and deep as the long-buried marble, to achieve the expression for Mary that emerged not only from her emotion but from the feeling of the whole sculpture. He stood with his head lower than Mary's, his hands opposite his forehead, the tools angled upward, carving as close as he could get to the drama of the Pietà. The block saw him face to face, the sculptor and the sculptured involved in the tender restrained sadness. He left far behind him the dark, unforgiving Pietàs, their message of love blotted out by blood. He would not sculpture agony. The nail holes in Christ's hands and feet were tiny dots. There was no sign of violence. Jesus slept peacefully in his mother's arms. Over the two figures there was a suffusion, a luminosity. His Christ awakened the deepest sympathy, not abhorrence for those who stood outside the sculpture and had been responsible.

His religious faith he projected in terms of the sublimity of the figures; the harmony between them was his way of portraying the harmony of God's universe. He did not attempt to make Christ divine, since he would not have known how, but exquisitely human. The Virgin's head emerged delicate, the features Florentine, the face of a maiden with silent pale composure. In her expression he made a distinction between divine and sublime; sublime, for him, meant supreme and perfect. He reflected, "The meaning of the figures lies in their human qualities; the beauty of face and form portrays the grandeur of their spirit."

He found that he was achieving a tactile richness, with the forms mirroring the loving days he had devoted to them.

Balducci brought him the news that Sansovino, his fellow apprentice in the Medici garden, had returned to Florence after working for a number of years in Portugal, and been commissioned to do a marble group of St. John Baptizing Christ for the Baptistery. He was looked upon as the logical choice to win the Duccio block commission.

"Sansovino is a good sculptor," said Michelangelo loyally.

"Better than you?"

He swallowed hard before he replied. "He finishes well everything he starts."

"Do you think he can win over you?"

Again Michelangelo struggled with his answer. "We both will do our best."

"I've never seen you modest before."

Michelangelo blushed. He was grimly determined to outdesign Sansovino and win the contest; but he would not talk Sansovino down.

"Leo Baglioni tells me I have few friends. Sansovino is a friend. I intend to keep him."

"Torrigiani is also entering the competition, and is telling everyone that he will get the Duccio marble because he was an anti-Medici man; and that, since you backed Piero, you won't be allowed to compete. Paolo Rucellai says you must return to Florence in time to make your peace with the Signoria."

This intelligence cost him several nights of sleep. He had occasion to bless Baglioni for his generous supply of goat tallow candles.

In mid-January snow began to fall, and fell heavily for two days, accompanied by wind from the north. The piercing cold lasted for several weeks. Michelangelo's enclosed courtyard was piled high with snow. Inside the rooms were frigid. There was no way to keep the icy boreal wind from coming in through the wood and linen shutters. The three braziers made no impression. Michelangelo worked with his hat and earmuffs on, and a blanket pinned around his shoulders. Again in February the snow and ice came. The city was still, the markets abandoned, the shops closed because the ice, sleet and frozen mud made the streets impassable.

Michelangelo and Argiento suffered. Michelangelo took the boy into bed with him to combine their warmth. Damp oozed through the whitewash on the walls. The leaks were slower under the compacted snow, but lasted longer. Coal was in short supply, the price went up so heavily that Michelangelo could buy only a minimum amount. Argiento spent hours scratching in the snow of the surrounding fields looking for wood for his fire.

Michelangelo caught cold, went down with fever. Argiento found two bricks at an interrupted building job, heated them in his fire, wrapped them in towels and alternated them on Michelangelo's feet to keep down the chill. He fed him hot beef broth. No work was done; for how many days Michelangelo lost count. Fortunately there remained only the polishing. He did not have the strength for the heavy manual labor involved in the cutting.

For his Pietà he hoped to achieve the highest polish of which marble was capable, a faultless velvety loftiness. On the first warm day he walked to Trastevere and bought several large lumps of pumice, divided them with a blow of the hammer, searching for flatter surfaces. Now he could grip the pieces in the palm of his hand, using the long, silky parallel strands to polish the broad planes of the Madonna's robe, of Christ's chest and legs: slowly, with infinite patience, over long days and weeks.

Now he needed sharper edges, split the pumice with his chisel, cut the appropriate shapes to reach into the recessions, cavities and undulations of hair, cloth, fingernails. Finally, he made sharp-edged slivers that looked like primitive arrowheads to polish the curves around Christ's nostrils. He did not finish the back of Mary since the statue was to sit in a niche, but left the marble lined and blocked, as were the rough rocks on which she was sitting. The white marble, polished and gleaming, lighted up the dingy room as though it were a stained-glass chapel. The homely artist had indeed created a work of beauty.

Sangallo was the first to see the finished sculpture. He made no comment on the religious aspect of the marble, but congratulated Michelangelo on the architecture of the triangular composition, the balance of lines and masses.

Jacopo Galli came to the studio and studied the Pietà in silence. After a time he said softly, "I have fulfilled my contract with the Cardinal of San Dionigi: this is the most beautiful work in marble to be seen in Rome today."

"I'm nervous about the installation," said Michelangelo. "Our contract doesn't say that we have the right to put the Pietà in St. Peter's. With the cardinal dead . . ."

"We won't ask any questions. We'll install it without a sound. What no one knows, no one can object to."

Michelangelo was aghast. "You mean, sneak my sculpture in?"

"Nothing furtive. Just discreet. Once the Pietà is sitting in its niche, no one will bother to have it removed."

"But the Pope was fond of the cardinal. He gave him a three-day funeral. He granted him permission to put a sculpture in the Chapel of the Kings. Why should anyone want to have it removed?"

"I'm sure they won't," said Galli reassuringly. "Suppose you hire those stoneyard friends of yours to help you. Tomorrow, after dinner, while the city is resting."

There were so many obtruding parts: hands, feet, folds, that he did not dare to entrust the moving of the marble to beams or crowbars, no matter how securely he wrapped it. He asked Guffatti to come to the workshop, showed him the Pietà and discussed the problem with him. Guffatti stood in front of the sculpture in silence, then said:

"I bring the family."

The family turned out to include not merely three husky sons but a variety of cousins. They would not allow Michelangelo to touch the piece, wrapping it in a half dozen mangy blankets and then, accompanied by a medley of cries, arguments and commands, lifting it on its base. They carried the Pietà, eight strong, to the ancient wagon with its bed of straw, and roped it in. With Michelangelo guarding the tailgate, they made their way cautiously along the cobbled Via Posterula, across the Sant'Angelo bridge, then down the newly opened, smooth Via Alessandrina, which the Pope had rebuilt to celebrate the Centennial Year. For the first time since he had come to Rome, Michelangelo had occasion to bless the Borgia.

The Guffatti stopped their wagon at the foot of the thirty-five steps. Only the fact that they were under a sacred burden kept them from cursing as they carried the heavy marble up the first three sections of seven steps, set it down to rest and wipe the perspiration from their brows, then picked it up again to carry to the atrium, past the splashing fountain and to the church door.

Here, while the Guffatti stopped once more to rest, Michelangelo had a chance to observe that the basilica was leaning even more sharply than when he had begun work. It was now so dilapidated it seemed beyond repair. He swallowed hard at the thought of putting his lovely Pietà in a basilica which had not long to remain upright. Surely the first wind to roar down off the Alban hills would flatten it? He had an image of himself crawling over the rubble to find the fragments of his shattered statue, was reassured only when he remembered Sangallo's architectural drawings which showed how St. Peter's could be counterpropped.

The Guffatti once again picked up the load. Michelangelo led them into the basilica, with its five corresponding naves and hundreds of columns assembled from all over Rome; then into the Chapel of the Kings of France, to the left of a huge figure of Christ enthroned. The Guffatti lowered their bundle carefully before the empty niche, unwrapped the blankets, wiped their hands clean of sweat, raised the Pietà reverentially to its place. Michelangelo straightened it to the position he wanted. The Guffatti family bought candles from an old woman in black, lit them before the statue.

They refused to take one scudo for their hours of backbreaking labor.

"We take our pay in heaven," said the father.

It was the best tribute Michelangelo could receive. It was also the only tribute he received.

Jacopo Galli came into the chapel, accompanied by Balducci. His head bobbed with pleasure. Guffatti, standing amidst his relatives, asked: "Is this all? No services? No blessing by the priest?"

Galli answered, "It was blessed in the carving."

The Guffatti and Argiento knelt before the Virgin, crossed themselves, murmured a prayer. Michelangelo gazed up at the Pietà, feeling sad and depleted. As he reached the door of the chapel and turned back for a last look, he saw that the Virgin too was sad and lonely; the most alone human being God ever put on earth.

He returned to St. Peter's day after day. Few of the city's pilgrims bothered to visit the Chapel of the Kings of France. Those who did hastily genuflected before the Pietà, crossed themselves and moved on.

Because Galli had advised discretion, few in Rome knew the statue had been installed. Michelangelo could get no reaction, even of the mixed kind he had received in Galli's garden from the poets and academicians. Paolo Rucellai, Sangallo, Cavalcanti visited St. Peter's; the rest of the Florentine colony, grieved over the execution of Savonarola, refused to go inside the Vatican walls.

After nearly two years of dedicated work, Michelangelo sat in his cheerless room, now empty, despondent. No one came to speak of sculpture. He was so exhausted that he could not even think of the Duccio block. Nor did Galli believe this the appropriate time to cry up a new job for him.

One afternoon he wandered into St. Peter's, saw a family with several grown children, from Lombardy, he guessed by their clothes and dialect, standing in front of his Pietà, making elaborate gestures of the hands. He went to their side to eavesdrop.

"I tell you I recognize the work," cried the mother of the family. "It is by that fellow from Osteno, who makes all the tombstones."

Her husband waved the fingers of both his hands loosely, shaking off this idea as a dog shakes off water.

"No, no, it is one of our countrymen, Cristoforo Solari, called 'The Hunchback,' from Milan. He has done many of them."

That night Michelangelo made his way through the streets, green sailcloth bag in hand. He entered St. Peter's, took a candle from the bag, put it in the wire loop of his hat, reached into the bag again for hammer and chisel. He raised his tools, leaned forward across the Christ so that the candle cast a steady glow on the Virgin's bosom. Onto the band going tightly between the breasts he cut in swift, decorative letters:

$$\text{MICHAEL AGLVS·BONAROVS·FLOEN FACEBAT}$$

Michelangelo Buonarroti of Florence made this.

He returned to his rooms, packed his things. The hundreds of drawings he had done for the Bacchus and Pietà he burned in Argiento's fire, while Argiento summoned Balducci. Balducci arrived, his shirt askew and hair tousled, promised to resell the furniture to the dealer in Trastevere.

Just before dawn, each carrying a sailcloth bag, Michelangelo and Argiento made their way to the Porta del Popolo. Michelangelo rented two mules, joined the pack train, and at first light set out for Florence.

BOOK SIX

THE GIANT

The warm June Florentine sun flooded his face as he gazed out the window at the tawny stone towerhouse of the superintendent of the Florentine Guilds. Returning from Rome with no commissions, and no funds, he had been obliged to send Argiento back to his family's farm outside Ferrara, and himself return to his father's board. However he occupied the front and best room of the commodious apartment in which the Buonarroti now lived, for Lodovico had invested some part of the Rome earnings to good advantage. He had bought a small house in San Pietro Maggiore, used the income from it to clear the title to the disputed Buonarroti property near Santa Croce, then raised the family's social position by renting this floor in this house in the more fashionable Street of St. Proculus, a block from the superb stone pile of the Pazzi palace.

The death of Lucrezia had aged Lodovico; his face was thinner, the cheeks sunken; in compensation he had allowed his hair to grow in a thick mass down to his shoulders. As Jacopo Galli had predicted, nothing had come of the business Michelangelo had hoped to set up for Buonarroto and Giovansimone. Buonarroto had at last settled down in the Strozzi wool shop near the Porta Rossa; Giovansimone was a crushed youth, apathetically taking jobs, then disappearing after a few weeks. Sigismondo, barely able to read and write, was earning a few scudi as a hired soldier for Florence in its present hostilities against Pisa. Lionardo had disappeared, no one knew into what monastery. His aunt Cassandra and uncle Francesco were beset with minor ills.

He and Granacci had clasped each other in a hilarious embrace, happy to be together. During the past years Granacci had come into the first half of his fortune and, as the gossip Jacopo of the Ghirlandaio *bottega* reported gleefully, was keeping a mistress in a villa in the hills of Bellosguardo, above the Porta Romana. Granacci still maintained his headquarters at Ghirlandaio's, helping out David Ghirlandaio after his brother Benedetto's death, in return for using the studio for his own work. He riffled through the sketches on Michelangelo's worktable.

"Open for business, I see."

"Best-stocked shop in Florence."

"Any customers?"

"None. I'm joining Soggi."

Granacci chuckled. "He's been quite a success. Just bought space for a butcher shop in the New Market."

"The Bertoldo method of carving calves."

They set out for an *osteria* under the trees, turned left on the Via del Proconsolo, past the gracious Badia church, into the Borgo dei Greci with its Serristori palace designed by Baccio d'Agnolo and into the Via dei Benci. Here were the ancient Ghibelline Bardelli palace and the first of the Alberti palaces, with its columned courtyard and capitals by Giuliano da Sangallo.

Florence spoke to him. The stones spoke to him. He felt their character, the variety of structures, the strength of their impacted layers. How wonderful to be back where *pietra serena* was the material of architecture. To some people stone was dead; "hard as stone," "stone cold," they said. To him, as he once again ran his fingers along its contours, it was the most alive substance in the world, rhythmic, responsive, tractable: warm, resilient, colorful, vibrant. He was in love with stone.

The restaurant was on the Lungarno, located in a garden shaded by fig trees. The owner, who was also the cook, went down to the river, raised a basket on ropes, wiped off a bottle of Trebbiano on his apron and opened it at the table. They drank to Michelangelo's return.

He climbed the familiar Settignano hills to see the Topolinos, found that Bruno and Enrico had married. Each had added a stone room for his new family on the far side of the house. Already there were five grandchildren, and both wives were again pregnant. He commented:

"The Topolinos are going to control all the *pietra serena* carving of Florence, if you keep up this pace."

"We'll keep up," said Bruno. The mother added, "Your friend, Contessina de' Medici, she too had another son, after her daughter died."

He had already learned that Contessina had been banished from Florence and lived in exile with her husband and son in a peasant's house on the north slope of Fiesole, their home and possessions having been confiscated when her father-in-law, Niccolò Ridolfi, was hanged for participating in a conspiracy to overthrow the Republic and bring Piero back as King of Florence. His affection for Contessina had not changed, though the years had passed without his seeing her. He had never felt wanted at the Ridolfi palace, and so he had not gone to visit; how then could he go to her after his return from Rome, when she was living in poverty and disgrace? Might not any visit, now that they were plagued by misfortune, be construed as pity?

The city itself had undergone many perceivable changes in the almost five years he had been gone. Walking through the Piazza della Signoria, the people bowed their heads in shame when they passed the spot where Savonarola's body had been burned; at the same time they were smothering their consciences under a tornado of activity, trying to replace what Savonarola had destroyed, spending large sums with the gold- and silversmiths, the gem cutters, the costume makers, the embroiderers, designers of terra-cotta and wood mosaics, the makers of musical instruments, the manuscript illuminators. Piero Soderini, whom Lorenzo de' Medici had trained as the brightest of the young men in politics, and whom Michelangelo had often seen at the palace, was now at the head of the Florentine Republic as *gonfaloniere,* or mayor-governor of Florence and the city-state. He had achieved a measure of harmony among the Florentine factions for the first time since the mortal battle between Lorenzo and Savonarola had begun.

Florentine artists who had fled the city had sensed the upsurge of activity and returned from Milan, Venice, Portugal, Paris: Piero di Cosimo, Filippino Lippi, Andrea Sansovino, Benedetto da Rovezzano, Leonardo da Vinci, Benedetto Buglioni. Those whose work had been stopped by Savonarola's influence and power were now producing again: Botticelli, Pollaiuolo, the architect, known as *Il Cronaca,* the storyteller, Rosselli, Lorenzo di Credi, Baccio da Montelupo, jester and scandal bearer of the Medici sculpture garden. They had organized a Company of the Cauldron, and while it was restricted to only twelve members, each was allowed to bring four guests to the monthly dinner meeting in Rustici's enormous sculpture studio. Granacci was a member. He had immediately invited Michelangelo to accompany him. Michelangelo had refused, preferring to wait until he had a commission.

The months since his return had contained little real pleasure. He had left for Rome a boy, returned a man, ready to carve mountains of marble; but as he turned to gaze sightlessly at his Madonna and Child and Centaurs, which he had affixed on nails to the side wall of his combination workroom and bedroom, he thought unhappily that as far as Florence knew he might never have carved the Bacchus or Pietà.

Jacopo Galli was still working for him in Rome: the Mouscron brothers from Bruges, who imported cloth from England into Rome, had seen the Pietà and were interested in a Madonna and Child. Galli thought he could secure an excellent contract on the Mouscrons' next visit to Rome. He had also interested Cardinal Piccolomini in employing Michelangelo to carve the figures needed to complete the family altar honoring his uncle Pope Pius Il, in the cathedral in Siena.

"Without Galli," he muttered, "I'm out of business. While the grass is growing, the horse starves."

Immediately on his return he had gone to the Duomo workshop to study the seventeen-foot Duccio column called by some a "thin piece," by others "emaciated," to search its innerness for ideas, testing it again and reiterating to Beppe:

"*Il marmo è sano*. The marble is sound."

At night he read by candlelight in Dante and in the Old Testament, looking for a mood and a heroic theme.

Then he learned that the members of the Wool Guild and the Board of Works of the cathedral had been unable to make up their minds about the carving of the giant block. It was just as well, thought Michelangelo, for he also had heard that many favored giving the commission to Leonardo da Vinci, recently returned to Florence, because of the magnificent reputation of his huge equestrian statue of Count Sforza, and his painting of the Last Supper in the refectory of Santa Maria delle Grazie in Milan.

Michelangelo had never met Leonardo, who had abandoned Florence for Milan some eighteen years before, after being acquitted on a morals charge; but Florentine artists were saying that he was the greatest draftsman in Italy. Nettled, curious, Michelangelo had gone to Santissima Annunziata when the cartoon for Leonardo's Virgin and Child and St. Anne was on exhibition. He had stood before the cartoon with his heart beating like a hammer. Never had he seen such power or authenticity of drawing, such forceful truth about the figure, except, of course, in his own work. In a folio on a bench he had found the sketch of a male nude seen from the rear, with arms and legs outstretched. No one had rendered the male figure in this fashion, so galvanically alive and convincing. Leonardo, he was certain, had dissected! He had pulled the bench up in front of the three figures and plunged into copying, had left the church chastened. If the Boards granted the commission to Leonardo, who could contest their decision? Could he, with only a few reports of his Bacchus and Pietà beginning to filter northward to indicate his stature?

Then Leonardo had rejected the commission. On the grounds that he despised marble sculpture as an inferior art, good only for artisans. Michelangelo heard the news in a state of turmoil. He was glad to have the Duccio block free, and Leonardo da Vinci out of the running; but he felt a resentment against the man for his belittling statement, which all Florence took up and was repeating.

One darkness before dawn he rose, dressed hurriedly, ran through the empty Via del Proconsolo to the Duomo workshop, and stood at the corner of the column.

The diagonal beams of first sunlight streamed across the marble, projecting his shadow upward the full seventeen-foot length of the column, magnifying his silhouette and turning him into a giant. He caught his breath, thought of David as he knew his story from the Bible. "This is how David must have felt," he told himself, "on that morning when he stepped forth to face Goliath." A Giant for the symbol of Florence!

He returned home, reread the David chapter with heightened perception. For days he drew from memory virile male figures, seeking a David worthy of the biblical legend. He submitted design after design to his former Medici palace acquaintance, Gonfaloniere Soderini; to the Wool Guild; to the Board of Works of the cathedral. But nothing happened. He was stalemated; and he was burning up with marble fever.

2

His father was waiting for him in a black leather chair in the family room at the rear of the apartment. On his lap was an envelope which had just arrived on the Rome post. Michelangelo opened it with a knife. Inside were several closely written sheets in Jacopo Galli's handwriting informing Michelangelo that he was about to get Cardinal Piccolomini's signature on a contract. "However I must warn you," Galli wrote, "that it is by no means the kind of commission you want or deserve."

"Read it to me," cried Lodovico, his dark amber eyes alight with pleasure.

Michelangelo's face dropped as he learned that he would have to carve fifteen small figures, all of them fully clothed, to fit into the narrow niches of an Andrea Bregno traditional altar. The drawings would have to be approved by the cardinal, and the marbles recarved if the final pieces did not please His Grace. The pay was five hundred ducats; Michelangelo could take no other contract for three years, by the end of which time the final figure had to be completed and approved.

Lodovico warmed his hands in front of his chest as though it were a brazier.

"Five hundred gold ducats for three years' work. Not as good as you did in Rome, but added to our rents, a modest living."

"Not really, Father. I must pay for the marble. And if the cardinal doesn't approve I must rework the figures or carve altogether new ones."

"Since when can't you please a cardinal? If Galli, a shrewd banker, is willing to guarantee you make the best statues in Italy, why should we be foolish enough to worry? How much are they paying in advance? 'He that gives quickly, gives twice.' "

"There is no advance."

"How do they imagine you are going to buy supplies? Do they think the money is coming from me?"

"No, Father, I'm sure they know better than that."

"Thanks to God! Galli must make it part of the contract that they advance you one hundred gold ducats before you begin work. Then we're safe."

Michelangelo slumped into a chair.

"Three years of carving draperies. And never once a figure of my own choosing."

He jumped up out of the chair, ran through the apartment and slammed out the door. He took the short cut past the Bargello and the Piazza San Firenze, through a narrow side street into the blazing light of the Piazza della Signoria. He turned aside from a pile of fine gray ash, put there in the deep of night by the faithful to commemorate the spot where Savonarola had been burned, went to the broad steps leading up into the Signoria courtyard. On the left was a stone staircase which he took three steps at a time, then was in the majestic high-ceilinged Council Hall where the meetings of the Florentine Council were held, with space for a thousand citizens to take their stand. The vast hall was empty and bare except for a table and a dozen chairs on a podium at the far side.

He turned to a door on his left admitting to the chambers which had always been occupied by the *podestà*, such as his friend Gianfrancesco Aldovrandi had been, but was now occupied by Piero Soderini, latest in the tradition of sixteen Soderini ancestors who had been Gonfalonieri before him.

Michelangelo was readily admitted to Soderini's office. It was a magnificent corner room overlooking the piazza and rooftops of much of Florence; elegant, paneled in dark wood, with a broad ceiling painted with the lilies of Florence. Behind a massive oak desk sat the chief magistrate of the Republic. On his last trip to Rome, Soderini had been told by the Florentine colony about the Bacchus, and been taken to St. Peter's to see the Pietà.

"Ben venuto," Soderini murmured, "what brings you to the seat of your government on this warm afternoon?"

"Troubles, Gonfaloniere," replied Michelangelo, "but I suppose no one comes up here to unburden his pleasures?"

"That's why I sit behind such a capacious desk: so that it can hold all the problems of Florence."

"It is your shoulders that are broad."

Soderini ducked his head deprecatingly: by no means a handsome head. At fifty-one his blond hair, covered by a strangely shaped cap, was bleaching white, his chin was long and pointed, his nose hooked, his skin yellowish, the eyebrows irregularly arched over mild hazel eyes that were devoid of audacity or cunning. Florence said that Soderini had three virtues not combined in any other Tuscan of the day: he was honest, he was plain, and he could induce opposing factions to work together.

Michelangelo told Piero Soderini about the proposed Piccolomini contract.

"I don't want this commission, Gonfaloniere. I'm on fire to carve the Giant! Can't you force the Boards of the Duomo and the Wool Guild to decide about the competition? If I don't get it, at least it will be out of my range of possibility. I could go on to this Piccolomini contract as something I can't escape."

He was breathing hard. Soderini gazed at him blandly across the broad desk.

"This is not a good time to force things. We're exhausted from our war with Pisa. Caesar Borgia is threatening to conquer Florence. Last night the Signoria bought him off. Thirty-six thousand gold florins a year for three years, his salary for serving as captain general of the Florentine forces."

"Blackmail," said Michelangelo.

Soderini's face turned red. "Many do kiss the hand they wish to see cut off. The city has no way of knowing how much more it will have to pay Caesar Borgia. The Guilds have to provide this money to the Signoria. So you can understand why the Wool Guild is not in the mood to discuss a sculpture competition."

An emotional silence filled the space between them.

"Hadn't you better be more receptive to the Piccolomini offer?" suggested Soderini.

Michelangelo groaned. "Cardinal Piccolomini wants to choose all fifteen subjects. I cannot carve until he approves the designs. And what wages: thirty-three and a third ducats for each figure, enough to pay rent, buy supplies . . ."

"How long since you've carved marble?"

"More than a year."

"Or been paid?"

"More than two."

Michelangelo's lips trembled. "You don't understand. This altar was made by Bregno. All the marbles have to be fully clothed; they must go into dark niches where they will be seen only as rigid still lifes. How can I tie up three whole years of my life filling Bregno's highly decorated altar with more decorations?"

His agonized cry hung heavily in the room.

"Do today what you must do today," said Soderini in an annealing voice. "Tomorrow you will be free to do what you must do tomorrow. We bought off Caesar Borgia. For you as an artist it is the same as with us as a city-state; only one law prevails: survival."

At Santo Spirito, Prior Bichiellini, sitting behind the desk in his manuscript-lined office, pushed his papers aside, his eyes blazing behind the spectacles.

"Survival on what plane? To stay alive as an animal stays alive? For shame! The Michelangelo I knew six years ago could never think, 'Better mediocre work than no work at all.' This is opportunism, fit for mediocre talent."

"I agree, Father."

"Then don't take the commission. Do the best that is in you, or nothing at all."

"In the long run, you are right; in the short run I suppose Soderini and my father are right."

"There are no long and short runs," the prior cried, his voice heavy with indignation. "There is only a God-given number of years in which to work and fulfill yourself. Don't squander them."

Michelangelo hung his head in shame.

"If I sound like a moralist," said the prior quietly, "please remember that it is my job to be concerned with your character."

Michelangelo went out into the bright sunlight, sat on the edge of the fountain in the Piazza Santo Spirito and splashed cold water on his face, even as he had on those nights when he had emerged from the dead room. He groaned aloud, "Three years! *Dio mio!*"

Back in his studio, Granacci barely listened to him.

"Without work, Michelagnolo, you are the most wretched creature alive. What does it matter if you have to carve dull statues? Your worst will be better than anybody else's best."

"You're maddening: you insult and flatter me in the same breath."

Granacci grinned. "Do as many figures as you have time for. Everybody in Florence will help you outwit Siena."

"Outwit a cardinal?"

Granacci grew serious. "I'm trying to face reality. You want to carve, ergo, take the Piccolomini contract and do the best you can. When something better comes along, you'll sculpture better. Come and have dinner with me and the Company."

Michelangelo shook his head. "No."

3

He returned to the drawing board, to sketches of the Madonna for the Mouscrons, attempts to capture saints for the Piccolomini contract. But he could think of nothing but the Duccio column and the Giant-David. In 1 Kings 16:17, he found himself reading:

> Meanwhile the Lord's spirit passed away from Saul . . . an evil mood came upon him that gave him no rest. When Saul said, "Find one who can play the harp well, and bring him to me," one of his servants replied, "I myself have met such a man, a skillful player indeed, a son of Jesse the Bethlehemite. He is sturdy besides and a tried warrior, well spoken and personable, and the Lord is with him . . .

Some time later, when Saul questioned the wisdom of David's meeting Goliath in battle, David replied:

> My Lord, I used to feed my father's flock; and if lion or bear came and carried off one of my rams, I would go in pursuit, and get the mastery and snatch the prey from their jaws. Did they threaten me, I would catch them by the throat and strangle them. Lion or bear, my Lord, I would slay them.

He sat staring at the lines: "lion or bear . . . I would catch them by the throat and strangle them." Was there any greater feat of strength or courage in the Bible? A young man, without weapons or armor, had pursued the most powerful of beasts, caught them and strangled them with his bare hands.

Could any of the Davids he had seen in Florence have conceived such an act, let alone executed it? In the morning he stopped before the Castagno painting, gazing at the youthful David, with slender arms and legs, small hands and feet, a mass of hair blowing about the delicate-featured, pretty face, somehow seeming halfway between man and woman. He next went to see Antonio Pollaiuolo's David Victor, somewhat older than Castagno's, with feet solidly on the ground, but with tiny, ladylike fingers crooked as though he were about to eat a custard. There was a well-developed torso and a determination about the stance, but he was dressed in the lace-trimmed coat with matching lace undershirt of a Florentine nobleman, the most expensively, aristocratically dressed shepherd boy on earth, mused Michelangelo.

He ran to the Palazzo della Signoria, mounted the steps to the Sala dei Gigli. Outside the door stood Verrocchio's bronze David, a wistful adolescent. Inside the Sala was Donatello's first David, carved in marble. Michelangelo never saw it but he gasped at the sensitivity and finish of the flesh. The hands were strong, the one visible leg under the long, luxuriant robe was heavier than in the paintings of Castagno and Pollaiuolo, the neck thicker. But the eyes were blank, there was a flaccid underchin, a weak mouth, a wreath of leaves and berries crowning the expressionless face.

He descended the stone steps to the courtyard and stood before Donatello's bronze David, with which he had lived for two years in the courtyard of the Medici, and which had been appropriated by the city after the sack of the palace. It was a sculpture he admired passionately, the legs and feet sturdy enough to carry the body, with strong arms and neck. Yet now that he looked at it critically he saw that, like the other Florentine Davids, this one had pretty features, an almost feminine face under the decorated hat, and long curls hanging down over the shoulders. Though it had the genitals of a young boy, it also had the budding breasts of a young girl.

He returned home, fragments of ideas racing through his mind. These Davids, particularly the two beloved Donatellos, were boys. They could no more have strangled lions and bears than they could have killed the Goliath whose head rested between their feet. Why had the best artists of Florence depicted David as either an adolescent or an elegantly garbed and groomed young dandy? Had no other artist read beyond the description of David as "red-cheeked, fair of face, pleasant of mien"; had they not gone on to, "Did they threaten me, I would catch them by the throat and strangle them. Lion or bear . . . I would slay them."

David was a man! He had accomplished these feats before the Lord chose him. What he did he did alone, with his great heart and great hands. Such a man would not hesitate to face a Goliath so gigantic that he could carry a breastplate of mail weighing a thousand pounds. What was Goliath to a young man who had mixed with lions and bears and beaten them in fair battle?

At dawn he walked streets still wet from their scrubbing, carrying his measuring equipment to the Duomo workyard. He computed his figures on the column, calculated to a hairsbreadth the distance between the deepest point of gouging to the point on the opposite side to see if it were possible to design a David whose thighs, the shortest distance across the body, could be fitted into the marble that was left.

"No good," commented Beppe. "For fifty years I watch sculptors measure across here. Always they say, 'Too bad. No figure will fit.' "

"It's a matter of invention, Beppe. Look, I'll draw *la sagoma,* the silhouette of the block, for you. This dot indicates the deepest point of gouging, halfway down the column. Now suppose we were to swivel the hips away from this narrow area, and opposite use a strongly outpushing wrist or hand to compensate . . . ?"

Beppe raked his behind.

"Ah," cried Michelangelo, "you think it might work! I can tell how pleased you are by what part of your anatomy you scratch."

The weeks passed. He learned that Rustici had decided that the project was too big for him. Sansovino required an added block of marble to get anything out of the Duccio column. The half dozen other sculptors in town, including Baccio, Buglioni and Benedetto da Rovezzano, had walked away from the column, saying that since the deep gouging had been done midway down its length it must certainly break in two at that narrow point.

A courier brought a packet from Rome containing the Piccolomini contract:

> . . . The most Reverend Cardinal of Siena commits to Michelangelo, son of Lodovico Buonarroti-Simoni, sculptor from Florence, to make fifteen statues of Carrara marble, which is to be new, clean, and white and not veined, but as perfect as it is necessary to make first-quality statues, each one of which should be two *braccia* high, and which should be completed in three years for the amount of five hundred large gold ducats . . .

Jacopo Galli had secured an advance of a hundred ducats by guaranteeing to return the money to Cardinal Piccolomini if Michelangelo died before he finished the last three statues. Cardinal Piccolomini approved Michelangelo's first sketches. But there was a line in the contract which carried the crowning indignity. "As a figure of St. Francis has already been sculptured by Pietro Torrigiani, who left the draperies and head unfinished, Michelangelo will complete the statue out of honor and courtesy, in Siena, so that the statue can stand among the others made by him, and anybody who sees it would say that it is the work of Michelangelo's hand."

"I never knew that Torrigiani started this contract," Michelangelo cried to Granacci. "Think of the ignominy of my scavenging after him."

"Harsh words," said Granacci. "Let's just say that Torrigiani was incapable of finishing even one figure adequately, and so Cardinal Piccolomini had to turn to you to make it right."

Galli urged that Michelangelo sign the contract and commence work at once. "Next spring, when the Mouscron brothers come from Bruges, I will get you that free-standing Madonna and Child to carve. There will be better things for the future."

He gathered up an armful of new sketches for the David and went again to plead with Piero Soderini. The commission must come to him if only the Gonfaloniere could force the Wool Guild to act.

"Yes, I might force it through," agreed Soderini. "But then the Boards would have acted against their will. They would resent you. They must want this piece carved and must choose you as their sculptor. You perceive the difference?"

"Yes," replied Michelangelo sadly, "it makes sense. Only I can't wait any longer."

Off the Via del Proconsolo, a few steps down from the Badia, was an archway that looked as though it led into the courtyard of a palace. Michelangelo had passed it innumerable times on his way from his house to the sculpture garden, and knew that it provided the opening to an artisans' piazza, a private world surrounded by the backs of palaces, truncated towers and two-story houses. It sheltered some twenty workshops of leather tanners, coppersmiths, carpenters, wool dyers, flax weavers, scissors makers preparing their products for the shops in the open markets and on the popular streets of the Corso and Pellicceria. Here he found a workshop for rent, one that had been occupied by a shoemaker, on the south side of the oval-shaped piazza, getting most of the day's sun. He paid three months' rent in advance, sent a letter in care of the Gesuati of Ferrara to Argiento telling him to come back to work, bought a truckle bed for the shop for him to sleep on.

In the June heat the craftsmen worked at benches in front of their narrow slots, the dyers' arms stained blue, green and red, the metalworkers in their leather aprons, bare to their burly waists, the carpenters sawing, planing, filling the air with clean-smelling shavings; all making the indigenous noises of their trade, blended together compactly in the closed-in area, creating the kind of companionable background music in which Michelangelo felt at home. Surrounded by simple workmen, the workshop afforded him the same busy privacy he had enjoyed from his worktable in Rome, overlooking the bustle of the Bear Hotel.

Argiento arrived, dust-covered and footsore, chattering straight through a morning as he scrubbed out the vestiges of the shoemaker's tenancy, unable to contain his relief at being off his brother's farm.

"Argiento, I don't understand. In Rome you walked into the *campagna* every Sunday to see the horses . . ."

Argiento raised his perspiration-streaked face from his bucket of suds. "Farms I like to visit, not to work."

The carpenter across the way helped them build a drafting table just inside the door. Argiento scoured the Street of the Ironmongers to find a secondhand forge. Michelangelo bought iron rods, baskets of chestnut wood to make his chisels. He found two blocks of marble in Florence, sent specifications for three more to Carrara. Then, without clay or wax models, without looking at the designs approved by Cardinal Piccolomini, he set up the four-foot blocks and in the sheer joy of having his hands back in marble carved first the St. Paul, bearded, with fine features bespeaking the first Christian missionary's Roman citizenship and contact with Greek culture, the body, though covered by voluminous robes, muscular and tense. Without pause he went on to the St. Peter, closest of Christ's disciples, witness of Christ's resurrection, a rock on which the new Church was founded. This statue was quieter physically and mentally, reflective in spirit, with an interesting arrangement of vertical draperies accented by a softly flowing horizontal scarf over the chest and arms.

The workmen of the piazza accepted him as another skilled artisan who arrived in laborer's clothes at dawn, just after an apprentice had washed down the communal square, and who quit at dark, his hair, face, nostrils, shirt, bare legs and feet covered with white marble dust, even as they were covered with wood shavings or dye or tiny strands of leather or flax. Sometimes one of them would call out in a full voice above the saws, hammers and scraping knives, while Michelangelo's chisels were singing through the white marble like plows through the spring earth:

"It's a miracle! All Florence swelters in the heat, and in our piazza we have a snowstorm."

He kept the whereabouts of his workshop a secret from everyone except Granacci, whose visit on the way home to his midday dinner brought Michelangelo news of the city.

"I can't believe it! You signed the contract on June 19; here it is only the middle of July, and you have two of the statues completed. They're quite good, in spite of all your moaning that you could carve nothing worth while. At this rate you'll be finished with the fifteen statues in seven months.''

Michelangelo gazed at his St. Peter and St. Paul, replied soberly: "These first two figures are not bad, they contain my hunger to carve. But once they're shoved into those narrow niches, they'll die a quick death. The next two statues are of Pope Pius II and Gregory the Great, in their full papal crowns and long stiff robes . . .''

"Why don't you go to Siena," Granacci interrupted, "and get rid of Torrigiani? You'll feel better.''

He left that day.

4

Tuscany is a state of grace. The countryside is so lovingly designed that the eye sweeps the mountains and valleys without stumbling over a single stone. The lilt of the rolling green hills, the upsurging cypresses, the terraces sculptured by generations that have handled the rocks with skillful tenderness, the fields geometrically juxtaposed as though drawn by a draftsman for beauty as well as productivity; the battlements of castles on the hills, their tall towers standing gray-blue and golden tan among the forest of trees, the air of such clarity that every sod of earth stands out in dazzling detail. Below him the fields were ripening with July barley and oats, beans and beets; on both sides of the road the grape-heavy vines were espaliered between the horizontal branches of silver-green olive trees, composing orchards of webbed design, rich in intimation of wine, olive oil and lacy-leaf poetry.

He had a sense of physical delight as his horse moved along the contours of a ridge, rising ever higher into the flawless Italian sky, the air he breathed so pure that his whole being felt ennobled, meanness and pettiness falling away from him: a rapture he experienced only when he carved white marble. Tuscany untied the knots in a man's intestines, wiped out the ills of his world. God and man had combined to create this supreme work of art. Pictorially, Michelangelo thought, this might be the Garden of Eden. Adam and Eve had departed, but to his sculptor's eye, scanning the undulating ranges which flowed backward in space with the lyricism of the green river winding through the valley below him, dotted with stone houses, sun-mellowed tile roofs, hayricks, Tuscany was paradise. He recited a verse from his childhood:

> Italy is the garden of Europe,
> Tuscany is the garden of Italy,
> Florence is the flower of Tuscany.

Toward sundown he reached the heights above Poggibonsi, the Apennines covered with virgin forest, rivers and lakes shining like rolled silver under the oblique sunset rays. He descended the long hill to Poggibonsi, a wine center, dropped his saddlebag in a scrubbed, bare-floored inn, then climbed the hill beyond the town to explore Giuliano da Sangallo's towering Poggio Imperiale, a fortress palace that Lorenzo had ordered built to keep invading armies from passing beyond this heavily fortified point which controlled the valley leading to Florence. But Lorenzo had died; the Poggio Imperiale had been abandoned. . . .

He scrambled down the rocky footpath. He was served supper in the yard of the inn, slept soundly, rose at cockcrow and set out on the second half of his journey.

Siena was a warm reddish-brown city, made of brick from its reddish-brown earth, even as Bologna was a burnt-orange city from its native earth. He entered the gate of the encompassing city wall, made his way to the Piazza del Campo, shell-shaped, running rapidly downhill from its top line of private palaces to the Palazzo Pubblico at the other end, and piercing the skies above it the beautiful and daring Tower of Mangia, a breath-taking stone sculpture.

He walked to the center of the piazza around which Siena ran its mad horse race each summer, to Della Quercia's lovely fountain, then mounted a steep flight of stone steps and came to the Baptistery, with its baptismal font sculptured by Della Quercia, Donatello and Ghiberti.

After circling the font to study the work of Italy's best sculptors, he left the Baptistery and climbed the mountain-steep hill to the cathedral. He stood gaping in awe at the black and white marble façade with its magnificent carved figures by Giovanni Pisano, its rose windows, black and white marble Campanile. Inside, the floor was a mine of marble slabs, inlaid with black and white marquetry depicting scenes from the Old and New Testaments.

Then his heart sank. Before him stood the Bregno altar, the niches shallower than he had imagined, each of them topped by a heavily incised shell-like dome, against which the heads and faces of his figures would have to be seen, draining their expression. Some of the niches stood so high in the air that no one on the floor would know what kind of sculpture they contained.

He measured the niches, revised in his mind the height of the bases on which his figures would stand, sought out the caretaker, a pleasant redfaced man of middle years who greeted him loquaciously.

"Ah, you're the Michelangelo Buonarroti we've been waiting for. The St. Francis arrived from Rome weeks ago. I set it up in a cool room off the Baptistery, forge and all. The Cardinal Piccolomini instructed me to take good care of you. Got a room all ready in our house across the square. My wife prepares the best Sienese *pappardelle alla lepre*, wide noodles with a hare sauce . . ."

Michelangelo swam into the river of words.

"Would you take me to the St. Francis? I must see how much work there is."

"Of course! Remember, you're Cardinal Piccolomini's guest here, and the cardinal is our great man . . ."

Michelangelo swallowed hard at the sight of Torrigiani's sculpture: wooden, lifeless, a plethora of flowing robes under which no part of a living, breathing human could be discerned; hands without veins, skin or bone; a rigid, stylized expressionless face . . . all these points he ticked off to himself as his eyes mercilessly tore through the unfinished block.

He vowed to give this poor marred St. Francis, whom even the birds would not recognize, all of the love and skill at his command. He would have to re-enter the block, shed its artificial trappings, throw out the committed marble and redesign the whole figure, recast the concept so that St. Francis might emerge as Michelangelo thought of him, the most gentle of the saints. But he would sleep on it first, then bring drawing materials and sit in this cool room carved out of the cathedral mountain, with diffused light from an overhead window, and search his mind until St. Francis emerged in his love of the poor, the stricken, the abandoned.

The next day he made his drawings. By nightfall he was putting new edges on old chisels, balancing them for his hand, getting accustomed to the heft of the hammer. The following dawn he began carving in white heat; and out of the now skinny block there emerged a travel-weary body beneath a slight robe, the emaciated shoulders down to bone, the hands touchingly expressive, the legs thin, knock-kneed, the feet that had trod the roads to give sustenance and to adore everything in nature, tired.

He felt an identity with St. Francis, and with this maimed block from which he was emerging. When he came to the head and face he carved his own hair, brushed in a straight line down the forehead, his own caved-in face as he had seen it in the Medici mirror the morning after Torrigiani stove it in: the nose squashed between the eyes, snaking downward in an S, a lump over the eye, the swollen cheekbone below; a St. Francis saddened by what he saw when he looked out at God's world, yet over the pained features a forgiveness, a sweetness and acceptance.

A mood of sadness pervaded him as he rode home through the Chianti hills. Wearily he dropped off his horse, made his way to his workshop, saddlebag over his shoulder. He found Argiento wiggling excitedly from one foot to the other, waiting for Michelangelo to look at him.

"Well, Argiento, what are you bursting with?"

"Gonfaloniere Soderini, he wants to see you, he sends a page every hour!"

The Piazza della Signoria was aglow with orange light from the burning oil pots that hung from every window and from the top of the crenelated tower. Soderini detached himself from his Council associates in the raised loggia and met Michelangelo at the base of Donatello's Judith. He was dressed in a plain silk shirt against the locked-in heat of the evening, but his expression was one of being coolly pleased with himself.

"Why the oil pots? What are we celebrating?"

"You."

"Me?"

"In part." Soderini's eyes twinkled wickedly in the orange light. "The Council agreed this afternoon on a new constitution. That's the official explanation. The unofficial explanation is that the directors of the Wool Guild and the Duomo voted you the Giant . . ."

Michelangelo went rigid. It was incredible. The Duccio column was his!

Soderini's voice continued gaily. "When we realized that our best Florentine carver was bound by a Sienese cardinal, we asked, 'Does Siena suppose that Florence does not appreciate its own artists? Or that we can't afford to employ them?' After all, we've spent years at war with the Sienese . . . !"

"But the Piccolomini contract . . ."

"Out of patriotic duty you must postpone the Piccolomini contract, and on September first take over the Duccio block."

Michelangelo felt the familiar stinging behind his eyelids.

"How do I thank you?"

Soderini slowly shook his elongated head with its yellow-streaked hair, murmured, "We are sons of *Il Magnifico;* we must observe that bond."

5

His feet carried him down the Borgo Pinti into the Via degli Artisti, then out a gate of the wall, along the Affrico River, and up the hills to Settignano. The Topolino family was in the yard enjoying the evening breeze from the hills.

"Listen," he called out, "I just heard. The Duccio column. It's mine!"

"We should be able to trust you now with a few window frames," teased the father.

Michelangelo spread his hands in front of him. "Thank you for the honor, *padre mio,* but a good *scalpellino* likes to shape building block."

He remained the night, sleeping on an old straw pad under the arches between the grandfather and youngest son. At dawn he rose to join the men chipping *pietra serena.* He worked for a few hours, while the sun climbed high in the valley, then went into the house. The mother handed him a jug of cold water.

"*Madre mia,* how goes it with Contessina?" he asked.

"She is frail. . . . But it is more. The Signoria has forbidden anyone to help them." She made the eloquent Tuscan gesture of hopelessness, her hands circling outward and down. "The hatred of Piero still poisons."

Michelangelo drank deeply of the water, went back to the workyard and asked Bruno:

"Can you spare a few pieces of iron?"

"There is always to spare."

Michelangelo put wood in the forge, lit it, fashioned a set of small chisels and hammers, the kind the Topolino father had made for him when he was six. Then he cut out an oblong of *serena,* carved the *scalpellino's* alphabet on it, from the herringbone to the lines of the dog's-tooth chisel.

He bade the Topolinos *"Addio."* The family knew, by some mystical system of communication, that he had come to them first after learning of his good fortune. His visit here overnight, the companionable work hours on the blocks, told them of his continued love for them.

The horse he had borrowed was old and tired. Halfway up the steep trail Michelangelo dismounted and led the animal. At the top of the ridge he turned west as the sun flooded the sky over the Mugnone Valley with rose and purple. It was a short haul into Fiesole, northern anchor of the Etruscan league of cities that began at Veii, just outside Rome, and that Caesar's legions had had a difficult time conquering. Caesar thought he had leveled Fiesole, but as Michelangelo started down the north slope, seeing Poliziano's Villa Diana in the distance, he passed Etruscan walls still cemented and intact, and new houses rebuilt of the original stones of the city.

Contessina's house was at the bottom of a steep, narrow track, halfway down the slope to the Mugnone River. It had formerly been the peasant's house for the castle on top of the hill. Michelangelo tied his horse to an olive tree, made his way through a vegetable garden and looked down at the Ridolfi family on the small stone-paved terrace in front of their cottage. Contessina was sitting on a cane-backed chair, the baby at her breast, a six-year-old playing at her feet. He called softly from the bank above:

"It is I, Michelangelo Buonarroti, come to visit."

Contessina lifted her head sharply, covered her breast.

"Michelangelo! What a surprise. Come down, come down. The path is over to the right."

There was a constrained silence as Ridolfi lifted his proud, hurt face. Michelangelo took the *serena* slab and tools from the saddle bag and made his way down the path. Ridolfi was still looking upward to him, standing stiffly. He set the toy chisels, hammer and slab at Contessina's feet.

"Yesterday I received the Duccio column. I had to come to tell you. *Il Magnifico* would have wanted it. Then I realized that your oldest son must now be six. It is time he started learning; I shall be his teacher. Just as the Topolinos taught me when I was six."

Contessina's peals of laughter rang out over the fields of olives. Ridolfi's stern mouth twitched with amusement. He said in a low voice, "You are kind to come to us this way. You know that we are pariahs."

It was the first time Ridolfi had ever addressed him; and it was the first time Michelangelo had been close to him since the day of Contessina's wedding. Ridolfi was short of thirty, but ostracism and bitterness were already ravaging his face. Though he had not been involved in the conspiracy to bring back Piero de' Medici, he was known to despise the Republic and to be ready to work for the return of an oligarchic control of Florence. His family fortune, based on world trade in wool, was now being used to help finance the city-state.

"Which makes it a doubly noxious brew for me to imbibe," said Ridolfi; "but one day we shall be returned to power. Then we shall see!"

He felt Contessina's eyes burning into his back. He turned to gaze at her, head on. Her attitude was one of calm acceptance of what was, even though they had just finished a plain dinner, were wearing threadbare clothes, and were housed in a peasant's cottage after having lived in the richest palaces of Florence.

"Tell us the news of yourself. Of the years in Rome. What have you sculptured? I heard about the Bacchus."

Michelangelo reached into his shirt for a sheet of drawing paper, took charcoal from his belt and sketched the Pietà, explaining what he had tried to accomplish. It was good to be with Contessina again, to gaze into those dark eyes. Had they not loved each other, if only with the love of children? Once you have loved, should not that love last? Love was so rare, so difficult to come upon.

Contessina divined his thoughts; she always had. She turned to her son.

"Luigi, would you like to learn Michelangelo's alphabet?"

"Can I help carve the new statue, Michelangelo?"

"I will come and teach you, the way Bertoldo taught me in your grandfather's garden. Now, take this hammer in one hand, the chisel in the other. On the opposite side of the stone I will show you how to spell. With a hammer and chisel we can write sculptures as beautiful as Dante's poetry. Is it not so, Contessina?"

"It is so," she replied. "Each of us has his own alphabet with which to make poetry."

It was midnight by the time he had returned the Topolino horse and walked down the hill. His father was awake, waiting in the black leather chair. This was apparently his second night of sitting up, and he was thoroughly exasperated.

"So! It takes you two nights to come home to your father with the news. Where have you been all this time? Where is the contract? What price are they paying?"

"Six florins a month."

"How long will it take you to carve?"

"Two years."

Lodovico figured rapidly, then turned a ravaged face upward to his son.

"But that adds up to only a hundred and forty-four florins."

"The Board agrees to pay more, when I'm finished, if they think I deserve a larger compensation."

"Who shall that decision be left to?"

"Their conscience."

"Conscience! Don't you know that a Tuscan's conscience stops short of his belt?"

"The David will be so beautiful they will want to pay me more."

"Even the Piccolomini contract is better: you earn three hundred and thirty-two florins in the same two years of work, more than double!"

Michelangelo lowered his head in despair. Lodovico did not consult his son's expression. He said in a tone of finality:

"The Buonarroti are not rich enough to make a charitable contribution of one hundred and eighty-eight florins to the Wool Guild and the Duomo. Tell them that the David will have to be postponed until you have earned the five hundred ducats from Siena."

Michelangelo knew better than to get angry. He replied quietly, "Father, I am going to carve the David. Why do you always bring up these futile arguments?"

Several hours later his brother Buonarroto commented:

"Not so futile. Before the argument, how many florins a month were you planning to pay Father?"

"Three. Half for him, half for me."

"And now you have agreed to give him five."

"I had to to quiet him down."

"So, for a few hours' argument, he has earned himself two extra florins a month for twenty-four months."

Michelangelo sighed wearily.

"What can I do? He looks so old and white. Since the Board is paying my costs, what do I need the other two florins for?"

Buonarroto groaned. "You were better off as an apprentice in the Medici palace. Then, at least, I was able to put away some savings for you."

Michelangelo gazed out the window at the figure of the night guard strolling down the Via San Proculo.

"You're right about Father: I'm his quarry."

6

Granacci launched a celebration party built around the meeting of the Company of the Cauldron. To salute Michelangelo's good fortune, eleven members of the Company showed up, Botticelli limping painfully on crutches, and Rosselli, of the rival studio to Ghirlandaio, so ill that he had to be carried in on a litter. Rustici received him heartily, Sansovino pounded him on the back, the others offered congratulations: David Ghirlandaio, Bugiardini, Albertinelli, Filippino Lippi, *Il Cronaca*, Baccio d'Agnolo, Leonardo da Vinci. The twelfth member, Giuliano da Sangallo, was away.

Granacci had been provisioning Rustici's studio all afternoon with chains of sausages, cold beef and suckling pig, figures carved out of pastry, demijohns of Chianti. When Granacci approached Soggi with the news, he contributed an enormous basin of pickled pigs' feet.

The food and drink was all needed, for Granacci had invited the town: the entire Ghirlandaio studio, including Domenico's talented son, Ridolfo, now eighteen; all of the Medici garden apprentices; a dozen of the better-known sculptors and painters including Donato Benti, Benedetto da Rovezzano, Piero di Cosimo, Lorenzo di Credi, Franciabigio, the young Andrea del Sarto, Andrea della Robbia, the maker of glazed terra cottas, the leading Florentine craftsmen, goldsmiths, clockmakers, gem cutters, bronze casters; the mosaicist Monte di Giovanni di Miniato; the illuminator Attavanti; wood carvers; the architect Francesco Filarete who was chief herald of Florence.

Wise in the ways of the Republic, Granacci had also sent invitations to Gonfaloniere Soderini, the members of the Signoria, the Boards of the Wool Guild and the Duomo, to the Strozzi family to whom he had sold the Hercules. Most of them came, happy to join in the fun, for the huge assemblage now spilled out of Rustici's jammed, noisy studio into the square, where Granacci's hired band of acrobats and wrestlers were entertaining, and musicians and minstrels were chanting songs for the young men and girls dancing in the square. Everyone wrung Michelangelo's hand, pounded him on the back and insisted upon drinking a toast with him, friend, casual acquaintance and stranger alike.

Soderini shook Michelangelo's hand, said, "This is the first major commission agreed upon by all of the city Boards since the coming of Savonarola. Perhaps a new era will start for us, and we can wipe out our deep-lying sense of guilt."

"Which guilt are you referring to, Gonfaloniere?"

"The mass guilt, the individual guilt. We have suffered bad times since the death of *Il Magnifico;* we have destroyed much that made Florence the first city of the world. The bribing of Caesar Borgia was only the latest in nine years of indignities. But tonight we like ourselves. Later, perhaps, we will be proud of you, when the marble is finished. But now it is ourselves we are proud of. We believe that great commissions for frescoes, for mosaics, for bronzes and marbles will be forthcoming for all our artists. We are seeing a rebirth." He laid a hand on Michelangelo's shoulder. "You happen to be the midwife. Handle the baby well!"

The party lasted until dawn; but before that, two incidents occurred which would affect the pattern of his days.

The first filled him with joy. The ill and aged Rosselli gathered the ten members of the Company about him, announced:

"It is not meat and drink, if you will forgive a pun, for a member of this Company of the Cauldron to be carried to these orgies on a litter. Therefore, much as I dislike promoting anyone from the Ghirlandaio studio, I herewith resign from the Cornpany and nominate Michelangelo Buonarroti to succeed me."

He was accepted. He had been no part of any group since the Medici sculpture garden. He remembered again his lonely childhood, how difficult it had been for him to make friends, to be gay. He had been skinny, unsociable, unwanted. Now all these artists of Florence, even those who had long waited to be invited into the Company, were applauding his election.

The second incident was to cause him considerable anguish. It was begun, though unwittingly, by Leonardo da Vinci.

Michelangelo was already angry at Leonardo by the first time he had seen him crossing the Piazza della Signoria, accompanied by his inseparable and beloved apprentice-companion, Salai, a boy with features straight off a Greek statue, a mass of curly hair waving around his head, with a small round mouth and soft round chin, dressed by Leonardo in an expensive linen shirt, a cloak rich in silver brocade. Yet compared to Leonardo, Salai was dull in appearance; for Leonardo's was the most perfect face to appear in Florence since the golden beauty of Pico della Mirandola. He carried his big sculptural head thrown back aristocratically, the magnificently broad forehead topped by a haze of reddish hair, softly curled and worn down to his shoulders; a chin carved out of the heroic Carrara statuary marble he despised; a flawlessly designed broad nose, rounded, full-blooded lips, the face dominated by cool blue eyes of a piercing penetration and intelligence; and the fair complexion of a country girl.

Leonardo's figure, as Michelangelo watched him cross the square followed by his usual retinue of servants and hangers-on, matched the flawless face: tall, graceful, with the broad shoulders and narrow hips of a wrestler, with the agility and strength as well, dressed in regal splendor and a disdain for convention: a rose-colored cloak barely covering his shoulders, and falling short at the knees, wearing his shirt and *calze* tight to the point of bursting.

He had made Michelangelo feel ugly and malformed, conscious that his clothes were inexpensive, ill fitting and worn. Leonardo's coiffured golden hair and scent of perfume, the lace about his neck and wrists, the jewels, the ineffable exquisiteness of the man's presence made him feel tattered and dirty by comparison.

When he had spoken of this to Rustici, who was Leonardo's friend, Rustici had reproved him.

"Don't be fooled by an elegant exterior. Leonardo has a magnificent brain. His studies of geometry are extending the work of Euclid. He has been dissecting animals for years, and keeping meticulous notebooks of his anatomical drawings. In his pursuit of geology he has discovered fish-shell fossils on top of the mountains of the upper Arno, proving that they were once under water. He is also an engineer and inventor of unbelievable machines: a multiple-barrel gun, cranes for lifting heavy loads, suction pumps, wind and water gauges. Even now he is completing experiments for a machine that will fly through the air as the birds do. The dazzling performance of imitating a rich nobleman is his effort to persuade the world to forget that he is the illegitimate son of a Vinci innkeeper's daughter. Actually he is the only man in Florence who works as hard and long as you do: twenty hours a day. Look for the real Leonardo beneath that defensive elegance."

In the face of this brilliant recital, Michelangelo could not bring himself to mention his anger at the man's outspoken deprecation of sculpture. Leonardo's hearty welcoming of him into the Company of the Cauldron this evening had also assuaged his uneasiness. Then he heard Leonardo's high-pitched voice behind him, declaring:

"I refused to compete for the Duccio block because sculpture is a mechanical art."

"Surely you would not call Donatello a mechanic?" asked a deeper voice.

"In some ways, yes," answered Leonardo. "Sculpture is so much less intellectual than painting; it lacks so many of its natural aspects. I spent years at it, and I tell you from experience that painting is far more difficult, and reaches the greater perfection."

"Still, for a commission as important as that . . . ?"

"No, no, I would never carve marble. It causes a man to sweat and wearies his body all over. The marble carver comes out of a day's work as filthy as a plasterer or baker, his nostrils clogged with dust, his hair and face and legs covered with powder and chips, his clothes stinking. When I paint I work in my finest clothes. I emerge at the end of a day immaculately clean and refreshed. Friends come in to read poetry to me, and play music while I draw. I am a fastidious man. Sculpture is for laborers."

Michelangelo felt his spine stiffen. He glanced over his shoulder. Leonardo's back was to him. Again a rage rose in his bowels. He yearned to spin Leonardo around, smash him in his beautiful face with the sculptor's fist he held in such contempt. Then quickly he moved to the other end of the room, hurt not only for himself but for all marble carvers. One day he would make Leonardo eat those words.

The following morning he awoke late. The Arno was down to a trickle. He had to go miles upstream to find a deep pool. Here he bathed and swam, then walked back, stopping at Santo Spirito. He found Prior Bichiellini in the library. The prior heard his news without expression.

"And the Cardinal Piccolomini contract?"

"When the two Boards sign this commission, I will be free of the other."

"By what right? What you have begun, finish!"

"But the Giant is my great opportunity. I can create something glorious . . ."

"After you fulfill your obligation," interrupted Bichiellini. "This is a worse variety of opportunism than led you to sign a contract you detested." His voice became more friendly. "I understand that you do not want to give your energies to figures which are unsatisfying to you. But you knew that to begin with. You may also be surrendering your integrity for no gain. Cardinal Piccolomini may be our next Pope, and then the Signoria will order you back to the Siena pieces just as they obeyed Alexander VI and put Savonarola on the rack."

"Everyone has the next Pope!" said Michelangelo caustically. "Giuliano da Sangallo says it will be his Cardinal Rovere. Leo Baglioni says it will be his Cardinal Riario. Now you say it will be Cardinal Piccolomini . . ."

The prior rose, abruptly left Michelangelo's side, made his way to the open archway overlooking the piazza. Michelangelo hurried after him.

"Forgive me, Father, but I've got to carve my David now."

The prior made his way across the corner of the piazza, leaving Michelangelo standing flat-footed in the merciless glare of the August sun.

7

Beppe gave him a raucous welcome. "So you own the Duccio block for free!" He grinned, scratching his bald scalp.

"Beppe, like it or not, you've got me under your wing for two full years."

The foreman groaned. "As though I don't have troubles enough keeping the cathedral from falling down. But the Board of Works say give him everything he wants: marble, chisels, pretty girls . . ."

Michelangelo laughed aloud, bringing the artisans running. They welcomed him to the yard.

The Duomo workyard ran the full width of the block behind the Duomo Works buildings from the Via dei Servi on the north side to the Street of the Clock on the south, bound in by an eight-foot brick wall. The front half, where the Duccio column had lain, was the quarters for the artisans maintaining the cathedral; the rear half was used for storage of lumber, brick, paving stone. Michelangelo wanted to be close to the workmen so he could hear the sound of their tools and voices, yet not be involved. In the center of the rear yard there was an oak tree, and behind it, in the wall admitting to a nameless passage, an iron gate, locked, rusted. The gate was exactly two blocks from his house. He could work nights when he wished, and holidays when the main yard would be locked.

"Beppe, is it permitted to use this gate?"

"Nobody forbids. I locked it myself, ten, twelve years ago, when tools and material were missing."

"Would it be all right if I used it?"

"What's wrong with the front entrance?"

"Nothing. But if we could build my workshop around this gate, I could come and go without bothering anybody."

Beppe chewed toothlessly on this idea to make sure Michelangelo was not repudiating him or his crew. Then he said:

"I do it. Draw me plans."

He needed thirty feet along the back wall to be paved for his forge and tools, and for keeping his wood dry; the brick wall would have to be raised another nine feet so that no one could see the column or watch him working on it when he mounted his scaffold. On each side, for a distance of about twenty feet, he wanted low plank walls, but the work area would be open to the sky for the nine dry months of the year, and at the front as well. The Giant would be bathed in the full sunlight of the southern arc as the brilliant Tuscan sun made its daily transit across the city.

He decided to keep the workshop in the piazza; it would be a place to go to when he wanted to get away from the large marble. Argiento would sleep there, and work with him here during the day.

The Duccio block was so seriously gouged in the center of its seventeen-foot length that any attempt to move it in its present state could prove fatal; a jarring motion or lurching impact would split the column in two. He bought several of the largest pieces of paper he could find, pasted them over the face of the horizontal column and cut out a *sagoma,* a silhouette, taking care to measure the deep cut accurately. He then took the sheets to the workshop in the piazza and had Argiento nail them up on the wall. He moved his workbench around to face the paper silhouette, began fitting together a second series of sheets on which to draw a design of the David, indicating which parts of the existing block would be discarded, which parts used. Back at the yard, he chipped out marble from the top and bottom corners, balancing the weight so that the column would no longer be in danger of cracking.

Beppe's workmen established a smooth path to the new work area. They used a block and tackle to raise the two-thousand-pound column and get rollers under it. The column was moved slowly; as each rounded beam fell out the back end, a workman ran ahead to reinsert it under the front end. By nightfall the column, though still in a horizontal position, was inside Michelangelo's enclosure. He and his Giant-David block were alone.

Now, for the first time, he realized that the drawings that had satisfied the Boards were no longer of any use to him. He had outgrown these elementary stages of his thinking. All he knew for sure was that his was to be the David he had rediscovered, that he would use the opportunity to create all of the poetry, the beauty, the mystery and the inherent drama of the male body, the archetype and essence of correlated forms.

He burned his earlier drawings, settled down to the simplest beginning, probing within himself.

The Greeks had carved bodies from their white marble of such perfect proportion and strength that they could never be surpassed; but the figures had been without mind or spirit. His David would be the incarnation of everything Lorenzo de' Medici had been fighting for, that the Plato Academy had believed was the rightful heritage of man: not a sinful little creature living only for salvation in the next life, but a glorious creation capable of beauty, strength, courage, wisdom, faith in his own kind, with a brain and will and inner power to fashion a world filled with the fruit of man's creative intellect. His David would be Apollo, but considerably more; Hercules, but considerably more; Adam, but considerably more; the most fully realized man the world had yet seen, functioning in a rational and humane world.

How to draw these convictions on paper?

During the early weeks of autumn he achieved only fragmentary answers. The more he was frustrated the more complicated he made his drawings. The marble lay silent and inert.

"Maybe nobody can bring it to life?" suggested Beppe, when Michelangelo seemed depressed.

"Fine time to tell me! Like asking a girl does she want to be a mother after she's in the family way. Beppe, I'm going to have to model in marble instead of clay. Could you buy me a piece, about a third as large as this one?"

"I dunno. They said give workmen, material. But a five-foot block, that's money."

He delivered, as always, a fair enough block. Michelangelo plunged into the marble, trying to rough his way through his problem with hammer and chisel. What emerged was a strongly built, primitive young man, the face idealized and indeterminate. Granacci, seeing the marble, said with a puzzled expression:

"I don't understand. He stands with his foot resting on Goliath's head; but at the same time he's got a rock in one hand and is reaching over his shoulder for his slingshot. You're of two minds: the upper half is about to use the slingshot, the bottom half is already resting triumphantly on its victim."

"You flatter me. I have no mind at all."

"Then why not spend a couple of days with me at the villa?"

Michelangelo looked up sharply; it was the first time Granacci had acknowledged that he had a villa.

"You will be diverted; you'll forget your David for a couple of days."

"Agreed. I can't remember smiling for weeks."

"I have something at the villa that will bring a smile."

He did indeed: a girl by the name of Vermiglia, blond in the Florentine tradition, with her hair plucked back to give her a higher brow, her breasts propped up in a gown of green taffeta. She proved a charming mistress of the villa, presiding over their late candlelit supper on a porch overlooking the Arno as it wound its way to the sea. When she had gone inside, Granacci said:

"Vermiglia has a wide variety of cousins. Would you like her to choose one for you? I think she's lonely here. You could have a suite overlooking the city. It would be a pleasant way of life for us."

"Thank you, caro. I have a way of life. As for casual encounters, Beppe says, 'What you put into the ladies at night, you can't put into the marble in the morning.' "

He sat by his window, sleepless, watching the towers and domes of Florence under a scimitar of moon, rising to pace through the series of three small rooms, then going back to his vigil by the window. Why had he carved two Davids into his five-foot block, one already triumphant over Goliath, the other just preparing to hurl the stone? No piece of sculpture could stand at two different moments in the realm of time, any more than it could occupy two different areas in the realm of space. He would have to take a stand, decide which of the two warriors he was going to sculpture.

By dawn he had worked his way back, step by step. Sharp light flooded his mind. Goliath had to go. His head, black, dead, blood-spotted, ugly, had no place in the realm of art. It should never have been included in the first place. The full meaning of David was obscured by having that horrendous head forever chained to his ankles. What David had done became a mere physical act ending in the slaying of an opponent. Yet to him this was only a small part of the meaning of David, who could represent the daring of man in every phase of life: thinker, scholar, poet, artist, scientist, statesman, explorer: a giant of the mind, the intellect, the spirit as well as the body. Without the reminder of Goliath's head, he might stand as the symbol of man's courage and his victory over far more important enemies.

David had to stand alone. Even as he had stood on the plains of the Valley of the Terebinth.

This decision left him exalted . . . and exhausted. He climbed between Granacci's fine linen sheets, fell into a deep sleep.

He sat in his shed before the column, drawing David's head, face and eyes, asking himself:

"What is David feeling at this moment of conquest? Glory? Gratification? Would he feel himself to be the biggest and strongest man in the world? Would there be a touch of contempt for Goliath, of arrogance as he watched the fleeing Philistines, and then turned to accept the plaudits of the Israelites?"

All unworthy emotions, none of which he could bring himself to draw. What could he find in David triumphant, he asked himself, worthy of sculpturing? Tradition portrayed him after the fact. Yet David after the battle was certainly an anticlimax, his great moment already gone.

Which then was the important David? When did David become a giant? After killing Goliath? Or at the moment he decided that he must try? David as he was releasing, with brilliant and deadly accuracy, the shot from the sling? Or David before he entered the battle, when he decided that the Israelites must be freed from their vassalage to the Philistines? Was not the decision more important than the act itself, since character was more critical than action? For him, then, it was David's decision that made him a giant, not his killing of Goliath. He had been floundering because he had imprisoned himself and David at the wrong moment in time.

How could he have been so stupid, so blind? David pictured after Goliath could be no one but the biblical David, a special individual. He was not content to portray one man; he was seeking universal man, Everyman, all of whom, from the beginning of time, had faced a decision to strike for freedom.

This was the David he had been seeking, caught at the exultant height of resolution, still reflecting the emotions of fear, hesitation, repugnance, doubt; the man who wished to follow his own ways among the hills of Jerusalem, who cared little for the clash of arms and material reward. The man who killed Goliath would be committed all his life to warfare and its consequence, power. The reluctance would still be fading from his face, this giving up of the pastoral life in which he had been happy for a life of courts and kings, of jealousy and intrigue, of control and disposition of other men's destinies. This was the dichotomy in all men: the reflective life and the active. David would know that the man who gave himself to action would have sold himself to an inexorable master who would command him all the days and years of his life; he would know intuitively that nothing gained as reward for action, no kingdom or power or wealth, could compensate a man for the loss of his privacy.

To act was to join. David would not be sure he wanted to join. He had been a man alone. Once he tackled Goliath there would be no turning back, far more true if he vanquished Goliath than if he were vanquished. It was what he sensed that he would do to himself, as well as what the world would do to him, that made him doubtful and averse to changing the pattern of his days. His had been a hard choice, indeed.

This concept opened wide vistas to Michelangelo. He soared, he drew with authority and power; he modeled in clay, eighteen inches high, his fingers unable to keep pace with his thoughts and emotions; and with astonishing facility he knew where the David lay. The limitations of the block began to appear as assets, forcing his mind into a simplicity of design that might never have occurred to him had it been whole and perfect. The marble came alive now.

When he tired of drawing or modeling he would join his fellow members of the Cauldron for an evening of talk. Sansovino moved into the Duomo workyard to begin carving a marble St. John Baptizing Christ for over the east door of the Baptistery, setting up his workshed between Michelangelo and Beppe's stonemasons. When Rustici became bored with working alone on his drawings for a Boccaccio head and an Annunciation in marble, he would come to the yard and sketch with Michelangelo or Sansovino. Next Baccio joined them in the Duomo workyard, to design a crucifix which he hoped the church of San Lorenzo was going to commission. Bugiardini would bring in a hot dinner in pots from a nearby *osteria,* and the former apprentices would spend a companionable hour, Argiento serving the food on Michelangelo's plank worktable against the rear wall. Soggi, proud of his former associates, visited once in a while, wheeling in a cart of cooked sausages for the communal dinner.

Every now and then he would climb the hill to Fiesole to give Luigi a lesson on *pietra serena,* which the six-year-old seemed to enjoy. He was a bright-faced, handsome child, resembling his uncle Giuliano, with Contessina's alert mind.

"You are wonderful with Luigi, Michelangelo," remarked Contessina. "Giuliano loved you too. Sometime you must have your own son."

He shook his head.

"Like most artists, I am a mendicant. When I finish one commission I must go in search of the next, work in whatever city it takes me to: Rome, Naples, Milan, or even Portugal, as Sansovino did. That is no life for a family."

"It goes deeper than that," said Contessina in her small, sure voice. "Marble is your marriage. The Bacchus, Pietà, David are your children." They stood close, as close as they sometimes had in the Medici palace. "While you are in Florence, Luigi will be as your son. The Medici need friends. And so do artists."

Cardinal Piccolomini sent a representative to Florence who demanded to see the statues for the Bregno altar. Michelangelo showed the agent the completed St. Peter and St. Paul, and the roughed-out figures of the Popes, promising to finish them soon. The next day Baccio came into the shed, his once again mischievous face wreathed in smiles. He had received the commission for the crucifix. Since San Lorenzo had no work space for him, he asked Michelangelo if he might share the shop in the piazza.

"Instead of paying rent, I could finish the two Popes from your drawings," he exclaimed. "What do you say?"

He did the pieces credibly. With four figures and the St. Francis completed, Michelangelo felt he would have a respite from Cardinal Piccolomini. When Baccio began carving his crucifix, Michelangelo was glad he had taken him in; the work was honest and full of feeling.

Argiento swept out the shop each evening when he returned from the Duomo. He too was content in Florence, working in the Duomo workshed all day, at night having the company of the other young apprentices of the piazza who also slept in their shops, each providing food for a common cookpot.

Best of all, Giuliano da Sangallo returned from Savona where he had completed a palace for Cardinal Rovere at the family estate. Leaving Savona, Sangallo had been intercepted and kept a prisoner for six months by the Pisans and had had to be ransomed for three hundred ducats. Michelangelo visited with him at the family home in the Quarter of the Sun, near Santa Maria Novella. He still insisted that Cardinal Rovere would be the next Pope.

"Tell me about your design for the Giant," he demanded. "And what have you heard of interesting architectural jobs in Florence?"

"There are several of great urgency," said Michelangelo. "A revolving table strong enough to turn a two-thousand-pound column of marble, so I can control the light and sun. A fifteen-foot scaffold, one in which I can change the height and work all around the block."

Sangallo was amused. "You are my best client. Let's get pen and paper. What you need is a series of four towers, with open shelves that take planks from either direction, like this. . . . As for your turntable, that's an engineering task. . . ."

8

There were heavy rain clouds overhead. Beppe and his crew built a wooden roof that arched upward at a sharp angle from the back wall, leaving space for the seventeen-foot column, then tiled it securely to keep out the rain.

His marble was still lying flat on the ground. He made a wooden lid to fit its length, with lead-weighted strings hanging over the sides to show at what level in the block he would be seeking for the back of David's head, the arm raised to take the slingshot, the hips swiveled away from the gouge, the rock inside the huge right hand, the tree trunk supporting the right calf. He marked these depths with charcoal and then, helped by Beppe's augmented crew of fifteen, roped the column, attached a block and tackle, slowly raised it to stand upright on Sangallo's turntable. He and Argiento then built the scaffold towers that had open shelves to take wide planks at any height he needed to work.

Now the column cried out to him, giving itself wholly. His tools tore into its flesh with a terrifying penetration, searching for elbows and thighs and chest and groin and kneecap. The white crystals that had lain dormant for half a century yielded lovingly to every touch, from the subtlest nuance to the driving "Go!" in which his hammer and chisel swept upward from the ankle through the knee and thigh without stopping, the routine count of seven for work, followed by four of rest, abandoned as he felt within himself the strength of a hundred men.

This was his most glorious experience in working marble; never had he had such an expanse of figure, such a simplicity of design; never before had he been so possessed by a sense of precision, force, penetration or depth of passion. He could think of nothing else now, could not bring himself to stop for food or change of clothes. He fed his marble hunger twenty hours a day, the acrid dust coagulating in his nostrils, his hair covered as white as old Ficino's, the vibrations of the marble consistency running from the chisels and hammer up his shoulders, then down his chest into his loins and thighs and knees, throbbing and vibrating through his body and brain long after he had thrown himself across his bed in exultant exhaustion. When his right hand tired of driving the hammer he shifted it to the left, the chisel in his right moving with the same precision and probing sensitivity. He carved at night by candlelight, in absolute quiet, for Argiento retired at sundown to the other shop. To Sangallo, who sometimes walked over after supper to check the turntable and scaffold, he commented:

"I'd like to carve for a year of days and nights, with no break at all."

"It's midnight, and freezing in this shed. Aren't you cold?"

Michelangelo flashed his friend a mischievous grin, the amber eyes shining as a cat's do at night.

"Cold? I'm burning with fever. Look how the tension of the torso is beginning to emerge. Another few days and life will break through."

He had met the challenge of the deeply gouged area by tilting the figure twenty degrees inside the column, designing it diagonally, on the bias, down the thickness of the marble, so that David's left side could be fitted into the remaining marble. Now it was as an engineer that he buried in his design a strong vertical structure beginning at the right foot, continuing up through the right leg supported by the short tree trunk, through the thigh and torso and the width of the giant neck, face and head. With this shaft of solid marble his David would stand erect; there could never be an inner collapse.

The key to the beauty and balance of the composition was David's right hand enclosing the stone. This was the form from which the rest of David's anatomy and feeling grew; as the key to the Bacchus had been the arm raised high to hold the wine cup, the Virgin's face the key to the Pietà. This hand with its bulging veins created a width and a bulk to compensate for the leanness with which he had had to carve the straight left hip opposite, even as the right arm and elbow would be the most delicate form in the composition.

As he became increasingly absorbed, Granacci could no longer persuade him to come to the villa for supper; he went rarely to the meetings at Rustici's, and then only if the night were too wet and raw to continue work. He could hardly concentrate on what was being said, let alone contribute anything to his friends. Leonardo da Vinci was the only one who complained, claiming that Michelangelo had no right to come to them in his filthy clothes and dust-matted hair. From the pained expression on Leonardo's face, the slight sniffing of the patrician nostrils, he saw that Leonardo thought he smelled bad. He imagined that he probably did, for he did not take his clothes off for a week at a time, even to sleep; but he was too involved to care. Easier to stop going to the Company of the Cauldron.

Christmas came, he accompanied his family to high mass at Santa Croce. The New Year he ignored, not even going to the celebration at Rustici's to help the Company usher in 1502. He stormed through the dark days of January, Argiento feeding coal to four braziers so that he would be warm enough to work, turning the table to catch the most light, moving the plank-platform up and down the David, forward and back as he worked the four sides simultaneously, keeping a heavy webbing between the legs and between the arms and the bulk of the body. The neck was so tremendous he could work it without fear of the head breaking off. He left considerable marble about the heroic head so that later he could carve a shock of short wavy hair.

Soderini came into the yard to observe progress. He knew that Michelangelo would have no peace at home until a price was set on the finished David. Toward the middle of February, after Michelangelo had been working for five months, he asked:

"Do you feel you have moved far enough along now for the Boards to see the work? I can have them meet here, and arrange a final contract . . ."

Michelangelo looked up at the David. His study of anatomy had strongly influenced his carving; in this early stage his chisel had roughed out the muscle movements of the calves, the thighs, the chest, pulling the inner action to the surface of the skin. He pointed out to Soderini how a muscle structure consists of fibers that run in a parallel direction; all action that took place in the David ran along these parallel fibrous lines. Then, reluctantly, he turned back to Soderini's question.

"No artist likes to have his work seen in this crude state."

"The Boards might pay considerably more if you could wait until it is finished. . . ."

"I can't," sighed Michelangelo. "No extra amount of money could compensate me for two more years of my father's misery."

"Two more years? Even with the figure emerging as well as it is?"

"This is the work that goes fastest."

"I'll bring the members as soon as we meet on a sunny day."

The rains vanished. The sun came out, clear and warm, to dry the stones of the city. Michelangelo and Argiento took the tiles off the roof and stacked them against the next winter, then removed the planks and let the full light bathe the shed. The David pulsated with life in every fiber of its body, beautiful bluish-gray veinings running up the legs like human veins, the considerable weight already firmly carried on the right leg.

Word arrived from Soderini that he would bring the members of the Boards at noon the following day. Michelangelo exclaimed, "Argiento, start cleaning! This must be two months of marble chips I'm walking on."

"Don't blame me," cried Argiento, "you won't keep out of here long enough to let me sweep. I think you like to wade through them, ankle deep."

"You're right, I do. But there'll be enough distraction for the Board members."

How much should he tell the men who were coming to pass judgment? If this concept of the David had taken him months of painful intellectual search, he could not expect to justify his departures from Florentine tradition in one short hour. Might not the men think of what his tongue was saying instead of what his hand had carved?

Argiento had everything scrubbed and orderly in the workshed. Soderini, with sixteen men, arrived just as Giotto's Campanile bells began to chime. Michelangelo greeted them warmly, remembering the names of Michelozzo, chancellor of the Wool Art Guild, Consuls Pandolfini and Giovanni di Pagno degli Albizi, Paolo de' Carnesecchi of the Board of Works, the notary of the Board, Bambelli, a number of others. The older men were still guarding against the cold by wearing full dark cloaks fastened at the neck and reaching their square-toed, thonged shoes, but the younger and more venturesome were saluting spring in particolored stockings patterned with the family blazon, and shirts with slashed sleeves.

They crowded around the half-born David, gazing up ten feet in the air with awe. Chancellor Michelozzo asked if Michelangelo would demonstrate to them how he worked the marble. He picked up his hammer and chisel, showed them how the back of his chisel sank into the hammer just as it sank into the marble, creating no explosion, but rather a gentle insinuative force. He indicated that the abrupt termination of each chisel passage caused a slight chipping as the tool was lifted, therefore the longer the "Go!" the fewer chippings.

He had them circle the David, pointed out its vertical structural strength, how the arms would be released from the protective webbing which ran at an angle into the torso, the tree trunk which would be the only object to support the giant nude. The figure was still tilted twenty per cent in the upright block, but he demonstrated how, as he discarded the negative marble now surrounding it, the David would stand head on.

The next afternoon Soderini came into the Duomo yard with an official-looking document in his hand, clapped Michelangelo on the back.

"The Boards were pleased. Shall I read? 'The Honorable Lord Consuls of the Wool Art Guild decided that the Board of Works of the Duomo can give the sculptor Michelangelo Buonarroti four hundred large golden florins in payment of the Giant called David existing in the Opera and that Michelangelo shall complete the work to perfection within two years from today.' "

"Now I can forget about money until I have finished. That is paradise for an artist."

He waited until Lodovico brought up the subject the next time. "The reward has been fixed, Father: four hundred large gold florins."

Lodovico's eyes sparkled, lighting his hollow cheeks.

"Four hundred florins! Excellent! Plus six florins a month for as long as you work . . . ."

"No."

"Surely they're adding the florins you've earned each month? They're not so niggardly as to take those back?"

"I continue to receive six florins a month for two more years. . . . ."

"Ah, good." Lodovico picked up his pen. "Let's see, twenty-four times six equals one hundred and forty-four, added to four hundred, equals five hundred and forty-four florins, a much better price."

Bleakly, Michelangelo replied, "No. Just four hundred florins. In toto. All the florins paid by the month are in advance. They will be deducted at the end."

The pleasure went out of Lodovico's expression as he saw himself losing one hundred and forty-four florins.

"It's not right," he muttered, "first they give you money, then they take it away."

And Michelangelo knew how it would be: Lodovico would go around with a wounded expression, as though someone had taken advantage of him. He had not earned his peace, after all. Perhaps there was no such thing as peace.

9

To mark the frontal projections, David's left foot, left knee, right wrist, the left elbow and hand at the shoulder, he affixed nailheads in the marble. With these fixed points established he was able to carve the upsurging line from the knee through the thigh and chest, delineating David's hard physical stamina; the flesh of the belly in which David was feeling quiverings of anxiety; the left hand holding the slingshot, the great right hand standing cocked, rock at the ready. To protect himself he had left half again as much marble at the rear as he would ultimately need, keeping in mind the fact that there were forty views of a statue as one walked around it.

He had designed David as an independent man, standing clear of all space around him. The statue must never be fitted into a niche, stood against a wall, used to decorate a façade or soften the harsh corner of a building. David must always be free. The world was a battlefield, man forever under strain, precarious on his perch. David was a fighter; not a brutal, senseless ravager, but capable of achieving freedom.

Now the figure became aggressive, began to push out of its mass, striving to define itself in space. His own pace matched the drive of the material, so that Sangallo and Sansovino, visiting with him of a Sunday afternoon, were staggered by his passion.

"I've never seen anything like it," cried Sangallo. "He's knocked off more chips from this hard marble in the last quarter of an hour than any three of his stonecutter friends in the quarry could cut in four."

"It's not the quantity that frightens me," added Sansovino, "it's the impetuosity. I've been watching fragments get hurled four feet in the air, until I thought the whole marble would fly to pieces."

"Michelangelo," cried Sangallo. "You've been shaving the line so closely that if you had overpassed it by a hairsbreadth, you risked losing all!"

Michelangelo stopped work, turned and faced his friends.

"Once marble is out of its quarry, it is no longer a mountain, it is a river. It can flow, change its course. That's what I'm doing, helping this marble river change its bed."

When the others had returned to their homes, Michelangelo sat at the David's feet and gazed up at him. He thought, "It takes as long for a marble column to bear, as it does a fruit tree." Yet each separate form within the sculpture was beginning to mirror the time and love he had lavished on it. Nor was he frightened by Sansovino's warning, for he identified himself with the center of gravity of the block, fitting himself into the core, feeling the balancing weight of the arms, legs, torso, head, as though they were his own. When he sliced off marble he did so with the precise knowledge of how much flesh he could safely spare.

The one thorn in this flesh, his own and the David's, was Leonardo da Vinci's belittling of the sculptor's art. To Michelangelo it appeared a serious threat. Leonardo's influence in Florence was spreading; if it should convince enough people that marble carving was a second-rate craft, when his David was completed it would be received with indifference. Growing within him was a need to counterattack.

The following Sunday when the Company of the Cauldron was meeting at Rustici's, and Leonardo made light of stone carving, Michelangelo said:

"True, sculpture shares nothing with painting. It exists on its own premises. But primitive man carved in stone for thousands of years before he began to paint on cave walls. Sculpture is the first and original art."

"By that very claim it is condemned," answered Leonardo in his high-pitched voice. "It satisfied only until the fine art of painting was developed. It is now becoming extinct."

Infuriated, Michelangelo struck back with a personal attack.

"Isn't it true, Leonardo," he demanded, "that your equestrian statue in Milan is so colossal that it can never be cast? And hence will never come into existence as bronze sculpture? And that your huge clay model is disintegrating so fast that it's becoming the joke of Milan? No wonder you talk against sculpture, you're not capable of bringing a piece to completion!"

There was an uncomfortable silence in the room.

A few days later Florence learned that, despite its payments to Caesar Borgia, he was marching on Urbino and helping to incite a rebellion in Arezzo against Florentine rule. Leonardo da Vinci joined Caesar Borgia's army as an engineer, to work alongside Torrigiani and Piero de' Medici. Michelangelo was outraged.

"He's a traitor," he cried angrily to Rustici, who was taking care of Leonardo's possessions while he was gone. "Caesar Borgia offers him a big salary, and so he will help conquer Florence. After we gave him hospitality, commissions to paint important pictures . . ."

"It really isn't that bad," said Rustici placatingly. "Leonardo is at loose ends, he can't seem to finish his painting of Monna Lisa del Giocondo. He's more interested in his new war machines than in art. He saw in Caesar Borgia's offer a chance to test out a lot of his inventions. He doesn't understand politics, you know."

"Tell that to the Florentines," replied Michelangelo acidly, "if his new machines batter down the walls."

"You're justified in feeling as you do, Michelangelo, but try to remember that he is amoral. He is not interested in right and wrong as it applies to people; only in the true and false in science and knowledge."

"I suppose I ought to be glad to be rid of him. He fled once before, for eighteen years. I hope we can count on as long this time."

Rustici shook his head wistfully.

"You two stand like the Apennines above the rest of us, yet you hate each other. It doesn't make sense. Or does it?"

The cycle of the seasons brought gloriously hot weather. Occasional showers did nothing to the David but wash the marble dust off him. Michelangelo worked stripped to his drawers and sandals, letting the sun beat down on his body and pour its strength into him. He scampered up and down the ladder as lightly as a cat, working the stout neck, heroic head and mass of curls from the top of the scaffold, carving the spine with great care to indicate that it carried and directed the whole body and was the mainspring of all movement. There could be no part of the David that was not palpable, and perfect. He had never understood why the erogenous zone had been represented as unbeautiful. If God made man as the Bible said he had made Adam, would he have made the area of procreation something to hide, something vile? Perhaps man had perverted the uses thereof, as he had managed to pervert so much else on earth; but what did that have to do with his statue? That which had been despised, he would make godlike.

He kept no track of time. He carved all day. Late of a stifling evening he might sit on the cool marble steps of the Duomo, where the young artists of Florence still gathered, to listen to improvised songs on guitars, exchange news of coming commissions throughout Tuscany, and listen to Jacopo discuss which of the passing girls were mattressable . . . even as he had fourteen years before. In June, Piero Soderini was elected to another two months as Gonfaloniere. People were beginning to ask why, since he was the best man in Tuscany for the job, he could not be allowed to govern longer.

When Michelangelo learned that Contessina was going to have another baby, he went to Soderini's office overlooking the Piazza della Signoria, to plead her cause.

"Why can she not return to her home for the birth of her child? She has committed no crime against the Republic. She was *Il Magnifico's* daughter before she was Ridolfi's wife. Her life is being endangered by this isolation in a cottage where there are no facilities . . ."

"The country people have managed to have their babies in those houses for a thousand years."

"Contessina is not country people. She's frail. She wasn't raised this way. Couldn't you plead to the Council of Seventy for justice?"

"It is impossible." Soderini's voice was flat, expressionless. "The kindest thing you can do is not bring up the Ridolfi name."

It was in the middle of Soderini's two-month term, with Arezzo and Pisa again in revolt, Piero de' Medici welcomed in Arezzo and promised help in conquering Florence, Caesar Borgia kept from attacking only through fear of French retaliation, and the city's gates kept locked during the day, with "all who lived along the river forbidden to lower ladders, to prevent anyone entering the town," that Michelangelo received a message to have supper with the Gonfaloniere at the Palazzo della Signoria. There was good work light until seven, after which he returned home to put on a linen shirt.

Soderini was sitting before a low table, his long yellow-white hair still wet from washing. They exchanged news on the state of the David, Soderini told that the Council of Seventy was about to change the constitution. The next man elected Gonfaloniere would have a lifetime position. Then he leaned across the table in a relaxed, confiding manner.

"Michelangelo, you have heard of Pierre de Rohan, the Maréchal de Gié? He was here in the 1494 invasion with Charles VIII, as one of his closest advisers. You may also recall that in the Medici courtyard Donatello's bronze David had the place of honor."

"The day the palace was sacked I was knocked into it so hard I had a lump on the back of my head."

"Then you know it well. Now, our ambassador to the French court has written that the Maréchal fell in love with the David while staying at the Medici palace, and would like to have one. For years we have been buying France's protection with money. Isn't it gratifying that for once we can pay for it with a work of art?"

Michelangelo looked at this man who had become such a good friend to him. It would be impossible to deny him. Instead he asked, "I am not to copy the Donatello?"

"Let's say that it would be safe to create minor variations, but not enough to disappoint the Maréchal's memory."

Michelangelo put a slice of cheese on a quartered pear.

"I've never had a chance to do anything for Florence. It gives me a good feeling. If only I had not been an idiot, and refused to learn casting from Bertoldo."

"We have good casters in Florence: Bonaccorso Ghiberti, the cannon maker, and Lodovico Lotti, the bell caster."

The sensation of being a patriot faded when he again stood in front of Donatello's David in the courtyard of the Signoria. He had come so far from this conception in his own figure! If he could not bring himself to copy it, and at the same time could not change it . . . ?

He returned to the courtyard in the morning, carrying a box to sit on, and sheets of old drawing paper. His David emerged several years older than Donatello's, more male and muscular, drawn with the inner tensions that can be transplanted to marble, few of which were present in the smooth-surfaced bronze youth before him. He set up an armature on the back bench in the workshed, used his occasional rest hours to transpose his drawings into a rough clay structure, slowly building up a nude with a turban binding up the hair. He was amused to think that, in the interests of Florence, he had to model a head of Goliath, on which David rested his foot in triumph. The Maréchal would never be happy without that head.

The perfect weather lasted through November first, when Soderini was installed as Gonfaloniere for life in a colorful pageant on the Signoria steps, with all of Florence in the piazza, and Michelangelo up front, feeling proud and secure. Then freezing winter clamped down. Michelangelo and Argiento put up the roof, reset the tiles. The four braziers could not cut the intense cold. He wore his cap with the earmuffs. Beppe hung a canvas over the side opening, but there was little light from the overcast skies and the canvas cut out that little. Now he suffered from darkness as well as cold. He worked by candlelight and lamp. Nor was spring much help; heavy rains began in early March and lasted for months.

Toward the end of April he received an invitation to dinner in the new apartment of the Signoria, presided over by Monna Argentina Soderini, the first woman ever permitted to live in the palace. The suite had been decorated by Giuliano da Sangallo and young Baccio d'Agnolo, the living, dining and bed rooms converted from first- and second-floor offices formerly used by the city notary and chancellor. The dining room was frescoed, the ceiling done in gilt, the cupboards and buffet of inlaid woods. The dinner table was laid before a fire, warm and cheerful. Michelangelo took off his green cloak, pleased with his appearance in his smocked woolen shirt. Soderini showed off his wife's flower pots in the windows.

"I know some people are complaining about the expense of the window boxes," he said shyly; "but actually I think it's their way of saying that women shouldn't live in the Palazzo della Signoria."

After dinner Soderini asked Michelangelo to accompany him to the Duomo.

"For years Florence has been talking of having the Twelve Apostles in marble for the cathedral. Larger than life size. Of perfect Seravezza marble. That would fill the cavernous space, would it not?"

"With the light of a thousand candles."

Soderini stopped at the back of the central altar, facing the Donatello and Della Robbia marble choirs.

"I've been speaking to the members of the Boards. They think it a magnificent idea."

Numbly, Michelangelo murmured, "It's a lifetime of work."

"So were Ghiberti's doors."

"That's what Bertoldo wanted for me: a body of work."

Soderini linked his arm through Michelangelo's, walked him down the long nave toward the open door.

"It would make you the official sculptor of Florence. The contract I have been discussing with the Boards includes a house we will build for you, and a studio of your own design."

"A home of my own! And a studio."

"I thought that would please you. You could do one Apostle a year. As each was delivered, you would own another twelfth of your house and studio."

Michelangelo stopped in the doorway. He turned about to look at the enormous and empty cathedral. Assuredly it could use the Twelve Apostles.

"Tomorrow is the monthly meeting of the joint Boards. They have asked you to appear."

Michelangelo's smile was sickly. He made his way, cold and shivering, through the streets toward the hills, glad that he had worn a warm cloak. When he began to climb to Settignano he perspired as heavily as though he had a fever. He could not concentrate his thoughts on any one aspect of Soderini's proposed commission. Then, as he reached the Settignano farmhouse, pride took precedence: he was only twenty-eight, and he was going to have a home of his own, and a sculpture studio adequate to carve heroic pieces. He stood on the terrace in the midst of the five Topolino men, began slicing *pietra serena* blocks into long slabs.

"Better tell us," said the father, "before you burst."

"I am now a man of substance."

"What kind of substance?" asked Bruno.

"I shall have a house."

He told them about the Twelve Apostles. The father brought out a bottle of old wine, reserved for marriages and births of sons. They drank a glass to his good fortune.

His anxieties rushed upward to drown out the pride. He descended the hill, jumped stones to cross the creek, climbed the opposite side to stand for a moment gazing at the house and rooms in which he remembered his mother. How proud she would be, how happy for him.

Then why was he not happy for himself? Was it because he did not want to carve the Twelve Apostles? Because he hesitated to lock himself into a commission that would consume the next twelve years of his life? Once again be obliged to handle fully clothed and draped figures? He did not know whether he could endure it, after the glorious freedom of the David. Even Donatello had done only one or two apostles in marble. How was he going to create something fresh and different for each of the twelve?

His feet carried him to Giuliano da Sangallo, where he found his friend at his drafting table. Sangallo already knew about the proposal; Soderini had asked him and *Il Cronaca* to appear at the meeting the following afternoon to witness the signing of the contract. *Il Cronaca* was to design the house.

"Sangallo, this project isn't anything I conceived for myself. Should a sculptor undertake a twelve-year task unless he's passionately eager to do it?"

Sangallo replied noncommittally, "It's a lot of years."

"As long as a sculptor lives from one commission to another he remains someone who is hired."

"Painting and sculpture have always been commissioned. Is there an alternative?"

"To create art works independently, sell them to whoever will buy."

"Unheard of."

"But not impossible?"

". . . perhaps not. But can you turn down the Gonfaloniere and the Boards? They are offering you the biggest commission since Ghiberti's doors. The members would be offended. That would put you in a difficult position."

Michelangelo sat with his head in his hands, glum.

"I know. I can't take it, and I can't turn it down."

Sangallo brought a hand down sharply on Michelangelo's shoulder.

"Take the contract, build your house and studio, carve as many Apostles as you can do well. When you're through, you're through; you'll pay off the rest of the house in cash."

"Another Piccolomini contract," said Michelangelo mournfully.

He signed the contract. The news spread through the city with the speed of a fresh scandal. Strangers bowed to him respectfully in the Via de' Gori. He nodded back, wondering what they would think if they could know how miserable he was. He reached home to find the Buonarroti in the family room, excitedly planning their new house. Uncle Francesco and Aunt Cassandra decided they wanted a third floor to themselves.

"Get it built quickly," said his father. "The faster we move in, the sooner we stop paying rent here."

Michelangelo turned away to gaze sightlessly into the street. He spoke without emotion.

"This is to be my home. And my workshop. It is not to be the family residence."

There was a stunned silence. Then his father, uncle and aunt all began talking at once, so that he could not disentangle the voices.

"How can you say such a thing? Your home is our home. We can save rent. Who will cook and clean . . ."

He knew better than to say, "I am now twenty-eight, and it is time I had my own house. I have earned it." Instead he replied, "The land is provided, but I am allowed only six hundred florins for building purposes. I need a huge studio to handle these marbles, with a thirty-foot roof, and a large outdoor paved court. There will be enough left for a small house, one bedroom, two at the most . . ."

The storm lasted the rest of the day, until everyone was worn out. Michelangelo was adamant; the least he could get out of the contract was private work quarters, a secluded island to live in. But he had to agree to pay the rent for this apartment out of his monthly advances.

When he had a clay model of the Maréchal's David he sent Argiento to Lodovico Lotti, the bell caster, and Bonaccorso Ghiberti, the cannon caster. The two artisans came from their foundries in clothes streaked with grime. The Gonfaloniere had requested them to help Michelangelo get the bronze ready. When they saw Michelangelo's model they looked at each other, Lotti wiping black soot from the back of his hand across his eyes.

"It won't cast," he declared.

"Why not?"

"Because you got to make a plaster mold," said Ghiberti.

"I know nothing of this confounded art."

"We can only cast what another man makes," replied Lotti.

Michelangelo sought help from Rustici, Sansovino, Bugiardini, to see if they had listened more closely to Bertoldo about bronze. From them he learned that he would have to make his clay statue full size and exact, then build over it with plaster, piece by piece, marking on every piece a numerical key for identification, oil the pieces where the edges had to be connected, set the plaster cast aside . . .

"*Basta!*" groaned Michelangelo. "No wonder I never learned."

The casters brought him back his David. He gazed dully at the ugly red bronze figure, streaked, bumpy, ridged, with protuberances of metal where it was not wanted. He was going to need punches, files, chasing tools to make it look human; then burnishers, metal chisels, polishers, pumice and oil to make it presentable. Even then, would the Maréchal's memory so fail him as to imagine this David resembled Donatello's? He doubted it.

10

The first fruit of his contract for the Twelve Apostles was a visit from a neighbor he had known in the Piazza Santa Croce, Agnolo Doni, his own age, whose father had made a beginning competence in the wool trade and bought a neglected palace near the Albertini palace in the Santa Croce quarter. Agnolo Doni had taken over his father's business and palace, earned the reputation of being the sharpest bargainer in Tuscany, made a fortune and remodeled the palace. He had come so high in the financial and social worlds of Florence that he was now engaged to Maddalena Strozzi.

Beppe brought Doni into the workshed with an apologetic expression. Michelangelo was high on the scaffold carving on the sling over David's left shoulder. He laid down his tools, climbed down the ladder. Doni was wearing an expensive doublet, from which a shirt puffed out at the shoulders, fastened at the breast and waist with golden clasps.

"I'll come straight to the point, Buonarroti," he said as Michelangelo reached the ground. "I want you to do a Holy Family as a wedding present for my bride-to-be, Maddalena Strozzi."

Michelangelo flushed with pleasure; Maddalena had been brought up with his Hercules.

"The Strozzi have good taste in the arts," he murmured. "A Holy Family in white marble . . ."

Doni's small mouth, framed between the vertical creases on either side, fell visibly.

"No, no, it is I who have the good taste! I thought of commissioning you, not Maddalena. And who said anything about marble? That would cost a lot of money. All I want is a painting, to be used as an inset in a round table."

Michelangelo picked up his hammer and chisel.

"Why should you come to me for a painting? I haven't put color on a brush for fifteen years."

"Pure loyalty. We are of the same quarter. Remember how we used to play football in the Piazza Santa Croce?"

Michelangelo smiled ironically. Doni pressed.

"What do you say? A Holy Family. Thirty florins. Ten for each figure. That's a generous sum, isn't it? Shall we call it a bargain?"

"I don't know how much the painters will charge you, Doni, but you can have your choice of half a dozen of the best in Italy: Granacci, Filippino Lippi. What about Ghirlandaio's son, Ridolfo? He's going to be a fine craftsman, and he'll do it cheap."

"Look, Buonarroti. I want you to paint a Holy Family. I don't want one by Lippi or young Ghirlandaio. I already have Gonfaloniere Soderini's permission."

"But, Doni, it makes no sense. You don't take your wool to a scissors maker to be woven . . ."

"It is well known that to carve marble is to be only a fraction of an artist."

"Enough," growled Michelangelo, furious at this repetition of Leonardo's denunciation. "I'll paint your Holy Family. For one hundred gold florins."

"One hundred!" screamed Doni, so that he could be heard the length of the Duomo workyard. "How can you cheat one of your oldest friends? The playmate of your youth. It's like stealing the purse off your brother's belt."

They compromised on seventy florins; but not until Michelangelo's eardrums felt broken. By the crafty smile in Doni's shrewd eyes, Michelangelo perceived that Doni had outwitted, or at least outshouted, him and would have paid the hundred florins. From the door Doni said not unkindly, "You were the worst *calcio* player in the neighborhood. That puzzles me: how could you be so bad at football and so good at sculpture? But you certainly are the artist of the moment."

"That's why you want me, because I'm fashionable?"

"What better reason could there be? When will I see the sketches?"

"The sketches are my business. The finished product is yours."

"You agreed to let Cardinal Piccolomini see your drawings."

"Get yourself appointed a cardinal."

When Doni had left, Michelangelo realized that he had been an idiot to let the man goad him into taking the commission. What did he know about painting? Or care? He could design a Holy Family, the drawing would be fun. But paint and color! Young Ridolfo could handle these better than he.

Yet his interest was piqued. He had dozens of drawings for a Madonna and Child that he had made for the merchants from Bruges, should the Mouscrons sign Jacopo Galli's contract. They were intensely spiritual, removed from the mundane world. For a Holy Family the concept should be the opposite in spirit: earthy, a family of simple people.

As always during the hot summer days when he permitted himself a rest, he tramped the roads of Tuscany, sketching the farmers in the fields, eating before their door in the cool of evening, the young country mothers nursing their young before putting them to sleep in cribs under the outdoor arches. Over the days he drew for the Doni portrait a strong-limbed, healthy young girl from one household, a plump, red-cheeked curly-haired child from another, a bald-headed bearded grand-father from a third, put them together in an affectionate grouping on the grass. The flesh tones of the arms, faces, feet, the naked *bambino* he had no trouble with, but the robes of the mother and Joseph, the blanket of the child, eluded him.

Granacci dropped by, amused at Michelangelo's bafflement.

"Would you like me to fill in the colors? You're making such an awful mess."

"Why didn't Doni honor you with the commission in the first place? You are of the Santa Croce quarter. You played football with him too!"

In the end he did a series of monotones, as though they were colored marble. The mother's dress he painted pale rose and blue, the child's blanket light to burnt orange, Joseph showing only a shoulder and arm of faded blue. In the foreground he painted a few simple bunches of flowers growing in the grass. The background was bare, except for the impish face of John looking upward. To amuse himself he painted a sea on one side of the family, mountains on the other; before the sea and the mountains he drew in five nude youths, sitting on a wall, glorious bronze figures with the sun on them, creating the effect of a Greek frieze.

Doni's face went the color of his red tunic when he answered Michelangelo's summons to see the finished picture.

"Show me one thing that is holy about this picture of peasants! One sentiment that is religious! You're mocking me!"

"Would I be such a fool as to throw away my work on a mockery? These are fine people, tender in their love of the child."

"I want a Holy Family in a palace."

"Holiness has nothing to do with surroundings. It's an inner spiritual quality."

"I cannot give this picnic on the grass to my delicate bride. I would lose cast with the Strozzi family. You have put me in the worst imaginable light."

"Might I remind you that you did not reserve the right of rejection?"

Doni's eyes narrowed to slits, then flew open at the same time as his mouth as he cried in horror:

"What are those five naked boys doing in my Holy Family?"

"Why, they've just come out from a swim in the sea," replied Michelangelo calmly, "and are drying themselves in the sun."

"You've been touched by the moon," screamed Doni. "Whoever heard of five naked youths forming a background for a Christian picture?"

"Think of them as figures on a frieze. This gives you both a Christian painting and a Greek sculpture, at no extra charge. Remember your original offer was thirty florins, ten for each figure. If I wanted to be greedy I could charge you fifty florins extra for the five youths. But I won't, because we are of the same quarter."

"I'll take the picture to Leonardo da Vinci," growled Doni, "and have those five obscene idlers painted out!"

Until now Michelangelo had been amused. Now he cried, "I'll sue you for defacing a work of art!"

"I'm paying for it, and I can deface it all I want."

"Remember Savonarola! I'll haul you before the Council."

Doni groaned, stormed out. The next day his servant arrived with a pouch of thirty-five florins, half the price agreed upon, and a release for Michelangelo to sign. Michelangelo sent Argiento back with the pouch. On a scrap of paper he scrawled:

> The Holy Family will now cost you one hundred and forty florins.

Florence enjoyed the contest, with bets on who would win. Michelangelo found himself on the short end of the odds because no one had ever bested Doni in a deal. However the time was growing short to Doni's wedding day, and he had bragged all over town that he was having Florence's official artist paint a wedding gift for his bride. Doni arrived at the Duomo workshed with a leather purse containing seventy florins, crying:

"Here's your money, give me my painting."

"Doni, that wouldn't be fair. You hate the picture, and I release you from your agreement."

"Don't try to outwit me. I'll go to Gonfaloniere Soderini and have him force you to fulfill your contract."

"I didn't know you loved the painting that much. Now I believe that you're a great art collector. Just hand over the hundred and forty florins . . ."

"You're a swindler! You agreed to paint the picture for seventy . . ."

". . . an agreement you threw open to renegotiation by offering me thirty-five florins. My price is now one hundred and forty."

"Never," screamed Doni, "for that mediocre peasant picture. I'll see youu hanged from the Bargello first."

Michelangelo decided he had had his fun, was about to send the painting to Doni when a barefooted *contadino* boy brought him a note which read:

> I hear that Maddalena wants your painting. She has said no wedding present will please her more.   C.

He had immediately recognized the handwriting. He knew that Maddalena Strozzi had been Contessina's friend; he was happy to realize that some of her old friends had remained in touch with her. He chuckled, sat down at his workbench, and wrote a note which he sent to Doni:

> I fully appreciate how expensive my painting must seem to you. As an old and dear friend, I will release you from any financial embarrassment by giving the Holy Family to another friend.

Doni came running on Argiento's heels; flung down a pouch with a clang loud enough to be heard above all the stone chipping in the yard.

"I demand the painting! It is now mine by legal right."

He picked up the leather bag, untied the thong and poured the hundred and forty gold pieces onto the worktable. "Count them! One hundred and forty pieces of gold! For a miserable peasant family sitting on the grass. Why I let you exploit me this way is beyond my comprehension!"

Michelangelo picked up the painting, handed it to Doni.

"My compliments to your wife-to-be."

Doni made his way to the door, grumbling, "Artists! Supposed to be impractical. Ha! You'd bankrupt the shrewdest merchant in Tuscany!"

Michelangelo gathered up the coins. He had enjoyed the whole affair. It was as refreshing as a vacation.

11

There was considerable rejoicing in August when the Borgia Pope, Alexander VI, died. When Cardinal Piccolomini of Siena was elected to the papacy, Giuliano da Sangallo was crushed, Michelangelo was apprehensive. He had done no further work on the Piccolomini statues, not even a line of drawing. One word from the new Pope, and Gonfaloniere Soderini would be obliged to take him off the David until the remaining eleven figures were completed and delivered.

He refused to allow anyone into the workshed for a month as he worked frenziedly, before the Vatican ax could fall. Most of David's body was realized, only the face and head remained. For the first time he realized the weight of the contract for the Twelve Apostles, which would also hang over his head for years. He wanted to throw himself into the Arno.

Cardinal Piccolomini lasted as Pope Pius III for one month, dying suddenly in Rome. This time Giuliano da Sangallo proved to be the prognosticator: Cardinal Rovere was elected Pope Julius II. There was an uproarious celebration at the Sangallos', where Giuliano told everyone he was taking Michelangelo to Rome with him to create great marble sculptures.

Leonardo da Vinci returned from Caesar Borgia's army, was given the keys to the Great Hall of the Signoria in anticipation of being awarded a commission to create a fresco for the wall just behind the platform on which Gonfaloniere Soderini and the Signoria sat. The payment was to be ten thousand florins!

Michelangelo was livid. This was the largest and most important painting commission given by Florence in decades. Ten thousand florins to Leonardo for a fresco which was to be completed in two years. Four hundred florins to him for the Giant-David! For the same amount of work! Given to a man who would have helped Caesar Borgia conquer Florence! Leonardo was to be paid twenty-five times as much as the city was paying him. By that very fact, he had again struck a mortal blow against sculpture.

He ran in his rage to Soderini's office. Soderini heard him out; it was part of his talent to let his people have their say. He also allowed a few moments of silence for Michelangelo to hear his angry words echoing off the walls before answering in the quietest possible voice.

"Leonardo da Vinci is a great painter. I have seen the Last Supper in Milan. It is tremendous. No one in all Italy can equal him. I am frankly covetous of Milan's fresco, and I am anxious that he paint one for Florence. If it is as fine, it will enrich us enormously."

Michelangelo had been reproved and dismissed, all in the same breath.

There began the final months of work, so highly pleasurable to him now that the two years of labor were coming into focus. He went to David's face, carved it tenderly, with all the love and sympathy in his being: the strong, noble face of the youth who would, in one more moment, make the leap into manhood, but at this instant was still sad and uncertain over what he must do; the brows deeply knit, the eyes questioning, the full lips expectant. The set of the features had to be of a whole with the body. The expression on David's face must communicate that evil was vulnerable, even though it wore armor weighing a thousand pounds. There would always be some spot in it which was undefended; and if the good in man were dominant it would find that exposed area and evolve a way to penetrate it.

The emotion must convey the idea that his conflict with Goliath was a parable of good and evil.

The head was to have a feeling of illumination about it, coming not only from within but from the aura around it. To achieve this, he left volume about David's lips, jaws, nostrils. For the eyes and nostrils he used an auger; for the eyebrows a small chisel. For the deep penetration in the ear holes and between the teeth he drilled with a small-size bit, then larger bits as the openings grew larger. Between the strands of hair he made a series of penetrations, the holes following one another, orderly, controlled, using a long thin needle, holding it between both palms, rotating it, exerting only the slightest pressure of the hands. He took the most exquisite pains with the skin creases on the forehead, the tense slightly drawn-in nostrils, the slightly parted lips.

With the last of the webbing slowly cut away, he began to polish. He did not want as high a sheen as he had achieved for the Pietà. What he wanted was the outward expression of blood, muscle, brain, vein, bone, tissue; true, convincing, lifelike, in beautiful proportion: David in the warm palpitant human flesh, with a mind and a spirit and a soul shining through; a David quivering with emotion, the cords in his neck pulled taut by the head turned hard to Goliath, yet withal knowing that to live is to act.

In early January of 1504 Florence learned that Piero de' Medici had acted for the last time. Fighting with the French army, because he hoped to secure help from Louis XII against Florence, Piero had drowned in the Garigliano River when a boat in which he was saving four pieces of artillery from the Spanish army overturned. A member of the Signoria exclaimed publicly, "We Florentines are much rejoiced to hear that news!" Michelangelo had a moment of sadness, then pity for Alfonsina and her children; he remembered Lorenzo on his deathbed, telling Piero how to rule Florence. Then he was conscious that Piero's death meant that Contessina was nearer to being released from her exile.

At the end of January, Soderini called a meeting of artists and artisans of Florence to decide where the Giant-David should be placed. Michelangelo was summoned to the Signoria and shown the list of people invited to the discussion. He saw that the painters included Botticelli, Rosselli, David Ghirlandaio, Leonardo da Vinci, Filippino Lippi, Piero di Cosimo, Granacci, Perugino, Lorenzo di Credi. The sculptors were Rustici, Sansovino and Betto Buglioni, the architects Giuliano and his brother Antonio da Sangallo, Il Cronaca, Baccio d'Agnolo. There were four goldsmiths, two jewelers, an embroiderer, a terra-cotta designer, an illuminator; two carpenters on their way to becoming architects, the cannon caster Ghiberti; the clockmaker Lorenzo della Golpaia.

"Can you think of anyone left out?" asked Soderini.

"Me."

"I don't think you should be included. The others might be constrained in speaking."

"I'd like to express my opinion."

"You already have," replied Soderini dryly.

The meeting was called for the following day in the upstairs library of the Duomo headquarters, before the supper hour. Michelangelo had not meant to hover, but there were windows in the library facing the workyard, and he heard the hubbub of many voices above him as the artists collected. He walked through the yard, climbed a back stair to a small adjoining vestibule. Someone rapped for order, silence fell, Michelangelo recognized the voice of Francesco Filarete, herald of the Signoria.

"I have turned over in my mind those suggestions which my judgment could afford me. You have two places where the statue might be set up: the first, where the Donatello Judith stands; the second, in the middle of the courtyard where the bronze David is. The first might be selected because the Judith is an omen of evil and no fit object where it stands; besides, it is not proper that the woman should kill the male; and above all, this statue was erected under an evil constellation, since we have gone continually from bad to worse since then. The David is imperfect in the right leg; and so I should counsel you to put the Giant in one of these places, but I give the preference myself to that of the Judith.''

That suited Michelangelo fine. Another voice started speaking, one he did not recognize. He peeked into the library, saw that the speaker was Monciatto, the wood carver.

''I say that the Giant was meant to be put on the pillars outside the Duomo, or spurs around the church. I do not know why it should not be put there, and it seems to me that it would look fine and as a suitable ornament to the church of Santa Maria del Fiore.''

Michelangelo watched Rosselli rise feebly.

''Both Messer Francesco Filarete and Messer Francesco Monciatto spoke all right. However I had originally thought that the Giant should be placed on the stairs of the Duomo, to the right side, and, according to my opinion, this would be the best place.''

Other opinions came fast. Gallieno, the embroiderer, thought it should be placed where the Marzocco, the Lion, stood, in the piazza, with which David Ghirlandaio agreed; several, including Leonardo da Vinci, chose the loggia because the marble would be protected. Il Cronaca suggested the Great Hall, where Leonardo's fresco was to be painted.

Michelangelo muttered, ''Isn't there one artist here who will say I should have the right to select the spot myself?''

Then Filippino Lippi said, ''I think that everyone said wise things, but I am sure that the sculptor will propose the best place, as he certainly has considered longer and with more authority the spot where the Giant should be placed.''

There was a murmur of agreement. Angelo Manfidi concluded:

''Before your magnificent lords decide where the statue ought to be placed, I suggest that you ask the advice of the Signori among whom there are some high intellects.''

Michelangelo closed the door noiselessly and went down the back stairs to the yard. Gonfaloniere Soderini would now be able to guide the Giant-David to the spot Michelangelo wanted: in front of the Palazzo Signoria where the Judith now stood.

Crusty Pollaiuolo, *Il Cronaca,* as supervising architect of the Duomo, was in charge of moving the David; but he appeared grateful for the offer of Antonio da Sangallo, as well as Giuliano, to design a carrier. Baccio d'Agnolo, the architect, volunteered his services, as did Chimente del Tasso and Bernardo della Cecca, the two young carpenter-architects, since they were interested in the problem of moving the largest marble sculpture ever to be carried through the streets of Florence. The statue must be anchored securely so that it would not topple, yet not so rigidly that a jolt, jar or sudden movement could damage it.

''The David will have to be carried upright,'' said Giuliano. ''The framework in which it is being transported must be moved so that the marble feels no motion.''

''The solution?'' replied Antonio. ''A carrier within a carrier. We won't fasten him down; we'll put him in a sling, inside a big wooden frame; then he'll sway gently back and forth with the movement.''

The two carpenter-architects built a twenty-foot cage of wood to the Sangallos' specifications, open at the top. Antonio devised a series of slip knots which ran easily on the ropes, becoming tighter under weight, loosening as the pressure slacked. The David was encased in a net of enormous ropes, lifted by grapples, moved inside the open cage, suspended and held in its web. The wall behind the workshed was ripped out, the cage raised onto round rollers, the roadbed made smooth. The statue was ready for its mile-long journey through the Florentine streets.

Il Cronaca hired forty men to drag the huge crate on its round logs, using windlasses turned by a bar. As the heavy frame inched its way forward the rear log was released, picked up by a workman who ran forward to put it under the front of the framework. David, secured at the crotch and upward along Michelangelo's columnar structure over the strong chest, swayed only along the distance of the slip knots.

In spite of the forty workmen, the statue was moved but a few feet an hour. By nightfall they had gotten it out of the wall, down the Street of the Clock to the corner, maneuvered the sharp turn into the Via del Proconsolo, with hundreds of people watching the procession, and then only half a block down the street before darkness settled.

Everyone cried their "Good night. Until tomorrow." Michelangelo went home. He paced the bedroom, trying to pass the hours. At midnight, uneasy, he left the house to return to the David. There it stood, gleaming white in the moonlight, unfettered in its roped-in security, still facing toward Goliath, the hand reaching for the sling, the profile chiseled and polished to flawless beauty.

He threw a blanket inside the cage, in the space behind the David where the right calf joined the tree trunk. There was room for him to lie on the wooden floor. He had fallen into a state halfway from wakefulness when he heard running feet, the sound of voices, then stones hitting the side wall of the frame. He sprang up, cried:

"Guards!"

He heard the running feet go down the Proconsolo, gave chase, calling at the top of his lungs:

"Stop! Night guards! Stop them!"

The half dozen fleeing forms seemed to be young boys. His heart pounding wildly, he returned to the David, found two guards standing there with lanterns.

"What's all the noise?"

"The statue was being stoned."

"Stoned? By whom?"

"I don't know."

"Did they hit it?"

"I don't think so. I heard only the sound on wood."

"You're sure you weren't having a bad dream?"

"I tell you I saw them. And heard them. If I hadn't been here . . ."

He circled the David, peering through the darkness, wondering who would want to injure it.

"Vandals," said Soderini, arriving early to watch the moving process resume. "But I'll put a guard out tonight."

The vandals came back, a dozen strong, after midnight. He heard them while they were still sneaking up the Street of St. Proculus, shouted a warning which made them unload their barrage of stones too soon. The next morning all of Florence knew that there was a movement to damage the David. Soderini summoned him to a meeting of the Signoria to ask who the attackers might be.

"Do you have enemies?"

"None that I know of."

"We should rather ask, 'Does Florence have enemies?' " said Herald Filarete. "Just let them try it tonight."

They did, at the bottom corner of the Piazza della Signoria, where Piazza San Firenze joined the big square. But Soderini had concealed armed guards in doorways and yards surrounding the David. Eight of the gang were captured and taken to the Bargello. Michelangelo, half dead from lack of sleep, scanned the list of names. There was not one he recognized.

In the morning the upper hall of the Bargello was jammed with Florentines. Michelangelo gazed at the culprits. Five were young, perhaps fifteen years old; they testified that they had merely joined in the adventure proposed by their older friends, and did not know what they were stoning. Their families were fined, the boys released.

The other three were older, resentful and vindictive in mood. The first said he had stoned the David because it was obscenely naked, that Savonarola would have wanted it destroyed. The second said that it was bad art, and he wanted to show that some people knew better. The third claimed that he was acting for a friend who wanted the David broken; but he would not mention the friend's name.

All three were sentenced to the Stinche by the judge, who quoted a Tuscan adage, "Art has an enemy called ignorance."

That evening, the fourth day of its journey, the David arrived at its destination. D'Agnolo and the young carpenters knocked down the cage. The Sangallos unslipped the knots, removed the rope mantle. The Judith was carried away, David installed in her place at the foot of the palace steps facing the open piazza.

Michelangelo drew in his breath sharply as he came into the piazza. He had not seen the David at such a distance. There it stood in all its majestic grace, lighting up the Signoria with pure white light. He stood below the figure, feeling insignificant, weak and homely, powerless now that the statue was out of his hands, asking himself, "How much of what I wanted to say have I managed to convey?"

He had stood guard for four nights, was only half conscious from exhaustion. Should he keep guard again tonight? Now that the David was completely exposed, at anyone's mercy? A few large stones, well directed, could tear off its arm, even the head. Granacci said firmly:

"Things happen while something is in transit that stop when it takes its permanent place."

He guided Michelangelo home, took off his boots, helped him into bed and put a blanket over him. To Lodovico who was watching from the door, he said:

"Let him sleep. Even if the sun goes twice around."

He woke feeling refreshed, and ravishingly hungry. Though it was not time for dinner he ate his way through pots of soup, *lasagne* and boiled fish that were supposed to feed the family. His stomach was so full he could hardly crowd himself into the wooden tub for a bath. He enjoyed the fresh white linen shirt, stockings and sandals, the first he could remember in weeks.

He turned off the Piazza San Firenze into the lower end of the Signoria. A crowd was standing below the David in silence. Fluttering from the statue were pieces of paper stuck to the marble during the night. He had seen this sight in Rome, when people had pasted up verses derogatory to the Borgia on the library door of the Vatican, or affixed their smoldering complaints to the marble torso of the Pasquino statue near the Piazza Navona.

He walked across the square, through the crowd. It fell back to let him pass. He tried to read their expressions, to see what was in the wind. They seemed big-eyed.

He came to the David, climbed up on the base, began taking off the papers, reading them one by one. By the end of the third, his eyes began to mist: for they were messages of love and acceptance:

You have given us back our self-respect.

We are proud to be Florentines.

How magnificent is man!

Never can they tell me man is vile; he
is the proudest creature on earth.

You have made a thing of beauty.

Bravo!

His eye caught a familiar paper, of a kind he had held in his hands before. He reached for it, read:

*Everything my father hoped to accomplish
for Florence is expressed in your David.*
Contessina Ridolfi de' Medici

She had made her way into the city at night, past the guards. She had taken the risk to come and see his David, had joined her voice to that of Florence's.

He turned, stood above the crowd gazing up at him. There was silence in the square. And yet he had never felt such complete communication. It was as though they read each other's thoughts, as though they were one and the same: they were a part of him, every Florentine standing below, eyes turned up to him, and he was a part of them.

12

A letter arrived from Jacopo Galli enclosing a contract signed by the Mouscron brothers, who agreed to pay him four thousand guldens, and saying, "You are free to do any Madonna and Child you can conceive. Now, after sweet meat, comes sour sauce. The Piccolomini heirs insist that you carve the balance of their statues. I prevailed upon them to extend the contract for another two years; that was the best I could do."

A two-year extension! He quickly dispatched the pieces to the back of his mind.

An immediate repercussion of the David was a call at the Buonarroti apartment by Bartolommeo Pitti, from the secondary branch of the wealthy Pitti who lived in a stone palace on the opposite side of the Arno. Bartolommeo was a shy and retiring man whose modest house on the Piazza Santo Spirito had a draper's shop on the ground floor.

"I am just beginning an art collection. So far I have three small paintings on wood, lovely, but not important. My wife and I would give anything if we could help a work of art to be born."

Michelangelo was taken by the man's simple manner, the mild brown eyes shining beneath the bald crown.

"In what way would you like to participate, *messere?*"

"We wondered if there were some small piece of marble you might have had in mind, or would take pleasure in thinking about, for us. . . ."

He took his very first sculpture off the wall, the Madonna and Child relief he had carved under Bertoldo's guidance. "For a long time, Messer Pitti, I have perceived how much I failed in this first bas-relief, and why. I should like to try again, but in the circular, tondo shape. I think I could bring whole figures out of bas-relief, create the impression of sculpture in the round. Would you like me to try this for you?"

Pitti wet his dry, ridged lips with his tongue. "I cannot convey how much happiness that would bring us."

Michelangelo escorted Bartolommeo Pitti down the stairs to the street.

"Something good will emerge for you, I feel it in my bones."

The Signoria passed a resolution urging *Il Cronaca* to get Michelangelo's house and studio built. Pollaiuolo had allowed the drawings to become lost under a pile of bric-a-brac on his cluttered desk that always contained a couple of dozen hard-boiled eggs, the only food he ate.

"Suppose I set up the structure and the room space?" he asked Michelangelo. "I imagine you will want to design the stone blocks?"

"I should like that. Could I make a few stipulations?"

"What client doesn't?" growled *Il Cronaca*.

"I'd like the kitchen upstairs, between the family room and my bedroom. A fireplace with the chimney built into the wall. A pillared loggia outside my bedroom, overlooking the back yard. Brick floors, good windows, a second-story latrine. A front door with a cornice over it of thin hewn stone. All interior walls plastered. I'll paint them myself."

"I can't see what you need me for," grumbled *Il Cronaca*. "Let's go over to the land and place the studio for light and sun."

Michelangelo asked if the Topolinos could do the stonework.

"Providing you guarantee the work."

"You will get the most beautifully carved blocks ever hewed in Settignano."

The open lot was on the corner of the Borgo Pinti and the Via della Colonna, forty-six feet on the Borgo adjoining the Cestello monastery, the Via della Colonna side considerably longer, ending at the shop of a blacksmith and carpenter. They bought some pegs from him, paced off the land and drove in the boundary stakes.

Il Cronaca returned in a couple of weeks with the plans for the house and adjoining studio, uncompromisingly square on the outside but designed for comfort within. There was an open loggia off the second-story bedroom where Michelangelo would eat and rest in warm weather.

The Topolinos were soon cutting *pietra serena* according to his specifications, the stones emerging a luminous blue-gray, with marvelous grainings. They cut the blocks for his fireplace, using the strings he brought them for length, the thin hewn stones for the cornice; and when the building blocks were ready the entire family built the house. *Il Cronaca* brought in the plasterers for the interior walls, the tilemakers to put on the roof, but at night Michelangelo could not resist going to the house to quench the lime with water from the well that had been dug in the yard, to temper the loggia, and to paint the interior walls the warm blues, rose and orange colors he had evolved for the clothes of the Doni Holy Family. The entire south wall of the studio admitted to the courtyard.

The furniture money had to come out of his own purse. He could buy only modestly: a wide bed, chest, single chair for his bedroom, for the loggia chairs and table which could be moved inside in wet or cold weather; a leather chair and bench for the family room, pots, bowls, frying pans, boxes for salt and sugar and flour for the kitchen. Argiento moved his bed from the workshop in the piazza, putting it in the small downstairs bedroom near the front door.

"You should put pictures of sacred objects in your house," his aunt Cassandra told him; "to look at them will be good for your soul."

Michelangelo hung his earliest Madonna and Child opposite his bed, put the Centaurs in the family room.

"Pure narcissism," commented Granacci; "your aunt tells you to put up sacred objects, so you hang your own work."

"They're sacred to me, Granacci."

He worked joyfully in the late summer sun flooding the open studio, his head and hands rich with ideas that came tumbling over each other in profusion: the wax figure of the Bruges Madonna, the sketches for the Pitti tondo, exploratory figures for the Apostle St. Matthew for the Duomo; filing the bronze David for the French Maréchal. When the five-foot block arrived from Carrara for the Madonna, Argiento helped him set it up on a turntable in the middle of the studio. Within the hour he was massing around the edges, feeling the figures stir inside the marble, baptizing the brick floor of the studio with its first snowstorm.

His personal fulfillment did not lead him to evolve a cheerful Madonna; on the contrary this Madonna was sad; she had already, through his sculptures, known the Descent. The tranquillity of his early bas-belief, when Mary still had her decision to make, could never be recaptured. This young mother was committed; she knew the end of her boy's life. That was why she was reluctant to let him go, this beautiful, husky, healthy boy, his hand clasped for protection in hers. That was why she sheltered him with the side of her cloak.

The child, sensitive to his mother's mood, had a touch of melancholy about the eyes. He was strong, he had courage, he would step forth from the safe harbor of his mother's lap; but just now he gripped her hand with the fingers of one hand, and with the other held securely to her side. Or was it his own mother he was thinking about, sad because she must leave her son alone in the world? Himself, who clung to her?

He worked as though he were on a holiday, the chips of marble flying, these smaller, compact figures coming almost without effort after the overpowering male massiveness of the David. His hammer and chisels had the weight of feathers as he evolved the Madonna's simple draperies, her long fingers, the rich braids over the long-nosed face, the heavy-lidded eyes, the boy's head of curls, powerfully shaped body, the plump cheeks and chin: an aura of compassion permeating the marble. He did not idealize the Madonna's face as he had before; he hoped to make her noble through her sentiment.

Granacci commented, "They will be the most alive beings in any chapel they may be put into."

Prior Bichiellini, who had made no comment on the David, came to give Michelangelo's new house the traditional blessing. He bent on his knee, spoke a prayer to the Madonna. Then he rose, put both hands on Michelangelo's shoulder.

"This Madonna and Child could not have evolved in such tender purity if you did not feel tenderly and were not pure in heart. Bless you and this workshop."

He celebrated the completion of the Bruges Madonna and Child by setting up a square block, rounding off its corners to give him the roughly circular tondo form, beginning work on the piece for the Pitti. The wax model on the armature took shape quickly, for it was an idyllic period for him, working in his own studio, wanted. This was the first circular sculpture he had attempted; by tilting the marble saucerlike, he was able to achieve planes-in-depth in which the Madonna, seated on a solid block, as the most important figure, emerged full-bodied; the child, though leaning on an open book in his mother's lap, receded to a secondary plane, John, peeking over Mary's shoulder, was buried deep in the saucer.

He used half a dozen different textures in his finish, almost the whole alphabet of the chisel; only Mary's face was polished in the high flesh tones of the Pietà, enriching the emotional tactility. He felt this Mary to be the strongest of his Madonnas, mature; the child embodied the sweetness and charm of a happy youngster; the figures moved freely within their circle.

Argiento wrapped the tondo carefully in blankets and, borrowing a barrow from the carpenter next door, wheeled the marble through the streets to the Pitti house. Michelangelo walked beside him. They carried it up the stairs above the draper's, set it on a high narrow buffet. The Pitti were speechless, then the parents and children began to talk and laugh all at once, to run about the room to see the piece from different angles.

The months that followed were the happiest he had known. The David, still called the Giant by most Florentines, was accepted by the city as its new symbol, mentor and protector. Things took a sharp turn for the better: Caesar Borgia, seriously ill, ceased to be a menace; Arezzo and Pisa seemed subdued; Pope Julius II, friendly to Florence, made Cardinal Giovanni de' Medici important at the Vatican. There was a spirit of confidence and energy in the air. Trade was booming; there was work for all, a market for every man's product. The government, with Soderini as its permanent head, was stable and secure, the last of the internecine Florentine feuds forgotten.

Much of this the city-state attributed to the Giant-David. The date of its installation marked a new era in the minds of the Florentines. Contracts and agreements were dated, "One month after the unveiling of the Giant." In conversation, time was divided by saying: "This was before the Giant," or, "I remember it well because it happened in the second week following the Giant."

From Soderini Michelangelo extracted the promise that Contessina, her husband and children would be permitted to go to the protection of Cardinal Giovanni in Rome, just as quickly as he could persuade the members of the Council of Seventy. He was friendly and companionable at the dinners of the Company, stopped attacking Leonardo, helped other sculptors with their designs when they were seeking commissions. He obliged Argiento to spend more time in training with him. He climbed the hills to Settignano to watch the pile of thin decorative strips for his front cornice grow, each carved as though it were a gem. From there he walked to Contessina's to give Luigi a lesson and play with the growing Niccolò. He was patient with his own family, listened quietly as Lodovico told of searching for more houses and farms to buy in order to build an estate for his sons.

The Pitti family sent him Taddeo Taddei, a Florentine intellectual who loved the arts. Taddei wondered if Maestro Buonarroti might be willing to carve him a tondo. Michelangelo already had a point of departure, born while working the Pitti piece. He sketched the fresh idea for Taddei, who was enchanted. Now he had still another delightful commission from a sensitive man who appreciated what he was going to sculpture for him.

A few months short of thirty, he seemed to have reached the full expression and acceptance for which he had yearned.

13

His period of grace was short-lived.

Every few weeks since Sangallo had been summoned to Rome by Julius II, he had sent encouraging word to Michelangelo: he had told the Pope about the David; he had urged His Holiness to look at the Pietà in St. Peter's; he had persuaded the pontiff that there was no equal master in all Europe. The Pope had begun to think about marble sculptures; soon he would decide what he wanted carved, then he would summon Michelangelo to Rome. . . .

Michelangelo passed several of these notes around at the Company of the Cauldron meetings, so that when Julius II summoned Sansovino to Rome to erect two tombs, one for the Cardinal of Recanati, the other for Cardinal Sforza in Santa Maria del Popolo, it stunned him. The Company gave Sansovino a noisy farewell party, in which Michelangelo joined, pleased over his old comrade's good fortune, hiding his own humiliation. He had suffered a severe blow to his prestige. Many in Florence asked:

"If it is true that Michelangelo is the first sculptor of Florence, why did the Pope not send for him instead of Sansovino?"

During the early months of 1504 Leonardo da Vinci had spent his time in a series of mechanical inventions, suction pumps, turbines, conduits for the rerouting of the Arno away from Pisa, an observatory under his skylight with a magnifying glass for studying the moon. Rebuked by the Signoria for neglecting his fresco, he had started in May to work on it in earnest. The cartoon became the talk of Florence: artists flocked to Leonardo's workroom in Santa Maria Novella to study, admire, copy, change their styles. Word went around the city that something startling and wondrous was in the making.

With the passing months the city became caught up in admiration of Leonardo and his cartoon, crying out about its marvels. It became the chief topic of conversation. The David was taken for granted now, as were the good times it had brought. Michelangelo began to perceive that he was being superseded. Admiring acquaintances and strangers who had stopped him on the street to pay their respects now nodded casually. He had had his day; it had passed. Leonardo da Vinci was the figure of the moment. Florence proudly proclaimed him "the first artist of Tuscany."

This was bitter medicine to Michelangelo. How fickle were his Florentines! Relegating him to second place so quickly! Knowing Santa Maria Novella from the months he had spent there with Ghirlandaio, he managed to see the Leonardo cartoon without anyone knowing he was there. The Battle of Anghiari was tremendous! Leonardo, who loved horses as dearly as did Rustici, had created a masterpiece of the horse at war, in violent combat, ridden by men in ancient Roman armor, savagely trying to destroy each other, striking, biting, slaying as though they were the furies, men and horses alike caught up in violent, bloodthirsty conflict, many individual groups designed to fit into the brilliantly integrated pattern.

Leonardo was a great painter, he could not dispute that; perhaps the greatest the world had yet seen. Instead of reconciling him, this inflamed him the more. At sunset, as he was passing Santa Trinita, he saw a group of men talking on the benches in front of the Spina banking house. They were discussing a passage from Dante, of which Michelangelo recognized the lines as coming from Canto XI of the *Inferno*.

> "Philosophy," my master answered me,
> "To him who understands it, demonstrates
> How nature takes her course, not only from
> Wisdom divine, but from its art as well.
> And if you read with care your book of physics,
> After the first few pages, you will find
> That art, as best it can, doth follow nature,
> As pupil follows master."

The man in the center of the group looked up.

"Here is Michelangelo," said Leonardo da Vinci; "he will interpret the verses."

Michelangelo looked so much like a laborer returning home from his day-long tasks that some of the younger admirers around Leonardo laughed.

"Explain them yourself," cried Michelangelo, blaming Leonardo for the laughter. "You who made a model of a horse to be cast in bronze, and to your shame had to leave it unfinished!"

Leonardo's face turned a flaming red.

"I was not mocking you, I asked in earnest. It is not my fault if these others laughed."

Michelangelo's ears were plugged with the bubbling hot wax of anger. He turned away without hearing, struck out for the hills. He walked all night, trying to put down his anger, humiliation, sense of frustration and shame. He could not reconcile himself to having been passed by, treated cavalierly by the city that now turned its eyes elsewhere.

He had walked a long way in the night, up the river to Pontassieve. At dawn he stood at the confluence of the Sieve and the Arno, on the road that led to Arezzo and Rome. He knew that there was only one answer to his problem: he could never surpass Leonardo in handsomeness, in regality of figure, in superiority of manner. But he was the best draftsman in all Italy. No one would believe him, merely saying so; he would have to prove it. And no proof would serve except a fresco, of the same proportions as Leonardo's.

Leonardo's fresco was going to occupy the right half of the long eastern wall of the Great Hall. He would ask Soderini for the left half. He would put his work up side by side with Leonardo's, prove that he could outpaint him, figure for figure! All the world could see and judge. Then Florence could say who was the first artist of the time!

Granacci tried to cool him down.

"This is a sickness, a fever. We must find some way to physic you."

"You're not funny."

"*Dio mio*, I wasn't trying to be. What you can't stand is Leonardo's proximity."

"The smell of his perfume, you mean."

"Don't be nasty. Leonardo doesn't use perfume, only scent."

Granacci looked at his friend's sweat-caked arms and legs, the shirt dirty from the smoke of his forge.

"There are times when a bath wouldn't kill you."

Michelangelo picked up a heavy beam, brandished it at Granacci and screamed, "Get out of my studio, you . . . you traitor!"

"I didn't bring up the subject of scents, you did. Why disturb yourself over his painting, when you have years of sculpture at hand? Forget him."

"He's a thorn in my foot."

"Suppose you come out second best, with a wall full of bandaged toes?"

Michelangelo grinned. "Trust me, Granacci, I'll come out first. I've got to."

Late that afternoon he presented himself at Gonfaloniere Soderini's office, bathed, barbered, wearing his clean blue shirt.

"Phew," said the Gonfaloniere, leaning as far away as he could, "what did the barber put on your hair?"

Michelangelo flushed. ". . . a scented oil . . ."

Soderini sent a groom for a towel. When it arrived he handed it to Michelangelo, saying, "Rub that stuff out. Stick to your own smells. At least they're indigenous."

Michelangelo told Soderini why he had come. Soderini was flabbergasted; it was the first time Michelangelo had ever seen him lose his presence.

"But that is unreasonable!" he cried, walking around his broad desk and staring at Michelangelo. "You've told me yourself that you never liked the fresco work at Ghirlandaio's."

"I was wrong." His head was down, his voice dogged. "I can paint fresco. Better than Leonardo da Vinci."

"Are you sure?"

"I'll put my hand in fire."

"Even supposing you can, why would you want to take the years away from marble? Your Madonna for the Bruges merchants is divine. So is the Pitti tondo. Your talent is a gift from God. Why should you throw it away for an art of which you want no part?"

"You were so thrilled, Gonfaloniere, to have Leonardo paint one half your wall. You said the world would come to see it. Why would not twice as many visitors come to two panels, one by Leonardo, the other by me? It would be a great *palio*, race, that would excite people."

"And you think you can surpass him?"

"I'll put my hand in fire."

Soderini walked back to the gold-emblazoned chair, dropped into it hard, shaking his head in disbelief.

"The Signoria would never approve. You already have a contract with the Wool Guild and Duomo to carve the Twelve Apostles."

"I'll carve them. But the other half of the wall must be mine. I don't need two years, the way Leonardo does, I'll do it in one year, ten months, eight . . ."

"No, *caro*. You are wrong. I won't let you get yourself into bad trouble."

"Because you don't believe I can do it. You're right not to believe, since I come here with only words in my hands. Next time I come back it will be with drawings, and then you will see what I can do."

"Please," said Soderini wearily, "come back with a marble Apostle instead. That's why we built you that house and studio, so you would carve Apostles."

Soderini looked up at the lilies on the ceiling.

"Why wasn't I content with two months as Gonfaloniere? Why did I have to take this job for life?"

"Because you are a wise and persuasive Gonfaloniere who is going to get the city to appropriate another ten thousand florins for the painting of the other half of the wall."

To excite the Signoria sufficiently to spend an additional sum, to delight the Wool and Duomo Boards enough to release him from his contract for a year, he would have to paint a scene of glory and pride for the Florentines. He did not want to paint horses covered with protective trappings, soldiers in their breastplate armor and helmets, sword and spear in hand, with the confusion of rearing animals, wounded and dying men. This was not for him.

But what was?

He went to the Santo Spirito library, asked the Augustinian monk in charge to recommend a history of Florence. The librarian gave him Filippo Villani's *Cronaca*. He read about the wars between the Guelfs and Ghibellines, the wars with Pisa and other city-states. His fresco did not necessarily have to be a battle, but it did have to be a triumph of some sort to puff the national honor. Where in Florentine history was he to find such a scene, of the kind that he could paint; and which would stand in dramatic contrast to Leonardo's battle spectacle? One from which he could emerge the victor?

It was not until he had read for several days that he came upon a story that quickened his pulse. The scene was laid at Cascina, near Pisa, where the Florentine forces had made camp on the bank of the Arno on a hot summer day. Feeling themselves safe from attack, a number of the soldiers had gone bathing in the river, others were coming out to dry themselves, while still a third group, having shed their heavy armor, was sun-bathing on the grass. Suddenly a guard burst into the group, crying, "We are lost! The Pisans are about to attack!" The Florentines scrambled out of the river, those on the bank hastily buckled on their armor, others went rushing for weapons . . . in time to beat back three Pisan attacks and to rout the enemy.

Here was a chance to paint a large group of men, young and old, with the water and the sun on them, galvanized into action, all of them at a moment of danger, of tension, of pressure, recorded not only on their faces but in the bending, reaching, straining to prepare for the attack and save their lives. Here was a chance to create something exciting. They would all be Davids; a complete portrait of mankind, startled out of its momentary Garden of Eden.

He went to the Street of the Stationers, bought the largest squares of paper he could find, colored inks, chalks, black, white, red and brown crayons, took them back to his workbench. Draawing swiftly, he organized the scene on the Arno at Cascina, in the center Donati crying to Captain Malatesta, "We are lost!", some of the soldiers still in the water, others trying to climb the steep bank, others throwing on a garment while reaching for a weapon.

Three days later he stood in Soderini's office. The two men stared at each other, wide-eyed. Michelangelo fitted together on the floor beside the desk the dozen large sheets with twenty male figures, some crosshatched with the pen, others outlined in charcoal or drawn with long bold slashing lines heightened with white lead, still others glowing with flesh colors.

He dropped into one of a row of tall leather chairs against the side wall, feeling tired and let down. Soderini studied the drawings in silence. When he looked up, Michelangelo recognized the affectionate regard in which Soderini held him.

"I was wrong to discourage you. To be an artist one must sculpture and paint and create architecture with equal authority. This fresco can be as revolutionary as the David, and bring us the same joy. I'm going to get you this commission, even if I have to fight every member of the Council."

And so he did, for a sum of three thousand florins, less than a third of Leonardo da Vinci's pay. It was Michelangelo's largest commission, though he felt disgruntled that the Signoria thought his work worth so much less than Leonardo's. They would change their minds when they saw the finished fresco.

Now people stopped to tell him they heard he was going to paint a forest of Davids.

"And so you have been repatriated," said Granacci, a touch caustically. "You are once again our first artist, providing the fresco comes out brilliantly. I only hope you're not paying too high a price."

"A man pays what he must."

14

He was given a long narrow room at the Hospital of the Dyers, a charitable hospital that had been founded by the Art Guild of the Dyers in 1359. It fronted on the Street of the Dyers, just a couple of blocks from his early home near Santa Croce; he remembered it because as a boy he used to walk in the gutters which ran blue, green, red and crimson. His room faced the Arno, south, so that he had sun all day; the back wall was larger than his half of the Hall of the Great Council. He would be able to mount his cartoon sheet by sheet, and see it whole before painting the fresco. He ordered Argiento to keep the street door locked.

He worked in an absolute fury, determined to show the city that he was a sure and swift master who did not need to be rebuked by the Signoria for dawdling over drawings of canal pumps and other mechanical engines. When the weather turned cold he sent Argiento out for wax and turpentine in which to steep the paper the Dyers used for windows. He drew his overall design on an oblong strip of paper, cut to scale, then divided it into the number of squares he would need to assemble to fill the twenty-two by fifty-eight-foot wall. In contrast to his early Battle of the Centaurs, the key figures would stand ten feet high; yet this scene would have a similar sense of a group of nude warriors crowded into a limited area, all of the arms, legs, torsos, heads intertwined organically, as though integral parts of a whole, engaged in a melodramatic melee to get out of the water, into their clothes, their armor and ranks before the enemy fell upon them.

He drew one young warrior, his back turned, wearing a cuirass and shield, a sword under his feet; naked youths who had picked up their spears and swords, ignoring their clothes; hardened warriors with powerful legs and shoulders, ready to spring at the oncoming enemy barehanded; three young soldiers just scrambling out of the river; a central group around Donati caught between consternation and the beginnings of preparation; a warrior shoving an arm powerfully through a shirt; an old soldier wearing an ivy wreath on his head, trying to draw his hose over wet legs, "so that all the muscles and sinews of his body are seen in strain," Michelangelo explained to Granacci, "the contortions of his mouth show his agony of haste, and how his whole frame labors to his toetips."

Worked carefully, the Cascina cartoon which he called the Bathers, would have taken a full year; done at the height of a young man's power and talent, it might conceivably have been done in six months. By New Year's Day of 1505, three months after he had started, driven by a force he could not contain, Michelangelo's cartoon was completed. Salvadore, the bookbinder, had spent the two previous days gluing the separate sheets together; now Argiento, Granacci, Antonio da Sangallo and Michelangelo stretched and tacked the cartoon to a light frame against the rear wall. It filled the room with fifty to sixty desperately challenged men. In the panel were contained fear, terror, hopelessness; and at the same time all the manly emotions surging upward to overcome surprise and disaster by swift purposeful action.

Granacci stood gazing at the overpowering force of this body of men caught between life and death, each reacting according to his individual character and resolution. He was stunned by the authority of the draftsmanship.

"How strange," he murmured, "that poor motivation can create rich art." When Michelangelo did not answer, he continued. "You must open these doors and let everyone see what you have accomplished."

"There has been grumbling over your closed doors," added Antonio; "even members of the Company have asked me why you should lock everybody out. Now that they can see the miracle you have wrought in three short months, they will understand."

"I'd like to wait another three months," grumbled Michelangelo. "Until I have the fresco completed in the Great Hall. But if you both say I must, then I must."

Rustici arrived first. Being Leonardo's close friend, what Rustici said would carry weight. He weighed his words carefully.

"Leonardo painted his panel for the horses, you for the men. Nothing as superb as Leonardo's has ever been done of a battle scene. Nothing as magnificently shocking as yours has ever been painted of human beings. The Signoria is going to have one hell of a wall!"

Twenty-two-year-old Ridolfo Ghirlandaio, who was studying at Rosselli's studio, asked if he might sketch. Andrea del Sarto, nineteen-year-old Florentine who had transferred from a goldsmith's shop to the painters' *bottega* of Piero di Cosimo, also arrived with drawing materials. Antonio Sangallo brought his twenty-four-year-old nephew, who was apprenticed to Perugino. Twenty-one-year-old Raphael Sanzio, a former apprentice of Perugino's, was brought by Taddeo Taddei, who had commissioned Michelangelo's second tondo.

Michelangelo liked Raphael Sanzio immediately. He had a sensitive, patrician face, with wide, gentle, perceptive eyes, a full-lipped but disciplined mouth; long, luxuriant hair, fastidiously kept: as exquisite a face as Leonardo da Vinci's, yet in spite of a creamy skin, altogether manly. He carried himself with an expression of gracious warmth. His strong face was imbued with confidence, but there was not the slightest trace of haughtiness. His clothes, too, were as fine as Leonardo's, with a white shirt and lace collar, richly colored cloak with tight-fitting cap to match; but he wore no jewels or scent. The beauty of the soft-spoken young man's face, figure and clothes did not make Michelangelo feel ugly, awkward or shabby, as Leonardo's inevitably did.

Raphael turned to the cartoon, spoke no word for the rest of the afternoon. When dark fell, he came to Michelangelo and said in a voice which lacked the slightest shred of flattery:

"This makes painting a wholly different art. I shall have to start back at the beginning. Even what I have learned from Leonardo is no longer sufficient."

The eyes he turned on Michelangelo were not so much admiring as incredulous; his expression conveyed the thought that it was not really Michelangelo who had done all this, but some outside force.

Raphael asked if he might move his materials from Perugino's studio and work before the cartoon. Sebastiano da Sangallo terminated his apprenticeship to Perugino to study the shape and movement of the muscles in the figures in the cartoon, while at the same time painstakingly writing down his theories of what had impelled

Michelangelo to draw the figures in such difficult positions. Without willing it, or even wanting it, Michelangelo found himself at the head of a school of talented young apprentices.

A surprise visitor was Agnolo Doni, who had been spreading the word that it was he who was responsible for having started Michelangelo on his career as a painter. Had not Michelangelo protested that he was not a painter? Had not he, Doni, perceived that all he had needed to start him on this glorious career was Doni's confidence in him? The story was plausible. Because some people believed it, Doni was becoming one of the more important art connoisseurs in Florence.

Now he arrived at the Dyers' to commission Michelangelo to paint portraits of himself and his wife. He said loftily, "This commission could be the making of you as a portrait painter."

Michelangelo was amused. In his basic tenet, Doni was right. He had badgered him into painting the Holy Family. And if he had not got the feel of brush and paint, he might still have thought himself a world removed, unwilling and unable to touch the medium. But he was still beyond portraits!

At that moment Raphael entered the hall. Michelangelo turned to Doni.

"Raphael will paint your pictures, with charm and likeness. Since he's just beginning, you can get him cheap."

"You are sure he can measure up to the high level of my art collection?"

"I guarantee it."

Toward the end of January, Perugino came to the Dyers' Hall, having been moved to do so by Raphael's enthusiasm. He was twenty-five years older than Michelangelo, with the lurching gait of a countryman, a face scarred with gullies from years of privation when he had had to go without food for lack of the meanest coin. Perugino had been trained in Verrocchio's studio and had carried forward the immeasurably difficult technique of perspective begun by Paolo Uccello. Michelangelo welcomed him warmly.

Perugino stood near the windows of the oblong hall in silence. After a time Michelangelo felt him advancing slowly toward the large cartoon. His face had turned charcoal, his eyes seemed glazed, his lips were fluttering as though in an effort to force out words. Michelangelo picked up a stool, put it behind Perugino.

"Please . . . sit down . . . I'll get some water."

Perugino knocked the stool out from behind him with a savage backward kick.

". . . beastly . . ."

Dumfounded, Michelangelo stared. Perugino thrust his left hand across his chest, fingers stiff as he swept away the cartoon before him.

"Give a wild animal a brush, and he would do the same. You will destroy us . . . all we have spent a lifetime to create!"

Sick at heart, Michelangelo could only murmur, "Perugino, why do you attack me? I admire your work . . ."

"My work! How dare you speak of my work in the presence of this . . . this filthiness! In my work I have manners, taste, respectability! If my work is painting, then yours is not. It is a debauchery, every square inch of it."

Ice-cold now, Michelangelo asked, "You mean the technique is bad, the drawing, the design . . . ?"

"You know nothing of such matters," cried Perugino. "You should be thrown into the Stinche and kept from destroying the art that decent men have created."

"Why am I not a decent man? Is it that I have painted nudes? That this is . . . new?"

"Don't talk to me of originality! I have done as much as any one man in Italy to revolutionize painting."

"You have done much. But painting does not come to an end with you. Every true artist re-creates the art."

"You go backward, before civilization, before God."

"You sound like Savonarola."

"You will never get one figure of this immorality up on the Signoria wall. I shall organize the artists of Florence . . ."

He stormed out of the Dyers' Hall, walking stiff-legged, his head held stiffly on his neck. Michelangelo righted the stool and sat down, trembling. Argiento, who had been hiding in a far corner, came forward with a cup of water. Michelangelo dipped his fingers, touched them to his feverish face.

He could not understand what had happened. That Perugino might not have liked his cartoon was understandable. But to launch so bitter a personal attack, to talk of putting him in the Stinche . . . of having his cartoon destroyed . . . Surely he would not be so foolish as to go to the Signoria?

He rose, turned his back on the cartoon, shut the door of the room, walked quietly with eyes on the cobblestones, through the streets of Florence to his house. He let himself into the studio. Slowly he became normal, the nausea passed. He picked up a hammer and chisel, worked the gleaming marble of the Taddei tondo. He turned his thinking upside down from the Pitti concept, creating everything in reverse: this would be a playful, joyous mother and child. He carved Mary on a secondary plane of depth in order that the son might dominate the scene, sprawled diagonally across her lap to avoid the goldfinch that John was mischievously thrusting toward him.

He had chosen a deep, resourceful block. With a heavy point he gouged out a background to give a sense of the deserts of Jerusalem, the white chips flying about his head as he happily stripped out marble with a claw-tool *gradina* to achieve the saucerlike effect, the bodies of Mary and John forming the circular rim, Jesus cutting across but connecting them, none affixed to the background, moving freely with every change of light. The smoky-smelling marble dust tasted as sweet in his nostrils as sugar on the tongue.

He had been a fool. He should never have left sculpturing.

The door opened. Raphael came in, quietly stood by his side. This was Perugino's countryman. Why had he come?

"I came to apologize for my friend and teacher. He's had a shock, and is now ill . . ."

Michelangelo gazed into Raphael's eloquent eyes.

"Why did he attack me?"

"Perhaps it is because for a number of years now Perugino has been . . . imitating himself. Why should he think he should change, when he is one of Italy's most famous painters, beloved for his work here in Florence, at home in Perugia, and even in Rome?"

"I admired his work in the Sistine Chapel."

"Then can't you see? When he saw the Bathers he felt exactly as I had: that this was a different world of painting, that one had to start over. For me, this was a challenge; it opened my eyes to how much more exciting an art I had entered than I had suspected. But I am not yet twenty-two. I have life before me. Perugino is fifty-five; he can never start over. This work of yours will make his art old-fashioned." He paused, thought hard. "It can make one ill . . ."

"I appreciate your coming here, Raphael."

"Then be generous. Have the goodness to ignore him. It won't be easy. He has already gone to the Signoria to protest, and he has called a special meeting of the Company for tonight, leaving you out . . ."

Michelangelo was aghast.

"But if he is organizing a campaign against me, I must defend myself."

"Surely you need no defense? Here in Florence, where the young painters look to you? Let him talk himself out; in a few days he will tire, it will blow away . . ."

"All right, Raphael, I'll hold my tongue."

It grew increasingly difficult to keep his promise. Perugino had begun what amounted to a crusade. His fury and energy were rising with the passing of time rather than abating. He had lodged complaints not only with the Signoria but with the Boards of the Duomo and Wool Guild.

By February, Michelangelo discovered that Perugino had not been ineffective; he had gained a small group of adherents, the most vociferous of them seventeen-year-old Baccio Bandinelli, son of Florence's most important goldsmith, an aspiring sculptor; and several friends of Leonardo.

He sought out Granacci. Granacci tried to preserve his usual calm.

"They are joining Perugino for various reasons. There was some murmuring when you, a sculptor, got a painter's commission. But for others, the cartoon is a point of departure. If it were conventional, or mediocre, I think they would not care. . . ."

"Then it is . . . jealousy?"

"Envy, perhaps. Of the kind you feel for Leonardo. Surely you should be able to understand that."

Michelangelo flinched. No one but Granacci would have dared say such a thing to him; or have known how true it was.

"I promised Raphael I would say nothing against Perugino. But now I'm going to strike back."

"You must. He's talking to people everywhere he goes: in the streets, the churches . . ."

As a start in his own campaign, Michelangelo went to see the Perugino paintings around town, a Pietà which he remembered from his home church of Santa Croce, a triptych in the convent of the Gesuati, a panel in San Domenico in Fiesole. He saved for last the Servite altarpiece in Santissima Annunziata for which Perugino had painted the Assumption. There was no question that his earlier work had line, brilliance in the use of clear, light color, that his landscapes were attractive; his later work seemed to Michelangelo to be flat, decorative, lacking vigor or perception.

That Sunday he went to the dinner meeting of the Company. The moment he entered Rustici's studio the laughing banter fell away; a feeling of restraint came over the room.

"You don't have to turn your eyes away and fall silent," he cried with a tinge of bitterness. "I didn't start this; I didn't want it."

"È vero," several voices answered. "It is true."

"Nor did I invite Perugino to the Dyers'. He came by himself, then launched into the worst attack I ever heard. You are my judges that I have not answered back."

"We are not blaming you, Michelangelo."

At that moment Perugino entered the studio. Michelangelo gazed at him for a moment, then said, "When one's work is in danger, one must protect himself. I have just studied Perugino's paintings here in Florence. Now I understand why he wishes to destroy me. It is to protect himself." There was a deadly silence in the room. "This I can prove to you," he continued, "canvas by canvas, figure by figure . . ."

"Not in my home," broke in Rustici. "A truce is herewith declared. Either party breaking it will be forcibly ejected."

The truce lasted until the following morning, when Michelangelo learned that Perugino had been so incensed by his statement before the Company that he was going before the Signoria to demand a public hearing on the decency of the Bathers. An adverse vote could mean the cancellation of the contract. His counterattack was harsh, but he could see no alternative. Perugino, he told Florence, had exhausted his talent. His present works were antiquated, still-life figures without anatomy, feeble rearrangements of earlier pictures.

A messenger summoned him to the Signoria: Perugino had accused him of slander. He was suing for damage done to his reputation and earning power. Michelangelo presented himself at Soderini's office at the appointed hour. Perugino was already there, seeming old and tired.

Soderini, pale and constrained behind his broad desk, with his fellow members of the Signoria ranged on either side of him, did not look at Michelangelo when he entered the room. He spoke to Perugino first, determined that Perugino had opened the attack, without provocation other than the sight of the cartoon. He asked Michelangelo if he had made certain charges against Perugino. Michelangelo admitted that he had, but claimed they were made to defend himself. The other members asked questions, then nodded to Soderini. Soderini spoke with considerable sadness.

"Perugino, you did wrong. You attacked Michelangelo without provocation. You attempted to do him and his work personal damage. Michelangelo, you did wrong to belittle Perugino's talent in public, even though you acted in defense of your interests. You have hurt each other. But your Signoria is less concerned with this than it is with the harm you have done Florence. We are famous all over the world as the capital of the arts. So long as I am Gonfaloniere we shall continue to deserve that reputation. We cannot allow our artists to indulge in quarrels that hurt us.

"The Signoria therefore orders that you both apologize; that you shall desist from attacking each other; and that you shall both return to the work from which Florence draws its fame. The case of slander against Michelangelo Buonarroti is dismissed."

Michelangelo walked back to the Dyers' Hall alone, sick with revulsion. He had been vindicated, but he felt hollow inside.

15

It was at this moment that the summons arrived from Giuliano da Sangallo: Pope Julius II wanted Michelangelo to come to Rome at once, and was providing him with a hundred florins travel allowance.

It was a bad time for him to leave, for it was important that he transfer the cartoon to the Signoria wall while the painting was fresh and glowing in his mind, before there could be other outside threats to the project. After that, he had to carve the Apostle Matthew, for he had been living in his home for a considerable time and must start to pay for it.

Yet he wanted desperately to go, to learn what Julius II had in mind, to receive one of those magnificent commissions that only Popes could grant. The aura of good will in which he had lived and worked these past five years had been broken by the Perugino quarrel.

He reported the summons to Gonfaloniere Soderini. Soderini studied Michelangelo's face carefully for what seemed a long time before he spoke.

"One cannot refuse the Pope. If Julius says 'Come!' you must go. His friendship is important to us in Florence."

"And my house . . . the two contracts . . . ?"

"We will hold these things in abeyance until you learn what the Holy Father wants. But remember that the contracts must be honored!"

"I understand, Gonfaloniere."

He walked up to Fiesole to see Contessina, whose baby had died in childbirth, and to ask permission to speak to Cardinal Giovanni in her behalf.

"But I am not a Medici any longer, I am a Ridolfi."

"He is still your brother . . ."

Her eyes, as they rested affectionately on him, still seemed larger than her face. "You are kind, *caro*."

"Have you a message to send to Giovanni?"
Her expression altered only a trifle.
"Tell His Grace that I trust he is enjoying Rome."

Michelangelo had only to enter the Porta del Popolo to see and smell the startling changes. The streets had been washed. Several of the stinking forums had been covered with crushed rock. Gaping walls and abandoned houses had been torn down so that the streets could be widened. The Via Ripetta had been repaved; the swine market cleaned out of the Roman forum. A number of new buildings were under construction.

He found the Sangallos living off the Piazza Scossacavalli, in one of many such palaces belonging to Pope Julius II, rather severely designed on the outside but with a spacious inner court surrounded by octagonal columns. When he was admitted by a liveried footman he found the interior richly hung with Flemish tapestries, the rooms decorated with costly vessels of gold and silver, paintings and antique sculptures.

The palace was teeming with people. A big music room overlooking the courtyard had been converted to a draftsmen's workshop. Here half a dozen young architects who had apprenticed themselves to Sangallo were working on plans for broadening the piazzas, building bridges over the Tiber, constructing new academies, hospitals, churches: the plans originally conceived by Sixtus IV, who had built the Sistine Chapel, neglected by Alexander VI, now revived and expanded by Julius, nephew of Sixtus.

Sangallo appeared twenty years younger than when Michelangelo had last seen him. His oriental mustaches had been trimmed to European length, his hair was immaculately dressed, his clothes of expensive cloth; he exuded the air of a man who was fulfilling himself. Sangallo led him up a broad marble staircase to the family apartment, where he was embraced by Signora Sangallo and their son Francesco.

"I have waited these many months to welcome you to Rome. Now that we have the commission formulated, the Holy Father is eager to see you. I shall go to the Papal palace at once and ask for an appointment for tomorrow morning."

Michelangelo sat down on a fragile antique chair that creaked beneath him.

"Not so fast," he cried. "I still don't know what it is the Pope wants me to carve!"

Sangallo drew up a second fragile chair, sat facing Michelangelo, their knees touching, overcome with excitement.

". . . a tomb. Not a tomb, the Tomb. The Tomb of the World."

". . . a tomb," groaned Michelangelo. "Oh no!"

"You don't understand. This tomb will be more important than the tomb of Mausolus or Asinius Pollio's Memorial, or the mausoleums of Augustus or Hadrian . . ."

"Augustus . . . Hadrian . . . Those are gigantic!"

"So will yours be. Not in architectural size but in sculpture. The Holy Father wants you to carve as many heroic marbles as you can conceive: ten, twenty, thirty! You'll be the first sculptor to have that many sculptured marbles in one place since Phidias did the frieze on the Parthenon. Think of it, Michelangelo, thirty Davids on one tomb! Never has there been such an opportunity for a marble master. This commission makes you the first *statuario* of the world."

Unable to assimilate the words, he said stupidly, "Thirty Davids! What would the Pope want with thirty Davids?"

Sangallo laughed. "I don't blame you for being dumfounded. So was I, as I watched the project grow in the Holy Father's mind. Statues as great as the David, I meant."

"Whose idea was this tomb?"

Sangallo hesitated for a moment before answering. "Whose inception? We evolved it together. The Pope was speaking of ancient tombs, and so I seized the opportunity to suggest that his should be the greatest the world had ever known. He thought that tombs ought to be built after a Pope's death, but I convinced him that such crucial affairs should not be left to the negligent hands of posterity; that only by utilizing his own fine judgment could he be sure to have the monument he deserved. The Holy Father grasped my reasoning at once. . . . And now I must run to the Vatican.''

Michelangelo made his way down the Borgo Vecchio to the Sant'Angelo bridge, crossed and went along the familiar Via Canale to the Via Florida. Every step brought memories of his earlier stay, some of them pleasant, some painful. He pulled up short in front of the Jacopo Galli home; the house seemed strangely shut up. As he knocked on the door he felt uneasy, realizing suddenly that he had not heard from Galli for many months.

He waited a long time in the drawing room, airless, unused, without any of the disarray of books and manuscripts that Galli always left strewn behind him. When Signora Galli entered he saw that she looked badly, with a sallow paleness draining the last of her beauty.

"What has happened, Signora?"

"Jacopo is desperately ill. He has been confined to his bed."

"But what . . . ?"

"This past winter he caught cold. Now his lungs are affected. Dr. Lippi has brought his colleagues, but they do nothing for him."

Michelangelo turned away, gulped. "Could I see him? I bring good news . . ."

"That will help. But I must warn you: do not show sympathy or mention his sickness. Talk only about sculpture."

Jacopo Galli lay beneath warm blankets, his body making only the slightest bulge. The flesh of his face was wasted away, the eyes sunken. They lighted with joy when Michelangelo entered.

"Ah, Michelangelo," he cried, "how good to see you. I have heard wonderful things of your David."

Michelangelo ducked his head deprecatingly, flushed.

"Plenty brings pride," said Galli. "I am happy to see you are still humble, as humble as you can ever be."

"Put not an embroidered crupper on an ass," Michelangelo quoted with a crooked grin.

"If you are in Rome, it can only mean that you have a commission. From the Pope?"

"Yes. Giuliano da Sangallo arranged it."

"What will you carve for His Holiness?"

"A monumental tomb, rich with marbles."

Galli's eyes were amused.

"After the concept of the David, which created a whole new world for sculpture! A tomb! From the greatest tomb hater in Italy."

"But this is to be different: a tomb to hold all the sculptures I can conceive."

"That should be quite a few!"

Was there a touch of twitting in Galli's voice? Michelangelo could not be sure. He asked, "Is His Holiness good to work for? It was he who commissioned the murals in the Sistine . . ."

"Yes, good to work for, providing you don't overemphasize the spiritual, or get him angry. He has an uncontrollable temper. He is a militant Pope, honest, decent: he issued a new constitution a few months ago which will do away with simony. There will be none of the scandals of the Borgias. But there will be more wars. Julius wants an army, which he will command himself, to recapture all of Italy that once belonged to the Church . . ."

"You must conserve your strength, *caro*," said the *signora*. "Michelangelo will learn these things soon enough."

Jacopo Galli fell back on his pillow.

"So he will. But remember, Michelangelo, I am still your manager in Rome. You must let me draw your contract with the Pope, so it will be right . . . ."

"I would not move without you."

That night there was a gathering at Sangallo's: high churchmen, wealthy bankers and traders, some of whom Michelangelo knew from Galli's garden, many of the Florentine colony. Balducci embraced Michelangelo with a shout of joy, arranged for them to meet for dinner at the Trattoria Toscana. The palace was aglow with hundreds of candles in high candelabra. Uniformed servants circulated among the guests with food and wine and sweets. The Sangallos were surrounded by admirers; it was the success for which Giuliano had waited for fifteen years. Even Bramante was there. He had not aged in the five years that had passed; he had the same curls at the base of his bald head, the pale green eyes still danced with laughter, the bull-like neck, muscular shoulders and chest had lost none of their wrestler's power. He seemed to have forgotten their argument in the courtyard of Cardinal Riario's palace. If Bramante were disappointed at the turn of fate that had made Sangallo the architect of Rome, he showed none of it in his manner.

As the last guest left, Sangallo explained, "It wasn't a party. Just our friends coming in. This happens every night. Times have changed, eh?"

Though Julius II hated the very mention of the Borgia name, he was obliged to occupy Alexander VI's rooms because his own quarters were not yet ready. As Sangallo led Michelangelo through the great hall of the Appartamento Borgia, he had time to take in the gold ceilings, silken hangings and oriental carpets, Pinturicchio's colorful murals of landscaped gardens, the enormous throne surrounded by stools and velvet cushions. Beyond was the smaller of the two reception halls, with its large windows framing green gardens and stretches of orange and pine trees as far as Monte Mario.

Sitting on a high, purple-backed throne was Pope Julius II, about him his private secretary, Sigismondo de' Conti, two masters of ceremonies, Paris de Grassis and Johannes Burchard, several cardinals and bishops in full regalia, several men who appeared to be ambassadors, all waiting their turn for a private word with the Pope, who was pouring out an uninterrupted flow of observations, condemnations and detailed instructions.

Michelangelo studied the sixty-two-year-old former Cardinal Giuliano della Rovere who, when deprived of the papacy twelve years before by the Borgia's purchase of the office, had had the courage to issue a proclamation for a council to depose "this false pontiff, betrayer of the Church." The act had forced him into exile in France for ten years; and had set Sangallo to mending church ceilings.

Michelangelo saw before him the first pontiff to wear a beard, a spare figure, lean from abstemious living, once handsome in a strong-featured fashion, but now with deep lines in his face, his beard showing streaks of white. What Michelangelo felt most was the enormous energy, what Sangallo had described on their walk to the Papal palace as Julius' "fiery impetuosity," echoing off the walls and ceiling. "Here is a man," Michelangelo thought, "who has been planning to be Pope for so many years, he will try to accomplish as much in a day as his predecessors have been content to do in a month."

Pope Julius II looked up, saw them standing in the doorway, waved them in. Sangallo knelt, kissed the Pope's ring, introduced Michelangelo, who also knelt and kissed the ring.

"Who is your father?"

"Lodovico Buonarroti-Simoni."

"It is an old Florentine family," Sangallo proffered.

"I have seen your Pietà in St. Peter's. That is where I wish my tomb to be erected."

"Could Your Holiness stipulate where in St. Peter's?"

"In the center," replied Julius coldly.

Michelangelo guessed that he had asked something wrong. The Pope was obviously a blunt man. Michelangelo liked his manner.

"I shall study the basilica. Would you speak, Holy Father, about your wishes for the tomb?"

"That is your task, to give me what I wish."

"And so I shall. But I must build on the foundation of Your Holiness' desires."

This answer pleased Julius. He began speaking in his rough-timbred voice, pouring out plans, ideas, bits of historical data, ambitions for the Church. Michelangelo listened as concenteratedly as he could. Then Julius struck terror into him.

"I desire you to design a frieze of bronzes to go around all four sides of the tomb. Bronze is the best medium for storytelling; through it you can relate the most important episodes of my life."

Michelangelo locked his back teeth, bowing low to conceal the expression on his face, wanting to exclaim, "To tell stories is for those who sing ballads."

16

When the last of the apprentices had left, Michelangelo sat on a stool before a drafting table in Sangallo's converted music room. The house was quiet. Sangallo set before him tablets of the size they had used to sketch Rome, seven years before.

"Tell me if I am correct," said Michelangelo. "First the Pope wants a walk-in tomb. Second, he wants the tomb to suggest that he will have glorified and solidified the Church . . ."

". . . brought art, poetry, scholarship back to Rome. Here are my notebooks on ancient and classical tombs. Here is one of the first, for Mausolus, in 350 B.C., in Asia Minor; here are my drawings of Augustus' and Hadrian's tombs, as described by the historians."

Michelangelo studied the drawings closely.

"Sangallo, in these drawings sculpture is used to decorate the architecture, to ornament a façade. My tomb will use the architectural structure merely to hold my sculptures."

Sangallo stroked his mustaches, seemed surprised to find them so short.

"Design a solid structure first, or your marbles will fall off."

He excused himself. Michelangelo was left alone to pore over the drawings of gods and goddesses, allegorical figures, all overwhelmed by the structural mass. He would keep his tomb smaller, design the sculptures larger, so that they would dwarf the architecture.

It was dawn by the time he put aside his pencils and charcoal. The sunless March morning sifted color into the room as though it were thin gray smoke. He made his way to the bed in the room next to Sangallo's son Francesco, climbed between the icy sheets.

He slept a couple of hours, awoke refreshed and walked to St. Peter's, overjoyed to see that it had been securely counterpropped. He went into the Chapel of the Kings of France to see his Pietà. Strong morning light was coming in from the high windows in the opposite wall, suffusing the faces of Mary and Jesus. The marble was alive with poignancy. Fragments of memory stabbed through him as he ran his finger tips over the two figures, the exquisitely polished marble warm and alive to his touch. How he had worked to achieve this!

He entered the main basilica, gazed at the altar in the center of the transept, under which was the tomb of St. Peter. This was where the Pope wanted his tomb to be. He then walked about the ancient brick building, with its hundred columns of marble and granite forming the five naves, wondering where in this central nave, which was three times as broad as the others and rose to a timbered ceiling, there could be a place for Julius' tomb to join the other ninety-two Popes buried there.

He stopped in to visit with Leo Baglioni and learned that, although Cardinal Riario had missed the papacy, he was as powerful as ever because Julius was his cousin; then he went on to the palace of Cardinal Giovanni de' Medici, near the Pantheon.

Cardinal Giovanni, plumper than ever, the cast in his eye more pronounced, had had good times with Cardinal Rovere while they were both in exile. Now Rovere was Pope Julius II and Giovanni enjoyed his friendship. He was genuinely glad to see Michelangelo, to hear about the David. Giuliano entered the room, a full-grown man now, as handsome as the portraits Michelangelo had seen of Lorenzo's brother, after whom he had been named. And, for the first time that Michelangelo could remember, Cousin Giulio greeted him without hostility. He too was changed; with Piero dead, and Cardinal Giovanni head of the house of Medici, Giulio no longer feared that he would be repudiated.

"Do I have Your Grace's permission to speak of a delicate matter?" Michelangelo asked.

Cardinal Giovanni still did not like delicate matters; they were usually painful. But he granted Michelangelo permission to speak.

"It is about Contessina. She suffers from the poorness of that little house. And almost no one dares visit or help her."

"We are getting money to her."

"If it would be possible, Excellency, to bring her to Rome . . . to her proper place."

A flush rose slowly on Giovanni's cheeks.

"I am touched by your loyalty to our house. You may be sure I have thought of this."

"The Florentine Council must not be offended," added Cousin Giulio. "We are only now becoming friends with Florence again. If we hope to regain the palace, all of the Medici holdings . . ."

Cardinal Giovanni waved a hand at him, lightly.

"All these things will be effected in good time. Thank you for calling, Michelangelo. Come as often as you can."

Giuliano took him to the door. Out of eyeshot of his brother and cousin, he seized his arm affectionately.

"It is good to see you, Michelangelo. And good to hear you plead for my sister. I hope we can all be together again."

He stopped at the Bear Inn, opposite his old rooms, rented an apartment at the rear overlooking the Tiber and the Castel Sant'Angelo, where he could have quiet and privacy, neither being available in the Sangallo palace.

Then he went on to meet Balducci at the Trattoria Toscana. Almost automatically he had slipped into his old routine. He had had a magnificent fulfillment in the David, a public acceptance. He had a house and studio of his own. Yet somehow as he walked the streets, their rough cobblestones not yet reset, he had the strange feeling that nothing had happened. Nothing had changed.

What kind of memorial could he design for Pope Julius II? With nothing to disturb his gaze but the muddy waters of the Tiber, he asked himself, "What do I want to carve? How many large figures can I use? How many smaller? What about the allegories?" The tomb itself did not take him long: thirty-six feet long, twenty-three feet wide, thirty feet high, the ground floor thirteen feet, the first story, which would carry his giant figures, nine feet, the recessed third story, seven feet.

Reading in the Bible he had borrowed from Sangallo, he found a figure vastly different from the David, but a figure that also emerged as a summit of human achievement and represented a model for man to seek in his own life: Moses, symbolizing the maturity of man, even as David represented man's youth. Moses, the leader of his people, the lawgiver, the bringer of order out of chaos, of discipline out of anarchy; yet himself imperfect, capable of anger, of weakness. Here was Lorenzo's half-man, half-god, who had triumphed for humanity, codified for the ages the concept of a single God, helped to create a civilization. He was a loving kind of figure, not a saint, but a loving kind of figure.

Moses would occupy one corner of the first story. For the opposite corner he thought of the Apostle Paul, about whom he had read when carving the saint for the Piccolomini altar. Paul, born a Jew, a well-educated, well-bred Roman citizen and student of the Greek culture, was also a lover of the law. He had heard a voice that said, "I am Jesus, whom thou persecutest," and had devoted his life to carrying the message of Christianity to Greece and Asia Minor, laying the foundations of a Church as widespread as the Roman Empire. These two would dominate the tomb. For other corners he would find equally interesting figures to carve; eight in all, massive in volume, eight feet high though seated.

Since these would be draped figures, he now gave himself the freedom to carve many nudes on the main level: four male Captives on each side of the tomb, with shoulders and heads towering over the columns to which they were bound: sixteen figures of all ages, build, spirit, caught in the anguish of the captured, the enslaved, the crushed, the dying. His excitement rose. There would be figures of Victors too, the uncrushables, the struggling, hoping, fighting, conquering. The tomb would have the scope of the Bathers in the three-dimensional, heroic character of marble.

Julius had asked for a bronze frieze, and Michelangelo would give it to him, but it would be a narrow band, the least part of the structure. The true frieze would be this band of magnificent nudes extending around the four sides of the tomb.

He worked in a fever of exultation for several weeks, nourished by the unending flow of sketches that were born in his brain and brought to life in India ink. He took his portfolio to Sangallo.

"His Holiness won't want a totally naked male tomb," said Sangallo, his smile somewhat forced.

"I was planning to make four allegories. They will be feminine, figures from the Bible, such as Rachel, Ruth, Leah . . ."

Sangallo was studying the architectural plan.

"You're going to have to have a few niches, you know . . ."

"Oh, Sangallo, not niches!"

"Yes. The Holy Father keeps asking what you are going to put in the niches. If, when you submit the design, he doesn't find a single niche on the entire tomb . . . His Holiness is a stubborn man; he gets what he wants, or you get nothing."

"Very well, I'll design niches . . . between each group of bound captives. But I'll make them high, eight or nine feet, and keep the figures well out in front of them: Victories, for example, and female figures. Then we can put angels up on this third level . . ."

"Good, now you're beginning to think the way the Pope does."

But if Sangallo grew more excited with the mounting pile of sketches, Jacopo Galli grew increasingly quiet.

"How many figures will there be in all? Do you intend to set up a studio, with helpers? Who is to carve these cherubs at the feet of the Victories? I remember you told me you couldn't design convincing *putti*, yet I see a good many of them indicated. . . ." He searched Michelangelo's face with sunken, burning eyes. ". . . these angels holding up the Pope's sarcophagus? Do you recall your lamentations about carving angels?"

"These are only rough sketches, to please the Pope, to gain his consent."

He brought Sangallo his latest drawing. The Captives and Victories on the ground level rested on a platform of marble blocks, each richly decorated. Starting from the second story, between the Moses and Paul, was a short pyramid form, an arched temple containing the sarcophagus, and hovering over it, two angels. He had designed the front in detail, indicating that the other three sides would carry out the Pope's concept of having the captured provinces represented as well as his homage to the arts.

By now he had between thirty and forty large sculptures indicated for the tomb, which left relatively little architecture to intrude upon his carvings.

Sangallo was enthralled by the magnitude of his concept.

"It's a colossal mausoleum! Exactly what the Pope envisaged for himself. I'll go immediately to make our appointment with the Holy Father."

Jacopo Galli was furious. Over Signora Galli's protests he called for a servant to get him up, wrap him in warm blankets and help him into the library to study Michelangelo's drawings on the same antique desk where Michelangelo had written his sonnet to Alexander VI. His ill-suppressed anger lent him strength, he again seemed seven feet tall. His voice, grown hoarse during his sickness, was burned clear.

"Even Bregno wouldn't have been this obvious!"

"Why is it obvious?" Michelangelo demanded hotly. "It will give me the chance to carve magnificent nudes, the like of which you've never seen."

Galli cried, "I would be the last to dispute that. But the good figures will be surrounded by so much mediocrity they will be lost. These endless chains of decorative sausages, for instance . . ."

"They're rows of garlands."

"You are going to carve them yourself?"

". . . well, no, I'll be too busy. . . ."

"Are you going to sculpture these angels?"

"I could make the clay models."

"And this figure of the Pope on top? You're going to carve that monstrosity?"

Michelangelo cried, "You're being disloyal."

"The best mirror is an old friend. Why are you intruding a bronze frieze on an all-marble tomb?"

"The Pope wanted it."

"And if the Pope wants you to stand on your head in the Piazza Navona on Shrove Thursday with your buttocks painted purple, you'll do that too?" Galli's manner softened. He said quietly, "*Caro mio,* you will carve a glorious tomb, but not this one! How many actual statues do you have indicated here?"

"About forty."

"Then you are dedicating the rest of your life to this tomb?"

"Why must I?"

"How long did you carve on the Bacchus?"

"One year."

"The Pietà?"

"Two."

"The David?"

"Three."

"Then by the simplest arithmetic, these forty figures on the tombs will take you between forty and a hundred years."

"No." Stubbornly. "I've learned my craft now. I can work fast. Like lightning."

"Fast, or good?"

"Both. Please don't exhaust yourself, my dear friend, I'll be all right."

Jacopo Galli shot him a piercing look.

"Will you? Let's make sure."

He opened a cabinet of the desk, took out a batch of papers tied with a thin leather cord, the name Michelangelo Buonarroti scrawled across the top.

"Here are the three contracts I drew for the Pietà, Piccolomini altar, and the Bruges Madonna. Pick up that pen, we'll write the best clauses from each."

Signora Galli came to his side. "The doctor ordered you not to get out of bed. You must conserve your strength."

Jacopo looked up at his wife with a shy smile, asked, "For what? This may be the last service I can render our young friend, and I cannot in all conscience let him go without it." He turned back to the contracts. "Now, if I know the Pope, he will want the tomb completed immediately. Hold out for ten years, more if you can. As for price, he drives a hard bargain because he wants his money to finance an army. Don't take a scudo less than twenty thousand ducats. . . ."

Michelangelo wrote as Galli dictated from the three earlier contracts. Suddenly Jacopo went deathly pale, began to cough, put the blanket to his mouth. Two servants half carried him back to his bed. He gave Michelangelo a fleeting "Farewell," tried to hide the bloodstained towel, turned his face to the wall.

When he again entered the Appartamento Borgia, Michelangelo was taken aback to find Bramante engaged in animated conversation with the Pope. He felt uneasy; why was Bramante present at this hour appointed for the examination of the tomb drawings? Was he to have a voice in the decision?

He and Sangallo knelt, were graciously received. A chamberlain set a table before Julius, who took the folio of sketches from Michelangelo's hand, spread them eagerly before him.

"Holy Father, if I may presume to explain . . ."

The Pope listened attentively, then brought his hand down sharply on the table. "It is even more imposing than I had dreamed. You have caught my spirit exactly. Bramante, what do you say? Will it not be the most beautiful mausoleum in Rome?"

"In all Christendom, Holy Father," replied Bramante, his green eyes boring into Michelangelo's.

"Buonarroti, Sangallo informs me that you wish to choose the marbles yourself in Carrara."

"Only in the quarries can I be certain of getting perfect blocks, Holy Father."

"Then set out immediately. One thousand ducats will be provided to you by Alamanno Salviati for the purchase of the stones."

There was a moment of silence. Michelangelo asked respectfully, "And for the sculpturing, Your Holiness?"

Bramante raised his eyebrows, threw a glance at Julius which to Michelangelo insinuated, "This stone carver does not consider it a sufficient honor to work in the service of Pope Julius II. He is grasping at this work for profit." The Pope thought for an instant, decreed:

"The Papal Treasurer shall be instructed to pay you ten thousand ducats when the tomb is satisfactorily completed."

Michelangelo gulped, heard Galli's voice crying, "Do not take a scudo less than twenty thousand ducats. Even that will be short pay for a task that will take ten to twenty years."

But how could he bargain with the Holy Father? Demand double what the Pope had offered? Particularly with Bramante standing by, a mocking expression on his face. The thousand ducats the Pope was advancing would barely pay for the major marble blocks and get them transported to Rome. But he wanted to carve these marbles! His need to sculpture had to come first. He shot a swift look at Bramante.

"You are generous, Holy Father. And now may I speak of the time for completion? If I could have a minimum of ten years . . ."

"Impossible!" thundered Julius. "It is my dearest wish to see the tomb completed. I will grant you five years."

Michelangelo felt his heart plummet, the way it did when he had accidentally knocked off a piece of marble. Forty marble carvings in five years! Eight a year! His Moses could not be less than a year's work all by itself. Each of the Captives and Victors should have half a year to a year for full realization, the Apostle Paul . . .

His jaw stiffened with the same obstinacy he had shown to Galli. One could no more bargain with the pontiff over time than over money. He would manage. . . .It was not humanly possible to create the entire tomb with its forty marble figures in five years, Jacopo Galli had been right about that. Then he would simply have to achieve the superhuman. He had inside himself the power of ten ordinary sculptors, of a hundred, if necessary. He would complete the tomb in five years, even if it killed him.

He bowed his head in resignation. "All will be done, Holy Father, as you say. And now that it is arranged, could I presume to ask that the contract be drawn?"

What he heard in response was a peculiar silence. Bramante lowered his head into his bull-like shoulders. Sangallo was stony-faced. The Pope glared. After what seemed to Michelangelo a tortured time, Julius replied:

"Now that everything is arranged, I should like you and Sangallo to visit St. Peter's to determine the proper place for the tomb."

Not a word about the contract. Michelangelo put his left hand across his chest, feeling in his shirt the paper Jacopo Galli had dictated to him.

He kissed the Pope's ring, started for the door. The Pope called, "One moment." He turned, his hopes flaring. "I wish Bramante to accompany you, to give you the benefit of his advice."

There simply was no room in the basilica, and no proper place for so imposing a marble tomb. It was obvious that his sculptures would be crowded in by pillars, without space around them in which to move or breathe. There would be no proper light from the small windows. At best it would be a bulking obstacle, a hindrance to all movement in the basilica.

He went outside, circled toward the rear where he remembered a half-completed structure outside the west apse. Sangallo and Bramante joined him before the six-foot-high brick wall.

"What is this, Sangallo?"

"According to my studies there was an ancient Templum Probi here. Pope Nicholas V had it torn down, and started a Tribune to house a platform for the bishop's throne. He died when the building had reached this height, and it has been left this way ever since."

Michelangelo jumped the wall, paced off the width and length.

"This could be a solution," he exclaimed. "There would be space around the tomb on all sides. We could build the roof at the height we needed, plaster the interior walls to set off the white marble, put in windows for light, break through the wall of the basilica for a square arch . . ."

"It has the prerequisites," Bramante commented.

"No," decreed Sangallo. "It would never be better than a makeshift. The roof would be too high for the width, and the walls would slant inward as they do in the Sistine."

Disappointed, Michelangelo cried, "But, Sangallo, we can't use the basilica!"

"Come with me."

In the surrounding area were a number of ill-assorted buildings, built over the centuries since St. Peter's had first been erected by Constantine in 319; chapels, choirs, altars, a miscellany thrown up in total confusion of whatever material happened to be available: black tufa, cream-colored travertine, dull red brick, peperino speckled with dark lava and white limestone.

"For a tomb as original as the one you are going to create," said Sangallo, "we must have a completely new building. The architecture of the building must be born of the tomb itself."

Hope revived in Michelangelo's bosom.

"I will design it," Sangallo continued. "I can convince His Holiness. Here on this eminence, for example, there is sufficient space if we clear out these wooden structures and a couple of those decaying shrines. It would be visible from the city below."

Michelangelo felt Bramante's eyes boring holes in his back. He spun around. To his surprise, Bramante's eyes were sparkling with approval.

"Then you like the idea, Bramante?" Michelangelo asked.

"Sangallo is completely right. What is needed here is a beautiful new chapel, with all these surrounding impairments swept away."

Sangallo beamed with pleasure. But when Michelangelo turned to Bramante to thank him, he found that the architect's eyes had gone opaque, there was a twitching at one corner of his mouth.

BOOK SEVEN

THE POPE

He had no way of knowing, during his stay in the mountains of Carrara, that his years of grace were over. He returned to Rome in time for Julius' New Year's reception of 1506, and to unload the boats as they arrived at the Ripa Grande, only to find that the war between himself and the Pope had begun. Bramante had persuaded Julius to abandon Sangallo's idea for a separate chapel to house his tomb; instead, a new St. Peter's was to rise on the hill where the chapel was to have gone, the best design to be chosen through public competition. Michelangelo heard of no provision for his tomb. He had spent the Pope's entire thousand ducats for marbles and shipping, but Julius refused to give him more money until he had seen one of the statues carved. When Julius provided him with a house behind the Piazza San Pietro, a papal secretary informed him that he would have to pay several ducats a month for its use.

"Could I wait until I am paid something by the Holy Father before I return his rent money?" he asked caustically.

He went to the docks in a gray January overcast, accompanied by Piero Rosselli, a Livorno muralist who was known as the best preparer of walls for fresco. A peppery, freckle-faced chap who had gone to sea as a youth, Rosselli walked along the quays with a swaying movement as though to accommodate a rolling deck.

"I've fought this current many times in winter," said Rosselli, looking downstream at the swollen Tiber; "it'll be days before a boat can make its way up here."

Back at Sangallo's house, Michelangelo warmed his hands before the library fire while his old friend showed him his finished designs for the new St. Peter's, incorporating the Old Basilica. Sangallo believed that he had overcome the objections of the Sacred College and the public to replacing the original church.

"Then you don't think Bramante has a chance to win the competition?"

"He has talent," replied Sangallo; "his Tempietto in San Pietro in Montorio is a gem. But he has had no experience in building churches."

Francesco Sangallo broke into the room, crying, "Father! They've unearthed a big marble statue in the old palace of Emperor Titus. His Holiness wants you to go at once and supervise excavating it."

A crowd had already gathered in the vineyard behind Santa Maria Maggiore. In a hollow, the bottom half still submerged, gleamed a magnificent bearded head

762

and a torso of tremendous power. Through one arm, and turning around the opposite shoulder, was a serpent; on either side emerged the heads, arms and shoulders of two youths, encircled by the same serpent. Michelangelo's mind flashed back to his first night in Lorenzo's *studiolo*.

"It is the Laocoön," Sangallo cried.

"Of which Pliny wrote!" added Michelangelo.

The carving was over eight feet in height and equally long, an awesome sight. When the news spread through Rome the vineyard and streets and steps of Santa Maria Maggiore became jammed with high church officials, merchants, noblemen, all hoping to acquire the prize. The farmer who owned the land announced that he had sold the statue to a cardinal for four hundred ducats. The Vatican's Master of Ceremonies, Paris de Grassis, offered five hundred. The farmer yielded. Paris de Grassis turned to Sangallo. "His Holiness asks that you bring it to the Papal palace immediately." Then, to Michelangelo, he added, "He requests your attendance this afternoon to examine the block."

The Pope had ordered the Laocoön set up on the closed terrace of the Belvedere pavilion, across a valley and on the hill above the Papal palace.

"I wish you to examine the figures minutely," said Julius, "and tell me if they are truly carved from one block."

Michelangelo began working the statue, front and back, with sharp eyes and sensitive finger tips, finding four vertical junctures where separate pieces of marble had been joined together by the sculptors of Rhodes.

He left the Belvedere, walked to the bank that had been Jacopo Galli's. How different Rome felt without Galli in it; how desperately he needed his friend's counsel now. Baldassare Balducci was the new manager-owner of the bank. His family in Florence had invested in Rome, as had many members of the Florentine colony; Balducci had seized the opportunity to marry the plain-faced daughter of a wealthy Roman family, with a considerable dowry.

"What do you do with your Sundays now, Balducci?"

Balducci flushed. "I spend them with my wife's family."

"Don't you miss the exercise?"

"I still go hunting . . . with a gun. The owner of a bank has to be respectable."

"Che rigorista! I never expected to find you conventional."

Balducci sighed. "You can't grow rich and amuse yourself at the same time. One's youth should be spent on women, his middle years on money, his old age on bowling."

"You've become quite a philosopher. Could you lend me a hundred ducats?"

He stood in the wind-driven rain watching the boat with his marbles struggle to make its way to the docks. Twice the prow went under the whitecaps. It seemed that the boat and its precious cargo would sink to the bottom of the swollen Tiber, carrying with it thirty-four wagonloads of his best quarried marbles. While he stood drenched on the riverbank, the sailors made a last frenzied effort; ropes were thrown from the docks, the boat tied up. The job of unloading in the torrential downpour was nearly impossible. He helped carry ten of the smaller blocks off the bobbing boat which the current whipped away from its lashing several times, but he was unable to move the six-, ten-, and twelve-foot columns until Sangallo came to direct the use of a loading crane.

Dark fell before the job was completed. He lay awake listening to the storm increase in fury. When he reached the docks in the morning he found that the Tiber had overflowed. The Ripa Grande was a marsh. His beautiful marbles were covered with mud and yellow silt. He waded through water up to his knees to clean off the loose debris, remembering the months he had spent in the quarries searching for the purest bed, supervising the cutting of the big blocks from the mountainside, lowering them down the precipitous slopes on cables and rollers, loading them on wagons which took them to the beach, rolling them gently over the sand onto the boats at low tide, all without a chip or crack or stain. And look at them now, after the barest few hours in Rome!

It took three days for the rain to stop and the Tiber to recede from the quay. The Guffatti sons came with the family wagon to carry the marbles to the rear portico of the house. Michelangelo paid them out of the loan from Balducci, then bought a large tarpaulin to cover the blocks, and some used furniture. On the last day of January, surrounded by his wet and stained marbles, he sat down at the plank table and wrote his father a letter, enclosing a note to Argiento, which he asked Lodovico to send on to the farm at Ferrara, where Argiento had gone when the Signoria reclaimed Michelangelo's house until he could resume work for them.

Pending Argiento's arrival, Sangallo recommended an elderly carpenter by the name of Cosimo, with a thin thatch of silver hair and rheumy eyes, who needed lodgings. His cooking tasted of resin and shavings, but Cosimo in a methodical fashion helped Michelangelo build a wooden model of the first two floors of the tomb. Twice a week young Rosselli would go to the fish markets at the Portico of Octavia to buy fresh clams, mussels, shrimp, squid and sea bass, cooking a Livornese *cacciucco,* or fish stew, over Michelangelo's fire. The three men mopped up the spicy orégano sauce with crusts of bread.

To buy a forge, Swedish iron and chestnut wood, it was necessary for him to visit Balducci's bank to borrow another hundred ducats.

"I don't mind making a second loan," said Balducci. "But I do mind your getting deeper into the hole. When do you expect to put this tomb on a businesslike basis?"

"As soon as I have some carving to show Julius. First I must decorate several of the base blocks, to establish models for Argiento and a stonecarver I'm planning to bring from the Duomo workshop. Then I can start massing the Moses . . ."

"But that could take months! What do you intend to live on until then? Be sensible, go to the Pope. From a bad paymaster, get what you can."

He returned home, measured Cosimo's wooden model for the size of the block at the corner of the tomb, then cut a marble to shape, carving a series of three masks, two in profile, a full face below, surrounded by flowing calligraphic lines. That was as far as he got: three structural support blocks. Argiento sent no word in response to his letter. The stonemason from the Duomo workyard could not come. Sangallo did not think it a good time to ask the Pope for money.

"The Holy Father is judging the plans for St. Peter's. The winner is to be announced on March first. At that time I will take you to His Holiness."

But on the first of March the Sangallo palace fell silent. When Michelangelo arrived at the house he found it deserted, not even the draftsmen having come to work. Sangallo, his wife and son were huddled together in an upstairs bedroom as though someone in the family had died.

"How could this have happened?" cried Michelangelo. "You are the Pope's official architect. You are one of his oldest and most loyal friends."

"All I hear is rumor: the Romans around the Pope hate all Florentines, but they are friendly to Urbino, and hence to Bramante. Others say he makes the Holy Father laugh, hunts with him, entertains him . . ."

"Clowns! Do they build great churches?"

"They ingratiate themselves . . ."

"I will get the truth from Leo Baglioni."

Baglioni gazed at him in genuine astonishment. "The truth? Don't you know the truth? Come with me."

Bramante had bought an old palace in the Borgo, close to the Vatican, torn it down and rebuilt it with simple elegance. The house was jammed with important personages of Rome: courtiers from the Vatican, princes of the Church, nobles, professors, artists, merchants, bankers. Bramante held court, the center of all eyes and admiration, his red face beaming, the green eyes crackling with excitement and triumph.

Leo Baglioni steered Michelangelo upstairs to a large workroom. Pinned to the walls and scattered about the worktables were Bramante's drawings for the new St. Peter's. Michelangelo gasped: it was an edifice to dwarf the cathedral of Florence, yet of an elegant, lyrical design, noble in its conception. By comparison Sangallo's Byzantine conception, a dome over a square, seemed ponderous and fortress-like.

Now Michelangelo knew the truth: it had nothing to do with the Romans hating Florentines or Bramante being an entertainer. It had to do with talent. Bramante's St. Peter's was the more beautiful and modern in every aspect.

"I'm sorry for Sangallo's sake," said Baglioni matter-of-factly, "but this was a competition, and there's no doubt in anyone's mind who won it. What would you do, if you were the Pope? Award the commission to a friend and build a church that was outmoded before it began? Or give it to a newcomer, and create the most beautiful church in Christendom?"

Michelangelo did not trust himself to answer. He fled down the steps, out into the Borgo, circled the Leonine Wall until he was drugged with exhaustion. If he, Michelangelo Buonarroti, had been Pope Julius II, he too would have been obliged to choose Bramante's plan. This church, far more than the paved streets and enlarged piazzas, could be the beginning of a new and glorious Rome.

That night, as he lay cold and sleepless in his bed, listening to Cosimo snore as though each breath were his last, it became obvious to him that Bramante, from the moment the Pope had sent him with them to find a proper spot for the tomb, had laid his plans to see that the special chapel would never be built. He had used Sangallo's idea for a separate building, and Michelangelo's grandiose plan for the mausoleum, for his own purpose: the securing of a commission to build a new cathedral.

There was no question but that Bramante's St. Peter's would be a glorious abode for the tomb. But would Bramante allow it in his church? Would he be willing to share credit and attention with Michelangelo Buonarroti?

2

By the middle of March the sun came out. Michelangelo had the Guffatti family set three giant columns upright. Soon he would be ready to remove the negative marble and probe for the Moses and the Captives. On April first it was announced that the Pope and Bramante would lay the cornerstone of the new cathedral on April 18. Paris de Grassis was busy establishing protocol. When the workmen began digging the wide hole which the Pope was to descend to bless the laying of the first stone, Michelangelo saw that the sacred old basilica was not to be included in the new structure, but would be demolished piecemeal to make room for the new church.

He was outspoken in his disapproval. He loved the columns and ancient carvings; he also felt that it was sacrilege to destroy the earliest temple of Christendom in Rome. He spoke of it with whomever he met, until Leo Baglioni warned him that some of Bramante's less savory hangers-on were saying that unless he stopped attacking their friend his tomb might be built before that of the Pope.

"I wouldn't want you turning up in the Tiber, my unpolitic young friend," laughed Leo.

He received a letter from the man who owned the boats in Carrara, advising him that another shipment of marbles would reach the Ripa Grande early in May. Michelangelo would have to make payment at the docks before the marbles could be released. The bill was for more ducats than he had. He washed, went to the

Papal palace. Pope Julius, his bristling beard protruding from a high ermine collar, was in his small throne room surrounded by courtiers. Beside him was his favorite jeweler. Julius turned on the man, cried:

"I do not mean to spend a *baiocco* more for stones, small or great."

Michelangelo waited until the gem cutter had retired and the Pope seemed calmer, then pressed forward.

"Holy Father, the next shipment of your marbles for the tomb are on the way. The boat charges must be paid before I can have them carried home. I am without funds to meet the bill. Could you give me expense money to secure the blocks?"

"Return Monday," said the Pope curtly, and turned away.

Rome was beautiful in the butter-yellow spring sunlight; but Michelangelo walked the streets blindly, a torrent raging in his head. He had been dismissed like the tradesman! Why? Because that was all an artist was, a skilled tradesman? But the Pope had called him the best marble master in all Italy.

He took his story to Baglioni, asking if his friend knew what had caused the change in the Holy Father. Leo had trouble keeping his voice matter-of-fact.

"Bramante has convinced the Pope that it is bad luck to build one's own tomb. That it could hasten the day when it has to be pressed into service."

Michelangelo sank onto a wooden bench, breathing hard.

"What shall I do?"

"Go back on Monday. As though nothing had happened."

He went back on Monday. Then on Tuesday, Wednesday, Thursday. Each time he was admitted, received coolly, told to return. On Friday the guard at the Papal palace refused him entrance. It was hot in the midday sun, but Michelangelo felt cold all over. Thinking there might be some misunderstanding, he again tried to enter the palace. His way was barred. At that moment the Pope's cousin, the Bishop of Lucca, arrived.

"What is the matter with you?" cried the bishop to the guard. "Do you not know Maestro Buonarroti?"

"I know him, Your Grace."

"Then why are you sending him away?"

"Excuse me, Excellency, but I have my orders."

Michelangelo walked home, his shoulders jerking as though in spasms. His brain was on fire. He quickened his pace, without actually running, bolted the door of his house, sat down and scrawled:

> Most Blessed Father, I have been turned out of the palace today by your orders; therefore, if you want me, you must look for me elsewhere than in Rome.

He addressed the letter to Messer Agostino, the Pope's steward, sent a neighboring boy to find Cosimo. The old man came hurrying.

"Cosimo, I must leave Rome tonight. Tomorrow send for a dealer and sell this furniture."

At the second hour of the night he rented a horse at the Porta del Popolo and left with the post for Florence. At the rise north of town, where he had caught his first glimpse of Rome, he turned in the saddle to gaze back at the sleeping city. Into his mind came a favorite Tuscan adage, born of centuries of feuding:

> How much the fool who goes to Rome
> Excels the fool who stays at home.

Early the second day he dropped off his horse at Poggibonsi at the inn where he had stopped on his way to Siena to recarve Torrigiani's St. Francis. He was washing in a bowl near the wall when he heard thunderous hoofs storming up the road. It turned out to be Baglioni at the head of a party of five couriers, their horses lathering at the bit from hard riding. He stood gazing at his fastidious friend's face, covered with dried perspiration, his clothes discolored by the dust of the road.

"Leo! What brings you to Poggibonsi?"

"You! The Holy Father knew we were friends. He ordered me to head the party."

Michelangelo blinked at the five armed men of the Pope's guard sitting their horses and glaring at him.

"What . . . party? I'm on my way home to Florence. . . ."

"No, you're not!" Baglioni dismounted, brushed the hair out of his eyes. He took a parchment from his saddlebag. "This is a letter from Pope Julius. He commands you to return forthwith to Rome under penalty of disgrace. . . ."

"I did not deserve to be driven from his presence."

"All will be set to rights."

"Permit me to doubt."

"I have the Holy Father's word for it."

"The Holy Father has lapses of memory."

A burly horseman asked, "Shall we truss him up, Messer Baglioni? We could sling him over his own saddle."

"I was not instructed to use force. Michelangelo, you're not the first to be kept waiting by a Pope. If Julius says, 'Wait!' you wait, if it takes a week, a month or a year."

"I'm going back to Florence for good."

"Not for good. Nobody leaves the Pope dangling! Upon my oath, the Holy Father is sorry about what happened. He wants you to return and resume work."

"I will not allow any man to treat me as dirt."

"The Pope is not 'any man.' " Leo came close, so the guards could not hear, said, "Bravo! You sound like the Florentine Marzocco. But now that you have asserted your independence, come back. Do not put me in a difficult position."

Michelangelo was silent; Baglioni had always been a good friend. But what about his own self-respect? No one should ask another man to surrender his pride. He told Leo so. Baglioni's face became stern.

"It is not possible to defy the pontiff. You will see. Now or later. And later could be worse. As your friend I urge you not to match your will against his. How could you win?"

Michelangelo lowered his head, crinkled his eyes and studied the pattern of the earth beneath his feet.

"I don't know, Leo. . . . But if I return now I lose everything. I'm going on to Florence to get my house and my contract back. If he wishes it, I'll sculpture the Pope's tomb . . . under the shadow of the Signoria tower."

3

His father was not pleased to see him; he had imagined Michelangelo to be earning large sums from the Pope in Rome. He took over his front room again, set Taddei's Our Lady on a workstand, checked his marble for the Apostle Matthew where it was stored in a Duomo workshed, carried home from the foundry the still unfinished bronze David. His cartoon for the Bathers had been moved from the Dyers' Hall, mounted on a fir-tree frame and attached to the wall of the gallery beyond the Great Hall of the Palazzo della Signoria.

The news of the exchange in the yard of the Poggibonsi inn took only a few hours to make its way over the mountain. When he and Granacci reached Rustici's studio for supper with the Company, he found himself a hero.

"What a tremendous compliment Pope Julius has paid you!" cried Botticelli, who had painted frescoes in the Sistine Chapel for Julius' uncle, Pope Sixtus IV, "to send an armed recovery party after you. When has this ever happened to an artist?"

"Never," growled *Il Cronaca*. "One artist is like another; if he vanishes, there are a dozen to take his place."

"But here is the Pope acknowledging that an artist is an individual," added Rustici excitedly. "With special talents and gifts, not to be found in exactly the same combination in anyone else in the world."

Michelangelo felt more put upon than a hero.

"What else could I have done?" he cried, as Granacci shoved a glass of wine into his hand. "I was barred from the Vatican . . ."

The following morning Michelangelo was awakened to the fact that the Florentine government did not agree with the Company of the Cauldron on the beneficent effects of his revolt. Gonfaloniere Soderini's face was grave when he received Michelangelo in his office.

"I'm apprehensive about what you did. At Rome, as the Pope's sculptor, you could be of considerable help to Florence. Defying him, you become a source of potential danger to us. You're the first Florentine to defy a Pope since Savonarola. I'm afraid your fate will be about the same."

"You mean I'll be hanged from a gibbet in the piazza, and then burned?" He shivered involuntarily.

Soderini smiled for the first time, wobbling the end of his nose.

"You are not guilty of heresy, only of disobedience. But in the end the Pope will have his way."

"Gonfaloniere, all I want to do is settle down in Florence. I'll start carving the St. Matthew tomorrow so that I can have my house back."

Soderini's skin went as yellow-white as his hair.

"Florence cannot renew your sculpture contract now. His Holiness would consider it a personal affront. No one can employ you, not Doni, or Pitti or Taddei, without incurring the Pope's enmity. Not until you complete Julius II's tomb, or the Holy Father releases you."

"Would it embarrass you if I were to complete existing contracts?"

"Finish the David. Our ambassador in Paris keeps writing that the king is irritated with us because we do not send the statue."

"And the Bathers; can I do the fresco?"

Soderini looked up at him. "You have not been in the Great Hall?"

"The groom brought me through your apartment."

"I suggest you go out that way."

He went directly to the east side of the Council platform where Leonardo da Vinci had painted the Battle of Anghiari. The back of his hand swung up to his mouth.

"Dio mio, no!"

The entire lower half of Leonardo's fresco was in ruin, the colors having run as sharply downward as though pulled by powerful magnets: horses, men, spears, trees, rocks, having flowed into each other in an indistinguishable chaos of color.

All the antagonism, the quarrels, the feuds washed away in whatever solvent had destroyed Leonardo's magnificent mural. Michelangelo felt only the deepest regret for a fellow artist who had created mightily for a whole year of his life, only to have the results wiped out. What could have gone wrong? Tuscans had been the masters of fresco for over three hundred years. He felt Soderini at his shoulder.

"Gonfaloniere, how did it happen?"

"Leonardo was determined to revive ancient encaustic painting. He took the recipe for the plaster from Pliny, used wax with a solvent, and then gum to harden the mixture. When he finished, he applied heat by lighting fires on the floor. He said he had tried it on a small mural in Santa Maria Novella, and it had worked well. But this mural is twenty-two feet high, and in order for the heat to reach the upper portion, he had to heap on the fuel. The intense heat on the lower half caused the wax to run . . . and pulled all the colors down with it."

Leonardo lived in the San Giovanni quarter. Michelangelo knocked on the clapper. A servant answered. He was ushered into a large, beam-ceilinged room filled with art works, musical instruments, tapestries, oriental rugs. Leonardo, in a Chinese-red robe, was writing in a notebook at a high ledgerlike desk. He looked up, saw Michelangelo, put the notebook into a drawer and locked it with a key. He came forward, limping markedly from a fall he had sustained in his flying machine on a hill near Fiesole. An edge of his shining beauty had faded from his face, his eyes held a touch of melancholy.

"Leonardo, I've just come from the Signoria. I want you to know how sorry I am about the fresco. I, too, have just wasted a year of my life, so I know what it must mean to you."

"You are kind." Leonardo's voice was cool.

"But that was not my main purpose in coming. I wanted to apologize to you . . . for my crustiness . . . for the wretched things I have said about you, about the statue in Milan . . ."

"You were provoked. I said slighting things about marble carvers."

Leonardo was beginning to thaw. Color had returned to the alabaster skin.

"I saw your cartoon for the Bathers while you were away. It is truly magnificent. I sketched from it, even as I did from your David. It will become a glory of Florence."

"I don't know. I've lost all appetite now that your Battle of Anghiari will not be fought beside mine."

If he had straightened out an enmity, he was endangering his most valuable friendship. Gonfaloniere Soderini sent for him two days later to read to him from a letter from the Pope, demanding that the Signoria return Michelangelo Buonarroti to Rome at once, under pain of pontifical displeasure.

"Looks as if I had better keep going north," replied Michelangelo mournfully; "maybe to France. Then I will no longer be your responsibility."

"You can't run from the Pope. His arm reaches over all Europe."

"Why am I so precious to the Holy Father in Florence? He locked me out in Rome."

"Because in Rome you were an employee who could be ignored. Having repudiated his service, you become the most desirable artist in the world. Don't push him too far."

"I'm not pushing anybody," Michelangelo cried in anguish; "I just want to be let alone."

"Too late. The time for that was before you entered Julius' service."

On the next post he received a letter from Piero Rosselli which made him feel as though the curls over his forehead were dancing on his head like snakes. The Pope did not want him back in Rome to continue work on the marbles; Bramante definitely had the Holy Father convinced that the tomb would hasten his death. His Holiness now wanted Michelangelo to paint the vault of the Sistine Chapel, the ugliest, most clumsy, ill-conceived and God-forsaken piece of architecture in all Italy. He read and reread Rosselli's lines:

> Last Saturday evening, when the Pope was at supper, he called for Bramante and said: "Sangallo is going to Florence tomorrow, and will bring Michelangelo back with him." Bramante answered: "Holy Father, he will not be able to do anything of the kind. I have conversed with Michelangelo, and he has often told me that he would not undertake the chapel, which you wanted to put upon

> him; and that, you notwithstanding, he meant only to apply himself
> to sculpture, and would have nothing to do with painting. Holy
> Father, I do not think he has the courage to attempt the work,
> because he has small experience in painting figures, and these
> will be raised high above the line of vision. That is something
> different from painting on the ground.''
>
> The Pope replied: ''If he does not come, he will do me wrong;
> and so I think that he is sure to return.'' Upon this, I up and gave
> Bramante a sound rating in the Pope's presence, and spoke as I
> believe you would have spoken for me; and for the time he was
> struck dumb, as though he felt that he had made a mistake in
> talking as he did. I proceeded as follows: ''Holy Father, Bramante
> never exchanged a word with Michelangelo, and if what he has
> just said is the truth, I beg you to cut my head off. . . .''

Michelangelo cried aloud, ''Me talk with Bramante? It's a fantastic lie! Why
would he want to tell the Pope such a story?''

The letter threw Michelangelo into deeper turmoil. He could do no work at all.
He set off for Settignano to sit silently and cut building blocks with the Topolinos,
then visited Contessina and Ridolfi. The baby, Niccolò, now five, insisted that he
too be taught how to ''make the marble fly.'' He put in an occasional hour filing
and burnishing the Maréchal bronze, went several times to the Great Hall in a
futile effort to whip up enthusiasm for his fresco. He knew even before Gonfaloniere
Soderini summoned him at the beginning of July that the coming months would be
torn by strong winds from the south. Soderini began reading at once from the Pope's
breve:

> ''Michelangelo the sculptor, who left us without reason, and in
> mere caprice, is afraid, as we are informed, of returning, though
> we for our part are not angry with him, knowing the humors of
> such men of genius. In order then that he may lay aside all anxiety,
> we rely on your loyalty to convince him in our name, that if he
> returns to us, he shall be uninjured and unhurt, retaining our
> apostolic favor in the same measure as he formerly enjoyed it.''

Soderini put the letter down. ''I'm going to have the Cardinal of Pavia write a
letter by his own hand, in which he will promise you safety. Will that satisfy you?''

''No. Last night at the Salviati I met a Florentine merchant by the name of
Tommaso di Tolfo who lives in Turkey. There is a chance for me to go out there
and work for the Sultan.''

His brother Lionardo asked to see him by the brook at the foot of their field in
Settignano. Lionardo sat on the Buonarroti bank, Michelangelo on the Topolino
side, cooling their feet in the narrow creek.

''Michelangelo, I want to help you.''

''In what way?''

''Let me first admit that I made mistakes in the early years. You were right in
following your course. I have seen your Madonna and Child in Bruges. Our brothers
in Rome speak reverently of your Pietà. You have been worshiping God too.
Forgive my trespasses against you.''

''You are forgiven, Lionardo.''

''I must explain to you that the Pope is the viceroy of God on earth. When you
disobey His Holiness you disobey God.''

''Was that true,'' Michelangelo asked, ''when Savonarola fought Alexander VI?''

Lionardo let the black cowl slip forward to mask his eyes. "Savonarola disobeyed. No matter what we think of any one Pope, he is the descendant of St. Peter. If each of us were to judge him, the Church would fall into chaos."

"Popes are men, Lionardo, elected to high office. I have to do what I feel is right."

"You're not afraid that God will punish you?"

Michelangelo looked across the brook at his brother. "Every man's courage is important. I believe God loves independence more than He does servility."

"You must be right," said Lionardo, his head lowered again, "or He would not help you carve such divine marbles."

Lionardo rose, walked up the hill toward the Buonarroti house. Michelangelo climbed the opposite bank to the Topolinos'. From the top of the ridges they turned, waved to each other. They were never to meet again.

The only one who was not frightened for him was Contessina, who was irreverent about Pope Julius. A daughter of one of the ruling dynasties of the world, she had seen her family driven out of the city it had helped make the greatest in Europe, had seen her home sacked by fellow townsmen who had loved and benefited from her family's efforts, had seen her father-in-law hanged from the Signoria, had been exiled for eight years in a peasant's cottage. Her respect for authority was fading.

Her husband did not share these feelings. Ridolfi wanted to get to Rome. Therefore he did not wish to offend the Pope.

"It is with reluctance, Buonarroti, that I must ask you not to come here again. It will be reported to the Pope. The Holy Father, through Cardinal Giovanni, is our last hope. We must not endanger it."

Contessina asked in a constrained voice, "Michelangelo could come here to visit during the years when he risked his position in Florence, but not now, when he is risking your position in Rome?"

"Not my position, Contessina, ours. If the Pope turns against us . . . After all, Buonarroti has a trade; if Florence banishes him he can ply his craft elsewhere. Rome is the only place we have left to go. Our future depends on it, and that of our sons. It is too dangerous."

"Being born into this world is the primary danger," observed Contessina, gazing head on at Michelangelo. "Everything after that is a game of seed cards."

"I will not come again, Messer Ridolfi," said Michelangelo quietly. "You must protect your family. It was thoughtless of me."

4

In late August Julius left Rome with an army of five hundred knights and nobles. He was joined by his nephew, the Duke of Urbino, at Orvieto, and made a bloodless conquest of Perugia. Cardinal Giovanni de' Medici was left in command of the city. The Pope was joined by the Marquis Gonzaga of Mantua with a trained army, crossed the Apennines to avoid Rimini, which was held by hostile Venice; bribed the Cardinal of Rouen out of the eight thousand French troops sent to protect Bologna by offering cardinalate hats to his three nephews; and publicly excommunicated Giovanni Bentivoglio, the ruler of Bologna. The Bolognese drove out Bentivoglio. Julius marched into Bologna.

Yet nothing sufficiently diverting had happened to Pope Julius II to make him forget his errant sculptor. At the Palazzo della Signoria, Soderini, flanked by the other eight members of the Signoria, shouted at Michelangelo as he entered:

"You have tried a bout with the Pope on which the King of France would not have ventured. We do not wish to go to war with the pontiff on your account! The Holy Father wants you to do some works in Bologna. Make up your mind to go!"

Michelangelo knew he was beaten. He had known for weeks, actually, for as the Pope advanced through Umbria, reconquering it for the Papal State, then Emilia, the people on the streets of Florence began turning their heads when he passed. Florence, which had no defense, so desperately needed the Pope's friendship that it had sent hired mercenaries, including Michelangelo's brother Sigismondo, to help him with his conquests. No one wanted the Pope's now swollen and confident army crossing the Apennines to attack. The Signoria, the townspeople, all were determined that he be sent back to the Pope, regardless of the consequences to him.

They were right. Florence came first. He would go to Bologna, make his peace with the Holy Father as best he could. Soderini did not abandon him. He gave Michelangelo a letter to his brother, the Cardinal of Volterra, who was with the Pope:

The bearer of this letter will be Michelangelo, sculptor, who is sent to you in compliance with the request of His Holiness. We assure Your Lordship that he is a good young man, and unique of his art in Italy, perhaps in the world. He is such that, using good words and kind manners, one can obtain everything from him; one must be tender and kind to him, and he will do such things that anyone who sees them will be amazed. Said Michelangelo comes upon my honor.

By now it was November. The streets of Bologna were crowded with courtiers, soldiers, foreigners in colorful costumes who had thronged to the court of the Pope. In the Piazza Maggiore a monk was suspended in a wire cage from the Palazzo del Podestà, having been caught coming out of a house on the Street of the Bordellos.

Michelangelo found a messenger to take his letter of protection to the Cardinal of Volterra, then mounted the steps of San Petronio, gazing in veneration at the Della Quercia Istrian stone sculptures of the Creation of Adam, the Expulsion from Paradise and the Sacrifices of Cain and Abel. How far he was from fulfilling his hope of carving these scenes in free-standing marble! He entered the church, where mass was being said, and was recognized by one of the Pope's body servants from Rome.

"Messer Buonarroti, His Holiness has been waiting impatiently."

The Pope was at dinner in a palace, surrounded by his court of twenty-four cardinals, the generals of his army, the noblemen, knights, princes, perhaps a hundred at dinner in the banner-strewn hall. Michelangelo was escorted the length of the room by a bishop sent by the Cardinal of Volterra, who was ill. Pope Julius looked up, saw him, fell silent. So did the rest of the hall. Michelangelo stood by the side of the Pope's big chair, at the head of the table. The two men glared at each other, their eyes flashing fire. Michelangelo threw his shoulders back, refusing to kneel. The Pope was the first to speak.

"You have delayed long! We have been obliged to come to meet you!"

Michelangelo thought grimly that this was true: the Pope had traveled a good many more miles than he had. He said stubbornly, "Holy Father, I did not deserve the treatment I received in Rome in Easter week."

The silence deepened in the big hall. The bishop, attempting to intervene in Michelangelo's behalf, stepped forward.

"Holiness, one must be indulgent toward this race of artists. They understand nothing, outside their trade, and often lack good manners."

Julius rose from his chair, thundered:

"How dare you say to this man things that I myself would not say? It is you who lack manners!"

The bishop stood dumfounded, unable to move. The Pope gave a signal. Several courtiers seized the terror-stricken prelate and ushered him from the hall with a rain of blows. Having received as close to a public apology as a Pope could proffer, Michelangelo knelt, kissed the Pope's ring, murmured his own regrets. The Pope bestowed his benediction, said, "Come to my camp tomorrow. We will arrange our affairs."

At dusk he sat before a fire in Aldovrandi's library. Aldovrandi, who had been sent as ambassador to Julius on two earlier occasions, and had been appointed by the Pope as a ruling member of the Council of Forty, could not stop chuckling at the happenings in the dining hall. His fair skin and jovial eyes looked as young as Michelangelo remembered them from ten years before.

"You're so much alike," he commented, "you and Julius. You both have a *terribilità*, terrifying awesomeness. I'm sure you are the only one in Christendom who would have thought of reproaching the pontiff after having openly defied him for seven months. No wonder he respects you."

Michelangelo pulled on the steaming mug of hot water flavored with brown sugar that Signora Aldovrandi had brought against the end-of-November cold.

"What do you suppose the Holy Father intends to do with me?"

"Put you to work."

"At what?"

"He'll think of something. You'll stay with us, of course?"

Michelangelo accepted with pleasure. Later as they sat over supper, he asked:

"How is your nephew Marco?"

"Quite well. He has a new girl, one he found in Rimini two summers ago during the *ferragosto,* the mid-August holiday."

"And Clarissa?"

"One of the Bentivoglio uncles . . . adopted her. When he had to flee with Giovanni Bentivoglio, she leased her villa to one of the Pope's courtiers for a handsome rental."

"Would you know where I can find her?"

"I believe in the Via di Mezzo di San Martino. She has an apartment there."

"Would you excuse me?"

Aldovrandi rose, murmured, "Love and a cough cannot be hid."

She stood in the open doorway of the roof penthouse overlooking the Piazza di San Martino, silhouetted against the orange glow of the oil lamps behind her, her face framed in the fur cowl of a woolen robe. They stared at each other in silence, as he and the Pope had, though with a rather different emotion. His mind went back to the first time he had seen her, when she was nineteen, slender, golden-haired, with an undulant softness of manner, her lithe, willowy figure moving with delicate sensuousness, the beauty of her neck and shoulders and bosom recalling Botticelli's Simonetta. Now she was thirty-one, at a lush peak of ripeness, only a little heavier, a little less scintillating. Again he was aware of her magnificent body through every pore of his own. She spoke with the same sibilance of voice that seemed to enter his every orifice, making it difficult for him to separate the words because of the pounding in his ears.

"The last thing I told you was, 'Bologna is on the road to everywhere.' Come in."

She led him into a small sitting room, warmed by two braziers, then turned to him. He slipped his arms inside her fur-lined robe. Her body was warm from the soft fur. He held her to him, kissed her yielding mouth. She murmured:

"When I first said, 'It is natural for us to want each other,' you blushed like a boy."

"Artists know nothing of love. My friend Granacci describes it as a diversion."

"How would you describe it?"

"What I feel for you?"

"Yes."

"As a torrent . . . that hurtles a man's body down through rocky canyons, sweeps him along at flood tide . . ."

"And then?"

". . . I can talk no more. . . ."

The robe came undone, slipped off her shoulders. She raised her arms, released a few pins and the long braids of golden hair fell to her waist. There was no voluptuousness in her movements, but rather the quality he remembered of sweetness, as though love were her natural medium.

Later, they lay in each other's arms under a double cover lined with azure cloth and filled with fine wool.

"The torrent . . . ?" she teased.

". . . and then, washes him out to sea."

"You have found love?"

"Not since you."

"There are available women in Rome."

"Seven thousand. My friend Balducci used to count them every Sunday."

"You did not want them?"

"It is not my kind of love."

"You never showed me my sonnets."

"One was about the silkworm:

> "Were it mine, that shaggy fleece that stays,
> Woven and wrought into a vestment fair,
> Around her beauteous bosom in such bliss!
>
> All through the day she'd clasp me! Would I were
> The shoes that bear her burden! When the ways
> Were wet with rain, her feet I then should kiss!"

She savored the lines.

"How did you know I had a beauteous bosom? You had only seen me clothed."

"You forget my craft."

"And the second sonnet?"

He quoted a few lines from his first agony-wrought stanzas:

> "What joy hath yon glad wreath of flowers that is
> Around her golden hair so deftly twined,
> Each blossom pressing forward from behind,
> As though to be the first her brows to kiss!"

"I have heard that you are a marvelous sculptor; travelers have spoken of your Pietà and David. You are a poet, as well."

"My master, Messer Benivieni, would be pleased to hear you say so."

They ceased talking, were together again. Clarissa murmured in his ear, holding his face down hard against her shoulder and neck, running her hand over the well-developed shoulders, the hard muscled arms like those that he had gone to sketch among the Maiano quarrymen, "To love for love. . . . How wonderful. I had affection for Marco. Bentivoglio wanted only to be entertained. Tomorrow I will go to church to confess my sin, but I do not believe this love to be a sin."

"God invented love. This is beautiful."

"Could the devil be tempting us?"

"The devil is an invention of man."

"There is no evil?"

"Ugliness is evil."

5

He reached Julius' military encampment on the bank of the Reno River, through heavy snows. Julius was reviewing his troops, wrapped in an enormous furred and wadded overcoat up to his chin, on his head a gray woolen hood which covered his ears, forehead and mouth. Apparently Julius did not like the condition of the soldiers, for he was abusing his officers in coarse language, calling them "thieves and villains."

Aldovrandi had told him stories about the Pope: how he had won acclaim from his admirers as "well fitted for the military life" because he spent long hours with his troops in wretched weather, equaling them in enduring hardships, outswearing them, looking like an Old Testament prophet as he stormed up and down his lines, shouting orders, causing the troops to cry, "Holy Father, we look upon you as our commanding officer!" and his detractors to murmur behind their hands, "Holy Father, indeed! Nothing is left of the priest but the frock and the name."

Julius led the way to his tent, hung with warm furs. Courtiers and cardinals gathered about the throne.

"Buonarroti, I have been thinking what I would like you to sculpture for me. A tremendous bronze statue. A portrait in my ceremonial robes and triple crown . . ."

"Bronze!" It was an agonized cry, wrung from his vitals. Had he thought it even remotely possible that the Pope would condemn him to bronze, he would never have returned to Bologna. He protested:

"It is not my trade!"

The peculiarly hushed silence he had heard in the palace dining hall the day before fell among the soldiers and prelates in the tent. The Pope's face flushed with anger.

"We are informed that you created a bronze David for the Maréchal de Gié of France. Is it your trade for him but not for your pontiff?"

"Holiness, I did that piece because I was urged to do it as a service to Florence."

"*Ecco!* You will do this statue as a service to your Pope."

"Holy Father, it is a bad sculpture! It is not completed. I know nothing of casting, finishing . . ."

"*Basta!*" The Pope's face was livid as he roared into a violent temper. "It is not enough that you defy me for seven months, refusing to return to my service! Even now you continue to pit your will against mine. You are incorrigible!"

"Not as a marble carver, Holy Father. Let me return to the blocks, and you will find me the most tractable worker in your service."

"I command you, Buonarroti, to stop issuing ultimatums. You will create a bronze statue of me for San Petronio which Bologna will worship when I return to Rome. Go now, and study the space above the main portal. We will build a niche for you, as large as the space between the portal and the window will allow. You will create as stupendous a bronze as the niche will hold."

Michelangelo knew he was going to have to do this miserable bronze in order to get back to his marbles. Yet perhaps it was no worse a penance than the seven months he had already thrown away in rebellion.

By midafternoon he was back at the Pope's camp.

"How large a statue can you fit there?" Julius demanded.

"For a seated figure, thirteen to fourteen feet."

"How much will it cost?"

"I think I can cast it for one thousand ducats, but it is not my profession, and I do not wish to take the responsibility."

"You shall cast it over and over until it succeeds, and I will give you enough money to make you happy."

"Holy Father, you can only make me happy by promising that if my bronze statue pleases you, you will permit me to resume carving the marble columns. If

Your Holiness would make that promise, I would have twenty fingers with which
to model the bronze.''

"The pontiff does not make bargains!'' cried Julius. "Bring me your drawings
in one week from this hour. Dismissed!''

Humiliated, he made his way back to the Via di Mezzo di San Martino, climbed
the stairs to Clarissa's apartment. Clarissa was dressed in a deep pink silk, with
low neckline and bucket sleeves, a pink velvet girdle around her waist, her hair
caught up in a garland of jeweled threads. She took one look at his pale, crushed
face, kissed him on the sunken bridge of the nose. Feeling returned to his numbed
mind and body.

"Have you eaten today?'' she asked.

"Only crow.''

"There is hot water on the fire. Would you like a bath to relax you?''

"Thank you.''

"You can take it in the kitchen, while I find some food for you. I will wash
your back.''

"I've never had my back washed.''

"Apparently there are a lot of things you have never had.''

"And may never again.''

"You are depressed. What is the bad news from the Pope?''

He told her that the Pope had demanded a bronze almost as large as Leonardo's
enormous equestrian statue in Milan, which could not be cast.

"How long will it take you to make the drawings?''

"To please Julius? An hour . . .''

"Then you have a full week free.''

She poured hot water into a long oval tub, handed him a scented cake of soap.
He dropped his clothes on the kitchen floor, stepped gingerly into the hot water,
then stretched his legs with a sigh of relief.

"Why don't you spend it here, the week,'' said Clarissa, "just the two of us?
No one will know where you are, you will be undisturbed.''

"A whole week to think only of love! Is that possible? Not one thought of clay
or bronze?''

"I am not clay or bronze.''

He reached wet soapy arms up to her. She leaned down.

"All these years I have said the female form was not beautiful to sculpture. I
was wrong. You have the most beautiful body in the world.''

"You once told me that I was flawlessly carved.''

"In pink Crestola marble. I am a good sculptor, but I could never capture you.''

"You have captured me.''

She laughed, a soft musical tone that dissipated the last of the day's humiliation.
"Here, dry yourself before the fire.''

He rubbed his skin hard and red, then Clarissa wrapped him in a second enormous
towel, sat him at a table before a steaming dish of thin sliced veal and *piselli*.

"I must send word to Gianfrancesco Aldovrandi. He invited me to stay with
him.''

She stiffened for a moment, as though confronted with a past that was far gone
from her mind.

"Non importa, cara. He knew I wanted you, ten years ago.''

Her body relaxed, resumed its feline grace. She sat across the table from him,
her face cupped in her hands, her eyes wide as she gazed at him. He ate ravenously.
Content, he pushed his chair back from the table, turned toward the fire to let the
flames lick his hands and face. Clarissa came to sit at his feet, her back against
his shins. The feel of her flesh through her gown burned him more fiercely than
the heat from the logs.

"No other woman has made me want her," he exclaimed. "How can it be explained?"

"Love is not to be explained." She turned, got on her knees, wrapped her long slender arms about his neck. "It is to be enjoyed."

"And to be marveled at," he murmured. He burst into peals of laughter. "I'm sure the Pope didn't mean to do me a kindness, but he has . . . the first."

On the last afternoon of the week, filled with a delicious lassitude, unable to feel any part of his body without a determined effort, oblivious to the cares of the world, he picked up drawing paper, a piece of charcoal, was amused to find he barely had the will to move it across the paper. He remembered the lines from Dante:

> Neither upon down
> Nor under coverlets, men come to fame;
> Without which, he who runs his course of life
> Leaves of himself on earth the selfsame trace
> That smoke leaves in the air, or foam on water.

With an effort he called to mind Julius sitting in the big throne room in the Appartamento Borgia in his long white robes. His fingers started to move. For several hours he drew Julius in a dozen tentative positions before catching a formal pose, with the Pope's left leg extended, the right leg bent inward, resting on a raised base for support, one arm reaching out, perhaps in benediction, the other holding some solid material object. The robes would cover the Pope's feet, so Michelangelo would be casting almost thirteen feet of solid bronze draperies. Two sets of fingers would be exposed, and whatever could be seen of Julius' features under the triple crown.

"What about the Pope's face?" Clarissa asked. "The Holy Father is not going to be happy unless he recognizes himself."

"The only thing I hate worse than making robes is making portraits. As my friend Jacopo Galli used to say, 'After sweet meat comes sour sauce.' "

At the appointed hour he appeared before Julius, sketches in hand. The Pope was delighted.

"You see, Buonarroti, I was right: you can make bronze statues."

"Begging your pardon, Holy Father, this is not bronze, it is charcoal. But I will do my best so that I may return to the marbles in Rome. And now, if you will direct your treasurer to pay out some money to me, I shall buy supplies and begin work."

Julius turned to Messer Carlino, his papal treasurer, and said, "You are to give Buonarroti whatever he needs."

The treasurer, a sallow, thin-lipped man, gave him a hundred ducats from a chest. Michelangelo sent a messenger for Argiento, only a few miles away in Ferrara, and wrote to Manfidi, the new Herald of the Signoria, asking if the two bronze casters Lapo and Lotti, who were employed by the Duomo, could be sent to him in Bologna to help cast the Pope's statue. He offered a liberal wage.

He rented a former carriage house on the Via de' Toschi, Street of the Tuscans, with a high ceiling, stone walls and an uneven orange-colored brick floor. There was a garden with a door at the back, and a walk-in fireplace for cooking. The walls had not felt a drop of paint in a hundred years, but unlike his rooms in Rome they were dry and unstained by watermarks. His next stop was at a used-furniture shop, where he found a Prato marriage bed, ten feet wide. On both sides and at the end was a low footboard which served as bench and chest. The bed came with a canopy, curtains and a striped mattress, old and lumpy, but clean. He also bought a kitchen table, some unpainted wood chairs.

Argiento arrived from Ferrara, explained that he had been unable to leave his brother's farm when Michelangelo called him to Rome in the spring, and set up his kitchen in the fireplace.

"I like to learn about bronze," he told Michelangelo while scrubbing down the walls and then the floor.

Lapo and Lotti arrived two days later, attracted by the offer of a higher wage than they were earning in Florence. Lapo, forty-one years old, considerably smaller than Michelangelo in stature, had such an honest face that Michelangelo put him in charge of all buying of supplies: wax, clay, cloth, brick for the casting ovens. Lotti, who had been trained as a goldsmith in the workshop of Antonio Pollaiuolo, was lean, purple-cheeked, a conscientious craftsman of forty-eight who served as master caster of the Florentine artillery.

The Prato marriage bed proved to be a godsend; after Lapo had bought supplies and Argiento had shopped for food and a few cooking utensils for his kitchen, the hundred ducats were exhausted. The four men slept together in the bed, which at ten feet was wide enough for them to be comfortable. Only Argiento was unhappy, protesting to Michelangelo:

"Everything costs too much! The shops are so crowded with courtiers and priests that a poor man like me isn't waited on."

"Patience, Argiento, I'm going to ask Messer Carlino for more money, then I'll buy you a haircut and a new shirt."

"Not worth it," replied Argiento, who looked like an unsheared sheep; "barbers are charging the double."

Messer Carlino listened to Michelangelo's request with darkly brooding eyes.

"Like most commoners, Buonarroti, you have a mistaken conception of the role of a papal treasurer. My job is not to give money, it is to be resourceful in ways of refusing it."

Michelangelo said doggedly, "I did not ask to make this statue. You heard me say that the bare cost would be a thousand ducats. The Holy Father said to pay me the costs. I cannot set up a bronze caster's workshop without funds."

"What did you do with the first hundred ducats?"

"None of your business. The Pope said he would give me enough money to keep me happy."

"There isn't enough money in the world for that," said Carlino coldly.

Michelangelo lost his temper, called the treasurer an incisive Tuscan name. Carlino winced, bit his underlip.

"Unless you hand over another hundred ducats," continued Michelangelo, "I shall go to the Pope and inform him that you are forcing me to abandon the statue."

"Bring me receipted bills for the first hundred, and written estimates of what you want to spend the second hundred for. I must keep the Pope's books accurately."

"You're like the gardener's dog, that neither eats cabbage himself nor lets anyone else."

A ghostlike smile was transferred quickly from the ledgers of the treasurer's eyes to the till of his lips. "It is my job to make people hate me. Then they return as seldom as possible."

"I'll be back."

Lapo quieted him. "I remember what I spent. I'll write up the bills."

Michelangelo walked through the Piazza Maggiore, then along the side of San Petronio to the open-sided gallery, flanked by the houses of bankers and the University of Bologna, crossed the Borgo Salamo and headed southeast to the Piazza of San Domenico. Inside the church, heavy with incense from a morning service, he went straight to the Dell'Arca marble sarcophagus, smiling to himself as he gazed at his own husky *contadino* boy with the wings of an eagle, ran his hands lovingly over the aged St. Petronius holding the model of Bologna in his arms, the face intelligent, saintly. He leaned down to sniff the clean white crystals of young St. Proculus, with his belted shirt, magnificently corded legs. Suddenly he straightened. The St. Proculus had been broken in two places, awkwardly repaired.

He felt someone staring at him, whirled, saw a man with an egg-shaped head, narrower at the top than at the base, a ragged shirt covering his chest, his bulging arms and shoulders orange-colored with the dust of the Bolognese earth.

"Vincenzo!"

"Welcome back to Bologna."

"You wretch, you made good your promise to break one of the marbles."

"The day it fell I was in the country, making brick. I can prove it."

"You saw to that."

"It could happen again. There are wicked folk who say your statue of the Pope will be melted down the day his soldiers leave Emilia."

Michelangelo blanched. "If I report that to the Holy Father, he will have you drawn and quartered in the public square."

"Me? I am a most devout man! I plan to kneel and cross myself before it. It's other sculptors who make threats."

6

He started work at white heat, driven by a fury to get finished almost before he began. Lapo and Lotti knew what could be cast, advised him on the technical structure of his armature under the wax model, the composition of the enlarged clay. They worked together in the cold carriage room, which Argiento's fire heated only for a radius of a few feet. Come warm weather, he would return to the enclosed courtyard at the rear of San Petronio where he had carved his earlier marble figures. He would need this kind of outdoor space when Lapo and Lotti began building the giant baking oven for the fourteen-foot bronze.

Aldovrandi sent him models, spread the word that those men most closely resembling Pope Julius would be paid a special wage. Michelangelo sketched from light to dark, Argiento cooked and cleaned, Lotti built a small brick oven to test the local metals for fusing, Lapo did the buying, paid off the models.

Tuscans say that the appetite comes while eating; Michelangelo found that craftsmanship comes with working. Though he did not consider clay modeling authentic sculpturing, since it was the art of adding on, he was also learning that there was nothing in his nature which would permit him to do a sleazy job. Much as he detested bronze, he was going to have to make the best bronze statue of the Pope that he could conceivably dig out of himself, even if it took twice as long. The Pope had not done right by him, either in Rome or here in Bologna, but that did not free him from doing right by himself. He would finish this giant bronze so that it brought honor on himself and the Buonarroti name; if it earned him neither the happiness the Pope had promised nor the creative ecstasy that came from carving marble, that was of secondary importance. He was a victim of his own integrity, which forced him to do his best, even when he would have preferred to do nothing at all.

His only joy was Clarissa. Though he often worked after dark, drawing and modeling by candlelight, he managed to steal off a couple of nights a week to spend with her. No matter what hour he arrived there was food by the side of the fire, ready to be heated, pots of hot water for the oval-shaped tub.

'You're not eating very much," she commented when she saw his ribs beginning to arc through the skin. "Is it because Argiento is a bad cook?"

"More because I have been turned away three times by the papal treasurer when I went for money. He says my costs are falsified, yet Lapo puts down every cent he spends . . ."

"Couldn't you come here each night for your supper? Then at least you would have one good meal a day."

She laughed as her words echoed in her ears.

"I have been talking like a wife. In Bologna we have a saying, 'Wives and wind are necessary evils.' "

He put his arms about her, kissed her warm, stirring lips.

"But artists do not marry?" she added.

"An artist lives everywhere. This is the closest I will come."

She returned his kiss. "We will have no more serious talk. In my house I want you to have only happiness."

"You are better at keeping your promises than the Pope."

"I love you. That makes it easier."

"I hope that when he sees himself in fourteen feet of bronze he will be so pleased he too will love me. Only in that way can I get back to my columns."

"Are they so exquisite?"

" 'How fair thou art, my true love, how fair! Eyes soft as doves' eyes, half-seen behind thy veil; the neck rising proudly, nobly adorned; graceful thy breasts as two fauns that feed among the lilies . . . Fair in every part, no fault in all thy fashioning.' So, too, my marble columns. . . ."

Mail from home came irregularly over the Futa Pass. Michelangelo looked forward to news of the family, but mostly he received requests for money. Lodovico had found a farm at Pozzolatico; it was good income property, but a deposit had to be paid right away. If Michelangelo could send five hundred florins, or even three hundred . . . From Buonarroto and Giovansimone, both working at the Strozzi wool shop near the Porta Rossa, there was rarely a letter without the lines, "You promised us a shop. We are tired of working for someone else. We want to make lots of money. . . ."

Muttering to himself, "Me too," Michelangelo wrapped himself in a blanket in the freezing carriage house while his three assistants slept in the Prato bed, and answered the family:

"As soon as I come to Florence, I will set you up in business by yourselves, or with a company, as you wish. I shall try to get money for your deposit on the farm. I think I shall be ready to cast my statue around the middle of Lent; so pray God that it turns out well; for if it does, I think I will be in luck with the Pope. . . ."

He spent hours following Julius about, sketching him in a variety of poses: saying mass, walking in procession, holding court, shouting in anger, laughing uproariously at a courtier's joke, fidgeting in his chair while he received deputations from all over Europe; until at length he knew through his drawing hand every muscle, bone and sinew of the Pope's body beneath his robes. Then he returned to the carriage house to model in wax or clay each characteristic turn and twist.

"Buonarroti, when do I see some work?" the pontiff demanded on Christmas Day, after saying mass in the cathedral. "I do not know how much longer I will keep the court here, I needs must return to Rome. Inform me when you are ready, and I will come to your workshop."

Spurred by this promise, Michelangelo, Lapo, Lotti and Argiento worked day and night, building the thirteen-foot-high armature of wood, then slowly adding on the clay, touch by touch, spatula by spatula, to create the model from which the bronze would be cast. He created the naked figure of the Pope, seated on his big throne, one arm raised, the left leg extended as he had envisaged him in his drawings. He derived keen pleasure from seeing the true figure of Julius emerge before him, vast in size, true in composition, line, mass, movement. He worked huge rolls of linen cloth over a duplicate model that Lotti and Argiento built for him, practicing with mud from the yard as he had with Tiber mud in Rome, to see how best to model the Pope's regal robes without concealing the fiery figure beneath.

Caught up in the heat of his own creation, he worked absorbedly for twenty hours a day, then threw himself on the bed between Argiento and Lotti. In the third week of January he waited on the Pope.

"If Your Holiness would come to my workshop, the model is ready to be approved."

"Excellent! I shall come this afternoon."

"Thank you. And could you bring your treasurer? He seems to think I am building the statue out of Bolognese sausages."

Julius arrived at midafternoon, accompanied by Messer Carlino. Michelangelo had draped a quilt over his one comfortable chair. Here the Pope sat in silence, studying his portrait.

Julius was pleased. He rose, walked around the model several times, commenting on its accuracy and lifelike qualities. Then he stopped in front of the statue, looking perplexedly at his right hand, which was raised in a haughty, almost violent gesture.

"Buonarroti, does this hand intend to bless or curse?"

Michelangelo had to improvise, for this was the Pope's favorite gesture while sitting on his throne ruling the Christian world.

"The right hand lifted, Holy Father, bids the Bolognese be obedient even though you are in Rome."

"And the left hand. What shall it hold?"

"A book?" asked Michelangelo.

"A book?" cried the Pope scornfully. "A sword! I am no scholar. A sword!"

Michelangelo winced.

"Could the Holy Father perhaps be holding in his left hand the keys to the new St. Peter's?"

"*Bravissimo!* We must extract large sums from every church for the building, and the symbol of keys will help us."

Glancing at Carlino, Michelangelo added, "I must buy seven to eight hundred pounds of wax to create the model for the oven. . . ."

The Pope authorized the expenditure and swept out to join his train waiting in the street. Michelangelo sent Lapo to shop for the wax. Lapo returned shortly.

"I cannot get it for less than nine florins and forty soldi a hundred. Better buy it at once, it is a good bargain."

"Go back and tell them that if they will knock off the forty soldi I'll take it."

"No, the Bolognese people would be the last in the world to take a lira off what they ask."

Michelangelo was disturbed by a strange note in Lapo's voice. "It can wait until tomorrow."

When Lapo was occupied Michelangelo said quietly to Argiento, "Go to the same shop and ask the price."

Argiento returned, whispered, "They are asking only eight and a half florins, and I can get off the brokerage charge."

"That's what I thought. Lapo's honest face has made a fool of me! Carlino was right. Here, take the money, get a receipt, and wait for their wagon to deliver."

It was dark by the time the donkey pulled up in front of the carriage house and the men brought in the wrapped bales of wax. When they had gone Michelangelo showed Lapo the bill.

"Lapo, you've been taking a profit from me. On everything you bought."

"Why shouldn't I?" the man demanded without change in expression. "When you pay so little."

"Little? I've given you twenty-seven florins in the last six weeks, far more than you earn at the Duomo."

"But we live so miserably! There isn't enough to eat!"

"You eat what we eat," growled Argiento, his heavy-knuckled fists clenched. "Food's expensive in the markets, the court and the visitors buy it up. If you had stolen less there would have been more for all of us."

"There's food in the restaurants. And wine in the wineshops. And women in the Street of the Bordellos. I would not live the way you live."

"Then return to Florence," said Michelangelo bitterly, "where you live better."

"You're firing me? You can't do that. I've told everybody that I am the artist on the job, and am in favor with the Pope."

"Then you go right back and tell them that you're a liar and a petty thief."

"I'll complain against you to the Signoria. I'll tell Florence what a miser you are. . . ."

"Kindly leave behind the seven florins I advanced you against future work."

"Never! It will be my travel money home."

He began packing his possessions. Lotti came to Michelangelo, said apologetically, "I'm afraid I must go with him."

"But why, Lotti? You have done nothing wrong. We have been friends."

"I admire you, Messer Buonarroti, and I hope I can work for you again sometime. But I came with Lapo, and I must go with him."

That night, alone in their empty, echoing carriage house, Michelangelo and Argiento were unable to eat the *stufato* that Argiento had thrown together. Michelangelo waited until Argiento was asleep in the enormous bed, then went to Aldovrandi's, wrote a full account to the Herald of the Signoria, and one as well to his father. He then walked the deserted streets to Clarissa's, found her asleep. Cold, nervous, shaking inwardly with frustration and rage, he got under the quilts, warmed his body by clasping her to him. But that was all. He was worried and upset, lay wide-eyed. Unhappiness is not the climate for love-making.

7

He lost not only Lapo and Lotti but Clarissa as well.

The Pope announced that he would return to Rome for Lent. This gave Michelangelo only a few weeks in which to perfect the wax model and get the Pope's approval. Without experienced helpers, without a bronze caster to be found in Emilia, it meant that he had to work through the days and weeks with no thought of food, sleep, relaxation. On those rare hours when he could tear himself away he had no time to sit companionably with her, to talk to her, tell her what he was doing. He went only when he could no longer contain his own passion, when hunger for her drove him blindly through the streets, to seize her, possess her, and then to leave at once. This vestigial shred was all that the demands of his job left for love. Clarissa was sad, she gave less of herself each time he came, until she was giving nothing at all, in an act that bore no resemblance to the full sweetness of their early love.

Leaving the apartment one night, he studied his fingers, discolored from the wax. "Clarissa, I'm sorry for the way things are."

She raised, then lowered her hands hopelessly.

"Artists live everywhere . . . and nowhere. You are inside that bronze statue. Bentivoglio has sent a groom from Milan. With a carriage to take me there. . . ."

A few days later the Pope visited the workyard for the last time, approved the model, the hand holding the keys of St. Peter's, the face at once fierce and benign. Julius liked this image of himself, gave Michelangelo his benediction, as well as an order on Antonmaria da Lignano, a Bolognese banker, to continue paying his costs.

"Farewell, Buonarroti, I shall see you in Rome."

Hope flared in Michelangelo. "Then we will continue on the tomb . . . I mean the marbles?"

"Only God can predict the future," replied the pontiff loftily.

Desperately needing a bronze caster, he wrote again to the Herald in Florence, asking him to send Master Bernardino, the best in Tuscany. The Herald wrote that Master Bernardino was not available. Michelangelo scoured the countryside until he found a French cannon maker who agreed to come, build the big oven and cast his statue. He returned to Bologna to wait. The Frenchman never arrived. He wrote again to the Herald in Florence. This time Master Bernardino agreed to come, but it would be weeks before he could finish his tasks in Florence.

Unseasonal heat struck early in March, killing the spring crops. Bologna the Fat became Bologna the Lean. The plague followed, invading forty families within a few days. Those who dropped in the streets were left exposed, no one daring to touch the bodies. Michelangelo and Argiento moved their workshop out of the carriage house and into the yard at the side of San Petronio, where there was an occasional breath of air.

Master Bernardino arrived in a blaze of May heat. He approved the wax model, built a tremendous brick oven in the center of the courtyard. There followed weeks of experimenting with the fires, testing the way the metals fused, making an enclosing envelope of ash, earth, horse manure and hair, applying them layer by layer, and enclosing the wax to the width of half a span. Michelangelo was filled with impatience to cast, and go home.

"We must not hurry," Bernardino warned him. "One untested step, and all our work will be for nothing."

He must not hurry; but it was already more than two years since he had entered the employ of Pope Julius. He had lost his house, his years, and he had not been able to save a single scudo. As far as he could gather he was the only one who did not profit from his contact with a Pope. He read again the letter that had arrived from his father that morning, crying for money for another wonderful opportunity to invest. The details Lodovico dared not write, they had to be kept secret for fear someone might steal them; but he had to have two hundred florins immediately or he would lose the great bargain, and he would never forgive Michelangelo for his stinginess.

Feeling put upon by both his Holy Father and his earthly father, Michelangelo went to the bank of Antonmaria da Lignano. He set down the figures and details of his two barren years in Julius' service, his urgent need. The banker was sympathetic.

"The Pope has only authorized me to pay out money as you need supplies. But tranquillity is an important supply too, for an artist. Suppose we compromise: I'll advance you one hundred florins against future needs, and you can send the money home today."

Aldovrandi came frequently to watch the preparations. "This bronze of yours is going to make me a rich man," he commented, wiping his brow as the testing of the oven turned the workyard into an inferno.

"How so?"

"Bologna is betting that your statue is too large to cast. Giving good odds. I'm taking all bets."

"It will cast," replied Michelangelo grimly. "I have watched Master Bernardino step by step. He could make bronze without fire."

But when they finally poured in June, something went wrong. The statue came out well as far as the waist; the rest of the material, nearly half of the metal, remained in the furnace. It did not fuse. In order to take it out it was necessary to dismantle the furnace. Aghast, Michelangelo cried:

"What could have gone wrong?"

"I don't know. This has never happened to me before." Bernardino was as wretched as Michelangelo. "There must have been something wrong with the second half of the copper and brass. I'm so ashamed."

Hoarsely, Michelangelo replied, "You are a good artisan, and you put your heart into the work. But he who works, at times fails."

"I feel ill. I'll start again tomorrow morning."

Bologna, like Florence and Rome, had its system of instantaneous communication. In a flash it was all over town that Michelangelo had failed to cast the pontiff's statue. Crowds started to pour into the courtyard to see for themselves. Among them was Vincenzo, who slapped the still warm bricks of the furnace triumphantly and cried:

"Only a Bolognese knows how to use Bologna brick. Or make Bolognese statues. Back to Florence, puny one."

Michelangelo whirled around to pick up an iron bar. Aldovrandi arrived in time to intervene, curtly ordered Vincenzo from the yard, then cleared the others out.

"How serious is the failure, Michelangelo?"

"Only half. As soon as we can rebuild the furnace we'll be able to pour into the mold from the top again. If the metal fuses we'll be all right."

"You'll make it next time."

When Bernardino entered the courtyard in the morning his face was green.

"What a cruel city this is! They think they have gained a victory because of our failure."

"They don't like Florentines, and I guess they don't like the Pope either. If we fail we kill two birds with one bronze."

"I can't raise my eyes in the streets."

"Let us live here in the courtyard until we can pour again."

Bernardino worked heroically, night and day, rebuilt the furnace, tested the channels to the mold, experimented with the metals that had not fused. Finally, under the blinding heat of the mid-July sun, he poured again. Slowly, as they nervously waited, the heated metal began to run from the furnace to the mold. With that, Bernardino said:

"There's nothing more you need me for. I leave for Florence at dawn."

"But don't you want to see how the statue comes out? Whether the two halves join well? Then you can laugh in the faces of the Bolognese."

Bernardino wearily pushed the thought aside. "I don't want revenge. Only escape. If you'll pay me what you owe me I'll be gone."

Michelangelo was left to discover the results himself. He had to sit on his hands for three weeks, while the country burned up in a drought and Argiento could find fewer fruits and vegetables in the market, until the mold cooled sufficiently for him to tear it down.

Bernardino had done his job. The two halves of the statue were joined without a serious mark. The bronze was red and rough, but there were no imperfections. "A few weeks of filing and polishing," Michelangelo thought, "and I, too, will be on my way."

He had misgauged the task. August, September, October went by, water became almost unavailable at any price, while he and Argiento went through the hateful manual labor, neither of them understanding the nature of bronze, their nostrils filled with the filings and scrapings, seemingly condemned to an eternity of cleaning up the tremendous statue.

Finally in November the bronze was finished, rubbed down to a shiny dark tone. It was a full year since he had come to Bologna. Michelangelo went to Antonmaria to ask him for a final inspection and dismissal. The banker was delighted with the result.

"You have surpassed the Holy Father's greatest hopes."

"I leave it in your care."

"You can't do that."

"Why not?"

"I have received an order from the Pope saying that you must install it properly on the façade of San Petronio."

"But my agreement says that I may leave it where I finish it."

"The Pope's latest order is the one to be obeyed."

"Does the Holy Father say that I am to be paid?"

"No. Only that you are to install."

No one quite knew why there were delays: the ledge was not yet finished; it had to be painted; the Christmas holidays were approaching; then the Epiphany. . . . Argiento decided to return to his brother's farm. As he bade Michelangelo good-by there was a puzzled expression on his face.

"An artist is like a *contadino;* his chief harvest is trouble."

He was not killing time, time was killing him. He rolled the full width of the Prato bed burning with marble fever, aching to have hammer and chisel in his hands, to be tearing through the white crystalline stone with the sweet acrid dust caking in his nostrils; his loins swollen and throbbing for Clarissa, longing to possess her; the two acts mystically cojoining in a continuous "Go."

At last a crew came, after the middle of February, to move the statue under its protective cloth to the front of San Petronio. Bells rang all over the city. The statue was hoisted into the niche, over the Della Quercia portal. The whole city assembled in the Piazza Maggiore, listening to the fifes, trumpets and drums. At the hour which the astrologers had told Julius was propitious, three in the afternoon, the covering was removed from the statue. The crowd cheered, then fell to its knees and crossed itself. That evening there were fireworks in the square.

Michelangelo, standing in his worn workman's shirt at the far end of the piazza, went unnoticed. Looking up at Julius in his niche, illuminated by shooting rockets, he felt nothing. Not even relief. He was dry, barren, used up, too exhausted from the long, senseless wait and waste to wonder if at long last he had bought his freedom.

He walked the streets of Bologna all night, hardly knowing where he was. There was a cold drizzle. He had exactly four and a half florins left. At dawn he knocked at Aldovrandi's door to bid his friend good-by. Aldovrandi loaned him a horse, as he had eleven years before.

Only a little way into the foothills the rain began to fall in torrents. It rained all the way into Florence, the horse's hoofs slopping through the wet earth. The road seemed endless. His hands loosened on the reins, his head began to spin, exhaustion overtook him . . . until he lost consciousness, fell off the horse and struck his head on the roadbed.

8

"My dear Michelagnolo," said Gonfaloniere Soderini, "it seems to me that you are more often covered with mud than with capon broth."

He sat back, let the brittle early March sunlight stream over his face. Michelangelo had learned in the several days since his return to Florence that Soderini had good reason to be satisfied with himself: through his brilliant roving ambassador, Niccolò Machiavelli, whom he had been training in the same manner that Lorenzo de' Medici had trained him, Florence had concluded a series of amiable treaties which should enable the city-state to live in peace and prosperity.

"All reports from Bologna and the Vatican tell us that Julius is delighted. . . ."

"Gonfaloniere, the five years I spent carving the David, the Bruges Madonna and the tondos were the happiest of my life. I hunger for only one thing: to carve marble."

Soderini leaned across the desk, his eyes sparkling.

"The Signoria knows how to express its gratitude. I am empowered to offer you a fine commission: a gigantic Hercules, to match your David. With one of your figures on either side of the main gate to the Palazzo della Signoria, ours will be the noblest entrance to a city-state government in the world."

Michelangelo drew in his breath. A giant Hercules! Representing all that was the strongest and finest of the classical culture of Greece. *Il Magnifico* had made Florence the Athens of the West; here was an opportunity to establish the connecting link between Pericles and Lorenzo, to follow through his early experiments with a Hercules. He shook with excitement.

"Can I have my house back? And my studio to carve the Hercules in?"

"It's rented now, but the lease expires soon. I will charge you eight florins a month rental. When you begin carving the Apostles, the house will become yours again."

Michelangelo sat down, suddenly weak.

"This is where I will live and carve all the rest of my life. May God hear my words."

Soderini asked anxiously, "What about Rome, and the tomb marbles?"

"I've written to Sangallo. He has made it clear to the Pope that I will go back to Rome only to revise my agreement and bring the marble columns back to Florence. I will work them all together: Moses, Hercules, St. Matthew, the Captives . . ."

His voice was full of the joy he felt inside himself. Soderini gazed over his wife's red geraniums to the roofs of Florence.

"It is not part of my job to interfere in family life, but the time has come for you to secure your freedom from your father. I want him to go with you to a notary and sign a legal emancipation. Up to now the money you have earned has been legally his. After your emancipation it will belong to you, and you can control it. What you give to your father then will be a gift, not an obligation."

Michelangelo was silent. He knew all of his father's failings yet he loved him, shared Lodovico's pride in the family name, the desire to rebuild its place in Tuscan society. He shook his head, slowly.

"It would do no good, Gonfaloniere. I would have to turn over the money to him anyway, even if it were mine."

Soderini persisted. "I shall make an appointment with the notary. Now, about the marble for the Hercules . . ."

"Could I select at Carrara?"

"I will write to Cuccarello, the quarry owner, telling him that you are to have the biggest and purest block ever quarried in the Apuan Alps."

Lodovico was heartbroken at being obliged to appear before the notary, Ser Giovanni da Romena, for under Tuscan law an unmarried son became free only at the death of his father. There were tears in Lodovico's eyes as they walked home, past the ancient church of San Firenze, and up the Via del Proconsolo.

"Michelangelo, you won't abandon us now? You promised Buonarroto and Giovansimone that you would set them up in a shop. We need to buy several more farms, to build our income . . ."

Because of a few lines on paper Michelangelo's relationship with his father had been reversed. Now he was the one in authority; he could no longer be badgered or driven. Yet, glancing out of the corner of his eyes, he saw that sixty-four-year-old Lodovico had aged ten years in the ten-minute legal ceremony; his head was bowed, his shoulders hunched.

"I will always do everything in my power for the family, Father. What else have I? My work and my family."

He renewed his friendships at the Company of the Cauldron. Rosselli had died, Botticelli was too ill to attend, and so younger members had been elected, including Ridolfo Ghirlandaio, Sebastiano da Sangallo, Franciabigio, Jacopo Sansovino, Andrea del Sarto, a talented painter. He was delighted with Granacci, who had completed two works that had absorbed him for several years: a Madonna with Infant St. John, and St. John the Evangelist at Patmos.

"Granacci, you acknowledged scoundrel! These are glorious. The color is beautiful, the figures fine. I always told you that you would become a great painter, if you worked at it."

Granacci flushed. "What do you say we have a party at the villa tonight? I'll invite the Company."

"How is Vermiglia?"

"Vermiglia? Married. To a clerk in Pistoia. She wanted to start a family. I gave her a dowry. I have a new girl: hair redder than Tedesco's, plump as a partridge . . ."

He learned that Contessina's lot was considerably better now; with the growing popularity and importance of Cardinal Giovanni in Rome, the Signoria had permitted the Ridolfi family to move up the hill to the main villa, far more commodious and comfortable. Cardinal Giovanni sent the supplies and money they needed. Contessina was permitted to come into Florence whenever she wished, but not Ridolfi. She would have been permitted to join her brother in Rome, but since Ridolfi was still an avowed enemy of the Republic the Signoria was not willing to let him out of its earshot.

She caught him flat-footedly gazing at his David.

"It is still good? You have not worn out your pleasure in it?"

He whirled at the sound of her voice, found himself gazing into the piercing brown eyes that had always been able to stab through his thoughts. She had high color in her cheeks from the walk in the brisk March air; her figure had filled out; she was growing a little matronly.

"Contessina! How well you look. It is good to see you."

"How was Bologna?"

"Dante's Inferno."

"All of it?"

Though her question was innocently asked, he flushed to the curls brushed down over his square brow.

"What was her name?"

"Clarissa."

"Why did you leave her?"

"She left me."

"Why didn't you follow?"

"I had no carriage."

"Then you have known love, some portion of it?" she asked seriously.

"In full measure."

Tears flooded her eyes.

"Permit me to envy you," she whispered, and was gone, walking quickly out the piazza before he could follow her.

Gonfaloniere Soderini advanced him two hundred florins against future work. He went to see young Lorenzo Strozzi, whom he had known since his family bought the Hercules. Lorenzo Strozzi had married Lucrezia Rucellai, daughter of *Il Magnifico's* sister Nannina, and of Michelangelo's cousin, Bernardo Rucellai. Michelangelo asked Strozzi if he could invest a modest sum in his brothers' names, so that they might begin to share in the profits of the shop.

"If the arrangement works well, Messer Strozzi, I could keep building the fund as I accumulate money, so that my brothers will earn more."

"That will be agreeable to my family, Buonarroti. And if at any time you wish your brothers to open an independent shop, we will provide them with the wool from our looms in Prato."

He walked to the Duomo workyard, was raucously welcomed by Beppe and his stonehewers. Only Lapo turned away.

"You want me to build another shop for you?" Beppe cackled toothlessly.

"Not yet, Beppe, not until I go to Carrara and find a block for the Hercules. But if you would help me move the St. Matthew so I won't be in your way . . ."

He had chosen St. Matthew because his was the first gospel in the New Testament, and because Matthew had not met a violent end. His early sketches of Matthew had envisaged him as a tranquil scholar, book in one hand, chin held reflectively in the other. Though he had broken into the front wall of the block, uncertainty had kept him from probing further. Now he understood why; he could find no historical Matthew. His was not the first gospel written, for he had absorbed much of Mark; he was said to have been close to Jesus, yet he had not written his gospel until fifty to seventy years after Christ's death. . . .

He took his problem to Prior Bichiellini. The prior's deep blue eyes had grown larger behind his magnifying lenses as his face shrank with age.

"Everything about St. Matthew is disputed," he murmured in the quiet library. "Was he Levi, a tax collector in the service of Herod Antipas? Perhaps, perhaps not. The sole reference to him outside the New Testament is in Greek, and in error; it says that Matthew composed the Oracles in the Hebrew language. But they were written in Greek, for Greek-speaking Jews, to prove to them that Jesus was several times predicted in the Old Testament."

"What am I to do, Father?"

"You must create your own Matthew, even as you created your own David and Pietà. Walk away from the books; the wisdom lies in you. Whatever you carve about Matthew will be the truth."

Michelangelo smiled as he shook his head up and down. "Father, your words are kind; no one has ever had so much faith in me."

He started over again, searching for a Matthew who would symbolize man in his tortuous quest for God. Could he carve Matthew in an upward spiraling movement, trying to break his way out of the marble block, even as man had struggled to release himself from the stone mountain of polytheism in which he had lain enchained? He designed Matthew's left knee to push forcibly against the stone, as though striving to release the torso from its imprisoning cowl, arms held close, head twisted agonizingly away from the body, searching for a way of escape.

At last he was back in the column, feeling whole again, and a master, the fierceness of his joy sending the chisel through the block like lightning through cumulus clouds. He carved in a heat as great as that of the forge in which his tools were tempered; the marble and the flesh of Matthew became one, with Matthew projecting out of the block by the sheer force of his will, to achieve a soul with which to rise to God. Did not every man strive to emerge from the womb to achieve immortality?

Thirsting for a more lyrical mood, he returned to Taddei's Our Lady, carving the round frame, the serene, lovely face of Mary, the textured skin of the infant Jesus stretched across his mother's lap. Then came word from Pope Julius that Florence was to celebrate a Jubilee of Guilt and Punishment in order to raise funds with which to build the new St. Peter's.

"I have been put in charge of the decorations," announced Granacci gleefully.

"Granacci, you're not going back to theater scenery again, after those fine paintings? It's a waste of your talent. I protest."

"My talent has plenty of time," said Granacci. "A man should have some fun."

A Jubilee to pay for Bramante's church would be no fun for Michelangelo. It was scheduled for April. He vowed to flee the city and spend the days with the Topolinos. Again the Pope interfered with his plans.

"We have just received a *breve* from Pope Julius," said Soderini. "You see, it was sealed with the Fisherman's ring. He asks you to come to Rome. He has good news for you."

"That can only mean he is going to let me carve again."

"You will go?"

"Tomorrow. Sangallo wrote that my second shipload of marbles has been lying exposed in the Piazza San Pietro. I want to rescue them."

9

His eyes bulged when he saw the marbles dumped like a cord of firewood, discolored by rain and dust. Giuliano da Sangallo gripped his arm.

"The Holy Father is waiting for you."

They passed through the smaller of the throne rooms of the Papal palace, filled with a variety of supplicants hoping for an audience. Once in the large throne room, he advanced toward the throne, bowing to Cardinal Giovanni de' Medici, nodding formally to Cardinal Riario. Pope Julius caught sight of him, suspended a conversation with his nephew Francesco, Prefect of Rome, and Paris de Grassis. Julius was dressed in a white linen cassock, his pleated knee-length tunic had tight sleeves, while the elbow-length scarlet velvet cape was trimmed in ermine, as was the scarlet velvet skullcap.

"Ah, Buonarroti, you have returned to us. You are pleased with the statue in Bologna, are you not?"

"It will bring honor on us."

'You see," cried Julius triumphantly, throwing out his arms energetically to include the entire room. "You had no confidence in yourself. When I made this splendid opportunity available to you, you cried out, '"It is not my trade!" The Pope's mimicking of Michelangelo's slightly hoarse voice brought appreciative laughter from the court. "Now you see how you have made it your trade, by creating a fine bronze."

"You are generous, Holy Father," murmured Michelangelo with a twinge of impatience, his mind occupied with the pile of stained marbles lying just a few hundred yards away.

"I intend to continue being generous," cried the Pope heartily. "I am going to favor you above all the painting masters of Italy."

". . . 'painting' masters?"

"Yes. I have decided that you are the best artist to complete the work begun by your countrymen Botticelli, Ghirlandaio, Rosselli, whom I myself hired to paint the frieze in the Sistine Chapel. I am commissioning you to complete my uncle Sixtus' chapel by painting the ceiling."

There was a light patter of applause. Michelangelo was stunned. Nausea gripped him. He had asked Sangallo to make it clear to the Pope that he would return to Rome only to begin carving on the sculptures for the tomb. He cried passionately:

"I am a sculptor, not a painter!"

Julius shook his head in despair.

"I had less trouble conquering Perugia and Bologna than I have in subduing you!"

"I am not a Papal State, Holy Father. Why should you waste your precious time subduing me?"

The room went silent. The Pope glared at him, thrust out his bearded chin, demanded icily, "Where did you have your religious training, that you dare to question your pontiff's judgment?"

"As your prelate said in Bologna, Holiness, I am but an ignorant artist, without good manners."

"Then you can carve your masterpiece in a cell of Sant'Angelo."

All Julius had to do was wave a hand at a guard, and he could rot in a dungeon for years. He gritted his teeth.

"That would bring you little honor. Marble is my profession. Let me carve the Moses, Victors, Captives. Many would come to see the statues, offering thanks to Your Holiness for making them possible."

"In short," snapped Julius, "I need your sculptures to assure my place in history."

"They could help, Holy Father."

There was an audible gasp from those around the throne. The Pope turned to his cardinals and courtiers.

"Do you hear that, gentlemen? I, Julius II, who recovered the long-lost Papal States for the Church and brought stability to Italy, who have cleaned out the scandals of the Borgias, published a constitution abolishing simony and elevated the decorum of the Sacred College, achieved a modern architecture for Rome . . . I need Michelangelo Buonarroti to establish my historical position."

Sangallo had gone deathly pale. Cardinal Giovanni stared out a window as though he were not there. The Pope loosened the collar of his cape against his own warmth, took a deep breath and started again.

"Buonarroti, my informants in Florence describe your panel for the Signoria as 'the school of the world' . . ."

"Holiness," interrupted Michelangelo, cursing himself for his envy of Leonardo that had led him into this trap, "it was an accident, something that could never be repeated. The Great Hall needed an accompanying fresco for the other half of the wall. . . . It was a diversion."

"*Bene*. Make such a diversion for the Sistine. Are we to understand that you will paint a wall for a Florentine hall, but not a ceiling for a papal chapel?"

The silence in the room was crushing. An armed courtier, standing by the Pope's side, said, "Your Holiness, give me the word and we will hang this presumptuous Florentine from the Torre di Nona."

The Pope glowered at Michelangelo, who stood before him defiant but speechless. Their eyes met, held in an exchange of immovability. Then a wisp of a smile drifted across the pontiff's face, was reflected in the tiny amber sparkle of Michelangelo's eyes, the barest twitching of his lips.

"This presumptuous Florentine, as you call him," said the Pope, "was described ten years ago by Jacopo Galli as the best sculpture master in Italy. So he is. If I had wanted him fed to the ravens I would have done so long ago."

He turned back to Michelangelo, said in the tone of an exasperated but fond father:

"Buonarroti, you will paint the Twelve Apostles on the ceiling of the Sistine, and decorate the vault with customary designs. For this we will pay you three thousand large gold ducats. We shall also be pleased to pay the expenses and wages of any five assistants you may choose. When the Sistine vault is completed, you have your pontiff's promise that you shall return to the carving of the marbles. My son, you are dismissed."

What further word could he say? He had been proclaimed supreme among his country's artists, made a promise that he would resume work on the tomb. Where could he flee? To Florence? To have Gonfaloniere Soderini cry out, "We cannot go to war with the Vatican because of you." To Spain, Portugal, Germany England . . . ? The Pope's power reached everywhere. The Pope demanded much, but a lesser pontiff might well have excommunicated him. And if he had refused to come back to Rome? He had tried that too, for a barren seven months in Florence. There was nothing to do but submit.

He kneeled, kissed the Pope's ring.

"It shall be as the Holy Father desires."

Later, he stood by the front entrance of the Sistine Chapel, his mind aswirl with revulsion and self-incrimination. Sangallo was just behind him, his face haggard, looking as though he had been whipped.

"I did this to you. I persuaded the Pope to build himself a triumphal tomb, and to call you here to sculpture it. All you have had is grief. . . ."

"You tried to help me."

"I could not have controlled the Pope. No. But I could have been more realistic about Bramante. Come to grips with his . . . charm . . . his talent. . . . Because of him I am no longer an architect and you are no longer a sculptor."

Sangallo wept. Michelangelo shepherded him inside the protective doorway of the chapel, put an arm about the trembling shoulders.

"Pazienza, caro, patience. We will work our way out of this predicament."

"You are young, Michelangelo, you have time. I am old. Nor have you heard the crowning indignity. I volunteered to erect the scaffolding for you, since I renovated the chapel and know it well. But even this I was denied. Julius had already arranged with Bramante to build it. . . . All I want now is to return to my home in Florence, enjoy a little peace before I die."

"Do not speak of dying. Let us speak instead of how we can tackle this architectural monstrosity." He threw both arms up in a despairing gesture that embraced the Sistine. "Explain this . . . edifice . . . to me. Why was it built this way?"

Sangallo explained that when it was first completed the building had looked more like a fortress than a chapel. Since Pope Sixtus had intended to use it for the defense of the Vatican in the event of war, the top had been crowned by an open battlement from which soldiers could fire cannons and drop stones on attackers. When the neighboring Sant'Angelo had been strengthened as a fortress that could be reached by a high-walled passageway from the Papal palace, Julius had ordered Sangallo to extend the Sistine roof to cover the crenelated parapet. Quarters for the soldiers, above the vault that Michelangelo had been ordered to paint, were now unused.

Strong sunlight was streaming in from three tall windows, lighting the glorious frescoes of Botticelli and Rosselli opposite, shooting strong beams of light across the variegated marble floor. The side walls, one hundred and thirty-three feet long, were divided into three zones on their way up to the barrel vault, sixty-eight feet above: the lowest area was covered by tapestries, the frieze of frescoes filled the second and middle area. Above these frescoes was a cornice or horizontal molding, projecting a couple of feet out from the wall. In the topmost third wall area were spaced the windows, on either side of them portraits of the Popes.

Taking a deep breath, he craned his neck and looked up the more than sixty feet into the air at the ceiling itself, painted a light blue and studded with golden stars, the enormous area he was to fill with decorations. Arising out of the third level of the wall and going up into the curved vault were pendentives, which in turn were based on pilasters, column-like piers buried in the third tier. These pendentives, five on each wall and one at either end, constituted the open areas on which he was to paint the Twelve Apostles. Above each window was a semicircular lunette, outlined in sepia; the outer borders of the pendentives formed triangular spandrels, also colored in sepia.

The motive for the commission now became crushingly clear to him. It was not to put magnificent paintings on the ceiling that would complement the earlier frescoes, but rather to mask the structural supports which made the harsh transition from the top third of the wall into the barrel vault. His Apostles were not to be created for themselves but rather to capture the gaze of people on the floor so that their attention would be diverted from the ungainly architectural divisions. As an artist he had become not merely a decorator but an obliterator of other men's clumsiness.

10

He returned to Sangallo's, spent the rest of the day writing letters: to Argiento, urging him to hurry to Rome; to Granacci, pleading with him to come to Rome and organize a *bottega* for him; to the Topolinos, asking if they knew of a stonehewer who might like to come and help him mass the marble columns. In the morning a groom arrived from the Pope, informing him that the house where his earlier marbles had lain these two years was still available to him. He went to the Guffatti stoneyard, hired the family to haul the marbles from the Piazza San Pietro to the house. Several of the smaller blocks had been stolen.

He could not find Cosimo, the carpenter; the neighbors thought he had died in Santo Spirito hospital; but that afternoon freckle-faced Piero Rosselli lurched in, laden with bundles, to cook his Livorno fish stew. While the *cacciucco* simmered in its orégano, Michelangelo and Rosselli examined the house, which had been unoccupied since Michelangelo abandoned it in haste two years before. The kitchen was of unpainted brick, small, but comfortable enough for cooking and eating. What had formerly been the family room could be converted into a tolerable workshop. The covered porch would hold all the marbles if they were carefully stacked; and the two unpainted brick bedrooms would sleep the *bottega*.

In May he signed his contract for the Sistine Chapel, was given five hundred large gold ducats from the papal purse. He paid his long-overdue debt to Balducci, returned to the furniture dealer in Trastevere to buy pieces that looked startlingly like the ones Balducci had sold back to the dealer eight years before. He hired a young Roman boy to take care of the house. The lad cheated on the market bills, so he let him go. The second boy stole several ducats out of Michelangelo's purse before he was caught.

Granacci arrived at the end of the week. He had stopped off at a barber's to have his blond hair cut. He had already found the elegant men's shops on the Piazza Navona and brought to Michelangelo's house a new outfit of black trunk hose, a shirt, gold-embroidered hip-length cloak and a small ribbed cap, worn on the side of the head.

"I never was so glad to see anybody in my life!" cried Michelangelo. "You must help me draw up a list of assistants."

"Not so fast," said Granacci, his light blue eyes dancing; "this is my first trip to Rome. I want to see the sights."

"Tomorrow I'll take you to the colosseum, baths of Caracalla, the Capitoline hill . . ."

"All in good time. But tonight I want to visit the fashionable taverns I've heard about."

"What would I know of such things? I'm a workingman. But if you're serious, I'll ask Balducci."

"I'm always serious about my pleasures."

Michelangelo drew two chairs up to the kitchen table.

"I'd like to assemble the painters we worked with at Ghirlandaio's: Bugiardini, Tedesco, Cieco, Baldinelli, Jacopo."

"Bugiardini will come. Tedesco, too, though I don't think he knows much more about painting now than he did at Ghirlandaio's. Jacopo will go anywhere on somebody else's money. But Cieco and Baldinelli, I don't know whether they're still in the art."

"Who can we get?"

"Sebastiano da Sangallo, first of all. He considers himself a follower of yours, copies before your Bathers every day, gives lectures on it to new painters. I'll have to search for a fifth. It's not easy to get five painters all free at the same time."

"Let me give you a list of colors to send for. These Roman colors are no good at all."

Granacci glanced shrewdly at his friend. "It appears to me that you don't find anything good in Rome."

"Does any Florentine?"

"I'm going to. I've heard about the sophisticated and beautiful courtesans who have the charming villas. As long as I must stay here to help you get that vault plastered, I'm going to find an exciting mistress."

A letter brought him news that his uncle Francesco had died. Aunt Cassandra, after living with the family for forty years, had moved back to her parental home, starting suit against the Buonarroti to oblige them to return her dowry and to pay Francesco's debts. Though there had never been any real friendship between Michelangelo and his uncle, he had a strong blood-loyalty. He was grieved to see the next to last of the elder Buonarroti go. He was also worried. His father obviously intended him to fight Cassandra's lawsuit, hire a notary, see it through the courts. . . .

The next day he summoned up the courage to return to the Sistine. He found Bramante there, directing carpenters who were hanging a scaffolding from the ceiling by means of forty pipe-poles that had been driven through the cement vault and lashed together with ropes interlocked through the soldiers' quarters above.

"There's a scaffolding that will hold you securely for the rest of your life."

"You'd like to think so, Bramante, but actually it will only be a matter of months." Bramante stuck in his throat like a half-swallowed fly. The Pope by himself would hardly have thought of inflicting this ceiling on him. He inspected the scaffolding, knit his brows. "Just what do you intend to do with the holes in the ceiling after the poles come out?"

"Fill them."

"How do we get up to the holes to fill them after the scaffolding is down? Ride on an eagle's back?"

". . . I hadn't thought of that."

"Nor of what we are to do with forty ugly cement fills in the middle of my painting after I have finished the job? Let's discuss it with the pontiff."

The Pope was dictating *breves* simultaneously to several secretaries. Michelangelo laid out the situation in a few clear words.

"I understand," said Julius. He turned a puzzled expression to Bramante. "What *did* you intend to do with those holes in the ceiling, Bramante?"

"Just leave them, the way we leave holes in the sides of buildings when we pull out the poles that hold up the scaffolding. It can't be helped."

"Is that true, Buonarroti?"

"Assuredly not, Holy Father. I will design a scaffold which will never touch the ceiling. Then the painting will remain perfect."

"I believe you. Take down Bramante's scaffold and build your own. Chamberlain, you will pay the expenses for Buonarroti's new scaffold."

As Michelangelo turned away he saw Bramante biting the corner of his lip.

He ordered the carpenters to take down the scaffold. When all of the timber and rope had been lowered to the floor of the chapel, Mottino, the hunchbacked foreman of the carpenters, said:

"You will be using these materials for your own scaffolding?"

"Not the rope. You may have it."

"But it is valuable. You could sell it for a considerable sum."

Mottino was ecstatic "This means I will have a dowry for my daughter. Now she can be married! They say in Rome that you are a difficult man, Messer Buonarroti. Now I see it is a lie. May God bless you."

"That's precisely what I need, Mottino. God's blessing. Come back tomorrow."

That night he tackled the problem inside his own head, which he found to be his best workshop. Since he had never seen such a scaffolding as he had promised the Pope, he would have to invent one. The chapel itself was divided into two parts, separated by Mino da Fiesole's carved screen: the half for laymen, which he was going to paint first, the larger division, or presbyterium, for cardinals. Then came the altar and the Pope's throne. On the rear wall was the fresco of the Assumption of the Virgin by his erstwhile enemy Perugino. The walls were thick and strong; they could stand any amount of pressure. If he built with planks that were solidly wedged against them, then the more weight put on his scaffold the more pressure it would apply and the more secure his framework would be. The problem was how to anchor the ends of his planks, since he could not cut niches into the walls. Then he remembered the projecting cornice; this ledge would not be strong enough to carry the weight of the scaffolding and men, but it could give his planks anchorage.

"It might work," said Piero Rosselli, who frequently had to build his own scaffolding. He directed Mottino in the bolting of the planks and construction of the bridge. Michelangelo and Rosselli tested it, summoned the carpenter crew, one by one. The more weight on the trestle, the stronger it became. They were jubilant. It was a tiny victory, really; yet it provided the impetus to begin the detested chore.

Argiento wrote that he could not leave his brother's farm until the crops had been harvested. Neither could Granacci assemble a crew of assistants by mail.

"I'll have to go to Florence and help them finish their commissions. It may take a couple of months, but I promise to bring back everyone you wanted."

"I'll do the drawings. When you get back we'll be ready to start the cartoons."

Summer clamped down. Miasmic vapors moved in from the marshes. No one could breathe. Half the city became ill with clogged heads and pain in the chest. Rosselli, his only companion during these stifling days, fled to the mountains. Michelangelo climbed the ladder to his trestle at dawn, savagely tormented for want of hammer and chisel in his hands. Instead he spent the airless days drawing scale models of the twelve pendentives where the Apostles would be painted, cutting out paper silhouettes of the lunettes and spandrels, which he would also have to fill with what the Pope had called customary decoration. By midmorning the vault was like a furnace, and he was gasping for breath. He slept as though drugged through the heat of the afternoon, then worked at night in the back garden, evolving designs for the nearly six thousand square feet of sky and stars that had to be replastered and made pretty.

The hot days and weeks passed in lonely suffocation, broken only by the arrival of a former Settignano stonecutter whom his father had found in Florence, Michi by name, who had always wanted to visit Rome. Michi was about fifty, gnarled and pock-marked, sparely spoken, with the chipped, staccato accent of the stonehewer. Michi knew how to cook a few Settignano dishes; before his arrival Michelangelo had gone for days on bread and a thin wine.

In September Granacci returned with a full *bottega* in tow. Michelangelo was amused by how much the former apprentices had aged: Jacopo was still slim, wiry, with darting black eyes to match the remnants of oily dark hair, and deeply etched laugh wrinkles; Tedesco, sporting a bushy beard several degrees more carroty than his hair, had become thickset, with a ponderous manner that made him the natural butt for Jacopo's jokes. Bugiardini, still moonfaced and round-eyed, showed a center patch of baldness that resembled a tonsure. Sebastiano da Sangallo, newcomer of the group, had developed a serious mien since Michelangelo had last seen him, which earned him the nickname of Aristotle. He wore luxuriant oriental mustaches which he grew in honor of his uncle Giuliano. Donnino, the only stranger to Michelangelo, had been brought by Granacci because "he's a good draftsman, the best of the lot." He was forty-two, looked like a hawk with a high-bridged thin nose in a long face with negligible slits for eyes and mouth.

That evening, after Granacci had made sure that his mistress, whom he had supported over the summer, was still waiting for him, the new *bottega* held a party. Granacci ordered in flagons of white Frascati wine and a dozen trays of food from the Trattoria Toscana. After three long pulls on the Frascati flagon, Jacopo told the story of the young man who went each evening to the Baptistery in Florence and prayed aloud for St. John to tell him about his wife's behavior and his son's future.

"I hid behind the altar and called out, 'Your wife's a bawd, and your son will be hanged!' Do you know what he replied? 'You naughty St. John, you always did tell lies. That's why they cut your head off!' "

When the laughter subsided, Bugiardini insisted on drawing Michelangelo's face. When he had finished, Michelangelo exclaimed, "Bugiardini, you still have one of my eyes in my temple!" Next they played the drawing game on Donnino, letting him win so that he would have to buy the next day's dinner.

Michelangelo bought a second large bed in Trastevere. He, Bugiardini and Sangallo slept in the room off the workshop, while Jacopo, Tedesco and Donnino slept in the room down the hall. Bugiardini and Sangallo went out to buy sawhorses and planks, set up a worktable in the center of the room long enough for all six of them. At ten o'clock Granacci arrived. Jacopo cried, "Careful, everybody, don't let Granacci pick up anything heavier than charcoal, or he'll collapse in a heap."

Officially baptized by this buffoonery, the studio set to work in earnest. Michelangelo laid out on the table before them the scale drawings of the ceiling. The large pendentives at either end of the chapel he reserved for St. Peter and St. Paul; in the five smaller pendentives on one side would be Matthew, John and Andrew, Bartholomew and James the Great, on the opposite wall James the Less, Judas called Thaddaeus, Philip, Simon and Thomas. He sketched one complete Apostle, sitting on a high-backed throne, pilasters on either side; above were winged caryatids on C-shaped volutes, with medallions in square fields and scroll-like ornaments.

By the first week in October the house had fallen into chaos, for no one thought to make a bed, wash a dish or sweep a floor. Argiento came in from Ferrara, was so delighted to find that he was to have six companions in the house that he washed and scrubbed and polished for days, in addition to cooking the meals, before he got around to being unhappy about Michelangelo's commission.

"I want to work stone. Be a *scultore.*"

"So do I, Argiento. And so we shall, if only you'll be patient and help me get that ceiling splashed with paint."

To each of his six assistants he assigned a division of the vault for decoration: rosettes, *cassettoni,* circles and rectangles, trees and flowers with spreading foliage, wavelike movements of undulating lines, spirals. Michi, he discovered, was adept at grinding colors. He himself would do the final cartoons for most of the Apostles, but Granacci could paint a couple of them, and perhaps Donnino and Sangallo could each do one. He had already spent five months getting to this day, but now that he had them all together and started, he felt certain he could cover the whole ceiling in seven months. That would be another year out of his life. A total of four since he had first come to Rome to confer with Pope Julius. He would finish by May, and then either go to work on the marble figures for the tomb or return to the Hercules block which Gonfaloniere Soderini had brought to Florence for him.

It did not quite work that way. Donnino, though he was as fine a draftsman as Granacci said, lacked the courage to venture past his sketches into the colored cartoons. Jacopo kept them entertained but did no more work at thirty-five than he had at fifteen. Tedesco painted poorly. Sangallo dared anything Michelangelo put him on, but he was still inexperienced. Bugiardini was solidly reliable, but just as at Ghirlandaio's he could paint only flat walls and windows, thrones and pilasters. Granacci's cartoon for his Apostle came out well, but Granacci was having a good time in Rome. Since he had refused to take a salary, how could Michelangelo oblige him to put in more work hours? Michelangelo worked twice as hard as he had thought he would have to, and made slow progress through the weeks of November.

At last the time arrived, during the first week of December, when they were ready to fresco a major zone of the ceiling. One of the Apostles was his, the St. John on the side; opposite, Granacci was to paint St. Thomas. The others on the scaffold, led by Bugiardini, were to paint the decorations on the barrel vault between the two Apostles. Piero Rosselli had laid a heavy coat of intonaco on the area the day before, hatching a rough surface on which, this morning, he would plaster the precise area to be painted by dark.

At dawn they set out for the Sistine, Michi driving the donkey, the cart loaded with pails, brushes, tubes of paint, cartoons, bundles of sketches, charcoal bags, pots and bottles for color, with Rosselli sitting in the midst of sand and lime. Michelangelo and Granacci walked ahead, Bugiardini and Sangallo just behind them, Tedesco, Jacopo and Donnino bringing up the rear. Michelangelo felt hollow at the pit of his stomach, but Granacci was in a gay mood.

"How do you feel, Master Buonarroti? Did you ever imagine you would be walking at the head of your own *bottega* to begin a fresco commission?"

"Not in my wildest nightmares."

"Good thing we were all so patient with you. Remember how the Ghirlandaios taught you to use the instruments for squaring up? How Mainardi showed you to tint flesh in tempera, and David showed you how to make brushes from white pigs . . . ?"

"And Cieco and Baldinelli called me a fraud because I wouldn't paint wings on an angel? Oh, Granacci, what have I got myself into? I'm no fresco painter!"

11

The group worked well together, Michi mixing the plaster on the scaffold after hauling the sacks up the ladder, Rosselli expertly laying the daily area to be painted, remaining to watch its drying rate and to keep it sprinkled. Even Jacopo worked hard to copy the cartoon colors into the designs that Bugiardini had outlined with red ochre.

After the paint had had time to oxidize and dry, Michelangelo returned alone to study the result. With a seventh of the vault completed, he was able to see what the entire ceiling would be like when they had frescoed the rest. The Pope's objective would be accomplished; no one would be disturbed any more by the projecting spandrels, loomingly empty lunettes or the broken-up vault with its monotonous circles of gold stars. The Apostles on their thrones, the thousands of square feet of brightly colored designs would conceal and divert.

But what about the quality of the work? It was in the marrow of his bones to create only the finest he could produce; to create far beyond his abilities because he could be content with nothing that was not new, fresh, different, a palpable extension of the whole of the art. He had never compromised with quality; his integrity as a man and an artist was the rock on which his life was built. If he split that rock by indifference, by giving less than the exhausting best of himself, if he were content merely to get by, what was left of him?

He could have done the bronze statue of Pope Julius twice as fast had he been satisfied with a merely adequate statue; no one would have criticized him, since bronze was not his trade, and the commission had been forced upon him. But he had spent energy-draining months determined that his work must bring honor upon himself and his family and all artists. Had he been willing or able to do an immediately conceivable bronze of Julius it would perhaps be easier now to do this conceivable ceiling fresco. He and his group could apply the remaining paint without much trouble. But he could not deny that the quality was mèdiocre. He told Giuliano da Sangallo so.

"You have done your best under the circumstances," replied his friend.

Michelangelo paced the Sangallo drawing room, hugging his arms about him, perturbed. "I'm a long way from convinced of that."

"No one will blame you. The Pope gave you a job, and you did as you were told. Who could do otherwise?"

"Me. If I walk away from this ceiling as it is, I'll despise myself."

"Why must you take things so hard?"

"If there is one thing I know for sure it's that, when I hold a hammer and chisel in my hands and start that 'Go,' I need my full assurance that I can do no wrong. I need my complete self-respect. Once let me know that I can be content with inferior work . . ." There was agony in his voice, a pleading with Sangallo to affirm this concept. ". . . and as an artist, I'm through."

He kept the *bottega* busy designing the cartoons for the next area of the ceiling. He said nothing of his dilemma. Yet a crisis was impending; he could not take the studio up to the top of the scaffold and cover another area with paint which he knew would not remain. They were only ten days away from blowing up the next cartoons to full size. He would have to reach a decision.

He was temporarily spared by the advent of Christmas. The Rome celebrations, starting considerably in advance, gave him a reason to suspend work without revealing the turmoil going on within him. The studio was overjoyed at the vacation.

He received a note from Cardinal Giovanni. Would Michelangelo join them for dinner on Christmas Day? This was the first word he had heard from Giovanni since his monumental battle with the Pope. He bought himself a handsome brown woolen shirt, the first in several years, a pair of matching hose and a cloak of beige camlet that lightened the color of his amber eyes. He went to mass at San Lorenzo in Damaso, where his Christmas spirit was shattered at seeing the church so forlorn now that it was stripped of its glorious stone columns.

A groom with Florentine lilies embroidered on his livery admitted him to Cardinal Giovanni's palace on the Via Ripetta. As he passed through the spacious entrance hall with its majestic stairway, and then a drawing room and music room, he was able to perceive how greatly Cardinal Giovanni had profited from his benefices. There were new paintings on the walls, ancient sculptures from Asia Minor on pedestals, cabinets of antique coins, carved gems. He moved slowly, studying the recent acquisitions, marveling that of his father's formidable genius Giovanni should have inherited only this one facet: flawless good taste in the arts.

He came up sharp at the entrance to the smaller of the drawing rooms. There, sitting before a log fire, her hands extended to the flames, and high color in her alabaster cheeks, sat Contessina. She looked up.

"Michelangelo."

"Contessina."

"*Come va?*"

"*Non c'è male.*"

"As the Settignano stonecutter says."

"I don't have to ask how you are. You look beautiful."

The color mounted higher in her cheeks.

"You've never said that before."

"But I've always thought it."
She rose, came close to him. Her scent was the one she had used as a child in the Medici palace. Nostalgia for those happy years swept over him.
"You are a deep part of me. From the days when my life began. In the sculpture garden."
Her eyes filled with pain and joy in equal measure.
"As you have always been a part of me."
He became aware of the others around them, changed his tone.
"Luigi and Niccolò, they are well?"
"They are here with me."
"And Ridolfi?"
"No."
"Then you are not staying?"
"Giovanni has taken me to see the Pope. The Holy Father has promised to intercede with the Signoria for us. But I cannot hope. My husband is committed to the downfall of the Republic. He never loses an opportunity to make his views known . . ."
"I know."
They smiled at each other, wistfully.
"That is not discreet of him, but it is his resolve." She stopped abruptly, studied his face. "I have talked about myself. Now I want to speak of you."
He shrugged his shoulders. "I fight, but always I lose."
"The work does not go well?"
"Not yet."
"It will."
"Are you sure?"
"I'll put my hand in fire."
She held her hand out toward him as though it were already in the searing heat of the flames. He longed to take it in his own, if only for a moment. Then she threw back her head in laughter at the drastic Tuscan phrase of affirmation. Now their laughter joined together, seized each other and held close, harmoniously, intertwined through each other's fabric and substance. This too, he knew, was a kind of possessing; rare, beautiful and sacred.

The *campagna romana* was not Tuscany; it did not fill him with an all-absolving lyrical grace. But it had power, and history: the flat, fertile plains rolling for miles, traversed by the remains of Roman aqueducts that had brought clean water down from the hills; Hadrian's villa, where the Emperor had re-created the glory of Greece and Asia Minor, and where Michelangelo watched the excavators unearth marbles that went back to the generations of Pericles; Tivoli, with its majestic waterfalls, favorite holiday village for the Romans of the Empire; the Castelli Romani, a series of towns located on the lava and tufa slopes of the volcanic Alban Hills, each village on its separate peak in a series of peaks surrounding an enormous crater, with other ranges, covered by dark green forests, rolling back sculpturally as did the mountains beyond Settignano: Frascati, Tusculum, higher into the hills, where he wandered among the ruins of Cicero's villa, the amphitheater, forum, buried temple; the hills dotted with tiny stone villages whose origins were lost in obscure ages of history: before the Romans, before the Etruscans; the Temple of Fortune at Praeneste, whose walls included an entire village, with a Cave of Destiny and crypts that dated from who knew what distant age of man?
He walked deeper and deeper into the past, circling the enormous rim of the volcano, coming across carved building stones that had been spilled over the ground like milk, beneath which lay ancient settlements. Each night he stopped at a tiny inn or knocked on the door of a *contadino* family to buy his supper and space on a bed to rest, gripping the magnificent mountains between his legs, the irresilient

tufa beneath his feet, filled with the delicious pulsating fatigue that beat up from his soles and ankles and calves and knees and thighs into his groin.

The deeper he penetrated into the eon-old past of the volcanic hills and civilizations, the clearer his own problem became for him. His helpers would have to go. Many marble masters had permitted their apprentices and assistants to hew the marble block to within a safe margin of the central figure, but he had to hammer off the corners, mass the edges, work the four flat sides, remove every last crystal himself. He did not have the nature of a Ghirlandaio, able to do the main figures and focal scenes, allow the *bottega* to do the rest. He had to work alone.

He paid no attention to passing time; the days seemed so infinitesimal among the lost ages of the lava rock. In lieu of time he was conscious of space, trying to fit himself into the core of the Sistine vault as he had into the center of the Duccio block, so that he would know its weight and mass, grasp what it might hold and what might break off in imbalance. He had cleared the fields, plowed, seeded, stood with his head in the sun and the rain. Nothing showed; the thin, bright green miracle announcing the beginning of new life remained below the surface of his mind.

On New Year's morning, with his country hosts celebrating the first day of the Year of Our Lord 1509, he left their stone hut in the mountains, mounted higher and higher along the sheep trail until he came to the summit. The air was sharp, clear and cold. As he stood on the peak, muffler wound around his mouth to keep his teeth from freezing, the sun came up behind him, over the most distant range to which his eye could travel. As the sun rose in the sky the *campagna* plains came to life in pale pinks and tawny browns. In the distance stood Rome, sparklingly clear. Beyond and to the south lay the Tyrrhenian Sea, pastel green under a brittle blue winter sky. The whole landscape was flooded with luminosity: forests, the descending ranges beneath him, the hills, towns, the fertile plains, the somnolent farms, the stone-pile villages, the mountain and sea roads leading to Rome, a ship on the ocean. . . .

Reverentially he thought, "What a magnificent artist was God when He created the universe: sculptor, architect, painter: He who originally conceived space, filled it with His wonders." He remembered the lines from the beginning of Genesis:

> God, at the beginning of time, created heaven and earth. Earth was still an empty waste, and darkness hung over the deep. . . . Then God said, Let there be light. . . . God said too, Let a solid vault arise amid the waters. . . . a vault by which God would separate the waters which were beneath it from the waters above it. . . . This vault God called the Sky. . . .

. . . vault . . . God too had been faced with the need to create within a vault! And what had He created? Not merely the sun and moon and heavens of the sky, but a whole teeming world below it. Sentences, phrases, images flooded his mind from the Book of Genesis:

> . . . God said, Let the waters below the vault collect in one place to make dry land appear . . . the dry land God called Earth, and the water, where it had collected, He called the Sea. . . . Let the earth, He said, yield grasses that grow and seed. . . .
> . . . God said, Let the waters produce moving things . . . and winged things that fly above the earth under the sky's vault.
> . . . And God said, Let us make man, wearing our own image and likeness; let us put him in command of the fishes in the sea, and all that flies through the air, and the cattle and the whole earth, and all the creeping things that move on earth. So God

made man in His own image, made him in the image of God.
Man and woman both, He created them. . . .

And Michelangelo knew, just as clearly as he had known anything in his life,
that nothing would suffice for his vault but Genesis itself, a re-creation of the
universe. What nobler work of art could there be than God's creating of the sun
and moon, the water and the earth, the evolving of man, of woman? He would
create the world on that Sistine ceiling as though it were being created for the first
time. There was a theme to conquer that vault! The only one that could so overwhelm
it that all of its ugliness and clumsy architecture would vanish as though it never
existed, and in its place would come the glory of God's architecture.

12

He asked Chamberlain Accursio if he might see the Pope alone for a few moments.
The chamberlain arranged the meeting for late in the afternoon. Julius was sitting
quietly in the small throne room with just one secretary remaining, dictating a letter
to Venice, the Vatican's strongest opponent in Italy. Michelangelo kneeled.

"Holy Father, I have come to speak to you about the Sistine vault."

"Yes, my son?"

"I had no sooner painted one section than I realized it would turn out meanly."

"Why so?"

"Because the placing of the Apostles alone will have but a poor effect. They
occupy too small an area of the total ceiling and become lost."

"But there are other decorations."

"I have begun these decorations, as you instructed me. They make the Apostles
seem poorer than ever."

"This is your best judgment, that at the end we will emerge with a poor effect?"

"I have given the matter a great deal of thought, and that is my honest opinion.
No matter how well the ceiling may be painted under the original plan, it can bring
little honor to either of us."

"When you speak quietly this way, Buonarroti, I hear truth in you. I can also
tell that you have not come to ask permission to abandon the work."

"No, Holy Father. I have a composition that will cover the entire vault with
glory."

"I have confidence in you, and so I shall not ask the nature of your design. But
I shall come often to the chapel to watch your progress. You are involving yourself
in three times as much work?"

". . . or five or six."

The Pope stirred on his throne, rose, paced up and down the room, then came
to a halt before Michelangelo.

"You are a strange one, Buonarroti. You screamed that fresco was not your
profession, and almost knocked me down in your rage. Yet now, eight months
later, you come back with a plan that will entail infinitely more time and labor.
How is one to understand you?"

"I don't know," replied Michelangelo ruefully. "I hardly understand myself. I
only know that since I must paint that vault I cannot bring you something mediocre,
even if it is all you have asked for."

Julius shook his white-haired, white-bearded head in amused puzzlement. Then
he put his hand on Michelangelo's head, blessed him.

"Paint your ceiling as you will. We cannot pay you five or six times the original
three thousand ducats, but we will double it to six thousand."

His next task was more delicate and more difficult. He had to tell Granacci that the *bottega* was finished, that the assistants would have to go home. He took him step by step along the tortuous trail.

"I will keep Michi to grind the colors, and Rosselli will lay the wet plaster. The rest I simply must do by myself."

Granacci was staggered. "I never really thought that you could manage a studio as Ghirlandaio did. But you wanted to try, and so I helped you. . . . But working alone on top of that scaffolding to re-create the story of Genesis will take you forty years!"

"No, closer to four."

Granacci put his arms about his friend's shoulders, quoted softly, " 'If a lion or bear came and carried off one of my rams, I would snatch the prey from their jaws. Did they threaten me, I would catch them by the throat and strangle them.' As an artist, you have David's courage."

"I am also a coward. I can't bear to tell the others. Would you do it for me?"

He returned to the Sistine to look at the vault with sharper eyes. The architectural structure did not accommodate his new vision. He needed a new vault, a completely different ceiling which would appear to have been constructed solely for the purpose of showing his frescoes to their best advantage. But he knew better than to return to the Pope and ask for a million ducats to tear down brick, plaster, soldiers' rooms above, solid roof beyond. Serving as his own architect, he would have to rebuild that tremendous vault with the sole material available to him:

Paint.

Through sheer invention he must transform the ceiling, utilizing its shortcomings even as he had the gouge in the Duccio block, to force his creative powers into channels they might not otherwise have taken. Either he was the stronger, and could displace this vault space, or the force of the vault to resist would crush him.

He was determined to get a teeming humanity up on the ceiling, as well as God Almighty who created it; mankind portrayed in its breathless beauty, its weaknesses, its indestructible strengths: God in His ability to make all things possible. He must project a throbbing, meaningful vitality that would invert the universe: the vault would become the reality, the world of those looking at it would become illusion.

Argiento and Michi built a workbench for him in the center of the icy marble floor. Now he knew what the vault must say and accomplish; the number of frescoes he could paint would be determined by his architectural reconstruction. He must create the content and the container simultaneously. He stared at the ceiling above him. The center space running the full length of the vault he would use for his major legends: Dividing the Waters from the Earth. God Creating the Sun, the Moon. God Creating Adam and Eve, Expelling Them from the Garden, the legend of Noah and the Deluge. Now, at long last, he could pay his debt to Della Quercia for the magnificent biblical scenes carved in Istrian stone on the portal of San Petronio.

Architecturally he must frame this crucial middle section; he must also make the long narrow vault visible as a unified whole, with a single impact. For all practical purposes he had not one ceiling to paint, but three. He was going to have to be a magician to achieve a unifying force which would embrace every portion of the walls and ceiling, tie the elements together so that each supported the other, and no figure or scene would be isolated.

It took weeks of concentration, but at length the solution emerged from the severest limitation of the ceiling: the eight heavy, obtruding triangular spandrels, four on each side, their apexes coming a third of the way into the vault, and the four double-sized spandrels at the ends, with their inverted apexes in the corners. He spent a hundred hours trying to design them out, so that they would not dominate the ceiling, before he saw that he had been thinking in reverse. He must transform them into assets by decorating them with rich sculptural designs; then they would constitute a continuous frieze, an outer frame for the whole of his inner design!

Ideas now came tumbling over each other so tumultuously that he could hardly move his hands fast enough to set them down. The twelve pendentives between the apexes of the spandrels on the ends and sides he would preserve for his Prophets and Sibyls, sitting each one on a spacious marble throne. Connecting these twelve thrones would be a marblelike cornice going around all four sides of the chapel; this strong architectural cornice would serve as a cohesive interior frame to encompass his nine central stories. On either side of each throne would be marble-appearing *putti;* above them, enclosing the panels at the corners, would be the glorious male youth of the world, twenty nudes, their figures facing away from the giant panels toward the smaller panels, filling the released corners.

When Rosselli mounted the scaffolding with a claw hammer to tear out the plaster already frescoed, with Michi holding a canvas catchall below, Argiento came to Michelangelo. There were tears in his muddy brown eyes.

"Argiento, what's wrong?"

"My brother is dead."

Michelangelo put a hand on the young man's shoulder.

"I'm so sorry."

"I have to go home. The family farm is mine now. I must work it. My brother left little children. I'll be a *contadino.* I marry my brother's wife, raise the children."

Michelangelo laid down his pen.

"You don't like living on the farm."

"You'll be up on that scaffold a long time. I don't like paint."

Michelangelo rested his head wearily on his hands. "Neither do I, Argiento. But I'm going to paint those figures as though they were carved out of a stone mass. Every one of them will look as though they could move right off that ceiling and come down to earth."

"It's still paint."

"When will you leave?"

"Today, after dinner."

"I will miss you."

He paid Argiento's back wages, thirty-seven gold ducats. This was almost the last of his funds. He had received no money from the Pope since May, nine months before; he had bought his furniture and paints, plastered a section of the ceiling and frescoed it, paid the wages and travel expenses of Jacopo, Tedesco, Sangallo, Donnino, Bugiardini, fed them for four months. He could not even consider asking the Pope for more funds until he had an important section of the ceiling finished. Yet how could he paint even one complete panel until he had designed the entire vault? That meant months of drawing before he could start his first fresco. And now, just when he would become most involved, there would be no one to cook a meal, sweep a floor or wash a shirt.

He ate his soup-of-the-country in the silent house, thinking back to the month that it had been so noisy and gay, with Jacopo telling stories, Aristotle giving a lecture on the Bathers, Bugiardini singing love songs about Florence. It would be quiet here now; but it would be lonelier still, all alone on the scaffolding in the barren chapel.

13

He began with the Deluge, a large panel toward the entrance of the chapel. By March he had the cartoon blown up and ready to be transferred to the ceiling. Winter had not released its grip on Rome. The Sistine was bitterly cold. A hundred braziers could not heat its lowest areas. He wore his warm wool stockings, *brache* and shirt.

Rosselli, who had left for Orvieto for a profitable commission, had trained Michi in the mixing of the plaster and the method of applying it. Michelangelo helped him carry the sacks of lime, sand and *pozzolana,* volcanic tufa dust, up the steep wall ladders to the top of the scaffolding. Here Michi made his mix. Michelangelo was dissatisfied with the tawny color caused by the *pozzolana,* adding more lime and ground marble. He and Michi then climbed the series of three receding platforms that Rosselli had built so that they could plaster and paint the top of the rolling vault. Michi laid an area of intonaco, then fixed the cartoon. Michelangelo used the charcoal bag, red ochre for connecting lines.

Michi descended, set to work grinding colors below. Michelangelo was now on his top platform, sixty feet above the floor. He had been thirteen when he stood for the first time on the scaffolding in Santa Maria Novella, alone on a peak above the chapel and the world. Now he was thirty-four, and now, as then, he suffered vertigo. The Sistine seemed so hollow from up here, with his head just one foot below the ceiling. He smelled the wet plaster, the pungence of his freshly ground paints. He turned from his view of the marble floor, picked up a brush, squeezed it between the fingers and thumb of his left hand, remembering that he would have to keep his colors liquid this early in the morning. . . .

He had watched Ghirlandaio paint enough panels to know that he should begin at the top and work his way downward on either side; but he lacked experience to paint professionally, and so he began at the dominant point, the one that interested him the most: the extreme left end, the last piece of green earth showing above the flood, the trunk of a storm-twisted tree extending toward what would later be Noah's Ark, with the last of perishing humanity climbing the banks: a woman carrying a child in her arms, an older one clutching her leg; a husband carrying his distraught wife on his back; a vanishing trail of heads, old and young, about to be submerged in the rising waters; and above them all, a young man climbing and clutching at the tree trunk in a desperate effort to gain the highest vantage point.

He painted with his head and shoulders pulled sharply back, his eyes staring straight up. Paint dripped onto his face, the moisture of the wet plaster oozed out and dripped in his eyes. His arms and back tired quickly from the strain of the unnatural position. During the first week he allowed Michi to lay only modest areas of intonaco each day, proceeding cautiously, experimenting not only with the contortions of the figures but with a wide variety of flesh tones and the colors of the blue, green and rose robes of those who still retained their clothing. He knew that these small areas caused too many seams, that at this rate Granacci's estimate of forty years would prove more accurate than his own resolution of four. Yet he learned as he went along; this panel of life and death in violent action bore little relation to the Ghirlandaio still lifes. He was content to feel his way slowly until he had mastered his medium.

At the end of the first week a biting north wind arose. Its whistling kept him awake most of the night. In the morning he walked to the Sistine with his scarf wound around his mouth, not sure, even as he climbed the ladder, whether he could get his hands warm enough to hold a brush. But when he reached the top of Rosselli's highest platform he saw that there was no need to do so: his panel was ruined. His plaster and paints were not drying. Instead, there was a moist dripping at the edges of his stormy tree, the man mounting the bank, a bundle of clothes on his shoulder. The oozing moisture was creating a mold which was creeping over the paint, slowly absorbing it. Behind him he heard Michi ask in a choked voice:

"I made the plaster bad?"

It was a long time before he could reply; he felt too sick.

"It was me. I don't know how to mix paints for fresco. It's been too many years since Ghirlandaio's. Granacci and the others did the work on my first prophet; all I did was apply the paint."

He stumbled down the ladder, tears in his eyes, made his way blindly to the Papal palace, waited for an interminable time in a cold anteroom. When he was admitted he stood forlornly before Julius.

"What is it, my son? You look ill."

"I have failed."

"In what way?"

"What I have done is spoiled."

"So quickly?"

"I told Your Holiness it was not my art."

"Lift up your head, Buonarroti. I have never seen you . . . crushed. I prefer you storming at me."

"The ceiling has begun to drip. The moisture is causing spots of mold."

"Can't you dry them?"

"I know not how, Holiness. My colors are disappearing into the mold. They are being consumed by the salty edges."

"I can't believe that you would fail. . . ." He turned to a groom. "Go to Sangallo's house, tell him to inspect the Sistine ceiling at once, and bring me his report."

Michelangelo retreated to the cold outer room and the hard waiting bench. This was the worst defeat he had ever suffered. Much as he hated giving his years to fresco, he had nonetheless evolved a masterly conception. He was not accustomed to failure; it was the only thing in his lexicon that was worse than being forced to work in alien mediums. That the Pope would be through with him there could be no doubt, even though his collapse as a fresco painter had nothing to do with his qualities as a marble sculptor. He would certainly not be allowed to carve the tomb. When an artist failed this abjectly, he was finished. The news of his failure would be all over Italy in a matter of days. Instead of returning to Florence in triumph he would creep home like a beaten dog, the tail of his pride between his legs. Florence would not like that. They would consider that he had undermined their position in the art world. Gonfaloniere Soderini would feel let down; he would have been a liability at the Vatican instead of an asset. Again he would have wasted a full year of his productive life.

He was buried so deep in his gloom that he did not see Sangallo come in. He was hustled into the throne room before he had a chance to collect himself.

"Sangallo, what have you found?" the Pope demanded.

"Nothing serious, Holiness. Michelangelo applied the lime in too watery a state, and the north wind caused it to exude."

"But it's the same composition Ghirlandaio used in Florence," Michelangelo cried. "I watched it being prepared. . . ."

"Roman lime is made of travertine. It does not dry as readily. The *pozzolana* Rosselli taught you to mix with it stays soft, and often breaks into an efflorescence while drying. Substitute marble dust for *pozzolana,* use less water with this lime. All will be well."

"What about my colors? Must I tear out that part of the ceiling?"

"No. In time the air will consume the mold. Your colors won't be hurt."

Had Sangallo come back and reported that the ceiling was ruined, he would have been on the road to Florence by noon. Now he could return to his vault, though the events of the morning had given him an excruciating headache.

The wind died down. The sun came out. His plaster dried. It was Sangallo who traveled the long road of defeat back to Florence. When Michelangelo went to the house on the Piazza Scossacavalli he found the furniture covered with sheets, the family's personal possessions stacked in the downstairs hall. Michelangelo was heartbroken.

"What has happened?"

Sangallo shook his head, lips pursed tightly.

"No commissions have come in, not the Palazzo Giuliano, the Mint, the new palaces. Do you know the only assignment I have now? Laying sewers under the main streets! A noble job for a papal architect, no? My apprentices have joined Bramante. He has taken my place, as he vowed he would."

The next morning Sangallo and his family were gone, their departure unnoticed by the Vatican. High on his scaffold, Michelangelo felt more alone in Rome than ever; as though it were he who was lying melancholy and hopeless on the last gray rocks still above the sea, opposite the last bit of green earth.

The Deluge took him thirty-two days of consecutive painting. During the last weeks he was completely out of funds.

"We don't know whether we're rubbing the skin of our belly or the bone of our back," commented Michi.

His former earnings, invested in houses and farms to increase the family income, helped him not a scudo's worth. On the contrary, every letter still brought laments: why wasn't he sending his brothers money to open their shop? Lodovico money to buy fertile farms he had located? Why wasn't he arranging to have Aunt Cassandra's suit transferred to Rome, where he could defend it? At this point he felt like one of the naked men in the center of his panel, trying to climb into Noah's boat where other agonized men, fearing for the safety of their last refuge, were standing above him with clubs raised.

How was it that only he did not prosper from his papal connections? Young Raphael Sanzio, recently brought to Rome by Bramante, his fellow countryman from Urbino, and an old friend of the Sanzio family, had immediately secured a private commission. The Pope had been so delighted with the grace and charm of the work that he had commissioned Raphael to fresco the *Stanze*, the rooms of his new apartment, into which he was moving from the detested Borgia apartment. The frescoes that had already been started by Signorelli and Sodoma the Pope ordered painted out, so that Raphael's work alone would be seen. Paid a generous retainer by the Pope, Raphael had rented a luxuriously furnished villa, installed a beautiful young mistress and a staff of servants to care for them. Raphael was already surrounded by admirers and apprentices, garnering the ripe fruits of Rome. The Pope included him in his hunting parties and private dinners. He was to be seen everywhere, petted, loved, everyone bringing him new commissions, including the decorating of a summer pavilion for Chigi, the banker.

Michelangelo gazed at the unpainted brick walls of his house, drab, without curtains or carpets, just the few pieces of used furniture he had bought. When Raphael arrived in Rome, Michelangelo had expected him to come and say hello. But Raphael never bothered to walk the few steps to the Sistine or to the house.

One evening when Michelangelo was crossing Piazza San Pietro, returning from the vault with his hair, face and clothes bespattered with paint and plaster, he saw Raphael coming toward him, surrounded by a full train of admirers, apprentices and hangers-on. As they passed, Michelangelo said dryly:

"Where are you going, as surrounded as a rector?"

Raphael did not stop but replied tartly:

"And where are you going, as lonely as an executioner?"

The remark rankled. The fact that his isolation was self-imposed did not help. He went to his drafting table, burying his hunger and loneliness in work, sketching the next fresco, the Sacrifice of Noah. As the figures came alive under his swiftly moving fingers and mind, Noah and his wife, the three nude sons of Noah, their wives, the ram to be sacrificed to the Lord, his workroom filled up with energy and vividness, vitality and color. His hunger, his sense of isolation receded. He felt secure among his companions in this world of his own creating. To the silent house he murmured:

"I'm never less alone than when alone."

And he sighed, for he knew himself to be a victim of his own character.

14

Pope Julius had been eagerly waiting a chance to see the first fresco, but destitute as he was, Michelangelo took another ten days to paint the Delphic Sibyl and the Prophet Joel on their thrones in the pendentives on either side of the smaller fresco of Noah's Drunkenness. He wanted the Pope to see good examples of the figures with which the central panels would be surrounded.

Julius climbed the ladder, joined Michelangelo on the scaffolding, studied the fifty-five men, women and children, a few showing only heads and shoulders, but most of them fully presented. He commented on the magnificent beauty of the dark-haired Delphic Sibyl, asked questions about the white-maned father carrying his dead son onto the rocks, Noah's Ark in the background looking somewhat like a Greek temple, inquired about what was going to be painted in the other areas. Michelangelo avoided direct answers; he needed freedom to change his ideas as he moved along. Julius was too pleased to mind. He said quietly:

"The rest of the ceiling will be as good?"

"It should be better, Holy Father, for I am still learning about proper perspective at this height."

"It is wholly unlike the frescoes below us."

"The differences will grow greater as I proceed, rather than less."

"I am pleased with you, my son. I shall order the treasurer to pay you another five hundred ducats."

Now he was able to send money home to still the outcries, to buy food for the house, needed supplies for the job; now there would be quiet months ahead, during which he could paint his way toward the Garden of Eden, God Creating Eve, and then the heart of the ceiling, God Creating Adam.

The months proved anything but quiet. Warned by friendly Chamberlain Accursio that his Pietà was being moved out of St. Peter's so that Bramante's army of twenty-five hundred workmen could tear out the south wall of the Basilica to make room for the first of the new piers, he ran up the long flight of stairs to find his Pietà already moved next door to the little chapel of Mary of the Fever, but undamaged. Relieved, he stood watching Bramante's foremen locking cables around the south row of ancient columns; then, unbelieving, and with a sickening sinking of his innards, he saw the ancient marble and granite columns shatter to bits as they fell to the stone floor, be swept up as rubble and hauled away. Monuments built into the south wall were destroyed as the wall collapsed, smashing the antique mosaic tiles of the floor. At so little cost they could have been removed to safety!

Two mornings later a paper was pasted on the door of Bramante's palace, changing his name to Ruinante. A story circulated through the city that Bramante, knocking at the gates of paradise, was refused admission by St. Peter, who asked, "Why did you destroy my temple in Rome?" In reply, Bramante asked whether St. Peter would like him to tear down heaven and rebuild it.

As far as he knew, no one but himself and Chamberlain Accursio had a key to the Sistine. He had insisted upon this, so that no one could spy, or intrude upon his privacy. While painting the Prophet Zacharias on the huge throne over the layman's end of the chapel, he had a feeling that someone was coming at night. He had no tangible evidence, nothing was touched or moved out of place; but he sensed that not everything was quite the way he left it. Someone was mounting the ladder.

Michi hid in a nearby doorway, brought back word that it was Bramante and, he believed, Raphael. Bramante had a key. They came in late, after midnight. Michelangelo was furious: before he could get his vault completed and open to view, his new techniques would be on the walls of Raphael's *Stanze,* even as Raphael's work now reflected his study of the Bathers. Raphael would have created the revolution, and Michelangelo copying him!

He asked Chamberlain Accursio to arrange a session with the Pope. Michelangelo made the accusation: there would be nothing new, no point of departure that Raphael would not know about. . . .

Bramante stood silent. Michelangelo demanded that the key be taken away from him. The Pope requested Bramante to surrender it to Accursio. Another crisis had been met. Michelangelo returned to the vault.

The next day there came a summons from a niece of Cardinal Piccolomini, who had so briefly been Pope Pius III. The Piccolomini family insisted that he begin carving on the remaining eleven statues for the Siena altar, or return the hundred-florin advance secured for him by Jacopo Galli. He could not spare a hundred florins now. Besides, they still owed him for one of the figures he had already delivered.

Next a letter from Lodovico informed him that, while he was making some repairs to the house in Settignano, Giovansimone had quarreled with his father, raised his fist and threatened to beat him, then had set fire to the house and barn. The damage was small, since both structures were built of stone, but the experience had made Lodovico ill. Michelangelo sent money to make the repairs, along with a blistering letter to his brother.

The four incidents upset him severely. He had to stop work. A marble hunger seized him with such palpable force that he felt weak. He made for the *campagna,* walked for miles with long ceaseless strides, breathed in heavy gulps of air to prove to himself that he was three-dimensional. In the midst of his despair he received a message from Cardinal Giovanni, summoning him to the Medici palace. What else could have gone wrong? Giovanni was dressed in his red robes and biretta. His pale plump face was freshly shaved, smelled of a familiar Florentine perfume. Giulio stood behind him, dark of face and fiercely serious.

"Michelangelo, as a former companion under my father's roof, I have the warmest of feelings for you."

"Your Grace, I have always felt that to be so."

"That is why I want you to become a regular of my household. You must come to dinner, be at my side during my hunting parties, and ride in my train when I cross the city in procession to say mass at Santa Maria in Domenica."

"Why must I do these things?"

"I want Rome to know that you are of my intimate circle."

"Could you not tell Rome that?"

"Words mean nothing. Churchmen, nobility, wealthy merchants come to this palace. When these people see you here they will know you are under my protection. My father would have wanted it."

He blessed Michelangelo, left the room. Michelangelo looked over at Giulio, who stepped forward and spoke with warmth.

"You know, Buonarroti, Cardinal Giovanni never makes enemies."

"That takes genius in Rome today."

"Cardinal Giovanni has that genius. He is the most beloved in the College of Cardinals. He feels you need his kindness."

"In what way?"

"Bramante blames you for the Ruinante story. Every day he makes new enemies for you."

"And Cardinal Giovanni wants to fight for me?"

"Not by attacking Bramante. If you become an intimate of this house, the cardinal, without saying one angry word to Bramante, will silence your detractors."

Michelangelo studied Giulio's slender, handsome face; for the first time he felt a liking for Giulio, even as Giulio was manifesting this first friendship toward him.

He climbed the winding trail up the Janiculum, then gazed down on the jagged, tawny rooftops of Rome, the Tiber snaking through the city like a continuous S. He asked himself whether he could join the train of Cardinal Giovanni and paint the Sistine ceiling at the same time. He was grateful to Giovanni for wanting to help him; and he needed help. But even if he were not working night and day, how could he become a hanger-on? He simply had no talent for social amenities, nor any liking for society. Hard as he had striven to raise the status of the artist above that of the artisan, he still believed that the artist was a man who had to work all the time. The years were so short, the frustrations so numerous, that unless he labored at the top of his capacity he could never achieve a body of work. How could he paint for a few hours in the morning, go to the baths, walk to Giovanni's house, talk charmingly to thirty guests, eat a delicious dinner over several hours . . . ?

Cardinal Giovanni listened carefully to his gratitude and his reasons for being unable to accept.

"Why is it impossible for you, when Raphael does it so easily? He too turns out considerable work of high quality, yet he has dinner at a different palace each day, supper with intimate friends, goes to the plays, has just bought a gem of a house in Trastevere for his newest mistress. His is a full life, would you not say? New commissions come in every day. He refuses none. Why he, and not you?"

"I honestly don't know the answer, Your Grace. For Raphael, the creating of a work of art is a bright spring day in the *campàgna;* for me, it is the *tramontana* howling down the valley from the mountaintops. I work from early morning to dark, then by candlelight or oil lamp. Art for me is a torment, grievous when it goes bad, ecstatic when it goes well; but always it possesses me. When I have finished with a day of work I am a husk. Everything that was inside of me is now inside the marble or the fresco. That is why I have nothing to give elsewhere."

"Not even when it is to your best interest?"

"My best interest can only be my best work. Everything else passes."

15

He returned to his scaffold determined that nothing should further divert him, neither troubles in Rome nor in Florence. His sketches for the vault were fairly complete now, and they called for three hundred men, women and children, all imbued with the potency of life, displacing space as three-dimensional as those who walked the earth. The force to create them must come from within himself. It would take days, weeks, months of demoniacal energy to imbue each individual character with an authentic anatomy, mind, spirit and soul, an irradiation of strength so monumental and outpouring that few men on the earth below could match them for power. Each one had to be pushed out of his artistic womb, pushed out by his own articulate frenzied force. He must gather within himself his galvanic might; his burgeoning seed must be generated each day anew within his vitals, hurtled into space, projected onto the ceiling, given life everlasting. Though he was creating God the Father, he himself was God the Mother, source of a noble breed, half man, half god, inseminated each night by his own creative fertility, carrying until the dawn, and then, on his lonely truckle bed high in the heavens, going through parturition to deliver a race of immortals.

God Almighty creating the sun and the moon, the earth and the water, the plants, the cattle, the crawling things, man and woman, even He had been exhausted from this torrential creativity. "God saw all that He had made, and found it very good." But "On the seventh day, He had come to an end of making, and rested." Why then should he, Michelangelo Buonarroti, a small man, only five feet four, weighing a hundred pounds, no heavier than one of Florence's society girls, laboring for months without adequate food and rest, why should he not be exhausted? When he prayed, "Dear God, help me!" he was praying to himself, beseeching himself to have fortitude, to be invincible of body and spirit, to have the stamina and will to create mightily in a vision of a more heroic world.

For thirty days he painted from light to darkness, completing the Sacrifice of Noah, the four titanic male nudes surrounding it, the Erythraean Sibyl on her throne, and the Prophet Isaiah in the pendentive opposite, returning home at night to enlarge the cartoon of the Garden of Eden. For thirty days he slept in his clothes, without taking off even his boots; and when at the completion of the section, utterly spent, he had Michi pull his boots off for him, the skin came away with them.

He fed off himself. When he grew dizzy from standing and painting with his head and shoulders thrown back, his neck arched so that he could peer straight upward, his arms aching in every joint from the vertical effort, his eyes blurred from the dripping paint even though he had learned to paint through slits and to blink them shut with each brush stroke as he did against flying marble chips, he had Rosselli make him a still higher platform, the fourth on top of the scaffolding. He painted sitting down, his thighs drawn up tight against his belly for balance, his eyes a few inches from the ceiling, until the unpadded bones of his buttocks became so bruised and sore he could no longer endure the agony. Then he lay flat on his back, his knees in the air, doubled over as tightly as possible against his chest to steady his painting arm. Since he no longer bothered to shave, his beard became an excellent catchall for the constant drip of paint and water. No matter which way he leaned, crouched, lay or knelt, on his feet, knees or back, it was always in strain.

Then he thought he was going blind. A letter arrived from Buonarroto, and when he tried to read it he could see nothing but a blur. He put the letter down, washed his face, ate a few forkfuls of the overcooked *pasta* Michi had made for him, went back to the letter. He could not decipher a word.

He threw himself on his bed, sorely beset. What was he doing to himself? He had refused to paint the simple commission the Pope had requested, and now he would come out of this chapel a gnarled, twisted, ugly, blind dwarf, deformed and aged by his own colossal stupidity. What Torrigiani had done to his face, the vault would do to his body. He would carry its scars to his dying day. Why couldn't he have let well enough alone? He would have made his peace with the Pope, been back in Florence long since, enjoying dinner with the Company of the Cauldron, living in his comfortable house, carving the Hercules.

Sleepless, racked with pain, homesick, lonely, he rose in the inky blackness, lit a candle, and on the back of an old sketch tried to lighten his mood by pouring out his woes:

> I've grown a goitre by dwelling in this den—
> as cats from stagnant streams in Lombardy,
> or in what other land they hap to be—
> which drives the belly close beneath the chin:
>
> My beard turns up to heaven; my nape falls in,
> fixed on my spine: my breast-bone visibly
> grows like a harp: a rich embroidery
> bedews my face from brush-drops thick and thin.

My loins into my paunch like levers grind:
my buttock like a crupper bears my weight;
my feet unguided wander to and fro;

In front my skin grows loose and long; behind
by bending it becomes more taut and strait;
crosswise I strain me like a Syrian bow: . . .

        Come then, try
to succor my dead pictures and my fame;
since foul I fare and painting is my shame.

Word reached him that his brother Lionardo had died in a monastery in Pisa.
There was no information as to why he had been moved to Pisa, or whether he
had been buried there, or the nature of his illness. But as Michelangelo walked to
San Lorenzo in Damaso to have a mass said for the repose of Lionardo's soul, he
felt that he knew the answer: his brother had died of an excess of zeal. Might not
that also be the cause of his own death?

Michi found a colony of stonemasons in Trastevere with whom he spent his
evenings and holidays. Rosselli traveled to Naples in the south, Viterbo and Perugia
in the north to build his master walls for frescoing. Michelangelo went nowhere.
No one came any more to call or to invite him out. His conversations with Michi
were confined to the subjects of grinding the colors and material needed on the
scaffold. He was living as monastic and secluded a life as the brothers in Santo
Spirito.
He no longer went to the Papal palace to confer with Julius, though the Pope,
after a second visit to the ceiling, had sent him a thousand ducats to carry on the
work. No one came to the Sistine. When he walked from his home to the chapel
and back he did so almost totally blinded, barely able to stagger across the piazza,
his head lowered, seeing no one. Passers-by no longer called attention to his paint-
and plaster-stained clothes, face, beard, hair. Some thought him crazy.
"Crazed would be the better word," he muttered; "after living up in that valhalla
of gods and goddesses all day, how do I make the transition back to this mean
earth?"
He did not even try. For himself, he had accomplished his primary objective:
the life and the people on the ceiling were real. Those living on earth were phantoms.
His close friends, his intimates were Adam and Eve in the Garden of Eden, the
fourth majestic panel in the line. He portrayed Adam and Eve not as tiny, timid,
delicate creatures, but powerfully built, alert, handsome, as primordial as the boulders
which sheltered them from the serpent-entwined apple tree, taking temptation in
calm accepting strength rather than weak stupidity. Here was a pair to breed the
race of man! And when they were banished from the Garden to the barren earth
on the opposite side of the panel, with the archangel's sword pointed at their heads,
they were frightened, but not cowed, not destroyed, not reduced to crawling things.
This was the mother and father of man, created by God, and he, Michelangelo
Buonarroti, brought them to life in noble mien and proportion.

16

In June 1510, a year and a few weeks after he had shown Julius the Deluge, the
first half of the vault was completed. In a small central panel God in His rose-
colored robe had just raised Eve from the rib of the sleeping Adam; in the corners,

framing the drama, were four nude sons that would arise from this union, with beautiful faces, powerful bodies carved out of warm flesh-colored marble; directly below on either side were the Vulcanlike Cumaean Sibyl and the Prophet Ezekiel on their thrones beneath the binding cornices. Half of the vault was now a flood of glorious color: mustard yellows, pale sea greens, dust rose and azure blues against the mighty parade of sun-flooded flesh tones.

He had not told anyone the vault was half completed, but the Pope knew at once. He sent word to Michelangelo that he would be in the Sistine at midafternoon. Michelangelo helped Julius up the last rungs of the ladder, took him on a tour, pointing out the stories of David and Goliath and Judith and Holophernes, the four stories from the Ancestors of Christ in the side spandrels.

Julius demanded that the scaffold be taken down so that the world could see how great a thing was being executed.

"It is not yet time to take the scaffold down, Holy Father."

"Why not?"

"Because there are so many things to be finished: the children playing behind the thrones of the Prophets and Sibyls, the nudes filling either side of the spandrel apexes . . ."

"But I had heard that the first half was completed."

"The major panels, yes, but there is so much detail still to be done . . ."

"When will it be ready?" insisted the Pope stubbornly.

Michelangelo was irritated. He answered shortly:

"When it is ready!"

Julius went red in the face, satirized Michelangelo's voice harshly as he cried, "When it is ready! When it is ready!" raised his walking stick in a fury and brought it down across Michelangelo's shoulder.

There was a silence while the two antagonists glared at each other. Michelangelo went cold all over, too shocked to feel pain in the shoulder. He bowed, said formally in a voice from which all emotion had been smitten:

"It shall be as Your Holiness desires. The scaffolding will be down by tomorrow, the chapel ready to be shown."

He backed away, leaving the space open for the Pope to descend the ladder.

"It is not for you, Buonarroti, to dismiss your pontiff!" cried Julius. "You are dismissed."

Michelangelo backed down the ladder almost without touching the rungs, left the chapel. So this was the end! A bitter, degrading end, to be beaten with a stick like a *villano,* peasant. He who had vowed he would raise the status of the artist from that of skilled laborer to the highest reaches of society, whom the Company of the Cauldron had acclaimed when he defied the Pope, he had now been humiliated and degraded as no other reputable artist he had known!

Waves of nervous revulsion swept over him as he stumbled and jerked his way blindly along unfamiliar streets. He had re-created the world. He had tried to be God! Well, Pope Julius II had put him in his place. Julius was God's viceroy on earth, even as his brother Lionardo had told him; and he, Michelangelo Buonarroti, was a laborer in the fields. Strange, how one blow of a stick could dispel illusion.

"Foul I fare and painting is my shame."

Bramante's triumph was complete.

What did he do now? Julius would never forgive him for inciting him to strike the blow, and he would never forgive Julius for inflicting this ignominy on him. He would never pick up a paintbrush, never again touch that vault. Raphael could decorate the other half.

He made his way home. Michi was waiting for him, silent and owl-eyed.

"Pack your things, Michi," he said. "Get a head start on me. We'd better not leave Rome together. If the Pope orders my arrest, I don't want them taking you too."

"He had no right to hit you. He's not your father."

"He's my Holy Father. He can put me to death if he wants to. Only he'll have to catch me first."

He filled one canvas bag with his drawings, another with his personal things. It took him only a moment to pen a note to Rosselli, bidding him good-by, and asking him to sell his furniture back to the dealer in Trastevere. Just as he finished there was a knock on the door. He froze. Michi's eyes went to the back door. It was too late for flight. He was caught, before he could get away. What would it be now, what new punishment, humiliation? He smiled grimly. After his fourteen months in the vault, the prison of Sant'Angelo would have its comforts!

There was a second sharp knock. He opened the door, expecting to see soldiers. Instead there was Chamberlain Accursio.

"May I enter, Messer Buonarroti?"

"Have you come to arrest me?"

"My good friend," said Accursio gently, "you must not take these little matters so hard. Do you think the pontiff would bother to strike anyone he was not deeply fond of?"

Michelangelo closed the street door behind Accursio, stood with his palms on the table, staring wide-eyed at the Pope's agent.

"Are you suggesting that the blow was a mark of His Holiness' favor?"

"The Pope loves you. As a gifted, albeit unruly son." He took a purse from his belt, laid it on the worktable. "The pontiff asked me to bring you these five hundred ducats . . ."

". . . a golden salve to heal my wound?"

". . . and to convey his apologies."

"The Holy Father sent apologies to me?"

"Yes. The moment he returned to the palace. He did not want this to happen. He says it's because you both have a *terribilità*."

"Who knows that the Pope sent you to beg my pardon?"

"Is that important?"

"Since Rome will know the pontiff struck me, I can only go on living here if people also know that he apologized."

Accursio rolled his shoulders, subtly. "Who has ever been able to conceal anything in this city?"

Julius chose the week of the Feast of the Assumption to unveil the first half of the vault. Rosselli directed Mottino and his crew in taking down the scaffold and storing it. Michelangelo spent the intervening weeks at home, drawing and making the cartoons for the prophets Daniel and Jeremiah, the Libyan and Persian Sibyls. He did not go near the Sistine or the Papal palace. Julius sent no word. It was an uneasy truce.

He kept no track of time. He knew what season he was in, and sometimes the month, but little more. When he wrote home he could not date his letters, saying, "I know not what day it is, but I think yesterday was Friday," or "I do not know what the date is today, but I know that yesterday was St. Luke's Feast Day." The Pope did not order him to the chapel for the ceremonies. The first he knew of the gathering in the Sistine was when Michi answered a knock at midday, bringing Raphael into the workroom. Michelangelo was crouched over his table sketching Haman and the Brazen Serpent for the spandrels.

He looked up at Raphael, saw that the younger man's face had aged considerably, with dark circles under his eyes, the flesh a little flaccid. He was dressed in expensive mauve satin embroidered with costly jewels. Commissions flooding into his *bottega* included everything from designing a dagger to building great palaces; his assistants completed whatever Raphael had no further time for. Only twenty-seven, he looked ten years older. Even as Michelangelo's hard, grueling labor had taken its toll of him, so Raphael's fine looks were dissolving in his too-muchness of everything: food, drink, women, pleasure, company, praise.

"Messer Buonarroti, your chapel staggers me," said Raphael with admiration in his voice and eyes. "I came to apologize for my bad manners. I should never have spoken to you as I did in the piazza. You deserved better of me."

Michelangelo remembered going to Leonardo da Vinci to apologize for his own bad manners.

"Artists must forgive each other their sins."

No one else came to congratulate him, no one stopped him on the street, no one approached him with a new commission. He was as solitary as though he were dead. The painting on the ceiling of the Sistine was outside the pale of Rome's life, a private duel between Michelangelo, God and Julius II.

And, suddenly, Pope Julius was deep in war.

Two days after the unveiling, Julius left Rome at the head of his army to drive the French out of northern Italy and to solidify the Papal State. Michelangelo watched him leave, riding a fiery charger, followed in procession by Spanish troops provided by the King of Spain to whom he had given control of Naples; Italian mercenaries under his nephew, the Duke of Urbino; and Roman columns led by his nephew-in-law, Marcantonio Colonna. His first objective was to besiege Ferrara, ally of the French. To help him in his conquest he was to have fifteen thousand Swiss troops, bolstered by the considerable Venetian forces. On the way north there were independent city-states to be reduced: Modena, Mirandola, family seat of the magnificent Pico. . . .

Michelangelo worried; the French were the sole protection of the Republic of Florence. If Julius could drive the French troops out of Italy, Florence would be vulnerable. It would be Gonfaloniere Soderini's and the Signoria's turn to feel the papal stick across their backs. He had also been left stranded; or he had stranded himself. The Pope's chamberlain had brought him money and an apology, but he had not brought him specific permission to put back the scaffolding and commence work on the altar half of the vault. Julius had waited for him to appear at the Vatican. He had waited for Julius to summon him. The Pope could be gone for months. What did he do in the meanwhile?

A letter from his father informed him that his brother Buonarroto was seriously ill. He would have liked to make the trip to Florence to be at his side, but did he dare to leave Rome? He sent money instead, out of Julius' apology purse. He considered seeking a commission, anything in marble or paint that would occupy and support him until the Pope's return. But he had never sought a commission. He did not know how to go about it.

When he heard that the Papal Datary, a Florentine by the name of Lorenzo Pucci, was leaving to join the Pope in Bologna, he sought him out and asked if he would speak to Julius in his behalf, try to collect the five hundred ducats still owed him for the half of the vault he had completed, secure permission to begin the second half, money to erect the scaffold. The Datary said he would try. He would also see if he could find an outside commission for Michelangelo to tide him over.

Then Michelangelo sat down to write a sonnet to the Pope:

I am thy drudge and have been from my youth—
Thine, like the rays which the sun's circle fill,
Yet of my dear time's waste thou thinkst no ill.
The more I toil, the less I move thy ruth.

17

It was not until after New Year's, 1511, that he was able to start painting again.

During the intervening months he had added to his fund of aggravation and frustration. Unable to stand the inactivity any longer, he had followed the Pope to Bologna, only to find the Bentivoglios regaining power, Pope Julius too immersed in his troubles to see him. He had gone on to Florence to visit Buonarroto, resolved to take some of his past savings which had been deposited for safekeeping with the *spedalingo*, business manager of the hospital of Santa Maria Nuova, rebuild his scaffold and return to work without permission or the Pope's money. He found Buonarroto recovered, but too weak to work; and that his father had received the first political appointment tendered by Florence to a Buonarroti in Michelangelo's lifetime: as *podestà* in the village of San Casciano. Lodovico had taken with him some of the savings from the *spedalingo* without Michelangelo's knowledge or consent, money to which he no longer had a legal right. An apologetic letter from his father explained:

> I took them with the hope that I should be able to put them back before your return to Florence. Now I see that I did wrong. I am awfully sorry. I did wrong in following other people's advices.

He had returned to Rome empty-handed. And it seemed that Pope Julius too would return empty-handed. For Julius, the general, everything had gone wrong: though his troops had taken Modena, he had found Bologna meagerly garrisoned and low on food supplies, with the Bentivoglios at one gate, the French army entrenched a few miles away. Ferrara had driven off his army in a serious defeat; the Swiss troops had been bribed by the French to return home; he was ready to send Pico della Mirandola's nephew to negotiate his surrender to the French when the Venetian and Spanish troops finally arrived to save him.

Now the Datary returned with the money owed Michelangelo, permission to place his scaffold under the second half of the chapel, across to the Pope's throne at the end, and the money to pay for it. Now Michelangelo could come to grips with God: God Creating Adam, Creating the Sun and Moon, Dividing the Waters from the Earth, Separating Light and Darkness; strive to visualize a God of such transcendence that everyone would cry out, "Yes! That is the Lord God! None other could be!" These four panels were the heart of the vault. Everything depended upon them. Unless he could create God as convincingly as God had created man, his ceiling would lack the focal core from whence sprang its reason for being.

He had always loved God. In his darkest hours he cried out, "God did not create us to abandon us." His faith in God sustained him; and now he must make manifest to the world who God was, what He looked and felt like, wherein lay His divine power and grace. His God must not be special or peculiar or particular, but God the Father to all men, one whom they could accept, honor, adore.

It was a delicate task, yet he did not doubt that he could achieve such a God. He had only to set down in drawings the image he had carried with him since childhood. God as the most beautiful, powerful, intelligent and loving force in the universe. Since He had created man in His own image, He had the face and body of a man. The first human whom God created, Adam, had surely been fashioned in His likeness. By setting forth Adam, the son, true creature of his Father: magnificent in body, noble in thought, tender in spirit, beautiful of face and limb, archtype of all that was the finest in heaven and on earth, there would be reflected God, the Father. God, in clinging white robe which matched His virile white beard, had only to hold out His right arm to Adam, to reach one infinitesimal life-breath more, man and the world would begin.

While Michelangelo remained high in the heavens painting the smaller panel of God Dividing the Waters from the Earth, Julius reversed positions with his fresco painter, plunging into the special inferno reserved for warriors who suffer a rout. He failed in his siege of Ferrara, failed in his efforts to break the alliance between the Holy Roman Empire and France; went down so badly with gout that he had to be carried to Ravenna in an oxcart. His papal and Venetian forces were severely defeated by the rampaging Ferrarese, his funds so exhausted that he had to raise eighty thousand ducats by selling eight new cardinalates at ten thousand ducats each. The French and Ferrarese recaptured Bologna and reinstated the Bentivoglios. Julius lost his armies, artillery, baggage, the last of his resources. Crushed, making his way back to Rome, he found nailed to the cathedral door at Rimini a summons of all rebellious churchmen to a General Council at Pisa to conduct an inquiry into the official behavior of Pope Julius II.

Julius' defeat was a defeat for Michelangelo, for his life had become inextricably interwoven with his pontiff's. The moment the Bentivoglios returned to power, the Bolognese had thronged into the Piazza Maggiore, torn his bronze statue of Julius from its niche, and thrown it to the paving stones. The triumphant Duke of Ferrara had then melted it down and recast it into a cannon, which he named *Julia*. Fifteen months of his time, energy, talent and suffering now sat on the cobbles of the Piazza Maggiore in the form of a cannon that was the butt of coarse jokes from the Bolognese, and would surely be used against Pope Julius if he were rash enough to lead another army northward. Vincenzo had triumphed.

Here in Rome, it seemed to Michelangelo, the same pattern of overthrow must inevitably continue. During the warm, light days of May and June he spent seventeen consecutive hours on the scaffold, taking food and a chamber pot up with him so that he would not have to descend, painting like a man possessed, the four glorious nude males in the corners of the panels, then the young Prophet Daniel with an enormous book on his lap; opposite, the old Persian Sibyl in her white and rose robes, then the single most powerful portrait on the ceiling, God in deeply dramatic action, creating the golden ball of the sun . . . hoping, praying, striving desperately to complete his Genesis before the collapse of its protector, before outraged successors came in, clerical or military and, wanting to wipe out all traces of Pope Julius II's reign, sent a crew into the Sistine to spread coats of whitewash over its ceiling.

It was a race against death. As a result of his internecine warfare, Julius had returned to Rome the most hated man in Italy, his resources so exhausted that he had to carry the papal tiara to the banker Chigi's house under his robes, ostensibly going to dinner but actually to borrow forty thousand ducats on the jewels. His enmities extended to all the city-states he had defeated and punished: Venice, Bologna, Modena, Perugia, Mirandola. . . . Even the Roman nobles, some of whom had led his defeated armies, were now in league against him.

Bound to each other, understanding defeat, Michelangelo felt that he must call on his Pope, the only obligation that could take him off the scaffold.

"Holy Father, I have come to pay my respects."

Julius' face was ravaged by frustration and illness. Their last face-to-face encounter had been a stormy one, yet instinctively Julius sensed that Michelangelo had not come seeking revenge. Julius' voice was friendly, intimate; they felt strongly drawn to each other.

"Your ceiling, it moves along?"

"Holiness, I think you will be gratified."

"If I am, you will be the first to bring me gratification for a long time."

"It is no simpler in art than in war, Holiness," said Michelangelo firmly.

"I will come to the Sistine with you. This very moment."

He could hardly make it up the ladder. Michelangelo had to haul him the last few rungs. He stood panting at the top; and then he saw God above him, about to impart the gift of life to Adam. A smile came to his cracked lips.

"Do you truly believe that God is that benign?"

"Yes, Holy Father."

"I most ardently hope so, since I am going to be standing before Him before long. If He is as you have painted Him, then I shall be forgiven my sins." He turned his face toward Michelangelo, his expression radiant. "I am pleased with you, my son."

Basking in the rays of the hot sun and the Pope's hearty acceptance of his labors, Michelangelo was reluctant to relinquish the happy mood. Wanting to hold its warmth and tranquillity for a little while longer, he crossed the piazza to where the piers and walls of the new St. Peter's were beginning to rise. As he got closer he was surprised to find that Bramante was not building in the traditional manner for cathedrals, of solid stone and concrete, but was erecting hollow concrete forms and filling them with rubble from the Old Basilica, and other debris. The bulky mass would give the appearance of being solid, but was it not a dangerous way to support so heavy a structure?

This was only the beginning of his astonishment. As he circled the works and watched the men preparing the concrete, he saw that they were not following the sound engineering precept of one portion of cement to three or four of sand, but were using ten and twelve portions of sand to each one of cement. There was no question in his mind that this mix could be fatal under the best of circumstances, but to hold the vast St. Peter's with uncompacted debris between its piers, it could be catastrophic.

He made straight for Bramante's palace, was admitted by a liveried footman into the elegance of the foyer, with its rich Persian carpets, priceless tapestries and furniture. He had not been invited, but the message he had to deliver was urgent. Bramante was working in his library, clad in a silk robe with gold clasps at the throat and waist.

"Bramante, I will pay you the compliment of believing that you do not know what is going on," he began without preamble or salutation. "However, when the walls of St. Peter's crumble, it will make little difference whether you were stupid or merely negligent. Your walls will crack."

Bramante was annoyed at the visit.

"Who are you, a ceiling decorator, to tell the greatest architect in Europe how to build piers?"

"The same one who showed you how to build a scaffold. Someone is cheating you."

"*Davvero?* It is true? How?"

"By putting in the mix considerably less cement than the minimum requirements."

"Ah, you're an engineer!"

Michelangelo ignored the remark.

"Bramante, watch your foreman prepare the cement. Somebody is taking advantage . . ."

Bramante went purple with rage, his bull-like shoulders hunched up around his jowls.

"Whom else have you told this to?"

"No one. I hurried here to warn you. . . ."

Bramante rose, clenched both fists in front of his jaw.

"Buonarroti, if you run to the Pope with this scandalmongering I swear I'll strangle you with my bare hands. You're nothing but an incompetent trouble-making . . . Florentine!"

He spat out the last word as though it were a deadly insult. Michelangelo remained calm.

"I shall watch your cement mix for two days. At the end of that time, if you are not using safe proportions, I shall report it to the Pope and to everyone else who will listen to me."

"No one will listen to you. You command no respect in Rome. Now get out of my house."

Bramante did nothing to change his materials. Michelangelo sweated out the paint from his pores in the Piazza Scossacavalli baths, put on his brown shirt and *calze,* went to the Papal palace. Julius listened for a time, then interrupted. His voice was impatient, though not unkind.

"My son, you should not bother yourself with other people's affairs. Bramante has already warned me of your attack on him. I don't know the cause of your enmity, but it is unworthy of you."

"Holy Father, I genuinely fear for the structure. The new St. Peter's grew out of Sangallo's idea for a separate chapel for Your Holiness' tomb. I feel responsible."

"Buonarroti, are you an architect?"

"To the extent that every good sculptor is an architect."

"But you are not as good an architect, or as experienced, as Bramante?"

"No, Holy Father."

"Is he interfering in the way you are painting the Sistine?"

"No, he is not."

"Then why can't you be content to paint your ceiling and let Bramante build his church?"

"If Your Holiness would appoint a commission to investigate . . . I came out of a sense of loyalty."

"I know that, my son," replied Julius. "But St. Peter's is going to take many years to build. If you come running here in hot blood every time you see something you don't like . . ."

Michelangelo knelt abruptly, kissed the Pope's ring, left. The Pope was right. Why could he not mind his own business? Yet he could not be neutral about St. Peter's. It had been the cause of unseating his friend Sangallo, had given Bramante the ascendancy in the Pope's mind which led to the cancellation of the tomb marbles, to his being locked out of the Papal palace, to the months of irresolution in Florence, the more than a year of wasted work in Bologna, and now more years of servitude in the vault.

He was also sorely puzzled. Bramante was too good an architect to put his most important creation in danger. There must be an explanation. Leo Baglioni knew everything; he knocked on his door.

"It's not hard to explain," replied Leo casually. "Bramante is living beyond his means, spending hundreds of thousands of ducats. He has to have more money . . . from any source. Right now the piers of St. Peter's are paying his debts."

Aghast, Michelangelo cried, "Have you told the Pope this?"

"Assuredly not."

"But how can you be silent in such a matter?"

"You told the Pope the facts. What did it get you, besides an admonition to mind your own business?"

18

In August, while Michelangelo was beginning his panel of the Creation of Eve, Julius went hunting at Ostia, returning home with malaria. He was reported to be at the point of death. The rooms of his private apartment were sacked, down to its linens; the Roman nobles organized to "evict the barbarian from Rome"; from all over Italy the hierarchy hurried to Rome to select a new Pope. The city buzzed with gossip. Would Cardinal Riario at long last have his turn, and Leo Baglioni become the Pope's confidential agent? Meanwhile the French and Spanish hovered on the borders, hoping to conquer Italy during the confusion. Michelangelo became anxious. If Pope Julius died, what happened to his payment for the second half of the Sistine? He had only an oral agreement with Julius, not a written contract which his heirs would have to honor.

The only calm area in Italy seemed to be Florence, thanks to the genius of Gonfaloniere Soderini, who had kept his city-state out of the quarrels, alliances, wars, resolutely holding to the middle ground, offering refuge to both the papal and French soldiers, refusing to house the Pisa Council of protest over Julius, but not attempting to keep it out of Pisa by force. Michelangelo knew that that was where he should be right now, and forever, out of this capital of chaos.

Julius fooled Rome: he recovered. The nobles fled. The Pope took firm control of the Vatican, money started coming in, he paid Michelangelo another five hundred ducats. Michelangelo sent a modest sum home, but the greater part of the payment he kept in Rome.

"I'm flattered!" cried Balducci when Michelangelo brought in the money. Balducci, grown portly with good and quiet living, had already sired four children. "Didn't you always believe that a dishonest Florentine bank was safer than an honest Roman one?"

"Balducci, I could have saved myself endless aggravation if you had been in charge of my affairs from the beginning. But artists are endlessly inventive in their ways of being stupid about money."

"Now that you're independently wealthy," teased Balducci with his perennial good humor, "won't you come to dinner on Sunday? We entertain all our biggest depositors."

"Thanks, Balducci, but I'll wait until I'm a part owner."

When Michelangelo made a second sizable deposit, and again refused Balducci's invitation, the banker walked over to Michelangelo's house late of a Sunday afternoon, bringing a cake his cook had baked. He had not been in the house in two years; he was shocked at its shabby meanness.

"For heaven's sake, Michelangelo, how can you live like this?"

"I can't help it, Balducci. I keep hiring apprentices who swear they want to learn and will take care of the house, but they're lazy and incompetent."

"Then hire a servant, one who knows how to cook and clean, who can give you a few of the amenities of life."

"What would I do with a servant? I'm never here; I don't come home at midday for dinner . . ."

"What would you do with a trained servant? You would live in a clean house, eat decent food; come home at night to a tub of hot water for your bath, have freshly washed linens laid out for you, a bottle of wine properly cooled . . ."

"*Piano, piano* Balducci, softly, softly, you talk as though I were a rich man."

"You're stingy, not poor! You earn enough to live well. Not like a . . . a . . . You are destroying your health. What good will it do you to be a rich man in Florence if you kill yourself in Rome?"

"I won't kill myself. I am of stone."

"Isn't your life hard enough, up on that scaffold, without making it worse by penury?"

Michelangelo flinched.

"I know you're right, Balducci. I must have some of my father in me. But right now I have no patience to live well. As long as I'm on that vault, there's nothing I can salvage in terms of pleasure or comfort. The time to live well is when one is happy."

"When will that be?"

"As soon as I get back to marble."

He pushed rigorously into the autumn, painting Sundays and religious holidays. A young orphan apprentice by the name of Andrea came to help each afternoon, and to take care of his house. Michelangelo let him paint a few decorative rams' heads and doorframes, flat walls or floor surfaces that Bugiardini had done at Santa Maria Novella. He allowed Michi to fill in some of the exposed surfaces of the thrones and cornices. Young Silvio Falconi, who asked to be considered as an apprentice, and who had a talent for drawing, he permitted to do a few of the color decorations buried in the end spandrels. All the rest, the entire reach of the vault, he painted himself: every figure, every robe, every face, every limb of every nude, every expression, emotion, every *putto,* every child behind the Prophets and Sibyls, the exquisitely beautiful Sibyls, the powerful and glorious Hebrew Prophets, every last touch he did himself: a gigantic lifetime of labor jammed into three apocalyptic years.

There was new trouble abroad. Pope Julius, strong again, turned against Gonfaloniere Soderini, put an interdict on the Republic of Florence for not siding with him, for not providing troops and money when he had been in trouble, for giving refuge to enemy troops, for not crushing the Council at Pisa. Julius appointed Cardinal Giovanni de' Medici as papal legate at Bologna, with an eye to bringing Tuscany under the rule of the Vatican.

Michelangelo was invited to the Medici palace at the end of the Via Ripetta. Cardinal Giovanni, Cousin Giulio and Giuliano were gathered in the drawing room.

"You have heard that the Holy Father has appointed me papal legate to Bologna, with authority to raise an army."

"Like Piero's?"

There was a strained silence.

"I hope not," replied Cardinal Giovanni. "Everything will be peaceable. We want only to be Florentines again, to have our palace and banks and lands back."

"Soderini must go!" interjected Giulio.

"Is that part of the plan, Your Grace?"

"Yes. Pope Julius is outraged at Florence, and determined to conquer it. If Soderini goes, a few irreconcilables on the Signoria . . . ."

"Who is to rule Florence in Soderini's place?" He tried to keep down his rising emotion.

"Giuliano."

Michelangelo looked across the room to Giuliano, saw the color mount in his cheeks. The choice seemed a stroke of genius: for Giuliano, now thirty-two, tall, with a slight beard and mustache, said to have weak lungs, yet to Michelangelo's glance seeming robust, Giuliano was close to *Il Magnifico* in mind, spirit and temperament. He had put in years of disciplined study, tried to prepare himself in the image of his father. He was handsomer than Lorenzo, though his nose was long and flat, his large eyes heavy-lidded, and had inherited most of Lorenzo's finest qualities: a gentle soul, with a touch of wisdom in him, and no violence. He had a reverence for art and learning, a deep love for Florence, its people and traditions. If Florence had to have a ruler, over and beyond its elected Gonfaloniere, Lorenzo's youngest and most gifted son seemed perfect for the job.

The men in the room knew Michelangelo's affection for Giuliano. They did not know that a fifth person was present, standing in his robes of office in the center of the floor, his long homely face, wobbly nose, bland eyes and yellow-streaked white hair all corporeally present for Michelangelo: Piero Soderini, elected lifetime Gonfaloniere of the Republic of Florence.

Looking down at his cracked and paint-stained nails, Michelangelo asked, "Why have you told me this?"

"Because we want you on our side," replied Cardinal Giovanni. "You belong with the Medici. Should we need you . . ."

He threaded his way as through the eye of a needle to the Piazza Navona, took a series of right angles to the Piazza Venezia, then went down the street of the ancient Roman forums with their scattered columns standing upright, and entered the colosseum, brightly lit in the full moonlight, for a thousand years Rome's quarry for home builders needing hand-hewn stone. He climbed to the topmost tier, sat on the parapet of the gallery overlooking the vast theater from its lowest, darkest pits with its cells where Christians, warriors, slaves, animals had been herded, up to its top sections of stone seats where the multitudes of the Roman Empire had sat, screaming for battle and blood.

. . . battle and blood, blood and battle. The phrase kept going through his mind. It seemed to be all that Italy was to know. All that he had known in his lifetime. At this very moment Julius was gathering another army to march north. If Florence resisted, the Pope would send Giovanni's troops against its walls. If Florence did not resist, Gonfaloniere Soderini would be driven out, as would all the members of the Signoria who did not consent to the loss of their independence. Now he too was being asked to become a part of it.

He loved both Gonfaloniere Soderini and Giuliano de' Medici. He felt a strong loyalty to *Il Magnifico,* to Contessina, yes, to Cardinal Giovanni too. But he had a faith in the Republic, which had given him his first recognition. To whom was he to be unfaithful, ungrateful? Granacci would tell him, "If anyone asks what side you're on, answer 'On the side of sculpture.' Be courageous in art, and a coward in the world of affairs."

Could he be?

19

During the gray winter months of 1512, while he painted the lunettes over the tall windows, his eyes became so badly afflicted that he could not read a line unless he threw his head back sharply and held the letter or book high in the air above him. Though Julius had remained in Rome, his wars had started. His armies were commanded by the Spaniard, Cardona of Naples. Cardinal Giovanni left for Bologna, but twice the Bolognese, bolstered by the French, fought off the Pope's troops. Cardinal Giovanni never got into Bologna. The French then chased the Pope's army into Ravenna where, on Easter, the decisive battle was fought; ten to twelve thousand soldiers of the papal troops were reported to have died in the field. Cardinal Giovanni and Cousin Giulio were taken prisoner. The Romagna fell into French hands. Rome was in panic. The Pope took refuge in the fortress of Sant'Angelo.

Michelangelo went on painting his vault.

Again the tide of fortune turned: the winning French commander was killed. The French fought among themselves. The Swiss came into Lombardy to fight the French. Cardinal Giovanni, having saved Giulio by a ruse, himself escaped and returned to Rome. The Pope returned to the Vatican. During the summer Julius recovered Bologna. The French were driven out of the country. The Spanish general Cardona, an ally of the Medici, sacked Prato, just a few miles from Florence. Gonfaloniere Soderini was forced to resign, fleeing with his family. Giuliano entered Florence as a private citizen. Behind him came Cardinal Giovanni de' Medici with Cardona's army, returning to his old palace in the quarter of Sant'Antonio near the Faenza gate. The Signoria resigned. A Council of Forty-five was appointed by Cardinal Giovanni, a new constitution adopted. The Republic had come to an end.

During all these months the Pope kept insisting that Michelangelo complete his ceiling quickly, quickly! Then one day Julius climbed the ladder unannounced.

"When will it be finished?"

'When I have satisfied myself."

"Satisfied yourself in what? You have already taken four full years."

"In the matter of art, Holy Father."

"It is my pleasure that you finish it in a matter of days."

"It will be done, Holy Father, when it will be done."

"Do you want to be thrown down from this scaffolding?"

Michelangelo gazed at the marble floor below.

"On All Saints' Day I shall celebrate mass here," declared the Pope. "It will be two years since I blessed the first half."

Michelangelo had wanted to touch up some of the draperies and skies *a secco*, in gold and ultramarines, as his Florentine predecessors had done below him. But there would be no time now. He had Michi and Mottino take down the scaffold. The next day Julius stopped by.

"Don't some of the decorations need to be brightened with gold?" he demanded.

Useless to explain that he had wanted to do this. Nor was he going to reerect the scaffold and go back up into the vault.

"Holy Father, in those times men did not bedeck themselves with gold."

"It will look poor!"

Michelangelo planted his feet stubbornly beneath him, his teeth locked, his chin stiffened. Julius gripped his fist over his walking stick. The two men stood before the altar beneath the heavens and glared at each other.

"Those whom I have painted were poor," said Michelangelo, breaking the silence. "They were holy men."

On All Saints' Day official Rome dressed itself in its finest robes for the Pope's dedication of the Sistine Chapel. Michelangelo rose early, went to the baths, shaved off his beard, donned his blue hose, blue wool shirt.

But he did not go to the Sistine. Instead he walked out under the portico of his house, pulled back the tarpaulin, stood ruminatively before the marble columns he had waited these seven long years to carve. He walked to his work desk, picked up a pen, wrote:

> The best of artists hath no thought to show
> Which the rough stone in its superfluous shell
> Doth not include; to break the marble spell
> Is all the hand that serves the brain can do.

Standing on the threshold of his hard-earned freedom, disregarding his costly hose, the fine wool shirt, he took up his hammer and chisel. Fatigue, memory, bitterness and pain fell away. Sunlight streaming in the window caught the first shafts of marble dust that floated upward.

BOOK EIGHT

THE MEDICI

Pope Julius II survived the completion of the Sistine vault by only a few months. Giovanni de' Medici, the first Florentine to be elected to the papacy, was the new Pope.

Michelangelo stood in the Piazza San Pietro among the Florentine nobles who were determined to make this the most lavish procession ever to be seen in Rome. Ahead of him were two hundred mounted spearmen, the captains of the thirteen regions of Rome with their banners flying, the five standard-bearers of the Church carrying flags with the papal arms. Twelve milk-white horses from the papal stables were flanked by a hundred young nobles in fringed red silk and ermine. Behind him were a hundred Roman barons accompanied by their armed escorts, the Swiss guards in uniforms of white, yellow and green. The new Pope, Leo X, mounted on a white Arabian stallion, was shaded from the warm April sun by a canopy of embroidered silk. Next to him, dressed as the standard-bearer of Rhodes, was Cousin Giulio. The lone figure in mourning was the Duke of Urbino, nephew of Julius.

Gazing at Pope Leo X, his heavy bulk perspiring from the weight of the triple tiara and heavily jeweled cope, Michelangelo thought how inscrutable were the ways of God. Cardinal Giovanni de' Medici had been in Florence when Julius died, so ill with ulcers he had had to be carried to Rome on a litter in order to cast his ballot. The College of Cardinals, sealed into the airless Sistine Chapel, had spent nearly a week battling between the forces of Leo Baglioni's Cardinal Riario and Cardinals Fiesco and Serra. The one member who had no enemies was Giovanni de' Medici. On the seventh day the College had unanimously settled on mild-mannered, modest, friendly Giovanni, fulfilling *Il Magnifico's* plan when he had had Giovanni consecraraed in the Badia Fiesolana at the age of sixteen.

The trumpeters sounded for the beginning of the march across the city from St. Peter's, where Leo had been crowned in a pavilion in front of the wrecked Basilica, to St. John in Lateran, earliest home of the Popes. The Sant'Angelo bridge was covered with brilliant-hued draperies. At the beginning of the Via Papale, the Papal Way, the Florentine colony had erected a giant triumphal arch bearing the Medici emblems. Throngs lined streets covered with sprigs of myrtle and box.

Riding between his cousin Paolo Rucellai and the Strozzi who had purchased his early Hercules, Michelangelo watched Leo, beaming with joy, raising his pearl-encrusted gloved hands in benediction, his chamberlains walking beside him throwing handfuls of gold coins to the crowds. Every house had brocades and velvets hung from its casements. The antique marbles of Rome lined the Via Papale: busts of the emperors, statues of the apostles, saints, the Virgin, placed side by side with pagan Greek sculptures.

At midafternoon Pope Leo descended from his horse by means of a ladder, stood for a moment by the ancient bronze equestrian statue of Marcus Aurelius in front of the Lateran. Then, surrounded by his College of Cardinals, flanked by Cousin Giulio and the Florentine and Roman nobles, he entered the Lateran and seated himself on the Sella Stercoraria, ancient seat of power occupied by the first Popes.

Michelangelo ate little of the elaborate banquet served in the hall of the palace of Constantine, restored for the feast. At sunset he remounted his horse to follow in Pope Leo's train back to the Vatican. By the time they reached the Campo dei Fiori night had fallen. Torches and tapers lighted the streets. Michelangelo dropped off his horse at Leo Baglioni's house, handed the reins to a groom. Baglioni had not been invited to ride in the procession; he was alone in the house, unshaven, gloomy. This time he had been certain Cardinal Riario would be elected to the papacy.

"So you made it to the Vatican ahead of me!" he grumbled to Michelangelo.

"I'd be happy never to see the inside of the Papal palace again. I cede my place to you."

"This is one game in which the winner can't cede. I'm out; you're in. There'll be glorious commissions."

"I have years of carving ahead for Julius' tomb."

It was late when he returned to his new home which sat in a sea of centuries in the valley between the Capitoline and Quirinal hills, near the foot of Trajan's column where the Macello dei Corvi, Slaughterhouse of the Crows, dribbled into the crowded square. Just before his death Pope Julius had paid him two thousand ducats to settle the Sistine account and to commence carving the tomb marbles. With Gonfaloniere Soderini and the Signoria in exile from Florence, his commission to carve the Hercules for the front of the Signoria had vanished. When this property, consisting of a main building built of yellow firebrick, a shaded veranda along one side, a cluster of wooden sheds in the rear, a stable, tower and overgrown garden with shady laurel trees, had come on the market at a reasonable price, he had bought it and moved his marbles in. Trajan's market, a tiered, abandoned ruin rising just across from him, had once housed hundreds of merchants in separate stalls, attracting buyers from all over the world. Now the piazza was quiet, there were no shops, only a few small wooden houses remained in the shadow of the undomed church of Santa Maria di Loreto. During the day people passed through on their way to the Colonna palace or the Piazza del Quirinale on the one side, or to the Anibaldi palace and San Pietro in Vincoli on the other. At night it was as silent as though he were living deep in the *campagna*.

The house had two front doors, both facing the Macello dei Corvi, for it had formerly been rented as two separate apartments. His living quarters consisted of a good-sized bedroom facing the street, behind it a dining-sitting room, and behind that, feeding out to a garden pavilion, a low-ceilinged kitchen of the same yellow brick. In the second half of the house he had taken out the wall separating its two rooms, making himself as large a workshop as he had built in Florence. He bought a new iron bed for himself, woolen covers, a new mattress stuffed with wool, sent money to Buonarroto for fine Florentine bed sheets, tablecloths and towels which he kept with his store of shirts, handkerchiefs and blouses in a wardrobe standing next to his bed. He acquired a sorrel for traveling the rough cobbled streets of the city, ate his meals at a well-set table, went abroad in warm weather in a cape of black Florentine cloth lined with satin. Silvio Falconi was proving to be a good apprentice-servant.

In the clapboard houses and stone tower at the rear of his garden were assistants helping with the tomb. Michele and Basso, two young stonemasons from Settignano; a foundling and promising draftsman who had asked permission to call himself Andrea di Michelangelo; Federigo Frizzi and Giovanni da Reggio, making models for the bronze frieze; Antonio from Pontassieve, who had agreed to bring his crew to Rome to shape and ornament the building blocks and columns.

He felt easy about his future. Had not Pope Leo X announced to the courtiers about him: "Buonarroti and I were educated together under my father's roof"?

For the first time since he had fled from Julius in April of 1505, eight years before, he was carving. Not one marble but three heroic columns, all at once. There was a natural rhythm between the movement of his breath and the movement of his hammer arm as he pounded the chisel across a cutting groove. This tactile joining with marble again made him swell with joy. He recalled the first lesson the Topolinos had taught him:

"Stone works for you. It yields itself to skill and to love."

He threw himself into the three blocks with passion yet with an inner calm and surety. The three white columns surrounded him in his workshop like snow-covered peaks. He desired intensely to breathe the same air his blocks did. He carved for fourteen hours a day, until his legs felt as though they were up in his body; yet he had only to leave the solid image before him, go to the door and gaze restfully into the void of sky to be refreshed.

He was plowing a straight furrow.

Carving the Moses, mounds of white dust caked in his nostrils like tranquillity settling into the marrow of his bones; he felt a man of substance because his own three-dimensional force became fused with the three-dimensional stone. As a boy on the steps of the Duomo he had been unable to prove that sculpture was superior to painting as an art; here in his studio, moving smoothly from the Moses to the Dying Captive to the Heroic-Rebellious Captive, he could demonstrate the truth with irrefutable crystalline fact.

Moses, holding the stone tablets under one arm, would be eight feet tall and massive even though seated. Yet what he was after was not an awareness of volume but of inner weight and structure. By pushing one leg sharply backward he set into action a dynamics of balance, creating a space-famine which was nourished by the monumentality of the right knee and calf, the outward thrust compensating for the vertigo caused by the withdrawn leg. His chisel hand flew unerringly to the point of entry in the four-foot-thick block: under the sharply pointed horizontal left elbow and corded forearm. He carved his line of flow through the wrist to the index finger pointing to the stone tablets under the opposite arm.

At midnight he reluctantly took off his paper cap with its goat-tallow candle. There was no sound except the distant barking of dogs scavenging behind the Colonna kitchens. Moonlight splashed in through the rear garden window, enveloping the block with a transcendent light. He pulled up a bench and sat before the roughed-out mass, musing about Moses as a human being, a prophet, a leader of his people who had stood in the presence of God and been given the Law.

The sculptor who did not have a philosophic mind created empty forms. What point was there in his knowing precisely where to enter the marble block if he did not know which Moses he intended to project? The meaning of his Moses, as much as the sculptural techniques, would determine its value. He knew where Moses sat in space; but where did he stand in time? Did he want to present the passionate angry Moses, returned from Mount Sinai to find his people worshiping the Golden Calf? Or the saddened, embittered Moses, fearing that he had arrived too late with the Law?

As he sat drinking in the almost liquid flow of the issuing figure he understood that he must refuse to imprison Moses in time. He was seeking the universal Moses who knew the ways of man and God; the Lord's servant on earth, the voice of His conscience. The Moses who had been called up to the heights of Mount Sinai, had hidden his face because he dared not look upon the open sight of God, and received from Him the carved tablets of the Ten Commandments. The fierceness of soul which would burn outward through the cavernous depths of his eyes could not be motivated by despair, or the desire to punish. What had moved Moses was the passionate resolve that his people must not destroy themselves, that they must receive and obey the Commandments which God had sculptured on the stone tablets, and endure.

His reverie was interrupted when the front door was unceremoniously thrown open by Balducci, who was advising him on the revision of the tomb contract. Pope Leo was using his good offices to persuade the Duke of Urbino and the other Rovere heirs to make the agreement more equitable for Michelangelo, to allow him more time and more money. Michelangelo glanced at his friend in amusement as he filled the doorway, for Balducci, who had been exactly Michelangelo's build when they first met on the streets of Rome in 1496, was now double Michelangelo's size in everything but the extremities of head and feet.

"Do you get fat from making profits," Michelangelo teased, "or do the profits come from getting fat?"

"I have to eat for you and for myself," boomed Balducci, patting his big stomach with both palms. "You're just as much a runt as you were when you tried to play football against Doni in Piazza Santa Croce. Have they agreed to the new terms?"

"They've raised the price to sixteen thousand, five hundred ducats. Seven years to complete, more if I should need it. . . ."

"Let me see the plans for the new tomb."

Reluctantly, Michelangelo dug a batch of papers out of a stained parchment folio. Balducci cried disapprovingly:

"You told me you were reducing the size!"

"So I have. Look here, the front side is a half less in length. I no longer have to build a walk-in chamber . . ."

Balducci had been counting on the sheets.

"How many statues are there?"

"*In toto?* Forty-one."

"What are their sizes?"

"From life size to twice normal."

"How many do you intend to carve yourself?"

"Perhaps twenty-five. All but the angels, *putti* . . ."

Even in the flickering light of the single candle Michelangelo could see Balducci's face turn purple.

"You're *pazzo!*" he cried. "All you've reduced is the structural framework which you weren't going to build anyway. It was bad enough that you didn't listen to Jacopo Galli eight years ago, but you were younger then. What conceivable excuse can you have for contracting a second time to do the impossible?"

"Julius' executors won't settle for less. Besides, I'm getting nearly the price and the time allowance Galli wanted for me."

"Michelagnolo," said Balducci softly, "I can't take Jacopo Galli's place as a man of culture, but he respected my talents sufficiently to make me manager of his bank. This is stupid business. Twenty-five giant figures must take you twenty-five years. Even if you live that long, do you want to be chained to this mausoleum for the rest of your days? You'll be more of a slave than these Captives you're blocking out."

"I have a good *bottega* now. Once the new contract is signed I'll bring more stonemasons from Settignano. I have so many of these figures already carved in my mind, not to bring them to life would be a cruel waste. Watch, and you will see marble flying around here like coveys of white doves in the spring."

2

The Sistine ceiling had produced an effect equal to the unveiling of the David in Florence. From artists of every medium who had flocked to Rome from all over Europe to help Leo celebrate his elevation to the papacy, Michelangelo had rewon the painting title first earned by the Bathers: "Master of the World." Only the group centered around Raphael continued to fight the vault, calling it anatomy rather than artistry, carnal, exaggerated, overwrought. But they were hampered now, for Bramante was no longer art emperor of Rome. Cracks of such serious dimension had shown in his piers of St. Peter's that all work had been stopped and extensive studies undertaken to see if the foundations could be saved. Pope Leo had been too kind to remove Bramante officially as architect; but work on the Belvedere above the Vatican was also in abeyance. Bramante's hands had become so crippled with palsy that he had been obliged to turn over the drawing of his plans to Antonio da Sangallo, nephew of Michelangelo's friend and architectural teacher, Giuliano da Sangallo. Over Bramante's house there now hung the slight odor of decay that had settled over Sangallo's the day Bramante won the prize for his design for St. Peter's.

One dusk Michelangelo answered a knock on his door, impatient with any intrusion. He found himself gazing into the amiable hazel eyes of a young man in an orange silk cloak, with a fair complexion and blond hair that brought Granacci to his mind.

"Master Buonarroti, I am Sebastiano Luciani of Venice. I have come to confess . . ."

"I am not a priest."

". . . that I have been a simpleton and idiot. This knock, these words, are the first time my hand or tongue have made sense since I arrived in Rome. I brought my lute so that I could accompany myself while I tell you my bathetic story."

Amused by the Venetian's infectiously light manner, Michelangelo bowed him in. Sebastiano perched on the highest stool in the room and ran his fingers across the strings of the lute.

"Sing and everything passes," he murmured.

Michelangelo dropped into the one padded chair in the workroom, sat with his legs stretched out stiffly before him, hands behind his head. Sebastiano sang a scanned improvisation of how he had been brought to Rome by the banker Chigi to paint his villa, had joined in the idolizing of Raphael by proclaiming that Raphael's brush was "in attune with the techniques of painting, pleasing in color, ingenious in invention, charming in all its expressions and designed like an angel." Buonarroti? "Admittedly he can draw, but his colorings? Monotonous! His figures? Bumpy anatomy. His scenes? Without grace . . ."

"I have heard these charges before," interrupted Michelangelo. "They weary me."

"As well they might! But Rome shall hear this dirge no more from me. From now on I sing the praises of Master Buonarroti."

"What has brought this change of heart?"

"The eclectic Raphael! He has picked my bones. Absorbed all I learned from Bellini and Giorgione, so that now he is a better Venetian painter than I! And so humbly thanking me for teaching him!"

"Raphael borrows only from the best. He does it well. Why are you abandoning him?"

"Now that he has become a magic Venetian colorist he is getting more commissions than ever. While I . . . I get nothing. Raphael has swallowed me, all except my eyes, which have been feasting on your Sistine ceiling these past days."

Sebastiano lowered his head over his lute, heels locked in the top rung of the stool. His voice filled the room with a robust gondolier's song. Michelangelo studied the Venetian before him, wondering why he had really come.

Sebastiano dropped in often for music and talk. An inveterate pursuer of pleasure and pretty girls, he needed money for the hunt. He was living on portraits while longing for one of the big commissions that brought a steady income. His draftsmanship was weak, he had no sense of invention. But he was loquacious, full of fun, refusing to be serious even about the illegitimate son who had just been born to him. Michelangelo continued to work while half listening to the amusing chatter.

"My dear *compare,* godfather," said Sebastiano, "don't you get mixed up, carving three blocks all at once? How do you remember what you want to do with each of them when you move from figure to figure?"

Michelangelo chuckled. "I wish I could have all twenty-five blocks standing around in a great circle. I would move from one to the other so fast that in five years I'd have all of them completed. Have you any concept of how thoroughly you can hollow out blocks of marble by thinking about them for eight years? Ideas are sharper than chisels."

"I could be a great painter," said Sebastiano in a flat tone. "I have all the techniques. Put a painting in front of me, and I'll copy it so exactly you'll never recognize it from the original. But how do you get the idea in the first place?"

It was a wail, almost of anguish, one of the few times Michelangelo had seen Sebastiano serious. He ruminated while chiseling out the two Tablets of the Law.

"Perhaps ideas are a natural function of the mind, as breathing is of the lungs? Perhaps God puts them there? If I knew the origin of men's ideas, I would have solved one of our deepest mysteries."

He moved upward to Moses' wrist and hand resting on top of the tablets, the fingers leading into the long-flowing, waist-length beard.

"Sebastiano, I'm going to make some drawings for you. Your use of color and shadow is as fine as Raphael's, your figures are lyrical. Since he has borrowed your Venetian palette, why should you not borrow my designs? Let's see if we can't supplant Raphael."

He enjoyed sketching at night after a full day of carving, thinking up new variations on old religious themes. He introduced Sebastiano to Pope Leo, showed the pontiff scenes from the life of Christ beautifully transformed by Sebastiano. Leo, who cherished all musical entertainers, made him welcome at the Vatican.

Late one night Sebastiano burst in crying, "Have you heard the news? A new rival to Raphael has arisen! The best of the Venetians, equal to Bellini and Giorgione. Paints with the charm and grace of Raphael! But is a stronger, more imaginative draftsman."

"Congratulations!" said Michelangelo with a wry grin.

When Sebastiano was given the fresco commission for San Pietro in Montorio, he worked hard to bring Michelangelo's designs to glowing life in his cartoons. Rome assumed that, as part of Michelangelo's *bottega,* Sebastiano was learning to draw with his master's hand.

Only Contessina, newly arrived in Rome with her family, thought there was something more involved. She had spent two years of evenings sitting by Michelangelo's side watching him draw; she knew his calligraphy. When he attended her elaborate dinner for the Pope and his court, for Contessina was determined to become Leo's official hostess, she took him into a small study that was so faithful a replica of Lorenzo's *studiolo* with its wood paneling and fireplace, cases of cameos and amulets that it brought nostalgic tears to his eyes. She gazed at him head on, her dark eyes flashing, demanded:

"Why do you allow Sebastiano to parade your work as his?"

"It does no harm."

"Raphael has already lost an important commission to Sebastiano."

"It's a godsend to the overworked, harried man."

"Why should you stoop to a hoax like this?"

He returned her gaze, thinking how much she was still the Contessina, Little Countess, of their youth; but at the same time how greatly she had changed since the election of her brother to the papacy. Now she was the Big Countess, brooking no interference from her two elder sisters Lucrezia Salviati and Maddalena Cibo, who had also moved their families to Rome. Contessina fought for papal appointments, benefices for the members of the Ridolfi family, working hand in glove with Cousin Giulio, who was in control of the business and politics of the Vatican. In her spacious gardens she had had a stage built on which were performed plays and musicals for the nobility of the Church and city-states. More and more the laity of the Christian world wanting favors and appointments were coming to Contessina. This grasping for power and the wielding of it was understandable, Michelangelo thought, after the years of exile and poverty; but it had made a change in Contessina which left him uncomfortable.

"Since I finished the Sistine," explained Michelangelo, "certain people have been saying, 'Raphael has grace, Michelangelo has only stamina.' And since I will not stoop to fight the Raphael clique for my position, I find it amusing to have a talented young painter do it for me. Without getting myself involved, Rome is beginning to say, 'Raphael has charm, but Michelangelo has profundity.' Isn't it amusing that fun-loving Sebastiano could have accomplished this transition by improvising verses of praise to my vault, accompanying himself on the lute?''

Contessina clenched her fists at the irony in his voice.

"It is not amusing! I am the Countess of Rome today. I can protect you . . . officially . . . with dignity. I can bring your detractors to their knees. That is the way. . . .''

He reached forward, took her two tightly clenched fists between his stonehewer's hands.

"No Contessina, it is not the way. Trust me. I am happy now, and working well.''

In place of the anger came the lightninglike, radiant smile he remembered from their childhood clashes.

"Very well, but if you do not come to my parties I shall expose you and Sebastiano as a couple of humbugs.''

He laughed.

"Who ever got the better of a Medici?''

Without thinking he placed his hands on the puffed shoulders of her silk gown, drew her close, searching for the fragrance of mimosa. She started to tremble. Her eyes grew enormous. Time dissolved: the *studiolo* in the Via Ripetta in Rome became the *studiolo* in the Medici palace in Florence. They were not the great countess and the great artist, with half of their years already gone; but for a fleeting instant, at the threshold of life.

3

Swiss guards in green, white and yellow arrived at his house early in the morning with what amounted to a *breve* from Pope Leo to dine at the Vatican palace that day. It was a hardship to walk away from his work, but he had learned that one did not ignore the summons of a Pope. Silvio laid fresh linens over his arm, Michelangelo went to the baths of the Via de' Pastini, soaked the caked dust out of his pores, and arrived at the Vatican at eleven.

He began to realize why the Romans were complaining that "Rome has sunk to a Florentine colony,'' for the Vatican was filled with triumphant Tuscans. Moving through the throng of more than a hundred dinner guests assembled in the two throne rooms, he recognized Pietro Bembo, the Vatican Secretary of State and humanist-poet; the poet Ariosto, who was writing his *Orlando Furioso;* the neo-Latinist Sannazaro; Guicciardini, the historian; Vida, author of the *Christiad;* Giovanni Rucellai, writing one of the first blank-verse tragedies, *Rosmunda;* Fracastoro, physician-author; Tommaso Inghirami, diplomat, librarian, classicist and improviser of Latin verses; Raphael, now painting the Stanza d'Eliodoro in the Papal palace, and occupying a place of honor just below Pope Leo; the woodcarver Giovanni Barile of Siena, who was decorating the doors and shutters of the palace with Medici emblems. Michelangelo spied Sebastiano and was pleased that his protégé had been invited.

Having bought back from the Republic of Florence most of his father's great library, Leo had experts searching the world for important manuscripts. He had also brought to Rome Lascaris, his father's Greek manuscript hunter, to edit and print the jewels of Greek literature. The Pope was also in process of reorganizing the Roman Academy for classical studies, which had been neglected by Julius, and was giving new hope of learning to the University of Rome. Michelangelo heard this new court of Leo's described as "the most brilliant and cultured since Imperial Rome."

Throughout the long sumptuous dinner, of which the Pope could eat little because he suffered from bad digestion and gaseous disturbances, Leo waved his white, bejeweled, plump hands while he accompanied Gabriel Marin of the remarkably beautiful voice, the master violinist Marone of Brescia, and Raffaelle Lippus, the blind balladier. Between the musical performances buffoons kept Leo amused. His court jester, *Il Magnifico's* former barber, had a fund of anatomical witticisms which he unleashed between bouts of eating forty eggs in a row, and then twenty capons, while nearsighted Leo gazed at him through his magnifying glass, emitting peals of laughter at the gargantuan gorging.

The four-hour dinner seemed endless to Michelangelo. He was incapable of absorbing but the most modest amount of salted trout, roast capon, sweet rice cooked in milk of almonds. He writhed in his seat over the many wasted hours, wondering how soon he would be released. For Pope Leo the dinner was but a preliminary to an afternoon and night of pleasure. Now came some of Italy's finest poets to read their new verses, then a ballet, then a masque, then another buffoonery at the expense of Camillo Querno, called the Arch-Poet, who read from an atrocious epic poem while Leo crowned him with cabbage leaves. The entertainments would continue until Leo could no longer keep his eyes open.

Walking home through the dark and deserted streets, Michelangelo recalled Leo's line to Giulio immediately after his coronation:

"Since God has seen fit to give us the papacy, let us enjoy it."

Italy was more peaceful than it had been for a number of pontificates. True, money was pouring out of the Vatican at an unprecedented rate; several times that day Michelangelo had seen the delighted Leo fling purses containing several hundred florins to singers and performers, which had caused one of his sober neighbors to comment:

"The Pope could no more save a thousand ducats than a stone could fly up into the sky."

Leo was going to need money: millions upon millions of ducats, an even more incredible fortune for the pleasures and the arts than Julius had needed for war. When he begged Cardinal Pucci, in charge of the Vatican's resources, to be sure that nothing was done that would bring dishonor on the Church, no simony, no sale of cardinalates or benefices, the cardinal shrugged and said:

"Holy Father, you have assigned to me the task of financing this worldwide business. My first obligation is to keep it solvent."

Michelangelo reached the Macello dei Corvi as the midnight chimes rang out. He changed into his work clothes, so thick with the accumulation of stone dust and impregnation of sweat from the hot summer sun they had become an extra layer of his own skin. With a sigh of relief he picked up hammer and chisel, juggled them in both hands to feel their accustomed weight. He determined grimly that this was the last time he would be persuaded to waste an entire day. His sympathies went to pale, puffy-faced Raphael, who was summoned at all hours of the night and day for the most trivial of the Pope's errands, to give an opinion of an illuminated manuscript or design a wall decoration for Leo's new bath chamber. Raphael was always polite, interested, though forced to waste his work hours and to go without sleep.

This was not for him. He was not a charming man. He would be eternally damned if he ever became one!

He could lock out Rome, but the world of Italy was now the world of the Medici, and he was too closely allied to the family to escape. Defeat overcame Giuliano, the only one of *Il Magnifico's* sons he loved. Letters from the family and Granacci told of how magnificently Giuliano was governing Florence: abstemious, gentle, warmhearted, walking the streets unaccompanied, opening the Medici palace to scholar and artist, reviving the Plato Academy, leaving the administration of government and justice in the hands of the elected councils. But these qualities did not appeal to Cousin Giulio or to Pope Leo. Leo recalled his brother from Florence, and now in September Michelangelo was dressing to go to the ceremony in which Giuliano was to be made a Baron of Rome.

The ceremony took place on the ancient Capitoline, just above Michelangelo's house. He sat with the Medici family: Contessina and Ridolfi with their three sons, Niccolò now twelve, and to be named a cardinal on achieving sixteen; the older sisters, Maddalena Cibo, with her husband and five children, including Innocenzo, also to be made a cardinal, and Lucrezia Salviati with her numerous family, and her son Giovanni, in line for a cardinalate. Leo had had a stage built over the ruins where Sangallo had taken Michelangelo sketching to recreate the glories of ancient Rome. The jagged earthen piazza had been covered by a wooden floor and hundreds of seats. Michelangelo listened to speeches of welcome to Giuliano from the heads of the Roman Senate, epic poems in Latin, a series of masques and satires in the Florentine tradition, watched as a woman wrapped in cloth of gold, personifying Rome, was carried to Giuliano's throne to thank him for condescending to become commander of the city. After a bawdy comedy by Plautus, Pope Leo bestowed privileges on Rome, such as a reduction of the salt tax, to the thunderous applause of thousands of Romans thronging the bare hillsides. Then began a six-hour banquet with a profusion of dishes not seen in Rome since the days of Caligula and Nero.

At the end of the orgy Michelangelo made his way down the Capitoline through the throng that was being fed from the leftovers of the Saturnalia above, and locked both street doors of his house behind him. Neither he nor Giuliano nor Rome had been fooled by this performance, which was designed to conceal the fact that scholarly Giuliano, who loved the Republic of Florence, had been replaced by Lorenzo, twenty-one-year-old son of Piero and the ambitious Alfonsina. Young Lorenzo had been sent to Tuscany with a letter of instructions formulated by Giulio telling him how to control elections, appoint his own Council, absorb the functions of government.

Giulio's power as the figure behind the Pope was growing. A commission appointed by Leo had declared Giulio of legitimate birth, on the grounds that *Il Magnifico's* brother had agreed to marry Giulio's mother, and that only his murder in the cathedral had kept the marriage from taking place. Now that he was legitimate, Giulio was appointed a cardinal; he would have the official power to rule the Church and the Papal States.

Nor was Leo's and Giulio's desire to extend the Medici control throughout Italy remote from Michelangelo's affairs. They had been trying to drive the Duke of Urbino, a Rovere nephew and heir of Pope Julius, out of his dukedom. Today Pope

Leo had deposed the duke as standard-bearer of the Church, in favor of Giuliano. Ultimately Leo would seize his lands. The Duke of Urbino, a violent man, was the one to whom Michelangelo would be responsible for Julius' tomb. The war that had been brought into the open between the Medici and the Roveres could mean nothing but trouble for the Buonarroti.

Over the mild winter he secured a reprieve from Contessina's receptions by bringing her to the workshop to see his three emerging figures; and from Leo's entertainments by a series of excuses which amused Leo sufficiently to grant him the high favor of abstinence. His only associates during the long productive work weeks were his assistants in the garden, his solitary diversion an occasional supper with a group of amiable young Florentines whose friendship was based on a nostalgic longing to be within sight of the Duomo.

Only once did he break his fast: when Giuliano came to the studio to urge him to attend a reception for Leonardo da Vinci, whom Giuliano had invited to Rome and installed in the Belvedere.

"You, Leonardo and Raphael are the great masters of Italy today," said Giuliano in his quiet way. "I should like the three of you to be friends, perhaps work together. . . ."

"I'll come to your reception, Giuliano, of course," said Michelangelo. "But as for working together. . . . We are as different species as are birds, fish and fowl."

"Strange," murmured Giuliano, "I should have thought that all artists would be brothers. Come early. I'd like to show you some of the experiments in alchemy Leonardo is conducting for me."

Entering the Belvedere the next day, Giuliano took him through a series of workrooms extensively renovated for Leonardo's purposes: windows made taller to give higher light, the kitchen built to take care of boiling alchemy pots, a paved terrace overlooking the valley, Papal palace and Sistine, furniture built by the Vatican carpenters, trestle tables, stands for mixing paints. Giuliano had persuaded Pope Leo to give Leonardo a painting commission, but as Michelangelo was led through the workshops, including that of a German ironworker who was to help Leonardo with his mechanical inventions, he saw that Leonardo had not yet begun to work at his art.

"Look at these concave mirrors," exclaimed Giuliano, "this metal screwcutting machine, all new. When I took him out on the Pontine marshes he located several extinct volcanoes, and sketched plans for draining the fever-laden area. He won't let anyone see his notebooks, but I suspect he's completing his mathematical studies for the squaring of curved surfaces. His work on optics, his formulations of the laws of botany—amazing! Leonardo feels he will be able to tell the age of trees by counting the rings on the trunk. Imagine!"

"I would rather imagine him painting beautiful frescoes."

Giuliano led him back toward the drawing room.

"Leonardo is a universal man. Has there been such a scientific mind since Aristotle? I think not. Art he conceives as only one aspect of human creativity."

"It is beyond my comprehension," growled Michelangelo stubbornly. "When a man has such a rare gift he should not spend his days counting the rings on trees."

Leonardo emerged, followed by his lifetime companion, the still exquisite and youthful Salai, dressed in an elaborate red blouse with lacy sleeves. Leonardo himself, Michelangelo thought, looked tired and old, his magnificent flowing beard and shoulder-length hair now white. The two men, who understood each other not at all, exchanged expressions of pleasure at the reunion. Leonardo in his high-pitched voice told Michelangelo of the time he had spent studying the Sistine ceiling.

"After analyzing your work I have written corrections to my treatise on painting. You have proved that the study of anatomy is extremely important and useful to the artist." His voice became impersonal. "But I also see a grave danger there."

Nettled, Michelangelo asked, "Of what kind?"

"Of exaggeration. The painter, after he studies your vault, must take care not to become wooden through too strong an emphasis on bone, muscles and sinews; nor to become too enamored of naked figures which display all their feelings."

"And you think that mine do?" Michelangelo's gorge was rising.

"On the contrary, yours are close to perfection. But what of the painter who tries to go beyond you? If your use of anatomy makes the Sistine so good, then he must use even more anatomy in order to be better."

"I cannot hold myself responsible for later exaggerations."

"Nor are you, except that you have brought anatomical painting to its outside limits. There is no margin for others to perfect. Consequently, they will distort. Observers will say, 'It is Michelangelo's fault; without him we could have refined and improved anatomical painting for hundreds of years.' Alas, you have started it, and you have ended it, on one ceiling."

Other guests began to arrive. Soon there was a hubbub in the rooms. Michelangelo stood alone at a side window overlooking the Sistine, not knowing whether he was perplexed or hurt. Leonardo was astonishing the guests with new contrivances: animals filled with air which sailed over everyone's head; a live lizard to which he had attached wings filled with quicksilver, and whose head he had decorated with artificial eyes, horns and a beard.

"The mechanical lion I made in Milan could walk several steps," he announced to the guests who were congratulating him on his inventiveness. "And when you pressed a button his breast fell open, exposing a bunch of lilies."

To himself Michelangelo muttered, *"Questo è il colmo!* This is the limit!" and rushed home, trembling to get the substantive feel of marble between his hands.

4

In the spring Bramante died. Pope Leo ordered an elaborate funeral for him at which artists spoke of the beauty of his Tempietto, the Cortile of the Belvedere, the Castellesi palace. Pope Leo then sent for Giuliano da Sangallo, his father's favorite architect. Sangallo arrived; his former palace on the Via Alessandrina was returned to him. Michelangelo was there within a matter of minutes to embrace his old friend.

"We meet again!" cried Sangallo, joy shining in his eyes. "I survived dismissal, you the years in the Sistine vault." He paused, knit his brows. "But I found a strange communication from Pope Leo. He asks if I mind making Raphael my assistant at St. Peter's. Is Raphael an architect?"

Michelangelo felt an involuntary twinge. Raphael!

"He has been directing the repairs at St. Peter's, and is seen on the scaffolding at all hours."

"But it is you who should take over my work. After all, I am nearly seventy."

"Thank you, *caro;* let Raphael help you. It gives me freedom with the marbles."

Pope Leo borrowed heavily from the Florentine bankers Gaddi, Strozzi and Ricasoli for the continuation of St. Peter's. Sangallo resumed the building.

Michelangelo allowed few visitors to his studio: former Gonfaloniere Soderini and his wife, Monna Argentina, who had been forgiven by Pope Leo and permitted to live in Rome; three men who offered him his first private commission since Taddeo Taddei had requested the circular Our Lady. Metello Vari dei Porcari, a Roman of ancient blood, and Bernardo Cencio, a canon of St. Peter's, said:

"We would like you to do a Risen Christ for us. For the church of Santa Maria sopra Minerva."

"I am pleased to have the request," declared Michelangelo; "but I must tell you that my contract with Pope Julius' executors does not permit me to take commissions. . . ."

"This would be a single piece, sculptured at your leisure," exclaimed Mario Scappucci.

"A Christ Risen?" Michelangelo was intrigued by the idea. "Beyond the Crucifixion? How do you envisage the piece?"

"Life size. With a cross in his arms. In an attitude that will be determined by you."

"Could I think about it?"

He had long felt that most Crucifixions did a grave injustice to Jesus, portraying him as crushed and defeated by the weight of the cross. He had never believed that for a single instant: his Christ was a powerful male who had carried the cross on the road to Calvary as though it were the branch of an olive tree. He began to draw. The cross became but a puny thing in Jesus' grasp. Since his commissioners had reversed tradition by asking for a cross after the Resurrection, why could he too not depart from the accepted concept? Instead of the cross crushing Christ, Jesus would stand triumphant. The first rough sketches crosshatched, he gazed intently at his drawing. Where had he seen this Christ before? Then he remembered: it was the figure of a stonemason he had drawn for Ghirlandaio in the first year of his apprenticeship.

Though he managed to keep the peace in Rome, his family in Florence kept his cup of anxiety overflowing. Exhausted by Buonarroto's badgering for money to open his own wool shop, Michelangelo took a thousand ducats from the funds provided by his new Rovere contract and had Balducci send them to Florence. Buonarroto and Giovansimone opened their shop, promptly running into trouble. They needed more capital. Couldn't Michelangelo send them another thousand? He would soon be earning a profit on his money. . . . In the meanwhile, Buonarroto had found a girl he would not mind marrying, her father having promised a sizable dowry. Did Michelangelo think he should marry her?

He sent Buonarroto two hundred ducats, which Buonarroto never acknowledged. What had happened to them? For that matter what had happened to the money Lodovico took from Michelangelo's account and had promised to return? What about his funds on deposit at Santa Maria Nuova hospital; why did the *spedalingo* delay in paying out the money as Michelangelo demanded? What was the good of owning five farms if the share tenants were stealing him blind?

A severe blow was word from Buonarroto that Mother Topolino had died. He put aside his work and walked to San Lorenzo in Damaso to say a prayer for the repose of her soul. He sent money to Buonarroto with instructions to ride up to the church in Settignano and have the priest say a mass for her there.

He locked the gates of his mind, as he had locked the gates of the garden. Working the marble was not only a delight, it was a consolation. How rarely a good piece of marble went bad! He spent the ducats advanced to him by the Roveres, hiring additional crews of master carvers, bronze casters, carpenters, all crowding his yard from dawn to dark, building the architectural base and the front façade while he sketched steadily to complete the drawings for the remaining sculptures, turning the Settignano *pietra serena* masons into marble *scultori* who could mass a dozen giant blocks so that he could get to the carving of the Victories.

The months passed. His apprentices brought him the local gossip. Leonardo da Vinci had fallen into serious trouble, spending so much time experimenting with new oils and varnishes for preserving the work that he failed to do any painting on Leo's commission. The Pope had cried mockingly at court:

"Leonardo will never do anything, for he commences by thinking about the end before the beginning of the work."

The courtiers spread the jest. Leonardo, learning that he had become an object of ridicule, abandoned Leo's commission. The Pope heard through informers that Leonardo was dissecting in the hospital of Santo Spirito, and threatened to drive him out of Rome. Leonardo, fleeing the Belvedere to continue his studies in the marshes, came down with malaria. When he recovered he found that his ironmonger had destroyed his mechanical experiments. When his protector, Giuliano, left at the head of the papal troops to drive the invading French out of Lombardy, Leonardo could no longer remain in Rome. Where to go? France, perhaps. He had been invited there years before. . . .

Sangallo too was stricken, with such a severe case of gallstones that he could do no work at all. For weeks he was bedridden, his eyeballs becoming mustard yellow, his strength ebbing. He was carried back to Florence on a litter. His repatriation had come too late.

Raphael became the architect of St. Peter's, and of Rome.

Michelangelo received an urgent note from Contessina. He hurried to the palace, was received by her son Niccolò, taken upstairs to her bedroom. Though the weather was warm, Contessina was covered by several quilts, her pale face lying exhausted on the pillows, her eyes cavernous.

"Contessina, you are ill."

Contessina beckoned him to her bed, patted a place for him to sit. He took her hand, white and fragile, in his own. She closed her eyes. When she opened them again there were tears moistening the warm brown pupils.

"Michelagnolo, I remember the first time we met. In the sculpture garden. I asked, 'Why do you work so furiously? Doesn't it exhaust you?' "

"And I answered, 'Cutting stone does not take strength out of you, it puts it back in.' "

"Everyone thought I was soon to die, as my mother and sister had . . . You put strength in me, *caro.*"

"You said, 'When I am near you, I feel strong.' "

"And you answered, 'When I am near you, I feel confused.' " She smiled. "Giovanni said you frightened him. You never frightened me. I saw how tender you were, under the surface."

They stared at each other. Contessina whispered:

"We have never spoken of our feelings."

He ran his fingers gently over her cheek.

"I loved you, Contessina."

"I loved you, Michelangelo. I have always felt your presence in the world."

Her eyes lighted for a brief instant.

"My sons will be your friends. . . ."

She was seized with a coughing spell that shook the big bed. As she turned her head away from him, raised a handkerchief to her lips, he saw the red stain. His mind flashed back to Jacopo Galli. This would be the last time he would see Contessina.

He waited, gulping the salt of unshed tears. She refused to turn her head back to him.

He whispered, *"Addio, mia cara,"* wheeled silently, left the room.

The death of Contessina shook him deeply. He concentrated on the head of the Moses, striving to bring it to a state of completion: upward through the beard to the intense, full lower lip, the mouth so expressive that a sound might emerge at any moment; to the sharply protruding nose, the passionate outburst of expression in the forehead, the creased muscles about the cheekbone, and finally, to the eyes set deeply in the head, creating dark accents to contrast with the highlights he would file onto the bone and flesh structure of the face.

Then he turned to the exquisitely sensitive, agonized figures of the two Captives, one resisting death, one yielding, pouring into their flesh his own grief and sense of loss. He had known that there could never be a life together for Contessina and himself. But he too had always been aware of her presence, had been nourished and gladdened by it.

Laying aside his hammer and chisel, he made models for the bronze frieze, bought twenty thousand pounds of brass, summoned additional stonecutters from Settignano, speeded up the work of the Pontassieve crew in squaring and decorating the structural stones, wrote a barrage of letters to Florence to locate a marble expert who could go to Carrara and buy him more blocks. He had all the ingredients for a sustained drive to complete in another year the all-important front wall, the Moses and Captives mounted in place, Victories installed in the niches, the bronze frieze set above the first floor. He would work like a man possessed; but since he was to be possessed by marble, it seemed good and natural.

Pope Leo had been determined to reign without war, but that did not mean he could avoid the incessant attempts on the part of his neighbors to conquer the rich country; nor the internecine strife which had been the city-states' history. Giuliano had not been able to subdue the French in Lombardy. He had been taken ill in the attempt, and moved to the monastery of the Badia at Fiesole where, it was rumored, he was dying, even as had Contessina. . . . The Duke of Urbino had not only refused to help the papal army but had become an ally of the French. Pope Leo himself rushed north to make a treaty with the French, which left him free to attack the Duke of Urbino.

Immediately on his return to Rome he summoned Michelangelo to the Vatican. Leo had been kind to the Buonarroti family while in Florence, naming them counts palatine, a high honor on the road to nobility, and granting them the right to display the Medici crest of six balls.

Leo, sitting at a table in his library with Giulio, was examining through his magnifier a number of gems and carved cameos he had brought back from Florence. His travels seemed to have done him good, for he had lost some of his flatulence, there was color in his usually chalk-white cheeks.

"Holy Father, you were most generous to my family."

"Not at all," said Leo. "It is many years now that you have been of our house."

"I am grateful, Holiness."

"Good," said Leo, laying aside the glass. Giulio also came to attention. "Because we do not want you, a Medici sculptor, spending your time creating statues for a Rovere."

"But the contract! I am obliged . . ."

A silence fell. Leo and Giulio looked at each other for an instant.

"We have decided to present you with the greatest art commission of our age," cried the Pope. "We wish you to undertake a façade for our family church, San Lorenzo . . . as my father thought of it . . . a glorious façade . . ."

Michelangelo stood staring sightlessly out the window, over the chaotic jumble of tawny rooftops. He heard the Pope speaking behind him though he could not discern the words. He forced himself back to the table.

"But, Holy Father, the tomb for Pope Julius! You recall the contract signed only three years ago. I must finish what I have contracted for, or the Roveres will prosecute me."

"Enough time has been given to the Roveres." Giulio's manner was abrupt. "The Duke of Urbino made a treaty to help the French against us. He was partly responsible for the loss of Milan."

"I'm sorry. I did not know. . . ."

"Now you do!" Cardinal Giulio's dark, sharp-featured face became less grim. "A Medici artist should serve the Medici."

"And so it shall be," replied Michelangelo, also relaxing. "Within two years the tomb will be complete. I have everything organized . . ."

"No!" Leo's round face was flushed with anger, a rare and frightening sight. "There will be no two years for the Roveres. You will enter our service at once."

His manner quieted.

"Now, Michelangelo. We are your friends. We will protect you against the Roveres, secure a new contract which will give you more time and money. When you have completed the façade for San Lorenzo you can return to Julius' mausoleum. . . ."

"Holy Father, I have lived with this tomb for ten long years. I have every inch of its twenty-five figures carved in my mind. We are ready to construct the front wall, cast the bronzes, mount my three big statues . . ." His voice had been rising; he was shouting now. "You must not stop me. It is a crucial moment for me. I have trained workmen. If I have to dismiss the men, leave the marbles lying about. . . . Holiness, on the love I bore your noble father, I implore you not to do this terrible thing to me. . . ."

He dropped on one knee before the Pope, bowed his head.

"Give me time to finish the work that is planned. Then I can move to Florence and to the façde in peace and happiness. I will create a great façade for San Lorenzo, but I must not be tormented in mind and spirit. . . ."

His only answer was a crosshatched silence in which Leo and Giulio, from a lifetime of communication, were expressing to each other by the look in their eyes what they thought of this difficult artist bowed before them.

"Michelangelo," said Pope Leo, shaking his head, "you still take everything so . . . so . . . desperately."

"Or is it," asked Giulio, "that you do not wish to create the San Lorenzo façade for the Medici?"

"I do, Your Grace. But it is a huge undertaking. . . ."

"You are right!" cried Leo. "You must leave for Carrara at once, choose the blocks yourself, supervise the cutting. I will have Jacopo Salviati in Florence send you a thousand florins to pay for them."

Michelangelo kissed the Pope's ring, left Leo's presence, descended the steps of the Vatican palace with the tears streaming down his face. Courtiers, prelates, ambassadors, merchants, entertainers thronging up the stairs to begin their day of merriment, gazed at him in amazement. He did not know that they saw, nor did he care.

That night, lonely, miserable, he found himself walking in the quarter where Balducci had searched among the prostitutes. Coming toward him was a young girl, slender, her blond hair plucked back to give her a high brow, dressed in a semi-transparent blouse, a string of heavy baubles about her neck causing a deep declivity between her breasts. For a startling instant he thought he caught an image of Clarissa. It passed quickly, for the girl's features were coarse, her movements angular; but even this fleeting memory of Clarissa had been sufficient to awaken his longing.

"*Buona sera. Vuoi venire con me?* Would you like to come with me?"

"I don't know."

"*Sembri triste.* You seem sad."

"I am. Can you cure that malady?"

"*È mio mestiere.* That is my trade."

"I will come."

"*Non te ne pentirai.* You won't regret it."

But he did, within forty-eight hours. Balducci listened to the description of his symptoms, cried:

"You've caught the French sickness. Why didn't you tell me you wanted a girl?"

"I didn't know I wanted one. . . ."

"Idiot! There's an epidemic in Rome. Let me summon my doctor."

"I contracted this by myself. I'll cure it by myself."

"Not without mercury ointment and sulphur baths, you won't. It sounds like a light case, you might be able to cure it quickly."

"I have to, Balducci. Carrara is a rough life."

5

The Apuan Alps loomed like a dark wall beyond his window. He slipped into his shirt, stockings and hobnail boots for the climb, left his apartment at the rear of the apothecary Pelliccia's house, went down the courtyard steps and into the Piazza del Duomo where an agent and quarry owner slipped past him in the darkness, the shawls over their shoulders tied at the waist. On the wooden bridge over the piazza two priests crossed from the sacristy to the choir loft of the cathedral for early mass. Carrara was asleep inside its horseshoe-shaped walls, the semicircle of stone closed toward the sea, open on the steep mountain side. He had not wanted to leave Rome, but being at the heart of his source material assuaged the pain.

Tucking his dinner of bread under one arm, he walked up a narrow street to the Porta del Bozzo, remembering the proud line of the inhabitants that "Carrara is the only town in the world that can afford to cobble its squares with marble." In the ash-gray light he saw the marble houses with their delicate marble window frames and columns, for everything that Florence did so superbly with its *pietra serena* the master masons of Carrara did with their marble from the quarries in the mountains above.

Michelangelo liked the Carrarini. He felt at home with them because he was a stone man himself; yet there could be no question but that they were the most inbred, suspicious, insular group he had encountered. They refused to be identified with the Tuscans to their south or with the Ligurians to their north; few left this mountain area, none married outside it; the boys were in the quarries alongside their fathers by the time they were six, and left only at their death. No farmers were permitted to bring their produce to the Carrara markets except those who had been admitted within the walls for generations; when a quarry needed a new man he was selected from the known farming families. Carrara and Massa, the largest of the neighboring towns, had fought each other since time before memory. Even the tiny surrounding villages were raised in the tradition of *campanilismo,* each group for his own tower or town, and against everyone else.

Carrara was a one-crop town: marble. Each day the Carrarino lifted his eyes to the reassuring white slashes in the hills, the patches that resembled snow even in the blinding heat of summer, and thanked God for its sustenance. Their life was communal: when one prospered, all prospered; when one starved, all starved. Their life in the quarries was so dangerous that when they parted from each other they did not say, "Good-by" but *"Fa a modr,* go carefully."

He wound along the Carrione River. The September air was sharp, good for climbing. Below him he could see the fortress-tower of the Rocca Malaspina and the cathedral spire standing guard over the elbow-to-elbow houses wedged into tight walls that had not been expanded for centuries. Soon the mountain villages began to appear, Codena, Miseglia, Bedizzano, each cluster pouring out its male population, feeding rivulets of quarriers into the human stream flowing upward. These were men more like him than his own brothers: small, wiry, tireless, taciturn, with the primordial power of men who work stubborn stone. They pushed upward, *matalò* or jacket hung on their right shoulder, through Torano, Station of the Bulls.

Sleep had their tongues. As first light sifted beyond the peaks they began speaking in clipped monosyllabic hammer strokes, the compact Carrarino language Michelangelo had had to learn, for the Carrarino dialect broke off words the way chips were chiseled off a block, *casa* becoming *ca; mama* becoming *ma; brasa,* embers, becoming *bra; bucarol,* canvas, becoming *buc;* a swift efficient language of one-syllable words. They were asking him about yesterday's search through the quarries of Grotta Colombara and Ronco.

"You find?"

"Not yet."

"Comes today."

"I hope."

"Go to Ravaccione."

"Heard news?"

"Break out new block."

"I try."

Pale yellow sunlight silhouetted the rugged cliffs ahead. The milky ravines of marble chips, dumped for centuries from the *poggio,* or work level below the quarry, emerged like winter drifts of snow. They were up a thousand feet now, moving effortlessly through primeval stands of oak, beech, fir, thorny bushes called *bacon* and then higher up, through a grass for grazing sheep in the summer, called *paleri.* Beyond the trees and San Pellegrino flowers, the trails cut across exposed rock with marble cropping to the surface.

The stream of two hundred quarriers, fathers and sons, split into rivulets again, making their way up the three main canals or marble draws, each of which had its favored diggings: the Ravaccione, which included the Polvaccio quarry, the Canale di Fantiscritti, which the ancient Romans had opened; and the Canale di Colonnata. As they parted, each murmured:

"*Fa a modr,* go carefully."

"*Se Dio 'l vorà,* God permitting."

Michelangelo continued with a group on to the Polvaccio where he had found his best marble for Julius' tomb eleven years before. The Polvaccio, at the extreme end of the Poggio Silvestro, produced good statuary white, but the surrounding quarries of Battaglino, Grotta Colombara and Ronco contained ordinary marbles with slanting veins. As the sun edged over Monte Sagro they reached the nearly mile-high *poggio* where the crew dropped their jackets and were at work as swiftly as they could raise a hammer. The *tecchiaioli,* steeplejacks of the quarries, descended their ropes from the precipices above, cleaning the ledges of loose stone, clearing away with their *subbie* and *mazzuoli* as they dangled several hundred feet in the air, to protect those working below from falling debris.

The owner of the quarry, called The Barrel from his enormous round torso, greeted Michelangelo heartily. Though he was as illiterate as his workmen, his contact with buyers from England, France, Germany and Spain had taught him to speak a near-full sentence.

"Ah, Buonarroti, today we have your great block."

"Permit me to hope."

The Barrel grasped him by the arm, led him to the area where water-soaked wooden pegs had been driven into a V-shaped incision and, in the natural course of swelling, had forced an opening in the solid marble cliff which the quarriers were now attacking with levers and sledge hammers, driving the pegs deeper to dislodge the marble from its bed. Since marble was quarried vertically, the topmost blocks were being pried out. The foreman cried, "Fall below!" Workmen sawing blocks with sand and water fled to the edge of the *poggio.* The topmost block ripped from its hold with the sound of a falling tree, landed with tremendous impact in the level work space below, splitting according to its *peli,* cracks.

When Michelangelo came forward and studied the huge jagged block he was disappointed. Heavy rains soaking through the bare foot or two of earth that had covered the marble for a millennium had carried with them enough chemicals to vein the pure white. The Barrel, looming in front of him, had cut this particular block hoping Michelangelo would be satisfied.

"A beautiful piece of meat, no?"

"It is good."

"You accept?"

"It is veined."

"The cut is near perfect."

"I must have perfect."

The Barrel lost his temper.

"You cost us cash. A month we quarry for you and not one *soldo* we see."

"I will pay you much money . . . for statuary marbles."

"God makes marble. Complain to Him."

"Not until I am convinced there are not whiter blocks behind these."

"You want me to cut down my whole peak?"

"I will have thousands of ducats to spend for the façade of San Lorenzo. You will have your share."

The Barrel turned away, a scowl on his face, grumbling something which Michelangelo could not catch, but which sounded as though the owner were calling him "The Big Noise." Since he had not raised his voice, Michelangelo was sure he had misunderstood.

He picked up his jacket and dinner, struck out for Ravaccione, using an old goat trail that gave him but a few inches of security as he moved down the cliff. He reached the quarry at ten o'clock. On the *poggio* level, teams were two-manning long whipsaws across marble blocks with the *bardi,* apprentices, keeping a stream of sand and water under the teeth. At a chanting call from the foreman, the quarriers who were widening a fault in the stratified marble cliffs above came down to a wooden shed for their dinner. Michelangelo joined them on a plank stretched across two blocks, took out his thick slices of bread flavored with olive oil, vinegar, salt and berry seed, dipped them into the communal bucket of water and ate hungrily. Monna Pelliccia had offered him *companatico,* a covering for his bread, but he preferred to eat what the quarriers ate.

This was the best way to get along with the Carrarini; for the Carrarini were special. They said proudly of themselves, "So many heads, so many ideas." During his stay in 1505 when he had been gathering blocks for Julius' tomb he had been received with as much reserve as any of the other foreign sculptors who came to buy marble for their commissions. But as he had spent his days in the quarries, detecting intuitively the hollows, bubbles, veining, knots; as he had worked with the teams to bring his twenty-ton blocks down the steep slopes on rollers with nothing to hold back the oblong cargo but a few ropes tied around nests of wooden stakes, they came to believe that he was not only a sculptor but a quarryman. Now, returning to Carrara, he was accepted as a Carrarino, invited to the taverns on Saturday night where the men gathered to drink the Cinqueterre wine and gamble at *bastoni,* cards with varying numbered sticks, the winners and losers drinking after each hand until the tavern was drunk with fun and wine.

Michelangelo was proud to be accepted at a table where the gambling chairs passed from father to son as a family inheritance. Once, seeing an empty building on a rise above the town where a half dozen marble shops lined the Carrione, the front wall open to the river, he had thought to himself, "Why should I go back to Rome or Florence to carve my statues when here in Carrara it seems natural rather than peculiar if a man wants to give his whole life to sculpture?" Here in Carrara there were expert *smodellatori,* men who did the massing from the model; he would never lack for trained assistants. Crossing Florence or Rome after a day of furious carving, covered from head to foot by marble dust, he had been an object of concern if not derision. Here he looked and felt no different from all the other men returning home from the quarries or marble shops. He belonged.

At Ravaccione he found himself disappointed for a second time that morning: a new cut, ripped out of the white mountain wall and falling to the *poggio* below, showed soft fissures. He could not use it for one of his giant figures.

"A beautiful block," said the owner, hovering near. "You buy?"

"Perhaps. I will try."

Though he had replied courteously, the owner's face set in a grim expression. Michelangelo was about to move on to the next quarry when he heard the sound of the horn coming from the Grotta Colombara, a number of ridges away, echoing up and down the valleys. The quarriers froze in their positions. Then they laid down their tools, draped their jacket over their right shoulder, began a wordless climb down the trail.

One of their members had been hurt, perhaps killed. Every quarrier in the Apuan Alps made the hour-long descent to his village, there to await word of the fate of his companion. No further work would be done until the following morning, and none then, if there should be a funeral to attend.

Michelangelo descended by the path along the river, watched the women washing their clothes in water the color of milk from the marble workshops that swept their dust and chips into the stream. He circled to the bottom of the town, entered the Market of the Pigs, admitted himself to his two-room apartment at the rear of the apothecary's house which sat on a level midway between the shop and the flat of the Pelliccia family above. Apothecary Francesco di Pelliccia, fifty-five, bigger in stature than most of the Carrarini, was the second best-educated man in town, having been trained at the neighboring University of Pisa. He was one of the few men who had set foot outside Carrara, to buy potions from the Near East, and had seen the David in Florence, as well as the Sistine ceiling and the Moses in Michelangelo's house in Rome. Michelangelo had rented these rooms before; the men had become friends. Pelliccia owned important marble quarries, yet he did not use his friendship as an excuse to press his output upon Michelangelo.

Pelliccia had gone to attend the injured man. There was a doctor in Carrara but few of the quarriers used him, saying, "Nature cures and the doctors collect." When someone fell ill a member of the family came to the apothecary shop, described the symptoms, and then waited while Pelliccia concocted a prescription.

Signora Pelliccia, a busty vigorous woman in her early forties, set the table in the dining room overlooking the Piazza del Duomo. She had saved Michelangelo some of the fresh fish from their midday dinner. He was finishing the *minestrone* when a groom arrived from the Rocca Malaspina with a note from the Marquis Antonio Alberico II of Carrara, lord of the Massa-Carrara area, requesting that Michelangelo come at once to the castle.

6

The Rocca was a short walk uphill, a fortress bastion which served as the mountain anchor for Carrara, the opposite wall of the horseshoe fortifications being impregnable because of the Carrione River flowing below it. Built in the twelfth century, the Rocca had crenelated defense towers, a moat and thick stone walls to withstand siege: for that was one reason the Carrarini hated all outsiders, they had been overrun continuously for five hundred years. Only lately had the Malaspina family been able to sustain the peace. What had originally been a crude fortress had been converted to an elegant marble palace, with frescoes and furnishings from all over Europe.

The marquis was waiting at the head of a majestic flight of stairs. Even while exchanging greetings Michelangelo could not resist admiring the splendid marble floors and columns ringing the stair well. The marquis was tall, courtly, commanding in mien, with a long thin face, high cheekbones and a luxuriant beard.

"It was kind of you to come, Maestro Buonarroti," the marquis said in his low patriarchal voice. "I thought you might like to see the room where Dante Alighieri slept when he was a guest of my family here."

"Dante was a guest here?"

"Indeed. He wrote some lines of *The Divine Comedy* about our country. This was his bed. And here the plaque with his verses:

> That man whose back is close behind his belly
> Is Arunas, who once dwelt on Luni's mount,
> Near where Carrara's toilers work below;
> And from his cave among the snow-white marbles
> He could observe the galaxy of stars,
> And glimpse the azure of the ocean wave. . . ."

Later, in the paneled library, the marquis got down to business. First he showed Michelangelo a letter from Monna Argentina Soderini, who was also a Malaspina:

Master Michelangelo, a sculptor whom my husband deeply loves, and who is a very honest, polite and kind person, of such a value as to make us think that today there is no man in Europe who is similar to him, has gone to Carrara to work a certain quality of marbles. We warmly wish that you offer him every possible benefit and assistance.

The marquis gazed at Michelangelo. "There is some beginning unpleasantness," he murmured.

"Unpleasantness? On what score?"

"Do you remember a name that the owner of the quarry called you?"

"I thought I heard him call me 'The Big Noise.' What can it mean?"

"In Carrarino it means to be a complainer, not to accept what is handed to you. The owners say that you don't seem to know your own mind."

"They're partly right," Michelangelo admitted ruefully. "It has to do with the façade for San Lorenzo. I have a suspicion that Pope Leo and Cardinal Giulio concocted the idea just to take me off the Rovere tomb. They have promised me a thousand ducats to buy marbles, but nothing has arrived. For that matter, I too have been remiss: I promised them scale models, but I have not drawn a line since leaving Rome. A troubled mind, Marquis, makes a poor draftsman."

"May I make a suggestion? Sign two or three modest contracts for marbles to be delivered in the future. The owners will be reassured. It seems that a number of them who have quarried blocks just for you fear they have cut too much and may have to idle the men. These *gente,* people, have little reserve. A few weeks' beans and flour separate them from hunger. Threaten this thin margin and you become their enemy."

"It is a narrow precipice. I will do as you suggest."

Within the next weeks he signed two contracts, one for eight pieces of marble over eight feet high, plus fifteen smaller ones, with a deposit of a hundred florins; and then bought from Mancino, Left-handed, three pieces of white marble from his quarry at Polvaccio. Two witnesses signed the contract in the Piazza del Duomo. Tension vanished as he promised The Barrel and Pelliccia to buy heavily as soon as money arrived from the Pope.

He had dissipated the tensions for the Carrarini, but he could not do as much for himself. Although the Rovere heirs had buckled under to the Pope's demands, writing a third contract which further cut down the size of the tomb and extended the time limit from seven to nine years, Michelangelo knew that they were outraged.

Pope Leo had blandly assured the Roveres that he could continue to carve the tomb marbles while he did those for the façade; but no one, least of all Michelangelo, was fooled by this promise. From now on he would work for the Medici as long as there was a Medici Pope in the Vatican. The unfinished tomb was a canker eating at the lining of his stomach. Sebastiano had promised to keep a careful watch over his house in the Macello dei Corvi; still he worried about his marbles, and the decorated blocks.

News from Florence was equally joyless. The city's pleasure in elevating its first Pope had been soured by the fact that the election had cost the city its freedom. Giuliano had died. The Republic was gone, the elected councils banished, the constitution outlawed. The Florentines did not like being ruled by twenty-four-year-old Lorenzo, son of Piero, whose smallest act was dictated by his Roman mother and by Cardinal Giulio. Nor did the arrival of Giulio in Florence to tighten the Medici control do anything to raise its spirits. Buonarroto's shop was operating at a loss. It was not Buonarroto's fault, these were not good times for a new business venture. Buonarroto needed more money, which Michelangelo could not spare.

His brother had brought his wife, Bartolommea, into the family house to live. He kept expressing the hope that Michelangelo would like her. She was a good woman. She had nursed Lodovico during a recent illness and was managing the house quite well with only the elderly servant, Monna Margherita, who had been caring for Lodovico since *Il Migliore's* death. Michelangelo gathered that she was not especially attractive of face or figure, but had brought a substantial dowry, and had a quiet sweetness.

"I will like her, Buonarroto," Michelangelo told his brother. "Just let us pray that she will produce sons. With Sigismondo living like a nomad, and Giovansimone unwilling to support even a cricket, your good Bartolommea is our only hope to continue the Buonarroti name."

Lodovico had become a real problem. He had grown cantankerous, blaming Michelangelo for squandering his funds on the Rovere tomb without completing it; for taking the Medici façade without a contract or guarantees; for not pouring more funds into Buonarroto's shop; for refusing to buy the additional houses in Florence and farms in the surrounding countryside which Lodovico spent months tracking down. The old man barely let a post go by without demands, reproaches and recriminations.

Winter rains turned the mountain trails into flooding river beds. Then the snows fell. All work stopped in the mountains. The quarriers in their oozing, cold stone houses in the foothills settled down to remain as warm as possible while consuming as little beans and *pasta* as possible. Michelangelo bought himself a wagonload of logs, set up his worktable in front of the fire and surrounded himself by letters from Baccio d'Agnolo, who was going to help him build a wooden model of the façade, from Sebastiano telling him that a dozen sculptors, including Raphael, were trying to take the façade commission away from him; and from Domenico Buoninsegni in Rome, an honest and able man in the tradition of Jacopo Galli, who was devoting time to getting a façade contract negotiated, imploring him to come to Rome because Pope Leo was clamoring to see the designs.

Michelangelo paced the cold room, his hands snuggled under his armpits to keep them warm, saying to himself, "I must get back to that wonderful feeling I had when *Il Magnifico* walked me to San Lorenzo and said, 'One day you will carve a façade that will be the wonder of all Italy.'"

He reached Rome as the city was preparing for Christmas. He went first to his house and was relieved to find everything as he had left it. His Moses seemed nearer to completion than he had remembered. If only he could steal off a month . . .

He received a hearty reception at the Vatican. Cardinal Giulio appeared to have grown surer of his control of the Church. As Michelangelo knelt to kiss the Pope's ring he noted that Leo's double chin was again cascading over the collar of his ermine robe, the fleshy cheeks almost hiding the small sickly mouth.

"It gives me pleasure to see you again, my son," said Leo as he led Michelangelo to the papal library.

The aromatic scents of parchment manuscripts took Michelangelo back to the library in the Medici palace; he saw *Il Magnifico* standing with an illuminated volume bound in purple leather. The sharpness of this vision, as though he were recalling a scene enacted only a week instead of twenty-five years before, enhanced the illusion that he was designing the façade for Lorenzo.

He spread his sheets of paper on a desk. There was an outline of the unfinished brick of San Lorenzo, then the façade, divided into two floors and a tower, the lower floor with a dividing cornice over the three entrances to the church. Flanking the doors he had drawn four large figures representing the saints Lawrence, John the Baptist, Peter and Paul on the ground floor; in the niches of the second floor, larger than life-size statues of Matthew, Luke and Mark; and on the tower, Damian and Cosmas, represented as physicians, which was what the word "medici" meant. He would carve these nine major figures himself; the rest of the façade was architectural. The nine-year plan would afford him the time to complete Julius' marbles. At the end of the contract both the Medici and the Roveres would be happy.

"We are prepared to be generous," said the Pope.

"But one thing must be changed," added Giulio quietly.

"What is that, Your Grace?"

"The marbles must come from Pietrasanta. They have the finest statuary marble in the world."

"Yes, Your Grace, I have heard. But there is no road."

"A matter of labor."

"The Roman engineers were said to have tried to open such a road and failed."

"They did not try hard enough."

There was a look of finality on Cardinal Giulio's hollow, dark face. Michelangelo surmised that something more than the quality of marble was involved. He turned to Leo with a questioning glance.

"You will do better in Pietrasanta and Seravezza," the Pope explained. "The Carraresi are a rebellious lot. They have not co-operated with the Vatican. The people of Pietrasanta and Seravezza consider themselves loyal Tuscans. They have signed over their quarries to Florence. Thus we shall secure the purest statuary marble for only the cost of labor."

"I don't believe it is humanly possible to quarry in Pietrasanta, Holiness," protested Michelangelo. "The blocks would have to come out of stone precipices a mile high."

"You will make the trip to the top of Monte Altissimo and report on what you find."

Michelangelo did not reply.

7

He returned to Carrara, to his rooms behind Pelliccia's apothecary shop. When the Pope's thousand ducats were at last sent to him by Salviati, he put out of his mind any worry about the Pietrasanta quarry and began buying marble almost in a fever: from Jacopo and Antonio three blocks that were on display in the Market of the Pigs, seven blocks from Mancino. He went into partnership with Ragione, Reason, to finance the quarrying of a hundred wagonloads.

That was as far as it went. He rejected the wooden model he had hired Baccio d'Agnolo to make, declaring that it "looked like a childish thing." He made one himself . . . which was no better. He paid La Grassa, a *pietra serena* hewer from Settignano, to make a clay model . . . and then destroyed it. When Salviati wrote from Florence, and Buoninsegni from Rome, that the Pope and the cardinal were disappointed that he had not yet poured his foundations, he made a contract with Francesco and Bartolomeo from Torano for another fifty cartloads of marble, despite the fact that he had designed nothing more than the sizes and shapes of the blocks he wanted the *smodellatori* to mass.

The Marquis of Carrara invited him to Sunday dinner at the Rocca, served the traditional Carrarino cake, *focaccia,* made of sifted wheat flour, eggs, pine nuts and raisins. Afterward he asked about the Pope's plan for opening quarries in Pietrasanta, news of which had seeped through from Rome.

"Be reassured, *signore,*" said Michelangelo. "No work will be done in those mountains."

Then came a stinging letter from Buoninsegni:

> The Cardinal and Pope think you are neglecting the marble at Pietrasanta. They believe you do it on purpose. . . . The Pope wants Pietrasanta marbles.

He told no one of his destination, arranging to have a horse ready at dawn to take him down the coast road. Pietrasanta had once had considerable importance as a boundary stronghold, but unlike the Carrarini, the Pietrasantans no longer enclosed themselves within walls they could not hope to defend. Their houses were built around a spacious square where the markets and festivities were held; the western side was open to a superb view of the Tyrrhenian Sea; the Pietrasanta farmers died in their beds of the incurable malady of old age.

He tarried for a moment at the morning market to buy an orange. Above him towered Monte Altissimo, named Highest Mountain by the people of Pietrasanta and Seravezza because its awesome bastion of sheer rock, jutting jaggedly a mile into the skies, dwarfed and intimidated those who lived in its portentous presence. The Carrarini pointed out disdainfully that Monte Altissimo was not the highest mountain at all; Monte Sagro, Pizzo d'Uccello and Pisanino above Carrara were taller. The Pietrasantans made the rejoinder that the Carrarini could live with their peaks, traverse them, quarry them, but that Monte Altissimo was impregnable. The Etruscan, genius with stone, and the Roman army had not conquered its implacable gorges or precipices.

There was a narrow wagon road between Pietrasanta and the hill town of Seravezza, used for transporting farm products. Michelangelo started up the deeply rutted path to the site of the defending fortress for the hundred families farming the valleys and knolls. Here everything was unrelieved stone, the houses interlocked around a cobbled piazza. He found a room for the night, and a guide in the husky young son of a cobbler. His name was Antonio, called Antò, and he was the possessor of a height of pale pink gums which showed above his stubby teeth when he spoke.

"What you pay? Agreed! We start at first light."

They left Seravezza in the pitch-dark. The first hour's walk in the rising foothills was not difficult, for Antò knew the terrain. But where the trail ended they had to cut through thickets of underbrush with knives taken from the cobbler's shop. They climbed straight up dark stone ranges, rock formations that looked as though they had been made as steps for the gods, half scrambling, half falling down precipitous gullies, keeping from plunging over cliffs by grappling an occasional tree trunk. They descended deep into gorges as dark as Antò's shop in Seravezza, clammy cold from centuries without sun, then climbed on hands and knees up the next range rolling backward, with Monte Altissimo towering in the background still several uncharted miles away.

By midmorning they emerged at the top of a shrub-covered promontory. Between Michelangelo and Monte Altissimo was only a sharp hogback, and beyond this a canyon at the foot of the *monte* where they would have to cross a river. Antò took from his leather pouch two loaves of heavy-crusted bread, the soft insides scooped out and refilled with fish in tomato sauce. They ate, then went down into the valley before this next to last hogback, worked their way toward a low division where the cascading ranges sloped downward to expose the wall of Monte Altissimo.

Michelangelo sat on a boulder looking upward at the fearsome Alps.

"With the help of God, and the whole French army, one might get a road built to this point. But how could anyone build a road up that perpendicular wall?"

"Not possible. Why try?"

"To get marbles out."

Antò gazed at Michelangelo, moving his lips up and down incredulously over the field of pink gum.

"You never said marble. That's *pazzesco!* Nobody brings blocks down."

"*È vero*. True."

"Then why you come?"

"To make sure. Let's start climbing, Antò. I want to see how good the marbles are that we can't bring down."

The marbles were not only good, they were perfect: outcroppings of purest white statuary. He found a *poggio* where the Romans had dug, fragments of a marble block they had excavated. After the battle to keep their footing up the rocky ravines and gorges until they had passed the snow line, and the struggle to dig the rest of their way up with fingernails and toes, it was clear to Michelangelo why the emperors had used Carrara marble to build Rome. Yet his whole body ached to set hammer and chisel to this shining stone, the purest he had ever seen.

It was dusk by the time he reached Carrara. As he came up the road from Avenza he noted that the farmers in the fields did not appear to see him. When he entered the Porta Ghibellina the townspeople in front of their shops suddenly became busy. In the Piazza del Duomo a group of men talking in a tight circle hunched their shoulders toward each other as he passed. He walked into the apothecary's shop where Pelliccia and his son were grinding medications on a slab of marble.

"What has happened? I left yesterday morning a Carrarino. I return tonight a Tuscan."

Pelliccia said nothing until he had dumped his mixture into the handkerchief of an old woman in black and bade her a *"Fa a modr."*

"It's your trip up Monte Altissimo."

"So your townspeople have adopted the Roman law that a man is guilty until proved innocent?"

"They are frightened. The opening of quarries in Pietrasanta could destroy them."

"Please report that I was ordered up Monte Altissimo by the Pope."

"They claim it's your doing."

"Mine! How?"

"They trace it to your demand for flawless blocks; say that 'The Big Noise' was heard in Rome."

"But I have been buying Carrara marbles."

"The Carrararini feel that in your heart you have been searching for the *sanctum sanctorum*, the pure white soul of the mountain; and that that was why Pope Leo ordered you to open Pietrasanta: to find the perfect marbles that would satisfy you."

For the moment Michelangelo could not answer. He knew that the Pope and Cardinal Giulio had assumed ownership of Monte Altissimo, that they were punishing the Carrarini who were anti-Vatican. But were the Carrarini instinctively right about him? Not once in the past seven months, even after he had paid out good money for their blocks, had he been satisfied that he had secured the best statuary white.

Had he been yearning for the Pope to open the Pietrasanta quarries, even while he proclaimed the feat impossible?

"I shall report to His Holiness that no marbles can be brought down from Monte Altissimo."

"They can rely on you?"

"I give them my word of honor."

"That will be good news."

He was more amused than concerned when he learned that Baccio d'Agnolo and Bigio had been granted five hundred ducats to go into the Seravezza mountains and lay out a road. He knew them both; they could not lay out a corpse.

It was a prosperous spring for Carrara, with sculptors coming in to buy marbles, staying in the parish house across the bridge from the Duomo: Bartolomeo Ordoñez from Spain, Giovanni de' Rossi and Maestro Simoni from Mantua, Domenico Garé of France, Don Bernardino de Chivos working for Charles I of Spain. He too felt prosperous, for the Medici had agreed to pay him twenty-five thousand ducats for the façade.

Jacopo Sansovino, apprentice to his old friend Andrea Sansovino from the Medici garden, arrived in Carrara on a rainy afternoon and stood with his back to Michelangelo's fire to get dry. Jacopo was an attractive chestnut-haired man of thirty who had taken his master's family name and appeared to have talent. Michelangelo had seen him at Sansovino's studio on and off for a number of years.

"Jacopo, it's good to see a Florentine face. What brings you to Carrara in this bad weather?"

"You."

"Me? How?"

"Pope Leo has promised me the frieze."

"What frieze?"

"Why, on your façade, of course! I submitted my design to the Pope and he was enchanted."

Michelangelo turned his face away so that Jacopo would not see his astonishment.

"But I have indicated no frieze."

"The Pope opened a competition for anyone wanting to make a contribution. I won. With a continuous bronze band above the three portals, showing scenes from the life of the Medici."

"Suppose your frieze does not fit into my design?"

"You do your work, and I'll do mine."

Jacopo's tone was not insolent, yet it admitted of no argument. Michelangelo said quietly:

"I have never collaborated, Jacopo."

"What the Holy Father says, is done."

"Assuredly. But under my agreement I am bound to correct the faults in anyone else's work."

"There will be no faults. Trust me. You have more to worry about with Baccio and Bigio."

"What about Baccio and Bigio?" Michelangelo felt his spine stiffen.

"They are to do all the decorated stones and columns."

He did not sleep that night. He kept logs on the fire, pacing the two rooms of his apartment while he tried to grapple with the depths of his mind. Why had he let these months go by without completing a model which the Pope and Cardinal Giulio could approve, without designing the major figures, or returning to Florence to lay the foundations? By giving himself a sense of motion, by buying hundreds of marbles, he had created the illusion of direction. The visit of Jacopo Sansovino with the news that the façade was being drained away from him proved he had been wrong. He had been standing still; for an artist, one of the more painful forms of death.

There was no more time to spare. Since he had to carve this façade he might as well start at once and carve the whole of it: squares, columns, cornices and capitals as well as saints.

He wrote to Rome:

I promise you, Holy Father, that the façade of San Lorenzo will be a mirror of architecture and sculpture for all Italy.

8

He returned to Florence in the spring, in time to celebrate the birth of Buonarroto's daughter Francesca, whom he nicknamed Cecca. He invited his friends to the house on the Via Ghibellina for *vin santo*, holy wine and cake, then went out to buy a piece of land on the Via Mozza, near Santa Caterina, on which to build a studio large enough to house the big blocks for the façade and for Julius' tomb. He had to deal with the canons of the Duomo, who charged him three hundred large gold florins for the land, sixty more than Michelangelo knew it to be worth. When he protested, the canon replied gravely:

"We are sorry, but we cannot deviate from the papal bull concerning sales."

"Then let me have that extra piece at the back for the sixty florins you have overcharged."

"Would you have us go against an order of the Holy Father?"

He worked for several weeks to finish the design from which he would build his wooden model. As he expanded his concept, adding five half-relief histories in square frames, two in circular frames, he expanded his costs so that it would be impossible to create the façade for less than thirty-five thousand ducats. The Pope retorted through Buoninsegni, who wrote:

They like your new plan, but you have raised your price by ten thousand ducats. Is this for extensions of the façade, or a miscalculation of your earlier plans?

Michelangelo replied, "This will be the architectural and sculptural marvel of Italy! When will payments be forthcoming?" Buoninsegni answered:

Money is tight, there is very little available, but do not be suspicious, your contract will be signed. Start work at once on the foundations. His Holiness is disturbed that you have not built them yet.

Jacopo Sansovino, informed by the Vatican that the new model showed no bronze frieze, came to Michelangelo and launched into a scathing attack.

"May the day be cursed on which you ever said anything good about anybody on earth!"

"Now, Jacopo, I have spoken highly of your work. I tried to tell you in Carrara . . ."

"You tried to tell me that there was no room for anyone but yourself. That's all that was involved."

"Jacopo, don't let us part as enemies. I promise to help you get a commission. Then you will understand that a work of art cannot be a symposium; it must have the organic unity of one man's mind and hands. Anything else is a Livornese fish stew."

Lodovico chose this time to reproach him for not making available to him the *spedalingo* funds at Santa Maria Nuova.

"Father, if you don't stop this eternal nagging, the house will no longer be big enough for the two of us."

By nightfall Lodovico was gone, his room empty. The following evening Buonarroto returned with news that Lodovico was telling everyone he had been driven out of his own house.

"Where is he staying?"

"In the peasant's cottage behind our house in Settignano."

"I'll send a note to him at once."

He sat down at Lodovico's pie-shaped account desk, which looked strange in this conventionally square room, and wrote:

Dearest Father—I hear you are complaining about me and saying that I have driven you from the house. I marvel, for I am quite sure that from the day I was born till now my mind has never harbored a thought, great or small, that was detrimental to you. Every labor I have undertaken has been accepted by me for love of you . . . and you know that I have bestowed all I possess upon you.

You have had thirty years' experience of me, you and your sons, and you are well aware that I have ever thought and acted, when I was able, for your good. How can you go about saying I have turned you out of doors? Do you not see what a character you are giving me? . . . This is all that was wanting to complete my tale of troubles. You repay me well.

But let it be as it may: I am willing to accept the position that I have brought you nothing but shame and disgrace. . . . I implore you to forgive me, like the scoundrel I am. . . .

Lodovico returned to the Via Ghibellina, forgave him.

Florence was depressed, the Florentine pleasure-loving tradition having moved to Leo's court in Rome. His own joylessness was increased when he learned that his cartoon for the Bathers had vanished.

"Destroyed would not be precisely the right word," said Granacci gravely. "Traced, written on, worn out, cut apart, stolen."

"But how? It belonged to Florence. Why wasn't it protected?"

Granacci gave him the details. The cartoon had been sent to the Hall of the Popes near Santa Maria Novella, then to the upper hall of the Medici palace. A hundred artists passing through Florence had worked before it unsupervised, some cutting out portions to take with them. His enemy from the Perugino quarrel, the sculptor Baccio Bandinelli, was alleged to have appropriated a number of sections. The only fragments still in Florence were those purchased by his friends the Strozzi.

"So I join Leonardo," he observed morosely. "My cartoon is gone. Just like my bronze of Julius."

The only one who was able to put his troubles into perspective was Prior Bichiellini, so old and frail now that he was confined to his bed in Santo Spirito.

"Try to think of your whole life as a unity, rather than a series of unrelated fragments," counseled the Father. "That way each period grows out of the last, and you know there will be another to come."

He concentrated on the façade, built a solid model, grooving the columns, decorating the capitals, blocking out the niches which would carry his marbles, making wax figures to represent his final sculptures. Pope Leo signed a contract for forty thousand ducats: five thousand a year for eight years, four thousand forthwith for expenses, and a free dwelling near the church of San Lorenzo. However . . .

"His Holiness wills that all work to be done on the façade of San Lorenzo shall be carried out with marble from Pietrasanta, and no other."

He stood bareheaded in the cemetery of San Lorenzo listening to the last rites for Prior Bichiellini, and feeling that he had lost the dearest and best man on earth. For the saintly prior another period would grow out of the last: his reward in heaven.

For Michelangelo, watching his friend being lowered into the grave, the "other period to come" could be pure inferno.

Within an hour of his return to Carrara a crowd began to gather in the Piazza del Duomo, pouring in from the plains below the Market of the Pigs, down the road along the Carrione River and through the Porta del Bozzo, down the mountainsides from Torano, Colonnata, Forestieri, from the quarries in Polvaccio, Fantiscritti, Grotta Colombara, Battaglino. The Carrarini were several hundred strong now, fitting closer and closer in the square beneath the apothecary's windows, spilling under the overhead bridge into the space before the Duomo.

The apothecary's dining-room windows were of floor-to-ceiling height, the center pair being glass doors. Though there was no balcony, the doors could be opened; outside was a low wrought-iron railing. Michelangelo stood behind the curtained doors listening to the murmur grow in intensity as the quarriers continued to jam into the square. Then someone spied him behind the curtains. A movement went through the crowd. They began shouting.

"Big Noise! Big Noise!"

Michelangelo glanced at his host's distraught face, torn between loyalty to his people and to his guest.

"I'd better go into the square," Michelangelo declared.

"Too dangerous. When they're frightened, they're ugly. They could trample you to death."

"I'll have to talk to them."

He threw open the glass doors, stepped before the two-foot railing. A shout came up from below:

"*Figiol d'un can'*. Son of a female dog!"

Fists were clenched upward to him. He held his arms out, trying to quiet them.

"Your words of honor are droppings of sheep."

"This is not my doing. You must believe me."

"*Bastardo*! Bastard! You have sold us."

"Have I not bought marbles from you? I have new contracts to give. Trust me. I am Carrarino!"

"You are servant of the Pope!"

"I will suffer more from this than you."

A silence fell over the crowd. A man in front cried in ill-suppressed anguish:

"You will not suffer in the belly!"

The cry acted like a signal. A hundred arms were raised. Stones filled the air like hail. Fragments of white marble broke one glass door, then the other.

A large stone struck him on the forehead. He was stunned; more from the impact than the pain. Blood began to trickle down his face. He felt it wet his eyebrow, circle and seep into the corner of his eye.

He made no move to stanch the flow. The crowd saw what had happened. Murmuring swept the piazza.

"*Basta!* We have drawn blood."

The mass began to liquefy, streams flowing past the cathedral out the streets from which they had come. Within a matter of minutes the piazza was deserted, with only the white stones and broken glass to tell what had happened. He rubbed the palm of his hand across his eye, looked at the dark matted ooze. He had bled from marble before: chips from his too frenzied chiseling had sometimes hit him in the face, piercing the skin. But this was the first time he had been stoned.

9

He rented a house on the sea side of the Pietrasanta piazza, with a view of the mile-wide marsh he was going to have to traverse to make a port, retaining the elderly couple who owned the place to take care of him. Cardinal Giulio had informed him that he must also dig marbles for the building of St. Peter's and for repairs to the Duomo in Florence. The Wool Guild was sending an expert to build his road.

It was March, he had about six months of good weather before snow and ice closed down the mountains. If he could start the marble columns flowing out of the quarries and onto the beach by October, his job would be done . . . if it could be started at all! He would have the first blocks shipped to Florence where he would spend the winter carving them. When good weather came again, a foreman and crew could return to run the quarry.

He listed his needs, set out for Carrara and made directly for the supply shops above the town and outside the walls. He entered a hemp store, the first in the row of provisioners along the river.

"I need stout rope."

The owner did not look up from his cording.

"Have none."

He continued up the street to an ironmonger. The smith was pounding metal on his anvil.

"I want to buy a forge and some iron bars."

"All out."

The tool shop next door was the best in the area.

"Could you sell me some picks, axes, two-man saws . . ."

"Short supply."

He went into the mountains seeking out the owners with whom he had signed contracts and to whom he had paid big sums of money.

"Come to Pietrasanta with me, Left-handed."

"Big contract. Can't leave."

In the next canal he urged Reason:

"Lend me your foreman for six months. I'll pay you the double."

"Can't spare."

He climbed higher, heading for the remote quarries whose men centered around their own campanile instead of Carrara.

"Work my quarry instead of yours. I'll pay you the same profit, plus a contract for blocks from your quarry for next year. What do you say?"

The proprietor's eyes gleamed at the thought of the extra cash; but the enthusiasm quickly faded.

"I don't want the horn to blow for me."

Since he had no chance in the quarries he dropped down the trace quickly to town, entered the apothecary's house through the rear garden and sought out his friend.

"You have been hiring and training foremen all your life. Send one to me. I need help. Everyone else has refused me."

Pelliccia said sadly, "I know. I am your friend. Friends should not desert each other."

"Then you will help?"

"I can't."

"You mean you won't."

"It's the same. No man would go. They stand by their campanile. This is the gravest danger our commune has faced since the French army overran us. And this shop? It would be as though someone fingered the sign of the plague in ashes on the front door. I ask your forgiveness."

Michelangelo averted his eyes.

"The error was mine, to come."

Feeling more fatigued than if he had carved for twenty hours, he once again went through the marble-paved streets, passing the housewives wrapped in their *scialima,* shawl, until he reached the Rocca Malaspina. The marquis was not only the owner of much of Carrara but the sole government of the marquisate. His word was law. The marquis welcomed him in a manner grave but not hostile.

"The Pope is powerless here," he explained. "He cannot force men to dig marble out of the mountain. Not even if he excommunicates the whole province."

"Then, by implication, neither can you order them to quarry for me?"

The marquis smiled thinly. "A wise prince never issues orders which he knows will not be obeyed."

There was a lacerated silence in the room, until a servant came in to serve wine and *pasmata,* baked rolls, an Easter specialty.

"Marquis, I have spent a thousand ducats for marbles that are still sitting in the quarries. What about them?"

"Do your contracts call for the marbles to be taken to the shore?"

"They do."

"Then you may rest assured that they will be delivered. We fulfill our contracts."

The blocks and columns were brought down from the mountains on marble carts, heavy stones dragging on the rear wheels as brakes. But when they had all been deposited on the beach the Carrarini boatmen refused to transport them to Florence.

"Not in the contract."

"I know that. I'm willing to pay a good fee. I want them taken to Pisa, then up the Arno while it is still high."

"No bottoms."

"Your barges are sitting here, idle."

"Busy tomorrow. No space."

Michelangelo swore, mounted his horse and made the long hard journey through Spezia and Rapallo to Genoa. Here were plenty of shipowners eager for work. They figured out the number of barges that would be necessary. Michelangelo paid in advance, made an appointment to meet them at Avenza to direct the loading.

Two mornings later, when the Genoese barges came into sight, a Carrara rowboat put out to meet them. Michelangelo waited on the beach, chafing at the delay. At last the rowboat returned, carrying the Genoese captain. He glanced at Michelangelo's blocks and columns, said out of one corner of his mouth:

"Can't carry them. Too big."

Michelangelo went white with rage.

"I gave you the number, weights, sizes!"

"Too many."

The captain tossed a money pouch at Michelangelo, departed in the rowboat. The Carrarini on the beach stood expressionless, then turned and trudged up the long plain.

The following day he rode down the coast to Pisa. As he approached the city, saw the tower leaning against its background of blue sky, he remembered his first trip here with Bertoldo when he was fifteen, and his teacher had taken him to the Camposanto to prove that he had not copied the ancient Roman Battle of the Centaurs. Now he was forty-three. Could it be only twenty-eight years since he had studied the marvelous Nicola Pisano sculptures in the Baptistery? The longer he lived the farther he got from Bertoldo's sternest admonition: "You must create a great body of work."

"How?" he wondered, tiredly.

He found a reliable captain, paid a deposit, returned to Pietrasanta. The boats did not come on the agreed day . . . nor the next . . . nor the next. He and his costly, rigidly selected marbles had been abandoned. How was he going to get them off the Carrara beach?

He knew nowhere else to try. He had a quarry to open. He would simply have to leave them there. Later he could try again.

The *pietra serena* quarriers of Settignano knew that whatever fame Michelangelo had achieved had been purchased at a high price. They did not envy him as they watched his lean figure trudging up the road. But as he came in view of the open cliff, saw the angled strata of blue-gray stone, the men working the face, his spirits revived, he broke into a broad grin. Below, a crew was sledge-hammering the jagged cuts into salable sizes. It was time for dinner; small boys arrived with branches across their shoulders, a pot of hot food balancing at either end. The stonemen assembled at the mouth of their cave.

"Anyone know where there's a quarry short on orders?" he asked. "I could use some good men at Pietrasanta."

They would not want it said that they had refused an old companion; yet the quarries were working, and when there was work a man could not leave.

"That is fortunate," he exclaimed. He refrained from adding, But not for me. "Do you think I might try in the neighborhood? Behind the Pitti palace? At Prato?"

The men gazed at each other in silence.

"Try."

He visited other stone diggings, a *pietra dura* pit, the Cava di Fossato, Coverciano, the *pietra forte* quarry at Lombrellino. The men were working; there was no reason to leave their homes and families; there was serious apprehension about the mountains above Pietrasanta. In desperation he trudged back to Settignano to the Topolinos. The sons were running the yard, with seven mingled grandsons ranging from seven years upward, learning their craft. Bruno, the oldest, with close-cropped, shot-gray hair, negotiated the contracts; Enrico, the middle brother, trained by the grandfather for the most delicate work, columns and lacy carved windows, was the artist of the trio; Gilberto, the most vigorous, squared and beveled with the speed of three stonehewers. This was his last chance; if his Topolino family would not help him, no one would. He laid out his situation fully, omitting none of the hardships or dangers.

"Could one of you come along? I must have someone I can trust."

He could hear the three of them pool their silent thinking. Finally all eyes rested on Bruno.

"We can't let you go alone," said Bruno slowly. "One must come."

"Which?"

"Not Bruno," said Enrico; "there are contracts to discuss."

"Not Enrico," said Gilberto; "only he does finish work."

The two older brothers looked at Gilberto, said together:

"That leaves you."

"That leaves me." Gilberto scratched the bushy hair on his chest while looking at Michelangelo. "I have least skill but most strength. I will do?"

"You will do. I am grateful."

"Do not stir gratitude into family soup," replied Enrico, who had absorbed his grandfather's supply of folk sayings along with his skill at the grinding wheel.

Over the next days Michelangelo assembled a crew: Michele who had worked with him in Rome, the three Fancelli brothers: Domenico, a tiny fellow but a good sculptor, Zara, whom Michelangelo had known for years, and Sandro, the youngest. La Grassa of Settignano, the mason who had made a model for him, agreed to come, as well as a group of assorted stonemen who were tempted by his offer of a double wage. His heart sank when he assembled them to give instructions for leaving in his hired farm wagon the following morning: twelve stonecutters. Not one quarrier in the lot! How could he tackle a savage mountain with this inexperienced crew?

While pondering his way home he passed a group of stonehewers laying new blocks in the Via Sant'Egidio. Among them he was astonished to see Donato Benti, a marble sculptor who had worked in France on successful commissions.

"Benti! In the name of God, what are you doing here?"

Benti, though only thirty, had been born with an old face; he had purple pockets under his eyes, a seamed face with the lines culminating in a crosshatch on his chin. His manner was solemn. He wrung his hands in silent supplication, replied:

"Making small sculptures for people's feet to trod on. While little I eat agrees with me, I still have to swallow some food occasionally."

"I can pay you more in Pietrasanta than you can get in the street. What do you say? I need you."

"You need me," repeated Benti, his owl-eyes batting up and down in disbelief. "Those could be the most beautiful words in the Italian language. I'll come."

"Good. Be at my house in the Via Ghibellina at first light. There'll be fourteen of us going by wagon."

That evening Salviati came to Michelangelo's house with a gray-eyed man with thinning hair, whom he introduced as Vieri, a seventh cousin, once removed, of Pope Leo.

"Vieri will go to Pietrasanta with you as your commissary. He will arrange for food, for supplies, for transportation, and keep the records. The Wool Guild will pay his salary."

"I've been worried about who would keep the figures."

Salviati smiled. "Vieri is an artist with accounts. His books will be balanced as perfectly as your David, with never a *baiocco* out of place."

Vieri spoke in the constricted voice of a man who had little liking for words. "It's the columns of figures that are the masters . . . until they balance. Only then have I made them obey."

It was a happy departure, after all, for his sister-in-law Bartolommea was delivered of a healthy boy, whom they named Simone; and at long last the Buonarroti-Simoni name was safe for the future.

Vieri, Gilberto Topolino and Benti moved into the Pietrasanta house with him, Vieri taking one of the bedrooms for his office. Michelangelo then found a larger house in Seravezza for the remaining nine workers. He marked out the most promising route to the quarry area, set the men to work with picks and shovels to cut a trail up which the burros could carry supplies. A number of farm boys came to work under Antò's supervision, wielding sledge hammers to break out the mountain stone and form a safe ledge for passage. When it became evident that the one smith in Seravezza could not handle their needs, Benti sent for his godfather, Lazzero, a squat, neckless, bull-torsoed man who set up a forge to serve both the quarry and the road, and to build the special iron-supported wagons for transporting the marble columns down to the sea.

Michelangelo, Michele, Gilberto and Benti went prospecting, found several strata of variegated marbles on the lower levels of Monte Altissimo; and then, just one jutting crag below the summit, unearthed a formation of pure statuary marble, breath-takingly crystalline white, flawless in color and composition.

"It's true!" Michelangelo cried to Benti; "the higher the mountain, the purer the marble."

He summoned his crew, had Antò's men help him carve a level area on the peak from which they could mine. The marble ran straight back in a solid white sheet, an entire cliff of marble to be removed, the surface slightly weathered by snow and wind and rain, but below this outer skin, absolute purity.

"All we have to do now," he exclaimed exultantly, "is strip out great blocks that have been here since Genesis."

"And get them off this mountain," added Benti, gazing downward the five or six miles, past Seravezza and Pietrasanta to the sea. "Frankly, I'm more worried about the road than the marble."

The first weeks of quarrying were a total waste. Michelangelo showed the men how the Carrarini drove in their wet pegs along the seams and faults, how the pegs swelled until the marble cracked, and were then hewn out with giant levers. But marble and its quarriers were like lovers, they knew each other's every mood, transition, disposition to oppose or give in. Marble had always been the temperamental queen of hard mountain formations, yet the most easily shattered because of its delicacy: an obstinate gem demanding devotion and tenderness.

Of these things the Settignano stonemasons knew nothing. Nor did Benti or Domenico, even though they had carved statues. Michelangelo learned by trial and error, leaning heavily on his years of watching the Carrarini work the blocks, trying to absorb generations of skill in a few months. His crew of stonemasons did their best, but they made mistakes. The *pietra serena* on which they had been trained was infinitely more durable. They were not equipped to handle the Shining Stone; it would have been as well if he had brought in a dozen carpenters or blacksmiths.

As foreman, Gilberto Topolino was a volcano of energy; he hustled, bustled, attacked the mountain violently, kept the others going at a fearsome pace; but Gilberto knew only how to fashion *pietra serena* building stones held between his knees. The nature of the marble infuriated him by its arrogant toughness when it should have been as crumbly as sugar, and by dissolving granularly under his *subbia* and *mazzuolo* when it should have had solid substance.

Burly La Grassa complained:

"It's like working in the dark."

After a week of work at a lower outcropping where Domenico said they had found something good, they cut a block which turned out to have swirling circles of dark veins, useless for their purposes.

Vieri proved to be an excellent commissary, getting the lowest possible prices for food and supplies, keeping costs down. He had a receipt to show for every denaro laid out, but at the end of the month the immaculate accounts were of small comfort to Michelangelo. He had not yet quarried one ducat's worth of usable marble.

"You see, Buonarroti, my figures balance beautifully," said Vieri.

"But how much marble have I to balance the one hundred and eighty ducats?"

"Marble? My task is to show where every scudo went."

"And mine is to have marble to show for the expenditures."

By now it was close to June. The Wool Guild had not yet sent a superintendent to build the road. Michelangelo knew from the steepness of the terrain, and the fact that it would have to be cut through solid rock much of the way, that unless it was started immediately it could not be completed before the winter storms shut them down. At last the builder arrived: Bocca, Mouth, an illiterate laborer on the roads of Tuscany in his youth, who had had the extra energy and ambition to learn how to draw maps, to boss road crews, and finally to contract for building roads between farm villages. The Wool Guild had chosen Bocca, a brute of a man, hairy from his skull to his toes, because of his reputation for pushing through contracts in record time. Michelangelo showed Bocca his drawings for the projected route.

"I see the mountain myself," broke in Bocca. "Where I find a good place I build a good road."

Bocca had trained himself well. Within ten days he had mapped the simplest possible route to the base of Monte Altissimo. The only trouble was that the road was not directed toward those places where the marble was to be found. After Michelangelo had lowered his twenty-ton blocks down the ravines of Monte Altissimo by hand, he would still be a considerable distance from Bocca's road!

He insisted that Bocca accompany him to the topmost quarries, Polla and Vincarella, then down the ravines he would have to use to lower his columns.

"You see, Bocca, I could never get my blocks to your road."

"I took contract to build to Monte. This is where I build."

"What purpose will the road serve if I can't get the marble out?"

"I'm road. You're marble."

"But there is nothing at the other end of your road except marble," cried Michelangelo, exasperated. "I will have a thirty-two-bull team hauling the wagons . . . we are not hauling hay! The road must be the best route from the quarries. Like this, for example. . . ."

When Bocca was agitated he pulled on the inch-long hairs growing out of his nostrils and ears; he took a clump of black tendrils between his thumb and forefinger, massaging them downward.

"You build or I build. Not both."

It was a warm night, the stars hanging low over the sea in brilliant clusters. Michelangelo walked for miles south on the coast road, passing sleeping villages while he wrestled with his problem. What purpose would the road serve if it could not move his marble? Would it not be considered his fault if he did not get his columns down to the sea? Bocca's route would be worthless, for it went nowhere! What to do about the man?

He could complain to Pope Leo, Cardinal Giulio, Salviati, have another road builder sent in. But what assurance would he have that the second contractor would follow the course he himself thought best? The Pope might even say that this was his *terribilità,* that he could not get along with anyone.

What was his alternative?

He must build the road himself!

A tortured groan racked the warm night air. He looked about him, saw only the dark marsh between himself and the sea. How could he take upon himself the building of a road in some of the wildest country of Italy? He had never built a road. He was a sculptor. What did he know of such matters? It would put him under crushing hardships. It would mean summoning and supervising still another crew as they filled the marsh, cut down trees, blasted a passage through solid walls of rock. He knew what Pope Leo and Cardinal Giulio would say, the same thing that Pope Julius had said when he had fought so bitterly to avoid painting the Sistine vault, and then had conceived a plan which quadrupled his work.

He had cried to Leo and Giulio, "I am not a quarrier!"

Now he wanted to be an engineer.

Leo would exclaim:

"How is one to understand you?"

That was one question he could not answer. Though he had not yet brought forth so much as one usable base block, he had seen the glorious meat of Monte Altissimo. He knew that he would eventually quarry its statuary marble. When he did, he had to have a proper road.

Had he not learned over the years that a sculptor had to be an architect and engineer as well? If he could carve the Bacchus, the Pietà, the David, the Moses; if he could design a mausoleum for Pope Julius and a façade for San Lorenzo, why should a five-mile road be more difficult?

10

He used the rutted farm tracks into Seravezza, swung to the north of the village to avoid the Vezza River and gorge, then mapped the road to make straight for Monte Altissimo despite the fact that huge boulders sat astride his route. He laid out stakes up the valley of the Sera to the cluster of stone houses at Rimagno, crossed the Sera River at a shallow ford and followed the contour of the bank up the steep gorge. At two points he chose to tunnel through solid rock rather than try to push the road up a hogback and then serpentine down into the valley again. For a terminus he chose a spot at the base of the two ravines down which he planned to lower the blocks from Vincarella and Polla.

For two ducats he bought a walnut tree, and had a Massa wagonmaker build a two-wheeled cart with iron fitted over its wheels to carry the cut rock to the marsh between Pietrasanta and the sea. He made sad-faced Donato Benti superintendent of road construction from Pietrasanta to the base of the Monte Altissimo canal; Michele was given charge of the marsh fill; Gilberto Topolino remained as foreman of Vincarella, the quarry some forty-five hundred feet high in the Alps, at the last possible footing in the sheer precipice where a *poggio* could be dug to provide work space for excavation.

By the end of June Vieri presented him with a stern face.

"You'll have to stop building your road."

"Stop . . . but why?"

"There's no more money."

"The Wool Guild is rich. They're paying the costs."

"All I have received is one hundred florins. They have been spent. Here, see how the columns balance."

"The only columns I want to see are those of marble. And I can't get them to the port without a road."

"Peccato. Too bad. Perhaps the money will arrive soon. Until then . . ." Vieri arched both hands outward in an eloquent gesture of defeat. ". . . *finito,* finished."

"I can't stop now. Use my other money."

"Your private money for marbles? You can't spend it on the road."

"It's the same. No road, no marbles. Pay the bills out of my eight-hundred-ducat account."

"But you may never get them back. You will have no legal hold over the Wool Guild . . ."

"I don't have any hold over anybody," Michelangelo replied hoarsely. "Until I get the marbles out, the Holy Father won't let me be a sculptor. Spend my money for the road. When the Wool Guild sends in cash, pay me back."

From sunrise to dark he was up and down the mountains on a surefooted mule, watching progress. Benti was doing a fast job on the road, except that he was leaving the heaviest rock work for the end; Gilberto had removed the earth from the Vincarella strata of marble and was driving wet pegs into the faults; the local *carradori,* cart owners, were dumping tons of loose rock into the marsh, slowly building up the base to the beach where Michelangelo planned his harbor. With a hundred long hot workdays of summer ahead, he estimated he would have several columns for the master figures of his façade lowered down the canal to the loading platform by the end of September.

By July, according to Vieri's accounts, he had spent over three hundred of his eight hundred ducats. On Sunday after early mass he sat with Gilberto on the wooden railing of the Ponte Stazzemese, the hot sun beating on their bare backs while they gazed across the hamlet of Stazzema to the sea.

Gilberto glanced sideways at his friend's face.

"I want to tell you . . . so you won't be there when they leave . . ."

"When who leaves?"

"Half the crew: Angelo, Francesco, Bartolo, Barone, Tommaso, Andrea, Bastiano. When Vieri pays them they go back to Florence."

"But why?" Michelangelo was shocked. "They're well paid . . ."

"They're frightened. They think the marble get us, instead we get the marble."

"That's foolishness! We have a good block going. It'll be pried out in a week."

Gilberto shook his head. "A strong veining has shown. The front is waste. We have to drive deeper into the cliff . . .''

"How?" Michelangelo cried. "With half a dozen men who don't know what they're doing?"

Gilberto hung his head. "Forgive me, Michelangelo. I have failed you. Nothing from what I know of *pietra serena* is of any use here.''

Michelangelo put an arm about Gilberto's dejected shoulders.

"You're doing the best you can. I'll find new masons. You see, Gilberto, I don't have the privilege of quitting.''

By mid-September they were ready to tunnel through the three huge rocks they had by-passed: one at the edge of Seravezza, the second just beyond Rimagno, and the last where the river ran into an old trail. His road would be finished. He had dumped enough rock into the marsh to fill the whole Tyrrhenian Sea, but the constantly sinking and shifting roadbed was at last secure to the beach. Up in Vincarella, though it had cost an extra six weeks of hewing back into the mountain the whole thickness of the column to avoid the vein, he had at last managed to bring out a magnificent block. He also had a column at the edge of the *poggio*. Though some of the new men had drifted away, grumbling about how hard he worked them, he was happy with the results of the summer.

"I know it has seemed endless to you, Gilberto; but now that we have established a *modus operandi*, we'll get out another three or four columns before the rain closes us down.''

The following morning he started to move the enormous column down the ravine, well filled over the months with marble chips to provide a smooth sliding base. The column was roped half a dozen times around its width, several times around its length, crowbarred onto wooden rollers, then pushed and dragged to the edge of the *poggio*, its nose turned over the edge of the canal. Down the length of the draw, on either side, nests of stakes had been driven into the ground, angling outward. The ropes from the column, tied around these stakes, were the only hold the crews would have on the marble.

Down it went, held by some thirty men. Michelangelo, imitating the calls of the Carrara crews, a series of sung and shouted notes, directed the men handling the rollers to run with the one at the rear, when the end of the marble had passed, and put it under the front; and the men at the stake nests, holding the ropes with all their might until the column had slid past them, to run down the trail to the next stakes to tie up their ropes and apply the brake. Hours passed, the sun rose high in the heavens, the men sweated, swore, strained, complained that they were starving.

"We can't stop to eat," Michelangelo cried. "There's no way to secure the marble. It could get away from us.''

Down the long steep ravine the column slid, the crew exerting all its strength to hold it back, to slow its movement. It inched forward a hundred yards, two hundred, three, four, five, down almost the entire face of Monte Altissimo, until by late afternoon they were only thirty-five yards from the road. Michelangelo was jubilant; very soon now they would slide the column onto the loading platform, from which it would be moved onto the special wagon drawn by the team of thirty-two bulls.

He never quite knew how the accident happened. An agile young Pisan named Gino, who was running the rollers forward, had just kneeled to put another roller under the front of the column when suddenly there was a cry of alarm, something snapped, and the column started to move on its own.

There were shouts: "Gino! Get out! Quick!''

But it was too late. The column rolled over Gino, swerved toward Michelangelo. He threw himself over the side of the ledge, rolling a number of feet before he could break his fall.

The men stood paralyzed as the flawless column picked up speed, smashed its way downward, hit the loading platform and broke into a hundred pieces on the road.

Gilberto was leaning over Gino. Blood stained the marble-choked draw. Michelangelo went on his knees before the boy.

"His neck is broken," said Gilberto.

"He is still alive?"

"No. Killed instantly."

In his mind Michelangelo heard the mournful sound of a horn echoing from peak to peak. He picked up Gino's dead body, stumbled blindly the rest of the descent down the white passage. Someone brought his mule to the loading station. Michelangelo mounted, still holding Gino, while the others led the funeral procession into Seravezza.

11

The death of the boy lay heavy on his conscience. He took to his bed, sick at heart. Torrential rains inundated the piazza. All work was shut down. Vieri closed his books. The crews returned home. Michelangelo's accounting showed that he had spent thirty ducats beyond the eight hundred advanced to him at the beginning of the year for marble. He had loaded not a single block. The lone consolation was the attendance of a group of Carrarini quarriers and owners at Gino's burial. Apothecary Pelliccia linked his arm through Michelangelo's as they left the cemetery.

"We're deeply sorry, Michelangelo. The death of the boy brought us to our senses. We treated you badly. But we too have suffered from the loss of contracts from agents and sculptors waiting to buy from the Pope's quarries."

Now the Carrarini boatmen would transport his blocks, still sitting on the beach at Carrara, to the docks in Florence.

For several weeks he lay ill. The future looked blacker than the slate sky. He had failed in the task assigned to him; spent the monies advanced, used up the year fruitlessly. What happened now? Neither Pope Leo nor Cardinal Giulio had much patience with bunglers.

It took a letter from his friend Salviati, late in October, to set him back on his feet:

> I am sorry to hear that you are so distressed about this thing; in such an undertaking you might happen to meet much worse accidents. Believe me that you are going to lack nothing, and God is going to repay you for this accident. Remember when you complete this work, our city will be gratefully obliged to you and to all of your family, and will be under eternal obligation. Great and honest men take more courage in adversities and become stronger.

His fear that the Pope and cardinal might condemn him for the failure was allayed by a letter from Buoninsegni in Rome, who wrote:

> The Holy Father and His Lordship are very satisfied that there is a large quantity of marble. They wish the matter hurried as much as possible.

A few days later he made the trip alone on horseback to the end of his road, then climbed Monte Altissimo to Vincarella. The sun had come out, the air was filled with autumnal scents. At the quarry he found tools in the wooden shed, marked vertically with hammer and heavy chisel the four columns to be dug out of the mountain as soon as he could return with quarriers. He returned to Pietrasanta, put his few personal possessions in a saddlebag and made his way down the coast to Pisa, then through the rolling valley of the Arno, the Duomo displacing space on the horizon from miles away.

Florence knew about the accident, but only as a delaying mishap. Though some of the returning workers had complained about his driving them too hard, others praised him for the speed with which he had completed the road and extracted the first marble block ever quarried above Pietrasanta. He was still too shaken to attempt even the simplest carving, and so he settled for a more salutary work, the building of his new studio on the land he had bought on the Via Mozza. This time he did not design a house with a workshop attached, but rather a spacious high-ceilinged studio with a couple of small rooms added for living purposes.

When his plan grew too large for the lot he went to Fattucci, chaplain of Santa Maria del Fiore, and again tried to get the piece of land at the rear. The chaplain replied:

"The Pope has issued a bull saying that all church lands must be sold at the highest possible price."

He returned home, wrote to Cardinal Giulio:

Now if the Pope makes bulls enabling one to steal, I beg Your Lordship have one made for me also.

Cardinal Giulio was amused; but Michelangelo ended by paying the full price for the extra strip. He plunged into the building of his house with hurricane activity, hiring workmen, buying his planks and nails from Puccione, the carpenter, mortar from Ugolino, the kiln man, his roof tiles from Maso, fir trees from Capponi. He hired *contadini* to bring his sand, gravel and stone, remained on the job all day to supervise. At night he kept his accounts as straight as Vieri had kept the books in Pietrasanta, jotting down the names of witnesses who were present when he paid Talosi for putting in the stone window frames, Baggiana, the sand-bearer, Ponti for five hundred large bricks, the widow who lived next door for half of her protecting wall.

Trying to be, for once, as good a businessman as Jacopo Galli, Balducci and Salviati would have liked, he took over from the ailing Buonarroto the listings of the modest income from the properties he had bought over the years. . . .

I note hereafter the income I had in three years from the *podere* tilled by Bastiano called Balene (whales), *podere* that I purchased from Piero Tedaldi. In the first year: twenty-seven barrels of wine, eight barrels of oil and four bushels of wheat. In the second year: twenty-four barrels of wine, no oil, eight bushels of wheat. In the third year: ten barrels of oil, thirty-five barrels of wine, five bushels of wheat.

The winter was mild. By February his tile roof had been set, the doors hung, the high northern windows framed, the bronze caster had delivered four bronze pulleys for the studio. He brought half a dozen of his nine-foot Carrara blocks for Julius' tomb from the Arno storehouse, set them upright so that he could study them. His workshop completed, he had only to return to Pietrasanta, excavate the columns he needed for San Lorenzo; then he could settle down on the Via Mozza for years of concentrated work for the Medici and Roveres.

He did not ask Gilberto Topolino to go back to the quarries, that would have been unfair; but most of the others agreed to join him, including a new group of stonemasons. Rather than being frightened by Pietrasanta, the masons felt that with the road completed and the quarries opened the hardest work was already done. He took with him from Florence the needed supplies: heavy-duty rope, cables, sledge hammers and chisels. Still disturbed by the unexplained accident that had killed Gino, he evolved a system of iron lewis rings which could be driven into the surface of the block, giving the crews a surer grip on the marble as it was

brought down the ravine. Lazzero said he could make the rings on his forge.
Michelangelo sent Benti into Pisa to buy the best iron he could find.

In good time they detached the marble from the mountain vertically, letting the
blocks roll onto the *poggio*. The Pope had been rightly informed: there was enough
magnificent marble here to supply the world for a thousand years. And now with
the white walls exposed, all loose earth, rock, dirt, shale cleaned from above by
two *tecchiaioli*, the crystalline cliffs yielded superbly.

He hesitated to take the columns down the slide without the iron grips, but
Pelliccia came to the diggings, recommended that he double his nest of outspread
stakes along the trail, use heavier rope, and impede the downward movement by
lessening the number of rollers.

There were no more accidents. In the ensuing weeks he directed five superb
blocks down the canal, onto the wagon, down the road behind the thirty-two bulls,
past Seravezza, Pietrasanta, across the marsh, and onto the beach. Here the low
barges would be brought up close, their decks filled with sand until they sank low
in the water; the columns would be raised onto the sand fill, then the sand washed
out through the scuppers until the marble blocks settled down securely on the deck.

At the end of April, Lazzero finished his set of rings. Michelangelo, in a state
of exultation over the beauty of his glorious white columns, was relieved at this
added protection. Now, with the sixth column ready to be moved, he saw to it that
the iron rings were firmly attached to hold the massive weight, making it possible
to lessen the bulk of rope.

The improvement was his undoing. Halfway down the ravine a ring snapped,
the column got away, picking up so much speed that it jumped the bank of the
ravine and went crashing down the steepest slope of Monte Altissimo to the river
below, breaking to bits on the stony bed.

Michelangelo recovered from his moment of stupefaction, saw that no one was
hurt, then examined the broken ring. It had been made of poor iron.

He climbed swiftly up the side of the ravine, took a heavy hammer and hit the
iron connections of the hoisting cranes Lazzero had made. They broke under his
blows like dry clay. It was a wonder the entire crew had not been killed long before
this.

"Benti!"

"Yes?"

"Where was this iron bought?"

". . . in Pisa . . . like you said . . ."

"I gave you money to buy the best. There is not as much iron in here as there
is in the rib of a knife."

". . . I . . . I'm sorry," stuttered Donato Benti, "butI . . . I didn't go. Lazzero
went. I had faith in him."

Michelangelo turned toward the shed where the smith was working a bellows
over his forge.

"Lazzero! Why did you not buy the best iron, as I ordered?"

". . . this was cheaper."

"Cheaper? You charged me the full price."

Lazzero shrugged. *"Mah!* What would you? Every man uses a chance to make
a few scudi."

"A few scudi! To smash a column worth a hundred ducats. To endanger the life
of every man working here. How could you be so . . . so venal?"

Lazzero shrugged again; he did not know what venal meant.

"What is lost? One column. There are a thousand more just like it. Dig out
another."

As quickly as the news could reach the Vatican, and a letter of instructions be
sent to the Board of the Wool Guild, Michelangelo was recalled to Florence. A
foreman from the Duomo was sent to replace him.

Michelangelo rode his horse into Florence late the following afternoon. He was to report at once to Cardinal Giulio in the Medici palace.

The palace was in mourning. Madeleine de la Tour d'Auvergne, who had married Piero's son Lorenzo, had died in childbirth. Lorenzo, rising from a sickbed to ride from the Medici villa at Careggi to Poggio a Caiano, caught a fever, and had died only the day before. This removed the last legitimate heir descended from the male side of the Cosimo de' Medici line, though there were now two more illegitimate Medici: Ippolito, son of the dead Giuliano, and Alessandro, rumored to be the son of Cardinal Giulio.

The palace was also sad because rumor had it that Pope Leo's extravagances had nearly bankrupted the Vatican. The Florentine bankers financing him were in serious trouble.

Michelangelo put on fresh linens, packed his ledger and took the beloved walk through the Florentine streets, up the Via Ghibellina to the Via del Proconsolo, past the Duomo into the Street of the Watermelons with the House of the Five Lamps on the left, into the Via de' Calderai with its coppersmiths and cuirass-makers, across the Via Larga to the Medici palace. Cardinal Giulio, sent by Leo to take over the reins, was saying a requiem mass in the Benozzo Gozzoli chapel. When it was concluded, and everyone had filed out, Michelangelo expressed his regret at young Lorenzo's death. The cardinal did not appear to hear him.

"Your Grace, why have you recalled me? In a matter of months I would have had all nine of my giant columns on the beach of Pietrasanta."

"There is enough marble now."

Michelangelo was unnerved by an undertone of hostility in the cardinal's voice. "Enough . . . ? I don't understand."

"We are abandoning the façade for San Lorenzo."

Michelangelo turned white, speechless.

Giulio continued: "The floor of the Duomo needs repaving. Since the Duomo and Wool Guild Boards paid the cost of the road, they are entitled to the marbles you have excavated."

Michelangelo felt as though the cardinal had walked over his prostrate body in boots covered with dung.

"To pave the Duomo floor? With my marbles? With the finest statuary marbles ever quarried! Why do you humiliate me in this way?"

Cardinal Giulio answered icily, "Marble is marble. It should be used for what is needed next. Right now the cathedral needs paving blocks."

Michelangelo clenched his fists to stop his trembling, gazed at Gozzoli's exquisite portrait of *Il Magnifico* and his brother Giuliano, on the wall of the chapel.

"It is nearly three years now since His Holiness and Your Grace took me off the Rovere tomb. In all that time I have not been able to carve one inch of marble. Of the twenty-three hundred ducats you have sent me, I have spent eighteen hundred on the marbles, quarries and roads. On the Pope's instructions I had the marbles for Julius' tomb shipped here, so that I could carve them while I worked the San Lorenzo façade. To send them to Rome now, the shipment will cost me more than the five hundred ducats' difference! I do not reckon the costs of the wooden model I made; I do not reckon the three years I have wasted in this work; I do not reckon the great insult put upon me by being brought here to do this work, and then having it taken from me; I do not reckon my house in Rome, which I left, and where marbles, furniture and blocked-out statues have suffered upwards of another five hundred ducats. I will not reckon all these things, regardless of the terrible loss to me. I only want one thing now: to be free!"

Cardinal Giulio had listened carefully to Michelangelo's catalogue of complaints. His thin, smooth face grew dark.

"The Holy Father will review these doings at the proper time. You are dismissed."

Michelangelo stumbled down the long hallway, his feet carrying him to what had been *Il Magnifico's studiolo*. He thrust open the door, entered, stared at the room. He cried aloud to the long-departed spirit of Lorenzo:

"I am ruined!"

BOOK NINE

THE WAR

Where did a man go when he had been destroyed? Where else but to work, bolting the door of his studio, standing the dozen blocks around the walls as though they were armed soldiers guarding his privacy.

The new studio was a pleasure: ceilings thirty-five feet high, tall windows to the north, spacious enough to allow him to carve several of the tomb figures at the same time. This was where a sculptor belonged, in his workshop.

Since he had signed a contract with Metello Vari in Rome to do the Risen Christ, he decided to do this single piece first. His drawing hand revealed that he could not design a Risen Christ because in his mind Christ had never died. There had been no crucifixion and no entombment; no one could have killed the Son of God; not Pontius Pilate, not all of the Roman legions stationed in Galilee. Christ's corded muscular arms held the cross lightly, its transverse beam too short for man or even child to be nailed to; the symbols were there, the bamboo rod poetically curved, the sponge soaked in vinegar, but in his white marble there would be no sign of anguish, no reminder of the ordeal. He walked to Santa Maria Novella by way of the central market in the Via Sant'Antonio, went to the choir stalls and gazed up at the robust Christ of Ghirlandaio for which he had drawn the sketches. He had never believed that spirituality had to be anemic or aesthetic.

The small clay model shaped itself easily under his hands, then the studio was christened with the first flying white chips, seeming to Michelangelo as pure as holy water. A group of old friends came to celebrate his entering the block: Bugiardini, Rustici, Baccio d'Agnolo. Granacci poured the Chianti, raised his glass and cried:

"I drink to the three late lamented years. *Requiescant in pace.* Now let us drink to the years to come, when all these brave blocks shall spring to life. *Beviamo!*"

"*Auguri!* Best wishes!"

After his three-year fast, the Risen Christ surged out of its column. Having persuaded Vari to contract for a nude figure, his chisel sang out the contours of the standing male in an equilibrium of proportion, the head gazing downward lyrically upon man, the sweet calm tranquillity of Jesus' virile face saying to all who looked upon him:

"Have faith in God's goodness. I have surmounted my cross. I have conquered it. So can you, yours. Violence passes. Love remains."

Because the statue had to be shipped to Rome he left the webbing between the left arm and torso and between the two feet; nor did he attempt to articulate the hair, since it might break off, or give the face a high polish that could be scratched on the journey.

The day it was shipped, Soggi came to visit the studio, fairly bursting out of his own tight red sausagelike skin.

"Michelangelo, I just held a world competition for sculpture."

'Oh. And where did you hold it?"

"In my head. I'm happy to tell you that you won."

"What have I won, Soggi?"

"The right to carve a calf for the front of my new butcher shop."

"Of marble?"

"Certainly."

"Soggi, I promised myself that I would never sculpture a calf unless it was of pure gold. Like the one the Hebrews were worshiping when Moses came down from Mount Sinai."

Soggi's eyes bulged. "Gold! That would be spectacular. How thin a plating could we use?"

"Plating? Soggi, I'm shocked. Do you put only a plating of meat in your sausages? To do your shop justice the calf must be solid gold, from the tip of its nose to the last hair in its tail."

Soggi, his face dripping perspiration, cried:

"Do you know how much a solid gold calf would cost? A million florins."

"But it would make you famous."

Soggi moved his head back and forth mournfully.

"No use to cry over spoiled meat. I'll just have to start a new competition. You're not eligible!"

He would earn little in the coming years, since the Risen Christ netted him less than two hundred ducats, and the figures for Julius' tomb had been paid for in advance. Yet he was still the sole support of his family. His brother Buonarroto now had two children and a third on the way. Buonarroto was sickly, could work little. Giovansimone spent his days in the wool shop but had no business sense. His brother Sigismondo had not been trained for any trade except war. When Lodovico became ill there were constant doctor and apothecary bills. The income from the farms seemed to trickle away. He was going to have to cut his costs.

"Buonarroto, now that I'm back in Florence don't you think your time would be better spent in handling my affairs?"

Buonarroto was crushed. His face went gray.

"You want to close our shop?"

"It's not making money.

"Only because I've been ill. As soon as I'm better I can go to business every day. What would Giovansimone do?"

And Michelangelo realized that the business was necessary to maintain Buonarroto's and Giovansimone's social position. With it they were merchants; without it they were dependents, living off their brother. He could do nothing to hurt his family name.

"You're right, Buonarroto," he said with a sigh. "The shop will make money one day."

The tighter he bolted his studio door against the intrusion of the outside world, the more evident it became that trouble was man's natural state. News reached him that Leonardo da Vinci had died in France, unwanted and unhonored by his countrymen. A letter from Sebastiano in Rome told him that Raphael was ill and exhausted, obliged to turn more and more of his work over to apprentices. The Medici were beset by difficulties: Alfonsina, suffering from ulcers over the loss of her son and the control of Florence, crept away to Rome to die. Pope Leo's political judgment had proved unsound in the backing of Francis I of France against Charles V, now the newly elected Holy Roman Emperor of Spain, Germany and the Netherlands. In Germany, Martin Luther was challenging papal supremacy by crying:

"I don't know if the Christian faith can endure any other head of the Universal Church on earth . . . save Christ."

After immuring himself for weeks, Michelangelo attended a dinner of the Company of the Cauldron. Granacci came to the studio so they could walk to Rustici's together. He had inherited the family fortune and was living in austere respectability with his wife and two children in the ancestral home in Santa Croce. When Michelangelo expressed surprise at Granacci's devotion to his business affairs, Granacci replied formally:

"Each generation is the custodian of family property."

"Perhaps you'll become serious about your talent as well, and do some painting?"

"Ah, well . . . talent. You have not neglected your talent, and look what you've been through. I'm still intent on enjoying life. What else is left, after the years have passed? Bitter reflections?"

"If I don't have wonderful sculptures to show that the years have passed, then my memories will be truly bitter."

Rustici still had the same studio in the Via della Sapienza, where they had celebrated the David commission. While passing through the Piazza San Marco, Michelangelo saw a familiar figure. He went faint, grabbed Granacci's arm. It was Torrigiani, talking to a nineteen-year-old goldsmith and apprentice sculptor, Benvenuto Cellini, laughing heartily and throwing his arms wide. They had no sooner arrived at Rustici's than Cellini came in, made straight for Michelangelo:

"That Torrigiani is an animal! He told me that you used to go together to the church of the Carmine to learn drawing from the Masaccios, and that one day when you were bantering him he gave you such a blow on the nose that he felt the bone crumble beneath his knuckles."

Michelangelo's face became grim.

"Why do you repeat his story to me, Cellini?"

"Because his words begat in me such a hatred for the man that although I was considering going to England with him—he's looking for several assistants for a commission there—I know now I could never bear the sight of him."

It was good to have a group of his friends and fellow Florentines about him in the closely knit Company. He had recommended Jacopo Sansovino for an important commission in Pisa, and Jacopo had forgiven him for not being allowed to participate in the now defunct façade. So had Baccio d'Agnolo, who had become famous for the beauty of his inlaid wood mosaics. Bugiardini, with a commission from Palla Rucellai to do an altarpiece of the Martyrdom of St. Catherine for Santa Maria Novella, was having trouble with his drawing. Michelangelo had spent several evenings with his old friend outlining in charcoal a design of nudes, wounded and dead, falling forward and backward, to catch a variety of light and shadow on their strong figures.

The only sour note was Baccio Bandinelli, who would not look in Michelangelo's direction. Michelangelo studied the man who had been fighting him ever since the Perugino quarrel; thirty-one, with a nose that was wire-thin at the bridge but flared wide at the nostrils; heavy-lidded eyes that were deceptively lethargic, and the nimblest, fastest-talking lips in Tuscany. He had been awarded several commissions by the Medici. Cardinal Giulio had recently given him an Orpheus and Cerberus to do.

"What is it that he can't forgive me?" Michelangelo asked Granacci. "The fact that he destroyed my cartoon for the Bathers?"

"That you were born, live, breathe and carve. The very fact that there is such a person as Michelangelo Buonarroti poisons the air for him. If you didn't exist, he believes he would be the first marble master of Italy."

"Would he be?"

"He made an incredible botch of the Hercules and Cacus for the *ringhiera* of the Signoria. But he's a skilled goldsmith, and favorite of the Medici because his father saved their gold plate during the sack. You can become as bad a sculptor as he is, or make him as good as you are. Nothing short of this will ever placate him."

Agnolo Doni, for whom he had painted the Holy Family, had wangled an unofficial membership in the Company by sponsoring a number of their more expensive parties. As Michelangelo's fame had grown, so had the legend of their friendship. Doni had them being an unbeatable combination on the Santa Croce football team; Michelangelo had lived as much in Doni's home as his own; Doni had encouraged him in his art. What Michelangelo now grasped was that, over the fifteen years of expanding and telling, Doni had come to believe his own tall tales. When Doni was relating to Aristotile da Sangallo how he had forced the rear door of a palace late one night and held the candle while Michelangelo sketched from a fresco which the owners had forbidden anyone to copy, Granacci winked at Michelangelo and drawled beguilingly:

"What a wonderful story, Michelangelo. Why did you never tell me?"

Michelangelo smiled wryly. He could not call Doni a liar in public. What would it accomplish? Better to regard it as a measure of his success.

As the months passed he broke into four nine-foot blocks simultaneously, creating advanced sculptural forms at one corner of each block, then tipping them over clockwise to work the other side.

These were to be part of his Captive theme for the tomb. Eager to define the muscular body forms, he measured the distances between anatomical areas and drove stubby bronze nails into the outer marble. He walked around the columns with a point in his hand making chips here and there, nicking the planes to familiarize himself with the density of the stone. When he started the detail work on any one section he would know how much marble lay behind it. Only with a hammer and point could he grasp the interior weight, the depth he could bite into.

He knew in his carver's eye the details of the sculptures. In his mind they were not four separate figures but parts of a unified conception: the somnolent Young Giant, trying to free himself from his imprisonment in the stone of time; the Awakening Giant, bursting forth from his mountain chrysalis; the Atlas, full in years and power and wisdom, holding God's earth on his shoulders; and the Bearded Giant, old and tired, ready to pass the world along to the Young Giant in a continuing cycle of birth and death.

He too lived as far outside the realm of time and space as these demigods twisting and spiraling their tortured way out of their encasing blocks. He carved tirelessly through the autumnal and winter days, kept warm by a log fire, eating a little soup or veal when Monna Margherita carried it through the streets in a pot for him, throwing himself on the bed fully clothed when he could no longer follow the tracks of his punch or claw chisel. He awakened after a couple of hours refreshed, put a candle in his cap and continued to work, hewing the fronts of his figures, drilling holes between the legs, modeling the four bodies with pointed chisels, keeping them at the same stage of development.

By spring the four Captive-Giants were viable. Though the Young Giant's body was still embedded in the marble womb from which he was emerging, his feet unformed, and only the outlines of the features suggested in a head shielded beneath the upraised arm, the body lived by its own anatomical weight, the blood coursing through it. The Atlas, his head totally encased in a roughhewn, overhanging clifflike boulder held up by his gigantic arms, was pulsatingly alive, feeling intensely the bulk of the world he held. The Bearded Giant, his back and buttocks crosshatched, leaned heavily against a base deep-scarred by the vicious pounding of the point.

The Awakening Giant's head pushed forcibly to one side, his arms thrown out in an encircling movement, one leg bent violently at the knee, the other still buried in the block.

He stood among his Giants, the nine-foot blocks dwarfing him. Yet all four bowed beneath his superior force, his driving power, the flying hammer and chisel which were creating four pagan gods to hold up the tomb of a Christian pontiff.

Granacci cried:

"You've already made up the three lost years in the quarries. But where do they come from, these mysterious creatures? Are they Olympians from ancient Greece? Or prophets from the Old Testament?

"Every work of art is a self-portrait."

"They have a tremendous emotional impact; it's as though I must project myself into their unfinished forms, complete them by my own thinking and feeling."

If Granacci did not mean to suggest that Michelangelo leave his four Captives unfinished, Pope Leo and Cardinal Giulio did. They decided to build a sacristy onto San Lorenzo in which to bury their fathers, *Il Magnifco* and his brother Giuliano. The walls of this new sacristy had been started on two earlier occasions. Michelangelo passed the masons without looking up at them, for he had no intention of getting himself involved in another stillborn Medici scheme. Unembarrassed by the fact that they had canceled his contract for the façade, Pope Leo and Cardinal Giulio, who was back at the Vatican after having left the Cardinal of Cortona in charge of Florence, sent Salviati to Michelangelo with an offer to make sculptures for the new *cappella*.

"I am no longer their sculptor," cried Michelangelo when Salviati appeared at his door. "Baccio Bandinelli now holds that exalted position. By the end of the year I will have these four Captives out of their blocks. Another two years of such work and I can complete Julius' tomb, assemble it, be done with the contract. The Rovere family will owe me some eighty-five hundred ducats. Do you know what that means to a man who has not earned a scudo for four years?"

"You need the good will of the Medici."

"I also need money . . . which I don't get from the Medici. They still think of me as a fifteen-year-old who is left three florins each week on the washstand for spending money."

As the walls of the sacristy rose so did the Medici pressure on him. The next overture came in a letter from Sebastiano in Rome.

Michelangelo went on carving his Giants, the twisted tension-packed thigh and knee of the Young Giant, the squat trunklike legs held in bondage by thongs, the expression turned inward. These were the realities of his life during the late spring days, the still, hot summer, the first cool breezes down from the mountains in September.

When his brother Buonarroto, now the father of a second son who was named Lionardo, walked over to the studio to complain that they had not seen him, and ask if he didn't get lonely working night and day without family or friends, he replied:

"The Giants are my friends. They talk not only to me but to each other. In debate . . . like the Athenians used to carry on in their agora."

"Who wins? You, I hope."

"*Dio mio*, no! Sometimes they conspire, and overwhelm me."

"They're so enormous, Michelangelo. If any one of them should drop his arm on your head . . ."

". . . it would break open like an egg. But there is no violence in them; they are victims, not aggressors, trying to hold up the world rather than tear it down."

Why did he accede? He was not sure. By October the pressure from the Vatican had become intense. By October Buonarroto's accounts showed that he had spent more cash in the past year than he had taken in in rents from the properties in the

Via Ghibellina, and from the sale of the wine, oil, barley, wheat, oats, sorghum and straw of his farms. By October he had poured out his strength so prodigiously on the nine-foot Captives that he was vulnerable. The news of Raphael's death had shocked him, made him aware of man's short span, the limited time for creativity. He became sad, thoughtful. The memory of *Il Magnifico* and his untimely death returned to haunt him.

"What would I have been without Lorenzo de' Medici?" he asked himself. "And what have I yet done to repay him? Would it not be ungrateful of me to refuse to carve his tomb?"

Although he again would be saddled with tomb sculptures, he could demand the freedom to carve some highly imaginative pieces, ideas for which began to catch fire in his mind like the autumn burning of the shepherd's *paleri* in the mountains above Carrara.

The final impetus was provided by Pope Leo's open expression of hostility. Sebastiano, striving desperately to get the commission to paint the Hall of Constantine in the Vatican, assured the Pope he could do wonders with the frescoes if only he had Michelangelo's help. Leo cried:

"I do not doubt it, for you all belong to his school. Look at Raphael's work; as soon as he saw Michelangelo's, he left Perugino's style. But Michelangelo has a *terribilità*, and listens to no reason."

Sebastiano wrote:

I said you were only so because you had important works to finish. You frighten everybody, including Popes.

This was the second pontiff in a row who had accused him of having an awesomeness. Even if it were true, who but they had been the cause of it? When he wrote to Sebastiano to complain, Sebastiano replied soothingly:

I do not esteem you terrible, except only in art; that is to say, in being the greatest master who ever lived.

Soon he would complete enough of the figures for Julius' tomb to satisfy the Roveres. Where did he go from there? He could not afford to be in disfavor at the Vatican. It controlled all the churches in Italy; even the nobles and rich merchants would heed its voice. Florence was also governed by the Medici. Either he worked for the Medici, or he might not work at all.

He reassured himself with the fact that since the walls of the new sacristy were almost completed the small, intimate chapel would be a limiting force, restricting the number of sculptures he might envisage. Jacopo Galli would approve of the scope of this commission!

2

Pope Leo and Cardinal Giulio were happy to have him back in the family. Ill feelings over the Pietrasanta quarries and road were forgotten, perhaps because the crews from the Duomo workyard had been unable to get out any additional marble. The quarries were shut down. His five white columns lay neglected on the beach. Salviati, on his way to Rome on papal business, offered his services in setting up a workable agreement.

"If such a thing is possible," exclaimed Michelangelo resignedly. "Tell the Pope and the cardinal that I will work for them on contract, by the month, by the day, or even as a gift."

Early the next morning he went to the new sacristy, entering through a workman's portal. The interior walls were of rough cement. The dome had not yet been added. He thought how delightful it might look if he designed the interior of *pietra serena* from the quarry in Maiano. He could pick the most luminous slabs, convert the cramped chapel into a shrine of white marble against blue-gray *pietra serena,* the two materials he loved best in the world.

Florence was flooded by wind-driven rains. He moved his worktable to the front of the fire and drew exploratory plans. The Pope had now decided that there must also be tombs for the younger Medici, his brother Giuliano, and Piero's son Lorenzo. Michelangelo's first idea of a free-standing tomb with four sepulchers in the center of the chapel was declined by Cardinal Giulio on the grounds that the chapel was too small to hold the tombs and sculptures as well. The cardinal's idea of a series of arches with a tomb in the walls above each arch, his own sarcophagus to be in the center, was rejected by Michelangelo as unworkable.

He drew a new concept: one austere sarcophagus on either side of the chapel, each holding two reclining allegorical figures: Night and Day on one, Dawn and Dusk on the other; two male, two female; great brooding figures of intense emotional and physical beauty, which would represent man's cycle within the days of his life.

This plan was accepted.

He thought of his five white columns on the beach of Pietrasanta. But they belonged to the Duomo. Simpler to send the two hundred ducats advanced by the Vatican to his favorite quarry, the Polvaccio in Carrara, providing detailed drawings for their size and massing. When the blocks arrived he was gratified to find that they were of high statuary quality and had been accurately dressed.

He spent the spring and summer months designing the interior walls and dome, drawing for the Night and Day, Dawn and Dusk, the two life-size figures of the young Medici for the niches above the sarcophagi, a Madonna and Child for the wall opposite the altar. Cardinal Giulio came through Florence on his way to Lombardy to join the Pope's army, once again fighting the invading French. He sent for Michelangelo, received him warmly in the Medici palace.

"Michelangelo, how can I see with my eyes and touch with my hands the exact chapel as you will finish it?"

"Your Grace, I will give you actual drawings of the *pietra serena* doors, windows, pilasters, columns, niches, cornices. Then I will build models in wood exactly the size the tombs are to be. I will put on them the proposed statues in clay, made to size and finished exactly as they are to be."

"That will take considerable time. The Holy Father is in a hurry."

"No, Your Grace, it will take only a short time and cost little."

"Then it's settled. I will leave with Buoninsegni an order to give you the money as it is needed."

The cardinal did no such thing; but this neither surprised nor diverted Michelangelo. He proceeded to make the models at his own expense. He then turned his attention to the architecture, making sketches and building plans for the dome. He also decided to close in a number of the windows. The only time he stopped work was to celebrate the birth of Buonarroto's third son, Buonarrotino; with three male heirs the name of Buonarroti-Simoni was now secure.

In late November Pope Leo returned from a hunt at his villa at La Magliana and caught a chill. By December 1, 1521, the first Medici Pope was dead in the Vatican. Michelangelo attended the requiem mass in the Duomo, standing next to Granacci, remembering his years with Giovanni in the palace and Giovanni's first big hunt; Giovanni's kindness and loyalty when he had become an influential cardinal in Rome. He joined in the prayer for Leo's soul. Later, he whispered to Granacci:

"Do you suppose that heaven can offer any part of the entertainment Leo provided himself at the Vatican?"

"I doubt it. God would not spend that much money."

The *tramontana* blew icily through the streets. No amount of logs could heat the studio. With Leo dead, the project of the Medici chapel became equally cold and wind-swept. In Rome half a dozen factions of the College of Cardinals fought for supremacy, until they finally compromised on sixty-two-year-old Adrian of Utrecht, a practical-minded Fleming who had been tutor to Charles V.

Cardinal Giulio half fled to Florence, for Pope Adrian was a highly moral churchman who had disapproved of the Medici pontificate and knew Giulio to be responsible for a considerable portion of it. Pope Adrian set out to right the wrongs of Pope Leo and to redress the grievances of all who had been injured. He started by returning sovereignty to the Duke of Urbino, ended by listening sympathetically to the complaints of the Rovere family, agreeing that they should file suit against Michelangelo Buonarroti for failure to fulfill his contract with Pope Julius' heirs.

Michelangelo found himself twitching nervously as he walked through the streets to the house of Raffaello Ubaldini, a notary. Ubaldini had just returned from an audience with Pope Adrian.

"Why should they want to take me into court?" Michelangelo cried. "I haven't abandoned the tomb."

Ubaldini was an intense, serious little fellow with a blue skin where he shaved.

"The Roveres claim you have."

"There are four Captives in my studio . . ."

"In your revised contract you agreed to complete the tomb last May. You agreed not to take any new projects, yet you accepted the Medici sacristy."

"I have only made drawings for the sacristy. . . . Given another year . . ."

"The Duke of Urbino has no more faith in your promises. They showed Pope Adrian that it is seventeen years since you made the agreement, and yet you have delivered nothing."

Quivering with rage, Michelangelo protested, "Did they tell Pope Adrian that it was Julius who stopped me originally by refusing to finance the tomb? By wasting fifteen months of my life forcing me to do his figure in bronze in Bologna? That Julius stuck me in the Sistine vault for four years of painting . . .?"

"Piano, piano, gently, gently. Here, sit down at my desk."

Michelangelo asked hoarsely:

"If Pope Adrian favors their suit, I am defeated?"

"Probably."

"What will they want of me?"

"First, all their money to be returned."

"I'll return it."

"Over eight thousand ducats."

"Eight thou . . . !" He sprang up as though a fire had been started beneath the leather chair. "But I've only had three thousand."

"They have documents, receipts . . ."

Ubaldini showed Michelangelo the accounting. Michelangelo went green.

"The two thousand ducats Julius paid me before he died was for the Sistine."

"Can you prove that?"

". . . no."

"Then the court will grant them eight thousand ducats, plus interest on the money over all these years."

"How much will that be?"

"Not more than twenty per cent. They are also asking monetary damages for your failure to fulfill the contract. That can be any amount the court sees fit to levy. Pope Adrian has no interest in art; he considers this purely a business matter."

Michelangelo blinked hard to force the tears back under his lids.

"What am I to do?" he whispered. "All of my farms and houses put together are hardly worth ten thousand florins. I'll be bankrupt, my life savings swept away . . ."

"Frankly, I don't know. We have to find friends at court. People who admire your work and will intervene with Pope Adrian. In the meanwhile may I suggest that you complete your four Captives and take them to Rome? If you would assemble as much of Julius' tomb as you already have carved . . . ?"

He returned blindly to his studio, his body pervaded with nausea. News spread over Florence of the catastrophe hanging over him. Friends began arriving: Granacci and Rustici carrying purses of gold; members of the Strozzi and Pitti families offering to go to Rome in his behalf.

He was trapped. The Roveres did not care about the money, they were out to punish him for abandoning the Rovere tomb in favor of a Medici façade and chapel. When he wrote to Sebastiano offering to come to Rome and complete the tomb, the Duke of Urbino rejected his offer, declaring:

"We no longer want the tomb. We want Buonarroti brought into court and judgment passed on him."

And he learned that there were degrees of being ruined. Three years before, when Cardinal Giulio had recalled him from Pietrasanta and canceled the façade, he had been seriously hurt, but he had been able to return to work, to carve the Risen Christ and begin the four Captives. Now he faced genuine disaster; forty-seven years old, he would be stripped of his possessions and publicly discredited as a person unable or unwilling to complete a commission. The Roveres would brand him as a thief for taking their money and giving nothing in return. There would be no work for him as long as Adrian was Pope. As an artist and a man his life was behind him.

He wandered the countryside talking to himself, conjuring up conspiracies against him, the intrigues and machinations of blind fate, often not knowing where he was as his mind veered from one fantasy to another: flight to Turkey with his friend Tommaso di Tolfo, who had invited him a second time; escape from Italy in disguise to take up life at the French court under another name; revenge against those who had injured him; diatribes about his tormentors, with visions of doing them violence: all the mental aberrations of the sorely afflicted. He was unable to sleep at night, to sit at table during a meal. His legs moved him to Pistoia or Pontassieve, while his mind was in Rome or Urbino or Carrara or Florence, quarreling, accusing, shouting, hitting, unable to absorb the injustices and indignities.

He watched the harvests being taken in, the wheat flailed on cobbled farm courtyards, the grapes brought from the vines and squeezed for wine, the hay shaped into ricks and covered for the winter, the olives picked and trees cut back, the trees begin to turn yellow. He became emaciated, could hold down no more food than during his nights of dissection at Santo Spirito. He asked himself over and over again:

"How could it have happened? When I started out so full of love for marble, so consumed to carve, to work at my craft? When I have never wanted anything else in this world? What has happened to me? How have I become displaced?

"What has been my crime, O Lord?" he cried aloud. "Why hast Thou forsaken me? How can I be going through Dante's Inferno if I am not yet dead?"

As he read the *Inferno* he came across passages that made him feel that Dante had written the book to describe his, Michelangelo's, life and lot:

Am I a thief, to be tortured by serpents?
Must I be part of "that wretched crowd"?

* * *

Each one seemed to be most strangely twisted
Between the chin and where the chest begins
The face of everyone turned to his back;
So ever backward they were forced to walk.

* * *

> I had come among that wretched crew
> Which God and all His foes abominate.
> These abject cowards who had never lived
> Were naked, and were stung incessantly
> By monstrous flies and wasps that swarmed about them.

He stayed off the streets during the day, away from the populous piazzas with their noisy, colorful markets and fairs; for it was just as when he had been painting the Sistine ceiling and walked home through the Piazza San Pietro: people seemed to look straight through him as though he were not there. He had the eerie feeling that he was moving like a ghost among the living. He sought out Granacci, demanding:

"What is it that I lack? I have been affiliated with Popes, given stupendous commissions. I have talent, energy, enthusiasm, self-discipline, singleness of purpose. What am I missing? *Fortuna,* luck? Where does one search for the leaven of luck?"

"Last out the bad times, *caro,* then you will be alive to enjoy the good. If you burn yourself out, like a rotted tree trunk set on fire . . ."

"Ah, Granacci, your favorite word: survival. What if one's work is done?"

"How old is your father?"

"Lodovico? Almost eighty."

"You see! Your life is only half spent. So your work is only half done. You just don't have enough faith."

Granacci proved to be right. God alone rescued him. After twenty-two agonizing months He gathered Pope Adrian to his everlasting reward. In the College of Cardinals there followed seven weeks of bargaining, dealing, promises and commitments . . . until Cardinal Giulio de' Medici garnered enough votes to get himself elected. Cousin Giulio!

Pope Clement VII sent word immediately after his coronation: Michelangelo must resume work on the chapel.

He was like a man who has been through a dangerous illness and has gazed into the visage of death. From this vantage point he came to a realization that everything that had happened to him before this had been a journey upward through time, everything that occurred after it a descent. If he could not control his own fate, why be born? The God of the Sistine vault, about to hand on to Adam the spark of life, had implicit in His glorious being the promise of freedom to accompany that life. He began to carve his allegories for the sacristy as creatures who had experienced the hardship and tragedy of life, who knew its wastefulness, its futility. The *contadini* said, "Life is to be lived." Granacci said, "Life is to be enjoyed." Michelangelo said, "Life is to be worked." Dawn, Day, Dusk and Night said, "Life is to be suffered."

His David had been young, knowing he could conquer everything he set out after; Moses was ripe in years, but with the inner strength to move mountains and form nations. These new creatures of his making had an aura of sadness about them, of pity; they were asking the most painful and unanswerable of dilemmas: for what purpose are we put on earth? To live our cycle? To perpetuate it? A continuous chain of living flesh, binding the burden of one generation to another?

Before, his concern had been with the marble and what he could extract from it. Now his concern shifted to human emotion and what he could portray of the philosophic meaning of life. He had been a man with marble; now he achieved an identity of man and marble. He had always wanted his figures to represent something important, but his David, his Moses, his Pietà, all had been solitary pieces, complete within themselves. In this Medici chapel he had an opportunity to portray a unified theme. What his mind evoked about the meaning of the carvings would be more important than the movements of his sculptor's hands over the marble surfaces.

On March 6, 1525, Lodovico gave a dinner at the family home to celebrate Michelangelo's fiftieth birthday. Michelangelo awakened in a melancholy mood, but as he sat down at the table, surrounded by Lodovico, by Buonarroto, his wife and four children, by his brothers Giovansimone and Sigismondo, he was content. He had come into the autumn of his life: a man had his seasons, even as had the earth. Was the harvesting of autumn less important than the seeding of spring? Each without the other was meaningless.

3

He drew, modeled and carved like a man released from prison, to whom the only remaining joy was the freedom to project himself in space. Time was his quarry; from it he would excavate the pure white crystalline years. What else was there to mine in the craggy mountains of the future? Money? It had eluded him. Fame? It had entrapped him. Work was its own reward; there was no other. To create in white marble more glorious figures than had ever been seen on earth or in heaven, to express through them universal truths, this was the payment, the glory of the artist. All else was illusion, vanishing smoke on the horizon.

Pope Clement put him on a lifetime pension of fifty ducats a month, assigned him a house across the piazza from the church of San Lorenzo as a workshop. The Duke of Urbino and the other Rovere heirs were persuaded to drop their lawsuit. He was now to design a single-wall tomb for which he had all the figures except a Pope and Virgin already carved. It had taken him a full twenty years to reach the practical conclusion about Julius' tomb which Jacopo Galli had known from the beginning.

For the sacristy he contracted with the Topolino family to handle the cutting and installing of the *pietra serena* doors, windows, Corinthian columns and architraves which divided the chapel walls into three levels, the giant pilasters of the lower level giving way to the delicate fluted columns and slender niches of the second, the lunettes and pendentives of the third supporting the dome. What he tried to achieve in his dome was a combination of the man-made form of the Duomo and the bulbous form of the ripe fruit all about him. It was somewhat compacted because it had to be set onto walls already erected, but he enjoyed finding out that there was as much sculpture in architecture as there was architecture in sculpture.

Orders and commissions began coming in, everything from windows for palaces to a tomb for Bologna, a villa for Mantua, a statue of Andrea Doria for Genoa, a palace façade for Rome, a Virgin with Archangel Michael for San Miniato. Even Pope Clement offered him a new commission, this time a library to house the Medici manuscripts and books, to be built above the old sacristy of San Lorenzo. He drew some rough plans for the library, again using *pietra serena* for the decorative effects.

His new young apprentice was Antonio Mini, a nephew of his friend Giovan Battista Mini, a long-faced lad with eyes and mouth too round for his thin cheeks, but with a well-modeled bone structure and a serene attitude toward life. He was honest and reliable in delivering models, copying drawings, making and repairing chisels in the forge; as loyal and delightful a helper as Argiento had been, but with considerably more talent. Since Michelangelo now had a woman servant, Monna Agniola, to do the housekeeping in the Via Mozza studio, the romantic Mini was free to spend his spare hours on the Duomo steps with the young boys of the town, watching the girls parade past the Baptistery in their high-necked dresses and puffed sleeves.

Giovanni Spina, merchant-scholar of the noble line of Jacopo Galli, Aldovrandi and Salviati, was named by Pope Clement to handle Michelangelo, the sacristy and

Medici library. He was a rangy man, stoop-shouldered, cold even in mild weather, with an intelligent face, and eyes that were not wide but very long. He introduced himself at the studio door by saying:

"I met Sebastiano at court in Rome. He admitted me to your house in the Macello dei Corvi to see the Moses and the two young Captives. I have always worshiped Donatello's work. You are like father and son."

"Grandfather and son. I was the heir of Bertoldo, who was the heir of Donatello. We are a continuous Tuscan bloodline."

Spina smoothed the hair which he combed downward over his ears. "When the Pope has no funds in Florence, you can count on me to get them . . . from somewhere." He approached the four unfinished Captives, circling, weaving in and out, studying, eyes opened to their full length in astonishment.

"This Atlas, holding on his shoulders the top of the block where his head will eventually emerge . . . is he saying that every man who carries a head on his shoulders is carrying the full weight of the world?"

They sat on the workbench discussing the Della Quercias in Bologna and the Laocoön in Rome. Spina asked:

"The Rucellai don't acknowledge that you are a cousin, do they?"

"How did you know?"

"I checked the records. Will you come to their palace gardens for our meeting? We are all that's left of the Plato Academy. This Thursday Niccolò Machiavelli is reading the first chapter of his history of Florence, which the Signoria commissioned."

Inside the unfinished sacristy he worked on the blocks of Dawn, Dusk, the Virgin and young Lorenzo. During the warm fall evenings he sat by the open doors to his yard, making clay models for the River Gods, symbolic of tears and suffering, for the base of the young Medici figures. Later, tired from carving or fashioning clay, but without desire for sleep, he lay wide-eyed hearing the surrounding church bells toll off the hours toward dawn. He saw Contessina's piquant face before him, heard the timbre of her voice; and at the same time felt Clarissa lying by his side, his arms twined tightly about her to hold her close to him; somehow, after the years of lovelessness, the two images merging until they became one, the figure of love itself. He wondered if he would ever know love again, in whatever form or guise. He rose, took sheets of drawing papers covered with crosshatched studies for Dawn and Dusk, arms, hips, breasts, legs, and spent the rest of the night pouring out his feelings in poetry:

Love's Furnace

So friendly is the fire to flinty stone
That, struck therefrom and kindled to a blaze,
It burns the stone, and from the ash doth raise,
What lives thenceforward binding stones in one;

Kiln-hardened this resists both frost and sun,
Acquiring higher worth for endless days—
As the purged soul from hell returns with praise,

E'en so the fire struck from my soul, that lay
Close-hidden in my heart, may temper me,
Till burned and slaked to better life I rise.

If made mere smoke and dust, I live today,
Fire-hardened I shall live eternally;
Such gold, not iron, my spirit strikes and tries.

With the first light he put away the papers, walked to the mirror over his washstand and studied his visage as though it belonged to a characterful model he had hired to pose for him. His entire physiognomy appeared to have deepened: the lines across his flat forehead, the eyes retreating from the world under the bony brows, the nose, which now appeared to be wider than ever, the lips pulled tight as though to lock in word and thought. The eyes were darkly amber. Only his hair had resisted change, remaining rich in color and texture, curling youthfully across his forehead.

With the return of a Medici as Pope, Baccio Bandinelli was given the commission to carve the Hercules for the front of the Signoria, the one Michelangelo had been offered by Gonfaloniere Soderini some seventeen years before. Knowing that Michelangelo had been upset, Mini ran all the way home, burst into the studio crying:

"The block for the Hercules just arrived . . . and sank in the Arno. People standing on the bank are saying that the marble tried to drown itself rather than be carved by Bandinelli!"

Michelangelo laughed heartily, picked up his chisel and made a long "Go" from the bony knee of the *Crepuscolo,* Dusk, to the groin.

The next morning a canon from Rome brought him a message from Pope Clement.

"Buonarroti, you know the corner of the loggia of the Medici garden, opposite where Luigi della Stufa lives? The Pope asked if you would like to erect a Colossus there, eighty feet high?"

"A marvelous idea," Michelangelo replied sarcastically, "only it might take up too much of the roadway. Why not put it in the corner where the barbershop stands? We could make the statue hollow inside and rent out the ground floor to the barber. In that way his rent would not be lost."

He went of a Thursday evening to the Rucellai palace to hear Machiavelli read his *Mandragola.* The feeling of the group against Pope Clement was bitter; he was referred to as the Mule, Bastard, "the dregs of the Medici." The Plato Academy was at the center of the plot to restore the Republic. Their hatred was intensified by the fact that the two illegitimate Medici were living in the palace, being groomed to take over the government of Florence.

"That would be the bottom of the trough for us," commented Strozzi, about Clement's son, "to be governed by the mule of a mule!"

Michelangelo heard stories of how Clement was strengthening the cause of the anti-Medici party by making fatal errors of judgment, even as Leo had. In the incessant wars among the surrounding nations he consistently backed the wrong side; his allies, the French, had their armies destroyed by the Holy Roman Emperor, whose overtures Clement had rejected . . . though, truth to tell, Clement changed sides so often that neither Michelangelo nor Europe could keep up with his intrigues. In Germany and Holland thousands of Catholics were abandoning their religion for the reformation which Pope Clement refused to carry out within the Church, and which Martin Luther's ninety-five theses nailed to the door of the castle church at Wittenberg in 1517 had enunciated.

"I am in an awkward position," Michelangelo told Spina as they sat over a supper of roast pigeon served by Monna Agniola. "I long for the return of the Republic, but I am working for the Medici. The whole fate of the sacristy depends on the good will of Pope Clement. If I join a movement to drive out the Medici, what happens to the sculptures?"

"Art is the highest expression of freedom," replied Giovanni Spina. "Let the others fight over politics,"

Michelangelo locked himself inside the sacristy, burying his head in marble.

But Cardinal Passerini of Cortona ruled Florence autocratically. A foreigner, he had no love for Florence; nor did Clement seem to have any, for he rejected all appeals from the Signoria and the old families to replace the man whom the Florentines found crude, greedy, contemptuous of their elected councils, bleeding them with excessive taxes. The Florentines were waiting only for an advantageous moment to rise, seize the necessary arms and once again drive the Medici out of the city. When the army of the Holy Roman Empire, sweeping southward to invade Rome and punish Pope Clement, marched thirty thousand strong on Bologna, after which it planned to conquer Florence, the city rose in a mass, stormed the Medici palace and demanded arms to defend itself against the coming invasion, shouting:

"Guns! Guns to the people!"

The Cardinal of Cortona appeared in an upper window and promised arms. But when the cardinal learned that the Pope's army, commanded by Michelangelo's erstwhile opponent, the Duke of Urbino, was approaching Florence, he ignored his promise and rushed out with the two young Medici boys to meet the duke. Now Michelangelo joined Granacci and his friends at the Palazzo della Signoria. In the piazza crowds were calling:

"*Popolo, libertà!* The people, liberty!"

Florentine soldiers guarding the Signoria made no attempt to prevent a committee of citizens from entering the government palace. A meeting was held in the Great Hall. Then Niccolò Capponi, whose father had led the earlier movement to drive out Piero de' Medici, stepped onto a balcony and announced:

"The Florentine Republic is re-established! The Medici are banished! All citizens are to be armed and summoned to the Piazza della Signoria!"

Cardinal Passerini arrived with a thousand of the Duke of Urbino's cavalry. The Medici party opened a gate for them. The committee inside the palace bolted the doors. Urbino's cavalry attacked the doors with long pikes. From the two stories of windows, and from the crenelated parapet above, there rained down on the duke's soldiers everything that could be pried loose inside the building: desks, tables, chairs, crockery, armor.

A heavy wooden bench came hurtling down from the parapet. Michelangelo saw that it was headed straight for the David.

"Look out!" he screamed, as though the statue might dodge.

He was too late. The wooden bench struck. The left arm holding the slingshot snapped off below the elbow. The arm fell to the stone of the piazza, broke.

The crowd drew back. The soldiers turned to stare. All movement from the windows and parapet of the Signoria palace stopped. A hush fell over the throng. He felt himself moving toward the sculpture. The crowd opened, murmuring:

"It is Michelangelo. Let him pass."

He stood below the David, gazing up into the pensive, resolute yet beautiful face. Goliath had not scratched him; but the civil war inside Florence had come within inches of destroying him completely. Michelangelo's arm ached as though it too had been amputated.

Out of the crowd Giorgio Vasari, one of Michelangelo's young apprentices, and Cecchino Rossi sped toward the David, picked up the three marble fragments of the arm and hand and disappeared down the narrow side street.

In the stillness of the night there was a tattooing of finger ends on Michelangelo's door. He opened it to admit Vasari and Cecchino. They began talking at once.

"Signor Buonarroti . . ."

". . . we have the three pieces hidden . . ."

". . . in a chest in Rossi's father's house."

"They are safe."

Michelangelo gazed at the two shining young faces before him, thinking:

"Safe?" What was safe in a world of war and chaos?

4

The Holy Roman Emperor's army reached Rome, breached the walls. The horde of mixed mercenaries overran Rome, forcing Pope Clement to flee along the high passageway to the fortress of Sant'Angelo, where he remained a prisoner while the German, Spanish and Italian troops looted, ravaged and burned Rome, destroying sacred works of art, smashing altars, marble statues of Mary, the prophets and saints, melting bronze figures for cannon, stained-glass windows for lead, lighting fires on the inlaid marble floors of the Vatican, putting out the eyes in paintings, dragging a statue of Pope Clement into the street and hacking it to pieces.

"What of my Pietà? My Sistine ceiling?" groaned Michelangelo. "What of my studio? The Moses and the two Slaves? They can be lying in a thousand pieces."

Spina arrived late at night. He had been to a series of feverish meetings at the Medici palace, and then at the Signoria palace. With the exception of a core of die-hard Medici adherents, all Florentines were agreed that the Medici must be deprived of their power. With Pope Clement a prisoner, the Republic could once again be proclaimed. Ippolito, Alessandro and the Cardinal of Cortona would be allowed to leave peacefully.

"And that," concluded Spina thoughtfully, "should be the end of Medici rule for a very long time."

Michelangelo was silent.

"The new sacristy?"

Spina hung his head.

"It must be . . . locked. . . . ."

"The Medici are my nemesis," he cried in agony. "All these years of work for Leo and Clement, and what have I to show for them? Six roughhewn blocks, the half-finished interior of a chapel. . . . With Clement a prisoner, the Roveres will descend on me again. . . ."

He sat down hard on his workbench. Spina spoke softly.

"I shall recommend you for an office of the Republic. Once our government is secure we can persuade the Signoria that the chapel is for *Il Magnifico*, whom all Tuscans revere. Then we will get permission to unlock the doors and start work again."

He boarded up the house across from San Lorenzo, with its drawings and clay models, returned to the Via Mozza and plunged abruptly into a block to define a Victory, one of the original concepts for Julius' tomb. It emerged as a classic Greek youth, well proportioned though not as muscular as others he had carved. He worked well with his hands, the chisels plowing the pliant marble; but before long he realized that his head was not working at all.

Victory? Over whom? Over what? If he did not know who was the Victor, how could he determine who was the vanquished? Under the feet of the Victor, defeated and crushed, he carved the face and head of an old man . . . himself? As he might look ten or twenty years from now, with his beard grown full and white. What had defeated him? Age? Was youth the Victor, since it was the only period in which one could imagine that one could be a Victor? The defeated one had experience, a deep knowing and suffering in his face, bent under the knee of the youth. Was that what happened to experience and wisdom? Was it always crushed and destroyed by time in the guise of youth?

Outside his studio the Republic of Florence was triumphant. Niccolò Capponi was elected Gonfaloniere to govern in the Soderini tradition. For its protection the city-state had adopted Machiavelli's revolutionary plan for a militia of citizens trained, armed and equipped to defend the Republic against invaders. Florence was ruled not only by its Signoria but by a Council of Eighty, which represented the old families. Trade was active, the city prosperous, the people happy in their regained freedom. Few cared what happened to Pope Clement, still a prisoner in Sant'Angelo, defended by a few adherents, among them Benvenuto Cellini, the young sculptor who had refused to be apprenticed to Torrigiani. But Michelangelo was vitally interested in Pope Clement. He had put four years of loving work into the sacristy. There were partially finished blocks in the now locked and sealed chapel to whose future he was dedicated. He kept a close watch on Clement's fate.

Pope Clement was in danger from two sides. The Church was being broken up into national units, with power drained away from Rome. It was not merely that the Lutherans were sweeping through mid-Europe. Cardinal Wolsey of England proposed a council of free cardinals in France to set up a new government for the Church. The Italian cardinals were meeting at Parma to establish their own hierarchy. The French cardinals were setting up papal vicars. Charles' German and Spanish troops quartered in Rome were still sacking, destroying, demanding ransom to get out. From Sant'Angelo Clement tried to raise the money, forced to sacrifice hostages to the enemy: Jacopo Salviati was dragged through the streets to the gallows and almost hanged. The months went by, intrigue grew in every country for a new distribution of power, for a new Pope, a council, a reformation.

At the end of the Year of Our Lord 1527 the tide turned. A virulent plague decimated the Holy Roman Emperor's armies. The German troops hated Rome, were desperately anxious to return home. A French army invaded Italy to fight the Holy Roman Empire. Clement agreed to pay the invaders three hundred thousand ducats within three months. The Spanish army was withdrawn from the base of Sant'Angelo . . . and after seven months of incarceration Pope Clement fled, disguised as a merchant, making his way to Orvieto.

Michelangelo promptly received a communication from Clement. Was Michelangelo still working for him? Would he continue to sculpture in the new sacristy? If so, Pope Clement had five hundred ducats on hand which he would send to him by messenger to cover the immediate costs.

Michelangelo was deeply moved: the sorely harassed Pope, without funds or followers or prospects of regaining power, had sent words of affection and continued trust, as he would have to any other member of his family.

"I can't take Giulio's money," Michelangelo said to Spina as they conferred in the Via Mozza studio; "but couldn't I carve sometimes? If I slipped in unseen, at night? It could not hurt Florence."

"Patience. In a year or two. . . . The Council of Eighty is apprehensive about what Clement may do. They would consider your working on the chapel an act of disloyalty."

With warm weather, the plague struck Florence. People came down with crushing headaches, pain in the back and limbs, fever, vomiting, and in three days were dead. If they dropped in the streets they were left there; if they died in their houses their families fled. Thousands of Florentines perished. The city became a morgue. Buonarroto summoned his brother to the house on the Via Ghibellina.

"Michelangelo, I'm frightened for Bartolommea and the children. Could I move up to our house in Settignano? We'd be safe there."

"Certainly. Take Father with you."

"I won't go," growled Lodovico. "When a man is in his mid-eighties he has a right to die in his own bed."

Fate was waiting for Buonarroto at Settignano, in the room where he had been born. By the time Michelangelo reached there Buonarroto was delirious, his tongue was swollen and covered with a dry yellowish fuzz. Giovansimone had moved Buonarroto's wife and children to safety the day before. The servants and *contadini* had fled.

Michelangelo drew a chair up to his brother's bed, thinking how much alike they still looked. Buonarroto's eyes lighted in alarm at the sight of his brother.

"Michelagnolo . . . don't stay . . . the plague . . ."

Michelangelo wet his brother's parched lips with a damp cloth, murmured, "I will not leave you. You're the only member of our family who has loved me."

"I always loved you. . . . But I've been . . . a burden. Forgive me. . . ."

"There's nothing to forgive, Buonarroto. Had I kept you by my side all during the years I would have been much better off."

Buonarroto managed a weary smile.

"Michelagnolo . . . you always were . . . good."

By sundown Buonarroto was dying. Michelangelo encircled him with his left arm, his brother's head resting on his chest. Buonarroto woke only once, saw Michelangelo's face held close to his own. The pain-caused furrows eased, resignation spread its calm unguent. In a few moments he was dead.

Michelangelo carried his brother in a blanket to the graveyard behind the church. There were no coffins, no diggers. He dug a grave, lowered Buonarroto into the hole, summoned the priest, waited until Buonarroto had been sprinkled with holy water and blessed; then he shoveled earth into the grave, filled it.

He returned to the Via Mozza, burned his clothes in the back yard, scrubbed himself in his wooden tub in water hot as he could stand. He did not know whether this helped against the plague, nor did he greatly care. Word was brought to him that Simone, his oldest nephew, was also dead of the plague. Michelangelo thought:

"Perhaps Buonarroto is the fortunate one?"

If he had caught the disease he had but a few hours to put his affairs in order. He drew up a paper paying back to Buonarroto's wife the dowry she had brought with her; a young woman, she would need it to get a second husband. He arranged for his eleven-year-old niece, Cecca, to be put into the Convent of Boldrone, providing for her keep and education by assigning produce from two of his farms. He set aside assets to pay for the education of his nephews Lionardo and little Buonarrotino. When Granacci banged on the locked door Michelangelo cried:

"Go away. I've been exposed to the plague. I may have caught it."

"Don't be *sciocco*, silly. You're too crusty to die. Open up, I've got a bottle of wine to ward off evil spirits."

"Granacci, go home and drink by yourself. I'm not going to be the cause of killing you. Maybe if you stay alive you'll paint one more good picture."

"Now isn't that an inducement!" laughed Granacci. "*Allora*, if you're still alive tomorrow, come finish your half of the Chianti."

The plague abated. People filtered down from the surrounding hills. Shops reopened. The Signoria returned to the city. One of its first resolutions was to commission Michelangelo Buonarroti to carve the Hercules which Soderini had ordered twenty years before, out of the block that Bandinelli had massed up to its navel.

Once again Pope Clement interfered. Having returned to the Vatican by making an alliance with the Holy Roman Emperor, he resumed power over the renegade Italian, French and English cardinals, formed an army out of the forces of the Duke of Urbino, the Colonna and Spanish troops. This army was being sent against independent Florence to wipe out the Republic, punish the enemies of the Medici and once again restore the family to power. Spina had underestimated Pope Clement and the Medici. Michelangelo was summoned before the Signoria, where Gonfaloniere Capponi sat at Soderini's desk, surrounded by his Eight-in-Office.

"Since you are a sculptor, Buonarroti," he said in a rushing voice, "we assume you can also be a defense engineer. We need walls that cannot be breached. Since they are of stone, and you are a man of stone . . ."

Michelangelo gulped. Now he would really be involved on both sides!

"Confine yourself to the south of the city. We are impregnable from the north. Report at the quickest possible moment."

He explored along the several miles of wall that began on the east with the hillside church of San Miniato, and snaked its way westward before returning to the Arno. Neither the walls nor defense towers were in a good state of repair, nor were there ditches on the outside to make the enemy approach more hazardous. Stones were loose, badly baked bricks were crumbling, more towers for cannon were needed, additional height to make scaling a longer task. The anchor of the defense line would have to be the campanile of San Miniato, from whose height the defenders could command most of the ground over which the enemy troops would have to charge.

He returned with his report to Gonfaloniere Capponi and the Signoria, laying out before them the number of stonemasons, brickmakers, carters, peasants he would need to make the walls defensible. The Gonfaloniere cried impetuously:

"Do not touch San Miniato. There is no need to fortify a church."

"There is every need, Excellency, for if we do not the enemy will not need to break down the walls. They will turn our flank here, east of the San Miniato hill."

He was given permission to prove that his plan was the best one possible. He pressed everyone into service: Granacci, the Company of the Cauldron, the masons from the Duomo workyard. Where before he had scoured the countryside seeking a figure, or face, a husky arm or elongated sunburnt throat for a statue or painting, now he searched for stonemasons, quarriers from Maiano and Prato, carpenters, brickmakers, mechanics, to stem a war. Work went ahead at full speed, for the Pope's army was reported moving on Florence from several directions, a formidable force of trained men and weapons. Michelangelo built a road up from the river for his men and supplies, began his bastions at the first tower outside the gate of San Miniato, toward San Giorgio, closing in the vital defense hill with high walls of brick made of pounded earth mixed with flax, or tow, and cattle dung, a hundred contadini working in teams, throwing up the walls as fast as they could get the bricks squared. The stonemasons cut, chipped, shaped, shoring up weak stretches, adding height to the walls and towers, erecting new areas at the more vulnerable spots.

When the first phase of his work was completed the Signoria made an inspection. The next morning when he entered the corner office overlooking the Piazza della Signoria and the tight-knit roofs of Florence, he was greeted with smiles.

"Michelangelo, you have been elected to the Nove della Milizia, the Militia Nine, as Governor General of the Fortifications."

"It is a great honor, Gonfaloniere."

"And a greater responsibility. We want you to make an inspection trip to Pisa and Livorno, to make sure our defenses from the sea are secure."

There was no further thought of sculpture. Nor could he cry, "War is not my trade." He had a specific job to do. Florence had called on him in its time of crisis. He had never imagined himself a commander, an organizer, but now he found that evolving intricate works of art had taught him how to co-ordinate each mounting detail to accomplish a finished result. He might even wish he had a little of Leonardo da Vinci's inventiveness with machines.

On his return from Pisa and Livorno he began a series of ditches as deep as moats, using the excavated earth and rock to form a further series of barricades. His next move was to secure permission to level all buildings between the defense walls and base of the encircling foothills a mile to the south, terrain over which the papal army would have to attack. The militia used battering rams of the kind the ancients used, to knock down the farmhouses and village homes. The farmers helped to level houses that had been in their families for hundreds of years. The wealthy protested against the wrecking of their palaces; not without reason, Michelangelo acknowledged, since they were so beautifully built. Only a few of the soldiers could be induced to level the several small chapels. When he himself came to the refectory of San Salvi and saw Andrea del Sarto's Last Supper shining in all its brilliance on the half-razed walls, he cried out:

"Let it be. It is too great a work of art to be destroyed."

The leveling job was just finished when he received word that the Via Mozza studio had been broken into. Models were thrown to the floor, folios of drawings and sketches scattered in wild confusion, many missing, as well as four models in wax. He saw the glitter of metal on the floor. Leaning over, he picked up a chisel from among a pile of papers. It was the kind used in a goldsmith's shop. He walked to the home of his friend Piloto, who knew the local goldsmiths.

"Do you recognize this chisel?"

"Yes. It belongs to Bandinelli."

Very discreetly the sketches and wax models were returned; Michelangelo instructed Mini to see that the studio was kept guarded.

The Signoria dispatched him to Ferrara to study the Duke of Ferrara's new fortifications. The note he carried with him read:

> We send to Ferrara our celebrated Michelangelo Buonarroti, as you are aware a man of rare endowments, for certain purposes which he will explain to you by word of mouth. We greatly desire that he should be recognized as a person highly esteemed by us and cherished as his merits deserve.

The Duke of Ferrara, a cultivated man of the Este family, and an enthusiast of painting, sculpture, poetry, the theater, urged him to be a guest at the palace. Michelangelo graciously declined, staying at an inn where he enjoyed an uproarious reunion with Argiento, who brought in his nine children to kiss Michelangelo's hand.

"Well, Argiento, have you become a good farmer?"

Argiento grimaced. "No. But the earth makes things grow, no matter what I do to it. Children are my main crop."

"And mine is still trouble, Argiento."

When Michelangelo thanked the Duke of Ferrara for revealing his defense structures, the duke said:

"Make me a painting. Then I shall be rewarded."

Michelangelo grinned. "As soon as this war is over."

Back in Florence he found that General Malatesta of Perugia had been brought to Florence to serve as one of the commanding generals. He quarreled immediately with Michelangelo's plan to throw up stone supports in the manner he had learned in Ferrara.

"You have already burdened us with too many walls. Take your peasants away, and let my soldiers defend Florence."

Malatesta seemed cold, devious. That night Michelangelo roamed the base of his ramparts. He came upon the eight pieces of artillery that had been given to Malatesta to defend the San Miniato wall. Instead of being placed inside the fortifications, or on the parapets, they lay outside the walls, unguarded. Michelangelo awoke the sleeping general.

"What do you mean by exposing your artillery pieces that way? We guarded them with our lives until you arrived. They could be stolen or destroyed by anyone who stumbled upon them."

"Are you the commander of the Florentine army?" demanded Malatesta, livid.

"Just of the defense walls."

"Then go make your cow-dung brick, and don't tell a soldier how to fight."

Returning to San Miniato, Michelangelo encountered General Mario Orsini, who demanded:

"What has gone wrong, my friend? Your face is on fire."

Michelangelo told him. When he had finished, Orsini replied sadly:

"You must know that the men of his house are all traitors. In time he will betray Florence."

"Have you reported this to the Signoria?"

"I am a hired officer, like Malatesta, not a Florentine."

In the morning Michelangelo waited in the Great Hall of the palace until he could be admitted to the Gonfaloniere's office. The Signoria was not impressed.

"Stop concerning yourself over our officers. Confine yourself to your new plans for the walls. They must not be breached."

"They won't need to be, with Malatesta guarding them."

"You are overwrought. Get some rest."

He returned to the walls, continued to work under the broiling September sun, but he could not put Malatesta out of his mind. Everywhere he went he heard stories against the general: he had yielded Perugia without a battle; his men would not fight the Pope's troops at Arezzo; when the armies reached Florence, Malatesta would surrender the city . . .

In his mind he went back time and again to the Signoria, pleading that Malatesta be removed, seeing his labors in building impregnable walls going for nothing as Malatesta opened the gates to the Pope's army. Or was it really to Gonfaloniere Capponi that he was protesting? . . . Wasn't it to Pope Julius . . . about Bramante's walls for St. Peter's . . . which were made of weak cement and would crumble? . . . Had Malatesta demanded, "Are you the commander of the army?" Wasn't it Pope Julius who had asked, "Are you an architect?" . . .

He became agitated. He envisaged the Pope's troops destroying Florence even as Rome had been, sacking, pillaging, smashing the works of art. Sleepless, unable to eat or to concentrate on directing his stone crews, he began to overhear shards of sentences which convinced him that Malatesta had gathered the officers on this south wall in a conspiracy against Florence.

He went six days and nights without rest or nourishment, unable to control his anxieties. One night a voice spoke to him. He whirled about on the parapet:

"Who are you?"

"A friend."

"What do you want?"

"To save your life."

"Is it in danger?"

"Of the worst kind."

"The Pope's army?"

"Malatesta."

"What is he going to do?"

"Have you killed."

"Why?"

"For exposing his treason."

"No one believes me."

"Your corpse will be found at the base of the bastion."

"I can protect myself."

"Not in this mist."

"What should I do?"

"Flee."

"That is treason."

"Better than being dead."

"When must I go?"

"Now."

"I'm in charge here."

"You haven't a moment."

"How can I explain?"

"Hurry!"

"My command . . . the walls . . ."

"Hurry! Hurry!"

He descended from the parapet, crossed the Arno, took a back route to the Via Mozza. Figures emerged from the thick fog half formed, like massed marble blocks. He ordered Mini to put clothes and money in their saddlebags. He and Mini mounted their horses. At the Prato gate they were challenged. A guard cried:

"It is Michelangelo, of the Militia Nine. Let him by."

He headed for Bologna, Ferrara, Venice, France . . . safety.

He was back after seven weeks, humiliated and in disgrace. The Signoria fined him, and barred him from the Council for three years. But because the papal armies were now camped thirty thousand strong on the hills beyond his southern defense walls they sent him back to his command. He had Granacci to thank for his reprieve; when the Signoria outlawed him, along with others who had taken flight, Granacci had secured a temporary commutation for him and sent Bastiano, who had helped Michelangelo repair the walls, in pursuit.

"I must say the Signoria was lenient," commented Granacci sternly, "considering that you have returned a full five weeks after the Rebel Exclusion Act. You could have lost all your property in Tuscany, and your head too, as Ficino's grandson lost his life for stating that the Medici seemed more entitled to rule than anyone else, considering their contribution to the city. You had better take a blanket up to San Miniato and enough victuals for a year's siege. . . ."

"Don't worry, Granacci, I can't be that stupid twice."

"What possessed you?"

"I heard voices."

"Whose?"

"My own."

Granacci grinned.

"I was helped by the rumors of your reception at the court in Venice, the offer from the Doge to design a bridge over the Rialto, and the French ambassador's efforts to get you to the French court. The Signoria thought you were an idiot, which you are, but a great artist, which you are. They weren't happy about your settling in Venice or Paris. Just thank your stars that you know how to chip marble, or you might never again have lived in sight of the Duomo."

Michelangelo looked out the third-floor window of Granacci's study to where Brunelleschi's glorious red tile dome stood in its spatial majesty against a stormy sunset.

"The finest architectural form in the world is the bowl of the sky," he mused, "and do you know, Brunelleschi's dome is equally beautiful!"

5

He settled his effects in the tower of San Miniato, gazed through the powdery light of a full moon at the hundreds of enemy tents with their pointed cones set up a mile away, beyond the ground he had cleared on the hills that formed a semicircle to enclose his protective line.

He was awakened at dawn by artillery fire. As he had expected, the attack was concentrated against the tower of San Miniato. If it could be knocked down, the Pope's forces would pour into the city. One hundred and fifty pieces of artillery fired steadily. Whole sections of brick and stone were blasted out by the exploding cannon balls. The attack lasted for two hours. When it was finished Michelangelo let himself out by a tunnel and stood at the base of the bell tower, surveying the damage.

He asked for volunteers among those who knew how to handle stone and cement. Bastiano directed the work inside, Michelangelo took a group outside and in full view of the papal troops refitted the fallen, shattered stone into the walls. For some reason beyond his comprehension, perhaps because they did not know how much damage they had inflicted, the enemy troops remained in camp. He ordered his carters to bring in Arno sand and sacks of cement, sent out runners to collect the crews of masons and quarriers, at dusk set them to rebuilding the tower. They worked all night; but it took time for cement to harden. If the enemy artillery opened fire too soon, his defense would be leveled. He gazed up at the campanile, its crenelated cornice wider by four feet all around than the shaft of the tower. If there were a way to hang something from those parapets, something that could absorb the impact of the iron and stone cannon balls before they could strike the tower itself . . .

He made his way down the hill, crossed the Ponte Vecchio, obliged the guards to awaken the new Gonfaloniere, Francesco Carducci, explained his device, obtained a written order and a company of militia. By first light they were beating on the doors of the wool shops, the warehouses and the customs sheds where wool was held for taxing purposes. Next they hunted the city for mattress covers, in shops and in private homes, then requisitioned carts to carry the material. He worked fast. By the time the sun was up he had dozens of his stoutest covers stuffed with wool and suspended by ropes across the face of the tower.

When the Pope's officers learned what was going on and turned their artillery on the campanile, it was too late. Their cannon balls struck the heavy paddings which, although they gave with the impact, had four feet of leeway before reaching the wet stone walls. The mattresses served as a shield for Michelangelo's newly cemented blocks. The cannon balls fell harmlessly into the ditch below. After firing until noon, the enemy abandoned the attack.

The success of his ingenious wool buffers won him repatriation. He returned to his studio, had his first night of peaceful sleep in months.

Heavy rains began to fall. The open mile of cleared fields between his walls and the enemy became a bog. There could be no attack now. Michelangelo began to paint in tempera a Leda and the Swan for the Duke of Ferrara. Though he worshiped the physical aspects of beauty, his art had been permeated with a sexual purity. Now he found himself indulging in a robust carnality. He portrayed Leda as a ravishingly beautiful woman, lying on a couch, with the swan nestled between her legs, the "S" of his long neck cupping one breast, his lips on hers. He enjoyed portraying the lusty fable.

The raw overcast continued. He spent the days on the parapets, at night waited his opportunity to slip into the sacristy and carve by candlelight. The chapel was cold, full of shadows; but he was not alone. His figures were familiar friends: the Dawn, the Dusk, the Virgin: for although they were not fully born, they were alive in the marble, thinking, telling him what they felt about the world, just as he spoke to them and through them, of art as man's continuity, the eternality that ties together the future and the past; a means of conquering death: for as long as art lives, man does not perish.

In the spring the war was resumed, but none of the battles except the one against starvation took place in Florence. Restored to his position on the Militia Nine, Michelangelo received reports each evening. By capturing small fortresses on the Arno, the papal army had cut off supplies from the sea. Spanish troops arrived from the south and Germans from the north to swell Pope Clement's troops.

Food grew scarce. Meat vanished first, then oil, greens, flour, wine. Famine took its toll. Michelangelo gave his own daily ration to Lodovico to keep his father alive. People began eating the city's asses, dogs, cats. Summer heat baked the stones, the water supply failed, the Arno dried up, the plague struck again. Men panted for air, dropped and never rose. By mid-July five thousand were dead within the city.

Florence had only one chance to survive, through its heroic general Francesco Ferrucci, whose army was near Pisa. Plans were laid for him to attack by way of Lucca and Pistoia and lift the siege. The last sixteen thousand men within the walls who were able to fight took the sacrament, vowing to storm the enemy camps on both sides of the city, while General Ferrucci struck from the west.

General Malatesta betrayed the Republic. He refused to help Ferrucci. Ferrucci hit hard, was on the verge of victory, when Malatesta treated with the Pope's generals. Ferrucci was defeated and killed.

Florence capitulated. Malatesta's troops opened the gates. Pope Clement's representatives entered the city to take control in the name of the Medici. Florence agreed to hand over eighty thousand ducats as back pay to the papal armies. Those members of the government who could, fled; others were hanged from the Bargello or thrown into the Stinche. All members of the Militia Nine were condemned.

"You'd better get out of the city this very night," Bugiardini urged Michelangelo. "The Pope will show no mercy. You built the defenses against him."

"I can't run again," replied Michelangelo wearily.

"Take refuge in the attic in my house," offered Granacci.

"I will not endanger your family."

"As official architect, I have the keys of the Duomo. I can hide you there," cried Baccio d'Agnolo.

Michelangelo was thoughtful. "I know a tower on the other side of the Arno. No one will suspect it. I'll take refuge there until Malatesta clears out with his troops."

He bade his friends farewell and made his way by back passages to the Arno, crossed the river and slipped silently to the bell tower of San Niccolò, knocking at the house next door, which belonged to the stonemason sons of old Beppe of the Duomo workyard, to let them know he was taking refuge. Then he locked the door of the tower behind him, climbed its circular wooden staircase and spent the rest of the night staring over the hills at the deserted enemy camp. At sunrise he was still leaning against the stone walls gazing sightlessly at the terrain he had leveled to protect the city-state.

Looking inward and backward, his own fifty-five years seemed as torn down, and uselessly so, as the mile of leveled ground below him. He reckoned the account of the years since Pope Leo had forced him to abandon the work on Julius' tomb. What did he have to show for those fourteen years? A Risen Christ which, Sebastiano had tearfully reported from Rome, had been injured by the inept apprentice who had removed the webbing between the legs and feet, and who had idiotically overlicked the face while polishing. A Victory which today, even more than the day he finished it, seemed confused. Four Giants still writhing in their blocks in the Via Mozza. A Moses and two Young Slaves in a house in Rome that had been plundered by an invading army.

Nothing. Nothing finished, nothing put together, made whole, delivered. And a one-armed, crippled David standing as a symbol of the vanquished Republic.

Not only cities were besieged and sacked. Man too was beleaguered.

Lorenzo had said that the forces of destruction were everywhere, overtaking everything and everybody within their range. That was all he had known since the days of Savonarola: conflict. Perhaps his father and uncle Francesco had been right to try to beat some sense into him. Whom had he enriched or made happy? He had spent a lifetime tearing himself apart, enduring the *terribilità* of his own nature in an attempt to create beautiful marbles, meaningful statues. He had loved the sculptor's art since he was born. He had wanted only to revive it, recreate it, bring to it newer, greater conceptions. Had he wanted too much? For himself, and for his time?

So very long ago his friend Jacopo Galli had told Cardinal Groslaye of San Dionigi, "Michelangelo will make you the most beautiful marble to be seen in Rome today, such that no master of our own time will be able to produce a better."

And here he was, a self-incarcerated prisoner cowering in an ancient bell tower, afraid to come down for fear he would be hanged from the Bargello as he had seen so many hanged during his youth. What an inglorious end for the pure bright fire that had burned in his bosom.

Between midnight chimes and cockcrow he walked along the upper marshes of the Arno, returning to find that food and water had been left for him, and the news of the day jotted down by Mini. Gonfaloniere Carducci had been decapitated in the courtyard of the Bargello. Girolami, who had succeeded him as Gonfaloniere, had been taken to Pisa and poisoned. Fra Benedetto, a priest who had sided with the Republic, had been taken to Rome to be starved to death in Sant'Angelo. All who had escaped were outlawed, their property confiscated.

Florence knew where he was hiding, but the somnolent hatred for Pope Clement, his generals and troops was so intense that he was not only safe from exposure but had become a hero.

Lodovico, whom Michelangelo had sent to Pisa with Buonarroto's two sons during the worst stage of the siege, returned without Buonarrotino. The boy had died in Pisa.

On a mid-November day he heard someone calling his name, loud and clear. Gazing downward from the bell tower, he saw Giovanni Spina huddled in a huge fur coat, hands cupped to his mouth as he cried upward:

"Michelangelo, come down!"

He took the circular wooden stairs three at a time, unbolted the door, saw Spina's long narrow eyes gleaming.

"The Pope has pardoned you. He sent word through Prior Figiovanni that if you were found you were to be treated kindly, your pension restored, and the house by San Lorenzo . . ."

". . . why?"

"The Holy Father wants you to return to work in the sacristy."

While Michelangelo gathered his things Spina surveyed the tower.

"It's freezing up here. What did you use to keep warm?"

'Indignation,'' said Michelangelo. "Best fuel I know. Never burns out."

As he walked through the streets in the late autumn sun he let his fingers trail over the *pietra serena* blocks of the houses; slowly they imparted their warmth to him. His breath came fast at the thought of returning to the *cappella*.

His studio in the Via Mozza had been thoroughly ransacked by the papal troops who had searched for him; even the chimney and chests had been looked into. Nothing had been stolen. In the chapel he found the scaffolding removed, probably to keep the clergy of San Lorenzo warm; but none of his marbles had been disturbed. After three years of war he could resume work. Three years . . . ! As he stood in the center of his allegorical blocks he divined that time too was a tool: a major work of art required months, years for its emotional elements to solidify. Time was a yeast; many aspects of the Day and Dusk, the Madonna, which had eluded him before now seemed clear to him, their form matured, their definition resolved. A work of art meant growth from the particular to the universal. To a work of art, time brought timelessness.

After a light supper with Lodovico he returned to the Via Mozza studio. Mini was out. He lighted an oil lamp, walked about the studio touching familiar pieces of furniture. It was good to be home again, among his few possessions: the Battle of the Centaurs and his Madonna of the Stairs hanging on the back wall; the four unfinished Captives still facing each other in an intimate circle in the center of the studio. He took out his folios of drawings, leafed through them approvingly, or made a stabbing correction line with a stubby pen. Then he turned over a drawing sheet and wrote with deep emotion:

> Too much good luck no less than misery
> May kill a man condemned to mortal pain,
> If, lost to hope and chilled in every vein,
> A sudden pardon comes to set him free.

Beauteous art, which brought with us from heaven,
Will conquer nature; so divine a power
Belongs to him who strives with every nerve.

If I was made for art, from childhood given
A prey for burning beauty to devour,
I blame the mistress I was born to serve.

Baccio Valori, new governor of Florence for Pope Clement, sent for him to come to the Medici palace. Michelangelo wondered: Valori had helped drive Soderini out of Florence in 1512. But Valori was all smiles as he sat behind the desk from which *Il Magnifico* had guided the destinies of Florence.

"Buonarroti, I need you."

"It is always good to be needed, *signore*."

"I want you to design a house for me. So I can build at once! And along with it, one of your great marble sculptures for the courtyard."

"You do me too much honor," muttered Michelangelo as he descended the broad staircase. But Granacci was delighted.

"It's your turn to woo the enemy. Valori loathes the Company. He knows we were anti-Medici. If you do as he asks we'll all be reprieved."

Michelangelo walked to the house on the Via Ghibellina. In a wool-padded storage bin in the kitchen stood the experimental David he had carved from the marble Beppe had bought for him, the David whose foot rested on Goliath's black, bloody head. With a little chiseling the head of Goliath would disappear, and in its place would be a round sphere . . . the world. David would become a new Apollo.

The family home seemed empty and forlorn. He missed Buonarroto. Sigismondo, who had been part of the Florentine army for the past three years, asked permission to live on the family farm in Settignano. Giovansimone was determined to have Michelangelo finance the reopening of the wool shop. Lodovico had grown feeble, so stricken by the death of his young grandchild Buonarrotino that he was unable to recount what had happened to the boy. Eleven-year-old Lionardo was the remaining hope and satisfaction of the Buonarroti family, inheritor of the family name. Michelangelo had paid for his three years of education.

"Uncle Michelangelo, could I be apprenticed to you?"

"As a sculptor?" Michelangelo was aghast.

"Aren't you a sculptor?"

"Yes. But it is not a life I would wish on my only nephew. I think you would be happier apprenticed to the Strozzi for the wool trade. Until then, suppose you come to the studio and take over your father's account books. I need someone to make the entries."

The boy's brown eyes, with the amber flecks so similar to Buonarroto's and his own, lighted.

Returning to the Via Mozza, he found Mini entertaining a lavishly gowned emissary from the Duke of Ferrara.

"Maestro Buonarroti, I have come to collect the painting you promised to my duke."

"It is finished."

When he brought out the Leda and the Swan, the emissary stared at it in silence. After a moment he said:

"This is but a trifle. My duke expected a masterpiece."

Michelangelo studied the tempera, gazing with satisfaction at the voluptuous Leda.

"May I ask what your business is, *signore?*"

"I am a merchant." Haughtily.

"Then your duke will find you have made a bad bargain for him. Be so kind as to remove yourself from my studio."

6

He resumed work in the chapel, again hiring brickmasons and cement men. Instead of working his Allegories on turntables to catch the changing light, he had them propped with wooden blocks at the angle at which the figures would rest on the sarcophagi, and in the position in the chapel they would ultimately occupy. In this way he would make the most effective use of the actual light and shadow they would absorb.

In designing the four reclining figures for the two tombs his problem was to hold the visual attention and not let it drain downward off the arc of the curved tomb cover. To this end he created a countercurve in the torso, with one leg of each figure bent upward in high projection, the other with outstretched toes extending to the farthest edge of the block. The abrupt upward thrust into space of the leg would hold his shoulder-to-shoulder figures on their precarious ledges.

It was cold in the chapel from the outside rains, and penetratingly damp from the water oozing out of the slow-drying cement of the bricked-up windows. He sometimes felt his teeth chattering even when moving with high speed through the marble. At night when he returned to his own studio he found his head filled with mucus, his throat raw. He ignored the difficulties, grimly determined that this project must not become another Julius' tomb.

Sebastiano continued to write from Rome: the Pietà had been exposed to danger in its chapel, but no man had dared injure the dead Jesus on his mother's lap. The Bacchus had been buried by Jacopo Galli's family in the orchard outside his old workshed and had now been set up again. He, Sebastiano, had been appointed the Pope's Keeper of the Seals, become a friar, with a handsome salary, and was now known as Sebastiano del Piombo. As for the house on the Macello dei Corvi, the plaster of the walls and ceilings was crumbling, most of the furnishings had vanished, the buildings around the edge of the garden had been torn down for firewood. His marbles were safe, but the house was in desperate need of attention. Couldn't Michelangelo send money to have the repairs made?

Michelangelo had no money to send. Florence had not recovered from the war; food and materials were scarce, trade was so poor that his outlay for the family shop was lost each month. Valori ruled with a harsh hand. Pope Clement kept the various factions of Florence at each other's throats. The city had hoped that Ippolito, the gentle, sweet-natured son of Giuliano, would replace Valori; but Pope Clement had other plans. Ippolito was made a cardinal, against his strongest wishes, and sent to Hungary as commander of the Italian forces against the Turks. Clement's own son, known as Alessandro the Moor because of his swarthy skin and thick lips, was brought to Florence with great ceremony and made sovereign of the city-state for life. A dissolute, ugly youth of low intelligence and rapacious appetites, with his father's troops on hand to enforce his slightest wish, Alessandro murdered his opponents in broad daylight, raped and debauched the youth of the city, wiped out its last semblances of freedom, and quickly brought it to a state of anarchy.

Equally quickly, Michelangelo fought with Alessandro. When Alessandro asked him to design a new fort above the Arno, Michelangelo declined. When Alessandro sent word that he wished to show the chapel to the visiting Viceroy of Naples, Michelangelo locked the sacristy.

"Your conduct is dangerous," cautioned Giovanni Spina.

"I'm safe until I complete the tomb. Clement has made that clear, even to his thick-skulled son . . . or I would have been dead long ago."

He laid down his chisels, wiped the marble dust from his face and eyebrows, looked about him and exclaimed with gratification:

"This chapel will outlive Alessandro, even if I don't."

"You won't, I'm sure of that. You are emaciated, you have a racking cough. Why don't you walk in the hills in the warm sun, cure your cold, put some merciful flesh on your bones?"

Michelangelo sat on the edge of a plank placed between the two sawhorses, answered thoughtfully:

"There is nothing left of the good in Florence, of order, except its art. When I stand before this marble Day with a hammer and chisel in my hands I feel that I am fulfilling the law of Moses through an art form, to compensate for the spiritual degradation of Alessandro and his bullies. Which will survive, these marble sculptures or the debauchery?"

"Then at least let me move the marbles to a warm, dry room."

"I have to carve them here, Spina, where the light is exactly what it will be when they are on the sarcophagi."

In the studio that evening he found a request from Giovan Battista, Mini's uncle: the boy had fallen hopelessly in love with an impoverished widow's daughter and wanted to marry her. His uncle thought he ought to be sent out of the country. Could Michelangelo help?

When Mini returned from the night's diversion Michelangelo asked him, "Do you love this girl?"

"Passionately!" said Mini.

"Is it the same girl you loved passionately last summer?"

"Of course not."

"Then take this painting of Leda and the Swan. And these drawings. The money from them will set you up in a studio in Paris."

"But the Leda is worth a fortune!" exclaimed Mini, astonished.

"Then see that you get a fortune for her. Write to me from France."

Mini had no sooner headed north than a young man of about twenty presented himself at the door of the studio, introducing himself as Francesco Amadore.

"Though I am called Urbino," he added in a quiet voice. "The priest at San Lorenzo told me you needed someone."

"What kind of job are you looking for?"

"I seek a home, Signor Buonarroti, and a family, for I have none. Later, I should like to marry and have a family of my own; but I must work for many years first. I come of humble people and have only these clothes on my back."

"You wish to become a sculpture apprentice?"

"An art apprentice, *messere.*"

Michelangelo studied the man standing before him, his clothes threadbare but neat, lean to the point of boniness, with a convex stomach that had never known its fill; steady gray eyes, dust-gray teeth and light, ash-gray hair. Urbino needed a home and employment, yet his manner had dignity, an inner quietude. Apparently he respected himself; and this Michelangelo liked.

"Very well, let us try."

Urbino had a nobility of spirit which illuminated everything he did. He was so overjoyed to belong somewhere that he filled the house with his own happiness, treating Michelangelo with the reverence due a father. Michelangelo found himself growing attached to the young man.

Pope Clement again urged Julius' heirs to negotiate a release. The Roveres, though they felt insulted and put upon, agreed orally to accept the single-faced wall tomb, ornamented by the figures which Michelangelo had already carved. He was to relinquish the Moses and two Slaves, finish the four Captives, and ship them with the Victory to Rome. All that remained for him to do was make drawings for the other figures and raise two thousand ducats to return to the Roveres, who would pay it over to another marble master to complete the sepulcher. After twenty-seven years of worry, and eight major sculptures for which he was not to receive one scudo of wage, he would be freed from his self-imposed hell.

He could not sell any one of his farms or houses for the necessary two thousand ducats. No one in Tuscany had any money. The only building for which he could get a fair offer was the Via Mozza studio.

"I'm heartbroken," he cried to Spina. "I love this *bottega.*"

Spina sighed. "Let me write to Rome. Perhaps we can arrange to have the money payment postponed."

Giovansimone chose this moment to come to the Via Mozza for one of his rare visits.

"I want the big house in the Via di San Proculo," he announced.

"For what?"

"To set myself up in style."

"It's rented."

"We don't need the rent money."

"Perhaps you don't, but I do."

"For what? You're rich enough."

"Giovansimone, I'm struggling to pay a debt to the Roveres . . ."

"That's just your excuse. You're stingy, like Father."

"Have you ever lacked for anything?"

"My proper place in life. We are noble burghers."

"Then act nobly."

"I haven't the money. You keep hoarding it."

"Giovansimone, you're fifty-three years old, and you have never supported yourself. I have supported you for thirty-four years, ever since Savonarola's death."

"You get no praise for doing your duty. You speak as though we were vulgar artisans. Our family is as old as the Medici, Strozzi or Tornabuoni. We have been paying taxes in Florence for three centuries!"

"You sound like Father," replied Michelangelo wearily.

"We have the right to display the Medici crest. I want to set it up in front of the Via di San Proculo house, hire servants. You're forever protesting that everything you do is for our family. Well then, prove it, dig out the words and fill the hole with gold."

"Giovansimone, you couldn't see a black crow in a bowl of milk. I don't have the resources to make a Florentine nobleman out of you."

He heard that Sigismondo had moved into the peasant's quarters in Settignano and was working the land. He rode up the hill to find Sigismondo behind a plow guiding two white oxen, his face and hair under a straw hat wet with perspiration, manure caked on one boot.

"Sigismondo, you're working like a *contadino.*"

Sigismondo took off his hat, wiped his forehead with a heavy clublike movement of his forearm.

"I just plow the field."

"But why? We have tenants here to do the manual labor."

"I like to work."

"But not as a laborer. Sigismondo, what can you be thinking of? No Buonarroti has worked with his hands for three hundred years."

"Except you!"

Michelangelo flushed. "I am a sculptor. What will people in Florence say when they hear my brother is working like a peasant? After all, the Buonarroti have been noble burghers; we have a coat of arms . . ."

". . . coat of arms won't feed me. I'm too old to fight now, so I work. This is our land, I raise wheat and olives and grapes. . . ."

"Do you have to walk in dung to do it?"

Sigismondo looked down at his crusted boot.

"Dung fertilizes the field."

"I've worked all my life to make the Buonarroti name honored throughout Italy. Do you want people to say that I have a brother in Settignano who tends oxen?"

Sigismondo gazed at his two handsome white animals, replied with affection, "Oxen is nice."

"They are beautiful animals. Now go take yourself a bath, get into clean clothes, and let one of our renters plow the furrows."

He lost both arguments. Giovansimone spread the word in Florence that his brother Michelangelo was a miser and a vulgarian who refused to allow his family to live according to their high rank in Tuscan society. Sigismondo spread the word in Settignano that his brother Michelangelo was a snob and aristocrat who thought his family had become too good for honest labor. As a result both brothers got what they wanted: more money for Giovansimone to spend; the land for Sigismondo to tend.

He concentrated on the two female figures, Dawn and Night. Except for the Madonnas, he had never sculptured a woman. He had no desire to portray young girls at the threshold of life, he wanted to carve fertility, the bounteous body which brings forth the race of man, mature women who had labored and been in labor, with bodies fatigued but indomitable. Did he have to be androgynous to create authentic women? All artists were androgynous. He carved Dawn as not yet awake, caught in the transition between dream and reality, her head still resting wearily on her shoulder; a band drawn tight under the breasts to emphasize spatially their bulbous quality; the stomach muscles sagging, the womb exhausted from bearing, the whole arduous journey of her life in the half-closed eyes and half-open mouth; the left arm bent and suspended in air, ready to fall as soon as she lifted her head from her shoulder to face the day.

He moved the few steps across the chapel to work on the sumptuously voluptuous figure of Night: still young, fertile, desirable, cradle of men; the exquisite Greek head resting on its delicately arched neck, eyes closed in resigning to sleep and darkness; tension reflected through the long-limbed figure in plastic manipulations of flesh to give a quality of sensuality which he would heighten with a high polish. Light moving freely on the contours of the milky marble would intensify the female forms: the hard ripe breasts, fount of sustenance, the magnificently robust thigh, the arm pulled sharply behind the back to turn the breast proudly outward: every man's dream of the beauteous, bounteous female body, ready for sleep? love? fecundation?

He polished the figure with straw and sulphur, remembering how his ancestors, the Etruscans, had carved reclining stone figures for the lids of their sarcophagi.

He finished Dawn in June, and Night in August, two heroic marble carvings in the nine months since he had left his tower, pouring out his inner power over the hot dry summer, then turned to the male figures of Day and Dusk, leaving strong calligraphic textures about the head, doing no filing or polishing because the tool markings in themselves denoted vigorous masculinity. With Day, a wise, strong man who knew every aspect of life's passing pain and pleasure, he carved the head sweeping out over its own massive shoulder and forearm, reflecting in its muscled torso a back that had lifted and carried the weights of the world.

Dusk was a portrait of his own sunken-eyed, bony-nosed, bearded face, the head diagonally reclining like the sinking sun as it dipped toward the horizon, the gnarled expression of the features reflected in the labored hands, the strong-modeled knees

raised and crossed, leg extending outward on its thin shelf of marble beyond the
tomb itself.

He had studied anatomy to acquaint himself with the inner physical workings of
man; now he treated the marble as having an anatomy of its own. In this chapel
he wanted to leave something of himself, something which time itself could not
erase.

He finished Dusk in September.

The rains started, the chapel became cold and raw. Again his flesh vanished, he
was down to bone and gristle, under a hundred pounds as he picked up hammer
and chisel to siphon the blood of his veins, his marrow and calcium into the veins
and bones of the Day, the Virgin and Child, the statue of a seated, contemplative
Lorenzo. As the marbles grew throbbingly alive, vibrant, powerful, lusty, he became
correspondingly drained; it was from his own inner storehouse of will, courage,
daring and brain that the marbles were infused with their eternal energies. His last
ounce of strength he poured into the immortality of the marbles.

"It won't do, you know." This time it was Granacci who reproved him, a
Granacci who himself had grown lean over the misfortunes of his city. "Death
from overindulgence is a form of suicide, whether it's from work or wine."

"If I don't work twenty hours a day I'll never finish."

"It's the other way around. If you would have the good sense to rest you could
live forever."

"It's been forever."

Granacci shook his head. "At fifty-seven you have the *forza,* force, of a man
of thirty. Me, I'm worn out . . . from pleasure. With your luck, why should you
think that dying is going to be any easier than living?"

Michelangelo laughed for the first time in weeks.

"Granaccio *mio,* how poor my life would have been without your friendship.
It's your fault . . . this sculpturing . . . you took me to Lorenzo's garden, you
encouraged me."

Granacci chuckled.

"You never wanted to do tombs, yet you've spent most of your life on marbles
for tombs. All your years you said you would never do portraits, and here you are
stuck with two of them, life size."

"You're dreaming."

"You're not going to carve the portraits for the niches?"

"Assuredly not. Who will know a hundred years from now whether my marbles
are good likenesses of young Lorenzo and Giuliano? I'm going to carve universal
figures of action and contemplation. They will be nobody, yet everybody. A subject
is a farm wagon to carry a sculptor's ideas to market."

Urbino had been taught to read and write by the priests at Castel Durante; slowly
he slipped into the position of steward of both the household and the studio. Now
that his nephew Lionardo was doing well as an apprentice to the Strozzi, Michelangelo
gave Urbino the books to keep. Urbino paid the wages and bills, assumed the role
Buonarroto had played when he was young, became a protector who could make
Michelangelo's life smoother, take the petty annoyances off his shoulders. Michelangelo
came to have a feeling of permanence about the relationship.

He rested by moving into clay models, mixing in cloth frayings to make the clay
fattier so that it would be more responsive to his manipulation, kneading the composition
to adhere to the armature. The dampness of the clay was so similar to the dampness
of the chapel that he felt he was shaping the wet raw interior space of the sacristy.
Transferring from the clay to the marble block, he carved the statue of young
Lorenzo for the niche above Dawn and Dusk, using an architectonic approach,
designing this figure of contemplation to be static, tight, withdrawn, involved in
its own interior brooding. For contrast he evolved an action-composition of Giuliano
for over the tomb holding the Day and Night on the opposite wall: loose, with a

circulation of tension and a continuous state of motion. Lorenzo's head was well set and compressed into his shoulders; Giuliano sat with a sudden thrust of the neck into space.

It was the Madonna and Child from which he took his joy. He longed to the very fibers and roots of his soul to give her a divine beauty: her face glowing with love and compassion, the birthplace and the resurgent future, instrument of the godhead through which the human race, in the face of its adversities and tragedies, endures.

He saw the mother-and-child theme all fresh and shining, as though he had never carved it before: intense desire and intense fulfillment: the child twisted about on his mother's lap, vigorously seeking nourishment; the elaborate folds of the mother's gown heightening the agitation, externalizing her feeling of fulfillment and pain as the greedy, earthy child sucked. He felt lightheaded, somehow as though he were back in his first studio, carving the Madonna for the merchants of Bruges . . . back in his period of grace.

It was only a high fever. When it passed he was so weak his legs could barely hold him.

The Pope sent a carriage and driver to Florence, ordering Michelangelo to come to Rome to recuperate in the warmth of the more southerly sun, and to hear about an exciting new project he had envisaged. Clement invited Michelangelo's friends in the Florentine colony for dinner at the Vatican, had several comedies played to amuse him. Clement's solicitude for his health was genuine, almost like that of a beloved brother. Then the Pope revealed his desire: would Michelangelo like to paint a Last Judgment on the vast altar wall of the Sistine Chapel?

At the dinner Michelangelo met a young man of singular beauty, like that of the Greek youths he had painted behind the Holy Family he had made for Doni. He had eyes of a luminous *pietra serena* gray-blue; a classical nose and mouth carved out of flesh-colored marble by Praxiteles; a high, rounded forehead in perfect plumb with the big-boned, curved chin; chestnut hair; long, symmetrically carved cheeks with high cheekbones; and the rose-bronzed skin of the youths who competed in the Stadia of Greece.

Tommaso de' Cavalieri, twenty-two, well educated, serious, was the heir of a patrician Roman family. Ambitious to become a first-rate painter, he asked eagerly if he might become an apprentice. The admiration in Tommaso's eyes amounted almost to idolatry. Michelangelo replied that he must return to Florence to finish the Medici chapel, but there was no reason why they could not spend some part of his time in Rome drawing together. The young man's intense concentration as he watched Michelangelo achieve his volatile effects was enormously flattering. Michelangelo found Tommaso to be a talented, conscientious worker, delightful and *simpatico*. Tommaso had the welcome faculty of making the thirty-five-year difference between their ages dissolve, so that in Tommaso's presence he felt young, was able to laugh, to be taken out of himself. When they parted they agreed to write to each other. Michelangelo volunteered to send special drawings from which Tommaso could study, and to send word when he had arrived at his decision for the Pope.

Back in Florence he returned to the sacristy refreshed. By spring he had forgotten about dying. In achieving his skin finishes on the two male figures he used the crosshatching method first taught him by Ghirlandaio with a pen: one set of calligraphic lines made by a two-toothed chisel superimposed over a set of *ugnetto* lines, at right angles so that the finer tooth marks of the chisel would not fall into the heavier and more prominent tracks of the *ugnetto*. He emerged with textures of skin that had all the tension and pull of living tissue. On the Madonna's cheeks he achieved a soft, pebbly texture.

The beauty of her face was sublime.

7

Time was not a mountain but a river; it changed its rate of flow as well as its course. It could become swollen, overflow its banks, or dry to a trickle; it could run clean and pure along its bed or become laden with silt and throw up debris along the shore. When Michelangelo was young, every day had been particularized; it had had body, content, shape, stood out as an individual entity to be numbered, recorded and remembered.

Now time was a soluble: the weeks and months merged in a continuous flow at an ever accelerated speed. He was getting as much work done but the very texture of time had altered for him, its arbitrary boundaries become indistinct. The years were no longer individual blocks but Apuan Alps which man in his need broke into separate peaks. Were the weeks and months really shorter in duration, or had he stopped counting, adopted a different measure? Formerly time had had a hard brittle quality, been a solid. Now it was a fluid. Its landscape had become as different for him as was the Roman *campagna* from Tuscany. He had imagined time to be absolute, the same always, everywhere, to all men; now he saw that it was as variable as human nature or the weather of the skies. As 1531 became 1532, as 1532 began contracting and converging on 1533, he asked himself:

"Where does time go?"

The answer was plain enough: it had been transmuted from the amorphous to the substantive by becoming part of the life force of the Madonna and Child, of the Dawn and Dusk and Night, the young Medici. What he had not understood was that time became foreshortened, just as space did. When he stood on a hill looking across a Tuscan valley the front half was visible in all its lucid detail; the more distant half, though as wide and broad, was compacted, compressed, jammed up, seeming to be a narrow belt instead of widely extensive fields. This happened to time in the more distant area of a man's life as well; no matter how closely he peered at the hours and days as they went by, they seemed shorter when compared to the wide-flung first portion of his life.

He carved the two lids of the sarcophagi in severely pure lines, the descending curves ending in a chaste convolute, a few simple leaves sculptured at the top of the supporting columns. He did nothing about the River Gods or about symbols of Heaven and Earth, ideas he had developed in a preliminary stage. He carved a mask below the outward shoulder of Night, and put an owl in the right angle formed by her raised knee; that was all. For him the beauty of man had always been the beginning and the end of art.

Word of what he was essaying in the chapel spread through Italy and then Europe. He welcomed serious artists, who sketched and made notes while he worked, but the increasing flow of sightseers got under his skin. One elaborately gowned nobleman demanded:

"How did you come to make that astonishing figure of Night?"

"I had a block of marble in which was concealed that statue which you see there. The only effort involved is to take away the tiny pieces which surround it and prevent it from being seen. For anyone who knows how to do this, nothing could be easier."

"Then I shall send my servant to look for statues in the stones."

He made a journey to San Miniato al Tedesco to visit with Pope Clement, who was on his way to solemnize the marriage of Caterina de' Medici, daughter of Piero's son Lorenzo, to the Dauphin of France. He had a happy time with Cardinal Ippolito, now attached to the Pope, and with Sebastiano del Piombo, still a favorite of Clement's.

For the rest, he remained within the quadrangle formed by the Medici sacristy where he carved, the house across the street where he made his models, and the Via Mozza studio where he lived and was cared for by Urbino. As drained of suet and sinew as he knew himself to be, he considered himself fortunate in having surrounded himself with good sculptors who were helping him conclude the chapel: Tribolo, who was to carve the marble Heaven and Earth from Michelangelo's models; Angelo Montorsoli, who was going to do a St. Cosmas; Raffaello da Montelupo, son of his old friend Baccio, clown of the Medici sculpture garden who had finished his two Piccolomini Popes. Sometimes at night he refreshed himself by picking up drawing materials and surveying his mind to see what it might have to say about a Last Judgment.

Bandinelli finished his Hercules for Clement. Duke Alessandro gave the order to have it installed opposite the David, in front of the Palazzo della Signoria, which he had renamed the Palazzo Vecchio because Florence was to have no more ruling council. The public outcry against the statue was so great that Bandinelli had to go to Rome to get a papal order to have it set up. Michelangelo walked with Urbino through the Piazza della Signoria to see the Hercules, the pieces of paper stuck to it during the night fluttering in the wind. He winced as he looked up at Bandinelli's meaningless muscle-bulges. After reading a few of the verses he commented with a grimace:

"Bandinelli is going to be unhappy when he reads these tributes."

Then he remembered Leonardo da Vinci's prophecy in the Belvedere:

"The painter, after he studies your ceiling, must take care not to become wooden through too strong an emphasis on bone, muscle and sinews. . . . What do painters do, when they try to go beyond you?"

He understood now what Leonardo had been trying to tell him.

"Don't complete your own revolution. Leave something for those who follow you." But even if he had understood Leonardo earlier, what could he have done about it?

Like the Carrarini, he had been a *campanilista,* rallying around the base of Giotto's bell tower as though it were the center of the universe. But Florence was supine now, its freedom strangled by Alessandro. Since art was being strangled in the same bloody bed with political liberty, most of the Company of the Cauldron had moved to other cities. The Florence of the early Medici had vanished. The Verrocchio and Donatello marbles still stood majestically in the niches of Orsanmichele, but Florentines walked the streets with their heads bowed; after the interminable wars and defeats, the "mule of the mule," the "Moor," was the final blow. When he passed the Marzocchi in the Piazza della Signoria, Michelangelo turned his head away. He could not even bring himself to repair David's broken arm; not until the Republic, the greatness of Florence as an art and intellectual center, the Athens of Europe, had been restored.

Lodovico's ninetieth birthday fell on an exhilarating day in June 1534. The air was warm but piercingly clear. Florence glistened like a precious stone in its prong of mountains. Michelangelo gathered the remnants of the Buonarroti family. At the dinner table there were Lodovico, so feeble that he had to be propped with pillows, Giovansimone, wan and thin from a protracted illness, silent Sigismondo, living his life alone on the family farm where they had all been born; Cecca, Buonarroto's seventeen-year-old daughter, and young Lionardo, who was completing his apprenticeship to the Strozzi.

"Uncle Michelangelo, you promised you would reopen my father's wool shop as soon as I was ready to manage it."

"So I shall, Lionardo."

"Soon? I'm fifteen now, and I've learned the business quite well."

"Yes, soon, Lionardo, as soon as I can get my affairs straightened out."

Lodovico ate only a few spoonfuls of the soup carried to his lips with trembling hands. In the middle of dinner he asked to be taken to his bed. Michelangelo picked his father up in his arms. He weighed no more than the tied bundles of sticks

Michelangelo had used to protect his walls at San Miniato. He put his father in bed, tucked a blanket around him. The old man turned his head slightly so that he could see the pie-shaped desk with its account books, neatly stacked. A smile came over his ash-gray lips.

"Michelagnolo."

The pet name. Lodovico had not used it for years.

"*Messer padre?*"

"I wanted . . . to live . . . to be ninety."

"And so you have."

". . . but it was hard. I have . . . worked . . . every minute . . . just to stay alive."

"It's as good a work as any I know."

"But now . . . I'm tired . . ."

"Rest. I'll close the door."

"Michelagnolo . . . ?"

"Yes, Father?"

". . . you will take care of . . . the boys . . . Giovansimone . . . Sigismondo?"

Michelangelo thought, "The boys! In their middle fifties!" Aloud he replied, "Our family is all I have, Father."

"You'll give . . . Lionardo . . . his shop?"

"When he is ready."

"And Cecca . . . a dowry?"

"Yes, Father."

"Then all is well. I have kept my family . . . together. We have prospered . . . gained back . . . the money . . . my father lost. My life . . . has not been lived . . . in vain. Please call the father from Santa Croce."

Lionardo brought the priest. Lodovico died quietly, surrounded by his three sons, grandson and granddaughter. There was so much color left in his cheeks, and his face looked so peaceful, that Michelangelo could not believe his father was dead.

He felt strangely alone. He had been without a mother all his life; and without love from his father, without affection or understanding. Yet none of that mattered now; he had loved his father, just as in his flinty Tuscan way Lodovico had loved his son. The world would seem empty, even forlorn, without him. Lodovico had caused him endless anguish, yet it had not been Lodovico's fault that only one of his five sons had been an earner. That was why he had had to work Michelangelo so hard, to make up for the other four who had added nothing to the account books on the pie-shaped desk. Michelangelo was proud that he had been able to fulfill Lodovico's ambition, enable his father to die a success.

That night he sat in his studio, the big doors open to the garden, writing under an oil lamp. Suddenly the garden and his room were invaded by thousands of small white moths, called "Manna from the Hebraic Desert," weaving a net around the lamp and his head, flying in patterns like birds. In a few moments they were dead, leaving the studio and garden looking as though a light snow had fallen. He brushed the thick layer of ephemera off his workbench, picked up a pen and wrote:

> Death is less hard to him who wearily
> Bears back to God a harvest fully ripe,
> Than 'tis to him in full and freshest mind.

> But cruel were the heart that did not weep,
> That he should see no more about this earth
> Him who gave being first, and then support.

Our grief's intensity, our weight of woe,
Are less or more, according as each feels;
And all my utter weakness, Lord, thou knowest.

He stood alone in the sacristy under the dome he had designed and built, surrounded by the *pietra serena* and marble walls so lovingly co-joined. Lorenzo, the Contemplative, was in his niche; Giuliano was sitting on the floor, not quite finished. Day, the last of the seven figures, was propped under the shoulders with wooden blocks, the back of the powerful male body unfinished where it would stand against the wall. The face, poised behind the high-raised shoulder, was that of an eagle, gazing stonily at the world through deep-sunk eyes, the hair, nose and beard rough-chiseled, as though cut out of granite, a strange, primordial contrast to the highlighted skin of the massive protective shoulder.

Was the chapel finished? After fourteen years?

Standing midst his exquisitely carved sarcophagi on either side, each to hold its two giant figures, Dawn and Dusk, Day and Night, the beauteous Madonna and Child sitting on her ledge against the spacious side wall, he felt that he had carved everything he had wanted to carve, and said everything he had wanted to say. For him the Medici chapel was complete. He believed that *Il Magnifico* would have been gratified, that he would have accepted this chapel and these marble sculptures in place of the façade he had envisaged.

He picked up a piece of drawing paper, wrote instructions for his three sculptors to mount Day and Night on their sarcophagus, Dusk and Dawn opposite. He left the note on the plank table under a piece of scrap marble, turned and went out the door without looking back.

Urbino packed his saddlebags.

"Do you have everything, Urbino?"

"All except the folios of drawings, *messere*. They will be ready in a few moments."

"Wrap them in my flannel shirts for protection."

They mounted their horses, crossed the city and went out the Porta Romana. At the top of the rise he stopped, turned to look back at the Duomo, Baptistery and Campanile, at the tawny tower of the Palazzo Vecchio glistening in the September sunlight, at the exquisite city of stone nestled under its red tile roof. It was hard to take leave of one's city; hard to feel that, close to sixty, he could not count on returning.

Resolutely he turned the horses south toward Rome.

"Let us push on, Urbino. We'll stay the night at Poggibonsi, at an inn I know there."

"And will we be in Rome by the following nightfall?" Urbino asked excitedly. "What is Rome like, *messere?*"

He tried to describe Rome, but his heart was too heavy. He had no idea what the future held for him, though he was certain that his own interminable war was at last over. If the astrologists who centered around the Porta Romana had cried out to him as he passed that he still had before him a third of his years, two of the four loves of his life, the longest, bloodiest battle, and some of his finest sculpture, painting and architecture, he would have remembered *Il Magnifico's* contempt for their pseudo science, and he would have laughed, tiredly.

But they would have been right.

BOOK TEN

LOVE

He rode his horse through the Porta del Popolo. Rome, after its latest warfare, seemed in a worse state of ruin than when he had first seen it in 1496. He walked through his own dilapidated premises on the Macello dei Corvi. Most of the furniture had been stolen, along with the mattresses and kitchen utensils, and some of the base blocks for Julius' tomb. The Moses and the two Captives had not been injured. He surveyed the rooms, looked around the overgrown garden. He would have to plaster and paint the walls, put in new flooring, refurnish the entire house. Of the five thousand ducats he had earned over the past ten years for the Medici chapel he had managed to save and bring to Rome only a few hundred.

"We must put our house in order, Urbino."

"I can handle the repairs myself, *messere.*"

Two days after Michelangelo reached Rome, Pope Clement VII died in the Vatican. The city poured into the streets in a paroxysm of joy. The hatred of Clement, which continued to manifest itself during the elaborate funeral ceremonies, was based on his responsibility for the sack of Rome. Only the day before Michelangelo and Benvenuto Cellini had visited with Clement. He had been in good spirits, discussing with Cellini a new medal he was to strike, and with Michelangelo the design for the Last Judgment. Although Cousin Giulio had sometimes caused him suffering, he felt a considerable sense of loss for this last of his childhood friends from the Medici palace.

During the two weeks it took for the College of Cardinals to assemble and elect a new Pope, Rome stood still. But not the Florentine colony. When Michelangelo reached the Medici palace he found that only the outside was draped in mourning cloth. Inside, the *fuorusciti,* exiles, were jubilant. With Clement dead there would be no one to protect his son Alessandro; he could be replaced by Ippolito, son of the beloved Giuliano.

Twenty-five-year-old Cardinal Ippolito stood at the head of the Medici steps to receive Michelangelo, an affectionate smile lighting his pale countenance with its patrician features and jet-black hair. He was wearing a dark red velvet coat and cap, a band of bold gold buttons across his chest. An arm was placed about Michelangelo's shoulder; he turned to find Contessina's son, Cardinal Niccolò Ridolfi, with his mother's slight figure and flashing brown eyes.

"You must stay with us here in the palace," said Ippolito, "until your house is repaired."

"My mother would have wanted it," added Niccolò.

A dozen of his old friends thronged to greet him: the Cavalcanti, Rucellai, Acciajuoli, Olivieri, Pazzi, Baccio Valori, Clement's Commissary of Florence, Filippo Strozzi and his son Roberto, Cardinal Salviati the elder, Cardinal Giovanni Salviati, son of Jacopo, Bindo Altoviti. The Florentine colony in Rome had been swollen by those families from whom Alessandro had stripped all property and power.

With Clement dead there was no further need to be discreet. What had formerly been an underground plot to get rid of Alessandro was now an open movement.

"You'll help us, Michelangelo?" asked Cardinal Giovanni Salviati.

"Most certainly. Alessandro is a wild beast."

There was a sharp murmur of approval. Niccolò said, "There is only one further obstacle: Charles V. With the Emperor on our side, we could march on Florence and overwhelm Alessandro. The citizens would rise and join us."

"How can I help?"

It was Florence's historian, Jacopo Nardi, who replied:

"The Emperor cares little about art. However we have heard reports that he has expressed interest in your work. Would you carve or paint something for him, if it would help our cause?"

Michelangelo assured them that he would. After dinner Ippolito said, "The stables that Leonardo da Vinci designed for my father are completed. Would you like to see them?"

In the first stall, under the high-ceilinged beams, was a white Arabian steed. Michelangelo stroked the animal's long neck, warm under his hand.

"He's a beauty. I've never seen so perfect a piece of horseflesh."

"Please accept him as a gift."

"Thank you, no," said Michelangelo quickly. "Only this morning Urbino tore down the last of our old barn. We would have no place to keep him."

But when he reached home he found Urbino standing in the garden gingerly holding the animal by the reins. Michelangelo again patted the horse's elegant white neck, asked:

"Do you think we should keep him?"

"My father taught me never to accept a gift that eats."

"But how can I turn back such a beautiful animal? We must buy some lumber and build a new barn."

He asked himself over and over again whether he was relieved to have the crushing burden of the Last Judgment off his shoulders. The altar wall of the Sistine would have required a minimum of five years to paint, for it would be the largest wall in Italy ever essayed in a single fresco. Yet as his ducats poured out for the repairs and refurbishing of his house he saw that he would soon be in need of money.

Balducci, as wide as he was tall, but of hard flesh and red cheeks, now raising grandchildren in profusion, exploded:

"Of course you're in trouble! Spending all those years in Florence without my financial wizardry. But you're in safe hands now. Turn over to me the money you earn, and I'll invest it so that you'll be independently wealthy."

"Balducci, there is something about me that seems to alienate money. Ducats say to themselves, 'This man will not give us a secure home in which we can multiply. Let us go elsewhere.' Who is going to be the next Pope?"

"You guess."

From Balducci's he went on to Leo Baglioni, in his same house on the Campo dei Fiori. Leo, with a leonine mane and unwrinkled face, had flourished as confidential agent to Popes Leo and Clement, a job Michelangelo had helped secure for him.

"I'm ready to retire now," Leo confided to Michelangelo over a dinner in the exquisitely furnished dining room. "I have had nearly all the money, women and adventure any man could ask. I think I will let the next Pope run his own errands."

"Who is that Pope going to be?"

"Nobody knows."

Early the next morning the Duke of Urbino came to call, followed by a servant with a box containing the four contracts for Julius' tomb. The duke was a ferocious-looking man, with a trench-lined battlefield for a face. He carried a lethal dagger at his side. It was the first time since Leo's coronation twenty-one years before that the two antagonists had met. The duke informed Michelangelo that the wall had been prepared for Julius' tomb in San Pietro in Vincoli, which had been Julius' church when he was Cardinal Rovere. He then took from the top of the leather box the latest agreement, that of 1532, which "freed, liberated and absolved Michelangelo from all contracts made previously," and flung it at Michelangelo's feet.

"There will be no more Medici to protect you. If you do not complete this last contract by May of next year, as specified in the agreement, I shall force you to fulfill the 1516 contract: twenty-five statues, larger than life. The twenty-five we have paid for."

The duke stormed out, right hand clasped on the handle of his dagger.

Michelangelo had not arranged for the four unfinished Giants or the Victory to be brought from Florence. He had welcomed the release afforded by the change from the original walk-in monument to a single-wall tomb; nevertheless he had been disturbed because these enormous statues would now be out of proportion on the marble façade. For the additional three carvings he owed the Roveres, he decided to sculpture a Virgin, Prophet and Sibyl, the blocks for which were stored in the garden. These figures would be neither large nor difficult. He was certain the Roveres would be as well pleased; in any event his own sense of design demanded the change. By next May, as specified in the contract, he would be finished with the three smaller figures and his workmen could assemble the wall in San Pietro in Vincoli.

In the matter of completing the Rovere tomb the fates were as much against the Duke of Urbino as against Michelangelo. On October 11, 1534, the College of Cardinals elected Alessandro Farnese to the papacy. Farnese had been educated by Lorenzo, but he had already left the palace for Rome before Michelangelo's time. From *Il Magnifico* he had acquired a lifelong love of art and learning. When his ravishingly beautiful sister Giulia had been taken by Pope Alexander VI as his mistress, Farnese had been made a cardinal, and entered into the dissolute life of the Borgia court, siring four illegitimate children by two mistresses. Rome had satirically called him the "petticoat cardinal," because he had received his appointment through his sister's position. However in 1519 when he was ordained a priest he renounced the pleasures of the flesh and began to live an exemplary life.

Pope Paul III sent a courier to the house on the Macello dei Corvi: would Michelangelo Buonarroti come to the Vatican palace that afternoon? The Holy Father had something of importance to communicate. Michelangelo went to the baths in the Via de' Pastini, where a barber trimmed his beard, washed and brushed his hair forward over his brow. Gazing at himself in the mirror of his bedroom as Urbino helped him into a mustard-colored shirt and cloak, he noted with surprise that the amber flecks in his eyes were beginning to fade, and that the crushed declivity at the bridge of his nose no longer seemed so deep.

"It's odd," he groused, "now that it no longer matters to me, I'm not as plain as I used to be."

"If you're not careful," said Urbino, observing the self-appraisal with a grin, "you'll grow to look like a Michelangelo sculpture."

When Michelangelo entered the small throne room of the Vatican he found Pope Paul III talking vivaciously to Ercole Gonzaga, Cardinal of Mantua, son of the cultivated Isabella d'Este, and a man of superb taste. Michelangelo knelt, kissed the Pope's ring, his eyes quickly sketching the new Pope's face: the narrow head, eyes incisively shrewd, the long thin nose jutted over the snowy white mustache; the hollow cheeks and thin-lipped mouth speaking of the voluptuary turned æsthete. It was a strong face.

"My son, I consider it a good omen that you will be working in Rome during my pontificate."

"Your Holiness is kind."

"It is a matter of self-interest. Several of my predecessors will be remembered largely because of the art works they commissioned you to create."

Michelangelo bowed humbly before the compliment. The Pope added warmly: "I wish you to enter our service."

Michelangelo paused for the stonemason's rest count of one two three four.

"How can I serve Your Holiness?"

"By continuing your work on the Last Judgment."

"Holy Father, I cannot take so large a commission."

"Why not?"

"I am bound by contract to the Duke of Urbino to complete Pope Julius' tomb. He has threatened me with disaster if I do not labor exclusively to that end."

"Is the Holy See to be intimidated by a war lord? Put the tomb out of your mind. I wish you to complete the Sistine Chapel for the glory of our pontificate."

"Holy Father, for thirty years now I have been tortured for the sin of signing that contract."

Paul rose on his throne, his slight body trembling under the bright red velvet, ermine-trimmed cape.

"It is thirty years for me, also, that I have desired to have you in my service! Now that I am Pope, am I not to be allowed to satisfy that desire?"

"Holiness, it is your thirty years against mine."

With a fiery gesture Paul pushed the red velvet skullcap back off his eyebrows and cried:

"I am determined to have you serve me, come what may."

Michelangelo kissed the Pope's ring, backed out of the small throne room. Returning to his house, he sank into an old leather chair. A sharp knock on the door straightened him up from his collapsed position. Urbino admitted two Swiss guards, tall blond giants in identical yellow and green costumes, who announced that Michelangelo Buonarroti would receive, the following midmorning, a visit from His Holiness Paul III.

"I will find charwomen, *messere*," announced the imperturbable Urbino. "What refreshment does one serve the Holy Father and his train? I have never seen a Pope before, except in procession."

"I wish that that was the only place I had ever seen one," grumbled Michelangelo. "Buy *passito* and *biscotti*, raisin wine and cookies. Use our best Florentine tablecloth."

The Pope arrived with his cardinals and attendants, causing considerable excitement in the Piazza del Foro Traiano. Paul smiled benignly on Michelangelo, went quickly to the Moses. The cardinals surrounded the figure in a field of red cassocks. It was obvious from the glance Pope Paul stole at Ercole Gonzaga that the Cardinal of Mantua was the acknowledged art authority of the Vatican. Gonzaga drew back from the Moses with his head cocked forward, eyes blazing with excitement. He declared in a voice compounded of awe, pride and gratification:

"This Moses alone is sufficient to do honor to Pope Julius. No man could want a more glorious monument."

Pope Paul said wistfully, "Ercole, I wish I had said that."

Then, turning to Michelangelo, he added, "You see, my son, I was not being unreasonable. Paint the Last Judgment for me. I will arrange for the Duke of Urbino to accept the Moses and these two Captives from your hand."

Michelangelo had not lived through four pontificates without learning when he was outmaneuvered.

2

When he was young his mind had leaped to herculean projects. Once in Carrara he had wanted to carve a whole marble peak to guide the sailors on the Tyrrhenian Sea. But as he twisted restlessly in his bed that night he demanded of himself, "Where am I to get the strength to cover a wall larger than the Sistine panels of Ghirlandaio, Botticelli, Rosselli and Perugino put together?" He would not have to lie on his back and paint above him on the ceiling; but the wall would take as long, and drain him as utterly. How to summon at sixty the cyclonic powers he had enjoyed at thirty-three?

Haggard from sleeplessness, he rose and went to early mass at San Lorenzo in Damaso. He bumped into Leo Baglioni, en route to his house on the corner. After each had confessed his sins and taken communion, they left the church and stood in the Campo dei Fiori with the pale November dawn on their faces.

"Leo, you've been out carousing, and I've been wrestling with my immortal soul; yet it took you less time to confess than it did me."

"My dear Michelagnolo, to me anything that gives pleasure is good, while anything that brings pain is sinful. Ergo, my conscience is clear. From your wan look I would say you had put yourself through much suffering last night; ergo, you had much transgression to be forgiven. Come inside for a cup of hot milk, we'll toast Cardinal Gonzaga's tribute to your Moses. Rome is talking of little else."

The hour of comradeship was relaxing. He left Baglioni's, walked slowly through the empty streets to the Pantheon, circled its majestic dome, then along the Via Recta to the Tiber and up the Via Alessandrina to St. Peter's. Antonio da Sangallo, nephew of Giuliano da Sangallo, and Bramante's assistant, had inherited the title of Architect of St. Peter's. As far as Michelangelo could tell, little had been accomplished in the eighteen years since he had left Rome except the repair of the giant piers and the building of the lowest foundation walls. Two hundred thousand ducats from all over Christendom had been poured into the concrete; but mostly, Michelangelo had learned, into the pockets of a ring of contractors who were erecting St. Peter's as slowly as was humanly possible. At the present rate, Michelangelo mused, St. Peter's would have trouble getting itself completed by Judgment Day.

The tiny chapel of Mary of the Fever had not yet been removed to make way for the transept. He entered, stood before his own Pietà. How beautiful Mary was. How exquisite and tender. And the son on the mother's lap, how sensitive the face.

He fell to his knees. For a moment he wondered if it were wrong to pray before his own creation; but he had carved these figures so long ago, when he was only twenty-four. Though there flooded over him waves of emotion from those distant days when he had first become a marble sculptor, he could not remember any of the actual detail of carving the block. It was as though someone he had known ages ago had done the work.

Rome was in the streets in holiday clothes, for today was a feast day in which twelve triumphal carts would start from the Capitoline hill and be driven ceremoniously to th Piazza Navona. This year it was to be a race between buffalo and horses, then twenty bulls would be attached to carts at the top of Mount Testaccio and driven down the steep slope to where they would be slaughtered as a spectacle, even as had the little pigs he had watched with Balducci.

Without knowing that he had so directed his steps, he found himself before the residence of the Cavalieri family. The palace was in the Rione di Sant'Eustachio, facing its own piazza and surrounded by extensive gardens. Square-cut, battlemented, the Cavalieri mansion had served for several hundreds of years as the center of continuous generations of Cavalieri "Conservators," Roman citizens who volunteered to conserve the Roman antiquities, old Christian churches, the fountains and statuary of the city.

It had taken him three weeks to achieve what could have been a ten-minute walk from his house in the Macello dei Corvi, along the narrow Via di San Marco and Via delle Botteghe Oscure, to the Cavalieri palace. As he dropped the heavy clapper against its metal base on the ponderous front door he wondered why it had taken him so long to call on Tommaso de' Cavalieri when in the back of his mind, during that last exhausting year in Florence, he had known that one of the reasons he looked forward to returning to Rome was the presence there of this charming young friend.

A servant opened the door, led Michelangelo into the high-ceilinged salon on the left which contained one of the best private collections of antique marble sculptures in Rome. As Michelangelo walked from a faun with a bunch of grapes to a child sleeping on a rock with some poppies in his hand, to a sea horse in half relief with a woman sitting on it surrounded by dolphins, he recalled the affectionate letters that had passed between himself and Tommaso, and the drawings of Ganymede and Tityos which he had made for Tommaso to study.

He heard footsteps behind him, turned . . . and gasped aloud. In the two years since he had seen Tommaso, he had made the transition from an attractive youth to the most magnificent male figure Michelangelo had ever laid eyes on: more beautiful even than the ancient marble Greek discus thrower that stood between himself and Tommaso: with broad, muscular shoulders, slim waist, straight slender legs.

"You've come at last," said Tommaso in a quiet voice, so surprisingly grave and courtly for a twenty-four-year-old.

"I had not wished to bring you my troubles."

"Friends can share troubles."

They met halfway across the salon, gripped each other's arms in a tense welcoming salute. Tommaso's eyes had deepened to a cobalt blue, his features slimmed to a finer mold.

"Now I know where I've seen you before," cried Michelangelo. "On the ceiling of the Sistine!"

"And just how did I get up onto the ceiling of the Sistine?"

"I put you up there myself. Adam, about to receive the spark of life from God. Even to the way your light chestnut hair tumbles back onto your neck."

"You painted Adam a long time ago."

"About twenty-four years. Just as you were being born. You have made my portrait come true."

"Do you see to what extent I will go for my friends?" said Tommaso with a chuckle. "I will even believe in miracles."

"Miracles may not be impossible. I came through your front door heavy-footed and heavy-hearted. I spend ten minutes with you, and ten years drop off my life."

"As your drawings have added ten years to my maturity as a craftsman."

"How wonderful that an old man and a young one can exchange years, as though they were gifts on Befana's Day."

"Do not call yourself old," cried Tommaso. When he grew angry his eyes became dark as ink. "I am shocked to find you thinking so conventionally. A man is as old as the creative force within him."

A warm smile spread over Michelangelo's features. The knots in his head and chest came untied.

"You know I am to do the Last Judgment for Pope Paul."

"I heard at mass this morning. It will be a grand completion for the Sistine, to match the vault."

Michelangelo turned his back on Tommaso to conceal the upsurge of emotion, stood running his hands over the exquisite posterior cheeks of an undraped marble Venus. A wave of happiness swept over him. He turned back to his friend.

"Tommaso, up to this moment I had not thought I could summon the courage to create a Last Judgment. Now I know I can."

They climbed a broad flight of stairs. On the balustrade the Cavalieri had mounted some of their smaller and more subtle carvings: the head of a woman with a basket on it, a Roman sculpture of the Emperor Augustus, an open sea shell inside of which was a nude figure. Tommaso de' Cavalieri spent half of his day working for the tax commission and as curator of public works, and the other half drawing. His workshop was at the back of the palace, overlooking the Torre Argentina, a room stripped bare except for long planks on wooden horses. On the wall above the table were the drawings Michelangelo had made two years before, as well as those he had sent from Florence. Spread out over the planks were dozens of sketches. Michelangelo studied them, exclaimed:

"You have a fine talent. And you work hard."

Tommaso's face clouded.

"In the past year I have fallen into bad company. Rome is full of temptations, as you know. I have drunk and whored too much, worked too little . . ."

Michelangelo was amused at the somber seriousness of his friend's self-reproach.

"Even St. Francis was wild as a young man, Tomao," he said, using the diminutive to cause a smile.

"May I work with you, if only for two hours a day?"

"My studio is yours. What could bring me greater happiness? See what your faith and affection have done for me already. I am now eager to start drawing for the Last Judgment. I shall serve not only as your friend but as your master. In return you shall help me blow up the drawings, share my models. We will develop you into a great artist."

Tommaso went pale, his eyes fading to the luminous powder-gray. He replied stiffly:

"You are the personification of art. The affection you show me is that which you would show to those who love art and wish to devote themselves to it. I can tell you this: never have I loved a man more than you, never have I desired a friendship more."

"It is an infinite sorrow to me not to be able to give you my past as well as my future."

"I have so little to give in return."

"Ah," said Michelangelo softly, "there you are wrong. As I stand opposite you at this worktable I feel neither age nor the fear of death. Do you know anything more precious that one man can bring another?"

They became inseparable. They walked arm in arm around the Piazza Navona for a breath of air, sketched on the Capitoline or in the Forum on Sundays, had supper in each other's homes after the day's work, then spent the evenings in stimulating hours of drawing and conversation. Their joy in each other gave off a radiance that made others happy in their presence; and now that they were acknowledged companions, they were invited everywhere together.

How did he define his feeling for Tommaso? Assuredly, it was an adoration of beauty. Tommaso's physical being had a strong impact on him, gave him a hollow feeling at the pit of his stomach. He realized that what he felt for Tommaso could only be described as love; yet he was hard-pressed to identify it. Of the loves of his life, where did this one fit? To which did it compare? It was different from his dependent love for his family, from the reverence and awe he felt for *Il Magnifico*, his respect for Bertoldo; his enduring though tenuous love for Contessina; the unforgotten passion for Clarissa; his friendly love for Granacci, the fatherly love he felt for Urbino. Perhaps this love, coming so late in his life, was undefinable.

"It is your lost youth you revere in me," said Tommaso.

"Not even in my dreams did I look anything like you," replied Michelangelo scoffingly. They were sketching at a table before a log fire. He was blocking out his first plan for the Sistine wall: using counterbalancing figures for the side portions, some floating upward toward heaven, others falling downward toward hell.

"You speak of your outer shell," retorted Tommaso. "My inner visage is plain. I would gladly exchange my features for your genius."

"You would be foolish, Tommaso; physical beauty is one of the rarest of God's gifts."

The color faded from Tommaso's face.

"And one of the most useless," he added in something of anguish.

"No, no," cried Michelangelo. "It brings joy to all people. Why do you think I have given my life to creating a race of glorious creatures in marble and paint? Because I worship human beauty as God's most divine attribute."

"Your people are beautiful because you have imbued them with souls. Your Pietà and Moses and Sistine characters, they feel and think, they know compassion. . . . That is why they live and have meaning for us."

Michelangelo was humbled by the passionate outburst.

"You have spoken with the wisdom of a man of sixty, while I have uttered the foolishness of a youth of twenty-four."

He was up at first light, eager to get to his drawing board. By the time the sun hit the top of Trajan's Column, Tommaso had come with a packet of freshly baked rolls for his midmorning refreshment. Each day a different model arrived, hired by Urbino in his search for the types designated by Michelangelo: laborers, mechanics, scholars, noblemen, peoples of all races and all sizes. Since there would be many women in the Last Judgment they had female models, the women from the baths, the bordellos, some of the more expensive hetaerae who posed in the nude for the adventure.

He did a portrait of Tommaso, the only time he had paid anyone such a compliment: in black chalk, with his smooth cheeks, the finely modeled bone structure dressed in ancient costume and holding a medallion in one hand.

"Do you recognize yourself, Tommaso?"

"The drawing is superb. But it is not me."

"It is you, as I see you."

"It discourages me . . . it proves what I have suspected from the beginning: I have taste, I can recognize good work from bad, but I do not have the creative fire."

Michelangelo stood above Tommaso, who was sitting hunched over a bench. His love for Tommaso made him feel fifteen feet tall.

"Tomao, did I not make Sebastiano a fine painter, and secure him important commissions? You have a thousand times his talent."

Tommaso set his jaw squarely. He had his own convictions.

"From your teaching I gain a deeper understanding of what is involved in this art; but no greater power to produce it myself. You waste your time thinking about me. I should not come here any more."

After supper Michelangelo sat at his long table and began writing. By morning he had completed two sonnets:

Love the Light-Giver

With your fair eyes a charming light I see,
For which my own blind eyes would peer in vain;

Stayed by your feet, the burden I sustain
Which my lame feet find all too strong for me;

Wingless upon your pinions forth I fly;
Heavenward your spirit stirreth me to strain;
E'en as you will, I blush and blanch again,
Freeze in the sun, burn 'neath a frosty sky.

Your will includes and is lord of mine;
Life to my thoughts within your heart is given;
My words begin to breathe upon your breath:

Like to the moon am I, that cannot shine
Alone; for lo! our eyes see nought in heaven
Save what the living sun illumineth.

When Tommaso arrived at the studio Michelangelo handed him the first sonnet. As Tommaso read, his face flushed. Michelangelo took the second sheet from his workbench, said, "This is the second poem I wrote."

I saw no mortal beauty with these eyes
When perfect peace in thy fair eyes I found;
But far within, where all is holy ground,
My soul felt Love, her comrade of the skies. . . .

Tommaso stood with his head bowed, remaining that way for a long moment. Then he raised eyes that were clear and radiant.

"I am unworthy of such a love; but I shall do everything possible to deserve it."

"Let us not get our just desserts," said Michelangelo with a gentle smile, "or Judgment Day will be unbearable."

3

He stood alone in the Sistine Chapel, the tumultuous army from Genesis overhead, making a detailed survey of the altar wall. Jonah, presiding at the end of the ceiling on a marble throne, would sit as an Old Testament prophet over the judgments of the New Testament Christ.

The fifty-five-foot-high wall, forty feet wide, was busy and chopped up; in the bottom zone were painted tapestries similar to the ones on the long side walls; above the table-altar were two Perugino frescoes, the Finding of Moses and Birth of Christ; in the next area were the two tall windows corresponding to those on the side walls, with portraits of the first two Popes, St. Linus and St. Cletus; and then, in the topmost, or fourth compartment, his own two lunettes in which he had painted the early ancestors of Christ.

The wall was fire-blackened at the bottom, pitted and broken at the second height; above, there was spoilage from damp, and an over-all soiling of dust, grime and smoke from the candles burned on the altar. He disliked destroying the Perugino frescoes, but since he was also obliterating two of his own lunette paintings no one could think him vengeful. He would seal up the two diverting windows, build a new baked-brick wall which he would engineer to slant outward a foot from ceiling to floor so that dust, dirt and smoke would no longer adhere.

Pope Paul readily gave his consent to Michelangelo's building plans. Michelangelo found himself liking the Farnese Pope more and more, developing a feeling of friendship for him. Having lived through the excesses of youth, Paul had become a Latin and Greek scholar, a fine speaker and writer. He intended to avoid the wars of Julius, the orgies of Leo, the international blunders and intrigues of Clement. He also was blessed with an astute sense of humor, as Michelangelo learned when he called at the Vatican. Noting the pontiff's good color and bright gleam of the eyes, he remarked:

"Your Holiness is looking well today."

"Not so loud," said Paul with mock whisper, "you'll disappoint the College of Cardinals. They only elected me because they thought I was on my deathbed. But the papacy agrees with me, and I shall outlive them all."

He was happy during these months of steady drawing in the studio that Urbino had redone with a touch of color in the walls. Drawing, like food, drink and sleep, puts strength back into a man. Through the medium of his drawing hand he was beginning to catch the tail of some germinal ideas. The Last Day had been promised by the Christian faith to coincide with the end of the world. Could that be? Could God have created the world in order to abandon it? The decision to create man had been God's alone. Then was not God powerful enough to sustain the world forever in spite of wickedness and evil? Would He not want to? Since every man judged himself before death, either in confessing his sins or dying unrepentant, could not the Last Judgment be a concept of a millennium which God held forever in reserve, with Christ just arriving among the nations of men, about to begin judgment? He did not believe he could paint the Last Judgment as something that had already happened, but only at the moment of inception. Then he might portray man's agonizing appraisal of himself. There could be no evasions, deceits. He believed that each individual was responsible for his conduct on earth, that there was a judge within. Could even a blazingly angry Christ inflict greater retribution? Could Dante's Charon in his rowboat on the river Acheron whip the miscreants into a deeper, more everlasting hell than man's unvarnished verdict on himself?

From the moment his pen touched the paper he sought the contour of the human form, a single line for each figure, nervous in quality to denote the desperate urgency behind its movements. Repeatedly he dipped the quill in the ink, impatient to have to interrupt the continuity of his linear passage, wanting to achieve a simultaneity of form and space. Inside the contour lines he used a system of parallel blocking and crosshatching to describe the play of muscles in their various states of stress as affected by the nervous tensions of the contours. What he sought was a sharp delineation of the human body from the crisp air about the figure; this he achieved by probing into the bare nerves of space. Every man, woman and child was to stand out in stark clarity, to achieve his full human dignity; for each was an individual and had worth. This was the key to the rebirth of human learning and freedom that had been sired in Florence, after the darkness of a thousand years. Never would he, Michelangelo Buonarroti, a Tuscan, be responsible for reducing man to an indistinguishable part of an inchoate mass, not even en route to heaven or hell!

Though he would not have admitted it, his arms were weary after the ten years of continuous carving on the Medici chapel. The more he studied his vault in the Sistine, the more he came to think that painting might become a noble and permanent art, after all.

He found himself the center of a group of young Florentines who met in the refurbished studio of the Macello dei Corvi house each afternoon to implement their plans for the conquest of Alessandro. The leaders were the brilliant, vital Cardinal Ippolito, who was sharing with Cardinal Ercole Gonzaga the leadership of Rome's high society of artists and scholars; the gentle and lovable Cardinal Niccolò; Roberto Strozzi, whose father had helped Michelangelo put Giovansimone and Sigismondo in the wool business, and whose grandfather had bought Michelangelo's first sculpture; the sons and grandsons of the long-established Florentine colony into whose homes he had been invited on his first visit to Rome, while Cardinal Riario was keeping him dangling. When he went visiting of a Sunday evening he found himself the focus of an attentive and excited group of young people: Pierantonio, the sculptor; Pierino del Vaga, most popular stuccoworker and decorator in Rome, and his disciple, Marcello Mantovano; Jacopino del Conte, a young Florentine pupil of Andrea del Sarto, who had followed Michelangelo to Rome; Lorenzetto Lotti, an architect of St. Peter's and son of the bell caster who had worked for Michelangelo in Bologna. The young people believed him a man of courage who had stood up to Popes; a worthy son of Lorenzo the Magnificent. At a time when Florence had descended to the depths, when its children despaired, they took comfort from the idea that Michelangelo towered above Europe like a Monte Altissimo. He made them proud to be Tuscans; singlehanded he had created more works of pure genius than all other artists combined. If Florence could create a Michelangelo it could survive an Alessandro.

Michelangelo realized with a pang that he had never enjoyed this kind of acceptance before; nor, for that matter, would he have been receptive if it had happened.

"My nature is changing," he commented to Tommaso. "While I was painting the vault I talked to no one but Michi."

"Was it a period of unhappiness for you?"

"An artist working at the top of his powers exists in a realm beyond human happiness."

He knew that this change in his nature had been brought about, in part, by his feeling for Tommaso. He admired Tommaso's handsomeness and nobility of spirit as though he were a young man falling in love with his first girl. He had all the symptoms: an overwhelming joy when Tommaso came into the room, a sense of forlornness when he left, pain-frought hours until he could see him again. He gazed over at Tommaso, who was drawing concentratedly with charcoal. He dared not tell him how he felt, and so late at night he wrote sonnets instead:

> Love is not always harsh and deadly sin:
> If it be love of loveliness divine,
> If it leaves the heart all soft and infantine
> For rays of God's own grace to enter in. . . .

News reached Rome that Charles V planned to marry his illegitimate daughter Margaret to Alessandro; that would mean an alliance between the Emperor and Alessandro, which would keep Alessandro in power. The hopes of the Florentine colony were dashed. A more personal disappointment for Michelangelo was Friar Sebastiano, round as a butterball, just returned after a journey.

"My dear *compare*, how wonderful to see you again! You must come to San Pietro in Montorio to see how well I transformed your drawings to oils."

"Oils? You were supposed to work in fresco."

Sebastiano's blush flooded downward through a large quantity of jowl.

"Fresco is for you, dear master, who never make a mistake. Oil is better for my temperament: if I make a dozen mistakes, I can wipe them off and start over."

They mounted to San Pietro in Montorio, which overlooked Rome. The air was pellucid, the waters of the Tiber as it wove through the tile roofs a clear blue under the winter sky. In the courtyard they passed Bramante's Tempietto, a jewel of architecture which always wrung an exclamation of praise from Michelangelo. Inside the church, Sebastiano proudly led Michelangelo to the first chapel on the right. He saw that Sebastiano had done a masterly job of blowing up his, Michelangelo's, drawings; that the colors had remained fresh and unchanged. Former artists who had painted with oil on walls, even such masters as Andrea del Castagno, Antonio and Piero Pollaiuolo, frequently had had their figures fade or turn black.

"It's a new method I invented," explained Sebastiano proudly. "I use a rough cast of lime mixed with mastic and resin, melt them together over a fire, then smooth them on the wall with a white-hot trowel. Aren't you proud of me?"

"What else have you painted since this chapel?"

". . . not much . . ."

"But if you were so proud of perfecting a new method?"

"When Pope Clement appointed me Keeper of the Seals I no longer needed to work. I had all the money I wanted."

"That was the only reason you painted?"

Sebastiano turned on Michelangelo and stared, as though his benefactor had suddenly been bereft of his senses.

"What other reason could there be?"

Michelangelo started to grow angry, then realized that he was dealing with an amiable child.

"Sebastiano, you're entirely right. Sing, play your lute, amuse yourself. Art should be practiced only by those poor wretches who can't help themselves."

The halting of St. Peter's was a more bitter potion. Though hundreds of men had been employed and tons of cement mixed during the months since his arrival in Rome, his experienced eye told him that no progress had been made in the body of the construction, or fabric of the church. The Florentine colony knew about the waste of money and time; but not even his three young cardinal friends could tell him whether Pope Paul suspected. Antonio da Sangallo had become so firmly entrenched during his twenty years as architect of St. Peter's that no one dared attack him. Michelangelo realized that it was the better part of discretion to keep still. Yet he burned inwardly, for he had never gotten over the feeling that St. Peter's was his own project because he had been part of the cause of its inception. When he could be silent no longer he found a moment to tell the Pope what was going on.

Pope Paul listened patiently, smoothing down his long white beard.

"Did you not make the same charge against Bramante? The court will say that you are jealous of Antonio da Sangallo. It puts you in a bad light."

"I've been in a bad light most of my life."

"Paint the Last Judgment, Michelangelo, and let Antonio da Sangallo build St. Peter's."

When he reached home, frustrated, he found Tommaso waiting for him with Cardinals Ippolito and Niccolò. Each was pacing his own orbit of floor.

"You look like a delegation."

"We are," replied Ippolito. "Charles V is coming through Rome. He will visit with only one private person, Vittoria Colonna, the Marchesa di Pescara. He is a long-time friend of her husband's family in Naples."

"I do not know the marchesa."

"But I do," replied Tommaso. "I have asked her to invite you to her gathering this Sunday afternoon. You'll go, of course?"

Before Michelangelo could ask, "But how do I fit in?" Niccolò, with Contessina's somber brown eyes, said, "It would mean a great deal to Florence if you became friends with the marchesa and could be introduced by her to the Emperor when he comes to Rome."

When the two cardinals had gone Tommaso said, "Actually I have wanted you to meet Vittoria Colonna. In the years since you last lived here she has become the first lady of Rome. She is a rare poet, one of the finest minds in Rome. She is beautiful. She is also a saint."

"Are you in love with the lady?" asked Michelangelo.

Tommaso laughed good-naturedly. "Oh no, she is a woman of forty-six, has had a wonderful romance and marriage, and has been widowed for the past ten years."

"Is she a Colonna from the palace on the Quirinal, above me?"

"Yes, a sister of Ascanio Colonna, though she rarely uses the palace. Most of the time she stays at a convent where they have the head of St. John the Baptist. She prefers the austere life of the mothers and sisters."

Vittoria Colonna, daughter of one of the most powerful families in Italy, had been engaged to Ferrante Francesco d'Avalos of Naples, the Marchese di Pescara, when each had been four years old. They were married in a lavish wedding in Ischia when they were nineteen. The honeymoon was short-lived, for the marchese was a general in the service of the Holy Roman Emperor, Maximilian, and had had to leave for the wars. In the sixteen years of their marriage Vittoria had seldom seen her husband. In 1512 he had been wounded in the Battle of Ravenna. Vittoria had nursed him back to life but he had returned to his command, and thirteen years later was killed at the Battle of Pavia in Lombardy after heroic action on the field. The lonely Vittoria had spent the long years of separation in a disciplined study of Greek and Latin, and had become one of the best scholars of Italy. At her husband's death she had attempted to take the veil, but Pope Clement had forbidden it. She had spent the last ten years giving her service and fortune to the poor, and to the building of convents, thereby enabling the innumerable young girls who were without dowries, and hence could not find husbands, to enter the nunnery. Her poems were considered to be among the most important literary events of the time.

"I've seen only one saint walking around in shoe leather," commented Michelangelo; "that was Prior Bichiellini. I shall be interested to see what the female version looks like."

That was the last he thought about Vittoria Colonna, Marchesa di Pescara, until late Sunday afternoon when Tommaso called for him and they walked up the Via de' Cavalli past the Colonna gardens on one side and the Baths of Constantine on the other, to the top of Monte Cavallo, named after the two marble Horse Tamers which Leo Baglioni had taken him to see on his first day in Rome. The gardens of the convent of San Silvestro al Quirinale were filled with warm spring sunlight, there were laurels for shade, and old stone benches against walls covered with green ivy.

Vittoria Colonna, sitting in the midst of half a dozen men, rose to greet him. Michelangelo found himself considerably surprised. After Tommaso's description of her deprivation and sorrow, of her saintliness, he had expected to meet an old lady in black, showing the ravages of tragedy on her face. Instead he found himself gazing into the deep green eyes of the most vitally lovely woman he had ever seen, with high color in her cheeks, warm lips parted in welcome, the expression of a young woman enormously excited by life. She had a regal bearing, though without hauteur. Beneath the lightweight cloth of her simple robe he envisaged a ripe figure to complement the large expressive eyes, the long braids of honey-gold hair looped low on her neck, the strong white teeth between full red lips, the straight Roman nose, slightly and amusingly turned up at the end, and the finely modeled chin and cheekbones which lent her face strength to match its beauty.

He felt so ashamed at undressing the defenseless woman, as though she were a hired model, that there was a roaring in his ears, and he could not hear her greeting. He thought:

"What a dreadful thing to do to a saint!"

His repentance caused the noise in his ears to abate; but he could not take his eyes from her. Her beauty was like the noonday sun, filling the garden with its light but at the same time blinding him. With an effort he acknowledged an introduction to Lattanzio Tolomei, a learned Sienese ambassador; the poet, Sadoleto; Cardinal Morone; the papal secretary Blosio, whom Michelangelo knew from court; and a priest who was discoursing to the group on the Epistles of Paul.

Vittoria Colonna spoke in a richly melodious voice:

"I welcome you as an old friend, Michelangelo Buonarroti, for your works have spoken to me for many years."

"My works were more fortunate than I, Marchesa."

Vittoria's green eyes clouded.

"I had heard that you were a blunt man, *signore,* who knew no flattery."

"You heard correctly," replied Michelangelo.

His tone left little room for argument. Vittoria Colonna hesitated for a moment, then continued:

"I have been told that you knew Fra Savonarola."

"No. But I heard him preach many times. In San Marco and the Duomo."

"I could covet that experience."

"His voice thundered through the vast spaces of the cathedral and bounded off the walls against my ears."

"It is too bad the words did not strike Rome. Then we would have had our reforms inside the Mother Church. We would not now be losing our children in Germany and Holland."

"You admired Fra Savonarola?"

"He died a martyr to our cause."

Listening to the intensity about him, Michelangelo realized that he was in the midst of a revolutionary group, highly critical of the practices of the Church and seeking a means to begin its own reformation of the clergy. The Inquisition in Spain and Portugal had taken thousands of lives on charges far less serious. He turned back to the marchesa, admiring her courage; her face was shining with dedication.

"I do not mean to sound disrespectful, *signora,* but Fra Savonarola martyred a good deal of fine art and literature on what he called 'a bonfire of the vanities' before he himself came to grief."

"I have always regretted that, Signor Buonarroti. I know one does not cleanse the human heart by wiping clean the human mind."

The conversation became general. They spoke of Flemish art, which was highly respected in Rome, and its sharp contrasts to Italian painting; then of the origins of the concept of the Last Judgment. Michelangelo quoted from Matthew 25:31–33:

> When the Son of Man comes in his glory, and all the angels with him, he will sit down upon the throne of his glory, and all nations will be gathered in his presence, where he will divide men one from the other, as the shepherd divides the sheep from the goats; he will set the sheep on his right, and the goats on his left.

As they walked down Monte Cavallo watching the sunset deepen the colors of the city below them, Michelangelo asked:

"Tommaso, when can we see her again?"

"When she invites us."

"We have to wait until then?"

"We have to wait; she goes nowhere."

"Then I will wait," cried Michelangelo, put out, "like a silent supplicant, until the lady deigns to send for me again."

An amused smile twitched the corners of Tommaso's lips.

"I thought you would be impressed."

That night it was Vittoria Colonna's face that glowed in the room. It was many years since a woman's presence had so completely taken possession of him. The poet's lines that had been roaming through his skull replaced Tommaso de' Cavalieri with the Marchesa di Pescara; and at cockcrow he rose to write:

Well may these eyes of mine both near and far
Behold the beams that from thy beauty flow;
But, lady, feet must halt where sight may go:
We see, but cannot climb to clasp a star. . . .

Clogged with mortality and wingless, we
Cannot pursue an angel in her flight:
Only to gaze exhausts our utmost might.

Yet, if but heaven like earth incline to thee,
Let my whole body be one eye to see,
That not one part of me may miss thy sight!

4

It was two weeks before he received a second invitation. Somehow in the interval he had begun to identify the sculptural beauty of her figure, the strong but tender face, with his marble statue of Night in the Medici chapel. It was a warm May Sunday when the marchesa's servant, Foao, arrived with the message from the marchesa.

"My mistress bade me tell you, *messere*, that she is in the chapel of San Silvestro al Quirinale; that the church is closed and pleasant. She asks whether you would care to come and lose a little of the day with her so that she might gain it with you."

He was excited as he refreshed himself in a tub of cold water which Urbino set out on the garden porch, then dressed in a dark blue shirt and stockings he had bought against just such an invitation, and made his way up the hill.

He had hoped to be alone with her, but as Vittoria Colonna came to greet him, gowned in pure white silk, with a white lace mantilla over her head, he saw that the chapel was filled. He recognized illustrious members of the Vatican court and the university faculty. A Spanish painter was complaining that there was no good art in Spain because the Spaniards considered painting and sculpture of little worth and refused to pay for it. The men began speaking of the art of their own city-states: in Venice the portraits by Tiziano; in Padua the frescoes of Giotto; the singular painting of the municipal chamber in Siena; in Ferrara the works in the castle; in Pisa, Bologna, Parma, Piacenza, Milan, Orvieto . . .

Michelangelo knew most of these works, and only half listened, for he was watching Vittoria, sitting motionless beneath a stained-glass window which threw a sheen of variegated color over her flawless skin. He found himself wondering about her; if her marriage to the Marchese di Pescara had been such a great love match, why had they been together only a few months out of the sixteen years? Why had the marchese remained in the north of Italy during the long rainy winters when no war could be waged? And why had an old friend looked away when he had asked under what heroic circumstances the marchese had been killed?

Suddenly he became aware of a silence in the chapel. All eyes were turned on him. Cardinal Ercole Gonzaga politely repeated the question: would Michelangelo tell them of his favorite works of art in Florence? With his face slightly flushed, and his voice a little off key, Michelangelo spoke of the beauties of the sculptures of Ghiberti, Orcagna, Donatello, Mino da Fiesole; of the painting of Masaccio, Ghirlandaio, Botticelli. When he had finished, Vittoria Colonna said:

"Knowing Michelangelo to be a modest man, we have all refrained from speaking of the art of Rome. In the Sistine he has done the work of twenty great painters.

Surely all of mankind will one day see and understand the Creation through his painting?''

Her enormous green eyes engulfed him completely. Now when she spoke, it was directly to him; quietly, chastely, yet her voice had a peculiarly throaty quality, her lips seemed only a few inches from his.

''Michelangelo, do not think that I overpraise you. In point of fact, it is not you I praise at all, except as a faithful servant. For I have long thought that you have a divine gift and were chosen by God for your great tasks.''

He searched his mind for an answer but no words formulated themselves. He wanted to speak only of how he felt about her.

''His Holiness has done me the favor of allowing me to build a nunnery for young girls at the foot of Monte Cavallo,'' continued Vittoria. ''The site I have chosen is by the broken portico of the Tower of Maecenas, where it is said that Nero watched Rome burning. I would like to see the footprints of such a wicked man wiped out by those of holy women. I do not know, Michelangelo, what shape or proportion to give the house, whether some of the old work may be adapted to the new.''

''If you would care to descend to the site, *signora,* we could study the ruins.''

''You are indeed kind.''

He had had no idea of being kind, he had merely hoped that he and Vittoria could descend to the old temple alone and spend an hour together while going over the piles of stones. Vittoria invited the entire group to accompany them down the hill. Michelangelo salvaged the right to walk by her side, churned by her closeness, the physical, spiritual and intellectual emanation that engulfed his senses. He emerged from his emotional cloud long enough for the architect to break through, to make an estimate of where the convent could best be placed.

''Marchesa, I think this broken portico might be converted into a campanile. I could make you some drawings for the convent.''

''I did not dare to ask for so much.''

The warmth of her gratitude reached out like two arms to embrace him. He congratulated himself on his stratagem in breaking down the impersonal barrier which Vittoria kept high between herself and the others.

''I will have some sketches in a day or two. Where may I bring them to you?''

Vittoria's eyes turned opaque. When she spoke her voice was constrained.

''There is much work to do at my convent. Could Foao bring you word when I am free? In a week or two?''

He returned to his studio in a fury, began knocking things about. What kind of game was this woman playing? Was she paying him these extraordinary compliments merely to bring him to her feet? Did she admire him, or did she not? If she wanted his friendship, why was she refusing it? Shunting him off . . . for another two weeks! Could she not tell how completely he was taken by her? Did she not have human blood in her veins, and human feelings in her breast?

''You must understand,'' Tommaso explained when he saw that Michelangelo was disturbed. ''She is dedicated to the memory of her husband. For all these years, since his death, she has loved only Jesus.''

''If the love of Christ prevented a woman from loving mortal man, the Italian people would have died out long ago.''

''I have brought you some of her poems. Perhaps you will learn more about her from them. Listen to this one:

> 'Since a chaste love my soul has long detained
> In fond idolatry of earthly fame;
> Now to the Lord, who only can supply
> The remedy, I turn.

Me it becomes not, henceforth, to invoke
Of Delos, or Parnassus; other springs,
Far other mountaintops, I now frequent
Where human steps unaided cannot mount.'

And this from another:

'Would that a voice impressive might repeat,
In holiest accents to my inmost soul,
The name of Jesus; and my words and works
Attest true faith in Him, and ardent hope. . . .' ''

Michelangelo chewed on the words for a few moments, running his index finger through the furrows of his brow.
"She sounds like a woman deeply hurt."
"By death."
"Permit me to doubt."
"What then?"
"My instinct tells me something is wrong."
When Tommaso had departed, Michelangelo asked Urbino to refill the oil lamp, and sat quietly before the sheaf of papers, studying their content. He read from the poem written to her husband:

Thou knowest, Love, I never sought to flee
From thy sweet prison, nor impatient threw
Thy dear yoke from my neck; never withdrew
What, that first day, my soul bestowed on thee.

Time hath not changed love's ancient surety;
The knot is still as firm; and though there grew
Moment by moment fruit bitter as rue,
Yet the fair tree remains as dear to me.

And thou hast seen how that keen shaft of thine,
'Gainst which the might of Death himself is vain,
Smote on one ardent, faithful breast full sore.

Now loose the cords that fast my soul entwine,
For though of freedom ne'er I recked before,
Yet now I yearn my freedom to regain.

He was puzzled. Why had Vittoria described her love as a prison and a yoke? Why would she "yearn my freedom to regain" from a love to which she had devoted the whole of her life? He had to have the answer: for he knew now that he loved her, had loved her from that first blinding moment he had laid eyes on her in the garden of San Silvestro.
"There are ways of getting information," resourceful Leo Baglioni assured him, "among the Neapolitans in Rome, particularly those who fought alongside the marchese. Let me see who among them owe me favors."
The material took five days to assemble; when Leo came to the studio he seemed weary.
"The facts started raining on me as though someone had pulled a stopper in heaven. But what tires me, even in my cynical old age, is the amount of myth that passes for truth."
"Urbino, be so good as to bring Signor Baglioni a bottle of our best wine."

"First of all this was no lyrical love affair. The marchese never loved his wife, and fled from her a few days after the wedding. Secondly, he wenched the whole way from Naples to Milan. Third, he used every excuse known to inventive husbands never to get into the same city with his wife. And fourth, the noble marchese pulled one of the most dastardly double treasons in history, betraying both his own Emperor and his fellow conspirators. Rumor has it that he died by poison, a very long way from anybody's battlefield."

"I knew it," cried Michelangelo. "Leo, you have just made me the happiest of men."

"Permit me to doubt."

"What the devil do you mean?"

"Knowledge will make your life harder, rather than easier. I feel that if Vittoria Colonna learned that you knew the truth about her marriage . . ."

"Do you think I'm an idiot?"

"A man in love will use any weapon against a woman he is importuning . . ."

"Importuning! I have yet to get an hour alone with her."

He was drawing at his long table piled high with paper, pens, charcoal, a copy of Dante's *Inferno* opened to the story of Charon, when Vittoria's servant Foao entered to invite Michelangelo for the following afternoon to the gardens of the Colonna palace on the hill above his house. The fact that she had summoned him to her ancestral home rather than a church garden or chapel led him to believe that they might be alone. In a fever of expectancy he wrestled with a stub pen:

> Nay, prithee tell me, Love, when I behold
> My lady, do mine eyes her beauty see
> In truth, or dwells that loveliness in me
> Which multiplies her grace a thousandfold? . . .

The Colonna gardens occupied an important part of the slope of Monte Cavallo, thickly planted with trees whose greenery Michelangelo could see from his house. A servant led him along a trail heavy with jasmine in bloom. From a distance he heard a babble of voices and was keenly disappointed. He came in sight of a summerhouse shaded by plane trees, with a waterfall and lily pond to keep the air cool.

Vittoria came to meet him. He nodded to the men in the pavilion and sat down abruptly in one corner, leaning against the lacy white latticework. Vittoria sought his eyes, tried to bring him into the discussion, but he declined. Into his mind there flashed the thought:

"That is why she refuses to love again. Not because the first love was so beautiful, but because it was so ugly! That is why she gives her love only to Christ."

He looked up, gazing at her with an intensity that could have pierced the tissue of her brain and the marrow of her bone. She stopped in the middle of a sentence, turned to ask solicitously:

"Is something wrong, Michelangelo?"

Then he sensed something else:

"She has never known a man. Her husband never consummated that marriage, either on their honeymoon or when he returned injured from the wars. She is as virginal as the young girls she takes into her nunneries."

He ached with compassion for her. He would have to accept the legend of the immortal love, and from that starting point try to persuade this courageous and desirable woman that he had a love to offer that could be as beautiful as the one she had invented.

5

His love for Vittoria in no way changed his feelings for Tommaso de' Cavalieri, who continued to arrive early each morning carrying a jug of cool milk or a basket of fruit to get in his two hours of drawing under Michelangelo's critical eye before the sun grew hot. Michelangelo made him do his sketches over a dozen times, never appearing satisfied, but in truth well pleased with Tommaso's progress. Pope Paul had accepted Tommaso at court and appointed him Conservator of the Fountains of Rome.

Tommaso looked up from the drafting table, his expression intent, the blue eyes serious.

"Michelangelo, there's not an engineer in Rome who knows how the ancients brought all that water down! Or would dare to rebuild the aqueducts. How can a people so completely lose their talents? I think I no longer want to become a painter. I should like to become an architect. My family have been Romans for eight hundred years. The city is in my blood. I want not only to conserve it but to help rebuild it. Architects are what the city needs most."

The over-all design for the Sistine wall was now complete. He was able to count more than three hundred characters he had integrated from his original drawings, all of them in motion, no one still: a tumultuous horde of humans surrounding Christ in inner intimate circles and outer remote ones; vertical shafts of bodies rising upward on one side, descending on the other, the clouds below Christ presenting the only emptiness. On the bottom to the left was the yawning cave of hell, with the burial ground of the ages; the river Acheron was on the right. He set himself a schedule of painting one normal-size figure on the wall each day, with two days allotted to those larger than life.

The Virgin emerged as a harmonious blend of his mother, the Pietà and Medici madonnas, his own Eve, six panels down the ceiling, taking the apple from the serpent, and Vittoria Colonna. Like Eve, she was a young, robust, life-containing female; like the others, she was glorious of face and figure. Mary was tactfully turned away from her son's merciless judgment of mankind, since she herself was not being judged. Was she also withdrawn in compassion because man must be judged, however just his fate might be? Did God judge the sheep, the oxen, the cattle, the birds? As a mother, would she not feel pain for the doomed souls cowering under her son's arm upraised in righteous wrath? Could she free herself from responsibility for him, even though he were the son of God? She had carried him in her womb for nine months, given him the breast, healed his wounds. Her son was judging other mothers' sons! The good would be saved, the saints return to heaven; but the elect seemed so few in comparison to the endless hordes of sinners. Everything her son did was perfection; yet she could not help but be anguished at the awful suffering that must follow.

Charles V did not come to Rome, but instead prepared a fleet to sail from Barcelona against the Barbary pirates. The Florentine exiles sent a delegation to him, urging him to appoint Cardinal Ippolito as ruler of Florence. Charles received the delegation in encouraging terms . . . but delayed his decision until he should have returned from the wars. When Ippolito heard the news he decided to join Charles in his expedition and fight by the Emperor's side. At Itri, where he was waiting to board ship, he was poisoned by one of Alessandro's agents and died instantly.

The Florentine colony was plunged into the profoundest gloom. For Michelangelo the loss was especially poignant; in Ippolito he had found everything he had loved in Ippolito's father, Giuliano. It left him with only Contessina's son to carry on the continuity of his love for the Medici. Niccolò seemed to feel the same way, for they sought each other's company during the dread-filled days.

By fall, one year after he had reached Rome, his Sistine wall was rebricked and dried; his cartoon of more than three hundred "men of all races," as Matthew had put it, ready to be blown up to wall size. Pope Paul, wishing to give him security, issued a *breve* which declared Michelangelo Buonarroti to be the *Sculptor, Painter and Architect of All the Vatican,* with a lifetime pension of a hundred ducats a month, fifty from the papal treasury, fifty from the benefice of the ferry over the Po River at Piacenza. Sebastiano del Piombo stood with him before the scaffold in the Sistine, asking eagerly:

"Would you like me to put the intonaco on, *compare?* I'm an expert."

"It's a tedious job, Sebastiano. Are you sure you want to?"

"I would be proud to say that I had a hand in the Last Judgment."

"All right. But don't use Roman *pozzolana,* it stays soft; put in marble dust instead, and not too much water with the lime."

"I will lay you a flawless surface."

So he did, structurally; but the moment Michelangelo approached the altar he smelled something wrong: Sebastiano had mixed mastic and resin with the lime, brewed them together, applied the plaster with a mason's trowel heated over fires.

"Sebastiano, you have prepared this wall for oil paints!"

"Isn't that what you wanted?" Sebastiano asked innocently.

"You know I work in fresco!"

"But you didn't tell me, Godfather. I did our San Pietro in Montorio wall in oil."

Michelangelo surveyed the Venetian from the crown of his bald head through the middle layers of his now frightened fat.

"And that made you qualified to paint part of this wall . . . ?"

"I only wanted to help."

". . . to paint the Last Judgment?" Michelangelo's voice was rising. "Since you know how to work only in oil, you prepared an oil wall so that you could collaborate with me. What else have you done?"

"Well, I . . . I spoke to Pope Paul. He knows I am of your *bottega.* You've been complaining that I don't paint any more. Here is your opportunity . . ."

"To throw you out!" shouted Michelangelo. "I ought to pull the entire plaster down over your ungrateful head."

But even as Sebastiano scurried away, Michelangelo knew that the surface would take days, weeks to scrape off. Then the brick wall would have to be allowed to dry again before a genuine fresco base could be laid. It, too, would take time to dry. Sebastiano had wasted months of his time.

The wall would be repaired by the capable Urbino; but the breach caused between Michelangelo and Antonio da Sangallo by Pope Paul's *breve* would last for the rest of his life.

Antonio da Sangallo, now fifty-two years old, decorated his thin face with a replica of his uncle Giuliano's luxuriant oriental mustache. He had joined Bramante as an apprentice on St. Peter's and, after Bramante's death, had worked as an assistant to Raphael. He had been part of the Bramante-Raphael clique that had attacked the Sistine vault. Since Raphael's death, with the exception of a few years when Baldassare Peruzzi of Siena had been forced on him as co-architect by Pope Leo, Sangallo had been the architect of St. Peter's, and of Rome. For fifteen years, while Michelangelo was working in Carrara and Florence, no one had risen to challenge his supremacy. . . . The Pope's *breve* made him raving mad.

Tommaso first brought the warning that Sangallo was growing increasingly violent.

"It's not so much that he fights your being named the official sculptor and painter of the Vatican palace. He laughs that off as a colossal piece of bad judgment. It's the appointment as official architect that has him half out of his mind."

"I didn't ask Pope Paul to put that in the *breve.*"

"You could never convince Sangallo of that. He claims you're conniving to take St. Peter's away from him."

"What St. Peter's? Those piers and foundations he's been pouring for fifteen years?"

Sangallo showed up that very night, accompanied by two of his apprentices who lighted him across the Piazza del Foro Traiano. Michelangelo invited them in, tried to propitiate Sangallo by recalling memories of their early days together in his uncle's house in Florence. Sangallo refused to be placated.

"I should have come here the very day I heard you had made accusations against me to Pope Paul. It was the same kind of wicked slander you used against Bramante."

"I told Pope Julius that Bramante's mix was bad and that the piers would crack. Raphael spent years repairing them. Is that not true?"

"You think you can turn Pope Paul against me. You demanded that he declare you the Vatican architect. You want to push me out!"

"That is not true. I am concerned for the building. The fabric has already been paid for, and no part of the church proper is yet apparent."

"Listen to the great architect talk! I've seen that miserable dumpy dome you inflicted on the Medici chapel." Sangallo pressed his clenched fists against his bosom. "Get your bashed-in nose out of St. Peter's. You've been a meddler in other people's affairs all your life. Even Torrigiani couldn't teach you any better. If you value your life: *St. Peter's is mine!*"

Angry for the first time, distressed at the mention of Torrigiani's name, Michelangelo compressed his lips, replied coldly:

"Not quite. It was mine in its inception, and it may very well be mine in its completion."

Now that Sangallo had announced open warfare, Michelangelo decided he had better see Sangallo's walk-in model. Tommaso arranged to take him to the office of the commissioners of St. Peter's where it was lodged. They went on a religious holiday when no one would be there.

Michelangelo was aghast at what he saw. Bramante's interior in the form of a simple Greek cross had been clean and pure, full of light and isolated from its surroundings. Sangallo's model included a ring of chapels which deprived Bramante's concept of all its light and provided none of its own. There were so many ranges of columns one upon the other, so many innumerable projections, pinnacles and subdivisions that the former serene tranquillity was lost. Sangallo had been building fortresses and defense walls; he had no sense whatever of how to create a spiritual church, one that was envisaged as the Mother Church of Christendom. If Sangallo were allowed to continue, he would erect a heavy monument, cluttered and in bad taste.

Walking home, Michelangelo said ruefully to Tommaso:

"I was wrong to tell the Pope about the waste of money. That is the least of the danger."

"Then you will say nothing?"

"It's clear from your voice, Tommaso, that you hope I won't. In point of fact, the Pope would tell me, 'This puts you in a bad light.' So it would. But St. Peter's will be as dark as a Stygian cave."

6

All the Last Judgments he had seen had been sentimental, unrealistic child's tales, rigid, without movement, stratified as much in space as in spiritual category, with an aloof still-life Christ sitting on a throne, his Judgment already passed. Michelangelo had always searched for the moment of decision, which was for him the eternal womb of truth: David, before the battle with Goliath; God, before giving the spark of life to Adam; Moses, before sustaining the Israelites. Now too he sought a Last Judgment not yet made, with Christ arriving on the scene in a burst of force, while all the nations of earth and time made their way toward him wondering in the starkest fear:

"What is to happen to me?"

This would be the most powerful of all his Christs; he made him Zeus and Hercules, Apollo and Atlas, while realizing it was he, Michelangelo Buonarroti, who would be judging the nations of men. He pulled back into space the right leg of Christ, even as he had the Moses, to cause an imbalance of weight and set the whole figure in a state of tension. The wall would be dominated by Christ's *terribilità*, his terrifying awesomeness.

On the vault he had painted his Genesis in bright, dramatic colors; the Last Judgment would be confined to quieter monotones, flesh tones and brown. On the ceiling he had worked in sharply delineated panels; with the Last Judgment he would have to perform the magician's trick of making the wall vanish and infinite space appear.

Now, ready to begin the fresco itself, all feeling of spent years, of fatigue and uncertainty about the future, vanished. Comfortable and warmed by his love for Tommaso, confident in the pursuit of his love for Vittoria, he tackled the wall with vigor.

"Tommaso, how can a man be happy painting the judgment of the world when so pitifully few will be saved?"

"Because it's not the damnation itself that your happiness derives from. Ecclesia supporting the young girl in her lap, and this condemned sinner, are as fine as anything you painted on the vault."

He was attempting to capture naked truth through nakedness, to express everything the human figure could articulate. His Christ would wear a wisp of a loincloth, the Virgin a pale lilac robe; yet as he painted her beautiful legs he could bring himself to veil them with only the sheerest of lilac-colored silk. All the rest, men, women, children, angels, were nude. He was painting them as God made them . . . and as he had wanted to paint them from the age of thirteen. He eschewed conventional iconography to achieve his emotional responses; there was little of the ritualistic vocabulary of religious painting. He did not conceive of himself as a religious painter, or of the Last Judgment as a religious fresco. It was spiritual, having to do with the eternality of the human soul, with the power of God to make man judge himself and hold himself accountable for his sins. He portrayed a single naked humanity struggling with the same fate, the peoples of all races. Even the Apostles and saints, holding forth their symbols of martyrdom, frightened lest they not be recognized, seemed stunned by this image of Christ, the "most high Jupiter," as Dante described him, about to cast fierce thunderbolts at the guilty.

By day he locked himself into the world of the Sistine, with only Urbino by his side on the high scaffold, painting first in the lunettes from which he had obliterated his early work. Just below was the figure of Christ, on the rock of heaven, the golden sun for a throne behind him. Standing on the floor of the chapel, looking upward, he felt a need to impart greater visual impact to Christ's raised arm. He ascended the scaffold, added more volume by extending the paint beyond the outline delineated in the wet plaster. Then he painted Mary beside Christ, the hordes of humans on either side.

At night he read the Bible, Dante, and Savonarola's sermons sent to him by Vittoria Colonna; all fitted together as parts of a whole. He could hear Savonarola's voice as he read sermons he had heard the friar preach forty years before. Now, even as Vittoria had told him, the martyred priest stood forth in his full glory as a prophet. Everything that Fra Savonarola had predicted had come true: the division within the Church; the setting up of a new faith within the framework of Christianity;

the low estate of the papacy and the clergy; the decay of morals, the increase of violence:

> Rome, a mighty war shall strip thee of thy pomp and pride, a mighty pestilence make ye cast aside your vanities.
> Behold, O Florence, thy fate, if thou wouldst have a tyrant. Thy tongue enslaved, thy person subject to him, thy goods at his disposal . . . debased in all ways.

On the outside, it looked as though Judgment Day had arrived for Pope Paul. Cardinal Niccolò, now one of the most influential cardinals at court, brought the news to Michelangelo: Charles V of Spain and Francis I of France had once again declared war on each other. Charles was traveling north from Naples with his army, the one that had sacked Rome and crushed Florence. Pope Paul had no army or means of resistance; he was preparing to flee.

"But where?" demanded Tommaso hotly. "To Sant'Angelo, while Charles's troops pillage again? We cannot stand another sack; we will become just another pile of stones, like Carthage."

"What will he fight with?" Michelangelo asked. "I watched the Emperor's army beyond the San Miniato walls. They have cannon, cavalrymen, lancers. . . . What would you use to defend yourselves?"

"Our bare hands!" Tommaso was livid with rage, the first time Michelangelo had ever seen him this way.

Pope Paul decided to fight . . . with peace and grandeur. He received the Emperor on the steps before St. Peter's, surrounded by the hierarchy of the Church in their splendid robes, and three thousand valiant young Romans. Charles behaved graciously, accepted the Pope's spiritual authority. The following day he called on Vittoria Colonna, Marchesa di Pescara, friend of his family, who summoned her friend, Michelangelo Buonarroti, for the meeting in the garden of San Silvestro al Quirinale.

The Holy Roman Emperor, a formal and haughty monarch, acknowledged Vittoria's introduction with considerable sanguinity. Michelangelo pleaded with Charles for the removal of Alessandro as the tyrant of Florence. The Emperor did not appear to be greatly interested but, when Michelangelo had concluded, leaned toward him and said with unaccustomed heartiness:

"I can promise you one thing when I get to Florence."

"Thank you, Excellency."

"That I shall pay a visit to your new sacristy. People of my court, returning to Spain, have declared it one of the marvels of the world."

Michelangelo looked toward Vittoria to see if he might continue. Vittoria's face was calm; she was willing to risk the Emperor's displeasure to allow Michelangelo to speak for his country.

"Excellence, if the sculptures of the new sacristy are good, they are so because I was raised in the art capital of Europe. Florence can continue to create noble works of art only if you rescue her from under the boot of Alessandro."

Charles maintained his pleasant mien, murmuring, "The Marchesa di Pescara says that you are the single greatest artist since the beginning of time. I have seen your Sistine Chapel ceiling; in a few days I shall see your Medici chapel sculptures. If they are all that I have heard, you have our royal promise . . . something shall be done."

The Florentine colony ran wild with joy. Charles V kept his word; he was so deeply stirred by his visit to the new sacristy that he ordered the wedding ceremonies of his daughter Margaret to Alessandro to be held in Michelangelo's chapel. The prospect made Michelangelo so ill he could not work. He walked in the *campagna* along the tomb-lined Via Appia, revulsion sweeping over him as he tried to vomit forth the noxious nature of the existing world.

The marriage proved to be short-lived; Alessandro was murdered in a house next to the Medici palace by a Popolano cousin, Lorenzino, when he thought he was keeping a tryst with Lorenzino's chaste sister. Florence was freed of its rapacious tyrant; but not Michelangelo. Alessandro's body, loathsome to all of Tuscany, was clandestinely dumped in the dark of night into the chastely sculptured sarcophagus under Dawn and Dusk.

"All Florentines are rid of Alessandro . . . except me," he said to Urbino morosely. "Now you see what a marble carver is good for: to provide tombs for tyrants."

Revulsion passes, as joy does. Each bad blow kept him out of the Sistine for a week or two. Such good news as the marriage of his niece, Cecca, to the son of the famous Florentine historian, Guicciardini, or the election of Vittoria Colonna's father confessor and teacher, Reginald Pole, to the cardinalate, which gave a strong boost to the reform faction, sent him back renewed to paint the compact group of saints pictorially beyond Christ's wrath: Catherine, with part of a wheel, Sebastiano, with a handful of arrows, attenuated forms wafting upward in the firmament, glorious female figures among the intermeshed maze of males. He used his spare energies to propitiate the still outraged Duke of Urbino by making a model of a bronze horse for him, as well as a richly decorated salt cellar. He took comfort from the fact that Cosimo de' Medici, a descendant of the Popolano branch of the Medici, a humble, decent seventeen-year-old, was in the Medici palace, and many of the exiles were returning home, the young sons of his friends coming to bid him an affectionate *A rivederci.*

He was shattered when the malign fates which had begun the enveloping of Florence since the untimely death of Lorenzo, *Il Magnifico,* moved on inexorably to inflict a culminating tragedy: Cosimo, though well behaved morally, was developing into a tyrant reducing the newly elected councils to impotence. The young men of Florence organized an army, bought arms, appealed to Francis I of France to lend them troops to defeat Cosimo's supporters. Charles V did not want a republic; he loaned his army to Cosimo, who crushed the uprising. The leaders were executed, hundreds of the finest minds and spirits of Tuscany, with every family suffering severe losses: Filippo Strozzi run through with a sword, his son killed; Baccio Valori and his son put to death; a dozen more of the young exiles who had thronged his studio, who had been bold and eager to return and fight for their city-state, dead, dead in the beauty and glory of their youth.

"What was their sin?" Michelangelo cried. "For what were they judged, that they had to be murdered in cold blood? What kind of jungle do we live in that such brutal, senseless crime can be committed with impunity?"

How right he had been to put up on that wall a fierce and wrathful Jesus on Judgment Day!

He redrew the lower right-hand corner of his cartoon, opposite the dead arising from their graves on the left; and for the first time pictured a group already condemned, being driven by Charon into the mouth of hell. Now man seemed just another form of animal life cropping his way along the surface of the earth. Was he possessed of an immortal soul? Precious little good it had done him: it was just another appendage he was going to have to carry down to the inferno with him. Perhaps this soul would help him to climb back up to purgatory, and eventually even to paradise. At the moment he would have said, "Permit me to doubt" . . . for Vittoria Colonna too had come into troubled times.

Giovanni Pietro Caraffa, long suspicious of her activities as an inquirer into new doctrines and a challenger of the faith, had been elected a cardinal. A religious fanatic, Cardinal Caraffa began his efforts to bring the Inquisition into Italy to wipe out the heretics, the freethinkers, the unbelievers . . . and in the case of Vittoria Colonna, those who were working from outside the Church to oblige the Church to reform itself from within. He made it plain that he considered her, and the little group around her, dangerous. Though they rarely had more than eight or nine at their meetings, there was an informer in their midst; Cardinal Caraffa had a complete record by Monday morning of the Sunday afternoon discussions.

"What will this mean to you?" Michelangelo asked Vittoria anxiously.

"Nothing, so long as some of the cardinals are in favor of reform."

"But if Caraffa gains control?"

"Exile."

Michelangelo was shocked. He stared at her alabaster face, himself turning pale. "Should you not be careful?"

The thought had made his voice harsh. Was he asking it for her, or for himself? She knew how important her presence in Rome was to him.

"It would do no good. I might issue the same warning to you." Her voice too seemed sharp. Was she asking it for herself, for him? Had she not shown him that she wanted him near? "Caraffa does not like what you are painting in the Sistine."

"How could he know? I keep it locked."

"The same way he knows what we say here."

Though he had allowed no one but Urbino, Tommaso and the Cardinals Niccolò and Giovanni Salviati into his studio since he had begun blowing up his cartoon, and not a solitary soul but Urbino into the Sistine, Cardinal Caraffa was not the only one who knew what he was putting on the wall. Letters began to arrive from all over Italy, commenting on it. The strangest came from Pietro Aretino, whom Michelangelo knew by reputation as a gifted writer and unscrupulous wretch who lived by blackmail, obtaining the most astounding favors and sums of money, even from princes and cardinals, by showing them how much damage he could do by flooding Europe with evil letters about them, couched in such vivid and witty terms that the courts of Europe repeated his slanders as amusing anecdotes. Sometimes cast down by his greed and concupiscence into poverty and disgrace, he was at the moment a man of importance in Venice, intimate friend of Titian and consort of kings.

The purpose of Aretino's letter was to tell Michelangelo exactly how he should paint the Last Judgment:

I see in the crowd the Antichrist with features which you alone could imagine: I see terror on the countenances of the living. I see the signs of the extinction of the sun, moon and stars; I see the elements melt and disappear, and I see exhausted Nature become sterile. . . . I see life and death scared by the fearful anarchy. . . . I see the arrowy flight of the words of judgment, issuing from the mouth of the Son of God, amidst tremendous thunderings. . . .

Aretino ended his long letter with the comment that, although he had vowed never to return to Rome, his resolve was broken by the desire to pay honor to Michelangelo's genius. Michelangelo answered satirically, thinking to rid himself of the interloper:

Do not change your decision not to come to Rome just for the sake of seeing my work. That would be asking too much! When I received your letter I rejoiced; yet I grieved at the same time because, since I have completed a large section of my story, I cannot put to use your conception.

Aretino began a barrage of letters which importuned drawings, sections of cartoons, models: "Does not my devotion deserve that I should receive from you, the prince of sculpture and of painting, one of those cartoons which you fling into the fire?" He even sent missives to Michelangelo's friends, to young Vasari whom he had known in Venice, and others who frequented the studio on the Macello dei Corvi, determined to have their help in getting some of the sketches which he could then sell. Michelangelo answered evasively, grew bored and ignored Aretino completely.

It was an error: Aretino saved his venom until the Last Judgment was completed, then struck with two inky ejaculations, one of which almost destroyed his five years of painting, the second, his character.

7

Now time and space became identical. He could not swear how many days, weeks, months passed as 1537 gave way to 1538, but before him on the altar wall he could tell precisely how many figures he had floating upward through the lower cloud levels to the rocky crags on either side of the Madonna and Son. Christ with his arm raised above his head in outraged denunciation was not here to listen to special pleading. No good for sinners to cry for mercy. The wicked were already damned, and terror was in the air.

Yet never were the forms of the human body more lovingly and pulsatingly portrayed. How could so mean a spirit live in so noble a castle? Why was the flesh so much more perfect in structure, power, beauty, than anything these frightened mortals had been able to accomplish with their minds and souls?

Each morning Urbino laid the needed field of intonaco; by nightfall Michelangelo had filled it with a body tumbling downward toward hell, or the portraits of the now elderly Eve and Adam. Urbino had become as expert as Rosselli at joining each new day's plaster so that the lines could not be seen. Each day at noon he had the woman servant, Caterina, bring hot food which he reheated on a brazier on the scaffold before serving Michelangelo.

"Mangiate bene, eat well. You need your strength. It is a *torta,* like your stepmother used to bake, chicken fried in oil and ground into sausage with onions, parsley, eggs and saffron.''

''Urbino, you know I'm too wrought up to eat in the middle of a day's work.''

''. . . and too tired to eat at the end of one. Look what I have here, a salad that sings in the mouth.''

Michelangelo chuckled. To indulge Urbino, he ate, and was surprised at how good it was, how like *Il Migliore's.* Urbino was pleased with the success of his stratagem.

When Michelangelo began to falter, after months of intensive work, it was Urbino who made him stay at home, rest, divert himself by massing the blocks for the Prophet, Sibyl and Virgin for the Roveres. When the Duke of Urbino died, Michelangelo was immensely relieved even though he knew he would have to confess the sin of rejoicing over another man's death. Before long the new Duke of Urbino arrived at the studio on the Macello dei Corvi. Michelangelo took one look at him standing in the doorway in his father's face.

"Dio mio," he thought, ''I inherit the sons of my enemies as well as my friends.''

But he was wrong about the young duke.

''I have come to put an end to the strife,'' he said quietly. ''I have never agreed with my father that your failure to complete my granduncle's tomb was totally your fault.''

''You mean that I can now call the Duke of Urbino my friend?''

''And admirer. I often told my father if you had been allowed to continue your work you would have completed that tomb even as you did the Sistine Chapel and the Medici chapel. You shall be harassed no more.''

Michelangelo sank into a chair. ''My son, do you know from what you have just delivered me . . . ?''

"But by the same token," continued the young man, "you will readily understand our earnest wish to see you finish the holy monument to my uncle, Pope Julius. Because of the reverence we bear Pope Paul, we shall not interrupt you while you are completing your fresco; but, being finished, we ask that you give yourself to the monument, doubling your diligence to remedy the loss of time."

"With all my heart! You shall have your tomb!"

During the long winter nights he made drawings for Vittoria: a Holy Family, a Pietà, exquisitely conceived; while she returned his feelings by presenting him with a first copy of her published poems, *Rime*. For Michelangelo, desiring to pour out the whole of his passion, it was an incomplete relationship, yet his love for her, and his conviction that she felt deeply for him, kept his creative powers at the flood while he painted husky *contadini* angels on a floating bastion several clouds below Christ, blowing their trumpets with such hell-let-loose loudness that all the dead below would hear and rise from their graves.

His brothers, his nephew Lionardo and his niece Cecca kept him posted on family afairs. Lionardo, approaching twenty, was showing the first profit at the family wool shop. Cecca presented him with a new nephew each year. Occasionally he had to write irritated letters to Florence, as when he received no acknowledgment of money sent, or when Giovansimone and Sigismondo quarreled over who should get how much wheat from which farm; or Lionardo, requested to send him some fine Florentine shirts, chose three which proved to be "so coarse a peasant couldn't wear them."

When Lionardo sent good pears or *trebbiano* wine, Michelangelo took a portion to the Vatican to give to Pope Paul as a present. They had become fast friends. If a long period went by without Michelangelo's visiting him, Paul summoned him from his work to come to the throne room, asking in an injured tone:

"Michelangelo, why do you never come to see me?"

"Holy Father, you do not need my presence here. I believe that I serve you better by remaining at work than do others who stand before you all day."

"The painter Passenti presents himself here every day."

"Passenti has an ordinary talent that can be found without a lantern in the market places of the world."

Paul was proving to be a good Pope; he appointed honorable and able men as cardinals, was dedicated to reform within the Church. Though he found it necessary to pose the authority of the Church against Charles's military power, he brought neither wars nor invasions down upon himself. He was devoted to the arts and learning. Nevertheless his heritage from the Borgia regime held over, making him a target for attack. As sentimentally attached to his sons and grandsons as the Borgia Pope had been to Caesar and Lucrezia, there was almost no piece of chicanery he considered despicable if it helped found the fortune of his son Pier Luigi, for whom he was determined to carve out a duchy. He appointed his fourteen-year-old grandson, Alessandro Farnese, a cardinal, and another young grandson he married to Charles V's daughter, the widow of Alessandro de' Medici, creating a place for him by taking the Duchy of Camerino away from the Duke of Urbino. Because of these acts his enemies called him base and ruthless.

By the end of 1540, when Michelangelo had completed the upper two thirds of the fresco, he hired the carpenter Ludovico to lower the scaffolding. Pope Paul heard the news, arrived at the locked Sistine door unannounced. He had given up the use of his personal chapel so that Michelangelo might have his privacy. Urbino, who answered the banging on the door, could not refuse to admit the pontiff.

Michelangelo came down from the new, low scaffold, greeted Pope Paul and his Master of Ceremonies, Biagio da Cesena, with cordial words. The Pope stood facing the Last Judgment, walked stiffly toward the wall without removing his eyes. When he reached the altar he sank to his knees and prayed.

Not so Biagio da Cesena, who stood glaring up at the fresco. Paul rose to his feet, made the sign of the cross over Michelangelo and then the Last Judgment. There were tears of pride and humility on his cheeks.

"My son, you have created a glory for my reign."

"It is disgraceful . . . !" spat out Biagio da Cesena.

Pope Paul was astounded.

"And totally immoral! I cannot tell the saints from the sinners. There are only hundreds of nudes showing their private parts. It is shameful."

"You think the human body shameful?" asked Michelangelo.

"In a *bagno*, bath, no. But in the Pope's chapel! *Scandaloso!"*

"Only if you wish to create a scandal, Biagio," replied Paul firmly. "On Judgment Day we shall all stand naked before the Lord. My son, how do I express my overwhelming gratitude?"

Michelangelo turned to the Master of Ceremonies with a conciliatory gesture, for he wanted to make no enemies for his fresco. Biagio da Cesena broke in roughly.

"One day this sacrilegious wall will be annihilated, even as you destroyed the beautiful Peruginos beneath it."

"Not while I live," cried Pope Paul, furious. "I will excommunicate anyone who dares touch this masterpiece!"

They left the chapel. Michelangelo stood rubbing a sorely painful area under his left breast. He asked Urbino to mix some intonaco and lay it on the blank spot on the extreme lower right-hand corner of the wall. This done, he painted a caricature of Biagio da Cesena, representing him as the judge of the shades of Hades, with the ears of an ass, and a monstrous snake coiled around the lower part of the torso: a lethal likeness, the pointed nose, lips drawn back over buck teeth. It was a poor revenge, he knew, but what other was open to an artist?

Word leaked out somehow. Biagio da Cesena demanded a second meeting before the fresco.

"You see, Holy Father," cried the Master of Ceremonies, "the report was true. Buonarroti has painted me into the fresco. With some kind of repulsive serpent for my genitalia."

"It's a covering," replied Michelangelo. "I knew you would not want to be portrayed wholly naked."

"A remarkable likeness," observed the Pope, his eyes twinkling. "Michelangelo, I thought you said you could not do portraiture?"

"I was inspired, Holiness."

Biagio da Cesena hopped up and down on either foot as though it were he instead of his picture standing over the fires of hell.

"Holiness, make him take me out of there!"

"Out of hell?" the Pope turned surprised eyes on the man. "Had he placed you in purgatory, I should have done everything in my power to release you. But you know that from hell there is no redemption."

The following day Michelangelo learned that no one ever got the last laugh. He was on the lowered scaffolding painting Charon with the protruding eyes and horns for ears, whipping the damned out of his boat and into the fiery depths, when he felt dizzy, tried to grasp a support rail, fell to the marble floor. There was a moment of excruciating pain. He revived to find Urbino splashing cold, sandy water from the bucket onto his face.

"Thanks to God, you're conscious. How badly are you hurt? Is anything broken?"

"How would I know? If I'm so stupid, I should have broken every bone in my body. For five years I work on this scaffold, and at the very end I fall off."

"Your leg is bleeding where it struck this piece of lumber. I will find a carriage."

"You'll find nothing of the sort. Nobody is going to know what an idiot I am. Help me up. Now put an arm under my shoulder. I can ride the horse home."

Urbino put him to bed, pressed a glass of *trebbiano* to his lips, then washed out the wound. When he wanted to go for a doctor Michelangelo stopped him.

"No doctor. I'd be the laughingstock of Rome. Bolt that front door."

Despite all that Urbino could do by way of hot towels and bandaging, the wound began to fester. Michelangelo developed a fever, Urbino was frightened and sent word to Tommaso.

"If I let you die . . . ."

"The thought has its compensations, Urbino. I wouldn't have to go climbing scaffolds any more."

"How can you tell? Perhaps in hell a man has to do forever the thing he most hated to do in life?"

Tommaso went for Dr. Baccio Rontini. When Michelangelo refused to allow them to enter the front door they forced a back door of the house. Dr. Rontini was irate.

"For sheer perverse idiocy, no one can rival a Florentine." He probed the infected wound. "Another day or two . . . ."

It took a week to get him back on his feet; he felt like a bag of meal. Urbino helped him up the scaffolding, laid a patch of intonaco in the sky just below St. Bartholomew. Michelangelo painted a caricature of his own drained, woebegone face and head, suspended in the middle of an empty skin, and held aloft by the hand of the saint.

"Now Biagio da Cesena doesn't have to feel too badly," he observed to Urbino as he gazed at his empty, hanging carcass. "We've both been judged, and recorded."

He painted the bottom third of the wall, the simplest part since there were fewer figures: the symbolic graveyards and hell, with the long dead rising from their tombs, one of them a skeleton trying to join those in the sky; and the too long alive, being driven into the fires.

It was at this moment that Vittoria's troubles came to a crisis. The most influential and talented of women, praised by the great Ariosto for her poetry, by the Pope for her saintliness; the closest friend of Emperor Charles V in Rome, a member of the wealthy Colonnas, and the D'Avalos by marriage, she was nonetheless about to be driven into exile by Cardinal Caraffa. It seemed impossible that a woman of such high position could be so persecuted.

Michelangelo called on Cardinal Niccolò at the Medici palace to ask for help. Niccolò tried to reassure him.

"Everyone in Rome now acknowledges the need for reform. My uncles Leo and Clement were too highhanded, they tried to bring the dissenters back by disciplining them. But Paul is sending the marchesa's friend, Cardinal Contarini, to negotiate with the Lutherans and Calvinists. I think we shall succeed in time."

Cardinal Contarini was on the verge of a brilliant success at the Diet of Ratisbon when Cardinal Caraffa had him recalled, accused him of collusion with Emperor Charles V, and had him exiled to Bologna.

Vittoria sent Michelangelo a message; could he come at once? She wished to say "Farewell."

It was an intoxicating April day, the buds bursting forth in the Colonna gardens, the wild scents of spring enclosed within the walls. Michelangelo had expected to find her alone for so personal a moment, but the garden was full of people. She rose, greeting him with a somber smile. She was dressed in black, a black mantilla covering the golden hair; her face seemed carved out of Pietrasanta statuary marble. He went close to her.

"It was good of you to come, Michelangelo."

"Let us not waste time on the formalities. You have been exiled?"

"I have been given to understand that it would be advisable to leave Rome."

"Where are you going?"

"To Viterbo. I lived in the convent of St. Catherine there. I consider it one of my homes."

"When will I see you again?"

"When God wills."

They stood in silence, probing deep into each other's eyes, trying to communicate.

"I'm sorry, Michelangelo, that I shall not be able to see your Last Judgment."

"You will see it. When do you leave?"

"In the morning. You will write to me?"

"I will write, and send you drawings."

"I will answer, and send you poems."

He turned abruptly and left the garden; locked himself in the studio of his house, bereft. It was dark by the time he roused himself from his torpor and asked Urbino to light him to the Sistine. In the Florentine district oil lamps were glowing in the windows of the houses. The Castel Sant'Angelo loomed up at the other end of the bridge like a cylindrically carved stone mountain. Urbino unlocked the Sistine door, went ahead with the taper to let warm wax drip onto the scaffolding and make a base for the two candles he was carrying.

The Last Judgment sprang cyclonically to life in the flickering half-world of the chapel. Judgment Day became Judgment Night. The three hundred men, women, children, saints, angels and demons, many of whom had been submerged in the full light of day, pressed forward to be recognized and to play out their portentous drama in the open spaces of the chapel itself.

Something drew his attention to the ceiling. Looking upward, he saw God creating the universe. Lines from Genesis came into his mind:

> The earth yielded grasses that grew and seeded, each according to its kind, and trees that bore fruit, each with the power to propagate its own kind. And God saw it, and found it good.
>
> God made the two great luminaries, the greater of them to command the day, and the lesser to command the night; then he made the stars. All these he put in the vault of the sky, to shed their light on the earth, to control day and night, and divide the spheres of light and darkness. And God saw it, and found it good.
>
> So God made man in his own image, made him in the image of God. Man and woman both, he created them.
>
> And God saw all that he had made, and found it very good.

Michelangelo turned his attention back to his painting on the altar wall. He saw all that he had made, and he found it very good.

BOOK ELEVEN

THE DOME

On All Saints' Eve, exactly twenty-nine years after Pope Julius had consecrated the ceiling with a special ceremony, Pope Paul said high mass to celebrate the completion of the Last Judgment.

On Christmas Day, 1541, the chapel was thrown open to the public. Rome streamed through the Sistine, terrified, shocked, awe-stricken. The studio in the Macello dei Corvi was thronged with Florentines, cardinals, courtiers, artists and apprentices. When the last of the guests had disappeared Michelangelo realized that two groups had not been represented: Antonio da Sangallo and the artists and architects who centered around him, remnants of the Bramante-Raphael coterie; and Cardinal Caraffa and his followers.

Very soon war was declared. An unfrocked monk, Bernardino Ochino, censured Pope Paul by demanding:

"How can Your Holiness allow such an obscene painting as that of Michelangelo's to remain in a chapel where the divine office is sung?"

But when Michelangelo returned to the Sistine the following day he found half a dozen artists sitting on low stools sketching and copying. The Pope rallied to his support by asking him to fresco two virtually twenty-foot-square walls of the chapel named after him, the Pauline, designed and recently completed by Antonio da Sangallo between the Sistine and St. Peter's. The chapel was ponderously topheavy, the two overhead windows affording insufficient light, but the walls were attractively set off by reddish Corinthian pillars. Pope Paul wanted a Conversion of Paul on one wall, a Crucifixion of Peter on the opposite.

While thinking through the imagery of the Conversion, Michelangelo spent his days with hammer and chisel. He sculptured a head of Brutus, which the Florentine colony had been urging. He articulated the thick curls on Moses' head, carving at the forefront the two horns, or rays of light, which the Old Testament attributed to Moses. With the heat of midsummer, he moved two marbles out to the bricked garden terrace from which to carve a Rachel and a Leah, Contemplative and Active Life, for the two niches alongside the Moses; niches which, in his redesigning of Julius' single-wall tomb, had become too small to hold the Heroic Captive and Dying Captive. He finished the sketches for the Virgin, Prophet and Sibyl which would complete the monument, then sent for Raffaello da Montelupo, who had carved the St. Damian for the Medici chapel, to sculpture them. With the two Captives no longer part of the design, and the four unfinished Giants and Victory still in Florence, it was Ercole Gonzaga who was proving to be the prophet. The Moses alone would be the majesty of Julius' tomb, and represent his best carving. Was it, as the Cardinal of Mantua had said, "sufficient monument for any man"?

Michelangelo wondered what Jacopo Galli would have said about his finishing the tomb with only one major work of the original forty he had contracted for.

He decided that Urbino had earned his independence.

"Urbino, you're past thirty now, and it's time you began making money for yourself. The Pope has agreed to pay you eight ducats a month for grinding the colors when I paint his chapel. Would you like also to contract for the construction of the tomb wall?"

"Yes, *messere*, for I must begin putting away money against my marriage. The family that bought my parental home in Urbino, they have a little girl . . . in about ten years she will make a good wife. . . ."

He sorely missed Vittoria Colonna. In the deep of night he wrote her long letters, frequently sending a sonnet or a drawing. At first Vittoria replied promptly, but as his letters became more urgent she answered less frequently. To his anguished cry of "Why?" she replied:

> Magnificent Messer Michelangelo:
>   I did not reply earlier to your letter, because it was, as one might say, an answer to my last: for I thought that if I and you were to go on writing without intermission, according to my obligation and your courtesy, I should have to neglect the chapel of St. Catherine here, and be absent at the appointed hours for company with my sisterhood, while you would have to leave the chapel of St. Paul and be absent from morning through the day. . . . Thus we should both of us fail in our duty.

He felt crushed, chagrined, as though he were a small boy who had been reproved. He continued to write passionate poems to her . . . but did not send them, contenting himself with scraps of news brought by travelers from Viterbo. When he learned that she was ill and rarely left her room, his sense of mortification turned to anxiety. Did she have good medical attention? Was she taking proper care of herself?

He was depleted, tired, at loose ends; yet all the loose ends had to be tied together securely. He laid a new plaster wall in the Pauline chapel; deposited fourteen hundred ducats in the bank of Montauto to be paid out to Urbino and Raffaelo da Montelupo as they made progress with the tomb. He drew a modest design for the Conversion of Paul, with some fifty figures and an additional number of faces surrounding Paul as he lay on the ground, having been struck by a shaft of yellow light coming down from heaven, the first New Testament miracle he had ever painted. He carved the Rachel and Leah, two tender, lovely young women, heavily swathed in robes, symbolic figures; and for the first time since the Piccolomini statues he was carving marbles in which he had no genuine interest. They appeared to him watered down in emotional intensity, without the throbbing, self-contained core of energy to grip and dominate the space about them.

His studio and garden had been turned into a busy workshop, with half a dozen young people helping Urbino and Raffaelo da Montelupo to finish the tomb. He was delighted to find a number of the Jews of Rome, some of whom reported that they were sons or grandsons of the men who had posed for his first Pietà, asking permission to come to the studio to see the Moses. They stood before their great teacher caught between pride and wonder, their lips silently murmuring something which Michelangelo knew could not be prayers, since the Ten Commandments forbade it.

The present and future had shape for him only in terms of work to be done. How many more works of art could he live? The Conversion of St. Paul would take so many years, the Crucifixion of St. Peter so many more. Better to count the projects ahead than the days; then he would not tick off the years one by one as though they were coins he was counting into the hands of a wary merchant. Simpler to think of time as creativity: the two Pauline frescoes, then a Descent from the Cross he wanted to carve for his own pleasure from the last of his magnificent Carrara blocks . . . God would not be inclined to interrupt an artist in the midst of begetting.

He consumed time as smoothly as he drank a cup of water: a few days represented a servant trying to restrain Paul's frightened horse; a week involved a wingless angel, a month conceived Paul, stricken by the light from Christ's hand; a year meant the massing of figures on one side of Paul, soldiers and companions, some terrorized, some trying to flee, some gazing upward in their consternation. What better way to tell time than through the body of content?

A Committee of Inquisition had been established in Rome. Cardinal Caraffa, who had lived a morally upright life as a priest in the corrupt court of the Borgia Pope, Alexander VI, had attracted power against the will and wishes of those who served him. Though he boasted that he never made himself agreeable to anyone, that he turned away roughly everyone who asked favors; though he was choleric in temperament and painfully thin of face and body, his burning zeal for the dogma of the Church was making him the most influential leader of the College of Cardinals; respected, feared and obeyed. His Committee of Inquisition had already established an Index which said what books could be printed and read.

Vittoria Colonna returned to Rome and entered the convent of San Silvestro in Capite near the Pantheon. Michelangelo did not think she should have left the safety of Viterbo. He pressed for a meeting. Vittoria refused. He accused her of cruelty; she replied that it was a kindness. Finally, from sheer persistence, he gained her assent . . . only to find that her strength and her beauty had been ravaged. Her illness and the pressure of the accusations against her had aged her twenty years. She had passed from a lovely, robust, vibrant woman to one whose face was lined, lips dry and pale, the green eyes sunk in their sockets, the rich copper gone from her hair. She was sitting alone in the convent garden, her hands folded in her lap, her head veiled. He was overcome.

"I tried to save you from this," she murmured.

"You think my love so shallow?"

"Even in your kindness there is a cruel revelation."

"Life is cruel, never love."

"Love is the cruelest of all. I know . . ."

"You know only a fragment," he interrupted. "Why have you kept us apart? And why have you returned to this dangerous atmosphere?"

"I must make my peace with the Church, find forgiveness for my sins against her."

"Sins?"

"Yes. I disobeyed, indulged my own vain opinions against the divine doctrine, harbored dissenters. . . ."

His throat locked. Another echo from the past. He remembered the anguish with which he had listened to the dying Lorenzo de' Medici pleading for absolution from Savonarola, the man who had destroyed his Plato Academy. He heard again his brother Lionardo's disavowal of Savonarola's disobedience to the Borgia Pope. Was there no unity between living and dying?

"My last desire is to die in grace," Vittoria was saying, quietly. "I must return to the bosom of the Church, like a child to the bosom of its mother. Only there can I find redemption."

"Your illness has done this to you," he cried. "The Inquisition has tortured you."

"I have tortured myself, inside my own mind. Michelangelo, I worship you as God-given among men. But you too, before your death, will have to seek salvation."

He listened to the noise of the bees as they buzzed in the cups of the flowers. His heart ached for her despair. They were still alive on the face of the earth. She spoke as though they were already dead. He said:

"My feelings for you, which you would never allow me to express, have not changed. Did you think I was a young boy who had fallen in love with a pretty *contadina?* Do you not know how great a place you occupy in my mind . . . ?"

Tears flooded her eyes. She began breathing rapidly.

"Thank you, *caro*," she whispered. "You have healed wounds that go . . . very far back."

And she was gone into a side door of the convent, leaving him on the stone bench which suddenly was cold beneath him, in a garden cold about him.

2

When Antonio da Sangallo began pouring his foundations for the ring of chapels on the south side of the tribune of St. Peter's, the long smoldering feud between them became full-blown. According to Michelangelo's measurements, the corresponding wing to the north, toward the Papal palace, would of necessity replace the Pauline chapel and part of the Sistine.

"I simply cannot believe my eyes," cried Pope Paul when Michelangelo drew him a plan of what was going on. "Why would Sangallo want to tear down a chapel he designed and built himself?"

"His plans for St. Peter's keep expanding."

"How much of the Sistine would his chapels replace?"

"Approximately the area covered by the Deluge, the Drunkenness of Noah, the Delphic Sibyl and Zacharias. God would survive."

"How fortunate for Him," murmured Paul.

The Pope suspended work on St. Peter's on the grounds that there was insufficient money to continue. But Sangallo knew that Michelangelo was the cause. Sangallo did not attack directly. He entrusted this to his assistant, Nanni di Baccio Bigio, with a long tradition of hostility to Michelangelo absorbed from his father, who had been excluded from the architectural work on the abortive façade of San Lorenzo, and from his long-time Florentine friend, Baccio Bandinelli, Michelangelo's most vocal opponent in Tuscany. Baccio Bigio, who aspired to succeed Sangallo as the architect of St. Peter's, had an inexhaustible set of vocal cords which he now employed in a retaliatory attack on the Last Judgment as giving comfort to the enemies of the Church and causing converts to Luther. Sangallo and Bigio succeeded in getting a statement issued through Cardinal Caraffa that all works of art, like all books, must first be approved by his committee.

Yet travelers coming into the Sistine fell on their knees before the fresco, even as Paul Ill had, repenting of their sins; such a dissolute poet as Molza of Modena underwent conversion. Michelangelo grumbled to Tommaso:

"When it comes to me, there is no middle ground. I am either the master or the monster of the world. The Sangallo crowd have formed an image of me out of the stuff of which their own hearts are made."

"Mice," replied Tommaso reassuringly, "trying to undermine the Great Wall of China."

"More like flies," retorted Michelangelo; "they bite deep enough to draw blood."

"You have blood to spare."

Bindo Altoviti, who had served on the last Florentine Council and was a leader of the exiles in Rome, chose this moment to declare at court that Michelangelo's defense walls of San Miniato had been "a work of art." Pope Paul sent for Michelangelo to join a conference on the defenses of the Vatican with the already appointed commission. His son Pier Luigi was president, Antonio da Sangallo architect; it included Alessandro Vitelli, an officer experienced in warfare, and Montemellino, an artillery officer and engineer.

Sangallo glared. Michelangelo kissed the Pope's ring, was introduced to the others. The Pope pointed to Sangallo's model, said:

"Michelangelo, we seek your opinion. We have a serious problem here, since our defenses proved so inadequate against Charles V."

A week later, having studied the terrain, Michelangelo was back in the Pope's study. The commission assembled to hear his verdict.

"Holiness, I have spent the days analyzing approaches to the Vatican. My opinion is that Sangallo's walls could not be defended."

Sangallo jumped to his feet.

"Why can't they be defended?"

"Because they are drawn to protect too large an area. Some of your positions in the hills behind us, and the walls going to Trastevere along the Tiber, could be breached."

"May I remind you," replied Sangallo, coldly sarcastic, "that people call you a painter and sculptor?"

"My bastions in Florence were never breached."

"They were never attacked."

"The Emperor's armies respected them too much to attack."

"And on the basis of one small wall at San Miniato you are an expert who will replace my fortifications!" shouted Sangallo.

"That will do," said Pope Paul sternly. "The meeting is adjourned."

Michelangelo left behind him his criticism of Sangallo's plan, along with detailed drawings to show what alterations should be made to give the Leonine City, or Vatican area, adequate protection. Pier Luigi Farnese and Montemellino agreed with the analysis. The Pope permitted a few of Sangallo's curtain walls to the river to be completed, as well as his lovely Doric gateway. The rest of the work was suspended. Michelangelo was appointed consulting architect to the defense commission, not to succeed Sangallo but to work alongside him.

The next foray came when Sangallo submitted his design for the third-floor windows and cornice of the Farnese palace which he had been building in sections over a long period of years for Cardinal Farnese before he became Pope Paul. Michelangelo had frequently seen the palace under construction, for it faced a piazza just a block from Leo Baglioni's house. He had thought the design ponderous, belonging to the fortresslike bastions of another age, with stubborn strength in its solid stone bulk but without the soaring beauty that such a formidable pile required to give it wings. Now Pope Paul asked Michelangelo to write him a candid criticism of the palace. Michelangelo marked a chapter in Vitruvius' book on architecture, sent it to the Vatican with Urbino, then wrote several blistering pages to prove that the Farnese palace had "no order of any kind; for order is a quaint suitability of the elements of the work separately and universally placed, coherently arranged." Neither did it have disposition, elegance, style, convenience, harmony, propriety or "a comfortable apportionment of places."

If designed brilliantly, he concluded, this top row of windows and cornice could be its saving grace.

As a result of his letter the Pope threw open to competition the design of the top floor and the decorative cornice. A number of artists, Giorgio Vasari, Pierino del Vaga, Sebastiano del Piombo and Jacopo Meleghino, announced that they were setting to work. And so did Michelangelo Buonarroti.

"It is beneath you to compete against the kind of artist one finds without a lantern in the market places of the world," protested Tommaso. "Suppose you were to lose? The humiliation would be a blow to your prestige."

"I won't lose, Tommaso."

His cornice was sculpture, carved and brilliantly decorated. The arches and slender columns of the windows gave the palace the elegance it needed to carry its ponderous body of stone.

Pope Paul studied the designs side by side on his breakfast table in the presence of Sangallo, Vasari, Sebastiano, Del Vaga. He looked up and announced:

"I wish to praise all of these drawings as ingenious and very beautiful. But surely you would agree that it is most true of the divine Michelangelo?"

Michelangelo had saved the Farnese palace from mediocrity and dullness, but gossip had it that he had done it to replace Sangallo as architect of St. Peter's; that now all he had to do was to walk into Pope Paul's throne room and announce that he wanted to take over the fabric.

"I shall do nothing of the sort," Michelangelo told Cardinal Niccolò at the Medici palace, when he had ridden there of a Sunday afternoon on his white Arabian stallion.

Cardinal Caraffa's Commission for the Inquisition began rewriting the classics and preventing new books from being printed. Michelangelo was astonished to find his poetry being regarded as serious literature, his sonnets on Dante, Beauty, Love, Sculpture, Art and the Artist being copied and passed from hand to hand. Some of his madrigals were set to music. Reports reached him of lectures being given about his poetry in the Plato Academy of Florence, and by the professors at the universities in Bologna, Pisa and Padua.

Urbino assembled the single-wall tomb of Pope Julius in San Pietro in Vincoli. He placed the Leah and Rachel in the lower niches, the Virgin, Prophet and Sibyl of Raffaello da Montelupo in the wall above. Michelangelo considered the monument a failure; but the Moses sitting in the central bay of the marble wall dominated the church with a power equaled only by that of God in the Genesis and Christ in the Last Judgment.

He set up an architectural office in a spare room of the house and put Tommaso de' Cavalieri in charge of the working drawings for the Farnese palace.

He completed the Conversion of St. Paul, Christ leaning downward from the sky, cleaving the heavens, with a multitude of wingless angels on either side of him. Paul, fallen from his horse, was dazed and terrified by the revelation, some of his company trying to raise him up, others fleeing in panic. The strong figure of the horse divided the two groups of travelers and soldiers on the ground, as Christ divided the angels above.

He had Urbino lay a fresh coat of intonaco for the Crucifixion of Peter. While it was drying he closed out the world, massing for the Descent, a Christ supported on one side by the Virgin, on the other by Mary Magdalene, and behind a portrait of himself as Nicodemus, who had helped take Christ down from the cross.

Reputations in Rome were made and broken in the time it took a man to crack a walnut. When Michelangelo refused to take advantage of his victory to force Sangallo out of St. Peter's, the city forgave him for criticizing the Farnese palace.

Then a letter arrived from Aretino, sent from Venice. Though he had never laid eyes on the man, Michelangelo had received a dozen letters from him during the past years, in which Aretino had coupled obsequious flattery with threats of destruction if Michelangelo continued to deny him a gift of drawings. He was about to throw this new epistle unopened into the fire when something wild in the way Aretino had splashed his name across its face arrested his attention. He broke the seal.

The letter began with an attack on the Last Judgment. It was too bad Michelangelo had not taken Aretino's advice to represent the world and paradise and hell with the glory, honor and terror sketched in his earlier letters. Instead "You, who are a Christian, you so subordinate belief to art that you have made the violation of modesty among martyrs and virgins into a spectacle, such as we should only venture to contemplate with half-averted eyes in houses of evil repute."

From there he went on to call Michelangelo "avaricious" for agreeing to build a tomb for an unworthy Pope, and then a fraud and a thief for having taken "the heaps of gold which Pope Julius bequeathed you," and given the Roveres nothing in return. "That is robbery!"

Repulsed but fascinated by the violent ranting and alternate begging tone of the long letter, Michelangelo then read: "It would certainly have been well if you had fulfilled your promise with due care, had it been only to silence the evil tongues who assert that only a Gherardo or a Tommaso know how to allure favors from you!"

Michelangelo was swept by a cold chill. What evil tongues? What favors? Drawings were his to give where he liked. They had not been "allured" from him.

He dropped the sheets from Aretino's pen, began to feel ill. In his seventy years he had been accused of many things, of being cantankerous, arrogant, unsociable, snobbishly unwilling to associate with any but those who had the greatest talent, intellect, excellence. But never had such an insinuation been made as this one. Gherardo was a former Florentine friend to whom he had given a few black chalk drawings more than twenty years ago. Tommaso de' Cavalieri was as noble a soul, as finely intelligent and well bred a person as there was in Italy! It was unbelievable. For fifty-odd years, since Argiento had come to him, he had taken apprentices, assistants and servants into his home; there had been at least thirty young men who had lived and worked with him, grown up with him in this traditional relationship. Never in his association with young art apprentices, starting with Ghirlandaio's *bottega*, had there been a word breathed against the propriety of his conduct. What a target for blackmail he would have been had he ever put himself at anyone's mercy!

The charge of blasphemy in his concept of the Last Judgment, the accusation that he had defrauded the Rovere family, could be simply fought. But to be confronted at this time of his life with this false imputation, a charge not unlike the one for which Leonardo da Vinci had been publicly prosecuted in Florence so long ago, seemed to him as devastating a blow as he had received in all his stormy years.

It did not take long for Aretino's poison to seep into Rome. A few days later Tommaso arrived with his face pale, his lips compressed. When Michelangelo insisted on knowing what was wrong he brushed the fingers of his right hand across the palm of his left, as though to rid his hands of offal.

"I heard last night," he said, more in sadness than anger, "from a bishop at court, about Aretino's letter."

Michelangelo slumped into a chair.

"How does one deal with such a creature?" he asked hoarsely.

"One doesn't. One accedes to his demands. That's how he has prospered in the world."

"I'm sorry, Tommaso. I never meant to cause you embarrassment."

"It is you I am worried about, Michelangelo, not myself. My family and companions know me well; they will scoff at this canard and ignore it. . . . But you, my dear friend, are revered all over Europe. It is you that Aretino means to hurt, your work and position. . . . The last thing in the world I want is to hurt you."

"You could never hurt me, Tomao. Your love and admiration fed me. With Marchesa Vittoria ill, it is the only love I can count on to sustain me. I also will ignore Aretino. As one should all blackmailers. If he can destroy our friendship he will already have achieved some part of his purpose of inflicting injury on me."

"Rome's tongue would rather wag over a fresh scandal than a *scaloppina*," warned Tommaso.

"Let us continue with our lives and our work. That is the proper answer to scandalmongers."

3

In his drawings for the Crucifixion of St. Peter he struck out boldly to find a new expression for painting. In the center of the design he pictured a hole being dug to hold the heavy cross. Peter was nailed to it, upside down, while it lay angled across a giant boulder. Unharmed as yet by his impaling, Peter glared out at the world, his elderly bearded face fiercely eloquent in its condemnation not merely of the soldiers about him who were directing the crucifixion, or of the laborers who were helping to raise the cross upward, but of the entire world beyond: an indictment of tyranny and cruelty as piercing as that of the Last Judgment.

As he was completing the sketch of the two Roman centurions and wishing he could draw their horses with the genius that Leonardo da Vinci had had with them, church bells started tolling mournfully over the city. His servant woman burst into the studio, crying:

"*Messere*, Sangallo is dead!"

". . . dead? He has been building in Terni. . . ."

"He caught the malaria. They just brought his body back."

Pope Paul gave Antonio da Sangallo a spectacular funeral. His coffin was carried through the streets with great pomp, followed by the artists and craftsmen who had worked with him over the years. In church, Michelangelo stood with Tommaso and Urbino listening to the eulogizing of Sangallo as one of the greatest architects since the ancients who had built Rome. Walking home, Michelangelo commented:

"That eulogy is word for word the one I heard for Bramante; yet Pope Leo had stopped all of Bramante's work, just as Pope Paul had halted Sangallo's on the Faraese palace, the defense walls . . . St. Peter's . . ."

Tommaso stopped in his tracks, turned to look sharply at Michelangelo. "Do you think . . . ?"

"Oh no, Tommaso!"

The superintendent of the fabric suggested that Giulio Romano, sculptor and architect, disciple of Raphael, be called from Mantua and appointed architect of St. Peter's. Pope Paul cried:

"It shall be Michelangelo Buonarroti. None else!"

Michelangelo was summoned by a groom, rode his stallion to the Vatican. The Pope was surrounded by a contingent of his cardinals and courtiers.

"My son, I am herewith appointing you architect of St. Peter's."

"Holiness, I cannot assume the post."

There was a twinkle in Paul's fading but still shrewdly discerning eyes.

"Are you going to tell me that architecture is not your trade?"

Michelangelo flushed. He had forgotten that Pope Paul, then the Cardinal Farnese, had been in this same throne room when Julius commissioned him to decorate the Sistine vault, and he had cried in anguish, "It is not my trade."

"Holy Father, I might have to tear down everything Sangallo has built, dismiss Sangallo's contractors. Rome would be solidly against me. I have the Crucifixion of St. Peter to complete. I am over seventy years old. Where will I find the vital force to build from the ground up the mightiest church in Christendom? . . . I am not Abraham, Holy Father, who lived one hundred and seventy-five years. . . ."

Pope Paul was singularly unaffected by Michelangelo's tale of woe. His eyes gleamed.

"My son, you are but a youth. When you reach my august age of seventy-eight you will be allowed to speak of your years. Not before! By that time you will have St. Peter's well on its way."

Michelangelo's smile was on the wan side.

He left the Vatican grounds by the Belvedere gate, made the long climb to the top of Monte Mario, and after resting and watching the sunset, descended the opposite side of St. Peter's. The workmen had gone home. He went over Sangallo's foundations, the lower walls for the ring of chapels extending to the south. The numerous and heavy piers, on which Sangallo had meant to build a nave and two aisles, would have to be leveled. The huge cement bases for the two steeples, or bell towers, would have to go, as would the supports being built for the heavy dome.

His tour of inspection ended just as night closed down. Finding himself in front of the chapel of Mary of the Fever, he went in and stood in the dark before his Pietà. He was torn by inner conflict. Every move he had made since he had first denounced Bramante's cement mix to Pope Julius had pushed him toward the inevitability of his taking over this task. He truly wanted to rescue St. Peter's, make it a glorious monument to Christianity. He had always felt that it was his church; that if not for him, it might never have been conceived. Then was he not responsible for it?

He also knew the dimension of the task, the depth of the opposition he would meet, the years of grueling labor. The end of his life would be harder driven than any portion that had gone before.

An old woman came into the chapel, placed a lighted taper before the Madonna. Michelangelo reached into the long basket of candles, selected one, lighted it, placed it beside the other.

Of course he must build St. Peter's! Was not life to be worked, and suffered, right to the end?

He refused to accept any pay for his services as architect, even when Pope Paul sent his Keeper of the Wardrobe to the Macello dei Corvi with a packet of one hundred ducats. He painted from first light until dinnertime in the Pauline chapel, then walked the few steps to St. Peter's to watch the leveling. The workmen were sullen and ill disposed toward him . . . but they followed the schedule he set. To his dismay he found that Bramante's four major piers, which had been repaired over a period of years by Raphael, Peruzzi and Sangallo, were still defective and would not support the tribune and dome until more tons of concrete were poured into them. The disclosure of this still evident weakness further infuriated the superintendent of the fabric and the contractors who had worked under Sangallo. They put so many obstacles in his path that Pope Paul had to issue a decree declaring Michelangelo superintendent as well as architect, ordering everyone employed on St. Peter's to follow his orders implicitly. Those contractors and artisans who remained unfriendly, Michelangelo dismissed.

From that moment the fabric began to grow with a momentum that startled and then amazed Rome as people came to look at the two spiral ramps he had built on either side of the slope so that both animals, carrying materials, and men on horseback, carrying supplies across their saddles, could climb to the top, speeding up the provisioning process fiftyfold over the workmen walking up and down with materials on their backs.

A committee of Roman Conservators, impressed, came to ask if he would rescue the Capitoline hill and downslope called the Campidoglio, which had been the seat of religion and government of the Roman Empire, with its Temples of Jupiter and of Juno Moneta. This glorious spot, just above his own house, where he had sat with Contessina to watch Pope Leo declare Giuliano de' Medici a Baron of Rome, was a shambles, the old temples reduced to piles of stone, the Senate building an archaic fortress, animals feeding off the site, the level area a sea of mud in winter and of dust in summer. Would Michelangelo undertake to restore the Campidoglio to its former grandeur?

"Would I?" cried Michelangelo to Tommaso, when the Conservators had left him to consider their offer. "If only Giuliano da Sangallo could know! This was his dream. You shall help me, Tomao. We can make your hope of rebuilding Rome come true."

Tommaso's eyes were dancing like stars on a windy night.

"Thanks to your training, I can do the job. You will see that I shall become a good architect."

"We will plan big, Tomao, set up work for the next fifty years. When I am gone, you will complete everything according to our plans."

Now that he was working as a full-fledged architect, he appointed Tommaso as his assistant, assigning additional architectural work space in the house. Tommaso, a meticulous draftsman, was rapidly developing into one of the ablest of the city's young architects.

Vittoria Colonna's brother Ascanio had become involved in a quarrel with the Pope over the salt tax, and his private army attacked by the papal forces. Ascanio had been driven out of Rome, all of the Colonna family properties confiscated. Cardinal Caraffa's antagonism to Vittoria was heightened. Several of her former associates fled to Germany and joined the Lutherans . . . which further convicted her in the eyes of the Committee of Inquisition. She now took refuge in the convent of Sant'Anna de' Funari, buried deep within the gardens and colonnades of the ancient Theater of Pompey. When Michelangelo visited her of a Sunday afternoon, she sometimes did not utter a word. He brought sketches with him, trying to interest her in the works he had projected, but she came alive only when she told him of the special permission she had received to visit the Sistine Chapel and stand before the Last Judgment, and when he spoke of the dome for St. Peter's, still vague and illusive in his mind. She knew of his abiding love for the Pantheon, and the Duomo of Florence.

"Because they are pure sculpture," he said.

"And what of St. Peter's dome? Will that be only a top to keep out the rain?"

"Vittoria, it is good to see you smile, and to hear you tease me."

"You must not think me unhappy, Michelangelo. I await with trembling joy my reunion with God."

"*Cara*, I should be angry with you. Why are you so eager to die, when there are those of us who love you dearly? Is it not selfish of you?"

She took his hand between hers. In the early flood of his love this would have been a portentous moment; now he could only feel how sharp her bones were beneath the skin. Her eyes burned as she whispered:

"Forgive me for failing you. I can forgive myself only because I know you have no real need of me. A new Descent from the Cross in marble, a regal staircase for the Campidoglio, a dome for St. Peter's: these are your loves. You created majestically before you met me, and you will create majestically after I am gone."

Before there was time for another Sunday meeting he was summoned to the Cesarini palace, home of a Colonna cousin who had married a Cesarini. He crossed beyond the Torre Argentina, was met at a gate and led into a garden.

"The marchesa?" he asked of the doctor who came out to greet him.

"She will not see the sunrise."

He paced the garden while the heavens moved in their cycle. At the seventeenth hour he was admitted to the palace. Vittoria lay on her pillow, her faded copper hair enclosed in a silk hood, dressed in a shirt of finest linen, with a lace collar fastened at the throat. She looked as young and beautiful as the first time he had met her. Her expression was one of sublimity, as though she had already gone beyond all earthly troubles.

Speaking in a low voice, Donna Filippa, Abbess of Sant'Anna de' Funari, ordered in the coffin. It was coated with tar. Michelangelo cried:

"What is the meaning of this tar-covered coffin? The marchesa has not died of an infectious disease."

"We fear reprisals, *signore*," the abbess murmured. "We must get the marchesa back to the convent and buried before her enemies can claim the body."

Michelangelo longed to lean over and kiss Vittoria on the brow. He was restrained by the knowledge that she had never offered him anything but her hand.

He returned home, aching in every joint of his body and cranny of his skull. He sat down at his workbench to write:

> If being near the fire I burned with it,
> Now that its flame is quenched and doth not show,
> What wonder if I waste within and glow,
> Dwindling away to cinders bit by bit?

Vittoria in her will had directed the abbess to select her grave. Cardinal Caraffa forbade burial. For almost three weeks the coffin was left unattended in a corner of the convent chapel. Michelangelo was at last informed that she had been buried in the chapel wall, but when he went to the church he could find no sign of the immurement. The abbess looked about cautiously, then answered to his question:

"The marchesa was removed to Naples. She will lie next to her husband, in San Domenico Maggiore."

Michelangelo trudged wearily homeward, chewing on the bitter herb of irony: the marchese, who had fled his wife during his married life, would now have her by his side for all eternity. And he, Michelangelo, who had found in Vittoria the crowning love of his life, had never been permitted to fulfill it.

4

He did not lack for projects. In the eyes of the world he was truly the "Master." He was assigned yet another task by Pope Paul, who asked him to undertake the design and building of the defense works which would give him greater security within the Leonine City, and to engineer the erection of the obelisk of Caligula in the Piazza San Pietro. Duke Cosimo urged him to return to Florence to create sculptures for the city. The King of France deposited money in a Roman bank in his name against the day when he would carve or paint for him. The Sultan of Turkey offered to send an escort party to bring him to Constantinople to work there. Wherever an art commission was to be granted, in Portugal a Madonna della Misericordia for the king, in Milan a tomb for one of the distant Medici, in Florence for the ducal palace, Michelangelo was consulted about the theme, design, the proper artists for the job.

He spent the better part of the daily hours in the Pauline, painting the amazed and terror-stricken faces of the women who were watching Peter on the cross, then the portrait of the elderly bearded soldier, grief-stricken over his part in the execution. Tiring of paintbrushes, he returned home to pick up hammer and chisel, glorying in the sheer freedom of being able to carve to satisfy his inner needs. Only marble carving gave him a sense of his own three-dimensional fullness. He had been unhappy about the Leah and Rachel, ashamed of presenting second-rate work to the world; he had been afraid that he had grown too old for the vigorous art of marble sculpture. But now his chisel sang through the shining stone in a continuous "Go!", creating the collapsed Christ and behind him Nicodemus with his own white beard, deep-sunk eyes, flattened nose, a cowl over his head, the mouth sensitive, poetic.

He allowed no one in the Pauline chapel while he painted, but his studio was thronged with artists from all over Europe whom he employed, encouraged, taught and found commissions for.

Then, after weeks and months of lavishly outpoured energy, he would suddenly fall ill, with what he could not tell: a pulling in his thighs, a piercing pain in the groin, a weakness in the chest that kept him from breathing, a kidney ailment. At such times he would feel his brain shrink, he would grow cranky, fractious with his closest friends and relatives, accuse his nephew Lionardo of making a trip to Rome during his illness to make sure he would inherit all the properties, and his manager of selling copies of an engraving to make money for himself. Realdo Colombo, Italy's greatest anatomist, who was writing the first book on the subject, spent his spare hours in the Macello dei Corvi, flushing Michelangelo with spring water from Fiuggi. He would recover, his brain seem to expand, and he would cry to Tommaso:

"Why do I behave so cantankerously? Because my seventies are fleeing so fast?"

"Granacci said you were already crusty at twelve, when he first met you."

"So he did. Bless his memory."

Granacci, his oldest friend, had died; so had Balducci, Leo Baglioni and Sebastiano del Piombo. With each passing month he seemed closer to the vortex of the birth and death cycle. A letter from Lionardo brought him the news that his brother Giovansimone had died and been buried in Santa Croce. He reproached his nephew for not sending the details of Giovansimone's illness. He also broached the subject of his nephew's marriage, suggesting that since Lionardo was approaching thirty it was time he sought a wife, and had sons to carry on the Buonarroti name:

I believe in Florence there are many noble but poor families with whom it would be a charity to form a union, and it would be well there should be no dowry for there would then be no pride. You need a wife to associate with, and whom you can rule, and who will not care about pomps and run about every day to parties and marriages. It is easy for a woman to go wrong who does these things.

Nor is it to be said by anyone that you wish to ennoble yourself by marriage, for it is well known we are as ancient and noble citizens of Florence as any other house.

Tommaso de' Cavalieri was married. Tommaso had waited until he was thirty-eight, then proposed to the young daughter of a noble Roman family. They were married in a sumptuous wedding, attended by the Pope and his court, the entire roster of Roman nobility, the Florentine colony, the artists of Rome. Within the year Signora Cavalieri presented her husband with his first son.

The birth was quickly followed by a death: that of Pope Paul, grieving over the incorrigibility of his grandson, Ottavio, and the murder of his son, Pier Luigi, whom he had foisted on the Duchy of Parma and Piacenza. In contrast to Clement's funeral, the people of the city showed genuine grief over the loss of Paul.

When the College of Cardinals met there was expectant joy in the hearts of the Florentine colony, for they believed it was the turn of Cardinal Niccolò Ridolfi, Contessina's son, to become Pope. He had no enemies in Italy except the small group sharing power with Duke Cosimo of Florence. However, Niccolò had a powerful enemy outside of Italy: Charles V, the Holy Roman Emperor. During the conclave in the Sistine Chapel, with the election all but settled in favor of Niccolò, he became suddenly and violently ill. By morning he was dead. Dr. Realdo Colombo performed an autopsy. At its completion he came to the house on the Macello dei Corvi. Michelangelo looked up with dazed eyes.

"Murder?"

"Beyond any doubt."

"You found proof?"

"If I myself had administered the poison I could not be more sure of the cause of Niccolò's death. Lottini, Duke Cosimo's agent, could have had the opportunity."

Michelangelo lowered his head, stricken.

"Once again it is the end of our hopes for Florence."

As always, when he was made desolate by the events of the outside world, he turned to marble. Now in the Descent, which he was carving in the hopes that his friends would place it on his own tomb after his death, he encountered a strange problem: Christ's left leg was hampering the design. After careful consideration he cut the leg off in its entirety. Christ's hand, extending downward and clasped in the Madonna's, adroitly hid the fact that there was only one leg left.

The College of Cardinals elected sixty-two-year-old Giovan Maria de' Ciocchi del Monte, who became Pope Julius III. Michelangelo had known him at court for countless years; he had helped to rewrite the contract for Julius' tomb several times. Three times during the siege of 1527 Cardinal Ciocchi del Monte had been seized by the Emperor's army and taken to the gallows in front of Leo Baglioni's house in the Campo dei Fiori; three times he had been reprieved at the last moment. His main interest in life was pleasure.

"He should have taken the name Leo XI," Michelangelo confided to Tommaso. "He will probably paraphrase Leo's statement by saying, 'Since God saved me three times from the gallows just to make me Pope, let me enjoy it.' "

"He will be good for artists," Tommaso replied. "He likes their company best. He plans to enlarge his small villa near the Porta del Popolo into a sumptuous palace."

Very quickly Michelangelo was summoned to dinner at the Villa di Papa Giulio, already filling up with ancient statues, columns, paintings; and with artists in all media, most of whom already had commissions, including Michelangelo's friends Giorgio Vasari, the new architect for the villa, and Cecchino Rossi, who, with Vasari, had saved the David's arm; Guglielmo della Porta, successor to Sebastiano, Annibale Caracci. As yet the new Pope had not discussed the continuation of St. Peter's. Michelangelo waited anxiously.

Julius III had a long nose that drooped downward, about the only feature to emerge from a matted gray beard. He was a prodigious eater, stuffing large quantities of food into an opening in the beard which seemed to entrap it. Suddenly the Pope called for silence. The diners became still.

"Michelangelo," he cried in his rough, hearty voice, "I have not asked you to work for me out of respect for your age."

"It is a mere twelve years' difference, Holiness," replied Michelangelo with mock humility. "Since we all know how hard you are going to strive to make your pontificate outstanding, I do not think I dare claim exemption on that score."

Julius enjoyed the sarcasm.

"You are so valuable to us, dear Master, that I would gladly give years off my life if they could be added to yours."

Michelangelo watched the Pope dispatch a plate of richly stuffed goose, thought, "We Tuscans are lean eaters, that is why we live so long."

Aloud, he said, "I appreciate your offer, but in all fairness to the Christian world I cannot let you make the sacrifice."

"Then, my son, if I survive you, as is probable in the natural course of life, I shall have your body embalmed, and keep it near me, so that it shall be as lasting as your work."

Michelangelo's appetite vanished. He wondered if there were some way to be excused. But Julius was not through with him.

"There are a few things I would like you to design for me: a new staircase and fountain for the Belvedere, a façade for a palace at San Rocco, monuments for my uncle and grandfather. . . ."

But no word of St. Peter's.

The Pope gathered his company in the vineyard for music and plays. Michelangelo slipped away. All he wanted from Julius was to be confirmed as architect of St. Peter's.

The Pope procrastinated. Michelangelo kept his designs and plans secret, providing the contractors only with those specifications for the next segment of the job. He had always had this need for privacy with work in progress. Now he had a valid reason for working in secrecy; but it got him into trouble.

A group of the ousted contractors, led by the persuasive Baccio Bigio, interested Cardinal Cervini, in charge of the bookkeeping for the fabric, in their claims. A written document was presented to the Pope. Michelangelo was summoned to the Villa di Papa Giulio.

"You are not afraid to face your critics?" asked Julius.

"No, Holiness, but I want the meeting to take place inside the fabric itself."

It was a large crowd that assembled in what was to become the new chapel of the Kings of France. Baccio Bigio opened the attack by exclaiming:

"Buonarroti has pulled down a more beautiful church than he is capable of building."

"Let us proceed to your criticism of the present structure," replied the Pope amiably.

An official cried, "Holy Father, immense sums are being spent without our being told why. Nor has anything been communicated to us of the manner in which the building is to be carried on."

"That is the responsibility of the architect," replied Michelangelo.

"But, Holiness, Buonarroti treats us as if the matter did not concern us at all. We are completely useless!"

The Pope repressed a half-formed quip. Cardinal Cervini threw his arms upward to indicate the arches that were being built.

"Holiness, as you can see, Buonarroti is building three chapels at each end of these transverse arches. It is our opinion that this arrangement, particularly in the southern apse, will permit too little light to reach the interior . . ."

The Pope's eyes peered over the edge of the matted beard.

"I'm inclined to agree with the criticism, Michelangelo."

Michelangelo turned to Cervini, replied quietly, "Monsignor, above those windows in the travertine vaulting there are to be three other windows."

"You never gave a hint of that."

"Nor was I bound to do so."

"We have a right to know what you are doing." Cardinal Cervini was now furious. "You are not infallible."

"I will never bind myself to give Your Lordship, or anyone else, information of my intentions. Your office is to furnish money and take care that it is not stolen. The building plan concerns me alone."

A bruised silence adumbrated through the vast construction, its walls, piers, arches reaching to the open sky. Michelangelo turned back to the Pope.

"Holy Father, you can see with your own eyes how much excellent building I am getting for the money. If all this work does not tend to the saving of my soul, since I have refused to accept any pay, I shall have expended considerable time and trouble in vain."

The Pope placed his hand on Michelangelo's shoulder.

"Neither your eternal nor your temporal welfare shall suffer. You are the supreme architect of St. Peter's." Turning to the ring of accusers, he said sternly, "And so shall he remain, as long as I am Pope!"

It was a victory for Michelangelo. In the process he had incurred a new enemy, Cardinal Marcello Cervini.

5

To placate Baccio Bigio, Pope Paul took away from Michelangelo the reconstruction job he had started on the Ponte Santa Maria. Bigio removed the ancient travertine supports to lighten the bridge, finished it with cement and pebbles. Michelangelo, riding over the bridge on horseback with Vasari, said:

"Giorgio, this bridge is shaking under us. Let us spur our horses or it may fall while we are on it."

Vasari spread the quip around Rome. Bigio was livid with rage.

"What does Buonarroti know about bridges?"

At the beginning of 1551 Julius III finally issued his *breve* making Michelangelo official architect of St. Peter's; but in a few months he had to shut down all work on the fabric. Julius was pouring such a vast fortune into the Villa di Papa Giulio and entertaining himself on such a lavish scale that he used up the income stipulated for St. Peter's.

It was now Michelangelo's turn to be livid. He demanded of Tommaso, as they hunched over their drawing boards:

"How can I go to Julius and cry, 'Holiness, your insatiable appetite for pleasure is bankrupting us. Restrain yourself so that we can complete St. Peter's'?"

"He would have you thrown into a dungeon of Sant'Angelo."

"Then I will keep silent, painful as it may be."

He was still agitated when he began to carve on the Descent later in the day. He struck emery in Christ's forearm. The sparks flew under his chisel. Angrily he struck the forearm a series of harsh blows . . . only to have it shatter and fall to the floor. He put down his hammer and chisel and left the house.

He walked past the stalls of Trajan's market like black holes in a cliff as they climbed the hill, toward the Temple of Mars. Unhappy about smashing the arm, he decided to start all over again. This time on an Entombment. He entered a stoneyard just beyond Caesar's forum, came across an ancient block that had been part of a cornice, a marble-colored limestone from the Palestrina area. Despite the fact that the stone had deep hollows he had it sent to the studio, began searching his mind for a concept. In his new version there would be no Nicodemus; Christ would be a giant head and arms and torso with foreshortened legs falling away, crushed under their burden, only Mary's head and hands visible as she tried desperately to hold up the weight of her massively dead son.

Relaxed and refreshed, he returned to the Macello dei Corvi. Urbino was waiting for him with a worried expression.

"*Messere,* I do not like to bring you further problems, but I must now leave you."

Michelangelo was too astonished to answer.

"Leave me?"

"You remember the girl I chose, in Urbino, ten years ago? . . ."

Michelangelo shook his head in disbelief. Was it already ten years?

"She is eighteen today. It is time for us to marry."

"But why go? Bring your wife here, Urbino, we'll fix up an apartment for you, buy furniture. Your wife can have her own maid . . ."

Urbino's eyes were round as Giotto's O.

"Are you sure, *messere?* For I am forty now, and I should have children as quickly as possible."

"This is your home. I am your family. Your sons will be my grandsons."

He gave Urbino two thousand ducats in cash so that he could be independent, then an additional sum to fix up a room for his bride and to buy a new bed. In a few days Urbino returned with his wife, Cornelia Colonelli, a sympathetic girl who took over the management of the household and ran it well. She gave Michelangelo the affection she would have brought to her husband's father. Nine months later they named their first son Michelangelo.

He urged his nephew in Florence to "purchase a handsome house in town, to cost from fifteen hundred to two thousand ducats, in our quarter. As soon as you have found it, I shall forward the money." Once Lionardo had settled in a proper house, he was to find a wife, and go about the serious business of having sons.

Lionardo chose Cassandra Ridolfi, a distant member of the family into which Contessina had married. Michelangelo was so delighted that he sent Cassandra two rings, one diamond and the other ruby. Cassandra sent Michelangelo eight lovely shirts as a return gift. They named their first-born son Buonarroto, after Lionardo's father. The next son they named Michelangelo, but he died very quickly, and Michelangelo grieved.

To recreate the Campidoglio he took the ancient Roman stone salt tax office, which a few hundred years before had been turned into a bastionlike Senatorial building, and converted it into a regal official palace with lyrical flights of steps rising from either end to a center entrance. He then planned two palaces, identical in design, for either side of the square which for centuries had been a market. He leveled the piazza, to be paved with patterned stones, searched his mind for a flawless work of art for the middle of the square. He thought of the Laocoön, the Belvedere torso, the gigantic stone head of Augustus. None of these seemed right. Then he remembered the bronze equestrian statue of the Emperor Marcus Aurelius which had stood unharmed in front of St. John in Lateran all through the centuries because the Christians had believed it to be Constantine, the first Christian emperor. He placed it on such a low platform that the gloriously lifelike statue would appear to be on eye level with the people coming in and out of the palaces on either side; Marcus Aurelius seemed to have just come down the Senatorial steps and mounted his horse to ride across Rome.

In March 1555, Tommaso, Vasari, Raffaelo da Montelupo, Ammanati and Daniele da Volterra gave him a party for his eightieth birthday. The walls of the studio were lined with drawings and projects for another eighty years ahead. . . .

Two weeks later Pope Julius III died, unable to spare any years off his life for his friend Michelangelo. To Michelangelo's consternation, Cardinal Marcello Cervini, erstwhile accountant for the fabric, was elected Pope. He took the title of Marcellus II.

And that, reasoned Michelangelo quite calmly, was the end for him. He had told Cardinal Cervini that the plan of St. Peter's was none of his business. As Pope, it would now be very much his business!

He spent no time in bemoaning his fate. Instead, he began winding up his affairs in Rome, making arrangements to transfer his bank account and marbles to Florence. He was leaving Urbino in the house, since his wife Cornelia was again pregnant. He burned his early drawings for St. Peter's and the dome, was about to pack his saddlebags when, after a three-week reign, Pope Marcellus died.

Michelangelo went to Church, offered thanks to God for giving him the strength not to rejoice over Cervini's death. After another three weeks he decided that it might have been just as well for him to have returned to Florence: Cardinal Giovanni Pietro Caraffa became Pope Paul IV.

No one knew quite how he had been elected. He was a thoroughly disagreeable man, violent of nature, intolerant of all about him. Pope Paul IV, knowing how completely he was hated, said:

"I do not know why they elected me Pope, so I am bound to conclude that it is not the cardinals but God who makes the Popes."

Announcing that it was his ambition to wipe out all heresy in Italy, he unleashed on the Roman people the horrors of the Spanish Inquisition. In a fortresslike structure near the Vatican his Board of Inquisition tortured and condemned accused people without trial, locked them in dungeons in the cellars, burned others in the Campo dei Fiori . . . at the same time the Pope was making a corrupt nephew a cardinal and establishing duchies for others of his relatives. Michelangelo considered he would be fit fuel for the fires burning outside Leo Baglioni's house; but he made no attempt to flee. The Pope did not molest him . . . until the day of reckoning.

Pope Paul IV received him in a small, monastic room with whitewashed walls and a minimum of uncomfortable furniture. His expression was as severe as his robe.

"Buonarroti, I respect your work. But it is the implicit will of the Council of Trent that heretical frescoes such as your altar wall be destroyed."

". . . the Last Judgment?"

He stood before the Pope's wooden chair feeling as though he were a corpse in the dead room of Santo Spirito and a dissector had just chiseled off his skull, lifted out his brain, and let it slip to the floor. He half slid to the corner of a bench, sat staring blindly at the whitewashed wall before him.

"Many in our hierarchy feel that you have blasphemed; they are confirmed by an article written by Aretino of Venice . . ."

"A blackmailer!"

". . . a friend of Titian, of Charles V, Benvenuto Cellini, the late Francis I of France, Jacopo Sansovino. . . . Here is one of the copies passing from hand to hand in Rome. I'm convinced the Council of Trent has also studied it."

Michelangelo took the paper from the Pope, began to read:

> Is it possible that you can have represented in the sacred temple of God, above the altar of His Son, in the greatest Chapel in the world, where Cardinals and Bishops and the Vicar of Christ, with Catholic ceremonial and sacred ritual, confess, contemplate and adore the body and blood of Jesus . . . so lofty a subject, with angels and saints without a remnant of modesty and denuded of all celestial ornament!

He jerked his head up abruptly.

"Holiness, this attack was written when I refused to send Aretino some of my drawings and cartoons. It was his way of striking at me . . ."

"Decent people are shocked by the nakedness of saints and martyrs, of hundreds of men and women fully exposed . . ."

"They are the narrow-minded, Holy Father, ignorant of the true nature of art."

"Would you call your Holy Father narrow-minded, Michelangelo? And ignorant? For I am one of them."

"The fresco is not evil. Never has there been a wall more permeated with a love of God."

"Very well, I will not demand that the wall be torn down. We will simply give it a coat of whitewash. Then you can paint something over it, a theme that will make everyone happy. Something simple and devout, that you can do quickly."

He was too crushed to fight back. Not so, Rome. His friends, adherents, his old associates at court, including a number of cardinals led by Ercole Gonzaga, began a campaign to save the wall. Tommaso brought him daily reports of new friends gained: an ambassador from France, a bishop from Venice, a noble Roman family.

Then an anonymous intermediary came up with what Rome believed to be a brilliant compromise. Daniele da Volterra, trained in painting under Sodoma and in architecture under Peruzzi, now one of Michelangelo's most enthusiastic followers, came to the studio with high color in his cheeks.

"Master, the Last Judgment is saved."

"I can't believe it. The Pope has agreed?"

". . . not to destroy it. There will be no coat of whitewash."

Michelangelo collapsed onto his leather chair, breathing hard.

"I must go out and thank personally every last person who helped me. . . ."

"Master," interrupted Daniele, with eyes averted, "we have had to pay a price."

"What price?"

". . . well, to mollify the Pope . . . he agreed not to destroy the wall providing breeches were put on everybody's nakedness."

"Breeches? You mean . . . *calzoni*?"

"And petticoats on the females. We must cover every erogenous zone. Only a few women may remain bare above the waist. All must be clothed from the hips to the knees, particularly those whose bottoms are facing the chapel. His favorite saints must be robed, as well as St. Catherine, the Virgin's skirt made heavier . . ."

"If in my earlier years I had given myself to make sulphur matches," swore Michelangelo, "I should now suffer less."

Daniele shivered, as though struck.

"Master, let us try to be sensible about this. The Pope was going to call in a court painter . . . but I persuaded him to let me do the job. I will injure the wall as little as possible. If we let some stranger . . ."

" 'Adam and Eve sewed fig leaves together, and made themselves girdles.' "

"Don't be angry with me. I am not at the Council of Trent."

"You are right, Daniele. We must offer up these private parts to the Inquisition. I have spent a lifetime portraying the beauty of man. Now he has become shameful again, to be burned in a new bonfire of vanities. Do you know what that means, Daniele? We are returning to the darkest, most ignorant centuries of the past."

"Look here, Michelangelo," said Daniele placatingly, "I can blend in gauze, bits of cloth to match your flesh tones. I will use so thin a paint that the next Pope can have all the breeches and robes removed without harming anything beneath . . ."

Michelangelo shook his head.

"Go then, and wrap their winding sheets about them."

"Trust me. I shall outwit the Pope at every point. This task is so delicate that it will be months, years before I even dare begin." Daniele was a hard worker, without originality, and so painstakingly slow that he had earned the reputation of never completing a commission during the patron's lifetime. "Perhaps by that time Caraffa will be dead, the Inquisition over. . . ."

The best way to shut out terror was to pick up hammer and chisel and start carving. He had recently bought an irregular column, protruding at top and bottom. Instead of straightening the block, he decided to make use of this odd shape to achieve a crescent profile. He started massing inside the center, wondering if the block could tell him what he wanted to create. The marble remained aloof, unyielding, silent. It was asking too much of raw material, even though it was shining stone, to create a work of art all by itself; but the challenge of the characterful column excited new energy in him.

It was just as necessary to survive at eighty as at thirty-five; but a little more difficult.

6

Sigismondo died in Settignano, the last of his brothers. He had outlived his generation. Equally sad was the illness of Urbino, who had been with him for twenty-six years. The nobility of Urbino's spirit shone forth when he whispered to Michelangelo:

"Even more than dying, it grieves me to leave you alone in this treacherous world."

Urbino's wife, Cornelia, gave birth to her second son at the moment her husband was being buried. Michelangelo kept them with him until Urbino's will was settled. He was named guardian and tutor of the two boys; when their mother left with them for her parents' home in Urbino, the house seemed desolate.

He pushed ahead the work of the rising tribune of St. Peter's; he carved his new Pietà; he bought another farm for Lionardo, sent Cornelia Urbino seven spans of a lightweight black cloth she had asked for; began searching for worthy poor whom he could help for the salvation of his soul. Then he had to let the work on St. Peter's grind to a halt once again because of the threatened invasion of the Spanish army.

The eighties, he decided, were not the most pleasant decade in the span of man. When he left Florence at sixty he had feared that his life might be over; but love had made him young again, and the sixties had flown by. During his seventies he had been so deeply immersed in the Pauline chapel frescoes, the carving of the Descent, his new architectural career, and St. Peter's, that no day had been long enough to accomplish his tasks.

But now, as he became eighty-one, and moved toward eighty-two, the hours were like hornets, each stinging as it passed. He could no longer see as well as he used to; his step was not as firm; stamina was giving way to a series of minor disturbances, sapping his strength, interfering with his drive to finish St. Peter's, to create a glorious dome for it.

Then he went down with a severe attack of kidney stones. Dr. Colombo pulled him through with the aid of Tommaso's untiring care; but he was confined to his bed for several months and was obliged to turn over the designs for one of the chapels to a new superintendent. When he recovered, and laboriously climbed the scaffolding, he found that the new superintendent had misread his plans, making serious errors in construction. He was overcome with shame and remorse; this was his first failure in the ten years of building. And at last he had handed Baccio Bigio a fulcrum on which to rest a new attack: an error of grave proportions which he could neither excuse nor explain away.

He called on the Pope at once; but quick as he was, Bigio had been there before him.

"It is true?" Pope Paul asked as he saw Michelangelo's face. "The chapel will have to be pulled down?"

"Most of it, Holiness."

"I am saddened. How could such a thing happen?"

"I have been ill, Holy Father."

"I see. Bigio claims you are too old to carry such a heavy responsibility. He feels that for your own sake you should be relieved of the crushing burden."

"His solicitude touches me. He and his associates have been trying to get this 'crushing burden' off my shoulders and into their own hands for a lot of years now. But didn't Bigio's Ponte Santa Maria just collapse in the flood? Can you believe that Baccio Bigio is better on his good days than I am on my bad?"

"No one is questioning your ability."

Michelangelo was silent for a moment, thinking backward.

"Holiness, for thirty years I watched good architects pour foundations. They never got St. Peter's off the ground. In the ten years I have been the architect, the church has risen upward like an eagle. If you dismiss me now, it will be the ruin of the edifice."

The Pope's lips twitched.

"Michelangelo, as long as you have the strength to fight back, you shall remain the architect of St. Peter's."

That night there was a meeting in the house on the Macello dei Corvi. Because he had nearly died, Tommaso, a group of his oldest friends, and the Cardinal of Carpi, who had become his protector at court, insisted that he build a complete model of the dome. Up to now he had made only fragmentary sketches.

"If we had lost you last week," said Tommaso flatly, "how would anyone have known what kind of dome you envisaged?"

"I have heard you say," added the cardinal, "that you wanted to progress the fabric so far that no one could change its design after your death."

"That is my hope."

"Then give us the dome!" cried Lottino, an artist disciple. "There is no other way."

"You are right," replied Michelangelo with a sigh. "But I have not yet conceived the final dome. I shall have to find it. Then we shall build a wooden model."

Everyone left except Tommaso. Michelangelo walked to his drawing table, pulled up a wooden chair. He mused aloud, as his pen roamed over a fresh sheet of paper. The Pantheon and the Duomo in Florence had two domes, one inside the other, interlaced structurally to give each other support. The interior of his dome would be sculpture, the exterior architecture. . . .

A dome was not a mere covering; any roof would serve that utilitarian purpose. A dome was a major work of art, the perfect blending of sculpture and architecture in displacing space and adding to the firmament. It was a vault of man, created in the image of the vault of heaven. The perfect dome went from horizon to horizon in man's mind, covering it with grace. It was the most natural of all architectural forms, and the most celestial, for it aspired to recreate the sublime form under which humanity spent the days of its years.

A dome of a church was not in competition with the dome of the sky; it was the same form in miniature, as a son to his father. Some people said the earth was round; for a man like himself whose travels had been confined between Venice and Rome, that was hard to prove. In Master Urbino's school of grammar he had been taught that the earth was flat, ending where the dome of heaven came down to its circular boundaries. Yet he had always observed a peculiar facet of that supposedly anchored-down horizon: as he walked or rode to reach it, it receded at an equal pace. . . .

Just so, his dome. It could not be finite. No man standing beneath it must ever feel that he could reach its boundaries. The sky was a perfect creation; whoever stood on the earth, wherever he might be, was centered at its heart, with the dome of heaven spread equidistant about him. Lorenzo, *Il Magnifico,* the Plato Four, the humanists had taught him that man was the center of the universe; and this was never more demonstrable than when he stood looking upward and found himself, a lone individual, serving as the central pole holding up the tarpaulin of sun and clouds, moon and stars, knowing that, lone or abandoned as he might feel, without his support the heavens would fall. Take away the dome as a shape, an idea, the symmetrical roof which sheltered man, and what was left of the world? Only a flat plate, the kind on which his stepmother, *Il Migliore,* had sliced her breads, hot out of the oven.

No wonder man had placed heaven in the sky! It was not because he had ever seen a soul ascend thereto, or caught a glimpse of the vistas of paradise above; but because heaven simply had to be housed in the most divine form known to man's mind or senses. He wanted his dome too to be mystical, not a protection from heat or rain, thunder or lightning, but of a staggering beauty that would reassure man of His presence . . . a sentient form which man could not only see and feel but enter. Under his dome a man's soul must soar upward to God even as it would in the moment of its final release from his body. How much closer could man come to God, while still on earth? With his vast cupola he meant to paint His portrait just as surely as when he had painted Him on the Sistine ceiling.

The saving of his own soul became part of the creation of the dome for St. Peter's. For his last great work he had assumed the most difficult task of the sixty-eight years since Granacci had taken him past the Street of the Painters, to the studio on the Via dei Tavolini, and said, "Signor Ghirlandaio, this is Michelangelo, about whom I told you."

His mind and fingers were moving with force and clarity. After drawing for hours he turned for refreshment to his crescent-shaped block. He changed his original concept of a Christ with head and knees turned in opposite directions for a version in which the head and knees concurred, but were contraposed to the Virgin's head above Christ's shoulder, affording a more dramatic contrast. He hollowed out a large figure from the crescent of the block before faltering. Then he returned to his dome.

7

He was after absolute balance, perfection of line, curve, volume, mass, openness, density, elegance, the profundity of endless space. He aspired to create a work of art that would transcend the age through which he had lived.

He laid aside his charcoal and drawing pens, started modeling, thinking that the maneuverability of the damp clay might bring him more freedom than the rigidity of the drawn line. Over the weeks and months he made a dozen models, destroying them, moving on to new designs. He felt he was coming closer to revelation, for he first achieved monumentality, then dimension, then majesty, then simplification; yet the results still derived from artistry rather than spirituality.

At last it came, after eleven years of thinking, drawing, praying, hoping and despairing, experimenting and rejecting: a creature of his imagination, compounded of all his arts, staggering in size, yet as fragile as a bird's egg in a nest; soaring, lilting heavenward, constructed of gossamer which carried effortlessly and musically upward its three-hundred-and-thirty-five-foot height, pear-shaped, as was the breast of the Medici Madonna. . . . It was a dome unlike any other.

"It has arrived," murmured Tommaso ecstatically, when he saw the completed drawings. "Where did it come from?"

"Where do ideas come from, Tomao? Sebastiano asked that same question when he was young. I can only give you the answer I gave him, for I am no wiser at eighty-two than I was at thirty-nine: ideas are a natural function of the mind, as breathing is of the lungs. Perhaps they come from God."

He hired a carpenter, Giovanni Francesco, to build the model. He made it of linden wood, one fifteen-thousandth of the projected size. The giant dome would rest on the piers and on the arches that the piers supported, and on a circular drum, or wide cement base. The drum would be built of brick with a sheathing of travertine; the external ribs of the dome would be of Tivoli travertine, the buttresses held to the drum by a framework of wrought iron, while the columns and horizontal entablatures would also be of travertine. Eight ramps along the lower drum would afford a means of carrying materials on the backs of donkeys up to the dome walls. The engineering plans took months to draw, but Michelangelo had the skill, Tommaso had become an expert.

All work was done at the Macello dei Corvi studio, in the strictest privacy. The interior dome Michelangelo molded himself; the exterior one he let Francesco indicate with paint. The festooned carvings and decorations were made of clay mixed with sawdust and glue. He called in a reliable Carrara woodcarver by the name of Battista to cut out the statuettes and capitals, the bearded faces of the Apostles.

Pope Paul IV died suddenly. Rome burst into the most violent insurrection Michelangelo had yet seen at the death of any pontiff. The crowd knocked down a newly erected statue of the former Cardinal Caraffa, dragged its head through the streets for hours while the citizenry heaped imprecations upon it, then threw the head into the Tiber before storming the headquarters of the Inquisition to release all prisoners and destroy the mass of papers and documents assembled to convict the accused of heresy.

Wearied of strife and bloodshed, the College of Cardinals elected sixty-year-old Giovanni Angelo Medici, from an obscure Lombardy branch of the Medici family. Pope Pius IV had been trained as a lawyer, was judicious of temperament. As a professional advocate he was a brilliant negotiator and soon came to be trusted in Europe as a man of integrity. The Inquisition, foreign to the Italian character, was ended. Through a series of legalistic conferences and contracts the Pope brought peace to Italy and the surrounding nations; and to the Lutherans as well. Guided by diplomacy, the Church achieved peace for itself at the same time that it reunited Catholicism in Europe.

Pope Pius IV reconfirmed Michelangelo's position as architect of St. Peter's, providing him with funds with which to push the arches upward to the drum. He also commissioned him to design a gate for the city walls, to be called Porta Pia.

It was clearly a race against time. He was approaching his mid-eighties. With a maximum of money and workmen he could reach the drum in perhaps two or three years. It was not possible for him to estimate just how long it would take to complete the dome, with its windows, columns and decorative frieze; but he thought he could do it in ten to twelve years. That would bring him to a round century mark. Nobody lived that long; but despite his attacks of the stone, pains in the head, a colic which brought disorders of the stomach, occasional aches in the back and loins, intermittent bouts of dizziness and weakness when he had to lie abed for a few days, he did not feel any true diminishing of his power. He still took walks in the *campagna*.

As he gazed into the mirror he saw that there was good color in his face. He had a vigorous shock of black hair on his head, albeit generously streaked with white, as was his forked beard. His eyes were clear and penetrating.

He would get that dome built. Had not his father, Lodovico, achieved ninety? Was he not a better man than his father, by at least ten years?

He had to go through yet one more ordeal by fire. Baccio Bigio, who had worked himself up to a high administrative position in the superintendent's office, had a documented set of figures to prove how many ducats Michelangelo's illness had cost the fabric because of the faulty chapel. He used his information to its fullest advantage, even convincing Michelangelo's friend, the Cardinal of Carpi, that St. Peter's was going badly. Bigio was putting himself into position to succeed to the job on the day Michelangelo took to his bed.

When Michelangelo no longer had the strength to climb the scaffolding each day, one of his able young helpers, Pier Luigi Gaeta, was appointed as assistant to the Clerk of the Works. Gaeta brought Michelangelo detailed reports each night. When the Clerk of the Works was murdered, Michelangelo proposed that Gaeta be promoted. Instead Baccio Bigio got the appointment. Gaeta was dismissed entirely. Bigio began to remove structural beams, take down scaffolding, and prepare the fabric for a new design.

Michelangelo, crawling painfully up the scaffolding of time, past eighty-seven toward eighty-eight, was too stricken by the news to get out of his bed, which he had had moved into his studio.

"But you must," cried Tommaso, trying to wake him from his lethargy, "or Bigio will undo the work you have done."

"He who contends with the worthless achieves no great victory."

"Forgive me, but this is not a time for Tuscan adages. It is a time for action. If you cannot go to St. Peter's today, you must send a deputy in your place."

"Would you go, Tommaso?"

"People know that I am as a son to you."

"Then I will send Daniele da Volterra. He has so long outwitted the court with the breeches for the Last Judgment, he should be able to handle the conspirators in the superintendent's office."

Daniele da Volterra was turned away. Baccio Bigio was given full building powers at the fabric. When Michelangelo encountered the Pope crossing the Campidoglio at the head of his train, he shouted crustily:

"Holiness, I insist that you make a change! If you do not, I shall return to Florence forever. You are letting St. Peter's be torn down."

In his astringent courtroom manner Pope Pius IV replied:

"*Piano, piano,* Michelangelo, let us go into the Senatorial palace where we can talk."

The Pope listened carefully.

"I shall summon the members of the fabric who have been opposing you. Then I shall ask my relative, Gabrio Serbelloni, to go to St. Peter's and investigate their charges. Come to the Vatican palace tomorrow."

He arrived too early to be received by the Pope, wandered into the Stanza della Segnatura which Raphael had painted during the years when he himself was up in the Sistine vault. He gazed at the four frescoes, first the School of Athens, then Parnassus, then the Dispute and Justice. He had never before allowed himself to look at Raphael's work without prejudice. He knew that he could never have conceived or painted these idealized still lifes; yet seeing how exquisitely they were done, with what integrity of craftsmanship, he realized that for lyricism and romantic charm Raphael had been the master of them all. He left the Stanza in a philosophic frame of mind.

When he was ushered into the small throne room he found the Pope surrounded by the fabric committee which had dismissed Gaeta and refused to accept Daniele da Volterra. In a few minutes Gabrio Serbelloni entered.

"Holiness, I find not an iota of truth in this report written by Baccio Bigio. It is fabricated . . . but unlike the great fabric of Buonarroti, it is pasted together maliciously, with no discernible purpose except self-interest."

In the voice of a judge handing down a decision Pope Pius decreed:

"Baccio Bigio is herewith dismissed from St. Peter's. In the future, the plans of Michelangelo Buonarroti may not be altered in the smallest detail."

8

While the cathedral structure rose through its giant columns, arches and façades, Michelangelo spent his days in his studio completing the designs for the Porta Pia and, at the Pope's request, converting part of the ruins of the stupendous Baths of Diocletian into the lovely church of Santa Maria degli Angeli.

Several years had passed since he had carved on his crescent-shaped marble. One afternoon while resting on his side in bed, the idea dawned on him that what he needed to mature the block was not merely a new form for the figures but a new form for sculpture itself.

He rose, picked up his heaviest hammer and chisel and removed the head of Christ, carving a new face and head from what had been the Virgin's shoulder. He then dissected Christ's right arm from the body, just above the elbow, though the detached arm and hand remained as part of the supporting marble that went down to the base. What had previously been the left shoulder and part of the chest of Christ he converted into the left arm and hand of the Virgin. Christ's magnificent long legs were now out of proportion, constituting three fifths of the entire body. The new attenuation created an emotional effect of limpidity, youth and grace. Now he began to be satisfied. Through the distortion of the elongated figure he felt that he had achieved a truth about man: the heart might tire but humanity, carried on its ever young legs, would continue to move across the face of the earth.

"If only I had another ten years, or even five," he cried to the statues standing about him, "I could create a whole new sculpture."

Suddenly darkness flooded over him. After a lapse of time he regained consciousness; but he was confused. He picked up his chisel, gazed at the limpid Christ. All continuity of thought was gone. He could not remember just what he had been doing with the marble. He knew that something had happened, but he could not collect his thoughts. Had he dropped off to sleep? Was he not quite awake? Then why did he feel a numbness and weakness in the left arm and leg? Why did the muscles on one side of his face feel as though they were sagging?

He called his servant. When he asked her to summon Tommaso, he noticed that his speech was slurred. The elderly woman gazed at him, wide-eyed.

"*Messere*, are you all right?"

She helped him into bed, then put on a shawl to go through the streets. Tommaso returned with the Cavalieri doctor. Michelangelo could see by their expressions that something serious had occurred though they pretended that he had just overtired himself. Dr. Donati gave him a warm drink, stirring in a foul-tasting medicine.

"Rest cures everything," said the doctor.

"Except old age."

"I've been hearing about your old age too long now to take it seriously," replied Tommaso, putting an extra pillow under his head. "I'll stay here until you sleep."

He awakened to find deep night outside his window. He lifted himself gingerly. The headache was gone, and he could see all too clearly the work that was still required on the crescent Pietà. He rose, put a goat candle in his cap, returned to his carving. The confusion was gone from his mind. It was good to have the feel of marble at his fingertips. He blinked his eyes to stave off the flying chips as he made a slashing "Go!" up the right side and around the shoulder, his calligraphic strokes pulsating on the marble torso and melting into space.

At dawn Tommaso opened the street door cautiously, burst into laughter.

"Why, you rogue! You pretender! I left you at midnight, deep enough asleep to stay for a week. I come back a few hours later, and find a snowstorm."

"Delicious smell, isn't it, Tomao? When the white dust cakes inside my nostrils, that's when I breathe the best."

"Dr. Donati says you need rest."

"In the next world, *caro*. Paradise is already replete with sculptures. There'll be nothing for me to do but rest."

He worked all day, had supper with Tommaso, then threw himself on the bed for a few hours of sleep before rising to fix another candle in his cap and begin polishing, starting with pumice and sulphur, then going to straw, giving the elongated legs of Christ a finish like satin.

He forgot all about the attack.

Two days later, as he stood before his marble, deciding that it was now safe to cut away the superfluous arm and hand to further release the elongated figure in space, he was struck again. He dropped his hammer and chisel, stumbled to the bed, fell on his knees, with his face sideways on the blanket.

When he awakened the room was full of people: Tommaso, Dr. Donati and Dr. Fidelissimi, Gaeta, Daniele da Volterra, a number of Florentine friends. Facing him was the disembodied forearm of the statue which throbbed with a life all its own. On the inside of the elbow was a vein, bulging with blood and life; though suspended in space, it existed. He had not been able to destroy it, any more than the centuries of being buried and trod upon had destroyed the Laocoön. Gazing at his own vein on the inside of his elbow, he saw how flat and withered it appeared. He thought:

"Man passes. Only works of art are immortal."

He insisted on sitting in a chair before the fire. Once when he was left alone he slipped a robe over his shoulders and started walking in the rain in the direction of St. Peter's. One of his newer apprentices, Calcagni, met him in the street, asked:

"Master, do you think it right to be about in such weather?"

He allowed Calcagni to take him home, but at four the next afternoon he dressed and tried to mount his horse for a ride. His legs were too weak.

Rome came to bid him farewell. Those who could not be admitted left flowers and gifts on the doorstep. Dr. Donati tried to keep him in bed.

"Don't hurry me," he said to the doctor. "My father lived to his ninetieth birthday, so I still have two weeks to enjoy this salubrious life."

"As long as you're feeling so intrepid," commented Tommaso, "what about a carriage ride in the morning? The last work on the drum is complete. To celebrate your ninetieth birthday, they're going to start the first ring of the dome."

"*Grazie a Dio*, thank God. No one will ever be able to change it now. But all the same, it's sad to have to die. I would like to start all over again, to create forms and figures I have never dreamed of." His amber-speckled eyes were unwavering. "I like best to work in white marble."

"You've had your *divertimento*, fun."

That night, as he lay sleepless in bed, he thought, "Life has been good. God did not create me to abandon me. I have loved marble, yes, and paint too. I have loved architecture, and poetry too. I have loved my family and my friends. I have loved God, the forms of the earth and the heavens, and people too. I have loved life to the full, and now I love death as its natural termination. *Il Magnifico* would be happy: for me, the forces of destruction never overcame creativity."

He was swept by a massive wave of darkness. Before he lost consciousness he said to himself, "I must see Tommaso. There are things to be done."

When he next opened his eyes Tommaso was sitting on the edge of the bed. He put an arm under Michelangelo and raised him up, holding his head against his chest.

"Tomao . . ."

"I am here, *caro*."

"I want to be buried in Santa Croce with my family . . ."

"The Pope wants you buried in your own church, St. Peter's."

"It is not . . . home. Promise you will take me back to Florence . . . ?"

"The Pope will forbid it, but the Florentine merchants can smuggle you out the Porta del Popolo in a caravan of goods. . . ."

"My will, Tomao." His strength was ebbing. "I commit my soul into the hands of God . . . my body to the earth, and my substance to my family . . . the Buonarroti . . ."

"It will all be done. I shall finish the Campidoglio, exactly as you planned. With St. Peter's at one end, and the Capitol at the other, Rome will forevermore be Michelangelo's as much as Caesar's, or Constantine's."

"Thank you, Tommaso. . . . I am tired . . ."

Tommaso kissed Michelangelo on the brow, withdrew weeping.

Dusk was falling. Alone in the room, Michelangelo began to review the images of all the beautiful works he had created. He saw them, one by one, as clearly as the day he had made them, the sculptures, paintings and architecture succeeding each other as swiftly as had the years of his life:

The Madonna of the Stairs and the Battle of the Centaurs he had carved for Bertoldo and *Il Magnifico*, with the Plato group laughing at him because he had made them "pure Greek"; Sts. Proculus and Petronius that he had made for Aldovrandi in Bologna; the wooden Crucifix for Prior Bichiellini; the Sleeping Cupid with which he had tried to fool the dealer in Rome; the Bacchus he had carved in Jacopo Galli's orchard; the Pietà that Cardinal Groslaye di Dionigi had commissioned for St. Peter's; the Giant David for Gonfaloniere Soderini and Florence; the Holy Family teased out of him by Agnolo Doni; the cartoon for the Battle of Cascina, called the Bathers, to compete with Leonardo da Vinci's; the Madonna and Child for the merchants of Bruges, carved in his own first studio; the ill-fated bronze portrait of Pope Julius II; Genesis, painted for Julius II on the vault of the Sistine; the Last Judgment for Pope Paul III to complete the chapel; the Moses for Julius' tomb; his four unfinished Giants in Florence; the Dawn and Dusk, Night and Day for the Medici chapel; the Conversion of Paul and the Crucifixion of Peter for the Pauline chapel; the Campidoglio, Porta Pia, the three Pietas sculptured for his own pleasure . . . and as the pictures came to a stop and stood still in his mind's eye, St. Peter's.

St. Peter's. . . . He entered the church through its front portal, walked in the strong Roman sunshine down the wide nave, stood below the center of the dome, just over the tomb of St. Peter. He felt his soul leave his body, rise upward into the dome, becoming part of it: part of space, of time, of heaven, and of God.